THE ODYSS[illegible]

NATH DRAGON

BOOKS 1-5

EXILED

ENSLAVED

DEADLY

HUNTED

STRIFE

CRAIG HALLORAN

The Odyssey of Nath Dragon Books 1-5
By Craig Halloran

Print Edition

TWO-TEN BOOK PRESS
P.O. Box 4215, Charleston, WV 25364

ISBN eBook: 978-1-946218-55-1
ISBN Paperback: 978-1-724403-62-9
ISBN Hardback: 978-1-946218-56-8

www.craighalloran.com

Publisher's Note
This book is a work of fiction. Names, characters, places, and incidents either are the product of the author's imagination or are used fictitiously, and any resemblance to actual persons, living or dead, events, or locales is entirely coincidental.

Table of Contents

NALZAMBOR
Faalum Sea
Urslay
Huskan
Marlun
Artus
Riegelwood
THRAAG
Pool of the Dragons
QUINTUKLEN
Riverlynn
Shale Hills
NARNUM
MORGDON
Valley of Bones
The Ruins
ELOME
The Settlement
Stonewater Keep
Advent
DRAGON HOME
Old Hen
Lost City of Borgash
Slaver Town
Cherlon
Abblyn
Berglon
Karl Vesterberg 2017

THE ODYSSEY OF

NATH DRAGON

BOOK 1

EXILED

CRAIG HALLORAN

Chapter 1

With the cool air of the higher altitude in his face, Nath let out a joyous howl. "Wooooweeeeeee!" He was flying. Not under his own power, but something vastly bigger and more powerful, with great wings that spanned over a hundred feet. Those wings flapped with mighty strength, propelling them higher and faster. They were dragon wings. The wings of his father. "Go faster, Father! Higher!" Nath's strong voice was almost drowned out against the wind that rushed through his hair.

"If we go too high, you'll get too cold," Balzurth, the dragon beneath him, said. His voice was easily heard, rich, loud, and full of wisdom. "I can't have you freezing to death on your one-hundredth-year celebration."

"I'll be fine!" Nath slapped his father's broad neck. Balzurth's scales were red, some flecked with gold, and shone like newly polished armor. Two grand horns adorned the top of his head. He was huge, magnificent, and most importantly, the king of the dragons. Nath climbed up between the two horns. Standing on the top of Balzurth's skull, he wrapped his arms around one of the horns, which was much taller than him. "Higher, Father! Higher!"

"It's *your* celebration day." Balzurth's long neck bent, turning his face in Nath's direction. His golden eyes were bigger than Nath's own head. "Hold fast, son. I don't want to lose you."

"I will. I promise."

Balzurth gave a nod. His wings pounded the air in slow, monstrous strokes, lifting them higher and faster. He punched through the clouds, plunging them into a sea of mist. Seconds later, they broke through the mist, and the clouds stretched out like a field of cotton below them. He skimmed the top of the clouds then rose even higher.

Nath's flame-red hair whipped like a banner behind him. The wind stung his eyes. His heart raced like a team of horses. Tingling with energy from head to toe, he spread one arm out wide and let out another elated cry at the top of his lungs. "Wooooooo-weeeeeeeeeeee!"

Balzurth continued upward.

Nath's teeth chattered. His nose and ears felt like icicles. He didn't care. He loved flying with his father. Nothing in all the world thrilled him more. But he dreamed of flying on his own one day. To soar through the heavens on his own—nothing could be more wonderful.

"Are you getting cold yet?" Balzurth asked.

With his teeth clacking together, he replied, "No."

"Hah!" Balzurth's huge body shuddered with rumbles from laughter. He turned his head slightly and puffed out a blast of steam.

The gust of hot air warmed Nath up instantly. "Ahhh," he moaned. "That felt so good."

Together, they rode the skies for hours. Balzurth blasted through flocks of birds. He dipped, dived, and barrel-rolled. Nath clung to his father like drying paint. Nothing in the world could wipe the smile from his face.

"Father, will you take me over the cities? I haven't seen them since I was very little," he said.

Balzurth's scales rippled beneath Nath's feet. For a moment, his wings skipped a beat. "You are still little."

"No, I'm not. I'm a hundred years old." Nath pulled a lock of his hair from his mouth with his finger. "That's older than most people live."

"How do you know that?"

"Maefon told me."

"That elf has a big mouth," Balzurth grumbled.

"She said elves, aside from dragons, live the longest, as much as a thousand years or so. The dwarves and gnomes live for centuries, but humans and orcs whittle away long before they are one hundred. She says that is because they are so inferior. She says they live foolishly and lack self-control."

"Maefon says a lot that she should not be saying," Balzurth said. "I need to have a talk with her."

"Why?"

"Well, there are many things that I prefer are not mentioned in Dragon Home. The elves are our guests, and they need to follow the rules of the dragons." Balzurth's head dipped. He scanned the forests and grasslands miles below them. "The world of the races is very complex, Nath, and I don't want the elves telling you about them. The elves that serve us have proven good and trustworthy, but their view of the other races can be jaded. I prefer to teach you myself, when the time comes. Do you understand?"

"Is now the time?"

"Soon."

"But I want to know now. They sound exciting. Maefon says I look like a human. She says I look like a young man or old child, but I'm man size. You know, big."

Balzurth shook his head. "You still have growing to do yet. Be patient."

"Ugh!" Nath rolled his eyes. "But you sleep sometimes five and ten years at a time. Can't you tell me more now? I'm one hundred. That's older than most people ever live. I'm ready to know, Father. You've even said yourself..." Nath imitated Balzurth's deep voice, "'You're never too young to be ready.' At least you say that in regards to my chores."

"We'll talk about it later," Balzurth said. Beating his wings harder and faster, he picked up speed.

Swept away in the moment, Nath closed his eyes as they dipped down and went higher, and spread out both arms. For several moments, it felt like he was flying on his own. His body spun in the air, and he plummeted toward the earth. He caught a glimpse of his father. Balzurth was going up. Nath was going down. He stretched out his arms and yelled, "Father!"

Chapter 2

Back facing the ground rushing to greet him a few thousand feet below, Nath looked skyward to his father. Balzurth's humongous frame had become little more than a speck. He called out again, shrieking in the wind. "Father! Father!" He lost sight of his father when he passed through the blanket of clouds. Spreading his arms and legs out, he twisted in the air, rotating himself so that he faced downward. The trees seemed so far away at first, but they were getting larger.

Guzan! This is bad!

His efforts slowed his fall as he cupped his hands while keeping his chest toward the world. Everything below him that had once appeared beautiful and peaceful now rushed upward, ready to destroy him.

"Father!" Nath's cheeks flapped against the gusting air. The wind roared in his ears. He spun out of control. The green treetops of the forest no longer appeared like somewhere he could make a soft landing. The trees spread apart, revealing seams and cavities of sharp rocks waiting like gnashing teeth that would swallow his broken corpse whole. "Faaaatherrrrrrrr!"

Seconds from being dashed on the rocks, four small metallic-blue dragons, half the size of Nath, darted in from nowhere. They latched their talons onto his wrists and ankles. Their claws dug deep into his skin as their wings beat, slowing Nath's death-defying fall.

"Ow!" he said, wincing. "You don't have to wound me, though I am thankful, little brothers." The group of dragons flew Nath upward, making a straight line for Balzurth, who'd just burst through the clouds. The dragon king's golden eyes smoldered like cauldrons of boiling gold. "Uh-oh."

"Take him to the ground, my life-saving blue razors." Flying alongside them, Balzurth glared at Nath. "You and I are going to have a long talk!"

Twenty feet above a clearing in the forest, the blue razors' talons released. "Whulp!" Nath landed hard on his feet and fell down. Eyeing the dragons who'd just saved him, he said, "You could have been a little gentler!"

The blue razors flew in a tight circle, flicked their tongues at him, then darted away with alarming speed. In two seconds, they were out of sight. He dusted off his hands. A tremendous shadow fell over his shoulders. Tree branches popped and snapped beneath Balzurth as he landed right behind him. Unlike most dragons, Balzurth's arms and legs were longer, giving him a more human-like appearance when he stood. "Heh, that was a close one, wasn't it, Father?"

Sitting on his rear legs, with his front arms crossed, Balzurth said, "You could have died!"

"I know I'll never die if you are around." Nath dusted off his knees.

Balzurth's tail swept Nath off his feet. He flipped head over heels, landing hard on his rear end. "I do not command power over life and death. Who will protect you when I am not around? Hmmmm? Would you have pulled off such a stunt if I was not there? Hmmmm?" He snorted out a hot blast of air. "No! Of course not, so why do it at all? You did this the last time, and the time before that. And you wonder why I don't take you flying more. I wouldn't have even considered it today if it wasn't your hundredth year of celebration." Balzurth's tail rose over his head. It hung there for a moment, swaying a little from side to side, then *wham!* It came down like a great cedar. "I thought you would have wised up more by now! I am disappointed!"

Nath shrank beneath his father's heavy stare. The hard scales on Balzurth's heaving chest heated to a brilliant orange color. At any moment, Nath expected flames to explode out of his father's mouth. He'd seen those flames before. The purifying, scalding heat destroyed anything it touched in an instant. With his head down and trembling, he said, "I'm sorry, but I just want to fly like my brothers and sisters."

"You still have a defiant tone, Nath. You lack patience. And you know, Sultans of Sulfur, you know that you cannot fly without wings. Do you see the wingless red rock dragons try to fly?" Balzurth poked him in the chest with a massive talon. "Do you? No, because that would be foolish."

Nath's trembling stopped. He sat up cross-legged. "Well, that's only because all they do is bask in lava. They are the laziest dragons I've ever seen."

"They do more than that. You just don't pay attention."

Nath rolled his eyes. "I know, I know, the red rocks protect the border and enrich the soils." He picked at the grasses, plucking out handful after handful and tossing it aside. "I don't think they are capable of much more."

"They serve their purpose."

"And what is my purpose? I don't even know that. You won't tell me. I know I'm a dragon born a man. The only dragon who talks to me in the Mountain of Doom—"

"Don't call Dragon Home that."

"Fine then." Nath held up a finger. "Let me rephrase. The only dragon that talks to me in the Mountain of Boring is you. All of the other dragons ignore me. Why that is, I don't know, and you won't tell me, but I'm positive that it's because I don't have any scales and they do."

"I've seen you engage with the other dragons plenty of times. You wrestled quite well against them. It makes me smile when you do that."

"They don't like me. None of them do. They treat the elves better."

"Friendships and trust take time to build. Dragons can be very picky and peculiar."

"That's an understatement." Nath hopped up. "When do you see it, when you sleep, one, five, ten years at a time. And look at this." He showed Balzurth his wrists. They were bleeding where the blue razors latched onto him. "They didn't have to dig in to me like I'm some varmint they snatch from the trees."

"That's the thanks they get?" Balzurth shook his head. "That's hardly a scratch. And don't try to deflect this argument away from the subject at hand. You did something foolish, and you will be punished for it."

"I'm sorry… and I'm glad I'm saved, just surprised. I didn't think other dragons really cared." Nath picked up a rock and chucked it high over the trees. "But it's my celebration day."

"Yes, and you need to make the most of it, because tomorrow, you will reap what you have wrought."

"And what will that be?"

Balzurth lowered himself and said, "Get on. You'll find out tomorrow."

With his shoulders slumped, Nath climbed onto his father's back. *Please, please, please don't let this day end.*

Chapter 3

With sweat on his brow and running down his back, Nath dug the shovel into a pile of coins. They clinked together with a distinctive metallic sound unique to the precious metal. He dumped the hundreds of coins into a half-empty wooden wheelbarrow. This was the twentieth load of the day, and the huge pile of treasure didn't look any smaller now than when he started. He kept digging, dumping in shovelful after shovelful of gold and silver coins, accented by countless precious stones such as diamonds, emeralds, rubies, and pearls. It wasn't all loose coins and gems either, but necklaces, bracelets, tiaras, chalices, silverware, and gilded china plates.

Shirtless, Nath stopped shoveling and dabbed his face on a towel woven from gold-colored cotton. "I hate this punishment. It's boring. I'd rather have the dragon switch taken to me a hundred times than this." His eyes swept the massive chamber. Treasure was stacked almost as high as his chin from one side of the chamber to the other. Back in the corners, it was stacked up even higher. His father once told him that this treasure throne room had more treasure than all of the kingdoms combined times a hundred. Nath never had a hard time believing it. But now, the treasure just seemed to sit there, useless.

He shoveled until the wheelbarrow was filled over the brim, dropped the shovel, lifted up the handles, and started pushing. The front wheel squeaked as he went down the paths between the piles. The sound echoed off the towering arches of the vaulted ceiling. The chamber had to be plenty big for the largest dragon of all, Balzurth, and there was ample room for him in there, even when he was standing. The chamber could hold two dozen dragons the size of Balzurth if needed.

Rolling by Balzurth's throne, Nath came to a stop. It was a huge armless and backless seat made from polished stone. It was more than big enough for Balzurth. Its design was simple, all stone, with some precious stones that twinkled in the ancient engravings. It was the most dominating object in the room, but out of place somehow. It seemed lonely. Balzurth used to sit on the throne and tell Nath stories that lasted for hours. The dragon king was a grand storyteller. They were some of the best times, but as he became older, the stories became old and a little boring. Balzurth, once he started, was very long winded. And the names he spoke of seemed to get longer and take forever.

Nath patted the leg of the throne. "Don't run off anywhere. You might be my seat one day, though I find it hard to believe that I'll be so impossibly big at the rate I'm growing." He eyed the grand murals on the walls behind the throne. The painted images showed dragons of all sorts and kinds—flying through the skies, nestled in caves, or snaking through the willowwacks. All the images seemed to move ever so slightly with life of their own. It wasn't an illusion. He could leave and come back days later, and all of the images would have moved elsewhere completely. This was where he came when he was younger and his father taught him about the dozens of kinds of dragons. Nath learned about their powers, too. The only thing he never learned was how to get them to like him.

He sighed through his nose and resumed his trek to the other side of the throne room. Coming to the end of the path, he dumped out the treasure and sat down. "Twenty loads down, nine hundred and eighty to go. That should do it, anyway." He picked up a coin and flicked it with his fingers. It shot across the room, hitting an adjacent pile. A waterfall of coins skidded down, revealing the edge of a picture frame. There were plenty of paintings in the chamber. The largest ones, even bigger than Nath, were propped against the walls. Some of them hung from the gigantic pylons and pillars that held up spots in the vaulted ceiling.

Nath crossed the path, climbed up the pile of treasure, and wiggled out the painting. It was wider than his shoulders were broad and even longer than he was tall. He held it out. It was a portrait of a lovely woman against the backdrop of a star-filled sky. Her wavy platinum locks framed her fair skin. Her soft, pale lips smiled slightly as her head tilted a little to the side. Her extraordinary eyes sparkled like diamonds. The detail was so realistic Nath found himself trying to find his breath. He'd seen plenty of elves and some pictures of humans, but no woman was anything like this.

"Whoa. She's a gorgeous thing, isn't she?" a playful woman's voice stated.

Nath jumped and dropped the painting. "Maefon, quit sneaking up on me! You aren't even supposed to be here!"

"Oh, it looks like someone is in love with the pretty woman in the painting. Kissy-kissy."

Nath frowned at her.

"Oh, Nath, don't be mad. She's very fetching for what appears to be a human woman. And the work is extraordinary." She squatted down with her dark eyes fastened on the picture. Maefon's flaxen hair was pulled back in a braid. She seemed about Nath's age and had been his closet companion since she arrived a few decades ago. In a way, they had grown up together, though she was more mature. She had a teardrop face, cat-shaped eyes that caught everything, and a dazzling smile that a blind man could see. Her sleeveless shirt was buttoned up to her neck just below the chin, and she wore all black from neck to toe. It was a casual ensemble that fit snugly on her elven frame. She cocked her head. "Do you love her, Nath?"

"Stop being silly. How can I love her? I just saw her." He picked up the picture. "But she certainly is worthy of my attention. If I didn't know better, I'd say that she is almost as striking as me."

Holding her stomach, Maefon erupted with laughter. "Oh, you are so vain. You, good looking—now that's rich. Why, you are the most unhandsome dragon I ever saw."

He tossed his hair. "That's only because I look like a human."

"You are only an average human at best." She climbed to the top of the pile and stuck her face in front of the picture. "Unlike me, who is the prettiest of the elves."

"You always say that, and I know you don't mean it. Your eyes stay glued to me even when you think I don't know you are looking." Eyes narrowing, he said, "I wonder who this is?"

Maefon grabbed the painting. Trying to pull the picture out of his grip, she said, "It's nobody real because no human looks like this. It's inhuman. Something from a dream. Trust me."

"You don't know. I think it's real. It could only be real, even if it is otherworldly. Maybe she lives beyond the murals."

"Maybe she's been dead millennia already. Who cares?" She yanked the frame out of his grasp.

"Careful," Nath said with a smile.

Maefon's eyes grew big. She fought for balance and footing. Coins slid beneath her feet. "Whoa! This is heavy!" She fell backward and slid down the hill of coins all the way to the bottom. An avalanche of coins covered her completely. Only her hands were still stuck out, holding the picture frame. There was a muffled "Help me!" coming from under the pile.

Nath slid down the pile, picked up the picture, and gently set it aside. Kneeling, he dusted treasure from her face. "That picture frame was heavy, wasn't it?"

She spit out a ruby as big as her knuckle. "I hate you."

He reached into the coins, grabbed her hand, and pulled her out. "I know. I hate you too."

They both burst out laughing.

Chapter 4

"NATH, ARE YOU FINISHED YET?" Maefon sat at the edge of Balzurth's throne, legs crossed and kicking. "I'm getting bored watching you work."

"You are welcome to help." Nath finished loading up another wheelbarrow and tossed the shovel aside. He wiped off his sweaty face on a towel. "I only have a few dozen more loads to go." He gestured to the treasure that had dwindled down to a manageable pile. "See? You can handle this."

"Oh no. This is your punishment, not mine. Watching you is my punishment." She made a playful smile as her eyes grazed over his muscular body. "Sort of."

If Nath noticed her attention, he didn't show it. Instead, he pushed the wheelbarrow down the path. As he passed her, he said, "If you get caught sitting on my father's throne, you're going to be punished, too."

"Oh, he doesn't care. Balzurth is gentle and wise. We are just children to him. He would forgive me, don't you think?"

"Eh, I suppose." Nath ambled down the path and dumped the treasure on the new pile he'd created. He stretched his aching back and groaned. "Oh, I can't wait to rest. This is awful. Who would think being in a chamber filled with such wonderful treasure could be so miserable."

"It is a burden," Maefon replied. "True treasure comes from simpler things."

Nath made his way back to the pile. "Such as?"

"Well, having friends to share time with. Working in the gardens. Nurturing the young dragons." Her eyes lit up. "Oh, how I enjoy that."

"They try to bite me."

She giggled. "They do not. You exaggerate."

"No, I don't. They hate me. All of them."

Maefon hopped off the throne, landing lightly on her feet. She followed after Nath. "Now, are you feeling sorry for yourself again? Hmmmm? Pouting is not an admirable quality for a king's son."

Nath picked up the shovel and got to work. "How can I be the prince of the dragons when I look like this? If it's absurd to me, then it's absurd to them. You know it." He dumped a shovelful in the wheelbarrow. "And I know it. What if you had to go and live among men? Wouldn't you feel out of place?"

"Oh no, I am certain they would worship me." She untangled her honey-colored hair from the braid. The bouncy locks fell perfectly over her shoulders, somehow further enhancing her natural beauty. "Don't you agree?"

Nath swallowed. He thought *yes*, but said, "I don't know. I haven't been around any humans to know. Maybe they would be frightened to death of you."

"Hah! They would not be frightened. In awe, yes, but not scared like little children."

"You really are a piece of work." Nath refilled the barrel. He enjoyed Maefon and her wit. If it weren't for her, he might go crazy. The other elves who served the dragons were friendly, but more as a matter of courtesy. Maefon was a true friend. She cared for him. "Have you spent any time with the humans?"

"I studied all about the other races in Elome. I know all that I need to know."

"You don't think that gave you a jaded point of view? After all, what you've learned would be from an elven perspective." He grabbed the handles of the wheelbarrow and moved on.

"The elves are the purest of the races," she said, following behind him with her hands behind her back. "What they record is a neutral view of things. Hence, I believe what I read. The orcs are stupid, the dwarves are difficult, humans are unpredictable, gnomes are impolite, halflings are childish, and ogres are smelly. Should I go on?"

"No, no, your research is beyond convincing. So deep, well thought out, and thorough. I am overwhelmed." He laughed. "And what does it say about dragons?"

"Well, there are many kinds, and we are still learning about them. That is what I'm trained for, being one of the Trahaydeen. So far, you are the most interesting."

He dumped the wheelbarrow. "I'm not even a dragon. How can I be interesting?"

"You are. And you are a good, obedient son. Not all dragons heed the dragon king's words. They seek their own purposes elsewhere." She put her hand on his wrist, and her voice lowered to a whisper. "Many wander far from home and become wicked. They serve themselves and not Dragon Home. Many others are lost, never to return home. It troubles Balzurth. We wonder why that is."

"Dragons, like any other race, can make their own choices. Nalzambor's a large world filled with many dangers and delights, the way I understand it. Dragons can make the most of their own lives, but they always have Dragon Home to come home to. Sometimes they just need help finding it. That's what Father says."

"The races fear the dragons. They hunt and kill them. They call Dragon Home the Mountain of Doom." She plucked an emerald-studded tiara from the treasure pile and placed it on her head. "How does it look?"

"It makes your head look really big."

"Oh, shut it." She slapped his arm then slung the tiara away. "Anyway, the races capture and torture dragons. They turn their scales into clothing. Sell dragon blood for potions. Their teeth, claws, eyes, or horns are used for decoration or jewelry. They are very nasty out there."

"How do you know these things?" He started pushing the wheelbarrow along.

"It's well known in the world, Nath. You are sheltered here. You only know what Balzurth tells you. I'm sure he only tells you what you need to know, and he is wise for it, I'm sure, but you should know more, just in case..." Her voice trailed off.

He stopped and looked down at her. Her head came to the top of his chest. "Just in case what?"

"Oh, nothing. I'm just rambling. Don't pay any attention to me. I've said enough already."

He grabbed her arm. "No, finish your thoughts. Out with it."

"I was just going to say, just in case something ever happens to your father. You'll have to know more about the world of men. What if he leaves to the land beyond the murals and does not return for a very long while? You would be in charge, wouldn't you?"

Nath's brow crinkled. He glanced at the mural behind the throne. It was a place where only dragons could go that his father said he'd learn all about one day. Usually, older dragons went to the land beyond the murals when their work in the world of the races was no longer needed. But only his father could go back and forth. It was something he didn't fully understand.

"No, the dragons have a council. They run things when he's gone. I just do whatever."

"I think you should be in charge of things. After all, you are the prince."

Nath shook his head and started pushing the wheelbarrow down the path. "You really need to temper your imagination before it becomes a dangerous thing. Why don't you run along, Maefon? I'll find you later. I just want to finish this on my own."

"I'm sorry, Nath. Have I offended you?" Her big, dark eyes were sad.

"I said I'll see you later."

Chapter 5

A couple of days passed. Nath ran along the rocky ledges of Dragon Home. He hopped over chasms and gullies of the barren mountainside. The mountain was at least a league of walking if he went all the way around the bottom. Its rocky crevices and ledges led to a small flat on the tip-top that hovered just beneath the first layer of clouds in the sky. About halfway up, lava flowed in bright, burning seams of orange, down into the sulfurous springs below. It formed liquid pools at the bottom. One thing could always be said—Dragon Home never got cold.

Nath angled up to a ledge that jutted out several feet like a flat nose. He took a seat on the edge and stared out at the vast land in the distance. For some reason, he was agitated. Maefon's words bothered him deeply. Even though the dragons were nothing short of rude to him, he hated that the races hunted them. It didn't seem right. At the same time, when she suggested that his father might leave for some time, it went right through him.

It was just something about the way she said it that rankled him. And if Balzurth did leave, shouldn't Nath be in charge? Or at least he should be in the conversation. Of course, the dragon council could handle things in Balzurth's absence. They always did, but next time, perhaps, Nath should pay closer attention.

Next time Father goes, I'm going to attend all of the council's meetings. After all, it's my right… but I've been before, and they are so boring. He clenched his teeth. *And so long, not that I have anything better to do, but dragons talking takes forever.*

Nath sat a very long time. The sun hung high in the sky, just beneath the clouds, lowering an inch at a time until the bottom dipped behind the trees. The sky became a light purple, a little gloomy, but promising in an uncanny sort of way.

"I do love the sunset."

Tired of being out of place, Nath often considered leaving. His father told him that he could leave when he was ready but not before. What Balzurth didn't say was whether or not he would leave as a dragon or a man. Nath waited for the change to happen. He wanted wings and scales like his father, but they had yet to come. He wanted to see the world with his own eyes and find out what it had to offer.

I guess I'll just have to wait… forever.

A small winged dragon flew right in front of him. Its scales were orange, and it was little longer than the length of his arm. Its wings beat quickly as it chirped out words in dragonese.

"Training? Now?" Nath sighed. "Fine. I'll be there, little brother." The dragon snorted at him, narrowed its eyes, and flew away. "Nice talking to you too, you little winged rodent."

Inside the mountain, Nath walked down the main tunnel that spiraled and weaved through the mountain. It was a vast, hollowed-out channel, more than large enough for Balzurth to walk through, with smaller tunnels that broke off from it, creating an intricate network. Nath had walked them all.

Walking up the slope, a huge bull dragon headed his way. It was powerfully built with brick-red scales, somewhat reminiscent of Father's, but not nearly as big. Still, it was a huge dragon, and Nath marveled. A smaller group of dragons, all bulls, trailed behind it. "Hello, mighty one," Nath said, moving aside as it passed. He didn't often see the larger dragons in Dragon Home. They liked the lands outside, which were more suited for them. "What brings you home? Taking the family for a visit?"

The bull dragon moved on without a look Nath's way. The pack behind him were the same.

Nath waved and said sarcastically, "Yes, very nice talking to you too, fat scaly lummox."

The bull dragon halted. Slowly, it turned toward Nath. The bull dragon's eyes had a deadly intent. "Did you say something, little dragon prince? Say it louder. I did not hear you. Something about a lummox?"

Nath touched his chest. "My, the lummox can talk. Why, that's almost as impressive as those horns on your head. And I didn't think bull dragons could talk. Something I read about them being very slow to speak. No, that's not it. That would be a compliment. No, bull dragons, those marvelous in size, are known to be dumb, or stupid, rather."

The bull dragon's chest swelled. Hot breath came from his mouth. Flames flickered behind his teeth.

"Only jesting, grand one," Nath said, lifting his hands up as he backed away. "I've always heard that bull dragons were known for their expansive sense of humor."

With the pack of smaller dragons behind him, the bull dragon approached. He stopped when he was face to face with Nath. The bull dragon's head was as high as Nath was tall. His orange eyes glared into Nath's. "No respect given, no respect received. No wonder you are thought so ill of."

"I offered courtesy. You didn't reply."

"Because you are not a dragon! You are a menace to our kind."

Nath blanched. The words stung. "I am not." The bull dragon turned and walked away. As he did so, the tip of his tail lashed out, knocking Nath's feet out from under him. He hit hard, lying on his side, gaping. "If anyone is a menace, you are!" The bull dragon and his family vanished around the next bend in the tunnel. "I am not a menace!" His words echoed back. "You are a menace."

Chapter 6

The Training Lair greeted Nath with sweltering heat. Torches and urns blessed with the everlasting dragon fire illuminated the large chamber-like cavern. Veins of lava flowed through the walls, giving it an eerie illumination. On the floor were racks of weapons such as swords, halberds, battle-axes, and spears. The cave floor was open, jagged rock formations spread out in random places. On the back wall, a lone dragon sat like a dog on a flat slab of stone. She was the size of a horse, and her scales were forest green all over, but her breastplate was a much lighter green. Her eyes, unlike male dragons', had long lashes. The horns were like the sharpened antlers of a deer.

Nath walked on his hands across the training floor. He climbed over the rock obstacles one at a time, leaving a trail of sweat as he did so. "Even if I didn't have my legs, I don't think I would walk this way, Dragon Master Elween."

The forest dragon's voice was sharp. "The purpose of this exercise isn't about walking on your hands. It's about discipline. Something you can never—"

"'Have enough of,' I know. But I do think I have this mastered. How about some sword play?"

"No," she said flatly. Her eyes slid over to the racks of weapons.

Nath followed her line of sight. It had been a while since he'd trained with steel. He hungered for it. It took his mind off things.

From out of nowhere, someone slammed into him. Nath dropped his shoulder and rolled. Before he could get to his feet, a shirtless elven warrior tangled up his legs. The slender man was a knot of well-defined muscle, with many braids in his hair. His size almost matched Nath's. Nath reached for the man. As he did so, a second elf caught him in a headlock. The elf cranked up the pressure. Nath's eyes bulged. He lost his breath.

"What's the matter, Nath? Having trouble speaking?" the elf who had Nath in a headlock said.

"I believe he's confounded." The other elf fought against Nath's kicking legs. "Choke him out, brother. Choke him out!"

Nath wedged his fingers between his neck and the arm of the elf on his back. He pushed through, breaking the elf's grip. The elf kicked away. "No you don't, Pevly!" Nath snatched the elf's quick feet. With a yank, he pulled Pevly to the ground. Hand over hand, he dragged Pevly toward him. "I've got you now!"

Pevly kicked him in the face. "That's going to leave a mark… I hope."

Nath glared at the elf. "You shouldn't have done that."

"What? This?" The elf executed another perfect kick to Nath's face. "Now that looked like it hurt. Did it?"

Nath's cheeks warmed. "Now you've asked for it!" He twisted Pevly's foot.

The elf cried out in pain.

"Yield!" Nath said.

"Never!" Pevly's face became a grimace of pain. "You won't break it! You won't break it!"

"I don't have to," Nath said, applying more pressure.

"Eeeoow! I yield! I yield."

Nath let go. He turned his attention to the elf fastened to his legs. He wrapped his arms around Tevlin's waist. In a tangle of limbs, the pair wrestled across the floor.

"Beat him, Tevlin! Destroy him!" Pevly shouted as he rubbed his ankle. "Avenge your brother!"

Tevlin executed move after move. His quick hands and feet battled to take Nath down. He landed short kicks to the ankles and stiff punches to the ribs. Elbows and knees pumped like an ironsmith's hammers.

Nath blocked, punched, and countered. The grapplers rolled over the floor. Finally, Nath shoved Tevlin onto his belly, drove a knee into his back, and pulled both of his arms backward. "Yield, Tevlin!"

Defiant, Tevlin shook his head.

Pulling harder, Nath said, "I'll yank your arms out of their sockets. I swear I will!"

Tevlin shook his head again.

"Pevly, talk some sense into your brother, will you? You remember what happened last time."

"Yes, I remember, but my brother is very stubborn and highly resistant to pain, as you know. So I don't think I'll be able to talk him into anything." Pevly pulled his knees to his chest. "I guess you'll have to call it a draw then. Tevlin, do you agree to a draw?"

With his nose on the ground, Tevlin nodded.

"What says you, Nath?" Pevly asked. "A draw then?"

Tevlin still wriggled against him. The elf was strong. Very strong. Nath was stronger. "We never had a draw before today. There won't be one now, either. Last chance, Tevlin. Yield or no yield?"

Again, Tevlin shook his head.

Nath tugged harder. Tevlin's shoulders gave. *Pop! Pop!*

Pevly jumped to his feet. "Nath, how could you do that?"

"It's been a bad day, and he should have yielded." He let go of Tevlin's arms. They flopped at the elf's sides. "Master Elween, is this match over?"

"You've incapacitated your opponent. Hence, it's over. But your training is not yet done."

"Of course not."

"Why?" Pevly moaned. "Why? You have crippled my brother, Nath! He's useless now! Just look at him."

With help from his brother, Tevlin sat up. His arms drooped heavily at the shoulder in unnatural positions. Tevlin's head was down. His long brown braids hung over his eyes.

Pevly pointed a stiff finger at Nath. Dramatically, he said, "You are cruel! Cowardly! Shameless, Nath! How can you live with yourself?"

"I guess because I can't live without myself," Nath replied. "And what is eating at you? This isn't the first time… Oh, I see what's going on. The Trahaydeen are preparing for the Showings, aren't they?"

Pevly crossed his arms and stuck his bottom lip out. "Possibly."

"And as always, your performance is incredible, Pevly. Very convincing. The dragons will like it. As for you, Tevlin, would you like me to help put your shoulders back in their sockets?"

Tevlin nodded.

"Permission to repair, Master Elween?"

"Yes, of course."

With the assistance of Pevly, Nath shoved both of Tevlin's shoulders back into their natural spots. Nath rubbed the mute elf's head. "All better?"

Tevlin gave him a stern look and a quick nod. The elf brothers were twins, each half a head shorter than Nath. Tevlin was expressionless, while Pevly's face always expressed a wide range of emotion. For elves, they appeared to be young adults and had been a part of the Trahaydeen for the last few decades. Like Maefon, they were some of Nath's best companions, even though he didn't see them all the time. The Trahaydeen rotated in their duties caring for the dragons. The dragons didn't need care, so to speak, but they enjoyed the attention. The elves massaged the dragons' scales, polished and filed their talons, rubbed the grit from their horns. They even grew special food in their gardens that helped clean the dragons' teeth. It was pampering, and the dragons delighted in it.

"So, Pevly, what are the Showings about this time?" Nath asked.

Pevly brightened. "It's called the Trap. It's about a young dragon, surrounded by enemies, but he doesn't even know about it. Danger lurks in every crevice and corner, waiting to strike until—" He smacked his hands together. "Whazmo!"

"Well, go on," Nath said, excited.

"I can't spoil it for you. Oh, and Nath, watch out behind you."

"I'm not falling for that. Seriously, what is—*ulp*!"

A serpent's tail coiled around Nath's neck. With a fierce yank, he was jerked from his feet.

Chapter 7

Nath found himself tangled up with a dragon. It was a gray scaler, little bigger than him, serpentine and nasty looking. The dragon's claws were pitch black. Its front paws locked around Nath's wrists. It eyed Nath, opened its mouth filled with rows of sharp teeth, and hissed.

Choking, Nath pulled the dragon in closer. He head-butted the dragon on the top of its snout. The dragon's tail and grip slackened. Nath twisted free. He slipped behind the dazed dragon, grabbed it, and body-slammed it to the ground. He put the dragon's serpentine neck in a headlock and squeezed with all his might. Entwined, they rolled and thrashed over the floor. The dragon twisted and jerked. Nath held on for dear life. Their bodies collided against the stones jutting from the floor.

"I'm not letting go!" Nath said. Muscles bulged in his arms. Veins popped up in his neck. "Yield!"

The gray scaler's tail tapped on the ground.

Nath released it. Panting, he said, "Thank goodness that's over."

Without a glance, the gray scaler slunk away with its head low and black wings folded behind its back. It vanished into a smaller tunnel in the rock.

Nath's eyes swept the room. Only Master Elween, Pevly, and Tevlin were there. "How did I do, Master Elween?"

"Horrible. You may have defeated your opponents, but you were surprised both times. If they wanted to kill you, they could have… easily."

"I suppose," Nath said, rising to his feet, "but this is only training, not the real thing. If it was, I would be ready."

Master Elween hopped from her rocky perch. Standing like a man, front arms up and tail on the ground, she walked on her hind legs to Nath. Fully upright, the forest dragon stood eight feet tall. Though dragons typically walked on all fours, some of the kinds were much like a man that could walk upright on its legs. Her probing stare seemed to size up everything there was to know about Nath with a look. She smacked Nath on both sides of his cheeks. "No one is ever ready for the opponent they have never seen. That is the one you must look out for."

Nath started to say, "I know," but he checked his tongue. Master Elween was one of the few dragons that did speak to him, thanks to the training. The Dragon Master had never been kind, but at least she conversed with Nath.

Looking into Nath's eyes, Master Elween said, "What is on your mind, Nath? Questions lurk in your eyes. Out with it."

"You speak as if I have an enemy that I don't know about already. You always have, to some degree, but lately, you've brought it up in all of my training. Is there something I should know that you are not telling me about?"

The elven brothers looked at each other briefly before turning their attention to Master Elween.

"I'm not teaching you any differently than any other."

"If that's the case, then why do I train with swords, knives, axes, and hammers?" Nath pointed to the weapons racks. "The other dragons don't train with them." Master Elween frowned at him. "Do they?"

"You are not here all of the time." Master Elween moved to the weapons racks. She lifted a longsword off its post and tossed it to Nath. She grabbed another one with a clawed hand much like a man's. "Let me show you what a dragon can do with a blade." She whipped the sword through the air, cutting with masterful strokes and precision.

Nath found the moves awkward, quick, but fluid. He'd never imagined seeing a dragon fighting with a sword before. Why would they? Dragons had claws as sharp as swords and other powers of their own. Eyes following the quick movements of Master Elween's steel, he said, "You are amazing."

"I've studied the weapons of the races for centuries. I should be." Master Elween held the sword up. The tip of her taloned finger tapped the blade. "Understanding your enemies' weapons helps you understand your enemies. Do you understand?"

"I never thought about that before."

"That's because you do little thinking at all, based off what I've seen," Master Elween replied.

Pevly giggled.

"Silence."

Pevly clammed up.

Master Elween continued, "Always have a plan of action in mind, Nath. Be ready." She set her feet in a fighter's stance. "On guard!"

Without hesitation, Nath attacked. He chopped at Master Elween. The dragon master parried the blow aside, countering with a slash of her own. Nath jumped backward. The tip of the dragon's sword missed his chest by an inch. "You are fast, Master Elween, but I am faster." Nath launched a flurry of strikes. He jabbed, stabbed, slashed, thrust, and cut. Steel collided with steel.

Clang! Bang! Clang!

Swordplay had been Nath's favorite training since he began. Over the past few decades, he'd trained on a regular basis. He'd mastered all the weapons, at least the best that his trainers knew how. They taught him different fighting styles. He'd learned to fight with two hand axes but swung them like a dragon attacking with claws. He spun a bo stick like a dragon's tail, sweeping enemies from their feet. It was the sword that he was the most fond of. Now, his skills were put to the test.

Master Elween's tail swept over the ground at Nath's feet. He jumped it. "Hah! I was ready for that, wasn't I?"

The dragon unleashed a hard swing. The metal striking metal jarred Nath's arms up to the elbow. Master Elween struck faster and faster. It took everything Nath had to parry. His arms ached. The muscles in his shoulders burned. Master Elween did not relent. She beat down Nath's sword. The blade fell from Nath's grip. He'd never been disarmed before. Now, the point of a sword pressed to his throat. He swallowed.

"My body was not created to fight with a sword. The body you have was. Yet here you are, defeated." Master Elween put her snout in Nath's face. "You have very much to learn, Nath. Very much. You are never as good as you think."

"I would be if you started training me like this twenty years ago," Nath said, not hiding his defiance. No matter what he did, it was never enough for Master Elween.

"So it's my fault?" Master Elween shook her head and put her sword back on the rack. "No, it's your fault. If I was not here, could you not have taught yourself? Ask yourself this—how did the first master master anything? Hmm? A shame. You've had a hundred years, and not once have you shown initiative in anything."

CHAPTER 8

"NATH! NATH!" MAEFON HOLLERED. SHE was dressed in her sleeveless all-black garb. Her honey-colored hair had been braided. Gold hoop earrings hung from the lobes of her pointed ears. Her sweet voice echoed down the corridor. "Wait up!"

Nath's stride didn't slow. He moved with determination into the lower levels of the mountain. His jaw was set. A lit torch was in hand.

Maefon ran in front of him and tried to bar his path, but he went around her. "Where are you going?"

"To the forges. And I'm going alone."

"The forges?" she said, catching up to him. "Why would you go there? And I don't even know where they are."

"I do. See you later." He left her standing alone with her mouth hanging open. He didn't want to be around anyone.

"Well, that was rude, and I am coming." She caught up with him again. "I don't know what you are pouting about this time, but if you talked about it, you wouldn't feel so mad."

"Not talking about it." Nath continued his descent, turning out of one of the main tunnels into a smaller one that split from it. The Mountain of Doom was like the inside of an anthill, twisting and turning into many paths. Every route he took had been paved with stones. The larger ones had light from urns and torches that ran along the sides, burning with the everlasting dragon fire. The side tunnels and narrow passages were often dark. The dragons didn't need light as much as men. Their keen senses more than compensated for it. When Nath was younger, he'd traveled the tunnels in total darkness, exploring, alone, and honing his one superior sense. It was at least one thing he did have in common with the dragons.

"Your stride is too long, Nath. Slow down. And what is your hurry? Whatever it is you are looking for isn't going anywhere."

"I suggest that you keep up if you don't want to get lost."

"Are you being overbearing because Master Elween thrashed you at the Training Lair?"

"Who told you—never mind. Pevly can't keep silent about anything. If I didn't know better, I'd guess you were his sister."

"What are you implying, that I talk too much?"

"You haven't stopped talking since you arrived. And I told you that I didn't want to talk about it." He angled into another corridor. "And I didn't want you to come either. I want to be alone."

"Now Nath, you don't want to be alone. You complain about it too much, so I know better. And you shouldn't take a thwarting from Master Elween personally. She's supposed to do that." She wrapped her arms around his elbow. "That's why she's a master."

He tried to pull away, but she held him fast. "I know that. She's walloped me plenty over the years for this or that. She said I didn't have initiative."

"So you are going to the furnace to find initiative?" Her nose crinkled. "That doesn't make any sense. Care to explain?"

"No."

"Ugh!" She let go of him. "You are so hardheaded!"

Using only torchlight, he continued down the black corridors. After an hour of walking, with Maefon clinging at his side, he turned in to a chamber with a vast opening.

"Hello?" Maefon squinted toward the darkness. Her voice echoed for a moment and faded.

Nath lifted his torch toward another torch that hung on the wall. Flames spurted from it, leaping across the room, and jumped from one torch to another until all were lit. More balls of flame dropped from their perches into the stone urns below them. In seconds, the massive chamber was illuminated with a warm orange glow.

Maefon's dark eyes became giant pearls. "This is the biggest forge I've ever seen. Of course, I haven't seen many, but still... it's so vast." She scratched her head. "Nath, being a young Trahaydeen, and still learning your ways, I haven't devoted time to finding out why dragons would need a forge. Do you know?"

"Yes." Nath started down the stone staircase, which was as wide as the chamber's opening. Centered in the middle of the room were a dozen forges—every station fully equipped and ready to use. There were bellows to pump the fires, tongs, anvils mounted on stone stands, hammers, and cooling tanks of water. The coals in the mouth of the forge were cold and black. Nath stuck his fingers in one of the beds of coals. "They are warm still but don't burn."

"How can they be warm? Is there magic in them?" she asked.

"I suppose. They have always been warm since I remember. Father brought me here once and told me all about it. The forges were used by elves and dwarves to make metal to use in the wars against the orcs when they lost their lands to the brutes. That was millennia ago." On a nearby table, he looked at a mold made for a sword. He ran his finger through the groove. "The dragons, seeing the danger, came to an agreement with the elves and dwarves. They would aid them, so long as they kept the secrets of Dragon Home to themselves. But in their lust for greater knowledge, they stole the secret of Dragon Steel from the dragons. The elves blamed the dwarves, and the dwarves blamed the elves. Both races were banished. All of this happened before my father was king. Dragon Home has been a quieter place ever since."

Traipsing through the smithy, fingers touching everything she passed, Maefon said, "Have you ever seen Dragon Steel?"

"No." Nath picked up a pair of hammers. He banged on an anvil with them. "But it can only be made from metal of the mountain that flows in the veins of the lava. Father says the elves or the dwarves, possibly both, stole some of that metal along with the secret of how to shape it." He imitated his father's voice. "*That's why the races can never be fully trusted.* The forges have been cold ever since."

"But your father allows the Trahaydeen?"

Nath shrugged. "Again, it was a long time ago." He walked over to the bellows and started pumping it with his foot. The coals in the forge caught fire. Smoke wavered up into the hood.

"I don't think you should be doing that." Her slender arms were crossed over her chest. "Why are you doing that?"

"Master Elween says that I don't have any initiative. Well, she's right, but I'm taking initiative now. If I want to understand a sword, then I'm going to build one on my own."

Chapter 9

For days, Nath worked in the smithy, laboring away with long strips of metal, trying to shape them into any weapon he could. His hair was tied back behind his head. Sweat coated his face and dripped from his chin onto a heavy leather apron. His trousers were soaked, and his feet inside his boots burned from all of the standing.

"I'm getting better at this. I swear I'm getting better at this!" He pounded on a strip of metal that glowed orange on one end. He didn't know what was taking a worse beating, the anvil or him. With his arms throbbing, he struck blow after blow, flattening the end of the metal. A long edge began to form the more he battered at it. "Come on, metal. You are a sword, and you know it. Now be it!"

He wore heavy gloves on his hands. One hand swung the hammer, the other held a pair of iron tongs that fastened on the tang or grip of the sword. It took him days to master holding the tang by the tongs, and he wasn't even sure if that was the right way to go about it, but it worked for him.

The sword he made was long, edged on one side, with a curve on the tip. It wasn't going to be anything fancy. The only thing that mattered was whether or not it would hold up for cutting or striking. Hammering away, he noticed a bend in the main body of the metal.

Cooling on the anvil, it started to bow. "No!" He pounded on it a few more times. The bow popped back into shape. "Great Guzan! Warped again!"

Nath took the blade and stuck it back in the hot coals. From there, he moved to a workbench where several earlier sword versions rested. He picked them up one at a time, inspected them, and said as he set each and every one back down, "Bent. Bent. Bent. Cracked. Cracked. What in the world happened to this one? It's curvy. I've seen sidewinders that are straighter." He picked up a hammer. "Perhaps I should try something simpler, like this, or an axe, perhaps." He thumbed the perspiration from his eyes. "I don't know. Just when I think I'm getting better, it looks like I go backward."

"I think you are getting better," Maefon said. Nath whipped around. She'd snuck into the smithy and sat cross-legged on a table behind him. "After all, it would be impossible to do worse with all of this practice."

"Will you quit sneaking up on me? It's only proper that you announce yourself." He dropped the hammer on the table. "You could end up getting hurt."

"I keep my distance, and I'm always wary of your temper tantrums."

"That would be wise," he said. "Case in point." He poked his finger at a nearby wall. A sharp flange of steel protruded from the rock. "I wasn't looking when I threw it earlier."

She wiggled her shoulders from side to side. "Lucky for you, I'm an excellent dodger. And why so edgy, Nath? You make it sound like I'm an assassin creeping up behind your back."

"I know how those tickling little fingers of yours work. You've dug them into my ribs on countless occasions. You make me jumpy."

"You're never jumpy. Just flat footed. You are so absorbed in what you are doing that you make it easy. You're a deep thinker, Nath. If you aren't careful, you'll miss what is going on around you."

"Listen, I just want to build a nice sword. Are you here to help or drone on like my father or Master Elween?"

She untied the braid in her hair and combed it out with her fingers. "I was hoping you were going to give up on this experiment. There are more exciting things that you could do."

Nath walked over to a bin that sat on the floor with a variety of metal shafts stuck inside. Rummaging through them, he said, "What could be more exciting?"

"We could go for a walk. I'll even let you hold my hand like you used to. It's been a while since we walked. I miss it."

Nath wasn't about to admit that he missed it too. He liked Maefon, more than he cared to admit. There was no one he was closer with than her. She was beautiful, smart, witty, and understanding. It was easy to talk to her, and she got him to talk even when he didn't want to. She had a special soothing and pleasant way and a smile that could melt his heart. "You know that I would love to, but I'm focused on this right now. I'm making progress." He pinched his fingers together. "I'm this close. I can feel it. I just need to find the right metal to work with."

Maefon frowned as she picked up a metal file that lay on the table where she sat. With ginger fingers, she touched up her nails. "Nath, you are more prepared for things than you realize. Master Elween will never stop pushing you. And no one can be prepared for everything.

She tries to convince you that you can be. Nath, in the world of men, you would be nothing short of extraordinary, with or without a shiny sword."

"I don't know about that."

"You underestimate yourself." She slid off the table, walked over to him, took the metal shaft out of his grip, and set it aside. She grabbed his hands. "You are special, and as ready to handle anything as anybody. You can defeat many of Elome's finest elves in hand-to-hand combat. Your knowledge of language and the texts is as good or better than any of the Trahaydeen. Believe me, only the finest of the elves are sent here, and that's after decades of training. You are unlike any man I have ever seen. I just wish you were elven."

Nath pulled back his shoulders. A charming smile crossed his face. "Well, when you put it like that, I suppose that I am a bit of a marvel."

She looked into his eyes, rose on tiptoe and said, "You are beyond marvelous, Nath. You are perfect."

Nath's heart pounded. He put his arms around her waist, drew her in, and kissed her. Maefon's soft lips eagerly engaged. Her body melted in his arms. She moaned with passion.

NATH.

He broke the kiss off. Heart racing, he turned his eyes down the hall.

"What is it, Nath?" she said with dreamy eyes. Her lips started to pucker.

NATH.

Gently, Nath pushed her back by the shoulders. "Did you hear that?"

"No. All I hear is my heart fluttering like hummingbird wings."

"It's my father. I can hear him." Eyes searching, he said, "Yes, Father."

COME TO THE THRONE ROOM.

"Er, right away!" He peeled his hands from Maefon's sticky fingers. "See what you've done. Father saw us."

"You kissed me. I didn't kiss you, but I would have."

"I have to go." He dashed out of the chamber. *Oh Gads, I hope he doesn't banish her.*

Chapter 10

Nath stood outside the threshold of the doors that led into the throne room. The split doors were massive things, each standing over thirty feet tall and half as wide. The wood doors were framed with polished brass. The hinges were as long as Nath's forearm. Head down, he sighed. It wasn't the first time he'd been called to the throne room through a calling in his mind. It had been a while, though, and the last time it happened, it shook him. He'd drawn the anger of his father.

I never should have kissed her. I never should have kissed her. I knew I shouldn't have crossed that line. Why did I do that? Father's going to either kill me or have me shovel treasure from one side of the throne room to the other. He put his hands on the door. *Just suck it up and get it over with.* He pushed.

The door quietly swung inward. Nath stepped through a gap just wide enough for him and closed it. Straight ahead, his father sat on the throne, same as a man, great wings folded behind his back. His clawed hands were on his knees, and his eyes were closed. Behind him, his long tail coiled around the legs of the throne. Everything in the room seemed insignificant in his presence.

Nath walked forward. His feet scuffled over the loose treasure covering the floor. Metal clinked against metal, making it difficult for him to move in his preferred silence. He chose to abandon any subtlety and announced himself. "Father, I am here."

"I know," Balzurth responded in a low, canyon-deep voice. "I understand that you have been spending your time in the forges. You and Maefon."

"I can explain that." Nath rolled his thumbs behind his back. "It just happened. It won't happen again. I swear."

Balzurth's right eye popped open. The big orb had a golden flare to it. His chin, covered with short horns on the bottom, tilted. "Why would you stop?"

"Uh, it's forbidden."

Balzurth scratched his chin. "I don't recall making weapons being forbidden. Of course, it's been some time since the forges were used, but when I heard the news that you were hammering steel on your own, I admit, I was excited."

He doesn't know! Yes!

"Well, that's a relief," Nath said, rubbing the back of his neck.

Balzurth leaned toward him. "Unless, you were talking about something else? Were you?"

"Well, uh..."

"Out with it, Nath. Now is no time for secrets." Balzurth pressed him. "You are a hundred years old. You must be honest, forthcoming, and trustworthy if I am to rely on you. The bond between father and son should be like iron. Will it be, or won't it be?"

The last thing Nath wanted to do was get himself or Maefon in trouble. What he did was egregious. His father's eyes seemed to bore into him. *I think he knows. He has to know. He's toying with me.*

"Nath, look me in the eye. What happened?"

He avoided Balzurth's gaze for moments and finally, without looking at him, confessed. "I kissed Maefon, Father. I'm sorry. I... I just couldn't help it." Then Nath looked at his father. He wasn't certain, but Balzurth's thin lips seemed to be bent up in a smile at the corners. The smoldering eyes of judgment seemed almost approving. "Please don't punish Maefon. It was my doing. I swear it. She is innocent."

"So that was your first kiss?" Balzurth asked.

"Well, yes. And the last. I promise. I know it's forbidden."

Balzurth leaned back. He patted the side of his throne. "Climb up here, son."

Nath did as he was told and plopped down beside his father. Balzurth put his hand behind his back in support. *Oh, he's going to crush me.*

"Relax, son. You aren't in trouble, and you haven't done anything wrong, but we do need to talk about it. Even though that isn't what I brought you here for. But it's the perfect time to address this *unique* situation." Balzurth's finger patted him on the back. "To be clear, it is forbidden for dragons to be intimate with the races. For example, a dragon couldn't marry a human. They are of a different kind. But your circumstances are different, being a dragon born a man. You will have feelings like a man, and you will experience like a man and be tempted like a man. But what you must remember is that you are a dragon, and one day you will meet a dragon that is meant just for you."

"So it's fine that I spend time with Maefon?" he said, hopeful.

"She is Trahaydeen, Nath, and their relationships with dragons are limited. A more intimate relationship with her is not something that she should pursue. That is forbidden. They are caretakers, given much trust to live among the dragons. They should not break their word."

"What will happen if she does?"

"She will have to leave."

Chapter 11

Nath jumped up. "No, I don't want her to leave. It was my fault!"

"Easy son. Sit."

Nath complied.

"We'll let this one incident pass. I don't see a point in mentioning it. But you should be mindful of the consequences, and now you are. Do you understand?"

Head down, Nath nodded. "Yes, I understand." His heart twisted inside his chest. Now that he couldn't have her, he wanted her more, but he didn't want to lose her. "This won't be easy. She's my closest friend."

Balzurth nodded. "Yes, I know. It's good that you have one. We all need a friend we can rely on, and the Trahaydeen are here in part to make life easier for you, but even they can become infatuated with the dragons. If they are overcome by it, they are banished."

"Father, it might not be so bad if I wasn't shunned by the dragons. I just don't understand it. I'm your son. Why don't they like me?"

Sadly, Balzurth shook his head. He let out a sigh filled with his warm breath. Some smoke rolled from his nostrils. "It's not because of anything that you've done. I think it's because of something that happened long ago."

"What happened?"

"I wish I could share it, but we vowed to never speak of it in the mountain. However, it has to do with a betrayal from a man the dragons trusted."

Nath's back straightened. "It's not fair to judge me for someone else's works, is it?"

"Of course not. Listen, as I've told you, in time, you will earn their respect, but you are young. You just need to remain on the path you are on. The right one. The higher road must be sought when you deal with the world of the races. Some days, it's a delight, and others, it's a tightrope."

"I'm good on a tightrope." Nath looked to Balzurth. "So I'm going to deal with the races at some point? What do you mean?"

"Well, that's part of the reason that I brought you here. It's time for a talk, because soon I must go."

Nath made a puzzled look. "Go? Go where? You sleep most of the time."

"I don't," Balzurth said, stretching out his speech. "It's mostly meditating."

"No, it's sleeping. I've never seen a dragon snore when they are meditating." Nath punched his father in the thigh. "But if you want to call it meditating, that's fine. After all, you are the king. So where are you going?"

"To the land beyond the murals." Balzurth turned his head toward the massive mural behind him, filled with painted images of dragons in different parts of the lands. "It's something I do, part of my charge as the dragon king. I won't be gone long, a few years perhaps, depending on my duties."

"Is Mother there?" Nath asked. He never knew who his mother was, and Balzurth never talked about her. He saw the narrowing in Balzurth's eyes. He'd asked often, and it seemed to irritate Balzurth as if a deep pain reflected in his eyes.

"No," Balzurth replied, showing a frown.

"Father, if she is dead, then you can tell me. I can understand it."

"I've never asked this, but I'm going to ask now. Don't ever ask me about her again. When the time comes, you will know. You must trust me on this matter."

Nath's shoulders slumped. "You say that about everything. Just wait. Just wait. Just wait. I'm tired of waiting. I'm ready for anything."

"No, you are not!" Balzurth's outburst shook the throne room. Coins slid down their piles. In a stern voice, he continued, "You must learn patience, Nath. You have a long life to live; don't rush into it. If you do, you might find yourself on a path that you cannot recover from, one filled with malice, haste, regret, turmoil, lies, and deceit. That is the world out there, and that is the world I brought you here to speak about. Do I have your attention?"

"Yes, Father," Nath said, nodding. The temperature in the room went up. He was sweating again. "I understand."

"Your understanding is youthful. My understanding is ancient. There is a difference. That is what you need to understand. Time and experience bring wisdom. The dragons live long and have learned and experienced much. That is why you must learn from them. Don't be so eager to venture out with a full head of steam. It can be dangerous, and you are important."

"Father, I just, I just want to... live."

"And you will." Balzurth's voice lowered. "The time will come when you will be ready to leave Dragon Home. You need to be best prepared."

"I'll be leaving?" Nath said, feeling a tingling sensation running through his body. "Does that mean that I'll be a dragon soon? I'll get my scales?" He stood up, inspecting his arms with his eyes. "My wings?"

"No, you will be going just as you are, Nath. A man. It is out there that you will have to earn your scales, and it won't be easy. You'll be surrounded by the races. They are full of folly."

"How soon? I'm ready... er, I mean, I'll be ready when the time comes."

"In another century, on your two-hundredth celebration day, you should be fully ready."

"Two hundred!" Nath plopped down. His face sank into his hands, and he shook his head. "That's forever!"

"A hundred years is not even a drop in the pond when compared to forever. In time, you'll look back, and it will seem little more than nothing."

Nath groaned. He didn't think he could put up with another hundred years of being shunned by the dragons. And he certainly couldn't resist Maefon another hundred years. That would be impossible. "I'm sorry, Father, but I'm about to burst out of my skin. I won't gain my scales, and I guess I can't do anything different. It will all be the same day over and over again. I need a challenge. I want adventure."

"You have the forge. Mastering steel can take many years, even decades. Focus on that."

Nath hopped out of the chair. His feet hit the ground hard. He started walking away. "Suddenly, I've lost interest."

Chapter 12

"Nath, you aren't dismissed." Balzurth's tail slid out from underneath the throne and blocked Nath's path. "I haven't even told you everything that I brought you to hear. And you should know better than to walk away from me like that. It's disrespectful."

Throwing his arms up in the air, Nath said, "I don't know what could be so important now that you just can't share it with me later. After all, we have at least a hundred more years, assuming that I don't have to wait another hundred on top of that. I'll probably have a beard down to my toes by then. And what if my hair turns gray? Did you even think about that?"

"Your hair won't turn gray for a very long time, trust me." Balzurth lifted his head toward the ceiling and puffed out the armor-like scales on his chest. "Look at my scales—they are still as red as ever. Even the gold keeps its luster. Now sit and listen."

"I'll sit, but I might not listen." Nath took his seat on Balzurth's tail. He knew he was being disrespectful, but he couldn't help it—he was mad. His cheeks were hot from it. "Go ahead, and if you will, try to keep it short, seeing how I have to get back to nothing to do for the next century."

"If you keep it up, Nath, then I might not give you your present for your one-hundred-year celebration." Balzurth's clawed hand scratched at his chin. "It would be a shame to keep it all to myself, considering it was made specifically for you."

Nath leaned forward, his eyes wide. "You made me a present?"

"Yes, one that has been decades in the making. It took a little longer than I'd planned, but it's finally ready."

Nath's rigid demeanor shifted. His frown turned upward into a smile. Inching upward from his seat, he said, "Where is it?"

"Well, there's no fun in that, now is there? You know how we play this game. Your present could be anywhere in the throne room."

Nath's smile stretched all the way across his face. He took off running. Ever since he was young, he had come to the throne room and searched for his present among the treasure. It happened every ten years, but this year, he'd forgotten about it completely. He couldn't believe he was so distracted that he forgot about his celebration-day present. Running up and sliding down piles of treasure, he scanned for anything new. "Hot or cold, Father? Hot or cold?" He dug elbow deep in the piles. "Hot or cold?"

"Cold, but remember, I'm only giving you a fair amount of hints."

"Yes, yes, I know." Nath jumped from one pile to another. He had many unique treasures his father gave to him, but this was the first one that had been made by his father. "Is it buried?" he said, not hiding his excitement. "The last time you buried it. It was hard to find."

"Perhaps a little. Maybe half in, maybe half out."

Nath came across the painting of the radiant platinum-haired woman. He picked it up and said, "It's not this, is it?"

"No."

"Is this Mother?"

"No," Balzurth said, slowly shaking his head.

"Do you know who it is then? She's incredibly fetching. Even Maefon says she thinks she's beautiful, and you know Maefon doesn't think anyone is prettier than her."

"Yes, I know the unforgettable face, but the name is slippery in my mind. Trinity, Minos... Ah, it's been so long, but like any treasure, there is a story behind it."

Nath tossed the painting aside and kept searching. "Hot or cold? Hot or cold?"

"You are getting warmer."

Rummaging through every pile, Nath's eyes swept over the stacks. He was plenty familiar with the objects in the throne room. He'd played here often as a boy. And even though he hadn't seen everything, he certainly had a feel for most of it. Coins and gems sliding under his feet, he jumped the piles like a frog on a lily pad. He landed on the object he had his eye on. "Hot or cold, Father? Hot or—"

"Hot."

Nath's eyes seized on the sword handle protruding out of a treasure pile. The pommel was fashioned with the face of a dragon. A handle that could be gripped with two hands was a rich brown with the distressed look of dragon horn. The crossguard of the sword was two metal dragon heads plated with gold. Each had gemstone eyes, one with emeralds and the other rubies. Nath had never seen such intricate work on a sword. For a moment, he wondered if it was only part of one. He looked back at his father and said, "Is this it?"

Balzurth nodded.

Using both hands, Nath pulled the sword free. Coins chimed against the edge of the blade. The lighting in the room flickered. *Shing!* The double-edged blade looked as sharp and straight as any he'd ever seen. The metal was bright with a blue shine shimmering within the steel. "It's magnificent!" Nath said with awe.

"Thank you," Balzurth replied.

Nath cut the blade through the air using short strokes at first that became longer. He spun the blade with his wrist then fancifully behind his back. "The balance is perfect! It has heft without being heavy. Yet it's so big."

"It's dragon steel blessed by magic, son. It cannot break. It will cut anything. That sword does not have an equal, I assure you."

"Whoa! And you spent decades on it?" Nath said, flipping it from side to side between both hands. "Just for me?"

"Yes, and I enjoyed every hour and every day making it. Dragon steel is very hard work, and I had to be patient. If I had not been, the work would not be what it is today. It would be incomplete. With patience comes perfection."

Nath was only half listening. The sword was nothing short of an extension of his own arm. He was one with it. He chopped, thrust, parried, and sliced with lightning-quick movements. The shining steel whistled when it cut the air.

"How could you make this when you are so… vast?"

"I have my ways. Like Master Elween, I'm built differently than most dragons. But I'll teach you more about that—"

"I know, later." The blade handle shocked Nath. He dropped the sword. "Ow!"

Chapter 13

Before the sword landed, he caught it on the toe of his boot and kicked it back up. He snatched it with his other hand. "It stung me. Why did it sting me?"

Balzurth shrugged his wings. "Perhaps he thought you were being disrespectful."

"He? The sword is a *he*, like a person?"

"Yes, he has his own thoughts and enchantments and will keep your best intentions in mind. He will be a friend that you can count on."

"Well, I can see that already." Nath's eyes were still glued to the blade. "I can't thank you enough, Father. Do you have a name for him?"

"No, I left that honor for you."

"Hmmm… What is a good name?" He rubbed the palm of his reddening hand. "Sting might be a fine name. Do you like that?"

Balzurth shrugged. "Perhaps if it was a much smaller blade, but that is a great one."

"Ah, true." Nath glanced between the sword and his father. That was when he noticed his father's teeth jutting out over the side of his mouth. The name hit him like a hammer. "Fang!"

Balzurth gave an approving nod. "I like it."

"I think he does too," Nath said. "The handle is warm, like a living thing."

"I'm sure you and Fang will have much to learn in your journeys when the time comes, but for now, Fang must remain in the throne room."

All of the excitement in Nath's body deflated. The boundless energy within him leaked out of his toes. "Huh? I can't take my present with me? We will only be in Dragon Home.

And I want to share with Master Elween. I know she can't beat me if I have Fang. I need to train with him."

"There are a few more enchantments I have left to do before I turn you both loose in the world."

"Turn us loose?" Nath rested Fang against his shoulder. "What do you mean?"

"That is the second reason that I brought you here, though I'd wanted to do it in another order." Balzurth put his hands on his lap and cleared his throat. A puff of smoke came out. "We've talked about the races over the years and our relationships with them. You've studied in the Trahaydeen libraries about them. But the time will come when you will have to move out into the world of men, and it is there that you must earn your scales."

Nath returned to his seat on his father's tail. Balzurth had his full attention now. "So I will become a dragon then?"

"Of course. But you will face many trials in order to do so. Unlike dragons, you are born a man, and being such, the path you will take will be much harder. That is why I want you fully prepared for the journey. It won't be easy. Trust me."

"Well, what am I supposed to do?"

"You have many lost brothers and sisters who are suffering. The races trap them, hunt them, sell them. You will be charged with rescuing them. Protecting them. But you cannot get too close to the races. They have different ambitions than dragons. I'm not saying there isn't much good in them—there is plenty—but the bad in them is much worse. Time among them brings much temptation. You are too young. With time, you develop wisdom."

"But I want to save the dragons now." Nath shot to his feet and started pacing. "I mean, if they are in danger now, shouldn't I go and help them? They need me. And if I help them, they will like me. Yes?"

Balzurth shook his head. "Don't ever expect a thank you for your good works. Your works should come from your heart. That is all that matters. Do you understand?"

"No, not really."

"That's because you are still young. You might look like a grown man, but you are very youthful inside. You must pay attention and observe the actions of others. That is how you will learn." Balzurth's massive mouth opened like a cave full of teeth as he yawned. "Listen, I promise to talk to you more about all of this when I return. In the meantime, the High Dragon Council will be in charge. Don't give them any trouble. I want a good report when I return. Until then, keep yourself busy. I think Fang will need a scabbard. That would be a fine project for you. And take your lessons seriously. You still have much preparation to do."

"You're leaving now?" Nath said, watching his father ease out of his chair. The end of his father's tail brushed past Nath's leg. "You just can't leave me on the edge like this. Not now. I have so many questions."

"Son, there are affairs that I must attend to in the land beyond the murals. Duty requires my presence every few decades or so. Now, the time has come again. You will understand one day." Heading toward the mural, Balzurth looked at him. "Son, make the most of the mountain, and do not depart from it no matter what. You are not ready. Also, spend more time with your older brother, Slivver. He should be returning soon. And most importantly, remember, I love you, no matter what."

"I-I love you too." Nath's voice trailed off as he watched his father walk into the mural behind the throne. Balzurth became a part of one of the painted images in the mural, flying among the other dragons but clearly the greatest one of all. "Goodbye."

With his father gone, the throne room felt like a tomb. Nath instantly missed him. He stared at the mural for the longest time, the images moving with very slow and subtle changes. His father flew farther away until, hours later, his image was gone.

One of Nath's knees sagged. It stirred up his blood, waking him from a trance. There was so much running through his mind. He had Fang. Eventually, he would have scales. He wanted to do it all now. Traipsing through the treasure while swinging Fang from side to side, he said, "I can't wait one hundred more years. That's forever, Fang. Don't you think?"

Fang's blade shone in the light.

"I don't really think that any more work needs to be done to you, either," he said to the blade. "You look perfect to me."

"And you look perfect to me," Maefon said, peeking inside the throne room door. "I see you have a new friend."

"Yes, and I see that you have invaded my father's throne room without permission. You can't do that, Maefon."

Easing her way inside, she made a pouty frown. "I was worried about you. I've been waiting outside in case I needed to come to your defense. After all, none can resist me."

Nath marched toward her. "Yes, keep telling yourself that."

Peeking past him, she said, "So King Balzurth is gone now, right?"

"Yes." He halted her from going farther inside with his arm.

"I knew he was gone. There was a stir in the air. A chill. It was as if a great warmth had left the mountain." She clung to his arm. "I've never felt anything like that before, but with you here, I know that all will be right. What did your father say about us? Are you in trouble?"

"No," Nath said, forcing himself to look in her eyes. "But I'm sorry to say that it's best that we don't spend as much time together as before. You're Trahaydeen. You understand, don't you?"

Her eyes watered. She turned and ran away.

Chapter 14

Nath spent the next few weeks in the smithy. Even though he had Fang to look forward to using, he still needed to keep his mind off of things. He labored in front of the forge and hammered metal on the anvil, making small hammers, axes, and knives. He'd started off too big before, and now focused on mastering the smaller items first. At the same time, he was able to avoid Maefon. At least, it kept his thoughts occupied. It hurt seeing her storm out of the throne room, and he hadn't seen her since.

He pounded the sharp edge of a one-bladed battle-axe. Sparks flew from the hammer. *Bang! Bang! Bang!* He lifted it from the anvil. "Looking better. Much better. I think I'll be able to put a nice shine on it." He set it aside on the table where many handleless weapons lay. A lot of them were warped and cracked, but some were usable.

Nath rinsed his sweat-smeared face off with water from a bucket that sat on the floor. Flinging the water from his fingers, he made his way over to where the scabbard hung on a cold forge. He'd made it for Fang. He smiled at his handiwork. Fang was longer than a normal sword—too long to carry from his hip. So he'd made a sword belt that he could strap over his shoulders. As for the scabbard itself, that was a different animal altogether. Fang's blade was sharp enough to split hair. Sliding the blade in and out of the scabbard would damage it if it wasn't designed precisely. He shaped the scabbard out of hard wood he'd stained black. He made sure the neck opening was firmly made to guide the blade straight inside. Fang would snap in snugly to the lock at the top. Then to soften the exterior, he wrapped the scabbard in dyed leather. He took it to the throne room, tested it once, and seeing it worked perfectly, he brought it back to the smithy to add the finishing touches.

It might not be a sword, but knowing how to care for a sword is a big step.

Nath's stomach let out a growl. He'd become so consumed that he'd forgotten to eat for days. Deciding to call it a day, he shut down the forge, tidied up his work, grabbed the scabbard, and left. On his way to eat, he figured he'd put Fang in his new sheath. As he traversed the corridors, his mind started to wander. Images of Maefon came to mind. He missed her and hated the fact that he'd hurt her.

I should check on her. I'm sure she is well, but I have to see her.

Even though Nath had avoided crossing her path, he had a pretty good idea where she would be. If she wasn't with him, she spent her time in the Trahaydeen's inner sanctum. If she wasn't there, she would be in the dragon nursery. Maefon loved the nursery, and she was as happy there as anywhere.

Nath changed direction and headed to the nursery. Even though the scabbard wouldn't be something that interested Maefon too much, at least he could show her what he'd been working on.

A natural archway made with seams of pure gold let into the nursery. Inside the archway was another large, well-illuminated cavern. The stone walls were smooth and slick. Rocks made a trough at the bottom filled with water that ran along the edge of the cave. A natural spring ran over the high rocks, making waterfalls of clear water. It was a very peaceful place. Small dragons, newly born, scattered behind the rocks in the room the moment they saw Nath.

Kneeling down, Nath said, "Come now, there is no need to be afraid of me. You'll dislike me enough when you're older, I'm sure. I see no reason why we can't have a truce now."

The fledglings were an assortment of breeds. There were husky bronze and slender copper dragons. Green lilies with very long tails, and baby red rocks with no wings at all on their backs. A very cute crimson dynamo crawled toward Nath with its head low. "Hello, little one," Nath said, letting the dragon sniff his finger. "See, there is nothing to fear from—" The dragon bit him. "Ow! You little brat!"

The Trahaydeen in the cavern started laughing. There were five of them, men and women, each holding a dragon to their chest and petting them. One of the five remained still, her back to him. Her hair was bound up on top of her head. She dipped a hand in the pool of water surrounding her where baby dragons swam.

Nath waved to the Trahaydeen. "Greetings."

"Be well," they replied, each with a warming smile. The elves were gentle and kind, all dressed in similar fashion—dark robes with light-blue flower patterns sewn at the sleeves and bottom of their robes. For a change, Maefon was dressed in the same modest manner.

Nath sat down beside her. "Hello, Maefon."

Her eyes remained fixed on the dragons swimming in the pool of water. The water bubbled and swirled beneath them. Steam rose from the water. Finally, she said, "Hello, Nath. Did you come here to break my heart again?"

"Come now, Maefon. You know that I would never ever hurt you. And it's not as if this isn't hurting me too. You know I adore you. How couldn't I?" He rubbed her shoulder. She scooted out of reach.

"If you *adore* me and *care* for me, then why haven't I seen you in weeks? Hmmm?" Bitterness filled her voice. "That doesn't sound like an *adoring* and *caring* person to me. You are just fooling yourself."

Rubbing his neck, he replied, "I've been working on my blacksmithing skills, and time got away from me. Look, I made this… for Fang."

Her gaze drifted to the scabbard. "What is that, a stick wrapped up in leather? How delightful."

"Listen, I worked hard on this. There's no need to be insulting. I would never do that to you."

Maefon put her face in her hands and started crying. Her body trembled with every sob. "Oh, Nath, I am so sorry. I don't mean to be so spiteful, but it hurts so much knowing that I cannot be with you." She clutched her chest. "My heart aches."

Nath's eyes watered. He wiped them. His own heart turned in his chest. Maefon was always so strong and confident. He found himself stunned that she'd come undone all on account of him. Heart pounding, he swallowed the lump in his throat. "You know I would do anything for you, Maefon. Anything, not to hurt you. But I can't risk getting you banished from here. Then I would never see you."

With tears dripping from her pretty eyes, she said, "I love you, Nath, and if I can't be with you the way a woman should be with a man, then I can't live like this."

"What are you saying?"

Barely able to control herself, she stood up. "I'm leaving the Trahaydeen." Without another word, she departed, leaving Nath with his heart breaking.

Chapter 15

INSTEAD OF SITTING IN THE nursery with his jaw hanging, Nath got up and chased after Maefon. She was nowhere to be seen, and there were so many paths through the mountain she could have taken. Nath's nostrils flared. He caught the sweet fragrance of perfume lingering in the air. It was Maefon's, mild and pleasant. With his senses in full swing, Nath ran after her.

Maefon's bare feet slapped on the stones, echoing in the corridor. She was fast, as most elves were, but no match for Nath. He caught up with her and grabbed her by the wrist. "Maefon, stop. Please," he pleaded. "We have to talk about this. And you can't leave. You just can't. It's your dream to be among the dragons. You love it more than anything."

"Apparently not," she said with her chin down. "Just go, Nath. Leave me. It's all for the better." She jerked away and started walking from him with her fists balled up at her sides. "And don't chase after me anymore!"

Nath ignored it, catching up to her but keeping a little bit of distance. "I read in the Tomes of Alvareen that women like to be chased after and they get mad when you don't."

"Alvareen is a fool. And clearly he writes from a man's point of view."

"He's an elven sage. The great romancer. Certainly, in his thousands of years, he couldn't have been that far off base." He stepped in front of her and smiled. "Come now, you don't doubt the wisdom of such a grand philosopher, do you? You've read his words with your own lips to me, trying to woo me."

She pushed through him. "Don't joke about this."

Nath recited one of his favorite poems. Short but fluid, the elven words spun from his lips like silk from a spider's web. She stopped in her tracks.

There's flourish in the meadows where the cattle chew the hay,
The grasshoppers' legs sing the dance,
With moist lips, the young maiden serenades the moon,
And the stars in the sky delight,
On the sweet breath of the wind, the fairies spin a woven song,
Where the honey of the bees flows like gold.
Never tarry for love that waits from the reeds to the chasms on high.
Nothing fades, all comes aflutter, when the troubadours of mirth march on.

She turned with a glowering look. "That was not Alvareen. It was horrible."

"Horrible. I wrote that one. You said you loved it."

"Yes, and I suppose I lied. I shouldn't have, but I did because I didn't want to hurt your feelings." A ray of a smile started on her lips. "Did you steal it from an orc?"

"Now, that is unfair. I know you like it, or you wouldn't be smiling."

As the color returned to her cheeks, she said, "I'm only smiling because it's laughable. '*Never tarry for love that waits from the reeds to the chasms on high.*' What does that even mean?"

"It's poetry. It doesn't really mean anything. You just write what you feel, and it comes out a jumble. I don't know."

"Please, just don't say it again, at least in elven."

Playfully, Nath crept toward her with his fingers needling the air. "Someone needs a tickle."

"Don't you dare!" She ran. Nath pounced on her, tackling her to the ground. His fingers dug at her ribs. "Stop it, Nath! Top it!" She giggled so hard she couldn't get the words out. "Top it!"

"Are you saying *stop it*? Because I am hearing *top it*, and I don't know what that means. Top what?"

She elbowed him hard in the ribs. "Stop it!"

"Ow." Nath winced as he rolled away from her body. "I'm topping it. Gads, you didn't have to bust a rib. I was about to yield."

Catching her breath, she let out a long sigh with a bit of laughter contained within. "At least you can still make me laugh. It's another one of your irresistible gifts. You are growing into a fine man, or dragon. I guess that's why this is so hard for me. I'm drawn to you more than ever."

He reached over and held her hand. "I feel the same. Perhaps on my next century of celebration, when I leave, then you can come with me."

She looked at him with her brows lifted. "What? Another hundred years you must stay? That's a long time, and I'm only slated to be here another fifty years. But you are ready for the world out there now. I know this." She squeezed his hand. "You are ready for anything. I just think your father is very overprotective."

"Father is wise."

"Yes, I know, but you are wise too." She put her arms around his waist, snuggling up to him as she placed her cheek on his shoulder. "You know, I told you I didn't want you to chase me, but I did. You are very wise for a young man."

"Alvareen said some women like pursuit and few shun it. They want a man to work for it—"

She put her finger on his lips. "Sssh. I don't care what Alvareen says. Those are just books we read from some lonely old hermit that lived in a tower all of his life. He never married. How wise could he really be about women? But his poetry is quite splendid. No, Nath, you figured it out. You know my heart. I just wish I could give it to you. And thanks for pursuing me. Normally, I would shun that, but I know that you care deeply. You truly are a prince, and every woman in the land, whether they admit it or not, is looking for a prince, even me, and now I've found one that I can't have."

He kissed her hair. "Let's take it a day at a time and see what happens." A trio of silver dragons, sleek in build and stunning in color, moseyed down the corridor without giving them so much as a look. "And to think that I am prince. Hah, an outsider would never know it."

"Well, I do." She kissed his chin. "Oh, prince."

Chapter 16

Maefon casually made her way back to Covelum, the home of the Trahaydeen. She had a small spring in her step, and her long curls bounced on her shoulders after she let her hair down. Covelum was a mill of quiet activity. The elves who weren't busy tending to the dragons took care of the elven village built into the rocks. There were fountains in the plaza and a small outdoor theater for entertainment. Hutches for quarters had been dug out above storefronts. It was all carved out of the mineral-rich mountain rocks in the likeness of the homes in the elven city of Elome. The rock had been shaped and chiseled to look like trees. The branches and leaves had been painted, giving it all the strong illusion of reality.

"Hello," she said, waving as she passed by her friends. There were two hundred elves in all, living in quiet and humble service to the dragons. They required little but slept in facilities much like home. They ate fish that swam in the streams that coursed through the mountain. There was rich soil within the rock that the elves enchanted to harness the sun's light. Almost everything an elf would need was provided for through their cooperation with the dragons.

Hurrying up the steps, she slipped onto the terrace of her hutch. Covelum had been her home for a long time, and she was more than fond of it. She tousled her hair and arched her back, watching the elves steadily fulfill their duties. Not a single thing was ever out of place, it seemed. They moved in harmony, setting tables, preparing food, and cleaning up after one another. Every day was devoted to making things better, not worse. They sought perfection. Order.

A soft whistle caught her ear. She turned. A heavy, deep-blue curtain was drawn in the back. She pushed the curtain back. An elf with wavy black hair and long sideburns that came to a point lay on her bedding. Dressed in attire like hers, he'd propped himself up against a pile of colorful pillows of all shapes and sizes as he chewed on a lime-colored apple.

"What a surprise to find you here, Chazzan," she said, offering a welcoming smile. She crawled onto the bed with him and took a bite out of his apple. "You aren't supposed to be eating in bed. It's awful manners."

"I was sleepy, hungry, and tired of waiting, Maefon. You have been missed. And even though it's mostly my idea, I have to admit, I'm a bit jealous of the time you spend with the dragon man." Chazzan spoke with the slyness of a serpent. A cunning intelligence lurked behind his dark eyes. His elven features, sharp and distinct, seemed even more so than a typical elf, leaving him with an air of rigidness about him. "So how goes the seduction, my priceless treasure?"

She batted her eyes at him then made a sad face, allowing tears to stream down her face. "I turned on my geysers, and he ate it all up. I'm certain he would do almost anything for me at this point. He is strong but naïve, though I tell him otherwise." She palmed his chest with her hand, rubbing it back and forth. "It's not nearly like you and me, of course." She took the apple out of his hand and tossed it away. Crawling on top of him, she kissed him fully. "All of this deception increases my longing for you. It's hard to focus on him when I'm thinking about you."

"I can't say I blame you. Perhaps it would be the same for me, if I were in a like situation. Ho-hum, I was beginning to think that Balzurth would never leave, but now, the moment has arrived." Wrapping her up in his arms, he pulled her against his chest. "Decades of planning will finally be executed."

"I'm surprised the Trahaydeen have been deceived. There is no doubt among them. They, like Nath, trust us fully, as do the dragons."

Chazzan smelled her hair. "We are Caligin. Deception is what we are born to do. We are elves, the elves with ebony hearts in our chests. No one sees us coming until it is too late. Think about it, Maefon—we have infiltrated not only the Trahaydeen, but Dragon Home. The world is ours to master as the Lord Dark Day says. Once we execute his plans, we shall be united with him and rule at his side forever."

"I can taste victory on my lips."

"And I on mine, but I like the taste of yours better." He kissed her again, long and fully. "You ignite me."

"Chazzan, are you certain this is safe? We stand little chance against the dragons if caught. Actually, none at all. We'll be turned to ash."

"Nay, we'll be long gone. And with Balzurth gone, there won't be any pursuit. The Dragon High Council cannot depart from Dragon Home in his absence. The dragons will stay put and mete out justice later. They are patient, more so than elves. Only Balzurth can unleash them. Besides, they won't be prepared for what is coming. The chaos and misdirection we spread will be in place. They won't know what to do."

"And all of this is because of Nath?"

Chazzan shrugged. "Lord Dark Day wants him separated from the flock. That is all. It seems absurdly simple but at the same time brilliant. Sometimes, I think I must have thought of it myself."

"No doubt you could have, love," she said, toying with his sideburns. "Do you suppose he'll kill Nath?"

"I don't think he needs him dead. He just needs him out of Dragon Home. Lord Dark Day says the rest will take care of itself."

"He believes the world will consume Nath, doesn't he?"

"Don't you?"

Maefon nodded. "Yes, he won't stand a chance against the races." There was a dark flicker in her eyes. "And the races don't have a prayer against the Caligin."

CHAPTER 17

NATH SPENT THE NEXT FEW days working the metal in the smithy and training with Master Elween. Even though he couldn't show Master Elween Fang, he still took the scabbard he made. Master Elween gave a nod but said very little, as always. Instead, she had Nath do pushups and sit-ups until his arms and belly burned like fires. Then she sent him on a run, carrying a rucksack loaded with rocks. For whatever reason, the tormenting training didn't faze Nath so much as before. His outlook had brightened.

Drenched in sweat and panting after the laden run, he said to Master Elween, "Will you come to the throne room and at least let me show you Fang?"

Perched on her rock as if she were a part of the stone herself, Master Elween said, "No."

Hands on his knees, Nath replied, "Don't say I didn't invite you to anything. Oh, and you could come to the forge. My skill bending metal is improving. I've made knives shaped like dragon claws, and if I don't mind saying so myself, the handles are quite fetching."

Stone faced as a dragon could be with eyelids that never blinked, Master Elween said, "I'll summon you for the next lesson. You are dismissed." The forest dragon slunk off her rock and out of the Training Lair.

Dropping the bag of rocks from his shoulders, Nath said, "So much for impressing her." He shrugged. "Oh well, at least I can look forward to spending time with Maefon in Covelum tonight." He sniffed the air. "Whew! Either I smell as rotten as an onion, or it's this cave. Come to think of it, it's been a while since I bathed. I can't show up to Maefon like this."

Quickly, Nath tidied up the Training Lair and departed. He headed to one of the many hot springs in Dragon Home. The dragons were notorious for lounging in the hot waters. He headed to the spas in the rocks, thick in steamy vapors. Inside were several pools of burbling water. In the largest pool, an orange blaze dragon was stretched out from one end to the other. The long lashes of her eyes were closed as two elves waded in the waters, massaging her scales and filing her nails. She was a beautiful dragon with a body twice as long as Nath was tall and a long tail swishing slowly over the floor by the edge of her pool.

Nath crept in, grabbed a towel, undressed, and slipped into a small bubbling spring all to himself. "Ah," he moaned as he sank neck deep into the water. The bubbling mineral-rich waters massaged his skin and muscles. "Why don't I spend more time in here?" An image of Maefon came to mind. She was splendid in his imagination. "I wish I could be spending more time here with Mae."

When they were younger, they would play for hours in the springs together, but now, that innocence had become something that seemed inappropriate. Still, he wished she were there.

Thinking out loud, he said, "Oh well, I'll see her soon enough. I'm certain we'll figure things out. At least she's speaking to me and we have time carved out for tonight."

A slosh of water caught his ear. He opened his eyes. The orange blaze was leaving. She didn't hide the displeasure on her face either.

"Oh, come now, I can't even spend time in the springs with my brethren without them rudely abandoning me?" Nath grabbed his towel and got out of the water. "Just stay. I'll go. For the love of Balzurth, I've never done a thing to any single one of you."

Storming through the corridors, he headed to his personal cove. The stone staircase he took led into a cave made of smooth walls and floors. There were pillows and folded blankets on the floor, some leather-bound tomes, and a cupboard of dried fruit and meat. Nath didn't sleep much and had little need for things, but he did have some chests and a small wardrobe. They were things the elves of Covelum gave to him. He put on a pair of navy-blue trousers and an old gold cotton shirt. A long rectangular mirror leaned against the wall. Staring at the mirror, he combed his fingers through his hair a few times. He took a brush and comb to his flame-red mane. "Perhaps it's my glorious hair the dragons are so jealous of. After all, they might as well be bald, given they only have scales, and my flowing locks are nothing short of perfect."

He grabbed some dried spice fruit from a cupboard to freshen his breath and hurried out of his room and down the steps to meet Maefon. Jogging, he made it to Covelum a few minutes later. It appeared the majority of the Trahaydeen were present, dressed in the dark elven robes trimmed with blue lace. The light posts that always glowed with lantern light were decorated with colorful wreaths and streamers. Picnic tables had food stacked up high. Fountains of rose-colored elven wine flowed from their cisterns. A small group of elves milled through their brethren, playing flutes and string instruments in perfect harmony. Dragons surrounded the stands, sitting where they could comfortably see the stage.

"Hello, Nath." Maefon slipped in behind him and tickled his ribs. "I was beginning to wonder if you were going to make it. I thought you might have forgotten our budding romance."

"Hah! I'd never forget you, Mae," he said. "You should know better than to doubt that."

"I don't know, I see your eyes caressing the steel. You are obsessed with it." She held his hand with hers and walked him toward the stage. "But I forgive your boyish silliness. For now is the time of the Festival of Change. The celebration of the new elven spring begins, and I'm glad you are here for it."

"Your people are my people," Nath said, holding her hand tighter. "If it wasn't for the elves, it would have been a lonely childhood. When you like to talk, there is nothing worse than not having anyone to talk to. The elves have always been here for me, and I for them."

Maefon led him to a seat in the front, and they sat down together. Sitting hip to hip with him, she said, "I wish you had come early. I would have fed you. The dragon soil has been so rich this season, and the fruit tastes as if it was from Elome's very soil. Oh..." She sighed. "I do miss the sun so, Nath. The change of seasons, the breeze through the branches. I hope to take you to Elome someday."

"I would love that. Perhaps we should take more walks on the mountainside. We haven't done that for years. We can always watch the seasons change from there."

"A walk? Don't you think I can run with you?"

Showing a clever smile, he replied, "We both know you could not keep up with me."

"Hah! We shall see soon then, assuming you don't hide in the hot little dungeon, talking to your forges and irons."

He put his arm on the back of her chair. His fingers rested on her slender shoulder. "I'd never hide from you."

She locked her fingers with his. "You couldn't anyway." She giggled. "Oh look, there on stage. Chazzan—you remember Chazzan, don't you? He is the orchestrator of the shows."

"Of course. I know all the elves. Just because I don't see you often doesn't mean I forget."

Chazzan stood out among the elves. He was the tallest, oldest, and least talkative of them. He was on the stage, helping the actors with their costumes. Along with Maefon, Nath waved. Chazzan turned away. "He doesn't smile so much, does he?"

"He takes his charges very seriously. Just ask him, and he'll tell you. He's very devoted to our discipline. Perhaps too devoted. I think he wants to *be* a dragon. He talks about them as if they were his own people. It's almost offensive."

"Well, he's clearly an elf. Look at his prominent features. Though he's like no other Trahaydeen," Nath said as he caught Maefon's questioning stare. "Aside from you, naturally."

"Good recovery, Nath. And yes, he boasts he is of the purest elven bloodline and that most elves should look more like him. He says many of our features are too rounded." She gave a quick approving nod. "I'm not so certain I believe it because he reminds us so much."

"Come now, I'm sure he is proud of his heritage, as we all are. But if I were to guess, I'd say that you are a perfect example of everything an elf should be."

"Oh, Nath, you flatter me." She leaned on his shoulder. "Don't stop. Go on. Your words are like a soft summer breeze in my hair."

"Softer, I'd hope. So what is this play about?" He caught the brothers, Pevly and Tevlin, on stage and waved. They were dressed like jesters with golden star-shaped hats. They juggled knives and axes hand to hand. Nath gave a puzzled look. "Or is it a play?"

"No, this is a show of talents. Many participate with dance, song, and daring stunts. Chazzan made the change. Not all agreed with it, but it is in line with elven tradition. In Elome, they have plays, musicals, orchestras, and shows of skill and daring. Though I will miss the drama of the old plays, I admit, I'm looking forward to this."

Nath settled back into his chair. "Me too."

Chazzan appeared on the center stage. He lifted his arms. The elves fell silent, the lantern light dimmed. With a bow, he said, "Let the show begin."

Chapter 18

For hours, Nath was delighted with some of the most outstanding elfin showmanship that he'd ever seen. A female Trahaydeen started off by singing a ballad with words so sweet they would make a cave troll cry. And she was just one of many singers with voices that lifted hearts with sheer joy. But there were sad songs too, about lost loves from war, disease, and famine, and what seemed to be the worst of all, broken hearts.

Pevly and Tevlin each climbed their own length of pole twenty feet in the air. Loaded with a scabbard of knives and hatchets, they stood on one foot on poles narrower than their legs. With another twenty feet between them, they juggled razor-edged objects in full circles on their own. They did three blades one handed, and in harmony with one another, they switched to the other. With eight blades, they faced each other, passing them back and forth between them. Their arms and wrists pumped back and forth in a blur.

The elves in the audience roared.

On the edge of his seat, Nath watched a scene like he'd never seen before. The elves, normally calm and pleasant, had stepped out of their skins and gotten a little crazy this year.

They swilled their wine. Shoulder to shoulder, they howled gleeful jollies. They were having fun.

"I'm not used to seeing your people so worked up," Nath said to Maefon.

Behind her, an elf bumped her chair. She frowned. "This does seem a bit zealous, even for the Festival of Change. I never imagined the Showing would invoke so much passion among my kindred. I assure you, though, they are harmless."

"No, I have no fear. I just feel like a bit of a prude sitting here. I feel out of place not partaking in their reveling."

"Perhaps you would feel better with some elven wine to freshen your palate." She patted his thigh. "I think I could use some myself."

"Uh." Nath swept the happy faces in the seats behind him. "I suppose I could join in. But hurry. The next act is about to begin."

Getting up, she winked at him. "I'll be back before you can recite the entirety of your own name."

"The show will be over by then," he said as she went. Hands on his knees, he focused on the stage. There were so many surprises, he didn't know what to expect. A troupe of dancers came out in clothing sewn like bright dragon scales, horns, and claws. Somehow, they came together in a strange contortion the shape of a dragon. A mouth opened in the front, made from arms and hands, and flames erupted. Nath applauded and whistled. "Fantastic!"

Maefon returned with two goblets of wine. "Looks like I missed something."

"No, they are still going," Nath said, not containing his excitement. Absentmindedly, he took the goblet and drank. The elven wine was a sweet juice with a little burn to it. He swallowed it down. "Watch, Maefon, watch this!"

"I'm watching, Nath. I'm watching. But I'm not sure what I enjoy more, the show or watching your excitement." She took his empty goblet and handed him her own. "Here, take mine before you go hoarse from all of the shouting."

The show went through a few more acts, with one just as titillating as the next. Nath couldn't remember the last time he had so much fun. Finally, Chazzan appeared on the stage. His face was painted with dragon-like features. He stood two feet taller and wore pitch-black robes, and his shoulders were unnaturally broad. His hands and feet were covered in oversized dragon-like talons and claws.

Leaning forward, Nath said with a slur in his speech, "What is this? He looks terrifying."

"Chazzan has been telling us about singing an opera song he wrote. I never imagined it would be so showy." Maefon's legs were crossed. One foot was kicking. She bit into her bottom lip. "I think he wants to show off."

"I think you are right," Nath said with awe. "He does want to be a dragon. A scary elven one. No offense—*hic*—but he looks a bit abominable." His eyes were heavy as he stared at the elf. The dragon costume wasn't so complicated. He could tell the elf wore shoulder pads underneath his robes, and he stood on a short pair of stilts. All in all, however, it was a clever costume. "So he's going to sing?"

Maefon shushed him. The rest of the cajoling elves quieted.

Chazzan sang. His voice filled Covelum with a perfect pitch that became louder and more powerful the longer he went.

Goose bumps rose on Nath's arms. "I never would have imagined something so loud could come out of such a small head," he whispered and partly slurred to Maefon. "Is that magic?"

"Hush, Nath. You are being rude." Her eyes were fastened on Chazzan, almost as if she were spellbound.

Nath eased back into his chair and listened. Chazzan sang in old elven with lyrics that flowed like the wind whistling through the trees. Up and down his voice went, accenting the highs and lows of a dangerous journey. He sang of a world where the dragons abandoned men, and a dark life took over. Nath's hazy mind tried to keep up with the story. Sitting up, he said, "What is he singing about?"

"Nath, don't be rude. I am listening."

Chazzan's words darkened. His voice became a thunderstorm and heavy rains. He seemed to control the very elements around him as the lighting changed with his mood. There he stood, arms wide, a menacing terror, with a voice that swallowed all other sound from the room. Nath's goose bumps moved up his arms to the hairs on the back of his neck. With blurry eyes, he looked around at the audience. All of them sat on the edge of their seats with spellbound eyes and mouths half-gaping open.

There was a sound of thunder. Nath noticed Pevly and Tevlin bending a thin sheet of metal from behind the stage. The sound had such a realistic effect. Nath watched Chazzan sing. The elf's lips moved more slowly than the words that came out. Nath's stomach turned inside his belly. He wanted to look away but couldn't.

Chazzan held his arms high, mouth open toward the ceiling. In one hand, he held a clear crystal orb. He let out the last lyric. "There was only doom without the dragons. The days will be dark forever." His high note cracked. The crystal in his hand shattered. His voice halted, and he bowed. There was a long, quiet moment, then the audience was on their feet, erupting in laughter. Maefon clapped heartily. Tears came from the corners of her eyes.

Nath applauded with heavy hands. Something wasn't right. Watching Chazzan walk from the stage, hunched over, with the shifting appearance of some sort of demon, Nath said, "I think I'm going to be sick." He plopped back into his chair. Maefon was in his face, features twisting and saying words he did not fully understand. All he could do was repeat the words, "There was only doom without the dragons." Looking at Maefon, he said to her, "Why would he say that?"

"It's a tragedy. Life is full of tragedy. Come on, Nath," she said with words that finally became clearer. "I'll take you home."

"Why can't I feel my fingers or taste my tongue?"

"I suppose you have a low tolerance for elven wine. Either that, or you drank too much of it." She stood before him, holding him by the waist and keeping him steady. The elves were celebrating in Covelum in a swarm of excited activity. She wasn't smiling when she said her next words. "Nath, you should be more careful."

He scratched his head. "I suppose. I don't understand Chazzan's song. Did you?"

"It's a tragedy."

"It was beautiful but awful at the same time. I'm sleepy."

"Yes, I know." With Nath leaning on her, she led him out of Covelum, away from all of the noise and celebration. She took him to his home and led him up the steps and into bed.

"I love you, Maefon," he said, curling up in his bed and falling into a deep sleep.

"Yes, Nath, I know," she said, brushing his hair behind his ears. "But I love Chazzan."

CHAPTER 19

"MAAAAAAH-ROOOOOOO!"

Nath woke with his face buried in his pillow. His bloodshot eyes cracked open.

"MAAAAAAH-ROOOOOOO!"

He pushed his pounding head up and sat up, wiping the drool from his mouth. Dragons were crying out. Their wailings filled the tunnels. Nath's body quavered. "What in the mountain is going on?" he said, covering his ears.

"MAAAAAAH-ROOOOOOO!"

With his heart racing, he forced himself to his feet and staggered out of his room. Never in his life had he heard the sounds of dragons mourning. Numerous roars from different dragons echoed like thunder through the corridors. There was hurt, disbelief, confusion, and rage.

Nath picked up his pace. With a head that felt like it was filled with cotton, he tried to sort out the last thing he had done. He was at the Festival of Change with Maefon, having as good a time as ever. Chazzan performed a very dark ballad that haunted Nath's dreams. Maefon was there, leading him home. He'd become sleepy, and he rarely slept. He didn't remember anything after that.

I must have overindulged in that elven wine, but it's never affected me so before.

"MAAAAAAH-ROOOOOOO!"

What has happened while I slept?

He stumbled, bumped against the wall, and regained his balance. His legs were still numb. He pressed on, tracking after the harrowing dragon calls. The sound came from the direction of the dragon nursery. Taking a split in the corridors, Nath passed a train of dragons of all sorts and sizes lined up in the channel. They moaned, grumbled, and growled as he passed them. Nath didn't bother asking what had happened. None of them would even look at him. He swore he heard the word *traitor*.

He entered the archway into the nursery where the dragons' lamenting was the loudest. He covered his ears. Inside, dragons were huddled over the fledgling dragons. The baby dragons' bodies were broken and slashed. All of them, once so spry and lively, were dead. Nath's heart sank to his toes as he dropped to his knees. "No," he whispered. "How can this be?"

Dragon blood smeared the floor, wet and drying. It was nothing short of a cruel, inhuman massacre. Dozens of the fledglings had been killed. There were dead Trahaydeen too. They lay on the ground, in their own blood, unattended. Knives had fallen from their hands.

Nath tried to sort out whether or not the elves defended the fledglings or if they were responsible. His nostrils widened. With his dulled senses clearing, the foul odor of charred flesh caught his attention. Near the back of the cavern, a pile of flesh had become a smoking stack of bones. There was no doubt it was elven. Nath's eyes swept the room, looking for others. He didn't see any more bodies, but some of the weapons he'd forged himself were scattered on the floor.

No, it can't be.

Dragon blood was on the blades and handles. His stomach sickened. He lifted his hands toward his face. Caked blood covered his fingers. Dragon blood.

This is madness. It cannot be.

The dragons in the room surrounded Nath. Towering over him with teeth and claws bared, they crowded him. With narrowed eyes, they said, "Liar. Traitor. Murderer."

A twenty-foot-tall gold dragon pushed through the ranks. "Seize him."

"But I didn't do it," Nath said, trying to address them all at once. "I swear I didn't! I could not have—ever!"

A tail blindsided him. The blow knocked him flat on the floor.

Nath fought to get up. The tail's hard blows pounded him into submission.

Chapter 20

Two gray scalers with black wings bound Nath's ankles with their long tails. They were as big as he was but sulked on the ground on all fours. Nath rubbed his aching ribs. The dragons throttled him with their tails, but he was thankful he hadn't been burned to a crisp. The intent to kill him was certainly there.

Nath had been brought to the chamber of the High Dragon Council. It was a place of decision-making and judgment. He'd been to several sessions in his lifetime, and the meetings were renowned for taking days, even years. At the moment, the voluminous chamber was empty aside from him and his guards. There were seven flat boulders that circled the chamber. Each was big enough to seat a large dragon. Above, balconies overlooked the chamber. No dragons were there.

Nath sighed. He'd been under heavy guard for several days, isolated from the dragons in a cave. Aside from his guards, he hadn't seen anyone else. No Trahaydeen. No Maefon. He hoped she was safe. He knew that he couldn't have hurt the dragons, and even if he didn't remember anything from while he slept, he must have been set up. It could only have been the elves who'd done it, and if he had to guess one, it would be Chazzan. There was something sinister about the elf the night of the Showings.

Nath's temper rose every time he thought about the innocent fledglings being slaughtered. Even though Nath and the dragons didn't get along, they were his kin, and it hurt him as much as it hurt the dragons. He would find whoever committed the atrocious act and make them pay.

I'll avenge you, little ones. I swear it.

The High Dragon Council entered the chamber. All of the dragons were golden flares, with radiant gold scales that showed brilliantly when they moved. Their horns varied, curling like a ram's horns or flowing toward their backs in twisted spikes. On the left side, three females with long eyelashes and alabaster-colored bellies sat on their rocks. Across from them were three males with heavier-plated, darker, golden-brown chests. The last golden flare took his seat on the mound of rock in the middle. It was the same dragon as at the nursery. Karnax was his name. He nodded to the others. All together, the golden flares reared up on their hind legs and crossed their arms over their chests. All eyes were on Nath.

Karnax spoke dragonese with a pleasant yet stern voice. "Nath, you stand accused of slaughtering twenty-two fledglings. What is your plea?"

"My plea?" he said. "I should not be accused of anything. I would never hurt a dragon, ever. This is insanity!"

Karnax's tail picked up a round stone and banged it on a rock beside his pedestal. "Order! Order!" The other dragons growled in their throats. "I will ask again, Nath, what is your plea?"

"I don't even know what that means. Karnax, you know I did not do this. The real murderers must still be out there." Nath tried to move forward, but the gray scalers' tails were like steel coils around his ankles. "They should be on trial. Not me!"

"Lower your voice, Nath," Karnax's voice boomed throughout the room. "Your answer is very simple. Guilty or not guilty. Now, I will ask you again. What is your plea?"

"Well, not—"

"Don't answer that!" a voice cut in. An eight-foot-tall slender dragon, walking upright like a man, entered the room. His eyes were blue as ice, and he wore a small satchel around his waist. Of all the dragons, Slivver was the most human. He walked upright like a man, spoke in common more than he did dragon, and even sat at tables and ate with utensils.

"Slivver!" Nath said with a sigh. His brother had shown up at the perfect time. He tried to hug the approaching dragon, but Slivver held him off.

"Just be silent, Nath," he said eloquently, "and let me do the talking for a change."

Nath nodded. Balzurth had many children, but none like Nath. Slivver was one of Nath's many brothers and sisters who were full dragons hatched from eggs. Though Slivver was gone most of the time, he was one of the very few who spoke with Nath like an actual sibling, friend, or person, for that matter.

"High council dragons," Slivver said, pacing with his arms behind his back. "I would like to remind you that the evidence does not point to Nath. You are aware of this. Our findings have concluded that the Trahaydeen are solely responsible for this act and Nath, the son of Balzurth, the Dragon King, was framed. Poorly framed at that."

Karnax stretched his neck. "Regardless, he must enter a plea. That is our law."

Slivver lifted a clawed finger. "As Nath's representative, I will advise you that he will not be entering any plea. A guilty plea would certainly satisfy our tragically hurt and wounded brethren, with a swift and certain justice. But a not guilty plea will lead to a trial, building up more tension, unrest, and the appearance of guilt, and that would be wrong. Your charges against Nath are without foundation, and I move that they be dismissed."

"No!" Karnax said. The other dragons nodded in agreement.

Slivver spread out his arms and wings. "High council dragons, we have proven without a shadow of a doubt that Nath is not involved in this foul conspiracy. And you cannot try to hold Nath accountable for tragedies of the past."

Nath whispered at Slivver, "What tragedies?"

Slivver shooed him away. "Though I hate to put it this way, in more human terms, this is a witch hunt. Nath is not the witch. He is our brother and guiltless at that. All of you knew this before you even came in here, yet you are trying to pin the murder on him still." Slivver punched his fist in his hand. "It... Is... Wrong!"

The council of dragons conferred with one another in their own dialect. As they convened, Nath went to work on Slivver. "You know I'm grateful, but can you please tell me what in the mountain is going on? Why would the Trahaydeen kill the fledglings and pin it on me?"

Putting his clawed hands on Nath's shoulders, Slivver said, "They had bad seeds, brother. All races do, and you can never fully trust them. Even the dragons have bad seeds. But the important thing is that you are innocent. I know this, as does the council, and many others, but it's not so easy to convince all of the dragons. They don't trust you or the elves. As it turns out, the culprits not only slew the fledglings, but many of their own kind as well. They wanted it to look like you went into some sort of rage. They framed you as a distraction and fled the mountain."

"But why, Slivver? I just don't understand it. Elves killing elves. That is madness within madness." His jaws clenched. "It was led by Chazzan, wasn't it?"

"I can't say for certain, but he was one of the many who fled. The others are incarcerated but most likely will be banished."

"What about Maefon? Where is she? I need to see her."

"She is one of the ones who fled with the others. She is a suspect." Slivver patted Nath's head. "I can see the blood running from your face, Nath. Are you all right?"

Ashen-faced, Nath replied, "I don't know."

Chapter 21

As the High Council of Dragons deliberated, Nath's thoughts raced through the rapids of the tragedy. Never in his life had he seen anyone die. The Trahaydeen were always in good health, even though many came and went. As for the dragons, the most ancient of them were rarely seen, and when it was time, they would move on to the land beyond the murals. Now, the most innocent of creatures, fledgling dragons, had been slaughtered by the most trusted of the races, the Trahaydeen.

Maefon couldn't have done this. She just couldn't have.

Nath rubbed his temples. His head hurt, and his heart ached. But deep within him, an anger burned. He wanted vengeance for the dragons. Justice would have to wait.

Slivver nudged Nath, breaking his train of thought. "The council," Slivver said quietly.

The High Council of Dragons broke from their conversation and turned their attention to Nath. Karnax spoke. "We have deliberated. The votes are split as to whether or not to dismiss the charges against you or not."

"Split?" Nath said with shock.

Slivver cut him off with his hand. "Let me do the talking." He stepped toward the high council. "Split? That is the most absurd judgment I have ever heard or witnessed. We have proved without a doubt that Nath is innocent. We know who the murderers are."

Karnax banged the round stone of the rock. "Order! Order, I say! There will not be any more outbursts from you, Slivver, or the defendant. A decision has been rendered. And you will be silent so I can complete it."

Slivver looked back at Nath and shook his head.

Nath stopped breathing for a moment. Were they really going to put him on trial for murder? *Why are they always against me?*

Clearing his throat, Karnax continued, "Given the split decision, I will make the final call." His yellow eyes locked on Nath and narrowed. "Nath, you stand accused of murder. We have weighed all of the evidence, and I have given every detail heavy consideration. The charges against you will be... dismissed."

Frozen in place and not believing his ears, Nath said, "Slivver, did he say dismissed?"

Slivver's quick jovial nodding confirmed the news. "Yes. You are free, Nath. No case will be made against you!" They hugged.

Nath slapped the folded wings behind Slivver's back. "Thank you for being here for me. I didn't know what to do." A loud banging of rock on rock echoed inside the chamber. Nath, along with Slivver, faced the High Council of Dragons again.

"We have a very egregious situation on our hands, Nath and Slivver," Karnax added. "Given the vile nature of this incident, coupled with the absence of King Balzurth, the dragon council has decided to enact Pwaunlow. It is effective immediately."

"Pwaunlow? What is Pwaunlow?" Nath asked Slivver.

"Dragon Home will be locked down until King Balzurth returns," Slivver replied. He clicked his teeth. "Interesting."

"Interesting? What do you mean? I really don't know what a lockdown is."

Karnax bent his long neck toward Nath. "Pwaunlow means that no dragons may enter and no dragons may leave until King Balzurth returns. If they depart, they will be exiled. The remaining Trahaydeen will be banished immediately."

Scratching the back of his head, Nath said, "I don't understand. What about the pursuit of the Trahaydeen? Certainly, the dragons are hunting them down and bringing them to justice. How can they do this if the dragons are not allowed to return?"

"Pwaunlow is Pwaunlow." Karnax banged stone on stone. "This meeting is adjourned." He departed the room first, followed by the other dragons.

The gray scalers released Nath and left as well. Nath faced Slivver, gaping. He shook his head. "That's it? They are just letting the elves go free. No pursuit? That can't be, Slivver. It just can't be." He punched his fist in his hand. "They must be brought to justice."

"Nath, let's walk, and I'll do the best I can to make sense of this." Slivver nudged Nath along with his hands. Jaws clenched, Nath moved along with him. They exited the chamber into the tunnels. "First off, the Trahaydeen who fled the mountain are gone. And when I say gone, I say they vanished. Their trail went dead at the base of the mountain. There was no evidence. No scent. It was as if they vanished into thin air."

"Magic?" Nath said.

"Certainly. And for all we know, they could be anywhere in all of Nalzambor. As far as the east is from the west in regards to Dragon Home. It might take decades to find them." Slivver moved down the corridor at an easy pace. "But the dragons are patient, and they will have vengeance, and they will have justice. It will be very slow going. When our father returns, I have no doubt that he will act on this event immediately. The important thing is that you are not among the accused anymore. You need to be patient and wait until Father returns."

Nath shook his head. "Patient? I'm not going to sit here and wait while a pack of murderers is out there. They don't deserve to get away. And Maefon is out there. I bet she's scared. She will need me to clear her name. There is no way she could be responsible for this act. I would know it in my heart. No doubt Chazzan has something to do with this. He's deceived her. I know he has. He's a shady elf."

Slivver stroked a loose slab of skin under his chin that looked like a beard. "Yes, I suppose he is. There are many strange goings on among the races, always. I tell you, Nath, they fascinate me. In all truth, I envy you, born a man. I wish it had been me."

"Really? Well, that's the dumbest thing I've ever heard. You would give up flying, not to mention all sorts of other things."

"True, but as you have a strong fondness of Maefon, I too have a heart's desire for one much like her." Slivver's ice-blue eyes sparkled. His taloned hands covered his heart. "She is radiant."

"No offense, Slivver, but that is kind of weird." Nath took a split in the path that led him back toward his home. "I suppose I should understand it, but I don't. I adore Maefon, but I still want to earn my scales and become a dragon. Like my father. Like you." Nath eyed his brother. He was truly one of a kind. "I envy you."

Slivver sighed. "I don't suppose anyone will understand my predicament."

"Nope, probably not." Nath climbed the steps into his cave. Slivver waited at the bottom with a perplexed look on his face. "Are you coming up? You don't have to, because I'm coming right back down. I've decided I'm leaving." He went into his little home and opened a wooden chest on the floor. There were many special items Balzurth had given to him. He quickly examined them one at a time. A small lantern, some candles, a leather gauntlet, and some rope. *I can't wait to use these again. There has been little use for them here.* He tossed them into a smallish backpack with dark zigzag shapes and designs woven into the leather and headed back outside with the pack slung over his shoulders.

"Nath, what is on your mind?" Slivver said.

"I'm going after the Trahaydeen." Nath hustled down the steps. "And don't try to talk me out of it. My mind is made up. I'm not letting them get away with this, and Maefon needs me. I know it."

Slivver seized his arm. "Nath, you cannot do this. You will be exiled."

Nath shrugged him off. "It will only be until Father returns. Just a few years or so. That should be plenty of time to rescue Maefon and bring those murderers to justice."

"No, Nath, you don't understand. You cannot leave. If you do, you won't be exiled for a few years. You'll be exiled for a century."

Chapter 22

"What?" Nath said, lowering his pack to the ground. "Did you say a century?"

"Yes." Slivver nodded. "Nath, you are thinking with your heart and not your head. You are not ready to leave Dragon Home. Trust me. And the High Council of Dragons has ruled for our safety. Even if Father returns, he will not overturn their ruling. He trusts them. You must wait until Balzurth comes back. I'm sure he will release you on this hunt then."

Balzurth's last words echoed in Nath's mind. *Do not depart from the mountain, no matter what.* "I have to go, Slivver. I must know what happened. This is the right thing to do. Father will have to understand."

"No, Nath, this is the foolish thing to do. You are a dragon, and dragons can be patient. More patient than a man. When the time comes, we will have vengeance, and we will have justice." Slivver grabbed him and gave him a serious look. "There is more to this conspiracy, Nath. I can feel it. And I don't think it has anything to do with those dragons so much as it has to do with you."

Nath pulled away. He headed toward the throne room. "What do you mean?"

"First off," Slivver explained, "I believe the High Council of Dragons enacted Pwaunlow hoping you would leave. It's not what they all want, but it's what most dragons want. You saw how the council was split. Even though we know you are innocent, most of the dragons feel that you are guilty, and with Father gone, they are trying to get you to leave. Stay here and prove yourself. Show them you are a true, obedient, and just prince. You have a big enough burden, given what you are, on your shoulders."

Stopping in his tracks, Nath faced his brother. "Do you know why they despise me so? Is it just because I look like a man? Or is it something else? I can't help but feel like there is something that is not being told to me that I should know."

Slivver's dragon features had a long look about them. When he spoke, his voice was soft. "I always figured Father would have told you more by now. After all, you are a hundred, and it's time that things are revealed to you. Nath, you have a brother."

Making a puzzled look, Nath said, "Yes, I have you, as well as other dragon brothers and sisters that don't ever speak to me." Nath marched down the hall. "How is this news?"

"No, you have a brother that is just like you. He's... human."

"Don't jest with me, Slivver," Nath said with a feeble smile.

"I wish I was, but I am not."

"And you know him? You've seen him?"

"Neither. I just know *of* him. He was on the scene before my time."

Grabbing Slivver's arm, Nath asked, "Well, who is he? What is his name? What does he look like?"

"I know of him, but I know little about him. He is not spoken about in Dragon Home. In truth, I wouldn't have even known that he existed if not for our brothers and sisters who explained to me why the dragons shun you so. It seems that your brother, our brother, committed an atrocity in Dragon Home."

"What kind of atrocity?"

"He was accused of killing dragons, but it could never be proved that he did it. Sound familiar?"

Nath was at a loss for words at the stunning news. He had a brother, like him. He'd always wished he had a brother or even a sister the same as him. It would have made life much easier in Dragon Home if he did. But at the same time, maybe he wasn't so special after all.

Slivver continued in a grim tone, "You see, Nath, that is why the dragons shun you. They fear that you will turn out like him. And now, fledglings are killed, and if not for the elves, every talon and tail would be pointed at you. So yes, the dragons have always watched you with wary eyes and suspicion. They fear the worst in you."

Suddenly, all of the dragons' ire toward Nath made sense, but he just didn't understand why Balzurth couldn't have told him. If he had known, things could have been different. "Well, I am not my brother, whoever he is. My actions should have spoken for themselves. So what happened to him?"

"He left. I'm not sure if he was banished or if it was of his own accord, but as I understand it, no one has seen him since."

"And this was a long time ago?"

"Perhaps three hundred years, maybe longer. Again, the dragons' lips are as sealed as bark to a tree." Slivver patted Nath's back. "I wish I could have told you sooner."

"No, that's fine. At least now I know something, and in truth, it does give me some relief." Nath stood in front of the throne room doors. He pushed the one on the right open.

"What are you going in there for?"

"To get Fang."

"And why would you be getting this Fang?"

"Fang is the sword that Father made me. I'm taking him on my journey."

Slivver reached for Nath's collar. Nath evaded it. "You are still going? Why? Be patient. I'm telling you there is more to this than we know. You need to stay put. At least give it a few months, if not years. Nath, don't go."

Nath walked into the throne room. Fang was lying in front of Balzurth's seat, sheathed in his scabbard. He picked it up and slid the blade halfway out. "Hello, Fang. We have work to do."

"Please do not do this, Nath. You are too young to go on this journey. And you will be gone a hundred years, if you even last that long. I'm telling you, stay put until Father returns. You have been cleared of this matter, and it is not your responsibility. You need more time to develop."

"Develop what? I've been training all my life. And another hundred years of it? No, I can't just sit and wait while Maefon is out there. And I'm not going to let those murderers get away with what they did. They killed fledglings, Slivver. Fledglings! In cold blood. Doesn't that outrage you?"

"It wounds us all. But vengeance and justice will only come with patience and a best-laid plan. You have no plan at all." Slivver stood in a pile of treasure. He pulled a steel breastplate out of the pile and dumped the coins and gems out. "Or protection, for that matter. Put this on."

"I don't need that. It will just slow me down."

"You are in an awful big hurry for someone who has no idea where they are going." Slivver spun Nath around. With quick hands, he dropped the breastplate over Nath's head and buckled the leather straps tight. "Perfect. It fits like a glove."

Nath inspected it. "Well, it is light." He knocked on his chest. The steel plate had a dull shine to it. "What is it made of?"

"Moorite."

"Huh, that's dwarven. I've read about it. I find it strange that it was crafted for a man my size. I thought they didn't like to share." Nath slung Fang over his back and looked up at Slivver. "You aren't going to try and stop me?"

The silver dragon didn't hide the disappointment in his face. His frown was as big as ever. "Didn't Father command you to stay in the mountain?"

"I'm not sure that he specifically said that." Nath knew exactly what Balzurth had said. He was not to leave.

"Disobedience has consequences, Nath. You will face them."

"You can come too."

"As much as I'd like to, I'll await Father's return. Besides, you need to know that you won't have a ring of safety around you. You are protected here, and you won't be out there. This is your last warning."

Nath gave his brother a fierce hug. "See you in a hundred years."

Slivver pulled something from a leather pouch he kept around his waist and stuffed it into Nath's backpack. "When you find the time, read it. It might prove helpful. It's a theory of mine."

"Of course." He made his way out of the throne room. As he crossed the threshold, the doors quaked and groaned. The door closed behind him. Fang suddenly felt like an anvil on his back. Balzurth told him that he wasn't supposed to take Fang out of the throne room. It seemed that Fang didn't want to go either. He pulled Fang free with a grunt. Looking at the sword, he said, "Fang, I have to do this, and I'll need you. But if I have to leave you, I will. What will it be?"

Fang's blade hummed.

The heavy blade lightened in Nath's grip.

"Thank you, Fang. Thank you." He set his eyes on the path out of the mountain. "We have a mission to fulfill."

Chapter 23

Nath exited Dragon Home near the base of the mountain. He turned back, looking down the long corridor he'd just taken. Slowly, rocks filled in the gap until nothing but stone remained. An archway made up of glowing ancient runes etched in the rock faded. Nath touched the rock. The stone was cold beneath his palm. It was the door he always took to come and go when he'd sneak out onto the mountain to watch the sun rise and fall, though there were others vastly bigger.

"Am I banished or am I not banished? That is the question." Nath took a breath. He recited the ancient words that let him enter. Long and flowing, the words came freely from his mouth. When it ended, the mystic runes in the archway did not appear. The stone remained. There would be no coming. There was only going. Emptiness filled him, a longing to be inside the warmth of the mountain. A chill breeze rustled his hair. He faced the horizon, set his shoulders forward, and walked. "One hundred years, here I come."

Nath traveled north. His journey took him over narrow paths, crossing over a moat of lava that circled Dragon Home. From there he traversed the rugged terrain of the lakes of lava. It was a slippery trek that only seasoned mountaineers, bold adventurers, or wingless dragons with strong claws would take. Climbing out of one steamy ravine after another, he noted the red rock dragons half buried in the hot muddy banks of the lakes. Their green eyes were fixed on Nath like he was their next meal. Nath came to an halt. "Huh, I've never been this far out before."

Standing on the bank, Nath watched the boiling red waters surge by. There was a wide gap, over one hundred feet. The treacherous terrain wasn't meant to be crossed to the mountain. It was a barrier between mortal and dragon that kept the races away. Nath searched the lava rocks that jutted up out of the fiery stream. There was a fair distance between them, but he was confident he could hop from one to another.

"I should have known that leaving the mountain would be difficult. One slip, and I'll be charcoal." He considered going back and taking another way, but one way in would be as troublesome as another. The Mountain of Doom was laid out that way, to keep the races' curiosity at bay. He gathered his legs beneath him. "Here goes!" In a flat-footed hop, he jumped ten feet to the nearest stone. He hopped from one to another, going forward and backward in a zigzag pattern. Halfway across, he landed on a rock and slipped. His boot toes dipped toward the boiling waters. "Whoa!" He flailed his arms, regaining his balance. "Whew! That was close."

He sucked the blistering heat in as he swiped sweat from his brow. Rivulets trickled down his back. He peered through the steam, searching for his next spot. He jumped from rock to rock, still advancing, but his own youthful energy began to fade. The lava was draining him. "Come on, Nath, only a few more to go." He jumped to the next rock. There was one more ahead, and then he'd have plenty of room to make the final leap to the other side of the bank. He huffed out a breath of relief and wiped the stinging sweat from his eyes. "This would have been easier than walking if I didn't have all of this gear on me."

Nath jumped. His landing spot moved. It wasn't a rock. It was a red rock dragon. "Gah!" The wingless dragon was as big as a Haversham hippo he'd come across in his studies. Its massive jaws opened wide. Pulling his feet up, Nath landed on the tip of the dragon's snout. It snapped. Nath jumped. Timing it perfectly, he jumped as the dragon bit, landed on its closing jaws, and jumped again. It became a dance between the two in the swirling river of flame.

"Quit trying to eat me! I am not your enemy, brother!"

Out of the corners of his eyes, he saw red rock dragons close in.

"You mindless brutes! You aren't supposed to eat your own kind!" Nath jumped. The lava waters rippled as the dragon heaved upward and snapped at his toes. Nath landed once again. Thinking on his feet, he decided to use the brute strength of the dragon in his favor. The dragon surged upward again. Nath leapt, using the dragon's momentum to propel him. He landed on the back of another red rock. It bit at him. He jumped again, twisting in the air toward the awaiting back. He landed face first in the hot dirt and soft clay, exhausted. He pushed his face out and saw the red rocks closing in on his position. He scrambled up the steep bank and climbed over the rim, just as the nearest red rock dragon nipped at his toes. Its jaws clacked together. Nath kept running, not stopping until the brown ground turned green.

Finally, standing in a field of grass and wildflowers up to his knees, he turned back toward the mountains and sat down. Dragon Home loomed miles away. Lava seams flowed out of the stark mountain between the ridges. Its peak waited beneath the rolling clouds, daring them to draw closer and be swallowed up. It was Nath's home, or at least it used to be. And from where he sat, it didn't look very pretty. If he didn't already know better, he would have thought Dragon Home looked scary.

He picked at the grasses and plucked the wildflowers. Bees moved from flower to flower, making a gentle buzz. The wind rustled the high grasses. A flock of bright-blue birds streaked through the skies above. A huge vulture-like bird, with the appearance of two heads, fell out of the trees, gliding over the grasses before disappearing in the lazy fabric of the meadows.

A chill crept through Nath. His eyes swept over his surroundings. He felt as if he was being watched. Finally, it passed.

Nalzambor was full of vibrant life. Nath had never witnessed it before at close range. At least, not at length. Most of the time, he was in the sky with his father. Wiping the mud off the best he could, he said, "This doesn't seem like it's going to be a dangerous place. It's kind of nice, actually."

A large drop of water splattered on his head. He looked up. Storm clouds formed overhead. Thunder rolled in. The winds picked up. The sky flashed, and a downpour of rain began.

Chapter 24

Southeast of Dragon Home, far away and forgotten, a fortress of stone was dug out of the rocks. The fortress overlooked a rushing river of rapids. A suspension bridge, barely wide enough for two, swayed over the river as the chronic stiff winds tore at its planks. With the rain beating against their faces, Maefon, Chazzan, and four other Trahaydeen elves made the risky trek across the bridge.

"The last time I was here, it was storming," Maefon shouted against the wind. She stepped forward, right behind Chazzan, clinging to the bridge as she moved forward, hand over hand on the ropes. "It's been storming since we left. I hate being wet."

"It rains often here, but I don't imagine Lord Dark Day will let us take up residence. He'll have plenty of work for us. As he says, 'A Caligin's work is never done until all of his enemies lie dead.'"

"Yes, I know," she said, reaching the end of the bridge. She hopped on the ledge and looked up at the fortress. Water cascaded from its crevices like a waterfall. The face of the stone complex was a hundred feet wide and a hundred feet high. Stone balconies jutted out from its sheer face. An iron portcullis behind the archway entrance in the middle was closed. The elves gathered underneath one of its arches, out of the hard rain, but huge drops of water still dripped on them. Shivering, she said, "It better be dry in there. And a fire would be nice. For some reason, I am freezing."

From behind, Chazzan wrapped his arms around her waist. "Either way, I will warm you up."

She touched his cheek. "I know you will."

Still holding her, Chazzan kicked at the portcullis. "Hello? I know you are there. I can see you hunched over your lard-filled belly."

Sitting against the wall with his face between his knees sat an ogre. His head, as round as a boulder, lifted up. More shoulders than neck, the chinless brute got up. Wearing nothing but trousers made from animal skins, the greasy-haired brute strolled over. His arms swung at his sides, knuckles almost scraping the puddles on the stony ground. Standing a full nine feet tall, he glowered down at the group with a milkly yellow eyes. "I am Monfur, warden of the portcullis of Stonewater Keep. State your business," the ogre said in a voice that sounded more monster than man.

"Whew!" Chazzan covered his nose. "What do you eat? Manure pudding? Add some fruit to it or something. Foul, so foul."

Maefon pinched her nose and backed away. "I don't think fruit will do it. He's an ogre. He was born rank. He'll die rank. Not even the salt of the seas could wash his stench away."

"Anyway, I don't care who you are. We are Caligin, faithful servants of the Lord of the Dark in the Day, and without further delay, you need to let us in." Chazzan produced a neck chain on which hung a platinum ring with a black stone set in it. "Cast your eyes on our insignia, and open this gate with haste."

The ogre stared at the black rock. "Hmmm... you may enter." The ogre bent over and removed a pin from the floor with his fingers. With one arm, he lifted the heavy iron portcullis that would have taken a dozen elves to lift.

All of the Trahaydeen gaped as they hustled inside.

"You know, if the ogres were half as smart as they were strong, they could possibly rule the world," Chazzan said to Maefon. All of the elves tossed their heads back in laughter. The gate dropped down with a loud bang, cutting off their laughter.

"Take the stairs," Monfur said, securing the pin in the portcullis. "He stays up." He walked back to the wall where he came from and hunkered down in his seat. "I stay down, but I always remember, elves are delicious."

Stonewater Keep's stone walls were slick with green-gray moss and dripping from most of the crevices. Maefon's feet splashed in puddles of water as they traversed the damp interior and made their way up the stairs. The wood beneath the elves' light feet creaked and groaned beneath them. Many of the wood planks were soft and rotting as the staircase crossed over and up, floor by floor. Rain dripped from above into the gap in the middle. They passed different doors on their way up, each sealed shut. Finally, they made it to the top level. An oak door strapped together with iron banding blocked their entrance into the room.

Chazzan wrung out the sleeves of his dripping-wet robes, tossed his hair back, and said with a clever smile, "Our destiny awaits." He knocked on the door.

The metal door on the square portal slid open. The person on the other side had no face. Instead, their head was covered in a sack of dark-crimson cloth. The eyes were cut out like slits. The prying eyes inspected the six Trahaydeen elves.

Chazzan held up his signet ring. "Hail to the Lord of the Dark in the Day."

The person in the mask let out a snobby snort and slammed the portal door closed. A few seconds later, the door's locking bolt popped. The heavy door swung inward. The six elves were bathed in warm firelight as they entered.

The entrance led into a grand hall where two fireplaces were burning. A long table made of ancient mahogany and fit for fifty people ran the length of the floor. Standing at attention behind most of the empty chairs were the guardians in crimson hoods. The cut-out eyelets were different for all of them, designed in a self-gratifying, sinister way. They had no mouths or nose holes. They all wore a set of black leather armor. A long sword and dagger dressed all of their hips. They were elves, the same as Maefon and the others in her group, but they were disciples of the Caligin, going through training. A feast of food spread over the table. There were roasted beasts, dates, fruits, nuts, and crystal decanters of apple wine.

Maefon's stomach rumbled. She needed food to settle it. The journey hadn't been long, but the teleportation spell that whisked them away from Dragon Home's mountainside turned her belly upside down.

At the far end of the table, the Lord of the Dark in the Day was seated. A scenic mural of the entire world of Nalzambor covered the wall behind him. By far the largest person in the room, the big-boned man wore crimson robes that partially covered his muscular arms. A chrome mask fashioned with the sharp features of a frowning elf covered his face. In his left hand, he held an orb made of solid iron. His head was tilted to one side. He banged the orb casually on the table.

Chazzan glanced back at Maefon. Together, all of them took a knee. Heads down with arms up and fingers outspread, all together, they said, "Our service is yours, Lord Darkken. Now and forever."

Lord Darkken spoke in a commanding voice. "Welcome home, Caligin. Enter. Feast."

Chapter 25

Maefon and Chazzan sat at the very end of the table. The other four Trahaydeen were beside them. Quietly, they ate. Even the disciples lifted their hoods over their noses and indulged in the meal.

Lord Darkken broke the uncomfortable silence lingering in the foreboding room. "They can eat, but they can't talk. You remember those days, don't you, Chazzan? Maefon?"

"Those days were unforgettable." Chazzan toasted his crystal goblet in the air and drank. "Has much changed since I trained, Lord Darkken?"

"Please, you can dispense with the formalities, brother. Lord will do." He let out a rusty laugh. "Ah-haha."

Maefon dabbed the corners of her mouth with a napkin. She never could tell when Darkken was joking or not. "I prefer Lord Dark Day."

"Oh, how I have missed your wit, Maefon." Darkken reached over and squeezed her forearm with an iron grip. "Dark Day, hah. Honestly, it was a consideration, but Darkken is suitable. And you both have earned the privilege. But whatever you are comfortable with will do. The Caligin are not explicit on formalities unless needed. It's best to keep it casual among the races. Adopt their culture and win them over." He locked his fingers. "Hence, I like to keep our conversing more casual in nature. The Caligin want their enemy's guard to be down before we strike. As it turns out, the word *Darkken*, Maefon, is old dwarven for dark day. Besides, I like to condense words where I can, given my upbringing."

"Understood," she replied with a nod but not fully understanding Darkken's meaning. "The dragon recitals, though fascinating, almost made my ears bleed at times. It wouldn't have been so bad if they didn't fully recite their names at the end to give credit. I could hardly keep my eyes open."

Chazzan rolled his eyes. "Oh, those were dreadful. They could be such boring creatures on occasion, and they moved so slowly."

"Yes, truly a waste of time. Often that is what the dragons do, waste time." Darkken's coppery eyes flickered like light behind his mask. "So you have brought new recruits, I see? Only four, after what, eighty years of work, Chazzan?"

"The Trahaydeen were hard to crack. Given the mission, Lord Darkken, I focused on exactly what I needed for fear that I would arouse suspicion." Chazzan smiled from ear to ear. "The mission was pulled off to perfection. Though I started to wonder if Balzurth—"

Darkken slammed the iron orb on the table. *Bang!* "Do not say his name."

"Yes, yes, absolutely," Chazzan said, shifting in his chair as the smile vanished from his face. "Apologies, Darkken."

Maefon shifted in her seat. She and Chazzan only knew the mission, but they did not know its purpose. For whatever reason, Lord Darkken wanted to take the dragons down or do them harm somehow, and Nath was the link in the chain that needed to be broken. Why, she didn't know for certain as of yet, but Darkken clearly had a grudge against Balzurth.

"It's Lord Darkken," the dark lord warned.

Maefon's heartbeat skipped. The edge in Darkken's voice sent chills down her spine. She'd trained in the keep for a full five years before becoming a full Caligin. Darkken had a voice that would cut right through her. He pushed, prodded, and demanded excellence. Stonewater Keep was a training ground where the elves learned to spin lies and deceit. They learned how to use weapons of wood and steel, as well as the weapons of the mind. There were potions and poisons brewed. The physical training pushed her to the limit. The tests of the mind were anguish. The devotion was pure because, as the Lord of the Dark in the Day liked to put it, you were purified in darkness. Their mission was to spread chaos throughout Nalzambor and take over the world. There was no better way to spread the deception than through the blood of the most trusted race of all… the elves. Maefon, from the moment she met him, thought he was brilliant.

Lord Darkken pushed back from the table. The chair legs ground over the floor. He stood up, a tower of a man, seeming even bigger than he already was. "As you can see, many of the chairs at the table remain empty. Both of you know how customary that is. Many wash out. I begin with fifty, train them for five years, and finish with sometimes less than twenty. But this class, as you can see, with forty left, has been remarkable. The Caligin's numbers are growing. Over a thousand strong now poison the fields and sow the seeds of deception through the land."

"Does that include this class?" Chazzan asked.

"No." Darkken faced the huge painted map on the wall of Nalzambor. "But it only takes a few to topple a kingdom. And I have many." He pointed to a spot on the map where the home of the elves, Elome, was. The city blended in with the trees and natural rock. "In Elome, our brethren keep the elves divided, for they have penetrated the highest of councils. Their policies agitate the dwarves who could be potential allies, and the skirmishes with the orcs will never cease. Of course, that is a given." He paced back and forth, poking the different locations as he spoke. "In the human city of Quintuklen, elven envoys and minsters give bad counsel. In Narmum, the melting pot of most of the races is stirred. Bad trade deals, failing crops, goblin raids in foreign lands. It never ceases, and words cannot describe my delight in these matters. Eventually, all of the kingdoms will crumble from within. Self-destruction is in their nature, even the elves and dwarves—one just has to know how to ignite it." He leaned on the map with his hands. His chrome skull turned all the way toward them. "Oh, how I delight in causing trouble."

"We delight with you, Lord Darkken," Maefon said. Standing up, she lifted her goblet. "May I propose a toast?"

Lord Darkken turned. "Yes, Maefon, and please, didn't I tell you to call me Darkken?" He eyed her. "But I agree! A toast is in order, though it will be difficult for me to drink due to this finely crafted mask." He approached the table, leaned down, and removed the mask. Long locks of flowing hair that matched his rust-colored eyes spilled out over his shoulders. His handsome face, without blemish or scar, was perfection. He set the mask down, picked up a goblet, and showed a radiant smile of pearl-white teeth. "Go on, Maefon."

With bated breath, she lifted her goblet higher. Everyone at the table stood. Her eyes were fastened on Lord Darkken. The only man she'd ever seen who rivaled his enchanting looks was Nath. They were different, Nath something brighter, and Darkken something darker. Her heart fluttered before the captivating man. "To deception and conquest!"

"To deception and conquest!" all present replied.

"Long live Lord Darkken," she added. "May his new kingdom reign supreme forever!" She touched glasses with Darkken beside her and Chazzan across from her. The crystal made a loud *tinnng!*

"I enjoyed that toast," Lord Darkken said, after taking a long drink. "And speaking of deception, I look forward to hearing more about your seduction of Balzurth's son, Nath."

Chazzan's eyes grew big. As Darkken was about to continue his conversation, he interrupted, "Lord Darkken, no disrespect, but I was just given a stern impression that you don't like the dragon king's name mentioned. Did I miss something?"

"Of course not, Chazzan. I just wanted to build more tension. It was merely a lesson for the disciples. You remember those mind games, don't you? How to control the room?" Lord Darkken set his glass down, moved behind Chazzan, and placed his hands on his shoulders. His fingers massaged the elf's muscles. "So now that we have gone around the horn, tell me how you executed the demise of the fledglings."

"Certainly, Lord." Chazzan smiled at Maefon. "I'd be happy to share. After all, deceiving the races is one thing, but misleading dragons is quite another. I cannot express what an honor it has been to be chosen for this mission. And having Maefon at my side was a boon." He winked at her. "In more ways than one." Chazzan recounted at length everything that he planned and executed to the last detail. He started the story with all of the flair and intensity one would expect from a master storyteller and stage performer. It included luring away the dragons from the nursery and pinning the murder on Nath. With everyone in the room captivated by his words, he finished by saying, "We fled the Mountain of Doom, used the talisman at the bottom, and arrived within a league of the keep." He drained his goblet of wine. "And here we live, and here we breathe."

Darkken's eyes narrowed for a moment.

"An interesting choice of words, Chazzan." Darkken slapped the elf's shoulders on the sides. "And I owe you a *well done*. Now, not wanting to interrupt such a delightful story, I wanted you to go back. You said that you framed Balzurth's son, Nath. I clearly stated that the fledglings were to be killed. I know I didn't mention Nath's involvement."

"Yes, but I saw an opportunity to deflect attention from us by implicating him." Chazzan refilled his goblet. "I pride myself on that kind of forward thinking. And I did have decades to come up with it. I just wished I could have remained to see the dragon's son squirm."

"I see." Darkken resumed massaging Chazzan's neck. "But I was very explicit. Explicit in meaning that you shouldn't take any liberties with this carefully planned project. I sent you in decades ago, Chazzan. My plan was not to be altered."

"Apologies, Lord Darkken. Is something wrong? I'm confident that all will turn out in your favor as always." Chazzan winced. The shoulder rubs were getting deeper. "Has Nath not departed the mountain as you surmised? I just wanted to borrow more time. Keep the dragons off our trail."

"Yes, he has departed. My eyes have told me that. That is not the problem. The problem is you not following my explicit orders." Lord Darkken's brows knitted together. He massaged harder. "You risked destroying everything I planned for."

"Lord Darkken, I swear, I would never cross an order—*hurk*!"

Lord Darkken's hands closed on Chazzan's neck and squeezed. Chazzan's eyes bulged. He dropped his glass. His knees banged against the table. Darkken ripped the man out of his chair. He held Chazzan high in the air.

In a heated voice, Lord Darkken said, "My orders were explicit." His arms flexed. Chazzan kicked his legs. He clawed and pounded on Darkken's arms. His pleading eyes flitted to Maefon. There was a loud crack that sounded like a dry tree limb being broken. Chazzan's neck sagged. His toes kicked a few times and stopped.

"Open the door," Lord Darkken said. A hooded disciple opened the door. Lord Darkken marched through it. "Monfur! Incoming!" He dropped Chazzan into the gap between the stairs. A delayed *thud* followed a moment later.

"To the washout?" Monfur hollered back up.

"Yes, along with all the other washouts. And don't let it dam up the river this time." Lord Darkken reentered the room. The door closed behind him. He had Chazzan's signet ring and necklace in his hand. He set it in front of Maefon. "For you," he said.

Fighting her trembles, she said, "Thank you, Lord Darkken."

"You're welcome. And I hope that you won't miss him, Maefon. You won't, will you?"

"No, Lord Darkken." Using her fork and knife, she sawed into her slice of meat. Her hands trembled. She fought against it. Her heart pounded like galloping horses. She loved Chazzan, and now she'd lost him, forever. She forced a devilish smile. "Of course not. I have you, don't I?"

"Of course. Heh-heh-heh."

Chapter 26

Sitting on a stream bank, Nath took off his boots. The storms had passed, but the pathways through the forests were muddy. He'd learned that he didn't care for mud or the rain. It made him wet and his boots muddy. If he could avoid it altogether, he would have. He moved out to a flat rock, sat down, rinsed his boots off in the water, and dipped his toes in the cool depths. With the setting sun shining in his face, he said, "Ah!"

Nath was used to seeing the world from above, not below. His only time in the world came when he flew with his father, and they never landed. Things were different when they weren't from a dragon's point of view. The trees were bigger, the land vaster, and the signs of life were overwhelming. In the mountain, things were quiet, very quiet most of the time. But now there were bugs chirping, varmints slipping through the grasses and climbing the branches, and the constant sounds of birds calling, except at night when the owls would hoot, but not as frequently.

"Nature sure is busy." Nath set his boots on the rocks and watched the stream rush by. "I suppose I'll get used to it, though. After all, I don't have much of a choice." Looking down at his clothing, he noticed mud splatter all over it. "I don't think looking like a vagrant will make a very good impression on whoever I meet, either." He waded into the water and sat down. The waters massaged his neck. "This isn't so bad." He rinsed off his face and hair. "I like it. I wonder why swimming in the water is different than getting rained on. This is much more pleasant."

Closing his eyes, Nath went over his plans to find the Trahaydeen. He knew what they looked like and who they were. He would go from village, to town, to city and ask the people if they had seen them. He had no doubt that someone would have seen something. Elves would stand out anywhere that wasn't elven. And the murderers wouldn't be safe in Elome. The elves were a tight people, and if the banished Trahaydeen immediately went to Elome, there would be questions.

Nath's eyes popped open. "Wait a moment. Won't the elves be looking for them too? Ah, I'm so stupid." He hit the palm of his hand on his head. "Of course they will. At least, I would. But maybe, like the dragons, they take forever making a decision. Yes, I need to be doing what I am doing, because the longer I wait, the farther away they get. And I have to find Maefon. She's in danger. I can feel it."

Nalzambor had five major cities. Quintuklen, the human city in the North; Thraag, the home of the orcs in the northeast; Elome, the home of the elves; and Morgdon, the westward city in the rocks. Then there was Narnum, the free city, where all of the races were welcome, so long as they were tolerable. If there were elves abroad in places like Narnum, then that was where Nath would start. He'd try his fortune there, and if he didn't have any luck, there were hundreds of smaller cities and towns he could look into. Someone somewhere would know something. He just had to ask.

"Well, lounging in the water isn't going to find me anything but fish," he said. At that same moment, a salmon leapt up out of the water over the rocks. Nath snagged it out of the air. The large fish wiggled in his hands. Nath held on. "Oh, no you don't. I'm hungry, and I'm going to eat you." The fish squirted out of his hands. "Ah! Blast!"

Nath climbed out of the water, pulled on his boots, readied his gear, and started back upstream.

"Help! Help!" a voice cried out from the other side of the stream. A vision of a woman raced through a clearing in a weathered cotton dress that clung to her body. Behind her, a two-legged man with four hairy arms and the head of a beast chased after her. It closed in on the screaming woman, who vanished into the willowwacks, still screaming, "Heeelp!"

Chapter 27

Without giving it a thought, Nath crossed the stream and burst out of the water. He chased after the monster into the woodland. Cutting through the brush and forest, he heard the woman still screaming, "Help meeee!"

Nath followed the sound of her voice. Branches slapped his face, and briars dug at his legs as he pushed toward the woman's cry for help.

Where did she go?

The forest darkened the deeper he went. The leaves were a deep-green roof over his head. Losing the sound of her voice, Nath slowed down. He reached behind him and drew Fang. The blade hummed in his grip and gave off a very faint shade of blue. Hearing some scuffling in the bushes and branches, Nath advanced.

A loud grunt was followed by a woman's scream.

Nath took off in a straight line. He didn't stop until he entered a cove where the beastly four-armed man had the woman cornered against the rocks.

"Get away from her, monster!" Nath shouted.

The monster whipped around. Its four oversized hands with talons like metal spikes clenched in and out. Its wide, hairy face was like a dog. Its big ears pointed up into tips. Its earlobes almost touched the layers of brawny shoulder muscles, and it stood a full foot taller than Nath. Wide jaws slavered with drool. "Go away, or die, little man! She is my prize, my prey, my dinner if I wish."

Flanking the beast, Nath said, "You speak well for such an ugly thing. Now use those big ears of yours. I will turn your four arms into two quicker than you can blink. So back away from the woman. Otherwise, I won't hesitate to slay you, whatever you are."

"I am Rond, the bugbear. I do not fear your metal. You might cut off one hand, but I will crush you with the others." He bared his teeth. "Come on then, give it a try."

Nath circled around, coming between the woman and Rond. The woman's tattered dress did nothing to conceal her beauty. She was young, fair skinned, with salt-and-pepper-colored hair and a full and fetching figure. Over his shoulder, he said back to her, "Stay close, lady. I am here, and I will protect you from this beast."

Sobbing, she said, "You are so brave, warrior. I owe you my life. Thank you for protecting me. My hero!"

Flashing his sword from side to side, Nath said, "Rond, I will only warn you one more time. Flee, or suffer the consequences of a single lethal strike. You see, I could take your arms, which seems helpful, seeing how you have two too many, or I could bury my blade in your heart. That will resolve all of your problems, and hers, and one of mine." The woman wrapped her arms around Nath's waist. "I don't think you want that, so begone."

Hugging Nath from behind and nuzzling her cheek in his back, the comely woman said, "You are my hero. A great, great hero."

"Did you hear that, Rond? I am a great, great hero, and I aim to live up to that. So last chance. Back off, or die. What will it be?"

Rond's narrowed eyes ran the full length of Fang's blade. He looked Nath in the eyes, made a hawking sound in his throat, and spit snot on the ground. "I'm going to pull that flame hair from your head, one handful at a time." He beckoned Nath forward. "Come on, give me your best."

"Stay here, lady." Nath broke away from her. "And you might not want to watch this."

"You are so brave." The woman touched his arm. "And foolish. I never met a brave man that wasn't."

"Huh?" Nath said. A shock ripped through his body like a jolt of lightning. His teeth clacked together. Fang fell from his fingers, and his legs wobbled beneath him.

Chapter 28

Regaining his balance and trying to shake the stars from his eyes, Nath said, "What did you do to me?" Charges of energy flowed from the young woman's hand and into his arm again. "Ow!" Nath fought to stand on his feet, swaying from side to side.

"Why aren't you falling?" She slapped his arm again. *Zzzzt!* Nath still stood. Her arms grew bigger. "Fall, mind you, fall!"

As she reached for Nath again, he grabbed her by the wrists. With a thick tongue, he said, "What is woong with yooou? I'm trying tooo heeelp yoooo!"

"Rond! Rond!" she called out, trying to twist out of Nath's grip. "Get this stubborn fool off me."

"Nooo, nooo," Nath said. "I am trying to help you. Why are you trying to hurt—" Rond's shadow fell over Nath and the woman. The bugbear's big fist collided with the side of Nath's face. Pain exploded through his cheek. He hit the ground face-first. The taste of dirt and grass filled his mouth. He fought to stay awake. He couldn't push his sunken face out of the dirt. Between the shocking and the heavy-handed blow, his limbs had nothing left.

"Bind him to the tree." The woman rubbed her hands with a scowl on her face.

"Why not kill him, Calypsa?" Rond said in his gruff voice. He dragged Nath by the hair and pushed him into a tree then looked at Calypsa. "I don't have any rope. What shall I tie him to the tree with?"

"Just hold him still." She faced Nath. She was very pretty, with a tiara made from twigs in her hair. The cotton dress she wore had living leaves woven into the fabric. Holding her hands out with her palms to the ground, she chanted, "Evergreen, evergreen, lend me your root. Evergreen, evergreen, life flows from your shoots."

The ground came to life. Like a snake, roots crept out of the ground, slithered around Nath, and wrapped him tight to the tree. He grimaced. The small veinlike roots felt like steel coil. They bit into his arms. His face ached, his tongue was swollen, and his energy was sapped. It took everything he had to keep from blacking out.

Calypsa and Rond huddled over Nath's gear. His leather pack lay on the ground, and Calypsa emptied out the contents. With big eyes, she said, "What have we here?" There were some potion vials, a leather purse, a small hooded lantern that fit in the palm of his hand, candles, a coil of rope, and a gauntlet with a gem embedded into the leather. She held it before her. "That's a big stone."

Rond handed her a knife. "Let me dig it out. The leather is useless."

She pulled away. "You just keep your twenty sticky fingers back, Rond. Even though the glove is too big for my hand, it is quite fashionable." She petted her face with it. Her nose crinkled. "It stinks a bit." She held out her hand. "Let me see that knife. I'm starting to think that digging it out is the right call."

"Don't ruin it," Nath mumbled.

The bugbear stormed over to Nath and pulled two hands back for a backhanded slap. "Silence!"

"Oh, Rond, leave him be. He's incapacitated now." Calypsa bit her tongue as she tried to dig the stone out of the leather glove. "My, this thing is really mounted in there well. Rond, go ahead and take a crack at it."

As Rond headed toward Calypsa, Nath managed to lift his boot and trip the bugbear. The bugbear fell hard to the ground. He jumped back up, chest and shoulders heaving. "You'll pay for that!"

Calypsa giggled. "Now that was funny. Just leave him be, Rond." She opened up the strings on Nath's purse and dumped the contents into her hand. Gold, silver, and precious gemstones poured out. "Oh my!"

Rond turned toward her. His long ears wiggled. He came to her side and fell to his knees. "It's a fortune. I've never seen such treasure." He held up an emerald that looked like a pea in his fingers. "What a score! We are rich!"

"Yes," she said. "This is the robbery of a lifetime!" She punched Rond in the arm. "I told you our day would come."

"You are thieves?" Nath said as his head began to clear. "You tricked me with a false cry for help only to steal from me?" He was aghast. "What is wrong with you?"

"We are not thieves," she argued. "He is a bugbear, and I am a dryad." She inspected the treasure in her hands. "Actually, I'm part dryad—my mother was a dryad, and my father was a man." She winked at Nath. "Not so very different than you, handsome."

"What you are doing is wrong," Nath said. "You can't just lie to people and steal from them."

"Why not? It's what we do. After all, we have to use our gifts for something," she said.

"Yes, why not," Rond said flatly. He started shaking one of the ceramic potion vials that was colored orange with black specks. "What is this?"

Calypsa snatched it away. Every move she made was graceful. Her way was captivating. "Besides, how does a lone man like you come by such treasure? Hmmm? I'll tell you how. You stole it. You stole all of it. For you are too young to have all of this wealth. It's a princess's ransom."

Brows knitted together, Nath said, "It's mine. Gifts from my father."

She burst out laughing. "Ah-hahahaha. Who is your father, the king of Quintuklen? You are going to have to come up with a better explanation than that, but I don't have time to listen." She started putting all of the items back in the pack. "Rond and I will be going. But it was nice robbing you, uh... What is your name?"

"Nath," he said with a frown.

She walked up to Nath and slung his bag over her shoulders. "Well, Nath, next time you see a gorgeous woman screaming for help, perhaps you should avoid it." She gave him a sweet kiss on the lips. "Most heroes wind up dead. Don't be one of them."

Suddenly, Nath felt very sleepy. He started to yawn. "What did you do to me?"

"I gave you the dryad's kiss. Just go to sleep, have sweet dreams of me, and enjoy it."

"But I don't want to go to..." As his words trailed off, his lids became heavy, and Calypsa and Rond walked away with his belongings.

Chapter 29

"Stop," Nath moaned. He shook the cobwebs out of his head. "Don't leave. You are thieves." As his vision became clear, Calypsa turned toward him. There was confusion on her face. She marched toward him.

"Why are you not sleeping? You should be asleep!"

"I'm not tired anymore."

She got down on her knees, grabbed his face, and kissed him again. "You will sleep. Every man I kiss sleeps."

Nath closed his eyes for a moment then popped them open again. "Not me. Perhaps your kiss isn't as powerful as you think it is. Or as good, for that matter."

"What? There is no better kisser than me." She kissed him fully with her soft lips.

Nath returned the kiss. In truth, she was a great kisser. When she broke it off, he said, "You are improving."

She jumped to her feet and stomped them on the ground. "What kind of man are you? Are you a sprite? A trickster?" She shook the bag. "Is this treasure even real? Rond! Choke the truth out of him!"

Rond fastened his big hand on Nath's neck and started squeezing. "Tell Calypsa what she wants."

Gagging, Nath tried to spit out the words. "I can't talk if I can't breathe."

"Loosen it up, Rond. Now, tell me who or what you are." She shook her head. "And is this treasure real, or is it bewitched?"

Rond's fingers loosened on Nath's neck. Nath started to get the feeling that neither Calypsa nor Rond was very bright. Either that, or she was paranoid. He considered telling her a lie. Perhaps he could be a sprite or a trickster, but lying wasn't the way he wanted to go. He decided the truth would be better. In a hoarse voice, he said, "I'm a dragon."

"A dragon? Really?" She looked at Rond. The bugbear squeezed Nath's neck again. "And if you are a dragon, then where are your scales? Your tail? I don't see any sharp teeth in your mouth. What about the horns and wings? You are a liar."

Red-faced, Nath shook his head. "I'm not."

"Just let go of him, Rond," she said. "I want to hear more of what he has to say. I have to admit, I'm a bit curious about this golden-eyed man that I cannot shock or put to sleep. That is abnormal."

"We should kill him. Cut off his head and go."

"Just let go of him." She crossed her legs, put her elbows on her knees, and propped her chin up on her hands. "I could use a good story. It's been a while."

"I disagree, Calypsa. I say we go. He smells of trickery." Rond stepped away but kept a wary eye on Nath.

"Out with it, Dragon Man," she said.

Clearing his throat, Nath said, "I am from Dragon Home."

"You mean the Mountain of Doom?"

"I suppose."

"Hah, this fairy tale is getting richer. Go on."

"I am the son of Balzurth, the king of the dragons. Recently, I was exiled for a hundred years because I am hunting down a pack of elves, called Trahaydeen, that murdered over a dozen dragon fledglings." Nath shifted against his natural bonds. "You see, I was not supposed to leave, and when I did, I became banished. So I cannot return, but I will find the murderers and avenge my brethren."

A little smile played on Calypsa's lips. Her big chestnut eyes probed his.

"What?" he said.

"You really are convinced that this is truth. I have to admit, your words are convincing. Either you are the greatest liar I have ever met, or what you say is true, which is preposterous." She glanced at Rond. "What do you think?"

"He lies." Rond punched two of his fists into both of his other hands. "Let me kill him."

"But I'm not lying," Nath pleaded. "Think about it. Your magic has little effect on me. How can you explain that, Calypsa? I know it perplexes you. The only explanation is that I am what I say I am. And that treasure you have, it could only come from the mountain. After all, I know you have not seen the likes of that before. How can you explain that?"

Calypsa's eyes looked up to the left. Rond scratched his chin. Finally, she said, "I suppose some of the story is plausible. And don't you think for a moment that I haven't witnessed many wonders. I am a dryad who has seen many things. But your story about the elves is ludicrous. Elves would never do such a thing. All of Nalzambor knows this. They might be aloof, but cold- blooded killers? I don't think so." She patted Nath on the ankle. "Sorry, but whatever you are and whoever you are, I think it's best that I keep my distance from you. So long, Nath Dragon, and thanks for all the treasure."

Chapter 30

Maefon stood behind the battlements on the top of Stonewater Keep. The wind tore at her robes, but the rain had stopped. The chronic dampness in the air lingered. Still damp, she shivered. It was always damp at the keep. Always. Below, the river rushed over the rocks, creating dangerous rapids. Her eyes followed the water. It carried large sections of branches down the channel, where it bent away from the sheer face of the mountain before turning, where it ended in a waterfall that spilled into a chasm below.

That was the washout. It was where the Caligin disciples who failed wound up. They were never told about it until they had become Caligin or it was too late. Now Chazzan was the latest elf to take the plunge into a watery grave. She rubbed the signet ring. The black stone had the distinct features of an elf etched into it. It reminded her of Chazzan. She truly had loved him.

If that can happen to him, then it can happen to me.

She couldn't shake the memory of Chazzan's limp body dangling in the might of Lord Darkken's hands. Chazzan was the best. She'd trained with many Caligin and known others, but there were none like him. He was gifted and unique. Now those blessings were in the pit of the river where countless others had failed.

She slipped the ring on her slender finger. It was too wide to fit. She looped it back through the chain and hung it over her neck. "Good-bye, Chazzan," she whispered. "You were the love of my life." She wiped her eyes and turned away from the battlement. She gasped then said, "Lord Darkken!" She gave a quick bow. "I'm sorry, I didn't know you were here."

"That's because you weren't supposed to know that I was here, Maefon," he said without feeling. He was dressed in the same robes, but his hair was braided over his shoulders in a ponytail. "Mourning, are we?"

"I-Well..." she sputtered then got a grip on herself. "Yes, I was. I'm sorry, but my heart and thoughts deceive me. I know that I cannot fool you."

"No, you can't, but you should at least try to fool me. After all, that is what Caligin do." He draped the blanket in his hands over her shoulders. "Take a breath, Maefon. I'm only jesting with you. In truth, I want the Caligin to be cold, ruthless, and compassionless. Emotionless would be delightful, but it is those emotions that drive me, and you. I hunger for power, vengeance, and supremacy. You would probably kill for Chazzan because you have passion for him. Perhaps I killed him because I was jealous of the spark that he shared with you. Now, wouldn't that be something."

"I'm flattered that you are so fond of me," she said, pulling the blanket over her shoulders and offering him a smile.

"Please, don't be flattered. I was only using that as an example." He petted her cheek. "You see, Maefon, the world is run on emotion. The Caligin were created to use them and abuse them, turning one against another by pulling on heart strings and levers." He moved to the battlements, raised his arms to the skies, and lifted his voice to the air. "It's intoxicating!"

"I agree," she said, "and invigorating. I enjoyed leading Nath along. He was very naive."

"Yes," he said with a dashing smile. He leaned against the battlements. "Tell me more. I want to hear this story. All of the details. Don't leave out a bit."

"That will take hours."

"You've been working on this for decades. I have the time, and you have the time. Time is a Caligin's ally."

Maefon started with the day she was taken in as a Trahaydeen, and the moment she met Nath. "Aside from you, I never imagined a man could be so handsome." She went on, talking about the friendship they built over the years, and the longer it went, the easier it was to deceive him. "But it wasn't easy. If Chazzan wasn't there, I think I might have been swept away by Nath. Chazzan kept me grounded. I struggle with why you would kill a brother that was so instrumental to your cause."

"Ah." He lifted a finger. "You just answered the question yourself. You called Chazzan an instrument. Or more clearly in his case... a tool. A big one. You see, he was there to keep you grounded and focused on your mission. He accomplished that, and I didn't really have any more use for him. So I killed him."

"Are you telling me that his feelings for me were not sincere?"

"If he was as good a Caligin as we thought he was, then no, he didn't have any feeling for you whatsoever. Henceforth, you shouldn't miss him." He looked between the battlements. "I'm certain that he's not giving you any more thought these days."

"But—"

"Now, don't let your heart get all twisted up. This is a learning experience. You will have other elves, men, or who knows, maybe a precious halfling in your life. It's all part of the game. Just enjoy playing it."

The weight of his words was staggering. Her shoulders drooped, and she stared at the ground with glassy eyes. How could what Chazzan showed her not be real? It felt real. She was enthralled with him, and he with her. Quietly, she said, "I have a lot of learning to do."

Lord Darkken clapped his hands and spread them wide. "There you go! You see, you are learning."

Maefon stepped back. "But if I completed my mission, then—"

"Then why don't I scoop you up in my arms and pitch you over this wall? Well, I have thought about that, but purely for entertainment's sake, and that wouldn't be practical. Besides, the disciples foul things up often enough to keep me treated." He gave her a big hug. "No, I still need to keep you around. You are the reason Nath left the mountain, are you not?"

"I'm certain that he would be worried about me. He tires of life in the mountain. He just needed a reason to leave. I'm a good one. I planted the seed of friendship deeply."

Lord Darkken lifted his eyes, cupped his mouth, and let out a squawk. A huge vulture circled down from the sky and landed on top of the battlements. Big as a man, it had two bald heads with rough and ugly reddish skin. Its feathers were black as a crow's. The nasty-looking bird's eyes were burning emeralds. "This is Galtur. My eyes, my ears, my familiar. Handsome, isn't he?"

"For a vulture, I suppose."

"Ha, good jest."

"So now are you going to tell me what you want from Nath?"

Rubbing the bird's belly of ruffled feathers, Lord Darkken smiled. "Perhaps later."

CHAPTER 31

NATH BUTTED HIS HEAD AGAINST the tree. "I'm so stupid!" He'd been fighting against his bindings for almost an hour. The more he wriggled, the tighter the roots became. "Come on, her spell can't last forever." He closed his eyes, breathed deeply through his nostrils, and let his body relax. The roots slackened. Nath flexed his muscles. The entanglement of foliage tightened again. "Gads."

On and off, he tried to relax, exhale, and narrow his body. Slowly, he shifted his shoulders, trying to inch his way out. Like living things, the roots tightened with every move. "Oh, it's no use. By the time the spell wears off, if it wears off, they'll be long gone." He leaned back and sighed.

So far, his life abroad in Nalzambor hadn't gone too well. He was certain when he left that he'd fare better, but already he'd been duped by the first people he'd encountered. And he was trying to help them.

What kind of world is this, anyway?

He thought about Calypsa and her captivating smile. He'd read a little about dryads in Dragon Home. Dryads were wood nymphs, born of the trees through magic, but she claimed to be different. She said she was part-dryad, with a human father. It seemed strange, if not impossible. Regardless, she wielded enchantments, two of which failed against Nath, but the third, the roots, got him. As far as he understood magic, it didn't have a lasting effect. So the spell was bound to wear off sooner or later. But that might be hours, or even days. He couldn't wait that long. Not only did Calypsa and Rond have his belongings, but they had Fang too.

"I'm not going to just sit here!" Nath heaved against his bonds. "Hurk!" His biceps and shoulder muscles bulged. The veins in his temples pulsed. His jaws clenched as new sweat beaded on his forehead. He gave it everything he had. The roots tightened. "I can do this! Mind over matter, Nath. Mind over matter!"

The vines cut the circulation off in his arms. His fingers started to turn blue.

Nath gasped. His taut muscles slackened. "Fine, you win, snakes of the ground, you win!" Panting, he noticed a woodchuck saunter into the clearing. It was a big one, with its little black nose to the ground. It sniffed the grass and the shrubs, gave Nath a glance, found a tree, and chewed at the bark.

"Say..." Nath said out loud. When he was younger, he was told that dragons came from magic and magic was in them all. They all had varying abilities. One of those abilities, he recalled, was speaking with other creatures. Not sure how to go about it, he spoke in dragonese. "Excuse me, woodchuck, can you hear me?"

Coated in a healthy brown fur, the woodchuck stopped chewing on the bark in his hands and looked at Nath.

"You hear me, yes, you can hear me. Woodchuck, will you come over here and free me of these vines?"

The woodchuck dropped from its hind legs onto all fours and came at Nath.

"You understand me. Yes, keep coming," Nath said, feeling a thrill go through him.

The woodchuck stopped at his feet. It sniffed the toe of his boot then opened its jaws and bit into it.

"Ow! Don't chew me—chew the vines!"

The woodchuck scurried away.

"No, no, no, no," Nath said more politely, "please come back. I need you to chew these vines and roots." He nodded toward it. "Please, chew them."

Head down, the woodchuck waddled forward and passed Nath to the other side of the tree.

Nath couldn't see it. With his head twisted to the side, he said, "Are you doing it? Yes? Chew them. Chew them away." He didn't hear anything. Turning his head from one side to the other, he said, "Are you there? Woodchuck, are you there?" He turned his head left, right, left. "Gah!"

"Gaaaaah!" the woodchuck said back to him, except it wasn't a woodchuck. It was a small, very hairy little man, with big brown eyes and sharp ears that pointed downward.

"What happened to the woodchuck?" Nath said, recoiling from the weird-looking little man, who was so thick in hair he didn't need clothes but wore mud-red fur trousers that covered his knees. "Who are you?"

Jutting his head in and out like a clucking chicken, the little man said, "Who are you?"

Nath arched a brow. The weird little shaggy man didn't seem dangerous. He carried nothing in his little hands. The skin on his face was smooth, but his features were large. He had a triangular snout and wide mouth. "I am—"

"Yes, I heard, you are Nath Dragon."

"Just Nath," he said. "Uh, you heard all of that? You saw Calypsa and Rond rob me?"

The little man gestured with his hands when he talked. His voice was pleasant, somewhat husky, but shady. "Oh, yes, the nymph and the bugbear. I see them rob all the time. I listen. They are greedy but not as smart as they think they be. I watch. I know." He flicked his pointed earlobes and popped out his eyes. "I know all in the forest." He made clicking sounds with his mouth as he poked and prodded Nath with his fingers and bare toes. "I heard your story. Yes, very interesting. Son of the dragon king. I believe you." He made a giggle. "Very interesting."

"Then you'll free me? Please free me."

"I will free you, but first, you must tell me what my name is."

Chapter 32

Nath shook his head. "What? Is that a jest? There are a plethora of names out there. I couldn't begin to guess that. What sort of creature are you, anyway? I don't recall learning about something like you. Are you some mix of woodchuck and pixie?"

"Hahaha." The hairy man sat on Nath's thighs like they were a bench. "I'm no part woodchuck, though my pelt resembles them." He picked bark out of his chest. "I'm a hermix.

A part gnome, part hermit, part varmint, some say. Hee-hee. So guess my name, and I will free you."

Rolling his eyes, Nath said, "I don't have time for this. What you ask me is impossible."

"Nothing is impossible, and in truth, I want to help you out. So I will make it easy. My name is Rumple."

"You are telling me your name, and it is Rumple?"

The hermix's caterpillar eyebrows lifted as a smile full of teeth took over his face. "Is that your guess?"

Nath shrugged. "I'll bite. I guess Rumple."

Rocking back and forth and stomping his little hairy feet, the hermix said, "No, that is not it. It is Ruffle. Not Rumple. You are wrong. Tee-hee."

"Is anyone honest outside of the mountain? So far, everyone I've met has lied or deceived me in one way or the other. No wonder the dragons find this world amiss. This is ridiculous." Nath kicked his legs.

Ruffle bounced up and down. "Oh, that is fun. Like riding the rapids. Life is filled with troubled waters. *You* will always paddle against the stream."

"Just get off me if you won't help."

Ruffle stabbed a finger in his face. "Ah, ah, ah, I will help you, but you, dragon prince, must help me."

"Help you how?"

"I need your promise that you will help me when the time comes. Your word, Nath Dragon."

"It's just Nath, and I'm not going to agree to do something if I don't know what it is."

Ruffle cupped his ear. "Hear that?"

"No."

"Yes, it is the sound of Calypsa and Rond getting farther and farther away. Soon, they will be gone, and you will not find them. Heh-hee."

Nath's fingers fidgeted. Ruffle was right. The longer he waited, the more likely his belongings would be gone forever. And he didn't want to spend his time tracking them down. He wanted to focus on finding the betrayers. Besides, what demand could the silly little creature picking his ear while he sat on Nath's lap really want? "I won't kill anyone for you. Is that clear?"

"Oh yes, perfectly." Ruffle eagerly nodded. "So you agree?"

Unable to stand the thought of Calypsa getting away, he said, "I agree."

Ruffle clapped his hands. "Hah-hah! Perfect. I will see you in the future, Nath Dragon. Be ready." The hermix faded along with his voice. In a moment, he was gone, as if he'd never been there at all.

"Hey!" Nath said, narrowing his eyes on the spot where Ruffle vanished. "You need to free… me?" The roots and vines that had constricted him were gone. "Yes!"

In no time, Nath was on his feet and running. He moved through the forest, hopping fallen trees and creeks like a deer. As he recalled some of Master Elween's teachings that—at the time—he never thought would have any application, his keen eye followed the disturbed branches and bushes where Rond must have passed. There were big footprints in the soft ground too. There was no sign of Calypsa's footprints, but he had no doubt that she was with Rond. Rond's body odor still lingered. Nath ran for a full thirty minutes before he caught up with them. They were sloshing through an ankle-deep stream. Calypsa had Nath's pack slung over her shoulder. Rond clapped. She stopped and turned.

Nath sank behind the bushes.

CHAPTER 33

CALYPSA'S EYES PASSED OVER NATH. As Rond crossed to the other side of the stream, she looked away, started singing again, and finished crossing.

Nath let out a breath of relief. He wasn't going to rush into this. He would follow along and see where they went, and once he saw an opening, he would take it. All he needed to do was snatch his pack and sword. Once he did that, he'd run. He knew they couldn't catch him, and he wouldn't be dumb enough to let them trick him again either.

Patience, Nath, patience. They might fool me once, but they won't fool me twice.

Calypsa and Rond moved at a brisk pace. Neither of them seemed to have a worry in the world as they both walked with their arms swinging. No, the two bandits of the willowwacks seemed to have delusions of grandeur in mind as they talked back and forth, laughing at one another.

It rankled Nath as he darted between the elms and blueberry bushes. He would get them. He just had to wait for the right time and then pounce. At the same time, the longer they walked, the more he worried. He envisioned them having a hideout of some sort, perhaps a cave along the grounds or a fort in the trees where it would be difficult to sneak up on them.

When will they stop walking? They have to stop sometime, don't they?

Tirelessly, the odd pair kept going onward, upward, downward, through channels of moss-covered rocks and huge ferns that filled the forest. Nath's biggest issue would be retrieving Fang. The brute had the blade and scabbard strapped over his back. His pack wouldn't be an issue. Calypsa carried it over one shoulder, with her flowing hair tossed to the side of the other.

Finally, shortly after night had fallen, they settled down in a clearing and made camp. Rond stacked up sticks. He broke big sections of branches with his arms. Calypsa touched the wood with her fingertips. There was a loud pop, and the campfire came to life. With the warm glow of firelight on her face, she talked with Rond and left the pack beside her. Nath listened in from only a couple dozen feet away.

"Rond, do you suppose that Nath really was what he said he was?" She had a brush carved out of wood that she ran through her hair. "I can't get over him still standing after I sent a charge through him. Several times. And those eyes. No man has eyes like that."

"I don't care what he is." Rond's four hands were filled with different things. On the top left, he held a hatchet, and in the bottom left, he held big branches. He chopped them into pieces while with his hands and arms on the right, he ate dried meat and drank from a canteen. "I hope a wild thing comes by and kills him. I didn't like him. He had a smart mouth. Everyone thinks they are smarter than Rond, but they are not."

"No, of course not, Rond. You are, after all, the smartest bugbear I know." She smiled at him when he stopped doing what he was doing and cast a wary eye at her. "You're smarter than most people too. But you want to kill everyone you meet. You would make a fine murderer if you wanted to be."

"I am a warrior." Rond beat his chest with the cheek of his axe. He shrugged. "But being a bugbear, we do like to kill things. We are good at it. Strong. Mighty. Hah." He flexed all four of his arms. "I am mightiest of them all."

"I've never met one mightier. You are a true warrior, Rond. The best. Just think, now you can buy whatever you need thanks to this treasure." She patted the backpack. "It is a fortune, but didn't he say there is more where this came from? I'm curious."

Rond tossed his sticks into the fire. With his heavy, gravelly voice, he said, "Stop thinking about that man. He is trouble. A liar. He stole it the same as we stole from him. We will be the better for it."

"He seemed innocent, though. If not for that far-fetched story about the elves—"

"I hate elves." Rond sat down in front of the fire across from Calypsa. He sneered. "They think they are so perfect. Scrawny little men that run and dance like they have wings on their feet. Hate them very much. I agreed with the flame hair. They are evil. I'm not surprised one bit."

She laughed. "A bugbear calling an elf evil. Well, if that's not the pot calling the kettle black."

"I'm not evil, entirely." Rond's ears bent as he spoke. "Misguided, perhaps, but not evil. I like things my brethren don't, such as you. That's why I'm outcast."

"You are an outcast because you are not some mindless slayer that kills whatever he is told to kill. You thought for yourself, Rond. You should be proud of that. You are a gem."

His head sagged. "No, I am outcast. My kind hate me. I'll have no home in the rocks and caves again. Not with them."

"Some of them might come around to your way of thinking. You never know." She made her way over to him and wrapped her arms around his shoulders. "Don't give up on your people. People change. You did."

"No, I still want to kill people." His face clenched. "It's just not the same mindless urge. I think about it first. If it's me or them, I let them have it." He punched his hands several times. "I still like it."

Nath picked up a stone. He chucked it far over Calypsa and Rond. The stone crashed through the forest.

Rond came to his feet. Pushing Calypsa behind him, he said, "Wait here. Probably a critter, but you never know." He vanished into the woodland, leaving Calypsa alone and peering after him.

On cat's feet, Nath crept into the camp. With Calypsa turned away from him, he grabbed his bag. He pulled open the neck strings, reached inside, and fished out the leather gauntlet.

The leather was thick and supple. The tips of the fingers were cut off. The blue gemstone mounted on the glove above the wrist shone like the moon. He slipped it on. The gem glowed more brightly.

Calypsa turned. "You!"

CHAPTER 34

"NO, NATH. BUT I HAVE to say, I'm a bit offended that you've forgotten my name so soon." Nath stretched the gauntlet over his left hand and flexed his fingers. He shouldered his pack. "I believe this belongs to me."

Calypsa's fists balled up at her sides. "You put that back. We stole it honestly."

"What? *Stole it honestly?* How can you steal something honestly? That is preposterous. What is wrong with the people in this world?"

Calypsa gave a sad look. Clasping her fingers together, she came toward him, pleading. "Oh, Nath, we are hungry. That is why we steal. The world is harsh and cruel. Please, let us share it." She went down on one knee. "I am at your mercy, but don't leave us starving. We'll die out here. Let me have the sack."

Nath couldn't break her hypnotic stare. His mind wanted to give her what she wanted. The words that came from her mouth were so convincing. The forest became a blur around her. "I… I…" He shook his head. He wanted to break her stare but could not. "I can't."

"*You must give me the pack, Nath.*" Her words were a tapestry carried through the air, dropping an unseen blanket over Nath. "*It is the right thing to do. Just set it down.*"

Nath started to take the pack off his shoulders. He couldn't feel his body. Some unseen force moved his body on its own. Her suggestions turned what he came to do completely around. *Stop. Don't let her do this. This is my gear. My possessions.* He stared back in her eyes. "No."

"*Look at me, Nath. Listen to me. Nath, leave the pack and go,*" she said with big beautiful eyes that could make men's hearts waxen. "*It is for the best. Trust me.*"

He stood rigid, with sweat dripping down his face. He fought against her words, an inner war waging in his mind. She was so beautiful, pleasant, soft, and convincing. All he wanted to do was help her.

"*You don't really need it, Nath. This would be the right thing to do,*" she continued in words soft and warm like a fireside blanket. "*Help me.*"

The backpack slipped down his arm. Completely unaware of his surroundings, Nath let the pack fall to the ground. All he saw was her with a smile growing on her face.

"Thank you, Nath," she said, crawling toward the pack. She looked up and over his shoulders. "Be still, Nath."

The blue gemstone on his gauntlet shone bright as a star. Nath's thoughts became lucid, his awareness keen. Someone crept in behind him. Like a striking snake, he turned and punched Rond square in the chest. The four-armed bugbear's entire body left the ground. He flew back twenty feet and slammed hard into the trunk of a tree.

Calypsa snatched the pack.

Before she could dart away, Nath grabbed her arm. "You aren't going anywhere with this." He ripped the pack free of her grip and slung it over his shoulder. "And I think I've had enough of you."

"Look at me, Nath," she pleaded as she tried to pull away. "Look at me."

Nath looked her dead in the eye. "I'm looking." Her hypnotic stare was there, but it had no power over him. "And I don't like what I see." He dragged her by the wrist toward Rond. The bugbear was sitting on his behind, rubbing the back of his head and chest. "Give me my sword, Rond, or I swear I'll punch you so hard next time that you won't land until tomorrow."

Grimacing as he moved with shaky limbs, Rond laid the sword and scabbard down at Nath's feet.

"You tricked us, Nath Dragon. You used magic." Calypsa's cheeks were rosy, and her hair hung in her eyes. She strained to break Nath's grip. "Let go of me!"

"I will when I'm ready." Nath held her with his right hand and looked at the gauntlet on his left. The fires in the blue gem died. "Thank you."

"What is that?" she said, shooting a glance at his glove. "Tell me. You are a warlock, aren't you?"

"No, I'm a dragon. And this," he said, holding up his left hand and spreading his fingers, "is the Gauntlet of Goam, a gift from my father. Though I never had any use for it before today. Frankly, I wasn't even sure of the full extent of its strengthening power." His brows lifted. "I think I know now. Hah! I'm glad I brought it." He swung a look behind him. "Aren't you, Rond?"

Rond clutched his ribs with all four arms. He feebly shook his head.

Nath released Calypsa. As she stood beside him, flatfooted and gaping, he slung Fang over his back, adjusted the strap, and put the pack on top of it. He looked down at Calypsa. "We are finished here. I wish we could have met under better circumstances, Calypsa. What you do is wrong. You should use your gifts for a greater purpose."

"That's just silly." She crossed her arms over her chest and turned her nose up. "You are no better than we are. You tricked us all the same."

"I didn't trick anybody." He shook his head. "I'm leaving now. Don't follow me. Don't chase me. I don't want to see either of you again. I won't be so merciful next time. I hope I'm clear." Giving them both a lasting look, he said, "This is normally where I'd say goodbye, but it doesn't seem appropriate for thieves and robbers."

Chapter 35

Not wanting to be followed, Nath ran on and off through the night and through the day, never stopping to rest. He crossed the highland plains and ran by herds of cattle. He wanted as much distance between him and the thieves as he could get. He'd been tricked and cheated, but he'd learned his lesson.

Making his way down a hillside, he finally stopped at an overlook. The rising sun settled on his face. Down in the valley was a large city with streets paved in stone and tall buildings over three stories tall. The main city was built by large cut stones, and outside of its border were homes made of logs, surrounded by miles of farmland where crops were growing and livestock grazed.

Nath tingled. It was clear to him that this city was rather big, with tens of thousands of people living together. From where he sat, a mile away, he could count the farmers in the fields. Men and women worked together, along with halflings, and even though he wasn't completely sure, possible part-elves too. The men wore wide-brimmed straw hats and had their sleeves rolled up. The women were in modest dresses and white cloth hats decorated with flowers. Wagons pulled by horses came and went on the main roads to the city.

"I suppose the time has come to dip my feet in the city." He headed to the bottom of the hill and angled toward the dirt road. Passing by the farmhouses and fields, he came to a huge wooden sign mounted on a boulder that read Riegelwood. There was a crest with an oak tree growing out of a rock. Shields were in the leaves.

Nath politely waved to everyone he passed. Most of the people waved or smiled. Others didn't look his way. The actual city started where the dirt road became paved with stones. Buildings stretched into the distance as far as he could see. Most of them were made from stone with wooden porches and walkways. There were decks on the top of the roof. People leaned over the rails. Flowers decorated the windows, and clothing was hung on lines on the very top roofs.

Nath nodded and said hello to a group of women who were walking toward him. They all blushed, giggled, and walked on by. One of them tripped over her dress as she passed. She spilled a basket of apples on the road, but she still couldn't take her eyes off Nath.

"Will you quit gawking, Candice?" A woman who seemed like the young lady's mother helped her daughter up. "You are making a fool of yourself."

Nath came over to help. "Let me lend a hand." He picked up the apples and loaded them into the basket. The other women giggled as he handed the basket to the girl. "Here you go. Sorry for the trouble. Could you tell me—"

The mother cut in front of him. "She's spoken for, lad. Now move it along." She gave Nath a long look up and down. "Quickly, before I forget I'm spoken for as well."

"Mother!" the young lady said, embarrassed.

"Well, I might be older, but I'm not blind. Let's go, girls. We have fantasies… I mean chores to do."

Nath waved as they hurried away. He turned and found himself face to face with two soldiers. They wore metal skull caps and a red tunic with the city crest sewn on the front over chainmail armor. Their hands were on the pommels of their swords. One was tall, black-haired, and had a short thick beard, and the other younger, shorter and clean shaven.

"Hello," Nath said.

"What brings you to Riegelwood, traveler?" the older soldier said.

"Just passing through." Nath could tell by the soldier's tone that he took his business seriously.

"I see." The bearded soldier's eyes landed on Fang's handle. "That's quite a length of steel you have strapped on your back. Are you a soldier or another one of those adventuring types who likes to create a ruckus in our city?"

"Yes, well, neither, I suppose," Nath replied as the younger guard moved behind him. "My father made this sword, and I'm a bit of a blacksmith myself. It's the last gift I have from him, and I go everywhere with it. That said, I'm just looking for a place to settle for a bit. I have money, and I won't be any trouble. If you could show me where I could find a place to eat and sleep, I'd be grateful."

The soldier clawed at his beard. "What do you think, Kevan?"

"He sounds honest, Hartson." The young man reached toward Fang's handle. "This craftsmanship is astounding. Look at the crossguard's detail. I swear, the little dragons are staring at me. May I touch it?"

"Uh, I wouldn't," Nath said, but it was too late. The young soldier's fingers were on the crossguard.

"That isn't real gold, is it?" Kevan said.

"Of course not. No fool of a blacksmith would make crossguards out of gold. It's too soft."

"It's gold plated," Nath said.

"It will chip," Hartson replied, "but that's probably more of a decorative sword, right? It's too fancy and big for fighting."

"Well, I haven't had to use it yet."

"Good. See to it that you keep it that way." Hartson knocked on Nath's breastplate. "What kind of metal is that?" He rubbed his knuckles. "Oh, never mind. Listen, you seem decent enough. Take this road five blocks down, turn left, and you'll find the Oxen Inn. Tell them Hartson and Kevan sent you. But don't make me look bad. Understand?"

"Yes, sir. Thank you, sir."

Hartson pointed at him. "I mean it. The city lord won't tolerate troublemakers, and I won't either. Come on, Kevan. We have work to do."

Chapter 36

The Oxen Inn was a quaint establishment. Men sat out on the porch underneath the deck, rocking in rockers and smoking tobacco made from polished wrynnwood pipes. They made small talk about the weather and the trades they represented. Nath gave them a nod on his way up the steps. Some of the men glanced his way but continued on with their lively conversations. Entering the tavern, Nath nearly bumped into a waitress. She slipped by him with a tray of food on her shoulder and kept on going.

Almost every chair at the tables was filled. Men and women were talking, laughing, and eating. There was a small stage in the corner near a fireplace. Three red-headed halflings sat on tall stools. One sang to the melody the others played on the violin and flute. The song was peppy, and several patrons clapped to the beat.

The day they robbed the dragon is the day the dread men died...
Fire came and swallowed them up, no water could quench the flame.
The disgraceful men of Run Tilllamill, were brave and bold, not wise.
For the day they robbed the dragon, is the day the foul men died.
The dragon took the treasure back,
The men's coffins were filled with ash...
Cause the day they robbed the dragon is the day the unwise died.

Nath gave a winsome smile as he made his way over to a lone stool at the bar. Men hunched over their food, gobbling up piles of steamy eggs covered in cheese, thick strips of bacon, and slabs of ham. Biscuits the size of Nath's fist were smothered in gravy. Nath scooted the stool back. His belly roared.

A very heavy man in nice clothing, tastefully wearing a lot of gold jewelry, cast a tired eye at Nath. "If you're hungry, this is the place to be." The man let out a belch. "Pardon me. Best food in the little kingdoms. Always stay here in my travels and try to stay as long as I can." He spied Nath's sword. "Uh, that's a big sword. Are you a henchman? Henchmen eat in the back."

"No, I'm checking in." Nath watched the women and men coming and going from the kitchen. The place was a hive of activity. Behind the bar, three women were working. Their hair was in buns, and they wore powder-blue aprons. They refilled coffee and switched out empty plates with plates loaded down with food. Nath waved at them. They paid him no mind. "Sir," Nath said, but the man turned his back and crammed half a biscuit into his mouth. Nath felt a tap on the shoulder. He turned. "Oh my."

A woman as tall as him and built like a blacksmith stood in front of him. Her brown hair was back in a ponytail, and her muscular arms were crossed over her chest. She wore an apron like the others but seemed more menacing than the rest. She cast a wary eye on Nath. "Excuse me, but we don't allow the adventuring types here. No offense, but this is a different kind of place of business. As you can see, our customers aren't loaded down in weaponry, just money, and we keep it that way." She took Nath by the elbow. "Try the Fox's Pit. Out you go."

Nath tried to ease his arm out of her grip. She held him fast. "I was told to tell you that Hartson and Kevan sent me."

Her grip eased. "They did, huh? Tell me, what did Hartson and Kevan look like?" He gave a quick, accurate description of the two men. "I see," she said. "Well, I'm Nina. I run the Oxen, and I won't have any trouble. You look like trouble with that hardware on your back." She let go of his elbow and gave him a friendly pinch on the chin. "But *you* don't look like trouble—anything but, actually." She smiled and stared right in his eyes. It went on for an awkward amount of time.

"Excuse me, Nina?" he said, sitting back down.

"Oh, oh yes," she said, blushing as she flattened out her apron with her hands. "Were you wanting to stay or eat?"

"Both, actually."

"Well, listen, you can't be down on the floor with that sword and wearing the stove door on your chest. I'll get you a room, but you need to change."

Scratching the back of his head, Nath said, "I don't have another shirt."

"You have money, correct?"

He nodded.

"I'll send a shirt up." Nina searched the room. She caught a tiny girlish woman as thin as a stick crossing the floor. "Little Shirl, get him a room and a shirt, and bring him down here while I fix him up."

The little woman nodded and hurried away.

Nina helped Nath out of his seat and sat down. "I'll save your stool and have a plate of hot food ready for you. Make it quick."

Chapter 37

Upstairs, Nath's room had a single bed with two quilts stacked up at the foot of the bed and a pillow. There was a small chest of drawers, and an oil lantern on a nightstand. He dropped all of his gear on the bed, closed the window, locked it, and drew the curtains.

"Here is your key and shirt," Little Shirl said, holding up the key while her eyes stayed focused on the floor. "You should change quickly. Nina doesn't like to wait. She is very demanding."

"Yes, well, this looks like a very busy place." He removed his breastplate and shirt and set them on the bed. Little Shirl stole a glance at him. "I believe I can find my way back, Little Shirl."

"Of course," she said flatly. "But do hurry." She opened the door, stepped out, and closed it behind her.

Nath slipped on a royal-blue tunic, adjusted the leather strings at the neck, and stared at the length of the sleeves. "This is a fine fit."

He took out his coin purse, exited the room, locked the door, and put the key in the purse. Heading down the hallway, he noticed Little Shirl waiting at the top of the stairs, adjusting the bun in her hair. "I told you I could find it, Little Shirl."

She held out her hand. "Yes, but you forgot my gratuity."

"Your what?"

"Have you ever stayed in an inn before? I could tell by the look about you, you hadn't. You seem as innocent as a sheep." She spoke in a spooky, quiet, and dull manner. "A gratuity is when you pay someone like me for the little help I do for you."

"You handed me a shirt and key."

"Yes, but I'll always clean and care for your room. Look after other needs. Just ask. It's how I make my living."

"Oh, I see. Please, excuse my ignorance. I haven't been to a city so big before."

"I could tell."

Nath fished out a gold piece from his purse. "Will this be adequate?"

Little Shirl's unblinking eyes hung on the coin like it was a diamond of comparable size. She swiped it out of his hand. "Yes. Thank you." She hurried down the steps and vanished through the doors leading into the kitchen.

Nath joined Nina at the bar. The man in the stool beside her had cleared out, and she switched to it.

Patting Nath's stool, she said, "I kept it warm for you." She snapped her fingers. A girl brought over a plate of steaming food, a wooden tankard filled to the brim with milk, and a glass cup and saucer of coffee. "Little Shirl hustled into the kitchen with a smile, I think," Nina said. "I'm curious as to why."

Nath stuffed bacon and ham inside his biscuit. "She introduced me to gratuity. I think she was pleased with what she had earned."

"Which was?"

Taking a bite out of his biscuit, he said, "Just a gold piece."

Nina's eyes grew big. "Nath, that is excessive. Only a silver at most. A few copper pieces would have been more than adequate."

"I don't have any of those." He drank his milk. "Ah, all of this is wonderful. Sometimes I forget to eat, but when I do eat, I eat a lot in a single sitting. You might have to keep the plates coming."

"Yes, well, that won't be a problem." She dusted the crumbs off his chest. "Nath, if you don't mind me asking, where do you come from? I've seen people from all over Nalzambor, but you are not like any of them."

"Why is that?"

Nina eased back against the bar. The gruff exterior she had carried earlier had been replaced by a lovely woman who carried herself in a very polite manner. "For starters, I've never seen a man with eyes the color of gold. Your hair, well, I'll just say, would make a princess jealous."

Smiling, with a mouthful of food, he said, "It would, wouldn't it?"

"Oh yes. Listen, it's not my business where you are from. After all, we are strangers. But I am glad that Hartson sent you here." Her legs were crossed, and hands clasped on her knees as she kicked her foot. "Are you going to be staying long?"

"Possibly." He dipped his biscuit into his gravy and ate the whole bite. "I'm from the south, and from a place that isn't a large city such as this. I want to get a feel for how life operates in a place like this, and I'm looking for some people. The truth is, I don't even have any idea where to find them. I'm just looking." Nath didn't want to say too much. He didn't know much about Nina, but she did seem friendly. He didn't want to make her suspicious either. He decided to fill her in a little more. "You see, I have some friends that ran away. I need to find them."

"Did you stop to think that they might not want to be found? Do you even know why they ran away?"

Nath told a half truth. "They were scared."

"Now that is interesting. Of what? I hope not you."

Nath wiped his hands on his cloth napkin. "No, not me. I feel that one of them was forced to flee because of the actions of the others. I want to make sure they are safe."

"A kidnapping?"

"Maybe."

"Nath, I've been dealing with people for over twenty years. The Oxen Inn is my family, and it is my home. And when you mingle as much as I do, you get a deep understanding of people." She took his hand in hers.

"This person you are looking for, it's a woman, isn't it?"

He gave a terse nod.

"And you love her, don't you?"

Feeling a little foolish, he said, "Yes."

CHAPTER 38

ONCE THINGS SLOWED DOWN IN the Oxen Inn, Nina offered to take Nath through the city. They strolled down the streets together. People stepped aside as she passed, even the men. Nina carried an air about her, and her towering presence was formidable as she stood a couple inches taller than Nath. She filled him in on Riegelwood and its people.

"The five major cities have kings and queens that rule them," she said, "but even though Riegelwood is vast, we don't have kings and queens. Instead, we have city lords and ladies. Our city lord is Jander, a fair-minded man whose family has been in charge for centuries. He keeps Riegelwood in order, but there is only so much he can do. We aren't without our problems, the same as any other town, municipality, or province."

Nath noticed beggars in the corners and men huddled in the shadows of the alleys. His nose crinkled when they passed certain places in the city. "Yes, there are some odors that I'm not accustomed to."

"Yes, the safest place to be is the places that don't stink, unless it's a barn, or something. It's understandable there." Nina walked with her arms behind her back. She was heading toward the castle that stood out at the end of the road. The stonework was white, and it had three ivory towers behind its walls with red roofs made from baked-clay tiles. The flag of Riegelwood billowed on the tops of all of them. From the main road, scaffolding held up workers that labored on the castle's wall. "That is Lord Jander's home. They are always building on it. It's a big family, but they really don't need that much room. My inn holds one hundred comfortably, but that castle could hold a thousand."

"I thought you said he was fair-minded."

"There have been worse than him. Jander hasn't become completely power hungry yet, but he is paranoid. That's why you can't be wandering around this city, asking questions. Adventurers pass through all of the time and are tolerated, but if they step out of line, they can easily wind up in the dungeons. If you don't like the stink up here, then you'll be in for a real shock when the stink greets you down there."

A flock of pigeons flapped away when they walked by. "I'm just looking for a friend. Certainly, there have been lost people in this city before."

"Yes, lost people and kidnapped ones as well." She led them to a small garden park across the street from the castle. Small trees and bountiful flowers flourished, and an assortment of colorful winged chirping birds fluttered about. They sat on a black marble bench. "There is a lot of wealth that flows through this trade city, and it's not all honorable. Things happen behind the scenes. People can be robbed, killed, or even disappear altogether. Gone without a trace. The city lord has to take care of his people, but there are always threats to his castle. Recently, one of his own daughters went missing. She was returning home from Quintuklen when tragedy occurred. She didn't make it. Her armed escorts were found dead less than a league from here. They had no wounds. They stood where they were, as solid as stone. There was no sign of Lord Jander's most beloved daughter, either. He called her Princess. Janna is what we like to call her."

"That's very sad," Nath said, watching the soldiers who were posted on the castle walls. "So are they still looking for her?"

"Certainly, but the more time passes, the colder the trail gets. I haven't seen Lord Jander in quite some time. I fear he is brokenhearted. Janna was very special to him." She sneezed. "Sorry, sometimes the flowers get me. Where was I? Yes, Lord Jander, I hear, secretly blames a rival family. He thinks they are trying to take him down and took Janna to wound him. Anything is possible. If she's not found, it's possible that a feud between the families will break out. That can get very ugly as well as bloody."

"There was no sign of her at all?" Nath asked. "Someone must know something."

"The trail went cold. I don't know how much you know about Nalzambor, but—"

"I know plenty if you are going to mention magic, Nina. When you mentioned the princess vanishing, it reminded me of what happened to my friend. She vanished very much the same. My brethren had no sense of what happened to her."

Nina shooed a bird off the side of the bench. "Go away, little nibbler. I don't have seeds today. Sorry, Nath. I come here often and feed them. They know me." She gasped. "Nath!" Small birds who had perched themselves on Nath's shoulders and legs scattered. "How did you do that?"

He shrugged. "I don't know. I just thought the birds liked me. Is that not ordinary?"

"No." She let out a laugh. "But I don't think you are ordinary either. You have a very charming quality about you. I think you will be well accepted by people."

Nath pulled his shoulders back. "Thank you. Nina, do you think you could take me to the place where the woman vanished from? The princess?"

"I don't see why. Listen, what you are talking about is adventuring, and that's a very risky affair." Nina stretched out her fists and yawned. "Excuse me. As I was saying before, adventurers, heroes for hire, henchmen, fortune hunters, and mercenaries are a dangerous and often sordid lot. They claim good intentions, but what they do, they do for treasure and glory. And it can be very competitive. You see, Nath, there is a reward for the princess, and there are men and women, around and about, that are trying to solve this mystery. You don't want to cross them."

"But I want to help," he said. Sincerely, he did, but he remembered his father's stern warning about getting mixed up in the affairs of men. *They will tempt you, and they will try you, and there is little honor among most of them.* "I at least want to look. Perhaps it will give me some new perspective on things. After all, it sounds like the city lord is dealing with the same kind of circumstance. Will you take me?"

She stared at the highest tower in the center of the castle. "I'll tell you what. We can ride out in the morning, but I want to hear more about this woman you are determined to find. I want to know your story. You don't have to tell me all of it, just something to delight me. Besides, your words are so pleasant when you speak. I'd enjoy more of your company."

Nath didn't see any reason to tell the domineering woman no, and he did like her company. He nodded. "I'll see you in the morning then."

"Meet me in the stables behind the inn." She kissed his cheek. "See you then."

Chapter 39

NATH SAT ON HIS BED in the Oxen Inn with his pack on his lap and his eyes closed as he leaned against his headboard. He'd been trying to sleep, or at least get a little catnap, but his excitement about the coming day was overwhelming. He couldn't wait to see where Nina took him. He opened his eyes. The oil lantern burned low, leaving the room very dim.

"I can't wait hours until the morning. I'm ready to go now." He moved to the window, drew the curtains, and opened the window. His window overlooked the back side of the inn. The barn roof was below him. In the star-filled sky, the bright white moon was at its zenith. "Great Guzan, the morning birds won't be out for hours still."

Nath paced the room. Typically, a few hours meant very little to a dragon. He'd seen dragons spend hours just yawning, and they were very slow about doing things. Since they lived so long, they tended to operate as if they had all the time in the world. Growing up in Dragon Home, Nath was used to it, though it did annoy him from time to time. There were very long stories, lectures, conversations, and training lessons. But outside of the mountain, inside the cities of men, life moved faster. The people moved about as if the sands in the great hourglass of time were about to empty out.

He plopped on his bed. The backpack rattled with the distinct clinking of the potion vials inside. He emptied out the contents by removing each item one by one. There were three potion vials in tubes made from a clear, thick glass, a thin coil of golden-brown rope, and some wax candlesticks. He held the hooded lantern in his palm. It looked like something that was more decorative, being so small that it could be hung from a tree like a seasonal ornament. The last thing was the Gauntlet of Goam. The soft, durable leather was broken in. The blue sapphire set in the leather showed a wink of fire burning deep within. All of the items were gifts from his father, but they wouldn't be anything that an actual dragon would ever use. Instead, Nath had come to the conclusion that the items were gifts that were brought to the dragons by the races long ago when dragons and men were friends.

Nath had some other common supplies in the bag too that he fished out. Among them were strips of cloth he used to wrap around the potions so they wouldn't rattle. He bound the vials up together all as one. Stuffing them back inside the pack, he felt something scratch against his knuckle. He pulled out a sheet of parchment rolled up like a scroll.

"Oh, Slivver, I'd forgotten about this." He unrolled the parchment. There were words written that only a dragon could read and a drawing in the corner. It showed a picture of a face with very sharp and distinct elven features carved into a black gemstone. The elven face had a deep scowl etched in it. Slivver's handwritten words read, "In my ventures abroad, I have discovered that there are elves that have aligned themselves with evil. They call themselves Caligin. Operating from the dark of the night and the shadows of the day, they strike from anywhere and at any time. Be wary, Nath. The friends you make might not be what they seem. Beware of the dark in the day. Slivver."

A chill breeze rustled the curtains. Goose bumps rose on Nath's arms. He studied the image and read the note again.

"What is he saying? Is he saying the Trahaydeen were Caligin? Maefon is Caligin?" The note slipped from his fingers. "She couldn't be, could she? No, that couldn't be what he is saying." He combed his fingers through his hair. Maefon was so beautiful and always loving toward him. She was his best friend. Then he thought of Chazzam. "He must be the Caligin."

CHAPTER 40

MAEFON ENTERED LORD DARKKEN'S STUDY. Like the rest of the keep, it was a dreary octagonal room made from the dark stone. The walls were bare aside from a single wooden bookshelf ten feet tall and over half full with leather-bound tomes. Lord Darkken stood in the center of the room, looking down into a large copper bowl that sat on a stone pedestal.

"Please, Maefon, come and gaze into the Pool of Eversight with me." Lord Darkken faced her from the other side of the bowl. The rims of his eyes glowed like shiny copper. "I've been looking forward to your company all day."

"And I yours, Lord Darkken," she said, stepping up to the Pool of Eversight. The copper bowl was bigger than she could get her arms around. The water in the bowl was clear as glass, showing the copper basin at the bottom. "What do you require of me?"

"A drop of your blood, and repeat my incantation, and you will then see all that I can see." He handed a dagger handle first over the bowl, which looked like it was carved from either a dragon's tooth or dragon bone. Taking the dagger, she quickly pricked the tip of her index finger. Fresh drops of blood plopped into the waters, making ripples and staining the clear liquid. "Close your eyes. Repeat after me."

The ancient incantation she repeated were words from a time long forgotten. The eloquent words took life of their own, lending new strength to her body. A spring of energy coursed through her the moment the incantation ended.

"Open your eyes. Gaze into the pool, and tell me what you see," Lord Darkken said.

The waters swirled, shimmered, then formed a clear image. "I see fertile lands as if a bird flies over them." She held her stomach. "My tummy twists."

Darkken let out a chuckle. "That will subside. If it does not, perhaps this duty is not something that you are suited for. There are others who might prove more capable if I give them a try."

"No, I'm fine, lord."

"Of course you are. I knew you would be. What you are seeing is indeed a bird's-eye view. This is what Galtur, my vulture, sees. Though sometimes he doesn't like it. It gets his feathers *ruffled*, so to speak, and I end up having to use other methods. Linking to him is one of the uses of the Pool of Eversight. Using Galtur, I have learned, gives me more flexibility. You see, I can command his actions from where I stand. Soon you will learn to command him as well. Have you been practicing your magic, Maefon?"

"Yes," she said, leaning farther over the pool. The image barrel-rolled, dove down toward the tall grasses, and swooped up again. Her knees buckled as her stomach turned. "Uh, it's all coming back to me, and I'd forgotten how much I'd missed it. It's good to have the magic back on my lips and fingertips."

"Indeed." Lord Darkken waved his entire arm over the bowl. The image faded. The spell broke off.

Blinking, she said to him, "Have I done something wrong, lord?"

"Of course not. The pool is power and takes some getting used to." He put his arm around her waist. "You did well. You didn't faint. I knew that you had the strength in you to withstand the power. Of course, if you had collapsed, I probably wouldn't have any use for you whatsoever."

Maefon felt like a child in his arms as he led her in front of the bookcase. Some of the books were as thick as the breadth of her hand. The spines were lettered in many different languages. "It's an impressive collection. Are they all spell books and histories?"

"History books are elsewhere," he said. "No, these are books of magic in every language and from every race that I can get ahold of. Of course, most of it is miniscule, and filled with a variety of concoctions and silly spells. Primitive, one might say, but every culture has something to offer. Most particularly the elves and humans." Up on tiptoe, Darkken grabbed a book from one of the higher shelves. He handed it to Maefon. "Heavy, isn't it?"

She nodded at the tome that now filled her arms. The muscles in her back pulled a little. Unlike the other books, this one wasn't bound in leather. It was bound with black dragon scales and skin. With awe, she said, "Where did you get this?"

"I made it. I want you to study it. There is much about dragons and men that you need to learn. I put it all together in there. Spells and lore. But the book remains in here."

"I'm honored."

Putting his hands on her shoulders, Darkken said, "I know you are." He took the book and put it back on the shelf. "You may come to this study as you please, when time away from your duties permits. But for now, there is another place I want to take you. I've gotten a bit bored, and I want to play around a little. Close your eyes."

The moment she closed her eyes, a warm breeze stirred her hair and clothing. Her stomach felt like it spun a full circle. Dizziness assailed her. The only things that kept her from falling were Darkken's strong hands.

With assurance, he said, "Open your eyes, Maefon."

With the sun on her face, she squinted. They stood on rolling grass hills as far as the eye could see. Darkken gave a handsome smile. He was dressed like a commoner, wearing a cotton white shirt under a brown vest. The shirtsleeves were rolled up over his forearms. His forest-green trousers were held up by a belt with a copper buckle. He wore leather traveling boots too. "Is this the field we saw?"

"Yes," he said, taking her hand and leading her through the meadow. "You look very pretty in your new clothing."

Maefon wore a pale-yellow blouse and forest-green skirt that covered her ankles. "I'm dressed like a milk maiden."

"I know. We need to blend in where we are going. Have you ever milked a cow before?"

"No," she said, frowning. Maefon touched the white cotton cap on her head, which was tied underneath her chin. She might be Caligin, but she preferred to maintain a certain style about her attire. Dressing like a human wasn't something she cared for. In addition to that, her mind raced. Darkken had just transported her across the countryside and changed her and his clothing in the wink of an eye. She knew he was powerful, but she never imagined his abilities were so vast. It scared her and thrilled her at the same time. A hunger for knowledge built inside her. She squeezed his hand. "But I'll milk a thousand for you if I have to."

"Good, because it will probably come to that."

CHAPTER 41

JUST BEFORE DAWN, ARMED AND ready to go, Nath headed to the barn. As he entered the barn, a horse nickered and another whinnied. Nina led two horses by the reins. Harnessed and saddled, the beasts were ready to go. So was Nina. The long strands of braided hair were curled up on the top of her head. She wore a leather tunic over a coat of chainmail. A broadsword and dagger were belted onto her full hips. She smiled at Nath. "Good morning. I hope it's not too early of a start for you. Is something wrong?"

"Er… no, it's just that you look like a warrior. I thought you were an innkeeper, but I'd swear by the looks of you, you are an adventurer."

"Who? Me?" she said, touching her hands, covered in leather riding gloves, to her chest. "Why, I'd never!"

Nath batted his lashes at her. Approaching the horses, he said, "What are you up to?"

She climbed into her horse's saddle. "We'll talk about it on the way. Have you ever ridden before?"

"Ridden what?"

She gave him a funny look. "A horse, of course. What else would you have ridden?"

Nath was thinking about riding dragons, but he said, "No, I haven't ridden a horse, but I'm fairly good with animals and get the hang of things quickly." He stuffed his foot in the stirrup, mounted, and turned the horse toward the barn exit. "Is this this how you do it?"

"Yes, that is how. Just be sure to keep up." She led the way out of the city at a trot. They headed northwest, following the roads to Quintuklen. As Nath got a better feel for his horse, Nina did the talking. "So you figured me out. I'm not just an innkeeper. I do my fair share of adventuring too."

"So you deceived me."

"No, you didn't ask. I just keep a very low profile, and given the notoriety of adventurers, I have to. After all, the Oxen Inn is my family business, but I'm not married to it." Her forehead wrinkled. "I'm not married to anyone. Are you mad at me?"

As the horses crossed over a small creek, he said, "No, I understand your reasons. And why would you be forthcoming with a stranger? You know little about me. I'd probably do the same."

"Speaking of forthcoming, tell me more about this woman you seek. I imagine she is very beautiful. A possible wife, perhaps?"

"No, I don't believe so. You see, she is an elf."

"An elf?" Nina said, unable to hide her shock. "Why would you chase an elf? They are the snobbiest race in the realm."

"Sorry, but I haven't been around many other people," he said.

"Raised by elves, huh?" she said, shaking her head. "Now I've heard it all. So what happened to your own parents? Clearly, you are not an elf. What did you become, a charity case they took on? The ones I've known are picky and often try to make things better."

"What's wrong with making things better?"

Red-faced, she said, "And you defend those pompous pointed-eared fiends." She took a breath. "Sorry, Nath, I had a bad experience with them. It still sticks. If I were raised by elves, perhaps I'd side with them too. So you have elven parents?"

"No, I don't have elven parents. I don't know my mother, but I've been with my father all of my life—until now, that is, since I left home to find Maefon."

"Hmph. Tell me more about her."

"She's elven, blond, and very friendly. She likes to joke a lot, and her laughter is delightful. She makes these little dimples when she smiles."

"That's enough. I get the picture. Come on, we're close." Nina dug her heels into her horse and snapped the reins. "Yah!"

Nath gave chase. Finally, Nina came to a stop at a bend in the road where the tree branches hanging over the road on both sides formed a tunnel. Nina dismounted. She led her horse off the road. "Did I say something to offend you?" he asked.

"No, I just don't care for men blustering over women unless it's me. Now, are you going to sit up there all day, or are you coming along?"

Nath hopped off his horse. "I'm coming."

Together, they entered the forest. Just inside the rim of the brush was a clearing. There were statues of soldiers in a circular ring, facing inward. In some cases, weapons were drawn. Shock and horror crossed their faces. Fear filled their wide eyes.

Nath's neck hairs rose. "I thought what you said about them being turned to stone was just a figure of speech. I never imagined…" He touched a man's face. "I've never seen faces so scared before. They are absolutely terror-stricken. Look, this man has goose bumps still standing on his arms."

"I know. I want to believe they aren't real, but I know better. They were found on the road just like this." She kneeled down. The forest had overtaken the stone men's feet. "They were dragged over here and made into this creepy memorial. I don't get it, but Lord Jander wouldn't allow them in the city. He's still investigating. He keeps leaning toward the rival families who want to take his scepter. Personally, I think the Riverlynn monks had something to do with it. I just can't prove it."

There was a wreath made from twisted sticks embedded with flowers hanging from one man's neck. The flowers had withered. Nath plucked wildflowers from the ground and began replacing them. Nina did the same. "So who are the Riverlynn monks?"

"Well, that's what they call themselves, but in truth, they are nothing more than a motley band of brigands and rogues pretending to be holy men. The lowest of the low are among them. And they are notorious snatchers," she said then shrugged. "But Lord Jander won't touch them without cause. If we could find some evidence, I'm sure he'd challenge them. Until then, he blames the other rival families. No one is as blind as he who will not see."

Snap.

Nath and Nina looked up as a dozen brigands dropped out of the branches.

CHAPTER 42

NATH DREW FANG.

Nina snaked her sword and dagger from their scabbards. "Stay in the circle, Nath! Stay with me."

One statue lay on the ground at Nath's feet. He stepped over it, coming back to back with Nina as the brigands closed in. Nath's eyes swept over them. This wasn't some motley band of wayfarers, but a well-organized group, dressed in clothing and armor that blended in with the woodland. Twigs and leaves were pinned to their garments. They carried swords, spears, and crossbows. There were twelve hard-eyed men, part-elves, and halflings. They lurked behind the cover of the statues, weapons poised for destruction.

A somewhat pleasant, even-keeled speaking voice with an edge to it cut through the tension. "Let's make this easy, shall we?" From behind the rank and file of bandits, a tall, broad-shouldered man came forward. He had more beard than face, piercing eyes, and a crossbow in his hands. "All we want is your steel, your purse, and your horses. Put the metal on the ground and drop your pack, and we won't put fresh holes in you. Do you understand?"

"I won't be surrendering anything to you." Nath turned the tip of his sword toward the ranging man, who stood even taller than Nina. "I've lost once, and I swear I won't lose again."

"Son, you've lost already. Look around you. Heh?" the leader said. "Not even the finest soldiers can escape from this. Not when we have a bead on you. No, do what makes sense and drop your weapons. Both of you."

"You lawless curs!" Nina said. A brigand poked through the statues and took a stab at her legs. She knocked the jab aside and chopped at the man. Quick on his feet, he sprang backward behind the statues, giggling hysterically. "Come back, you cowering, mangy dog! I'll split you like a log."

With one hand, the leader pointed his crossbow at her head. "You won't be splitting anything if you have any sense about you. Let me be clear. This is a robbery. I have no intent to kill you, but I will kill you if that is what it takes to achieve my goal. I'll do anything for my brothers, and they for me. Blood stains all of our hands. The less I feel, the better. What will it be?"

"He's bluffing," Nath said, searching their eyes. "I can see fear lurking in their eyes. They are uncertain. Doubt swells in their loins. Thieves are liars, and I bet this bearded fellow hasn't even butchered a cow."

Thwack!

A crossbow bolt tore into the back of Nath's thigh. "Argh!" He glared at the halfling behind him. His little fingers were reloading a crossbow. Another halfling, with a crossbow and bolt ready, stepped in front of the other.

"Nath!" Nina cried, looking down at his leg. "You're wounded. It looks bad."

Grimacing, he reached behind him and yanked the bolt out. "It's not as bad as theirs is going to be."

The brigands cast a few nervous glances between themselves.

The leader gave a lazy shake of his head. "I warned you, and now you bleed. You are a foolish young man. Lady, you seem reasonable. I asked, in exchange for your life, for your goods, all of which are replaceable. I'll tell you what. I'll even let you both keep your armor. I don't think it will fit any of us. That way you can return home with your britches on."

Nath's knuckles were white on his sword. "I'm not giving up my belongings. You'll have to kill me first."

"No, Nath, I can't let you do this." Nina tossed her sword and dagger down. "I'm not having your blood on my hands. Let them take it. Whatever you have, I'll replace it."

"You can't replace this," Nath said of Fang.

"It's only a sword," the brigand leader said. "Who knows, maybe you'll be able to acquire it one day after we sell it. It's very distinctive. It shouldn't be too difficult to track down unless some knight acquires it."

"Nath, please," she said, "just let this go. I'll make it right somehow. I'll help you find your friend."

The lot of brigands snickered.

Nath swallowed down his pride. Red faced, in pain, and sweating, he lowered the blade. "I'm sorry, Fang."

"You see, you are wiser for the robbery," the brigand said, giving an approving nod.

Fang's tip hit the stone statue of the man on the ground.

TIIIIIIINNNNNGG!

A shockwave of sound carried out of the blade like a tuning fork being struck. Pushing down the grasses, the sound slammed into the statues and the surrounding brigands. The grubby bandits dropped their weapons. They fell to their knees, clutching their heads. They screamed against the growing sound.

Nath lifted the sword. He stood over top of Nina, who lay on the ground, curled up in a ball. He could hear the distinctive sound, but it didn't have any effect on him. It was just a low ringing. Before his eyes, Fang's blade quavered. Blue light coursed through it. "I don't know what you've done, but I'm glad you've done it."

The leader of the brigands begged, "Make it stop! Make it stop!"

TIIIIIINNNNGGG!

Even if Nath could make it stop, he wasn't so sure that he would. As for Fang, what he was doing, he seemed to be doing on his own. "You'll think again before you ever cross me, won't you?"

The brigand leader shook his head, turned his back, and on jittering limbs, ran away. The other brigands staggered away, falling over and scrambling to regain their feet. The farther they got, the faster they moved. Without looking back, one and all disappeared into the forest.

The ringing sound ended. Fang's glowing metal cooled. One handed, Nath flipped him around a few times then sheathed him. "Well done." Nina lay sprawled out at his feet. Her eyes were closed. Her body spasmed. "Nina!"

CHAPTER 43

KNEELING, NATH SHOOK THE WOMAN, calling her name. "Nina! Nina! Can you hear me?"

Suddenly, her eyes snapped open. She gasped for breath. Broken out in a cold sweat, she panted. "What was that? I felt like I was trapped in a ringing bell tower. Oh, thank the lord it has ended." She clutched Nath's arm. "Tell me that won't happen again."

"That's not up to me. That's up to Fang." He put a waterskin to her lips and let her drink. "I didn't even know that he could do that. Sorry."

"You speak of your sword like it's a person," she said, wiping her mouth with her hand.

"Is that out of the ordinary?"

"I suppose not. I've known many warriors who talk to their weapons like friends." She searched the woodland. "Are they gone?"

"As far as their clumsy feet will take them." Nath glanced at the abandoned weapons on the ground. "I don't think they'll be coming back for them anytime soon."

"They won't be here when they do," she said, holding out her hand. "Help me up."

Nath hauled her to her feet, grimaced, and helped her steady herself. Nina swayed a bit. "Maybe you should sit longer."

"No, I'll be fine. Just embarrassed. And you need a bandage! They shot you," she said, red-faced.

"I'll manage," he said, taking a potion vial longer than his finger out of his pack. He drank down the clear bubbly contents in the little glass flask. "Ah," he said, able to feel the skin, muscle, and sinew in his leg beginning to mend. He put the half-empty vial back in the pack. "Much better. I might limp a little bit."

"Another surprise," she said. "Nath, I truly feel ashamed. Nothing has ever taken me down like that before. I just wasn't ready." Her eyes swept over their surroundings. She picked her sword and dagger up and slid them back into their sheaths. "You are full of surprises. I thought they had us for certain. I apologize for letting you down."

"Don't be silly. I think you were right to tell me to stand down. My actions could have gotten either one of us killed."

"I suppose we should go," she said, holding her stomach. "I'll gather up their weapons."

"That sounds like a good idea, but I'm not ready to go back yet. We still need to search around a bit." Nath reopened his pack. "Perhaps something was left behind that the others missed." He took the small hooded lantern with a brushed-nickel finish and green lens out of his pack. "This might be of some help."

"I don't see how a lantern is going to be of any help in broad daylight. And it's so small." Nina picked up swords, daggers, and crossbows and put them in a stack. Her eyes kept scanning the woodland. She glanced at Nath. "Even for a halfling."

"I haven't used it before, but it's a gift from my father. It was my thirtieth celebration day present. He called it Winzee's Lantern of Revealing. Supposedly, it's an all-seeing eye. If something was missed, we should find it."

"Who is your father that bestows upon you such magic?" Nina asked. "Was he a wizard?"

"Er... well, I suppose you could say that. But this has been in our family quite some time." Nath twisted the key on the lantern's side. A watery green light spilled out, casting new light around Nath in a ten-foot radius. "Whoa, now that is interesting." He picked up a silver piece hidden in the ground near his feet. "I didn't notice that before. And I have a very keen eye."

Nina's eyes were the size of saucers. "Nath, that is incredible. Can I use it?"

"I believe anyone can." He passed it to her. She took it by the handle. "I'll follow you."

"I'm going to start at the road where the scrum occurred." She pushed through the brush, back toward the road, and picked up several coins and a rusted horseshoe along the way. "This is impressive. I bet this little lantern would come in handy locating secret doors and passages. I wish I had it years ago. Huh, I might have avoided falling into a pit."

"You fell in a pit? Where did this happen?" Nath said, limping to catch up with her.

"It happened in an abandoned dungeon. We were treasure hunting. I'm just glad we made it out alive."

"You were a prisoner?" Nath asked.

"No, just searching ruins from cities abandoned long ago." Nina started on the dirt road and walked in a slow outward circle. With her eyes scanning the green hue covering the ground, she said, "This is like seeing the world with a new pair of eyes. Magic eyes. I've dealt with mystic items before, but never one such as this. Or your sword. This is fascinating."

"I'm glad you are enjoying it. It makes me happy."

"You have no idea how this thrills me. The uses are countless. The possibilities endless." She took a knee on the edge of the road, across from where they'd first entered the forest. Her fingers brushed over the dirt.

"What is it?" Nath asked, leaning over her shoulder.

"A button," Nina said, holding it up to his face. It was a steel button the size of a knuckle. Three wavy lines, like water, were engraved in the metal. "But not just any button." The lantern's light dimmed. "No!" she exclaimed. She slapped the lantern's side. She twisted the key. "Nath, what happened?"

"I suppose its use is limited." He took the lantern from her and twisted the key. Nothing happened. "I don't know."

Standing up, she gave him a serious look. "This is horrible." She kicked the dirt. "We need more proof than this button."

"What is so special about that button?"

"It's from the robes of the monks of Riverlynn."

CHAPTER 44

Back at the Oxen Inn, Nath waited to hear from Nina. He sat on a tall stool on the wraparound deck that overlooked the barn outside his window. The back of his wounded thigh still burned beneath him. He'd been sitting for hours, waiting for a knock at the door, but one never came. After Nina found the button and the lantern went out, they spent another couple of hours searching for more evidence. Nath found lizardman skin that had peeled. Nina found a strip of leather cord. She said she thought it might have been used to tie someone up and that she'd run it by Lord Jander, but it was unlikely, given the lack of evidence, that he'd support a mission.

The drifting clouds blotted out the sun on and off throughout the day. The sun set, the moon came. Nath was still sitting. He'd gotten a feel for the city and made a friend. He liked it. Nina was an interesting person. She wanted to help people. Nath wanted to help people too. He'd convinced himself that if he could find Janna, then he'd be better prepared to find Maefon. He could make new friends and allies. Nalzambor was a big place, and after getting jumped by the brigands, he realized having some allies and friends could make a difference.

Little Shirl appeared on the deck. The tiny lady walked up to Nath, head down. "Nina says you need to come with me. You can bring your arms."

Smiling, Nath said, "Well, I never go anywhere without my arms."

"You know what I mean," she said flatly.

"Yes, of course." Nath reached inside his room and grabbed his sword, belt, and pack. He closed the window. "After you, young lady."

"I'm not as young as I look," she said, walking down the deck and heading down the stairs at the end. "I'm as old as Nina but look much younger. I don't do those things that she does. You should not either. It will fill your comely face with wrinkles well before their time."

"I'm more worried about scales than wrinkles," Nath said.

Little Shirl shot him a confused glance. "Scales?"

"It's an odd condition that runs in the family."

"Sounds horrible."

"I guess it depends on one's perspective. Anyway," he said, catching up with her brisk pace, "where are you taking me?"

"I'm taking you where you need to go," the spooky girlish woman replied. "Keep up now."

The Oxen Inn was located on the eastern side of the city. Little Shirl took him west. The burning oil in the streetlamps gave the city a warm, shadowy illumination. The people who strolled over the cobblestone roads were lively. After a hard day of working, they walked arm in arm, some singing, and others staggering. On the balconies, women with long lashes and colorful cheeks, wearing silks and flimsy linens, waved and whistled at Nath.

"Traveler," they called. "Come visit. We want to greet you!"

Five of them were hanging over the balcony rail, waving their silk sashes and scarves and giggling.

"Yes, Red Hair, we welcome all who come here!" The women blew kisses and winked at him.

Nath waved back with a smile. "Perhaps later, when I return."

Little Shirl pulled his hand down. "Have you no sense at all? You don't consort with those women. They are trouble."

"Trouble how? They seem very friendly."

"Stay away from the ladies with the painted faces. I told you once. I won't tell you again." With both hands, she held his hand. "It's best I keep you close. We don't have far to go." She stayed on the main road, took a corner left and the next corner right. With storefronts on both sides, she stopped halfway down the street where an alley split the stores on the left. She pointed. "At the end is a door. They will meet with you inside."

"They?" Nath said, peering into the darkness of the alley. His nostrils flared. "And there is a stench."

"Yes, you are very observant. There is a stink, but that is very common in most alleys. More so in this area of the city. Good-bye, Nath. I bid you farewell." Little Shirl bowed, turned, and quickly walked away.

As Little Shirl faded into the crowd, Nath said, "That was a little cryptic." He stepped out of the streetlamp's light and into the alley. He let his eyes adjust to the darkness and crept forward. A rat darted across his toes. A cat chased after it. He weaved his way through the abandoned wooden crates piled up on the sides of the building. He made out the outline of the door at the end. Stopping at arm's length of the door, he gave it closer study. The door was made of metal and painted brick red. Extinguished torches covered in webbing hung on the sides.

Why would Nina want to meet me here? This is deplorable.

Nath took a backward glance. He peered up both sides of the walls. He'd learned a hard lesson from the brigands who ambushed them. He should have been more alert. He survived, but he had a limp to show for it. He wouldn't make that mistake again. Seeing no immediate threats, he faced the door and lifted his fist.

The door swung open, hard and fast. An unseen force yanked him inside, and the door slammed hard behind him.

CHAPTER 45

NATH'S ENTIRE BODY SLAMMED INTO the wall of a pitch-black room. Shaking his head, he fought his way back to his feet and reached for Fang's handle. A hard punch to the jaw sent him sprawling again. Lying flat on his belly, someone jumped on his back. Heavy as an anchor, the man locked his hands under Nath's neck and pulled.

"He's strong as a young bull," the person on his back said in a gruff voice. "But I can hold him."

"Just hold him still, Cullon, while we kick him all over." The person speaking made a high-pitched giggle. He kicked Nath in the legs with a hard-toed boot. "Did you feel that? Huh? Did you feel that?"

Muscles bulging in his neck, Nath fought to pull his chin down. He pushed up on his hands. "Auugh!"

"Be still," the person on his back said. "Stop wriggling, or we'll hurt you more!"

Nath heard the shuffle of more feet and others breathing. He guessed there were at least four people inside the room, plus him. One was kicking the daylights out of him. Another, whom he thought was called Cullon, had strong, calloused hands locked underneath his chin, trying to pull his head off. He made out four warm bodies in the darkness. Pitch black or not, Nath could make out the warmth of the living in the dark as if it were day. "Get off of me, thieves. I'm warning you!"

Cullon let go of his chin.

Nath's face hit the floor. His lips busted. He tasted blood in his mouth. He twisted to his back, threw a punch, and connected with a jaw as strong as iron. With pain shooting through his fingers, he unleashed a flurry of punches. His hard blows smacked into Cullon's face.

"That's enough of that!" In the dark, Cullon grabbed him by the collar of his breastplate and jerked him up. He head-butted Nath right between the eyes. "How does that feel?"

Bright spots exploded in Nath's eyes. Pain streaked down his neck. His temper boiled. Hearing a soft scuff of a boot near his head, he lashed out. He grabbed someone by the boot and yanked them down. They landed hard on the planks. "Ow!" the person said. "Let go of me!"

"You let go of me!" Nath hollered back. He pulled them closer and punched them in the ribs.

"Ulf." The person groaned.

Nath hit Cullon in the chest with everything he had.

Cullon made a low chuckle. "You'll have to hit harder than that."

In a swift move, Nath brought up his feet, hooked Cullon by the shoulders, and thrust him down. He pinned Cullon on his back. Cullon tore free and flipped to his belly. Nath put him in a headlock. He couldn't clamp down on the neck the way he wanted. Cullon was covered in hair. He hip-tossed Nath.

Nath hit the ground. Before he could get up, he felt the sharp edge of a weapon on his neck. "Stay down," a calm voice said. "Virgo, may we have some light, please?"

"As you wish," a woman with a velvety voice said.

A greenish glow filled the room as candles in an iron candelabrum hanging in the center of the ceiling caught fire, the flames a dark-emerald color. He was in a large storage room with many shelves loaded with boxes, jars, and wooden vegetable crates. There was a second door, and he could hear the faint rumblings and movements of other people. He was certain there was music too. Nath locked eyes with the man who held a dagger to his throat. "What are you waiting for?"

"Introductions, actually," the man said. He offered a nice smile with perfect white teeth. His brown hair, moustache, and sideburns were neatly trimmed. His chest and shoulders were covered in deep-brown leather armor. "I'm Tobias. Believe it or not, we are friends of Nina, who sent you. She'll be along shortly." He tucked his dagger into its scabbard. "This was a bit of a test. We wanted to see how you would handle yourself in a dangerous situation."

"I could have killed you," Nath said, propping himself up on his elbows.

"Not likely. We held back, way back."

"Aye!" Cullon's voice was loud and harsh. He was all dwarf, standing just shy of five feet tall and built like a rock. The very top of his head was bald. His black hair came to his shoulders, and a thick beard covered most of his chest. Belts of knives crisscrossed under his beard, hand axes hung on his hips, and a white scar crossed the side of his prominent nose. "I could have killed you. He's too young, Tobias. Soft. We don't need him."

"What's he talking about?" Nath said, coming to his feet. "I'm not soft." He pointed at the wiry man wearing a loose-fitting gray outfit who lay on the floor, holding his ribs. "He's soft. Look at him, squirming like a worm with ribs."

Slapping Nath on the back, Tobias let out a delightful laugh. "Ah-haha. I couldn't have put it better myself. Worm with ribs. It's perfect! Nath, meet Worm."

The scrawny man on the floor waved. He didn't look much older than Nath, but it was hard to tell because his messy light hair covered his eyes. "You have quick hands. You surprised me."

"He is really named Worm?" Nath said, slipping out from Tobias's hand.

"Yes," Tobias replied. "And last of all, meet Virgo. She is the one that so skillfully whisked you in here. Dashing, isn't she?"

Virgo, older than the rest but without a wrinkle, had straight, silvery hair down to her back. She leaned against the doorframe with her arms crossed. Her hypnotic eyes soaked Nath in. She wore a long black gown made from nicely woven cotton, giving her pale and slender figure a fuller look. She had a little smile as she seemed to glide across the room toward Nath. She took his hand. "I hope I didn't hurt you when my powers flung you into the wall." She made a pouty face. "But I do what I am told to do." She kissed his hand.

"You have very cold hands," Nath said, unable to break her stare or grip. "Not that it is a bad thing. I heard that cold hands make—"

"Warm hearts?" she said. "That's something cold and old women say. But I can assure you, my heart is very warm now." She brushed Nath's bangs aside. "Your hair and eyes are like nothing I've ever seen. You are dazzling."

"Yes, I think it's fair to say that he has above-average qualities, Virgo." Tobias, who was a good-looking man himself, peeled her fingers from Nath's and nudged her aside. "But we didn't bring him here to be fawned over. Nina thinks he'd be a welcome addition to our party." Studying Nath, he combed his moustache with his fingers. "But I agree with Cullon. He seems too soft. Too young."

CHAPTER 46

"I AM NOT TOO YOUNG," NATH exclaimed. "I'm older than you." He caught himself as the others started laughing. Aside from the dwarf, he was certain that he was older than the rest. He pointed at Worm. "Well, him, anyway."

"Don't be so sure of yourself," Worm said in a silky voice. "I am much older than I appear." He cackled. "But I coat myself in rare silks and oils when I slumber." He glided over to Nath. Staring at his face, he said, "May I?"

"I suppose," he replied.

Worm ran his fingers down Nath's face. "I've never seen one without blemish. His skin is smooth, yet there is thickness to it." He rubbed a lock of Nath's hair between his fingers and thumb. "My, the wig weavers would give a fortune for this. It has more sheen than even Virgo's."

"When did you stick your dirty little paws in my hair?" Virgo said to Worm.

Worm cackled. "Ah-hah, most likely it happens when you snore so soundly."

Arms crossed over her chest, Virgo rolled her eyes.

Nath brushed Worm's hand aside and stepped back. "When I say I'm old enough, you must believe me. And I'm a fine warrior, as good as any."

"Hah!" Cullon laughed. "Tobias, I say that we be done with this redheaded rogue. I say we vote now. My gut tells me that we need to move on. And we don't need him to do what we do." He clawed at his beard. "Saying he's older than us. There is something foul about that."

"Appearances aren't everything." Tobias combed his hair over a distinctive ear with a point on it.

"You're part elf?" Nath said.

"Quarter elf would be more accurate," Tobias said. "My grandfather on my father's side was full-blood elf." He motioned to a long table at the edge of the room. "Let's all have a seat, shall we?"

Sitting at the table, Nath asked, "Where are we? And where is Nina?"

"She'll be along." Virgo took a seat beside Nath and scooted close to him. "Don't worry, you have me to keep an eye out for you. And don't let Cullon bother you. He's a dwarf, born with a poor disposition chockful of rotten as his manners."

"Aye." The dwarf took a small wooden keg off the shelf, plucked out the wooden plug, tipped it up, and started drinking. Ale splashed all over his face and beard as he guzzled it down. "Ahh!" He replaced the plug and sat down at the table. His sausage fingers beat the barrel like a drum. "Go on, keep talking about how rotten I am. I like it."

Tobias sat across from Nath, leaning forward with one elbow on the table. "Have no fear, Nath. Nina will be along. She most likely will enter from the front entrance of this tavern. There are many types that haunt this not-so-refined establishment. That's why we had you come through the back—to avoid prying eyes. You tend to stand out a bit, like a candle flame on a dim night. It can stimulate provocation in a place such as this."

"So this is an adventurers' cove?" Nath's fingers tapped on the table.

"There are many sordid people in this den. Trust me when I say you are in good company, for there is a rotten brood out there."

"And in here." Cullon pulled the keg plug and drank more.

Tobias kept his eyes fixed on Nath. "Tell me a little more about yourself, Nath. You are from the south, as I understand it. Do you have a family name? We are all seasoned travelers. Perhaps we would recognize your family name?"

"Uh, I doubt that. There are thousands of names, and you couldn't possibly know them all," Nath said. *Or say them, for that matter.* Dragon names tended to be as long as a river, not to mention in an entirely different language. "Nath should be fine. I don't see a need for so many formalities."

"Nath, to be a part of this, we need to know much about one another. It's called trust." Tobias leaned back in his chair. "But if you really aren't that interested in saving Janna or receiving our help, I can't fault you for going it alone." He got up from his chair. "So sorry for all the trouble we put you through. I'll inform Nina that she was wrong. It was nice meeting you, Nath whoever-you-are."

Chapter 47

"No, wait, please sit back down, Tobias," Nath said. "It's not that I don't want to share my last name. It's just I'm a bit embarrassed about it."

All eyes were fixed on Tobias, who sat back down. "All right, I'm listening. Though I can hardly think of a last name that would be so embarrassing."

"Orc would be an embarrassing last name," Cullon said. "Are you Nath Orc?"

"No." Nath shook his head. If these people could really help him find Janna, he wanted to be a part of their group, and he didn't want to disappoint them. Thinking of the first thing to come to mind, he made up a lie. He recalled a long word that he'd learned in one of the books he read in Dragon Home. "Olifflinursagewahn. It's hard to say, and we would typically go by Olifflin, but it's meaning is even worse."

"Yes, it is a mouthful. It must be from a very old tongue," Tobias said, scratching the corner of his mouth. "So what does it mean?"

Nath could have given it any meaning, but he said the truth. "Dragon."

Cullon erupted in laughter. Holding his stomach, he said, "That is worse than orc!"

Worm cackled insanely. He banged his fist on the table. "Nath Dragon. Oh, that is rich!"

"Well, they don't call me that," Nath argued. His cheeks turned rosy. "Stop laughing. It's just a name."

Virgo rubbed his arm. "Well, I like it. It fits."

"I concur." Tobias rapped his knuckles on the table. "Nath Dragon—it has a nice ring to it."

"I don't want to be called that. Can we just stay with Nath?" he said.

Virgo laid her head on his shoulder. Batting her eyes at him, she said, "I'll call you whatever you like."

"Please, Virgo," Tobias said with a frown, "give this young warrior some space." He pushed back from the table and glanced at the door that led into the tavern. "Nina should be here by now. Anyway, Nath, I don't question your heart, but I don't want to endanger you right away. And frankly, my gut says you aren't ready. I say we have a preliminary vote, as Cullon requested. Do I have a second?"

"Aye," Worm said with a grin.

"Good." Tobias nodded. "All in favor of allowing Nath into this group, on a probationary basis, raise your hand." Virgo and Worm lifted their left hands briefly, the greenish light glinting off their fingers eerily, and dropped them down on the table. Their palms were both tattooed black. "And those not in favor?" he continued, lifting his left hand. His palm too was black. Cullon raised the same hand. It was black on the palm as well. "It seems the decision is split at this point, and I'm fairly sure where Nina the tiebreaker will lean."

"You can't cast a vote on account of her absence," Cullon growled. He glared at Virgo and Worm. "The both of you are ignorant. All you will do is get this boy killed."

"I'm no boy!" Nath said, looking at Tobias's hands. "I do have a question. Why are all of the palms of your hands stained black?"

Tobias showed a clever smile. "That is who we are, Nath. We call ourselves the Black Hand."

"So my hand will be tattooed?"

"Again, it's a probationary basis."

The door from the tavern opened. Nina hustled inside. The tall woman closed the door behind her and caught her breath. "Sorry I'm late. The city lord was being very chatty. He was quite interested in what I had to say, for a change. Then he slipped me out. He's so paranoid about who comes and goes. Hello, Nath. Are my friends treating you well?"

"I suppose," Nath replied.

"We took a vote, Nina," Tobias said. "The decision is split. Are you ready to cast your vote?"

"I think he's ready. At least, I've never seen a man so young and able, or well-equipped," Nina said, taking a seat at the table.

"I concur," Virgo said, keeping her eyes on Nath.

Cullon shoved the table. "I don't care what kind of equipment he has! He ain't ready, and I don't like him. You have too much of a thing for newcomers, Nina. It's a weakness. The Black Hand requires veterans."

"Worm is hardly a veteran. And none of us were perfect when we came along," Nina argued. "Every initiate is new."

"He's green." The dwarf slammed the keg back onto the shelf. "Green, I say."

"The only one that is green is you. Green with envy," Virgo quipped. "Not that I blame you."

"Speaking of equipment, Nath, now that you are part of the Black Hand, do you care to show us what equipment you have to offer?" Tobias said as he got up and walked to the nearest corner behind the table. A sword belt hung on a peg. He drew a falchion blade with a curved end and razor-sharp tip from the scabbard. The brass pommel was fashioned like a wolf. "This is Splitter, an enchanted blade passed down to me from my grandfather." He twisted it from side to side and made some quick cuts. "Splitter never slips from my grip. It's a marvelous piece of work, the same as my armor." He tapped his chest. "Leather from the weavers of Rodingtom. It can't be cut."

"Fascinating." Nath looked at Virgo, who was right in his face. "And do you carry a weapon?"

"You'll have to search me yourself, Nath Dragon," she said.

"I can just take your word for it."

"Oh, that is a shame," Virgo replied. "But I have a staff. I don't carry it always. It makes me look old."

"It's the wrinkles, not the staff," Nina said. "The staff is more polished than you."

Virgo shot a look at Nina. "I don't have wrinkles! Watch your tongue, you overgrown innkeeper!"

"Ladies! Let's not get into this again, please," Tobias said as he sheathed his sword. "We are the Black Hand, planners, not squabblers."

"I have many interesting items, Nath," Worm said. He had a parchment under one hand and three potion vials in the other. They were Nath's items from his pack. "And I thank you for them."

Nath flung his body at Worm. "Those are mine!"

CHAPTER 48

WORM VANISHED. NATH CRASHED INTO the young man's chair. Rolling to his feet, he found Worm sitting in Nath's chair beside Virgo. "You trickster!"

Cackling, Worm said, "I wouldn't call me that." He looked up. "I prefer prankster." He looked at the parchment Slivver had given Nath. "This is intriguing. Are you an artist? Virgo is an artist. Aren't you, gorgeous?" He planted a kiss on her cheek.

Virgo slapped at Worm. He vanished a split second before she made contact. "You dirty little rogue. I'll have you."

Worm reappeared behind Nath. He started stuffing Nath's items back into his pack. Quickly, he said, "I was only toying with you, Nath. Just fun."

"No one steals from me!" Furious, Nath spun around, launching a punch as he did so. Worm ducked underneath the swing. "Hold still." Nath threw several haymakers. Worm slid away from them all.

"Enough!" Tobias said, standing eye to eye with Nath and coming between them. "Apologize, Worm, and make this right. Offer the left hand of honor." He turned his attention to Nath. "You have to understand, Worm has very sticky fingers and an alley cat's curiosity. He's plucked us all more than a time or two."

Peeking from behind Tobias's shoulder, Worm said, "Yes, you just saw me steal a kiss from Virgo. And I'll steal one again." He held out the parchment from Slivver. "Here is your paper."

Tobias took the parchment. His eyes grew big when he glanced at it. He cleared his throat, rolled up the parchment and handed it to Nath. "Uh, sorry, but that's an interesting image on the paper. You can share all with your comrades here. Our lips will be as sealed as a boat that's watertight."

Nath snatched the parchment. Turning his back, he took out his items and placed them on the table. "There is all you need to see of me." He lifted the coil of rope and the lantern and showed them the Gauntlet of Goam that he'd put on his hand. He had the three potion vials again and his candles. "Wait a moment, where is my—"

Clink!

His purse of coins landed on the table. Nath looked inside the small sack. All of the coins and gems appeared to be intact. He turned and stabbed a finger at the rogue. "Worm, you better never steal from me again."

The slender young man slid out from behind Tobias with his head down. "I wasn't stealing. It was a prank. A jest." He looked up into Nath's eyes. "I can't help myself. It's what I do."

"Steal? I don't want to be in the company of thieves," Nath said with his eyes sweeping over all of their faces. "There is no honor in that."

"No, Nath, you don't understand," Tobias explained. "We all have different skills that we rely on to get us through the horrors that await us in tombs, caves, and ruins. Worm can find traps and disarm them. He has a very special gift for that. We need him. We need each other."

Worm offered his hand. "It won't happen again."

In the blink of an eye, Nath locked his fingers around Worm's throat. Squeezing, he lifted the young man up on tiptoe. Looking the rogue right in the eyes, Nath said, "No, it won't." He shoved Worm into Tobias's chest. Tobias couldn't hide the shock on his face. No one could.

Coughing and wiping his watery eyes, Worm said, "That was fast. Very fast."

"Yes, I'm very, very fast. What would you expect from a man named Nath Dragon?"

"Breathing fire would be a good trick," Cullon remarked.

Nath shook his head. "These are my belongings. Well, this and my sword and breastplate. Is there anything else you would know of me?"

All eyes were glued on the items on the table. The three other men in the room came closer with a glint in their eyes.

"Those appear to be very serviceable magic resources," Tobias said, looking at Virgo. "Am I correct?"

She spread all ten fingers out, closed her eyes, and began to hum an incantation. The skin on her hands illuminated with radiant light. She passed her hands over the items one at a time. Opening her eyes, she said, "It's all magic. Very strong magic."

"I told you what the hooded lantern could do," Nina said, standing up. She put her arm over Nath's shoulders. "I think our items and skills, combined with Nath's, are just what we need to rescue the princess. It will give us the edge we need. If Nath truly wants to help, we will succeed. What do you say, Nath? Do you want to be a part of the Black Hand?"

Nath gave an affirmative nod. "I believe I do. But how is it that your hand is black now when it was not before?"

"I can explain that," Virgo said with a playful smile on her lips. Getting up from her chair, she moved under the candelabrum and passed her hand beneath it. Arcane words spun from her lips. The candles' fires flickered. The colors shifted from an ambient green to natural orange. Holding up her hand, she turned and winked at Nath. Her black palm was the color of natural flesh again. "It's a little spell that I created to identify those who are marked. Your time will come, I hope."

"Everything seems to be in order, then," Tobias said to them all. "Black Hand, it's time to rescue a princess."

"Oh, there is one more thing I need to mention," Nina said. Her brows creased. "Lord Jander wants this done quietly, and he wants it done now. I suggested we leave at first light."

"Agreed," Tobias said. "We'll just have to make plans on the way to Riverlynn then." He smiled. "Dismissed."

The three men departed, leaving Nath alone with Nina and Virgo.

"Let's go, Nath," Nina said, yawning. "I need some rest. We'll get up early and have the horses ready."

"I'm not tired," he said. "The truth is, I'm tingling. I won't be able to sleep tonight. I don't sleep much anyway."

"Me either," Virgo said, hooking her arm in his. "Nina, please, go ahead. I'll walk him back to the inn later."

Casting a wary eye at Virgo, Nina said, "Remember the code, Virgo."

"Yes, I know the code. No romance among members."

Yawning, Nina gave a nod and departed.

Once the tall woman was gone, Virgo giggled. "But you're not a full member yet, are you?"

CHAPTER 49

NATH SAT ON A STOOL inside Virgo's apartment. Her place was nicely furnished, smelled of fresh flowers, and was very warm. Framed paintings hung on the wall in an assortment of sizes. Others were leaned against each other along the walls. Some of the paintings were of the trees in the woodland, snowy and sunny, and others were groups of people, in a tavern, or a parade or celebration, gathered together. But most of them were portraits of people, posing the same as Nath was.

"Sit up straight, Nath, and lift your chin a little higher. And a smile would be nice, you know. Flash a few teeth. You have a dashing smile. I want to capture it." Virgo had put her silver hair up in a bun and stood behind a canvas on an easel. She looked younger with her hair up, revealing more of the rich features of her beauty. She painted with easy strokes. The board with a palette of paints was in her left hand. "You might be my masterpiece, Nath. I can feel it. You are the one I've been waiting for."

Nath stuck his chest out and smiled. "I didn't imagine that when you brought me up here, it would be to paint me."

"Really, and what did you imagine, Nath?"

"Er… well," he said, wiping his sweating palms on the thighs of his trousers. "I thought you wanted to kiss me."

She laughed softly. "Well, the thought did cross my mind, believe me. But there is a code. Are you disappointed that I haven't acted on my passions?"

"Well, no, I'm more relieved, actually," he said.

"Relieved? That's not at all what I expected you to say."

"No, no, it's not you. You are divine. It's just that I haven't kissed many before, and well, I'm spoken for, sort of."

"Chin up," she said sharply. She chewed on the end of her brush as she eyed her painting. She took a few glances between the canvas and Nath. "This isn't turning out so well after all. Something is missing."

"I'm sorry, Virgo, have I offended you? I didn't mean to. I just, well, I don't really have much experience in the company of women. And—"

"Oh, stop it, Nath. It's refreshing having you in such a naive and innocent state of mind. So often, the men I paint can't stop begging for my attention. They grovel for my hand and my time. They vow to leave their families and offer me their fortunes. Shameless, they are. I just want to paint them."

Keeping his head still, Nath scanned the portraits on the wall. The details were incredible. There were many handsome men with strong lines in their features, and women, each a different kind of beauty, varying in their gorgeous hair, lovely eyes, or perfect smiles. "You have an amazing talent. They are so realistic."

"Indeed, but I feel I am falling flat on this effort." She approached Nath, palette and paint brush in hand. Eyeing his chest, she said, "Your armor. It is so… bland. Would you be offended if I were to paint a design on it?"

"Er… I don't see why not. It wouldn't be too showy, would it?"

"No, I just think it needs a bit of flair. Everything about you stands out, but the armor is dull. It doesn't fit. It needs some splash to it."

Nath shrugged. "If it makes you happy, then it makes me happy to let you do it."

"Breathe easy, but be still," she said as she began painting.

Nath could hear the soft brush strokes on his chest. Virgo's perfume filled his nose. Her soft breath kissed his neck. His mouth became dry. His eyes searched for hers. They found her soft pink lips, which had a glossy look on them. *I really do want to kiss her. She is so exquisite.*

"Just a little longer," she said. Her paintbrush moved with a quick and gentle ease in her hand. She carried on a few more minutes. "There, that will do it."

Nath let out a breath he hadn't realized he'd been holding. "So you are finished. May I see?" He looked down at his chest. He flexed one eyebrow. "What is that?"

"Come over here and look in this mirror," she said, walking over to a full-length mirror standing up in the near corner of the studio. She stepped alongside it. "Take a look."

Nath stood in front of the mirror. Two black lines, like partial wreaths, partially enclosed a brick-red design of a sword and a dragon. The sword resembled Fang, with the dragon crossguards, and the dragon profile was a large face with a smaller tail. They overlapped one another. He tilted his head to one side, then the other.

"Do you like it?" she asked.

"I think so."

"I can remove it," she said, frowning. "I understand if you don't care for it. But I really do like it."

"It looks like the symbols form a *D*."

She giggled. "Yes, it's subtle, but it is a *D*. A *D* for dragon. Nath Dragon."

His mouth hung open.

"You hate it. I'll take it off."

Eyes frozen on the symbol, he said, "No. No, don't." The corners of his mouth started to rise. "I actually think I do like it. It's flattering in an odd sort of way."

"Then I shall seal it!" Virgo said, setting down her brush and palette. She put her hands over his chest. "This might get a little hot, but only for a moment. It will keep the paint from peeling or chipping off." She closed her eyes and muttered an incantation. Her hands turned the color of fire.

Nath's chest warmed. Perspiration broke out above his brows. There was a sizzling sound, and a puff of stinky smoke rose from his chest.

"It is finished," she said. "Did that hurt?"

"A little, but I'm fine."

Virgo draped her slender arms over his neck and gave him a quick kiss. "Go back to the tavern and rest, Nath. I'll see you in the morning. We have an important journey ahead."

"But your painting of me. Don't you need to finish it? I'm not sleepy."

She broke off the embrace. "I have to prepare for tomorrow myself. And a little rest does keep away the wrinkles. You can find your way back, can't you?"

"Yes. See you in the morning, Virgo. I look forward to it." He backed toward the painting. "However, I would like to take a quick look."

"No, no, no!" Virgo rushed into his path. Pushing him back, she said, "You cannot look until it is complete, Nath. Now go."

"You're sweating all of a sudden," he said, wiping the perspiration running down the side of her temple. "It can't be that bad. You are a great painter."

"Nath, just go. I need to prepare for tomorrow." She pushed him toward the door. "In the morning, then?"

"In the morning." As he passed through the doorway, he turned back to say good night. The door slammed shut in his face. "Uh… good night."

Chapter 50

Late at night, Maefon watched a bridge that tied one side of the creek to the other burn. Men and women rushed from their village cottages in a mad scramble. They filled buckets of water from the nearby shallow river and passed them along a row toward the fire. The people hollered back and forth at one another. Lord Darkken stood among the villagers, talking with encouragement, passing the filled buckets from hand to hand. The bridge was consumed in flames. The timbers cracked and popped. A black plume of smoke darkened the sky, making a thick haze between the desperate people and the passing clouds.

"Maefon! Maefon!" a woman cried out, swing her arms wildly. "Lend a hand. Fetch more buckets from the storage houses!"

Maefon nodded. She sprinted toward the streets of Ferly. Dashing into a barn, she swung open the storage door and fetched three more milking buckets. For the past few days, she'd been helping out in the barn, milking cows and cleaning stables. Lord Darkken lent a hand to the men who built the bridge. The bridge tied two feuding villages, Ferly and Starnly, together. They'd finally come to terms and agreed to work with one another, opening up a road for trade and expanding commerce. The bridge, a sturdy wooden structure, not even a hundred feet long and wide enough for two wagons, was a symbol of the communities coming together. Now, it burned.

She ran back to the river and handed the buckets down to the crowd. The woman who had called out to her shook her head. Tears streamed down her cheeks. "It's too late. Too late," she said.

From one end to the other, the bridge became an inferno. The black cloud of smoke blossomed in the night.

The coughing and crying men and women's efforts to extinguish the flames came to a stop.

Flaming hunks of wood collapsed into the water.

A man clutched his head. "No, no, noooo."

On the other side of the stream, the people from Starnly shared the same distraught reaction. They had been working together for weeks, building a bridge that now had been burned down. Lord Darkken came over to Maefon. "You did a fine job setting that bridge on fire. And no magic. Impressive."

"I mixed hay and tar with oil," she said as they walked back toward the abandoned village. "I packed it underneath the joists last night. It was a simple thing, really. These people really took a shine to me."

"Yes, well, you are elven and often fascinate many people. You did well in your seduction of them. But not everyone slept," he said. "I, for one, didn't, and I witnessed the entire event." Lord Darkken stopped and turned toward the stream. "You see, a man spied you from the other side of the river. He was out wandering, drunken and smoking a pipe. I killed him. I used one of this village's marked chisels to complete the authenticity." He pointed to the bank south of the bridge on their side and made a little motion with his hand. "They should find their brother's body any moment now."

From her elevated position, she saw a bulk detach from the bank and float down the stream. The bloated body arrived among the squabbling people. A woman let out a bone-chilling scream.

The dead body was dragged out of the river and onto the bank. A woman from the other side of the bridge dropped to the ground, and from her hands and knees, she wailed, "My husband! My husband! They murdered my husband!"

Angry village folk waded through the stream toward one another. Shouts echoed over the burbling stream but quickly turned into an exchange of heated words, pushing and shoving, and punches thrown. Within seconds, the men and women from both villages were going at it.

Lord Darkken smiled down at Maefon. "I think that should create a grudge that will last a few generations. Don't you?"

"Agreed. You've created a fine stream of discourse."

He put his arm over her shoulders. "In this case, we both did. Now, let's go find another peaceful community with hopes and dreams we can destroy."

Chapter 51

On horseback, Nath rode with the Black Hand southeast from Riegelwood. In the distance, two mountain ranges merged together, forming a V-shape in the rocks. Stormy skies were beyond the vast gap. Flocks of birds flew over them in waves, every hour or so. Riding tall in their saddles, Nina and Tobias led, with Nath and Virgo in the middle, and Cullon and Worm brought up the rear.

Aside from Worm cackling from time to time, the journey had been very quiet. Nina and Tobias's eyes were fixed ahead or scanning from side to side. Their horses were loaded with plenty of gear, including bedrolls and saddle bags. Swords hung in scabbards off their saddles. Tobias also had a bow and quiver of arrows.

Riding beside Nath, Virgo carried next to nothing. She rode with her gown up over her bare knees, and a bedroll behind her. She looked at Nath and smiled from time to time. Aside from greeting her in the morning, she hadn't said a word to him. The Black Hand seemed to be all business.

Worm cackled.

Nath looked back at him. Worm wore loose-fitting clothing and showed nothing else of use. The young rogue made big eyes at him and laughed again. Even Cullon chuckled.

"Is there something that I should be aware of?" Nath asked.

"Oh no, of course not, Nath Dragon," Worm said, trying to hold back his laughter. His eyes drifted to Nath's chest, and he started laughing out loud again. "Bwah-ha-ha-ha-hah!"

Tugging the reins, Nath turned his horse around to face the man and dwarf. "I don't know what your problem is, Worm, but if you are laughing at me, I demand to know why."

"Just let it go, Nath," Virgo said, coming along his side. "Worm has a very twisted sense of humor. He laughs at and teases everyone. Don't take it personally. We all put up with it by ignoring it."

"I don't like it," Nath said, staring the man down. Worm had already stolen from him and tried to make a fool of him. Now, his cackling was getting under Nath's skin. "I want him to stop."

"I can't," Worm said, trying to look away, but his eyes remained on Nath's chest. Pointing at Nath's breastplate, he made a circle motion with his fingers. "It's that."

"My paint? What about it?"

"It's a bull's-eye," Cullon growled. The bushy-bearded dwarf with a bald top rode a horse loaded down with hand axes, short swords, a crossbow, saddle bags, two quivers, a coil of heavy rope, and a morning star. He spit black juice on the ground. "What kind of adventurer puts a mark like that on his chest? It's red. It has 'aim here' all over it. Hah!"

Glancing at the mark, Nath frowned. "No, it doesn't."

Cullon and Worm looked at each other and began laughing again.

Virgo touched Nath's bare arm with ice-cold hands. "Don't let them bother you. They are envious of the attention I've shown you. Especially Worm. He begs for me to paint him, but I don't." Worm stuck his tongue out at her. "He is childish, and Cullon should know better than to encourage him."

"And you should know better than to paint a bull's-eye on Nath Orc's chest," Cullon fired back. He unhitched his crossbow and pointed it at Nath. Closing an eye, he said, "Too easy. Of course, those bright-red locks aren't doing him any favors, either. Heh. That's two bull's-eyes in one." He squeezed the trigger. *Click.*

"Let's keep it moving!" Nina hollered back at them. "Or do you want Tobias and me to handle this all alone?"

"That would be fine by me," Worm said.

"What was that?" Nina yelled back.

"Nothing, Nina. We're coming." Worm led his horse by Nath, snickering along the way. Cullon did the same, leaving Nath and Virgo behind.

"I'm sorry, Nath. I didn't think my little design would create such a stir. I honestly don't think it stands out so much. I can make it duller," Virgo said, holding up her hand. Her fingers turned into a rainbow of alternating colors.

"No," Nath said, offering a smile. "I like it the way it is. Very original, and I wouldn't change a thing. I should have handled it better."

"Yes, be the bigger man, Nath." She squeezed his forearm. "And don't worry about Worm and Cullon. They are reliable, even if they are difficult to get used to. Believe me when I say that we have all had our bouts. What we do is a dangerous business, and it makes us all edgy. We all release it in one way or another."

Nath nodded. Following the leaders, they moved on. Nath wasn't very used to dealing with actual people. All of his life, it had been dragons and the Trahaydeen. All of them tended to go about their business in a very orderly fashion. Dragon Home was peaceful. Every day, Nath knew what to expect, but that all changed the day he left to find the murderers of the fledgling dragons. The people in Nalzambor, so far, had proven to be unpredictable. He was determined to get used to it. He wanted to be a part of people that he could count on. He might need someone's help to find Maefon and avenge his brethren.

Nina and Tobias led the group to a stop about a hundred yards from where the dirt road entered the narrow channel through the mountains. All of the riders made a row beside Nina. The dark passage between the rocks rose hundreds of feet high. Black birds with bright-yellow beaks flew in and out, sometimes landing in their nests high on the ridges. Addressing them all, Nina said, "This is the Channel. On the other side lies Riverlynn, where we shall find the monks and, hopefully, Janna. But the Channel is not without its dangers. Over the mountain is much longer," she added, pointing where the road split off and eased up the mountains in a long and winding path. "Does anyone object to taking the shortcut?"

"Quit trying to frighten the boy," Tobias said with a smile. "We've navigated the Channel dozens of times without incident. There's no need to be dramatic, Nina."

"Aye, let's just go," Cullon said, moving forward. "It's not the Channel—it's what lies on the other side that is a problem."

"I just want Nath to be wary. Anything can happen, and you seem to forget there was that one time," Nina added. "That I'll never forget."

"That was an accident," Tobias said, leading his horse forward, "and we swore to not speak about it ever again. Now, let's get moving before that storm hits."

Shaking her head, Nina looked at Nath. "Just stay alert."

"Always," Nath said. They rode into the Channel, and the day seemed to turn to night.

Chapter 52

The Channel bent left and right in ridged angles. A light rain started to fall. The rock enclosing them was sheer in many places. Any climb up to the mountain would be steep and require the skilled hands of a mountaineer, or climbing equipment. It didn't take Nath long to understand the concern of traveling the Channel. Fifty feet above their heads were overlooks and ledges. Heavy in thick brush from the mountain terrain and showing the natural cover of boulders, it was clear it was the perfect place for an ambush.

Birds darted through the gulch, zipping over the tops of their heads. The horses climbed up steep banks and through narrow passes barely big enough for a wagon to pass through. Thunder rolled in the distance, louder than normal as it echoed throughout the canyon. Nath's horse whinnied.

"Easy," Nath said, petting the beast's neck.

The Channel widened again, big enough for ten wagons side by side. The walls were as sheer as they'd passed in any part of the canyon. A few spots sloped steeply upward. On the other end of the expansive stretch was another narrow neck leading out. Nath surmised they were a mile deep with at least another mile to go. Nath adjusted his gear and subtly patted down the items in his pack. He slid a glance Worm's way. Concerned the thief would try something sly, earlier, Nath had also slipped the candles from his pack into his trousers, as they were small, no bigger than a finger and easy to conceal.

All items accounted for.

Nina raised her arm as she led her horse to a stop. She cast her eyes all over the upper ledges. A mountain lion prowled the upper ledges. It vanished over the rim.

"What's the holdup?" Nath said to Nina. "The big cat doesn't worry you, does it?"

"No," she said. Her eyes narrowed as she cast a glance toward the neck in the canyon ahead. "Do you hear that? Someone comes."

"Don't get so antsy, Nina," Tobias said in a whisper. "We aren't the only travelers in the Channel. We should always expect someone. I'm sure it's just some merchants not wanting to get caught up on the mountain during the storm. It gets a bit slippery, and sudden mudslides have sent many off the mountain only to perish in the Channel." He pointed toward the walls where the debris of wagons had crashed long ago. "Whoever it is, I'll do the talking."

"Well, don't take too long. We know how you like to gab," Virgo said, placing a cloak over her shoulders. Droplets of water splatted down around them. "I'd like to find shelter before I get soaked. You know I hate getting wet. It tampers with my spellcasting. Not to mention my hair and clothing."

A jackrabbit darted out of the narrowing passage. In a blur of brown fur, it hopped right at them. Nath and Nina's horses reared up as it weaved through the beasts' legs. The long-eared rabbit bolted for the passage where they just came from and disappeared through the rocks.

Nath fought at his reins, steadying his horse.

Worm cackled.

"Thanks for the warning, Nina," Cullon commented in a dusky tone. "That little rabbit just about made me brown my britches."

Everyone started to laugh.

With deep creases in her forehead and a new rosy hue on her cheeks, she said, "That certainly wasn't what I expected." She fought to control her horse, tugging the reins from side to side. All of the horses snorted and nickered. "What has possessed these beasts?"

On horseback, a barrel-chested orc with a lumpy face and coarse, stringy hair rode out of the passage. The horse was the biggest Nath had ever seen, at least half a head taller than the one he rode. Coming to a stop, the horse snorted and clawed at the ground. Its hooves were covered by hair that grew from its ankles. Behind the orcen rider, another group filed out of the passage on horseback, splitting to either side of the orc. They were a multitude of races with faces that Nath recognized. It was the same hard-eyed brigands from the encounter at the memorial of statues. Nath's blood ran cold as he reached for his sword.

Chapter 53

"Be still, Nath!" Nina commanded. Her hand was on the pommel of her sword, as was Tobias's, but none of them moved. Her eyes were fixed on the brigands on horseback easing out of the passage and spreading out before them. "Let Tobias do the talking."

Nath had his arm over his back on his pommel, with Fang slid out a few inches. "These are the men who tried to rob us. I won't go through that again." He scanned their faces. There was the orc, brawny and ugly, who carried an air of command that came with his great size and girth. The big steed beneath him made him even more formidable. Beside the orc was the tall, slender brigand who did all of the talking when they were robbed. He had his loaded crossbow leaned back against his shoulder and a cocky look on his face. There were part-elves and orcs, the wiry rogue who cackled much like Worm, and three red-haired halflings who seemed familiar. Nath eased his sword out of his scabbard a little farther. "We can take them."

Moving his horse between the orc and Nath, Tobias looked back to Nina, who was beside Nath. "Settle down our new addition, please, Nina, while I talk us through this."

Nina grabbed the reins of Nath's horse. "I'll handle it," she said in a dangerous voice.

Cullon and Worm backed behind Nath and Nina. They turned their horses to face the enemy. Virgo stayed to the left of Nath, Nina on the right, and Tobias in front, facing the orc less than thirty yards away.

Nath counted twenty brigands in all, excluding their leader. All of them were dressed in soiled woodsman garb, many with traveling cloaks covering their shoulders. Three of them skirted the edge and trotted to the other narrowing in the passage, blocking off any avenue for escape. The Black Hand was closed in. Nath's muscles tightened between his shoulders. Something was wrong, more wrong than what was seen. He couldn't put his finger on it.

Tobias approached the orc, stopping as their horses stood nose to nose. With beady eyes, the orc glowered down at the smaller man. Tobias spoke quietly.

"Why is he talking so low?" Nath said, leaning over his saddle horn. He wasn't certain, but it sounded as if Tobias was speaking in orcen. "I find that strange."

"Be silent, Nath. He's bartering for our safe passage." Nina grabbed his sword arm. "Let go of your weapon and relax. Tobias is a polished communicator. We just want to move through here without any blood spilled."

"But these men are thieves. They should be jailed if not killed," Nath retorted. He found the slender-bearded brigand holding a crossbow staring right at him with a knowing look. He winked at Nath. "Something is not right."

Nina took a quick glance over her shoulder at Cullon and gave him a quick nod. The dwarf's crossbow was in his lap. With two strong fingers, he locked back the string and loaded a bolt. Nina eased her sword a little further from her sheath. Virgo's hands and fingers made very subtle motions in the open air by her sides. Worm sank into his saddle with his hands hidden in his clothing. The drizzling rain came down harder. Virgo sighed.

The orc looked past Tobias, right at Nath. The look sent a chill through Nath. He scanned the faces of the brigands. In almost every case, they were looking right at him. He swallowed. Under some strange compulsion, he grabbed Nina's hand that held his horse's reins and tried to peel her iron-strong fingers free. The fingers did not give. "Let go, Nina."

"Nath, what are you doing? Be still," Nina demanded. "This is almost over with. Trust me. Just look." She tipped her chin at two more riders coming out of the passage. A man on one horse led out a young woman with long, wavy, honey-colored hair on another. Her eyes, ears, and mouth were bound by cloth. Her elegant robes were torn and tattered. Dirt smudged her face and hands. "Janna," Nina said, acting a little too surprised.

"I don't understand," Nath said under his breath. "What is she doing here? It doesn't make any sense."

"Perhaps you are good fortune, Nath Dragon," Virgo said, giving him a quick smile. "The kidnappers are moving her, and now they have run right into us. Our timing couldn't have been better."

On the back of one of the horses, Nath caught a red-haired halfling peeking out from behind the rider he'd doubled up with. At first, Nath wondered if it was the halfling who shot him in the back of the leg. He wasn't sure, but he remembered there were two. Searching faces, he noticed that there were three halflings in all, each sitting behind a different rider. All three had rooster-red hair. His stomach twisted into a knot. Perspiration broke out on his forehead then was quickly washed away by the rain. Every halfling face became crystal clear. They were the trio sitting on the tall stools, singing songs, the first time he set foot in the Oxen Inn. He swallowed. "Nina, let go of my horse."

"Nath, what is wrong with you?" she said. "You look like you have seen an apparition. Just be still a few moments longer. You have to trust me. Let this play out. The Black Hand knows what it is doing."

He shook his head. With every fiber of his being on pins and needles combined with a sinking feeling of the walls closing in, he ripped her fingers free from the reins. "You've lied to me!"

Nina's aghast expression turned calm, cruel, and collected. "Of course I did. We are the Black Hand. Lying is our business." She glanced at his chest. "And yes, that is a target."

Chapter 54

Nath went for his sword.

Thwack!

A crossbow bolt fired by Cullon lodged itself in the hindquarters of Nath's horse. The beast reared up, throwing Nath to the ground. Landing flat on his belly, he rolled to one knee and started to draw his sword. Nina thundered into his path. She kicked him in the side of the face. Nath kissed mud again. Something heavy landed on his back. Boots stomped him into the ground.

"Get down and stay down!" Cullon said, locking a thick arm around his neck. "Worm, get that sword off him!"

In a blink, Worm disappeared from his horse and appeared over Nath. Nath thrashed against Cullon while Worm slit the straps for Nath's pack and slung it aside. "What's yours is mine as always," the rogue said with a bubbly cackle. He fastened his fingers around the pommel of Fang and slid it out. "What a pretty, pretty sword. Certainly worth a fortune. What did you name it? Fang?" Holding it up before his eyes, Worm said, "I think I'll rename it Money. Gah!" Worm dropped the great blade. His face turned ashen. "The cursed thing burned me!"

"Good!" Nath pushed his face up out of the mud, his temper surging. Dragon heart pumping, he pushed against Cullon's dwarven strength. "Let go of me, you bearded bird's nest!"

"Hah!" Cullon shoved him down. "You're strong, boy, but you ain't that strong!"

A wellspring of endless strength flowed through Nath's left arm. The mud-covered Gauntlet of Goam's gem burned with the fire of starlight. Jaws clenched, Nath broke free of Cullon's grip.

Cullon's jaw hung. His dark eyes widened. "Impossible! How did you do—"

Nath punched Cullon in the chest. The burly dwarf flew backward, knocking Nina out of her saddle. His eyes slid over to Worm, who stood wide eyed over top of Nath's sword.

With a nervous smile, Worm said, "It's a pretty sword. You can have it."

Nath stormed the little man. Worm blinked out of sight. Nath snatched up his blade. Filled with boundless strength, he faced off his circling enemies. "Liars and thieves! Now you will face the wrath of Nath!"

From behind, lightning erupted from Virgo's fingertips. The streaks of white-hot light blasted into Nath's body.

"Gaaaaaaaaaah!" Nath screamed, jaws wide as pain lanced through his body. His limbs juddered, and his teeth clacked together. Fang fell from his fingertips. His knees splashed into the mud. He stood on his knees, shaking and wooden, as Virgo, on horseback, came into view.

"Sorry, Nath," Virgo said with wisps of lightning still glowing on her fingertips. "But that painting on your chest is a target indeed." She tossed her head back and laughed.

Nath's vision blurred. The words she spoke became garbled. Light-headed and full of blinding pain, he tipped forward, splashing face-first in the mud.

CHAPTER 55

NATH PUSHED HIS FACE OUT of the sloppy clay and rolled to his side, groaning. With one eye cracked open, he watched Cullon come to his feet. A beet-red face glowed behind his beard. Holding his ribs in one hand, he helped Nina to her knees with the other. Dashed with mud, she glowered at Nath. Cullon stormed right at him. "He broke my ribs! He'll pay for that!" Cullon launched a kick into Nath's armor-covered gut. "Get that breastplate off him so I can crush him!" Furious, he started kicking Nath again and again.

Tobias cut in with a sharp voice. "That's enough!" Still mounted, he said, "He's not to be damaged, Cullon. If he is, there's no deal, so back yourself off!"

"I don't care!" Cullon gave Nath one more stiff kick. "I'm going to bust him!"

Even though Nath wore the armor, he could still feel some of the sting from the blows. The strength behind them rattled his aching bones, shooting more pain through his body. He made a left-handed gauntlet-covered fist with the gauntlet still glowing.

"No, you don't," Worm said, appearing beside him and slipping the gauntlet from Nath's fingers. "It's a bit big and clumsy for the likes of me, but I know who it would be perfect for." He tossed it over to Nina, who plucked it out of the air. "Enjoy."

Nina slipped it on with a broad smile.

"Put that sword in its scabbard too, Worm," Tobias said.

"But it burned me," Worm said, rubbing his hands. "My precious fingers still ring like a bell." Tobias's hard stare changed the rogue's mind. "I'm on it then." Worm cut away Nath's scabbard and managed to push the sword back in place from the ground. He picked it up and handed it to Tobias. "All yours."

"Why me?" Nath groaned. His body spasmed. "Why, Nina, Virgo? Why?"

"He still speaks," Virgo said with a raised eyebrow. "Such remarkable constitution. I have to admit, Nath, I am very impressed."

"Yes, he is full of surprises," Nina quipped. She dismounted, marched over, squatted down, and pulled his face up by the hair on his head. "But as for why, well, Nath, this is what the Black Hand does. We are a guild of slavers, liars, thieves, and cheats, operating in a veil of good intentions. And our influence is very deep. For example, Lord Jander, a good man, believes we are helping him, when really we're going to trade you for his daughter in order to get the reward. Isn't that something? We have so many fooled, including the soldiers who you met on your way in. They sent you right to us."

"I trusted you," he said with another fierce shiver. The feeling began to return to his hands. The pain was subsiding. As his strength built, Nath chose to keep her talking while he searched for an exit plan. "Why me? I was just passing through."

"Look at you. You're practically a walking sunflower. And that sword, it's worth a fortune. I'm just glad none of our rivals got to you first," Nina continued. "But when you walked into my inn, I was thrilled. I gained your confidence, told you a story about a kidnapped princess, which, by the way, though true, wasn't anything we wanted you involved in. It was just some frosting for the cake when we needed to seduce you. So I took you to those statues in hopes of robbing you of your belongings quietly. These brigands, you see..." She twisted his head to face the brood. "Often work with the Black Hand. But you beat them. You beat us all with that sword of yours." She rubbed her left ear. "My ears are still ringing. It created quite a dilemma. All we wanted were your goods, and we would have sent you away, but you made it more complicated, didn't you?"

Nath shrugged as it all came together. "I think you are the one that made it complicated."

Nina continued. "As it turns out, we have discovered there is a desire in the slave markets for one such as you. Of course, it should have been obvious at first, but I must have been blinded by the sight of you. Look at you, a young man without scar or blemish, with rich red hair as if it was spun from silk. And those eyes... I don't believe there is another pair like them in all of the world. You alone are worth a fortune. The only thing I can imagine being of greater desire would be an actual dragon. So we hatched another plan by inviting—well, maybe lured is a better way of putting it—you into the Whistler, another home of the Black Hand, much like the Oxen. It was there we got a better understanding of your strengths and weaknesses and hatched another plan to bring you here. We get your goods and the girl, and they get a valuable slave."

"You could have just killed me," Nath managed to say.

"True, but we aren't murderers. We are slavers and thieves," Nina said as if it made her a better person, "and we like to execute our plans with style. We enjoy practicing deceit, and you made for excellent practice. It will serve us well in the coming days." She pushed Nath down and rose to full height. "It's been nice knowing you, Nath. But now it's time to turn you over to Prawl the slaver."

The rain came down harder. Thunder cracked. Water poured down in streams from the upper rim of the Channel.

"Wait." Nath tried to get up on his hands and knees. Cullon shoved him down again. "So you're taking the princess back to Riegelwood?"

"No, she'll stay with us at another location," Nina said, stuffing her boot into the stirrup of her horse and climbing into the saddle. "We will bleed the city lord's vaults and increase his concerns better that way. When the time comes, the Black Hand, as heroes, will return her home to her father safely. But this isn't something that you need to think on, Nath. Think to your future, for I am certain our paths will never cross again."

We'll see about that.

"Nina." Toblas gave a chin nod to the orc who approached. "We are ready to make the exchange. One person for another, Prawl."

"One person, yes," Prawl said in a gravelly voice, "and one gauntlet."

"What?" Nina said, pulling the gauntlet to her chest. "We already agreed that the mark's treasure would be ours, Prawl."

Prawl looked at her with fire in his beady eyes. "Tobias, do you let your mouthy woman speak for you?"

"You dare!" Nina pulled her sword free.

"Don't start it, orc." Tobias's hand fell to his pommel. "Nina, control yourself. Listen, Prawl, I don't know what game you are playing, but an agreement is an agreement. You will be paid when we receive the ransom. You'll be paid again when you deliver this man, Nath. In the meantime, the exchange is for the princess, and we'll handle it from there." He leaned over his saddle. "Give us your word, Prawl."

Prawl lifted his big face and grunted. "You voided the agreement when you deceived me. I will have the gauntlet and the man, or you won't have a princess."

"Only a fool would cross the Black Hand," Nina said, shooting daggers from her eyes. "Don't listen to him, Tobias."

"I'm not." Tobias moved his horse closer to Prawl and offered his hand. "The Black Hand will double your share of the ransom."

"What?" Nina, as well as the other members of the Black Hand, exclaimed. "Don't you dare agree to one coin more. These brigands failed us once already!"

Prawl showed a mouth full of ugly teeth and extended his hand. "Body for body, double the ransom and the gauntlet."

Tobias's expression darkened. "Now you're just insulting us, Prawl."

Prawl looked Tobias dead in the eye. "You insulted me first." He grabbed Tobias's arms, jerked him forward like a child, and popped him in the face with his fist. Tobias crashed to the ground. Prawl turned on Nina. "I'll have that gauntlet now!"

Chapter 56

Nina jumped off her horse and collided with Prawl. Prawl, the taller of the two, tried to wrap his big hands around her. Nina, the quicker of the two brutes, slipped behind him, picked him up, and body-slammed him into the mud.

The brigands erupted in a chorus of cheers as the big orc and brawny woman wrestled in a tangle of limbs all over the muddy ground. The gemstone of the Gauntlet of Goam glowed brightly as Nina let loose a punch at Prawl. The orc took it in the shoulder, let out a roar, and stuffed his boot in her gut. Nina skidded over the rugged ground. She came at him in a fury.

Nath gathered his senses as the two titans clashed and thrashed on the ground. At the passage's exit, the princess sat in the saddle, slumped over and abandoned. Taking advantage of all the attention Nina and Prawl were getting, Nath summoned his reserves, reaching deep, with a single-minded focus.

Rescue the princess. Escape.

On stiff legs, he ambled as fast as he could toward the princess. A lone brigand stood watching the fight, holding the horse by the bridle. The brigand turned just quickly enough to catch a hard fist in his face. The man sagged to the ground. Nath took the man's dagger, slit the ropes from the woman's wrists, and climbed into the saddle.

The princess pushed and slapped against him. Sitting in the front, he wrapped her arms around his waist and shouted in her covered ear, "Hold on, princess. I'm here to rescue you!" She wrapped her arms tightly around his body and held on for dear life. Taking ahold of the reins, Nath dug in his heels. "Eeyah!"

The horse lunged forward, galloping into the passage at full speed. Nath rode on, turning and weaving through the rocks with the wind and rain in his face. Water cascaded from the rocks above, filling the Channel.

"Who are you?" the princess shouted in his ear.

Nath took a quick glance back. Janna had removed the cloth that bound her eyes, ears, and mouth. "Hello," he said, "I'm Nath."

She shouted over the wind and rain, "I take it my father sent you?"

"Yes, you could say that, in a roundabout way!" The horse leapt a tree that had fallen across the path. Janna bounced out of the saddle and landed hard on the path. "Princess!"

"Break it up! Break it up!" Tobias yelled at Prawl and Nina. He managed to hook Nina's arms from behind and pull her away. The brigands made a wall between Prawl, Nina, Tobias, and the rest of the Black Hand. "Listen to me, idiots!"

"Mind who you are talking to," the tall, slender brigand leader said. He pointed his crossbow at Tobias's head. "She started this, not us!"

"Shut it, Andee!" Tobias said. "Look at what you fools have done. Have you not noticed the princess and Nath are gone?"

All eyes moved to the spot where the knocked-out brigand lay flattened on the ground.

Prawl pointed at Nina. "We'll settle this later. But that gauntlet will be mine. You are not worthy of it, woman!"

Wiping blood from her mouth, Nina said, "You'll sleep in the grave long before you'll have this, Prawl."

"We'll see who sleeps forever first." He climbed onto his horse. The huge beast reared up. "Men of Whispers! Let us ride!"

Led by Prawn, the band of brigands thundered into the passage after Nath and the princess.

Getting back on his horse, Tobias shouted at Nina, "Well done, hothead!"

Mounting her horse, Nina fired back, "Me! You are the one that caved into that belligerent orc's ego! If I didn't intervene, you would have given him all of our horses and the rest of Nath's treasure."

"I had it under control. He just has to be worn down! You played right into his hands." Tobias slung his muddy hair out of his eyes. "Let's get after them then, before he winds up with Nath and the princess too."

"Shall we stay back," Worm suggested, "in case either one doubles back?"

"Fool, it's impossible to double back in this Channel," Cullon said.

"Oh, is that so? Perhaps it's impossible for you, but not the likes of me. I can slip by anything, and he's proven to be slippery before."

"He's not getting away," Tobias said. "He doesn't know the land or the terrain. He'll be caught soon enough, and we need to be there. Agreed?" The small group nodded. With water running over the horses' hooves, he added, "Then let's ride before we all get washed out of this place."

CHAPTER 57

THE RAIN CAME DOWN HARDER. Nath dismounted and rushed to Janna. She was lying on her side, holding her ankle. "Are you hurt?" he said.

Anguished, she said, "Yes, no thanks to you! Why did you have to ride so fast?"

"Because we are being chased. Here, let me help you up." He took her hand and pulled her up.

"Ah!" she said. "My ankle. I can't put any weight on it." She sat back down. "I'm not going anywhere!"

"You just have to be able to hang on. Come now, please, we need to get out of here."

She pulled away from him. "I'm not riding with you! You're dangerous."

Nath stepped back. The princess sat in the soaking rain with her bottom lip stuck out, rubbing her ankle. It reminded him of a defiant child. He squatted down in front of her. "Janna—"

"It's Princess Janna to you, servant."

The sudden shift in her disposition tempted Nath to leave her right where she was. After all, he didn't owe her anything, and eventually, the Black Hand would return her for ransom. But he couldn't do that. "Listen, *Janna*, if we don't get moving, you will be captured again. You don't want that, do you?"

With her face turned away, she said, "No."

"Please, trust me, once again, and I promise to ride slower." Horse hooves thundered up the Channel toward them. "But we really, really need to get moving. It's imperative."

She looked at him with her gorgeous, spacy eyes. "Do you think I'm pretty?"

"Huh?"

"I said, do you think I'm pretty?" she said, blinking her long lashes.

"What? Uh, you are beyond compare!" he said, looking back over his shoulder. The thundering horse hooves were getting closer. Princess Janna's personality was shifting like the wind. Instead of acting like she was being chased, she was acting like she was in another world. *They have done something to her.*

"That's what I thought." She held out her arms. "You may carry me then. But ride slowly. My rump and hip are sore from the fall you already caused."

He picked her up in his cradling arms and hurried to his horse.

Looking him in the face, she gave a glowing smile. "Tell me more about me. I like hearing how pretty I am."

Helping her into the saddle, he said, "You have a smile beyond compare and a wealth of golden hair."

"Ooh, I like that."

Nath climbed in the saddle. He wrapped her hands around him and clamped them together. "Hang on!" The horse lurched forward, taking the next turn in the Channel just as the brigands came up behind him.

Prawl, the orcen leader, shouted out, "There he is!"

Nath dug his heels into his horse. The horse bolted forward. With his free hand, he held fast to the princess's hands, which were gripped tight around his waist.

Shouting in his ear, she said, "You promised you would go slower!"

"It's either this or get caught! You don't want to get caught, do you?"

"I don't know!"

Nath spurred the horse forward. Hard rain smacked his face, and thunder roared overhead. "Just hang on!" he shouted back to her. "You're getting rescued whether you like it or not!"

The Channel broadened and narrowed, twisted and turned as it filled with rushing water that rose up to the horse's ankles. Waterfalls gushed off the higher ledges. They rode underneath one that was entirely unavoidable, giving them an unwanted bath.

Janna let out a bone-chilling scream. "What did you do that for? Isn't it bad enough that I'm soaked already?"

Nath ignored her continuous complaints. He wanted out of the Channel. Even though he didn't know the terrain or where he was, he was certain he could find help on the other side. He just needed to keep riding and hope he made it somewhere before they caught up with him.

"What did you say your name was?" she asked.

"Nath!"

"Gnat?"

"No, Nath. N-A-T-H!"

"Oh," she said. "Nath, they are gaining on us. Go faster!"

"I am. Hang on, we have a jump!" He gripped her hands. The horse jumped a fallen pine, landed hard, and kept on running. The princess was still with him. "Whew!"

They angled out of a narrow passage into a widening area of the ravine. The watery Channel split into two separate paths.

"Go left!" the princess said.

"Why?" Nath said.

"Just trust me!" she said.

Not wanting to slow, Nath veered left, into another narrow passage that sloped upward. It was like crossing a downhill stream as the horse labored against the torrential ankle-deep current. Nath had a good feeling that they were heading up onto the mountain. It would get them out of the rushing rain waters, but he wasn't so sure about the change in terrain.

He needed help. He needed to find people. He found neither as he charged toward the huge mouth of a cave dripping water. "Gads!"

CHAPTER 58

"WE AREN'T GOING IN THERE, are we?" Janna said.

Nath rode toward the vast cave mouth, which opened up fifty feet high and was just as wide. Stalactites hung down from the upper rim of the cave like teeth. "You said to go left."

"What do I know? It was just a suggestion. You should have gone right."

"Then you shouldn't have said left." Nath passed through the sheets of water as he entered the cave. "We don't have a choice now."

"Nath, we need to turn back. I don't like this place. It's chilly," she said with a shiver. "Not to mention as black as a witch's heart."

"So you've met a few witches before, have you?" he said, easing them deeper into the blackness.

"I have sisters. Ew, what is that smell? It's rank." She coughed and cleared her throat. "Nath, we have to go back. We can't stay here. It's pitch black." She seemed to be coming out of the strange lull she was in.

Nath's nose crinkled. Goose bumps popped up all over his soaking-wet arms. He led the horse deeper into the cavern. "Trust me, I know a few things about caves."

Deeper inside the cavern, his keen eyes made out the straight edges of rectangular columns chiseled out of the rock, giving it the face of an entrance to a building.

"Nath, I can't see anything," Janna said, looking behind her, "except a way out. Take me back, please. Just let them have me, and I'll wait to have my ransom paid. This place scares me."

"There's nothing to be afraid of," he said, moving closer to the wall inside the cave. It was a huge flat front, thirty feet high, with a stone archway entrance.

"If there is nothing to be afraid of, then why aren't our pursuers chasing after us?" she said.

Nath glanced back. "They just haven't caught up with us yet. Come on, now, we don't have a choice. Besides, every entrance must have an exit."

"My father's dungeons don't."

Something slithered beneath the horse's feet. A stone rattler struck, sinking its venomous fangs into the horse's leg. The horse bucked, took several steps, and collapsed. Nath and Janna tumbled off, landing side by side. She let out a scream. The stone rattler slithered right at her.

Nath snatched the snake by the neck before it could sink its fangs in her. Its body coiled around his arm and constricted. His fingers started to turn purple.

"Kill it!" she said, wide eyed and scooting back. "Kill it, Nath!"

Tilting his head, Nath stared at the evil creature with his golden eyes. "You're a wicked little serpent, aren't you?" He crushed its neck and flung it aside. "You're safe now."

"Maybe from the snake, but what about them?" She pointed to the cave entrance.

Led by the orc, the brigands passed through the sheets of water into the cave. Prawl said, "Surrender. There is certain death beyond the Wall of Hozam. None escape from there."

Nath picked up Janna and headed for the entrance.

"What are you doing?" she said, pushing against him. "Didn't you hear him? Nath, it's certain death. Release me!"

Nath passed through the entrance and into the chilly pitch blackness.

Chapter 59

Inside the cave, the Black Hand was in a heated exchange with Prawl. Sword in hand, spit came from the angry orc's teeth. "This is your doing! Not mine! I should split your skulls for it! And I will have my ransom!"

"You are the fool who got greedy, Prawl," Tobias fired back. He had his sword, Splitter, in hand. The even-tempered swordsman was red-faced now. "Had you stuck with our original arrangement, all of this could have been avoided, and we would be eating, drinking, and making merry right now. You are a fool of an orc! Now, take your men inside that hole," he said, pointing to the Wall of Hozam's entrance, "and bring back our ransom!"

"Hah! They are dead already! And you owe me that gauntlet and my share of the ransom, Tobias. It will be that, or the Men of Whispers will be at war with the Black Hand."

"That is outrageous!" Nina said, whisking her sword from her scabbard. Veins bulged in her neck. Her sinewy arms flexed as she squeezed her sword in a death grip. "You owe us! We don't owe you!"

"Huh-huh-huh," Prawl laughed. "We shall see."

"I'm going to kill you," Nina said. The gemstone in her gauntlet burned bright. "I challenge you to a fight."

"No!" Tobias said, wedging himself between Nina and Prawl once again. "No more distractions. For now, I say we wait. There is always a chance that they will be back out shortly. Everyone, catch your breath. An even-keeled mindset will serve our needs better." He sheathed his sword. "Nina?"

She stuffed her blade back in her sheath.

Prawl rested his sword on his shoulder. "None come back from behind the Wall of Hozam. None. You are welcome to find them if you will." He tipped his chin at the brigands. "I suggest you make good on this loss, Tobias. Now we depart from you." He eyed Nina. "And I will have that gauntlet. Men of Whispers, let's ride." Prawl led all of his men out of the cave, leaving the Black Hand all alone.

"Good riddance!" Cullon shouted after them. "I can't stand the stench of the orc anyway. I warned you."

"Not now, Cullon," Nina said. "I'm in no mood for your complaints."

"I say get in the mood then, Nina. Because they are coming. I warned you about aligning with the Men of Whispers. I said we need to keep our operations small, like we used to. But you got greedy."

"Oh, stop it!" Nina said. "We are thieves. We are all greedy! Especially you!"

"Har! You are the master planner of this caper, not me." Cullon shook the rain from his bushy beard like a dog. "You and your grand schemes. We should have just robbed Nath, like I said, and left him for dead."

Raising his hand, Worm said, "If I could say something, I would like to go on the record and say that I am the greediest, and I like Nina's devious plotting and planning. They are vastly more fashionable than the dwarven style of clubbing someone over the head and running. But I am the greediest. I just want to make that clear."

Virgo rolled her eyes. "Tobias, what are we going to do now? I'm drenched and freezing. I say we cut our losses and go home, where the wine flows from the presses and the fires warm cheeks. We have Nath's items. They alone are worth a fortune."

"And his purse," Nina said, looking at Worm. "Take it out, rogue, and don't open it. I'm watching your slippery hands."

Worm held up Nath's purse and gave a crooked smile. "I would never steal from my mates." He tossed it to Tobias.

Tobias's eyes grew big when he opened the sack, spilling part of the contents into his hands. Pieces of gold were mixed with emeralds, rubies, and diamonds. "Zanthar's toes! We wouldn't get this much for the princess! Who is this Nath Dragon that carries a hoard in his pocket?"

"He's from the south is all that I know." Nina eyed the entrance to the Wall of Hozam. "I think we should go after him."

"Are you mad?" Cullon said. "They are dead already."

"You are taking the orc's word now, Cullon." Nina shook her head. "You don't know what lies in there. You've never been. All any of us know are rumors and legends. For all we know, there might not be anything in there but spiders and cobwebs."

"And snakes," Worm said. He'd dismounted and wandered near the entrance. The stone rattler hung limp in his hands. "This skin and venom will fetch another small fortune," he said, stuffing it into a sack. "I say we take a vote, Tobias."

"I second the motion," Virgo added.

With eyes locked on the treasure in his hand, Tobias said, "All right, all in favor of pursuing Nath and Janna, say *aye*."

"Aye," Nina said with a frown.

Worm cackled.

"Sorry, Nina," Tobias said, putting away the purse of treasure, "but we go where the wine and warmth awaits."

With a lasting look at the entrance, she said, "So be it."

The Black Hand rode out of the cave, through the Channel, and never looked back.

Chapter 60

Standing just outside of the cornfields near a small rural town, Lord Darkken and Maefon watched it blaze. The straw roofs of the stone cottages burned. The people of Tilly scrambled back and forth, carrying buckets of water from the creek. The effort did little to no good. The stiff night winds carried the scorching flames from one haven to another, consuming all with fire.

With the fires reflecting in her eyes, Maefon said, "Did I do well, Lord Darken?"

"It burns. That's what I expected." He put his arm over her shoulder. "Though your execution could have been better. I would have preferred that you waited a little longer into the night, to catch more of them sleeping."

"You wanted them to die?" she said, keeping her glassy stare on the growing inferno. "I thought the goal was simple discourse that would spread like fire."

"True, but the death of the innocent will brew bad blood for generations. And I like to hear the lamentations of the women. Their woe-filled cries are song to me. Besides, it's important that I see you have such killer instinct in you, Maefon." He hugged her with an iron grip. "The Caligin must be ruthless. When the time comes to kill, you must do so without remorse. It's our icy hearts that allow us to move forward and conquer."

"If I had known, I would have done more to please you," she said, trying not to wince under the pressure of his arm. "I killed the fledglings. Is that not enough?"

"I wasn't there, Maefon. I can only believe what I have seen for myself. After all, how fully can I trust a Caligin when I've trained them all to be excellent liars?"

She smirked. "Understood. But if you require fresh blood spilled—"

"Nay, you have proven much to me." He let go of her and gently caressed her back. "I just wanted to get you out, abroad, so you can experience how I prefer for the Caligin to operate. After all, you have been closed in on a single mission for a long time. Now that you are out, I want you to be fresh. Besides, I want you to focus on growing your magic skills. They will serve a greater purpose down the road."

"Again, I am glad to execute any order that you command, Lord Darkken." She took his hand and kissed his copper rings. "Any."

He shrugged his brows. "We'll see, eh…"

There was a jangle of armor and the clopping of hooves coming at them. Three riders rode up to Lord Darkken and Maefon. The riders wore faceless helmets, with one rider having a cross and eagle fashioned on the top. Soldiers. Wearing full suits of shining armor, breastplate with chainmail underneath, and a tunic over top embroidered in sky-blue and gold colors, they stopped several feet from Lord Darkken and encircled them.

"Good evening, Knight Commander," Lord Darkken said with a slight dip of his chin. "What brings the legionnaires of Quintuklen outside of the small town of Tilly?"

In a serious tone, the commander leaned forward in the saddle. "I'm curious as to why you are standing in this field while a village burns."

"I could ask the same of you," Lord Darkken said. "Aren't the knights of Quintuklen sworn to protect and serve their interests in the lesser lands?"

"You speak with a sharp tongue, stranger," the commander said as he dismounted. He approached with his hand on his sword handle. "As a matter of fact, I am serving these smaller establishments. It is my charge to protect them, as you say. Currently, I am investigating some bizarre troubles that have overcome many of the small towns under my watch."

Lord Darkken nodded. "I'm sorry to hear this news. Maefon, are you aware of any troubles?"

"No, none, aside from Tilly collapsing to the ground." With her fingers locked together, she pled, "Knight Commander, we weren't meaning to stand here stupefied. By the time we arrived, we knew our efforts were too late." She grabbed Lord Darkken's hand. "We were on a stroll, alone, the two of us, celebrating our renewed devotion to one another."

"Yes, of course, a man and an elf. How delightful for the two of you. I'm sure your family in Elome will be thrilled by your decisions." He twisted off the lid of his canteen and drank deeply. Putting the cap back on, he said, "Ah!" He combed his long moustache with his fingers. "A funny coincidence, though, now that you mention it. You see, my investigation has revealed at every tragic event, there was a man"—he looked at Lord Darkken—"and an elf"—he glanced at Maefon—"that perfectly fit your description. I just can't rule out the likes of the two of you and these tragic occurrences as coincidental. And they say that the elf called herself Maefon. Isn't that your name, young lady?"

Lord Darkken stepped in front of Maefon. "Commander, are you accusing us of something?"

"I've been doing this a long time, and I know when something's awry. You two might look like roses, but you stink of trouble." He drew his sword. "I'm going to need you to come along with me, back to the outpost, for some questions. A lot of them."

"And if we refuse?" Lord Darkken said.

"It is within my purview to bring you in dead or alive if I have to. I trust my instincts. I know the fire starters and murderers are you two," the commander said. "I've been privy to these secret dealings for a long time. I suspected it was elves, but it was hard to explain because people would think I'm mad. But now, I've caught you red handed."

Lord Darkken's copper-colored eyes became slits like a serpent's. "You couldn't be more right, Commander. Please, try and take us in."

"Demon spawn!" The knight commander rushed Lord Darkken and delivered an overhanded chop. The bright steel came downward in a flashing arc of steel.

Lord Darkken caught the sword blade with his molten red hands. His fingers melted grooves in the metal. His snake eyes were fire. "I'm impressed. You have strong powers of deduction, or should I say had?" He grabbed the knight by the back of the neck and hoisted him high in the air. The man's body shriveled to char and ash. His armor became molten and dripped sizzling to the ground.

One of the other knights rammed a lance in Darkken's back. It quivered in his grasp, not penetrating even half an inch, and snapped halfway down the shaft. Dropping out of the sky, Galtur the two-headed vulture snatched the man out of the saddle. Wings beating, Galtur hauled the man into the sky, over the fires in the village, and dropped the legionnaire in the flames. As it all went down, Maefon climbed up behind the last knight, slipped a dagger between his ribs, and pushed his dying body out of the saddle.

Lord Darkken's glowing snake eyes cooled. A smile crossed his face. "It's been quite some time since that has happened. It seems some of my Caligin need to be more careful." He stared at the pile of molten metal and human ash. "Oh, how I enjoy letting loose my powers. Come, Maefon, it's time to return to Stonewater. We've been found out." He reached up and took her hand, and they both vanished.

Chapter 61

With Janna cradled in his arms, Nath eased inside the Wall of Hozam. Air, like a stale, cold breath, tickled his neck. A few feet inside, he stopped and turned. The exit back into the cave was gone. "Not good," he whispered.

"What's not good?" Janna clung to him as if her life depended on it. Her fingernails dug into his skin. "Where's the door? Nath? Where did the door go?"

"Ssssh, keep your voice down. We don't know what's in here."

"Don't say that!" Her voiced echoed.

"Will you be quiet? Just give me a moment while my eyes adjust."

Her warm body shivered. A very faint enticing fragrance still lingered in her damp locks of hair. Her breath was on his neck.

"We will be fine, I promise. Are you feeling better?" he asked, seeing how she seemed more alert.

"Those kidnappers poisoned me with a strange water to keep me calm, I believe. The truth is, I wish I had more of it now." Her big eyes swept the area. "I don't like this place. It stinks."

Even inside Dragon Home, in the darkest places that Nath explored, there'd been more light. The great mountain always had warmth on account of the fiery streams of lava that flowed through it. This place was cold and deathly, like some sort of void with a foul, stagnant stench. Nath crept forward, sliding on his feet an inch at a time. Even his own keen sight couldn't make out the outline of the walls. Left, right, up, or down, he didn't see anything.

"I don't like this, Nath. I want to go back," Janna said with her face buried in his neck. "Please take me back. I can't see anything. Even when I was blindfolded, I could at least feel the sun and rain. Here, I feel as if I'm in nothing. Are we dead?"

"You are warm as a morning biscuit, so I'd say not."

"A biscuit? Really, is that what I feel like to you? A lumpy, clumpy hunk of baked dough?"

"You are a little lumpy," he said, smiling in the dark. She pinched him. "Ow!"

"I'm not lumpy."

"It was intended to be a compliment," he said, sidestepping as he tried to feel the ground along the darkness.

"I don't see how. You don't have much experience with women, do you?" she said.

"More so of late," Nath said, still searching through the dark. He felt like he was standing on the ledge of an overlook. He made sure as he moved that he kept his feet in touch with the ground.

"Have you ever rescued a woman before?"

"Actually, I tried once, but it turned out she didn't want to be rescued. She wanted to rob me."

"That's no surprise these days. It seems everyone is robbing everybody. Was she pretty?"

Nath shrugged. Pretty was an understatement when it came to Calypsa. She carried an enchanting beauty that could make an elf jealous. "Fetching would be a more apt description."

"More fetching than me?"

Nath rolled his eyes. "It's hard to say. I haven't gotten a full look at you. Once we find a source of light, I'll render my comparison."

"You know, at times like this, the smart thing to say would be no. Goodness, were you raised in a cave?"

"Sort of. It's a long story." The ground beneath his feet shifted. "Did you feel that?"

"The only thing I feel is you."

The faint sound of stone rubbing against stone caught his ear. It happened every time he moved. Something weird was going on right beneath him. Nath felt something rub him beside his breastplate and chest. "Zophar's candles," he exclaimed in a whisper.

"Who is Zophar?" she asked.

"A wizard from the ages." Nath fished out a candle—four-sided in shape and little bigger than his finger, he'd tucked them inside his trousers. "This was a gift from my father. Its flame will not go out."

"How will you light it?"

"Hah," he said in the darkness, "the same way you extinguish it. I just put my lips together and blow." With the candle before him, he put his lips together and let out a huff of air. The candle wick ignited with a bright-orange flame.

With her eyes squeezed half shut, Janna let out a sigh. "That's much better." The little candle created a large radius of light. "Can I hold it, Nath, while you carry me?"

"Uh, sure," he said, absentmindedly handing her the candle. "Just don't drop it."

Eyeing the flame, she said, "I feel better already. Don't you?" Her comment was met with silence.

Nath's jaw hung. His eyes were fixed on the moving parts of the floor. He stood on a slab of rock, suspended over a bottomless chasm of blackness. He had no idea how it had gotten there. Other slabs of stone floated quickly by, like logs floating on a black river. They moved about like stone tiles, quickly rushing by one block at a time and bumping lightly into each other before gliding away. It reminded him of when he was trying to cross the moat of lava outside of Dragon Home, but this seemed worse. "Princess, whatever you do, don't drop the candle. And please, keep your eyes on the flame."

"Why?" she said, peeling her eyes away from the candle. She stared right down into the abyss. She flinched. The candle fell from her fingers, bounced on the stone, and teetered on the edge. "Oh my!"

"Don't move a muscle," Nath said, bending at the knees. He reached for the candle. It fell into the chasm and vanished, leaving them enveloped in blackness again. "Gads!"

Chapter 62

Nath took out one of the remaining two candles. With a huff of breath on the wick, the candle ignited.

"Oh, thank goodness," Janna said, reaching for the candle.

"You can't drop this one," he said. "Do you understand?"

"I'm sorry, but the shock got to me. I swear I won't drop it again." She studied the rocks that swirled around them. "How are we going to cross this? I can barely walk, so I can't jump."

"I know, but I guess I'll have to make like a frog and jump from lily pad to lily pad."

"You can't jump with me."

"You aren't very heavy. I can do it. Just whatever you do, don't drop the candle again."

"I won't." She kissed his cheek. "Good luck."

Nath couldn't even see to the other side of the abyss. He didn't even know if there was one. All there was were random rocks floating around the one where he stood, which remained solid beneath his feet. The question was, how did he know if the rocks that he jumped on would hold him, let alone her and him? There was only one way. Forward. Like the lava moat around Dragon Home, he would have to go at it quickly. "Here goes everything." He jumped to the next passing rock. To his surprise, it was solid as the earth beneath him, though it moved quickly among the others of the expanse. He smiled at her.

"Well done. Keep going. I want to get out of this plaayyaace!"

The stone platform wobbled. It started to sink.

Propelled by very strong legs, Nath jumped to the next rock he could find. The stone he just came from dropped out of sight in the abyss. His eyes swept the chamber. None of the rocks that floated by came close. The slab he stood on began to wobble.

"Na-ath! Do something!"

"There's nowhere to jump," he said. Finally, a rock, a bit small, zoomed by. Timing it, he leapt. He landed on the ledge of the moving slab with his toes hanging over the edge. He bent back and forth and shuffled back, regaining his balance. He wasn't on the slab for two seconds when it started to sink. Nath made a quick calculation. As the stones glided by, he saw what he thought was a pattern and leapt. Without stopping, he jumped from one slab to the other, planning three jumps ahead as he passed.

"I can't watch! I can't watch!" Janna squeezed her eyes shut. "Please don't get me killed!"

He didn't stop. A ledge revealed itself on the other side. He made three more leaps, and his feet landed on the ledge. Panting and sweating, he backed to the wall. Only a handful of stones still floated above the abyss. All of the slab tiles he touched had dropped from sight. "You can open your eyes now, Janna. We are safe," he said.

She cracked an eye open. "Oh, thank goodness. I think you can put me down now. I want to walk on my own two feet."

He let her down. She put some weight on her leg and winced.

"I can still carry you."

"No, no, I can manage. Most of the sting is gone." Her knuckles were white around the candle. Her hand still shook like a leaf. "Where do we go now?"

"There's only two ways to go," he said, pointing over her shoulder. "Through that tunnel." He hitched his thumb over his shoulder. "Or that one."

"I think we'll go that way," she said, eyeing the exit behind Nath.

"No, you picked the last time. This time, we go my way." He grabbed her by the wrist and dragged her along behind him. She limped, so he didn't move too fast. The arch in the rock let them into a dry and musty corridor. The tunnels split off in many directions. Nath stayed on the path that angled upward.

"I heard stories from my father, but I never imagined there really were places such as this," Janna said. Her eyes were big as a moon. "And why does it smell so bad? Nothing could possibly live in here, could it?"

"It's a cave. Many creatures dwell in the earth. Like dragons." Nath led the way, moving from tunnel to tunnel, passing cove after cove. There were corpses, skeletons lying dead in their armor, and ragged clothing covering others. One skeleton's legs had been bitten clean through.

Shielding her mouth and nose with her hand, Janna said, "That is dreadful. What happened to them?"

Nath picked up a dragon tooth lying on the dusty ground, and one of the torches that lay nearby. "I'd say they ran out of light, couldn't find their way out, and then a monster came and got them. Either that, or they died first. I can't tell. Let's keep moving."

For hours they walked, winding through tunnel after tunnel. The light flickered, revealing the same bodies and broken bones as when they'd begun. Nath scowled. They were right where they'd started. Janna sat down. "I can't walk anymore. My feet are burning, and my ankle and hip are sore. What kind of madness is this? Will we ever get out of here?"

"We will," he said, putting his arm over her shoulder. "Just rest while I think about this." Nath wished he had his pack. It was times like this when he could use Winzee's Lantern of Revealing. He was certain there was something he was missing. Additionally, he could feel the walls closing in like a steel trap. He figured out why the other adventurers died. Wandering and lost, eventually, they ran out of flame. If it weren't for Zothar's candles, Nath and Janna would be doomed. Its flames would not extinguish, not by water, not by wind. The wick burned everlasting. He stroked her hair. "Don't worry. I'll find a way out of here."

Princess Janna gently snored.

A rumbling roar echoed through tunnels, stirring the cobwebs.

Janna's bleary eyes snapped open. She sat upright. "What was that?"

"I'm not sure," he said, coming to his feet, "but it sounded hungry."

Chapter 63

Rummaging through the rotting corpses, Nath searched for a weapon. He pulled a longsword out of a deteriorating sheath. The blade was coated with dirt, webbing, and grit. He banged the steel on the hard rocks, knocking the ancient debris free, and thumbed the keen edge. He turned it over in his hand a few times. "This will do." With a sword to match the dagger he'd taken earlier from the brigand, he said to Janna, "We need to move."

"What was that thing I heard? Tell me I was dreaming. Sometimes sounds in dreams are louder than they really are."

"I don't know what it was," he said. Nath suspected it was a dragon, but even dragons had different kinds of roars. It could have been a bear or a lion. There was no telling with the way sound traveled in the tunnels. One thing he did know was that whatever made that sound came from somewhere else, meaning there must have been another path he'd missed. "We just need to keep moving."

Janna clung to his elbow with her hand. She kept the candle before her. Hard creases appeared in her forehead. "This is going to give me wrinkles. I don't want to die."

"You won't." He moved down the same path he'd crossed a dozen times. It broadened into wide caverns only to narrow back down again. The walls were slick with bright deposits of mineral specks, making a smooth and glistening surface. There were flecks of gold and silver within, mixed with copper, brass, and other bright flecks made from rocks and minerals.

The strange roar thundered throughout the chamber, sending a chill down his spine.

"Nath," Janna said with a shaking voice, "I can't move. My knees are frozen."

"I'm with you. Whatever that is, it won't find us if we find a way out first." Nath tried to pull her along, but she hunkered down. "Come on, Janna, we must keep moving."

"I can't!"

With his sword and dagger in hand, Nath managed to scoop her up in his arms. "I can move for the both of us." He moved on, using the light of the candle that quavered in her trembling hand. Poor Janna shook like a leaf. Her delicate body quaked in his arms. He picked up the pace as he entered a cavern covered in broken stone. He weaved through the rocks. A stir caught his ears. Ahead, at the far end of the cavern, Nath caught a glimpse of small men scurrying into the field of stones.

Nath tensed. He started backward, not stopping until he stood underneath a rocky canopy of mineral stone. He set Janna down. "Stay here."

"Where are you going? What is out there?"

"I'll be right here," he said, looking from side to side. He made out hairy men dashing from rock to rock, coming toward him. Covered in black fur, they had big bulging eyes that were illuminated like the hot coals of a fire. Some crept forward on all fours. Others jumped silently from rock to rock. The bestial men skulked only a few yards away. Gooey spittle dripped from their lantern-shaped jaws, revealing large carnivorous teeth. Nath cut his sword through the air. "Stay back."

The bestial men slid from the rocks and crouched to the ground, creeping closer like prowling animals. Their long toe- and fingernails made scratching and clicking noises on the floor.

Cowering behind Nath, Janna said, "I'm frightened, Nath. Don't leave me!"

"I promise I won't. Just stay right where you are." Nath swung his sword through the air. If he ever missed Fang, he missed his magnificent blade the most right now. His dragon blood rushed like whitewater rapids. His heart pounded. "Back off, you hairy demons. I'll use this sword and dagger to put an end to you."

The smallish bestial men crept right at him with wide jaws that clacked and bit. One of them rushed Nath from the right.

Nath charged.

CHAPTER 64

NATH TURNED HIS HIPS INTO his swing. The longsword whistled through the air, delivering a fatal chop that took the beastman's head from its shoulders. A guttural howl erupted from the surrounding orange-eyed savages. All at once, they came at Nath in a wild frenzy. Sword in hand, he recollected Dragon Master Elween's endless lessons. Nath lashed out. His sword seemed to move with a life of its own.

A beastman howled when the sword sank into its chest. A second savage fell to a quick strike from Nath's dagger. Fingers were severed from hands. The beastmen came at him in a savage knot of brute strength, long, clawlike fingernails reaching out and teeth gnashing. The undisciplined lot's efforts were spoiled by the sting of Nath's longsword.

Slice! Chop!

The beastmen fell beneath the skill of Nath's singing blade. The battle raged. The sword flickered like the tongue of a striking snake. "Back off, monsters!" Nath shouted as he plunged his dagger in the heart of a beastman swatting at him from behind. Woozy, it staggered away, clutching its chest before falling to the ground.

Nath didn't let up. The beastmen didn't either. Howling like ravenous wolves, they came at him in desperation. Quick and powerful, they charged him as one. Nath cut and stabbed. The hairy brutes rushed forward, maimed and bleeding, and overpowered Nath. Their sheer weight and numbers knocked him from his feet and drove him to the ground.

"Get off me!" Nath cried out. Thrashing and kicking for his life, he cracked them in the face with the butt of his sword. Bone gave way, but their flesh did not. Teeth sank into Nath's arms. Claws scraped his face. Strong, thick hands clamped under his chin, squeezing his neck. "Now!"

The beastmen, though smaller, worked like a relentless hive of bees. They clubbed Nath with the hard knuckles of their fists. Howling and grunting, they beat on Nath's breastplate, trying to crack him open like some kind of egg. Teeth bit into Nath's ankle. He let out a scream. "Aaaaaaah!"

The beastmen wrapped him up in a coarse, hairy blanket made of constricting muscles. His arms and legs were seized, his weapons torn from his grip.

"Nath!" Janna called out in a high-pitched voice. "Help me, Nath! Help meeeeee!" Her voice trailed off.

Nath caught a glimpse through the brawny builds of the wiry men. Another group hauled Janna off by her wrists and ankles as they skittered away. "Janna! Janna! I'm coming! Let go of me, demons!" He broke their grip with one hand and landed a solid punch on a beastman's nose. It let out a howl, drew back its fist, and walloped Nath in the jaw. Somehow, Nath got hold of it by the chest hair. He ripped a fistful out and screamed, "Jaaanna!"

A beastman clocked Nath in the head with a stone.

"Guh!" Nath's taut muscles loosened. Blurry purple spots appeared in his eyes. He flexed against the rank horde again. Stone still in hand, the little brute struck him a second and third time. The lone light from the Zothar's candle went dim. Nath's thoughts for survival swam. The beastmen hauled him away with soft steps and heavy breathing. Nath hung suspended in their grip, fighting the darkness that crept over his consciousness.

Chapter 65

Nath woke with a throbbing headache. His blood had begun to dry and cake on his face. His eyelids hurt. He rubbed his swollen forehead and jaw. Lying flat on his back, he grunted and turned on his side.

"Trespasser. Thief. Arise," said a voice that was as ancient and cold as the winter wind.

Racked with pain from toe to forehead, Nath made it to his knees. He felt his heart beating in his tongue. His blurry vision cleared. Warm light illuminated the room like the sun from a hazy day. Small urns with green-blue flames burned around the outer edges of a chamber made from chiseled-out stone. The beastmen squatted by the urns, one on each side with their knuckles on the ground.

"Who are you?" the cold voice said.

Nath twisted his head around and realized he was facing the wrong direction. The person who spoke sat behind him in a throne chiseled from a black block of solid marble. The man was covered in loose cloth wrappings that wound around his limbs and body. Stringy strands of dry hair hung down past his shoulders. Ancient and dry skin covered the few spots able to be seen, and his eyes burned like the rising sun. He wore a crown made from entwined silver serpents on his head. He held Zothar's candles in a very bony hand covered with age spots and deep wrinkles.

Janna lay on the ground between them, passed out on the stone floor. A blue dome of mystic energy shielded her.

On impulse, Nath moved to the dome. "Janna! You better not have hurt her!" He attacked the dome with his fist. A jolt coursed through his body, standing his hairs on end and throwing him backward.

"Ah-hah-hah," the venerable man sitting on the throne said. "It's been quite some time since I've had a laugh." He coughed. Dust and moths came out of his mouth. "Pardon me." He waved his hand. A female beastman wearing a tattered blue dress brought over a tray with a golden goblet. The ancient man took the goblet with a steady hand and drank. He flicked his wrist at the female beastman, and she hurried away, disappearing into the darkness behind him. "I am Hozam, thief. Who are you?"

Nath stood. "I'm no thief, and you better not have hurt my friend. Let her go."

"Heh. She is quite safe, and you test my patience." Hozam set his goblet on the arm of the chair and waved the candle before his eyes. "This is a very valuable acquisition. This candle got you this far, but now your journey of robbing and stealing has come to an end. Now, tell me who you are."

"I am no thief," Nath replied, shaking out his fingertips. "My name is Nath."

"Nath." Hozam leaned back. With his free hand, he rubbed his chin. "A lousy name for a thief. Tell me, why did you dare seek out the treasure of the great Hozam? Is there not enough elsewhere in Nalzambor?"

"We didn't come to rob you. We came seeking refuge." Nath eased closer. "We were chased inside this... tomb."

Hozam's neck popped and cracked as he moved it from side to side, his eyes boring into Nath. His voice rose like thunder. "Hah-hah-hah... I have heard every lie from those that venture within. They all stretch wild tales as they plead for their lives. At least have the courtesy to tell me something original. I become quite bored down here."

"It is the truth. I was chased within by the Black Hand and the Men of Whispers. They sought to ransom this princess to her father and make a slave of me. I didn't come here by choice."

Hozam scratched the scabbing skin from his cheek. "Not very colorful or rich. It almost sounds believable. But you and this woman will die, unless you would prefer to be converted into one of my children—my precious beastmen, many of which you have slaughtered. Trying to steal my treasure is one transgression, but slaughtering my family is another."

"I didn't mean to kill them. But they attacked me—"

"Silence!"

Nath's hair bristled.

Hozam continued, "You are the trespasser. The thief. The liar. But a clever one, I must say. Not many make it as far as you did. Most perish in the abyss of slabs that you traversed. Others fall prey to the darkness, unless they have magical light, of course." He held up the candle. "Like this. That is when I send the beastmen. Most don't make it farther than that, but a few have. They face the great beast that lies within. You heard him, didn't you... Nath?"

"I heard a growl, yes."

"Yesss, that is my precious pet, the devourer of the dark. It can smell your fear. It feeds on it. It is the guardian of my treasure." Hozam placed the candle in his mouth and swallowed it. "Mmmm... delicious. I feed on magic." He coughed out yellow smoke.

"It looks more to me like you waste it," Nath commented.

"Heh." Hozam pushed out of his chair and started to stand. He became tall as a tower.

At full height, he stood eight feet tall. Standing at the top of the steps, he glowered down at Nath.

Nath felt like he was shrinking under the withered wizard's white-hot stare. He leaned backward as Hozam approached. The great wizard stood over the mystic dome of energy that surrounded Janna. "I don't mean to show disrespect, Hozam, but are you dead or alive?"

"Behind the wall of Hozam, I live. Beyond, I die. That is the price for my omnipotent power and immortality." He put his huge bony bare foot on the dome over Janna. "I am the last of my kind from long, long ago. Yet I still thrive, as ruler, in my city in the darkness. It's not often that I have guests. I relish in it." He took a deep breath. "You have an odd smell about you for a man. What race are you?"

"I'm not sure what you mean. I am what you see." Nath said, holding back the full truth while at the same time not lying.

"No, you are more. But we shall see." Hozam lowered his gaze to Janna. "I think this one is ready to transform. She is soft. She is weak. I shall make her stronger than ever before and make her life everlasting." The dome over the young woman swirled with scarlet. Janna bucked. Gasping, she came out of her sleep. Her little fists beat against the energy field. She screamed, but her voice was not heard. The hair on her head, arms, and face started to grow and thicken.

"What are you doing to her?" Nath charged Hozam. Hozam shot a bolt of energy out of his palm. The bright blast knocked Nath from his feet. His chest armor smoked. He stood up.

Janna's face was in agony. She stared wide-eyed at her hairy hands.

"Stop it!"

"No. I won't stop it, but you can, trespasser." Hozam pointed to an opening that appeared on the chamber wall. "Kill the devourer in the dark that guards my treasure, and you shall find a cure for her there. Then you and she can leave." The roaring sound of a beast came out of the opened portal. "I'll be waiting."

Chapter 66

"You are sending me to my death!" Nath's temper flared. His voice rose. "You expect me to fight a monster, and I don't even have a weapon. You play games, Hozam!"

"It's what I do. It's very boring down here. Of course, you are always welcome to stay if you willingly give yourself over to me." Hozam patted the dome of energy. "It isn't as painful when you don't resist. Your fellow thief resists. The more you resist, the more you suffer. But she will break, and when she does, there is only one way to save her. But you still have time. In the treasure chamber is a potion. Only one. Fetch it, before the devourer of the dark fetches you. He hungers. It's been a long time since he's fed, and he's tired of beastmen."

"This is a rotten game. You send me to a certain death. I need something to fight it with, at least."

"You cannot kill what you cannot see, but you can run from it, quickly. Now, stop wasting time. Your comrade needs you."

Nath hustled over to Janna. He put his hands on the dome. She put her hands to his. Her face had begun to change toward the likeness of the beastmen. Hair had sprouted on her face and chin. Her eyes bulged. Her frightened gaze was wet with tears. "I'll be back for you!"

He could read her lips as she said, "Help me, Nath! Help me!"

Hozam shoved Nath away with an ice-cold hand. "Stop wasting time, fool! My mercy will quickly end!"

"This better not be a lie, Hozam! If it is, I'll finish you!" He ran for the portal in the wall. He could hear Hozam's icy words as he crossed the threshold.

"Not when the devourer finishes you first."

The portal plunged Nath back into the pitch blackness. His fingertips grazed the wall. He crept forward, slowly at first, heart racing until his dragon senses homed in on the new environment. The walls were solid, made from rough stone. Tunnels spread out around him. It wasn't long before he had the distinct feeling that he was inside a city built inside of the mountain. He sniffed the stale air. His eyes searched for warmth and light. The only thing he heard were bugs that crawled on the walls and floor. As his eyes adjusted, he saw small centipedes and other bugs that glowed. Their small crawling bodies outlined the walls and floor.

"That's helpful."

A hungry roar shattered the silence, surrounding him.

Nath froze. It sounded close. "And that's not helpful."

Using the glowing centipedes as guides, Nath picked up his pace, hoping that he was moving in a direction opposite of whatever prowled the caverns with him. He came to a landing with a broad stone staircase that spiraled downward. Taking two steps at a time, he moved downward, quiet as a cat, hoping that somehow, some way, he was heading toward the treasure room. Of course, there was no way of knowing if there was even any sort of treasure at all. Hozam was an evil thing, and evil was prone to lying. Most likely, all the ancient wizard had done was send him to a certain death in the jaws of the devourer.

Nath tried to stay focused. His head hurt. The jolt Hozam sent through him still stung. Fists and jaws clenched, he fought through his pain and frustration with determination coursing through him. *I must do this!* The Black Hand duped him. They made him look like a fool. At the same time, he was mad at himself for letting it happen. Since he'd left Dragon Home, he hadn't done one single thing right. He'd been robbed twice, but the second robbery was sticking. To make matters worse, doubt crawled in his belly. Perhaps he made the wrong decision by crossing through the Wall of Hozam. The princess would have been better off in the hands of the kidnappers. At least they wouldn't have gotten her killed. They would have just turned her over for ransom. Nath could have dealt with that later.

I'm such a fool!

Step after step, he moved on, determined to make it right. He had to save Janna. He couldn't shake the horror of her beauty being slowly turned into an abomination. Even if

Hozam had lied about a potion, he had to take a chance that he didn't. He had to move on with hope.

Suddenly, the glowing bugs spotted on the walls and floors went black. The air turned icy cold and felt like a fetid breath on his neck. Something made a distinctive *sssssz* sound. Nath's flesh crawled. He spread out his arms and reached out. A presence was there, filling the gap behind him. Then it was gone. The bugs illuminated again. Nath could breathe again.

What in the world was that?

A few steps up, a centipede crawled over a scorched and smoking spot on the stone. As the bug crawled over the surface, it coiled up like it just passed through fire. Its inner light dimmed forever. Something had just been there, right behind Nath, that could have gobbled him up, but didn't. He had no doubt that it was the devourer, and it was toying with him. He took a deep breath and started back down the steps. His aching body throbbed, and his senses were on edge.

Onward, Nath, onward.

Chapter 67

At the bottom of the steps, Nath heard water trickling down and splashing into a pool. The floor was wet and slick beneath him. The light from the bugs on the walls and floor had gone cold. Nath stood in the pitch blackness again, but this time there was a cool, damp mist on his face. The splashing and dripping water he heard gave him a little hope. Perhaps it was from the rainfall seeping through the mountain and it would provide another way out if he could just find its source.

He felt something digging into his ribs under his armor. He fished it out. "I'm such a fool!" he uttered. He held the last of Zothar's candles in his hand. He intentionally didn't tell Janna, since she'd dropped the first one. So much had been happening that he'd forgotten all about the last one. He blew on the wick. The flame flickered on. The warm candlelight might as well have been a sunray. Nath couldn't contain his jubilation. "Ha-hah!"

A huge reservoir of water filled the chamber. On the far side was a broad row of steps. Above, water dripped from a chasm in the ceiling. Standing at the edge of the pool, Nath put his fingers in the water. Small, white, glowing fish scattered. As far as he could see, there wasn't a way around the pool, but the water smelled as fresh as rainwater. Nath climbed over the rim of the stone basin and lowered himself into the water. Thigh deep in the waters, he began to cross. The waves he created sloshed over the edge of the pool, splashing loudly on the floor. He moved more quickly toward the steps on the other side. The pool became deeper the farther he went. Something snaked around his ankles. "Gah!"

He plunged the candle into the water. The wick of the magic candle still burned brightly, but nothing was there. Moving onward, Nath found himself neck deep in the waters and started to paddle over. His breastplate dragged him down to where his feet touched bottom. He walked across the soft mud that clung to his feet. The fully submerged glowing fish started to circle. Baring sharp teeth, they darted in and bit him. Nath screamed underwater. Covered in biting fish, he climbed over the bottom, pulling himself toward the other side, hand over hand. His lungs burned. He needed air. When the pool became shallow enough, he burst out of the water and raced toward the steps on the other side. He flung the fish clamped onto his body aside as he did so. "Get off me!" The fish were still snapping once he made his way onto the steps. He picked them off and slung them across the pool. "What kind of fish eats you?"

He sat on the steps, panting and bleeding from a dozen small wounds. The fish remained in a frenzy where the steps and water met. Nath climbed up farther. He combed his hair out of his eyes and noticed a small skiff tied up at the end of the steps. "I'll use you next time."

Slowly, he traversed the steps to the top. He stood underneath another archway. On the left and right of the entrance were two stone statues of knights in full suits of armor. Beyond them, the floor to the room sloped downward. A crevice of golden light showed the way. Nath ventured past the knights and down the slope. Something moved out of the corner of his eye. The knights jumped down from their pedestals and attacked. One drew a sword, and another jabbed with a spear. They moved quickly for men made from granite.

Nath slipped to the side of a jabbing spear. He ducked underneath a sword swing and let out a savage war cry. "EEEEEE-YAAAAAAH!" Shoulders down, he plowed into the spear-wielding guardian and lifted the one-ton monster onto his shoulders. With a tremendous heave, he slammed it down on the ground. The stone knight burst into several large pieces. Nath rolled aside, dodging a deadly chop from the sword-wielding knight. He scrambled back to his feet.

The stone knight came at him on wooden limbs but stabbed at Nath with swift, powerful cuts that would split a man in two. Nath backpedaled toward the steps of the pool. He took a few steps down, standing out of the stone fighter's range. "Come on, what are you waiting for?"

The mindless automaton chopped at him, but the edge of the sword was nowhere close. It looked down and came forward.

Fast as a big cat, Nath raced up the steps, slipped behind the stone knight, and shoved it forward. Unable to keep its balance, the stone knight hit the steps with a resounding crack. Its stone sword snapped. One arm and leg broke off, and it lay still.

"Whew," Nath said, backing away from the scene. "I guess it's true. The bigger you are, the harder you fall."

Sssszz…

Nath spun around. He found himself face to face with a dark-scaled dragon with a bat-like face. Its ruby-red eyes bored into him. Its scales were hard as stone. It had no horns but was as big as a horse. It opened its jaws wide. Saliva dripped from its razor-sharp rows of teeth and sizzled on the floor. Its rancid breath was cold as death. Unlike other dragons, it didn't have any front arms, but small hands on the ends of its black wings like a bat. On reflex, Nath punched it in the nose. It didn't flinch. "Uh-oh."

Chapter 68

Twin scaled prehensile tails coiled around Nath's ankles and yanked him from his feet. The dragon's small hands clamped around Nath's neck. Its saliva dripped on Nath's breastplate in white-hot globs. His candle fell from his fingers. Nath had seen hundreds of dragons in his time, but never a shadow dragon. He'd only read about them. They were known to be one of the most vicious and deadliest dragons of all.

Nath grabbed the dragon's hands at the wrists and twisted with all his might. The dragon slung him aside and pounced on his back. It kicked him all over the floor. Swatting and slapping him, it beat Nath senseless. Nath crawled out of its grip only to be dragged back by its tails. It slapped his face, roared, and burned his arms and legs with its saliva.

Nath pushed himself up from lying on his belly. He'd studied all of the dragons and remembered most of what he learned. All dragons had a weakness. Sometimes, it was something as simple as pollen from a flower, or a soft spot not protected by their scales. With the shadow dragon, he wasn't certain, but he kept trying, kicking and swinging back, aiming for another spot every time he punched.

The dragon just kicked him around like some sort of toy. Nath skidded over stone and slammed into support columns. When Nath's weary limbs reached their limits, he finally shouted out in dragonese, "Will you quit playing around and just kill me!"

The shadow dragon pounced. Pinning Nath down, it glared into his eyes.

Nath tried to worm free, but his own strength finally faded. Spittle from the dragon's maw dripped and sizzled on his armor. The scales on the dragon's chest were a creamy white, unlike the hard, granite-colored scales covering the body. There were long eyelashes over its burning red eyes.

"Go ahead, sister, kill me."

The dragon put its snout in Nath's face and breathed deeply. Speaking mind to mind, in a harsh female voice, it said, "*You leak the blood of a dragon. You are no man. What are you?*"

"*I'm a dragon, born a man. I'm Nath, the son of Balzurth.*"

"*Balzurth!*" the dragon hissed in his mind. "*You speak lies!*" The dragon pushed down harder on Nath's shoulders. "*Who are you?*"

Nath was shocked that she was speaking to him, but he fired back. "*I told you, I am Balzurth's son! I come from Dragon Home! Search your own heart—you know it is true. No man can speak dragonese, especially mind to mind like me and you.*"

The dragon eased back. Head tilting from side to side, she said, "*I don't understand, but I know you speak truth, for the dragon blood runs through you.*" The dragon sat back. "*Why have you left Dragon Home to come here? And be specific. Very specific.*"

Fighting his way to his knees with a groan, out loud Nath quickly recounted everything that had happened since he left Dragon Home. If there was one thing he knew about dragons, it was that they enjoyed a good story. "And that's why I am here, trying to save Princess Janna from becoming one of the Hozam's cursed beastmen, as well as myself."

The shadow dragon stretched out her wings and folded them behind her back. "*It is a wondrous story thus far, and the ring of truth is with it. It's been a very long time since I've spoken to my brethren. I've been alone since Hozam made me his prisoner.*"

Rubbing his stiff neck, Nath asked, "I would be honored to help you, uh…"

"*You may call me Obsidian, little brother. Come.*" She turned her back and headed down the slope that led toward the glare of golden light.

With a wooden effort, Nath followed behind her. When she called him little brother, it put his mind at ease. It gave him comfort that he didn't have with the other dragons who'd ignored him. She didn't pass judgment on him like the rest of his brethren did.

At the bottom of the slope, lit by torches of endless fire, were a vaulted room and an open dungeon door. Inside was a small kingdom's treasure, not anything like Balzurth's throne room, but very ample for a city. There were golden plates, chalices, and silverware. Small chests full of coins and precious gems. Marvelous paintings were stacked against the walls, and the floor was covered with rare pelts and furs. In the rear of the vault, a jade decanter sat on a marble pedestal.

"*That is the potion you seek,*" Obsidian said. Nath advanced. She blocked his passage with her arm. "*Do not be so hasty. This does not work as you believe it does. Hozam has lied to you.*"

"What do you mean?" Nath said, trying to push by. Obsidian shoved him back. "Let me pass!"

"*Don't be a fool!*" Obsidian spoke from her lips now. "The potion will work, but you must understand the proper application." She stuck her head in his face. "*And do you really think that Hozam is going to let you use it to serve your own purpose? I would laugh if I still remembered how.*"

"He gave me his word," Nath said, "and we do not have a quarrel with him. It's a chance I have to take."

"*This place where you now dwell once thrived with life with a small race of renowned men who kept to themselves. Hozam killed them all in his quest for immortality. He only achieved it in part. He lives, but he cannot leave. He still searches for more power, that I fear your own blood could provide.*"

"What will my blood do?"

"*Feed him. Make him stronger. He will leave and take more lives—the more he takes, the more power he has. He will not only be a threat to man, but to dragons. He will figure out what you are soon enough, Nath. That is why we must act quickly.*"

"Let me take the potion then."

"*No.*" She fully blocked his path. Her tone darkened. "*I did not bring you here to help you. I brought you here to help me. I long for my wings to caress the open sky once more. You are my only hope since I was captured. I will not pass up on this chance. Look upon my neck. There is an entanglement of serpents. It is how Hozam controls me.*"

For the first time, Nath noticed the silver collar fashioned like entwined snakes on Obsidian's neck. Her scales grew over it in part as it bit into her skin and appeared uncomfortable, if not painful. It was the same craft as Hozam's crown. "I can try to remove it."

"*No. There is only one way. You must take the crown from Hozam's head and destroy it. That will free me and weaken him enough to kill. Once we have done that, I will show you how to heal your friend and let you out of this hole.*"

Nath shook his head. "I don't know that I can trust you."

"*You don't have a choice.*"

Chapter 69

Obsidian carried Nath in her jaws. It wasn't what Nath had in mind when he agreed to help the dragon, but it made sense. He couldn't waltz back into Hozam's chamber and hope to negotiate. It would end in failure. No, his best chance was to put his trust in Obsidian and hope that they could fool the ancient wizard. Soon, Hozam would see them. As the dragon crept up the steps and slunk toward the wizard's throne room, Nath lay limp. The dragon dragged him by the arm with sharp teeth that almost broke the skin. He did his best to stay loose and play along.

Using thought, Obsidian said to him one last time, "*Trust me and don't move. I will handle this. Strike when I say strike.*"

Nath felt the light on his eyelids the moment they entered the chamber. He could smell the rank dander of the beastmen and hear their grunting and scratching.

"What is this that my pet brings me?" Hozam's hollowed-out voice said. "Why did you not eat him? Are you not hungry, my pet?"

Obsidian dropped Nath on the floor. "This one is not edible," she said out loud. "He has a very unique blood that runs through his veins. It is the kind of blood that you require to achieve the immortality you desire."

"Do not toy with me, Obsidian. Explain."

The dragon picked Nath up by the armpits and held him in a standing position. She coiled one of her prehensile tails around his neck. "Can you not smell his blood? It's all over him. That is not man's blood—that is the immortal blood of a dragon."

Nath could hear Hozam's crusty robes dragging over the ground. The wizard stopped short. His foul and icy breath hit Nath's face. Nath remained limp, fighting the urge to strike. A finger cold as an icicle swiped over Nath's bloody skin. It sounded like Hozam was tasting it.

"Mmmm, this blood is strong, Obsidian. You have done well," Hozam said.

"Anything for my master." Obsidian pulled Nath closer to her body. "But I require a favor before I give this jewel into your hands. I want my freedom in exchange, or I will kill him where he stands. He will be no good to you dead, Hozam. The bargain is freedom for freedom."

A sliver of doubt suddenly crawled into Nath's belly. If Hozam gave Obsidian what she wanted, she wouldn't need Nath at all. Once the dragon had freedom, she would be gone. Shadow dragons weren't noble creatures. They marched to their own drum. And how good could a dragon be with the word *shadow* in it? If anything, they would be the perfect vessels of evil.

"Certainly, Obsidian," Hozam said, "whatever you wish. But I cannot release you until I have taken possession of his life force, for there is no guarantee that it will work, and where would I be here, without you, for all eternity?"

Obsidian's tail constricted more tightly on Nath's neck. "He is barely alive now. Don't tempt me to finish it. Remove this collar from my neck, for I have nothing else to live for."

"Heh, neither do I. It seems that we are at a standstill. No freedom for me, and no freedom for you. I think I can wait longer. Can you?"

To Nath, it sounded as if Hozam was turning away and moving on. *No, this can't be happening!*

"No, wait," Obsidian said. "Give me your word, and you can do what you do while I hold him still. Is it a deal, Hozam?"

Obsidian, you lying traitor!

"We agree. Now hold him higher. I need eye-to-eye contact to drain him." The wizard put his icy-cold fingers on Nath's shoulders. "Let's wake him up, shall we?"

"Yes," the shadow dragon said. "Let's wake him." She lifted Nath's toes from the ground. "Have at him. I want my freedom." Then with thought, Obsidian said to Nath, "The moment he speaks again, strike with all of your heart."

Hozam's cold, dead hands clasped Nath's face. His thumbs pushed his eyelids open. "Yes, yes," he said with hungry vigor. "I can feel the power of his blood within him. It will be mine."

Nath snapped his eyes open fully. "Surprise!" With a closed fist, he hammered Hozam underneath the jaw. The giant wizard's teeth clacked together. The serpent crown popped off the top of his head.

As Obsidian released Nath, she said, "The crown!" She pounced on Hozam. "Destroy the crown!"

"What is this? You dare betray me!" Hozam shouted with rage. "You will suffer for all eternity, lying dragon!" Bolts of energy fired out of the wizard's hands and into the dragon's body. Her scales smoked, but she clung to the wizard.

The crown rolled away from Nath with a life of its own. He chased it down and snatched it up with one hand. The ring came to life. The silver snakes bit his hands and fingers. "Argh! I've had enough of this!" Squeezing the snakes that coiled around his hands, Nath stretched them out to full length. They were one body with three heads on each end. Hissing and snapping, they writhed in his grip. Nath tried to pull them apart. It was like stretching steel. He put every ounce of strength he had into it. "Hurk!"

"Nooooo!" Hozam screamed. He punched Obsidian in the jaw with a flaming fist. The dragon fought to hang on.

The snake stretched in his hands, getting longer and longer. Its scales spread out, revealing flesh underneath, but it wasn't dying. It was growing.

"You fool! The crown lives. You cannot kill it. You cannot!" Hozam shouted as he pounded Obsidian's face harder and harder. "You will fail!"

"No! I won't!" On impulse, Nath bit down on the snake's body. It snapped into two pieces as it tore clear apart. An energy wave blasted across the room. Nath found himself on the other side of the room, head ringing, searching out Obsidian and Hozam.

The shadow dragon had the rotting wizard pinned down once more. The dragon's chest expanded. A geyser of flame erupted from the dragon's mouth, engulfing Hozam. His flaming arms flailed and burning legs kicked. He let out a scream that shook the room. "I will have vengeance!" he shouted. There was a loud pop, and his ashes filled the room.

Obsidian swiped her tails through the smoking ashes. "No, you won't. Great Guzan, that felt good. I haven't been able to use my flame in over a millennium because of that collar. I am in your debt, Nath. I won't forget this."

"What about the potion, and how do we get out of here?" he said.

"Pour the potion in the pool below. It will cure them all. The way out is the way you came in. With Hozam gone, the path will be revealed now. Goodbye, Nath." She slapped him on the back with her tails. "You did well. Balzurth would be proud." Obsidian spread her wings and rose into the cavern, fading from sight.

Nath rushed over to Janna and scooped her up in his arms. She had transformed in part to a beast. Her delicate features now bulged with ugliness. Hair covered most of her body like a coat of fur. He raced out of the room, through the portal, and down the steps. The night bugs lit up the corridor, scurrying away from his feet as he passed. The beastmen chased after him, but they did not attack. They moved about, hooting and grunting like frightened animals.

Outside of the pool, the jade decanter waited, alongside the still-burning candle. Obsidian had set it aside there when they hatched their plan to take down Hozam. She told Nath it would be ready when it was over. Now it was. Nath picked up the decanter and poured it into the pool. The water bubbled and foamed. As the surface cleared, a soft light shone through the blue waters. Nath carried Janna into the waters and submerged her fully. With a shimmer, her face and body transformed back into the radiant woman she was before. Her eyes fluttered open as he brought her out again.

"Janna," he said, "how do you feel?"

Her stare was blank and glassy. As he held her, the other beastmen climbed into the pool's waters. One by one, dozens of men and women of all races transformed back into their natural forms. Before Nath could bat an eye, a fight broke out among them. They fought and clawed their way toward the treasure.

"Are you mad?" Nath shouted. The greedy fools didn't even stop to thank him. After centuries of captivity, their greedy nature chose treasure over freedom. Nath carried Janna away in his arms and shouted back as he ascended the steps, "Have at it then! Fools!"

Chapter 70

Exhausted and on stiff legs, Nath carried Princess Janna in his arms through the Channel. The rain had stopped, but the ground was thick with sloppy mud. Water still poured from the mountain's ledges above. He stumbled, fought for footing, and splashed through the mud. Still standing, he rested his back against the canyon's wall. His back and shoulders burned. Janna wasn't heavy, but Nath was tired. Plus, nightfall had started to descend, turning the already-darkening chasm black.

"Can't stop now," he said, half talking to himself and half talking to Janna. She hadn't said a word, but her hands were locked tight around his neck. She kept her face buried in his chest and her eyes squeezed shut. She shivered the entire time as if she was trapped in a nightmare. Nath felt bad for her. She'd been through too much. The transformation into a beastman must have shocked her. "I'll get you home, Janna. I promise."

With his jaw set, he limped on, forcing himself forward one heavy step at a time. His boots stuck in the mud, making a sucking sound every time he pulled them out. Finally, covered in mud, he exited the mouth of the Channel. The road stretched before him, surrounded by green trees and thick in brush.

"Thank goodness."

Night had fallen. The air was damp and cool. Owls hooted from the trees as Nath continued down the road. On foot, it would probably take until morning to make it back to Riegelwood. Determined not to stop, Nath kept going forward, aching all over with his body burning. His belly moaned. He could eat a cow if he had one.

Two things kept him going: getting Princess Janna home and finding the Black Hand. They embarrassed Nath, and worst of all, they had Fang and the rest of his belongings. He would get them back, expose the Black Hand to City Lord Jander, and move on to his quest to find the Trahaydeen and Maefon. It seemed like an age had passed since he began his quest. So much had happened. Rogue Trahaydeen killed fledgling dragons. Nath had been exiled from his home to avenge them, and he couldn't return for a hundred years. It was all sinking in at once. For the first time, he truly missed home and his life among the dragons. The world outside had so far been inexplicably worse than he imagined.

I will see this through even if it kills me.

Fields of farmland appeared on the horizon, spreading out for miles outside of Riegelwood. Nath passed by barns where roosters crowed. Men and women stirred, hustling out of their cottages and tending to the livestock and the fields. They paid Nath no mind as he moved along the road, not stopping until he made it to the city's cobblestone streets just as dawn broke over the hillside horizon. Just outside of the city lord's gates, he dropped to his knees. "Help," he said.

Two soldiers approached. "What seems to be the problem, son?"

Nath barely managed to look up. It was the two soldiers he met when he came into the city—Hartson, black bearded, and Kevan, clean shaven. They were the ones who sent him to the Oxen Inn where he met Nina. He shook his head. "Nothing. We just got caught in the storm. We'll be fine. Just tired. It was a very long night."

"You're all muddy and covered in blood. It looks like you've been in more than just a storm. More like an awful fight." Hartson's hand went to his sword. "Say, you're that fella who came through a few days ago. Who's this woman with you?"

"A friend." Nath forced himself up to one knee. "I'll be taking her home now."

Kevan whispered in Hartson's ear. Hartson's eyes grew big. He took a hard look at the woman in Nath's arms. "That's Princess Janna," Hartson said. "Isn't it?"

"Yes," Nath said, "but you—"

"Kidnapper!" Hartson roared. He drew his sword while his son blew a whistle.

"I didn't kidnap her. I rescued her from the Black Hand!" Nath said, coming to his feet.

Hartson put his sword to Nath's neck. Kevan held a spear at his back. "Don't you dare move," Hartson said.

"You must listen to me, Hartson. I need to take the princess back to City Lord Jander. I have to explain all about the kidnappers, the Black Hand. I must warn him about them."

"Stop with your gibberish, man! I'm just doing my job." Hartson's eyes narrowed on Nath. "If you were wise, you never would have come back, stranger. The city lord doesn't like troublemakers."

The castle's barbicans opened up. More soldiers ran from within the castle archways. A commotion of people chattering started in the streets. Within seconds, Nath was surrounded by hard-eyed soldiers brandishing their weapons. As they took Princess Janna from his arms, her fingers brushed his cheek. Looking him in the eyes, she said, "Thank you, stranger." She vanished behind a wall of armored soldiers.

"Stranger?" Nath said to himself. Scanning the faces of the soldiers, he said to them as they crowded around him with numbers and sharp weapons, "I'm not the kidnapper! I saved her!"

"Take him to the dungeon." Hartson glowered at Nath. "Don't fight, or you'll die."

Nath didn't have the strength to fight anything. They shackled him and hauled him away as the third rooster crowed that day.

Chapter 71

For three days, Nath sat in a dingy dungeon cell on a bed of rotting hay, mulling over how the Black Hand betrayed him. The guards brought him food once a day. Outside of the cell were a wooden ladle and a bucket of water that he could drink from. With his back to the stone wall, he looked through the bars. He gently beat his head against the wall, saying, "I'm stupid, stupid, stupid."

The most disturbing part of the entire predicament was Princess Janna. When she was torn from his arms, she didn't recognize him. She called him stranger. He worried that part of her was lost. So far, he hadn't been accused of anything, but the guards wouldn't say a word to him. It was possible that he might be left to rot forever.

The main door to the dungeon opened. A lone set of hard-soled footsteps approached. It wasn't the same soft scuffle that the guards made. This was someone different. Nath rose to his feet as the door closed the newcomer inside.

Nina stood right in front of him. She was nicely dressed, wearing new gold and jewels on her arms, wrists, and neck, with a pelt of wolf hair over her shoulders. Her hair was in braids on the top of her head, and her bare muscular arms had a silky sheen to them. The tall woman never looked better. "Hello, Nath. You look horrible."

"You!" He thrust his arms through the bars, fingers clutching, but she stood too far away.

She let out a delightful little laugh. "Settle yourself. You have a long journey ahead, and you will need your energy."

Hands on the bars, he yanked on them. Arms shaking, he sighed. "What are you talking about now?"

"First, let me catch you up on your present situation. Currently, you are accused of kidnapping Princess Janna."

"That's a lie, and you know it! The Black Hand did it. You did it!"

She held out her hand. "Compose yourself, please. Or I will leave." She looked at her black-painted nails. "Do we have an understanding?"

"Yes."

She approached the bars and smiled. "You never fail to surprise me. I told Tobias when we left you behind the Wall of Hozam not to be surprised if we saw you again. He laughed. Anyway, we returned to the city with news that we believed Princess Janna had perished and we couldn't recover the body. I have City Lord Jander's ear, so he bought into the story where we chased you into the Channel and lost you and her behind the Wall of Hozam. But we did pin it all on you, Nath. And I put the word out that you might return with her and try to dupe City Lord Jander. He bought it all.

"Then you actually did show up," she said, incredulous. "And with the princess in your arms. You could have very well exposed us if she were able to tell the truth. As it turns out, to your misfortune, and our good fortune, she struggles to even remember who she is. I would love to know what happened behind that wall, but now I'm filthy rich, and I don't really care."

"You have one thing right," Nath said with a snarl.

"Oh really? What is that?"

"You're filthy."

"Hmph." She stroked the wolf pelt. "Listen to me, Nath. You would do well to not agitate me. Frankly, it is disappointing that you didn't join with us. But we all agreed that there was too much good in you to do the dirty deeds that need to be done, and it has cost you. However, I want to thank you. Since you did return the princess, we were able to convince Lord Jander of our efforts and collect her ransom. He trusts us deeply. We will use that to get back in the good graces of Prawl and the Men of Whispers. You're a part of that too."

"You collected the reward for someone that you kidnapped?" He kicked the bars. "That is madness."

"No, that is good business. And you should be thankful for us as well. Kidnapping the city lord's daughter is punishable by death," she said. "But because we need you alive, I talked City Lord Jander out of it. Plus, there really wasn't much evidence that you did it."

"Because I didn't do it," he said, hanging his head.

"That hardly matters. Only what the city lord and the people of this blinded city believe matters. Anyway, today, you will ride out of here and be delivered to Prawl as part of our original agreement. His needs will be satisfied, and so will ours. We can go back to business as usual."

"As kidnappers and slavers," he said, shaking his head. "Don't you have enough money now?"

"One can never have enough money or power, Nath. It's how we control people." She touched his hand. "It's been nice knowing you. I wish your circumstances could have been a little better, but not at the cost of mine. I'd wish you well, but I really don't want that to happen."

As she walked away, Nath said, "Can you tell me one thing?"

She turned on her heel. "Perhaps."

"Who has my sword, Fang?"

"Tobias. I'm certain that he plans to sell it for a fortune."

Chapter 72

Later that day, Nath was led out of the city lord's castle in a prison wagon. His wrists and ankles were in irons and chains. A metal collar bit into his neck. The citizens of Riegelwood lined up along the streets, booing and cursing him as they hurled rotten food at him. Nath sat inside the bars, swaying as the wagon rattled down the cobblestone streets. A squad of twelve soldiers accompanied him out of the city. Half of them were on horseback and the other half on foot. Nath knew their faces. They were the Men of Whispers. They stared at him with gloating faces.

How big of a fool can City Lord Jander be?

He felt worse for Janna as he watched the castle banners fade in the distance. She would be blinded, too. The entire city, it seemed, was secretly controlled by the Black Hand.

Finally, the wagon came to a stop several miles out of the city. The transport cell was opened, and Nath was led out. Farther up the hill stood six more horses and riders. One of them was Prawl. The other five were the Black Hand. Tobias, Nina, Virgo, Worm, and Cullon all sat tall in their saddles, smirking at Nath as he was pushed toward them. Nath didn't see Fang or any of his other items. As he walked by the group toward Prawl, he said, "This isn't over."

The Black Hand chuckled. Tobias spoke. "It was over the moment you walked in the Oxen Inn, son." He had a leather bag that appeared heavy with gold. He held it out to Prawl. "Your full share of the reward, or ransom, whatever you want to call it."

"Give it to Andeen. He'll cut out my share." Prawl nodded to the slender brigand leader among the Men of Whispers. Prawl dismounted, grabbed a coil of rawhide rope, and approached Nath.

"Iron cord, eh," Tobias said of the rope. "Good stuff."

Prawl bound up the irons on Nath's wrists and tethered Nath to his huge horse. "This is the one that I want. You made good, Black Hand. It's a good thing that you did." He glared at Nina. "I will have that gauntlet one day, woman, one way or another."

"We'll see," Nina said.

Tobias leaned over his saddle. "The slate is clean, then?"

Prawl and Andeen nodded.

"Until next time we do business." Tobias turned his horse away and looked at Nath. "Except for you, obviously. May you never show up again."

One at a time, following Tobias, all of the members of the Black Hand rode by Nath. Cullon spat on his feet. Worm cackled as he went. Virgo gave him a flirty wink, but Nina didn't even glance at him. Slowly, they shrank into the countryside. Andeen, dressed as a soldier of Riegelwood, led the other disguised brigands manning the cell cart after them. That left Nath and Prawl all alone. Prawl's horse let out a nasty nicker. Dark clouds blotted out the sunlight overhead.

Nath looked at Prawl. "Where are you taking me?"

The big orc didn't reply. Loaded down with weapons and gear, Prawl urged his horse forward. The big beast chugged along, pulling Nath behind them. Nath hustled, trying to keep pace with the horse's big stride. He took a long, lasting look over his shoulder. His enemies were gone.

Chapter 73

The stormy skies brought a hard and steady rain. The cloud cover was a blanket of darkness that turned the day to night. Raindrops splattered on the muddy road. Nath's worn leather boots sank beneath the mud with every step. The strapping young man had reached his limits. His strong frame, bruised and scabbed, was broken down. The fire in his tireless eyes barely flickered. With his wrists and ankles in irons, he trudged along, chin down and shoulders slumped. He clinked with every step.

Ahead, a big horse, dark as coal, with muddy ankle hair that covered its hooves, let out a monstrous snort. Nath's arms were yanked forward. He stumbled forward, fighting for his footing. A length of durable rope called iron cord tethered him to the saddle. The horse moved on, pushing through the rain, a juggernaut not affected by the stiff winds or the storm's fury.

With his voice cracking, Nath said, "Do you think we could rest for a spell?" He brushed his soaked red hair out of his eyes. "My feet are aching, not to mention my wrists, neck, and ankles. And this collar on my neck is chafing my skin. Especially right underneath my chin." His grubby fingers dug at it. "I'm not sure who designed this contraption, but if it were a little leaner, it would still have the desired imprisoning effect. Unless, of course, discomfort is part of the design. In that case, it's fairly well done."

Prawl didn't reply. The horse snorted, however. The rugged mount's snorts, whinnies, neighs, and disruptive nickering were the only communication Nath had had with anyone in over a day.

Nath summoned the reserves of his aching limbs and sped up his pace. The heavy weight of the chain and short length between his ankles cut his lengthy stride in half. He shuffled up alongside his captor and looked up to him as rain pelted his swollen face. "Please, I beg of you, Prawl. I am exhausted. Can we rest, just a short span? And eat. I'd really like to eat."

The orc's beady yellow eyes remained set on the road ahead. His head was thick with matted black hair, and he had a broad face lumpy with scars, and flaring nostrils like tunnels. The hood of his worn traveling cloak was down over his broad shoulders. Chain-mail armor covered his barrel chest, tight, like it was part of his body. A broadsword hung from the belt on his hip. Another pair of swords was strapped to the saddle. There were hand axes, rope, saddle bags. A bedroll was tied down on the back of the saddle. He smelled... bad, as if he hadn't bathed in over a year and had spent most of that time sweating.

"At least tell me how far we're going?" Nath pleaded. If he'd asked once, he'd asked a dozen times. He wasn't trying to be weak. All he wanted was to know something new about his situation. He understood well enough how he got here. He'd been betrayed, igniting a chronic anger burning inside of him, giving him the strength to go on. "Can you hear me?" Nath yelled at the top of his lungs. His voice rose higher. "Where exactly in Nalzambor are you taking me?"

Prawl turned in his saddle and glowered down at Nath with beady eyes like simmering coals. He showed a twisted smile of broken teeth. He dug his heels into the horse. The horse reared up on two legs and bolted forward.

"No! No! Nooooooo!" Nath cried out. He ran as the horse took off in a full gallop. He kept up for a few seconds before he was yanked off his feet. He hit the ground chest first, slipping and sliding down the muddy road. Mud filled his mouth. His eyes were covered in wet slop. Spitting mud out of his mouth, he rolled to his back. The gravel road ripped at his back. It burned. He tucked his chin into his chest and flipped back over. The breastplate he wore saved his skin. "Stop! Please stop!" he shouted.

The horse continued its gallop down the mud-soaked road. It went on minute after agonizing minute. Nath's arms were stretched out to their full length. His shoulders burned. He locked his fingers on the iron cord. Straining, he pulled, somewhat righting himself. It was all he could do to keep his arms from popping out of their sockets. His strength faded. Finally, when his arms were about to give, the horse came to a stop.

"Oh, Great Guzan, thank you." Nath rolled to his back. Rain pelted his muddy face. His chest heaved beneath his breastplate. He used his numb fingers to wipe more mud from his eyes. "That was awful."

The orc dismounted. His huge boots splashed through the puddles. He strolled over to Nath and stood over top of him for moments. He took a knee and said in a very gravelly voice that was difficult to understand, "Still hungry?"

Nath knew what he should say, but instead he said, "Very much so. Thanks for asking. A couple of roasted quail would be delightful. And some milk. The long journey's made my tummy queasy and—"

The orc slugged him in the face. He grabbed Nath by the back of the hair, pulled it back, and looked him in the eye. "How about some mud stew instead?" He stuffed Nath's face into the muddy road and held him down.

Nath kicked and squirmed. The orc's powerful hand pushed his face deeper into the road, grinding his face into the mud.

The orc pulled Nath up.

Nath gulped in a lungful of air.

"Still hungry?" the orc said.

"Yes!" Nath tried to pull away after he said it.

With bearish strength, the orc shoved his face back into the mud.

Nath pushed up on his arms. Straining with all he had left, he couldn't get his face out of the mud. *Gads, he's strong!* He pushed until he couldn't push anymore. He kicked out to no avail. The husky orc felt like he was an ogre.

The orc pulled him out of the mud again. "Still hungry?"

"Yes…" Nath managed to say, spitting out dirt at the same time.

The orc plunged his face into the sopping sludge again and again. Nath replied yes, every time, until he didn't have the energy to reply anymore. The orc shoved his head down, one last time, then stood.

Nath looked at him.

The orc busted him in the jaw with the boot of his toe. The world spun once before it went black.

CHAPTER 74

PINE NEEDLES PRICKED NATH'S FACE, his head pounding as he woke. He caught the sound of a crackling campfire and, groaning, turned in its direction. There it was. The warming flames of a fire roasted two hunks of meat on the spit. His mouth watered. His stomach moaned. Sitting up, he rubbed his sore jaw. At least, that was the sorest part of his busted-up body at the moment. His legs were scraped up and his trousers torn through. The toe of one of his boots was missing. He crawled toward the flame.

"Urk!" He gasped.

The metal collar on his neck snagged. He looked back to see that he was tethered to a pine tree by the iron cord. He reached around, grabbed it, and gave it a fierce yank. He was strong, but the iron cord was much stronger.

Nearby, the black horse stood on the other side of the fire, chewing on a bush in the glade. It was night, and the rain had come to a stop, but the ground was still soft and muddy beneath Nath. He turned back, faced the fire, crossed his legs, and licked his dirty, busted lips. The hunger pangs were the worst he'd ever had. Never in his life had he been at the brink of starvation. Not to mention thirst. His parched lips were cracking. The tongue he'd already bitten more than once was swollen. Yet there was nothing he could do about it. He was a prisoner.

How did I not see this coming? I'm so stupid! I could kick myself!

The scrunch of footsteps caught his ear. Prawl emerged from the darkness of the forest.

Large, dark, and dusky, he stood with four dead rabbits clasped by the ears in one hand. Nath had only encountered a few orcs before, at a distance, but none like this one. He was bigger, and even uglier with his misshapen face shadowed in the fire's light. Not only that, but the way the orc carried himself was formidable. A snarl remained fixed on his face. The seasoned orc carried many weapons. The handles were polished and the blades oiled. The orc pulled out a knife with a handle made from elk horn and a keen curved blade. He began skinning the rabbits.

"I suppose one of those rabbits is for me?" Nath said politely. "I'd be more than happy to prepare one for myself, even yours, if you like. It's the least I can do since you fetched it."

The big orc kept skinning.

"That dagger you have has a very clever design. I'm curious. Did you make it yourself? I'm a bit of a blacksmith myself."

Prawl tore the skin off the rabbit. "I made it to silence things that annoy me, such as you."

"So rabbits annoy you? Interesting. I'd probably be a lot more content to be quiet if I had some food and maybe a little more information." Nath combed his hair out of his eyes. "You aren't going to kill me, it seems. We both know this, so at least give me a hint as to what is in store for me. Who wants to buy me, or do you know?"

Prawl finished skinning the other rabbits and placed them on the same spit where the other two rabbits had finished cooking. He tore off a leg, stuffed it in his mouth—bone and all—and started chewing.

Nath grimaced. The crunching of bone gnawed at his ears. "I promise I'll save you my bones when I'm finished eating."

Looking Nath in the eye, the orc ate the entire rabbit. A few moments later, he belched. "South," Prawl said.

"What's that?" Nath leaned forward.

"You asked where. I gave it." The orc tore into the other hunk of cooked meat. "South, very south. That's where I take you."

"Ah, Prawl, thank you. As if the sun didn't tell me that already." Nath offered a smile. "And please, call me Nath."

"I don't care what your name is."

"Of course you don't. I was just offering a proper introduction." Nath moved his hands back and forth. "Now that we are formally acquainted, we can dine together."

Prawl continued to chew with his pronounced lower jaw jutting out. Rabbit flesh hung from tusk-like teeth on his bottom jaw.

"You say we are going south, very south. Is there a name for it? Perhaps I'm acquainted with it? Cherlon maybe? I heard that is one of the fairest cities on the inland sea. They say the castle spires are gilded in gold and decorated in abalone."

"The more you talk, the less you eat," Prawl said. He waggled a rabbit leg at Nath. "Less."

Nath's mouth started open. Prawl pulled back the leg. Nath sealed his lips.

The orc tossed the leg over.

After snatching the meat out of the air, Nath quickly ate. There was little meat, but it tasted wonderful—so good, in fact, he considered eating the bone. Instead, he snapped the bone and sucked on the juicy marrow. "More, please."

"Hah," Prawl said. "I shouldn't have fed you at all. Slaves are troublesome with a full belly. It gives them strength to escape, and I have to track them down again. I'd rather not."

Sucking his fingers, Nath said, "Just a little more, please. I'm no good to you if I'm so weak that I can't walk."

"You'll manage. You don't look it, but you're tougher than ogre's hide. You'll do well, heh-heh."

"Do well at what?"

The orc stuffed the rest of the meat in his mouth, crunched it up, swallowed it, and washed it down with water from a skin. He wiped his hands on the dirt. His expression darkened as he picked up the knife in his hand. "Stop talking. I won't say it again."

Nath pulled his knees to his chest. He looked away and stared into the campfire, where the broken limbs were turning to ash. Small blue flames burned in the middle. Even though he knew that Prawl wouldn't kill him, he'd learned firsthand that Prawl wasn't one to be trifled with.

Hang on, Nath, hang on.

As the rabbit meat sizzled on the spit and grease dripped into the fire, Nath, still starving, focused on something else. The gloating faces of his betrayers burned forever in his mind. They tricked him, lied to him, stole every precious thing from him, and sold him to a slaver. His gold eyes glowed as hot as the flames.

I will survive this! I will hunt my enemies down and make them pay.

CHAPTER 75

NATH'S VENGEFUL THOUGHTS WERE INTERRUPTED by Prawl crunching on rabbit bones. The orc sucked his dirty, greasy fingers clean. There was one last rabbit burning on the spit. Nath's mouth watered. One rabbit leg wasn't enough. He needed more.

"Go ahead, take it," Prawl said, tossing the last bit of meat on the ground before Nath.

Nath walked on his knees as far as the length of rope would take him. Collared and tied to a tree like a dog by the iron cord, he stretched out his fingers. He grabbed the meat with his fingertips. Steaming-hot rabbit meat stung his bound hands. He juggled the meat between his fingers the best he could.

"What is the matter? Don't you like my hot food?" Prawl growled. Up on his feet, moving with alarming speed, he crossed over the campfire in a single stride and tried to snag the rabbit from Nath's fingers. Nath bit down hard on a rabbit leg just as Prawl ripped the creature from his grasp. The orc swatted Nath hard in the face.

Nath ate hungrily every bit he had, licking it clean to the bone. Prawl kicked him as he stuffed the entire rabbit in his mouth, crunched it up, and swallowed.

"You weren't really going to give me that entire thing anyway. You just play games."

"I like games." Prawl crossed back over to the other side and sat down. He propped himself up on his elbow and stared at the fire. "I like torture better. It's like games, but deadlier."

Savagely, Nath licked his own fingers clean. "You've certainly had your fair share of games recently. I can't help but wonder why you let the Black Hand take you like they did. They took a fortune in coins and gems from me that made that reward money look like a widow's purse. I'd be very angry if I were you. How much could I be worth, anyway?"

Prawl narrowed an eye on him. "More than that."

"That doesn't make any sense," Nath said.

"Some things are worth more than precious pieces. That's the Black Hand's loss and my gain. Now, shut your mouth and rest. The journey is many days, and I will ride in silence, unless you don't want to be fed."

"If I'm to be sold, I'm certain my buyer doesn't want me hungry and bruised." Nath swatted at a mosquito that buzzed in his face. "He or she would be angry."

"You're to be delivered alive and fully limbed. That's what the slave lords expect. That's what I deliver." Prawl closed his eyes.

Nath worked at the ropes on his wrists. The more he fidgeted, the more the coarse bindings bit into his wrists. He considered running, but Prawl secured his legs with more iron cord the moment they camped. He wasn't running anywhere if he didn't want to cut off the blood supply that fed his extremities. He closed his eyes for a moment, and before he realized what happened, he was fast asleep, dreaming of all the horrors of Nalzambor that he'd already faced.

Prawl woke him with a stiff kick. The early glow of dawn showed on the leaves of the trees. The orc undid the rope that tangled Nath's legs. He didn't understand how Prawl could tie it and untie it, but he could. It was as if the iron cord had one lock on it that only orcs had the key to. With Nath tethered again to the horse, they moved on. Every time Nath spoke, the orc would spur his horse into a gallop and drag Nath a half mile over the rugged plains. Tired of eating dirt and grass, he gave up speaking entirely. He hated Prawl. He hated all obnoxious orcs. He hated the Black Hand too. He kept his burning legs churning.

Judging by the sun, they moved southeast at a brisk pace, taking paths almost overcome with vegetation. There was a moment as they crossed the plains when Nath could see the very tip of Dragon Home in the far distance. His heart ached to be home again. He never imagined that he would miss it so much. With a long and suffering heart, he had to look away.

Five days later, beyond broken from travel, they ventured down a road deep into the lush southern hemisphere. Ahead, a city-like establishment sat on a hill behind walls made out of wood. Prawl and Nath weren't the only ones on the busy road. Merchants were coming and going. Like Nath, there were people bound by rope or chains on their hands, feet, and neck, bringing up the rear behind horse and wagon. Nath walked by at least a dozen slaves with their heads down. Grubby and scrawny, they walked on rickety limbs with blank stares on their faces. He stopped. A hard tug of his rope towed him forward.

There was a sign written in common mounted in rocks just outside the city's wooden gates. "Slaver Town: You bring the gold, we bring the slaves."

Nath ground his teeth. His fists balled up as he was led inside the gates. Lavishly clad men and women haggled over an assortment of people of all races and creeds, standing up on auction blocks. There were at least a dozen going on all at once. *What is wrong with this world?*

Prawl dismounted. He untethered Nath from the saddle, found a young boy, and had him stable his horse. The orc led Nath through the filthy streets into a huge barn-like structure made of stone. Inside the barn were rows of stables that had been converted into prisoner cells. People were stuffed inside the cells in twos, threes, and fours. Judging by appearances, the slaves were fed like animals. Many desperate stares hung on Nath. Others looked down and away.

A human jailer with bulging and sweaty rolls of fat on his neck and wrists sauntered over to Prawl. "This is a fine one. You continue to impress as always, Prawl. Our purchasers will be pleased." He smacked his lips. "Very pleased."

"He gets his own cell. No one touches him until the buyer who contracted me to get him comes," Prawl warned.

"No, of course not. This one will be well provided for in his own cell." The jailer reached for Nath's hair. Nath flinched away. "That hair will make the wig weavers sing."

Prawl poked the jailer in his flabby chest. "Don't touch him."

"Yes-yes," the man said nervously. "Come, come." He led them to the very back of the barn, separated from the rest of the barn by heavy curtains. It was a dark, dank room busted out of the rocks with metal bars walling off the front. Prawl untied Nath and shoved him inside. The jailer closed the door. He extended his hand. "All is in order."

Prawl nodded.

"Then I shall send word out to your buyer. Come with me, Prawl. We'll go over the papers and get your payment prepared." The jailer looked at Nath. "I'll have food sent."

"No," Prawl said, glowering at Nath. "Not until after I leave. The journey has been long. I plan on enjoying myself for a bit."

"As you wish," the jailer said. He pushed the curtains aside, and they left.

Ravenous, Nath gripped the bars of his new home and screamed, "Praaaaawlll!"

Epilogue

Months later, back at Stonewater Keep, the home of the Caligin, Lord Darkken and Maefon stared into the Pool of Eversight. The waters swirled with a phantasmagoria of colors, but there was no image. Maefon had a film of sweat on her forehead. Her eyebrows were knit together.

Dressed in all-black clothes that enhanced Lord Darkken's domineering demeanor, he said to her, "You've been training very hard, Maefon. You should have mastered the pools by now."

"I know." She waved her hands over the waters. She'd been at it all morning, trying to link to the pool's mighty powers, but her extensive training left her exhausted. She did not dare disappoint Lord Darkken. Failure was the equivalent of death. "I will make it happen. I swear it." The waters heaved for a moment then calmed. The prism of swirling colors cleared. She immediately took a knee and bowed. "Apologies, Lord of the Dark in the Day. I've failed you."

"No," he said with the soothing voice of an all-knowing father, "you have only failed yourself. You can learn from that, Maefon." He took her hands. "Rise." She did. "Look at me, Maefon. Your hard work has not gone without notice, and I admit, I have neglected you over the last several weeks. But now, I am here to guide you through this. Tell me, what image were you trying to summon from the pool?"

"The town, Tilly, that I burned. I was curious to see how it fared since the disaster."

"Do you feel connected to those people that suffered at your hand?"

"No, I swear it. I was more curious than anything."

Lord Darkken put his arms over her shoulders and turned her toward the pool. "Easy, Maefon. I have more faith in you than you realize. My point is that because you don't have a strong connection, for you it will be difficult to summon the power of the waters. That comes later. For now, you need to think of something or someone that you are strongly connected with. The Pool of Eversight can relate to that. Open yourself to it, and it will open itself to you." He spoke right in her ear with his hand on the small of her back. "Who do you care for most, aside from me, of course? Who comes to your mind first?"

Nath came to mind the moment Lord Darkken asked the question. She didn't want to say it—it seemed like the wrong answer—but Lord Darkken would know she was lying if she claimed any other. "Nath."

"Let it all out, Maefon. Trust the pool, and the pool will trust you. Besides, I am very curious to observe his condition. You should be too. After all, he is looking for you."

She took a deep breath and gazed into the waters. With her fingers tapping over the pool, she let her own mystic energy out. At the same time, she recalled her times with Nath. There was a lot of laughter with Nath, and his share of frowns too when he didn't get what he wanted. It all flowed out of her, as if she were feeding the pool what it wanted. In an instant, she felt herself being rocketed over Nalzambor. She soared over the trees and hilltops and flew by flocks of birds. She slowed in the southern lands where the forests were thick with vines and leaves. A city in the hills, defended by wooden walls and battlements, was nestled on the rocks.

"Ah, how refreshing. Slavertown," Lord Darkken said, as if he was surprised, but it came across as if he already knew it.

The pool showed the city from a bird's point of view. It hovered by droves of depraved people. There was a crowd gathered around muddy fields, hooting and cheering with vigor. Their hungry eyes were in the field where the action was. Men pulled sleds with rocks piled on top across the muddy field. Halflings sat on the rocks, cracking whips at the men's backs. Like beasts of burden, the men's hands clawed at the mud as they pulled with all of their might. Covered in mud up to his elbows, the sled puller in the lead was Nath.

Maefon let out a little gasp. The image in the pool quavered.

"Concentrate, Maefon," Lord Darkken said, hugging her tightly around the waist. "I want to see who wins this."

Nath's golden eyes were full of anger and anguish. She had never seen him in such condition. It was a shock to see him, once so perfect, now sticky in mud and blood from superficial wounds. He surged ahead of the other men with the whip cracking on his back, pumping his knees with all of his might.

"As I recall, the winner of this type of event gets to eat while the others starve. It looks as if Nath is very, very hungry." Lord Darkken passed his hand over the image in the pool. Ripples took the image away, and the waters cleared.

Maefon fell back into Lord Darkken's arms, panting.

"That is enough. Your first connection will drain you. You'll be stronger after that. You did well. A good thing... for you."

Straightening up, she faced him. "What is Nath doing there of all places? Is he enslaved?"

"Of course he is. I had him enslaved."

"But why? I don't mean any disrespect by asking, but I can't help but be curious." She closed her eyes and rubbed her temples. A nagging headache had come on. "I'm having trouble understanding the end game."

"Certainly, you've earned the answer." Lord Darkken put his hands on the rim of the basin and stared into the waters. "I'm making him tougher. I want him to hate this land and hate its people. It is the only way to break the good that is in him."

"Wouldn't killing him do the trick?"

He showed a clever smile. "Of course, but he is of no use to me dead. I need him alive. I will be vastly more powerful with my brother by my side than with him dead."

Maefon paled. "Brother?"

"Yes. You see, I am Balzurth's other son, a dragon born a man. But I despised the dragons from the start." The Pool of Eversight came to life. A new image started to form. "Like you, I slaughtered the fledglings, my own kind." He shrugged. "For sport. But in Balzurth's heart of hearts, he could not kill me. He banished me instead, to walk along in the dust of men forever. I'll never fly, but I'll never die so long as I can turn Nath to my side."

"So you are the one the dragons would not speak about."

"Yes."

It all came together for her. "And that's why they despised him so?"

"That's how I planned it all along. My little brother was doomed from the start, and thanks to you, Maefon, and your work among the Trahaydeen, my master scheme is set into motion. I will turn Nath, or he will die."

A new image formed in the pool. It was the same field of mud in Slaver Town. Nath's sled was stuck in the mud. He hadn't finished. The others did. People were booing and throwing stones at him.

"It looks like he lost. Tsk. Tsk. What a shame."

"Can't he die?"

"Of course, but he's a lot tougher than even he can imagine. Trust me when I say that, Maefon." He passed his hand over the pool. The waters cleared again. "I'm hungry. How about you?"

"Famished, actually." She put her hands around his waiting elbow. "So how much stronger would the two of you be together?"

"Powerful enough to rule the world and ruin the dragons forever."

THE ODYSSEY OF

NATH DRAGON

BOOK 2

ENSLAVED

CRAIG

HALLORAN

Chapter 1

A hazy sun hung high in the sky. The glaring light beat down on Nath's back. Sweat ran down his bare chest and spine. It was one of the hottest days he could remember. Humid, muggy, and steamy air amplified his crowded surroundings. The irons around his wrists and ankles jangled as he swung his sledgehammer, breaking apart the heavy rocks in the quarry. Chips of stone flew away. His lower back burned like fire. It all started days after Prawl, the orc slaver, took him into Slaver Town. That was four hundred and twenty-five days ago. Nath had been suffering ever since.

With arms as hard as iron and corded in muscle, Nath brought the hammer down again. The rock split in two. He wasn't the only one hard at it. A handful of men swung heavy hammers on shaky legs. Hope had long ago fled their faces as they tried to pace themselves. One man, standing close to Nath, with arms little bigger than the hammer's handle, brought down his hammer. It skipped off the rock into the man's foot.

"Guh!" The man went down, wincing in pain as he held his foot. Tears swelled in his eyes. "I don't deserve this. I don't."

"Get up," Nath said in a harsh whisper. His eyes swept over the quarry. Burly orcs were posted throughout the vast pit of rocks as slave guards. They wore dyed black leather armor, and had scourges in hand and black clubs on their hips. At the moment, their backs were turned toward the ogre pushing a huge wheelbarrow up a ramp to the top level. Nath crouched down by the man. "You have to stand, no matter how much it hurts, or they will whip you."

The haggard man looked into Nath's eyes. "I don't care. I can't do this. I'm not meant for it. See these fingers," he said, holding them up to Nath's face. "I am a musician. I play the strings and keys. My music brings peace."

"The only music you are going to hear today is the crack of a whip on your back if you don't hustle up," Nath said, looking around. The other laborers were pounding away, oblivious to anything surrounding them but their own misery. The man on the ground wasn't very old, maybe thirty. His hands and features were delicate, his eyes as soft as his skin. He was new to Slaver Town, or at least to the rock quarry. Nath hooked him under his arms and lifted him. "Stay up."

"I can barely stand," the man moaned. "I think my foot is broken. Surely, the guards will understand."

"No, they won't," Nath said. "Stand and swing. You must." Normally, Nath would ignore someone else's trouble. The laborers came and went, and most of them were never seen again. Some of them died in the quarry, either by accident or at the hands of the guards. Nath had seen it all. Merciless cruelty. It defied reason. He looked at the man. "What is your name?"

"Homer," the man said, offering Nath a shaking hand. "And you?"

"Nath. Listen, Homer, you have to pick up that hammer, no matter how bad it hurts, and swing. You can deal with your foot tonight. Be strong, Homer, be strong."

Homer swallowed and nodded. "Aye, I will." He picked his sledgehammer up to the waist and landed a solid shot on the boulder. "I can do this." He half swung again, grimacing as he leaned on his stronger foot. His halfhearted swings were pitiful, but at least Homer was moving.

Nath lifted his hammer high and brought it down hard. He paced himself, stealing glances at Homer. The man was pitiful. All of the slaves were. They were brought in and broken down with hard labor, and barely enough food and water to sustain them. Many cried in their cells at night. The biggest and most rugged of the men cried the worst. Others, it seemed, became sick with fever, gave up, and died. Scores of men and women had been hauled off dead since Nath had been there. He'd dug the graves of many of them.

Vengeance burned inside him. He pictured Prawl's pitted and lumpy orcen face on the rock. He brought the hammer down hard and busted the rock into pieces.

"You swing with anger," Homer muttered. "I have no fire in me. I'll die here, won't I? I don't want to die, Nath, but I cannot bear this."

"Then don't die, Homer," Nath said, taking another swing. "The ones who live are the ones who want to live. The ones who die give up."

"I don't want to be a slave. I can't do this. I don't deserve this. I need to use my gift."

Nath shook his head. He didn't want to hear it. He'd heard it all before. A lot of people were brought to Slaver Town to be bought and sold as slaves. Among them were many beautiful women, all of which were well cared for. Among the others were men of different skills and crafts. They were broken down and sold on the auction blocks, desperate for any kind of freedom that would be better than living in Slaver Town.

But there was another group that came into the fold as well. The undesirables. Men of ill repute. Thieves that had been caught. Family that was betrayed. People that the societies of the world didn't want so they were turning into slaves. They worked day and night in the prison-like conditions, creating items that the slave lords would sell for profit on the markets. It made Nath sick.

He drew up a picture of Cullon in his mind. The dwarven member of the Black Hand had been nothing but nasty to Nath. He smote the hammer in the imaginary image of the dwarf's bearded face. "Hate the Black Hand."

"What's that?" Homer said. He was sitting down now, holding his foot and rubbing it. "The black what?"

"Homer, get up!" Nath said. Out of the corner of his eye, he caught a slave guard's fixed glance on Homer. "Quick, get up, they are coming."

"I don't care," Homer said. "I'll just have to make them listen to reason."

The slave guard marched right at Homer, brandishing a scourge of many tails in his hand.

"Homer, listen to me, they don't know what reason is. Get up now!" Nath whispered.

"I'll just have to teach them then."

The orc soldier didn't say a word. He stood over top of Homer, glowered at him, and swung. The lash slapped hard into the flesh of Homer's back. The fragile man let out a bloodcurdling scream. The orc lashed Homer repeatedly with hard overhand swings.

"Please stop!" Homer begged in a cracking voice. He clung to a rock as if it would save him. "Please!"

The orc didn't let up.

Fire ignited in Nath's veins. He cocked back his sledgehammer and swung.

CHAPTER 2

NATH'S HAMMER CONNECTED WITH THE orc guard's chest. A loud *crack* of bone giving way followed. The orc stumbled backward, snorting and wheezing. His eyes were wide as the scourge fell from his hairy fingers.

There was a sharp whistle. All at once, the other guards converged on Nath. They came at him all at once, brandishing their scarred-up clubs made from wood as hard as stone. Nath deflected a club on the handle of his hammer. He put his boot in the orc's gut. Confined by the irons on his legs, he shuffled out of harm's way as best he could. He blocked a few more shots and ducked his head away from a swing that would have busted him in the ear. He jabbed the hammer hard in a heavy orc's bulging belly.

"Get him on the ground!" a husky voice shouted from somewhere. "Quit swinging like fools! He's too quick for you!"

Using his irons to his advantage, Nath hopped like a frog out of harm's way. Moving quickly, he hopped behind one guard, whacked him in the back, hopped away, and hit another.

"Ha! Ha!" Nath said with glee. It had been a while since he'd taken a shot at the guards. It felt good to bring them down to the ground. An orc rushed him with a snarl on its sweating lips, its little tusk teeth protruding from its mouth. Nath busted it square in the jaw with his hammer. It fell. He hopped over it onto another.

All around him, the other slaves cheered. They let out raucous cries of encouragement. They made a clamor by beating their hammers on the rocks. Even the ogre, pushing the wheelbarrow up the ramp, started to clap. Then, suddenly, it picked up its full wheelbarrow and threw it down on the guards.

"Fools!" the same orcen voice of command called out in a now-booming voice. "Do I have to handle everything myself?"

Nath's neck hairs stood on end. He spun toward the source of the voice. A jolt of energy blasted through his entire body. His irons turned white hot, burning the flesh on his neck, wrists, and ankles. "Yeee-argh!" Unable to move his wooden limbs, he fell to his knees. He swore his eyebrows simmered. Burnt hair smelled of icky smoke. A guard slipped into view, swinging a club. Stunned, Nath couldn't move. The club connected with the side of his head. *Chok!* He fell over on his side and lay there, motionless, in a body that felt like it was filled with sand. "It hurts… bad."

The guards got in a few more licks, hammering at his body, before the sharp voice called them off. "Enough! He isn't to be maimed unless I say he is to be maimed. Did I say he was to be maimed?"

The orcs backed off, heads down and shaking.

Nath blinked and with a painful grunt rolled onto his back. Fuzzy, colorful spots obscured his vision. He managed to prop himself up on his elbows. A man appeared behind him. Medium in height and slender in build, the man had an orcen nose with big nostrils and the coarse black hair, tied back in three ponytails. He wore the customary ringmail with a brown tunic over it. In his hand, he carried a black-handled sledgehammer with runes woven in the head. With a thick tongue, Nath said, "Oh, it's you, Foster. I thought I recognized your rotten voice, but I wasn't sure until the smell came over, and even then, I had my doubt until I saw your face. Boy, those eyebrows sure do like each other."

"Your tongue does you more harm than good, prisoner," Foster said, pointing the hammer at Nath's bare chest. "You must learn respect, or die from a lack of it."

"I like your hammer. Are you going to help me pound rock too?" Nath said, looking right at the foreboding tool. "Uhn, as for respect, for what? Orcs and slavers? Tell me you are–"

A charge of energy flared from Foster's hammer. *Ssszap!*

Nath's teeth clacked together. Pain lanced through his entire body. He flattened out on his back, trembling. All he could smell was the singed stink of his own hairs. Foster looked down on him with a crooked smile on his face. Nath tried to speak, but he had no control over his body.

"You are a glutton for punishment, prisoner," Foster said, sneering at Nath. He spit dark juice on the rocks. It dripped down his chin. He wiped it on the sleeves of his robes. "Thanks to your reckless efforts, all the rest of the prisoners in the quarry will suffer as well. Especially that sappy friend you defended. He'll have the worst of all. In the end, he will feel the whipping would have been worth it. He will hate you for it. They all will. Put him in the hold."

Nath tried to speak, but only a sound that was like a creaking door came out. Two guards picked him up by the arms and legs and carried him away like a rolled-up carpet. He caught glimpses of the other slaves being corralled and beaten. The ogre was controlled by a special collar that glowed with blue stones around its neck. The ogre sat against the wall on the ramp, sucking its thumb like a baby. It sniveled and let out a cry.

Tremors ran through Nath's body. *That hammer Foster carries kicks like a mule. Gads! That hurts! Where did it come from? He didn't even touch me with it.* He was carried beyond the barn-like slave barracks where Prawl had brought him initially to a stone building behind it guarded by more orcs. It was the Pen, the place where prisoners and unruly slaves were taken. Inside, the walls were thick with grime, covered with cobwebs in the corners, and reeking so badly he almost didn't dare breathe. Carried down one level of steps, Nath was tossed into a small stone cell. The orcs each gave him a stiff kick in the ribs. They hustled out of the pen and slammed the steel door behind them.

Darkness closed over Nath. Lying on a smelly, sticky bed of hay, he groaned.

CHAPTER 3

An outline of gray light framed the cell door that barred Nath's escape from the small hold. Since he'd been imprisoned, he'd become very familiar with his cramped surroundings. He counted every block and ran his fingers over the lines of cracking mortar. None of the heavy stones budged. He wasn't going anywhere if the slave lords didn't let him.

Nath had pushed up the straw in the dry back corner of the cell. The rest of the floor was wet and slimy. Water seeped through the walls and ran across the floor of the small cell that didn't have enough room to stretch out in. He'd managed to get some of the straw to dry, giving himself a place to lay his head down when he slept. His slumbers were restless, however. Moans of misery carried down the halls. Little bugs crawled all over him. His wrists and ankles were swollen inside the iron. The metal collar always bit into his neck. All he did was sigh, every few hours or so, long, lengthy, and heavy.

Punishment was something Nath had gotten used to. He'd been imprisoned for over a year, and he'd tried to escape several times. His efforts were thwarted each time. Everywhere he went, the slavers watched him, but he managed to slip them a few times. He'd made it as far as the inside of the outer wall before the guards piled on him the last time. Usually, he was put in the stockades, not fed a few meals, and was whipped a few times. But it was him, and him alone. Him and his noisy shackles. This time, his punishment was new. No light, and little food or water.

He crawled toward the cell door. A plate and cup made from baked clay sat near the door. Water from the ceiling dripped into the cup. Nath flicked off a bug from the cup's rim. Swishing it around a few times, he discovered he had at least a swallow. He wet his parched lips with it.

"Ah, that was delicious. Water straight from the moldy rock. It couldn't be any better," he said deliriously. He pounded on the door. "I bet it doesn't get any better out there than it does in here! Your well water stinks! This water is good as gravy! Hah-hah!"

Nath lined the cup back up underneath the water and crawled into his dry corner. He brushed his bangs away from his eyes. He wondered how Homer was faring. The musician might be dead for all he knew. Perhaps Nath did make it worse for the man by getting involved. One thing he'd learned was that the slaver Foster was a man, or half-orcen man, of his word. He'd dogged Nath almost daily since he'd been there. Every punishment Nath received was a result of Foster's intervention. He could see the gloating orc's face in his mind.

I hate orcs. All of them. Always.

The orcs secured Slaver Town with an iron fist. The merciless brutes poked, prodded, and harassed every human they could find. There were other races too, no full elves, but a few unlucky part elves that got the worst of the harassment. There were some dwarves, halflings, and gnomes, all of which seemed to have given up on life. There was a forever lingering emptiness behind their eyes. Nath tried to speak with many of them, but they avoided him the best they could. Nath, out of all of them, got the worst treatment. Perhaps that was why they wanted to avoid him.

With his head wedged in the corner of the wall, Nath muttered, "Why me?"

He knew why he was there. The Black Hand sold him to Prawl to get rid of him forever. All the while, they had his magic items and Fang. But Nath was certain when he came to Slaver Town he would be sold, or at least, had been sold, according to what Prawl had said. But his buyer had yet to show up. He had no idea who owned him, not that he could be owned, but whoever did, didn't seem interested in him. Nath thought he was sought out for his grand looks, but he was coated in nothing but dirt and grit. The locks of his lustrous red hair were brown. He hadn't washed since he'd been there. He was as soiled and filthy as a pig in mud. Forgotten.

It didn't stop him from stirring conversation when he could. He tried to talk to the others, but even in his cell above, he was isolated. He poked at Foster, hoping the half-orc would give him some kind of information. Foster's only concern was that Nath wasn't hurt or damaged too much. He protected Nath for somebody. Nath wanted to know who that somebody was. It kept him going. The Black Hand gnawed at him. Prawl's face angered him. And then there was still the entire reason why he left the sanctuary of Dragon Home in the first place. He needed to find Maefon and the murderous Trahaydeen. He needed to find the Caligin. But until he escaped, all of that had almost been set aside and forgotten.

Nath closed his eyes and slept. He saw Dragon Home in his dreams. From within, it burned.

Bang!

Nath jerked. Soaked in sweat, he wiped the perspiration from his face.

Bang!

It sounded like someone was hitting the metal door with a sledgehammer.

"Stay back!" a gruff voice said on the other side of the door. "Stay back!"

"I am back!" Nath fired back. Normally, the guards tapped on the door when they brought food and water. This time it was different. The banging on the door was even offensive for them. *Bang!* He yelled at the top of his lungs, "I said I'm back, you obnoxious brutes!"

The locking mechanism on the door popped and cracked. The door—groaning on the hinges—swung outward.

Nath shielded his eyes. Even though the outside light was dim, it glared like a burning sun.

An orcen guard ducked inside. He pushed Nath against the wall with a long stick with a man-catcher end on it. The metal jaws collapsed around Nath's arms. "Stay back!"

"I'm not going anywhere. You have my arms pinned, idiot. Isn't that the purpose of a man-catcher?"

"Bring him in," the orc said.

Nath assumed someone was coming to speak to him. Perhaps his buyer. His hopes fled the moment the fattest, ugliest man he'd ever seen was shoved inside the door. The fat man got stuck in the frame. With a hard shove, he stumbled inside.

"Who's this?"

The orc squeezed by the fat man as he backed out of the hold. "Your cellmate. Heh-heh. Have fun sharing your meals with that one."

Chapter 4

Nath caught a solid glimpse of the puffy man before the cell door closed them in. He had short brown hair and a head that looked like the size of an antelope's on his bloated body, and a grimy apron hung over his clothing. The man squirmed around, wheezing, as his hands pawed all over the cell. He squeezed Nath's ankle.

"Pardon me?" Nath said.

"Gah!" the man hollered in a shrill voice. In the dark, the full weight of his hefty body slammed into the door. The clay glass and plate somehow crunched underneath his girth. With a shaky voice the man said, "Who said that?"

"I did," Nath replied dully.

"Are you a ghost?"

"What? No, I'm Nath. Didn't you hear me speaking when you were brought in?"

"I couldn't hear anything but the blood rushing through my ears," the man said. "Are you going to hurt me?"

"I don't know. I'll have to think about it."

Meaty hands pounded on the door. "Guards! Guards! Help me! There's a ghost threatening to kill me in here. Guards!"

"I'm not a ghost, fool," Nath said, completely unable to hide his irritation. As bad as his situation was, he never imagined it could have gotten any worse. Now he was smashed inside his cell with a man who every time he moved bumped into Nath. "You felt my leg. I'm flesh and blood, like you, just not as fleshy. Try not to panic. It will only make matters worse."

"Oh-oh-oh, I don't like the dark. I get night terrors, you see. I-I-I can't do this," the man said. "Guards! Please! Let me out!"

"You haven't been in here a minute. Trust me, they won't let you out anytime soon." Nath shifted away from the man the best he could. "Eh, what is your name?"

"I-I'm Radagan. What is your name, spirit?"

"I told you."

"Oh, you did, uh, I don't recall, well, sorry, but my thoughts are so distorted. Could you repeat it again?"

"Nath."

"Eh, nice to meet you, Nath. I wish I could see you. Are you sure you won't hurt me? No, better yet, will you promise you won't hurt me?"

Nath's eyes adjusted. He could make out the warm body and outline of Radagan's features clearly. The hefty man trembled like a nervous mouse. His head swiveled side to side on the meaty folds of his neck. Nath said, "I promise I won't hurt you."

"Oh goodness, that is wonderful." Radagan crawled across the cell. His searching hands touched all over Nath. "Oh, sorry, is that you?"

"Yes, and you need to keep your hands to yourself, Radagan. I hate to break them."

Radagan froze. "But you said you wouldn't hurt me?"

"I could have lied. This place is full of liars, as I'm certain you know, and I must be an awfully terrible person to be put in this hold."

"Oh my, I never thought about that." Radagan scratched his head. "Oh, please don't hurt me!" he whined.

"Just stay on your side, Radagan. Can you do that?" Nath used his hands to guide the man toward the other side of the wall. "That's your side. This is my side. Do you understand?"

"Yes." Radagan moved to the other side of the wall, but their hips were still touching. "It's squishy and wet over here. Is your side dry?"

"Radagan, you are in my cell. I am not in yours. I make the rules."

"I bet I'm bigger than you. Where I come from the big guys make the rules."

"Is that so?" Nath popped the man in the shoulder with his fist.

"Ow! What did you hit me for?"

"To make it clear who the boss of this cell is."

Droning, Radagan said, "But that hurt. You said you wouldn't hurt me?"

"Hurting you by my definition would be causing you painful and irreparable damage. Do you want that?"

"No."

"It's settled then. I'm the boss, right?"

"Yes, the boss."

"Good." Nath leaned his head back and took a breath. The cell, normally cool, had become warmer. He shifted. "Can you scoot over more?"

"I'm against the wall now. I'll try." Radagan grunted and groaned. "Is that better?"

"No, just be still. Radagan, I have to ask, how is it that you came to be put in here? For all intents and purposes, you seem rather harmless."

Radagan' s voice became sinister. "Well, appearances can be deceiving."

"What?"

"Just jesting. I really am harmless, but sometimes I try to convince the others otherwise. Anyway, I'm one of the cooks, and, well, they caught me stealing the slave lords' cream cakes. You know the ones they served at the auctions with the raspberry and blueberry glazed toppings. Well, I made those." Radagan' s belly let out a rumble that sounded like a roaring lion. "Excuse me. I get excited when I talk about the cream cakes. Anyhow, I'm stuffed in here for the time being, to teach me a lesson."

"No offense, Radagan, but it looks to me that you've been eating cream cakes for quite some time. And only now, they are cracking down on you?"

"Yeah, you make a good point. I don't know. They just got mad at me all of a sudden and brought me in here. It just… happened." He sobbed. "Nath, I'm scared. What if they don't let me out of here? I don't deserve to be in here over a few cream cakes."

"A few?"

"Well, maybe I overdid it, but I was born here. I've been eating like this all my life. They never minded before. Besides, I was never skinny. Right out of the womb, I was a husky baby. My mother and father are the same. We are just big people."

"Huh," Nath remarked. "Well, if you say so, I believe you. So Radagan, you've been here all of your life?"

"I've never even seen the trees outside of the walls."

"Interesting. How about I ask you a few questions?"

Radagan started snoring. It was the loudest snore Nath had ever heard. He pushed on the man who kept on snoring. "Radagan? Radagan?" The big man teetered on top of him. "Radagan!"

Chapter 5

Miserable, Nath sat, fully awake thanks to Radagan's heavy snoring, trying to sort his thoughts. It made little sense that the man was in the cell because of cream cakes. If anything, Foster was tormenting Nath. He recollected the orc's sniggering when they brought the food. Nath's suffering was their pleasure. By the time Radagan woke, at least a full day had passed. The disoriented man tried to prowl the cramped cell like a wild cat in a cage. "Where am I? Where am I?" He crushed into Nath and screamed. "What are you?"

"Calm down, Radagan! It's Nath. And you are in a cell below the dungeons."

"Oh geez, I was hoping all of that was a nightmare and I would wake back in my bed." He boo-hooed. "I can't believe this is really happening. They need me. After all, I make the cream cakes, as well as other things. My riblet stew is unsurpassed."

"I'm sure they'll come around." Nath pushed Radagan aside and moved back into his spot. When the man slept, it was all but impossible to move him, and he'd flattened out on the cell floor, snoring like a bear. "Let's just try to think about other things, shall we?"

"Like what?" Radagan's belly groaned. "Oh, I'm so hungry. I feel as if I haven't eaten in a week. Nath, I eat all the time. I can't not eat."

"Just settle yourself. The guards brought some food while you slept. You can even have my share."

Radagan sniffed. "Is that meat? Bread?"

"It's duck and flat bread. Not much, but it might tide you over for a few—" In the dark, Radagan snatched the plate of food from Nath's fingers. "You are quick for a big fellow."

Grunting, Radagan gobbled up the food. He ate as if he was the only person in the entire world. He nibbled the bones clean and sucked the grease from his fingers.

It reminded Nath of Prawl eating roasted rabbits.

I hate Prawl. I hate them all.

Radagan finished the food and water with a hearty belch. He thumped his chest a few times. "Thank you, Nath. I appreciate you saving me some."

"That was all of it."

"You didn't eat?"

Nath shrugged. "I'm getting used to being hungry. Besides, I wasn't really hungry anyway." His belly rumbled.

"You show mercy where mercy is not shown. I swear, Nath, once I get out of here, I will bake you a cream cake and get it to you. Somehow. I have ways, you know."

Nath's brows lifted. "About that, Radagan, you say you have been here all of your life?"

"Born and raised."

"So, given that there are only several thousand people behind these walls, I wonder, has anyone ever escaped?"

"We aren't to speak of such things," Radagan whispered. "They'll flog me."

"So, someone has?"

"No, no, no, I don't know."

Nath could tell from the tightness in the man's voice he knew something. "I will let you have the entire next meal if you tell me more about what you know; otherwise, I just might eat it all."

"That is cruel. Besides, one has been trying to escape, but the guards always catch him. He's a striking man with golden eyes. I spied him in the stockades once or twice. Trust me, you don't want to go through what he does."

"That's me, Radagan!" Nath slapped the man on the shoulder. "I'm the one that tries to escape and gets caught time and again. These shackles slow me, and the guards' eyes are everywhere."

"Not everywhere."

"What?"

"Nothing. I didn't say nothing." Radagan balled up. "Oh, please don't ask me any more. It will only lengthen my sentence. I had no idea you were the one they called the Special."

"Special?"

"Yes, that is what they say. Oh, I did not know that it was you I shared the cell with. I should seal my lips, forever, and I would, if I didn't need to eat."

Nath reached over and put his hand on Radagan's shoulders. "Tell me, what do they say about me? I must know. Who has bought me? What are they planning to do with me?" He shook the man. "Tell me."

"I don't know. I mean, for one such as you, with divine looks, I would think you would be put in auction and fetch a very high price. Perhaps the highest price. But, you are being put through a grinder. Busting the rocks in the quarry, churning in the plow races. It's as if they are tormenting you in spite of yourself. Someone wants to break you, methinks." Radagan smacked his lips. "Of course, I'm just saying that from the top of my head. You asked me so quickly that was all I could come up with. In truth, people like me enjoy seeing what they will put you through next. People bet on whether or not you can take it."

Nath sat back in his corner. "Who in Nalzambor is so out to get me? I don't even know anybody. Well, not that many at least." The only people he could think of were the Black Hand and Prawl. But Prawl said that someone would pay a high price for someone like him. He went to great lengths to take Nath into slavery. The only other people he could think of that would know about him were the Trahaydeen. But they couldn't have known that he left Dragon Home. He put his face in his hands. "This is so confusing. I need to get out of here and find answers."

"Well, if you want to get out of here, you are going the wrong way about it," Radagan said. "Achoo! Oh goodness, I have gooey all over my hands. You wouldn't have a handkerchief, would you?"

"No," Nath said, aggravated.

"Well, it's a good thing I still have my apron," Radagan said, wiping his hands on his covering.

"What were you saying about going about this all wrong?" Nath asked.

"The more determined you appear to want to get out, the closer they will watch. Let them think you are broken. You go at everything like an angry bull. All you will do in the long run is wear yourself down for real." Radagan sneezed again. "Pace yourself. Perhaps that is what your new owner wants to see. They need to see that you are broken."

"I don't know if I can do that. I can't stand to see what is going on all around. The slavers, they are so cruel."

"Hah, you haven't seen the half of it, but keep it up and you're going to."

Chapter 6

Over the next several days, Nath suffered inside the sweltering cell with Radagan. If the baker wasn't moaning, his belly was groaning, and he whined and complained from the time he woke until the time he slept. Radagan wasn't a bad person, perhaps a little jaded by the sordid lot he was brought up with, but all in all, he was harmless. The worst thing about him was his snoring, plus he took up over half of the cell when he flattened out on the floor and became immovable.

Finally, the guards started letting Nath and Radagan out of the cell once a day, giving them enough time to stretch out and relieve themselves. Pigeons roosted in the barred windows that let the daylight in from the outside. A fresh breeze tickled the hairs in his nostrils. He took long, lasting breaths. The guards even let them clean out the cell and place a fresh bed of straw inside. So long as neither one of them spoke or made eye contact with the guards, they didn't have any problems.

On their tenth day together, after they'd finished their time outside and were sealed back into the hold, Radagan said, "Did you see that, Nath?"

"No." Nath squeezed his way back into his corner. He was still in irons, but Radagan was not. "What are you talking about?"

"My hips! My hips made it through the door without rubbing. Isn't that something?"

"I guess that's what happens when you go without cream cakes for a while. And you know, it does seem like there is a bit more room in our cell than when we started," Nath added.

"Isn't that something?" Radagan said, lying down on his straw bed. "I even feel lighter."

"Good." Nath ran his finger around the collar on his neck. He'd do anything to have it taken off. Even though he'd gotten used to being in the hold with Radagan, it was still miserable. It was hot, he sweated all the time, and the shackles that dug into his skin were a chronic reminder that he was a prisoner. Good sleep was impossible to come by, and there were other unforeseen circumstances. His nostrils flared. His eyes popped wide. He pinched his nose. "Ew… Radagan, not again."

"Pardon my flatulence, but you think you'd be used to it by now."

"We were just outside, couldn't you let it out then?"

"It sneaks up on you. Besides, it's not like you don't do it."

Nath squeezed his eyes shut. "Mine are not so rank that they burn your eyes."

Fanning the air, Radagan said, "Oh, it's not that bad. The orcs are far worse, and the ogres, oh my, they leave a stink you don't forget."

Shaking his head, Nath tried to block it out. There was nothing good about the dungeon. Damp or musty, it reeked. He kept his eyes closed and tried to forget about it. Using his quiet time, he considered his next course of action. He actually liked Radagan's plans to pretend as if he'd given in. But he had to sell it, that's what Radagan said. He said it would take some time to convince the slavers, too. They were seasoned masters of cruelty, and they knew what made their slaves tick. They'd be wise to whether or not Nath was faking it, if he wasn't careful. Finally, he let out a yawn, and to the loud rhythm of the baker's snoring, he fell asleep.

Bang!

"What in the heavens was that?" Radagan said.

Nath's eyelids lifted. The orcs always pounded the door to wake them, and it startled Radagan every time.

Bang!

"Get back from the door," one of the guards said.

"We're back," Nath replied.

The door groaned open. An orc guard holding a lantern peered inside. "Radagan, get your flabby husk out of there. Your punishment has ended."

"Me! Really!" Radagan was on his hands and knees, crawling toward the door. "Oh, thank the slave lords." He slid outside and vanished into the hall, outwardly thanking the slave lords. "Thank you, thank you, thank you!"

"What about my time?" Nath said.

"Heh," the guard replied. "Your time has just begun." He slammed the door shut.

Nath sat with his jaw sagging. He didn't even hear a goodbye from Radagan. It was as if the baker had forgotten him already.

Chapter 7

MONTHS PASSED. NATH WAS FED once a day and let out once a day, but only for a few minutes. When he was let out it was night, and he saw no sunlight to warm his face. Once a week, they allowed him to lay a new bed of straw and shovel the old damp straw out. That was it. It was just him, alone in the hold, where his mind wandered. There were times he doubted whether or not Radagan had even been in the cell with him. Had it been a dream or a nightmare? Suffering in his solitude, he found himself missing the portly baker and his musings to the point where he had conversations with the funny man who wasn't there.

"Cream cakes, cream cakes, I want cream cakes," Nath said as he scratched on the wall with a stone. He marked the days he'd been put away by making lines on the wall, even though he could barely see them. "Huh, if Radagan wasn't real, then where did I come up with cream cakes? I've never had a cream cake before."

He considered other things that Radagan had told him. The baker told him much about the layout of Slaver Town. He described the buildings and dwellings. Slaver Town operated like a military complex. The slave lords had their own special dwellings, and the guards stayed in barracks. Many of the higher-ranking officials even had cottages for their families, but it was all located on the other side of Slaver Town, and Nath had barely seen a glimpse of it. Radagan said they had their own taverns and lodging there. There were stores like any other city. It was a fairly big and bizarre place. Radagan knew about it because he was a baker that prepared food for the people. He, in a sense, was a slave, but had gained citizenship, in an odd sort of way, by serving the higher-up people. All in all, Slaver Town was what it was, a prison set up like a city.

Radagan also said that the slave lords came and went as they pleased. And even though they didn't leave often, they didn't go through the main gate either. He said there was a separate tunnel at the south side of the town. He hadn't seen it, but it was rumored to be there. Based off the descriptions given, Nath pictured it all in his mind. Now, all he had to do was plot a way to escape, but he needed to get out of the pen first. And then, find a way out of his irons. He was confident if he could lose the shackles, he could run and they would never catch him.

Bang! Bang! Bang!

"Stay back from the door," the guard on the other side of the cell door said.

Nath pushed his face up from the bed of straw. For the first time in a long time, he'd actually been in a deep sleep. His eyelids were heavy. He sat up, picking strands of straw from his face. "I'm back," he replied. It seemed like an odd time for the guards to feed him. They'd been doing it in the evening, but there was a warmth that carried through the air that his dragon senses could tell was daylight.

The door opened. An orc crouched just outside with a lantern in one hand and a man-catcher in the other. "Scoot back."

Nath complied.

The orc set the lantern aside then pinned Nath's arms in the jaws of the man-catcher. "On your feet, slowly."

Nath stood.

The orc guard in black leather armor pulled him out into the hall. There were several more guards out there. One of them, a fish-eyed orc with tangled locks covering his forehead, held a burlap sack. The guard looked at Nath. "Time to go."

Squinting, Nath said, "To where?"

The orc punched him in the belly. Nath buckled over.

"Don't ask questions!" the orc said. He placed the burlap sack over Nath's face and pulled it tight around his neck. He punched Nath in the gut again. "That was for the question you were thinking of asking." The orcs sniggered.

CHAPTER 8

WHEN THE GUARDS REMOVED THE sack from Nath's head, he saw Foster. The stalwart half-orc slaver sat behind a desk, looking at a ledger. They were inside an office where the slaves were checked and searched on their way in and out from their prison-like quarters in the barn. The Barn, as they called it, was a prison of cages in a barn-like building where Nath spent most of his stay in his cell, isolated like some sort of prize behind the heavy curtain.

Foster wrote in the book, and without looking at Nath said, "Search him."

"What?" Nath said. "I just came out of the hold. What would you be searching me—*gah*!" A guard clubbed Nath in the back of his legs. He dropped to his knees. Two guards searched him all over. They even opened up his mouth and looked inside.

"He's clean, Slaver Foster. And the irons hold firm," the fish-eyed orc said. "But he still seems feisty for a man in the hold. Shall I take more fire out of him?"

"No." Foster closed the leather-bound book. His hand moved to the dark hammer that he smote Nath with months ago. He scooted his chair over the floor to face Nath and laid the sledgehammer across his legs. "If he acts up, I'll deal with him. Dismissed."

The orc guards left but remained just outside the doorway, posted on each side of the frame. The door remained wide open.

"Close the door, idiots!" Foster said, fanning a buzzing fly from his face. Sneering, he watched the fly with beady eyes. He lifted his hands and smacked them together, smashing the fly between them, and wiped them on his trousers. The door closed. "Now, it's just the two of us, prisoner. Did you miss me?"

"Of course not." Nath noticed his breastplate armor propped up in the corner of the room. His eyes slid back to Foster.

"I'm so hurt to hear that. Ha. Ha." Foster glanced at Nath's breastplate. "Yes, it's very nice. Light. I think I'll paint the banner of Thraag on it and wear it on my journey."

"Suit yourself," Nath replied.

"I have to admit, you aren't as worse for wear as I expected. Over three months in the hold, and you don't sneeze, or twitch." Foster's brows crinkled. "There is something to that. I'd expect it from an ogre perhaps, but you, a man, seem little weakened. Your hair is still thick with color, even though there is slime in it. I think I see lice crawling in there too. It's customary that we shave it."

"I don't feel any creatures on my head," Nath said, flicking his locks back with his fingers.

"Foster, to be up front, I don't want to go in the hold again. I would really like to bathe. I don't know what you have in mind for me, but I swear, I've learned my lesson."

Foster leaned forward. "Have you? Because, I'm not convinced. Believe me when I say that I have heard the finest testimonies from the best liars, and you are no good at it. No, you rebel. You cringe. I can see you hate the sight of me."

"I hate the sight of all of you. You are slavers. Tormentors. Liars and thieves. You know it. You're proud of it." Nath's jaws clenched as he fought the urge to spit. "But, you are in charge, and I am not. I don't like you, you don't like me, but that doesn't mean I can't get along. When I say I've learned my lesson, I mean it. If there is anyone in this den of vipers whose word you can take, it is mine."

Foster took his hammer in his fist and tapped the end in his hand, making light smacking sounds. "Clever."

"I just want to go back to where I was," Nath said, scratching his cheek. "If that means I have to bust rocks until my owner takes me, then so be it. I'll mind my own business. When I say I don't want to go back in the hold, I mean it."

"Your owner, huh?" Foster made an ugly smile. "What makes you think that you have an owner? As I understand it, you are the property of Slaver Town. All of the slave lords, including me, own a piece of you."

Nath shook his chin. "I don't believe you. I was brought here for a reason, because someone wants me, or someone like me. Not that it matters. I'm a slave either way and you have to protect me, don't you, Foster?"

The half-orc's eyebrows knitted together. His nostrils flared. He pulled back the hammer, stopped, tossed back his head, and let out a gusty laugh. "Bwah-hahaha!"

Nath perched an eyebrow. Part of him wanted to laugh with Foster for some compelling reason. He started laughing himself.

"Silence!" Foster lifted the hammer with deadly intent in his eyes. "You don't want another kiss from Stone Smiter, do you?"

Clamping his mouth shut, Nath looked at the hammer. *No, please no. It's been a bad enough day.*

"Listen to me, prisoner. I don't like you. You are a thorn. Strong and defiant. How many times have you attempted to escape? Three times." He jerked toward Nath. Nath didn't blink. "You see. You don't budge. You don't fear, and that makes you a danger. You will try to flee again and again, and I cannot kill you. But that doesn't mean accidents can't happen either." He pulled the club back and eased into his chair. "I think it's time that you had more hazardous duties, further isolated from the other prisoners. After all, you wouldn't want any more deaths on your hands."

Nath's back straightened. "What deaths?" He immediately thought about the instrumentalist, Homer.

"Yes, it seemed that his fragile human body wasn't equipped to handle the flogging my men gave him when you departed to the pen. I believe his heart gave out after forty lashes."

"You monster!" Nath lunged forward. With a flick of the wrist, Foster pointed the hammer at Nath. The rune stone on top of the hammer flared. A bolt of light shot into Nath's face.

Sssszap! Painful stars exploded in Nath's head. Crumbling to the ground, unable to control his body as he twitched, the last thing he heard was Foster saying, "Guards, take him away."

Chapter 9

Nath felt someone dabbing his throbbing head with a damp cloth. He seized their wrist. The person gasped, and the wet cloth fell on his face. Nath flung it off and sat up. His eyes grew big. "Homer?"

"Yes," the man said, wincing. "Please, let go of my wrist. You are breaking it."

Nath let go. "You're alive!"

Rubbing his wrist, Homer said, "Yes, but my fingers don't feel like it. You are strong as an orc."

"And you, gentle as a flower, apparently." Nath sat up on his cot. He was back inside his cell behind the curtain in the barn. A blanket was over his shoulders, and his hair was wet. "Did it rain?"

"Heh, no. The guards rinsed you in the stream before they brought you here. You must have been awfully rank for them to bathe you."

For the first time in months, Nath felt clean. He touched the knot on his head. "Ooh, does it look as bad as it feels?"

"Probably worse. What happened?"

"Foster took after me with his hammer when I came at him. Energy shot into my eyes and filled my body like needles of lightning. I'd just gotten out of the hold, and he told me that you'd been flogged to death." Nath made a weak smile. "Glad you live."

"Well, if it makes you feel any better, I was flogged." Foster turned his back and lifted his shirt. The skin was chewed up on his back. "I can still feel the sting when I sleep sometimes. Wakes me up in the sweats."

"I'm sorry, Homer. It's my fault."

"Oh, don't you go apologizing to me, Nath. You told me to stand firm, and I wish I had. Neither one of us would have gone through this if I wasn't careless." He extended his hand, offering a warm and friendly smile. His soft, slender hands were hardened with callouses now. His face was hard-lined and chiseled. "But your words made me tougher. I finally got through it."

Nath shook his head. "So, you aren't angry?"

"By the sky, no. I'm relieved you're back. I thought when you went to the pen you would not return. They say that many don't, especially when they are gone so long. How awful was it?"

"Small, dark, damp, and quiet. And the food is even worse. Speaking of which, do we have anything to eat? I'm beyond famished."

Homer scurried to the end of the cell. He lifted a cloth napkin off a plate that had a small loaf of bread and a hunk of cheese. He offered it to Nath. "Here, it's yours."

Nath ate with vigor. With his mouth half full, he eyed a second cot in the cell. "Homer, is that your cot?"

"Er, well, yes, I've been assigned here for the last couple of months. I hope I won't crowd you. I like it better here."

"No, believe me, there is plenty of room. I welcome the company. It's been a while since I've been around anyone. Tell me, how did you wind up in this place?"

Homer swallowed. His soft eyes started to water. "You don't want to hear my sorry tale. It's inexcusable."

"You said you were a musician. Why don't you tell me about that?"

"May I sit?" Homer said, eyeing the end of Nath's cot.

Nath nodded.

"Well, I'm a fine instrumentalist, a master of strings, with fingers as nimble as the elves. Some would say, that is. I played and sang in Quintuklen, and even caught the king's attention. I entertained him and the queen many times in their courtyard." He gave a dreamy smile. "But, I fell."

"You fell? From a horse, or something."

"No, I fell for the queen, and she fell for me." Homer grinned. "I swear it, Nath. She said my music delighted her inside and out. One day, I went to play for her inside her very chambers. Oh, you should have seen the curtain and felt the linens. No bed of cotton is so soft." Head down, he rubbed the back of his neck. "Well, one thing led to another, and without getting into the details, I wound up here. But at least I still had my head on my shoulders."

Straight-faced, Nath said, "You aren't supposed to do that, Homer."

"Well, don't you think I know that? And what was I supposed to do, tell the queen no?" His voice reached a higher pitch. "She's the queen!"

"You still should have told her no. You might still have ended up here, but at least you would have your honor."

"Don't you know anything about a woman scorned, Nath?"

Nath pictured Maefon, blond, elven, and beautifully featured. The half-dryad Calypsa, with piles of hair covering her bare shoulders and a figure that was unforgettable. Then came the Black Hand. Nina, a very tall, athletic, and attractive woman with arms like a blacksmith's, and Virgo, a platinum-haired enchantress with eyes that shone like diamonds. He'd never spurned any of them. "Have you ever heard of a man being scorned?"

"Well, no one really cares about that side of things," Homer puffed. "Anyhow, Nath, I'm ashamed to say that I am what I am, and perhaps I had this coming."

"Did you love her?"

"I suppose I did in one sort of way. The excitement dancing in her eyes when I played, well, it made me feel so wanted." Homer slapped his hands on his knees a couple of times. "But it wasn't love for either of us the way it should be. At least, it's not the same as the love I have for my wife."

"Homer! You too were married?"

"I really wish I hadn't mentioned that. It's embarrassing. And I feel all the more a failure. But, she was the queen, Nath. I couldn't tell her no."

"You could have if you wanted to," Nath said, lying down on his back. He felt disappointed, but he wasn't sure why. After all, the men were there for crimes they had committed. They were criminals, all of them, the wretched of society. He caught Homer limping over to his cot on the other side of the cell. Nath rolled to the side. "Homer, your foot did not heal well?"

"No. I can barely walk. I think that's why they put up with me. Nath, I'm sorry if I've let you down."

"Don't be. I haven't met anyone that hasn't let me down so far." He turned his back. "I suppose it's time I lowered my expectations in this world apparently filled with rotten people."

Homer sobbed.

Chapter 10

For several weeks, Nath spent his time in the rock quarry, busting stones from sunup to sundown. His back burned, and his shoulders ached. By the time he ambled back into his cell, he barely had enough energy to eat. Soon, he was fast asleep, only to wake up what seemed to be a few minutes later to face the same misery again.

Few words were exchanged between him and Homer. He didn't have the energy for it. The older musician had been assigned a lighter duty, playing the strings in the slave lords' taverns. "I'm working on my citizenship," Homer commented. "I might as well. Then, at least I can play my music."

Nath didn't care. For the time being, he was keeping his head low and his mouth shut. Over the next few days, he turned his eyes away from the cruelty that his tormentors inflicted on the prisoners. The guards would whip the prisoners, beat them, and toss them into the pen or lock them in stockades. They did it all for little more than a casual look in their direction. It was clear that they were going to have their wills broken.

At midday one day, underneath the hot glare of the sun, Nath pushed a wheelbarrow laden with stone up the ramp and out of the pit. The hunks were larger than a man's head. At the top of the quarry pit, more prison laborers would take the stones and put them on work tables, where in an assembly line they would chisel them down into rectangular bricks. From there, the bricks were loaded into wagons, pulled by a train of four mules, and hauled away. They headed toward the main gate of Slaver Town that was too far away to be seen. It gave Nath an idea for escape that he kept to himself.

He finished unloading the rocks on the tables, wiped the sweat from his brow, and headed down the ramp. He took his time, keeping in the shade provided by the wall of the quarry. A breeze cooled his sun-bronzed skin. At the bottom, one of the guards met him with an empty bucket in his hand.

"Go to the well and fill it," the guard said, stuffing the bucket in Nath's chest. "It's for us. Not you."

Eyes downcast, Nath said, "Right away."

"Make it quick, prisoner. We are thirsty."

Nath wanted to tell him that if he was so thirsty, he could fetch his own water. He kept his lips sealed and scurried away. He tried to make it look faster than he was actually moving, as he zigzagged across the quarry. On the far side, the stony crater steps led up and out of the quarry. He angled up four flights of steps, faced another guard, and said, "I need water, for the guards in the quarry."

With a grunt, the guard led Nath over to a natural spring that flowed through the little town, providing an endless supply of fresh water. There were steps cut out of the natural stone that led to a natural dock. Nath dipped the bucket in and filled it to the rim. It was horrible that the slaves begged for water every day, especially when there was a more than ample source.

None should thirst here. None should thirst anywhere.

He lifted the bucket out of the water, allowing it to sprinkle his thighs and legs. With a nod to the guard, he moved away from the spring and offered the guard a drink from the ladle.

"Get moving," the guard said.

Still in irons, Nath headed back into the quarry. He was crossing to the other side when the ogre stepped into his path. The brute was eight feet tall with a big, hard belly that came up to Nath's chin.

"Torno thirsty," the ogre said, reaching for the bucket. His huge hands were almost big enough to enclose the bucket.

Nath shuffled backward. He took another angle and walked away from the hairy brute.

Torno cut into his path. "Give me drink!"

Shaking his head, Nath said, "No. This is for the guards." He could see the guards closing in. They had their hands on their clubs. There were ten guards on the quarry's bottom level and even more spread out along the rim. In a large wooden chair, Foster sat underneath the shade of an open tent. His eyes were intent on Nath.

"Just give him the water," one of the guards said to Nath. "Go ahead."

It wasn't the same guard who sent Nath after the water. He knew them all. "No, I'll do as I was instructed to do. If you don't mind, please keep Torno at bay."

"Don't tell me what to do, prisoner." The orc guard marched right up to Nath, slapping his club in his hand. He got right in Nath's face. "I don't like you."

"Torno want drink now!" All of a sudden, the ogre picked up the guard who stood in front of Nath and flung him aside. He reached for the bucket again. "Give me drink, red-haired man!"

Nath skipped away, careful not to let water slosh out of the bucket. Torno came at him, but the guards were doing nothing. "Turn his collar on!" Nath said, shuffling backward and away.

"Don't you spill a drop of that water!" Foster yelled down into the pit. "That's for the laborers. You drop it, then they don't drink for the rest of the day."

The other workers in the yard stopped working. They licked their cracked lips. They put their hammers and splitters down and watched as Nath, fully shackled, danced away from the ogre. It was a setup. It was all done to make him look bad, or get him in trouble. He'd been a model prisoner for weeks, and now Foster wanted to get to him. He managed to make it to the orc guard who sent him after the water in the first place. "Here, take it. Take the bucket," he said.

"That is for the prisoners. Get it away from me." The guard moved up the ramp.

"Give me the drink!" Torno came at him. He squatted down, pulled his arms back, and opened his huge jaws wide. "Now!"

Moving away from the ramp, back into the quarry, Nath tried to reason with the ogre. "Torno, let these men have their share first and you can have what is left. How does that sound?"

"No! Torno wants it all." He beat his chest. "Torno works the hardest."

"Don't you dare give him that bucket, prisoner," Foster yelled from his chair. "Not a drop!"

The guards encircled Nath and Torno. They sniggered in their evil way. They'd put Torno up to this. The ogre, though not smart, was somewhat peaceful. He never got stirred up unless he was incited. Torno must have been threatened if he didn't do what he was told. Nath gave in. He looked beyond the guards and set the bucket down. "Sorry, men. Torno, it's yours."

Torno picked up the bucket. He put the bucket to his lips. His collar glowed. There was a distinct *bzzzzitt* sound. The bucket fell from his fingers. All of the water spilled into the ground. A snarl formed on the ogre's face. "Red hair trick Torno! Red hair will die!" He lunged at Nath.

CHAPTER 11

NATH SKIPPED JUST OUT OF Torno's reach. As he did so, he plucked a sledgehammer from the ground, and faced off against the monstrous man. "Torno, listen to me, I'm not your enemy. Just stop!"

Slather dripped from Torno's jutting jaw. He charged.

Putting his hip into his swing, Nath busted Torno in his outstretched fingers. The ogre jerked his hand back and wailed. He threw a fist with the other. Torno's fist pounded Nath in the shoulder. The blow sent him spinning to the ground. He looked up. The ogre's fists came down.

"Torno kill!"

Nath scrambled out of harm's way. Torno came at him with rage-filled eyes. The ogre swung wildly. Nath crawled, hopped, and slid out of the way, stirring up the dust. "Foster, cut off this madness." He coughed and ducked another wild swing. "Now!"

Torno picked up a rock the size of a cantaloupe and threw it at Nath. He flattened on his belly. The rock smashed into another slave's ankles. The man went down wailing.

"Blast it! This has to stop!" Nath launched right at Torno. Aiming as if he was being watched by Dragon Master Elween, he let Torno have it. Using the sledgehammer, he popped the ogre with hard raps to the elbows and knees. The metal head crushed into hard bone. He put all he could into it. The shackles restrained his swings. "Back off, Torno!"

"Raaaaawwwrr!" Torno bull-rushed Nath.

Nath tried to dash out of the way, but his ankle snapped on the short length of chain between them. He fell. On his knees, he tried to crawl away. Torno scooped him up in his massive arms and bear-hugged him.

"Torno crush! Torno kill!"

Nath dropped the sledgehammer. His eyes bulged. His body turned beet red. He strained against the mighty arms that constricted like pythons made of iron. The ogre might have had a thick coat of fat, but Torno was nothing but burgeoning muscle underneath. "Let go, Torno!" Nath blurted out. "You're killing me!"

Something inside Nath's body popped and cracked. Pain lanced through his ribs.

"Torno kill!"

Nath looked upward at Slave Master Foster. The half-orc sat on the edge of his seat with a clenched fist in his lap. A triumphant look sparkled in his dark eyes. The other guards were howling and urging the ogre on.

"Crush him! Kill him!" they said. Even some of the other prisoners were into it.

Nath kicked at the air. He took a sharp, painful breath and flexed his arms and shoulders. "Nooooo! I will not die like this!" Another rib snapped. With each second now a painful and eternal moment, his strength faded. His vision blurred. The sky darkened.

Bzzzzzzzzt! Bzzzzzzzt!

A shockwave passed through the ogre and into Nath. The ogre's limbs gave way as Torno howled like a wounded beast. He dropped Nath, scurried to the wall, curled up into the fetal position, and sucked his thumb.

Body tingling with shards of pain, Nath passed out to the sound of the guards' rumbling laughter.

Chapter 12

Something poked Nath hard in a busted rib. "Guh!" He blinked, taking in the stockades. The scorching sun blistered his bare back. Every inch of his body hurt. The water bucket he'd carried lay on the ground, broken. He turned his head but couldn't see who was behind him. Still, he had a pretty good idea.

"You owe me a bucket." Foster came from behind to stand in front of Nath. "And the work of three wounded men. It will be a very long time before you pay that debt off."

"I'm fairly certain my debt will never be paid," Nath replied. "At least, not so long as you are in charge."

Foster grabbed Nath's chin and tilted his head up. "You have a sharp tongue. That is your undoing. You need to learn silence." The half-orc eyed him. "Silence."

Despite his circumstances, Nath couldn't hold his tongue, even though he wanted to. To make matters worse, Foster was wearing Nath's breastplate. The half-orc was bigger than him, but it fit him like a glove. His tongue became unfettered. "You really need to take my armor off."

"This, why, no?" Foster said, almost cheerfully. He spun in a slow, tight circle. "It fits so well. But for some reason, I can't scrub this paint off. I plan to mark over it at some point in time, but for now, it will do. At worst, I'll put my tunic over it."

"You're just wanting to make me mad."

"Is it working?"

"Yes." Nath thrust against the boards that held his neck and wrists fast in the stockade.

Foster tossed his tawny locks back with his hands and snorted a laugh. "That is your problem. There is too much fire in you. I knew when the ogre came after you, you would fight. You should have played dead."

"And take a chance and let that brute kill me? I think not. He would have crushed my head." The collar pinched him. He turned his head left and right, trying to ease the discomfort. He couldn't believe they actually put him in the stocks with his irons still on. The outfit gave him little room to wiggle. "You would have done the same. Any person would have."

"Not the broken. They will give up and die. I've been here all of my life, and I have seen it with my own eyes. Many pass away in their sleep. Some die in the quarry. Others—"

"You kill for sport," Nath remarked.

"Don't take up the cause of the broken. The wretched. They don't care about you or what you can do for them. The world doesn't want them anymore. We give them a purpose here. You should be able to see that."

"You make it sound as if the people volunteered," Nath said. "I've heard their stories. You stole them from their homes and families. Others were kidnapped from raids on merchant trains. I have good ears, I know what is going on. Don't try to make it sound noble."

Foster patted Nath on the head. "I am what I am. So are the others. This is what we know. People are either born slaves or slave lords. Heh-heh. Like me."

Nath ground his teeth. He hated everything about Foster and his ilk. They were cold, cruel, and compassionless.

If I had Fang I would end them all.

"The sooner you are broken, Nath," Foster said, for the first time calling him by name, "the sooner you will be turned over. But as I've said, you won't fool me. I'll know when that golden flicker in your eye goes out. Of course, from what I've seen, you are like a wild mule. Difficult to break, which is a surprise for such a young man. Normally, one such as you is broken in days."

"I guess that's what makes me special." Nath set his eyes on the slaver. "You know, Foster, we've been at this a while already. Perhaps it's me that's going to outlast you. Did you ever think about that? I noticed a little gray over your ears. They weren't there when you started on me."

Foster stiffened. He waved some of his men over. "Take the scourge to him. Twenty lashes a day until I say you are through." He glared at Nath. "I will break you." He slugged Nath in the jaw and stormed away.

Nath waved goodbye with his fingers, and just as he was about to say it aloud a *crack* erased his thought. Fire exploded over his back nineteen more times. Nath didn't scream once. He held it all in. Dripping sweat from his chin and eyebrows, he said under his breath, "Gads, I hate orcs!"

Chapter 13

Alone, Maefon stood inside Lord Darkken's study, staring into the Pool of Eversight. The full-blooded elven woman's wavy blond hair lay over her shoulders. She wore a sleeveless black tunic and leather leggings. Sensual and exotic, her painted fingernails rested on the magic basin's rim. She watched the image in the waters.

The entry doors to Lord Darkken's study parted. Two elven sentries, wearing red hoods made from satin, entered. The eyelets in the hoods were cut out in different designs. They wore the dark leather armor of the Caligin. A sword and dagger hung from their belts. The two stepped aside and bowed as Lord Darkken entered. Tall, athletic, and with the flowing rust-colored hair of a gallant knight, he approached Maefon. His chiseled features were handsome, and his copper eyes burned bright. He wore the same black garb and equipment of the Caligin, but being a man, he filled out his attire with hard muscles.

Maefon gave him a quick bow. "Good morning, Darkken."

He offered her a warm smile and clasped her hands. "Good morning to you as well, my darling."

She slipped her hands out of his firm grip. Her fingers climbed up his broad chest and locked around his neck. Rising up on tiptoe, she kissed him. "I've missed you."

"Of course you did." He put his arm around her waist and looked into the pool. "Ah, what do we have here?"

"It seems that the slavers are scourging your little brother again," she said. "But aside from that, little has changed. He remains... obstinate."

"As he should. After all, he is a dragon. If he'd been broken sooner I would have been disappointed." He moved away to a high-backed leather chair that sat adjacent to a fireplace. He took his boots off and tossed them on the hearth. With a flick of his fingers, the logs inside caught fire, creating a warming crackle. "I might need to turn the heat up on him, so to speak."

Staring into the pool, she said, "I thought we would be patient. Wear him down through attrition."

"Perhaps, but we don't want him to get too used to something. He'll build up a resistance to it. And frankly, I'm looking forward to meeting him." He laid his head back against the soft leather of the chair and sighed. "Ah, this feels good. So good that I could almost get used to it. But I'm too selfish with my intent to destroy the dragons. Of course, once that is done, I'll rest."

"You'll never rest," Maefon said.

"Oh really? Why is that?"

She crossed the room and sat down on Darkken's lap. Caressing his hair, she said, "Because no power will ever be enough for you. You said it yourself, there is always more power to be had. Power that created the world itself."

"Yes, I did say that, didn't I?" He took her hand and kissed her fingers. "You know me as well as any, Maefon, and lucky for you, I find you worthy. It would be a shame to cast you aside like all the others."

"Others?"

"Oh, don't worry about them. Focus on the future. Your future."

"Of course. I am as always." She noticed bloodstains on the shoulder of his armor. "Darkken, when you were gone, did you do battle?"

"Oh, the blood. Well, it had been a long time since I swung a blade, so I went and got myself into a skirmish."

"Really," she said, sounding interested. "Tell me more about it."

"Well, as you know, I like to take very long walks. On my journey, I came across a small bridge that crossed a barren gulch. Well, there was a group of dwarves on the other side, coming back from laboring in the mines. Seven in all. They wanted to cross the bridge, and I told them no. If you could have seen their faces. Talk about angry." He opened his eyes. "Did you use the pool to search for me?"

"I did. But I had no fortune finding you."

"Good, that's the way it should be. Now, where was I?"

"The dwarves."

"Yes, the dwarves. They came right at me with shovels, picks, and axes. I think they thought to bowl me over, but I was too quick. My blade slid from the sheath and cut the first one through his beard into his neck. Now that really incensed them. Like angry hornets they came on. I chopped them down one by one." He patted the pommel of his longsword. "I forgot how good I was with this thing. Anyway, those dwarves are dead, aside from one. I let him live with a severely wounded leg that will give him a stiff limp on his stubby lump for the rest of his life."

"By the sound of it, I'm surprised that there isn't much blood on you," she said, rubbing the stain with her thumb. "So, who did you blame this slaughter on?"

"I was wearing an elven tunic, which the dwarven blood ruined. I did a little dabbling with myself as well." He combed his hair back over his ear, revealing a pointed tip. "The spell still lingers, but I'm pretty sure I was one of the biggest elves they ever saw. Of course, I wanted to leave an impression."

"You leave an impression on everybody." She hugged his chest. "I missed you, Darkken. And I want to hear all about everything else that you did."

Lord Darkken petted her back. "I dispatched the last class of Caligin and gave them new assignments. My army grows. Our intentions spread. It won't be long before one kingdom can't stand another. It will be so bad they won't even do business with one another. Their lust for money is what really gets them riled up, at least among the men. The dwarves have hoarded theirs, and the elves are indifferent about it. But there are ways to get to them." He kissed her forehead. "We'll keep chipping away, one day at a time, slow and steady. Eventually, the dam will break and waterworks will flow."

"So, you think there will be war soon?" she asked.

He showed a winning smile. "I'm counting on it."

Chapter 14

The months dragged on, one agonizing day at a time. There was nothing that Nath did right in the eyes of Slave Master Foster. The orc kept Nath under his scrutinizing gaze from the moment he left his cell until the moment he returned. If he wasn't whipped for some reason, he was starved. He even spent another short spell in the hold. Aside from the hold in the pen, and his cell in the barn, the rock quarry was his home. He spent the majority of his time there.

The rock quarry stretched out one hundred yards and was about half as wide. It was a solid bed of stone that the slaves had been busting out for decades, perhaps centuries. Now, it was about three stories deep, and it would take decades more to make it three more stories deep at this rate. Nath carried a boulder the size of an ogre's head. He waddled over to an oversized wheelbarrow and dumped it in.

On the other side of the wheelbarrow, Torno twisted around and looked at him. They hadn't tangled since their last encounter, but Torno's big hands clenched every time Nath came close. Nath turned his back and shuffled back to his spot. He picked up his sledgehammer, thumbed the sweat from his brow, and started swinging.

Two orc guards stood on either side of him, sharing a bucket of water between them. They drank heartily, letting the water spill down their jutting chins onto their ringmail and leather tunics.

"Laugh it up, dirt balls," Nath said under his breath, not paying them a lick of attention. Every day was the same. He worked. They taunted. If he looked at them, they stung him on the backside with the tails of their scourges. The only purpose it served was to slow him down. Bringing the hammer high, he brought it down hard and fast. Stone chips busted off in all directions.

"Gack!" One of the guards wiped his eyes and glared at Nath. "Watch what you are doing, human!" He pulled back his scourge.

Nath turned his bare back and tensed. The leather tails slapped against his back. *Crack!* Nath went down on a knee. He never got used to the biting sting that ran from his back to his chest. Using the hammer handle as a cane, he slowly came back to his feet, cringing somewhat, waiting for another kiss from the lash. It didn't come. The guards walked away, chuckling.

With arms that felt like lead and a back that felt like it was on fire, Nath banged away on the rocks. As he did so, he stole a glance at Foster. The slave lord sat in his tall chair, underneath a tapestry of shade, with two small slaves fanning him with wooden leaves. Foster's eyes were right on Nath. Nath averted his gaze.

He watches me like a hawk.

Foster was in charge of the guards who watched the slaves, but what Nath hadn't seen were the people who pulled Foster's strings. They were the real force behind Slaver Town. And even after two years in the camp, he'd not seen them once. He snatched glimpses down the roads on his way to the barn. He spied the wall and the watchtowers. He saw the auction blocks, the gallows, the stockade, and the road that led to the main gate. But that was only half of the city. Radagan had told him more. Of course, he wasn't even certain Radagan was real.

The day of labor ended at dusk. Nath got his final drink of water from the bucket and fell into line. They were told to keep their heads down as they were all marched back to the barn. Foster checked them all in at his office. He filled out the ledger as the guards patted them down and took them back to their cells, except for Torno. Torno was too big. He remained in the quarry. The guards patted Nath down. He kept his eyes on the floor. He heard the quill and ink scratching his marking on the ledger.

"Anything to say, prisoner?" Foster asked Nath. It was the first thing he'd said to Nath in weeks.

"No, slave master," Nath replied.

Foster studied Nath with probing eyes. He leaned back in his chair and grunted. "You've been very quiet, lately. I'm not used to it."

"I'm just trying to do what the slave master wishes," Nath said.

"I'm almost convinced." Foster grunted. "Take him away."

Back in his cell, Homer was already inside and lying on his cot. His arms covered his face. The guards shoved Nath inside, slammed the door behind him, and locked it. They departed through the curtain. Homer sat up. His eyes were bright. "How was your day?"

"Lousy," Nath said, arching his back. He took a seat on his cot. "I hope you weren't expecting a different answer."

"No, but I might just change yours." Homer took a quick glance at the curtain, then reached under his cot. Underneath a blanket, there was a plate with a bowl flipped over on the top. He picked it up and took it to Nath. Excitedly he said, "For you."

"Me?" Nath held the plate in his hand. "What is it?"

"Just take it, quick, before a guard pokes his head in."

Nath lifted the bowl off the plate. A round cream cake with a honey-and-raspberry glaze sat in the middle just as Radagan had described. The sugary aroma wafted into Nath's nostrils. His mouth watered. "Where did you get this?"

"You won't believe this, but one of the guards brought it. Just an hour ago." Homer smacked his lips. "Hurry, eat it. That smell will drift, and the hounds will be on us."

Nath fingered the spongy golden crust. "An orc brought this?"

"No, it was a man, dressed like a guard. He was very discreet."

"Was he very fat?"

"No. Just a man, the same as any other. I found it odd myself, but I was so surprised I didn't pay any attention. He said it was for you. You'd know who sent it." He took another quick glance at the curtain. "Eat it, will you? It's been gnawing at my gut, and now that I see it again, I can barely stand it." Homer's eyes were ravenous. "Hurry."

Nath heard footsteps outside of the curtain and a rattle of metal armor. He flipped the bowl over the cake, put the blanket over it, and set it on the end of his cot.

A barrel-chested guard passed through the curtain. Club in hand, the orc approached the cell. "Time for a cell inspection."

Chapter 15

The big-chested guard stuck his key inside the cell lock. "Get back."

Homer scooted to the end of his cot. Nath pressed his back to the wall while still holding the blanket, saucer and bowl in his lap. Just as the key turned inside the tumbler, another guard, holding a club, came through the curtain. His face was flushed.

"You have to see this new prisoner," the new guard said. He had a white scar on his chin. "Just walked in with a train of our brethren."

"If you've seen one, you've seen them all," the barrel-chested guard said. "I'm not missing anything."

"Oh yes, you are." The second guard came at the first and hooked his arm. "Come on, we might need you. This one's big."

A commotion of prisoners banging on their cells started up. Something or someone crashed into what sounded like a wooden table. The sharp crack of splintered wood caught everyone's ear. Clubs in hand, both guards headed for the curtain.

The guard with the scar on his chin said, "I told you!" They vanished behind the curtain. It sounded like a group of men were fighting a wild beast. Something let out an inhuman howl. There was smack of fist on bone.

Nath and Homer's eyes hung on the curtain. It billowed a little. He fully expected to see something crash through the curtain at any moment. There was the sound of clubs whacking and guards hollering. They were trying to wrestle a prisoner down. A very big, very angry prisoner by the sound of it.

"It's not our problem, Nath," Homer said, scooting back to the end of his cot. "Go ahead and eat your cake."

"Now?"

"It's not as if you can see anything. And that guard will be back here when it's over. And it will be soon, I imagine." Homer's eyes were pleading. "Hurry. Eat."

Eyes on the curtain, Nath uncovered the pastry. He picked it up with two hands and broke it in half. He put one half in the bowl and gave it to Homer. "I've a feeling that you'll enjoy it more than I will, even though I'm certain I'll enjoy it."

"Oh, thank you, thank you, thank you, Nath!" Homer bit into it. His eyes grew like saucers. He chewed as if he was eating something made from the bakeries in heaven. "Mmmmm..."

Nath bit into half of his cake. It was warm, sweet, and buttery. He instantly wished he had more of them. "My, that is good!"

"I can't remember something so exquisite in my life. I've even tasted morning pastries made by the queen's own bakers."

"Let's not go there," Nath said.

"Oh, of course not. Perhaps it's been so long since I've tasted anything but gruel I can't remember, but I swear this is truly unique." Homer stuffed the rest of his cake in his mouth and licked his fingers. "Thank you again, Nath. I know I don't deserve your generosity, being the wretch that I am."

"I've been too hard on you, Homer. You could have eaten this and not told me, but you are a true friend." He ate his cake while Homer licked his bowl clean. As Nath chewed, he bit into something dull and tasteless. He pulled a small piece of folded paper out of his mouth.

"What's that?" Homer said, setting his bowl down.

Nath unfolded the strip. "There's lettering on it. In common. 'You have allies. Use them. R.'"

"Who is R?"

Nath smiled. "It must be Radagan. I suppose he was real."

"You mean the baker who made these cream cakes? I must meet him and tell him what a talent he has. Incredible—"

Bzzzzzt!

The clamor of wrestling bodies on the other side of the curtain came to an abrupt end.

Nath felt sharp, familiar tingles running through his body. "I know that sound."

"Ew... sounds like the new prisoner just got kissed by Foster's smiting stick. I bet that hurts really bad, doesn't it?"

Nath grimaced. "It's worse than it sounds." He looked at the note again. "What allies is he talking about?"

"You are the Special. I think the other prisoners like you. At least that is what I have heard." Homer offered his hand as he looked at the note. "May I?" Nath handed Homer the note. The musician's eyes scanned it. He put it in his mouth and swallowed it.

"Fool!" Nath glared at Homer. He clamped his hand around the man's neck. "Why did you do that?"

CHAPTER 16

WITH A RASPY VOICE AND bulging eyes, Homer said, "Because. Because." He pointed at the curtain. Just as he did so, the broad-chested orc pushed through the fabric. With his keys in one hand and a club in the other, he limped to the cell.

Nath released Homer.

"Both of you get back in the corner." The orc wasn't even looking at them. Nath and Homer moved where the guard said. He put the key in the lock, twisted, and flung the door open. He knocked over the cots and waved the blankets. Kicking the straw strewn on the floor, he noticed the saucer and bowl. He picked them up. "Where did this come from?"

"One of the guards brought it, in error, I presume," Homer offered. "I thought it was odd that he brought clay over the wooden."

"Prisoner scum don't get earthenware," the orc said. He spit black juice on both Nath and Homer's cots and blankets. "I'll look into this. If I find out you're lying, I'll bust your heads open just like Foster did the new prisoner."

"Is he dead?" Homer inquired.

The orc stuck the end of his club in Homer's gut. Homer collapsed on the ground. "None of your business!" The orc marched out of the cell, slammed the doors, ripped out the keys, and headed through the curtain.

Nath helped Homer back to his feet. "You shouldn't talk so much."

Holding his gut, Homer said, "I wanted to push his buttons. He was hurt. Did you see it?"

Nath tilted Homer's cot back over and helped the man to sit. "Yes, something got the best of him. I hope to see what it was."

"Me too." Homer lay down.

"Sorry I choked you, Homer."

"You have a wee bit of a temper, but you need that fire to keep you going. You can't let them break you, Nath. You are the Special."

Nath straightened up his own cot and sat down. "What were you saying about other prisoners liking me? I don't even see any prisoners."

"No, but I do. I've been working the laundry when I'm not playing the strings for the slave lords. They ask about you. They think you can free them?"

Nath sat up. "Why would they think that? I can't even free myself. And why didn't you tell me this before?"

"You haven't been talking to me, that's why. I thought I'd keep my distance. But lately, it seems things are stirring. And that cream cake, I think it's a sign." Homer coughed. His forehead made thick wrinkles as his face reddened. "Woo-boy, that club to the belly smarts. But as I was saying, I think the prisoners want to rise up. They talk as if you are going to lead them."

"That's absurd. They don't even know me."

"What's to know? You are the Special that Foster can't break. They cling to hope that you will free them." Homer rolled on his side. "Nath, these men, they need something to cling to. It gets them through the night. Besides, I knew the moment I met you that you would get out of here. Maybe the rest of us won't, but you will."

"I'll leave when my buyer takes me," Nath said. "And then I'll make my mistake."

"Nath, you have no master. You never will. The rest of us are just dogs in a kennel, whipped and beaten until we are ready to serve our master. If we get one." Homer scratched the scruff on his jaw. "But not you. You are meant for something greater. Everyone knows that… but you."

Nath slept more in the prison than he'd ever slept in his life. Even though dragons were known for long slumbers, Nath required little sleep. That all changed during his time in Slaver Town. His body was broken, bruised, and exhausted. From the time he fell asleep, he slept like a stone until the guards stirred them early before dawn. The last several weeks had been the worst. Nath used to wake at the sound of the guards' scuffle of boots. Now he didn't wake until they hammered into the cell bars, making sounds like ugly bell chimes.

"Wake up, dirt! Wake up, maggots!" the guards hollered.

Nath used his fingers to peel his eyes open. His limbs felt like they were made from boards as he sat up. His wounded back made a sticky ripping sound as he peeled it from his cot. Coming to his feet, he rubbed the sandy grit from his eyes. Homer ambled out of the cell, limping with a painful expression on his face. Nath followed.

Beyond the curtain was the main courtyard of the prison. There were three levels of cells that went all the way around the inside of the barn. A wooden deck walkway was built out in front of the cells. Guards were posted on all decks. The first wave of prisoners had already headed outside. Many remained in their cells. In the courtyard, prisoners were standing behind tall wooden tables, digging their spoons into lukewarm bowls of bland porridge.

At the serving table, Nath and Homer picked up their bowls. An ugly man with a hunchback and bulging eye plopped spoonfuls of porridge in the wooden bowls. They took them to the table, where they stood and ate.

Nath noticed many of the prisoners were stealing glances at him. He'd paid little attention before—he was too tired to care—but they all had curious looks on their faces. Nath and Homer ate alone with a guard standing at either end of the table. There was no conversation, just heavy breathing and wooden spoons scraping in their bowls. As they quickly ate, Nath made a quick count of the cells. He'd done it dozens of times, but he couldn't help but do it almost every day.

Two hundred and two. The same as the day before yesterday.

There were two hundred cells. Sometimes there were two to a cell, maybe even three, he wasn't sure. But, there were at least three hundred prisoners if he had to guess. The guards within numbered forty. There were more than enough prisoners to overpower the guards, but they'd have to act as a single unit. He wondered if they were willing to do that. There were still hundreds of well-armed guards on the outside to consider. They were a small army, well trained and well equipped for any kind of trouble. The slave lords guarded prisoners like priceless treasure.

"Get moving," the guard said to Nath.

Nath gave Homer a quick nod and fell in line with the handful of prisoners who went to the quarry with him daily. Homer was taken out with another group with more delicate builds. They marched down the dusty road. The morning sun had just lifted over the outer wall. They approached the quarry, and the loud sound of metal heads striking the rock echoed through the town. Roosters crowed.

Taking the ramp down into the dark pit of rock, Nath's back started to ache. His feet were already burning when he took a hammer from one the guards. Someone in the pit was hammering away all alone in the middle of the quarry. The huge person had a broad, muscular back and a monstrous head of shaggy hair. He wasn't bigger than an ogre but towered over most men.

Nath approached the prisoner.

The prisoner alternated between swinging two sledgehammers at a time using four arms. Its powerful arms rotated between swings, busting the rocks to bits.

Nath's jaw hung open. It was the bugbear, the beast of a man who had once robbed him. He was the one teamed up with Calypsa, the half-dryad Nath had first run into when he left Dragon Home. "You!" Nath said.

Rond stopped hammering and turned. The bugbear's eyes ignited. He charged.

Chapter 17

Biceps pumping, Rond chopped downward with two overhand hammer swings. Nath crouched down, slipped inside of Rond's overextended swings, and punched the head of his sledgehammer into Rond's groin.

"Ooooooof!" the bugbear gushed out in pain.

Nath snuck underneath the bugbear's legs. He popped up behind the seven-foot-tall bugbear and hooked the hammer around Rond's neck. He pulled back on the handle, choking the life out of Rond. "What are you doing here, thief?"

Somehow, Rond choked out raspy words. "I'm going to kill you…"

"Not if I kill you first!" Nath pulled back hard. Rond's neck muscles were cords of iron. The beast of a man didn't give easily. Rond thrashed back and forth, slinging Nath side to side. Nath held on for his life. "Go down, monster!"

Rond went down all right, but it wasn't what Nath had in mind. The bugbear hopped up and pancaked Nath underneath his broad back.

Nath's breath came out in a gust. His healed-up ribs cracked again. The hard gravel and debris cut into his back. He held on. He wasn't sure what it was about Rond that sent a fire through him, but he only saw red now.

Rond rolled over the ground, taking Nath with him.

The prisoners and guards cheered.

Scraped up from head to toe, the two warriors went at it with all of their might. Rond dropped one of his hammers. With his two top hands, he grabbed the handle of Nath's sledgehammer and pulled it away. "You are not stronger than Rond! Redheaded weakling!"

"Hurk!" Nath yanked back on the handle. His strength seeped out of his trembling limbs. He didn't eat enough or rest enough to keep going on like this. His entire body had been exerted to its limit. He pulled back one last time. His fingers lost grip on the handle. "I hate you," he said in Rond's ear as his hammer slipped from his grasp.

Rond flung Nath onto the ground. Looming over Nath, he brought the hammer up high overhead.

The ground quaked.

Crack-Thoom!

Arms flailing, Rond fell backward. A seam split through the rock bottom between the two. All of the prisoners scattered, leaving Nath and Rond lying in the dust.

Nath rolled to his side. Foster stood several feet away, feet spread over the crack he'd just created in the bedrock. The mystic sledgehammer, Stone Smiter, rested on his shoulder. The arcane runes in the hammer's head coursed with red light. The gemstones on top of the hammer glowed brightly. Eyebrows buckled, in a threatening tone he said, "If either one of you move a muscle, I will turn your bones into dust."

Nath had already felt a kiss from Stone Smiter before. That was just a shock. He had no idea the hammer had even more power. He swallowed and dipped his chin twice.

"I said not a muscle, prisoner!" Foster walked over to Nath. His hands squeezed the hammer's handle and twisted. "Just give me a reason."

Nath knew that Foster would not hurt him, but there was murder in the half-orc's eyes. He looked at him for moment then looked at Rond.

"Bugbear, do you know this man?" Foster took the hammer off his shoulder and walked up to Rond. "It seems as if you know each other."

Sitting on his backside, leaning on all four hands behind him, Rond scowled. "I robbed him, long ago."

"Ah." Foster rested the sledgehammer back on his shoulder. "That is an interesting story. A bugbear that is a thief, whose past has caught up with him, not once but twice." Foster slung his three ponytails over his back. "The best way to stop a thief from stealing is to cut off his hands. And you have four of them. Listen to me, bugbear. Settle yourself, or I will take my hammer and smash those greedy paws of yours into gravy. Do you understand?"

Rond nodded.

Foster turned back on Nath. "As for you. I can only imagine how precious something must have been to you for you to act out like this. It gives me a chuckle. What was stolen? I know it wasn't your ego. No, you still have plenty of fire in you. And I'd begun to suspect it had died. Too bad for you. So, what was it, prisoner?"

"My gold," Nath said, keeping his eyes averted.

"Hah! Good! The bugbear probably spent it on all of the cattle and ale he could eat and drink. Guards, put them both in the stocks!"

One of the guards said to Foster, "But, the bugbear has four arms."

"Then chain the other two hands down, idiot!"

Chapter 18

Clamped in the stockades, Nath glared at Rond. The bugbear was in the stockade across from his, staring right back at him. The brute's neck and wrists were tight in the stocks. His fingers were swollen and red and his ugly face flushed. Nath had no sympathy for the bugbear's discomfort. His bonds pinched all the same. Even the drenching rain didn't bring him comfort. The hard drops needled on his back. Finally, Nath broke the silence. "This is your fault."

Rond snarled at him.

Normally, the guards would be right on top of Nath for speaking, but now, they took shelter from the rain, on a porch not so far away. There were two guards sitting in chairs. One reached his hand out, filling a bucket full of rain water. He set it down off the porch and resumed talking to the other.

At the moment, Nath would rather be busting rocks. Instead, he was back in the stocks again, suffering as much as ever. In truth, he couldn't blame Rond for it. When he saw the bugbear, he just snapped. The bugbear and the dryad were his first encounter out of Dragon Home, and they tricked him and stole from him. He got back what he'd lost, but there had been nothing but trouble ever since.

Water dripped from his face. Puddles formed on the muddy ground. He pulled against his stocks. The effort bit into his wrists. "Gads!"

To make matters worse, he revealed to Foster the fire that still burned in him. He'd been docile, and it allowed him to get into a routine. Now, he'd blown that. "I'm such a fool," he said out loud. The heavy rain drowned his words so that even he could barely hear them. "Such a fool."

"You are a fool, for certain." Rond's large, pointed ears were flared out and wiggling. Metal hoop earrings were pinned in his ears. His face was more like a dog than a man. Hair covered his chin and face like a pelt of fur. His beady eyes were bright as a night demon's. "A fool indeed," he said in a gravelly voice.

"Excuse me. You dare call me a fool, Rond!"

"You said it yourself, and I agree, fool."

"I wasn't talking to you. I was talking to myself. But with you having ears the size of paddles, I suppose I shouldn't be surprised that you heard me. And I'm not a fool, just... never mind."

Rond's neck twisted in the stock. He let out a hollow laugh. "You are a fool and you know it. You are here, aren't you? Only fools wind up in a place like this."

"Then you are as big a fool as I am."

"No, I wasn't made to come here, unlike you. You were captured by Prawn. I allowed myself to be captured by the slavers."

"How did you know about Prawn?" Nath demanded. "Is this more trickery? More lies? You must have overheard that."

"No, I was there outside of Riegelwood when the Black Hand released you to Prawn. We saw the exchange." Rond managed a quick shake of his face. "Bloody rain. I hate rain."

For the moment, all of Nath's irritating agonies faded. His mouth hung open. He was stupefied. Once again, it seemed as if everyone knew what was going on but him. He wondered if perhaps Rond was a part of the Black Hand, or something else. After sorting his thoughts in the soaking rain, his temper ignited again. "Why didn't you help me?"

"Hah! We don't care about you. We want those items you stole from us."

"Stole from you? You stole them from me! You thief! Robber! Liar!"

The guards on the porch were leaned in their chairs with two legs on the planks. They leaned forward, putting all four legs on the deck. The one that had the bucket stood, peering at Nath through the rain. The stare lasted several seconds. The orc guard picked up the bucket, sat down, and the guards shared a drink.

"Those items belong to whoever has them, the way I see it," Rond said. "Either way, they are the Black Hand's now."

"For all I know, you and that little trickster, Calypsa, are members of the Black Hand. How else would you know about it?"

Rond didn't reply.

"Where is your little partner in crime? Is she taking up quarters somewhere with the slavers? Perhaps, she is a Black Hand member, or one of their mistresses."

Rond thrust his frame against the stock. The boards groaned but held fast. His two free arms strained against the chains that tethered them down. The fingers on his hands flexed. "Don't you talk about her like that. I will tear your head off for it."

The angry expression on Rond's face said it all. He'd found a soft spot in the bugbear. Nath considered drilling down on the bugbear's emotions, but if he did, he'd never find out why Rond would get caught on purpose. He remembered a saying Balzurth said.

Words can be used for weapons, but that is never wise. Soothing words can gain the favor of even the most troublesome man.

Leveling off his tone, Nath said, "Rond, I grudgingly apologize. Calypsa is your friend, I respect that."

The bugbear's hard stare could crack a mirror, but the wrinkles in his clenched face softened.

"Why are you here, Rond? And where is Calypsa?"

"She was captured with me, for a stupid reason."

"You really allowed yourself to be captured?" Nath managed to shake his head a little. "Why in Nalzambor would you do that?"

Rond looked right at Nath and said with disdain, "We are here to rescue you."

Chapter 19

"THAT'S THE BIGGEST LIE I'VE ever heard," Nath said. "It's insulting that you would expect me to believe it."

"You are a self-admitted fool, but what I say is truth," Rond replied. "And I'm a fool for going along with it. She's a crazy dryad. She doesn't think the way that she should."

"Most likely, the both of you were captured for stealing, and now you want me to get you out of this. Well, it's not happening. You are on your own, and when I escape it will be without you. I'll do it on my own." Nath stretched his fingers out absentmindedly. He wanted to wipe the water from his eyes. His hand was fastened down over a foot from his head. "I hate the stockades! Great Guzan, I've had enough of this!" He rocked against the contraption. "Blast!"

"You won't make it out of here without us. Not with those irons. You would have made it out by now if you could have."

Nath didn't have a hard time not believing a word Rond said. He'd been lied to by everyone he'd met thus far, and bugbears certainly didn't have any credibility. They were an evil brood that Nath had studied about in Dragon Home, though Rond seemed different. Still, Rond's words did have a ring of truth about them that he couldn't shake. "What do you mean that she is a crazy dryad?"

"She wants to rescue you, doesn't she? We are in Slaver Town, aren't we? Who does that?"

"I think why is the question," Nath said. "Why would she want to rescue me? She must need something, right? And why now? I've been here two years."

Rond mumbled something.

"What?" Nath said.

The bugbear sighed. "Calypsa fancies you."

"Fancies me?" Nath perked up. "You mean to tell me that she is going to all of this trouble because she likes me?" He belted out a laugh. "Hahahaha."

Rond shrugged his arms that were chained to the ground. "It is laughable, and it stinks. She's not been the same since she met you. She says you are special. That we need to help you."

"Special?" Homer had been telling Nath that the other prisoners were calling him that. They seemed to see something in him that he didn't see in himself. He didn't understand it. He knew he was different, but what was it that other people saw? "So, I'm so special that she wants to save me for nothing in return?"

"It's lovesickness. A madness that must overcome dryads. That's what I tell her. I've been trying to move on, but she won't stop speaking of you. After we failed to retrieve our items from the Black Hand, she became even more convinced that we needed to find you."

"You went up against the Black Hand? To steal my items that were stolen from me?"

"Aye." Rond's ears tilted forward and back. "Caly spent months planning it. She tried to infiltrate their ranks. They became wise to her, and she almost died before she finally escaped. That's a wicked brood. Thieves and killers. She said if she was going to die, she'd die doing the right thing for a change. She said she wanted to try and save you." Rond's ears sagged. "And I'd die to save her, even if it meant trying to save you."

"That's quite a change in disposition," Nath said as his heart softened. As crazy as it all sounded, he believed Rond. "Where is Calypsa now?"

"She's slated for the slaver's blocks, I'm certain. A woman as radiant as her will fetch the highest of prices, but no one can keep her. She has her way of escaping anything. You'll see."

"Do you really think that she'll be able to get us all out of here? Even if we overtake the wall, they'll give chase. They have hundreds of soldiers, and let's not forget the hounds. We'll need a long head start, at least you will. I'm pretty sure none of them can catch up with me."

"She's working on it. She's been in here for a month now. When everything is in order, be ready to go."

"A month? But you just came here."

"That was the plan."

"But certainly they would have sold her by now. Perhaps she's gone. How do you even know she is here?"

The rain subsided.

"I know. I've seen her. She's here." Rond's gravelly voice carried.

The orcs came out from under the porch with scourges in hand. They gave Nath and Rond both a couple of licks on the back of their legs. Nath still had a hundred questions for Rond, but eyeing the lashes, he bit his tongue.

Chapter 20

Nath stayed in the stocks until the evening of the next day, when he was taken back to his cell. He hadn't been able to say another word to Rond either. The bugbear only spent one full day in the stocks before he was taken away. It was late when his cell door was opened. Homer lay fast asleep but stirred when the door slammed shut. Once the guard cleared the room, he slowly sat up.

"How are you, Nath?"

Lying back on his cot, Nath said, "Other than feeling like my back is on fire, I couldn't be much better. You?"

"Just worried about you. Sorry to hear that you were put in the stockade. I heard you put up quite a fight with that four-armed bugbear. He's quite a sight."

Nath closed his eyes. "You saw him?"

"I saw both of you buttoned up in the wood when I crossed through to my duties. It was just a long peek." Homer sat with his fingers locked together, rolling his thumbs over top of one another. "I felt for you."

"Well, better me than you, I suppose." Nath yawned. All of his life he'd never been tired. He rested some, yes, but always felt as spry as a woodland deer. Now, he was exhausted, always. "You have to forgive me if I pass out on you again. I'm bushwhacked. It's so bad, I fear to fall asleep because I know I'll be woken the moment I close my eyes. Do you feel as tired as I am?"

"Doing the laundry isn't as backbreaking as busting stones, but these bags under my eyes aren't signs of good rest. At least your eyes aren't tired. You are young. I suppose it keeps you together."

Nath wanted to mention he was one hundred years old, but held his tongue. He was actually one hundred and two years old, but who was counting? Every day had become an eternity of agony. The nights were like winks between the days. Life in Slaver Town was truly miserable. Now, after his talk with Rond, he was too exhausted to even think about all the bugbear had said. He summoned a little more energy and asked Homer something anyway.

"Homer, have you seen any suspicious women when you are out and about executing your charges?"

"I see a few women being taken to the blocks sometimes." Homer scratched the scruff on his chin. "Others work in the homes of the slave lords, doing chores, like I do. They cook, clean, and gather for the slave lords. They run the shops and stores. You know, this would be a suitable city if not for these foul lords. With the natural spring it could be a sanctuary. It's a shame that these orcs and slavers run it. Nath?"

Nath barely caught the man's soft words. He snuggled down a little more in his cot and pulled a blanket over him. "You talk too much, Homer. Listen, there is a woman named Calypsa. You would know her if you saw her. Her face is beautiful, and her chestnut hair flows down in piles on her shoulders. She has a rich tan, with wine-colored lips as soft as rose petals. A true natural beauty as if she was birthed by nature." He smiled. "Unforgettable."

"I can't say I've ever seen a woman such as that." Homer looked up at the top corner of the cell, squinting. "Why would she be here?"

"She's going to help me escape," Nath said as he dozed off.

Homer shook his head and covered up under his blanket and lay back down. He said, "Poor Nath. Now he's delirious from a lack of rest. Now, he's dream talking."

Nath dreamed. He fell through the sky, passing through portal after portal, seeing different parts of the world as he passed. He screamed the entire time. It was the fear of falling and hitting the ground; it was the fiery flying beast that pursued him. He'd lose the flaming dragon-shaped monster in one portal, only to see it chase him down again in the next. There was no way for Nath to run or change direction. All he could do was fall and scream as the beast bore down on him, getting closer and closer.

A warm jolt woke him. He sat up. "Gah!" He found himself looking right at Calypsa, who was sitting on his cot.

With a warm and inviting smile, she said, "Hello, Nath Dragon. Did you miss me?"

Nath blinked. At first, he thought he was dreaming, but he felt fully alert and revitalized. He noticed her hand was holding his. Energy flowed from her into him. "Calypsa? It's really you?" he asked, trying to pull his hand away.

She held his hand in a strong grip. "There is only one me, obviously. So, it couldn't be anyone else but me. Do you feel better?"

"Much," Nath said. He felt better than he'd felt in two years, actually. He flexed his arm. "Much better. Thank you."

"You looked so worn out. I just had to help you." She crawled into his lap and put her hands over his neck. "Did you miss me?"

Her warm, alluring body seemed to merge with his. She nuzzled her face into him. Her soft lips brushed against his neck. His heart started pounding in his chest. Calypsa nuzzled his neck. It felt so good having the curvy woman in his lap. Her hair tickled his nose. But now, with his strength back, he managed to control his own passion. "Not to be without thanks, but I've been so miserable, I hadn't been able to think about you or anyone. I just want out of here."

She stopped nuzzling his neck and looked at him with a straight face. "You haven't thought of me at all?"

"I have, some, but I never thought I would see you again," he admitted.

"And when you thought about me, what did you think about?" she said.

Nath didn't want to say what he thought. He was mad at her for robbing him in the first place. That's when his entire life started to slide downhill. He changed the subject. "Calypsa, how did you get in here?" The door to his cell was locked shut. "And what about the guards? What if they find you in here?"

"Then we will die together," she said. Just as she finished, a guard came through the heavy curtain. Calypsa waved at the man. "Hello."

Nath couldn't believe his ears. *Rond was right. She's crazy!*

CHAPTER 21

"TELL ME THIS IS A dream," Nath said, as the guard marched right up to him. The guard wasn't an orc, but a man. The ringmail and tunic he wore fit loosely on his body, and his shoulders were broad, making his head look smaller. He seemed familiar. Nath swallowed then said, "Tell me you don't see a woman on my lap."

"Well of course I do. A very fetching one at that," the guard said in a friendly voice.

Nath's head tilted. "Radagan?"

The man grinned. "You remember?"

"Well, of course I remember, but you shrank."

Radagan slapped the small belly he still had with his hands. "I still keep a little bit of the old me around. As a reminder of how big I was." He hitched his thumb over his shoulder. "I could have dressed myself in that curtain back in the day. So, how have you been, Nath?"

"I've been rather miserable until now," he said. Calypsa lay against his chest with her eyes closed, breathing in and out deeply. "How did you get so small, Radagan? And why are you a guard?"

Casually, Radagan leaned against the cell bars. "Well, being in the hold broke me of my bad eating habits, it seemed. I don't know, but I just changed. The fat fell off me after that, but I still indulge a bit in the kitchen, but mostly on the slow days. You see, once I got fit, I told them I wanted to join the guards. Isn't that something. Look at me, I have armor and a club." He pulled his club out of his belt and dropped it on the floor. It made a loud clatter. "Whoops." He reached down to pick it up and kicked it away. Finally, he grabbed it and stuck it back in his belt. "Sorry, I get excited."

"I thought only orcs were guards," Nath said, staring at the curtain. Given the amount of racket going on, he expected more guards to come in at any moment.

"They are increasing the force," Radagan said. "A few men, born and raised in Slaver Town like me, have been added. That happens time to time. I guess I'm one of the lucky ones. And the orcs have their training outside in the fields, so they need to leave another force behind. They have more training coming on soon. That's when they ride the horses, take the dogs, and hunt after prisoners they have loosed. I hope I get to do that soon."

Nath tapped Calypsa on the shoulder.

"Yes?" she said, looking at him with dreamy eyes.

"I think you have some explaining to do. Both of you. How am I to escape again?"

Radagan's eyes grew big. "Escape? Caly, you didn't say anything about escape. You just said you wanted to see him. I can't be privy to any escape plan. I'll lose my position."

She shooed Radagan away with her hand. "Just go away and make sure no other guards hear your blathering. I'll explain it all to Nath and to you later."

With a little grunt, Radagan shuffled away, stepping beyond the curtain.

"So, what is the plan, *Caly*?" Nath asked.

"Oh, I like it when you call me Caly. It's very personal." She walked her fingers up his bare chest. "Say it again."

"One more time, and you explain, Caly?"

"You have such a soothing voice, Nath Dragon. I love it."

Homer stirred. He looked right at Nath and Calypsa, blinked a few times, shook his head, pulled the blanket over him, and started snoring.

"Out with it, Caly," Nath said.

"The prisoners and slaves are ready to revolt. They are convinced that you will lead them," she said, looking at her fingernails. "The day after the guards head outside to train for the slave hunts, the slaves within will be ready to act. There will be a sign. The slaves will turn on their masters and on the guards, and during all of the commotion of battle, we, you and I, will make our escape."

"You've told these people I am leading a revolt? Are you insane?" Nath clamped her wrists in his hands. "Innocent people will die."

"Pfft. These people are criminals. Who cares what happens to them? All that matters is that you and I are free to be together forever." She batted her eyes at him. "And ever."

Nath wanted out, but he wasn't willing to risk the lives of others to do so. It wasn't right. People like Radagan, born in Slaver Town, could be hurt or even killed. The same could happen to Homer. "Caly, you can't do this. I don't want others to suffer on my account."

"Don't be silly, Nath. They are already suffering, and they are choosing to do this." She looked him dead in the eye. "Would you not risk your own life for freedom, Nath? Or the freedom of others? Don't deny the others the same opportunity."

"These people are broken. They will not fight."

"They will when they have something to fight for. Nath, you are not here by chance. You are here to be their liberator. At least, I've convinced them of that. You are the Special."

"So, that is what you have been doing since you've been here? Getting their hopes up in me?" Nath said, exasperated.

"You have to admit it is an excellent plan."

"It's a horrendous plan."

"How is freeing you a horrendous plan, Nath Dragon?" She scowled. "I'm risking everything for you, and this is the thanks I receive. These people are nothing. But you are something. They all can see it, but you can't. Maybe you don't want to get your hands dirty, but there is no other way out of here unless you do. As for slaves, do you really think they want to be slaves?" She got on her feet. "At least I've given them something to believe in. You."

"My idea of leaving was slipping out on a wagon loaded with block. Not by distracting the slavers with a war. These people are too weak to fight, Caly. They'll be slaughtered."

"Then so will you," she said. Somehow, her body shimmered, and she squeezed through the narrow bars like a rubbery cat.

Nath moved to the bars. "Calypsa," he said, marveling. "How did you do that?"

"I can do many things. You should trust me." Standing on the other side of the bars, she said, "There will be a riot, Nath Dragon. And there will be an exit. Whether or not you take it is up to you."

"I'm not going anywhere with these irons on. And they watch me like a hawk."

"Don't you think I've thought of that?" She shook her head, frowning, turned, and left the room.

Scratching his head, Nath said to himself, "What just happened?"

CHAPTER 22

OVER THE COURSE OF THE next several days, Nath spent his time busting rocks in the quarry. It was just him and about twenty other slaves, the same as always. The bugbear kept his distance. He didn't look Nath's way, not once.

With a steady rhythm, Nath's sledgehammer came down on the rock. Chips of stone flew. Rock split off in chunks. A bald, broad-backed dwarf would dig the hunks of stone out of the crevices with his hands and haul them away. The dwarf, who never spoke a word, now hummed. He even glanced at Nath a few times with his hard eyes.

Nath peered around, checking his surroundings. Unless he was going crazy, the slaves had a bit of a spring in their step. At the same time, the guards were oddly quiet. Even Foster, who sat at the top on his tall chair, didn't have much to say. It was as if they were all going through the motions, waiting for something to happen.

With the sun at its zenith, the prisoners were taken into the shade and given a water break. They sat along the wall and passed oak buckets down the row to one another. Hard loaves of bread were passed between them. Nath's eyes swept the upper rim of the quarry. He was hoping to see Calypsa. He hated the way things were left.

But she's crazy.

He'd mulled over her plans and even shared them with Homer.

"Women will go to great lengths when they are in love with a man. I'd be flattered, if I was you."

That wasn't all of the conversation either. When Nath asked Homer if he would risk his life to be free, he was surprised at the musician's answers. "Wouldn't death be better than a life such as this? At least the slaves can die fighting for themselves, rather than dying weak and withered, like a sun-scorched flower, at the hands of their cruel masters. I think they would be with you, Nath."

The plan wasn't for Nath to lead a fight, however. The plan was for the fight to allow Nath to escape. He couldn't do that. But again, Homer surprised him.

"If the slaves can free one prisoner among them, then it is a victory for them. They want to stick it to the guards, to Foster and the slave lords, and make fools of all of them," Homer said. "Perhaps, Nath, now is not the time to free all of us. Perhaps you can be freed, come back, and put an end to this place. All days are the same for us, you know that, but give us hope for a new day, when the sunshine and rain can be enjoyed again."

"Break's over," one of the guards said. It was a man. The guard force was down to half of their number. Where there used to be twenty, there were only ten. In the barn, there were less than twenty, as opposed to the forty Nath normally counted. It made Nath nervous. There was tension in the air, like the calm before the storm. He got up, grabbed his hammer, and got back to work.

The slave hunt training was going on somewhere beyond the wall. If Nath were to guess, at least half of the orcs were gone. He figured there were five or six hundred guards in all, and even though men had replaced some of them, it only appeared to be a couple of dozen at most. At this point, the slaves vastly outnumbered the guards, at least three, if not four to one.

Now would be the perfect time to do it. If the slaves wanted, they could take over the entire city, bar the guards on the outside by defending the walls from within. Heh, it would work if it were well coordinated.

Lost in thought, Nath pounded away at the rock, with several scenarios playing through his mind. In midswing, he heard the crunch of a foot stop on the rocks behind him. He checked his swing and turned.

Foster stared down Nath with his head tilted slightly. He held his sledgehammer, Stone Smiter, in front of his waist with two hands. A pair of guards flanked Foster from behind. They had swords on their hips, not clubs. "It's awfully quiet," Foster said to Nath, "too quiet. I have a feeling that something is going on, Nath."

Nath's blood froze. Foster never called him by name. Something else occurred to him too.

The guards didn't have their clubs, just the lash, but swords were now strapped on their hips. Nath had been so tired and preoccupied he'd missed it. He could only think one thing. *Oh gads, he's on to us!*

CHAPTER 23

NATH RESUMED HIS SWINGING. THE hammer head struck stone.

Bang!

How can he be on to me when I haven't even done anything? It had eaten at Nath that if Calypsa did indeed stir up the slaves, then they would be talking. What were the chances that the guards wouldn't overhear them? Certainly, they knew the slaves and their habits. If something was up, the guards would know. *You don't know anything. You haven't heard anything, Nath. Everything with Caly was just a dream.*

"I don't know what you are talking about, Foster," he said while swinging. *Bang!* "If something is going on, I'm sure you'd be certain that I'm the last to know. Besides, I thought you knew all that happened in your slave yard."

"Oh, but I do." Foster licked his puffy lips. "You see, even though there is a lot of orc in me, I have a very calculating mind. You might be interested to know that my father was an engineer on the towers in Narmum. A brilliant man who would lay block that will not fall. That is where these stones go. He taught me a few things when I was young. He said, 'Pay attention. There are always signs before a change. You will feel it in your bones, so long as you always pay attention.' My bones quaver, Nath. I want you to tell me what is going on."

Nath kept hitting.

Bang! Bang! Bang!

"I don't know what you want me to say. You have your guards, though I guess some of your men are away for training during the slave hunt." He brought the weapon high overhead and brought it down. *Bang!* "I didn't want to tell you I knew that because you would punish me for knowing. But Homer, my cellmate who does laundry, shares what he hears with me." He drew the hammer back over his shoulder.

Foster grabbed the sledgehammer by the handle with an iron grip. "Stop swinging and keep talking."

Fighting the urge to glance around, Nath continued. Mopping the sweat from his brows on his forearm, he said, "Fine, I could use the rest. Where were we? You were telling me about your mother, weren't you?"

"My mother? I don't speak about my mother. She was an orcen tramp who abandoned me and my father."

"I can't say that I blame her. You were probably a very rotten son. Did you have any other brothers and sister—"

Foster slugged Nath in the stomach.

"Oof!" Nath landed on his knees. "I guess that's a no," he sputtered out.

"Stop delaying, fool! Keep talking about the prisoners. What do you know?"

Catching his breath and holding his stomach, Nath said, "I don't know why you are interrogating me. You should ask them. I don't even consort with any of them." Foster drew back. Nath put his hands up. "Listen, I think that they are excited that the orcs are gone. They would see it as an opportunity to escape while your numbers are weakened. But, it's purely fantasy. I'm sure that you've dealt with this before, during times like this."

"True, but not with you here. Not with the one they call the *Special*."

Nath's heart skipped. Cleary, Foster had his ear to the ground, and he knew exactly what was going on. If anything started now, it would be a disaster. He glanced at the guards' swords. "You are amply equipped for any sort of riot." He lifted his chained wrists. "And I'm not a threat. I just want to get away from you and serve my master, whoever that might be."

"You lie. You want to escape. Of course, you want to escape." Foster stuck the head of his hammer in Nath's face. "But the only escape from here, for anybody else but you, is death. And that will include your cellmate."

Angered, Nath said, "Foster, I have learned my lesson. I'm following my orders, biding my time until the master I serve comes. Leave others out of this thing that you created." He caught the ogre, Torno, pushing the huge wheelbarrow their way. There was a half full load in it. He came to a stop a few feet behind the guards that came with Foster. "Eh, I think your big pet wants something."

Foster turned his head and gave Torno a look. "What do you want, ogre? Load your rocks and go away." He turned toward Nath. "I should have let him kill you. Oh, I wish I would have."

"Why do you hate me so much?" Nath asked.

"Because you are you, and I am me. I hate everybody." Foster rested his hammer back on his shoulder. With his free hand, he reached into his belt pouch and produced a rock the size of an egg. It was made of cinnamon-red crystal that matched the small stones embedded in Torno's collar. "Torno, you don't want to draw my ire today, do you?" The stone flickered in his palm. "Now, take those rocks up the ramp before I have you sucking your thumb like an ape."

Nath looked at Torno. The towering ogre lifted a huge maul that was sitting in the wheelbarrow. His brow crinkled. That's when Nath saw it. Or didn't see it. The ogre's restraint collar was gone.

Foster must have seen a curious look in Nath's eyes. The half-orc suddenly twisted around. "Torno, where is your collar?"

With the suddenness of a thunderclap, the ogre unleashed a hard, powerful, bone-breaking swing. The massive maul collided with the two guards, sending them flying head over heels.

Foster lifted Stone Smiter and charged. "Tooorno!"

CHAPTER 24

ON INSTINCT, NATH DOVE ON top of Foster's legs. The half-orc collapsed on the ground. Nath climbed up the half-orc. He tried to get the chain connecting his wrist irons over the slaver's neck. Foster threw a hard elbow into Nath's chin. The stunning blow rocked Nath's head backward. At the same time, the half-orc hooked his arm, flipped him, and rolled on top of him.

Foster put Nath in a one-armed headlock and started punching his face. "I knew you were behind this!"

In the background, Torno fought against the guards who surrounded the brutish ogre. The enraged ogre swung the maul in long, sweeping blows. The guards dove to the ground.

Nath grabbed Foster's hands. "I wasn't part of this, but I'm in it now!" Foster wouldn't let go of his hammer, so Nath used his own skill against the man. Without thinking, he punched Foster in the gut, only to have his fist bust into his own armor.

"Heh-heh," Foster sniggered as they wrestled over the ground. "It's good armor, isn't it? I feel impervious in it."

"Impervious? That's an awfully big word for someone with such a little mind." Making his fists into one, he swung an awkward strike into the slaver's face.

Foster's head snapped back. Blood spilled from his nose. He spit it from his teeth. "Now you're just making me mad." With a heave, the half-orc shoved Nath aside. The gemstone on top of his hammer ignited. A ray of light shot out of the hammer into Nath's body.

Bzzzzaat!

Nath convulsed on the ground. Burning needles raced through his bloodstream. The hair on his arms stood up and smoldered.

Foster loomed over him with his mystic hammer in hand. "Once I kill the ogre, I'll deal with you next. I'll deal with all of you!" He marched right at Torno. "Get away, all of you! I'll deal with this beast!" Foster faced off with Torno.

The ogre lifted the maul over his head. Aiming at Foster, he brought the maul down with all of his might. Foster ran inside of the ogre's swing and turned loose a swing of his own. The sledgehammer hit Torno in the chest, making the sound of cracking thunder. Torno's body, limbs and all, quavered like jelly. His eyes rolled up in his head. He staggered a few steps on wobbly legs, hit the ground with a thump, and died.

"No," Nath muttered. Seeing the ogre die sent a charge right through him. All around him, the slaves had engaged the guards in a fight. Rond was among them, heaving stones and swinging hammers with all his might. Rocks busted into the soft bodies of the men. The sledgehammers busted into bones. But up on the ramps, more guards were coming with their swords drawn and fire in their eyes. The slaves were about to be slaughtered. "I can't let this happen. Not because of me."

Foster fixed his eyes on Rond. With the hammer glowing, he made a straight line for the bugbear.

Fighting through the pain, Nath picked up a sledgehammer and rose to his feet. He yelled the half-orc's way, "Foster, where are you going? We aren't finished."

The half-orc turned. He said to his guards, "Deal with the bugbear! I'll take care of this one… permanently." The slave guards drew their swords and took after Rond and the other prisoners. Foster advanced on Nath. "You shouldn't even be on your feet after that jolt from my hammer. Your fortitude is surprising. But now, you are going to feel the full wrath of me and my hammer. I'm no longer going to preserve you for your master. Your fate is sealed."

Nath wasn't sure if he had gotten used to the hammer's jolts or if it was from Calypsa healing him, but one thing was for sure, he'd had enough of it all. If Foster wanted a fight, he was going to get it. He locked his eyes on the master slaver. "Foster, only one of us is going to leave this pit. It's time to find out who it is."

"Come! Greet your doom, then, you redheaded fool!" Foster hoisted the sledgehammer over his shoulder and charged.

With a foot-length of chain tethering Nath's ankles together, he advanced with short, stiff, wooden steps. He lifted his sledgehammer handle to parry just as Foster's hammer came down. Nath hopped aside. Foster's hammer slammed into the stone, sending hunks of stone exploding out of the ground. Nath swung at the half-orc's back. Quick for a big man, Foster turned into Nath's swing. Nath's hammer head bounced off the armor on Foster's chest. Nath's arms shook up to his shoulders from his own strike.

"This armor is a wonder!" Foster said. "Your little hammer can't harm me, but my hammer will squash you like a bug. You'll die the same as Torno, but unlike him, I'm going to make you suffer first."

"You can't kill what you can't hit!" Nath jabbed his hammer at Foster's face. The slaver's head snaked back. Foster was not only strong, but he was quick, and skilled for a fighter. It was clear by the calluses on his hands and scars on his face that he'd been in many battles in his lifetime. Nath backed away, swinging the sledgehammer in wide arcs, keeping the advancing half-orc at bay.

"I'm going to enjoy breaking you one bone at a time," Foster said. His nostrils flared, and his chest heaved. Keeping his eyes fixed on Nath's, he cocked Stone Smiter behind his hips and turned loose a swing. The burning gem on the top of Stone Smiter made an arcing streak like a star.

The hammer heads clacked together. *Kraaang!* A heavy soundwave knocked Nath from his feet. His sledgehammer flew from his fingers. He landed hard on the ground with his ears ringing. He lay flat on his back. Tilting his chin, he caught Foster rushing him. The hammer, at its full height above the half-orc's head, glowed with angry fire.

Gads, he's really going to kill me! Move, Nath, move!

Not knowing what to do as his mind went blank, his body lay still, awaiting the hammer's last call.

Stone Smiter came down.

CHAPTER 25

NATH'S LIFE FLASHED BEFORE HIS eyes. He saw his friends' and enemies' faces. His father, Balzurth, and last of all, Dragon Master Elween. The forest dragon sat perched on her stone in the training room, lecturing Nath. The words Master Elween spoke a hundred times before came to life.

"Make your weakness a strength, and your enemy's strength a weakness."

In the past, those words passed through Nath's ears like the wind in a tunnel, but today, they registered loud and clear. A spark of thought ignited. His dragon-quick reflexes went into action. Seated, he hopped backward a full body length. At the same time, he spread his ankles wide apart.

Stone Smiter crashed down on the chains between his irons, making a loud *crack-chink* sound. Stone chips flew into Nath's eyes. He tasted the rocky gust and a bit of metal on his tongue. As Foster's hammer rose again, Nath caught a glimpse of the chains on his ankle. The metal was bent and busted. His legs were free. "Haha! You missed, you clumsy half-orcling!" From his knees, Nath laid his head on a slab of stone. "Here's my face. I bet you can't squash it like a melon. But you can try if you like."

Stormy-eyed and spitting, Foster let out a growl. He took aim at Nath's head and unleashed another fierce swing. "Raaaawh!"

Quick as a hummingbird's wings, Nath moved his head and replaced it with the chains on his wrists. The sledgehammer pounded into the links and stone.

Kraaak-chink!

The rock exploded in a plume of dusty smoke. Nath couldn't see through the dust. He fanned the smoking cloud from his face and realized he had full motion in his arms again. He spread them wide. *Yes!* At the same time, he lifted one knee to his chest. The chains were broken. His plan worked. He was fully free. "Sweet dragons, I can run again!"

Foster coughed. The dust cleared.

Coated in stone powder, Foster spit juice on the ground and twirled his hammer in big rings like a toy. "Are you going to run like a coward, or finish this fight, red hair?"

Nath considered running for the gate. With all of the commotion going on, now would be the perfect time to disappear. No one would catch him. However, surrounded by the clamor of battle, he knew many would die if he did not act. The least he could do was finish Foster. He set his eyes on the slaver master. "Let's finish this."

"I'm going to crush your face!" Foster rushed Nath. He stopped short as the gemstone on the hammer head flared.

Nath sprang high. A bolt of light shot across the quarry, ripping through the place he once stood, and burst into the backside of one of the guards. Nath landed, ducked, and rolled from a series of short, powerful swings.

"Stand still and fight, coward!" Foster twisted the hammer back and forth, making whooshing sounds in the air. The hammer head made bright streaks of light, showing its power.

Springing away from one fatal blow after the other, Nath ducked and dodged. "You can't kill what you can't hit, orc!"

"You won't be killing anything, either. I'll wear you—"

Out of nowhere, Nath hit Foster hard in the face with a right cross. The half-orc shuffled backward, blinking. Nath poured it on. Unleashing his anger, he hit Foster's hard face with punch after punch, shouting, "Dragon! Dragon!"

Foster parried with the sledgehammer and shoved Nath back with a desperate heave of his handle. Lathered up in sweat, the slaver started panting. "Stop hitting me!"

"Like this?" Nath slipped by the hammer and socked Foster in the jaw. *Whap!* "Or like this?" He hammered Foster in the ear. It felt like he was hitting a bag of solid bones, but the hardened half-orc's flesh was giving. Foster lowered his arms. Nath hit him in the face half a dozen times. *Whap! Whap! Whap! Whap! Whap! Crack!* The last shot busted the half-orc's nose.

Foster swayed side to side. He used Stone Smiter like a cane to hold him up.

"I can't believe you haven't fallen." Nath grabbed the hammer by the handle. He tugged against Foster's iron grip.

"Never!" Foster said, holding on to the hammer with white knuckles on his hands. "You will not have it. Never!" He launched a kick into Nath's groin. Nath went down to a knee with a groan. "Ever!"

Nath held on. In a fierce tug of war, he put his boot in Foster's chest. "Listen, orc, you might be strong, but you aren't stronger than a dragon!" With a yank of his arms, he pushed off with his foot and ripped the hammer from Foster's grip. The half-orc stumbled to the ground and landed on hands and knees, dripping sweat and gasping.

"Take off my armor," Nath demanded. He held the hammer now. It was heavy, but not as much as the regular sledgehammer. The handle of the great hammer felt like it had a life of its own, sending little pulsations through his fingers. It was power. Great power. Nath cocked it back. "Now, Foster!"

"Yes, yes, you have won." With effort, the half-orc unbuckled the breastplate and shimmied out of it. He set it in front of Nath. "You will never get out of here. You will always be a prisoner. Heh-heh. You'll see."

Nath bent over to pick up his armor. As he did, a sharp crack of stone and bone caught his ear. He turned. Rond the bugbear pummeled guards with hands full of stones. A sudden sharp pain dug into his side. He looked back. Foster had a dagger in his hand. His blood dripped from the blade. The half-orc had stabbed him.

CHAPTER 26

FOSTER SNIGGERED. "I TOLD YOU that you were going to die."

Clutching his side, Nath felt the warm blood on his fingers. His anger turned to rage as the gloating half-orc stood up with the dagger in his hand. The gem top of the hammer burned bright as a red star. Foster's face paled the moment he looked into Nath's eyes.

Nath hit Foster with everything he could.

The half-orc skimmed over the ground and slammed against the wheel of Torno's wheelbarrow. The slaver, his tormentor, was dead. Nath had never killed a person he knew so closely before. Something didn't feel right about it. He grabbed his armor and buckled it over his chest. Calypsa was right. No one was leaving Slaver Town without blood on their hands. Not even him.

"Nath!" Rond yelled. He had a sledgehammer in each hand and fought off two guards who were swinging swords. "Are you going to stand there and gawk at the dead, or are you going to help us fight our way out of here?"

Grinding his teeth, Nath stared at his tormentor's corpse. It left a hollow feeling inside him. And there were questions unanswered. Who was Foster working with that put Nath through so much suffering? The slave lords would know, but they were sight unseen. He would have to deal with them later.

On the top wall of the quarry, Calypsa stood with her arm up, waving a golden sash in her hand. "Let's get out of here!"

"I've been waiting for you!" Rond batted the soldiers' swords aside. He crushed them both underneath heavy blows with the hammer.

Nath and Rond ran toward the ramp. The guards rushed into their path. Nath and Rond swept them aside with sweeping blows. Nath pulled back his swings as the might of the sledgehammer took the inexperienced men from their feet with ease. The guards, orcs and men, were no match for the bugbear, or Nath wielding Stone Smiter. They ran up the ramp and knocked the onrush of guards aside, sending them tumbling down to the next level.

Just as they were about to the top, Rond let out a scream. "Eeeyargh!" A crossbow bolt sank into the back of his shoulder. More bolts clattered into the ramp and walls of stone.

Nath swung his head around. "There!" Guards were in one of the small, two-story guard towers on the rim of the quarry, firing at them. "Keep going, Rond! I'll take care of them." Nath jumped from the ramp to one of the ladders. With biting pain in his side, he scrambled up one more level to the top. A bolt shattered against his breastplate. Nath ran right at the nearest tower. Three guards fired at him and the slaves still in the quarry. The stone workers were engaged in a battle with the guards at ground level.

A tower guard fired. The bolt streaked through the air. Nath slid his head aside as the bolt whisked by his neck. He dashed underneath the tower and took the sledgehammer to its support leg. The wooden leg cracked under the hammer's might. The tower at the top teetered. The inner framework crashed down. Nath skipped away, watching the tower fall over into the quarry.

He jumped aside as a team of four white horses pulled a wagon right up to him. Calypsa sat in the seat, reins in hand, with Rond riding in the back of the wagon among the cut blocks of stones. "Get up here, Nath," the dryad said. "It's time to go!"

Nath climbed onto the bench beside her. "Go where? Those watchtowers are still filled with guards, and the main gate is sealed shut. Unless these horses can fly, I don't see another way out of here."

"Leave that to me!" Without snapping the reins, she yelled, "Eeeyah!" The wagon lurched forward. The wheels clattered over the road as they raced through the dusty streets of the city. The guards chased after slaves who streaked through the maze of buildings. The ones they caught were hauled off by their hands and their hair. Horns blared from the watchtowers. Every soldier was on deck, battling against the rioters.

Rond picked up blocks of stone and hurled them at the guards. Two crossbow bolts now protruded from his back. He took several guards to the ground with stones that smashed into them as they passed. "It's good! Hahaha! How is that for accuracy?"

Out of the chaos, more guards came. They attacked the wagon at the turns in the streets. Galloping through the chaos, the horses plowed over a lone guard, sending the wagon jumping off its wheels. Laughing, Calypsa said to Nath, "How do you like my driving?"

"I'd say much better than that guard back there did."

"You're funny, Nath Dragon. I like it!" With her beautiful face set against the wind, she drove the horses onto the road that led toward the main gate. The gate's doors were closed. A score of guards stood their ground. The towers on either side fired bolts at them. She tossed her head back and laughed again as a bolt zinged by her face.

Gaping, Nath said, "Calypsa, what are you doing? We can't ram this wagon through that gate. This isn't escaping. It's madness."

"Oh, you dragon of little faith, just hang on and let the dryad do the driving." She gave him a quick wink. "And by the way, I am crazy! Eeeeyah!"

Chapter 27

With less than one hundred yards between the wagon and the main gate, the crossbow bolts came closer to the mark. A bolt embedded itself between Nath's legs in his seat. "We are going to get skewered, Caly! Turn away!"

"No! I have a plan! Take these and drive my horses straight for that gate!" Calypsa handed him the reins.

The horses galloped onward at full speed, snorting and puffing like fearless beasts. Nath instinctively snapped the reins. "Yah!" Beside him, Calypsa had her eyes closed. Her hands were clasped together, and she had a serene look on her face. "Whatever you are doing, you better do it now!"

Rond shoved Nath in the back of his head. "Leave her be, fool. Can't you see she is concentrating?" With the wagon jostling over the road, the bugbear reached behind his back with the top two of his four hands and pulled the two bolts out of his shoulder. "Urg!" He slung them out of the wagon. "Those things hurt, but I've felt worse. Have you ever been stung by a zethrene hornet? It swelled me up like a ball for days."

"What are you talking about?" Nath yelled back to Rond while keeping his eyes fixed ahead. Now was the worst time for a conversation. In front of him, a score of guards were posted in front of the gate with spears pointed right at them. The gate, made of hard wooden planks covered by bars that sealed it closed, might as well have been a wall of stone. They weren't going anywhere except straight for their doom. He pulled back on the reins. "I'm turning away!"

"No!" Rond put his hands on Nath's shoulders and squeezed. "You must trust her. She gave everything for you, now give everything for her!"

A crossbow bolt ricocheted off Nath's chest armor. At the same time, he caught a bolt sailing right at Calypsa. He snatched it, inches from her face.

"Good catch," Rond commented.

They were fifty yards away from the main gate. Thirty-five yards away. The guards with spears cast nervous glances at one another. Suddenly, from the main gate, came a sound of wood popping and bending.

Calypsa's eyes opened wide, a bright forest-green glow emanating from them. Sweat beaded on her face. Quickly, she chanted ancient, unintelligible mystic words.

The main gate groaned. The men in the watchtowers cried out. The guards on the ground turned. The wood planks in the gate came to life and twisted like snakes. The heavy wooden beam that barred the gate shut slithered out of the brackets and over the ground at the guards. One end coiled back like a snake. It struck, hitting a guard full in the face and knocking the man out cold. At the same time, the main gate doors twisted and peeled back, opening a gaping hole between them.

"She did it!" Nath shouted. "Ah-hah! She did it!" He snapped the reins. "Eee-yah!"

Many of the guards on the ground dove out of the way of the charging wagon team. Another trio of guards stabbed spears futilely into the wood beam that attacked them. The tips dug in but did no harm. A guard, gaping at the main gate with his backside to the oncoming wagon, was plowed over by the horses. The wagon wheels jumped and crashed on the ground hard, causing Calypsa to bounce out of her seat.

Nath grabbed her and reeled her back in as they roared through the main gate.

"We are through!" Rond said with a big smile that didn't seem to come naturally for the bugbear. "Haha! Freedom!"

Behind them, the stark wooden walls of Slaver Town faded in the dust. Nath stole a glance at one of the watchtowers that overlooked the wall. A guard was waving. Nath recognized the face of Radagan. He wondered if the baker, turned into a guard, had anything to do with Calypsa's plans. At the same time, he was worried about the battle that brewed within. He was free, but what about all of the other slaves? What was in store for them, and men like Homer?

"We made it," Calypsa said. The glow in her eyes was gone. She leaned against Nath's chest.

"We are out," Nath said. "You did it, Caly."

"We might be out of the fort, but we are not out of danger." Rond stuck both index fingers of his right hands forward. "Look! The guards from the slave hunts return!"

Several score of the Slaver Town guards were coming back from their training. The warning horns from Slaver Town had already alerted them that some sort of danger was going on. Many of the guards were on horseback. The rest on foot led several teams of dogs.

"Great Guzan! That's half of the slaver army!" Nath clutched his bleeding side with one hand. The blood from the stab wound was thick on his fingers.

Seeing the blood on his hand, Calypsa's eyes grew big. "You are wounded!"

"I'll live."

"That is bad, Nath Dragon. You need healing for it," she said.

"I'm wounded too," Rond commented. He pointed two of his thumbs at his back. "I have two holes in my back. He only has one."

"Your back is thicker than a horse's saddle," she fired back. Her fingers dug into Nath's side. He grimaced. "You need this stitched, now, Nath Dragon. Be still while I mend you."

Leading the horses at full speed down the road, not so far ahead, the Slaver Town forces gathered along the forest road. "There's no time to be still for anything," Nath said. "Our enemy is upon us."

Chapter 28

Orcen guards from the slave hunt charged right at the wagon.

"Don't slow down!" Rond said.

"I'm not!" Nath snapped the reins.

"Nath, you need to be still so I can mend this. You're bleeding all over the seat," Calypsa said.

"It's going to have to wait. We aren't stopping now!" He handed the reins back to the dryad. "You lead the horses while Rond and I fight." He picked up the sledgehammer and stood halfway up on the right side of the wagon. In the back of the wagon, Rond picked up two blocks and moved to the left. "It's time to fight!"

The slave guards hustled into the middle of the road, jamming it with their bodies. They hunkered down with spears and swords in hand.

"Hold on!" Calypsa said. "It's going to get bumpy! Real bumpy!"

Orcs on horseback, with their tangled black locks streaming behind their heads, rode up alongside the wagon. Nath took a poke at the one closest to him. The hammer cracked the orc in the knee, bringing forth a guttural cry. Spear in hand, the orc jabbed at Nath. He swatted the spear aside with a quick crack from his hammer.

On the other side of the wagon, Rond hurled stone after stone at the orcen riders. A squared block smote the orc in the chest, knocking the guard out of the saddle. One block at a time, the bugbear kept throwing. "I'm running out of blocks!"

As the horse and wagon thundered down the road, they closed in on the barricade of orcen guards. "This is it!" Calypsa said. "Hang on to something!"

Nath hooked his hand on the handle on the bench. He could see the yellow-whites of the orcs' eyes grow bigger a split second before the horse and wagon plowed into them.

There was a clamor of hooves trampling over the armor of orcs and their bones. The wagon pitched upward in a violent heave. The horse snorted angrily, thrusting through the ranks of the guards. The wagon slowed then surged forward as Calypsa urged the beast onward. "Eeeyah! Eeeeeyah!"

The wagon bumped, bounced, swayed, and jumped. The guards screamed underneath the bone-crunching horse hooves and wagon wheels.

Nath bopped an orc in the shoulder, knocking the guard clear off his saddle. With his foot in the saddle, the orc was dragged off by the galloping horse. As they cleared the tangled fray of orcs strewn in the road, Nath yelled out, "We're clear!"

With the slave guards hot on their trail, they raced down the road, distancing themselves from the guards on foot, but not the riders. There were at least a score of the riders left, running with a pack of hunting dogs that had been loosed from their leashes.

One of the orc riders led the pursuit. Black bearded and scruffy, the top brute barked commands in orcen to his men, keeping them out of Nath and Rond's range. "None escape Slaver Town. Those that do die." He pointed at four of his riders. "Take out their horses!"

The four horsemen spurred their horses after the wagon. They gained ground on the team of horses quickly. Two flanked one side, and two flanked the other. They held spears high in their hands.

"Don't let them pass, Rond!" Nath said. "We'll all go down if they get to our horses."

Calypsa shouted at the horses in words Nath did not understand. The laboring beasts gained speed.

Rond picked up stones two at a time. With a block over his head, he hurled it at the orc riders. His bottom set of hands handed up another block to the upper set of hands, then grabbed another block. The stones missed the mark. The orc riders started to pass.

"You're going to have to aim better than that!" Nath stretched out his hammer, trying to get a swing at the orcs passing by him. "Come closer, you cowards!"

Without a glance, the riders gained ground. They were seconds from striking out at the horses.

Nath climbed out of his seat and onto the team of horses. He rode bareback on one of them, eyeing the orcs who stabbed at the horses. He swatted their spear tips aside. "Get away!"

Rond knocked another rider from his saddle with a hunk of block. The second rider slipped up to the front. The orc jabbed its spear into the horse on the left rear side. The beast bucked and whinnied. The wagon lurched. All of the white horses let out a scream.

"Get away from my horses!" Calypsa said. "Stop hurting them!"

The wagon rumbled. For long minutes, Nath, Rond, and Calypsa managed to keep the orcs at bay. They were so preoccupied with defending the horses, they overlooked the other orc riders, who climbed into the back of the wagon. Two of the ringmail-wearing brutes rushed Rond and knocked him out of the wagon.

Calypsa screamed, "Rond!"

At that same moment, an orc rider jabbed his spear deep in the front horse's neck on the left. The white horse veered a hard left, leading the wagon off the road, down the bank, and into a steep rut. The wagon crashed. Wood snapped and broke. Nath flew off the horse and into the grasses on the side of the road. By the time he pushed up to his feet, he was surrounded by the wagon's wreckage and orcs.

Chapter 29

Rond hoisted an orc high over his head and threw the orc down hard on the ground. His big fists pumped like hammers, busting into the swarming slavers. Running through the grasses, Calypsa weaved her way through the enemy on nimble feet until she made it to the team of white horse. She started to unhitch the white beasts from the wagon. Three orcs came at her at once.

Without thinking, Nath sprang into action. Running swift as a deer, with the loose chains on his ankles and wrists clinking, he came on the orcs all at once. He turned his hip into his swing. Stone Smiter collided with the first orc that jumped over a busted wagon wheel trying to spear Calypsa. The blow sent the orc backward. The orc landed on the feet of another orc, tripping it. The third orc plunged his spear into Nath's chest. The metal tip broke off on Nath's breastplate.

A solid hit from the sledgehammer sent the burly orc to the grave.

"Help me get these horses free, Nath!" Calypsa shouted at him. Two of the horses were freed and galloping away. The last two were locked up in the harness. One of them had red blood on its hip.

"You free them, I'll fight," Nath replied, as he set his heel while more riders came at him. His first instinct was to let the horses be. They needed to abandon them and run, but he had a gut feeling Calypsa wouldn't have anything to do with that. There was hurt in her eyes. She'd give her life to protect them. "Just make it quick!"

"I can't unlock this harness. It's stuck!" she fired back. "Help me!"

"If I help you, who's going to help me!" An orc flung a spear through the air at Nath. Nath caught it with his free hand and flung it back. The spear hit the orc in the ribs. The slaver guard fell from his horse.

Calypsa rushed to Nath's side. "Free those horses. I'm too weak for it." Her eyes locked on the orcs. "I can handle these sweaty-nosed pigs." She put her fingers to her lips and made a shrieking whistle. The branches in the trees of the surrounding forest came to life with the quick flapping of bird wings. Birds, big and small, shot out of the leaves, descending on the orcs' faces in a massive flock.

Horses reared up. Bodies twisted and fell.

Nath worked on the harness. It was a metal contraption that twisted during the wreck. The wounded horse lay on its side, kicking. The other horse was on all four hooves trying to pull the wagon. Nath saw the problem. There was a pin that linked the horse harness to the wagon. There was too much pressure on it to be popped free. With the wagon and harness in place, the wounded horse was trapped underneath.

"I wish I had Fang," he said. The blade's keen edge would hack through the metal in a couple of swings. As the birds frenzied in the air like small feathery clouds, he looked at the head of the sledgehammer. The gem tip didn't glow so brightly. It was as if its power was gone.

"It looks like you have expended all of the hammer's charges," a voice said that wasn't at all familiar.

Nath's head twisted around. A little man was sitting on the blocks that had spilled out of the wagon. He was a grungy, hairy fella who looked like he was part gnome and part woodchuck. Nath instantly recognized the odd person. He was the part gnome, part varmint, part hermit that called himself a hermix. The hermix had helped Nath escape from the woodland tangles that Calypsa put him in. Nath had forgotten all about him. "Ruffle? What are you doing here?" He fixed his attention back on the pin and raised the hammer to strike it. "I hope you are here to help."

"Where did all of these birds come from?" Ruffle said, swatting at a blue jay with his little hands as it zoomed past his face. "Go away, you flying varmints!" Ruffle's bushy eyebrows crinkled when he spoke. He sounded like an old man when he talked. "Anyway, I am here to collect the debt you owe me?"

"Debt?" Nath started tapping the pin from the bottom side with the end of his hammer. He recalled an agreement he made with Ruffle saying he would help him in exchange for his freedom. "Yes, well, it's going to have to wait. As you can see, I'm very busy." Hammering away, with stiff strokes, the pin started to give. "Almost have it."

The birds, once as thick as storm clouds, started to dart away.

"Hurry, Nath, my power fades," Calypsa said as she stood beside the wreckage of the wagon. The orcs were regaining control of their mounts. Their leader barked out new commands, and the riders paired up and began to unfurrow nets. "Free my horses!"

With a strong final whack from the hammer, Nath popped the pin free. Setting the hammer aside, he grabbed the harness, maneuvered it, and worked it free. The standing horse bolted. The wounded horse came to its feet and trotted away, then looked back at Nath and gave what seemed to be a thankful whinny. Nath picked up the hammer. He saw the pleased look in Calypsa's eyes, and said, "Let's get out of here!"

"Ahem!" Ruffle said. The little man hopped off his pile of stone and teetered over. "Nath, it is time to leave. You agreed to help me when the time comes. Did you not?"

Looking down at the hermix, Calypsa said, "Who is this strange man?"

"It's Ruffle. He's a hermix," Nath replied.

Ruffle raised his little voice. "The *time* has come, Nath Dragon. You agreed to it!"

The orcs had their nets spread out. One pair trotted their horses toward Rond. Another set advanced on Nath and Calypsa. Ignoring Ruffle, Nath said to Calypsa, "We need to fight or run. I'm all for running."

She took his hand with trembling fingers. "We must make it to the woodland! I'm weak, but should have enough power to hide us. Rond! Let's go!"

Ruffle screamed, "The time has come, Nath. I mean now! You come!"

"If you want me, you're just going to have to keep up." Hand in hand, Nath and Calypsa aimed for the tree line. Just as Nath's knees started to churn, the air shimmered all around him. The scenery changed. He stood at the foot of a snow-covered mountain with icy winds in his face. "What just happened? Calypsa! Rond! Where are you?" he screamed.

"I'll tell you where they are; they are where I left them!" Ruffle said. The hermix was half sunk in the snow. "Nath Dragon, your time has come to help me, not them."

"You have to send me back, Ruffle! They might be captured."

"Not my problem or yours," Ruffle said. "Besides, what do you care? They stole from you before. They are thieves. They deserve where they are going."

Nath dropped on his knees. His voice echoed through the snowy valley, "Noooooooo!"

Calypsa froze in her tracks. Her hand was empty. Nath was gone. She slowly spun in a circle. "Nath, where are you?" All she saw was Rond rushing toward her. The riders bore down on the bugbear. They flung the weighted net over top of him. She screamed as another net was dropped on top of her. The orcs, using clubs, beat them down and dragged them all the way back to Slaver Town.

Chapter 30

Nath followed Ruffle into the forest tree line at the base of the mountain. The snow-covered branches rustled under the weight of the squirrels and other varmints that jumped from tree to tree. The brisk winds tore through the branches with a biting wind, dusting up the snowflakes from time to time. The hard ground beneath the pines, oaks, and elms was brown, covered in an icy sheet of snow over the pine needles and acorns that had fallen. The ground crunched underneath Nath's feet as he followed Ruffle up the steep hillside. His teeth clattered, and the wound in his side still burned. The blood from the wound Foster had given him had caked up over his ribs.

"Ruffle, you have to send me back," he said, trudging along after the spry little man that moved like a varmint himself. "My friends are in danger. I need to go back and help them. This is wrong!"

"The robbers?" Ruffle looked back over his shoulder at Nath with a sparkle in his dark eyes. "Why would you care about them? They are thieves. Trust me, I know. They only want to use you to get your items from the Black Hand. Nothing more than that." The hermix disappeared behind a tree, then he popped his head around. "Will you hurry? You move very slow for one with much longer legs than I. And much bigger feet too!"

"I'd like to take my feet to the back of your hind end!"

"You should be thanking me," Ruffle fired back. "I saved you from yourself."

Nath pushed his way underneath some low-hanging branches. A clump of snow fell onto his neck. He flinched. "Gads, that's cold! Ruffle, I don't know what you have in mind, but you're going to pay for this!"

Ruffle's short legs churned on. Up the slick slope he went, weaving through the trees only to vanish from time to time.

Nath trudged along, trying to make sense of what had just happened. He had no idea where he was, but he guessed it was far north. He'd flown on his father's back very far a few times and even passed fairly close to the snowcapped mountains, but he'd never touched snow before. It was pretty, but the chill it gave, he didn't care for. "How in Nalzambor did you bring me here? Wherever this is!"

Ruffle didn't answer.

There was a lot of confusion rattling around in Nath's mind. How did Ruffle, who for all appearances seemed rather harmless, manage to transport Nath from one side of Nalzambor to the other? The scruffy little man, covered in fur like some sort of animal, wore nothing but a shabby burlap robe that only covered his chest to his knees. He carried nothing and had tiny hands more like an animal. How could he have the power to transport Nath through space? And on top of all of that, how did Ruffle know where Nath was and how to find him?

Nath lengthened his stride and caught up with the hermix. "Ruffle, you aren't being honest with me."

"Oh, why do you think that? I haven't lied to you about anything." Ruffle scratched his chin. "At least, I don't think I have. We haven't had very many conversations."

"I don't know what a hermix is, but you don't seem powerful, yet you are. And how did you know about the Black Hand?" Nath grabbed Ruffle by the scruff of the neck and stopped his advance. He spun the hermix around. "What are you, really? A wizard? Some demented woodland enchanter? I want to know!"

"When you finish this quest, I'll answer your questions. Maybe." Ruffle twisted free of Nath's grasp with uncanny agility. "Now, keep up so we can get this over with. I've been waiting a long time."

"I don't care for all of the mystery, Ruffle. You haven't even told me where we are going or why." He slapped a branch. Snow fell, covering his head and shoulders. "Gah! That's cold!"

"Tee-hee-hee," Ruffle joyfully chuckled. "If you think it's cold here, wait until we get to the tip top."

CHAPTER 31

ON THE WAY UP THE mountain, Ruffle led them into a cleft in the rocks that formed a cave. Nath had gathered twigs and small branches. He insisted that they stop and make a fire. It wasn't warm inside the cave by any means, but it took him out of the stiff winds that whistled outside of the opening. On his knees, Nath started grinding sticks together to make a fire. He'd watched Prawl the slaver make a campfire, and he used the same tactics.

"You are wasting time," Ruffle said, pacing back and forth with his arms folded over his chest. "It's not that cold. It's not even winter, and there isn't even a foot of snow out there. You are acting like a child that needs the warmth of his mother. Nanny, nanny!"

"Whatever you need to have done can wait," Nath said, rubbing the sticks faster. Smoke started from the wood. "Yes!" He rubbed faster. The smoke faded. "What? No, give me my fire!" Nath chucked the sticks at the cave wall. "Blast it!"

Ruffle looked at him. "Good, now we can get going."

"We aren't going anywhere until you tell me where we are going." Nath hugged himself, rubbing his shoulders, which felt like frozen hams. "What is this all about?"

"You must follow. You gave your word."

Standing on one knee, and looking down slightly at Ruffle, he said, "Let me tell you something, you talking rodent." Nath shoved him. "If you were a good creature, and found me when I was entangled, then you would have freed me anyway. Instead, you made me make a promise under duress. What sort of trickster does that?"

Ruffle blanched, shuffled back, then retorted, "You speak wise words for one that was ignorant enough to wind up enslaved."

Nath walked up on him, backing the hermix toward the wall. "You need to tell me how it is that you know so much. How can you see where I've been and where I go? And if you needed me, why didn't you just take me out of Slaver Town sooner?" He stabbed his finger into Ruffle's chest. "Huh, you deceiver? Explain that!"

Ruffle's lips tightened. His eyes narrowed. "You will do what you promised to do, Nath Dragon. You said you would help me, so you will help, the same as I helped you."

"I shouldn't have to help you at the expense of others. That is wrong!"

"They are nothing in the grand scheme of things. You will forget them. Let their troubles be their troubles." Ruffle pushed Nath in the leg. "Let's get moving. All of this hot air you are blowing has warmed it up enough in here."

Nath held the sledgehammer out in front of him. "No. I'm not going to budge until you tell me what it is that you want me to do."

"Then you will be there a very long time, and you will never see your worthless robber friends again."

"How do you know that?" Nath shook his head, slung the hammer over his shoulder, and started out of the cave. "Never mind, I'll find them myself." He started out of the cave, not really wanting to face the harsh wind that swirled the snow just outside. At the same time, he wondered if Ruffle would just snatch him back like he did before.

I don't care. I'm not going to do something I don't want to do. My word or not. That would be foolish.

"Nath, wait," Ruffle said urgently. "Come back and I will quickly explain." He made a little grumbling sound. His feet scuffed the dirt. "I'll even make a fire, but a quick one. We must move. Time is pressing." He fluttered his fingers over the fire. The twigs and branches ignited. "There."

Nath hurried toward the warm caress of the small flames. He sat, letting the heat warm his cheeks as he rubbed his hands together. Within a few minutes, he was warm. "I've had the sun beating my back for two years, and thought I'd never miss a fire, but I was wrong. I'll take the hot over the cold any day."

"It won't matter to you over time. You are a young dragon. Eventually, you won't notice such trivial things." Ruffle sat down across from Nath and crossed his legs. "The birds and the critters do not wake wondering why it is cold or hot. They do what they are designed to do. So will you."

"Even varmints like a warm fire. If they like the cold so much, they would not hibernate.

Now, tell me, Ruffle, what is it you require of me?" Nath put his warm hands on his neck. "Oh, that feels so good."

"I need you to retrieve an object of my affection," Ruffle said, closing his eyes. "You see, in these northern peaks, there is a small temple city. It has no name; hence, people call it Nameless, but it was a sanctuary for a private and peaceful people that thrived there for centuries. Perhaps longer. It was not a grand group, but a mixed lot of all of the races, seeking a place to prosper in the quiet, sworn to never shed blood and to always abhor violence." He cleared his throat. "Sorry, but I've not spoken so much in a very long time."

Nath smirked. "So, I'm going to a place with no name called Nameless. This isn't very encouraging."

"Heh, these people didn't care for names or titles. They were very humble," Ruffle continued. "And private. Being a very private people, and casting themselves as far away as they could from trouble, they believed that no problems would come their way. But there is always trouble in the world. None can escape it." His voice became a dark whisper. "Especially when you try so hard to avoid it; it will find you and your secrets."

CHAPTER 32

NATH DROPPED A FEW MORE twigs and a couple of pinecones on the fire. "So, Nameless was more than a sanctuary? It was a sanctuary of secrets? What were they doing, mining gold and diamonds and then they woke a dragon? Hah."

"You are closer to the mark than you realize." Ruffle's bushy brows wiggled. "You see, even though the nameless society rejected violence, they still needed protection. They created an artifact of great power called the Star of Unity. It is a brilliant stone shaped in a smooth oval that was found in outer rocks already perfectly formed. They believe it came from the heavens, long ago, and they filled it with enchantments."

"What sort of enchantments?"

"If any transgressors came to Nameless with dark intentions, their thoughts would be changed, and they would be turned away. In some cases, it was rumored that the wicked stayed. Also, for those that would attempt to steal to fulfill their own selfish intents, they could be turned to stone." Ruffle looked upward. "Perhaps rays of power shoot forth. I'm not for certain. Much of it is legend, and legends are often forgotten."

"Am I to understand that you want me to retrieve this stone for you?" Nath rolled his eyes. "I'm not going to rob this nameless society. It's their stone; they can do what they want with it. I'm not going to meddle in their affairs."

Ruffle shook his little hands. "No, you misunderstand. I don't want the Star of Unity. For all I know, it is not even there. I want you to retrieve something far more precious than that." His eyes watered. "I need you to rescue my son, Nath."

"Your son? What are you talking about?"

"Listen to me, there aren't any people left in Nameless. It is abandoned. They either fled, died, or turned to stone. My son went there against my wishes, but he was a man with his own free will. I warned him. In life, there will be trouble, no matter where you go, but he did not listen. I've lived long, Nath, centuries, but all I have left is my son. I know he lives, and I need him back, but I cannot overcome the guardian of the Star of Unity."

"Maybe the star or this guardian is protecting your son from you?"

Ruffle sniffled. "I've worked too hard at this to be insulted, Nath. For decades, I have been trying to find a way to save him or at least find one that can. The one that can is you. The moment you left Dragon Home, I knew you were the one. The world quaked the moment you crossed the moat of lava." He clutched hands over his heart. "I knew then my hopes had been answered."

"And you knew this how?"

"I'm a hermix, born of the earth where we stand. A little of everything is in us. We do have special powers, like the druids and pixies, but we must store them up a long time in order to use them." He sighed. "I exhausted what I had to take you here. And I cannot fight what lies in the temple either. It will sniff me out."

"The Star of Unity will *sniff* you out?"

"No, the basilisk."

"What? A basilisk." Appalled, Nath said, "You never mentioned a basilisk!"

"I did mention one!"

"No, you mentioned a guardian, not a basilisk. A basilisk! That's different. Entirely!" Nath came to his feet and started pacing. He knew a lot about the creatures of the world, particularly ones with scales. A basilisk, for all intents and purposes, was a wingless dragon that no respectable dragon would ever claim as a dragon because they were so vile. There was no beauty in the basilisk. They were horse-sized scaly brutes with eight powerful legs, and sharp ridges and scales on their backs. Their bite and claws were lethal. A single stare from them was lethal. Nath wrung his hands. "What is it doing in there?"

"As I said, trouble will find you no matter where you go. The basilisk, they say, came upon them in the dark of the night. It wanted the star. It seemed to fall in love with it."

"Who said this again?" Nath asked.

"There were survivors, and I found one. It was a half-elf who outlived the rest. He resided outside of Narnum, near the rivers, and was difficult to reach. He lived in Nameless over a hundred years. He knew my son, Blust, who is very distinctive in appearance, the same as me. He was there when the basilisk came, clipping petunias in the gardens, he said. The moment the screams started, he fled." Ruffle sniffled and wiped his nose. "That was almost a hundred years ago, and the half-elf has died."

Taking it all in, Nath asked, "How do you know your son isn't dead?"

"Because, I would have felt it. And if he had escaped, he would have found me. We are very close. I'm certain that he is a stone. I know it. I at least have to know for myself."

"Can't you use your power to pop in and pop out? Couldn't your son have done the same?"

"If he had the chance, I know he would have, but my son would have protected the others. I'm certain of it. And he might have been surprised." Ruffle gave a sad shrug. "He was very young and little. I should not have let him go with those odd people trying to create their own utopia. All they did was attract more evil, not realizing their mistake until it was too late. Besides, I cannot go in. The basilisk will smell me, but it will pay no mind to one of its own kind, like you."

"It's not one of my kind, but I understand what you mean," Nath said. Even though he looked like a man, he had the blood of a dragon running through his veins. The basilisk wouldn't feel threatened by him or any other dragon for that matter, unless they came after it. It was the first thing that Ruffle said that made any sense. He picked up Stone Smiter. "I'll try to get in and out without any trouble. We'll see. So, Blust looks like you?"

"More like a hedgehog, but about half my size. He is very small for a hermix." Ruffle stood and approached. He touched the irons on Nath's wrists and ankles. The bolts cracked away. The cuffs fell to the floor. "Bend down," he said. Ruffle did the same to the collar on Nath's neck. "Nath, I am sorry it has to be this way, but I had to do what I thought was best. I hope you will understand one day and forgive me for it."

Nath turned his back and walked out of the cave. "Save it for the basilisk."

Chapter 33

NATH HAD TIRED OF THE talking. He'd tired of the cold too. Ankle deep in snow, he trudged up the slopes, wanting to get it over with. The higher he went, the scarcer the trees became. The snow started coming down in large flakes. He came upon a road half covered in overgrowth, almost a wagon wide, winding upward, toward the mountain's peak. He gazed up.

Why would anyone live in such a place? There is nothing up here but snow and ice.

With his eyes fixed on the road ahead, he moved along with an ache in his side, in his back, his jaw, ribs, and legs. Everything ached, and when his heart beat, he felt it in his fingertips. Calypsa had healed him some, but that had faded. Ruffle's words didn't fade, however. The hermix said that the dryad and the bugbear were robbers. He said they were setting Nath up to get his magic items, the birthday presents from his father. At the same time, Nath couldn't help but wonder why they would go to all of that trouble to save him. In his heart, he felt Calypsa had changed, but Ruffle's words echoed in his mind.

You can't trust anybody, Nath. Ever.

Taking his eyes off the road, he glanced over the mountain and caught another surprising sight. "Whoa."

Far away, the sea began and continued as far as the eye could see. Massive waves crashed against the rocky banks, splashing sea-foam into the air. There were settlements along the beach and back into the high green-blue grasses that hugged along the coast. Far out, he saw birds in flocks, diving for fish in the waters. At that moment, he felt as far away from home as he'd ever been.

I wish I had wings. I'd take to the winds and fly back.

He looked up the road and shook his face in the winds.

There will be no flying today, however.

Upward the road went, turning at hard elbows, zigzagging up the hill. The stretches between the bends became shorter the higher up he went. Finally, he made the last bend, the climb crested, and he stood face-to-face with a temple entrance covered in frost and ice. On a small portion of the face of the mountain, a temple of stone had been chiseled out. Eight round pylons twelve feet tall made a fence on both sides of the entrance. One the other side of the entrance, the daylight bathed the ground. The winds howled through the opening. There were steps leading up to the entrance. Its design wasn't anything remarkable. The fashioning was simple but elegant, with the face of a humble home.

Nath scanned his surroundings. Natural overlooks faced the sea and the cold grasslands, creating a beautiful view. Even though it was cold, it was peaceful.

Perhaps, in the summer, it wouldn't be so bad.

He glanced at the ground. The snow surrounding him had not been disturbed. The snowdrifts made layers of soft white waves. Not seeing any signs of the basilisk, Nath headed up the snow-covered stairs. The arch in the entrance had rows of long icicles at the top, giving it the appearance of a fang-filled mouth. He crossed to the other side and discovered a courtyard. A natural skylight in the rocks gave Nath full view of the oval courtyard, about fifty feet long and half as wide. Eyes sweeping the area, Nath's blood froze in his veins.

Oh my!

A statue of a woman with a look of horror in her wide eyes stood twenty feet away. She carried a clay jug in her arms. The pottery had cracked. The robes she wore were tattered by time. Nath approached her. She wasn't the only one in the courtyard. There were several more, standing, or in the motion of running. The woman had gentle features, now contorted with terror. Like the petrified men outside of Riegelwood, she seemed so real. He fanned his face in front of her eyes, expecting her to blink. He touched her. The skin was hard as stone.

"That is an awful way to go," he muttered to himself.

There was an elf on his knees with royal-blue robes peeling away from his back. His stony hands were held up inches from his face. A heavyset woman lay on her back, half covered in snow, with her knees drawn up and mouth wide open in a silent scream.

Nath's stomach turned upside down. He'd never seen such terror on a person's face. A part of him felt that they were still in agony. He bent down and touched the woman's cheek. "I'm so sorry."

There was another man, standing with his back straight, holding a lute over his head, poised to strike. His lips were pulled back over his teeth. With his back to the entrance, Nath stood in the courtyard. Smaller stone pylons seemed to hold up a rocky overhang, but they were only chiseled out. He could see that there was more than one entrance leading inside. He advanced, passing by one of the many stone urns in the courtyard that he assumed burned on a regular basis. There were stacks of wood beside them. Cold logs lay within the bowl, mixed with dark ash.

What I wouldn't do to light one of these up.

As he approached, a few feet from the rocky overhang, he stopped in his tracks. A foul odor wafted into his nostrils. He covered his nose. The musty smell of death was a slap in the face. "Pew," he said under his breath. His neck hairs rose. On the far side of where he was standing, something slunk out of the temple. Nath's heart jumped. It was a basilisk.

CHAPTER 34

A PRY BAR COULDN'T HAVE PEELED Nath's fingers from the handle of his hammer as he stared at the basilisk. It was a huge monster, covered in dark blue and red scales. Bigger than a horse, it slunk forward on eight powerful legs into the courtyard. Its long black tongue flicked out over the ground like slithering snakes. The spiny ridges on its back were folded backward as it moved over the grounds slow and low.

That is one nasty creature.

Nath crouched behind the pylon. His heart beat in his temples. The basilisk's head slowly swiveled side to side. The foul creature was all scales with hard muscle rippling underneath. It moved with purpose, and no need for grace. Gobs of saliva dripped from its jaws. It tossed its short powerful neck backward and let out a loud birdlike call.

Guzan! It's hungry!

Nath knew that there was a possibility that the basilisk might be sleeping. He'd hoped for it. The giant lizards were hunters though, and when they were hungry, they would be more than fierce.

The monster lizard weaved its way through the courtyard with its tail swishing over the snow behind it. Its body didn't touch a single statue. It stopped in front of the petrified woman that held the clay jug. Its tongue flickered over Nath's prints in the snow.

It knows I'm here!

The basilisk's black eyes swept over the courtyard. Its gaze turned Nath's way. He crept farther behind the pylon with his eyes averted toward the ground.

Don't look. Don't look. Don't look.

Nath squeezed his eyes shut. It took all of his willpower to not take a look at the scaly, eight-legged brute. All he could hear was his heart thumping inside his temples and chest. It was so loud he swore the basilisk would hear it. Doubt crept into Nath's mind. What if the basilisk did smell him? Its tongue went into his footprints; it had to know he was there. In his mind, he could see the saliva dripping from its jaws. It would rip him apart if it found him.

I should run. Ruffle will just have to find another son.

Clutching the hammer in an iron grip, Nath took a deep breath. He'd wrestled with dragons before, but none of them were so big. They didn't want to kill him or eat him either. He recollected Master Elween's instruction.

Calm yourself. Have a plan of action.

His thundering heartbeat quieted. Using his ears, he listened to what the basilisk was doing. There was a crunch of heavy footsteps in snow. He heard the sound of its mouth stretching open. He opened his eyes and peeked around the pylon. The basilisk's jaws were wide. Rows of small, sharp teeth filled its mouth. A fine mist came from its jaws, coating the statue of the woman.

What in Nalzambor is it doing?

The basilisk had a gaze that would paralyze with a glance. The lizard's breath would petrify the body. If they didn't devour the body at first, they would drag it off and eat it later. Perhaps it had to keep them petrified with its breath by coating them every so often. It was difficult to tell.

The spines on the basilisk's back glowed. Its eyes shone like stars.

Nath squinted.

That isn't normal! There was a sinking feeling in Nath's stomach. *Oh my, I believe it ate the Star of Unity. What else could cause that?*

The statue of the woman holding the clay jug blinked.

Nath tensed.

Her body slowly sagged to the ground.

Oh my goodness, she's alive!

The lizard's scales stopped glowing. Its teeth clacked together. The twinkle of starlight in its eyes went dim. It slavered over the awoken woman and opened its jaws wide again.

Without thinking, Nath ran at full speed toward the beast with his hammer raised up high. His lips were sealed, but his mind was screaming, "Dragon! Dragon!"

Chapter 35

Nath closed the distance between him and the basilisk in two seconds. He aimed at the hindquarters of the lizard. At the last second, the basilisk looked up. It turned its body away from Nath just as he unleashed his swing. The gem on the top of the hammer sparkled, making an arc of light in the air as he swung. He clipped the lizard's hindquarters.

The basilisk jumped off of all eight of its clawed feet. It scurried back into the temple, dragging its tail between its legs. Panting, Nath watched as it vanished into the darkness. His instincts were on edge.

That was easy. It can't be that easy. I might have scared it, but it will be back.

The woman lay on the ground with her teeth chattering. She shivered all over. Her eyes were spacey. Nath helped her to her feet. "You need to get out of here. Do you understand me?"

She shook her head as she shivered. "What happened?"

"I'll explain later, but now you need to go." He hurried her toward the entrance to the temple, taking quick glances over his shoulder. "Listen to me, get on the road, and keep going down. Don't stop no matter what you hear. You should find help along the way."

"But, what—"

"No time to explain, just go!" He gave her a little shove. "I'll help the others."

A terrible roar erupted out of the temple's inner sanctuary.

The woman took off, running frantically through the snow and out the front entrance. The moment she was gone, Nath rushed across the courtyard, back behind the overhang, fully expecting the basilisk to come back out. He considered two courses of action. Climbing above to the overhang and hoping he could get a clean shot on it from behind with Stone Smiter, or taking his chances in the temple within and trying to find Blust and slipping out of there.

He waited, considering all options. He'd hoped to not encounter the lizard monster at all, but now, minutes into it, he'd attacked it. Things couldn't have gone worse. Now, it seemed that the basilisk was even more than a terrible beast, but enhanced with powers that might come from the Stone of Unity. It was a theory, but it was the only one that made any sense. In addition to that, the people who were petrified, through some strange anomaly of magic and beast, could be revived. Nath wouldn't have believed it if he hadn't seen it with his own eyes. This compounded the problem. Not only did he need to find Blust, he needed to free them all, if possible.

If I can kill it, will that wipe out the chances of saving all of them? It's not my problem they are cast in stone. They should have been paying better attention! Heh, of course, who's going to remember people that don't have any names?

That's an awful way of thinking, Nath.

An unfamiliar sound caught Nath's ears. He lifted a brow. There were many dragons known for singing, not as people do, but with a gentle harmony that came from their throats. A similar sound permeated the air and the surrounding rocks. If Nath were to guess, the lizard was singing a song of its own. It was soothing and softened Nath's grip on the hammer. His rapid breathing eased. He remembered what Ruffle said about the Star of Unity. It could change the way people thought and take their violent intentions from their hearts. Nath's knees bent. The falling snowflakes became something from a dream. He lifted his hand and caught them.

This isn't so bad. It's pretty.

Nath wandered into the courtyard, dragging the hammer behind him as he caught a few snowflakes on his tongue. "Mmmm… snowflake. I guess snow isn't so bad. How can something so pretty be bad?" he said languidly.

Deep in a chasm within him, Nath's fighting spirit screamed, "Wake up, you fool! There is a basilisk out there that wants to eat you!"

"Oh, I'll be fine," Nath said to himself. He stubbed his toe on something buried in the snow. He dug the snow away and saw another person buried under the flakes. It was a little man that looked like a hedgehog, little bigger than a toddler. "My, your eyes are big. Are you Blust?"

His inner voice said, "Pick him up and run! Pick him up and run!"

As the airy harmony permeated the air, Nath set the sledgehammer down on its head, burying it in the snow with its handle sticking straight up. With misty thought, he reached down and tried to pick up the little man. Blust's body was frozen to the ground. "My, your backside must be awfully cold." He bent at the knees, lifted, and put his back into it. "Hurk!"

The husky little body ripped away from the frozen grasses. Nath held the young hermix up like a baby. "That's better," he said with a warm smile. "I think your father is missing you."

He spoke with moony cheerfulness. "I'm going to take you back to him and free the others." He had an idea. "Say, perhaps I can have the basilisk unthaw you right now. And the others as well. Wouldn't that be grand, little fella?"

Nath's inner voice shouted once again. "Run, you fool!"

With the hermix held up right before his eyes, Nath started to slowly turn. "I'm certain we will find him."

The dreamy sound of music ended. Nath's dreamy thoughts began to clear. Blinking, he stared at the hermix in his hands. His nostrils flared. A fetid breath was upon him. Something dripped and sizzled in the snow. He lowered the petrified hermix. Tucking it under his arm, he found himself face to massive face with the basilisk. Its hypnotic eyes fastened on Nath's.

"Grab Stone Smiter!" his inner voice said.

Nath's carnal reflexes acted. His hand grabbed the handle, but his eyes were locked with the basilisk. Terror gripped his heart. His limbs stiffened like stone. He couldn't even blink.

Nooooooooooooo!

Chapter 36

The basilisk roared in Nath's face. The inside of its mouth was a tunnel into a rank blackness. Rotted flesh and bone were wedged in its teeth. Nath, though paralyzed, could still smell, feel, and hear everything. The smell was awful as waste. Tiny little flies buzzed on the inside of the monster's mouth. It snapped its jaws shut with a loud clack of teeth.

Nath felt the wind on his face. His heart beat fast. The icy wind gave him hope as the terror caused by the monster's glaring eyes that sent his heart jumping began to wear off. So long as the monster didn't breathe on him, he wouldn't be petrified like stone. So he hoped. The basilisk's black, soulless eyes devoured Nath. Its tongue licked over his body, smacking his face, hair, and hands. If Nath were to guess, the giant reptile was confused about what he was.

I might look like a man, but I bet I taste like a dragon. His only hope was that he somehow confused the monster by being what he was. If anything, it gave him time. His fingers tightened on the handle of the hammer. Unlike mortal men, whose bodies would freeze under the deadly gaze of the basilisk, Nath recovered more quickly. The basilisk surprised him, but strength started to flow into his rigid limbs.

I just need a little more time. Please, don't breathe that mist on me!

As the basilisk inspected him, Nath couldn't help but think about the horrors of being eaten whole. Or alive for that matter. It seemed that the basilisk had been feasting on the people it had petrified for quite some time, and he didn't want to become one of them. Nath needed a distraction. He had to throw the monster off its game. There was only one way he could do it, and that was by doing what tripped him up in the first place. He needed to look into the eyes of the reptile again.

It snorted in his face.

Come on, look at me!

The basilisk fixed its soulless eyes on Nath again. Its probing stare locked on Nath's consciousness and sent slivers of terror underneath his skin. The monster's stare bent his will, trying to push it over like a tower of blocks that would fall and sink into a pit of despair. Deep inside, Nath let the anger within him unfurrow. He'd been enslaved, tormented, beaten, and abused. Everything that happened to him had been the fault of one monster or another. He pulled up the faces of his enemies. He saw them in the basilisk's eyes. The Black Hand. Prawl. Foster and even Ruffle had angered him. It fed fire into his veins, and something else came to mind in his thoughts of rage. He glared back at the monster. *I am the son of Balzurth! I am the Dragon Prince! And you, vermin with scales, are nothing!*

The basilisk reared back. Its mouth opened wide.

Nath thought for certain that a petrifying glaze would spew from its slavering mouth. Instead, a frustrated roar came out. *That's it, let it all out, monster!* Nath's powerful constitution, fueled by the dragon blood in his veins, restored the strength in his body. He remained still, channeling all of his focus into the hammer. Still eyeing the basilisk, he caught the hammer's gem glowing out of the corner of his eye. The handle warmed in his hand.

A gurgling sound came from inside the basilisk's gaping mouth. Back inside its throat were nodules of flesh that pulsated. A steaming mist burst forth.

Nath brought the hammer up out of the snow in an underhanded swing. The head of the hammer crashed into the lizard's bottom jaw. Its mouth clacked together. Chips of ivory-white teeth flung into the snow. Nath sprang backward just as the lizard's tail swiped right at him. The tip of the tail clipped his chest, spinning him halfway around. Using the momentum, Nath kept spinning, bringing around a defensive two-handed swing.

The basilisk moved fast with its head low.

Stone Smiter hit it flush in the side of the head. Its neck rocked left. All eight powerful legs wobbled. It staggered through the snow, moving in a slow circle, like an old dog chasing its tail. It shook its neck side to side. The lids on its black eye blinked. Then, sudden as a crashing wave, it charged Nath.

With the hammer over his shoulder, Nath brought it up and thrust it down like he was busting stone in the quarry. The lizard skidded in the snow, pulled back, and watched the hammer bust into the earth. It charged before Nath could lift his swing. The full weight of its body bowled Nath over. It crushed Nath into the snow, its front claws ripping at his chest. It bit at Nath.

Nath rolled his head aside. Mouth wide open, the monster struck again. He stuck the entire length of the sledgehammer in the monster's mouth, wedging its jaws wide open. The reptile reared up on its four back legs, shaking its head with fury. Nath rolled aside and scrambled to his feet. His eyes swept over the courtyard, looking for a weapon. Anything. The beast trampled recklessly through the courtyard, knocking the statues over as the ground quaked. Nath slid out of the wild beast's path time and again, hurdling urns and skidding over the snow.

What I wouldn't do to have Fang at my side.

With a hard shake of its head, it flung the hammer out of its mouth. The hammer flew end over end and landed squarely in Nath's awaiting hands. He gaped.

Zounds! What are the chances? Somebody somewhere must still like me!

The wild lizard tilted its head and lowered its belly to the ground. The spiny ridges on its back rose with a glow. Its dark eyes turned into the bright stars of the night. With a tongue flickering out of its mouth, it snorted in Nath's direction.

Brandishing his hammer with the gemstone aglow, Nath said, "I suppose it's too late to talk about this?"

The basilisk charged.

Nath ran at it swinging.

Chapter 37

The melee went back and forth with Nath fighting with everything he had in him. The hammer struck into the lizard's flexible iron hide, only to see the basilisk recoil briefly and spring back again. The hammer flashed. The eight-legged juggernaut of a monster hissed and roared. Its claws scraped over Nath's breastplate. Its tail slapped Nath to the ground. Rolling and spitting blood from his mouth, he bounced back up and rushed at the lizard.

Stone Smiter busted into the monster's hide. Hard bone snapped. The frenzied lizard tore into Nath with claws and teeth. He skipped and twisted away from the tips of nails and teeth. Nath's quickness saved his neck time and again. The monster, though not slow by any means, couldn't keep up. It chased him. Nath moved like a jackrabbit, evading its lethal swipes and biting jaws. Nath hit it again with the hammer, striking it above the tail. The blow skipped off.

Even this hammer cannot harm its hide!

With arms as heavy as lead, Nath kept swinging, keeping the brute at bay. A sword would be a more formidable weapon that could slice through its armor and pierce its inner flesh. Hitting it with a hammer was like beating a rug with a broom. All it did was knock the snow off it. And Nath didn't have time to put it all behind his swings. *I heard a crack though! I know I broke a rib. Or two!*

Nath and the basilisk went back and forth, exchanging blows and swipes. Its eyes still glinted like stars. The spikes on its back were ridges of mystic fire. Nath had no doubt that something was protecting and nullifying Stone Smiter's heavy-handed blows. Face-to-face, the lizard spit poison at Nath. He jumped aside. The poison burned into his arm. "Aaaugh!"

The behemoth charged.

Nath leapt. He struck it square on the tip of its nose. As the beast turned aside, Nath drew back and took another hard swipe into the ribs he hit before. The lizard moaned. Its eight clawed feet scraped up the snow and dirt. The glowing ridges on its back flickered. Nath gave chase, hitting the basilisk in the same spot again and again. More bone snapped inside its body. Its legs gave way.

It lurched forward, slinking toward the entrance into the temple, moaning a deafening, painful roar the entire way. Its spiny ridges flickered out. It pulled itself forward at an agonizing pace.

Nath climbed on the basilisk's back, straddling the upright ridges, lifted the sledgehammer high, and brought it down with all of his might. The hammer's head came down in a flash like lightning. The metal hit the skull, making a thunderclap. Bone caved in to the unyielding head of metal. The basilisk fell dead with its tongue halfway out of its mouth.

On shaking legs, Nath hopped down. He poked the beast a few times in the back with his hammer. "Thank the dragons that's over." He collapsed to a seated position in the snow. Steam came off his sweaty body. His arms and legs were caked with blood. He pushed his matted hair out of his eyes. "I can't believe I killed it. I didn't think it could be done. Even with this hammer."

He respected the monster and had no desire to kill it, but what had to be done, had to be done. It just didn't turn out the way that he hoped it would. But it was a basilisk. There was no good in them. All they did was kill, terrorize, eat, and move on once they'd destroyed everything and had no food left.

Glancing at the beast's gaping maul, he noticed a sea-blue light coming out of its throat. He pulled his hammer to his chest, fully expecting the beast to come to life again for another round of battle. "Oh, please be dead, I can't take any more." When nothing happened, Nath crawled closer. The glow came from deep inside the beast's smelly throat. He gagged. "Please, somebody or something give me a reason not to do this."

He wedged the hammer back inside the monster's slimy mouth. Careful not to poke himself on its teeth, he reached elbow deep in its throat. His fingers fished around and touched something warm as fire and smooth as a stone. Clasping it inside the palm of his hand, he pulled it out. The stone was three times the size of a hen's egg, oval, and glowed like lights beneath the city. The light inside swirled and sparkled like living things. "You must be the Star of Unity, but I think all you did was get a bunch of other people killed."

He tucked the stone inside his breastplate and searched the courtyard for Blust's body. He found the little hermix where he left him, still intact, and picked him up. "Thank goodness you aren't broken."

Nath ambled out of the temple's courtyard entrance. Standing beyond the arches, he looked back. There were more people within. It was possible he might have destroyed the cure. He just hoped that the woman he saved, or possibly Ruffle, could figure it out. Perhaps the Stone of Unity would do it, but he didn't care. He did his part. He was taking Blust to his father and heading back to Slaver Town.

He made it down to the cave and found the woman shivering inside. There was no sign of Ruffle, but the woman was warming herself by the fire. Her eyes widened when she saw Nath.

"You're safe," Nath said, creeping inside. "The basilisk is dead. I'm a friend. Do you remember?"

She nodded and huddled back up by the fire, shivering. Nath handed her the Stone of

Unity. "Here, perhaps this will warm your bones. It's yours, or your people's." He peered around. "Have you seen a furry little man who has the appearance of a groundhog?"

Holding the stone, she gave a quick nod. "Yes. He said he'll see you again at another time."

"What? But I saved his son, Blust." He held out the statue that looked more hedgehog than person. "Why would he leave?"

The woman gave him a curious look. "There is not a person called Blust in our temple. We have no names, but that statue you hold is just a statue."

"No, it's a person," Nath said.

The frigid woman shook her head. "No, it's just a hedgehog. I know. I chiseled it from the stone myself." She stood with the stone in her hands. "I thank you. Now, I must go and restore my brothers and sisters. I hope you find your friend." She kissed his cheek. "Please, return for a visit sometime, or if you like, you can help me restore my friends. I'm certain I could use your assistance, if it's even possible."

Shaking his head in disbelief, Nath said, "You might need the lizard's glands. I don't know. Are you certain that Ruffle left?"

She nodded, patted his cheek, and departed.

Moments later, Nath exited the cave and screamed at the top of his lungs, "Ruuuffffle!"

Chapter 38

Nath walked down to the base of the mountain, into the forest, and across the grasslands without stopping. He didn't stop for over a day, traversing the woodlands with a scowl on his face. He'd been duped. He had no idea why he was set up, but he knew how it happened. Ruffle did it. End of story.

The woman he saved from Nameless stated that Ruffle said they would meet again. Nath hoped that wasn't the case. If he saw the little groundhog of a man, he might be tempted to kill him.

Is there anyone in this world that I can trust!

The only good thing that happened was that when he left the mountain, he got out of the snow. His toes thawed out from the walking, and the sun warmed his face. He basically stayed warm by walking. He considered running, but he wasn't sure where he was, and given his situation, he wasn't in any hurry.

If Ruffle didn't really have a son, why did he send me there?

Did Ruffle want Nath to kill the basilisk and free the people of Nameless, or did the furry, impish man want the basilisk to kill him?

His stomach moaned. Nath didn't care. He scooped water out of the streams and drank a few times, but onward he went, one step at a time, weighing everything that happened.

Nath had left Dragon Home to pursue the murdering elves who killed the fledglings. The High Dragon Council banished him for one hundred years for leaving. Maefon, an elven woman of the Trahaydeen, fled with the elves. Nath loved her, and he found it hard to believe that she would have been involved in the atrocious act. He felt she was in danger. All of that seemed as if it happened ages ago. The closer he tried to get to their trail, the farther away he became. He had been completely lost in the new world. A ship without a rudder. He made one mistake after another.

He came upon a split in the streams. Standing between them, he contemplated his next move.

Nath, you are free now. Free to pursue the Caligin and find Maefon. Free to forget about all of the others that have brought you nothing but heartache and harm.

He picked at a scab on his forearm. The basilisk's claws had cut him up all over. The wounds burned. Squatting down over the stream, he rinsed the blood off his face. "I must look like I've been spit out of a dragon's mouth. I *feel* like I've been spit out of a dragon's mouth." He stood up, stretched his back, and groaned. At least his wounds were healing. The nagging from the knife blade Foster stuck in his side was almost gone. He considered himself fortunate that painful wound wasn't any worse. He was even luckier that the basilisk didn't get the best of him.

He followed the stream south, thinking about Calypsa, Rond, and Slaver Town. As far as he knew, it had only been a couple of days since he'd escaped. A lot of people risked their lives for him, including Homer and Radagan. Slaver Town was a wicked place. People were taken against their will and sold to others. Nath couldn't understand how people could do such a thing. At the same time, many people within were very sordid. He wanted to help his friends, but were they really his friends?

Did Calypsa and Rond only come to rescue him because they wanted his magic items? Did they even escape the slavers? Something ate at his gut. He felt the half-dryad woman was sincere.

But, I didn't ask her to rescue me. They are not my problem. Perhaps they do need to be punished for the crimes that they committed.

After two days of straight walking, he came upon a road that led to a small northern logging and timber city called Huskan. Despite his shabby attire, he walked down the main road, ignoring the suspicious stares from the men and women he passed. He stepped onto the porch of the first tavern that he saw. A pair of old men sitting on a bench in front of the window were whittling wood. One of them had a big head, was skinny, and had a wad of chaw in his mouth. He said to Nath, "Stop gawking. Can't you see we're busy?"

Nath pushed through the double doors of the tavern. The room was warm and smoky. The tables were half filled, and it smelled like cooked food. With his tummy gurgling, he moved to the bar and sat on a stool. He propped the hammer against the bar. A meaty older woman in a pink apron with a face so chubby he could barely see her eyes said, "What will you be having?"

Offering a smile, Nath said, "What do you have that is free?"

"Hacksaw!" she shouted. "We have another loafer!"

Chapter 39

A shadow fell over Nath. The floorboards groaned behind him. He looked back over his shoulder. His eyes moved up. The man behind him wore a white apron and had the scraggly graying beard of a woodsman. His eyes were heavy. He was built like a chimney with the thick forearms of a blacksmith. Respectfully, Nath said, "I take it you are Hacksaw?"

"The one and only," Hacksaw said, slapping a hard, calloused hand on Nath's shoulder. "We don't take kind to highwaymen, loafers, and drifters. We work hard in Huskan." He was well-spoken. "It's time you were going."

Nath lifted his hands up. "I don't want any trouble, but I was hoping for some charity. I'll be going."

The old woman behind the bar said, "I don't hear those feet shuffling. Perhaps Hacksaw needs to help you out of that seat."

Nath slid out of the stool. His stomach moaned so loud the woman's eyes appeared beneath her fleshy eyelids. He gave her a nod and grabbed his hammer. "If I had money, I'd be happy to pay." He looked around at the cozy establishment. The patrons were enjoying tall mugs of ale, hot bread slathered with butter, and slabs of ham and steak that made his mouth water. "I was robbed recently. I can work for it?"

"We have all the help we need and are going to need," Hacksaw said, pushing Nath toward the door. "Just keep walking. You won't find any more charity from the rest of this city either. They'll throw you in the jail and won't feed you there either. There's plenty of streams. Learn to fish." He caught a glimpse of Nath's hammer. His eyes popped open. He reached for Stone Smiter. "Eh… where did you get this?"

Nath pulled it away, cradling it to his chest. "It's my sledgehammer and not your concern. I guess I'll learn to fish with it."

The big man rubbed his beard. Looking down at Nath, he said, "I'm a fair man." He laid his hand on Nath's shoulder, more like a friend this time. "Why don't you tell me about that hammer over a bowl of Granda's meat stew?"

"Hacksaw, son, what are you doing?" the old woman said, shaking her head. The curly waves of short hair shook. "You are setting a bad precedent for our customers."

"Please, just fix this young man a bowl of your stew, Mother. I'm willing to pay for a good story. It's been a while since I've heard a good one." He looked Nath in the eyes. "What do you say? Granda's stew is really good."

"It smells good, but I think I'm going to take my business somewhere else. Sorry, but my story is a private matter. I'd rather not share it." Nath pulled away from the man's strong hand. He departed from the tavern with a shove through the doors. He'd shared enough with Nina in the Oxen Inn, and that got him in a heap of trouble. He didn't need any more. He was better off starving, but he could at least try to fish, eat berries, nuts, or something. Head down, he walked down the road, following the main road out of the timber city.

Hacksaw caught up with him. "Listen, stranger, I hate to see you run off without something to eat, regardless of whether or not you share your story." The bearded man offered a loaf of bread in a cloth napkin. Looking around for other prying eyes, he said, "Listen, we can't just let anyone wander in and feed them. We run a decent tavern. The people work hard. There's nothing they despise more than seeing someone take something for nothing. But I can see you are truly in need. Take this bread and best to you, young man. Just don't tell anyone that you received it from me."

Nath squeezed the soft round loaf of bread in his hands. "Thank you. I am grateful."

"Son, you looked like you wrestled a bear." Hacksaw walked alongside Nath. "What in the world have you been through?"

"A lot." Nath tore off a hunk of bread and put it in his mouth. "This is the best bread I've had in... years... oh, aside from Radagan's cream cakes. I did have one of those."

"Do you mind?" Hacksaw said, taking the cloth from the bread. He covered the sledgehammer head and tied it off. "It's less threatening. I bet you could use that sledge to bust up a lot of wood, even though I'm pretty sure that's not what it is made for."

"You sound like you are doing some fishing now, Hacksaw?"

The big man chuckled. "I can't help but be curious... uh, do you mind telling me your name, or is that private too?"

"Nath."

"Well, Nath, unlike these hatchet men and saw seers you see milling about in this town, I've been around this world a time or two. That hammer you carry, it's special"—he shrugged his brows—"isn't it?"

"You want it, don't you?"

"No, not at all," he said, lifting his hands. "Honestly, I just want the story. You know, I used to adventure, when I was younger. I have a sword that hangs over my mantel." He showed a full set of teeth behind his beard-covered mouth. "It's magic. Would you like to see it?"

"Is there more food involved?"

"Food, a place to sleep, and mead."

Nath nodded his chin. "I'll take it."

CHAPTER 40

NATH SAT IN AN ARMCHAIR crafted from the local timber, facing a stone hearth. Hacksaw sat adjacent to him, looking into the fire, smoking from a long-stemmed tobacco pipe fashioned from some kind of animal horn. The cottage was cozy and warm, made from logs of the local woodland. Flannel blankets and cushions padded the furniture as well as dressed the windows.

Hacksaw blew a long stream of smoke from his mouth. "Did you get enough to eat, Nath?"

"That's the best I've eaten in a very long time. I really am grateful." Nath glanced up at the sword that hung over the mantel. It was a cutlass, a one-sided blade with a slight curve at the end. It had a rounded steel crossguard and a handle made from either bone or horn. Nath wasn't sure. On the pommel was a jade-green face, fashioned like the face of some sort of goblin. "So, that's your blade, eh? It's quite remarkable."

"I call it the Green Tongue. When he's all worked up he gets a greenish shine to him. I put a lot of hurting on the goblin hordes back in the day." Hacksaw poked two fingers at the sword. "I took it from a goblin commander that tried to slay me. It was one nasty fight."

Granda came in from the kitchen with a mug of something that was steaming. "Are you still bragging about that sword? It could have killed you, you know." She shook her head. "He was always wanting to get into a scrap. All he talked about was adventuring, being a swashbuckler or legionnaire, ever since he was little. My other sons had more sense about them." She handed Nath the steaming brew. "That's what I get for taking to the coast for a spell."

"Look how big I am, Granda." He spread his arms. "This build is made for fighting."

"It's a big target, that's all it is!"

"Yes, you've told me a thousand and one times, including today. Granda, are you comfortable with Nath staying?"

Granda gave Nath a once-over. "He ain't hurting my eyes." She shuffled away, wiping her hands on her apron before disappearing into the kitchen. "Good night."

Hacksaw smiled. "I think she likes you."

"Good." Nath sipped the brew. It had a sweet, spicy flavor. "Is this mead?"

"Oh, heavens no, that's Granda's pumpkin cider. Would you rather have mead?"

"Actually, I'm enjoying this." The steam warmed his nose. "So, you're an adventurer?"

"Retired, so to speak." Hacksaw puffed out a ring of smoke. It drifted over the mantel and dissipated on the sword. "You say that as if it's a bad thing."

"I've encountered a few adventurers. They didn't turn out to be what I thought they were. It cost me."

Hacksaw's sausage fingers rubbed the hair on his cheeks. "Adventurers are often a sordid lot. I've traveled with many men and women like that myself. Generally speaking, we are driven by the challenge of facing the unknown and cheating death. But some, well, they are in it for glory, coins, and precious baubles. Look around." He tipped his chin. "All I have to show for my days of triumph is that sword that hangs on the wall. All of the other items didn't have so much meaning. But that sword you see, there are stories that come along with it. Stories and memories." His voice trailed off. "Good and bad." With a grunt, he leaned forward, grabbed a log, and tossed it in the fire. He eased back into his chair. Eyeing his sword, he said, "It's a marvel I'm still here."

The fire popped. Bright-orange sparks shot out from the crackling new wood. Nath breathed deeply through his nose. He liked Hacksaw. There wasn't anything pretentious about the man at all. He said what he said, and showed what he felt. It seemed very clear to Nath that he wasn't trying to hide anything. He picked up the hammer that was leaning against the arm of his chair and handed it over to Hacksaw. "Take a look."

Hacksaw took the cloth towel from the head of the hammer, revealing the dark head of metal. "That's an extraordinary size for a sledge. It has the feel of one of the usual girth." He balanced it behind the head with two fingers. "Remarkably balanced, but an unusual weapon for a man such as you. You have the build of a swordsman."

"I am a swordsman, but I don't have a sword. And I've only been with the hammer a few days. It's called Stone Smiter."

Hacksaw's eyes lit up. He traced the runes on the hammer with his finger. "That is a grand name! Very grand, indeed!" He stood up and spun it through the air. With awe, he held it up. "Stone Smiter!"

Nath scooted to the edge of his seat. "I take it you like it."

With a hungry glaze over his eyes, Hacksaw said, "Yes. I'm a warrior. What warrior does not adore weaponry, especially with a craft like this. I feel I could crack a giant's skull like a melon with it."

"Yes, well—" Nath started to stand.

Hacksaw froze. "Easy, Nath. I hope my getting carried away didn't frighten you." He handed the hammer back to Nath. "I understand your concern. I didn't like letting anyone touch Green Tongue either." He sat back down in his chair. "But you can if you like. Just be careful, you might fall in love with the blade."

"Would you trade?"

Hacksaw let out a hearty laugh. "Oh, I would be tempted, but I wouldn't want to live without those memories. Many wicked foes fell underneath the wrath of Green Tongue. I killed a wight, goblins, and their commander, as I mentioned. Spilled the blood of gnolls and orcs. I even faced a hill giant, but I wasn't alone on that one. You should have seen the brute. He had a belly as hard as iron and a slab of muscles up to his ears. I'll tell you this, we could have used the hammer."

Nath gulped down the cider. "Ah!"

"Don't go too fast on Granda's cider. It'll soften your bones."

"I don't care. I haven't felt this good in a while, so I might as well enjoy it." He burped.

Hacksaw rose from his chair. "I'll get more cider then." He left and returned with a big iron pot full of cider and another mug. He beckoned at Nath with his hands. "Here, here, let me refill you."

Nath handed over the mug. Hacksaw sank the mug in the cider, filling it up, let the excess drip off, and handed it over. "Granda would bust my knuckles if she saw me being sloppy like this, but lucky for us, she sleeps like she's petrified."

Blanching, Nath said, "I hope not."

CHAPTER 41

HACKSAW PUT NATH'S MIND AT ease as he moved on to talk about his adventures. He said the sword, Green Tongue, was taken from the commander of a goblin pirate ship he encountered on the Fallum Sea. The old warrior worked as a henchman and caravan guard, fought with the legionnaires, and even mined with dwarves. He went on and on, talking about many of the things he did and the people he'd met. Nath could have listened to him all night. He was fatherly, almost an uncle.

"So, do you have your own children?" Nath asked.

"Never married, though I was close once. She was a pretty little thing with silky hair and a voice as sweet as honey." His jaws sagged. "I think I scared her when I lost me temper once. Not with her, but with another man that became snide with me. I busted him so hard in the face he didn't wake up for days. It was never the same after that. There's a time and place when you let the beast out like that, and you shouldn't do it in front of a lady. They don't understand."

"Aye," Nath agreed. With a warm and fuzzy feeling inside, he said, "Well, I'm chasing after a woman myself. She's an elf as beautiful as you ever saw, but I've been nothing but sidetracked since I took after her." He tossed another log on the fire. "Nothing has been right since I left home."

Hacksaw packed more tobacco into his pipe. "And where might that be, if you don't mind me asking?"

"Eh, near Dragon Home."

"You mean, the Mountain of Doom? You are from the settlements?"

"Near there."

"I understand if you don't want to say."

"It's complicated." Nath took a long drink of cider. He looked at the hammer leaned up beside the hearth. "That hammer was taken from a slaver lord when I escaped from Slaver Town."

"Slaver Town!" Hacksaw sat up. "That place is real?"

"As real as you and me," Nath said. Without giving specific details, Nath filled the man in on everything he'd encountered. He told him about Calypsa and Rond. The betrayal he experienced by the Black Hand. How he rescued Princess Janna, only to be duped again and sold to the orcen slaver, Prawl. He went on at length about Slaver Town. Foster. His harrowing escape with Calypsa and Rond before being transported from the bottom of the world to the top by Ruffle. "After I killed the basilisk, I found myself here."

Hacksaw blew smoke. "You know, there are good storytellers and there are great ones. You, Nath, are a great one."

"You don't believe me?"

"I didn't say that, but I'd be inclined to call you a liar based off what I just heard. Still, your words ring true, and I consider myself a pretty good judge of character. I'll give you the benefit of the doubt, but I find it hard to believe that you single-handedly killed that basilisk in the Nameless Temple. That's the story of legends. And you're too young to be legend."

"So, you know about the Nameless Temple and the lizard then?"

"Well, sure, everyone does in the northwest. Anyone could say they slew it, because everyone is too scared to go up there and no one would believe them. At least, not without the monster's head. But no one can glance at a basilisk and live."

Nath wanted to say that he did in fact stare down a basilisk and live, but he thought better of it. "Well, have you ever seen a basilisk? How do you know?"

Hacksaw slapped his knee. "Ha-hah! You make a fine point, Nath. Who can really know for sure without seeing it with their own eyes, and that beast took over the temple more than a hundred years ago. But there was a man who lived here named Derek, and he claimed to have seen the beast. Told me all about it when I was a boy. He was old then, and died not long after he shared the story. The truth is, his story is all we have to go on."

Nath frowned. "I suppose, his and mine."

"I'm sorry to have offended you, Nath. But as I said, I'll give you the benefit of the doubt. Perhaps, you can go back to something that I can relate better to. Tell me about Riegelwood and these adventurers called the Black Hand."

CHAPTER 42

NATH DEPARTED HUSKAN. HE WASN'T alone either. He was on a horse equipped with saddlebags, a bedroll, rope, rations, and other supplies. Hacksaw rode with him. The big man rode tall in the saddle, leading the way with a sway in his broad shoulders. The old adventurer had geared up in a suit of leather armor. He wore bracers and had scuffed-up metal guards on his arms, shins, and shoulders. Green Tongue hung on his left hip. Two daggers were belted on the other side. A full quiver of arrows was on his back, and a short bow he said was for hunting crossed over his back.

With snowflakes drifting down from the gray clouds above, Hacksaw said, "It's a fine day for a long ride. And I haven't been south for a long time. I'm looking forward to the warmth."

Riding alongside the man down the dirt road that led into the grass-covered hills, Nath said, "I know we've been riding for a while, Hacksaw, but I wish you would let me talk you out of this. It's my problem, not yours."

With his eyes ahead, Hacksaw replied, "No, you are in need of a friend. And, well, I feel a calling. The truth is, I've been very restless the last few seasons. I still hunger for a trial. I just can't stand around and split logs all day. I need to do more. I was meant for it."

"Granda seemed very upset."

"She gets upset easily with me. She's always wanted me to stay home."

"Well, I was more worried that she was upset with me."

"Hah, I suppose she'll blame you." Hacksaw shook his head. "No, when I heard your story about the Black Hand and these Men of Whispers, I knew I had to help. I've crossed men of that foul ilk before. I can't stand the thought of them."

"How do you know that you have to help? I certainly don't owe you anything. I'm a complete stranger who wanders into your tavern looking for food, and now you're following me to Riegelwood."

"Actually, you're following me. I don't think you know where you are going." Hacksaw petted his horse's neck. "The Black Hand has crossed you up once, and they'll do it again if you don't have a good plan. Please, tell me, how do you suppose to get your precious items back?"

"Well, I haven't had time to plan it out, but I know where they will be. The Whistler or the Oxen Inn. I'll find them, and let them have it."

Hacksaw shook his head. "That's the worst plan that I've ever heard. Not to mention that they'll see you coming from a mile away. All you are going to do is wind up back in Slaver Town again."

Miffed, Nath replied, "I said I really hadn't had much time to think about it. I'll come up with something better."

"No, we'll come up with something better. Tell me something, Nath. Do you want your items back, or do you want vengeance?"

"I want both, actually."

Hacksaw turned his head and eyed him. "Are you willing to kill them for it?"

Nath swallowed. "Well, I don't know about that. They certainly need to be exposed or taught a lesson. They are thieves. They should be punished for it."

"I'm all for justice, but you'll have to decide how far you are willing to take this. If you go at them head-on, it's going to be a nasty fight that you might not be able to finish, but you could just steal back what you've lost. If they don't know that it was you, you might just get away with it."

"You're suggesting I steal my items back?" Nath looked up. A flock of geese flew in a v-formation moving south. "I never thought about it like that before. I just assumed that I would reclaim what is mine."

"You said you've been a slave for over two years, and you haven't put any more thought into this?" Hacksaw shook his head. "That's bad planning. If I'd been locked up, I'd be planning my strategy every day. I'd run it through my head to perfection."

"There were a lot of distractions."

"Don't take this personally, but based off what you told me last night, you haven't had a plan since you started. You are looking for this little elven girl without any idea in the world where to start looking. Am I right?"

Frowning, Nath said, "Yes."

"That's pretty stupid. To be honest with you, I'm not even sure how you made it this far, but you have, and that's what fascinates me."

The more Hacksaw talked, the worse Nath felt. Like a fool, he'd charged headlong into a world he knew little about. He'd read about it, heard about it, but it wasn't anything like experiencing it. He'd been miserable since the day he left, and he left with all of the right intentions. "Everything went backward on me," he mumbled.

Hacksaw cupped his ear. "What's that?"

"Nothing. So what were you going to say about stealing my items back? I'm listening."

CHAPTER 43

"NOW, DON'T GET ME WRONG Nath," Hacksaw said. "I prefer a straight-up fight, but sometimes, it's best to flank and blindside your enemy. One of the best ways to do that is to divide and conquer."

"I've heard about that," Nath said. He'd taken a spear out of a leather sleeve mounted on the horse's saddle. He eyed the leaf-shaped head. "Not to change the subject, but what is this spear for? Fighting or hunting?"

"Both, but in the case of this journey, hunting. Have you ever hunted with a spear? Or bow for the matter?"

"No."

"I'll show you how it's done. The woodland is filled with tasty varmints. We'll find us one and feast like kings."

Nath wasn't completely honest about his skills with the bow and spear. He'd been trained with most all weapons, but he'd never actually hunted with any of them.

"Tell me a little more about the Men of Whispers and this orc? What was his name? Crawl?"

"Prawl."

"Yes, Prawl. He sounds like a nasty one, not that any of them aren't, but some are formidable. Give me details. We'll need an angle."

"The Men of Whispers are common folk who work behind the scenes. Many of them are actual soldiers working for City Lord Janders. He was oblivious to their cause." He spun the spear in his hand and put it back in his sleeve. "Prawl is in charge of them. They work with the Black Hand, but they are not the same. I believe they have a rivalry of sorts. Prawl doesn't like them, and they don't like him, but they serve the same evil cause."

Spurring the horses to a brisk trot, they crossed a small stream. The horses whinnied as they clopped through the icy waters.

Hacksaw said, "I'd say they are still doing the same business. It sounds to me like the Black Hand chooses the people, and the Men of Whispers are the support system. It's all a clever setup that starts the moment a newcomer enters their city. It's a big operation. We won't be able to bust it up, Nath. So don't start feeling too heroic. We need to be focused on just one thing, getting those items back. The trick is to get one item, and then blame it on the other."

Nath's eyes brightened. "Ah, well, you know, I think I might have an angle on that."

"Let's hear it."

"One of my items is the Gauntlet of Goam. Prawl had his eyes on it, but Nina claimed it. He was very bitter that he didn't get it." He scratched his neck. It still itched from where he'd worn that collar; if there was one thing that he was thankful to Ruffle for, it was that his irons were gone. "On the trail to Slaver Town, I told him about my treasure and the items. His beady little eyes sparked. He knew he'd been duped."

Hacksaw's bearded smile went from ear to ear. He jabbed his index and middle finger at Nath. "Now, that's the smartest thing you've done since you began your trek."

"It is?"

"Yes, you planted a seed. We can work with that."

"So, what are you suggesting? For all we know, Prawl might have it already."

"Perhaps." Hacksaw shrugged. "But we know nothing, so it's best to plan based off what we know. I imagine they are still going forward with business as usual. We'll know quickly enough when I check out the Oxen Inn. That is where Nina is, correct? And she had this Gauntlet of Goam?"

Nath nodded.

"Tell me about the gauntlet. If we're going to use it to push a wedge between the groups, I should know what we're looking for."

"It's made of a supple leather, open fingers, with a blue jewel over the palm. I can punch like a mule kicks when I have it on." Nath clenched his fingers in and out. He didn't say any more about how it gave him greater strength, but that should have been obvious. He hadn't used it much, so he wasn't certain if it had any other powers or not.

"I've never heard of Goam, either," Hacksaw commented. "Is that a person or a place?"

"It could be either. I don't know, it was a gift to my father that was handed down to me." Nath reflected on Balzurth's throne room that was covered wall-to-wall with treasure. All of it was tribute given to the dragons from all of the races in the land for millennia. He missed the treasure room. Some of his best memories were playing there and being with Maefon.

I hope that I will see her again. I need to find the truth.

"Nath, when we get to Riegelwood, you are going to have to lay low. And if you see the enemy, you can't act out on it," Hacksaw said. "Remember, they have eyes everywhere and can certainly recognize you. That's why I have you covered up in that traveling cloak. But you still have to keep those eyes averted. I've never seen a man with eyes like that. No one would forget them."

"I will."

Hacksaw continued. "I'll search out Nina in the Oxen Inn. If she is there, I should be able to feel out her situation, but it might take a few days. You, in the meantime, will be squirreled away somewhere out of sight, while I handle it. And if the Men of Whispers work within that devious network, as you say, we'll find the gauntlet, steal it, and pin it on Prawl. This will bring all of the hungry rats scrambling out of their holes. In daylight, we will expose them."

"You make it sound easy."

"Hah! Not one single thing about it is easy, but if it was going to be easy then it wouldn't be any fun." He took the bow from his wide shoulders. "I'm getting hungry. We have rations, but let's preserve them. Besides, I'd rather hunt. Are you ready to learn?"

"No, I'm eager."

CHAPTER 44

MAEFON STOOD ON TOP OF Stonewater Keep, staring over the battlements at the rushing river below. It was early morning, and the fog hung over the surging waters roaring below. Dressed in black raiment with her arms and shoulders bare, she leaned farther over the edge. At the bottom, an elf lay still, his body dashed against the rocks. Crows and carrion birds were picking at it. It was one of the Caligin, a fine male who crossed Lord Darkken at the wrong place at the wrong time.

She rubbed her neck and swallowed.

Something sent a spark of rage through Lord Darkken over a week ago. Standing atop the keep with rain coming down in sprinkles, Lord Darkken addressed the Caligin. Maefon stood by his side, basking in his glory, nodding in agreement to everything he said. That's when it happened. A Caligin, standing in the second row, coughed. Maefon could see what happened next as plain as day. The Caligin was ripped out of the ranks by invisible hands. The elf came right into Lord Darkken's iron grip. The Lord of the Dark in the Day lifted the man over his head and, howling with rage, hurled the man clear of the battlements.

Maefon shivered.

There was a break between the battlements where a platform jutted out over the river. Bodies could be dropped from there, straight into the churning waters. That had happened before, but this was pure anger. She actually laughed when it happened. Not because she approved, but because she felt that was what Lord Darkken would want. She didn't want to show the fear that festered inside her chest. She hadn't felt that way in a long time. Lord Darkken departed shortly after that without a word, leaving them all in the cold.

Among the jagged rocks that crowded the riverbank, a large figure climbed over the rocks. It was Monfur, the nine-foot-tall ogre who guarded the entrance to Stonewater Keep. The birds feasting on the dead Caligin's body scattered from the hulking brute's approach. With one hand, the ogre picked the rotting elf's body up like a ragdoll and flung it in the river. One of the elf's arms fell off, landing at Monfur's feet. The ogre picked it up and started eating it.

Lips tight, Maefon turned away. Hands behind her back, she started to pace. She tried to block out the abominable sight. There were other problems. Ones that she wished she didn't know, that she was certain Lord Darkken would be angry about.

For two years now, she'd shared his bed on and off. She never knew for sure where she stood. Lord Darkken seemed to push her to her limits by merely showing a frown at her mastery of magic and new achievements. In one moment, he was imposing, and in the next, a sheer delight. Elves were very straightforward in their personalities. She was used to that, but she couldn't get used to Lord Darkken's unpredictability.

He's trying to control my emotions. I should be emotionless by now, but when he learns about what has happened to Nath, he'll fly into a rage.

That was the problem. Late yesterday she had been using the Pool of Eversight. She focused on Nath being in Slaver Town, but he wasn't there. There was a great stir among the orcs there as well. It seemed Nath had escaped. Not only that, it seemed that he had disappeared into thin air, and she wasn't sure where to start looking for him. She was rattled. Her concentration was lost. She couldn't sleep and had spent half of the night on the top of the keep, pacing.

Out of the corner of her eye, she caught something flying over the tops of the trees, coming right for her. It felt like her heart tilted side to side in her chest. It was the two-headed vulture, Galtur. She could see a glint of its emerald eyes from where she stood.

Lord Darkken must be close.

Wringing her hands, she turned and found herself face-to-face with Lord Darkken. Her heart sank to her toes.

His expression was grim. There were strange patches of animal fur that looked to be growing on his cheeks. Dressed in the black leather armor of the Caligin, he tilted his head. "Is everything all right, Maefon? Aren't you glad to see me?"

Without hesitation, she threw her arms around his waist and hugged him tight. "I'm sorry, my lord. I was in deep thought and you startled me. Of course, I missed you. The nights have been very cold without you."

"I told you that you should sleep closer to the fire," Lord Darkken said, pushing her away. "So, tell me, what have I missed since I've been gone?" He started picking the animal hairs out of his face a few at a time. "Drat this spell. It lingers."

Galtur landed on the top of the battlement. One head let out a hideous squawk, followed by the other. It was a huge bird, gaunt and ugly, with heads twice the size of a man's.

"Lord Darkken—"

He lifted his index finger. "Why so formal, Maefon? Is something wrong?"

"Sorry, Darkken, but I fear that I have some bad news to report."

"Are you leaving me?" he said in a friendly voice, coupled with a dashing smile.

It put her at ease. Touching her chest, she said, "Of course not. Ever. I just have to report about Nath."

"Oh, my little brother." He picked more hairs from his face and flicked them away. Galtur made a crowing sound. "How is the little dragon doing? Miserable, I would hope."

"He escaped from Slaver Town."

Lord Darkken's eyebrows buckled. He ripped more hair from his face. "You don't say."

Chapter 45

Maefon stopped breathing. All she could feel was the icy bits of rain on her face. She was certain that Darkken would hit her, if not pitch her over the wall at any moment. Then, without warning, Darkken said, "That's delightful news!" He patted her shoulders. "I knew that he had it in him. It was just a matter of time."

"So, you aren't angry?"

"At you, no, of course not. It's hardly your fault, Maefon." He threw his arm over her shoulder. "If anyone is to blame, it is the failure of the orcen slavers. I paid them to break

Nath, not bodily, but in spirit. It seems they failed in both cases. But you have to remember what you are working with. The orcs are quite stupid, but effective for what I had in mind."

Maefon had understood all along the reason for Nath's captivity. Darkken wanted him to suffer at the hands of others. He wanted Nath to see how despicable people could be. He wanted Nath to hate them all. "I'm glad you aren't upset, but I have more news to report."

"As long as Nath is not dead, I'll be fine. I assure you." He nodded toward the vulture as he turned Maefon toward the steps that led down into the keep. "Go, Galtur. Find some halflings to feast on or something. I'll summon you when the time comes."

Stretching its long skinny necks, it squawked. The bird turned away, spread its expansive wings, and launched itself off the wall.

"Let's go inside, and talk over a bottle of wine by the fire," he said, leading her down the steps by the hand. With his voice echoing in the damp and dreary stairwell, he added, "I'm thirsty. I'm rarely parched, but today, I feel my tongue needs to be drenched in the best elven wine from the finest vineyards." They entered the dining room, where there were fifty seats surrounding the table. She sat while Lord Darkken grabbed a bottle of wine from the wooden wine racks. He popped the cork, filled two crystal goblets, and joined her at the head of the table. "And do you know what makes this wine extra savory?"

"It's stolen."

"Precisely!" He hefted the goblet. "There's nothing more fulfilling than drinking the wine of conquered peoples. A toast?"

She lifted up her glass. "To the conquest of all enemies."

"No!" he said cheerfully. "To the conquest of Nath and all of the dragons."

They clinked glasses and drank.

"This is delicious."

"Yes, well, the elven vineyards are the best, and these bottles date back over one thousand years. They are priceless. So, tell me, where is Nath now?"

"I tried to find him using the Pool of Eversight. He's vanished without a trace."

Darkken set his crystal goblet down and started drumming his fingers on the table. "You can't locate him? That's very troubling, Maefon. I need to know where he is, at all times."

Her back straightened. "I will find him. I swear it!"

"No, that's quite all right. I will just have to locate him myself. Besides, there is a young Guardian of the Crimson Hood that is quite adept in magic. Perhaps I'll let her have a go at it. After all, I need to have someone that can assume your place in case anything happens to you. We can't have a letdown in our progression toward world domination."

"Darkken, I assure you, there is no need for that." She scooted her chair back and got up. "I'll go to the pool and find him now. No excuses."

"You have not been dismissed, Maefon. You overstep your boundary. Sit down!"

She obeyed.

"Maefon, I need you to be confident for the next step in our journey. You are now giving me doubt. I don't like that. You should have full mastery of the pool now."

"I might have had an off moment, but I am confident that I can find Nath. I will make it happen. Just let me have another chance."

"Your chance will be coming soon enough." He drank. "Relax, Maefon, let's just enjoy the wine. I need to unwind myself. Frankly, I'm relieved with all of this news. Nath proves to be formidable. I'll need that at my side. A brother in arms. Together, we will be invincible."

Maefon wanted to kick herself for being so weak. She should know better than to panic in his presence. The last thing she needed to do was cast doubt on herself. She took a chance and said, "You planned all of this, didn't you?"

"Me?" Darkken tossed his head back and laughed. "Are you accusing me of being a puppet master?"

"You are the grand puppet master." She shook her head. "I should have seen all of this. You orchestrated Nath's escape, didn't you?"

Checking his fingernails, he replied, "I might have had something to do with it. After all, he'd suffered enough. And I tired a little bit of waiting."

"Why don't you share these plans with me, Darkken?" She clasped her fist to her chest. "You wound me. I would like to see these events unfold, and not hear about them later."

"In due time. It's still early in the game, but the game is about to speed up, and you won't be watching from my study. You'll be watching with your own eye for a change."

"I'm looking forward to it." She leaned over the table with her hands clasped before him. "So, tell me, please, Darkken, and don't tease me, how did you orchestrate Nath's escape from Slaver Town?"

"The Caligin's eyes and ears are everywhere. Are they not?"

She nodded.

"It seems a dryad has taken a shine to Nath. She wanted to free him."

"A dryad?"

"Yes, these unsuspecting interventions are the things that you must watch out for. Faith, hope, and love can often get in the way of proper planning. It can be unpredictable, but it can serve to benefit us too." Lord Darkken drained his goblet. "Let's go for a walk. I'll explain."

Chapter 46

Back in Slaver Town, Calypsa sat on her knees surrounded by orc guards as she watched Rond. The four-armed bugbear had been locked in the stockades. Taking turns, the orcs whipped him. The bugbear had rivulets of sweat running down his back. His body shook with every crack of the lash.

"Stop it!" Calypsa tried to scream, but the cloth gag in her mouth made it inaudible. The slavers had come around in regards to what she was. They knew she was a dryad and had special powers. Now, her hands had been bound up in rags where she couldn't move her fingers, and her wrists and ankles were in heavy, painful irons. The lash cracked against Rond's back again. "Stop it!"

An orc leered down at her. He backhanded her in the face. She crumpled to the ground. Her face hit the dirt. It had been like this every day for four days. They locked her up in the barn in a cage made for a large dog. Several orcs kept watch on her day and night. They'd rise early in the morning and take her to the stockades where Rond was whipped. Then they locked her back in the cage.

Seeing Rond suffer was the worst of all of it. The muscular bugbear's mighty frame now sagged in his bonds. His chin hung toward the ground. The vibrant brute was nothing but a shadow of his former powerful self. And it was Calypsa's fault. All of it.

I'm so sorry, Rond.

She'd gotten hung up on Nath Dragon. Deeply. Calypsa tried to focus on her old way of life. She wanted to live off the land, and others, as she chose, the way she and Rond had done for years. But there was something about Nath that changed her heart. There was good in him, deeper than anything she'd ever encountered. She felt it the moment her lips touched his.

The orc that hit her lifted her back to her knees. "Quit falling. Heh-heh!"

Unable to get Nath out of her mind, she decided to entertain Rond's idea to steal Nath's items from the Black Hand. With those items, she could learn more about Nath, and keep Rond appeased. She infiltrated the Black Hand and worked with them for months, trying to become one of them. She learned about how they worked with the Men of Whispers and the slaver, Prawn. They bought and sold people for money. They deceived City Lord Janders. Every word they spun was a lie taken to be the truth. It sickened her, and she wasn't one to care for normal people.

As for Nath's items and his purse of treasure, it had all been locked up in a chest, secured in the backroom of the Whistler, the inn that was one of their hideouts. Using her charm on Tobias, she managed to seduce him enough that he showed her everything. Drunk, the braggart took her right back into their room in the Whistler and showed her the chest that was cleverly concealed behind a panel in the wall. It was a metal strongbox that would fill a man's arms and be difficult to carry away. There were five different key locks. Each member had a key, but Tobias winked at her and said, "Yes, we all have a key, but who do you think designed this chest?" He held up a small ring of keys and smiled. "I did."

Tobias opened the chest, revealing a hoard of treasure, including Nath's items. It was all there in her grasp for the taking, but she waited. For weeks she kept close to Tobias, building their relationship, then when he was drunk one night, she took the keys and slipped into the Whistler. Entering the room in the back, where the Black Hand met, she opened up the secret panel. Then, the candles in the candelabra above flickered from orange to green. Calypsa glanced back. All of the members of the Black Hand were in the room: Virgo, Cullon, Nina, Worm, and even Tobias.

Tobias took the keys from her hand with a grand smile. "That was a very entertaining game we played." He winked. "I enjoyed it." Out of nowhere, he socked her in the gut. "No one fools the Black Hand, you rogue from the woodland. No one."

The Black Hand took it to her after that, beating her savagely. They threw her in a cage and turned her over to the Men of Whispers.

"She'll make a fine slave. Take her to Slaver Town," Tobias said to a lean, bearded brigand named Andeen, who loaded her into a cage in a wagon. "Tell Prawl this one is on us."

Calypsa took one long look at all of the Black Hand's faces as Tobias handed them their separate keys. She spit through the bars of her cage just before Andeen covered her up and rode out of the city. But the half-dryad would have the last laugh. She never once revealed her powers to the Black Hand. A mile out of the city, she enacted her powers. With her hands and lips still free, she transformed into a chipmunk, slipped through the bars, and ran into the woodland.

The orc lifted her to her feet. "Time to go."

Passing by Rond, she cast him a long-lasting glance. His head was down, and his eyes were closed. Sweat dripped from his forehead in steady drips. Her heart ached. She made a bad deal, and it cost them both dearly. She'd been fooled, not once, but twice.

The orcs put her back in her cage inside the barn. There were several of them keeping their eyes on her at the same time. She couldn't use her powers, not gagged and bound. She could only transform with total freedom of her mouth and limbs. But even if she could, she wouldn't leave without Rond.

Tears ran down her cheeks as she huddled in the cell.

Why did I do this for a man I don't even know?

Chapter 47

At the ground floor of Stonewater Keep, Monfur, the ogre, lifted the portcullis. The ogre held it up with one hand, bracing it against his shoulder. Flies buzzed around the brute's skin. He stank of the dead. Flesh hung out of his teeth. Maefon covered her nose, fanning the flies away as she hurried after Lord Darkken. She wasn't two steps beyond the threshold when the portcullis slammed down behind her. She jumped forward, glaring back. Monfur waved at her and grinned. "Yum-yum."

Lord Darkken threw an arm over her shoulder. "Oh, don't let Monfur get under your skin. He leads a very boring life and relishes his moments of tormenting the Caligin when he can. Besides, he can't talk with them when he's eating them. They scream too much. I actually don't like that, so I feed him after they are dead, most of the time."

"Yes," she said with a shiver. They started to cross the bridge that connected Stonewater Keep to the lands beyond. The surging rapids splashed against the rocks, spraying them with misty water. "I saw him snacking on some elves that did not make it to the river from the top of the keep. I hate the sound of him crunching on bones. It twists my stomach."

"Hah! That is nothing, Maefon." He tousled her hair. "Wait until you see an earth giant get ahold of the living. Their mouths are cave openings that open and close like steel traps. I've even seen them eat an ogre. Once, I witnessed two giants pull one ogre apart and eat it like a cow chewing grass."

"The giants are that big?"

"Oh, certainly." Lord Darkken continued down an overgrown road that led away from the keep toward the grasslands. It was another cloudy day filled with drizzling rain. "But let's not talk about giants and ogres. They are so foul. Instead, let's talk about something beautiful, like me."

She leaned her head against his chest. "You are my favorite topic, but I'm curious to know about what happened in Slaver Town."

"Again, we are going to talk about me, and my uncanny ability to manipulate my surroundings and bend them to my favor." A box turtle with black and yellow scales was crossing the road. Lord Darkken picked it up and eyed it. "I've never understood the purpose of such a slow creature. Do you know?"

"Something has to be slowest," she said.

"Hah! I like that answer." He punted the turtle high in the air.

Out of nowhere, Galtur swooped in and snatched the turtle out of the sky with its talons. The two-headed vulture flew upward in a large loop. At the top of the loop, it dropped the turtle. With its left mouth open wide, it caught the turtle in its mouth at the bottom of the loop. Galtur's jaw clamped down.

"There's that crunching sound you hate so much. Sorry for that," Lord Darkken said.

"I suppose I shouldn't be discomforted by it. I should be stronger by now," she admitted.

"You are an elf, and it's only natural that you have an aversion to such things. Don't worry, Maefon, I won't hold it as a strike against you." He ran his hand down her backside and patted her on the rump. "But if I ever catch you crunching on chicken bones, I'll make you Monfur's bride."

She giggled. "I'm certain that won't ever happen. He's too handsome for me."

"Agreed. Anyway, about Slaver Town and Nath's escape. As we both know, our eyes and ears are everywhere, and dealing with the slave lords is a large part of what I do. They do a fine job at ripping families apart. Having this relationship, I put the word out on Nath. I gave a description, and the Caligin spread the word through Riegelwood. It didn't take long to send Nath to the deep southern land of Slaver Town. It was there that I purchased him, so to speak. My orders were to rough him up. Build his character. Make him hate everything that surrounded him. And I needed to make sure that he couldn't be broken, which he wasn't, and I admit, I'm proud of my little brother for that."

Maefon nodded. She wiped the rain from her face and was relieved that it had stopped. She'd felt damp since she'd come to the keep and enjoyed the moment of the sun breaking through the clouds and warming her face.

As they strolled down the path arm in arm, Lord Darkken continued, "In disguise, I kept a close watched on Nath."

She quickly looked up at him. "What were you disguised as?"

"Oh Maefon, I think you know by now that I can disguise myself as anyone. I could be one of the slaver guards, a buyer, trader, another prisoner. Whatever my needs require, it can be done," he said with a devilish smile. "You did know that, didn't you?"

"I haven't actually seen you change from one person to another," she said, shamefaced. "I've just seen your ears like an elf's, and that fuzz on your face from today. Oh, I do recall your nose being very wide at one time. I don't mean to be ignorant, but you've never explained it to me. You leave a lot for me to ponder." She looked back at him and gasped.

"Is something wrong, Maefon?" Lord Darkken said in his own voice, but he had the face and body of an orc.

Chapter 48

"How did you do that so fast?" Maefon said, marveling. She let go of his arm and stepped away. Lord Darkken's entire appearance had changed. He was a full orc, wearing a suit of ringmail covered in a black tunic. He carried a lash and a club just like the ones Maefon saw in Slaver Town, through the Pool of Eversight. "Your power astounds me."

"It is impressive, and it should be. After all, I have dragon blood in my veins, and with dragon blood comes magic, which has allowed me to master many mystic things." Lord Darkken shimmered, returning to his normal self. "Do you understand how I did it?"

"I've been studying your tomes, but I've yet to come across a spell such as that, at least one that you command with thought and not words." She hugged his arm. "That was a very powerful illusion, but I thought that you transformed and it faded gradually."

"I can do both. The illusions are quicker to execute, but easier to detect. A full transformation spell has the more lasting and realistic effect. But I like the illusion. It gets me through in a pinch."

Maefon squeezed his arm. "I want such power." Her mouth watered at the thought of being able to change form at any time. She would be the ultimate Caligin then. "Will you teach me?"

He lifted the index finger of his free hand. "Some things cannot be taught. Like faeries and pixies who are born of magic, it all comes very naturally. As for you, well, you are elven, and very adept in drawing from the mystic river, but it will take much more study and years of hard work. It comes much easier to me, but I've worked for it." His eyes narrowed. His angular jawline clenched. "Very hard for it. Centuries' worth."

"I have the time and the devotion," she said. "And I've grown so much in a short time."

Lord Darkken looked down on her with an arched brow. "Show me something."

"I'd be happy to." She stepped away from him to the other side of the road. A stone the size of her head lay at her feet. She spoke quickly, weaving magic elven words. Her body sucked in energy from the earth. A brisk wind came. The grasses alongside the road bent. Her hands showed a purple aura. The stone rose from the ground. With a flip of her left hand, she flung it high in the air. Pointing at it with her right hand, a ray of fire shot from her fingers, striking the rock. The stone exploded into debris and dust that the wind spread over the grasses.

Lord Darkken applauded. "A fine execution of a very offensive spell. I like it. You could kill many with that when the time comes, but I want you to try spells that are subtler but every bit as dangerous. We'll need it."

She nodded as the glow on her fingers went out. "It would be my pleasure." It felt good unleashing her power. Her body trembled. A hunger grew inside her to use more magic. She tired of holding it all in. She wanted more.

"Come along, now," he said, twisting one of the copper rings on his fingers. "I still need to finish telling my story about Nath. You see, as I observed him, suffering in the stockades, pounding rocks with hammers, and starving in his cell…" With his fingers adorned in copper, he spread them out before him, palms up, and shrugged. "I became bored. It happens to me, very often. Anyway, as I'm in the midst of gaining his confidence by feeding him cream cakes—"

"Cream cakes?"

"Yes, I enjoy baking, don't you know that?"

"Nooo," she said, stretching out the word. "I've never seen you do anything more than open a bottle of wine, and even that is beneath you."

"True, but I have to act the part from time to time. Anyway," he said, nonchalantly, "this dryad comes along. Or, a portion of a dryad. Now, listen to this, she has fallen in love with Nath and had herself, and a bugbear comrade, become captured, just to free him."

Maefon's heart hopped in her chest. "Fallen in love with Nath." A spark ignited the blood in her veins. Her breath quickened, and the palms of her hands glistened with new sweat. "A dryad?"

"Yes, women born of the trees in the wilderness, but I believe this one was the result of one mating with a human at some point." He glanced at her. "Maefon, you look pale. Did you drain yourself with that spell?"

"Perhaps," she said, wiping her palms on the side of her pants. But her heart was racing like a charging horse. The thought of Nath being with another woman infuriated her. She played it off by saying, "It was the first time I unleashed that spell. I think the excitement got the best of me, but I'm fine. Please, continue."

He patted her back with a heavy hand. "I understand. You work very hard to impress me, and I appreciate it. As I was saying, this dryad, an astonishing woman of great beauty, risked her own life to save Nath's. Or at least free him."

Maefon stumbled on the loose stones on the road.

Lord Darkken steadied her. "Are you well? Elves are always surefooted."

"Just finish the story," she fired back. "I've taken countless steps in my life; can't I slip once?"

"That is an interesting point. You've probably walked thousands of miles in your life, and the odds are that you are bound to slip once." He massaged his clean-shaven chin. "You've given me new perspective. Continuing. This dryad, Calypsa, as moony-eyed as a farm girl seeing her first legionnaire bristling in his shining armor, hatched a plan to free Nath. This little woodland minx turned Slaver Town inside out. She caught the orcs with their trousers down past their ankles, and made fools of them all. It was a total riot. Surprises like that make the best entertainment. There was a battle in the quarry, a wagon chase, skirmishes of slaves and prisoners against the guards and the slaver lords all over the town. It was a complete debacle. This dryad, whew, what she did that day made for great work that would rival that of the Caligin." He elbowed Maefon. "The elves couldn't have made a better mess themselves."

"So, what happened?"

"Eh, well, they escaped the city, only to crash a few miles from the town. Nath, they reported, was whisked away. The dryad and bugbear were captured."

"Good," she said, speaking of the dryad.

"Good to what?"

"Uh, that Nath escaped, how you wanted him to escape?"

"Yes, but it sounded like you were more concerned about the bugbear and dryad. That would be odd, seeing how they are irrelevant."

Maefon pushed in another direction. "So, you teleported Nath elsewhere? And you know where he is?"

"Not exactly, I just know where I left him, but I'm confident that I know where he is going."

Aggravated, she tried to stamp her own jealousy down. Why did the thought of another woman in Nath's life infuriate her? She felt cheated somehow, which didn't make any sense because she loved Chazzan, who Lord Darkken killed. For some reason, she just wanted that dryad, Calypsa, dead. At the same time, Lord Darkken angered her. He still hadn't told the entire story about what he did with Nath. She wasn't even sure if any of it was truth. *Just play along. He'll only show you what he wants to show you.* "So where is he going then?"

"The same place we're going now. Riegelwood."

Chapter 49

On a chilly, breezy day, Nath and Hacksaw hunkered down in the woodland. Nath had Hacksaw's bow in his hand. His eyes were fixed on a deer that stood prominently with a rack of horns with twelve points that almost touched the lower branches. Hacksaw reached an arrow over to Nath and under his breath said, "That's a long shot. We need to get closer before you take it."

"I don't think we are going to get any closer than this," Nath said, taking the arrow and notching it on the string. They were downwind, surrounded by the rustling of leaves. The deer stood at least seventy-five yards away. It bent its neck to the grass, then its eyes twitched. It froze and looked their way.

"Take it," Hacksaw said. "Quick."

Nath pulled back the bowstring and aimed.

The deer sprang away, vanishing into the willowacks.

"Ah, barnacles!" Hacksaw slapped his face. "Well, you wouldn't have hit it anyway. It was too far, and those lower branches would have altered the trajectory." He slapped Nath on the shoulder as he rose. "But, it's always a joy to try."

"I would have hit it, for certain," Nath said.

"No, you wouldn't have. Besides, how long has it been since you fired a bow?"

If Nath were to guess, it must have been over thirty years ago. Master Elween and the

Trahaydeen worked with him when he was younger. He learned about most kinds of weapons and how to use them. "It's been a few years, I guess. I was younger."

"Yes, well, next time I'll take the shot."

"I would have hit it."

"You need some practice first, but I don't want to waste arrows. You never know when you might need them." Hacksaw peered about. "But I'll give you one shot." He jabbed two fingers in the direction of where the deer once stood. "Can you see that red elm just behind where the deer once stood? It has a knothole in it. Aim for that."

"I see it." The red elm's bark had a crimson-like stain on its trunk. Nath closed an eye, took aim, and stretched the bowstring back.

"Whoa now, you need to ease your breathing. Only hold a little bit in," Hacksaw advised.

Nath exhaled through his nose and softly said, "I know." He pulled the string back farther, altered his aim a little upward, and focused on the knothole.

"Nice and easy."

"Do you mind? I'm trying to aim."

"Sorry."

Nath released. The arrow zipped across the woodland and vanished.

"Did you hit it?" Hacksaw said, squinting his eyes. "I didn't hear it hit."

"I hit it, dead center. But I'm not so sure that I killed it, and I don't think trees are very good for eating." He handed over the bow to Hacksaw.

"Let's take a look," Hacksaw said.

They marched across the forest, making a straight line for the red elm tree. Nath hopped over a dead tree and ducked underneath the low-hanging branches of another. He came right up to the tree that he shot. The feathered shaft was sunk almost dead center in the knothole. He opened his hand to it and smiled. "See, I wouldn't lie to you. And I could have made that shot at an even greater distance. I have great eyesight. Like a hawk."

"Yes, it's a fine shot. Perhaps a lucky shot." Hacksaw yanked the arrow from the tree and eyed it. "The tip is still good." He slipped it back into his quiver. His eyes narrowed. He placed one hand on the pommel of his sword.

"Is something wrong?" Nath asked.

"I have a feeling that it was something else that spooked that deer. Not us." Hacksaw's head turned, eyes slowing scanning the woods. "Do you hear that?"

"I don't hear anything."

"That's what I'm talking about."

Clatch-zip!

A crossbow bolt struck the red elm tree.

Thunk!

The surrounding woodland came to life. Small men with hatchets, wearing armor made from hide and skins, raced right at them.

Hacksaw drew his sword and screamed, "Goblins!"

Chapter 50

STANDING JUST OVER FOUR FEET tall, the wiry, fiendish-looking goblins were like smaller versions of Rond the bugbear, with large pointed ears and broad mouths with sharp teeth. Their ruddy skin was greenish brown, and their eyeballs were yellow. They attacked with the ferocity of wild dogs.

"Don't hold nothing back," Hacksaw said, brandishing his sword. Green Tongue's blade glowed with a rosy amber hue. "They'll tear you apart." He thrust his sword into a charging goblin's belly. "No mercy!"

Three goblins rushed Nath at the same time. Weaponless, he jumped over top of all three of them, doing a somersault in midair. The moment he landed, he kicked a goblin in the back, knocking it into the other two. "I could use a weapon!"

"You should always carry a spare, or two!" Slashing back and forth, keeping three goblins at bay, Hacksaw tossed him the bow. "Try this!"

Nath snatched it out of the air. He swung the bow downward, clocking a rushing goblin on the middle of the head. It winced, growled, and swung its hatchet at Nath's knees. The nasty, dirty little men, with their tangled hair tied up with bones, encircled Nath. One darted in, chopping, followed by the other. Nath parried with the bow, twisting left and right, catching their swings one at a time.

"Quit dancing with them and start killing them!" Hacksaw roared with a wild look in his eyes. He slashed with a long, broad stroke. Green Tongue removed a goblin's head from its shoulders. The goblins let out a frenzied *schreeeeeel* sound. "And remember, it makes them madder when you kill them. They take it personally."

"Good to know!" Nath said, blocking another attack. He'd left Stone Smiter with the horses when they went out hunting. He didn't even have a dagger on him. *Never again!* He jabbed the tip of the bow's edge into the biggest goblin's neck. It fell to its knees, clutching its neck. Suddenly, everything seemed to slow down for Nath. The moment of surprise passed. His natural speed and instincts kicked in.

The smallest goblin chopped at Nath's chest. Nath stepped into it. The hatchet banged off Nath's breastplate. Nath punched the goblin hard in its broad nose. The goblin staggered back, shook its neck, and came at Nath again. While blocking the blows of the third goblin, Nath quickly jabbed his fist into the smallest goblin's face half a dozen times. It fell flat on its back, holding its bloody nose.

Using the bow, Nath swept the legs out from underneath the third goblin. He kicked it in the ribs so hard they cracked. Rising to their feet, all three of the goblins who had attacked him scurried away, clutching their noses, necks, and ribs.

"Why did you let them get away?" Hacksaw said angrily. His face was covered in sweat, and he puffed for breath. Goblin blood dripped from his sword. "You're supposed to kill them!" He pointed two fingers at three dead goblins sprawled out on the forest floor. "See! Like that!"

"They fled. I'm sure they won't be back." Nath pushed his hair out of his eyes. "I'm pretty sure we scared them."

"Oh, they'll be back, and there will be more of them. You can count on that." Hacksaw cleaned his sword on the fur armor of the headless goblin. "You just can't let evil things like them go. It always comes back to haunt you. Come on, let's just get back to the road and ride toward Quintuklen. The greater the distance, the better."

"Am I supposed to apologize that I didn't kill them?"

"Those are goblin raiders. They hunt in small packs, but they are a part of a much larger one. I have to admit, I'm surprised that they are lurking this far north in the woods, but they move about like nomads, killing and stealing anything that they think they can overpower. And because they got away, they'll end up killing someone else." Hacksaw took his own dagger from his belt and handed it to Nath. "So, yes, you should apologize, not to me, but to the family of the dead that they will kill later." He slammed Green Tongue back in his scabbard. "Let's go."

As they made their way back to the horses, Nath pondered Hacksaw's words. He'd never deeply considered the ramifications of inaction. What if Hacksaw was right and the goblins did kill others and he could have stopped it?

I can't be responsible for that, can I? But it makes sense.

Ahead, Hacksaw walked with a limp. There was a bloody gash on his upper thigh. "Hacksaw, you are wounded?"

"Yes, that's what happens most times in a fight. I'll stitch it up." The bearded man pushed through leafy branches. "Huh! I'm just glad that my sword didn't freeze in my scabbard."

"What do you mean?"

"It's an expression that soldiers sometimes say. Sometimes, when battle erupts, some men quake in their boots. With tongues cleaving to their mouths, they stand as still as a post. Their extremities lock up, and they can barely breathe. Those fellas don't last long in a fight. I'm thankful my body didn't fail me today."

"You seemed more than prepared for those goblins. You made quick work of them. You're a fine swordsman."

"If you only saw me in my prime. I would have downed all six of them." Hacksaw stopped. Twenty yards away in a clearing, the horses nickered. "Nath, don't hesitate in a fight. If I ever second-guessed myself when I fought those little monsters, I'd be as dead as those little monsters. Do you understand me?"

Nath nodded.

"Good. Have you ever stitched a wound?"

"Uh… sort of."

"Well, today you are going to become an expert. I'd do it myself, but it's best that you learn as well. Besides, I'd like to smoke my pipe. It's a tradition I practice after battle, especially with no pumpkin cider around."

Chapter 51

THE REST OF THE JOURNEY greeted Nath and Hacksaw with warmer weather. They switched roads a few times, passing by caravans of people. Nath greeted them with a smile. Several women and young ladies giggled as they turned away from him. A little girl in a blue dress with flowers sewn all over it gave him a sunflower. She skipped away laughing.

Hacksaw shook his head at him. "You draw too much attention to yourself. Try frowning, keeping your head down or something."

"But I don't want to frown. I did enough of that in Slaver Town," Nath said, shifting in his saddle. He urged his horse forward alongside Hacksaw. "Listen, this is the most peace that I've had since I left home, and I want to enjoy it. So far, Nalzambor has been nothing short of a horrible place. How can this beautiful world be that way? The trees are filled with life that hums with its own special song. The water is fresh, the fish ample in supply, but just about everyone I've met has been a terror."

"Don't get too easy in your saddle, Nath. Sure, this world is a wonder, and it's not all full of trouble, but that's because good people fight to keep it so." Hacksaw took his pipe out of his pouch. "There is nothing like hunting, fishing, or a good hard day of work, rewarded by warming your sore feet by a fire, but we have to be vigilant to keep it so. Those goblins are only an itsy bit of the problems. Evil lurks in the shadows, ready to pounce like a lion at any moment."

Nath rolled his eyes. "Now you are depressing me."

Hacksaw chuckled. "The point is, we can't all be jumping and skipping around like a bushel of happy halflings. We have to work for peace and hold on to what we have. If not, someone else will take it away."

"I understand that clearly enough," Nath said, referring to what the Black Hand did to him when they robbed him. It stuck in his craw. "Is it wrong to be driven by vengeance?"

"Try not to think of it as vengeance. Think of it as justice. An unjust act robbed you and sent you into slavery. I wholeheartedly believe that you are justified in setting things right."

Nath gave an approving nod. "I like that. It sounds very much like something my father might say."

"I'm sure your father is very wise." Hacksaw stuffed his long-stemmed pipe with tobacco. He puffed on it a few times, creating a small cloud of smoke. "My father instructed me well. I still miss him to this day."

Nath cocked his head and stared at the smoke. "I just realized that when I sewed you up, you smoked the pipe, but I don't remember how you ignited the fire."

"Really?" Hacksaw lifted his brows. "I don't suppose that you would believe I'm a druid?"

"What?"

Hacksaw blew out a stream of smoke. "I'm jesting. No, this pipe was passed down to me from my grandfather, through my father. It has some magic in it and can light itself. Isn't that something?"

Nath nodded. He thought of his rectangular-shaped candles that were gifts from his father, and wondered if the same mage who made the ever-burning candles he'd used to light his way for many hours made the pipe. "What is that pipe carved out of?"

"Ah." Hacksaw held the pipe out on display. The material was bone colored with a twisting pattern along the stem and the bowl. "Have you ever seen a unicorn?"

"No." Nath gasped. "Is that unicorn horn?"

"Well, let's just say it might be. My grandfather was quite the storyteller, speaking of fantastic places and different worlds. He never said for sure about many things, but he often alluded to them as if they were the truth." Hacksaw put the pipe back in his mouth. "I've chosen to believe it is even though I've never seen a unicorn."

Nath had seen unicorns painted on many murals among the dragons inside of Dragon Home. For some reason, it prompted him to ask, "Have you ever seen a dragon?"

"Seen them? Certainly. But none of the big ones, though I do check the skies, and on more than one occasion I swear I've seen beasts far bigger than birds. Like the ones they talk about from the Great Dragon Wars."

"Where did you see the smaller ones?"

"Oh, when the poachers capture them, they make a big event of it as they parade the dead lizards though the streets," Hacksaw said. "Everyone comes out to see the dragons. There was a green one with scales that shone like gold. It had red claws like an eagle's talons, and horns curled around and behind its head like a woman's flowing hair." He glanced over at Nath. "No bigger than a man, it was something to see… Eh, Nath, are you well? You look like someone just stole that hammer of yours."

"You've seen this? Dead dragons? Paraded through the streets like a trophy, and you enjoyed it?"

"A dragon is the ultimate hunt for many men, but I don't agree with all of the butchering that they do to them. I find them to be noble beasts, to be respected, the same as a stag or a twenty-pointed red-tailed deer."

"A stag or a deer?" Nath exclaimed.

"Nath, your cheeks are getting red as roses. Did I say something offensive?"

"Yes! Yes, you did!" Nath rode away.

CHAPTER 52

NATH GALLOPED AWAY, DISTANCING HIMSELF from Hacksaw by at least a mile before veering off the road toward a small lake. Dismounting, he stormed to the pond, picked up flat stones, and skipped them several times over the calm waters. Many of the stones made it to the other side. Some of them sank after a few skips. On the far side of the pond, a frog jumped on one of the lily pads that dressed the bank. Nath skipped a stone at it. It slipped back into the waters. Nath let out a loud, "Guh!" His voice scattered a cluster of pheasants that nestled in the tall grasses. He sat down.

Hacksaw's callous words about the dragons infuriated him. He wasn't sure who he was angry with more—the hunters or Hacksaw. Dragons weren't monsters; they were people, just a different kind. The thought of them being hunted for sport, or as a prize or treasure, turned his blood hot. He panted.

A few minutes later, Hacksaw rode up behind him and dismounted. "What put a bur in your saddle, son?"

"Don't call me that, and go away." Nath pulled a wildflower from the bank and plucked the sun-yellow petals one by one.

The old warrior stood over top of him, scratching his head. "Listen, if you have a strange affection for dragons, I can respect that, but don't ever bull up on me like that again. It's childish."

"Do you even know what a dragon is?"

"What I know is that dragons almost wiped out every man and woman on this world a scant few centuries ago. Sure, they say some of them are good, and they fought alongside men, but I've never seen it." Hacksaw sat down beside Nath. "Those men who poach the dragons, they aren't a very good brood. If it makes you feel any better, I've never hunted a dragon myself. But I'm not saying I wouldn't either. If my family needed fed, I'd do what I need to do. It's just like hunting anything else."

"Have you ever hunted people? Why wouldn't you just eat them if you were starving?"

Aghast, Hacksaw said, "You don't eat your own kind. That would be a sickness. What in the world is going on in that head of yours? I don't understand it. Is there something you aren't telling me that needs to be said, because this is one of the oddest conversations I've ever had."

"I'm a dragon."

"Excuse me?"

Nath looked him dead in the eye. "I—am—a—dragon."

Scratching his hair underneath his chin, Hacksaw said, "Go on."

"I come from Dragon Home."

"The Mountain of Doom?"

"Yes, that place." Without telling the old warrior about him being the prince, he did tell him about being raised in Dragon Home and how it was his mission to save the lost dragons when he became older. Perhaps it was that part that ate at him most. He should be saving dragons and trying to find Maefon, but so far, he'd only been trying to save himself. "It's quite a story, isn't it?"

"You're full of stories," Hacksaw said. He'd propped himself back on his elbows in a comfortable position while Nath was talking. Smoke still puffed from the pipe in his mouth. "I believe them."

"You do?"

Shrugging, Hacksaw said, "It explains the things that I had questions about. Your eyes for instance. No man has eyes like that. And your arms were scarred up from that basilisk, but they've healed up nicely. You were worn down and starving, but now you appear bright-eyed and bushy-tailed. You're quicker than a jackrabbit too, by the way. Even if you weren't a dragon, you'd still be something." He tilted toward Nath. "I know good when I see it. You are good. So long as I'm around, I'll help you. If we have to rescue dragons, so be it, but they aren't so easy to find. For now, let's focus on the Black Hand." He extended his hand.

Feeling a great deal of relief, Nath shook the man's thick hand.

Late the next day, the heavily traveled roads began to widen. Coming around the bend of the tall hillsides, Nath caught his first glimpse of castle spires that overlooked the city of Quintuklen.

Hacksaw let out a whistle. "She's a sight, isn't she? The City of Kings always takes my breath when I see it. Every time is like seeing it for the first time."

Nath soaked the city in. Every building was made from large, rectangular blocks of white stone. The surrounding barrier wall formed a ring around the city layered with several inner walls in a circular maze. Birds swept across the spires, jetting from rooftop to rooftop. Quintuklen, vast and deep, was a breathtaking vision that made the steep hillside surrounding it seem small.

The wooden front gates of the outer wall opened outward. Knights in full suits of shiny platemail armor rode out on horseback four columns wide. The front ranks of knights wore full battle helmets with colorful plumes on the top. Each rode on a black horse. The knights behind them wore full helmets and no plumes. Every man's horse was equipped with two swords and a sleeve full of spears, similar to what Nath had with him. The horses stomping became louder as they emerged through the front gate. In perfect harmony, knights and horses rode as one, hooves clomping on a stone-paved road in a steady forward rhythm.

Hacksaw started whistling and waving his arms. "Bring the thunder, legionnaires! Bring the thunder!"

Nath counted over two thousand knights on horseback. Bringing up the rear were five hundred more riders in lighter armor, leading what looked to be wagons loaded with rations, supplies, and more weaponry. The ground quaked as they rode onward. Behind them, under light guard of men, were elves in gorgeously woven robes. Distinct from men, their slender faces with sharp handsome features were fixed ahead, with their backs straight and chins upward.

Leaning over his saddle horn, Hacksaw said, "That's odd. What are elves doing all the way up here in Quintuklen?"

A chill ran down Nath's spine. He hadn't seen a full-blooded elf since he was with the Trahaydeen. His grip tightened on the reins. "I don't know," he said, "but let's find out."

CHAPTER 53

AS THE LAST OF THE legionnaire army passed out of the gate and moved farther down the road, Hacksaw said, "Follow me, I'll do the talking. The soldiers on the wall are tight-lipped and won't hesitate to stick a person that noses in their business."

Nath's eyes followed the back end of the army. The elves he saw stirred him. They were all men, but they reminded him of Chazzan and Maefon. The elves he knew inside the mountain were very good people, as kind and gentle as a person could hope for, but his image of them was tainted now. "So, elves don't come this far north?"

"Well, it's not unheard of," Hacksaw said. "I've met with plenty of elves in my time, not so much as men of course. It was mostly commerce related. Every race has something to offer, at least, among the elves, dwarves, gnomes, and halflings. The orcs and such, not so much, but they aren't half bad at trading."

Hacksaw rode up to the main entrance where several guards were stationed along the wall. The wooden gates behind the huge archway remained open. A smaller pedestrian archway was set off to the right. Two soldiers in ringmail armor, covered in green tunics with a crown-and-lightning-bolt insignia on the chest, stood guard at the entrance. Their metal helmets with a small nose guard came down to the top of their eyes. Hacksaw lifted a hand. "Hail and well met."

Both soldiers nodded. The taller of the two, standing on the right of the entrance, spear in hand, stepped forward, eyeing Hacksaw's horse and gear. "Are you seeking entrance into the City of Kings?"

"No, not today," Hacksaw said, watching both men walking around both his and Nath's horses with the eyes of a hawk. "We are passing by and saw the legionnaires in full complement. It made my heart sing seeing those bright banners flapping. I was just curious, where would such a full complement be headed? Even if they were going to the field for training, that size of a force was quite excessive."

The soldiers grabbed Hacksaw's horse by the harness. "A legionnaire's business is a legionnaire's business. They don't share it with commoners, especially people just wandering through."

The soldier's disposition rankled Nath. He opened his mouth.

Without looking at Nath, Hacksaw held his hand up to him and looked down at the soldiers. "Once a legionnaire, always a legionnaire." He pulled his sleeve up past his elbow and showed it to the soldier. There was an eagle with spread-out black wings, carrying lightning bolts in its talons.

The soldier's eyes widened. "Forgive me, marshal. I had no way of knowing." He saluted. So did the other guard.

Hacksaw returned the salute. "At ease, soldiers. You did a fine job manning your post. I did the same thing back in my day. Anyway, do you feel a little more comfortable telling me what this is all about?"

"They are going to war with the dwarves."

"What?" Hacksaw's horse shifted beneath him. "That's the most outlandish thing I've ever heard. By the king's crowns, why would they do such a thing?"

"It's a land war. As I understand it, there is a conflict over mineral mines in the hills just south of our borders. The dwarves claim it and have dug in. They are prepared to die for it." The soldier stood up on tiptoe. "Did you see those elves? They are aiding our cause with this. I've never seen the likes of them before. We will flatten the dwarves, no doubt about it."

"I hate to say it, but have you ever tried to dig a dwarf out of a mountain?" Hacksaw said.

"No," the soldier replied.

"Do you know of anyone that ever tried?"

"No."

"Well, there's a reason for that." Hacksaw shook his head. "Thanks for the information, son."

"My pleasure, Marshal… uh, what is your name, sir?"

"Hacksaw."

Both guards quickly glanced at each other with big eyes. Their backs straightened. They saluted heartily. "Our pleasure, always, Marshal Hacksaw. It's been an honor to meet you."

Hacksaw saluted. "May you always ride on thunder."

Nath and Hacksaw rode in silence until Quintuklen disappeared behind the hills. Hacksaw had a somber look on his face and appeared to be in deep thought. Nath broke the silence. "Well, Marshal Hacksaw, it seems that you have a reputation about you. Those soldiers' eyes turned into moons when they heard your name. Care to explain that?"

"What… huh?" Hacksaw shook his head as if he was woken from a dream. "Sorry, but this talk about the legionnaires taking on the dwarves disturbs me. That's not a natural thing. I just hope it doesn't get bloody and they can come to an agreement. Or else, it will get really ugly. I have plenty of faith in my legionnaires, but separating dwarves from minerals is about as easy as giving an ogre a bath. Not our mission, but it troubles me. What did you ask me?"

"I was saying, those soldiers back at Quintuklen knew your name. They acted as if it was renowned or something." Nath raked his hair out of his eyes. "Care to explain?"

"I told you about how I came upon Green Tongue, didn't I?"

"You took it from a fallen goblin."

"Yes, well, that's because I was the only one left standing."

CHAPTER 54

ON THE DUSTY ROAD LEADING toward Riegelwood from Quintuklen, Hacksaw started telling a story in a low and easy voice. Nath rode beside him, listening intently. He'd heard many stories since he'd ventured out of Dragon Home. Most of them were lies, not to mention the tales he overheard in Slaver Town. The orc guards were particularly good at it, lying about everything they'd ever done with one always trying to top the other. One thing was for certain, he needed to be more careful about who he believed. He felt confident about Hacksaw, but he still didn't know the man that well.

Puffing on his pipe, Hacksaw said, "I was a lot younger when I rode with the legionnaires. I'd just been knighted weeks earlier, and it might have been the finest day of my life. Well, as it goes, the legionnaires patrol the lands all around the City of Kings, just up to the dwarven and elven and orcen borders and just about everything south of there. I headed out on my first patrol, a squad of four, led by Marshal McCracken. He had twenty years in, but looked like he'd put in forty. He wasn't a big man, but was stalwart as they come, and spoke in a voice deeper than mine. The other two were Matty and Sacks. They were a couple of southerners out of the settlements, lean and athletic, with dark skin and eyes as green as a bean. Brothers and veterans, with two decades served between them. I learned more from them in two weeks of patrolling than I learned anywhere else in my life.

"Anyway, we started getting word about the goblins ramping up their raids and heading into the Shale Hills southwest of Quintuklen. They'd attack in a pack of about four or five, swelling around people that traveled in twos or fours. The goblins, as you've seen, only attack when they have superior numbers to their prey. We tracked them, following sprinkles of blood on the ground and on the leaves. It seemed one of them had been wounded. Once we hit the Shale Hills, it got a little trickier. Those chips of rock do good to hide a trail, and it astounds me that the trees still grow in those areas at all. Higher up in the hills, the pine trees made a tall hedge line in front of a small wooden fort in the rocks, half covered in overgrowth. We could see the wood was rotting. It couldn't have held many, maybe twelve or twenty, by the looks of it. So, we hung back, spying from a distance, and waited for the yellowbacks to emerge again. McCracken, figuring for a dozen at most, thought we'd cut them down real easy once they came out and we got in behind him." His voice trailed off. "He was wrong."

Nath patted Hacksaw's shoulder. The man's eyes had watered up. Hacksaw sniffed and wiped his nose. "You can stop if you want."

"No, I need to tell it again. Even though it opens a wound in me, I feel it honors them." Hacksaw cleared his throat. "So, the yellowbacks—"

"Why do you call them yellowbacks?"

"It's just what we call those cowards. It's been a name since long before I came around, but I think it's because of that mustard yellowness in their skin."

Nath shrugged. "Sorry to interrupt."

"No worries. So, we waited outside of that fort for a few hours. A gate opened, and five goblins crept out. All they had on them were hatchets and some long knives. They wore bone jewelry and the worst excuse for hide armor I ever saw. And you know, there was a stink coming from the fort that I'd never forget. Goblins stink, that's for certain. So, we followed the scurrying yellowbacks halfway down the hill, keeping our distance, hoping to track them after we hit bottom. We found them, standing ankle deep in the shale, waiting on us with that putrid yellow gleam around their beady eyes. My neck hairs stood on end as I watched McCracken slide his spear out of its sleeve." Hacksaw shook his head. "The moment it came out, it happened." Hacksaw slapped his hands together. "Whack!"

Nath rocked back in his saddle. "What happened?"

"Trap," Hacksaw said out of the side of his mouth. "The goblins burst out of the shale right underneath our horses' feet. They gored our mounts by jabbing them right underneath their bellies. All four horses reared up, and all four of us knights went down. By the time I realized what was going on, I was looking up the hill. Goblins by the dozens were streaming down the hillside, howling like wild dogs. My limbs locked. I couldn't feel my fingers or toes.

You probably don't know this about knights, but we don't run from a fight. We fight until it's over or we are over."

Nath swallowed. His jaw tightened just from hearing the severity of the moment. "Dozens of goblins and only four men?"

"Three," Hacksaw said, talking in a long breath. "I looked back for Marshal McCracken. He caught a spear in the neck and was down on the shale, fighting for his last breath against the goblins who attacked us. I saw his eyes. He was gone, but his body still fought on. That left me, Matty, and Sacks. They were yelling. I couldn't hear a thing. Sacks stuffed a shield in my arms and drew my sword for me. He stuck it in my hand and screamed in my face, 'Fight!'"

The horses jumped.

Hacksaw continued, "It was all a bloody nightmare after that. Matty, Sacks, and I formed a defensive triangle standing back to back. Hiding behind our shields, we braced ourselves for the coming impact. It was Matty doing all of the talking, shouting, 'Stand firm! Strike swift!'" He coughed out a sob. "The goblins hit us in a tide of flesh. My feet were planted firm on the ground, but I was pushed back. To be honest, I didn't have any idea what I was doing. Those first moments were a blur. I snapped out of it when I tasted blood in my mouth for the first time that wasn't my own. I can still taste goblin blood now. I realized I was in a fight to the finish.

"Strike hard. Strike fast. Matty said that in a cadence. It's those first several moments that matter the most. I know my training and my armor saved me. I used to think that heavy armor was a waste, that it would slow you down, not to mention that it was uncomfortable, but I'll never, never complain about that polished breastplate again. It saved my hide.

"So, we were being pushed around, and the goblin bodies were stacked up to our waists, but more kept coming. My arms felt like they would fall off at any moment. I have no idea how I hung on. They say in the heat of battle, a man can do things beyond his means. By power that was not my own I sustained. I walled the yellowbacks off with my shield and kept thrusting. The sword pierced them, and they screamed like a forest banshee every time. I still wake to bad dreams, hearing that chaos ringing in my ears. I see their twisted faces trying to peel me out of my armor. With blood in my eyes and my body burning, I fought the battle of lifetimes.

"Then Matty's voice gurgled. He fell under a heap of the fiends. Back to back, Sacks quavered against me. I heard a blade slip though the links in his armor. His backside swayed into mine. Sacks yelled out one last cry, saying, 'Ride the thunder, Hacksaw. Ride the thunder from the sky!' Just as he died, I struck down the goblin who'd stabbed him with everything I had left. My longsword took half of its face off. I figured I was doomed after that. I expected something to run me through at any moment, but then thunder clapped, the wind twisted through the trees in a howl, and all of sudden, I felt the spirits of McCracken, Matty, and Sacks rush into me. Their voices were in my head, urging me to fight on. A silvery flame came upon me. I waded into the goblins with the ravenous speed of a panther. I dropped my shield, picked up another sword, and turned into a bushwhacker." Hacksaw's voice rose like a wave. "The goblins fell in twos and threes. Like the rain in a storm, nothing could stop me.

Goblins were sprawled out all over the shale, leaking blood like sap from a tree. The spirits of my brethren knights fled me.

"There was only two of us standing, if I could call it standing. It was just me facing against the goblin commander, and he wasn't anything like the rest. He was bigger than I, broader than oaks, with hardly a stitch of clothing on him. My swords hung at my sides. I couldn't lift them. The goblin commander held Green Tongue in his hand. The blade burned like a long green candle flame. I could see in his eyes that he was ready to whittle me down. He spit on the ground. I let the swords fall from my aching fingers and dropped to my knees. Sick to my stomach, I retched. The goblin stormed right at me, holding Green Tongue high overhead. With my last breath, I yelled at him, 'Ride the thunder!' Lucky for me, goblins are stupid, and he didn't see the spear half buried in the shale underneath my knees. Summoning everything I had in me, I snatched it up and buried it deep inside his heart. That goblin died, eyes wide open, standing, propped up by the spear. Green Tongue fell at my feet. I cried."

Nath wiped his eyes. He felt every word Hacksaw said as if he was there. After riding another half mile down the road, he finally asked, "How many were there?"

"A hundred goblins in all, including the big one. I told the other knights what happened. I asked them how McCracken, Matty, and Sacks became a part of me. They said legionnaires have tales about riding the thunder before they move on to the next world. It's a bond, born from blood and battle, that we all share. I never felt anything like that before, and I've never felt the likes of it since, but I rode the thunder that day, and the goblins felt every bit of it in my steel." Hacksaw sagged in his saddle. "Whew, it exhausts me to tell it."

Nath nodded. To him the words rang true, and he believed every one.

CHAPTER 55

ON A BLUSTERY DAY, LESS than an hour before sunset, Nath and Hacksaw arrived just outside of Riegelwood. Nath donned the hood of his traveling cloak and stooped in the saddle. Hacksaw let his shoulders sag, with his own hood down around the shoulders. He looked at Nath. "How do you feel?"

"Angry," Nath replied. All of his memories of the Black Hand swelled up inside him. His hands became clammy. It had been over two years, but it felt like a decade since he cast his eyes on the stony walls that surrounded Riegelwood like a hedge. They'd paraded him down the streets like a criminal to a chorus of boos from citizens who thought he'd kidnapped Princess Janna. He wondered if her mind ever recovered or if she even remembered him. He took a deep breath though his nose and exhaled. "Very angry."

"You're going to need a clear mind before we set into this," Hacksaw said. "If you go into this on all emotion, they'll catch on to you. I know you want to rush in there and start pounding on doors, but you need to be patient."

"I know," Nath said, shifting in his saddle. "And I'd like to think I have plenty of time, but I am worried about my friends in Slaver Town. I need to get them free of that place."

"One thing at a time, Nath. You can't take care of everyone. Sometimes, you have to do for yourself." Hacksaw clamped his cloak at the neck. "I've been thinking about Slaver Town. You escaped, so I'm fairly certain they are searching for you. There's been enough time for word to carry up here."

Nath rolled his eyes. "Ugh, I didn't even consider that, but they wouldn't look so far for me. Would they?"

"If it cost them money, I'm sure they would. That's what drives everything, and if they prized you as much as you told me, the slavers are looking for you." With two fingers, Hacksaw pointed at his eyes and ears. "They see all. Listen, I know it's going to kill you, but I'm going to ride in alone. They'll take little notice of an old northerner like me. Will that be fine by you?"

"Where are we going to meet when you come back?" Nath replied. "Am I supposed to wait in the chill?"

"Chill? You have plenty of grasses and a bedroll to keep you warm. Just keep out of sight." Scratching the back of his head, Hacksaw added, "Where are those statues you told me about? Where the brigands first robbed you?"

Nath pointed to another road. "That way, but that's too far. I'm just going to linger here. I'll be fine. I don't need much sleep, and I'll see you coming from plenty far away, even in the night."

"Do they patrol out here?"

"No, I don't think so. Soldiers do hug the city though. You might not want to go in there with Green Tongue either. They'll slaver over it."

"He's coming with me, but I can conceal him better."

Nath dismounted. He grabbed a bedroll, his warhammer, and some rations from his saddlebag. "Why don't you stable them both together? I sleep just fine without a fire, and not having a horse will draw less attention. So, you'll check into the Oxen Inn?"

"Yes, I'll see what Nina's situation is, if she's there. You gave a pretty clear description of them all. I'll ride back out in the morning and tell you what I know. Don't be surprised, Nath, if they've moved on. But we'll see." He turned his horse away. "So long."

Nath waved. He stood in the grass, watching Hacksaw saunter on horseback into Riegelwood with a sway in his shoulders. It was a little difficult watching him go.

I hope I can trust him.

Chapter 56

The moon shone like a bright star on the breezy evening. The crickets chirped, and small critters burrowed under the grasses. Sitting behind the thickets outside of the road, Nath lay on his bedroll with his eyes cast up. Streaking clouds rushed though the sky. He watched for dragons.

Oh, what I wouldn't do to be up there, where I could see anything, and have all of the freedom I ever wanted.

He closed his eyes and listened to the wind rustling through the grasses. Beyond the sounds of nature, he could hear voices shouting in the city of Riegelwood. Even though there was a chilling nip in the air, it was still a fine night, and it sounded as if some sort of celebration was going on within. Nath propped himself up on his elbows.

I bet Hacksaw is having a fine time in there. And here I am in the woodland. Though, I shouldn't complain. It's better than Slaver Town.

He rolled on his side and closed his eyes. He rolled back to his other side. He tried to sleep, but he wasn't tired. The last few days of riding had been easy, and he rested plenty when they camped at night. The truth was, he didn't need much sleep, and sitting in the woodland with nothing to do was agonizing. He was so close to his enemies. He didn't want to go the slow way about it either. He wanted to hit them when they didn't expect it. Hacksaw's plan sounded like something that would take forever. He sat up.

"I can't just sit here and do nothing," he said to himself. Something in the brush scurried away. "I'm going for a walk."

Nath picked up Stone Smiter and went on a stroll. Staying on the edge of the grasses, he headed back on the road to Quintuklen, but split off on the road where Nina took him to show him where Princess Janna had been kidnapped. It was a long walk, but he arrived at the spot where the princess's guards were all turned to stone. The men were at least half covered in overgrowth with their faces frozen in terror. It reminded him of what he saw when he encountered the basilisk. He ran his hand over one soldier's face. He could feel the man's gaping mouth and gruesome expression with his fingers. He tugged on the thick veins of ivy that covered up most of the body.

Nina had said these men were turned to stone but was very hazy on the detail. They had been dragged from the road into the grove. She claimed that the Riverlynn Monks did it, but in truth it was the Black Hand that kidnapped the princess. The question was, who or what turned the soldiers to stone? And giving them a closer inspection, noting the thicker vegetation around some of them, it was quite possible that these statues could have been in this condition for years, if not decades. But, the uniforms did match the ones of the soldiers for Riegelwood.

I'm such a fool! These soldiers probably have families that cut back the grasses from time to time. These bloody statues may have been here for years. There probably isn't such a thing as the Riverlynn Monks! Or Riverlynn for that matter!

He'd had plenty of time in prison to think about things, but he hadn't taken time to take it back as far as he was now. He just walked into a city, put his trust in the first person he had a full conversation with, and followed along like a puppy dog. For all he knew, the button with three wavy water lines she found on the road using Winzee's Lantern of Revealing was something she planted. Or it was just a button that could have come from anything else. It was all clear to him at this point. Everything he was told was a lie, but that didn't mean there wasn't a clue in it. It might serve him later. He needed to learn from his mistakes. Still, he wanted to scream.

Standing in the grove of statues sent a chill down his spine. An owl hooted, and the wind picked up. He felt sorry for the soldiers and wondered if there was a way to bring them back, like the people in the Nameless Temple. For all intents and purposes, a basilisk could have been the culprit. He started walking away.

They are not your problem, Nath. They'll have to remain someone else's.

He touched one of the statues on the shoulder. "Sorry, men."

A clamor of footsteps came from the road west of his position. A large group of men were talking and joking with one another. Women cackled among the gruff voices too as they cheerfully sauntered down the road toward Riegelwood.

Nath hid behind a thicket on the edge of the road. He hunkered down. Dark silhouettes of men came down the road, walking on soft feet, but making plenty of chatter. They carried no torches or lanterns. Their clothing hung loose on their bodies, and they all walked with an easy gait. Swords, knives, and daggers were belted on their hips. There was a sloshing of liquid from jugs that were being passed around. Bringing up the rear were two saddled riding horses.

Many conversations were going on all at once, but one man's distinct voice overpowered the rest. "Enjoy the Festival of the Coming Winter, but don't forget your role and this mission, Whisperers. And as always, wait for my signal."

Nath gripped Stone Smiter with white knuckles. He coiled back, eyes burning on the men that had a hand in abducting him. *Men of Whispers, prepare to pay!*

CHAPTER 57

UNABLE TO FIND A TABLE that suited him in the crowded Oxen Inn, Hacksaw settled in behind the bar on the farthest end. He drank mead from a very tall wooden tankard and took his time chewing the plate of food they served him. The mouthwatering cooked meat, slathered in gravy, with a mix of cheeses and buttered breads, took his thoughts away from why he was there. It was a bristling atmosphere, with the patrons full of celebration and joy as they sang song after song in honor of the Festival of the Coming Winter.

Hacksaw wiped the gravy from his beard on a maroon cloth napkin. A tiny young woman wearing a pink apron wiped down the bar, took orders, tapped kegs, caught his eye, and swung by. "Sir, how is your meal? Do you need anything else?"

"Perhaps," he said with a smile, "but not at the moment. Say, what is your name, young lady?"

The solemn little gal turned her back, wiping down his area. "They call me Little Shirl, and you?"

"I'm Hacksaw." He tipped his chin and pulled out his pipe.

"Where are you from, Hacksaw?"

"North," he said, proudly. "Huskan. Now, winter's really cold up there, and we don't celebrate it. We don't dread it either, we just keep chopping wood."

"I'll be back," she said, scurrying away to wait on two men who'd just wiggled their way into the bar. Little Shirl wasn't the only one behind the bar. There were three more young ladies, all attractive, with smiles on their faces and their hands full. Little Shirl returned. Wiping her face on her apron, she said, "Sorry, I didn't mean to end our conversation, but we've had many visitors from Huskan before, and they say the same thing as you."

"Forgive my lack of originality, Little Shirl. I'll try to put a little commentary on my comments next time," he said with a wink.

"No, I like your charm compared to the others I recall. I can tell you are a very warm man, and I'm sure your heart alone keeps you and your wife warm at night."

"I don't have a wife," he said.

"Really," she said, making a smile. "Are you a widower?"

"No, just never married."

"That is fascinating, Hacksaw." She touched his hand. "You are very handsome. What brings you to Riegelwood?"

With his cheeks warming under her glowing stare, he said, "Uh, just a little bored and lonely, I suppose. I thought I'd do some traveling. Take a break from logging. I've been around, but there are plenty of places in this world that I've never seen."

"That sounds exciting. I've never been outside of Riegelwood. I stay too busy." A patron four stools over called out for her. "Excuse me." She hurried away, took the man's order, then disappeared through the doorway that led back into the kitchen.

Hacksaw dabbed his forehead on his napkin. The thrill came over him as he was quickly reminded about his days of soldiering and adventuring. There were many taverns, inns, and an assortment of ladies who cozied up to him and sent his blood running. It was the innocent ones, like Little Shirl, that surprised him the most. He gulped down his mead and finished off his plate of food. He took out his pipe and started smoking.

Turning in his stool, he watched two halflings on the stage. Their locks of hair were almost as red as a cherry. They played lutes with fast fingers, working the strings vigorously, but their smiles were as broad as a rainbow as they sang. There was a third halfling, identical to the others, springing from table to table, playing a tambourine to the thrill of the crowd. Hacksaw's shoulders gently rocked side to side. His hand patted the bar in rhythm. Caught up in the moment, he listened to the words they sang in a rolling, bright, and cheery tune.

We'll never forget the day he came, the day the dragon came to town,

As quick as the wind, with fire on his chin, he stole the princess away,

So, we never forget the day he came, the day the dragon came to town.

The flames were bright, his teeth like swords, his scales as bright as flame,

It was the day he came, we'll never forget, he took the princess to his cave,

But the brave, the bold, the daring, the citizens of the wood, swore an oath to one another that they would take the dragon down.

They took to the Channel, where the storms of heaven roared, the floods came to swallow them the day they left the down.

The day after the dragon came to town… the day after the dragon came to town,

But armed with hearts of gold and chivalry, the brave warriors of the wood, armed with righteous power, sought the dragon to cut him down, the day after the dragon came to town.

Deep in a cave, black and cold, they hunted the cold-hearted beast, fought with a lion's ferocity and slew the dragon down... and slew the dragon down.

That was the day that we will never forget, the day the dragon came to town,

And on that day, the dragon sealed its fate, for stealing a priceless princess destined to be the ruler of our town.

So, we'll never forget the day it came, the day the dragon came to town. It tried to take our crown. Now it soils a dark, damp cave.

That's what the dragon gets for coming to our town, don't ever come to our town, don't ever come to our town, don't ever come to our town, don't ever come to our town.

Hacksaw started coughing, smoke from his pipe spilling out. He couldn't help but think that song was about Nath. Those halflings were exactly the ones Nath described. They were part of the Men of Whispers. The thing was, there wasn't any sign in the tavern of the woman, Nina, or any others for the matter. But, being so caught up in the moment, Hacksaw hadn't been looking really hard. He'd been enjoying himself.

I need to get my head on the mission. I'm here for Nath, not me, but this is nice.

He started coughing again. He picked up his tankard and drank the rest of his mead. A few more rumbling coughs came out. "Lords of Thunder, what's gotten into me."

A heavy hand started slapping his back. "Are you well, old traveler?" the person patting his back said.

Tapping his chest, he twisted his head over his shoulder. Hacksaw's eyes widened as he caught sight of the biggest woman he'd ever seen.

CHAPTER 58

A MOMENT FROM UNFURLING HIS RAGE on the Men of Whispers, Nath felt an invisible hand on his shoulder. He sank back into his crouch. No one was behind him, but his inner conscience spoke to him. "Don't do it, Nath. Not now. Patience."

The Men of Whispers sauntered right past without a single glance his way, showing no signs of care or fear. It was the swagger in their stride, the cocky cheerfulness in their forces that had Nath's fingers twisting on the leather bindings on the hammer. He took a deep breath. Once the brigands were out of eyeshot, but with their foul mutterings still tickling his ears, he set out after them.

If they are going to kidnap somebody, then I'm going to have to stop them.

Like a prowling panther, Nath followed, picking his way through the forest, careful not to reveal himself. The Men of Whispers might be a little careless, but they weren't stupid, and Nath wasn't about to do anything stupid himself. But following them into Riegelwood wasn't the best idea either.

Just outside of town, where the glow of torches and lanterns were specks in front of the buildings, the brigands gathered. The tallest of them stood in the middle. It was Andeen, a slender, bearded man, with a little charm in his cutting voice that ruffled the muscles underneath a man's skin. It seemed, after two years, none of the brigands had changed at all. And in the dark, Nath gave them closer study, memorizing their shapes, sizes, and how they walked.

Finally, in pairs and groups of three, the brigands spread out, entering the city from a different direction. Two brigands, along with the pair of horses, stayed back, just off the road. They were bundled up fairly well, pacing and rubbing their hands together. The riding horses nickered and snorted quietly. Their ears twitched.

So, that is the getaway plan for the kidnappers. We'll see about that.

Facing the city, the pair of surly men talked quietly, passing a bottle back and forth. One gruff voice said to the other, "It's going to be a bit."

"Don't be so sure," the other replied, speaking with an elven accent as he took a swig from the bottle. "Andeen acts fast when the moment comes."

"Nah, they won't do anything before the pyro-works scream in the skies. That's when I would do it."

The leaner brigand shrugged.

Nath was certain the man was part-elf, and possibly the second one was part-orc. They'd be a rough pair to overcome if he wasn't careful. Using the shadows cast by the trees from the moon, Nath moved in behind them on cat's feet. At the same time, the part-orc and part-elf went for their blades and turned. Nath grabbed them both by the back of their heads, filled his fingers with hair, and slammed their noggins together as hard as he could. The part-elf sagged. The orc stood on noodling legs, teetering. Nath slugged him hard in the jaw. The orc brigand spun to the ground in a heap.

Finding rope on the horses, Nath bound up both brigands, gagged them, and rolled them into the woodland. With a smack on their hindquarters, he sent the horses galloping away.

"That should put a kink in their plans. Now, it's time to hatch another plan of my own. There won't be any more kidnappings on my watch." Nath donned his hood. Using his sledgehammer like a cane, with the head in his hand, hidden by the sleeve of his cloak, and the handle on the ground, he sauntered into town disguised as an old man, completely oblivious of the two-headed vulture that now circled high above him.

Chapter 59

Hacksaw blinked at the sight of the mountain of a woman behind him. She was attractive, with a hard, angular jawline. Auburn braids of hair twisted up on her head. Fit with the rigorous build of a blacksmith, her arms were bare and muscular. She wore a weathered brown leather tunic, buttoned down the front. She kept patting his back with a calloused hand. "Are you well? You appear to have choked on your spirits."

Turning on his stool, Hacksaw swallowed. "Thanks, kind lady. I think the show had me worked up. It's a lively place." He extended his hand. "I'm Hacksaw. From Huskan."

She showed a little smile and took his hand with an iron grip. "I'm Nina. I run this establishment. So, you are enjoying yourself?"

"Am I ever," he said, pulling his hand free from her powerful grip. He'd never known a woman so strong before. "You sure do know how to run a business. This place has been jumping and hopping since I've come in, but it runs smooth as a sailboat on breezy waters."

"Why, thank you," she said, filling the stool beside him on the left. "I hope you don't mind, but when I have a moment to spare, I check in with newcomers. I take a keen interest in our customers at the Oxen Inn."

"That's just good business," he said, turning back toward the bar and facing her. She sat taller than him in her stool, but not as broad. "Back in Huskan, my mother and I have a tavern, but it's a far cry from this. It's mostly a place to get something hot to eat and warm your toes after a long day in the timbers. It's respectable, just not very fanciful."

"It seems we clothe ourselves in a similar cloth," she said, eyeing him up and down. "Hacksaw, you wouldn't take it the wrong way if I treated you to another round of mead, would you? I just appreciate a kindred spirit. And you have a salty demeanor that I like enough to share a cup with but nothing else."

"No, I'd be flattered, and please, no need to think I'd try to take advantage. You are a young and pretty woman, but I could pass for your grandfather." Hacksaw puffed on his pipe. "See, only old codgers smoke from a stem pipe. Just look around."

She made a delightful laugh. "I'm sure you know your way around the ladies. I can see it in you." She looked deep in his eyes. "I watch people all day. I know what they are thinking. I'm a very good judge of character like that."

Hacksaw leaned back. Nina had a deadly intent in her voice, but it came across in a very charming tone. She was attractive, just as Nath described, but there was a nasty streak lurking behind her eyes too. "Eh, I'm not sure what you are meaning."

Nina clamped her left hand down on his right forearm. "I've seen all types. I know a seasoned adventurer when I see one. There are other places in this town for men like you, and to keep my patrons and my reputation intact, I like making sure you aren't bringing any trouble."

Hacksaw winced. Her hand had the power of a vise in it. He looked down. She wore the leather gauntlet that Nath described as the Gauntlet of Goam. The blue gemstone was like the sky, a twinkle deep within. "It seems there has been a shift in the wind, and I don't follow. I thought you were buying a fellow tavern keeper a tankard."

"Sorry, but that steel on your hip doesn't look like anything an ordinary man carries. You are an adventurer, and those are troublemakers. I'm not very fond of their kind."

"Those days are decades gone," he said, pulling his arm out of her fingers. "I'm more soldier than adventurer, and all I have to show for it is this sword, if you don't mind. And I'm not going to cross one countryside to another without it." He dumped the ashes out of his pipe onto his plate. "And you should be a little less direct with your elderly patrons. I'll pass on the drink." He got out of his stool and put three silver talents on the bar. "I'll be enjoying the festival elsewhere."

Chapter 60

Using the sledgehammer as a crutch, Nath hobbled into Riegelwood, hunched over, and dragging a foot from time to time. Leaning heavily on the cane, he made his way down the festive streets. The celebrations in Riegelwood were in full swing. The townsfolk teetered through the streets, arm in arm, some dancing and others singing. They carried large canisters of ale or clay jugs of wine. There were bonfires in the middle of the streets. Hosts of people gathered around them. The lantern posts were decorated with blue and white colors, casting off a wintery glow in the streets. Colorful streamers crossed the streets, connecting one building to the other. Women, dressed in heavy cloaks trimmed in fur, squealed and giggled to the men who entertained them with songs and rugged acts of bravado as they wrestled bare-chested in the streets with one another.

Sneaking a peek from time to time, Nath thought to himself, *These people have lost their minds.* When he first came to Riegelwood, over two years ago, the thriving town had a wholesome sense about it. The people, in general, seemed openhearted, but now they were all caught up in revelry. He shoved his way onto the storefront porches, where many made a line between the posts, watching the wild parades carry on throughout the city. He caught a man breathing flames out of his mouth. Three acrobats jumped up and down as seesaws hurled them over the bonfire flames. The raucous crowd screamed in drunken jubilation.

What is wrong with these people? They seem as if they have gone mad.

An older woman and a young daughter, wearing heavy cloth dresses, and with their heads covered in a modest white raiment, scuttled Nath's way. The young woman's eyes were big as saucers as her head turned toward the activities. "Mother, why are the people being so wild? They scare me."

Head down and holding her daughter tightly by the wrist, the mother replied, "They are expecting a long winter. They are getting the orneriness out of them, I suppose. But I've never seen them so worked up before. Just don't look at them. We'll be to your grandmother's soon."

As the women passed Nath, he caught a couple of men sharing a bottle, leering at the women. They fell in step behind the mother and daughter, sniggering. They hustled to catch up to the women, making catcalls. Nath stuck his foot out. The first slob fell face-first into the planks. The second tripped over top of his friend. They both jumped up with faces as red as beets. In a shaky old voice, Nath said, "Pardon me, young ones. My sight is poor even for my age. You are not harmed, are you?"

"No," the burliest of the two said. He shoved Nath into the wall. "But you will be, old timer." The ham-fisted man punched Nath hard in the stomach. His knuckles busted on Nath's metal breastplate. "Eeeouch!" The drunk clutched his busted hand. "You're wearing some sort of armor. I'm going to kill you, trick—"

Nath whacked the man in the jaw with the butt end of the hammer. As the other drunk went after a dagger tucked between his belt and bulging belly, Nath slugged the man hard in the face. He caught the second one as he fell, and dragged the knocked-out man into a store doorway. Scanning his surroundings, not one person looked his way or appeared to have even noticed. The two women were gone.

There's another good deed done.

Keeping on the porches, Nath half-hobbled, half-moseyed through the town. He'd learned his way around enough in the short time he spent there before and had a good idea where he was going. Peeking through the crowds from time to time, he searched for the Men of Whispers, who could be lurking anywhere. The problem was, there were thousands of people milling about the streets, and despite the lanterns, torches, and bonfires, it was still dark, casting a lot of shade on people's faces.

Not far from the Oxen Inn, a huge stage had been erected out of wood that overlooked the crowd. Center stage, singers, acrobats, and dancers performed amazing feats as one. It reminded Nath of the showings that the Trahaydeen elves performed in Dragon Home. From a talent standpoint, it wasn't the same equivalent, but the effort was there. Seeing that was where the crowd was thickest, he wedged his way between some folks standing on the edge of the porch. Casting his gaze over the area, he listened to the conversations around him intently.

A pair of gusty women, half covered in animal furs mixed with cotton clothing, said, "I'm quite eager for the city lord's appearance. He's such a handsome man. His smile knocked me out of my loafers the first time I saw him, I swear it."

The second woman, with a thick head of hair hanging down past her shoulders, said, "You fall for any man that smiles at you."

"You don't think the city lord is handsome, Lila?"

"Of course I do, Sallie, but I don't lose my senses over it. Yes, he has the smile of an elf and the eyes of a dove, but I'm not going to slobber all over him, or throw my britches at him like you tried once."

Gasping, Sallie replied, "I never threw my britches at him. I was carrying my wash from the wellsprings, and the wind caught them. You make it sound like I threw them in his face. That's awful."

"Heh, heh, heh," Lila laughed. "I saw what I saw, and I'm sticking to it."

Sallie hit Lila in the shoulder. "Like you are beyond reproach. If he wasn't getting married, you'd be throwing yourself on the floor of the castle gate."

"Maybe you, but not me." Lila grinned ear to ear. An eruption of applause and cheering broke out as the act on stage came to an end and the entertainers, hand in hand, took a bow. They departed. A quartet of trumpeters in royal raiment came to the front and blasted their horns. "Ah, the city lord comes with his new bride to be." She nudged her friend. "Try to restrain yourself."

"I'll whistle all I want. I at least have to get him to look at me."

Nath turned his eyes to the activity on the stage. He was confused about the description of City Lord Janders. He didn't remember him as the women described, but he was glad to hear the man would marry again. Perhaps that was what Riegelwood needed to regain its civility. He peered around the edges of the stage.

I hope I see Janna and she is well.

Nath rose out of his stooped position when the crowd fell silent and the horns went quiet.

A man in formal winter garb stepped out to the front of the stage. He was very tall and lean and spoke in a strong voice. "Citizens of Riegelwood, please welcome with a hearty applause, City Lord Tobias and his bride to be, Lady Janna."

What?

Chapter 61

NINA HOOKED HACKSAW'S ARM AND pulled him back onto his stool. "Now hold on, Frosty Britches. I didn't mean to turn the table and seem rude, or disrespectful for that matter, but I was vetting you. It comes with the territory, and it's natural to me."

Hacksaw cast an inward smile to himself. Nina played right into his hands. She came at him like an attack dog, and he flipped it back on her. She felt guilty. He could see it by the creases in her face. Once again, he pulled free of her sticky grip. "I don't know. Once I'm ready to move, I'm ready to move. We don't treat people like that in the north, unless they are acting up or something. I don't think I've done anything but enjoy myself until now. You've ruined it for me."

"Hacksaw, just give me one more chance," she said, swinging her arm over his shoulder and leaning into him with her full body. "Little Shirl! Take this plate, bring two more tankards, and some pie."

Little Shirl broke away from the order she was taking, and quick as a mouse, she took Hacksaw's plate and tankard back into the kitchen.

"I bet you don't have a place to stay," Nina said, rubbing his back. "Do you? It's too crowded this year, but I always keep at least one room back in case someone relevant swings in. I want you to have it, no charge, tonight. I feel bad, and I want to make things right with you."

Her appealing smile made it easy to give in. With a nod, Hacksaw said, "I'll take the room, but I'd insist on paying for it."

"No, there is no need for that at all. Just let me make this right by you." She embraced him. "I'll feel better for it."

"I know better than to tell a lady no, twice. I thank you. Much obliged. The truth is, I thought I might have to sneak a sleep in the stables with the horses."

"Horses?"

"I have two. I'm a heavy packer when I travel 'cause I don't really know what I might get into. Plus, I enjoy hunting. I used to trap and sell skins for a bit, but I wasn't the best at it. I made my best living chopping wood and serving pumpkin cider."

Little Shirl reappeared with two tankards with frothy tops that seem too heavy for her arms. The mousy young woman lifted them onto the bar. "Here is your mead. I'll be back with the pie in a moment." She looked up at Nina. "Do you have a preference, Nina?"

Nina looked at Hacksaw. "What delights your tummy?"

Hacksaw thumped the bar with his hand. "Bring whatever you think is best!" With a nod,

Little Shirl vanished back in the kitchen. He grabbed his tankard. Nina did the same. He hooked his arm with hers. "Now, let's wet our lips, shall we?"

Nina smiled. "Indeed."

"To the Oxen Inn and the gorgeous young maiden that leads it!" Together, arms entwined, they drank deeply from the tankards. "Ah! That's fine mead," he said, wiping the froth from his beard.

Nina wiped her chin. "It's my own special mixture. I'm glad you like it."

Hands covered with mittens, Little Shirl set down a pie steaming from the top of its golden flaky crust. "Here is your pie. Let me know if you require anything else."

"I will," Hacksaw said.

"Little Shirl, see to it that our guest's horses are well tended to as well," Nina said. "You did use our stables, didn't you?"

"Aye, that I did," he said, waving the pie's aroma into his nostrils. "What is that pie filled with? I smell spiced apples, cinnamon, and pumpkin?"

"Yes, it's my family's recipe," Nina said, taking a fork and digging in. "It goes really well with the mead. I hope you like it." She filled his mouth.

He chewed it up and swallowed. "Delicious." Nina cut a full slice out and put it on the plate. "I like the nuts and the strawberry glaze. A fine mixture of ingredients that goes well with the coming winter. Can I have the recipe?"

She looked him in the eyes and patted his face. "Never."

Hacksaw talked Nina up after that, asking her about her tavern and the city of Riegelwood. He claimed to be an amateur historian and spoke a little about his days of soldiering in Quintuklen too, without giving too much away about himself being a legionnaire. The knights of Quintuklen were not often well received, as they were considered to be very arrogant by some. He emptied two tankards, and felt warmer and cozier in Nina's presence the longer he sat. Then, the room quieted a bit. A stir started in the tavern while the halflings were still singing. There were stairs that hugged the wall that led up into the rooms above. A group of elves in cloaked colors like a gray misty day came down the steps quietly. Eyes followed them. People spoke in quieter voices.

Hacksaw's stool groaned underneath him as he turned their way. Something about the elves unsettled him. They were so out of place. He said to Nina, "Interesting customers. I don't ever think I've seen elves in a place such as this."

"Times are changing," she said, squeezing his forearm. "I'll be back."

Chapter 62

Nath tingled from his fingertips to his toenails as he stared at the man who'd led the Black Hand. The radiant smile on Tobias's handsome face cut through him like a razor. He fully expected to see City Lord Janders, but instead, he got a surprise that took his breath in the worst way. He wanted to jump on the stage and strike the man down. Tobias, the strapping swordsman and Black Hand leader, stood tall, dark, and handsome. He gave a subtle wave to the cheering crowd. He had the appearance of royalty in the finest suit of dark leather armor. Black gloves covered his hands. His sword, Splitter, was belted on his side.

Blinking, Nath said under his breath, "I can't believe it." Beside Tobias stood Princess Janna. Her long blond hair was braided down her back. She wore a long outdoor cotton gown that would keep the snow warm. Her head was downcast, and she had a smile as long as a river. "This can't be happening." Nath pecked the gusty woman, Sally, on the shoulder and said in his fake scratchy voice, "Pardon. But it's been a while since I've been in the city. What happened to Lord Janders?"

Barely giving Nath a glance, Sally said, "He died two years ago, you old crone. Now, don't bother me. I'm basking in Tobias's glow."

A commotion started in the crowd, near the front of the stage. A group of men pointed their fingers at Tobias and chanted, "Murderer! Murderer! Murderer!"

The soldiers surrounding the rim of the stage converged on the chanting men's position and beat them down with clubs. They dragged the men off by their collars and out of sight. The praises for Tobias started again.

The lathered-up citizens shouted at the top of their lungs as Tobias lifted his arms to the sky.

Nath caught Janna looking away. His innards twisted inside him. There was definitely something wrong. Somehow, the Black Hand had fully overtaken Riegelwood, and he feared that his magic items had played a part in that. The stage had soldiers carrying spears spaced out along the perimeter. On the back end of the stage, more people had gathered as some sort of entourage. Nath rose higher on tiptoe, using the post for support. *Are those elves?*

There was no denying their distinct elven features. The pointed ears, graceful movements, and clothing as soft and splendid as clouds in the sky. There were only two, but they were accompanied by aristocratic men in similar winter refinery. Nath had the feeling they were merchants, businessmen, and guests for the upcoming wedding. But lurking nearby, standing close together, were the other members of the Black Hand.

Nath squeezed the head of the hammer. His jaws clenched.

I will have them. I will have them all!

Cullon the dwarf, black bearded and bald on the top, stood a mighty stump of a man. Belts of knives crisscrossed over his body. A scowl crossed his face as he scanned the crowd with narrow eyes. Beside him stood Worm, shifting his shoulders and giggling. The mop of sandy hair still covered the young man's eyes. A goofy grin broke out on his face from time to time. Virgo stood beside Worm, a sultry platinum-haired goddess. Dressed in a tight winter outfit with fox fur covering her neck and wrists, she shivered. Her lips were tight, and she looked as if she'd rather be anywhere else but on that stage.

Nath didn't see Nina. *She must still be in the tavern.* He looked back over his shoulder. He could clearly see the top level of the Oxen Inn. Patrons were outside, hanging over the railing on the porches, waving their arms, hats, and caps. *Something is really off with this place. How could they have ruined it so quickly?* He heard his father's voice in his head, saying, *"Weeds spread quickly if there is no good grass to choke them out."*

A shoving contest started in the crowd farther away from the stage. Nath caught sight of a few of the Men of Whispers he encountered on the road. He could tell it was them, just by how they moved, their voices, and their clothing. They were hassling some locals. That's when out of the crowd, three orcs joined in the shoving match.

Orcs are here? Why?

Nath noticed the black armor and chainmail uniforms they wore. They weren't any orcs. They were guards wearing the insignia of Slaver Town.

Gads!

CHAPTER 63

LITTLE SHIRL TOOK A SEAT on Nina's stool while Hacksaw watched Nina converse with the elves at the bottom of the stairs. "Did you find a moment to rest your feet? I bet they get sore from all of the walking and standing you do around here," he said to Little Shirl.

"My feet are fine. I don't think I'm heavy enough to make them sore."

"I wish I had that problem."

"I can prepare a bath for you and rub them later if you like," she said.

"Oh." Hacksaw's brows lifted. Bright-eyed, he said, "I think that offer tops the one Nina made me. But I'll pass. I'd hate for you to look upon my feet. They aren't a pretty sight." He drained the rest of his ale. It was a strong brew, but no match for Granda's pumpkin cider, so he still had his wits about him. So far, he had Nina under his spell. He could tell she was a sordid woman, but she hid it very well. It was no wonder that Nath was so easily crossed up with her. If Hacksaw wasn't already the wiser, Nina would have captivated him too. "Tell me, do you get many elves up here?"

"They've been passing through and staying for longer stretches." Little Shirl picked up his tankard and ran her dishcloth over the bar. "Do you want more mead?"

"No, not at the moment." He scratched his cheek. "I'm just not very used to seeing elves in a place like this. The ones I crossed always kept to themselves."

"They still keep to themselves," she said with a little fire in her voice. "They take their time when they order something to eat or drink. You serve them and they sneer a little. They talk to themselves in their own language, acting like you aren't even there. Then, when they do speak, they startle you. Or at least they startle me. I'm busy thinking about other things while I wait. But Nina insists that I give them my full attention. I'd rather watch water come to a boil."

"Ho-ho," he laughed. "I like your dry wit."

"Yes, well, I thought elves were very friendly, but they keep their noses turned up in the air too much for me."

"So, what are they doing here? Business?"

"A lot of them sell reams of cloth that I have to admit are very extravagant. The women in this town gobble it up, as well as their glassware." She folded up her towel and stuck it in her apron. "They make these little glass-blown figurines. Very decorative items. Then, they move on, but I think some of these elves are guests for the city lord's wedding. I get them mixed up sometimes because they often dress alike."

With his eyes fixed on the elves at the bottom of the steps, he said, "I can see that." There were four elves in all, standing on the stairs, chatting among themselves with their backs to Nina. Men were coming down the steps but couldn't get through. Nina's face had reddened. "Eh, you said the city lord is getting married?" Hacksaw asked.

"Yes, the full ceremony is being held in the castle tomorrow. Part of the celebration has been mixed in with the Festival of the Coming Winter. City Lord Tobias and Princess Janna will be wed." Little Shirl frowned. "His legacy will be cemented in Riegelwood forever after that."

Hacksaw knew who Tobias was because Nath told him all about the members of the Black Hand, but was careful not to show it. It was a twisted-up bit of information that Nath would need to know. He'd have to figure out a way to slip out, but until then, the old knight played along. "You don't sound like you care for this Tobias fellow."

"I like tradition. Tobias is not part of the bloodline here that the other houses are. He's an outsider. I'm not sure how he came to such power."

"What happened to the city lord before him?"

"City Lord Janders died from a failing heart. He was never healthy. After Princess Janna was rescued, he seemed much better, but then fell suddenly ill. He died a few weeks later. It's very sad."

"Indeed." Hacksaw scratched his beard. "Uh, as I understand it, wouldn't Princess Janna be the new city lord in her father's stead?"

"She's not strong, and the rival houses want to claim the city lordship. I think she's marrying Tobias to strengthen her reign. He's been at her side since she came back, and she named him city lord in her father's stead." Little Shirl retied the strings on her pink apron. It was without a drop of mead or flake of food on it. "It's been very tense and unsavory since he's taken power. The people think that the wedding will fix things, but I know it won't. I can feel it."

"You'll be fine, I'm sure. Politics and family matters such as this are just a part of life. The tides of change will shift many times in your life." He laid his hand on her shoulder. "Endure, but you can still enjoy."

She nodded. "I need to get back to work now. Don't forget about that foot rub. The offer is still good."

Despite being cold outside, the inside warmed considerably. Absentmindedly, Hacksaw pushed his sleeves up. Little Shirl had dropped a load of information on him that he didn't anticipate. It wasn't any of his business if Princess Janna married Tobias, but it could only be bad news for a city like Riegelwood. The place would be run by slavers and bandits, and more innocent people would be lost. His plan had been to separate Nina from the Gauntlet of Goam and somehow cast blame on the Men of Whispers. But it seemed like an impossibility now. Judging by his conversation with the stalwart woman, she probably slept with it on. He drummed his fingers on the side of his tankard. *We're going to need a new tactic. And I need to get out of here.*

"Did you miss me?" Nina appeared out of nowhere.

Hacksaw hopped in his stool. "You spooked me! Huh-huh. I was about to rescue you from those elves."

"No need. They are on their way," she said, taking her place on the barstool. She placed her hand on his knee. "So, did you miss me?"

"Er, of course, but Little Shirl chatted with me a bit."

"She did? About what?"

"Well, she talked about the elves, because I asked about them. And she told me there's a wedding tomorrow. I guess that explains all of your guests and this excitement. Seems like an important time for this city."

Nina rolled her eyes. "I'm sure Little Shirl's face was drowning in her frown when she told it." She scooted closer. There wasn't a hand's breadth between their faces. "Little Shirl's family lays claim to the city lordship, but it's not going to turn that way for them. So, she's a little bitter."

"I see."

"Hacksaw, that mead is getting to me, and I feel very drawn to you. It's not like me."

"Er, well, maybe we should get some fresh air before either one of us does something we might regret," he said. He needed to slip out and track down Nath. Nina coiled her arms around him. "Will you join me?"

With dreamy eyes, she said, "I suppose, but let's take a look from the balconies. We can see the events from there." She took him by the wrist with her left hand and locked her fingers tight. "The view is splendid."

She dragged him through the tavern. *Lords of Thunder. Her grip. I can't break it.*

CHAPTER 64

DON'T PANIC, NATH. JUST BECAUSE *the orcs are here doesn't mean that they are here for you.*

Moving at a brisk but still hobbled pace, Nath's hammer cane clicked down the porch front planks away from the stage. The sight of the orcs, wearing the iron-faced insignia of Slaver Town, shook him up. If they were in Riegelwood, then chances were that they told the Black Hand Nath had escaped. He crossed the street, splitting the bonfires where the people were gathered, and ducked into an alley. He pressed along the wall, catching his breath.

Think it through, Nath. Think it through.

Unlike the time he spent in Riegelwood before, the mixture of people had changed. There were dwarves, halflings, gnomes, elves, part-elves, orcs, and part-orcs. He was certain there were other people too that he hadn't encountered yet, but the town was wild in celebration. Listening to the raucous music and cajolers, he covered his ears.

This is madness.

He could feel his heart thumping in his ears. There was so much to take in. The Men of Whispers were primed to snatch more victims in the dark of the night. Nath could only imagine that person would be someone among the visitors for the wedding and winter celebration. In addition to that, Princess Janna was about to be wed to Tobias, leader of the Black Hand. If that happened, the entire city would be in a death hold. And worst of all, the Black Hand could possibly expect that he might be near. They probably had people searching the streets now.

I have to find Hacksaw. I need to tell him what is going on. Just keep your head down.

Nath took to the street, angling back toward the Oxen Inn. Revelers bumped him on more than one occasion, jostling him as they passed. One bumped into him hard. He felt a deft hand slip into his cloak. He grabbed the hand, squeezing the fingers until they cracked. The young man let out a gasp. Nath said, "Respect your elders, you filthy little pilferer." The young man scurried away.

Shoving forward, Nath finally found himself facing the front porch of the Oxen Inn. His stomach twisted the moment he looked up at the wooden sign hanging from two chains swaying in the wind. There was a painted picture of a pair of oxen pulling a plow. Horns were mounted on both sides. Men and women crowded the front porch, smoking pipes and swilling ale. He hoped to find Hacksaw among them, but there was no such luck. It was mostly waitresses in pink aprons seated in rocking chairs, or benches, or on men's laps with their hands draped over their necks.

I can't just wander in there like this. But I have to find him.

He considered asking one of the waitresses if they'd seen a man fitting Hacksaw's description when he had the urge to look up. The cajolers were in full swing on the porch above.

"No," he said with a sharp breath.

Out in the open, leaning against the rail, Hacksaw stood, pipe in mouth. He jabbed two fingers toward the stage. Behind him stood Nina, her arms wrapped around Hacksaw's waist. She affectionately talked with her lips to the burly knight's ear. She had a playful look in her eyes. Hacksaw was all smiles.

"Traitor," Nath said underneath his breath. He started straightening his back. His blood boiled over. Everyone he'd met had lied to him one way or the other. He couldn't believe Hacksaw had him fooled. The legionnaire was one of them. A part of the Black Hand. Out loud, Nath said it again, "Traitor!"

The people on the porch front looked right at him. Their faces tilted to one side. The ones on rockers stopped rocking. Their eyes became fixed on Nath holding out his hammer with a gem on the top that glowed like purple fire.

Nath pulled down his hood. Chest heaving, hammer gripped in both hands, he looked right up at Hacksaw and Nina. "Traitors!"

Nina's eyes grew as big as her biceps. "You!"

Nath's voice carried over all the commotion as he said with wroth anger, "Woe to the man that lies to a dragon!" With golden eyes full of fury, he cocked the hammer over his shoulder. Jagged tendrils of energy erupted from the gem in Stone Smiter. With a howl, Nath put his back into it and swung.

CHAPTER 65

HACKSAW WENT RIGID. HIS TONGUE clove to the roof of his mouth. He wanted to cry out to Nath and tell him to stop. But the misunderstanding he saw deep in Nath's eyes was clear. In a moment, the confusion in the youth turned to rage. Nath's golden eyes became molten storms. The head of the hammer sparked with fire. There would be no turning back the time. The young man exploded like an angry god. *Lords of Thunder, brace for the storm.*

The men and women standing on the Oxen Inn's porch scurried like rats. They trampled one another as fast as their legs would take them away from the voice of his wrath. Stone Smiter collided with the center post that supported the porch above. The wood shattered into one thousand splinters. Above, Nina, Hacksaw, and the porch came down. Patrons above tumbled through the gap, landing on top of one another. Nina and Hacksaw were buried underneath a tangle of limbs.

"Get up!" Nath shouted. He grabbed woozy men by the arms and slung them aside. He found Hacksaw's face, grabbed the man by the beard, and pulled him up. Choking up on the handle of his hammer, he stuck the glowing head of the hammer in the man's face. "You are a liar! I hate liars!"

"No, Nath! Listen to me, I did not deceive you! This is a misunderstanding. Focus on Nina!" Hacksaw pleaded as he tried to push Nath away.

"You are one of them!"

"No! I am not!"

There was the gusty sound of a woman's laughter as Nina pushed bodies aside and came to her feet. "There's no need to lie to him any further, Hacksaw. You led him right into our trap, just as we planned."

"She's lying, Nath!" Hacksaw pleaded. "Let go of me, so we can take her down. You have to believe me, I've never seen the woman, or been in this town before today."

"He's the best liar," Nina said, dusting off her elbows. "One of the best." She looked at the gathering crowd. "People, do you not remember this man named Nath, who two years ago kidnapped our precious Princess Janna? He's invaded our sanctuary again! It's time to take him!"

The crowd turned into a murmuring mob.

"Nath, listen to me, I've never lied to you, not once," Hacksaw said in a harsh whisper. "This woman is full of lies and deceit. If you want to kill me, kill me, but right now, you need to trust me. Have faith, and trust me. Let's ride the lightning."

Nath shoved Hacksaw to the ground. He raised the hammer over his head. "No more lies!" He started to bring down a strike that would pulverize the hardest stone. He adjusted his swing and turned it toward Nina. "You will pay!"

Stone Smiter whipped down on a collision course with Nina's skull. She grabbed the handle of the hammer just underneath the head, using the Gauntlet of Goam. The gemstone on the leather gauntlet blazed with wavering light. She tossed her head back and laughed. "Do you think you can defeat me with this little toy? I've mastered the powers of Goam, you fool. I am invincible with it!"

"No one is invincible!" With a grunt, Nath tried to rip the hammer from her grasp. Her vise-like grip didn't budge an inch. He heaved against her again. "Hurk!"

"You are still a young fool," she said, drawing him right into her face. "I don't know how you escaped, but you will not find vengeance today, you will only find death. Now, let me show you the full power of the Gauntlet of Goam!" She tried to rip the hammer from Nath's fingers. He would not let go. She turned her hip into her next effort and flung Nath and the hammer over the porch and through the tavern's bay window.

With a loud crash of glass, Nath landed in a heap of tables and chairs. The people spilled out of the doorway and scurried up the stairs. Women screamed.

Nath shook his head and sat up. He found himself face-to-face with Little Shirl. Not caught up in the chaos or commotion, she said to Nath, "I knew you would be back. I missed you, Nath."

"Little Shirl, uh, I'd like to talk, but as you can see, I'm very busy." He came to his feet and patted her head. "You need to find safety."

"As you wish," she said, making a big smile that showed no teeth. "Try not to let her hit that pretty face of yours."

"Pretty?"

Nina stepped through the front entrance. "Nath! You owe me a window! Now get out of my inn!"

Nath slung a chair at her. It skipped over the floor, and she caught it with her hands. "Oh, don't forget about the tables and chairs, Nina." He stomped on the wooden planks that were hollow beneath him. "Or the floor."

"What?" She tilted her head. "The floor's fine."

"You mean, it was fine. Now, it has a giant crack in it!" He lifted Stone Smiter over his shoulder.

"No, Nath!" she said, shaking her hands in front of her. "If you damage any more of this tavern, I'll kill you."

Tapping into his anger, Nath said, "Wrong answer!" He brought the hammer down. The planks burst. Nath kept swinging. *Whack! Whack! Whack!* The boards quavered and split. The floor bowed beneath them.

Nina screamed with rage, "Nooooooooooooo!" She flung herself at Nath.

Nath braced himself for impact. The brutish woman plowed him over. Pinned to the ground, Nina crushed him underneath her unnatural weight. *Gads! What is she made of?* In the recesses of his mind, he felt the Gauntlet of Goam had something to do with it, but he had bigger concerns. The wild-eyed Nina pounded her glowing fist into his chest like a hammer. *Wham! Wham! Wham!* Every blow jarred his limbs and rattled his bones. *Guzan! She's going to kill me!*

CHAPTER 66

SOLDIERS OF RIEGELWOOD SHOVED THEIR way onto the scene outside of the Oxen Inn. Using the shafts of their spears, they pushed the people back. "Back away! Back away!" They made a wall along the porch, beyond where the upper porch had collapsed. The sergeant in charge started asking questions, and the drunken people blurted their accounts of what occurred.

The inn shook from within. The soldiers' eyes grew as the porch shifted underneath their feet. One of the sergeants peeked inside through the busted window. He hollered back to the sergeant. "It's Counselor Nina. She's in a tussle with a stranger." The building rocked again. "He has a hammer that strikes like thunder. Oh, she's got him now! Giving him a beating!"

Hacksaw burst into action. The mead had slowed his blood, but the charge of battle fed him again. He needed to help Nath or die trying. He rushed through the crowd, making a beeline for the front door. The soldiers walled him off.

"Where do you think you are going?" The sergeant poked a spear at Hacksaw. "Step back or I'll skewer you and let the revelers roast you. Do you understand, old man?"

With three soldiers pointing their spears at him, Hacksaw replied, "When I want to go somewhere, no one will stop me. It's you that needs to step aside." There was something about the rugged soldiers that ate at him. Their tunics were unkempt and not as crisp as the soldiers he'd witnessed earlier. And their trousers were plain trousers, and not part of the city garrison's uniforms. "I warn you, I'll have no problem whittling down rogues like you today."

"Rogues? How dare you!" the sergeant said.

"You might fool the rest of these drunks, but you won't fool me. That insignia on your chest is upside down, and your clothing is sloppy. I know who you are, Men of Whispers. Now step aside, or taste my steel."

The sergeant's eyes narrowed on Hacksaw. "Kill him."

Tobias stood proudly with Princess Janna on his arm. In less than a day, he would be the most powerful person in Riegelwood. His seed would be firmly planted. Having full control of the local government, the Black Hand would be able to run their corrupt operations unhindered. He patted Janna's hand. "Tomorrow will be a grand day, Janna. You need to enjoy it. Your father would be glad to see you wed to the likes of me. We were great friends."

Janna held her tongue. She pulled away, but Tobias held her fast. Then, head down, she said, "My father would stretch your neck from here to Riverlynn if he only knew what I knew."

"Oh, come now, Janna, do you really think that your father was that blind to the Black Hand? We are the ones that kept him in power." Smiling for the crowd, he whispered in her ear, "Who do you think kept the other rival families at bay? Lord Janders always said, 'See to it my hands stay clean, but get yours as dirty as you want.'"

Janna looked at him, aghast. "He said no such thing."

"Regrettably, I must inform you that he did. Janna, there comes a price for power, but you will reap the rewards of it."

"And you will reap what you have sown."

"I know. That's why it's so wonderful to be me. Don't worry, you will get used to it. They all get used to it." He gave her a dashing smile. "Power is delicious." He waved to the crowd.

A commotion of voices started behind them. Janna and Tobias glanced behind them. One of the commanders was in an excited conversation with Cullon, Worm, and Virgo. All three sets of their eyes grew big. Cullon and Worm slipped off the back end of the stage. The commander started toward Tobias, but Virgo hooked the man's arm and pulled him back. Gracefully, she made her way to Tobias. She waved slowly to the crowd and motioned to the entertainers to begin another round of songs. The music began.

"What is it, Virgo?" Tobias said to her.

Virgo gave Janna a look.

"I'm not going anywhere, Virgo. Whatever you have to say to him, you can say to me. After all, I will soon be the lordship's wife and you are my subject underneath my full authority."

Coldly, Virgo replied, "Don't get carried away. But if Tobias approves."

He gave the sorceress a nod. "Out with it, Virgo. What has happened? Have the Men of Whispers botched another assignment?"

"That wouldn't surprise me, but no, there is trouble at the Oxen Inn," Virgo replied.

"What sort of trouble could there be that Nina couldn't handle? Lords of the River, men quake underneath her stare. Don't tell me Prawl walked into the tavern and demanded her precious gauntlet."

"No, I believe the situation could be direr than that."

Tobias's radiant smile dulled. "Really, how so?"

"Nath Dragon has returned with a hammer that calls thunder and strikes like lightning."

The blood drained from Tobias's face. "Commander!" he shouted to the soldiers behind him. He shoved Janna into the man's arms. "Lock her in her room, and post plenty of guards." He put his hand on the pommel of his sword. "I have some work to do."

Chapter 67

STUPID!

Nath couldn't believe he let the brunt of a woman's power drive him to the deck. Now, she hammered her fist into his armor. If not for the breastplate, his ribs would be jelly. He could feel it. He groaned. "You think you would have greeted me with a hug and kiss."

Nina pinned him down by the neck and aimed for his face. "I'm going to knock those pretty teeth out of your mouth and pulverize the rest of you!"

"Not with my gauntlet, you won't! And stop spitting when you talk. It's disgusting!"

Grunting like an animal, brows knitted together, Nina let loose a punch with all of her might.

Nath squirmed aside. Her fist punched through the planks. Still being choked, he said in a mocking way, "You missed."

She ripped her hands out of the busted floorboards. "I won't miss again!"

"Not with your spit, anyway." The boards below Nath groaned. Lording over top of him, Nina's eyes grew big. The floor collapsed underneath them. They plummeted into the wine cellar. Glass bottles busted. Nath squirted out of Nina's clutches. Wine spilled into the broken glass all over the floor. "You really have a lot of wine down here. I bet it's worth a fortune." He slugged the nearest wine rack with his hammer, shattering the bottles. "Whoops, I must have slipped. You weren't going to drink or sell those, were you? They looked so old and dusty."

"You!" Nina rose to her feet with her chest heaving. Her wine-splattered arms bulged with muscles. The veins in her neck rose up like snakes. "Don't you dare break one more bottle. I swear I will—" *Thunk*! A wine bottle skipped off her forehead and busted on the ground.

With another bottle in hand, Nath casually said, "I know, you will kill me." He flipped the bottle in the air and caught it. Checking the label, he said, "Say, this is elven."

"Leave that one alone, Nath! Listen to me! Just set it down. We can talk about this."

"Give me back my gauntlet and I'll leave your precious wine cellar alone." His eyes quickly swept through the basement. There were long rows of racks filled with wine bottles and keg barrels. There must have been enough to last for centuries. "Or I will take this hammer and destroy every bottle and barrel in this cellar."

"You wouldn't!"

"I've been in prison for over two years, thanks to you. I've had plenty of time to think about this. I seethe!" He glared right at her. "Give me my gauntlet and I'll show mercy. Fail to do so and perish."

Nina shrank under his hard gaze for a long moment. Then, her hapless expression turned back into a wicked snarl. "You'd never kill a woman. You don't even have it in you to kill a man."

"Prison changes a man." He tossed the bottle of elven wine up through the hole. "You better catch the bottle before it hits the floor. It's going to have to last you a while."

Nina looked up, eyes locked on the bottle, stretching her fingers upward. She caught the falling bottle. "You'll never make it out of this city alive, Nath. There are too many of us. Now, stop this madness!"

Stone Smiter in hand, Nath had backpedaled alongside one of the support beams. "Sorry, but the madness has just begun!" He swung the hammer into the eight-inch-thick post. The beam exploded. The roof sagged, groaned, and started to collapse.

"Noooooooooooooo!" Nina screamed. She raced toward Nath, who skipped away to the next post. She tried to hold the broken post in place. Using her mighty strength, she pushed the floor up with a grunt. Her muscular arms knotted up like tree roots. Layers of sinewy muscle heaved with life.

"You know what your weakness is," Nath said, spinning the hammer in his hand. "First, you love this tavern too much, and second, you can only be in one place at a time." He spun the hammer with a twist of his wrist and took it to the support post.

Crack!

The post splintered in half. The roof wobbled. Dust and debris showered down on Nath. It created a fine mist.

"Stop it! Stop it!" Nina shouted at the top of her lungs. "You're killing my tavern!"

"Exactly!" Nath ran from one post to the other. Stone Smiter flashed in streaks of purple fire. Every strike was a clap of thunder. The heavy posts, designed to hold like a rock, splintered one by one. Sections of floor came down in hunks. The entire inn swayed, but the outer walls of the building held. Cracks suddenly spiderwebbed along the walls. "Oh no," he said, looking at Nina. She was surrounded by rubble, trying to hold the roof up. "Nina, the tavern's coming down! Get out of there!"

"Never!" she said.

All at once, the Oxen Inn collapsed, top to bottom, burying the both of them.

Chapter 68

The soldiers converged on Hacksaw with jabbing spears. He snaked his sword out of the scabbard. Green Tongue flashed before the soldiers' eyes. All three spear heads were lopped off. "Do you lying fools still want to fight me?" Hacksaw said in a bold voice. The feel of battle was upon him. The old knight came to life. "Because I've plenty of fight left in me!"

The sergeant who'd hung back chucked a spear at Hacksaw. Hacksaw slipped his head out of the way. The spear sank into a man that had crept in behind the knight with a dagger in his hand.

"You dirty little backstabbing thieves!" Hacksaw roared. He stormed the porch as the brigands disguised as soldiers went for their swords. Hacksaw plunged his sword into the heart of the one in the middle. He hated liars, brigands, and thieves as much as he hated goblins and orcs. He detested men who didn't live by an honest day's work. "Come on then, worms! It's time to let the blades dance!" Shimmering like a metal blade of grass, Green Tongue flashed right past their noses.

The soldiers' eyes filled with uncertainty. They shuffled backward. The sergeant thrust at Hacksaw's belly.

Hacksaw banged the man's metal aside in a fierce parry. He chopped the man in the shoulder. The sergeant went down to his knees with a painful howl. The other two imposters fled the deck. "It's death for you, brigand!" Hacksaw put his sword to the man's neck. "You better ask for mercy! You have but a moment!"

The sergeant bled heavily from the wound. "I-I-mercy!"

Inside the Oxen, it sounded like a bucking bull had been turned loose. The building trembled to the sound of thunder. Hacksaw moved up on the porch and peeked inside. The main floor collapsed into the basement. The bar looked like a ship half submerged. "Lords of Thunder!" He called out, "Nath! Nath! Where are you, man?"

The walls bowed and bucked. The entire building swayed as if it had been hit by a swift wind. All of a sudden, the floor above came down with a resounding crash.

Hacksaw dove off the porch into the road. A blast of dust, glass, and wood splinters hit him in the face. The city folk stood around with their jaws hanging. Some were wiping their eyes. Many were crying.

The murmuring broke out from the dusty, drunken faces. "I hope everyone made it out."

"Where is Nina?"

"Who was that man that attacked her?"

"It was the man who kidnapped the princess. I saw his face. He is a demon."

"I hope he's dead."

"Where is Nina?"

Hacksaw got up on a knee. He spit dust from his mouth. Green Tongue flickered like a burning emerald in his hand. *The danger ain't ended yet!* Two men shoved through the crowd. One was a hard-faced dwarf, bald on top, with a look as mean as a rattlesnake. The other man was young, and moved with ease as he giggled at the collapsed building. Hacksaw knew immediately who they were—the Black Hand members Cullon and Worm. Their eyes fell upon him the moment the crowd said, "Councilman Cullon, this man killed our soldiers!"

Cullon glared at Hacksaw and pulled a battle axe from a sleeve on his back. "Is that so?"

Surrounded by darkness and half buried in the building, Nath pushed away the busted boards and debris. There wasn't a crack of light anywhere, but Nath's dragon vision helped him get his bearings. He pulled his hammer free and began crawling through clutter. The glow from the hammer's gem cast light on his surroundings. Even though the building had collapsed, there were still pockets of space everywhere. His nostrils flared at the strong aroma of wine and ale.

Food dripped from the kitchen that must have been above him. He could smell baked pies and hot stew. There was a greasy smell too. Smoke wafted by his nose. A flame flickered somewhere behind him. The distinct crackle of flames caught his ear.

Oh gads, Riegelwood is about to have its biggest bonfire ever.

Deep in the darkness came a moan.

Nina!

Nath forced his way through the wreckage until he found her body, half buried and huddled around the bottom end of a broken post. He could see the woman's chest rising and falling. Her breath was raspy. Nath might have hated Nina, but he didn't want her to die. Suffer, yes; die, no. He crawled over some broken boards and scooted toward her. He grabbed her.

"Nina," he said, "can you hear me?"

"Yes," she said in a raspy voice. "It's like poison in my ears. I wish you were dead. You destroyed my inn."

"This inn is the least of your worries now. We need to get you out of here before the entire building turns to flame."

"Let me burn with it. I have nothing to live for now. You win, Nath. My arms and legs are pinned down and I can't move. I'm drained."

"Don't be a quitter. I'm getting you out so I can see you put in prison." He started pushing away boards. He could see her body, but her arms and legs were covered underneath planks and beams. The glow from the Gauntlet of Goam was nowhere to be seen. "Don't try anything."

"Why would I go to prison?" she said without making so much as a wriggle. She just lay there, limp as a fox belt. "You escaped prison. You are an escapee. You kidnapped Janna." She let out a long, ragged sigh. "You come from nowhere, of nothing, and have no leg to stand on. I am a councilwoman here. You endangered all of our guests and patrons. Do you really think you will come out of this unscathed?" She coughed a laugh. "You are still naïve."

Looking her in the eyes, he said, "You make a very sound point. And I've given it plenty of consideration. But, regardless of your ill will toward me, I'm going to help you to safety."

"Why would you do that? You can't be that big of an idiot."

"Because it's the right thing to do. You're helpless, and what kind of man would I be to see a woman perish in the flames?" He unburied her left arm. The gem on the Gauntlet of Goam shone dimly on her hand. Nath looked in her eyes as he held his hammer in position for a quick strike. "Don't try anything."

"Oh, believe me, if I could knock those golden eyes out of your head, I would, but my shoulder is busted thanks to the fine timber that fell upon it. My arm's not moving, but at least I can feel my fingers."

Nath lifted the beams from her legs, uncovered the rest of her body, with a little push from her, and freed her from the debris. He put his arm around her waist, supporting her on her weaker side. "We're going to have to squirm out of here, but we can make it." He coughed as the burning smoke thickened.

"Stop talking and let's go. As if you didn't make it stuffy enough in here. And I can walk on my own. My shoulder's busted, but not the rest of me." Nina coughed.

"Just stand back." Nath swung the hammer left and right, clearing a path through the havoc. The choking smoke filled his lungs. His eyes burned.

"There," Nina said, coughing and choking, pointing her right arm over his shoulder. "That's the cellar exit to the outside, head that way. Hurry."

Nath knocked more boards aside. They stooped down into a small tunnel that led to stairs leading up. A pair of heavy wooden double doors waited. Nath shoved on them. "Locked from the outside."

"Well, there's nothing for anyone to steal now. Give it a whack with that hammer of yours before we both suffocate!"

Nath punched through the doors using the might of the hammer. Arm in arm they climbed out of the stairs, sucking in the fresh air. The crackling and popping fire spread over the tavern. Nath huffed out a breath as he came to his feet and helped Nina up to hers. "That was close."

Looking down in his eyes, she said, shame-faced, "I suppose I should say thank you for saving my life."

"It wouldn't hurt."

"Well, Nath, there is something that you need to know first."

"What's that?"

Her back straightened, her left arm cocked back. "I'm a great liar!" She busted him hard in the face, snapping his head back and sending him head over heels. "Fool!"

Nath crashed into a storage bin. Stars filled his eyes. He couldn't move. His vision was obscured as Nina stormed right at him. "My shoulder was not busted!" She grabbed him by the collar and hauled him up face-to-face. "Now, I'm going to do to you what you did to my tavern!"

CHAPTER 69

"THAT'S A FINE LENGTH OF steel you carry," Cullon said to Hacksaw.

Sword in hand, Hacksaw's eyes slid from Cullon to Worm. He shifted his feet into a fighting stance. Nath told him about Worm and his ability to displace. Hacksaw would have to watch the man carefully. He faced the dwarf. The scars on Cullon's bare forearms and forehead told him that the man was a seasoned warrior. He'd fought alongside many before in his time. They never stopped until the fight was over, with or without their limbs. "Why don't you come a little closer and I'll let you kiss it," Hacksaw replied.

"Bold words for a man whose bones rattle." Cullon advanced a step, flipping his battle axe from side to side. It was a cruel-looking device, double-bladed with razor-sharp batwing edges. A full squad of soldiers made a ring around the three men. "Back off! I'll handle this upstart!"

"As you wish, Counselor Cullon," the sergeant in arms replied. "Back away, men. Let our champions handle this. Perhaps you'll learn a thing or two."

Hacksaw pointed two fingers at Cullon. "You are a disgrace to your kind, dwarf. A thief. A slaver. Your time has come." Audible gasps came from the crowd. Confused glances were exchanged among the soldiers.

"He speaks lies," Worm said with a sneer. His hands were hidden inside his loose clothing. He paced smoothly, in a short walk, back and forth. "This stranger rides into town, kills our soldiers, and tells inflammatory stories. It will be a certain death for him if he does not surrender."

Hacksaw pushed up his sleeve, revealing his tattoo. "I'm a knight of the legionnaires. Everyone knows we don't lie."

The big-eyed soldiers leaned forward. Grumbling broke out among the people.

Cullon fired back in his gruff voice, "Infidel imposter! I'll cut your lying tongue out!" He charged Hacksaw. Their weapons clashed in a loud ring of steel. Back and forth in battle they went in a violent series of thrusts and parries.

Bang! Clang! Slice!

Cullon pressed the attack like a ravenous wolf. His chops came short and powerful. He thrust with ferocity. There was no error in his movement. The strokes he unleashed were fatal. Hacksaw's sword arm labored to bat the blows aside. He countered with quick slashes across Cullon's eyes. He stabbed at the stocky man's gut.

Cullon swatted the blow away and let out a grunt-like laugh. "You tire quickly, Gray Hair. Don't worry, you shall rest soon." He unleashed a double-handed side swing that would take a tree down.

Twisting his hips and sword around at the same time, Hacksaw blocked the blow. The collision of blades shook his arms to the shoulder. His fingers went numb. Cullon was right. Hacksaw hadn't had a hard fight in decades.

Lords of Thunder! If I were a younger man I'd have turned the bearded toad into dog food by now!

Fighting to keep up with the tireless dwarf's heavy-handed blows, he lost sight of Worm. The rogue would appear in the corner of his eye, only to disappear. On the defensive, he backpedaled. The crowd cheered the dwarf on.

"Slay him, Cullon!"

"Run your axe through him!"

"No, split his skull open!"

The harsh comments fueled Hacksaw's efforts. He stabbed, backpedaled, jab-stepped forward, and stabbed again. Green Tongue flickered back and forth, a striking snake, keeping the wary-eyed dwarf at bay. Hacksaw lunged, pulled back and away from Cullon's parry, adjusted his swing, and cut the dwarf in the shoulder. Cullon hopped back. Eyeballing his bleeding shoulder, he spit.

Hacksaw smiled. The moment gave him a breath too. The hair on his neck rose. A chill went through him. The air shimmered. *Worm!*

The rogue whispered behind the old knight's ear, "Surprise." He thrust a dagger down.

Hacksaw jerked away. The blade sank deep into the meat of his shoulder, right through his ringmail armor. The blade felt like it plunged to his abdomen. He flung his head backward. Skull cracked on cartilage. Worm squealed. Hacksaw turned, swinging at the same time, determined to cut the rogue in half.

Holding his broken nose, Worm vanished into thin air.

Hacksaw yanked the knife out of his back. He flung it to the ground and said to Cullon, "Let's finish this dance, dwarf."

A shrill voice cut through the wintery air. "Rebel Riders! Rebel Riders! Reeeeee-Bell!" Thundering through the streets came a group of men on horseback. Their faces were half covered by handkerchiefs. Carrying long bo-sticks like lances, they plowed into Riegelwood's forces, knocking flat-footed soldiers on the ground. A horse and rider cut between Hacksaw and Cullon. He lost sight of the dwarf. The horse reared up. The man in the saddle screamed. "Rebel Riders! Rebel!" The horse lunged forward. The space between man and dwarf momentarily cleared.

Cullon was gone.

Violent fighting erupted all over the streets.

Laboring for breath, Hacksaw dashed the sweat from his eyes. With heavy limbs, he stepped up on the broken porch of the Oxen Inn. A fire began to spread. He called down into the smoky basement, "Nath!"

He traversed the wreckage that burned in several places. Plumes of yellow smoke made chimneys in the air. The heat built as he searched for an opening in the floor or any sign of life. Crossing from one side to the other, he noticed that horses were being led out of the stables, away from the flames. A scuffle in the shadows caught his eyes.

Nath!

Nina had the young warrior pinned against the shed. Her gauntlet radiated with star fire. Hacksaw took off running at a full sprint. All he could see was Nath's face being busted by a giant woman who punched harder than a mule kicked. Nath's body sagged against the shed. His head was loose on his shoulders. The sledgehammer lay dim at his side.

"Say goodnight forever, Nath Dragon!" Nina launched the fatal punch.

Hacksaw closed the gap. He chopped Green Tongue down hard and fast. In a bright arc of light, the shimmering sword cut clean through Nina's forearm. *Slice!*

Nina gaped at the wound. She let out a bloodcurdling "Nooooooooooo!"

Nath saw a streak of green light, but it was the ear-wrenching scream that lifted him out of his haze. Strong arms pulled him to his feet. Those same hands stuffed his hammer and something else into his arms. As his senses quickly cleared, he said, "Hacksaw!" He pushed the man away.

"We don't have time for this. We need to get out of here, Nath," the old knight said.

Nath stole a glance at Nina. The distraught woman was clutching her decapitated arm. "Did you do that?"

"Yes." Hacksaw shoved him toward the stables. "You have your gauntlet back. Now, let's go."

Horses bolted out of the stables. The fires from the tavern spread. People shouted as they scrambled for buckets.

Nath couldn't take his eyes off Nina. He looked at the foreign object in his hands. "Gah! It's her hand!"

"And your gauntlet. Now, keep moving. They'll be upon us soon enough!" Hacksaw looked back at the inn that was fast becoming an inferno. "A shame. I was looking forward to a good night's sleep in there too. And the pie was wonderful." Horses raced by. They couldn't catch any of them. "Where are my horses?"

A wagon, pulled by two horses, rode right up on them. Two people were in the seats, heads covered by their cloaks. A bright, familiar voice said, "Nath, quick, get in the wagon!"

Nath stepped back. It was a woman speaking. Very elven. A big man held the reins. Shaking his head, he said, "Pardon, but who are you?"

She dropped her hood.

"Maefon!" Nath said with exasperated shock. The blond elven woman appeared as radiant and beautiful as ever. His heart stirred within. "Is it really you?"

With dire seriousness, she said, "Of course it is. Now you and your friend get into the wagon! Your enemies will be here soon enough."

"But," he said.

"Just get in, Nath. Whatever questions you have, I'll explain later. Right now, let's get to safety before they overcome us."

Nath could see back in the streets, on the other side of the flames, the soldiers appeared to be regrouping. He looked at Hacksaw. "Well?"

"She don't have to ask me twice." Hacksaw climbed into the wagon. He stuck out his hand. "I say we go."

Nath climbed in.

The driver snapped the reins. The wagon lurched forward, rumbling over the road and disappearing from sight in the cold, early winter darkness.

Chapter 70

"AUUUUGH!" IT WAS NINA SCREAMING. Cullon used a belt for a leather tourniquet around her severed arm. The dwarf stuck the stump inside the flames of her burning building. She screamed again. "Blast you, dwarf! Set your own self on fire!"

"Be still unless you want to lose the rest of your arm," Cullon fired back. "And stop crying. It's not dwarven."

Face beaded in sweat, she retorted, "I'm not crying, and I'm not a dwarf, you ugly stump!"

Cullon released her. "It's finished. It might stink for a while, but it will hold."

Nina looked at her smoking stump. "Isn't there magic for this sort of thing?"

"Not on hand," Cullon said. There was blood on his armor from the wound Hacksaw gave him in the shoulder. "You don't see me whining, do you? The truth is, I'm a bit jealous. Dwarves are revered for losing a limb only to keep on fighting. Back in Morgdon—"

'Shut your mouth, you bearded braggart. I don't want one of your stupid dwarven stories. I lost my hand! That's a problem!"

"At least it wasn't your sword hand," Cullon replied. "And I'm going to need my belt back. It was my father's."

Worm giggled.

Nina shot a murderous look at them both. They had gathered behind the burning inn where Nina was wounded. The streets were still in chaos. The Rebel Riders, a group Nina had never heard of, were riding roughshod through the streets and assaulting the city lord's guards. Nath and Hacksaw had departed several minutes ago. With unexplainable pain shooting through her body, she said, "Nath took the gauntlet. I can't believe I lost it."

"That legionnaire was a saint with a sword. A bit rusty, but a fine fighter," Cullon said to her. "There's no shame in falling to his steel. Green steel at that. Green as a shining snake."

"Is that so, Cullon?" she growled. "And where were you when he blindsided me? Huh?"

She shoved him backward with her good hand. Turning on Worm, she tried to shove him, but he slipped away. "Come back here, you… worm! I need to knock your heads together."

"That's going to be hard to do with only one hand," Worm said. Nina lunged at him. He slipped away on feet as light as a cat's, laughing. "Slow, so slow."

Tobias and Virgo approached from the streets. Four soldiers were with them. "What's going on?" Tobias asked.

"I'll tell you what is going on," Nina said, not hiding her rage. "Nath is back, and now my tavern is burned to the ground. Not to mention I've lost my hand and the Gauntlet of Goam."

Eyes on Nina's stump, Virgo said, "Ew, that is disgusting. You know we have salves and potions for that." The sensual sorceress's nose crinkled. "That stinks. Why would you do such a foolish thing?"

"Cullon did it because I was bleeding to death, maybe that's why?" Nina replied.

"Worm, don't you have any salve on you?" Virgo asked.

"Oh, well, maybe." Worm's slender hands rummaged through his deep pockets. A small blue jar appeared in his hand. "Do you mean this salve?"

Nina screamed, "Worm!"

"Give her the salve, Worm!" Tobias said. Worm tossed the jar to Nina. Tobias's brows were knitted together, his handsome expression gone. He addressed the soldiers. "I'll be fine, men. We need some privacy. Tend to that haphazard rebellion in the streets."

"Yes, city lord," the sergeant said. He wasn't one of the brigands disguised as a soldier, but a genuine soldier. He saluted, and all of the soldiers left.

Tobias continued saying to Nina, "What happened to Nath? Where is he?"

Applying a gob of blue salve to her wound, she said, "He and Hacksaw hopped in a wagon and rode south."

"Alone?"

"No, someone was driving two horses." Nina let out a sigh of relief. "Oh, that feels so much better"—she swung a look at Cullon and finished with a shout—"than burning it!"

"Charred limbs are an improvement if you ask me," Cullon replied.

"Go char yourself!" Nina replied.

"Focus, Nina!" Tobias said. "Who drove the wagon?"

"I don't know," she said with a sarcastic sneer. "I was busy dealing with my hand that had been lopped off!"

"Certainly you remember some detail, and who is Hacksaw?"

"A legionnaire I met in the tavern," she said. "I didn't know it at the time, as I was feeling him out, but he's some ally of Nath's. The people driving the wagon, I don't know. The big one was a man, covered up, but the woman was an elf. Blond. She called Nath out by name."

"See, you did know more than you realized."

"Yes, my thoughts are less clouded when I'm not in excruciating pain." Nina eyeballed her arm. The black skin started to mend and turn pink. She tucked the jar of salve in her clothing. "I'm keeping this." She noticed Tobias smiling. "What?"

"Nothing," he said, patting the pommel of his sword as he looked up into the sky.

"No, I know that look, Tobias. You know something. Did you know Nath was coming?"

"Of course not," he said.

Nina, Worm, and Virgo encircled Tobias.

"Out with it, Tobias. I know when you're lying through your teeth." Nina stuck her stump in his face. "If I lost my hand because of something that you didn't tell me, I will bust you into pieces."

Brandishing his axe, Cullon agreed, "That goes double for me."

"Listen, a couple of days ago I received word that Nath escaped Slaver Town, but I gave my word that I would keep it to myself."

"You knew and didn't tell us!" Nina said.

Virgo's face was aghast. Her fingers sparked. "I should blast your eyes out!"

"You are low," Worm commented.

Tobias pulled his sword partly from his scabbard. "You listen to me. All of you. First, I've been preparing for my wedding. And don't forget how big this is for all of us. And second, I gave my word to a man that I dare not trifle with. He is the one who wants Nath. We, in a twist of fate, are the bait, in this case. If it had gone smoothly, none of you ever would have known the difference. But Nath—"

"—has a way of making a mess of things," Nina said, finishing his sentence. "Tobias, who is after Nath?"

Tobias gave her a disappointed head tilt. "Don't be naïve. You know who it is."

"I don't know who it is," Worm said. "Who is it, Nina? Tobias? Don't keep me in the dark, or us in the dark for the matter."

Nina nodded at Tobias. "It's the Lord of the Dark in the Day, isn't it?"

Cullon and Virgo's tight expressions were replaced by concern. They eased away from Tobias.

"Yes," Tobias said. "And the less all of us know, the better. I'm certain he'll let us know if we are needed. In the meantime, I have a wedding to plan and some sort of rebellion to crush. I need to get some rest between now and tomorrow."

An elf in a charcoal-gray cloak approached from the south. He seemed to glide quietly over the grasses. A long sword and dagger were belted on his hips. Nina recognized him from her tavern. He was one of the elves she last spoke with at the bottom of her steps. Without a word, the elf handed Tobias a scroll, nodded, and departed back toward the distant woodland.

Tobias opened the scroll.

"What does it say?" Worm said, as all of the Black Hand members gathered around Tobias.

Nina looked over their leader's shoulder. She saw an elf with sharp elven features drawn in black at the bottom of the paper. The words were written by no ordinary hand.

Tobias read it out loud. "The trap is set. Nath will invade your wedding tomorrow. Be ready. We'll take him down there. Play along. Let the darkness rule the day." The parchment caught fire. The flames brightened their faces as everyone except for Virgo gasped. Now it was her turn to laugh.

"That is impressive," Virgo said.

"What, a letter that turns itself to flame? Isn't that easy?" Worm said.

"It's not the letter. It's the planning," the platinum-haired sorceress said. "The Lord of the Dark in the Day knows what happens before it happens. Once again, Nath Dragon will be easy prey, and all we have to do this time is sit back and watch."

CHAPTER 71

THE WAGON CAME TO A stop along the dark road a few miles south of Riegelwood. They'd been riding at full speed for several minutes. Maefon climbed into the back with Nath and Hacksaw. She threw her arms around Nath and hugged him tight. "I can't believe it's you."

Nath let her warm body melt in his arms. It felt so good to have his arms wrapped around her. He missed Maefon. He thought he'd never see her again. "I've been looking for you. It seems like it's been forever."

"I know. There is so much to tell," she replied.

"I hate to break up a fine reunion," the hooded man in the driver's seat said in a friendly but somewhat serious tone, "but I'm certain that there will be a pursuit. Hop out and I'll take the wagon further down the road. There's a good spot to hide back beyond the thickets. I'll meet you there in a bit."

Nath didn't really pay any attention to the man's words. He was caught up in Maefon's hug as they scooted together out of the wagon.

Hacksaw made it out with a loud grunt. "Oh, my back."

Maefon broke away from Nath to aid Hacksaw. Her fingers ran over the gash in his back. "You need sewn up."

The driver tossed her a leather satchel. "I'll be back." He snapped the reins. The horses took off with the wagon thundering down the road.

"Let's move, quickly," Maefon said. Taking Nath by the hand, she led him and Hacksaw into the trees. They shoved through the brush and kept going until they came to a clearing near a creek. She opened her satchel and pulled out some sewing materials. She wore a cloak and a well-designed leather tunic underneath it. She sat Hacksaw down. "Let's get this ringmail off your back. It will be quicker that way."

Nath rubbed his aching face. His head still rang from where Nina hit him. There was blood on his fingers. His blood.

Helping Hacksaw out of his ringmail, Maefon looked at Nath. "What's that?"

He lifted the hammer. "It's a sledgehammer."

Maefon shook her head. "I know what a sledge is. I'm talking about that… hand?"

"Oh!" Nath said, eyeing the thing. "It's, uh, the Gauntlet of Goam. It was stolen from me, and, well, Hacksaw and I just retrieved it. I guess that sounds gruesome, but Hacksaw chopped her hand off, not me."

"Her?" she said, deftly sewing Hacksaw's wound.

"If it makes any difference, she is truly evil," Nath said, "and was a moment away from caving my face in."

"We wouldn't want that, now would we," she said, biting off the excess string from the wound. Opening a very tiny jar, she applied a clear ointment to the wound. "That will hasten the healing. Just relax for a moment. Uh, what is your name?"

"Hacksaw."

"Nice to meet you, Hacksaw. I'm Maefon."

"You'd make a fine nurse. Never seen anyone stitch me up so fast, and I've been stitched up plenty."

"Thank you." Maefon approached Nath with smiling eyes. "I really don't know where to start. Should you go first, or should I?"

"I think I need to sit down," he said. Moving to a tree that fell over the creek, he sat. He pulled Nina's hand free of the gauntlet. "This is gross. Should I bury it?"

"Burn it," Hacksaw said.

"Well, not now." Nath tossed the hand in the water and looked away. He slipped the gauntlet over his left hand. The gem on the back sparkled. His blood churned through his arm. Flexing his fingers, he said, "That feels good."

She sat down beside him. "Nath, I think I should go first, if you don't mind. I'm very confused about many things, namely, why you are here and not at Dragon Home. I feel responsible."

"You are responsible," he said. Out of nowhere, anger swelled up inside of him. "The fledglings were killed. You and the Trahaydeen were gone, and now I find you here, in what could be a miraculous coincidence."

"I assure you, it is just that. You've been far from my mind the past couple of years, and I don't mean that in a mean way." She held his hand in both of hers. "I'm overwhelmed to see you. I just assumed you would be safe in Dragon Home. Your time to leave there was still a century away. Anyway, I ache over the fledglings. I swear, I did not kill them. That was the work of Chazzan."

Nath wanted to believe her, but he'd been lied to so much that it was difficult to trust anyone. "You blame Chazzan, but you fled with him. That is an admission of guilt."

"I found out about the fledglings later, Nath. After it happened. After we fled. Chazzan woke me from a dreamy slumber. He told me the dragon's wrath would soon be upon all of the Trahaydeen. He said that we needed to flee." She rubbed his hand. "What was I to do? Chazzan was my leader, our leader. If he said leave, then we had to leave. So, with a breaking heart I did."

Nath brushed the hair out of her eyes. Her silky flaxen locks were longer than they used to be. Her face showed dirt and creases from hardship that he'd never seen before. "They blamed me for it."

"You! That's absurd. Why would they do that?"

"Because it was made to look as if I did it. My weapons from the forge, they were there. Only you knew about that."

"Nath, I never would have, or could have done such a thing." She clutched his hand to her chest. "I swear it. Nath, I'm so sorry, but you must listen to me."

"I'm still listening to you. Out with it."

Maefon let out a sigh. "It was a horrible night. A group of us, led by Chazzan, slipped out of the mountain. Hemmed in at the moat of lava, I thought the dragons would soon be upon us. I don't know why, but I knew in my belly at that moment that Chazzan had done something very, very wrong. I could see it in his face. It was a dark grimace I'd never seen before, as if he was possessed. He removed a sapphire from his clothing the size of a bird's egg. I'd never seen it before. He told us to hold hands, which we did, he chanted in elven, and we were transported."

"To where?"

"I had no idea where we were at first. I didn't for weeks because we didn't go anywhere. It was a keep, far west, across the Foaming River, built into the rock. There were more elves there, but they weren't Trahaydeen, like me. No, they were just the opposite. They call themselves Caligin."

CHAPTER 72

NATH'S BROWS ARCHED. "CALIGIN," HE whispered. It was a shock to hear it from Maefon's own lips. It sent a chill through him. The Caligin were the elves Slivver, his dragon brother, warned him about. He wasn't certain they were real, until now. "Chazzan is a Caligin?"

She nodded.

"Where is he?" he asked.

"That is what I am trying to do. Find Chazzan. His trail led me to Riegelwood."

"Back up a second," Hacksaw interrupted. His breath was misty in the cold. He'd put his armor back on. "How did you get away from Chazzan?"

"It took me a while to understand what was going on and who the Caligin were. Chazzan was very insistent that the dragons received what was coming to them because of past atrocities they committed against elven kind. He was adamant that the Caligin were a force for good, trying to make life right for all in the world. But his ways were twisted, I could see it, but so many bought into it. I played along, learning about the Caligin and being part of their devious ways until I could find a way to escape."

"Humph," Hacksaw said. "You sew as good of a tale as you do stitches. What you are saying sounds a little too easy to me. You just escaped. And the Caligin didn't hunt you down?"

"No, they think I'm dead," she said.

"And why is that?" Nath asked.

Maefon stood. She opened up her cloak and lifted her tunic up over her belly. Two ugly white scars, like a knife wound, crossed over her belly. "Chazzan killed me, or so he thought. He tossed me in a gulch and rode away, leaving me to die in my own blood."

Nath's throat tightened. "Macfon, I'm sorry. How did you survive?"

"Good question," Hacksaw added.

"I made my way out of the gulch somehow and crawled on the road. I was certain I would die, but at least I would be found." Her eyes watered. "All I could remember thinking was what would you, Nath, think of me, if I could not clear my name. Then, he came."

"Who came?" Nath asked.

A stir came from the brush. Hacksaw whisked his sword out, and Nath readied his hammer. The cloaked driver appeared with his hands up. "Sorry to startle you, but I said I was coming." He puffed for breath. "And I ran. Been a while since I did that." He dropped his hood, revealing a handsome face with a strong, angular jawline. He had a sword on his hip and a saddlebag over his shoulder. He walked forward and extended his hand to Nath. "Hello, my name is Darkken."

Chapter 73

Nath stood and returned a firm handshake. Darkken was taller than Nath, imposing in size, but appeared much older than Nath, but much younger than Hacksaw. He had a nice, likeable quality about him and held Nath's stare with coppery rust-colored eyes. Underneath his cloak was leather armor dyed black. "Nice to meet you."

"Very well met," Darkken said, making his way to Hacksaw. They shook. "I'm sorry, I feel as if I interrupted something." He looked at Maefon's belly. "Oh. I hate to see you reliving that moment, dear. Is that necessary?"

Maefon pulled her tunic down. "I was telling them about what Chazzan did to me. Nath needed to know. I want him to understand."

"I'll tell you what you need to understand. That Chazzan is a real bastard, that's what he is!"

"Darkken!" Maefon exclaimed. "Control your temper."

Darkken let out a breath. "Sorry, but you know how I feel. Of course, I haven't met him, but I found Maefon dying in the road. She slept like the dead for a week before she opened those beautiful eyes again." He stretched his arm out and petted her face. "I swore I would never leave her side until she was avenged. The very story sickened me. Backstabbing elves that manipulate the world of men day and night. Who gives them the right?"

Maefon kissed Darkken's hand. "Easy, love. You'll have to forgive Darkken's passion."

"The two of you seem very close for an elf and a human," Hacksaw commented.

"We are inseparable," Darkken said as he threw his arm over her shoulder. He spoke words in perfect elven. "She is my sun and stars and moon all over." He smiled. "It might sound strange, but I was raised by elves."

Nath's blood stirred. He sank back down on the fallen tree. It bothered him that Maefon and this man were so close. He tried to block it out and focus. So much seemed to be happening at once. "So, Chazzan leads the Caligin?"

"No," Maefon said. She took her place by Nath. "Chazzan is a commander, but it is the Lord of the Dark in the Day that is in charge. He's a very powerful elven wizard who made it his mission to control the world. He struck at the dragons to break their trust with the elves.

This is how this dark lord does things. Now, the Trahaydeen are separated from the dragons." She looked at Nath. "I assume."

"Yes, you are right. That happened before I left." Nath took a look at Hacksaw. The old knight slowly nodded. His eyes were almost squinted shut. He wondered what Hacksaw was thinking. "No dragons are leaving the mountain until my father returns."

"Your father, Balzurth?" Darkken asked.

Nath looked at Maefon with concern.

"It's all right," she said to him. "I've told Darkken everything about you and your father. I still don't think he believes any of it."

"I would not if her descriptions were not so vivid," Darkken replied. "It all sounded like fairy tales to me." He smoothed his long hair, colored like the leaves of fall, back from his eyes. "But she's very convincing."

Incredulous, Nath said, "You told him the secrets of the mountains? You are sworn to never reveal what you have seen."

"Nath, I'm sorry, but if the Trahaydeen are no more, their word is bound to no one. And I only shared about you and what Chazzan did to the fledglings. Darkken could care less about the rest."

"I only care about what matters to you, and that is tracking down this host of fiends. We will find this Dark Day and kill him, and Chazzan," Darkken said.

"But you said they have a hideout in the west. Isn't this wizard there?" Hacksaw asked. "You seem to be a long way from the problem."

"We've been there," Darkken responded with a shrug. "And, like so many other places we have tracked them, once we get there, they are gone. They move like ghosts and are spread out all over. This Lord Day in the…how does it go, Maefon?"

"Dark in the Day."

"Yes, him or *it*. I don't think he should be considered a person of any kind, the misaligned bast—"

"Darkken, control yourself," Maefon warned.

"Ho-ho, you won't offend my ears," Hacksaw said. "I've heard my soldiers say words that would make an ogre's butt pucker."

Darkken tossed his head back in unbridled laughter. Holding his stomach, he managed to say, "I'd be curious about those words."

Nath, Hacksaw, and Maefon joined in the contagious laughter. Nath couldn't remember the last time he belly-laughed. With tears in all their eyes, they finally regained their composure, and Nath said, "Oh, I've laughed so hard I think I have a headache."

Chapter 74

On a chill, fireless night, it was the conversation that kept them warm. Nath did most of the talking. He told them about being banished from Dragon Home for a hundred years. Maefon sat against him with tears in her eyes as he went on.

"Like a fool, I put my trust in the Black Hand, only to be imprisoned for over two years. I escaped, but I fear my friends are in danger all on account of me." He was referring to Calypsa, Rond the Bugbear, Homer the musician, and Radagan the baker. The mention of Radagan brought a smile to Darkken's lips that Nath did not notice. "After I battled the basilisk and dealt with the mysterious hermix, Ruffle, I met up with Hacksaw in Huskan. Heh, we haven't even been here a day and it's been a disaster."

"At least you retrieved the gauntlet," Maefon said. "That's a start. Nath, I swear that I will help you with the rest. We will help you retrieve your presents. Especially Fang. I know how you adored it."

Darkken's ringed fingers tapped on the pommel of his sword that hung on his side. The rings were copper, and the pommel was fashioned like a dragon's head, but carved from ivory. "I believe our destinies are intermingled, Nath. Maefon and I have dedicated ourselves to tracking down the Caligin, and the likes of Chazzan, in hopes to bring the Lord of the Dark in the Day down. It is very difficult to convince people of the danger that these dark elves impose. They think elves are good, but this brood is evil. We happened upon Riegelwood because we followed the Caligin here. Thanks to Maefon's dealings with them, she knows what to look for. It is quite clear the Caligin are aiding the likes of the Black Hand. They put the city in chaos and keep them at odds with the neighbor cities. It's awful, but difficult to convince the people of that otherwise. There are only a few of us to do so."

"A few of us as in who?" Hacksaw said.

Darkken made a soft whistle. Twelve elves appeared among the trees, wearing the soft leather garb of a woodsman.

Chills raced over Nath's flesh.

"Great gargoyles!" Hacksaw slid his sword halfway out of his sheath. "Have they been there the entire time?"

"Most of the time. Didn't you notice?" Darkken said.

"I guess I was too caught up in our conversation. Shame on me for not being more vigilant."

Nath's fingers tingled at the sight of the mysterious elves who had appeared out of nowhere. *How did I miss that? Was I so distracted?*

"Don't be alarmed, Nath," Maefon said. "These are my brothers and sisters in elvenhood. We've been recruiting them, slowly, as they are convinced of the Caligin. Of course, we have to be careful who we choose. As one, we work to hunt down and stop the Caligin."

"I saw elves inside Nina's tavern. Were those Caligin?" Hacksaw asked.

"Most likely," Darkken replied. "They are very subtle, working as merchants and traders, but manipulating people's actions from behind the scenes. I'm certain many of them are guests for the wedding and they are here to see that things go through. If they control the Black Hand, then they control the city. They pull the strings of mankind from the shadows, but we can stop them." He punched his fist in his hand. "We must stop them. Brothers of the Wind, come with me," he said to the elves and led them deeper into the forest. "We must plan."

"Sorry, Nath, but my dearest becomes a bit emotional over all of this," Maefon said.

"Are the two of you together then?" Nath asked. "I grasp you have a very strong relationship."

"Yes, well, I don't know what the future holds for us, me being an elf and him a man, but we are inseparable. He saved me, and I adore him."

Nath frowned. "I understand. I'm just glad you are well and happy."

Maefon gave him a quick hug from behind. "I'll be happy when we avenge the fledglings and put an end to the Caligin menace, but I fear it's going to take a great deal of time to root them all out. We are small. They are many. But I say let's focus on getting your items back first. We can do that."

Nath stood. "We are going to need to do more than that. We need to put a stop to this wedding too."

"Let me go check on Darkken," she said, breaking away from Nath. "He tends to get overly excited about things, but he's a good planner. Just too aggressive from time to time. Besides, you two would probably like to talk."

"I'm about talked out." Hacksaw yawned and stretched his arms over his head. Approaching Nath, he said, "Those elves, Brothers of the Wind, really spooked the sweat out of me."

"You aren't alone in that statement. I got chills on chills."

"So, what are your thoughts?" Hacksaw asked.

"Funny, I was going to ask you the same question. I'm going to stay with what you suggested. I want to get back at the Black Hand. I want my sword. That's the mission." He held up his gauntlet. "I'm ready to take it to them."

Hacksaw grinned. "We are going to bust up this wedding, aren't we?"

"One way or the other. Besides, it's only Princess Janna that can clear my name. She was out of it the last time I saw her, but perhaps now she will remember. With Tobias out of the picture, she'll be in charge, won't she?"

Hacksaw shrugged. "I'm fairly certain, but every city's local politics varies. So, are you buying all of what your elven friend is saying?"

Nath sighed. Scanning the woodland, he said in a lower voice, "Let's just say I'm willing to see what happens, but I'm inclined to believe her."

"She's very convincing. I lean with them as well, but we won't know for sure until we see them in action, if we see them in action."

Nath stared at the cold rippling water in the creek trickling by. His life had been bad for so long that it was time that things turned in his favor. If Maefon was against him, certainly the Brothers of the Wind could have taken him and Hacksaw down. As for Darkken, he liked him. He put a heavy hand on Hacksaw's shoulder. "I forgot to thank you for saving me. Thank you. And I'm sorry for not trusting you."

"I don't blame you. I'm certain I would have thought the same. Now, let's go stick it to the Black Hand."

Chapter 75

Maefon and Darkken stood in the clearing. The elves surrounded them with their backs to them. The elves, well equipped with longswords and daggers, wore suits of fine chainmail or leather under their cloaks. Darkken called them the Brothers of the Wind, but they were in fact Caligin. The steely-eyed elves scanned the woodland, on guard, fine elven hair bristling in the chill wind.

"Nath seems to be taking to us quite well," Maefon said to Darkken. "What is your plan now that we have him?"

"He still has doubts about us; I can see it in his eyes," Darkken said. "Hacksaw is the bigger problem. He's a seasoned soldier, and not as easy to fool. This show we are about to put on might end up being fatal for him. But nothing is to happen to Nath. I'll stay close to him and handle it. You follow my lead."

Maefon shook her head. "You are being vague."

He showed a ravishing smile. "I know. Isn't not knowing what I'm going to do more exciting?"

"I suppose it has its mmmuh—" Darkken took her in his arms and kissed her fully. The passionate kiss stole her breath. He broke it off. She finished her word, "Merit." Her heart pounded in her chest. "*That* I liked."

"I saw the way you looked at him, and I felt a tad jealous. The time you shared together in Dragon Home created a strong link between you. I'd hate to think you have lingering feelings that could get in our way."

"Never. I'm enjoying the journey with you. I've never felt so alive."

"I will admit that you've done a fine job selling the story. I'm almost proud of you. But let's focus on the task at hand. I've already informed Tobias that I will be delivering Nath right into his arms. He'll be expecting us and the elves as guests. We'll be disguised among them." He opened his hand, revealing two small clear glass vials with orange liquid in them. "Including Hacksaw and Nath."

Maefon took the vials in hand. "Polymorph?"

"It's the best way. It won't be a problem for the rest of our elves, or me, for the matter. But they'll be looking for Nath and Hacksaw. The main thing is that Nath is convinced that we are on his side. Again, and let my orders be clear, I'll follow his lead and you follow mine. It will be a delicate situation dealing with the Black Hand."

"I understand."

"Good. Now, go back to Nath. Tell them to get some rest. I'll sell the rest of the story in the morning."

She nodded. "As you wish."

A strong hand shook Nath out of his slumber. He'd been in a deep sleep, which was rare for him, but the cold and the night, coupled with stress and exhaustion, took him. Blinking, he saw Darkken looking down at him. Dawn had come. The air around him was misty. Propped against the tree, he leaned forward.

"Sorry to wake you, but you were snoring, disturbing the others," Darkken said.

"I was?"

"No, of course not. I'm teasing you." Darkken squatted down. "I was hoping we could take a moment to talk before we dove into this mission. I want to be clear about what is about to happen. At least, I want you to know my approach."

"Of course. Let me get Hacksaw," he said. Hacksaw leaned by a nearby tree, snoring softly through his nose.

"He sleeps deep. You might want to give him a few more moments. He's turning gray, and trust me when I say he's not as spry as me and you." He put his arm over Nath's shoulder. "Let him be. I won't be long, and you can fill him in on what I say on the trail later."

"I suppose." Nath followed Darkken into the forest. "Where are the elves?"

"They've taken their stations in the city. They'll be changing into clothing appropriate for the wedding, and they'll be scouting for us in case of danger. The Black Hand I believe works with the Caligin, and would not fear them, or any other elf for the matter."

Nath nodded. "So, Maefon says we're all attending the wedding as guests?"

"True, but I'll act as an elven interpreter. My men I'm not worried about, but the other elves in the city I'm not so sure. Some are probably reputable merchants, while others will be Caligin. The Brothers of the Wind separate themselves from the others by a subtle design in their hair, such as a feather, or a beaded braid. The Caligin aren't so easy to identify. They dress in plain elven clothes, but you have to look for the darkness hiding in their eyes. They are very difficult to vet if you don't catch them in the act."

"I see."

Strolling among the trees with his hands behind his back, Darkken said, "Listen, Nath, I have a very direct approach. When I see an enemy, I want to attack—punch them right in the face, or chop their head off."

"You really don't fool around, do you?"

Darkken waved his hand. His long fingers spread out then clenched into a fist. "You can't give evil snakes a second chance. This world is full of evil. Every race, every creed, every subject struggles against it. The only way to defeat it is to stamp it out and burn it, so to speak."

"You sound like Hacksaw. He really hates goblins."

"At least you know what to expect from a goblin, but evildoers like the Black Hand, they are far worse. You never know what to expect from them." Darkken let out a puff of frosty breath. "Sorry, but some subjects rile me. I've said that, haven't I?"

"Yes, but I understand. Ever since I left home, I've been belted from every corner. I haven't found much good in people, or most people at least. They are selfish."

"And weak." Darkken ducked underneath some low branches into a grove thick in grass, clover, and winter wildflowers. He faced Nath. "I want to be up front, Nath. Unless you know another way, once you reveal yourself it will be a war with these people. There can't be any mercy. I won't risk Maefon or the Brothers of the Wind to get into a slap fight. This will be for blood."

"No, I understand completely. I want vengeance. I want my sword. I want what is mine, but mostly, I want my sword back. My father made it for me."

Darkken patted his sword's pommel. "I know how you feel. My father gave me a fine blade as well. May I show it to you? His name is Scalpel."

Darkken drew his sword, Scalpel. It was a wonderfully crafted blade made from the finest elven steel. The sword itself was a sleek one-sided blade, straight from the handle, making a clean linear line that curved slightly at the end of the blade. Decorative rune carvings dressed the white bone handle of the blade. Similar markings had been etched into the topside of the blade, enhancing its elegant design. He rolled it over his wrist a couple of times and twisted it through the hair. He stroked the flat of his thumb across the blade. The metal hummed quietly like a tuning fork. "Scalpel sings his own special song."

"It's beautiful," Nath said. His eyes ran up and down the length of the sword. At first appearance, it looked small in Darkken's hand. Upon a closer look though, Nath realized the sword fit the bigger man's hand perfectly. "I've never seen the likes of one before."

"My father, as I say, was elven, a blacksmith as a matter of fact. He made this sword for my hand. Most elven blades aren't so long, but I have a big grip and some additional length that makes me very dangerous when I find a shorter man, or elf." Darkken glanced at the ground. "Pick up those acorns. Just a couple."

Nath bent over and grabbed the acorns. He held them out in his hands.

Darkken eased into a sword-fighting stance. At the same time, he sheathed his sword. He winked at Nath. "I'm going to show off now. Toss the acorns up. In front of me. Just above my head."

With a flick of his hand, Nath tossed the nuts in the air.

In a flash, Scalpel snaked out of the scabbard. Darkken sliced through the left acorn at its zenith and the second acorn on its way down. He slid the sword back into his scabbard, snapping it into the locket. He reached down and picked up the acorns. Both were cut cleanly though the middle, in four semi-perfect pieces. He showed them to Nath. "Sharp, isn't he?"

Big-eyed, Nath said, "Extremely, but you're fast. I don't think I've ever seen a man move so fast. Your form is so smooth and fluid. The sword strikes as fast as a viper."

"Faster," Darkken said. "Nath, once again, I want to emphasize that when we engage, if we engage, I won't hold back."

"No, I understand. I don't suppose the Black Hand will surrender either. I'm ready to do this, Darkken, and I'm glad I have you at my side." Nath lifted his sledgehammer. "Stone Smiter and Scalpel have work to do. It's time to do it."

Chapter 76

Princess Janna sat behind her dressing table, facing the mirror. Behind her, two women combed the tangles out of her hair. It had been a long night, confined to her chambers like a prisoner, pacing the floor and tossing and turning in her bed. She nibbled at her fingers.

One of the maidens, young and dull-eyed, pulled Janna's hand away from her face. Softly, the young maiden said, "We need to paint them. If you chew them, we will have to file them again."

"Listen, you little crumb-eater," Janna retorted. "I am the princess, and if I want to chew my nails off, I will!"

The young maiden stepped back. The older maid stopped combing her hair.

Janna took a deep breath and slowly let it out. Today was supposed to be the most special day of her life, but instead, it was going to be a disaster. She was about to wed a murderer. In her heart, she knew Tobias had killed her father. She wanted to cry, but she spilled them all in her bed last night, soaking her favorite pillow, shaped like a bunny rabbit, that her deceased mother made for her long ago. She straightened her back. "I apologize. For the record, I don't want to do this, but I do what I do to protect the likes of you and my family. There is just no other way."

"We are grateful, Janna." The older woman resumed combing. "You don't need to say anything more, but our ears, hands, and feet are yours."

"Thank you," Janna said with a sob. She reached over and pulled the young maiden over. "I'll chew my nails off after the wedding. Probably my fingers too." She managed a smile.

The young maiden giggled. "At least he's handsome."

"Yes, but my father always said to marry for love, not looks, and to pray that I met a decent fellow fit to marry because I probably wouldn't be given many choices given the political climate. In this case, I didn't even get a choice. All I can hope for is that Tobias dies before we wed, and that's not likely to happen."

"You will endure," the older handmaiden said. "We all do. But there is always hope for the better."

Janna had had nothing but heartache since her rescue. She remembered being rescued by Nath, but the details were hazy. The wizard, Hozam, had turned her into some sort of cave-dwelling creature. She woke at night in a cold sweat, screaming sometimes, seeing the face of a hairy orange-eyed monster instead of herself in the mirror. As for Nath, she envisioned a young face and soft locks of flame-red hair. He seemed like more of a dream than a reality, but the moment Virgo brought up his name, her memories began to sharpen. She still struggled with whether it was all a bad dream or not.

Nath, if you are real, you rescued me once. Please rescue me twice.

She'd thought about him on and off over the past two years, but her mind was never clear. She never saw the people who kidnapped her, but they made her drink bitter toxins that kept her calm and dreamy-eyed. It lingered with her. Some moments she was very astute and sharp, but at other times, she could be in the middle of the conversation and her mind would slide somewhere else. She would usually wake up in bed after wondering what happened. Her handmaidens would tell her.

A third handmaiden came in with a tray loaded with a porcelain teapot, cup, and saucer. She set it on the dressing table and filled the cup. With a quick bow, the woman departed.

Janna took the cup in both hands and closed her eyes. "If it wasn't for this tea, I don't know how I would make it. It's the only thing that soothes me." She drank, not noticing the handmaidens' knowing looks exchanged with one another.

Chapter 77

Still in the woodland, Nath and Hacksaw drank the polymorph potion. Before one another's eyes, they were transformed into elves. Hacksaw rubbed his face. "I feel weird without my beard. Is it truly gone?"

"You look every bit an elf to me," Nath said, giving Hacksaw a once-over. He was a little broader than most elves, but it wasn't that noticeable. His face was smooth and his features uniquely sharp. "Honestly, it's an improvement."

"I bet."

Maefon fitted them both in some elven cloaks. "Wear these and don't do anything sudden or aggressive. The enchantment from the potion will wear off. Once we are allowed inside the castle, stay close to me." She tied the strings on Nath's cloak around his collar. "Just be patient. Darkken usually has a very good feel for things. He'll let us know what to do and when. The Brothers of the Wind will be ready too. And keep in mind, if we have to flee, then we have to flee, Nath."

"Why would you say that?"

"Because there are a great deal of visitors, including orcs and soldiers, and if we are outmaneuvered in our efforts, we will face superior numbers. I just don't want to see you hurt, or imprisoned again, on account of me." She gave him a quick hug and looked up into his eyes. "You know, you make a very handsome elf. And your red hair is still radiant. It's a shame your elven look is not permanent."

"I'm pretty sure my hair is always radiant," he said with a smile. "At least compared to yours."

She gave him a slap on the shoulder. "I have missed your sense of humor, and maybe your confidence a bit. I'm glad you're still cocky. Let's go get your sword back." She departed.

Hacksaw watched her vanish into the woods. "I'm staying close to you, and you better stay close to me."

"Why do you say that?"

"I'm a soldier. I just have the feeling in my fingers and a turn in my belly."

"Maybe it's the potion. My belly moves since I drank it," Nath replied.

"Aye, just keep your guard up." Hacksaw ran his finger over his collar. "We're following them into the fire."

The midday sun hid behind gray clouds. Castle Janders stood proudly in the northern end of Riegelwood. There wasn't a moat of water surrounding it, but instead, an empty gulch filled with beds of flowers. A drawbridge had been lowered across splendid beds of colorful winter daisies that bloomed year round.

Nath's nostrils flared. He walked in step with the squad of elves. They made up three columns, five rows deep. Nath and Hacksaw were in the middle. Maefon walked between them, making a complete group of fifteen, plus Darkken, who led the way from the front.

Maefon's hand brushed against his. In elven she said, "Nervous?"

He shook his head.

They passed under the portcullis and entered the courtyard. Soldiers in full chainmail and tunics, crossbows, swords, and spears ready to bare, were stationed throughout the castle yard, manning the doors, on the walls, and parapets. They stood at attention, eyes forward and expressionless. Darkken led them to a stop. He and the elves were surrounded by the soldiers.

Nath leaned forward, looking quickly at Hacksaw. The big man transformed into an elf gave him a shrug. *We are standing like toadstools right here.* Nath's hands clenched. He was feeling for his sledgehammer, but he'd slipped it through his belt loop like a sword. It dug into his side. He patted its head.

In elven, Maefon whispered, "Stop fidgeting."

He pulled his hand away. So many soldiers boxing them in stood his hair on end. His keen sight and sense of smell picked up on some other details about the men. His eyes swept through the ones he could see without turning his head noticeably. Not all, but many of them were from the Men of Whispers. Their uniforms were ruffled and their faces unshaven. They didn't match up with the other soldiers, who had polish on their buttons and a shine on their boots. Their itchy fingers drummed on crossbow triggers or the handles of the swords on their belts.

Nath inhaled deeply through his nose.

If I hear one click or the sound of steel scraping out of a scabbard, I'm taking Stone Smiter to them.

In front, Darkken and the castle commander began a heated exchange. The commander, holding a scroll, argued, "We have a full host of elves already. There are no more listed on the register. You may stay in the courtyard, but you will not be allowed inside."

"The elves bring a special gift to City Lord Tobias on his wedding day," Darkken replied. "And I assure you, he is expecting us. Commander, I respect your authority, but I assure you that you err. Is there no one that you can speak with?"

"This is the registers." The commander held the parchment to Darkken's face. "There is no mention of the merchant elves from Avaleen. Or a party of sixteen. You need to take your leave, or my soldiers will escort you—"

"Commander Holman!" Virgo entered the outside courtyard dressed in formal clothes.

Her neck, fingers, and wrists sparkled with jewelry. She marched right alongside Darkken. She had another scroll in her hand and gave it to the commander. "This is the updated register. Read it. I'm sure you will find their names on there." She gave Darkken a glowing smile. "We are honored to have the merchants of Avaleen among us. City Lord Tobias is eager to bridge new relationships with the elves."

Darkken kissed her hand. "We are honored to bring Lord Tobias and his bride a most precious gift."

Commander Holman looked over the scroll. "Aye, Counselor Virgo. I thank you for the register." He handed the old register back to his second-in-command. "Do away with this."

Virgo hooked her arm in Darkken's. "Allow me to escort you and the elves to your place."

Nath's skin crawled as they marched from the courtyard and into the castle hall. Darkken and Virgo whispered and laughed with one another, as if they'd known one another a very long time. His hands balled up into fists.

This doesn't feel right.

Chapter 78

The long hallway had been cut from white marble. Huge portraits hung on both sides of the wall, showing pictures of the city lords from generations long past. At the end of the hallway, at the top of a short, wide set of steps, were two large wooden doors that were open. Four orc soldiers were posted there, standing at attention on both sides of the door, carrying polearms.

Nath felt Hacksaw's eyes on him. This time, it was his turn to shrug. The orcs glowered at the elves. They were two races that hated one another with a great fervor and passion. Nath gave one a look as they went up the steps and started into the grand hall. The orc's bottom canine teeth stuck up to the side of his nose.

I hate orcs. How can these elves stand it?

Virgo led them into the grand hall. The guests were gathered on both sides of the aisle, but there weren't any pews or chairs. Less than five hundred guests and dignitaries stood facing the front of the grand hall. On a higher platform, there were two thrones, bright brass chairs padded with velvet pillows, one bigger than the other. Three well-dressed redheaded halflings formed a tiny orchestra of string instruments that played quietly in the background. Behind the throne was a massive fireplace made from blocks of stone just like the ones Nath busted up in Slaver Town. Fang hung over the mantel.

Nath's eyes enlarged. He broke out in a cold sweat. His mouth became dry. He slid into a row near the front with the other elves, feeling like he was about to burst from his skin. Fang was no more than one hundred feet away. Maefon held his hand and squeezed. "Patience." She tipped her chin at the sidewalls.

Standing between the portal windows shaped like rounded-off crosses were dozens more soldiers, men and orcs, equipped for battle. If Nath had to fight his way out of the castle, it would be a fight to the bitter end. The soldiers were as thick as flies in Castle Janders. He searched for an exit. The only way out that he could see were the portal windows, but they were long and narrow. He didn't think he could squeeze through them.

This is bad. Very bad.

He noticed Hacksaw shifting on his feet. The old knight cast a concerned look at him.

Aside from the heavy security, the guests talked quietly with one another in casual conversation. The ladies in the room politely commented on one another's gowns and jewelry. The men exchanged stories about what they saw in the streets last night. Most of it was about the Oxen Inn burning down. There were rumors of a man with flame-red hair striking the tavern with a hammer he spun like a whirlwind. Many of the men rubbed red rings around the rims of their eyes. They yawned, and the heavier ones' jaws were sagging. They also chatted about the strange rebellion that swept through the streets. The Rebel Riders. They chuckled about the strange horse-riding bandits who they considered nothing more than pests that showed up in the names of baseless causes from time to time.

For all intents and purposes, the people seemed normal, waiting to indulge themselves in a jubilant celebration, completely oblivious to the coming storm that Nath felt running through his fingertips.

Maefon squeezed his hand again. "It will be all right," she said in elven. "Just play along or else you'll give yourself away."

He nodded. On the left side of the aisle, in the same row, were fifteen more elves, similarly dressed in the fine elven robes. They stood with their backs straight, chins up, and eyes ahead on the platform. They did not have the bird feathers woven into the braids in their hair like the Brothers of the Wind. They paid no mind to the others around them. Their hands were tucked inside their robes. Nath wondered if they were Caligin.

A cleric in blue robes with silver embroidery and a very tall, fanciful hat entered from a side entrance behind the platform. He was old, pale, and wrinkling. His eyes barely seemed open, but he teetered across the platform with rickety limbs and stood in the middle.

Nath noted the side entrance. They were well concealed behind black curtains and could provide another avenue to escape. *Perhaps I should dash after Fang and run.* He started running through other scenarios. Now would have been the perfect time to slip into one of the Black Hand's hiding spots at the Whistler. He knew where their treasure box was hidden. No one would be guarding it now. He could take it, his treasure and items, and be gone. With everything in hand, he could start all over again.

Darkken eased his way into the end of their aisle. All of the elves scooted down one spot. He gave Nath and Maefon a warm glance and subtle wave.

The cleric lifted his hands over his head. The sleeves of his robes slid down, revealing his wrinkly tattooed arms. He dropped them quickly as if he was shedding water from his fingers. The halflings' music stopped. The talking in the grand hall ceased, and all of the guests turned toward the stage.

The cleric started off by saying, "Marriage… is why we gather." He spoke with a thick tongue, and marriage sounded more like a drawn-out *marewage* that drew a chuckle from quite a few people. "It is this matrimonial union that brings two people together, but binds the city in which it serves too." He gestured to the left and right entrances off to the sides of the platform. The curtains were pulled back. Tobias walked through the curtain wearing a smile as broad as a rainbow. He wore a fine suit of black leather armor that had an oily shine to it. His sword and daggers were belted on. He walked up on the platform followed by Nina, Cullon, and Worm. Nina had a bitter expression. Her left hand was tucked inside her clothing. Virgo, who had been standing in the front, made her way onto the platform and stood behind Worm.

Interesting.

Cullon wore his crisscross of knife belts. His battle axe hung between his shoulders. Nina had her sword, and Worm's hands were concealed inside his frumpy clothing. Aside from Tobias having a nice shine on his armor, the Black Hand was as ready for action as they ever were. They faced the cleric in a slanted line, customary for most weddings.

From the right side entrance, Princess Janna entered, wearing a trimmed white gown, no veil, with her bouncing silken blond hair down over her shoulders. The guests were awed by the truly gorgeous bride. They sighed and murmured excitedly as she walked up on the stage, carrying a small bouquet of flowers. The trains of four handmaidens dressed in blue were behind her. Janna's head was downcast. She took her spot across from Tobias, and her chest heaved gently from a sigh.

Nath felt sorry for the young princess. Her body language said it all with her slumped shoulders and doubt lingering in her beautiful eyes. She was lost and alone. He had been there before.

The cleric nodded to the bride and the groom. "It is time to light the fire of unity. Let this fire burn everlastingly as a sign of your new covenant to one another." He turned, walked between the two throne chairs, stumbled on his robes, caught his balance, and with a smooth recovery made his way back to the fireplace. He looked at the sword hanging over the mantel and scratched his chin. "That's new." With a wave of his hand, the logs inside the huge fireplace ignited. He returned to his spot in the front and looked at Tobias and Janna. "May your passion burn just as brightly for one another."

Smiling, Tobias gave an affirmative nod.

Janna lifted her eyes to him and gave a weak smile.

The cleric said, "Face your guests and let's join hands." Standing between them, the cleric held both of their hands. He closed his eyes. "Let me pray a blessing. Will the guests please close your eyes and join me?"

I'm not about to close my eyes!

Nath kept his head down, but he scanned the crowd. Everyone had their eyes shut, including the Black Hand, Maefon, Darkken, and the elves. Even Hacksaw closed his eyes. Confusion and doubt swelled inside him. Sweat beaded on his brow. Wasn't something supposed to happen? Wouldn't now be the perfect moment for Darkken to strike? Yet, the man did nothing. This time Nath squeezed Maefon's hand. As the cleric was praying she squeezed back in a series of pulses that he took to mean settle down or be patient.

The cleric continued, "As one river greets another, a greater river flows, the trees are bountiful and the harvest is sweet, please let this blessing be upon this young man and young woman."

Nath's stomach sank into his toes. He quickly relived the deception that Nina unleashed on him in the Channel, where they set him up and turned him over to Prawl. That put him through two years of unending torment and misery. He wasn't going to go through that again.

No, I have to get out of here. Something is wrong!

He tried to pull away from Maefon. Her sticky fingers held him fast.

"Amen," the cleric said.

Everyone opened their eyes. There was a rustle of clothing and scuffle of shoes on the floor as the suffocating silence was broken.

Nath started to breathe easier as things returned to normal, but the muscles between his shoulder blades were still tight. He glared at Maefon.

She glared back. Under her breath she said, "Wait."

The cleric spoke a few more ceremonial things and said, "This marriage will join House Janders with House Tobias. Tobias will become the new city lord of the throne. He is the chosen spouse of Princess Janna. This union is legal, binding, and longstanding. It will serve the best interest of Riegelwood and its citizens, and it is a great honor for both parties. What is done cannot be undone, as it shall all be witnessed in the eyes of the people."

Nath couldn't believe what was happening. The Black Hand was moments away from putting Riegelwood in permanent tyranny, and he was just standing there, doing nothing. He realized that they were outnumbered, but he couldn't just let this happen. His heart raced.

"Before I join these hands to recite the sacred vows," the cleric said, "as is customary, I will ask if anyone objects to this wedding. Even though there is nothing to object to. Both parties come willingly to the altar."

Princess Janna's sad eyes searched the crowd with a pleading look. She was a woman trapped, forced to make a decision best for others, but not for her. In the long, silent moment, she started to deflate. Her eyes watered then cleared.

The cleric cleared his throat loudly. "With no objections, and I didn't expect there would be" —the guests chuckled—"we will join their hands and complete this ever-binding ceremony."

Nath leaned forward. Darkken's rust-colored eyes were fixed ahead. He was as captivated as the rest of the audience. Anger building, Nath whispered to Maefon in elven, "We can't let this happen. We must strike."

"No," she said. "Be still. Now is not the time and place. It's too dangerous. The wedding will just have to be. Just focus on your sword. Janna will have to be liberated later."

"Tobias. Janna. Face me," the cleric said. "It is time to recite your vows."

Janna sobbed as she turned and joined hands with Tobias.

The deluded guests reacted as if Janna's tears were tears of excitement. The handkerchiefs were out. The ladies dabbed their eyes and noses.

I am not going to stand for this!

Bursting at the seams, Nath ripped his hand free of Maefon's grasp. He shoved his way through to the middle aisle. Brandishing Stone Smiter, with its gem burning like fire, he shouted at the top of his voice, "I object!"

All eyes locked on him. His elven disguise faded.

Tobias turned, tossed his head back, and laughed.

THE ODYSSEY OF

NATH DRAGON

BOOK 3

DEADLY

CRAIG
HALLORAN

Chapter 1

Within the walls of Castle Janders, inside the ceremonial hall where the wedding of Tobias and Janna was taking place, a bristling Nath stepped into the center aisle and shouted, "I object!"

Tobias turned and faced the young warrior. Shooting Nath a knowing look, he tossed his head back and laughed.

Nath shrank inside his clothing. Tobias's laughter was like a splash of ice water down his back. It cooled his burning veins. The curious stares of the guests bore into him. A moment earlier, he had been disguised as an elf, but now he'd transformed into a man. On the platform, the cleric performing the ceremony blinked. Next to the cleric, Princess Janna's back straightened. Her beautiful eyes widening, she moved toward Nath.

Tobias hooked her arm and pulled her back. "Be still, dear."

The other members of the Black Hand standing on the platform glared at Nath. Cullon, the grizzled, balding dwarf, unhooked his battle axe from his back and started down the steps. "I'll handle this intervener."

"Cullon, be still," Tobias ordered.

Janna wriggled against him.

He twisted her arm behind her back and shoved her into the arms of Nina and Worm, who held Janna fast.

Worm sniggered.

Tobias lifted his hands and addressed the guests. "Friends and citizens, I apologize for this abrupt interruption, but it seems that we have an uninvited guest, which, if you take a closer look, you will recognize as the man who kidnapped Princess Janna over two years ago."

There were many audible gasps and looks of confusion.

"You see, he recently escaped from Slaver Town, and it seems that he has returned to"—he tilted his head—"object to a wedding." He shrugged. "A very odd move for a fugitive."

"You are full of lies, Tobias!" Nath fired back. "Your words are poison. That goes for all of you!" He pointed the sledgehammer at the Black Hand members. The gem on the top of the hammer radiated brightly. So did the gemstone mounted on the top of his gauntlet. The flames that were momentarily doused inside him kindled again. "I'm here to set the record straight!"

Tobias rolled his eyes. The grand chamber fell silent. "Says the man who burned down our cherished Oxen Inn and cut our beloved Counselor Nina's hand off. This is comical. What do you expect to do? Take me out with that hammer?" Tobias's hand fell on his sword pommel. "You are surrounded by the finest soldiers and my most loyal hands. You will only bring destruction to yourself and possibly harm others. You should be wise and turn yourself in. For there is only one way out, and that is death."

The guests stirred. Faces beaded with sweat. Women clung to their husbands and escorts. Hands fell on weapons that hung from their hips. The soldiers on the outskirts of the room slowly crept toward Nath. He could hear more guards barring the doors in the back. Nath didn't want any innocent people getting hurt, but he was too close to his goal to turn back now. Still, something was bothering him. Darkken stood behind him, quiet as a mouse. The rest of the elves, the suspected Caligin on the left, and the Brothers of the Wind on the right, remained still as water. Even Hacksaw didn't budge an inch. Nath swallowed.

What is with Darkken and Maefon? They stand there doing nothing?

The old wizened cleric cleared his throat. He rubbed spittle from the corner of his mouth on his priestly robes. "It is in the written law that one man may challenge another in a ceremony of objection. They can cross swords or wrestle." A wrinkled smile formed on his lips. "I saw someone object once when I was a young acolyte. The men wrestled for hours over the bride's hand. She ended up marrying the challenger. I remember, he had long hair and fingers like sticks, but he wrestled like a snake."

Tobias gave the cleric a boorish look. "He can't challenge me. He's not a guest, he's a fugitive and a kidnapper. He's but a moment away from being locked in irons and being carted back to Slaver Town. I'm sure the orcs in the south will be very eager to see him again."

"Oh, I see." The cleric scratched his head. "Uh, should I carry on with the ceremony, or are you supposed to arrest him? He's just standing there, sort of interfering."

Tobias's fingers drummed on the pommel of his sword. He craned his neck, staring into the crowd as if he too was expecting something to happen. His eyes focused primarily on the elves, who didn't appear to blink, or even breathe for that matter.

"Let's just kill him, Tobias, and get it over with," Cullon suggested. "I'm ready to drink some ale and celebrate."

"Agreed," Worm chimed in, making a goofy giggle as he toyed with Janna's hair. Appalled, she shrank away.

Behind Nath, the soldiers slowly made their way down the aisle, shoulder to shoulder, three rows deep. More soldiers came around toward the front.

With a perplexed look on his face, Tobias said to Nath, "To be clear, are you going to surrender or not?"

Nath hefted the sledgehammer over his shoulder. The purplish gemstone shined on his face. He managed a smile. "You don't want to find out what this hammer can do. Trust me. I drop it down, and things are going to get really nasty." He looked beyond the thrones on the platform at his sword, Fang, that hung over the fireplace. His father had given him that sword, and Nath intended to get it back. "Give me my sword and Janna and walk away, and I won't make a mess of this place."

Tobias's shoulders shook as he laughed. "So, you came to steal my bride. Ha! Every moment becomes more ludicrous than the last. No, interloper, I won't be entertaining any more of your malicious ideas. Soldiers of Jander, take him!"

Chapter 2

Nath started into a downward swing.

Darkken stepped forward and said, "I challenge Lord Tobias for the hand of Princess Janna!"

Checking his swing, Nath turned to face Darkken. Underneath his breath, he said, "This is your plan?"

Talking quietly back, Darkken said, "No, but you ruined my plan."

Nath gave a quick unbridled reply. "Your plan was to stand there and do nothing while the fate of the city unfolded."

"We are outnumbered, severely, and you would get us all killed. Now let me try to get all of us out of this." Darkken stepped past Nath toward the thrones. "May I address Lord Tobias?"

"Frankly, I tire of this wedding being interrupted by fools. You can address me once Nath is in irons and on his way back to Slaver Town."

"The challenge has been made. It must be honored or be withdrawn," the cleric said. He fanned himself with his floppy sleeve. "It's getting toasty in here. We need to get on with whatever it is we are going to do before my voice becomes as dry as parchment. Eh, Darkken is it, do you withdraw your challenge?"

"In the name of peace, I hoped to do something ceremonial." Darkken cast a nervous look at Nath. "I didn't want to see what happened when he dropped that hammer into those stones. I merely wanted to delay and avoid danger. Not that I'm a coward of any sort, but I don't want to see innocent people get hurt."

"You've made your point, so withdraw the challenge," Tobias said.

Looking at Tobias dead on, Darkken snaked his sword, Scalpel, out of the scabbard.

The audience gasped.

The cleric stepped back. "Oh my." He searched out Princess Janna. "Milady, do you accept this man as your champion? It would be best to say no, then we could move on. I'm getting hungry and would like to eat soon."

"Er," Janna's stare fixed on Darkken. She made a pleasing look. "I do."

The cleric shrugged. "It's settled then. Let there be a test of steel, and to the victor goes the bride."

Darkken smirked.

Tobias let out a quick, scoffing laugh. "Have you gone mad, Darkken? You are an interpreter and a businessman. A bridge between man and elf. Your foolishness will cost you a century's worth of relationships."

Darkken slowly made his way up the steps with his sword poised to strike. "You can always withdraw and let your bride-to-be be mine."

"Withdraw? I'm the finest swordsman for a hundred leagues. I'll not back down to anyone." Tobias's brows buckled. He slipped his sword out of the sheath. "Today, it seems, there will be a wedding and a funeral."

Nath cast a quick glance at Maefon. Her mouth hung open, and her eyes were glued on the platform. Hacksaw stood beside her with his hand on his hilt. He'd come to life, still appearing like an elf but watching the advancing soldiers who circled the stage. Nath's blood rushed through his ears. The entire incident had become nothing but bizarre. He didn't know what to do.

On the platform, holding Janna around the waist, Nina said, "Tobias, what is going on? You shouldn't be fighting this man. Compose yourself!"

"He called it," the leader of the Black Hand said with murder in his eyes. "I'll finish it. Clear the stage."

Everyone on the platform moved down the steps except the old cleric, who sat down in one of the throne chairs, trembling from age. He closed his eyes and started praying.

Maefon eased beside Nath. All eyes were on the stage. The soldiers even stopped their advance, eyeing the two swordsmen who slowly circled one another. "I really have no idea what he is doing," she whispered to Nath, shaking her head. "I just don't know."

For the moment, Nath was safe. Darkken had taken all of the attention off Nath. There wasn't a single eye cast anywhere but on the stage. Tobias was a tall, well-built man with the sleekness of a natural athlete. Decorated in his black armor, he appeared deadly as a viper. Across from him, only a few feet away, Darkken stood in a fighter's stance that seemed out of place in the decorative attire he wore. There was a powerful allure about him that seemed to bristle around him.

Darkken's eyes hardened on Tobias. The easy tone in his voice was gone. "You think you're the finest swordsman within a hundred leagues? Well, let me tell you, you aren't even the finest swordsman in the room."

Quick as a snake, Tobias thrust his sword at Darkken's chest. Darkken backstepped and parried to the sound of ringing steel. The leader of the Black Hand pressed the attack, unleashing a flurry of slashes and thrusts. His expertly crafted blade flicked back and forth like a shiny snake's tongue, driving Darkken backward into the vacant throne.

Locking swords, they came breast to breast. "You fight well, but one of the best?" Darkken scowled at him. He shoved Tobias back. "I don't think so!"

Nath counted every stroke of steel that Tobias turned loose. He'd launched twenty attacks, and Darkken parried them all with perfect technique. Tobias's chest labored. Sweat drenched his brow. Darkken breathed easily.

Earlier, when Darkken had sliced the acorns that Nath tossed into the air, Darkken showed he had speed and skill. But Master Elween, the dragon weapon master, had taught Nath that many weapon masters could perform many tricks and master techniques, but that didn't translate into a real battle when one's life was on the line.

He's the real thing. They both are.

Hunkered down, the fighters circled once more. Tobias slid his foot forward. His sword arm cocked back. Darkken struck out with his sword. The blades clashed. *Clang!* Darkken's masterful sword strokes pushed Tobias backward. The black-haired man parried in a frenzy. He tried to counter the attacks, but Darkken's short thrusts cut in. Tobias slid his head to the side, dodging Darkken's sword tip. Tobias backpedaled, putting a gap between them and puffing for breath.

"You are out of shape, Tobias." Darkken paused his advance. "Perhaps there's been too much wedding planning and not enough practicing. And is that a little bulge protruding over your belt? Perhaps the wine you guzzle slows the blood in your veins."

Tobias's jaw clenched. He wiped the sweat from his face with his forearm. "Shut your mouth, interpreter!"

"Will the both of you stop this?" Nina shouted. "Tobias, yield. There is no need for this foolish display of ego!"

"Agreed." The exotic sorceress, Virgo, made her way up the steps with her elegant fingers glowing at her sides. "Darkken, you are our guest. What is the meaning of this madness? I insist that you withdraw this insane challenge for Janna's hand. Tobias is not the enemy." She pointed at Nath. "He is!"

Chapter 3

As all heads slowly turned toward Nath, Darkken cut them off. "I see you have your women fighting your battles for you, Tobias. Perhaps they should be swinging that sword, not you."

A few blasts of choking laughter sputtered throughout the room. Tobias's face turned red. "Nina! Virgo! Stay out of this!"

"You can always yield." Darkken spun his sword with his hand. "There is no dishonor in that. You can do something else, such as live."

Tobias glared at Darkken. "I don't know what is going on here, but there will only be one groom today, and that groom will be me." He held out his sword, squeezing the handle so hard that he shook. His sword blade shimmered with a deep-purple light. The guests gasped as the strange light passed into Tobias's body. His eyes glazed over with a purple haze. His voice became hollow and dark. "You fool, Darkken. You shall regret this! Now I've summoned my sword's power, and I will have your head!"

Nath's neck hairs stood on end. Tobias's voice drew shrieks from the women and some of the men as he advanced on Darkken like a hungry animal awakened from a long sleep. He'd become more than a man, powered by something ancient and mystic. Seeing Darkken's confident expression falter, Nath advanced a step.

Maefon held him back. "No."

Tobias attacked. His glimmering purple blade struck out like a flash of lightning. A shower of mystic sparks danced off the colliding blades. With a wild look in his eyes, Tobias attacked faster, using heavy thrusts and chops. With boundless energy, he pushed Darkken back across the floor.

Bang! Clang! Clang! Clang!

Laboring to block the attacks, Darkken landed on a knee in front of the throne where the cleric sat. The old man pulled his feet up into the seat and cowered. Ducking underneath Tobias's side swing, Darkken darted between the throne chairs. He distanced himself, puffing for breath.

"Look who runs now!" Tobias spat on the ground. "Now, you will feel the full wrath and power of Splitter!" Tobias wound his sword arm around and around in a windmill. The sword's energy formed a shield like fire. In midswing, he stopped the motion, pointing the blade at Darkken, who crouched in a defensive position. An arc of energy shot from the blade, slamming into Darkken, knocking him clean off his feet. He skidded across the floor and slammed into a low platform wall.

The guests went into a frenzied panic. They rushed for the exit door. The grand chamber became a sea of chaos as the terrified horde busted through the guards.

On the stage, Darkken lay on the floor, unmoving. Tobias, with triumph in his glowing eyes, advanced on the fallen man. He lorded over top of Darkken, mighty with power. "I told you there would be a funeral today." He lifted his sword to deliver the fatal blow. "Goodbye, Darkken!"

"Nath!" Maefon said in a helpless voice. "Do something!"

Stone Smiter came down hard on the stone floor, making a sound like a clap of thunder. The chamber shook. People fell to the ground, screaming. The members of the Black Hand stumbled on the stairs. Tobias staggered backward.

Maefon shouted, "Brothers of the Wind, protect Darkken!"

Chaos. Mayhem. There were no other words that could aptly describe the grizzly scene that unfolded. The guests fought their way back to their feet and surged through the exit door. The elven Brothers of the Wind slipped concealed short swords from their sheaths and attacked the castle guards. The elves on the other side of the aisle sprang into action, blades in hand, attacking the Brothers of the Wind. They didn't have special braids or feathers woven into their hair like the Brothers of the Wind. Nath knew instantly they were Caligin. Dark elves. The wreckers of his world. He slipped aside from a piercing blade aimed at his neck and cocked back his hammer. Maefon, dagger in hand, stabbed the dark elf in the heart.

"Are you going to stand there, or are you going to fight?" she said to Nath. Maefon darted away, locking arms with another dark-elf fighter.

"Fight!" Nath replied.

Three orc guards rushed down the aisle at him with halberds lowered.

Nath slid between the massive jabbing weapon heads. He punched an orc in the middle of the chest with the Gauntlet of Goam. The breastplate covering the orc's upper body dented. The orc collapsed on the ground, clutching his rib cage and sucking for breath. Using the sledge in close quarters, Nath popped the second orc in the chin with the end of the handle. The orc's head rocked back. He rammed the sledge's head into the chest of the third orc. The beast of a man wailed and collapsed.

Nath spun the sledge full circle with a flick of his wrist. "You ugly things are too slow for me." He turned toward the stage.

A mad rush of soldiers, men, orcs, and brigands plowed into him before he could turn loose a swing. Limbs flailing, Nath collapsed under the sheer weight of numbers. "Gads!"

Chapter 4

In all of his life, Hacksaw had seen many things, but he'd never seen elves fighting elves. Back and forth, the Brothers of the Wind battled what he could only assume were the Caligin Nath had talked about. The cat-quick fighters fought one another, blade against blade, with vicious intensity, while at the same time battling the swarms of guards all around him. Keen eyed, he still had trouble figuring out who was on whose side. With his sword, Green Tongue, in hand, he stabbed the first soldier that charged his way.

"Beware the green flicker!" Hacksaw said.

His elven form faded into the bearish form of a big man. Hacksaw battled his way through the fray of men, orcs, and elves, legs and steel driving toward the stage. It was the dwarf, Cullon, who caught his eye. They'd had a fight earlier that hadn't yet finished. The dwarf stood on the steps, battling an elf rushing the platform. Using his axe like the blade of a windmill, the powerful dwarf cut the elf down. Hacksaw shoved through the ranks at Cullon. "Let's finish our dance, backstabber!"

Cullon shoved the elf's corpse down the steps and gripped his axe in two strong hands. "Gladly."

Hacksaw charged at the dwarf. He sliced downward. The blade shone in a green flash. Axe and sword collided with a resounding *clang*. Back and forth, the towering man and burly dwarf fought, exchanging hard chops, thrusts, parries, and counterswings. Within moments, Hacksaw sucked in hard through his nose.

"You tire quickly, human." Cullon chopped hard and quick at Hacksaw, his dark eyes set with murderous intent. "I'm going to enjoy killing you as much as I enjoy killing the elves. Yah!" The dwarf turned loose a mighty two-handed swing at Hacksaw's leg.

Hacksaw parried. The jarring blow rang off Green Tongue, shaking his arms to the bone. *Lords of thunder! His arms are like iron!* Backpedaling, Hacksaw slid away from the heavy swings of the dwarf's deadly axe. Hacksaw was no slouch. His arms were as hard as oak from decades of chopping wood, but the dwarf was as stout as petrified black oak. *Finesse, Hacksaw. Finesse. Beat him with your mind, not your body. You're not a young man anymore.* He sucked in a quick breath. His lungs were burning.

"That's a pretty sword," Cullon said, gaining confidence and showing endless might behind his swings. "It will make a fine addition to my collection."

"And your beard will make a fine addition to mine." Hacksaw unleashed a series of quick thrusts. Cullon leaned back, flailing his battle axe at the flickering blade. Hacksaw changed tactics. He didn't slam his sword against the heavier axe. He slipped it away from the swing and shifted his feet, leaving Cullon swinging at air. Lunging forward, the dwarf overextended and lost balance, exposing his side. Hacksaw slashed the dwarf hard across the ribs.

Cullon let out a roar of anger. Seething, he said in a roar, "You'll pay for that!" Holding his hand over his bloody side, Cullon came at Hacksaw with renewed ferociousness. The wicked-looking, razor-sharp battle axe sliced at Hacksaw's belly.

The old knight hopped back. He countered with a downward swing. Cullon didn't parry but stepped under the swing, driving his shoulder like a battering ram into Hacksaw's chest. The charge knocked Hacksaw from his feet. He hit the ground on his back. Cullon chopped down at him. He rolled left. The axe bit into the ground and stuck. Hacksaw backhanded the dwarf in the jaw. It was like hitting a statue.

Cullon puffed a laugh as he ripped his axe free from the floor. "Only a fool punches a dwarf in the face."

Using his sword like a cane while he labored for breath, Hacksaw pushed himself back to his feet. He took a deep breath through his nose. Cutting trees had kept him strong over the years, but fighting for his life was another matter. This was life and death. His blood churned, but he was exhausted. Shoulders sagging, he squared up on Cullon. "Let's just get this over with."

Cullon set his hard eyes on him. "It's already over, human. You're just too dumb to know it."

Maefon watched a member of the Brothers of the Wind fly through the air and crash into a wall. The elf had been propelled by an unseen force. Her eyes swept through the chaotic sea of battling bodies. Elves, men, and orcs whacked at one another with rigorous strikes. There was confusion as they struck out at one another, uncertain of who was on whose side. Nath had disappeared underneath a heap of bodies in the aisle. *I need to help him.* Hands aglow with mystic fire, she spread out her fingers. Pointing her hands at the orc soldiers rushing right at her, she turned loose her mystic fire. Flame-like energy erupted from her fingertips, covering the enemy soldiers in a burning wave of energy. The soldiers screamed as the fire danced over their bodies. Their weapons clattered to the floor. Frantically, they tried to pat the flames out.

The fires extinguished underneath a powerful gust of wind. The soldiers moaned, wide-eyed, giving thanks to whatever they prayed to.

Maefon glared at the source that had canceled out her spell. It was the woman, Virgo. The beautiful woman with short platinum-blond hair stood on the steps, her body shimmering with light. She tipped her chin at Maefon. "Little elf, you crossed the wrong sorceress today." She winked. "Let's play." Shards of energy erupted from Virgo's fingertips.

As she crossed her arms in front of her, Maefon's mystic shield of green energy flared up in front of her body. The shards that Virgo fired skipped off the shield. Maefon sneered behind the translucent wall of protection. She didn't like the woman. There was something about how the woman carried herself that ate Maefon up. Perhaps it was knowing that Virgo had spent time with Nath and betrayed him that bothered her, even though that was what was supposed to happen. Whatever it was, she decided to let the anger feed her and turn it against the woman. "If that is your best, you are in for a very disappointing day." Using her powers, Maefon propelled herself through the air, right at the wide-eyed Virgo, and slammed into her.

Virgo screeched as they crashed into the steps. "What sort of sorceress are you that attacks with the flesh? Pathetic!" They wrestled over the floor and steps. Their entwined bodies, glimmering like the light of dawn, floated from the ground toward the ceiling. They went at it above while the fray of steel raged below. They bumped and rolled across the ceiling, trying to claw one another's eyes out. "I don't know what your game is, elven witch, but I'm going to kill you!"

Maefon watched the woman's eyes flicker like lightning. She tried to tear free of the woman's grasp. A charge of energy swept through her entire body. "Guh!" Her back arched. She fell toward the ground, hit hard, and lay still.

Chapter 5

Crushed underneath a pile of soldiers stabbing and punching at him, Nath thrashed and twisted. Daggers jabbed into his body armor and skipped off. Someone had ahold of his hair, yanking hard and snapping his head back. "Get off me!" he yelled at the sweaty soldiers that struck at anything that moved, sometimes hitting one another.

"I got him!" a brigand with droopy eyes said. He tried to rip Nath's hammer away. "And I'm taking this sledge once he's dead. Stab him, will you, somebody?"

Nath head-butted the man in the nose. The brigand yelped. The rogue was another one of the Men of Whispers who he'd seen disguised as a soldier earlier. The mere sight of the man made him angry. The orcs were even worse. Kicking and twisting like a wild animal, Nath kept his limbs free from being seized. In the close quarters, the sledgehammer was no good to him. But on his free left hand, the Gauntlet of Goam blazed like fire. "I've had enough of this!" He punched an orc soldier in the belly. A whoosh of air exploded out of the orc's mouth. It left its feet and sailed across the aisle.

The soldiers paused.

"Did you see that?" one of the men said.

Catching the soldiers with their mouths hanging wide open, Nath clobbered three at once with a haymaker swing. The men almost came out of their boots, flopping backward and colliding with the others. Back on his feet, Nath spun the hammer, creating a circle of light. "Who's next?"

Someone tapped him on the shoulder. "I am."

Nath spun around and found himself face-to-face with Worm. The young, disheveled rogue looked at him with the same dull eyes.

"You made a mistake coming after me, Worm!" Nath swung the hammer at him.

Worm vanished into thin air.

Nath shuffled around, expecting an oncoming rush of soldiers. Instead, he found himself face-to-face with Nina's fist. The punch in the face rocked him backward and sent him flat on his butt. The sledgehammer slipped from his fingers. Blinking, he shook his head and rubbed his jaw. He reached for the hammer. Worm reappeared over the sledge, snatched it up, and with a cackle tossed it to Nina.

The towering woman glowered down at Nath. "You're a dead man!" The hammer rose and fell.

Lying on his side, Darkken kicked out the moment Tobias approached. The sure-footed fencer hopped over Darkken's feet and laughed.

"You missed, you pathetic fool," Tobias said as he renewed his advance, sword and eyes glowing. He coiled back his arm for the final, lethal blow. "For the life of me, I'll never understand what foolishness got into you, Darkken, but you crossed the wrong swordsman today." He stabbed at Darkken. The blade sank inches into the man's chest, passing right through the hidden chain links of armor hidden underneath his clothing. "Goodbye."

Darkken smiled like a crocodile. With one hand, he grabbed Tobias's blade, squeezed hard, then wrenched it free of the man's grip. The glow in Tobias's eyes went out. His face turned ashen as Darkken rose. "I have no more use for you, Tobias."

"What are you talking about?" Tobias stood underneath Darkken's heavy stare like a wounded child. He looked at the stab wound in Darkken's chest. "You don't bleed."

"Oh, I can bleed, I just don't want to." Darkken snagged Tobias by his wrist, then locked the fingers of his free hand around the man's strong neck. In a dark, all-knowing tone, Darkken said, "I want you to know that I have appreciated your service."

Straining to yank his hand and neck free, Tobias sputtered out, "What do you mean?" Doubt mixed with fear built in his eyes. "Who are you?"

Darkken pulled the man up to his tiptoes. "Haven't you figured it all out yet? Certainly, you are smarter than that. I'd expect much better from the leader of the Black Hand." He squeezed the swordsman's neck more tightly.

Tobias choked. His eyes bulged, and he chopped at Darkken's arm with his hand. "You," he spat out. "Cal-i-gin!"

"I don't want you to say that too loudly," Darkken replied as his coppery eyes quickly swept the room. "And no, I am not Caligin. But seeing how dead men can't tell tales, I'll share my little secret." His now-glowing eyes met with Tobias's eyes as they began to flutter. "I am the Lord of the Dark in the Day."

Puffing out the words, Tobias said, "Why kill meee? I-I have served well."

"You have served your purpose. I don't need you anymore." Darkken squeezed harder. The muscles in Tobias's neck gave way. So did his spine. *Crack.*

Darkken let the dead man slip from his fingers and lowered him to the ground. He spied the cleric sitting in the chair, staring right at him. "You didn't hear that, did you?"

"No, no, of course not. I'm awful of hearing these days," the trembling cleric said. "Eh, is the wedding over?"

Strolling over to the feeble cleric, Darkken gently patted the man's scrawny shoulder. "Yes, I believe it is. As for you, not hearing what I said to Tobias a moment ago, I fear I can't take any chances. Besides, you are very old and don't have much left to live for these days." Darkken sent a charge of energy through his hand that raced through the cleric's body, stopping the old man's heart. The cleric sagged in the chair, dead. "Rest in peace. It's better than pieces."

Ignoring the ensuing battles all around him, he strolled toward the sword hanging over the burning fireplace. With admiration, he said, "Father, that's quite the masterpiece, but it was intended for me, not my brother." He reached for the sword and lifted it from the brackets. The handle warmed but did not burn. "Interesting." He sliced the great blade through the air. "Magnificent!"

Hacksaw and Cullon battled back and forth, exchanging heavy blows. The old legionnaire had hundreds of fights underneath his belt, but that was decades ago. Now it took all he had to keep up with the dwarf's relentless attack. He blocked and parried. His arms shook. His efforts to defend himself became wooden. Instinct saved him from getting skinned once and again. Sweat stung his eyes. His numb hands somehow held onto Green Tongue. The quivering green blade would be whacked down only to bounce up again.

"Time is short, old man," Cullon said. "If you have any last words, I'd say them now, even though you don't have the breath left in you."

"You are right about that," Hacksaw wheezed as he parried another thunderous blow. "Guh!" Green Tongue fell from his fingertips. In all of his years of battle, he'd never been so disarmed before. He'd never fought a seasoned dwarf, either. He stood there panting. His hand fell to the dagger inside his belt.

In a single quick step, Cullon put the head of his axe under the gasping man's throat. "Don't even touch it. Well fought, knight, but this bout is over. Kneel."

Hacksaw had lost. He knew it. Kneeling was the honorable thing to do when one was about to be vanquished. He kneeled. "Have my body taken back to Huskan, that's all I ask."

"You'll have to leave that to the vultures when they dump your body in the gulch. I won't be doing it."

"You have no honor for a dwarf," he replied.

"Yes, well, I'm a thief and a slaver at heart. What else would you expect?" Cullon lifted the axe over his shoulder. "So long."

Hacksaw triggered a sharp blade that shot out of his gauntlet. He lunged into the dwarf, burying the blade in the burly dwarf's heart. Cullon's eyelids opened wide, fluttered, and closed. His axe fell from his fingertips and clattered on the floor behind him. Hacksaw shoved him to the ground. Blood dripped from the hidden blade in Hacksaw's gauntlet. After he wiped the blade down, he pressed the trigger, and the blade retracted. It wasn't an honorable way to fight, but in the end, Cullon had no honor and wasn't worthy of a fair fight. Hacksaw crawled over to Green Tongue, picked it up, and headed back into the ongoing battle shouting, "Ride the Thunder! Ride!"

CHAPTER 6

MAEFON HIT THE GROUND HARD, banging her head and drawing stars in her eyes. Behind the blinking gems, Virgo, in her glorious white gown, came down, softly landing beside her. Mystic fire crackled on her fingertips. Maefon had been training with Darkken for years in dark sorcerous ways, but she'd yet to test her full powers. Seeing the gloating look in Virgo's eyes stirred the fires in her belly. She started to her feet.

"You should stay down, little elf, if you know what is good for you. My magic will rip you apart," Virgo said.

Maefon pulled her shoulders back, dark magic churning within. "And you are little more than an enchantress, far more skilled at keeping your skin from sagging than using it with any potency."

"You elven witch!" Virgo cast her arms at Maefon. A torrent of energy burst from her hands that lit the room up like the dawn of a new day.

As she threw her hands up, a shimmering shield of energy appeared, catching the full brunt of Virgo's energy. The channel of magic plowed Maefon into the ground. She pushed back with shaky arms. *She's strong!*

"*You are stronger.*" Darkken said to Maefon with thought. His voice was convincing and powerful. "*I prepared you to take more potent mages than this lowly sorceress. You are Caligin. Take her down!*"

Maefon's teeth ground. She pushed herself up to a knee and shoved back against Virgo's blistering tide of energy. Rising to her feet, she looked the woman dead in the eye. "If that's all you have, it's over."

Virgo laughed. "Over for you, little elf, not me." She spread her hands out. As she did so, the geyser of energy enveloped Maefon. Within a few seconds, Virgo covered her in constricting strands of energy. "Ha ha, how about a hug?"

Maefon wriggled against the mystic coils that pinned her arms to her sides. Her shield cracked, splintered, and, fleck by fleck, vanished. Then she unleashed her plan. Despite the lancing pain, Maefon spit out a powerful elven incantation. The bright energy blistered her body and seared her clothes. Her hair stood on end. The magic that constrained her was gone.

"Clever!" Virgo said with balled-up fists at her sides. "You think you can absorb my power, then let us see how much you can take!" She rushed Maefon. The two women locked fingers. Energy coursed through their bodies as they muttered enchanted words at one another.

Maefon reached deep inside her gut and summoned everything that Darkken had taught her. She felt Virgo's will pushing deep into her body, stinging her bones, threatening to tear her body apart from the inside out. Down inside Maefon, a deep, insidious anger lurked, creating a powerful manifestation of energy. She let the dark inner beast out. It pushed back against Virgo and devoured the woman's will.

Aghast, voice trembling, Virgo said, "What is this? What are you doing?" She tried to pull free of Maefon's locked fingers. The elf held her more tightly than a vise.

Maefon forced the woman to her knees. Filled with power, she said to Virgo, "I'm killing you." Radiant purple energy flowed down her arms in a river of power. It passed through Virgo's fingers, hands, and arms.

The gorgeous white gown started to smoke underneath the sleeves. The beautiful woman cried out in agony. "Aaaeyeeee!"

The shrill scream could have cracked glass. Drunk with power, Maefon turned on the awesome power unleashed by the spell of inner darkness. Virgo's skin hardened like sun-dried leather. She begged and pleaded. "No! No! Nooooo!" Her body convulsed. The skin cracked. Streaks of purple glowed underneath the cracking skin. All at once, her body turned into hot cinders and ash. The fibers of the gown caught fire. Her body became nothing but ash. Virgo was gone. The only things left of her were charred bones and some jewelry still clinging to her wrists and neck.

Maefon made a rueful smile. With exhilaration, she said, "I've never felt so alive!"

Nath rolled aside. The sledgehammer busted up the floor, shaking the ground. Face red with rage, Nina lifted the hammer again. Nath punched her in the gut.

A whoosh of air exploded from her lips. She collapsed to the ground, dropping the hammer, and clutched her belly. "Noooo," she moaned.

Nath's neck hairs stood on end. Behind him, he sensed a presence. He rammed his elbow backward. It connected with a rib cage. He spun around, catching Worm just as he fell. The rogue clutched a dagger in his hand. His face paled.

Worm started to mutter something. His body shimmered. Nath stepped on the hand that held the dagger. The thief moaned. His effort to vanish was nullified.

On instinct, Nath tore the man's cloak away. It tingled in his fingertips. "So, this is how you sneak around." He caught a scuffle behind him.

Nina tried to stand. Her good hand reached for the hammer.

"Don't move, Nina," he said. "You're surrounded."

Nina's eyes slid to the Brothers of the Wind who now surrounded her. Battered, bruised, and bloodied, they'd clearly been in a nasty scrap. They covered Worm too, pinning him down with their feet. Nina snarled and spat on the ground.

"Not very polite for a woman," Nath said as he picked the hammer up. It seemed the last of the fighting had ended. One elf, a Caligin, popped up from his spot where he played possum on the ground. He dashed to one of the windows and slid through. Two Brothers of the Wind gave chase. Wiping his hair out of his eyes, Nath scanned the room. Men, orcs, and elves, good and bad, had fallen. The brigands who didn't escape were lined up against the wall on their knees with their hands on their heads. The elves guarded them. Nath spied Hacksaw sitting on the steps, drenched in sweat, drying off his sword. He moved to the man. "Are you well?"

Hacksaw put his pipe in his mouth. "I live. That's always well." He shook his head, surveying the room. "That was nasty. I'm not even sure what happened."

"Neither am I," Nath said. He took a deep breath. It had all ended as fast as it happened. One moment, Darkken and Tobias were battling on the platform, then all chaos broke loose. He noticed that Cullon was dead. "You beat the dwarf?"

"Barely."

"I'm glad," Nath said. As his blood cooled, so did the gems on the gauntlet and hammer. There were so many dead on the floor. The odd thing that struck him hardest were the elves. Many of the Caligin had died. There were only eight Brothers of the Wind left standing watch over the soldiers and brigands that gave themselves up. That's when he spied Maefon sitting on the floor on the far-right side, kneeling over a pile of ashes. Her face was ashen. Tears streaked her face. Squeezing the old knight's shoulder, he said, "I'll be back."

"I'm not going anywhere," he said, puffing smoke out of the pipe. "My extremities won't let me."

Nath crossed the room and kneeled beside Maefon. Taking her trembling hand in his, he said, "Are you all right? You're warm as toast."

With her eyes transfixed on the ashes, Maefon sighed. "I'm drained. I felt like a titan a moment ago, but now, I can hardly feel a thing." She looked at Nath. "I killed her, Nath. I've never killed someone like that before."

Nath stared at the ashes. His brows lifted. "That was a person?" He started to ask who, but then he saw loose pearls and a bracelet scattered in the ashes. There were fragments of white satin cloth too. In awe, he said, "You did this to Virgo?"

"It was either that or she did the same to me." She gave him a somewhat worried and blank stare. "I didn't know I had that in me. I cast a spell, and a monstrous force came out. It was thrilling and scary at the same time. Did I do wrong, Nath?"

Nath rubbed his nose. The foul smell of disintegrated flesh hung heavy in the air. "I hate to see anyone die before justice is meted out, but so long as you are alive, that is all that matters. I'm just dumbstruck that you wield such power."

"It's my gift. But I never used it so much at Dragon Home. Since I've been gone, I've been training." She rubbed her hands. Wisps of energy flowed out of them. "I'm tired."

"I think we all are." Nath put his arm around her shoulders, lifted her to her feet, and led her toward the platform.

Darkken stood at the top with Fang gleaming in his hands. He walked down the steps and held out the sword, letting it rest on his forearms. He gave Nath a nod. "I believe this is yours."

Chapter 7

"Fang," Nath said in a barely audible voice. He took the sword by the handle and lifted it out of Darkken's arms. The heft of the sword felt like an old friend returning to his hand. They hadn't spent much time together, he and the gift made by his father, but having the blade back in his hand filled a big part of the void that was in him. His eyes watered. "I'm sorry I lost you. I swear, I'll never let it happen again."

"It's a magnificent piece of workmanship, the likes of which I have never seen," Darkken said, rubbing his shoulder and rolling it a few times. "I can certainly see why it means so much to you. A sword can be a true friend. One that always listens to what you say and never talks back to you."

Nath ran two fingers down the blade. "I don't know about that. Fang has a mind of his own sometimes."

Darkken tilted his head. "Really?"

Nath shrugged. "He's quiet, but I know he is thinking."

"That's very interesting." Darkken eyed his palm, clutching his fingers in and out. "You know, I felt something when I held it, or him, rather. His handle is warm, like a living thing. My sword, Scalpel, though elven, is cold in the grip, even on a warm day. Pure elven steel, forged with a single purpose, to cut, slice, and kill. But I failed against Tobias. His blade was a living thing, like yours. He almost got the best of me."

Nath noticed Tobias lying on the platform, dead. His neck was bent awkwardly. His hand was inches away from his sword, Splitter. Nath's stomach turned. "You choked him?"

With a heaviness in his voice, Darkken said, "He disarmed me. Desperate, I jumped him, drove him hard to the ground, and snapped his neck against the dais. The fall worked to my fortune; otherwise, I would have been lying dead the same as him."

Nath felt eyes on him. Hacksaw was sitting several feet away, puffing on his pipe. He gave Nath a doubtful look. Maefon sat down beside Darkken. She wrapped her arms around his broad shoulders. "We are all fortunate. We live, and we have each other. Nath, I'm glad you have your sword back. I hope it makes you happy."

He nodded, but it seemed like such a high price to pay to retrieve his blade. So many were dead, all on account of him wanting to regain his sword. That wasn't what he'd had in mind. He wanted to take the Black Hand down but not at the cost of so many. His stomach twisted. "You lost many elves. I feel awful about that."

"They were mine to command, and though I love them like brothers, they knew what we were getting into." Darkken leaned his head gently into Maefon's. "At least this dear one is well. And Nath, what we did here was meaningful. The Black Hand has been exposed. The people of Riegelwood will have a bright future, not a dark one. Their liberation was worth fighting for."

A choking sob interrupted the conversation. Princess Janna sat at the base of one of the thrones. Her arms were wrapped around the old cleric's knees. Nath went to her. "Janna."

She turned to look at him. Her tear-filled eyes were puffy. "He's dead. Cleric Carl is dead." She sniffed. "Why is he dead? He never would have hurt anybody. He's old, harmless, and feeble."

Nath's eyes grazed over the old man. There weren't any signs of him being hurt. No blood or wounds. Nath's heart sank, however. The fight might have been too much for him to handle. "Perhaps it was just his time. He appears to have died naturally."

Janna wiped her nose on the sleeve of her gown. "Do you really think so?"

"It doesn't appear that anyone hurt him." He helped Janna to her feet. Putting his arms around her tiny waist, he said, "Are you going to be well?"

She touched his face. "I knew you were real. I doubted, but deep inside, I somehow knew that you would come. But I can't marry you. It is Darkken that fought for my hand, and I must marry him. I'm sorry."

"Whoa, whoa, whoa," Darkken said as he sprang to his feet and made his way to Janna. He took her away from Nath. Looking deep into her eyes, he said in his charming manner, "As great an honor as it would be to be your beloved, sadly, I cannot commit to that. We came to put an end to this tyranny and avenge your father, but we still are in pursuit of old enemies, much like the Black Hand. It would be best if you married the man who is your heart's true desire. You are free to choose now. Make that choice when you are ready."

She stuck her bottom lip out. "Are you rejecting me? I don't like rejection."

"Even a blind man could not reject one as fair as you. I am just a man bound by duty." He spread her arms out and looked over her splendid figure. "And today, it wounds me."

Janna cracked a smile. "I will let you off the hook. And you are right, there is another that has eyes for me the same as I have for him."

"Janna! Janna!" a man cried out. He ran down the aisle with a sword in his hand. He was a handsome young noble, not a brown hair out of place, with soft eyes and a kind face. He took the steps up to the platform two at a time. Nath and Darkken walled him off. "Get out of my way before I cut the both of you down!"

CHAPTER 8

IN A BLINK, DARKKEN TOOK the sword out of the shorter man's hands and grabbed him by the neck with one hand. He lifted him up on his tiptoes. "You're interrupting our conversation."

"Darkken, no, let him down." Janna wedged herself between the two men and tried in vain to push Darkken's arm down. "This is Edwin, a friend from the house of Shirlwood. A true friend."

Darkken let go. "Sorry, Edwin."

Rubbing his neck, Edwin coughed a few times, then stuck out his hand. "Nice to meet you." They shook. He turned his attention to Janna. "Oh, I'm so glad you are well. I waited outside, praying this wedding would not take place. Then the pigeons burst from their perches. Your guests charged into the streets, screaming about a massacre." He couldn't take his eyes off Janna. "I fought my way inside, fearing the worst. Thank the moon and stars you are here. Eh, are you married?"

"Tobias is dead," she replied. "Thanks to Darkken and Nath making an objection."

"Yes, the mother of all objections," Darkken said. "But the lordship is back in the hands of a true Janders now. I believe, Princess Janna, that you are in command once again. What is your wish?"

Gripping Edwin's hands tightly in hers, she said, "To marry my true love, Edwin." Edwin took her in his arms, dipped her down, and they kissed.

Nath could see true love exchanged between the kissing couple. For the first time in a long time, he felt good.

With the help of Nath, Darkken, and a score of Edwin Shirlwood's men, Princess Janna took control of Castle Janders. Nath's mission was not complete, however, and with a few lingering items that he needed to take care of, he took to the streets with Darkken, Maefon, and Hacksaw in tow. The Brothers of the Wind, meanwhile, stayed back to help Princess Janna and Lord Edwin's men.

The stiff wind made for a bitter cold day as they traversed the cobblestone streets that were buzzing with gossip. The rumor mill spread the news about the upending of Lord Tobias. Nath could hear whispers about Tobias being assassinated by elves or poisoned from a goblet of wine. Most of the people liked Tobias, it seemed, and there were many people who sobbed on the porches.

"Slow down," Hacksaw said as he skip-stepped up beside Nath. "I'm not sure what the big hurry is. Whatever you are after isn't going to move. Now, where did you say we were going?"

"The Whistler," Nath replied. "It's the Black Hand's hideout. At least the only one I know of. They used to have some things of mine in there, and I will have them back. With these keys, I will have them." He opened his hand. Five keys were inside his palm. He had taken them from the dead bodies of Tobias, Virgo, and Cullon. Nina and Worm parted with theirs unwillingly, but they had little choice as they were hauled off to the dungeons.

"We are with you, Nath," Maefon replied.

A wooden cart loaded with hay blocked the entrance to the alley that led to the Black Hand's back door. Two donkeys were chewing on the hay. Nath squeezed by them and trotted down the alley. At the end, the heavy iron door waited, almost concealed by the outlying building's shadows. Nath gave the door's brass handle a tug. "Locked, but I expected that."

"I don't see a keyhole," Hacksaw said.

"No, but I brought a key that can open any door." Nath handed Fang back to Darkken, who handed him Stone Smiter in return. He spun the handle in his hand. The gemstone on top glowed with new light. He cocked the sledge over his shoulder. "Stand back."

Hacksaw, Darkken, and Maefon took a full backward step.

Nath swung. The hammer struck true, busting the lock wide open. He flung the door aside and entered the empty room. It was dark, but the hammer's gemstone offered light. The walls were lined with storage shelves, and a large round table and chairs were in the middle. Scrolls were laid out and weighed down with stone markers covering the corners.

All of a sudden, the chandelier about the candles flickered on. Maefon's hand glowed. She smiled at Nath. "You're welcome."

Hacksaw pressed his ear to the door that led back inside the tavern. Commotion from the kitchen workers could be heard through the wooden walls. "I'll keep an eye out for anyone coming."

Darkken moved in behind Nath. He helped Nath move sacks filled with grain and flour out of a nook in the back corner of the room. Nath popped open a false panel, reached inside, and dragged a treasure chest out.

"I'll be," Darkken said. "That looks like quite a haul."

"It's heavy." Nath fished out the keys and stuck them in the chest. The chest was about two feet wide, half as deep, and tall. It was made from polished blackwood with brass fittings and hinges. Nath started to turn the keys, but Darkken grabbed his wrist. "What?"

"Is it possible that the keys need to be turned in a particular sequence?" Darkken asked. "I've known pirates in the Faalum Sea who were very crafty when it came to the locks on their treasure. With five keys, I'd say they went to a lot of trouble with this chest."

"You make a good point. Uh…" Nath tried to recollect the sequence the Black Hand had put the keys in before. "I remember."

"You're certain?"

"I think you are overthinking it, but I'm certain."

Cullon's key was in the middle. Nina's, left of it, Cullon's, to the right with Virgo's key on the far left, and Worm's, the far right. Nath turned them in that order.

Click. Click. Click. Click. Click.

Darkken's brows arched. "Well done."

With Maefon standing nearby and Darkken kneeling beside him, Nath lifted the lid. The chest hinges creaked. *Click.*

Darkken shoved Nath hard in the shoulder, pushing distance between them. A small dart zipped out of the chest, impaling Darkken's forearm. "Gar!" Liquid oozed from its tip. Darkken's arm turned red. "Poison. Very dangerous. Lethal maybe!" He pulled the dart out. "It makes quite a sting!" His eyes fluttered. He teetered and collapsed.

Maefon rushed to the man's side. "Nath, do something!"

CHAPTER 9

DARKKEN'S WOUNDED ARM BLISTERED. HE groaned. Nath rummaged through the chest. He'd had potions before, ones that healed wounds. Shoving the coins aside, he found his vials. One had a golden-yellow liquid inside. He handed it to Maefon. "Try this!"

Drenched in sweat, Darkken stammered and moaned. His body twitched.

"Hold him still!" Maefon ordered.

Nath restrained the man's arms. Hacksaw rushed over and pinned down his legs. Maefon took the lid from the potion vial, plucked out the dart, and applied the liquid directly to the wound.

Darkken wriggled against them, body tightening in a ball of muscle, then he calmed. His eyes opened. Blinking, he said, "Oh thank you! Mercy on me, and thank you! I thought my arm was going to burn off." The blisters disappeared. The red skin tanned again. "So much better."

Nath let out a sigh. "That's another one I owe you. It could have been me if you hadn't knocked me out of the way."

"Your quick thinking saved my arm, I think. I don't think I would have perished," Darkken said, "but it sure felt like it. That poison, I think it's an acid, perhaps from a copper dragon's glands. I've dealt with it before." He eyed the chest. "So, are your items in the chest?"

"Well, one of my potions was. Let me see," Nath said. It almost seemed petty for him to be looking for the items that his father had given him, especially considering that so many had been placed in danger because of them. Darkken had risked his life, and Maefon too, on account of him. He felt that he owed them more. Inside the chest, he found his bags of precious stones, two of Zophar's candles, a tight coil of rope, and Winzee's Lantern of Revealing. The little bull's-eye lantern fit in the palm of his hand. "Small, isn't it?"

"Some of the most powerful things come in small packages," Darkken said. "So, is that all of it?"

Nath looked inside his pouch. The precious stones, gold, and silver coins rested inside. Some were missing, but it was a small amount by his estimate. "I think that is all of it." He scooped his hand into the chest, lifted up more coins, and let them sprinkle out from between his fingers. "The Black Hand have done quite well for themselves. I'm sure they have more elsewhere. But what shall we do with this?"

"I'll take it," Hacksaw said. His eyes were as big as saucers. "I've not seen so much since I last guarded the king's treasury. I even adventured for such a hoard and never came upon it."

Nath scooted the chest toward him. "Help yourself."

Hacksaw reached for the chest with hands like claws. He pulled back. "What about the two of you?" he said to Maefon and Darkken. "You need to fill your purses. After all, you have men to feed."

"We have plenty of means. Besides, we like to travel light," Darkken said. "Sometimes, treasure can weigh a man down." He put his hand on Hacksaw's shoulder. "Take what you need to return home, Hacksaw. You've earned it. If it makes you feel any better, I'll take a little for myself." He grabbed a handful of coins and loaded them into a purse. "There. I'm ready to blow it already."

"I'm not set on going home," Hacksaw said, giving Darkken a stern look. "Perhaps I'll roam where Nath roams."

"Of course," Darkken said, wincing. "I just assumed you'd make your way to Huskan now that this adventure is over, but I'm all for keeping this party together."

"Me too." Maefon giggled as she grabbed a strand of pearls made for a woman's wrist. She twirled it on her finger. "I like this. I suppose we earned it. We should celebrate today and ride out in the morning."

"Ride out where?" Hacksaw's brow furrowed.

"The Brothers of the Wind waste no time pursuing the Caligin. After all, many of them escaped the wedding. We need to get after them while the trail is hot," Darkken added.

Nath scooped out a handful of coins and handed them to Hacksaw. "Take this. I think I know what can be done with what is left." He shut the lid on the chest. "But I'm not going after the Caligin until I free my friends from Slaver Town."

Everyone looked at Nath with surprise on their faces.

"Why would you do that?" Darkken asked. "These friends of yours, are they not criminals? No offense, but I think you should forget about them. They are responsible for their own actions. You need to focus on the Caligin. Otherwise, the opportunity shall slip away. It could take years to find them again."

"So be it then." Nath stood up and picked up the chest. "If no one objects, I'm going to give a large share of this to my friend Little Shirl."

"Uh, well, er…" Darkken shrugged. "Do what you like. Who is Little Shirl?"

"A fine little gal," Hacksaw said in his gravelly voice. "I like this idea. She could build her own inn with it." He stood and faced Nath. "Let's track her down, you and me. We'll catch up with the two of you later."

"Meet at Castle Janders then," Darkken said as he and Maefon helped one another to their feet. "I need to get our brothers out on the hunt. They keep us apprised on the whereabouts of the Caligin."

Nath nodded. "See you soon."

Chapter 10

Nath and Hacksaw tracked Little Shirl down. She resided in a small stone cottage with a straw roof. Inside, a small fireplace burned, giving the sparsely furnished habitat a cozy feeling. Hacksaw sat on a three-legged stool in the corner, puffing on his pipe. Nath sat on a chair that creaked when he moved. On the floor, in front of the fireplace, Little Shirl gaped at the contents inside the chest. Her small hands combed over her braided ponytail. Finally, she said, "You entrust me with… all of this?"

"I don't know many people in Riegelwood and thought you might appreciate the gift," Nath replied. "Besides, you lost your job, no thanks to me. Perhaps you can build a new Oxen Inn and have a tavern of your own?"

She gave a weak smile, but it was big for her. "I like that idea. I think I could do it." She dipped her hands in the treasure. "But with so much, why would I need to work at anything?"

Nath and Hacksaw exchanged glances, then Hacksaw burst out laughing. "She's right. There's enough treasure there to last a long time. She could always trust it to the bankers and let them manage it for her."

"I wouldn't do that. The bankers are as much thieves as the Black Hand. Perhaps more so."

Nath didn't know anything about bankers or worldly affairs. Nalzambor and its intricacies were still very new to him. "Just do what you feel is best. It's your life, you can live it how you want, but I suggest that you do it with a good and proven purpose."

She closed the chest lid. "Perhaps I'll find a good purpose, though I do like the tavern idea. I'd hate not to work. It's all that I've known. I like being busy." She gave Nath a curious look. "What are you going to do?"

"Er… me? Well, I have to move on to Slaver Town and save some friends who saved me."

"Can I come?"

"As much as I'd enjoy the company, I don't think it would be safe."

Little Shirl's creaseless face and lack of expression made it hard to read her, but she seemed a bit sad. "You should take me. I'm a good helper."

"I know that, but please understand, I don't want to endanger those I care about." Nath patted her knee. Her cheeks turned rosy. "You are precious. It would wound me if anything happened to you because of me. Besides, I think this city needs you. You could run things one day."

"Well, my brother will be running things soon enough, thanks to you," she said.

"Your brother?" Nath exchanged a glance with Hacksaw again. "Who is your brother?"

"Edwin. Edwin Shirlwood. He'll be wedding Janna soon enough. Perhaps this treasure would make a fine wedding gift, or at least I could buy them one. A very nice one." She tilted her head. "You seem confused."

"Edwin is your brother?"

"Yes, remember I told you that Tobias had horned in on my family's right to lordship. He'd outright stolen it from our family. But now, it's ours again."

Nath did recall her mentioning it briefly when he saw her the last time. "If you are part of a powerful house, then why did you work for Nina?"

"I spied on Nina. We spied on all of them, but they were so crafty. I'll tell you a secret, but you must keep it. Will you promise?"

"Yes," Nath said.

"Of course, my honor as a knight," Hacksaw added.

"Good. My family leads the Rebel Riders. We've been a thorn in the Black Hand's side a long time, but thanks to you, now we have them. Edwin hoped the raid last night would have delayed or canceled the wedding, but it didn't. I'm just glad you came along. I knew you would for some reason."

"Perhaps you should share the treasure with them," he suggested.

Her face lit up. "That's a good idea. Perhaps I will."

Nath rose, helped her to her feet, and gave her a hug. "I wish you the best, Little Shirl. Take care."

Chapter 11

After Nath and Hacksaw departed, Darkken and Maefon spent time walking the streets. Her head was filled with questions that up to this point Darkken had been reluctant to answer.

"Hungry?" Darkken asked as they walked past a tavern where several customers sat in rocking chairs, talking excitedly.

She touched her stomach. "Famished, actually."

"You know, it's been a while since we've shared a bite. Let's go inside and have some pie and coffee. We need to remember to indulge in what this world has to offer more. After all, it's a very long road to world domination."

She nodded. Following him inside, they took a seat at a round table with two chairs and a view out the back window. The patrons were buzzing with conversation. The waitress hustled from table to table. Roasted spiced meat and vegetable scents lingered in the air. The waitress came, and they ordered hot apple pie and a carafe of coffee.

Darkken had a pleasant smile on his face as his eyes swept the room like a visitor entering a new and exciting place. "I truly love observing people. It's fun. They are so ignorant that I know what they are going to do or say before it happens. Predictable. It's all in their nature, whether it be men, orcs, or dwarves." Forearms on the table, he took her fingertips in his own. "I know what you are wanting to ask, so please, ask it, Maefon. But you should be able to answer your questions yourself."

"I don't understand why you took down the Black Hand. Won't we lose our grip on this city?"

"A good question," he said, nodding. He looked deep into her eyes. "Why do you think I did it?"

Looking up to the right, she thought about it for a moment. "I suppose you did it to convince Nath that we are indeed on his side."

"Well done."

"But the cost, Darkken. We lost allies and our brother Caligin. At least a dozen. And all for what, to lure Nath into our web? I thought we already had him."

The waitress returned. She placed a plate of steaming pie in front of each of them. "It's hot out of the oven," she said, then set down a coffee pot and filled the mugs. "The pot's fresh. Just flag me down if you need me. Enjoy."

"Oh, thank you. You are spot on with your service, young lady," Darkken said, but the seasoned waitress had moved on. "Now that is hustle. If more people in this world had that sort of ethic, we would all be better off. It's ambition that gets the best of them, however." He focused back on Maefon. "Where were we?"

"Dead brothers and allies," she said, taking a fork to her pie.

"Oh yes. First, let's not use the C-word out loud. We are a shadow society, remember. Second, you needed to see that our kin are faithful to the death. Brother fighting against brother, selling out for a deeper, darker cause. That's loyalty. Sure, my men are well trained and not easy to replace, but it's all about catching the bigger prize—Nath. We've weaved quite a deceitful tale, you and I. We must absolutely gain Nath's full trust."

"Is that why you took that dart in your arm?"

He made a rueful smile then started in on his pie. "Oh my, this is wonderful. The crust is flaky, and the apples sweet with a little tart still in them." He moaned with delight. "Simply wonderful. Now, let's try this coffee."

Between bites, she asked, "Are you not worried about losing your hold on Riegelwood? You just turned it over into the hands of good people."

With his mouth half full, he said, "Not at all. We will be around a long time, Maefon. The town's leadership is easily corrupted. Besides, we still have the Men of Whispers in our corner. The Black Hand can be replaced. Anyone can be replaced."

"Will I be replaced once Nath is in your hands?"

"Don't be silly, Maefon. I don't kill everyone that fulfills their purpose. Just most of them. But if I expect you to die for my purposes, you won't resist, will you?"

She swallowed. "Uh, no, I'm faithful to the end. I made my oath, and I shall keep it. I'll give my body and spirit for you."

Sipping his coffee, he winked. "Good answer. Good brew too. Maefon, you spent time among the dragons. Since you've been gone, have you seen anything in this world that compares to their magnificence and power?"

"Aside from you, no."

"Oh, you flatterer, you. You know my weak spot. But to stay on point, there is nothing more powerful than the dragons. Imagine if we controlled the dragons. You see, the dragons will follow their king, which is my father, Balzurth. Only one heir is destined to be king. It was me, but now it is Nath. If Balzurth is gone, Nath will take his place. I control Nath, and I control the dragons." His expression darkened. "We can put Balzurth in his place once and for all."

"So, the goal is to kill Balzurth and take over?"

"The first goal is to turn Nath against our father. Balzurth will be no match for two sons against him. He couldn't bring himself to kill me, and he won't be able to kill Nath, either. He's merciful. It's his weakness."

"It's deep."

"Yes, it is. We will rule all in Nalzambor. That is the goal. But enough of my grand plans. Enjoy your pie."

"I am. It is very good. So, what do we do now? Nath is going to Slaver Town, and we are chasing our own ghosts."

"No, we'll change our mind and accompany him to Slaver Town. It will give us time to build up our trust."

She nodded. "What about Hacksaw? I don't think he's easily convinced. His eyes are wary."

"True. The old legionnaire is a bit of a problem. He's seasoned and has an eye for deceit. If we can't fool him, then I'll have the brethren take him out. I hoped for such an outcome at the wedding. I really thought Cullon could take him, but Hacksaw proved more formidable. Speaking of which, once we are finished, I have another task for you to undertake."

"Certainly, what is it?"

Darkken drained his coffee. "Two members of the Black Hand remain alive in the dungeons. They are loose ends. I can't have them lingering around. I need you to kill them."

Maefon's food caught in her throat midswallow. Half choking, she washed it down with coffee. "As you wish."

Chapter 12

The next day, Maefon rose with her stomach turning. Her hands were clammy. *Why did he put me up to this? The other Caligin could have executed the Black Hand. Why me? I have proven my loyalty.*

She had tossed and turned most of the night, contemplating how she would kill Nina and Worm. She was Caligin, trained to kill in many different ways. She could kill with a dagger or poison food. She had spells that could choke them to death. The trick was to kill in such a way that neither she, Darkken, or any elf would arouse suspicion.

On a trunk at the end of the bed was an ordinary frumpy cloak. It was the one that Worm wore. The Cloak of Vanishing. She picked it up and slipped it over her shoulders. It was warm, like a living thing cradling her body. She closed her eyes and opened up her magic, connecting herself with the cloak. Her body tingled. "Ah, I see."

Envisioning herself moving from one side of her bed to the other, she passed through time and space to the other side in a blink, vanishing from the very spot where she'd stood before. Her knees buckled. She put her hand on the bedpost. "Impressive, but it's a good thing I haven't eaten."

Not wasting any time, she headed down the stairs to the main level, where the servants moved in a hive of activity, setting up the banquet room and doing other chores. The subterranean dungeons were positioned on the back side of the castle, opposite the stables. One soldier guarded the open doorway that led to the grim setting below the castle's splendid walls. His body filled the opening as he tossed a horseshoe up and down. Maefon cast a spell on the horseshoe. As the soldier tossed it up, it hung in the air above the man's widening eyes. Staring stupidly at it, he scratched his head. With a flip of her finger, the horseshoe came down, bashing the man between the eyes. He stumbled away from the doorway, cursing. Maefon lifted the keys from his belt and dashed down the stairs into the dungeon.

The stale air in the tunnel was rank. She covered her nose with her sleeve. With her head covered, she slipped past the cells. Behind the iron bars, a few prisoners were nestled under rotting blankets on their cots, some shivering against the chilled, damp air. Quiet as a mouse, she made her way down the row, searching for Nina and Worm. *Can't have any witnesses. They all might have to go.*

The last cell at the end of the row contained Nina and Worm. The young rogue was on his feet, hands locked on the bars, staring right at Maefon. Nina sat on one of the cots with her face in her remaining hand. "Interesting attire," Worm said, brushing his thick locks from his eyes. "I can only assume that you are returning it to me."

Maefon shook her head.

Nina rose. "You are the woman who killed Virgo. What game do you play?"

"I don't play games. I follow orders," Maefon replied.

Worm cackled. He licked his lips. "I like games. Like this cell. They think it can hold me, but nothing can. I don't even need *my* cloak to escape. And I would have it back."

"If you could have escaped, you would have done it already," she replied. "But that is not something that you should concern yourself with now." She approached the bars. "I'm here to give you a proper escape."

Worm stuck his slender hands through the bars and grabbed the cloak. His fingers toyed with the fabric. "Yes, that would be very nice. Let us go so we can sort this madness out."

"Of course," she said, touching his hand and caressing it in her own. "Soon, you will be reunited with the Black Hand, and all will be well."

"What do you mean?" he said, his eyes getting big. "Tobias and Cullon still live?"

"In a manner of speaking, yes. They are waiting for you on the other side of death's door." Maefon stabbed her concealed dagger into the young man's heart.

"Urk!" Worm's skin paled. His fingers slipped from the fabric of the cloak and back through the bars. He staggered backward with a glassy stare in his eyes. "I don't want to die—"

Nina caught him before he hit the ground. "Worm!" She turned her head toward Maefon with murder in her eyes. "You! You are Caligin, and you betray us!" Her face knotted with confusion. "Why?"

"The Lord of the Dark in the Day sends his regards."

Nina paled. "Guards! Help!"

Maefon grabbed Nina's throat with a telekinetic hand. Nina chopped at the unseen force. Her eyes bugged out, and choking, she dropped to her knees, fell over, and died. Reaching through the bars, Maefon wiped the blood from her dagger on Worm's pants leg. From where she stood, the other prisoners couldn't see her or into the cells beside them. They were walled off by stone. Her keen ears didn't hear a stir from the men lying on the cots.

Hmm… how can I make this look like an accident?

She got a better idea of what Darkken meant by loose ends. Leaving them alive could be trouble, but killing them seemed to make more. Now she had to bury her own tracks.

Someone always sees something. This is tricky.

The Caligin specialized in setting up accidents and making them fatal. An oil lantern hung on the wall behind her. She took it, opened the cell, and sprinkled the oil on Nina's and Worm's clothing. Whispering mystic words, she used her magic and set the bodies on fire. The clothing, hay, and cot caught fire. The flames and smoke spread. Covering her mouth, she said to herself, "It's not perfect, but if anyone pertinent asks, we'll just blame the Caligin."

Men started choking and coughing. They screamed for the guard. Heavy footsteps came running down the stairwell. The guard waded through the smoke, fingers fumbling for the keys. Maefon used the cloak's power and vanished from her spot to one behind the guard. She dropped the keys and dashed up the smoky stairwell. She vanished forward a few more times until she was back in her room, hoping no one saw a thing. She took off the cloak and flopped down on her bed. "Phew!"

CHAPTER 13

IN LITTLE OVER A DAY, Castle Janders had turned from a place of dark tragedy to a festive place true to Riegelwood's identity. Inside the banquet hall, Nath sat behind a long table with Hacksaw on his right and Maefon on his left. Darkken sat beside Maefon, talking with Princess Janna. Platters of food were spread out all over the tables. The servants kept every goblet filled with wine and mead. In the room's center, surrounded by more round tables, was a dance floor. The invited dignitaries danced gracefully in their flattering clothing while a small orchestra of men played in the corner behind Nath's table.

"By the looks of things, one would think that yesterday didn't even happen," Hacksaw commented as he sawed into a hunk of ham with his knife. "I suppose a free party dresses over more important issues. You'd think they'd be scared, but here they are, back again, as celebratory as ever."

Drumming his fingers on the table, Nath said, "I hadn't thought about that, but I suppose it's odd."

"Odd and spooky if you ask me," Hacksaw added.

"The pair of you need to enjoy yourselves. After all, this party is for us. They are celebrating a very important and heroic day," Maefon said. She was dressed in her sleeveless black-leather armor, the same as Darkken. Side by side, they looked like a formidable pair, even meant for each other. She hugged Nath's arm. "Enjoy this, Nath. I think Princess Janna is considering naming a day after you, well, all of us maybe, but especially you. You rescued her twice, and she seems very grateful." She drank from her goblet. "Live it up. You're a hero!"

"Well, I didn't say I wasn't enjoying myself. It's nice." Nath clinked his goblet with hers and drank a sip of wine. "I'm just not used to being comfortable yet. Given all that I've been through, I suppose it's hard to relax."

"Aye. I know that feeling," Hacksaw agreed. "I could hardly sleep after my soldiers died, and there would be goblins in my dreams. They still crawl around my mind at night." He slapped Nath on the shoulder. "But when you're among friends, let your guard down once in a while. You've earned it."

"Absolutely," Maefon agreed.

Nath frowned. "I don't know. The Black Hand is dead, but I don't feel overjoyed about it. I have my sword and items, but I feel empty. I just wanted to talk to them to find out why they did what they did to me."

"You want closure, but they are in the grave." Hacksaw pushed his plate back. "Nath, it's a war. Sometimes you don't get the answers or results you want, but you live, we all do. Be thankful of that."

"I just wish I could have spoken to Nina. I swear, I sensed some good in her." He looked at Maefon. "So, you heard they burned in a fire? In the dungeon? They are savvy people. It seems odd that they would perish like that."

Hacksaw leaned forward, casting his eyes on Maefon as well.

"I don't know, Nath," she replied. "That is just what I heard from Janna, well, through Darkken, who heard it from Janna. I didn't see any reason to investigate the details. I'm just glad they are gone." She drank. "You have to move on. We all do. Chazzan is out there, somewhere, and we must find him. At least, Darkken and I need to, though, I wish you would join us."

"I have to take care of my friends first."

Darkken joined the conversation. "Pardon my big ears, but I overheard your concerns about Chazzan. You know, I've been giving it some thought, Maefon, and I think we should join Nath and Hacksaw."

Maefon turned on him. "But we must pursue him before the trail grows cold."

"The Brothers of the Wind won't give up the chase. They'll keep us informed. I don't think a few weeks out of what might be a decades-long pursuit will kill us." He raised his eyebrows at Maefon and Nath. "What do you think?"

Elated, Nath said, "I think that would be great."

Surprised, Maefon added, "I, uh, agree."

"Good, it's settled then." Darkken rose and draped his long arms over both of their shoulders. "I think I can help out in Slaver Town. I know people that can assist. So, let's enjoy the music and dance." He offered his elbow to Maefon." Milady, will you give me the pleasure of escorting you to the dance floor."

"Certainly," she replied.

Nath watched Maefon and Darkken take the floor and gracefully dance in a waltz style. The pair moved as one, with Maefon almost disappearing in the rangy man's arms from time to time. It stirred Nath's blood seeing her with Darkken. Maefon was so beautiful and tempting. The love they had shared in Dragon Home was real, and he missed it.

"Don't let your feelings get too crossed up over a girl," Hacksaw said as he stuffed sweet tobacco into his pipe.

"Excuse me?"

"I see that look in your eye. You want her. Can't say I blame you. She's a gorgeous thing, but she's not the one for you. Be patient."

Nath turned his shoulders to Hacksaw. "How do you know she's not the one? She could be."

Hacksaw pulled on his pipe made from white unicorn horn and leaned forward. "Keep this between you and me, but I think something is off with the two of them. They make me edgy."

"What do you mean? They've been nothing but a help since we met them. Darkken has risked his life twice and his elves. The same for Maefon. I'm convinced they are sincere."

"I know, but it all seems too… eh, what's the word I'm looking for… convenient."

"How so?"

"Like you, I'm not so comfortable that the Black Hand is dead. The last two, Nina and Worm, well, they should have been taken to trial. They knew things, but the dead can't speak, can they?"

Nath nodded. "You are saying someone wanted them kept quiet?"

Hacksaw shrugged.

"Perhaps it was the Men of Whispers or the Caligin. That would make the most sense. The Black Hand could expose them."

"Or perhaps that is exactly what someone else wants you to think." Hacksaw blew out a long stream of smoke. "I know what you are thinking, Nath, I'm overly suspicious. Well, maybe I am, and I hope I'm wrong, but I'm not sold on the two of them yet. The timing of this matter is too remarkable."

"Perhaps." Nath's eyes drifted toward the two radiant figures on the dance floor. Darkken and Maefon stood out in their black armor, even though they weren't doing anything special to draw attention to themselves. With smiles on their faces, they exchanged words with one another. Darkken tossed his head back and laughed heartily. Nath's fingers balled into a fist.

"Are you enjoying the celebration?" Princess Janna draped her arms over Nath's shoulders and kissed him on the cheek. Tipsy, she took a seat in his lap and talked to him with dreamy eyes. Fingers crawling up his chest, she said, "You better save me a dance, Nath Dragon."

"Oh, certainly." He searched out Edwin. Janna's betrothed was busy talking with some dignitaries with his back toward them. Meanwhile, Janna was enticing in a powder-blue evening gown that showed off her hourglass figure. Her red lips looked as sweet as honey. Her eyes hung on Nath's. He swallowed. "Do you want to dance now?"

"No. I like my place right here," she said. "I want you to know that I love Edwin, but I'm wounded that you are not my betrothed. Actually, I thought it might have been Darkken, but though extremely handsome, he seems older. You are young and fair, and those eyes and that hair." She caressed his silky red locks. "They enchant me. Will you promise that you won't be a stranger to Riegelwood? You'll always be welcome at Castle Janders."

He patted her thigh. "I promise."

"You know, I'm not married yet. And you are my hero. Perhaps we can share a moment together later."

Not wanting to offend her, he tried to think of the right answer and stammered, "I-I…"

Edwin swooped in. He wore a forced smile, and his brows were crinkled. "There's my princess." He pulled her out of Nath's lap. "Dearest, I have some family that you've yet to meet. Will you join me?"

Her neck swayed from one side to the other. She grabbed a goblet of wine. "Certainly."

Edwin gave Nath and Hacksaw an affirmative nod. "Gentlemen. Thank you. I look forward to a long chat later." He pulled Janna away, but she turned and winked at Nath before she was hauled into the crowd.

Nath looked at Hacksaw. "Let's get out of here."

"Agreed."

Chapter 14

Early the next day, Nath, Hacksaw, Maefon, and Darkken departed Riegelwood accompanied by six elves. Maefon and Darkken drove a wagon, sitting hip to hip. Nath and Hacksaw were on the old knight's horses. The Brothers of the Wind easily kept pace, traveling on foot. Ahead was a long road that traversed the grassy wildflower-laden knolls underneath a dreary cloud-covered sky. The chill wind bit at Nath's ears, but otherwise, he was comfortable back in the saddle.

"Oh," Hacksaw groaned. He slumped forward, shoulders drooped. "I think I ate and drank too much last night. I should have known my limits, but instead, thinking like I was young again, I figured I didn't have any. The body really pays for a lack of wisdom when you're old." He rubbed the back of his head. "Feels like someone is chopping wood inside my skull."

"I echo your sentiments," Darkken replied. "That spring wine they make is a dandy. It goes down as smooth as water, fooling your senses. It's no wonder they call Riegelwood the city of festivals. It's festive."

Maefon rubbed Darkken's back. "You men just can't hold your spirits like an elf can. I feel as spry as a pixie and drank every bit as much as you. Possibly the both of you."

"I don't know about that," Hacksaw commented.

With a winsome smile, Nath rode along, enjoying their conversations. Last night at the banquet, he'd met a few score of people that showered him with adoration and thanks for his heroism. They offered him gifts, a place to stay in their homes, and exchanged warm hugs and kisses. There were many fine maidens who clung to his arms, fighting one another, trying to haul him away as they danced, sang, and drank into the night. He'd felt needed and appreciated.

It would be a long road to Slaver Town. He'd made the journey before, tethered to Prawl the orc. The trail brought back memories that haunted Nath. Prawl was every bit as cruel as he was ugly. His face burned an unforgettable impression in Nath's mind. That wasn't the only unforgettable orc, either. There was Foster, the quarry master, who Nath acquired the sledgehammer, Stone Smiter, from. The pair of them had tormented him with beatings, torture, and confinement with unfettered cruelty. Deep inside, a big part of Nath didn't want to return to Slaver Town, but at the same time, he wanted to burn it all down. Swaying in the saddle, he caught Darkken looking at him.

The older warrior waved him over. "Nath, why don't you and Maefon change places? I'd like a bit of your time to catch up on all that has happened. You don't mind, do you, Maefon?"

"Of course not." She stood up and arched her back. "I prefer the warmth of a leather saddle over this hard bench any day." With Nath's help, she sat in the saddle right in front of him. She pushed her supine body back into his. "Off you go now."

Somewhat reluctantly, Nath slipped into the supply-laden wagon and sat on the bench.

"Aren't the two of you a pair," she said with an approving smile. "I like seeing my favorite men together. If you don't mind, I'll take this beautiful beast for a gallop. I love a hard ride and the wind in my hair. Would that be all right with you, Hacksaw?"

"Gallop all you want, but don't overdo my steed. I might trot after you. A quick ride in the wind may clear my head a little."

Maefon put her heels to the horse. The beast lunged forward into a trot then broke out into a full gallop with the elves running in fast pursuit.

Hacksaw trotted past the wagon. "I'll keep an eye on them."

Darkken chuckled. "I suppose we could race this wagon down the road in case you are feeling left out."

"No, I'm quite fine, thank you." Nath felt a little awkward being alone with Darkken. It was as if he was vulnerable for some reason. "But if you want to race…"

"Of course not," Darkken said in his warm and friendly manner. His eyes were smiling like a caring friend. "So, tell me, how are you feeling?"

"How am I feeling? That's an odd question, isn't it?"

"Nath, you've been through a lot, and honestly, I didn't know what to say to you. I thought we should talk about your plans for Slaver Town, but"—Darkken lifted a finger—"I thought I would break the ice with simple conversation. Sometimes, when so much happens, your mind needs a break. You just need to talk and let it out."

"I see." Nath bobbed his chin. "Honestly, I feel… relaxed, but I feel guilty for feeling that way. I'm so used to being on edge or under fire." Blue jays flew right past the horses and into the tall berry bushes scattered along the road. "I'm not used to peace."

"I feel the same way. If you think for one moment I enjoy this pursuit of the Caligin, you would be dead wrong. Why, I'd much rather be back in the city of festivals being showered in gifts. But it would become stale after a while. That's why I just make the most of it when I can and then get back to the business at hand. Besides, I can't sleep well knowing the likes of Chazzan and the Caligin are out there. When I see that scar on Maefon's belly..." Darkken ground his teeth. His hands tightened on the reins. "It sends a fire right through me."

"I know the feeling."

The wagon bounced hard on the rocky road.

"See, it's like that," Darkken commented.

Nath gave him a funny look. "Like what?"

"In life, you'll be moving along, nice and easy, when all of a sudden, *boom*, something unexpected happens. You are jostled. If you aren't prepared for it, your entire life can be turned upside down." Darkken flipped the reins, alternating with each hand in rhythm but not disturbing the horses. "See how the reins ripple like waves in water. Life is like that. But if I snapped them hard, an untamed horse would bolt, but these horses expect it. It's the same as the big bumps in the road. We know they are coming. We are prepared but avoid them if we can. Many are never prepared. Some bumps are unavoidable. But you, Nath, are used to the bumpy road. Even the big bumps give you comfort. Life without those bumps is empty. Make sense?"

Nath rubbed the back of his head. "I think it does, but I don't feel empty."

"Oh, you will, give it a day or two of nothing happening. You'll be lost. Just imagine now, a life of honest work and three hot meals a day. Would you be satisfied with that?"

"I never thought about it that way, but I suppose not."

"It would be as boring as a conversation with a fence post. Life is fullest when it's filled with adventure. The days are longer, different, and full of surprises." He handed Nath the reins. "Do you mind?"

"No."

"Take Hacksaw, as he's a fine example. He's a seasoned man, past his prime, but you can see in his eyes there is excitement. He's spent a decade or more at home, doing the same chores, chopping wood, and probably eating the same bland food. But now, he tastes something different every day."

Nath nodded.

Darkken continued, pointing his finger at Nath and wagging his wrist. "Hacksaw didn't have to come with us. He didn't have to come with you from Huskan to Riegelwood for that matter, but he saw the empty road and wanted adventured. It's addictive."

"He just wanted to help, I'm sure. I needed it," Nath replied.

"Oh, no doubt. That's what most men tell their wives before they set out to do something foolish. Eh, does he have family?"

"No. Just his mother."

"Interesting. Anyway, he couldn't be happier that you came along to lead him out of the wagon-wheel rut of life. He might not show it, but he's as warm and pink as a piglet's belly within. I know it."

Nath huffed a laugh. "I think you are right."

Rubbing his hands together and blowing into them, Darkken said, "The point is, when adventuring such as this gets in your blood, it stays with you. You won't ever be a domesticated man, which, being what you are, I'm certain that's not what you are meant for. This kind of life is… addictive."

"I think I could have lived without the imprisonment and torture."

"Aha, yes, I suppose that was an awful situation, but at least now you know that you are a survivor. Most people break and stay imprisoned forever, even when they are free."

"Dragoni Sephner Phi."

"What does that mean?" Darkken asked.

"Dragons are always free. We say that back in Dragon Home."

"I see." Darkken's angular jawline tightened. "I suppose that has to do with flying."

"Well, not all dragons have wings."

"No, and apparently not all dragons look like dragons, either." He slapped Nath on the back. "Do you believe in destiny?"

Chapter 15

Maefon thundered down the road for about a half mile before she broke right into the tall wildflowers and grasses. The Brothers of the Wind raced one another at full speed behind her. They were all men, not nearly as tall as Hacksaw, but had long-legged strides. Hacksaw followed after them at a trot, keeping them in his line of sight. His gut gurgled, and the jostling ride, though slow, only made his headache worse. "This was a bad idea."

He was relieved to see that Maefon led her horse to a halt on a rolling hillside that overlooked a pond. The elves caught up with her, slowing as their long-braided hair fell to their shoulders. For some reason, Hacksaw was winded when he finally caught up to them. The Brothers of the Wind, wearing leather woodsman garb dyed green and black, didn't look his way or say a word to one another. They slipped behind him in a half circle, sliding their short hunting bows from their shoulders.

Maefon's eyes were on the pond, watching the geese skim across the surface. "A lovely place, isn't it?" she said without turning to look at him.

Hacksaw put his hand on the shaft of his spear that was in a leather sleeve looped to his saddle. The elves hemmed him in, standing quiet as deer. His heart pounded in his ears. "A fine day for hunting. Do you hunt, Maefon?"

She spoke with her chin up, "We all do, though I'm not as great a woodsman as the brothers. As you can see, they are eager to hunt." She pointed across the pond. Wild gazelle with twisted horns stood on the bank with their faces dipped to the waters. "They are a good sign. We should eat well tonight and probably tomorrow." She turned in the saddle. Eyes looking through Hacksaw, she motioned with her thumb side to side. "Whisk, whisk," she said.

Hacksaw's heart jumped in his throat. He started to pull out his spear.

The brothers split, slinking through the tall grass and making their way around the pond, arrows notched on their bowstrings.

Hacksaw let out a breath and sank into his saddle. *Thank goodness they went another way.*

"Did you want to join them, Hacksaw?" she asked. "I see you have your spear ready. Do you really think that you could take down a gazelle with that heavy shaft?"

"I could if those gazelles were goblins." *Or elves, for that matter.*

CHAPTER 16

"I KNOW WHAT DESTINY IS," NATH said to Darkken as the wagon rumbled over the roadway. In the far distance, his keen dragon sight could make out Hacksaw and Maefon, standing on a gentle slope, talking to one another. "Why?"

"I hope my question didn't come across as offensive," Darkken said. "That wasn't my intent. Obviously you know about destiny, seeing as how you are destined to be a king one day."

Nath's eyes narrowed. It was true that one day he would take his father's place on the throne, but that seemed like an impossibility now. After all, his departure from Dragon Home had led him to an exile that would last one hundred years. Taking the throne was the furthest thing from his mind. "I've never thought about my role as destiny. Rather, it seemed more like the natural order of things. I'm his son, therefore I take the throne when he's gone. Though, I don't see that happening for, well, at least another thousand years."

"Do you have any other brothers and sisters?" Darkken asked. He twisted one of the heavy copper rings on his finger.

"Many, actually, some of which I haven't even met. They are all dragons, however, and for the most part, they shun me."

"So, some of them are older, then?"

"Most of them, actually. Why?"

"I don't mean to pry, but doesn't the oldest usually assume the throne of the king?" Darkken reached into the back of the wagon and grabbed a canteen. "Drink?"

"No," Nath replied. "In Dragon Home, the heir to the throne is a dragon that was born a man. That's how I've been taught."

"So, at one time, your father was a man too, like you?"

Nath tilted his head, eyes fastening on the clouds. "I've never really thought about it, and he's never told me about that. I guess that would be true. Huh."

"It's pretty deep, isn't it?"

Nath nodded. "I suppose it is."

Darkken took a long drink of water from the canteen. "My point about destiny is that it seems that many things in life happen for a reason. The sages say that much of life is preordained. That we are living in pages that have already been written in some universal book." He tossed the canteen back into the wagon. "What I'm doing a horrible job at trying to explain is that I think that the crossing of our paths is destiny, Nath."

"You really think that?"

"Well, I gave it some thought last night, and well, Maefon and I have become affectionately close in our relationship. We've been going after the Caligin for some time, but in truth, our hopes of finding Chazzan and his brood have been dwindling. Then you came along, and well, it just seems that the tables have turned back in our favor. I don't know how to thank you, but I'm grateful."

Nath pondered the man's words. Destiny made for a fine antidote to Hacksaw's concerns. "Darkken, I agree with you, I think. So, you think that fate has tipped over in our favor."

"I just think about all that you have been through. Two years you spent suffering in a misaligned slaver hole. The scales were heavily weighted against you, but since you persevered, I think life is… eh, balancing out. It can't always be bad when you are doing the right thing. I feel strongly that nature's alignments will correct themselves. Now, you are back on track. We are back on track. Does that make sense, or am I just being silly?"

"Your words seem as wise as my father's. I never thought I'd miss them, but I like hearing someone that speaks with sense again."

"Ha! You flatter me." He shoved Nath in the shoulder. "I feel that I've found a kindred spirit in you. You are passionate about doing the right thing. When you objected at that wedding, well, it stoked the fires in me. I'm ashamed to admit, at that moment, I hesitated, uncertain what to do. I chose to play it safe, and that could have been fatal."

"It was fatal for many," Nath said, frowning.

"Don't feel guilty about the lost Brothers of the Wind. They would die for the Caligin. Or to take down the Caligin. We all would. I have to say, I really feel that with you and Maefon, we can turn this chase around."

"And Hacksaw."

"Of course, the legionnaire's stalwart presence goes without saying. I'm honored to have him on the trail with us, but he seems so rigid."

Maefon and Hacksaw waited on the road that gently snaked through the grass about a half mile away. "I think it's all happened very fast for him. I don't think he'd be easily sold on the destiny story. He's cautious," Nath said.

"And wise to be so. That all works in our favor. We can't take this journey lightly, which I can be guilty of on occasion." Darkken tapped his ring on the bench. "Give us some time, and we should win him over. That's what I like about a long journey. You can learn a lot about people on the trip. It can be very… revealing."

CHAPTER 17

THE NEXT TWO DAYS OF travel took them past the Settlement, located north of Dragon Home. Without venturing into the town, they refilled their water supply in a natural spring that flowed down from the mountains and fed into the city. From a lofty perch in the rocks, Nath could see the town called the Settlement spread across a rich green valley surrounded by farms and meadows. There weren't any buildings, such as wood shacks, barns, or stone cottages with clay tiles or straw thatched together to make a roof. Instead, the tens of thousands of people that thrived there lived in tents made from different colors of fabrics. They were scattered all over, with no organization at all. It was as if nomadic people wandered in, pitched a tent where they would, and lived. Many hammocks hung between the trees as well.

Hacksaw joined Nath on the top of the crag. "It reminds me of the days when I did a lot of soldiering campaigns. All of the legionnaires had tents, but we didn't pitch them all about like the wind scattering fallen leaves. Nice, neat rows. A perfect order. We could make camp or pick up and go in minutes. All you needed would fit on your horse. It was freedom." He pointed toward the middle of the odd establishment. "Those bigger tents can hold about six knights. We used ones like those, because I was a knight, you know?" he added unashamedly.

"You still are," Nath replied.

"Yes, once a Lord of Thunder, always a Lord of Thunder. I tell you what though, we didn't pitch any tents anything the size of those ones." Hacksaw was eyeing the monstrous tents that stood several stories high and were dozens of yards wide and just as deep. "They say it's like a small city inside those tents. The fabric is stretched out over a wooden framework. That's where the sultans live. They rule the Settlement. Strange folk."

"Perhaps our travels will lead us there," Nath said. A squirrel ran out of the woodland and stopped right in front of his toes. It looked right up at him with big brown eyes. "Well, hello there, little fella." He reached down and picked up the squirrel. It scrambled up the length of his arm and parked on Nath's shoulder. "It seems I have a new companion. Squirrel, meet Hacksaw. Hacksaw, meet squirrel."

"How do you… ack, what am I talking to a squirrel for?" Hacksaw said.

The squirrel jumped off Nath's shoulder, hit the ground running, and disappeared over the edge of the rocky crag.

"You scared him," Nath said.

"He's a varmint. Them elves was probably about to eat him. They've butchered about every varmint we've laid eyes on since we left Riegelwood."

"Oh, you're exaggerating."

"Don't you find it odd that elves, who place a high value on natural life, are slaughtering hooved beasts like hungry ogres? They've filled up a wagon of meat. No one needs that much meat."

"They are selling it. It's good for relations." Nath combed his fingers through his hair. "And all meat is good meat. Many don't have enough of it, and they are sharing."

"They are elves, and I'm saying it's odd."

"Have you not softened up on them yet? They haven't done anything wrong."

"No, but they don't speak. The elves I've met are always more than happy to blather about their customs and their amazing accomplishments in Elome. I'm not saying I don't like them, they are very polite about it, but it's still bragging."

"Then you should be glad they aren't talking, right?"

Hacksaw grunted. "Let's get moving."

Chapter 18

The small party of men and elves made it past the city of Advent during the next day and kept moving. Slaver Town was more than a day away, but Nath couldn't sleep when they stopped to camp that night. He'd stand watch while the others slept, keeping his thoughts to himself. There was a great concern that something bad could have happened to his friends enslaved in Slaver Town. Calypsa, the half dryad, had risked it all to save him. She'd even talked the very reluctant four-armed bugbear, Rond, into helping. There was Homer the musician too. The man was barely fit to survive in the harsh environment. Nath hoped he'd made it. There was also Radagan, once an overweight cook who turned into a burly guard, who aided him. All gave some on account of Nath.

With the late-evening winds stirring his hair, he felt a presence in the sky. He lifted his eyes skyward. Just below the clouds, a bird-like creature with two vulture-like heads glided in a broad circle above him. Its wings were long and feathered. The silhouette of its body was pitch-black in the darkness. Standing knee-deep in tall grasses, Nath watched it for a long time. It was the third time he'd seen it on their trip. It was always at night, and the flying beast was too far up for most people to see, except Nath's eyes were anything but ordinary. He swore he could feel the creature staring right back at him. It seemed familiar. It beat its wings, lifting its body into the clouds, and disappeared.

"Another fine evening, isn't it?" Darkken said. The sizable man stood just behind Nath's shoulder, staring at the clouds.

Surprised, Nath said, "Where did you come from?" He had very keen senses, but with the stiff winds rushing by his ears and his attention on the weird bird in the sky, he'd become distracted.

"It's easy to slip in on a man's back side when he faces the wind. I let nature create cover for me—a little skill I picked up from working with the elves over the years. The real trick is to make the move when your prey is distracted."

"So, I'm prey?"

"Of course not, but you made for good practice." Darkken yawned and rubbed his eyes. "Oh, I'm tired, but I could not sleep. I hope you don't mind me joining you?"

"No, never. It would be good to talk to someone other than myself."

"You sound like a man with much on his mind."

"Slaver Town is a place I had hoped to never see again. I'd be lying if I didn't admit that the closer we get, the more on edge I am." Nath clutched and unclutched his hand covered in the Gauntlet of Goam. "I'll be better equipped this time around, however, and all of those filthy orcs will feel me, but they won't see me coming until it's too late."

"So, what is your strategy, Nath?"

He looked Darkken dead in the eye. "Simple. We'll charge through the main gate, slay all of the slavers, and liberate the oppressed."

Darkken arched an eyebrow. "You're serious?"

"Of course. Why, with our swords, hammer, and the elves, I'm certain we can overcome the impossible odds. I've seen you swing your steel like a hummingbird flapping its wings. Twenty orcs can't handle you. We'll make mincemeat out of them."

Darkken scratched his head. "I like the brazen plan, I really do, but I'm not so sure that is the best course of—"

Nath started laughing. "I'm just jesting with you, Darkken. I'm eager, but I'm not that big a fool. I got you though, didn't I?"

"You did." Darkken tossed his head back. "Ha ha! I'm glad to see that you have lightened up a good bit. The time on the trail is good for that. But seriously, we need to plan, and I'm certain that you have something in mind."

"I hate to admit it, but I don't have the best plan in mind. I've been thinking about it every day. There are two sections to Slaver Town. The prisoners are kept on the northern side of the city. The Slave Lords and their families live on the southern side. Before I escaped, there was talk of a large washout that led out of the city from the south. I have a blind spot when it comes to that area." Nath resumed his walk with Darkken by his side. "The first thing I would do would be to slip inside and find out where Calypsa, Rond, and Homer are being kept. I don't think Rond and Homer will be difficult to locate. I'd say they are in the Barn."

"The Barn?"

"Well, the Barn is the prison for the slaves. It's a barn-like structure with prisoner cells inside. Slaver Town wasn't always Slaver Town. It used to be something else."

"I'm curious to see this place but not so eager at the same time."

Nath unslung his small pack from his shoulders and took a knee. It was the same pack he'd left Dragon Home with that carried his items. The rich red-brown leather woven with unusual zigzag patterns was soft to the touch as he opened up the flap. He was glad to have the pack back. He took out Winzee's Lantern of Revealing, the bull's-eye lantern that fit in the palm of his hand. "This might help find another way in. I have a couple potions in here that we can try too," he said as his fingers rummaged through the pack. He held up three potion vials. One was half empty. It was the one he had used to heal Darkken's forearm. "See, we have options."

"I see two healing potions, but what does the other one do? The orange one?" Darkken asked.

Nath shook the orange liquid. It sparkled inside the clear glass vial. "I'm not sure. Father never told me. Perhaps I should take a sip."

"Let's just wait until we get a little closer. We don't want to waste any resources if we don't need to. Anyway, if we put our minds together, I'm certain that we will figure something out. Tell me more about what you know."

"There are over two hundred slavers who guard the city. The outer wall is made from great cedar trees that look like they were pounded into the ground by giants." Nath put the items back in his pack and strapped it over his back. "Guard towers over thirty feet high surround the city. They will see anything coming. Believe me. The Slave Lords, whoever they are, guard it like a fort."

"The slave trade is big business. Certain people are worth more than their weight in gold. I've never trifled with the Slave Lords. In a way, they are like the Caligin, running covert operations in the darkness that the wealthy people do not care to talk about. That's why they stay to the south, where you have to go out of your way to get there. That way, people can act like such oppression does not exist, even though they all benefit from it, one way or another."

"It's a sick thing to do to people," Nath said, grinding his teeth. "We should free them all."

"Well, I agree, but that would take an army, and we don't have one."

"Shouldn't the other kingdoms do something about this?" Nath asked.

"Yes, they should, but the problem is, the other kingdoms are benefiting from the works of the Slave Lords too."

CHAPTER 19

IT WAS ANOTHER SWELTERING MORNING inside the timber walls of Slaver Town. The hot sun beat down on the rooftops. The slaves trudged over the mud-packed streets from working station to working station. The sound of hammers beating on the rocks in the quarry echoed out of the chasm and across the streets. The slaves, one and all, some shackled in heavy irons and others shackled by broken spirits, kept their heads down as the orc guards drove another line of slaves out of the Barn.

Calypsa the dryad's own cell was on the main floor. It was nothing more than a cage made for a large dog. Everyone could see her. That included the guards and the prisoners. All day and through the night, the vilest of prisoners would catcall at her. They would howl like wolves and make kissing sounds. She would ball up underneath her tattered blanket the best she could, hoping it would all end.

The half dryad with sun-browned skin and thick locks of flowing brown hair peeked out from underneath her blanket. A pair of orc guards stood outside her cage, watching the slaves being taken outside. One of the slaves was the bugbear, Rond. The four-armed monster had a host of guards carrying spears around him. Rond's eyes were downcast. His shoulders drooped. He had scars from being whipped all over his broad chest and back. Calypsa pressed her face to the bars. She wanted to call out to her shackled friend. Rond, however, kept going. He didn't even look her way.

A tear fell. She wiped her eye, sniffled, and curled back underneath her blanket.

"Ay, pretty one." One of the orc guards rapped on her cage with his fist. The orc was an ugly brute. They all were, with coarse black hair and broad, flat, sweaty noses with big nostrils that seemed abnormal. They all wore black tunics over chainmail armor. "Get out from under that sheet. It's time for you to stretch those pretty little legs of yours."

The guards sniggered.

The cage door was unlocked, and with a creak, the guard opened it. This was the part of the day that Calypsa dreaded most. The guards poked and pawed at her all the time, but according to them, it was all unintentional. On hands and knees, she crawled out of the cage and came to her feet.

The guards crowded her. "You won't be needing this." The orc who spoke earlier tore the blanket from her body and tossed it into the cage. "That's better. I don't want you getting too hot." His eyes dressed her up and down.

Calypsa's clothing was changed to something more pleasing to the guard's eyes. She wore a snug one-piece dress woven from white cotton. It had a plunging neckline and covered the tops of her thighs. It was made for attractive women who were sold on the slave block. She would do just about anything to be someone else's slave right now.

"That's better," the guard said, placing his hand on her hip.

"Get your filthy hands off of me, pigface!" She pushed the orc in the chest.

The orc grabbed the chains attached to her wrists and slung her across the floor. She skidded off her knees and came to a halt on the dirt floor. Not having full range of motion prohibited her from using her magic. She needed to be unfettered, but the iron made it worse. It was the one metal that tampered with her powers. She wasn't sure if the guards knew that or if it was an unfortunate coincidence, but it presented a serious problem that she hadn't been able to wriggle out of. Even if she could, she swore she wouldn't leave Rond behind.

Another orc guard pulled her up by the hair and shoved her forward. Fully bearded, the orc studied her with hungry green eyes. "Stretch those legs, pretty thing. We like to see you walk."

She made a few laps inside the Barn, taking her time, scanning her surroundings. Her steps were short, thanks to the shackles. She rubbed her aching lower back, passing the warden's office, where two more guards were hanging outside the door. One of them blew a kiss at her. She kept walking, circling back to her cage. Stomach growling, she said, "I would like to eat now."

"You would, would you? And what is in it for me?" the orc guard said as he picked at his chin with yellow fingernails. "A kiss?"

"Sure, just pucker up your lips," she replied.

The orc tucked his chin into his neck. "Don't play me for a fool. You split me lip the last time you said that."

"And yet, you ask again? I would have thought that you learned your lesson." *Stupid orcs!* She refrained from saying it out loud but only because she was hungry and determined to keep her strength. She walked up to the orc, rose up on her tiptoes, and said in a sweeter voice, "Can I please have my breakfast? I don't want any trouble. I just want to eat."

"Fine. You will eat. Fetch Homer! Tell him to bring a bowl to this hungry witch."

The bearded orc vanished behind the curtain wall that concealed the cages where Nath was once imprisoned. The orc pushed the curtain back open. Homer came out with a bowl in hand. He walked with a limp. His clothing was frayed and tattered. His graying locks hung in his eyes. Homer had the light duty of preparing food for the prisoners and cleaning up after them. He approached the orcs and Calypsa with his head down and held out the bowl with shaking hands. "Breakfast," he said.

They'd gone through the same routine for over two weeks. They woke her up, harassed her, and made her beg for breakfast before finally letting her eat. It was humiliating. As a woman, she shouldn't be in the Barn. The other female slaves were kept in another section of the city, with lighter security. She'd basically been thrown to the wolves. Calypsa looked at the senior guard. "Permission to eat?"

The orc rolled his neck and, with a grunt, finally said, "Make it quick."

"Good morning, Homer," she said, eyeing the rickety-limbed man as she took the bowl. "I hope this morning finds you well."

With a bit of a stammer, Homer replied, "We are fortunate to have such loving masters. Enjoy, Calypsa, enjoy."

She sat down and leaned her back against the cage. Using two fingers like a spoon, she ate the soggy oats. There was a touch of cinnamon and sugar that gave it flavor. It was a little something that Homer did for her. The act of kindness helped get her through the days and long nights.

CHAPTER 20

IT WAS MIDDAY WHEN NATH and company hoofed it on foot to a rocky bluff that overlooked Slaver Town. The fort city was miles away, tiny and harmless, surrounded by a backdrop of woodland. Maefon stood beside Darkken, who had a spyglass to his eye. Nath and Hacksaw stood side by side with four Brothers of the Wind on bended knee in front of them. The others stayed back with the horses and wagon.

"It's quite a fortress," Darkken said, slowly turning his neck. "On the back end, I can see that stream you are talking about crossing through. At night, that might make for a possible way in."

"We should be able to make a search at night," Nath said, his arms crossed over his chest. He scratched his elbows. He kept seeing the faces of Foster and the other slavers. It jangled his senses. "We should go in a small number, though. Two to slip in and two to look out."

"It's bare as a baby's bottom along those cedar walls," Darkken replied. "And I can see patrols and dogs running along the rim. I'm not sure about the back side, but if the slaver lords reside there, as you said, I'm certain it's much more heavily guarded than what we see."

Hacksaw marched over to Darkken and held out his hand. "May I?"

"Certainly. Your tactical input will be as valued as it is needed." Darkken handed Hacksaw the spyglass. "If the image is blurry, you may need to twist—"

"I know how to use a spyglass." Hacksaw put the spyglass to his eye and in his throat made low, guttural words. "Hmmmm. Hmmmm. Hmmmm." Finally, he said, "In a situation such as this, I'd prefer to have an army and lay siege upon the enemy. But with captives inside, they have the full advantage." He swung the spyglass to the left. "Not to mention, they do have a lot of patrols. Nath, you haven't been gone so long, so I imagine that they are still looking for you."

"True, but the last place they would expect me is back inside," Nath replied. "Maybe we could use another polymorph potion, if you have one at your disposal, and go inside under disguise."

"A wise idea, but sadly, we've used up what we had." Darkken rubbed his chin. "But you have given me a very grand idea that I think will work well."

Collapsing the spyglass, Hacksaw said, "I'm all ears."

"Me too," Nath said.

"It's very simple. Myself and Maefon will pose as customers, looking to buy a slave."

"Ha!" Hacksaw laughed. "No one is going to believe that an elf is going to buy slaves. That's absurd."

"True. Sorry, but I got ahead of myself. Maefon is not a good choice." Darkken patted her on the backside. "Don't take that literally, sweetie. Hacksaw and I can be the buyers. We'll take the wagon, the two of us, flash some gold, and we will be the buyers. If you are not comfortable with that, Hacksaw, I'll risk it myself. What do you say, old knight? Me and you?"

Hacksaw rubbed his chin. "I don't know. Being a knight, it's not going to be easy to go in there and be convincing. I'm one to defend the oppressed. I'm liable to explode in close quarters with those orcs. I doubt I can be very convincing. I hate to admit it, but I might pose a greater risk."

"I wish that I could go," Nath said. "That would be so easy. If I could just turn into something else. Are you sure there isn't any more of the polymorph potion left?"

Maefon took a vial of liquid out of her clothing. It was the same bottle Nath drank from before. She shook the contents. "To correct Darkken, there is a little bit left but not enough to have staying power. This smidgen might not last an hour, and you would need more time than that."

"I see," Nath said.

Darkken offered a smile. "Listen, everyone, this is a team effort. We don't have to try it this way. As Nath stated, we'll find a way in and locate Nath's friends. The risk is higher, but we are committed to whatever you decide, Nath."

Nath looked down at Slaver Town. The last thing he wanted to do was get anyone else in harm's way. And Darkken's hand was a good one. "Darkken, let's try it your way."

Chapter 21

From the same bluff where Nath and the group spoke earlier, he watched the road down in the valley that led into Slaver Town. Maefon stood hip to hip with him with her arm around his waist. Her eyes were fixed on the wagon, pulled by two horses, and the man driving it.

"He's so tiny," she said. "All of it is. One really gets a different perspective from a higher point of view, don't they?"

"Huh?" Nath had been lost in thought since Darkken left. The older man had been very convincing, and Nath had faith in his decision, but his fingertips still tingled. "Oh yes, it's different. When I rode on my father's back, sailing through the skies, I always viewed the world as something so tiny and simple. But it becomes really complicated when you are on the ground level."

Maefon's arm tightened around his waist. Her small face leaned on the side of his chest. "I always thought that when I was a Trahaydeen that I would get to fly on a dragon one day. I was very disappointed when I found out it would never happen, though the histories said that elves and men had flown on the backs of dragons in times past. I secretly hoped you would become a dragon and be able to take me for a ride."

"Yes, well, I had the same aspirations."

Darkken led the wagon up to the front of the main gate of Slaver Town. He was surrounded by several guards. An exchange of words went back and forth between Darkken and the orcs. They'd been watching the comings and goings of Slaver Town for over a day, and there was slow but routine traffic. A large part of it was slaver patrols on horseback that guarded the perimeter. There were supply wagons and customers who bought, sold, and traded in some cases teams of slaves.

Hacksaw had the spyglass to his eye. "Darkken doesn't seem to be having too hard a time chatting the orcs up. Does he speak Orcen?"

"He speaks many languages," Maefon said, "so I'd imagine that he'd use it with them."

"I'm glad I didn't go. I can't stand the sight or sound of orcs. They are so pushy and foul," Hacksaw said. "I really don't know how you survived them, Nath."

"He's tough." Maefon smiled up at Nath. "He can survive anything."

Nath rested his hand on Maefon's shoulder. "I don't know about that. Anyway, I just hope Darkken knows what he is doing. The last thing I want to happen is for him to wind up as a prisoner there. Then we'll have four to rescue instead of three." He sighed. "I hate standing here and waiting."

"They're taking his sword belt," Hacksaw said. "Ugh, nothing worse than being without your blade. It always made me feel naked when I was younger. When you're on the trail, you sleep with your steel. I got used to it. Even after I retired, I still slept with my sword for over a decade. Finally, my mom convinced me to hang Green Tongue over the mantel. I bet when I return, I end up sleeping with it again."

Nath and Maefon chuckled. Four of the Brothers of the Wind were kneeling nearby, stoic and silent, without the slightest expression on their faces. All of their eyes were fixed on the road. The other two elves of the group were gone, out on patrol, keeping tabs on the slavers who patrolled the nearby hills.

"He's going in," Hacksaw said.

The wooden doors that led into the city were opened halfway. Escorted by two orcs, Darkken, still sitting in his wagon, followed them inside. As he crossed the threshold, he turned his head slightly and gave a subtle nod. He vanished inside, and the doors were closed behind him.

"He gave a nod," Nath said, breathing a little easier. "That's the sign he promised that all was well." He could still see over parts of the wall from their elevated location, but as tall as it was, it obscured most of their view. Many walls and buildings made borders through the city. Some of it protected the Slave Lords from the slaves. There were even trees that shielded the slave town from outside prying eyes.

"Nath, why don't we go for a little walk?" Maefon said. "Darkken is liable to be in there for a few days."

"A few days. Yes, well, I wasn't very comfortable with him saying that. It shouldn't take that long for him to figure out where Calypsa and Rond are."

Maefon held his hands. "They aren't going to just divulge that information willingly. Darkken is going to do business, and he'll need to win the slaver lords over. Don't worry, when Darkken flashes your treasure from Dragon Home you gave him, they will become very agreeable. They'll start talking and showing off their prized possessions. But don't suppose they will drop away from their busy plans for him. It's a business."

"I suppose you are right, but I don't think I can wait several days. I just wish we could go in there and take them all out." Nath pulled his hand free from hers. It fell to his sword. "If I become the dragon king one day, I swear, I'm going to wipe this place out."

"I believe you," she said, "but for the time being, let's focus on recovering your friends. Come on now. Let's walk and talk. You spent more time talking to Darkken on our journey than talking to me. I was jealous. But now, I have you to myself, and I want to take advantage of it."

Nath cast a final look at Slaver Town. "Fine. Lead the way. I know Hacksaw will keep an eye on things."

"Aye," Hacksaw said. He'd started puffing on his pipe. "You walk. I'm going to enjoy the warmth of the south."

The four Brothers of the Wind stood up suddenly and turned to face the wood line at their backs. Nath caught a stir in the forest. The other two Brothers of the Wind appeared. One of the two approached Maefon and whispered in her ear. She gasped. "A slaver patrol comes our way."

Chapter 22

Hacksaw drew Green Tongue. "How far away?"

The elf whispered back in Maefon's ear. She said, "They are coming up the back side of the hill. Minutes away."

Hacksaw dumped the ashes from his pipe and put it away. "Is there some reason why these elves can't speak out loud instead of going through you or Darkken? It's getting aggravating."

Maefon fired back at Hacksaw, "It is their way. And you might not like what they have to say."

Hacksaw narrowed an eye. "And why would that be?"

"I don't think they like your smoking."

"What?"

"Enough," Nath said, moving toward the forest line. "We need to move."

"There's no way to go, aside from down the face of this hill. Those watchtowers will catch us there," Hacksaw said. "But I don't think those slaver lords own this hillside. Could be that we're just passing by."

"Elves and orcs are mortal enemies," Maefon said, watching all six Brothers of the Wind fan out along the forest line and face away. Each of them unslung their short bows and notched an arrow along the string. "There will be no peaceful conversation between us."

"Then hide. You elves are good at that, aren't you?" Hacksaw replied.

"It's not a bad idea," Nath suggested.

The elf whispered in Maefon's ear again. "They have dogs," she said. "They'll sniff you out, but the Brothers of the Wind have the ability to throw their scent."

"Of course they do," Hacksaw replied. "Look, you hide, all of you. I'll talk. The orcs, though orcs, don't have anything on me. I've got my spear. I'll just tell them I'm hunting game."

"I'll stay as well," Nath replied.

"Nath, don't be foolish. They will recognize you," she said.

"I suppose they might, but I'm not leaving my friend's side. I'll take the chance that they don't remember my face."

"You are being foolish!" Maefon said. "You put all we have worked for in jeopardy. Let Hacksaw work with his idea. We will be close by if he needs us." She stretched her hand out to Nath. "You must come, quick."

"I don't know. They might not know me if I keep my head down."

With reddening cheeks, she said, "Are you being serious? No one lays their eyes on you and forgets you! Hacksaw knows what is best. Trust him. Come, now!"

"She makes a valid point, Nath. You should go," Hacksaw replied.

"I'm big. I can't hide any better than you can," he said to Hacksaw. "No, I'm staying. I'll cover underneath my traveling cloak and pretend I'm sick or something."

"You are being preposterous," she said, fishing out the potion vial of polymorph from her clothing. "Take what is left of this. Hopefully, it will last you long enough that you don't get killed." She threw it at him.

Nath plucked it out of the air. "Thanks. And do me a favor, leave me a bow and quiver. Can't hunt without that."

The elf that did all of the speaking to Maefon tossed his bow and quiver at Nath's feet.

"Let's go," Maefon ordered the brothers. All at once the elves ducked underneath the branches and disappeared into the woods.

Nath drank down the potion. As he did so, Hacksaw knocked on his breastplate. "They'll know that sign on your chest. It's hot, but you best cover up."

"Agreed," he said, donning the cloak while the potion's syrup trickled down his throat. "It has a bit of cinnamon in the flavor and something not so pleasant." His face soured. "What was that flavor?"

"I don't know, but you best figure out what you want to turn into before you look just as you are."

"What should I do, look like you? Ha, we could be twins."

"I suggest something a little more to their liking, such as a half orc. Can you pull that off?"

"We'll see." Nath had seen his fair share of half orcs inside the cedar walls of Slaver Town. He focused on the one most familiar. The potion syrup worked its way down into his belly. Suddenly, his skin flexed and stretched.

Hacksaw's lips twisted. His expression soured. "Ew. I've never seen loose hairs and warts pop out of a face like that before. It's gross."

Nath touched his face. He could feel hard little bumps and coarse hairs that sprouted up on his skin. "Ugh… this better wear off."

The branches rustled in the woods. Dogs started barking loudly. They burst out of the woodland and rushed at Nath and Hacksaw. They stopped several feet away, heads low, hackles raised, and barking. They were big beasts, part wolf and part hound. Four riders on horses, all full-blooded orcs dressed in chainmail armor covered with the uniform black-leather tunics of the slavers, pushed through the trees out into the open. A smell came with them.

Nath's nose crinkled.

Hacksaw said, "*Shew*. I'm not sure if it's the dogs or the orcs."

"I'm certain it's the orcs," Nath replied.

Without a word, fingers still clutching the reins, the slavers formed a ring around Nath and Hacksaw. Another rider came out of the woodland. He was all orc with a big belly that covered the saddle horn and a head as round and lumpy as a pumpkin. Long, tangled hair spread out over his shoulders like a waterfall. His face and skin were ruddy and greasy. A sleeve of spears hung from his saddle, and a battle axe hung on the other side. He finished the circle, glowering at Nath with beady yellow eyes. He looked at Hacksaw then back at Nath. Flies buzzed around him. In Common, he said, "Silence, mutts!"

The dogs stopped barking and sat down.

He pulled a spear from the sleeve. The other orcs did the same. Clasping his hairy fingers around the shaft, he pointed the tip right at Hacksaw. "I am Ornthall, squad master of Slaver Town. Who in the realm are you, half-breed?"

Chapter 23

Hacksaw started to speak, but Nath cut him off. After all, Ornthall' s attention was directed at him. In his best gravelly voice, Nath replied, "We are hunters, squad master. I am called Thantis, and this is my helper."

"You trespass on the domain of Slaver Town," Ornthall said. "Many trespassers have been sentenced to days of hard labor, and in most cases, they don't end. Some die in the quarries, and others on the rack. Only a fool comes so close to the circle of cedars."

Hunched over a bit and head tilted to the side, Nath said, "I never claimed to be so smart, but I am a good hunter. There is a red-tailed stag, stands as high as your horse, and we've chased him to here from halfway to Advent."

"Aye," Hacksaw agreed. "Once on the trail of a great hunt, there cannot be any turning away. We must finish the—"

"Human, if you don't want your tongue cut out, then don't speak another word. I detest the pink skins as much as dwarves and elves." Ornthall let out a loud belch. "The mere sight of you upsets my stomach. You make me retch." He turned his eyes on Nath. "And you, half-breed, do you prefer the company of men or orcs?"

"I-uh, no, certainly not, but sadly, I'm not always welcome by my kind." Nath opened his coarse hands and shrugged. "He's a fair hunter."

"And I'm a fair hunter as well, and I don't have any recollection of red-tail stags that roam the local woodland. You are full of elk dung!" He poked a spear at Nath's chest. "Tell the truth or I'll put this spear through one ear hole and out of the other."

Nath fought the urge to rip Fang out of his scabbard and cut the orc out of his saddle, but the great blade lay aside in the grass.

"Please, give me a moment to explain, great squad master," Hacksaw said in a pleading voice. "We mean no deception."

"You admit deceit," Ornthall said.

"We hope that what we seek is a red tail, but in truth, we've not seen it, yet we search. Its skin and horns would fetch a fine price, and we have lofty goals," Hacksaw admitted. "In truth, we wander and have not been so far south before. Eh, we are fools."

"All that are not Orcen are fools. I've known this since before my fires were born, fool," Ornthall said. He lifted his spear upright. "I patrol the province. I know names and faces. Many hunt, most we run off and threaten. You should have known not to hunt so close to here. Slaver Town is a place of business, only friendly to pockets filled with gold."

Nath swallowed. "We will move along at a hasty pace if you will show mercy on us."

"Mercy is for the weak." Ornthall leaned back. "But I will ask, have you seen any lone wolves traipsing through the lowlands or hills?"

Nath and Hacksaw exchanged a glance. "No one in particular stands out," Nath replied. "Is there someone that you are searching for? A runaway slave, perhaps?"

"One is long missing. A price is on his head. Perhaps you should hunt for that. Any information would be helpful. He is well built, much like you." Ornthall pointed at Nath. "Drop your hood, half-breed. I need a clear look at your face, so I don't forget you. The pink skin I hope to forget. His bearded face is hideous."

Touching his face with his thumb as he lowered the hood, Nath felt the ruggedness of his skin. *Thank goodness.* He looked up at Ornthall and showed a smile of broken teeth.

"You have strange hair and eyes," Ornthall said, tilting his head to the side. "Never seen a half-breed with locks like that. You must have had an ugly mother."

"She was human," Nath replied.

Ornthall snorted. "Light hair. Light eyes. It's a sign of inferiority. No wonder you hide it. It would be better if you shaved it off. You would have more fortune with the true bloods of our kind. The sight of you would be more tolerable to bear." He spat on the ground. "The one we seek is a man. Young. Fair. Tall and rangy. He is a murderer and slave. He would be out of place anywhere he goes."

"Why would he stay close to here?" Nath asked. "Wouldn't he be far, far away?" The skin on Nath's face clenched. Ornthall's eyes narrowed. Nath turned toward Hacksaw. The old knight's eyes grew big. Nath started scratching his face. "Um, um, what were you saying about this slave again? How did he look?"

"What is wrong with your face? Why are you scratching it like a hound?"

Nath felt his skin tightening on his face. "I-uh, well, I haven't—"

"Squad master, Thantis has a touch of crimson fever!" Hacksaw interjected. "I've passed it to him, sadly. I retched for days, I did, until my stomach was tight as a drum. The heaving is awful."

"I've never heard of a crimson fever," Ornthall argued.

"It's awful. Very contagious." Hacksaw patted Nath hard on the back. "It makes you heave your guts out!"

Nath dropped on his knees, doubled over, held his stomach, and started to pretend to retch. "*Blecht! Blecht! Blecht!*"

The big-eyed orcs backed their horses away. One of the orcs said to Ornthall in a surprisingly high-pitched voice, "I don't want this crimson fever, squad master. I had something like that a season ago and was quarantined. We can't take the curse back to Slaver Town."

"Be silent," the squad master said, shifting his head side to side. "I don't see any vomit."

"Oh, you will. The dry heaves are just the first sign of it," Hacksaw said, excitedly. "It gushes like a sewer and smells like one too. My comrade is going to go down for days. It'll be awful. You wouldn't have any clean trousers you could spare, would you?" He patted Nath on the back. "He'll need them."

Ornthall tucked his chin into his neck, backed his horse away, and covered his nose. "You better be off of this mountain when we come back in the next few days." He made a sharp whistle. The dogs bolted into the forest. "Let's go!"

One by one, the orcs, covering their noses, rode into the forest and out of sight. The sound of the riders thundered through the woodland like frightened rabbits and down the hillside. Hacksaw let out a gusty laugh. "Ha ha! We sure fooled those superstitious stinkers! Crimson fever. There is no such thing."

Feeling his face, Nath chuckled. "So, I'm back to normal?"

"Sure, if you call golden eyes and hair like flames normal."

Chapter 24

Another day passed. Nath and company kept their watch from the bluff. No one said much. They didn't make a fire, as there was no need for it in the southern warmth, but they did need to keep the snakes and varmints away that would nuzzle up when they slept.

Nestled in the hillside, in a seated position, Nath sat alone. His eyes were intent on the road leading into and out of Slaver Town. A covered merchant's wagon entered late the day before. Now, it was midday, and the same covered wagon came back out. Pulled by a two-horse team, the wagon rattled down the road. A lone driver sat on the bench, flicking the reins from time to time. A man and a woman were tethered behind the wagon. They were skinny, walking on bare feet, and struggling to keep up. A heavy-set merchant, wearing bright clothing and a puffy hat, hung out of the back of the covered wagon, shouting at them.

Nath pulled grasses from the bank out of the ground. He wanted to run down there and put an end to the travesty against humanity that was taking place. It was sick that people would do such things to other people. There had to be a way to put an end to Slaver Town. But it would take a small army.

"May I sit with you?" Maefon asked. She'd crept in behind him.

"Of course." Nath scooted aside. "Plant yourself on the hillside. That's what I've done. It doesn't seem that I'm good for anything else."

Maefon plopped down beside him. She followed his stare. "You can't save them all, Nath. It's a big world, and there is travesty and injustice everywhere. You just have to learn to—"

"Pick my battles. Yes, I know that, but it doesn't make it any easier to sit here and watch it happen."

"But aren't most of those prisoners criminals?" she said. "Isn't Slaver Town part of their punishment?"

Nath shrugged. "I know. There's some bad fruit in there. No doubt. But many of the slaves were kidnapped against their will." He picked a mud clot up and flicked it down the hill. It busted up and fell away into the grasses. "It's run by orcs. Isn't that bad enough?"

She patted his thigh. "I know. Perhaps when Darkken returns, we'll have some helpful insight."

"I don't need insight. I have intimate knowledge of that sludge hole. We need to take down the slavers and wipe out the orcs. I've been thinking, and it's kinda sad, but if I had command of the dragons, this would be easy. Just imagine dragons streaking out of the sky and turning those guard towers into pillars of flame. They could turn those great cedar walls to ash in moments."

Maefon's brows lifted. "Well, you certainly have given this a lot of thought. Such an imagination." She massaged his thigh with strong fingers and closed her eyes. "I can see it. A bull dragon dropping out of the sky, squashing dozens of orcs underneath its massive girth. Flames like a waterfall coming out of its mouth. That would be something!" She pushed Nath down into the grass, climbed on top of him, and kissed him.

It was a long, passionate kiss. Nath wrapped his arms around her firm body. He pulled her closer, letting all of his pent-up passion come out.

Maefon broke off the kiss. She was panting. "I'm sorry, but I've been wanting to do that since I saw you again." She looked around. "I don't think anyone saw." She kissed him hard, then broke it off.

Nath's heart pounded like a team of galloping horses. His chest expanded and fell. "What's going on? What about Darkken?"

"I love him, Nath, but I love you too. I've missed you, longed for you." She stroked the damp locks of hair over the top of his ear. "You are different. You make me feel like I'm bursting all over."

"I know the feeling." He tried to pull her back down to his lips.

She pushed against his chest. "We can't. I'm just spun up over you, but I know this is wrong. Now is not our time. There may never be a right one." She chewed her lip. Her eyes watered. She lay down in his arms with her body quivering. "I love you, Nath."

CHAPTER 25

THE SUN FELL BEHIND THE westward hills. Maefon had scurried out of Nath's arms not long after their last embrace. His heart was still pounding as he sat on the bluff, staring into space. Hacksaw approached. The hard-eyed soldier puffed out a stream of smoke from his pipe. "What's wrong with you?"

"Nothing." Nath didn't meet Hacksaw's eyes.

"Oh, that means something. I can tell by the tight inflection in your voice that you are troubled by something."

"Of course I am. Darkken is on the inside, and we are on the outside." Nath turned away.

"Heh. I've been around the world a bit, and I know that look. Besides, I saw Maefon scrambling up that hill with cheeks like blossoming roses." Mirth built in his voice. 'The two of you shared a moment, didn't you?"

"No."

"Don't start lying now. It's a bad habit to get into." Hacksaw climbed up on the rock and sat beside Nath. "It's nothing to be ashamed of. Relationships tend to heat up on the trail. That's why you don't see many women soldiers. When the hot blood gets going in the wild woodland—"

"Stop. I don't need to know about hot blood and wild woodlands." Nath frowned. "Can we not talk about it? I feel guilty enough."

"Why?"

"Well, Maefon and Darkken have a thing. We lost control of ourselves. I don't want to come between them."

Hacksaw puffed on his pipe. "She'll decide for herself. Most women always do. I remember my love. She was something. She wasn't a curvy little thing like that elven vixen, built more like a good solid plank of wood, but she sure made me happy. And personality—straight as an arrow and very forthcoming. Even Granda approved of her." He winked. "And she's hard to please."

"What happened?"

Hacksaw's face sagged. "Goblins got her. I was in the field. Didn't find out until weeks later. It broke a part of me. She was the one."

Nath looked over at his friend. "I'm sorry."

Misty eyed, Hacksaw said, "I found those goblins, and I killed them all. And then I killed more of them. Just another reason why I hate the goblins."

Both men sat in the silence with the wind in their faces. Birds streaked across the sky, finding their nests before the sun went down. The crickets began to chirp the moment the last of the setting sun, like a closing eye, vanished in front of a dark-purple sky.

"Can I ask you something?" Nath said.

"Yes."

"How did you know, uh, well, you didn't give her name, but how did you know that she was the one?"

"I called her Tulip. It was short for Petunia, which she said she never liked. She didn't care much for Tulip, either, but it was easy to remember, and she stuck with it. The first time I met her, I felt the heavens shake. I never felt anything like that before. But with Tulip and me, there was just a natural familiarity, as if we'd known each other all of our lives. I tell you, I was a very brazen young man, full of bull and stubborn as an ox, but she understood me. Where my gruff exterior ran others off, she found comfort, somehow. And that gave me comfort. It settled my fighting spirit." He blew smoke into the sky. "I can't say for certain how you know for sure, but you just do. There's just a quiet understanding. Do you feel that way about Maefon?"

"In truth, she's about the only woman in my life that I've ever known well. She's certainly intoxicating, but I feel that as much as I want her, we are different." He sighed. "If I'm meant to be with another dragon, well, it will be a long time coming."

"True, but it will be worth waiting for. Trust me."

Looking up at the stars, Nath said, "Do you really think there is someone out there for me?"

With the silver shimmer of the stars in his eyes, Hacksaw said, "Yes, she's out there already, I'd say, and your paths will cross one day."

"So, after Tulip, you never tried to make a family again?"

"No, it just hurt too much. Losing Tulip felt like hot steel running into my heart. I couldn't go through that again."

"I think it would be fine if you did, though, wouldn't it?"

"Eh, I don't know."

The main gate of Slaver Town parted. A wagon and rider came out, escorted by half a dozen guards. Nath stood up. "Is that Darkken?"

"You're asking the wrong person. Let me grab the spyglass." Hacksaw moved away.

Even in the twilight, there was no mistaking Darkken's large frame or the wagon. Tied to the back of the open wagon were three more people. Their faces were covered in sackcloth. A scrawny man, a woman with an unmistakable figure, and a four-armed hulk. All of their hands and legs were in shackles. Darkken spurred the horses forward at a low walk. The ropes on the slaves grew taut, and with a jerk, they all shuffled forward.

Nath almost jumped out of his boots. He took off for the forest, running by Hacksaw, who was fishing the spyglass out of the pack, before running right into Maefon. She wrapped him up with her arms. "Slow down."

Busting with excitement, he said, "It's Calypsa, Rond, and Homer. Darkken has them!"

"Nath, look at me." She grabbed his chin and looked him dead in the eye. "We have a rendezvous point. You can't just run down there like you were shot out of a crossbow. You need to wait. The Brothers of the Wind will meet at the point and make sure it's safe. We'll head down there when we get the go ahead." She squeezed his chin. "Do you understand me?"

"Perfectly." Nath picked Maefon up by the waist and moved her out of his way. She gave a startled squeal. "But I'm not listening."

CHAPTER 26

MAEFON RACED AFTER NATH, BUT in two seconds, he disappeared into the woodland. She'd never seen a man run so fast. She was an elf, and the elves were extremely quick on their light feet, easily outdistancing most men. Nath, though young, was big for a man. Yet he moved with the power of a stag and the lightness of a deer. Not even the Brothers of the Wind could catch him before he hit the base of the hills.

He's not listening. That's not a good thing!

Ducking through the branches and hurdling the brush, Maefon raced down the hill. It was her job to keep Nath under control when Darkken was gone. Darkken might take issue with the fact that Nath showed up before he wanted him to. Darkken would want time to confer with the Brothers of the Wind. The goal was to stay several steps ahead of Nath. Darkken would want to tell them his plans so they would all be on the same page before Nath was included.

Two more Brothers of the Wind sprinted by Maefon. They didn't give her a look as they cut through the brush ahead of her. The long-legged men had an advantage, and though she was fleet of foot, she was not a natural-born hunter like many of the Caligin Darkken recruited. She focused on magic. Her thighs burned, and her breathing was labored. She called out in Elven, "Stay back with me."

The elven men fell back alongside her. As one, they navigated down the hill, dusting up the dirt and bounding over small chasms made by heavy rains. They hit the bottom of the hill at full speed, then slowed to a stop. There was nothing but an empty field of grass between them and the distant road. Maefon scanned left and right. Nath was nowhere to be found. The two elves beside her squinted.

The rattle of wagon wheels on a dirt road caught her ear. To her right, the hill sloped down toward the road. Maefon wondered if Nath waited on the road, where he could not be seen. Hands clenching in and out, she started for the road.

"I changed my mind," Nath said.

Maefon gasped as she whipped around, drawing her dagger. The Brothers of the Wind tore their swords out of their sheaths. They sprang in front of Maefon. Nath had a bit of a smile on his face, but his eyes were fixed on where the road started past the hillside.

"How did you do that?" Maefon said, catching her breath.

Nath shrugged. "I can be sneaky too."

"What do you mean by that?" she said, stepping between the elven men. "Put those swords away."

"I'm just imitating what I have seen from the Brothers of the Wind. I thought you would be impressed. I was about to stop and wait for you but thought I'd make a game of it." Nath looked at her for a moment and turned his attention back to the road. "I did good, didn't I?"

"You should be more careful who you sneak up on, Nath. You could get hurt." She took a deep breath and stuffed her dagger back into its sheath. It was a hot day. She had goose bumps on her arms. Nath had spooked her and the elves. *How did he do that?* If anything was to be learned, it was not to underestimate Nath. He indeed was a fast learner, and that could be a problem. The determined look in his golden eyes bothered her as well. "So, are you going to wait here with me?"

"We'll see."

"Nath, I think we should honor Darkken's wishes. He risked a great deal—"

"You aren't in charge of me, Maefon. No offense, but you came with me, and not I with you."

"Nath!" she exclaimed.

Over one hundred yards away, the horse-drawn wagon appeared on the road. Darkken sat easy on the bench with his shoulders hunched over. He glanced behind him at the slaves. All three of them trudged along behind the wagon. Their faces were covered in hoods. The irons on their ankles and wrists clinked. Dust from the wagon wheels rolled over their feet.

Nath started forward. Maefon hooked his arms with her own. "Wait a moment. I might not be in charge, but show some patience. There is too much at risk to blow it now."

He pulled his arm free.

"What is your problem?"

"I want to see my friends," he said. The Brothers of the Wind moved out in front of Nath, barring his path. They had stone-cold looks on their faces. Their slender hands rested on their pommels. Nath glowered at them. "Get out of my way."

CHAPTER 27

MAEFON RUSHED BETWEEN NATH AND the elves. "There's no need for this. Look." She pointed behind her. "Darkken comes."

Nath didn't know what it was, but a prickliness in his shoulders came upon him. The Brothers of the Wind got under his skin. He wanted to run right through them. *Let them try to stop me.* Behind the elves, he saw Darkken turn the wagon toward them. "We'll wait."

"A good idea," Maefon said, patting Nath on the hard metal of his chest. "Let Darkken do the talking, please. All may not be as it appears."

Nath couldn't imagine why it wouldn't be as it seemed. His friends were shackled. He was dying to see them. He wanted to tear off their hoods and get them out of those shackles. "I suppose I can wait a little longer."

Darkken led the wagon straight toward them. The prisoners trailed behind the wagon, all with their heads down. The strapping man lifted up his arm and waved. He also gave a hand signal to wait and stopped the wagon thirty yards away. He got out of the wagon, and with a finger to his lips, he approached. "It's all well. All well," he said in a low voice. He glanced at Maefon then focused on Nath. "Let me inform you of what is going on."

"Get them out of those shackles," Nath said, finding it difficult to keep his voice down. "Now."

Darkken slapped a heavy hand on Nath's shoulder. "You must listen to me. Those prisoners do not know what to expect. We must approach this with delicateness. They are safe, out of Slaver Town. Is that not what you wanted?"

"Yes," Nath said. It all happened so fast that he hadn't even had time to consider what had happened. Without even mounting a rescue, Darkken had somehow freed them. He craned his neck toward his friends. "What happened? How did you get them out?"

"They are slaves, and all slaves are for sale. I bought them all with your treasure."

Nath's jaw dropped.

"It was the best way. No one gets hurt. We own them now."

"I don't want to own anybody." Nath's eyebrows knitted together. "Free them."

"They are as good as free. Don't take it so literally," Darkken replied. "This couldn't have worked out for the better. Your friends have nothing to worry about from Slaver Town. And that's not all. There is no longer a price on your head as well."

"What?"

"There is an awful lot that needs to be discussed." Darkken gave Nath an easy smile and grabbed his shoulders. "This is good. Very good. A clean slate for all, though it did cost a great deal. I didn't think you would mind, but I turned over all of your treasure for them and you."

"All of it?" Maefon said, her jaw hanging open. "That was a fortune! We could have used those resources against the Caligin. Darkken, what were you thinking?"

"No, it's fine," Nath replied. "I would have done the same thing. I'm glad you did it, Darkken. Well done."

Darkken nodded. "I know slavers are some of the worst of the worst, but they are businesspeople. In the end, all they care about is money. If you have enough, you can buy anything." He cleared his throat. "But the negotiation was about more than your friends. There was your escape, the death of the quarry master, Foster, and several other guards. That was costly as well."

Nath arched a brow. "You told them about me?"

"I had to make a deal, so I filled them in on some of the details about the Black Hand and the troubles of Riegelwood." Darkken frowned. "They were not pleased to know that some of their resources were lost in Riegelwood, but these things happen in a dangerous business, and the fortune in your purse covered it. Why, their eyes grew as big as melons when I poured it out on the table. They slavered like starving hounds."

A loud rustle came from the hillside. Everyone turned to look.

Hacksaw jogged out of the woods, huffing and puffing. He had all of their gear slung over his shoulders and carried loosely in his hands. "Thanks for waiting."

Everyone looked back at Darkken. Hacksaw dropped the gear on the ground and took a knee.

Darkken held out a scroll made from brown parchment to Nath. "It's all official. Your friends are free. Just keep that document on hand in case anyone ever questions it."

Nath ripped up the parchment. He dropped the scraps of paper on the ground. "They don't need a parchment to say they are free. They are always free."

"Why did you do that?" Darkken said as Maefon picked up the paper. "Regardless of how you feel about it, your friends broke their laws when they attempted to free you. There are consequences for their actions. They will need that in case they get into trouble again."

"I don't care." Nath walked toward the wagon.

Darkken caught up with him. "Just go easy. They will be frightened, and there is no telling how they will react."

"I can handle it." Nath stood in front of the three people tethered behind the wagon. Homer sat on the grass. Calypsa stood perfectly still. Rond's big head tilted side to side. Nath approached Calypsa first. She recoiled from the sound of his approach. Then he said, "Calypsa, it's me, Nath. You are free now."

Rond lashed out, hitting Nath upside the head with his fist and sending him to the ground.

CHAPTER 28

ROND'S METAL RESTRAINTS DID VERY little to hold him back from trying to pummel Nath. The bugbear flailed about like a wild animal, trying to tear Nath apart. Darkken grabbed the rope that tethered the four-armed bugbear to the wagon and yanked hard. He pulled Rond backward. Nath slipped out from underneath the bugbear and sprang to his feet. He backed away, wiping the blood from his cracked lip.

From out of nowhere, all six of the Brothers of the Wind appeared. They dragged Rond to the ground and bound him up more tightly by throwing ropes over his massive arms.

Darkken looked at Nath. "Are you all right?"

"It was a glancing blow." Nath could see Calypsa struggling against her bonds. A desperate muffled chatter came out from underneath her hood. Homer cowered under the wagon. Nath tore Calypsa's hood off. Her eyes were wide. She moaned into her gag. Nath pulled the gag down out of her mouth. "Calypsa, I'm so sorry." He threw his arms around her body and held her tightly in his arms.

Her body quaked against his. "Am I truly free from that cage?"

"Yes," he said. "Yes!" He kissed her cheek.

She nuzzled her face into his neck, tears flowing from her eyes. "Thank you, Nath Dragon. Thank you for coming back." She managed to push away. "Now will you please get these nasty links off me."

"Of course." He looked around a bit stupidly. He was still captivated by Calypsa. The dryad, though disheveled, was still as magnetic as ever. "Darkken, do you have keys?"

"Certainly." Darkken tossed Nath a set of small keys.

Nath went to work unlocking the shackles, wrists first and then the ankles. From one knee, he looked up at Calypsa. "Better?"

Rubbing her wrists, she smiled down at him. "You have no idea." A brisk wind stirred her brown hair, pushing it away from her face. She was scuffed up all over, and her full lips were cracked. "I thirst. And I'd like to sit." She took a spot on the back of the wagon while Darkken handed her a water skin.

"Uh, let me take care of Homer," Nath said. Homer's hands were locked on the wagon wheel. Nath had to pull the man away from the wooden spokes that he clung to. "Homer, it's me, Nath." The musician continued to squirm. "What's wrong with him?"

"He's probably so frightened that he lost his reasoning," Darkken replied. He held out another skin of water for Calypsa. "More?"

"No, I'll save more for the others," the half dryad replied.

"We have plenty."

Nath jerked the hood off Homer's head. The man was pale as a sheet of cotton. He shook head to toe. "Homer, it is me, Nath. Your friend. You are safe now." Nath undid the irons, freeing the man entirely from his bonds. He tossed them aside. "Are you thirsty? Hungry?"

In a dry, raspy voice, Homer said, "It's hard to see in this poor light, but I can see your eyes, and I know the voice. Is it really you, Nath, or do my senses deceive me?"

"I know you once had an eye for the queen of Quintuklen," Nath said in a cheerful tone.

Homer threw his arms around Nath. "Oh, thank the kings, it really is you!" He squeezed Nath as tightly as he could. "I didn't know what was happening. They tossed a sack on my head, and I had the awfullest time getting a sense of things. All I could hear was my blood roaring behind my ears. Nath, how have you been?"

The scrawny, soft-eyed musician with delicate fingers looked as shabby as Nath had ever seen him. "I'm just fine now that my friends are free." Nath tousled the older man's hair. "I look forward to spending some time together. I want to hear you play, somewhere."

"I doubt I still even know how," Homer said, eyeing Calypsa's legs that dangled over the wagon, her water skin, and then her legs once more. "I'm very thirsty."

"Yes, even my throat is a little dry, suddenly," Nath replied. He caught the water skin Darkken tossed to him and handed it over to Homer. "Drink and be filled."

Nearby, Rond, muscles bulging all over, struggled against his bonds. The Brothers of the Wind ran rope through the links in his chains and pulled his arms and ankles together, tying him up like a pig. He growled inside his hood.

Calypsa hopped onto the grasses and rushed to the bugbear's side. "Rond!" She lifted the hood from his face and took the gag from his mouth. Petting his face, she said, "I'm sorry. I'm sorry, but we are free now. Nath saved us."

Rond closed his eyes and looked away from her.

"Are you still mad at me?" she said. "I know this was my fault, and I am sorry, but I need you to forgive me."

Hacksaw approached. He had a hard look about him. "I'm not a fan of letting a bugbear loose. They are nothing but oversized goblins. One and all. Killers."

"Rond is no killer." Calypsa fired a nasty look at Hacksaw. "Who are you?"

"Goblin killer. Bugbears too," Hacksaw replied.

Rond lifted his gaze to Hacksaw. "Take off these shackles, and we'll see who kills who, you withering bag of bones."

Darkken chuckled. He caught Nath's intense stare. "Sorry, what would you have me do, Nath? I mean, Hacksaw does make a good point about him being a bugbear, and they are very nasty folk."

"Rond isn't. He might look it, but he isn't," Nath replied. He threw the keys to Calypsa. "Free him."

Darkken gave the elves a shrug. They loosened their ropes and backed away. Everyone stepped back several feet, hands drifting to their sword handles, eyes narrowing on the bugbear.

Calypsa unlocked all of the shackles and tossed them aside. Without looking at her, the square-jawed bugbear rose to his full seven feet of height. He glared at Hacksaw. "Want to tangle now?"

"Anytime," Hacksaw replied.

Towering over them all, Rond gave a quick nod of his chin. "Hand-to-hand combat then?"

"I'm not a fool," Hacksaw replied.

"No, but you are a weakling." Rond stared them all down. "You all are." He finished, looking down into Calypsa's face. "Especially you." He turned his back on her and walked away.

CHAPTER 29

WITH MAEFON STANDING BY HIS side, Darkken watched the bugbear walk toward the woodland. "I don't suppose I'm going to get a thank-you."

Maefon shrugged. Her burning eyes were glued on the dryad, however.

"Rond, come back." Calypsa started after him. "Come back. Let's talk about this. We are a team, are we not?"

Lifting all four arms, Rond said in his gravelly voice, "Stay away. We are a team no more!"

"Nath, you must stop him." Her eyes watered. "He can't just leave me like this."

"The creature's mind is made up," Hacksaw interjected. "We are all better off without it. Trust me."

"What do you know?" Calypsa shouted at the old knight.

"I know plenty," Hacksaw replied.

"Fool! You don't know the hearts and minds of all. I've never had a better friend than Rond." Calypsa walked away from all of them, wiping the tears from her eyes.

"Don't go, Calypsa." Nath tried to reach for her, but she slipped his grasp.

"Just leave her be, Nath," Darkken said. "Trust me. She needs a little time."

With Rond going one way and Calypsa going the other, Nath became torn. That's when he spied the gear Hacksaw had brought off of the hill lying on the ground. He grabbed the sledgehammer, Stone Smiter, and jogged after Rond.

The bugbear turned around, legs and arms spread out, ready to grapple. Eyebrows knitted together, he glowered at Nath, baring part of his teeth like a hungry animal.

Nath tossed him the sledgehammer. "It's yours. My way of saying thank-you."

Rond caught the hammer with his top two hands. His eyes grazed the haft. "You can stuff that thank-you where the sun doesn't shine, but I'm still keeping this stick." He walked away, not stopping until he merged with the hillside.

Hacksaw, Maefon, and Darkken came alongside Nath. "Why did you give him that hammer?" Darkken asked. "It was a true treasure."

"I didn't need it, did you?"

No one replied.

When Nath turned to head back for the wagon, Calypsa was standing there. Dressed in her cotton clothing, she'd adorned her hair with flowers and rings of ivy, and flowers covered her neck and wrists like jewelry. She had the appearance of a queen that was one with nature. "That was a nice thing you did for Rond. Thank you."

"You're welcome." Rubbing the back of his neck, Nath said, "I'm sorry that he's angry."

"He feels betrayed. It's my fault, and I can't blame him for feeling that way." Calypsa checked out the people who stood behind Nath. "So, fill me in."

Chapter 30

Led by Darkken, the group traveled a few more hours into the night, leaving Slaver Town far in the distance. They made camp in the woodland, out of sight from the road, leaving the wagon on the edge of the forest. The elves made a campfire, and Nath spent the better part of the evening telling Calypsa and Homer everything that had happened since the moment he left them, in detail.

"I can't believe you killed the Black Hand." Calypsa lay on her side, basking in the firelight. Using her fingers, she toyed with chipmunks that huddled along her body. "I feel greatly relieved, and I'm thankful for all of you. When the slavers hooded me, I had no hope that I was moments from freedom. Darkken, I appreciate what you did, but I'm still astonished that you pulled it off."

Darkken sat with his back against a stump that a woodsman must have cut down years ago, whittling on a stick. "It was intense. In truth, I felt there was a strong chance I too might wind up in shackles. I've no care to go back. Ever. Slaver Town was downright depressing."

"Tell me about it." Homer lay flat on his back, staring up into the trees. "I've never appreciated nature so much as I do now. The air is fresh with a plethora of pleasant odors. So much better than those rank, sweating, oily prisoners who haven't bathed in years. It was awful, and I never got used to it."

"No one gets used to orcs aside from orcs." Hacksaw puffed on his pipe and stared into the fire.

"No, everyone smells bad, including me. I imagine that evil place still lingers on my tattered clothing," Homer finished. "Apologies."

"We'll get you cleaned up in Advent." Maefon put a blanket over Homer. "Just rest."

Homer opened his eyes. "You are very, very pretty."

"I know." Maefon smiled at him.

"So, Advent, aye?" Hacksaw said to Darkken.

"Just a place to get refreshed." Darkken tossed his stick into the fire and put away his dagger. "Now that we have completed our mission at Slaver Town, I'm ready to get back to chasing Chazzan. I've sent some of the Brothers of the Wind to scout after the Caligin. We need to find out if they have discovered anything new over the past few days."

"How many did you send?" Hacksaw said.

They hadn't seen any signs of the Brothers of the Wind since they made the campfire. Nath didn't see any signs of them anywhere, but it wouldn't surprise him one bit if they weren't lurking deeper in the woods.

"I sent two. We are way off course from what the others are doing, but we'll manage to catch up somewhere along the trail. It will be good to have the full body of brothers together again," Darkken said.

"Sounds like the beginning of a wild-goose chase," Hacksaw replied.

Darkken leaned back with his hands behind his head. "Not at all. We have a method to sniffing out the enemy. You should know that by now. But if you don't want to join us, I won't be offended. I'm sure the lumberyards in Huskan miss you."

"I'm going where Nath goes." Hacksaw's eyes slid over to Nath, who was sitting right behind Calypsa with his legs crossed. "But a lot has happened. Maybe we should take our time about things before we jump into another bloody river."

"The last one wasn't so bloody," Maefon replied. "Darkken brought everyone back without a scratch."

Hacksaw grumbled to himself. "Still... ah, forget it. I'm going to sleep. Just keep your chatter down, if you will. For some reason, all of your talking gives me a headache." He moved away and crawled into his bedroll.

"He just needs a good rack and pillow," Darkken said in a hushed voice.

Nath and company giggled.

Chapter 31

Rond marched up the hill and down the other side, shoving his way through the heavy brush and trees as he went. He didn't care about anything. He'd had enough. For over a decade, he and Calypsa had been a team. They roamed the lands, taking mostly what they needed, sometimes a little more if it was to be had, but they never really hurt anyone. Then Nath came along. It changed everything.

Shoulders sagging, he came to a stop, sat down, and braced his back against a red oak tree that was much broader than two of him. His arms were heavy, and his back burned from all of the whippings he'd taken in Slaver Town. Laying the hammer across his lap, he took a deep breath and slowly let it out. He was free. He wanted to delight in it, but he couldn't.

The sight of Nath and Calypsa together at the wagon burned a painful image in his thoughts. Her eyes lit up like the stars when she looked at Nath. He'd never seen Calypsa infatuated with any man before. If anything, in general, she hated them. That's where Rond had an advantage. He was more monster than man, an outcast bugbear, ostracized by his own people for being different. Calypsa liked that about him. They hit it off. Two misfits meant to be together forever, or so he'd thought.

Rond's grip tightened on the handle of the sledgehammer. He twisted his fingers over the hard wood. The hammer was a fine weapon. The runes in the metal head were illuminated by a faint glow of the gemstone on top. They seemed to speak to him. Rond didn't understand why Nath gave him the weapon. The last thing he wanted to do was like the man. He was jealous. He could admit it.

"I hate people," he grumbled.

With his eyelids becoming heavy, he slid down the tree a bit, cradled the hammer in his arms, and slept. He woke the next morning with his own drool dripping on his chest. Wiping his mouth, he blinked. The forest was oddly quiet. A hazy fog drifted all around him, hugging along the bushes and trees. He sat up, rubbed his eyes, and looked around. The hairs on his bull neck stood up. He grunted.

His imprisonment might have tainted his woodland senses that at one time were as keen as a deer's. His ears wiggled. Something crept through the willowwacks on soft feet. He could sense it more than hear it. Or were his senses tricking him? He'd been stuck in a cramped cell or tied down in a stockade with a lot of racket all around. Perhaps what he felt was fooling him.

Eyes narrowing, he scanned his surroundings. "Leave me alone."

He figured that Calypsa or Nath might be coming after him. Perhaps they would plead for him to stay, but he couldn't bear it. For now, he just wanted to be left alone, even though, after a decent night of sleep, he felt better about things. Using the hammer like a cane, head in his big paw of a hand, he pushed himself up to his feet.

Slowly turning, he clearly heard soft footfalls rustling by the ferns and disturbing the shrubbery. "I don't know who you are, but you better turn around. I want no part of anything you have to offer."

There was no reply. The morning birds were silent. The hairs on his neck remained as stiff as boards. His nostrils flared. Holding his hammer at the ready, he slunk out of the forest, eyes sliding left and right, ears perked. He stood in the tall grasses, facing west, where the morning fog rose off the top of the grasses and slowly drifted up. He couldn't see it, but water from a river churned through the channel and over the rocks. His stomach rumbled. Perhaps he could snare some fish and eat.

With one last look back at the forest, he trudged along, convinced that no one else was there.

I need to get my bearings again.

In long strides, he headed toward the sound of water. Cutting through the fog, he made it to a point where the forest behind him could not be seen and his vision was clear for about twenty yards. That's when he saw an elf standing in the grasses, holding a bow. Rond stopped in his tracks. It was one of the elves that was with Nath. The slender man wore the leather garb of a woodsman. His long hair was braided with feathers. His eyes were piercing as daggers.

"What do you want? I want no part of you. Go away."

The elf said nothing.

Rond cast his gaze around him. More elves, the same as the first, appeared another twenty yards away. Each had a bow in hand. They had encircled him. The hairs stood up on his corded forearms. The gemstone on his hammer flared. Rond's lips curled back over his teeth. "What is this? Huh? Does Nath want his precious hammer back, or do you?"

The first elf, the one standing directly in his path, tipped his chin. At the same time, the elf slipped an arrow out of his quiver and notched the arrow on the strings. Smooth as silk, the other five elves did the same. All of them took aim at Rond. His death was in their eyes.

Rond patted the head of his hammer in his hand. "So, this is the way it's going to be? Fine. I hate elves anyway." Recalling what he'd seen both Foster the slaver and Nath do with the hammer, he quickly lifted the hammer overhead and brought it toward the ground.

Bowstrings snapped. Six arrows zipped through the air. Each arrow hit the mark.

Arrows planted themselves deep in Rond's thighs, his abdomen, and his back. The hammer hung suspended in his hands overhead. His limbs seized up. Racked with pain, in a world that seemed to move in slow motion, Rond watched all of the elves reload and fire again. More arrows filled his herculean body. His pain-filled groans were choked. The elves were fast and smooth as silk. "No," he panted, watching the elves draw arrows once more. "Noooo!"

Rond reached deep into his reserves and brought the hammer down with wroth force. The head flashed downward in a mystic arc of purple light. The ground exploded beneath him. The wave of energy blasted out, pushing down the grasses and knocking all of the elves from their feet. The wiry men of the woodland started back to their feet.

Filled with arrows lodged in his chest, shoulders, belly, and legs, Rond ran toward the sound of water. Fighting his way through the pain, he forced his body forward, legs churning. Pushing his way through the fog, he bore down on the sound of rushing water. He took a swipe at an elf in front of him. He clipped the elf's shoulder and spun him around. Racing ahead, he felt more arrows thud into his back. Big but not so fast, the monster-sized bugbear slowed. More arrows whizzed by him and into him. Firing on the run, the fleet-footed elven devils turned him into a pincushion.

The fog lifted where a river appeared. The sound of a waterfall caught his ear. Rond ran down the soft bank, into the rushing waters. Blood mixed in the water that surged by his knees. The elves came upon him at once and stabbed him with daggers. Others tore at the hammer in his grip. Fighting like a wild tiger, Rond punched and flailed his big fists. He and six elves fought in a frenzy of striking limbs. Rond's great strength fled out of him the same as his blood in the water. The elves tore the hammer from his loosened grip. He let out a howl as they stabbed him once more. He splashed backward into the waters. Floating down the river, staring up into the sky, thinking of Calypsa and the danger, he plunged over the roaring falls, far below, into a watery grave of darkness.

CHAPTER 32

NATH AND COMPANY SAT ON the flat rooftop of an inn that overlooked the town of Advent. Many other guests were seated behind tables around them, enjoying their meals. The warm southern city was a bustling hive of activity. The people had year-round tans and a healthy luster about them. There were a few castles, much like Riegelwood, with banners that flapped in the warm air. Farmland stretched as far as the eye could see outside of the city. Many workers wore straw hats as they pushed carts and drove livestock and wagons over the plains. All in all, the scenery was nice.

Hacksaw dabbed his sweaty forehead with a cloth napkin then drank from a tankard. Calypsa sat between him and Nath, looking over everything without touching the plate in front of her. Nath had his arms resting on the back of his chair. Across from him sat Darkken, Maefon, and Homer.

With an elbow on the table, Darkken leaned forward. "Is everyone enjoying themselves? The food is good, is it not?"

Homer had been shoveling the food into his mouth since they sat down, and he was on his second plate. "I don't remember food being so delightful. I swear, I could eat for days." He put his hands together and looked to the sky. "Please don't let me end up in Slaver Town again."

"Everything is fine." Nath nibbled on his food and sipped from a glass of juice. "I just don't think everyone knows what to do with themselves. It's been a long time since I've caught my breath." He looked at Calypsa. "You should eat."

The half dryad shook her chin. "I have no appetite, and frankly, so many people make me uncomfortable."

"At least they are not orcs." Homer chewed on an ear of corn. "Just normal people without shackles or cracking whips. I'd be content to stay here forever, I think, and never complain about life or love again."

Darkken looked over at him. "That's an interesting statement."

Homer shrugged his brows. "Long story that I don't care to relive."

"Maybe Calypsa would be more comfortable staying outside of the city with the Brothers of the Wind." Maefon cast a frosty look at the ravishing dryad. "She is a *creature* of nature, not comfortable living among a world full of men."

"I would be more comfortable," Calypsa fired back, "and I'm certain that you would be more comfortable too."

"What is your grievance against me?" Maefon said.

Not hiding the edge in her voice, Calypsa said, "I don't have a grievance, but I think that you do."

Maefon's cheeks reddened. "That's ridiculous. I was trying to be helpful."

All of the men leaned back from the table except Homer, who kept eating but managed to imitate a cat's angry meowing sound.

As the women stared one another down with icy stares, Darkken broke the tension. "Ladies, let's put the claws back in their sheaths, shall we? This is a time of celebration. Let's use it to get to know one another better." He lifted his juice goblet. "To sunny days and the warm smiles it brings to friendly faces."

Maefon and Calypsa broke off their stares and turned away.

"Or not." Darkken dropped his glass back to the table.

Chapter 33

Nath searched out Maefon's eyes, but her chin was turned away. They had shared a long passionate kiss that was unforgettable, but the moment Calypsa came, that changed. Maefon barely looked at him. At the same time, she was showing jealousy, which might catch Darkken's attention. Nath didn't want to interfere with the group and what they had, but he liked Calypsa too, even though their history was short. He shifted in his seat and took his arm from the back of Calypsa's chair. His knee bumped the table, rattling the platters and goblets. "Excuse me," he said.

Maefon abruptly stood up and said to Darkken, "I'd like to go back to the room and lie down."

"Of course." Darkken showed her a rich smile, taking her by the hand and kissing it.

The elven woman glared at him. "I don't want to be alone, either."

Taken aback, Darkken replied, "Oh, of course not." He feigned a yawn, covering his mouth with his hand. "I think a nap is in order as well. I'll tell you what, everyone, let's give each other some space for the next day or so. I think it would be good if your group took some time to get reacquainted." He got up from his seat and dropped Nath's purse on the table. "I held a little back from the Slave Lords, so you still have a little jingle if you need it. Just don't spend it all in one place. And I know I shouldn't say it, but try to relax. Once we get on the hunt again, we'll be busy. Assuming, that is, that you want to continue the pursuit?"

Nath nodded as he retrieved his purse. "Of course."

Darkken and Maefon departed.

"Ah, smell the fresh air." Hacksaw vigorously began sawing into an inch-thick slab of ham.

"Agreed," Calypsa said. "That chill in the air is gone already."

"What do you mean?" Nath said to her.

The half dryad shrugged. "If that elf could murder me with a look, she would. It's perfectly clear that she hates me. I can't blame her, seeing I have the same eyes for you that she does."

Homer finished spooning out a bowl of fruit and meal. "Better watch yourself, Nath. Before long, you'll find yourself back in shackles like I was. Love will do that to a foolish man."

"Oh, be quiet." Nath's cheeks warmed. "It's not like that."

"Like what?" Hacksaw put his forearm on the table and leaned toward Homer. "Tell me this story."

The scrawny musician shrugged his narrow shoulders. "Did he not tell you about the history behind my incarceration? How I wooed the queen of Quintuklen, innocently, only to find my heart and body in the dungeon."

Hacksaw's eyeballs grew as big as the plates on the table. "That was you? You are *that* Homer? Ha!" He rapped his meaty fist on the table. "I never would have imagined that!"

Homer looked at Hacksaw. "What is that supposed to mean?"

"No offense, but you are as scrawny as a minnow and as threatening as a butterfly. I find it hard to believe that one so far from formidable could sweep the queen out from underneath the king."

The soft-eyed musician replied in a richer voice that came across as smooth as silk, "Never underestimate the power of the strings matched with a heart-winning voice. And those are only two of the instruments I have mastered." He held up his fingers and wiggled them.

"Homer the great, I'll be—"

"Sh," Homer said, cutting Hacksaw off. "I prefer to remain discreet. No doubt, I still have enemies among the kingship."

"As a retired legionnaire, I can testify you are indeed free, but I don't think you should return to Quintuklen anytime soon. Or ever. Kings hold grudges a very long time. A lifetime."

"I just wish I could see the queen once more," Homer said with his eyes turning sad.

"Best you keep your freedom and move on." Hacksaw swallowed down more mead. "So, Nath, are we going to sit on our hind ends, waiting for Darkken to make all of the calls?"

"I'm trying to relax," Nath said. "And do you have to ride the man so hard? He and Maefon have been nothing but helpful to me. The Black Hand are gone, and my friends are now freed. And now I have more friends than ever, aside from one that is always disgruntled about it."

"I like them both very much." Homer peeled the skin from a grape with a paring knife. "And Maefon, she is quite a dandy. I haven't been around many elves, but she is something special, that one."

"Have you been around many dryads?" Calypsa asked.

"Well, no." Shrinking under Calypsa's hot stare, Homer added, "You are both fascinating but in different ways. I meant no offence. I just like them both is all. I like all of you."

"I like them too," Nath replied.

"Listen, I'm just saying that things are working out too well. It makes me edgy," Hacksaw replied. He stuffed scrambled eggs into his mouth. "And hungry."

Nath shook his head. Hacksaw was getting under his skin. He couldn't let it go. "When you've had a run as bad as I've had, at some point it had to turn. I feel as if things have righted themselves since I left Dragon Home. For the first time, I have some comfort. Don't spoil it with doubt. Darkken and Maefon have been faultless. I trust them, Hacksaw. You should too."

"Maybe it's just the old soldier in me, but I don't. Listen, I get it, they are likable, and they stuck out their necks for you, but in truth, they've been in control of everything since they arrived. That's what unsettles me." Hacksaw started eating again.

Nath looked at the old knight. "If it bothers you so much, then perhaps you should return to Huskan. I'm grateful for all that you have done, but I see no reason for you to risk yourself any more on this quest."

Hacksaw's face sagged. Shock appeared on the faces of Calypsa and Homer. They sat still, not noticeably breathing. Then Hacksaw's jaw clenched. His brows buckled. He got up and threw his napkin on the table. "Fine. Perhaps I will go then!"

Chapter 34

Maefon stood on top of the bed, waiting on Darkken. He'd trailed behind her, only to get caught up in conversation with some patrons at the inn. Finally, he entered, saw her standing on the bed, and made a quizzical look. She beckoned him over with her finger.

He came. Standing on the bed, she stood almost the same height that he was. She threw her arms around his broad shoulders and kissed him.

Darkken's strong arms tightened around her waist. He reeled her body into his.

Unlocking her lips, the short-haired blonde looked down into his eyes. "So, how am I doing?"

"Well, the kiss wasn't quite as good as ones that you've given before, but it was one of your better ones."

She slapped him on the shoulder. "That's not what I'm talking about."

"Oh, you're talking about that little show of jealousy on the terrace." He scooped her up in his arms. She let out a delightful squeal. "You even had me convinced." Darkken dropped her on the bed.

"What?" Maefon said. "Are you upset with me?"

He looked down at her. "Perhaps."

She came to her knees, grabbed his hand, and kissed the knuckles. "You know that my heart is only for you, Lord Darkken."

"That is something that I cannot possibly know. I might know my own heart but never someone else's. That requires a much greater power." He pulled his hand away. "Your jealousy is true, Maefon. Don't treat me like a fool. I don't like that."

"I would never do such a thing." She tugged on his arm, pulling him toward the bed. "It's very easy to like Nath, and that dryad, with all of those flowing locks and curves all over, is someone that any woman would be jealous of, and she flaunts it in a total disregard for modesty."

"The Caligin do not care about such things. We are manipulators, so learn to use her assets to your advantage. Our advantage." He sat down beside her and put his hand on her lower back. "Don't let your passions for Nath control you. He's an engaging character and always will be, but you can't get crossed up between him and the Caligin. The goal is to make him one of us. Then you'll have him wrapped around your finger."

"I just don't like the dryad. She'll be trouble. I would just as soon kill her."

"I can still hear that jealous inflection in your voice. You really need to work on that. So, tell me more about you and Nath. What happened when I was in Slaver Town? Did you do what I required."

"Yes, I planted a kiss on him that he'll never forget. Does that make you jealous?"

Darkken tapped his copper ring on the bedpost with his free hand. "Hardly. You won't find me the jealous type. I've never been turned down by any."

"Oh," she said. "Well, I know that I could never turn you down." She tried to push Darkken down on the bed, but the big man didn't budge. "You are thinking deeply, aren't you?"

"Always. And don't get me wrong, I think the dryad is a problem, but she'll probably move on. Hacksaw is the bigger problem. He's weathered and wise. We haven't fooled him yet."

"We'll just have to convince him to leave. It shouldn't be too hard."

Darkken scooted back on the bed and laid against the bed board. He put his hand behind his head and locked his fingers. "I truly want to destroy that man with a touch of my finger. I would delight in that. There is nothing more dangerous to our mission than a hound that can sniff out evil."

"Maybe he needs to have an accident," she suggested.

"No, it has to be real. An event where we survive, but he doesn't. I really thought that Cullon would have cut him down, but the old knight is formidable. He is a thorn. I don't like thorns."

"Do you want me to set something up?" she offered.

"We'll go and sniff around Advent later. Certainly, there is a dangerous opportunity that we can turn to our advantage." He closed his eyes. "In the meantime, I think a nap is a good idea. Come, lay at my side."

Maefon eased into his body, resting her head on his shoulder and draping her arm over his broad chest.

Stroking her back, he said, "Now, let us dream together, watching our enemies fall, nations be crushed, and the king of the dragons and his loyal brood banished from Nalzambor forever."

Chapter 35

Still on the terrace, Nath sat in silence, quietly finishing his meal. Calypsa watched the people in the streets while Homer finally eased back in his chair and belched a few times.

"Boy, I actually ate myself into a lather," the musician said. "So, Nath, are you going to just sit there or go after your friend?"

"I don't know." Nath pushed his plate away. As much as he liked Hacksaw, Darkken and Maefon had grown on him. The last thing he wanted was to have division in the group. "Probably not."

Calypsa placed her hand on Nath's forearm. "You have me now, so you shouldn't miss him. Besides, I didn't really like him. He wanted to kill Rond."

"True, but Rond wants to kill me, doesn't he?"

"Well, Rond says a great deal of things, but he's not a killer, at least not in the sense that his kind is. He was born with some good in him," she said.

"I have to say that I was not frightened by Hacksaw. He might have been gruff, but there was warmth and strength to it. But the bugbear, well, a hard look from him would frighten the deer droppings out of me," Homer said.

"Nath, I will remain by your side, regardless of what you decide. I will tolerate these people for you, even though all of you leave me out of my comfort zone." She kissed his cheek. "And I'm not going to let that little elven minx have you, either. She'll just have to let her jealousy boil off. I'm staying with you."

Homer rolled his eyes. "And you thought Hacksaw was going to be trouble."

"All right. All right. I'll go after him." Nath stood up and struggled to pull free of Calypsa's strong grip. She was smiling up at him. "Can I trust that the two of you will stay out of trouble? I'll meet you back here later."

"Oh, but I don't want you to go. Please, let me come with you," she said.

"No, I need to talk to Hacksaw alone."

She nodded. "As you wish."

It didn't take Nath long to find Hacksaw in the stable behind the inn. The old knight had slung his saddle onto his horse and buckled it on. Now he was adjusting the bridle and reins. Without a glance at Nath, he said, "So did you come down to officially remove me from the party? It was a unanimous vote, I assume."

"Yes, it was," Nath replied, "but I wanted to come down and thank you for your services."

Hacksaw eyed him. "Are you serious?"

Nath laughed.

"Har-har." Hacksaw led his horse out of the stable. "So, where is the rest of the brood?"

"I came alone. I just don't understand why you are so against Darkken and Maefon."

"Don't forget those creepy elves."

Nath shook his head. "They've done nothing but aid us. I trust them."

Hacksaw's shoulders deflated when he said, "Perhaps I'm getting old, and being such, I'm too set in my ways. I want to like them, I do, but I can't. You are young, Nath, and what you don't understand is that with time comes wisdom. You get the ability to discern the truth from the lie. Not in all cases, but in the case of many senior legionnaires, it's a gift."

"I don't mean to sound arrogant, but I am much older than you."

"Only in age but not in your mind and body. Though, you make a good point." Hacksaw petted his horse's flank. "Just be careful. At some point, take command, push back on Darkken's decisions, and see how he reacts. You can keep the horse too. Consider it a gift."

"Wait. Are you really going to go, just like this?"

"I need to go back home before this warm southern land softens me up too much. Besides, my axes probably miss kissing the wood. I need to get back into the swing of things, so to speak."

"But—"

Hacksaw climbed into the saddle. He poked two fingers at Nath. "Best to you and your quest, Nath, and good luck dealing with those wildcats."

"Wildcats?"

"The women," Hacksaw said. "They both want to embed their claws in you, but they might rip each other apart first. I have to admit, I wouldn't mind seeing how that unfolds. If you make it north again, stop by and see me."

Feeling like he had just lost a dear brother, Nath numbly said, "I will." Hacksaw trotted his horse out of the stable. Nath, lifting his arm, waved and shouted, "Thank you!" The old knight merged with the traffic in the streets and was gone. Glumly, Nath shook his head. "What have I done?"

Chapter 36

Nath spent that next few hours milling about the town of Advent. The local people were a robust bunch that seemed to enjoy sunny days. The vendors in the streets worked from the shaded porches in the front of buildings. The marketplaces were full of yurts, carts, wagons, and tents, where anything from produce to livestock to jewelry was haggled over all day long.

Women rushed up to Nath, trying to get him to smell their perfumed arms. They showed him spools of silks, cotton, and fine linens. "For your lady. For your lady," they said to him.

He kindly shoved through them, moving on from one station to the next, eyeing all of the trinkets and baubles. One thing he noticed about Advent compared to Riegelwood was the freedom. He saw some soldiers in the streets, but there wasn't an overwhelming presence. They stayed in the background, keeping to themselves, and not one was jumpy because he carried a sword.

A heavyset merchant in garish purple-and-gold clothing caught Nath's eye. "You! You! Dragon man! Come, come!"

Nath stopped, looked at the man, and touched his chest. "Me?"

The merchant with a black handlebar moustache and turban on his head waddled over. The man barely came up to Nath's chest. "Yes, you. Come, come. I show you something. You like dragons, don't you? Eh?"

"I, uh, why would you think that?"

"Your sword. Your sword. It has dragon faces on it. Come, come." He grabbed Nath's arm and pulled Nath toward his stand. "I am Aric. I am Aric. I make a good deal for you."

"I'm not really looking for a deal."

"Good deal. You will like. Come, come."

Wanting to keep his mind off of things and not having anything else to lose, he decided to entertain the merchant. The chubby man hustled behind his stand. He had wooden boxes loaded with trinkets and jewelry. From wooden trees with dowel rods for limbs hung necklaces and bracelets that sparkled and glinted in the sun's light. Aric had a little bit of everything when it came to decorating women and men. Nath picked up a bracelet from one of the bins. It was made from links of onyx fashioned like turtles. "I don't really have a need for any jewelry, Aric. Or anything else for that matter."

"No, no, no. Aric has something for everybody. Always makes a sale." He placed a small wooden box full of ribbons on the table. He strung out a gold strand. "For your hair. Weave it into a braid to keep the hair out of your eyes. The ladies love this style for the men." He pushed it in Nath's face. "Very, very nice."

"Um, I'm going to have to say no to the ribbons in hair. I like my locks just the way they are." Someone bumped into Nath. He looked down. Some small children snaked their way through the crowd. Little hands patted down his trousers. "What in the—"

Aric burst out from behind his yurt, waving a heavy stick at the boys. The kids scrambled into the crowd. "Get out of here, you little thieves! I will break your dirty stealing little hands!" He spat on the ground and looked at Nath. "I hate the thief. Check yourself, eh, the halflings have feathery fingers with a snatching grip."

Nath patted himself down. His coin purse was in his backpack, and everything was accounted for. "Those were halflings, not boys?"

"Boy and girl halflings. They start earlier in the guild." Aric hustled back behind his table. He rummaged through his stock. "Now, let's find something that you like, eh. I have something for everyone. I pride myself on it. You like dragons, eh?"

Nath crossed his arms over his chest. "I think that's safe to say."

Half hidden behind the cart, Aric stepped up on one of his crates and held out a closed fist. "Look at this?" He opened his hand.

Nath leaned forward. Aric held a dragon tooth, bigger than a coin, inside his puffy hand. "A dragon tooth. Very rare. It will bring you luck."

"A lucky dragon's tooth? I've never heard of such a thing." Nath didn't care for seeing the tooth, either, but like other creatures, dragons could lose their teeth, so it wasn't half bad. Still, it was unsettling as he pondered how Aric acquired it. "What other dragon items do you have?"

Aric's round face brightened. "You do like the dragons. Aha, I'll make a sale now. Take a look at this." He tossed the box of ribbons aside and pulled another, smaller jewel box from underneath the table. He set it down and opened the lid. Using his finger like a hook, he lifted a necklace made from dragon scales into full view. The emerald-green scales glinted in the sun. "This," Aric said with awe, "is real. Magical. It will bring very much fortune to the bearer."

Nath's fists balled up at his sides. Inside the chest, he could see more teeth, scales, talons, and clear vials that looked like they were filled with dragon blood.

Displaying the necklace of scales in both hands, Aric pushed it in Nath's face. "Try it on. Try it!"

Nath swatted the necklace out of the man's hands.

"What did you do that for?" Aric said.

Taking Aric by the shirt, Nath shut the chest and held it up. "Where did you get this?"

Aric broke out in a cold sweat. "I am a merchant. I trade, I swap, I buy, I sell. It come from all over. It's business. Will you please let go of me? I'm afraid that you will hurt me."

Nath looked him dead in the eye. "Where did you get it? I need more details."

"I certainly didn't retrieve it from the dragon's lair. I'm not such a man of action. No, I trade with many. You can't expect me to remember all the faces. They come. They sell. They go."

"I find it hard to believe that a merchant like you would forget anyone."

"Look, the pilferers bring in the dragon items." Aric's eyes blinked rapidly. "It eventually makes its way to me, but I don't deal directly with them. Oh, I feel faint. I'm not made for violent activity. I have many wives and children to feed."

"Sure you do." Nath pushed the man back. He took the chest and flung it at the man. The contents spilled out on the ground behind the cart. Nath stormed away.

Aric shouted after him, "You are a bad customer. Very, very bad customer. Highly irrational! And I'm telling the Alliance."

CHAPTER 37

IF THERE WAS ONE THING that always set Nath's blood on fire, it was people who hunted dragons. Just like the slavers, the races did it for profit, but what made it worse was wearing dragon parts like trophies. Dragons were not animals. They were a race, highly intelligent, and capable of making decisions on their own. Anything that men could do, dragons could do better.

Aric's reaction was even more startling. The man was oblivious to what dragons were all about. He saw them as some sort of dumb animal, created only to be slaughtered and sold.

Poachers. I'm going to find them, and I'm going to finish them!

He made his way back to the inn, where a crowd had gathered on the porch. The people were pushed up against the windows and cramming the doorway. Powerful music grabbed Nath by the ears and reeled him in closer. *What is going on in there?* Standing taller than most people, he got a good glimpse through the window. Onstage, in front of a capacity-filled room, Homer played a stringed instrument, and the light-footed Calypsa danced to the rhythm. Her body swayed, and her neck slowly rolled as she spun elegantly over the floor to the delight of the patrons. Her moves were spellbinding. Nath scratched his head.

What has gotten into them?

Squeezing through the crowd, he made his way inside, toward the stage. Pushing up to the front, he took a knee. Homer's fingers plucked a lute of many strings as fast as spider legs running. In a cheery soprano voice, he sang to the beat of a one-armed drummer sitting on a stool, beating a tall wooden bongo.

They came from the hills, and they slunk from the caves…
In the darkness, they snatched the innocent and turned them to slaves…
With black hands and legions, they fooled all the brave…
And before long their plans started to cave.
For a hero with hair as bright as the sun
Would not stop fighting until it was done.
Dragons… Dragons… The stars in our sky.
Dragons… Dragons... They soar in the heights.
Dragons... Dragons… Mortals beware.
They have hot breath that will singe all your hair.
Run… Run... For cover you fool.
The dragons, the dragons are no mortal's tool.
You may just see one and not know it's there,
but you will know, if you have flaming hair.

Homer stopped playing. Calypsa swirled down into a bulb and stopped dancing. The crowd erupted into applause. "More! More! Encore!"

With an easy smile, Homer lifted his hand and nodded his chin. He handed the long-necked lute back to a man that was sitting behind him on the stage, applauding vigorously.

Calypsa stood back up, bowed to Homer, and he bowed to her. They held hands and lifted them up.

Nath clapped and whistled wholeheartedly. All of the anger brewing within him had fled. Homer's song lifted his spirits. The other band members who were sitting on the back end of the stage started playing again, and the crowd, with a sigh, started to disperse. Nath approached his friends. "That was wonderful! What brought this about?"

"I don't know." Homer dabbed his sweaty forehead with a handkerchief. "We passed through, heard this tiny orchestra, and I just couldn't control myself. I asked the man if I could play, and the next thing I knew, song was pouring out of me like sweat."

"Even I enjoyed myself," Calypsa said as she wrapped her slender arms around Nath's waist. "Homer's music inspires me. And I felt comfortable around the people. I think even Rond would have liked to hear it. Homer is very amazing."

"No doubt," Nath replied. "So, that song you were singing, where did you learn that?"

"I just made it up," Homer admitted. He tucked his handkerchief into his pocket. "You should have come earlier. I had many on the floor crying. I thought I better lift them up with a song that was brighter, but I do like songs full of sorrow. After all, that has been my life. So, where have you been? Where is Hacksaw?"

"Let's grab some chairs," Nath replied. They found a table with two chairs. Calypsa pushed him into one chair and sat on his lap. He looked at her. "Comfy?"

"Very." She lay her head on his chest.

Nath put his hand on her waist and said to Homer, "I found Hacksaw, but he left."

"A shame. I liked him," Homer replied.

A waitress strolled up to the table with a flirty smile on her face and set down several goblets and a carafe of wine. "Courtesy of the innkeeper," she said to Homer and gave him a wink. She walked away, giving him a lasting glance.

"I'll be," he said.

"Don't pretend to be surprised. You knew what you were doing with your words that made the women's legs wobbly," Calypsa said. "You wanted to make them swoon, and you know it."

"Well, maybe a little."

"Homer, you little charmer. You really did win the queen, didn't you?" Nath said.

"Sh… I don't want anyone to know who I am. Word travels fast, and I'd just as soon keep my name to myself. They've been asking, and I told them it was Romeh."

"Romeh." Nath made a puzzled look then said, "Ah, I get it. But I think just *Rome* would be better."

Rubbing his chin, Homer said, "Rome. I like it. Anyway, I'm sorry your friend is gone. The legionnaires are fine men. Stalwart. Faithful. One can never go wrong by having one in your party, unless, of course, the intentions are jaded."

"Hacksaw made his mind up. I respect it. I just feel empty."

"Let me fill you up, Nath Dragon," Calypsa said. "Don't let that bearded codger get you down. Give it a day, and you'll no longer miss him. Trust me." She held a goblet of wine to his lips. "Have a drink."

"No, I'm not thirsty. Besides, I came across a merchant in the marketplace that made my blood boil. He tried to sell me dragon parts. Me!"

"What did you do?" Homer asked.

"I slapped them out of his hands and stormed away. That's when I came back here. I want to find the Caligin, but I want to go after these poachers too. I can't turn my back on the dragons."

Homer sipped his wine. "I wish I could help, but I'm not an adventurer. I'm a man of peace, not seeking out any trouble. I can play a lute in my sleep but can barely swing a hammer. I'm only deadwood when it comes to what you are pursuing."

"Are you leaving me too?"

Chapter 38

Darkken stood gazing outside of the window in his room. Maefon lay on the bed. Without looking at her, he said, "It's a nice evening out. How about we take a stroll?"

"Certainly. Anything is better than sitting here waiting for tomorrow." She sat up on the edge of the bed and slipped her leather boots back on. She buttoned up her black-leather tunic. "I take it this *stroll* is a rendezvous?"

"You should know better than to ask."

"Sorry."

Darkken opened the door, letting Maefon out, and closed the door behind him. They headed down the steps into the lively scene of the tavern. It was late, and there wasn't any sign of Nath, Calypsa, or Homer. They exited the tavern, holding hands, crossed the porch, and headed into the city. He led them toward the castles that outlined the city, not stopping until the inn was far out of sight. He ducked into an alley and followed it to the end, where it opened up toward the farmlands.

Maefon glanced up. In the sky like a great bat, Galtur, the two-headed vulture, circled five hundred feet above. It had been a long time since she'd seen anything through the vulture's eyes, and she missed using the Pool of Eversight. It prompted her to ask Darkken, "Are you able to see through Galtur all of the time?"

"Without the Pool? Ha, now that would be something," he said.

"That's not a denial."

"Nor an admission. But I think you know by now that I'm powerful. Very, very powerful, but that powerful? Eh, I can only wish." Darkken pointed to a small barn made of graying wood that leaned toward a nearby cornfield. "There."

The barn didn't have a door and was pitch-black inside. They entered. Maefon saw the heat of six elves waiting within. All of them took a knee and dipped their heads. It was the Brothers of the Wind.

"Little servants, what do you have to report to me?" he asked.

One of the elves, with a sling on his arm, held out the sledgehammer, Stone Smiter. He stood it up on the bottom of the handle. "The bugbear has perished. This is your gift."

Darkken looked at the injured elf. "Well done, but I see that you are wounded."

"My shoulder is busted, but I recover quickly."

"I see." Darkken took the hammer from the elf. He spun it a few times. "A powerful weapon. It sends energy right through me." He shivered. "It gives me the tingles." The gemstone faintly pulsated like a purple heart. "In the case of weapons such as this, many never fully comprehend their full potential. A wizard or warlock often offers additional enchantments, but the user can never unlock them. He's not equipped for it." He spun and twisted the hammer around his body, creating circles of mystic light. "What else?"

The same elf spoke. "The old knight moves north, riding on one horse. He would be just as easy as the bugbear to take."

Darkken patted the head of the hammer in his large hand. "Hmmm… I really do despise the likes of Hacksaw, but out of sight and out of mind is a good thing. Too many dead bodies can come back to haunt you, and I'd hate for something odd to get back to Nath. The less blood on our hands, the better, in this case. What would you do, Maefon?"

"I hoped to see him die through the course of our adventures, but perhaps we can turn a brood of goblins after him. After all, he admires them so much. And if word was to return about his demise, it wouldn't draw any suspicion."

"That is a rich idea. I really like it. But where can we scare up some goblins? They aren't so thick in this area." He tapped one of his copper rings on the hammer head. "I think I'm going to give the old knight a pass. He moves one way. We shall move another. Besides, we'll be able to hear him coming from a mile away if he returns. We'll keep an eye on that."

Maefon nodded.

In a flash of light, Darkken brought the hammer down toward the wounded elf's head but stopped an inch from his skull. The elf didn't flinch. "Take this hammer back to Stonewater Keep. It'll be a fine addition to my treasury. And I'll need another Caligin in your place." He dropped the hammer on the ground. The gemstone went cold. "The rest of you, rendezvous with more Caligin, and tell them it's time to prepare the poachers' lair."

The elves nodded, stood, slipped out of the barn, and vanished into the cornfield.

Maefon looked at Darkken. "Poachers' lair?"

He draped his hand over her shoulder and walked her back outside. "I planted a little seed in Nath's head today. I arranged a meeting with a merchant named Aric. This merchant exposed Nath to some dragon contraband. Oh, it turned his eyes to flame. So, now that this seed has been planted, Nath will be ready to pursue it."

"What about his pursuit of the Caligin? I thought that was the goal?"

"I'll bundle the mission, but the important thing is that Nath thinks that he is leading it. You know, Hacksaw was no fool. He was right when he said that our intervention was more of a convenience than a coincidence. Things have worked out too perfectly. At some point, Nath will become privy to that. That's why I don't hesitate to cut off the loose ends like Rond and Calypsa as soon as I can. Loose ends can be like snakes that come back to bite you. Eventually, they'll figure it out and warn Nath, and we can't have that."

Walking along his side, she said, "I wish you would tell me these things before you plan them."

"You should have anticipated it, Maefon. You need to develop your foresight and vision. None of this should surprise you."

"I'm not surprised, I just thought we had a plan."

"The goal never changes, but there is always more than one way to achieve the end goal."

She stopped and looked up into his eyes. "You're going to kill Hacksaw, aren't you?"

"I have over a thousand Caligin, not to mention a growing network of other sources. So why not?"

"You've dispatched someone, haven't you?"

Darkken smiled. "Now you're thinking like a Caligin."

Chapter 39

The next morning, on the inn's terrace, Nath met up with Darkken and Maefon. Calypsa and Homer accompanied him. The group sat at the table having breakfast. With a long face, Nath said, "Hacksaw rode home, and now Homer is leaving us too."

"Nath, do you have to make me feel so guilty? I feel bad enough as it is. I'm very grateful for you and Darkken giving me my freedom," Homer replied. He'd been eating steadily and looked fuller in the face since last night. He even wore a new set of clothing he'd bought with tips he was given after his performance. "I'm not an adventurer. I'm just a musician."

"You're more than just a musician," Nath replied. "But I know you are not fit to travel the way that we do."

"So, that was your golden voice that I heard through the walls yesterday while I napped." Darkken nibbled on a strip of crisp bacon. "I swear, you made my limbs limp. I didn't want to move, I just wanted to listen. You clearly have an extraordinary talent. And being a musician, I am certain, is much more rewarding that being a manhunter. Women lose their senses over a talented instrumentalist. Why, you'll wake up to a new loving face every morning."

Maefon elbowed Darkken. "Shame on you."

Darkken chuckled. "Well, it's true."

"Maybe in the world of men but not elves." Maefon shook her head. She wasn't eating, either.

Homer wiped his mouth. "I really don't want to go through a long goodbye, so," he stood up, "goodbye."

"What?" Nath said. "You can't just leave, Homer. Not like this."

"Don't get up. I don't want to get sappy and have my eyes filled with water. I'm free, and I'm moving on." Making his way around the table, Homer shook Darkken's hand. "Thank you." He kissed Maefon on the cheek. "Thank you." He hugged Calypsa. "Thank you." And he patted Nath on the shoulders. "I'll never forget you. Be careful, Nath. If I thought I could help you, I would."

At a loss for words, Nath watched Homer walk away, hook his arms around two waiting ladies, and head down the steps, the women giggling gleefully.

"That's gratitude for you," Darkken said with his own mirthful chuckle. "One never knows for sure where the bird will fly once it's let out of its cage."

Shaking his head, Nath said, "You can say that again." Nath had spent two years in prison with Homer, and of all his friends, he knew that man best, at least so he thought. Seeing the man casually walk away poked at his heart. And with Hacksaw gone, everything seemed even worse. Hacksaw was the person Nath trusted most, aside from Maefon. "I guess what is meant to be is meant to be."

"A great outlook, Nath," Darkken said. "We can't control the hearts and thoughts of men. They must come willingly, but you have to admit, Homer was quite ill-equipped, considering what we are doing."

"Yes, I know."

"I'm sorry, Nath," Maefon added. "But given who and what you are, it's probably best not to get too attached to people."

Darkken turned toward Maefon. "I beg your pardon. Should you not be too attached to me?"

"In your case, I just can't help it."

"Ha. Good recovery, my sweet." Darkken kissed her lips. "Very sweet. Now, let's just move on. We have much to discuss about our upcoming journey. I haven't noticed anything out of place here in Advent, but with some sniffing around, something will turn up. After all, there are elves about. We'll just have to introduce ourselves."

"There's something I would like to look into," Nath said.

"What's that?" Darkken replied.

"I met a merchant yesterday in the marketplace. He was selling dragon parts. I don't want to get away from the mission, but it's been eating at me all night. If these men are hunting and killing dragons, I need to do something about it. I have to."

Maefon reached across the table and squeezed his hand. "Nath, we can't stop all that is wrong in the world. We need to stop what we can. That's Chazzan. He's the bigger picture, with a long-term goal of hurting all dragons. We must focus on the bigger fish."

"I know," he said.

"I'll tell you what. Nath, why don't you and I go visit this merchant and shake his bones a little," Darkken suggested. "It couldn't hurt to dig for a little more information."

"I've been considering paying him another visit, but I didn't want to jeopardize anything because of my personal feelings."

Darkken got up and said, "You lead. I'll follow. And it will give the ladies time to get to know each other better."

Maefon and Calypsa exchanged scornful looks.

Nath and Darkken walked away laughing.

CHAPTER 40

MAEFON AND CALYPSA SAT ACROSS from one another with eyes that could burn holes in the other's face. Calypsa had her arms crossed over her chest. Her legs were crossed, with the top leg kicking under the table.

Maefon's fingernails drummed on the table. "What are you, exactly?"

"I am Nath's woman. That is what I am, exactly," Calypsa replied.

Maefon laughed. "I don't think so. He's no more yours than he is mine, whatever you are."

"You are clearly jealous of what I am, elf. You are just a normal person. That's all. Normal."

"And you aren't a person at all," Maefon fired back. "You are a thing, born in a tree of all things."

"You, an elf, have disdain for that? I think you are envious. You are born of a contaminated race, and I am born of something innocent and blessed."

The corner of one side of Maefon's mouth turned up. "But aren't you a half dryad?"

Calypsa's lips tightened.

Maefon leaned back and rested one arm on the back of her chair. "I've known Nath for fifty years—since he was a boy. We played in the dragon king's throne room and soaked in Dragon Home's hot springs together. I know him better than anyone that ever lived. And didn't you rob him the moment you met him? And not to mention that you consort with a bugbear, whose kind is notorious for eating people."

"You are full of venom!" Calypsa said.

A bird darted down out of the sky and clipped Maefon's head. The elf screeched.

The dryad started laughing. "Did the little birdy scare you?"

"Try a trick like that again, and I'll rip your eyes out." Maefon checked the sky as she fixed her hair. "You are no match for me." Seeing a clear blue sky, she looked back down. A score of field mice had crawled onto the table and were nibbling on the food. Other patrons saw the rodents and all at once hustled away, screaming and kicking, as a wave of rodents scurried onto the terrace. As the panicked crowd cleared, Maefon grabbed a fork and stuck it into a field mouse. She wagged it in Calypsa's wide-eyed face. "Keep it up, and this could be you!"

"You are a horrible person. I can feel it in my guts," Calypsa fired back.

Maefon leaned forward. "You won't be feeling anything if you keep this up."

Calypsa let out a sighing breath. The rodents scurried out of sight, just as quick as they came. She pulled her hair over her shoulder and combed her fingers through it. "I will not leave Nath's side. I am for him, and he is for me."

"He is a dragon. He is not for either one of us. You should go back to your tree stump and wait for the next bugbear to come along." Maefon flicked the fork and critter over the terrace. "You are out of your element, dryad, and you know it. You should go away."

"He needs me. I will not go."

Maefon rolled her eyes. "Nath doesn't need a starry-eyed woman to distract him." She softened her tone and decided to change tactics. "Listen, I care deeply for Nath. I want him to return to Dragon Home and avenge those that were lost. I was there. But to do that, he has to be focused, because this is very dangerous." She gave Calypsa a thorough once-over. "And in truth, I am jealous. I'm an elf, and I'm not used to seeing one as fair as I am."

Calypsa leaned her chest over the table. "Fairer."

"Yes, well, there is more to you than that striking figure, but nevertheless, you are a distraction. You have to ask yourself, do you want what is best for Nath or what is best for you?"

Calypsa's lip quivered. "He is special. I want to be with him. I gave my life for him."

"And he would give his life for you. Don't you see what a distraction that is? Calypsa, we rescued you for him. It was a risk we didn't need to take, but we did it for Nath. He means that much to us. And me especially, because I feel so guilty for the harm that I caused. I want to make it right. So, maybe my jealousy is a mix of guilt too. I don't know. But what I do know is that I truly want what is best for Nath. And if you do too, then you need to think about that."

Chapter 41

In the marketplace, Nath and Darkken didn't have any luck finding Aric. The chubby peddler's cart was nowhere to be found. They asked around, but no one had seen him all morning.

"Maybe he sets up later," Darkken said to Nath as he was checking out some fresh fruit. "Purple plums. I like these. I think I'll buy one. Now, if I can just find one that isn't bruised."

"I don't understand where he could be." Nath's gaze swept the marketplace for the hundredth time. "He was a real hustler. I don't think he'd miss an opportunity to make money."

"Perhaps you scared him."

"Maybe." Nath felt the light fingers of a child cross over his waist. Halfling children snaked their way through the crowd, touching everything they passed. Nath snatched one of the little fellas by the wrist and lifted him off the ground. The tiny halfling appeared to be about ten years old but was so small, standing barely above Nath's knee. Nath had seen the same boy yesterday. "Listen, you little thief, I'll give you a coin if you can show me where the chubby man in purple is."

The grinning halfling child held up two fingers.

"Show me the way," Nath said, agreeing. The little halfling pointed through the marketplace. Nath tucked the boy under his arm like a bedroll and went where he pointed. He led them out of the marketplace, down a single block to where more merchants and peddlers were spread out in the streets and corners. He saw Aric chatting up everyone that passed by his cart. His back side faced an alley. Nath placed two coppers in the halfling's tiny hand.

The boy frowned and said, "Blecht," before he hustled away.

"I wouldn't have paid him." Darkken was eating a purple plum. Juice ran down his chin. "Do you want a bite?"

Nath shook his head.

"So, that is our merchant," Darkken continued. "An interesting array of clothing. It's plum. Plum purple."

Together, Nath and Darkken crossed the street, and when Aric wasn't looking, they grabbed him and dragged him back into the alley. Hooking the merchant underneath the arms, they pinned him against the wall. Darkken clamped his hand over the squirming man's mouth. Nath did the talking.

"Aric, I want to know where you got those dragon scales. And I want details," Nath said. "Do you understand me?"

The merchant's eyes slid side to side. He broke out in a profuse sweat. He shook his head and made muffled sounds.

Darkken said, "Let me see if I can convince him. You see, Aric, the longer we hold you in this alley, the more likely the guilds will pluck you clean. You know as well as I that those halflings have their eyes on everything. Why, you'll be cleaned out in a minute."

Nath peeked outside of the alley. "I think I see them. Yes, they are juggling and dancing through the street."

Aric strained against his captors. He let out loud, strenuous grunts.

Darkken looked at Nath. "I don't think he wants to cooperate. Should I knock him out while you turn his cart over to the halflings?"

"At this point, I don't care. All I wanted was a little bit of information, but if I can't get it, I'll just have to try something else." Nath nodded at Darkken. "So, to knock him out, do you hit him in the face or use some other means?"

"There's a variety of chokeholds, mostly painful."

Aric screamed into Nath's hand. In a muffled voice, he managed to say, "No! No! I'll talk."

Darkken got nose to nose with Aric. "Don't you dare start screaming for the Alliance. Nod if you understand me."

Aric nodded.

Nath took his hand away.

Aric said, "*Shew!* You didn't have to suffocate me, you know. And what is with all of the rough-handedness? If you want information, you don't have to jostle one's senses. Just pay for it."

"We don't have any money," Darkken said.

Aric looked him up and down. "Sure you don't." He peeked out of the alley. "Do you mind if I man my cart while we talk? I don't want those halflings pinching me." He looked at Nath. "I'll tell you what you want, but you can't ever admit that you heard it from me." He waddled toward his cart and slipped in behind it. "And what is your issue with dragon scales and the sort? Why did you have a child's fit on me?"

"Just tell me where you got them," Nath said.

Twisting one end of his handlebar moustache, Aric said, "All of the dragon supplies come from poachers. I think everyone knows that. It's hardly secret information. Well, it's a secret but not a secret."

"So, you bought those items from the poachers?" Darkken asked.

"Well no, not directly. Don't you know anything about trading? I never pay a dime for anything, I trade. But I sell to make money, which I'm not doing now because the both of you are stopping me." Aric watched a troupe of women walk by. He wiggled his fingers and said, "Come back and see me! Anyway, you are costing me money. So, I got the dragon parts through my supplier, who owed me a debt. She said she got them from her supplier that owed her, but I know better." He dabbed his glistening forehead with a napkin. "She got them from those black-eared elves that pass through. They are shady, those ones."

"What do you mean, black-eared elves?" Darkken asked.

"They have onyx pins in their ears. They come in small bushels, dressed really nice, quiet, but polite, and they always have something different to offer." Aric lifted a box of scarves up onto the cart. "Elven silk. A splendid array of colors woven into the fabric. They traded with me once for them. I gave them fabrics from Quintuklen, no, Narnum. Yes, Narnum. They don't really like the larger kingdoms, they said."

Nath shook his head. "Why would they have dragon parts, though?"

Wagging his stubby little fingers, Aric said, "Now, that's an interesting thing. You see, I get around Advent, and I see and listen in on conversations. Everyone knows who the dragon hunters are, at least we do. Well, I see the elves talking to them from time to time. Very discreetly. In other words, they do business, and the Alliance doesn't frown upon it."

"Why would they frown upon it?" Darkken asked.

"The dragon hunters are a jaded sort. The leadership doesn't like them hanging around. They make people nervous." Aric started reorganizing his cart. "And they don't like the dragon parts much, either. These aren't elk or bear skins we're dealing with but items from creatures of magic. It draws the wrong type of people too. Plus, many of the city lords are superstitious and fear the wrath of the dragons will come upon us one day. But I never see enough that warrants worry. Will you leave me alone now? You've cost me enough business today."

Darkken laid a hand on the merchant's forearm and squeezed it. "One more question: where do the poachers frequent?"

"They have hideouts all over. But the westward hills are nearest."

"Where is that?" Nath asked.

"I don't know. I never go there. It's just what I hear. West, I suppose." Aric held out a hand.

"We aren't paying you," Darkken said. "Let's go."

"And a good day to you too, kind customers!" Aric shouted after them.

"Do you think those black-eared elves are Caligin?" Nath asked.

"I don't want to jump to conclusions just because an elf is wearing black, but the jewelry in the ear is a unique touch. The ones I've seen do show some onyx from time to time."

Nath recalled the parchment that his brother, Slivver, the silver-shade dragon, had given him. It had a picture of an elf's face carved in a black stone. "It sounds like them to me. Let's ask Maefon."

They returned to the inn only to find Maefon sitting alone behind her table on the terrace. She was looking outward, facing the fields of farmland. Nath and Darkken blocked her light. Her head snapped around, and she said, "Oh, you startled me."

"So, where is Calypsa?" Nath asked as his eyes swept over the terrace.

"I'm sorry, Nath, but she's gone."

CHAPTER 42

THE EASIEST WAY HOME WAS to follow the river north, all the way from Advent to Quintuklen, and then take the main roads from there. Hacksaw did just that, riding his horse at a slow pace, stopping now and again to catch a drink of water. He puffed on his white, long-stemmed pipe and hummed a cheery song. The tune did very little to ease his restless spirit.

The horse clomped over the reeds along the riverbank and down onto a sandy shoreline. The sky was gray, and the air became misty. He was still south, but he could see that the colder days of the north lay ahead as the wintertime brought an icy chill to the water.

Hacksaw blew out smoke rings, one after the other, and the river's breeze carried them away. A gnawing in his stomach hadn't left him since he departed from Nath. He'd been talking to his horse about it. "Am I so set in my old ways that I am blinded by my pride?" he said.

The horse shook its neck as it nickered.

"Well, that's what I thought. I've been around enough devious vicars and viceroys, lordships and kings to know that some people say all the right things, but that is not what is in their heart. They just want to win you over. That's how I feel about Darkken and Maefon. And it's driving me out of my skull."

The horse nickered again.

"If you were me, what would you do?" Hacksaw asked.

The horse kept walking, moving closer to the river's edge, where its horseshoes made heavy prints.

Hacksaw spied both sides of the river valley that he traversed. The trees on both sides sprouted toward the sky. There was a variety of every tree he'd come to know. Birch, oak, cedar, dogwood, and maple. They were huge, in some cases well over one hundred feet high. Birds of many colors flew from tree to tree. Squirrels and other varmints played in the branches. Nuts had fallen over the ground, and the critters took them away. He passed several deer that drank from the other side of the river. One of them was a buck with a rack of horns as big as he had ever seen. From over one hundred feet on the other side of the river, the white-chested buck snorted at him.

"Yes, well, hello to you too, big fella." All at once, the deer pranced away up the riverbank and were gone. "Hmmm, something spooked them."

Hacksaw had gotten used to being back in the woodland again. The open air was nice and warm on his face, and he started to dread the cold that he would soon have to face. There was nothing better than a warm fireplace and Granda's pumpkin cider to keep him company. He'd gotten used to it. But that wasn't living, not like he was now. That was just sitting by a fire and dying. He still wanted adventure, and he worried about his friend.

He rode on another half of a mile. The river surged over the rocks where natural shoals made for shallow spots along the water. Standing on the shoals were some fishermen. As he got closer to them, he realized by their pointed ears that they were elves. A chill went right through him. Four elves slung their fishing lines into the waters. One of the elves looked at him and waved. Hacksaw made a feeble gesture back. Something lurked in the elf's dark eyes. It was a knowing look. It was the same look that the Brothers of the Wind gave him—a silent, deadly look.

The elf nodded to the other elves, then the four of them were looking right at Hacksaw. All of them wore common traveling cloaks, but black-leather sleeves, swords, and dagger handles bulged beneath their cloaks.

Hacksaw nodded at them. He blew more smoke from his pipe. In his heart of hearts, he knew these elves were Caligin, and they'd come to kill him.

CHAPTER 43

NATH LEFT IN A HURRY, trying to track Calypsa down. Darkken pulled back a chair and sat down by Maefon. She was sitting with a smile on her face that she couldn't help.

Darkken said to her, "So, you managed to send the dryad away of her own freewill?"

Maefon shrugged.

Darkken twisted one of the rings on his finger. "I didn't want to send the strange woman away immediately. I had a different plan." Twisting in his chair, he asked, "Where did all of the other people go?"

"Calypsa brought in a swarm of rodents when we chatted."

"I see." He cleared his throat. "As I was saying, I didn't want her to go just yet. Nath has lost enough people close to him in the last day. There's no need to take them all away. It would make him suspicious."

Maefon looked him in the eye. "It's the same goal, with more than one way to get there."

Darkken gave her an approving nod. "Touché. So, that is your plan, to just send her away, leaving Nath upset and distraught?"

"She isn't gone, my dearest." She patted his forearm. "We talked, and though I did convince her, I told her that she should not just leave without talking to Nath. I did put a lot of doubt in her head about her role in his future. They'll sort it out in the room, and if she still decides to leave, it will be on him."

"Bravo, my young seductress." He took her hand in both of his and kissed it. "You know, you are ravishing when you are devious."

"I know."

"And if she does decide to stay?"

"I'm sure you have a perfect plan in place for her to die, but I would prefer to kill her myself."

"If she leaves, she'll seek out the bugbear, and that will stir up more trouble." He kissed her hand one last time. "She'd need to be dealt with before that happens. Do you think you can handle that woodland minx? She's not of the mortal sort."

"I can handle it. Besides, I need the challenge."

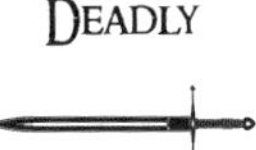

Nath tracked Calypsa to her room at the inn. She sat on the edge of the bed with her face buried in her hands, sobbing. Tears dripped between her fingers and dropped on the floor. Nath eased inside, closing the door behind him, and took a seat beside her. Softly, he said, "Caly, what is wrong?"

"I'm crying. Can't you see? That is what is wrong. I don't cry. I never cry. What is wrong with me?"

"I don't think there is anything wrong with crying. It's normal."

She sniffed. "Do you cry?"

"Dragons don't cry, but I hear that most women do."

"I'm not a woman, I'm a dryad."

"But part human too, right?" Nath grabbed a pillow and took the cotton case off. "Here, let me wipe those tears away."

With his help, she wiped her eyes. Letting out a long, shuddering breath, she said, "I feel so foolish behaving like this. I don't know what overtook me. I was angry and upset. That Maefon got under my skin."

Nath put his arm around her waist. "What do you mean?"

"I am not meant to be with you. It's just a silly dream. I really don't know what overcame me when I chased after you. I could have died. How foolish!"

In Nath's mind, he could understand Maefon's point of view. If Maefon wanted Nath, then Calypsa would only get in the way. It would be best to get Calypsa out of the picture. But would Maefon really do such a thing? "Don't listen to what Maefon has to say, Caly. I want you to stay. That is all that matters. I've parted with enough friends. I don't want to part with any more."

Sniffling, she stroked his cheek with her fingers. "You are sweet. The moment we met and I kissed you, I knew there was something special and different about you. My kisses would knock a man's boots off, but you made me tingle. That's never happened. Like I am a dryad, appearing as a human, you are a dragon, appearing as a man. Neither one of us is what we seem." She laid her head on his chest. "We are not meant for one another, no matter how much I would wish it. I got caught up in my own fantasy. But when I met you, you brought out the good that was buried deep within me, and I'm thankful for that."

"I'm glad, but what are you saying? Are you still leaving me?"

"You know in your heart that it is for the best. Your life has a different destiny than mine. A new path has been opened up for me. I adore you, and my heart splits to say this, but I must move on to the woodland, where I belong."

"No, Caly. No!"

She placed her fingers on his lips. "Sh. Don't make this any harder than it is. I must go. I need to find Rond. He was a true friend and very loyal to me. I know I've hurt him, and I have to make that right. Nath, I'm glad our paths crossed, and I'll always cherish our time. Perhaps we will meet again. Dryads live a very, very long time, and I am still young."

Nath crushed her in his arms. "I don't want this to happen. You're all that I have left."

"Just be careful, Nath. You are traveling down a very dangerous path. I hope you find the answers that you seek." She kissed him fully on the lips.

Tiny warm needles raced up Nath's spine. Calypsa slipped out of his grasp and exited through the window. He moved on numb legs toward the window. Calypsa walked on the grasses toward the fields. Except her feet weren't moving. The grasses under her feet seemed to be carrying her briskly into the farmlands, where she vanished into the cornfields. Nath wiped his eyes. "Dragons don't cry, my behind."

With a long face and feet as heavy as anvils, Nath headed back up on the terrace, where Darkken and Maefon were waiting. He slumped down in a chair. "She's gone."

Maefon rubbed his arm. "I'm sorry, Nath. Where did she go?"

He lifted his shoulders. "To find Rond."

With a quick glance at Darkken, Maefon said, "I see."

CHAPTER 44

After seeing the elves, Hacksaw continued to ride, moving farther upriver and taking casual glances behind him. There were four elves that he'd seen fishing back on the shoals, but in his gut, he knew there must have been more, waiting on him. He spied upriver as far as he could see. He scanned the trees left and right as he continued to puff on his pipe. His muscles tensed between his shoulders.

I knew those elves were rotten.

He played dumb when he passed the elves, acting as if everything was normal. He didn't want to tip them off that he was on to them. His only advantage was his horse. Elves might be fleet of foot, but they couldn't outrun a horse. The question was, assuming there were more elves, would they be upriver, waiting to cut him off? Were they watching him from the woodland now?

I need to warn Nath.

After decades of soldiering and training as a knight, Hacksaw had been imbued with a special sense of knowing good from evil. Evil, at its best, was often disguised as good. That was exactly what Darkken and Maefon had done. It was all as clear to him now as the beard on his face. There was no doubt. He thought of Darkken and Maefon. They wanted him out of sight, but they also knew that he would catch on. That's why they had to kill him.

They have to kill me just in case I make a decision like this.

He pulled the reins and turned the horse around. He headed back down the river.

A howl of a baying wolf came from somewhere in the woods, echoing throughout the river valley. To his left, in the tree line, elves appeared within the branches. They wore black-leather armor. Huge black wolves with slavering jaws stood by their sides with their hackles up.

Hacksaw bit down on his pipe. He grumbled to himself. "Who needs horses when you have wolves." He petted his horse on the neck. The mount was a riding horse, not meant for battle or racing. "I hate to do this to you, but I have no choice." He kicked his heels into the horse's ribs. "Eeyah!"

The horse bolted forward into a full gallop.

The wolves launched themselves after them.

Hacksaw sped his galloping horse down the riverbank. It was his best chance at survival, making a straight line, where the horse could outdistance the wolves. Taking to the woodland would be too risky. The wolves could snake their way through the foliage as quickly as the horse could. At the moment, Hacksaw had the advantage. The wind rushed by his ears as they stretched the distance, leaving the ravenous wolves behind them. He came upon a bend in the river where the shallow waters rushed over the rocks. Beyond the bend were the shoals where the other four elves were fishing. The question was, would they be expecting him or not?

The horse thundered around the bend. Hacksaw instantly saw the elves still standing on the shoals. Only one thing had changed. They no longer handled fishing rods. They had exchanged them for bows. "Kings of the River! I knew I should have brought my shield!" He kicked into the horse and pulled a spear from the sleeve and rode right at them. "Yah, beast! Yah!"

The elves took aim and fired. Arrows whistled through the air. Riding at them at a straight angle, the feather shafts whizzed by Hacksaw's face. He knew the best defense was to go right at them. It made him and the horse a smaller target. The elves reloaded. He hurled his spear with all of his might. The shaft rocketed out of his hand and into an elf's chest just as he notched an arrow.

"Ride the thunder! Ride the thunder!" Hacksaw bellowed. He snaked his sword, Green Tongue, out of its scabbard, a glowing line of green fire.

The last three elves fired the second volley as the horse and rider closed in.

Hacksaw chopped one arrow out of the sky. The second arrow missed, and a third hit the horse in the chest. "Don't go down! Don't go down! Avenge yourself!"

The horse thundered into the elves as they dived to the side. It trampled one of the elves underneath its powerful hooves and kept going. Hacksaw leaned over. He slashed at an elf crawling on hands and knees, sharp steel crossing the elf's back. "Wahoo! That's going to leave a mark!"

Without looking back, the horse and rider sped down the river. He'd made it. He pumped his sword in the air. "Yes!"

He came up on another bend in the river. With a glance behind him, he saw the wolves giving chase, followed by the elves. His horse labored and snorted. Hacksaw had ridden horses riddled with arrows before. The question was, could this horse make it all the way back to Advent without dying first? "Yah! Yah! Yah!" Horse hooves splashing through the water, he whipped around the bend in the river. Another half dozen elves and more wolves were waiting for him. The black-furred wolves came at him as if they were shot out of a crossbow.

Hacksaw pulled his horse to a halt and shouted a prayer, "Lords of Thunder, bless my steel one last time! Bless my gallant mount as well!" Hacksaw tightened his hands on the reins, hard leather biting into his palm. The horse snorted, reared up, and whinnied. Just as the first wave of wolves arrived, the horse came back down. Its hooves crushed a wolf beneath its weight. Hacksaw sang true, cleaving a wolf's large head in the skull.

With his sword glowing as green as flame, he hacked back and forth. The shimmering green steel found purchase against fur, flesh, and bone. The wolves' claws tore into the horse's flanks. Jaws bit and nipped at the horse's legs. The black wolves jumped at Hacksaw, knocking him loose in the saddle. He hung on, still swinging at anything that moved.

"Have at me, you mangy curs! Have at me!" Hacksaw chopped a wolf's head off. He thrust, hacked, and swiped with an arm as heavy as lead. He fought on. His laboring horse, clawed up and bleeding, reared up on its back legs and fell backward. Hacksaw jumped aside, falling face-first into the shallow waters of the river. He burst out of the waters, up on his feet, sword ready. His horse lay nearby, dead. A wolf was crushed beneath it. No more wolves came upon him. Instead, he found himself inside a ring of dark elves. With cold, dead eyes as dark as their armor, they stared him down.

Hacksaw gulped for air. "Which one of you elven devils dies first?"

The snap of a bowstring introduced him to a world of pain. He dropped his sword in the water. An arrow stuck through his forearm.

"You fight like cowards," he said, looking at the arrow sticking out of his arm. "Heh-heh."

More elves had their bows drawn on him. The others brandished swords and daggers. They were solemn. The only thing that stirred in them was the wind against their fine elven hair.

"You don't say much, do you? But I know you listen."

The elves pulled back their bowstrings and took aim.

"It would be a shame if you missed," Hacksaw said. At the same time, he saw his white pipe that had fallen into the shallow waters. He held two fingers up and pointed at it. "Let me die with one last guilty pleasure."

One of the elves shrugged an eyebrow and lifted his pointed chin.

Slowly, Hacksaw, with his wounded arm and hand, reached into the water and grabbed his long-stemmed pipe. He poured the water out and put it in his mouth. He started sucking on the end of the water-soaked pipe. Smoke puffed out of the bowl. "My last and final guilty pleasure. I just wish I had one last swallow of Granda's pumpkin cider." Hacksaw blew more smoke. "And if I see you fiends again, I swear I'll be ready to kill you." He started puffing more smoke.

The elves' narrowed eyes widened as they watched the smoke become thicker. Hacksaw let out a sharp whistle. The elves fired.

Thunk! Thunk! Thunk! Thunk! Thunk!

Arrow after arrow penetrated Hacksaw's armor and went straight into his body. The arrows were like shards of fire running through him. He dropped to his knees, surrounded by smoke, and faded away while his blood mixed in the waters.

Chapter 45

It was a rainy day in Advent. The streets were sloppy with puddles, and the gutters were overfilled. Darkken and Maefon were in their room, discussing their future plans.

Darkken buttoned on his leather armor over his muscular chest. "The dryad won't be easy to find, but with the help of Galtur, we should be able to guide you."

Looking out of the window, she turned back to Darkken. "We?"

"You know what I mean." He buckled on his sword belt. "Galtur and I are very close. He helps me keep an eye on things." He walked across the room and kissed her forehead.

"Would I be able to connect with Galtur without using the Pool of Eversight?"

"Ah, well, that is up to you. It's possible that you could master that. There is a spell for it. I could teach it to you."

"So, you can connect with Galtur and use his sight as yours?" She gave him a quick smile.

"I didn't say that, but possibly."

"You love these games, don't you?"

Darkken glowered at her. "Let's be clear, I don't love anything. I hate it all. As for you, quit worrying about me and worry about you. Ending the dryad will be a fine test. She possesses many witcheries that you are not accustomed to. Be ready for anything."

Maefon had a slender sword belt with two daggers that she fastened around her hips. "It shouldn't be too hard to kill someone that you hate."

"Why do you hate her?"

"I guess my feelings for Nath run deeper than I admitted. I'm jealous. Are you?"

"Of the dryad? Don't be absurd." Darkken checked his hair in a mirror and ran his fingers through his rust-colored locks. "Perfect."

"I was hoping to cause a stir in you," she said, "but I guess it's true that you don't love anything. Not even me."

"Love you? Don't be silly. You are a fine servant, one of my very best, and though I will admit that I enjoy your company and warm affections, it doesn't move me. I'm unflappable, not so easily charmed by those emotions that toss the races' hearts to and fro like a storm. Emotion is weakness. Controlling emotion is power." He clenched his fist. "True power."

"Revenge moves you, does it not?"

"I suppose I could admit to that. It gives me drive. Purpose."

Maefon kneeled, put on her boots, and laced them up. "You don't love, but you do hate, right?"

Darkken looked up. "Interesting. I suppose that I do hate. I hate my father, who turned his back on me. But perhaps it's his weakness that I hate, not him so much. After all, he is susceptible to emotion. I suppose I hate weakness. Feelings are weakness. They take control and cause irrational behavior. That's why I work so hard training the Caligin. I mold them into something stronger. Emotionless executioners. A beautiful creation, are they not?"

She rose. "I couldn't agree more."

"Maefon, come back to me after this is over. Let's make sure that we turn Nath together.

I can use you for that." He was still looking in the mirror. "And take a few Brothers of the Wind with you. At least one. I'll need that one to keep me apprised, just in case you don't make it back."

Maefon's heart sank as she departed the room. "Yes, Lord Darkken." She went down the stairs to the main tavern floor. Hungry people crowded the inn, staying out of the morning rain. She spied Nath sitting at a table for two. He stared out of the window with a glum look on his face. She crossed the room and sat down beside him. "Good morning, Nath."

He turned away from the window. "Oh, good morning."

The table had an iron kettle of coffee and a cup that was full of rich-brown brew. Maefon looked at him "Not eating or drinking?"

"Or sleeping," he said. "Sorry, Maefon. I'm just confused right now. I don't mean to hurt you, but I cared for Calypsa, just like I care for you. It's different, I suppose, but either way, I feel empty."

"It's not as if she is dead." *Yet.* "I'm certain you will see her again." *Never.* A waitress set down a coffee cup and filled it for Maefon. "Thank you," Maefon said. "Listen, I'm confused too. Having you back in my life has changed me, Nath. Deeply. And with Darkken, well, it's even more confusing. You've strummed up a lot of feelings in me. It's been awful, but in a good way. So, I understand. Listen, just let things be, and we will sort it all out when I get back."

"Get back?" Nath's brows knitted together. "Where are you going?"

"We talked about this last night, briefly, but I am going with the Brothers of the Wind to monitor the caravan trails while you snoop around here with Darkken. I envy you, given the weather and all, but we will all meet up in the same place. We'll sniff out the Caligin hideout."

Nath's head sank into his chest. "Fine. Just go, then. Everyone else does. Why not you?"

"Nath, pull that lip in and stop pouting. You aren't fifty anymore." She giggled and kicked him in the knee. "Now, let's enjoy this miserable morning before I go. Give me a proper send-off."

He lifted up his coffee cup and tapped its rim with hers. "To leaving."

"To leaving," she replied with a smile. *And killing that bark-kissing vixen.*

CHAPTER 46

TOGETHER, NATH AND DARKKEN DASHED across the rain-drenched street and hopped onto a covered porch. He let Darkken lead the way, jumping between the breaks between the buildings, avoiding the rain the best they could. By the time they reached their destination, a tavern known as the Merchant's Cove, they were soaked head to toe. Wringing out his hair, Darkken laughed wildly. "!"

Nath couldn't help but get caught up in the man's contagious laughter. He pushed his fingers through his hair, clearing his eyes. He leaned against a support beam and laughed harder.

"They say that every snowflake is different," Darkken said as he stuck his long arm out in the rain. His palm filled with splashing water. "Does that mean that every raindrop is different as well?"

Nath gave the man a dumb look. Then he blurted out, "Who cares?"

Darkken burst out in more gut-busting laughter. Nath, now laughing, wrapped his arms around the pole as the porch beneath him started to sway. "Why… why is the floor moving?"

"It's not moving." Darkken staggered side to side. "You're drunk."

"I'm not drunk," Nath replied. "I've never been drunk, so how can I be drunk?"

"Because," Darkken said, leaning over and shaking his shoulders. "You've had too much strong drink. It makes you drunk. And it makes your breath stink."

"My breath stinks?"

"I don't want to know. I'm just stating a fact." Darkken staggered toward the front door of the Merchant's Cove. "Come on. We'll dry out in here."

"Aye." Nath saluted the man and followed after him. For the last several hours, they had been moving throughout the city, tavern hopping. They were looking for Caligin, but there was a long-standing tradition in Advent that had gotten in the way of things. When it was too rainy to work, which wasn't often, the farmers, workers, and laborers took the day off and drank… heartily.

Nath was reluctant at first, but Darkken convinced him that he needed to blend in or else draw unwanted suspicion. Before long, Nath's belly warmed, and his spirits lifted. With all of his friends gone, he decided he might as well unwind, forget about things, and indulge. So drink after drink after drink, he did just that.

The Merchant's Cove was a one-level tavern with a great iron chandelier hanging above. The candles weren't candles at all but enchanted stones that glowed with an assortment of mystical light. In the center of the tavern was a mahogany bar shaped in an oval. Patrons sat in stools in a configuration that wrapped all the way around the bar. The exterior walls were lined with built-in sofas that were very cushy and made from rich brick-red leather. Tables and chairs filled the space between the sofas and bar. The place was crowded and humming with activity.

Nath coughed as he fanned the thick smoke from his face. He stayed behind Darkken, who waded into the room, saying hello and shaking hands with many of the people he passed. Nath did the same. The merchants were a lively bunch, quick to talk about their wares, invite them to drink, or share a smoke from their pipes. Their clothing was colorful and fanciful. Jewelry decorated necks, fingers, and wrists. Some of the men were pompous, fat, and overbearing, with purple wine stains soaked into their silken shirts.

Darkken found an open seat on the sofas on the opposite wall of the entrance and sat down. He let out a sigh. "Busy place, isn't it?"

Nath nodded. They had already been to several taverns in Advent, and all of them were pretty much the same with a different style or flair. The Merchant's Cove was bigger, though, and filled with a higher class of people. There weren't any farmers with muddy boots or laborers with calluses on their hands. These men and women were slick.

A pretty barmaid wearing an apron over a white blouse sat down on Nath's lap. Her long blond hair was tied back in a ponytail that hung over her shoulder. "Welcome to the Merchant's Cove, handsome. I haven't seen you here before." She looked deeply into his eyes. "You have beautiful eyes that remind me of the sun. We need more of that on a day like this. Can I take your order? The Merchant's Cove offers the finest wines and meads. If you want something stronger, we have that as well. You name it. It's my pleasure to serve."

"Um, I think I like you."

She pinched his cheek and grinned. "I like you too, and I'd like you more if you place an order. The sooner you do, the sooner I can leave and come back."

Nath nodded. "I'd like that." He stared at her with heavy eyes.

The barmaid looked at Darkken. "Perhaps you can place the order, sir."

"Certainly, miss. Do you have a barrel of a Lakeland ale called the Fitzgerald?"

"Yes, we do. Not many have requested it of late, but I will have Edmund fetch a barrel from the cellar." She hopped up and vanished into the crowd of people.

Nath blinked and rolled his neck toward Darkken. "I really liked her. She reminded me of Maefon but human."

A trio of dwarven merchants with beards down to their bellies, wearing tunics made from small bronze plates, marched right by them and climbed up onto stools at a small round table.

Nath glared at them. "I don't care for dwarves. They all look the same. Remind me of Cullon."

"They are a gruff race but not all bad, just difficult." Darkken stretched his arms over the back of the sofa. "I think you need to scale back on the local concoctions. Let's make this the last round. Besides, we need to concentrate on the mission. I believe we've gotten too carried away. Spying isn't supposed to be this fun."

The barmaid returned with two towels and tankards of ale on a serving tray. "Please, pat your dampness away with these towels, compliments of the Merchant's Cove." She tossed one towel in Nath's face. When he pulled it down, she was gone.

"She's fast," he said, toweling his hair dry. "I like fast."

"Yes, me too." Darkken bumped his tankard with Nath's. "This is the final round. Let's make the most of it."

Nath took a sip of ale. It was more bitter than the others but good. "I like the Fitzgerald."

"Yes, me too."

A band of men and halflings played from a nearby stage as the barmaids moved from patron to patron in concert with the music. As crowded and stuffy as the Merchant's Cove was, it moved in organized chaos. Nath eased back in his seat, scanning the room. Nothing seemed out of the ordinary, just a bunch of men and women huddled together and, in many cases, speaking in loud and excited whispers. He watched and drank for over an hour. He yawned. Darkken suddenly tapped him on the arm and pointed toward the front door. A group of elves in rain-soaked cloaks entered.

Chapter 47

Calypsa moved quickly south, staying in the woodlands and avoiding the roads. The last thing she wanted was any more encounters with people. She had had enough. Being around people, no matter who it was, always seemed to end up with her being hurt. It had been that way all of her life. She tried to fit in with humans, like her father, but only found herself running back to the woodlands. All she wanted to do now was find Rond, make sure he was okay, and then hibernate inside a tree for a while. Possibly a very long while.

She came upon a briar patch filled with little yellow flowers that barred her path. Not in the mood to go around, she spread out her fingers. The briars peeled back. She passed through the gap, moving onward, and the briars closed behind her. As a dryad, she had powers of nature that even the deftest of druids would take decades to master. For most of her life, she had taken her powers for granted and still did. She just didn't want to embrace who she really was. She'd been running from her own destiny.

The day that she met Nath, her life changed. Her heart was never the same after that. She felt something in Nath Dragon that she had never encountered with another person. He was truly good, and it restored her faith in humanity. Her experience with people had always been negative. Men wanted to take advantage of her beauty, skills, and powers. She would try to trust them but only find herself running from their selfish desires. It was different with Nath. She couldn't explain it, but it just was.

She picked up the pace, speeding up to a trot. She spied a deer and chased it south through the woodland. With the wind in her hair, she smiled. She didn't need anyone, just her friends in nature. They would take care of her. They always had. Finally, she slowed down and caught her breath. Holding her belly, she let out a "Wooo." The deer she'd chased came back to her and lowered its neck. She petted it.

The air stirred. The deer bolted away. The surrounding trees came to life. Their limbs ensnared her. "Nooooooo!" she screamed. "Nooooooo!"

On horseback in the pouring rain, escorted by three dark elves, Maefon headed south after Calypsa. She and the elves were well-trained trackers, but there was no trace of the half dryad passing anywhere. The half dryad had shown off her power on a few occasions. She had command of the critters and grasses, it seemed, and she wasn't someone to be underestimated. Maefon had prepared many spells and had them ready on the tip of her tongue. They were designed to kill, and she wasn't going to take any chances. She wanted Calypsa dead.

They remained on the main road. The Caligin who came with her had been there when Rond was killed. They already knew exactly where the dryad would wind up. They had to cut the woman off before she learned the truth. Otherwise, she would be able to warn Nath.

That was the tricky part. Being Caligin, they prided themselves on being a step ahead of everyone. In some cases, they were two or three steps ahead. But with Darkken, it seemed as if he was ten steps ahead of everyone. Maefon couldn't figure that part out, either. The Lord of the Dark in the Day seemed to be able to see the future. He was more cerebral than any person she'd ever known. Perhaps more than the dragon king, Balzurth.

Up in the sky, the great two-headed vulture soared through the drenching rain. With rain pelting her face, she stared up at it. One of its necks bent downward. The lowered head's emerald eyes glared back. She looked away and clenched her jaws.

Darkken can see through Galtur at all times. I know it! How did he acquire such power?

Maefon had spent countless hours studying stacks of mystic tomes back at Stonewater Keep. Even though there were spells that could be cast that would mimic the powers that Darkken had, that still didn't explain how he could do them all on command. And of the powers that he did execute on command, he was very tight-lipped about how he did it. Maefon ran through a checklist in her mind of things that Darkken could do. She'd never even seen him crack open a tome or read a scroll. He just did it.

To her recollection, without any noticeable aid, Darkken could see through the eyes of Galtur or somehow tap into the Pool of Eversight. He could shape-change into any living creature, and to top off all of that, he could teleport more than one person. It was the kind of power that would raise the hackles on an ogre's neck. Only the most powerful elven wizards could master one of those items, let alone all three. She could attempt it but only if she read from a scroll, memorized the spell, and uttered it perfectly. And Darkken did it all without breaking a sweat. It was just as easy as thinking.

I know he's a dragon, but does he really have such omnipotent power? And why does he really need Nath to kill Balzurth? Or is there something else to it?

She looked back at the elves riding with her. "It's time to pick up the pace." Maefon kicked her horse into a trot. With a lot on her mind, she still managed to be focused on one thing. Killing Calypsa. The last thing she wanted to do was fail Lord Darkken. Failure meant death, and she had no intention of dying.

Chapter 48

The elves who entered the Merchant's Cove moved deeper into the belly of the flamboyant flock. Many of the merchants gave quick nods and bows to them. Elves were good for business and known for not only buying high-quality products but selling them as well. The slender race was bunched up in a group of four. The waitresses cleared a table for them and handed them each a towel.

Nath leaned left and right as he tried to spy on the elves sitting on the other side of the bar. He started to get up. "I'll get a closer look."

Darkken grabbed Nath's arm. "Stay a moment. The elves are inclined to sense a disturbance in their surroundings, and we don't exactly fit in with the rest of the people here. Just wait and see what comes to you. Remember, we only need a peek."

Nath understood. The smoke-filled room made it hard for him to get a glimpse at the elves' ears. And from what he could see, their hair hung over the ears as well. All they needed to do was see an elf with a black pin in the ear. Or possibly some black onyx jewelry elsewhere on their bodies. He leaned toward Darkken. "Whatever you say. I can wait."

"And try not to stare at them, Nath. Elves are known for having eyes in the back of their heads. If they get suspicious, they'll scatter like rabbits, that is, assuming that they are, well, you know."

Caligin. Nath nodded. "I see." Even though his thoughts were hazy, they were still clear enough to understand Darkken's meaning. "If the elves are Caligin and if they're spooked, they would disappear back into the shadows from where they came. Right?"

Darkken touched his nose. "Try not to say it out loud. I'm pretty sure we are on the same page."

Nath put two fingers to his lips and wiggled them. "Yes, quiet. I'll act normal. Barmaid, another toxin, if you please."

Darkken rolled his eyes and shook his head.

Another few hours passed. Merchant patrons came and went, but the elves didn't move, and neither did Darkken or Nath. The front door flung open with a gust of wind. A sheet of rain came in with it. Two towering men entered the tavern wearing cloaks that covered their broad shoulders. Both men were at least seven feet tall and built like cedars. The music stopped. The tavern fell silent as all of the patrons looked at the colossal men. Behind them, a beautiful woman wearing golden robes stepped to the front. Wrapped around her waist was a scarlet-red sash. She had short brown hair, high cheekbones, tight features, and a commanding allure. All of the men in the room bowed. Others took a knee.

"Who in Nalzambor is that?" Nath asked Darkken.

Wide-eyed, Darkken replied, "I believe it's the Merchant Queen."

"Merchant Queen? I've never heard of such a thing."

"You haven't been around that long. There are many things that you have not heard. The title Merchant Queen is given to the merchant that is top in the class. This ravishing woman is top of the heap in all of the main cities. Something grand must be going on for her to make it out on a day like this. I believe her name is Sigourney."

"Huh." Nath's eyes followed after the woman. She had a beautiful teardrop face and eyes like a cat. She was tall too, like Nina, but slenderer and comely. As she strolled inside, she took command of the room. Her guardians stayed close. Very close. They made it over to the elves' tables and exchanged a greeting. The doors were closed, and the music started up again. Nath started to rise again. Darkken pulled him back into his seat. "What? Everyone is gawking. Why can't I?"

Darkken snapped his fingers. "You know, you are right. Everyone *is* gawking. I see no reason why we can't do it too. Go ahead. Just, well, try to be subtle. The elves will notice, but they'll think you are looking at her and not them. Once you get a good look, come back. No sense in overplaying our hand."

Nath gave a vigorous nod. "I'll be right back." He snaked his way across the room, making his way to the other side of the bar. Once he got close enough for a full view, he wedged himself between a couple of stools that were filled with husky men and ordered a drink. He craned his neck, getting a good look at the Merchant Queen and the elves. He wasn't the only one looking, either. Like vultures, many merchants crowded the table, bending their ears and hanging on her every word. The Merchant Queen, Sigourney, talked directly to the elves. She articulated with her hands, and she even spoke Elven.

Impressive.

Nath caught the Merchant Queen's guardian goons looking right at him. They were big-faced men with flat noses that appeared to have been broken on more than one occasion. There was something abnormal about them both. They appeared human, but for some reason, Nath felt that they weren't. Not wanting to stare, Nath looked away. When he glanced back, the goons' attention was on the surging crowd. The towering men shoved them back.

It took several minutes before many in the crowd lost their fascination with the Merchant Queen and moved on. With a little more breathing room, the Merchant Queen moved over to her guards. "My guardians, Reaver and Slaughter, are wearing something that I think you might be interested in."

Sigourney opened up their cloaks. Each man wore a vest of scale mail, one colored metallic blue and the other red—dragon scales. Nath crushed the metal head of the goblet in his hand.

Those mail vests are dragon hide. It would take a lot of dragon to cover up those men.

The huge men also wore necklaces of dragon parts made from teeth, bone, and horn. One of the goons set a dagger on the table that had been carved out of a huge dragon claw. Seeing red, Nath sauntered right toward the table of elves and merchants. He got an eyeful. There were dragon trinkets all over the table. Even small vials filled with blood in them. The Merchant Queen held a vial between her finger and thumb for all to behold. "It does wonders for wrinkles, but don't drink it, as it can be fatal."

The elves nodded as they talked among themselves and passed the items hand to hand.

Sigourney continued to talk it up in elvish words that the others couldn't understand. "I'm working with the city lords and top families, trying to tamp down their superstitions about the dragon trade. After all, the dragons are evil beasts that are better off hunted than trusted. They have a very potent magic that can be used for mankind's greater good." She picked up the dagger made from a dragon's claw. "Dragon armor is hard to penetrate, but this dragon claw, when shaved down, is sharper than mortal steel. We can use the dragons' own weapons and turn them against them." She glanced at her guardian goons. "Reaver and Slaughter can attest to that. They have killed many dragons their size and even bigger, all with cunning, strength, and using their own weapons against them. See their breastplate armor? It's impervious to dragon flames and other scorching attacks. It's literally saved their skins on more than one occasion."

The elves nodded.

Grinding his teeth and breathing heavily through his nose, Nath was about to launch himself at them when he caught one of the elves combing his hair over his ear. A black diamond-shaped stud was pinned in the elf's ear, made from onyx. He noticed the other elves had a similar onyx stone for cufflinks. His breath eased. He had what Darkken wanted. Proof that the elves were Caligin.

Focus on the mission, Nath. Focus on the mission.

Nath turned away, and that's when he heard the Merchant Queen say, "We've found a nest where a dragon roams hidden in the woodland. We are certain that there are eggs, if not babies, ready to be taken. Do you know how priceless that will be when I acquire them? They don't call me the Merchant Queen for nothing. Is that something that you elven gentlemen would be interested in?"

The elves nodded.

Nath's blood boiled. Pushing through the people, he made his way toward the men guarding the Merchant Queen. He firmly tapped one on the shoulder and said in Elven, "Do you mind? I would like to take a look at the dragon-scale mail you are wearing."

The giant man wearing red dragon armor turned. His arms were crossed over his broad chest. He looked at the Merchant Queen.

"Well, I see this handsome young warrior speaks Elven. How pleasant," the Merchant Queen said. "And you are a feast for the eyes too." She nodded at her goon, and he lowered his arms and pulled back his cloak, fully displaying the glinting crimson-scaled armor. "So, are you interested in a new set of armor? Something very special and very, very expensive?"

"No, I'm interested in justice." Nath hauled back, unleashed his fury, and slugged the brute square in the jaw with his bare hand. The man shuffled a half step back, spit out a tooth, and grinned.

Nath shook his aching hand and said, "Uh-oh."

Chapter 49

Before Nath could react, the seven-footer he'd punched grabbed Nath and slammed him back into the planks. Nath's head cracked hard into the weathered wood. Stars exploded before his eyes. Reaver dropped to a knee, cocked back his oversized fist, snarled, and punched.

Nath rolled aside.

Reaver's fist punched through the floor. He unleashed another vicious blow, hitting Nath full in the gut. The jarring punch shook Nath's body. His breastplate saved his ribs from shattering. He'd never known such power in a man before. Reaver was stronger than he appeared. Unnaturally so. With power, the seven-footer kept punching Nath's breastplate. The armor absorbed the blow. Reaver looked at his fist. His brows knitted together. He drew back once more.

Desperate, Nath planted his feet in Reaver's gut and kicked him backward. Reaver crashed into Sigourney and the elves' table, knocking it over. With mashed potatoes and gravy on his face, the enraged man rose back to his full height and wiped off his face. "I tear you apart!"

At that moment, Sigourney casually stepped in front of Reaver. "No blood can be shed in the Cove. Just get him out of here. We have business to attend to."

Shaking his head and catching his breath, Nath lifted his fists. "Let's dance, big one."

Reaver's knuckles cracked as he clenched his fist and came forward. The crowd shouted and cheered. Reaver waded in and turned loose a haymaker.

Nath ducked under the swing. He punched Reaver's ribs with an uppercut. It was like hitting a bag of sand. Nath dug his fists into the man's ribs with a flurry of hard punches. Reaver didn't flinch. *What is this man made of?*

Reaver filled his hand with Nath's hair in a mighty grip. He yanked Nath's head back and head-butted him forehead to forehead. Bone on bone cracked together.

Pain exploded in Nath's face. His limbs loosened. Seeing bright spots before his eyes, he felt the other monster man, Slaughter, snatch his arms and hold him by the wrists as his knees buckled. Reaver scooped Nath up by the ankles. With the crowd cheering wildly, Nath was marched through the open front doors and onto the porch. The pouring rain soaked him once more. With a heave, Reaver and Slaughter slung Nath across the road. He landed on the other side, skipped over the muddy waters, and slid into the edge of the adjacent porch. Peeking through his eyelids, he saw the seven-footers lumber back inside. The doors slammed shut behind them, leaving Nath out in the rain.

"Get up," someone said.

Nath looked up onto the porch behind him. Darkken stood on the edge with his arms out. His face was expressionless. Nath took his hands, and the stronger man lifted him to his feet. Blinking, he said, "Where were you? You could have helped me out."

"And make matters worse? I don't think so." Darkken pushed Nath down the street into an alley where the drains and gutters were overflowing. He pinned Nath against the wall. "What were you thinking?"

"Sorry, but they were covered in dragon parts and bragging about them. She even said they were going to capture some fledglings and eggs. I can't stand for that!"

"Patience! You don't ever want to let them know that you are coming. Anyway, I'll have to find a way to do some damage control. It's best they just think you are a drunken loon or something."

Holding his head, Nath replied, "I'm not a drunken loon. Gads, my head hurts. What was that man made of?"

"Those men are likely part giants or maybe really small ones." Darkken peeked out of the alley and came back. "So, what did you see?"

Rubbing his neck, Nath said, "Oh, the dark elves. Yes, they wore onyx. Plain as ugly on that goon's face.

Darkken nodded. "Well, believe it or not, your little outburst might have done us a favor. Assuming these Caligin know who you are, it's possible that they don't suspect that you know who they are. After all, you attacked the Merchant Queen, not them, and it is possible that the Caligin don't know about you anyway. That said, we should be able to keep an eye on them and the Merchant Queen. Let's wait and see what their next move is. Listen, go back to the inn, and get some food in you. I'll get word out to Maefon and the Brothers of the Wind." Darkken flashed a smile. "Now the real adventure begins."

CHAPTER 50

LEGS AND WRISTS CONSTRICTED, CALYPSA fought against the branches that held her. She yanked fiercely at the bonds and cursed loudly. "Let go of me, you fool! Let go of me now!"

The red oak groaned. A contorted face formed in the trunk of the grand tree and stared right at her. Its expression was ancient and lazy. In a deep, growly tone, the treant positioned her face to face with it. "Mother calls. Mother searches. I find."

Defiant, Calypsa replied, "Let go of me, treant, or I will turn your branches into flames."

Like a toothless old man, the treant screwed up its lips. "Mother calls. Mother searches. I find." A pair of chipmunks appeared inside the treant's mouth. They peeked at Calypsa with big eyes, jumped to the ground, and ran away. "Come home, child. Come home now."

"Tell Mother that I am not going home. Not now. Not ever." She kicked at the treant. Its limbs held her face. She was caught by many strands of branches like a fish in a net. "Now release me, else I release my power on you."

"You must come. Danger. Return home or pay the price," the treant moaned.

The treants in Nalzambor were weird creatures. They were more or less woodland spirits that inhabited trees and brought them to life. Their faces would form in the trunk of the tree, giving the bark life, and they controlled the limbs and roots like snakes. They were always creeping, and Calypsa had never cared for them. They were her mother's favorite spies.

The treant's limbs constricted.

Glaring at it, she said, "I cannot be forced to return. It must be of my own freewill. I strongly suggest you release me." She summoned her power. Her eyes shined orange as flames covered her arms, glowing with a fiery glimmer.

The treant's jaws widened. It shook her fiercely. "You have been warned, foolish daughter of the mother!" Its branches uncoiled. Its face in the trunk faded. The leaves in the branches shook, and the tree spirit departed.

Calypsa's shining eyes and arms cooled. She rubbed her wrists. Shaking her head, she said to the forest, "Just leave me alone, Mother." She resumed her journey, putting the warning behind her and focusing on finding Rond again.

Finally, after a long journey through the terrain, she made it back to the spot where she was towed behind the wagon away from Slaver Town. From this point, it wouldn't be difficult for her to find Rond. Nature saw everything, and she was part of nature. On bare feet, she moved west into the woods and up the hill. It wasn't the first time that she'd chased after Rond. He was a notorious pouter, inclined to sulking off when things didn't go his way. Still, with a smile on her face, she went after him, looking forward to mending fences. She looked forward to life being simple again, the way it used to be.

She connected with several woodland varmints who alerted her to Rond's passing through. The huge bugbear was hard to miss, and though the critters were vague on details, as they only communicated with little squeaking sounds, it was enough to send Calypsa in the right direction. Crossing through the rugged hillside, she made her way back down the other side to where the tall grasses met up with the willowwacks. A faint trail could be seen in the grasses that only appeared to be a couple of days old.

A chill breeze slipped through her clothing, causing her to shiver. The northern winds had come far south. Something felt wrong. She entered the field of grass, moving at a brisk pace. She called out in a worried voice, "Rond? Rond?"

It didn't take her long to arrive at a spot where the wildflowers had been crushed, and dried blood was on the grasses. Her blood went cold. She followed the trail where a big person had run roughshod through the field, leaving a blood-stained trail. She made it to the edge of the river. Huge footprints were pressed into the soft bank.

"Rond!"

She waded into the waters up to the waist, searching frantically for him. Studying the waters, the shriek of a bird of prey caught her attention. Where the river flowed south, she could see where it fell off in a waterfall. Just beyond it, vultures were circling. Charging through the surging waters, she raced to the edge of the waterfall and took the high rocks that overlooked the flowing edge. Thirty feet below, the cascading waters splashed into the river. Farther up about forty yards, she could see a hulking figure sprawled out over the rocks. It was Rond. His body was filled with arrows. He wasn't moving. Two vultures were on the ground nipping at him.

"Rond!"

She swan-dived off the waterfall and into the crashing waves below. She didn't stop until she made it to Rond. She shouted at the nasty birds, "Get away from him!" She patted Rond. "No, no, no. Don't be dead."

Rond's skin was pasty and sagging. Arrows had feathered him like a chicken. The wounds were nasty and gaping. His body smelled. Tears filled her eyes. "Noo," she sobbed. "Noo!" She lay across him, hugging him. "I'm so sorry. I'm so sorry. Don't be dead, Rond. You can't be dead!"

She wiped the tears from her eyes. Numb from head to toe, she tried to think of what she could do, but her mind was rattled. At first, all she could think of was him, then she found herself asking, "Who did this to you? Who?"

The answer to her question was right before her eyes as she stared at the arrows protruding from his body. The feathers on the wooden shafts were black and white, the same as the Brothers of the Wind. Then it all became crystal clear. The elves, Maefon, and Darkken were all Caligin, and they wanted her as far away from Nath Dragon as possible.

"They will pay for this," she said out loud. "I will avenge you, Rond, and all of your enemies shall die!"

Maefon and three elves stepped out of the nearby woodland. The elves had arrows notched on their bowstrings. Maefon twirled an arrow between her fingers. She looked right at Calypsa. "I wouldn't be so sure about that."

CHAPTER 51

CHEST HEAVING, CALYPSA STOOD UP and, in a voice that could kill, said, "You did this!"

Maefon showed a winning smile. Tapping the arrowhead in the palm of her hand, she said, "As much as I would like to take credit for it, I'm afraid I can't. You see, Lord Darkken is responsible. He's responsible for a great many things, but it's nothing that you need to concern yourself with now. You'll soon be dead."

"Don't bet on it." Calypsa eyed the elves.

Clad in traveling cloaks with black armor underneath, they spread out while keeping aim on her.

"I see you brought some friends. What is the matter? Do you fear that you cannot take me on alone?"

Maefon shrugged. "Just in case you slip through my fingers, their arrows will bring you to a permanent halt. The Caligin don't take chances. That is why we are so effective."

Calypsa wanted to smack the smug look off Maefon's face, but she wanted answers too. "What is this all about, elf? Why are you trying to kill us? Is it all because you want Nath to yourself?"

"Not me so much as the Lord of the Dark in the Day."

"Darkken?"

"Lord Darkken needs Nath for his own ambitious purposes. That is all you need to know."

Calypsa wasn't satisfied. She shook her chin. "It has something to do with the dragons, doesn't it? He's the reason that Nath left Dragon Home." Her eyes grew big. "He murdered the fledglings?"

"No, he ordered the murder of the fledglings, and there will be many more to come." Maefon came a few steps closer. She sniffed the air. "Your friend stinks."

"Not as much as you." Calypsa backed into the waters as she quickly began putting the pieces of the puzzle together. "You've set Nath up from the beginning. You've been pretending to be his friend all along, winning him over, when in truth, you are the enemy that he is looking for. Hacksaw was right all along."

"Yes, and now he sleeps comfortably in a cold, watery grave. Just like you will be."

"You've killed Hacksaw too?"

"We've killed everyone that Nath has ever known. Rond, you, the Black Hand, and Hacksaw." Maefon shrugged. "There will probably be a few more easy targets, but you, I want you all to myself." She tilted her head to one side. "What is the matter, dryad? Are you afraid?"

"No," she replied as she backed away. In truth, her stomach was turning upside down. Calypsa wasn't some street brawler. She was a woodland creature who, for the better part of her life, had managed to avoid conflict. Like an animal, she only fought when she had to. She backed deeper into the waters. Running might be the best option. A large shadow passed overhead. Something big splashed down into the shallow waters behind her. She turned and gasped.

A giant two-headed vulture taller than her stood behind her. Its ugly bent necks were stooped forward. Its four emerald eyes burned into her soul. It was a hideous thing with a bare, prickly neck and coarse black feathers. Its beaks clacked together, making a grinding, cracking sound.

Calypsa's heart raced. The ominous bird spooked her more than Maefon and the elves. There was something very off about it. She looked back at Maefon. "Who is this? Your father or mother?"

"Jest all that you like, but Galtur is just a little more assurance that you won't get away. Death is the only escape from the Caligin." Maefon's eyes started to glow with an inner fire. "But at least you'll get one chance at me."

"So, it's just me and you, then? To the bitter end?"

With a dark expression, Maefon nodded.

Calypsa tapped into the energy of nature. Its natural powers coursed through her body. Her fingernails twinkled with light. "This is for Rond."

Maefon sniggered. "And this is from me." With a flick of the wrist, the arrow shot out of her fingers and buried itself deep in Calypsa's midriff.

She dropped to a knee, groaning.

Maefon dusted off her hands. "That was easy."

CHAPTER 52

CLUTCHING HER BELLY, CALYPSA SWAYED and stumbled. Maefon came forward, sloshing coolly through the waters. She pulled out her daggers. "Don't fight death, Calypsa. It's inevitable. Just close your eyes and embrace it."

Calypsa held the arrow by the shaft with one hand. She sneered at Maefon. "I don't die that easily."

"You are only prolonging your pain." Maefon's eyes drifted to the arrow in the woman's gut.

Calypsa started pulling it out.

Maefon's stomach twisted. Her mouth hung open, then she stammered, "What... what are you doing?"

The dryad pulled the arrow out of her own body and pointed the tip at Maefon. "I'm not flesh and blood like you suspect, foolish elf." Her eyebrows knitted together. "I'm something entirely different." Her body flexed and heaved against her clothing.

Eyes widening, Maefon backed away.

The slender woman's neck thickened. Her muscles bulged all over her body. Thick brown hair sprouted all over her figure. She became taller and taller. An animal snout protruded from her face. In a matter of seconds, Calypsa had transformed from gorgeous woman into a silverback grizzly bear with hackles of silvery hair. Jaws slavering, the great bear rose to its full eight feet of height. The only things recognizable were its eyes. They were Calypsa's, dark and angry as storms.

Maefon's heart sank into her toes.

The wild bear charged.

Suddenly, the dagger in Maefon's hands seemed useless. She needed a spell, but there was no time. The bear bore down on her. She stuffed the daggers into her belt and started running away. "Caligin! Galtur! Attack!"

The three dark elves fired a volley of arrows into the bear's hide. The shaggy beast did not break stride.

Maefon's legs pumped as fast as they would go toward the shoreline. Fingers fidgeting, she chanted a spell. The savage bear plowed toward her. She stumbled over a log of driftwood and hit the sandy bank, landing flat on her back. She rolled up to the back of her elbows. The bear towered over her. Its huge paws were ready to rip her open. She cringed. "No, Caly, no!"

Galtur jetted over the waters and attacked the bear's head. Like an eagle snatching its prey from the water, it hovered over the grizzly, flapping wildly. It pecked and clawed at the bear's eyes.

Calypsa's great paws swatted the vulture across its ugly face. Claws dug into the big bird's body and ripped the feathers out. She slammed the smaller two-headed vulture into the bank. They wrestled and squirmed against one another, rolling over the ground and back into the edge of the waters. The bear pushed the vulture's heads underneath the surge. Galtur's wings flapped wildly.

Panting, Maefon gathered her thoughts and started summoning a spell. If Galtur died, that would be on her, and Darkken would have her head for it. Just as she started to cast her spell, the dark elves leaped into the fray. Swords in hand, the Caligin hacked at the colossal bear. The steel bit into the dark fur, shaving off hair, but no blood came.

Maefon withdrew her summons, watching as the battle unfolded. Calypsa turned to the elves. Her great claws hooked an elf underneath his arm. She reeled the elf into her massive body and crushed his body in a bear hug. Bone popped and cracked. The elf was slung aside like a dead fish.

Galtur fluttered out of the waters and took to the sky. Calypsa battled against the remaining Caligin. Flanking her, they attacked in turn, darting in and stabbing with their blades. She charged over top of one and mauled them while the last dark elf hacked into her back. She swatted the smaller elf aside with a single swipe that sent the elf head over heels into the water. From all fours, she rose up on two legs, searching for Maefon. Her eyes fastened on the female Caligin. She closed in.

Maefon pointed her hands at the great bear. A fiery glow pulsated between her fingers. She turned loose a stream of energy. "Die, you ugly bear woman, die!"

Calypsa let out a howl. Her singed fur smoked and smoldered. Snarling like a savage beast, she charged Maefon. Pawed feet pounding the sand and jaw hanging wide open, she roared.

"Noooo!" Maefon unleashed another stream of power. The grizzly's body slammed against the mystic stream and kept going. The great bear of a woman buried her underneath smoking fur and flesh. Suffocating underneath the great mass, Maefon squirmed. She was being squashed underneath the bear's singed belly. It rumbled. Calypsa was laughing. With her face pushed into the sloppy dirt, Maefon screamed again, "Noooooooo!"

With her great paw, Calypsa pushed Maefon's little face deeper into the bank. Her blood churned like it was streams of fire. Her body ached with pain from the fiery bolts the elf woman shot into her, but she withstood it. With hatred for the woman, she endured. Now she was going to finish Maefon and warn Nath Dragon. She spoke in a monstrous voice, "It's over for you, Maefon."

Something splashed down into the waters behind her. With the flailing Maefon smashed underneath her great body, she glanced over her shoulder. The two-headed vulture had returned. Its emerald eyes burned hot as coals. Both heads opened their beaks wide as a river. Green hellfire came out. The flames consumed Calypsa's body. She reared up and roared.

"The pain!" she moaned. "The pain!" She dove into the waters and rolled like a log. The flames were burning down to her flesh. She summoned her power, taking away the energy of being a grizzly to save herself from disintegration. Her body transformed. The flames that consumed her extinguished. The water bubbled and smoked around her. Sunk to the waist in the river, she found herself surrounded by the vulture, one elf, and Maefon.

Calypsa had no idea what the vulture was that burned her so, but she'd never felt anything like that before. Its eyes were still burning into her. It spread out its wings, blustering, squawking, and shaking off the waters.

Maefon was covered in mud. Chest heaving, she had her daggers in hand. She wiped her forearm across her mouth and waved a dagger at Calypsa. "You are going to pay."

"What's the matter? You can't finish me off by yourself?" Calypsa replied. Her energy was spent now. It took all she had left to fight off the vulture's fire. Her body trembled in the icy water. "I knew you were weak."

"I can kill you fine on my own, and I will." Maefon advanced.

Calypsa stood. "Me and you, then. I can't wait to get my hands around your bare throat and kill you!" She lumbered forward, summoning all the strength she had left.

Maefon came at her and stabbed.

Calypsa seized her wrists and head-butted her in the nose. She hip-tossed the smaller elf into the waters. Down they went.

Ripping free of Calypsa's grasp, Maefon stabbed the woman in the shoulder. The blade didn't break the skin.

Wrestling through the waters, Calypsa said, "Your metal can't hurt me." Back and forth they went, shoving, pulling hair, stabbing, and clawing at one another. Finally, Calypsa pinned Maefon down and choked her. Maefon stabbed futilely at her. "It's over," Calypsa said.

Maefon's lips twitched over quick little words. Her eyes turned coal black. Suddenly, the dagger blades she held stretched out like black flames. With a growl, she stabbed Calypsa in the neck with both blades. The blades sank hilt deep. Maefon pushed up out of the water, reversed position, and pinned Calypsa underneath her. In a voice full of triumph, she said, "No, woodland witch, it's over for you!" She shoved the blades in harder.

Calypsa let out an ear-splitting scream that scattered the birds from the branches. After a last ragged hiss, she said, "You are pure evil, but death will find you soon," and fell silent.

Maefon put her ear to the woman's mouth. Staring into Calypsa's glassy eyes, she said, "She's dead." She looked at the two wounded elves who had survived the grizzly attack. "Get a shovel and bury her and the bugbear." The black flame on her daggers extinguished as she stood. "Be sure to make it deep."

CHAPTER 53

On a sunny morning, Nath and Darkken headed north out of the city of Advent. On horseback, they took the dusty road to the covered bridge that crossed over a stream. The horses' hooves clomped loudly over the wooden planks. Nath looked through the openings and could see a young father standing on the bank, fishing with his three sons. The man tipped his chin at Nath while the three boys waved wildly. Nath waved back.

Riding right beside him, Darkken said, "The simple life is the best life. Do you fish?"

"Huh? Oh, well, no, I suppose." Nath's eyes lingered on the father and his sons. "It looks like a peaceful activity."

"There's always time for fishing on the trail. It helps one keep their sanity." Darkken's eyes glided up toward the rafters inside the covered bridge. There were birds nestled in the nooks of the beams, cooing and fluttering their wings. "I'd be honored to teach you how to fish. I think you'll enjoy it. It's a fine pastime but even better when you cook your own fish right."

"I'd like that," Nath said. Making it to the other side of the bridge, they were faced with a cross in the road. The road went north and south and straight ahead west. Darkken led the way north, heading toward the sprawling forest that stretched out over the hills for miles. There was nothing but green treetops as far as the eye could see. The massive greenery waited, ready to swallow them whole. "So, we should catch up with Maefon and the others soon?"

"We will. We have the advantage. Don't worry, Nath, our patience will pay off. It has to."

Nath nodded. They had spent the last four days in Advent, waiting for the dark elves and the Merchant Queen to make their move. They departed at separate times, with the elves going west but the Merchant Queen moving east. However, she circled back a day later and headed west again, into the forest. Nath watched them depart, but the rest of the information came by way of Darkken. The Brothers of the Wind kept a close eye on the Caligin, tracking their movements and getting back to Darkken. They did the same thing with the Merchant Queen.

As they entered the forest, the comfort of the bright warm sun quickly vanished. The woodland was dark and rich with heavy greenery. Strangely colored mosses climbed up the great trees. The critters darted from branch to branch. Birdcalls echoed through the branches. The dank forest had an eerie feel to it. The air was cold and damp.

Riding easy in the saddle, Darkken said, "It's chillier in the green fold, isn't it?"

"I suppose. But winter is coming."

"Yes, the northerners love that saying. As if a chilly season makes their kind any tougher. If they had any sense, they would just move farther south, where it's often warm and muggy."

Nath nodded. He missed the warmth of Dragon Home from time to time. The mountain home was always warm, making for a cozy environment. As much as he wanted to leave it when he was growing up, there was still comfort there. It was a one-of-a-kind place. He wondered about his father. Had Balzurth returned from the Land Beyond the Murals? Did he even miss Nath? Were all of the dragons still restricted to Dragon Home? Had they been released yet? He'd been so busy since he left, he hadn't given it much thought until lately. Now it seemed he had time.

I wonder how my brother, Slivver, is doing?

CHAPTER 54

THE FOREST HAD MANY TRAILS. On two occasions, Nath and Darkken passed some travelers, who had very little to say and didn't recall seeing any elves or merchants. Darkken led the way over the packed, hard dirt, pointing out any discrepancies along the trail.

"Check the ground and the trees. Sometimes a busted branch or an impression in the ground can give you a different direction." Darkken stopped on the trail where a low-hanging branch blocked the path. He lifted it with his hand. "Take a close look."

One of the smaller branches on the hanging branch had been broken, and there was a tear in one of the leaves. Nath cocked his head to one side. "That's intentional?"

"Yes." Darkken traced his finger over the small broken branch. "See where the wood is bright white? It's a clean break, recent, within a day or so. If it was much longer, the wood would be darker and faded. Someone is telling us something."

Nath looked at him. "It's the Brothers of the Wind, isn't it?"

Darkken smiled. "Very well done, Nath. Well done. Now, let's see how keen those eyes of yours are. I'll let you track them and the signs that they have left. How does that sound?"

"I'd like that."

They spent the next several hours following the subtle signs in the woodland. The signs led them farther off the main trails and deeper into the woods, where the pathways were mostly overgrown and covered. Darkken showed Nath a great deal of different signs that he would have overlooked before. There were soft impressions in the moss left by animals. When he looked closely enough, Nath could guess if it was a hoof or a paw. There were deer droppings and other kinds he learned to identify. Clusters of bugs on trees or in the dung were other signs that Darkken described. Nath got a pretty good feel for it by the time they were done. They found a clearing, and when the sun's light no longer fed the high tops of the trees, they made a fire.

Warming his hands over the fire and chewing on a hunk of dried beef, Nath said, "I think I could find more signs in the night. My vision is very strong."

Darkken lay on his side, staring into the flames. "There's no need for urgency." He yawned. "And I'm tired. I don't have your unique endurance or other gifts."

"You seem pretty gifted to me," Nath remarked. "The way you and the Brothers of the Wind work together is incredible. I never would have known such things if you had not shown me. I'm grateful."

"Oh, don't flatter me. You are just learning what many skilled hunters already know. Besides, you probably would have figured it out on your own. You are a sharp fella. Not very much escapes you."

"I don't know about that." Nath leaned closer to the flames. A wolf howl echoed from beyond. "Does that mean anything?"

"A howling wolf in the night? I think that just means it's bedtime." Darkken yawned again. "Oh my. It's not that late, and I'm sleepy. That's not like me. You'll have to forgive me if I doze off. Normally, at times like this, I make some coffee. Well, Maefon usually would. She enjoys making a warm mix of brown brew."

"Did I hear my name?" Maefon stepped out of the tree line right behind Darkken. Six Brothers of the Wind also emerged, forming a ring around the small camp.

Twisting around to see her, a delighted Darkken said, "You shameless forest devils. You could spook an apparition."

Maefon took a knee beside him and tousled his hair. "If you weren't so sleepy, you might have noticed." She gave him a quick peck on the cheek and looked at Nath. "How are you doing?"

Diddling his finger in his ear, Nath replied, "Going deaf, I suppose. I didn't hear a thing, either."

Maefon smiled. She was a vision in her dark armor. "Timing is everything. We just backtracked and came upon you moments ago. It's always best to arrive when one least expects it."

"Well said," Darkken replied.

"I learned from the best," she said. "So, you wanted some coffee?" She made her way to the horses. "It will be my pleasure."

"Honestly, I don't want to be up all night long. I'd rather sleep," Darkken said. "Your brew will keep me up."

Maefon dropped the flap on the saddlebag, gathered the rolled-up blanket from the saddle, and tossed it to him. "You'll probably need this."

The bedroll hit Darkken in the head, messing up his hair. He tucked the bedroll under his head and said, "At least you didn't throw the coffee mug."

Maefon chuckled. The Brothers of the Wind joined in, setting their gear aside as they crouched down around the fire.

Nath's eyes widened. He'd barely heard the Brothers of the Wind talk, let alone laugh. He didn't know what to make of it. "I didn't think they could do that. They hardly make a sound."

"The Brothers of the Wind have their moments," Maefon replied. She was gathering Nath's blanket from his horse. She brought it to him. "They are rare moments."

Taking the blanket, he said, "Thanks." That's when he noticed stitches on Maefon's bare arms. "Maefon, what happened?"

"Oh, well, a hungry little critter got the best of me."

"Little? Those look like pretty large claw marks." Nath grabbed her hands and looked over her arms. There were some bruises on her chin and cheeks too. "You've been mauled."

Darkken got to his feet and hopped over the fire. Squinting, he looked her all over. "Shame on me. I didn't even notice in the poor light. Are you wounded elsewhere?"

"Just my pride. I did something foolish. While the elves scouted, I decided to practice my spellcasting. I was in deep meditation and felt I was safe inside a small cave. I don't think the bear within took too kindly to an uninvited guest." She rubbed her battered arms. "It seems the bear hadn't hibernated yet, and well, you can see what happened. I'm blessed that the Brothers of the Wind came when they did, else I might have been dead."

Darkken gave her a stern look. "So, this *beast* is taken care of?"

"Yes, it's fertilizing the ground as we speak," she replied.

He wrapped her up in his arms. "Good."

CHAPTER 55

NATH AND COMPANY SPENT THE next few hours discussing their plans. Darkken yawned on and off throughout the entire conversation, even though he did most of the talking. Maefon offered to make coffee, but he continued to pass, and no one else seemed interested. Maefon filled them all in on some other interesting information. They'd followed the elves and the merchants to a fort nestled in the forest, and they weren't even a day's walk from it now.

"The fort is more or less a hideout for poachers," she said, tightening the blanket around her shoulders as she sat hip to hip with Darkken. "It's made from logs and stone, stacked horizontally, with towers on the front corners. It would be a challenge to get a look inside if we weren't invited. And the poachers, well, we saw some new faces going in and out. Gnolls and goblins. If I were to guess, no more than thirty. I got a good look at the Merchant Queen. She is striking."

"Yes, I suppose that's why they call her the queen." Darkken covered his mouth. "Oh my, I think my jaw is getting sore. Anyway, did you see any other elves?"

"Just the handful that went in." Maefon sneered. "It sickens me that elves would consort with gnolls and goblins. I don't understand how they can stay in the same room and not kill each other. There were some men too. Sorry I didn't mention that."

"No, I assumed there were some seedy men as well." Darkken looked at Nath. "Let's talk about our mission. On my side of the fence, I want to snare some of these elves and throttle information about Chazzan out of them, but I think Nath has a deeper concern. Please, speak what you are feeling."

"I don't want to be a burden. I want Chazzan too, but these hunters that go after dragons really rile me." Nath clutched his fingers in and out of a fist. His hand was still sore from hitting Reaver. "They said they knew where a dragon was and its fledglings. I feel compelled to protect it. I just can't let these butchers go after my kind and not do anything about it."

"I understand," Darkken replied. "I've been giving this a lot of thought too, and I strongly feel that the Caligin are behind these dragon issues. This is what they do. They bring a seedier element into the cities and expand it. Sometimes it's stronger wine or intoxicating foods and flowers, but I think they want to bend a fine town like Advent toward a lower level. Getting people to accept dragon merchandise is but another step in their game. It will draw a bad element and, at the same time, divide people. Those that are for and against."

Hugging Darkken's arm, Maefon said, "That's awful. Nath, I know this hurts you. It makes you think of the fledglings who died, doesn't it?"

"Yeah," he said with a sigh. He could see the fledglings that were slaughtered in Dragon Home clearly in his mind. He got up, stepped between two elves, and paced. "I gave up a lot. I will have justice."

Darkken agreed. "And we will help you. Perhaps we should stake out the fort. Nath, you said they were very clear about hunting down that dragon. Those monstrous goons, what were they called?"

"Reaver and Slaughter."

"Yes. Those two. I'm certain they will be going after this dragon and its nest. We can follow them there and rescue the dragon. Perhaps we can nab some Caligin at the same time—supposing that they work together to achieve the same task—but we risk exposing ourselves and might have to start the chase all over." Darkken shrugged. "I'm willing to take that risk for you, though. And I think I speak for us all."

Nath swallowed. He was moved that his new friends would come through for him like that. "I thank you. And I really do think this is the best course of action. After all, saving a dragon can only bring good luck."

"It should," Maefon replied.

Retaking his seat by the fire, Nath opened up his backpack and took out the Gauntlet of Goam. "I have a feeling I'm going to need this when it comes to dealing with these massive men. They felt like they were made of stone."

"Assuming they are true sons of giants, then they practically are made of stone," Darkken replied. "They are the offspring of giants that mixed with man is what they say. No one knows for sure how they come about. This Sigourney, the Merchant Queen, is privileged to command them. One couldn't ask for a better set of bodyguards. Those goons are practically one-man armies." He eyed Nath putting on the gauntlet. "You'll need that and then some, I imagine."

Nath held his hand before his eyes. The gem in the leather glowed with a warm inner fire. "Oh, I'll have something for them both, all right. I'll have the gauntlet and Fang."

"And us," Maefon said.

"Yes. That should be more than enough."

CHAPTER 56

On foot, Nath and company made it to the poachers' hideout late the next day. It was just as Maefon described, a sturdy construction made from stones and logs stacked up on one another. A road led up to the entrance that was mostly covered in grasses that were stomped down and muddy. A gate made from logs made up a portcullis that went up and down. The towers on either side stood thirty feet high, with a stony hillside in the background behind them. From the front, the rugged-looking fort was well protected, and the land behind it appeared impassable. If Nath were to guess, it could hold fifty to a hundred people. The massive logs reminded him of Slaver Town.

Hidden in the woodland but with a good view of the fort, Darkken pointed at the towers. In each, there was a big figure, a dog-face gnoll, standing with two goblins wearing metal skullcaps. They pointed crossbows down at the road. Their yellow eyes scanned the nearby foliage. "Well, we won't be sneaking up on them," Darkken said to Nath. "A good thing that we don't need to go in. Chances are they would butcher us."

"I think we could make it in if we had to. We'd just take the back side from the rocks and drop in," Nath replied.

"I'm sure they have some goblins stuffed in those nooks and clefts, but they are probably sleeping," Darkken quipped. "Anyway, Nath, no matter what happens, don't let your temper get the best of you like it did in the Merchant's Cove. We have to work as a team. Our very lives depend on one another."

"I know."

Darkken squeezed his arm. "You must know. Now, do you want to follow my lead, or do you want me to follow yours?"

"Yours."

"Good, but I'm open to suggestions. Again, we are a team."

Little was said between the group after that exchange. One and all, Nath, Darkken, Maefon, and six elves spied the fort from the woodland concealment. Darkness came, and it wasn't long before the next morning arrived.

As the morning birds began their songs, the portcullis opened. Nath slapped Darkken's shoulder, as the big man was curled up in a soft bed of ivy.

He sat up quickly, wiping his eyes and shaking his face. His gaze followed Nath's finger. Two wolf-faced gnolls came out with a small group of goblins wearing steel caps. They were towing a pair of pack mules loaded down with gear that included ropes, bundled-up nets, and sleeves of javelins.

Behind them came the towering goons, Reaver and Slaughter, donning heavy cloaks, showing a glint of dragon-scale armor covering their chests. Each colossal man had a two-handed sword resting on his shoulder.

They marched alongside Sigourney, the only person on horseback. She no longer wore the garish golden robes of a merchant but opted for leather riding gear with a red sash tied around her hips.

Behind them came four elves in dyed black-leather armor, carrying bows, full quivers, longswords, and daggers. They moved down the road at an easy pace. The fort's portcullis closed behind them.

"Mother of Mitra, those are some big swords they carry. Hmmm…" Darkken said, as he watched the formidable group make their way around the first bend in the road and disappear.

Nath eyed him. "What?"

Fanning a mosquito from his face, he said, "I just wonder how vulnerable that fort is with so many gone. It could be an opportunity, if that was our quest."

Maefon nudged up beside him. "I could stay back and keep an eye on things." She slapped her hands together, smashing the mosquito that hovered near Darkken. "Besides, they might have more living dragons in there. We'll never know if we don't take a peek."

Nath stiffened.

Darkken held a hand up. "I'm sure that isn't true, but if we capture someone, we can find out what is really in there. Let's get moving."

Silent as stalking panthers, the small group trailed after the party of dragon hunters. Keeping their distance, they followed them on a two-day journey north, where the forest terrain became rockier to climb. The dragon hunters made camp underneath a steep hillside that was riddled with caves half covered in brush. Spying from a distance, Darkken said, "Those holes look like a good place for a dragon to nest."

"Yes. Too good," Nath said. He understood dragons and knew that they thrived by burrowing deep into the ground and sleeping for a long time. Given the cold weather, he had no doubt that a dragon very well could be huddled inside the hillside, protecting its nest or fledglings.

"The caves aren't very big. I don't imagine there could be a very big dragon inside there, if there is one," Maefon said.

"Don't be surprised if one much bigger than you think comes out. They might ball up to the size of a boulder, but once they uncurl and stretch their claws and wings, they become much bigger than you would have imagined." Nath scanned the hillside. There was no way to tell which one the dragon would be in if he didn't get a closer look. "I need to get to the dragon before they do."

"It's broad daylight. Someone will see you," Maefon said.

"I can wait until nightfall," Nath replied.

Frowning, Darkken replied, "Bad idea, look. The poachers are already taking to the hills. I have a bad feeling that they already know exactly where this dragon is and are prepared to roust it out. I'm sorry, Nath, but we are going to have to wait and see what happens. Either that or have a full battle on our hands."

Pulling hunks of bark off a tree, Nath replied, "I can't just stand here and watch them kill it."

From a knee, Darkken replied, "Let's let it play out. There's no telling what they are getting into just yet. We can't overreact. And didn't you say they would try to take the dragon alive? That would be my guess, given all of the nets. Besides, dragons are worth more alive than dead, and all of those people are greedy."

The goblins scurried up the hillside. One by one, they darted into the caves, each carrying a coil of rope.

"They think the dragon sleeps. They are going to try to pull it out." Nath made a shaky laugh. "Ha, that will be difficult. The dragon will be wedged in there like a piece of stone itself."

"Not if they are using iron cord," Darkken said. "And those men, Reaver and Slaughter, I have a feeling that they could pull a horn out of a dragon's head if they wanted to."

Chapter 57

With avid interest, Nath watched the dragon hunters get to work. The goblins scurried from cave to cave, poking the points of their spears in the holes. The mouths of most caves were only a foot or two wide. Others were a lot bigger. After the goblins poked at the open mouths, they squeezed their wiry frames inside. They vanished and popped out moments later then moved on to the next hole. Near the base of the hill, the giant men, Sigourney, and the elves waited.

"A tedious process," Darkken said. He was on one side of Nath, and Maefon was on the other. They were well concealed in the ferns. "It might take all night long. It wouldn't surprise me a bit if they broke out torches right after nightfall."

"Perhaps they won't find any dragon, and they'll go home," Nath replied. "That would be a better option." His mind raced as he toyed with a plan of calling out to the dragon in Dragonese. But the sound would alert the dragon hunters, which certainly wouldn't fall in his favor. For now, he would have to wait it out, but at dark, he'd be tempted to sneak in.

A commotion broke out among the goblins. One goblin squeezed out of a bigger cave that had a four-foot opening. He had his coil of rope tied to something within. The other goblin was flagging down the people at the bottom of the hill. Reaver gave the two gnolls beside him a shove. The gnolls, bigger than most men, snapped their jaws at the giant. Reaver looked down at the bigger gnoll with cold, dead eyes. Heads dipping, both gnolls headed up the hill.

"Do you think they found a dragon?" Maefon's hands fastened on Nath's wrists.

"We'll see," he said.

The gnolls climbed their way up the steep hillside. They met the goblins at the mouth of the cave and took the rope in hand. Together, the gnolls braced their feet and started to pull. The muscular dog-faced brutes' arm muscles flexed. Hand over hand, they pulled together, hauling whatever was inside the cave out. The goblin team hovered over the cave mouth with spears poised to strike. A black mass came out. It was balled up, thick, and hairy.

Creeping up out of the ferns, Darkken said, "Is that a bear?"

"It is," Nath said with relief. The black bear was in a deep hibernating slumber. Its body lay lifeless, but Nath could see a very gentle rise and fall of its chest. He looked over at Maefon. She patted him on the back.

The gnolls confronted the goblins. They pushed the smaller men to the ground and barked at them. Using a garbled Common tongue, the gnolls called the goblins idiots. The goblins popped back up, pushing the gnolls. Before long, more goblins came over and started squabbling with the gnolls.

"Heh-heh. I love it when they fight with one another. It shows their stupidity," Darkken said. "It always gives us an advantage, especially when a goblin doesn't know the difference between a dragon and a bear."

One of the gnolls punched a goblin square in the face. The blow knocked the goblin's helmet from his head and sent him sprawling to the ground. The other gnoll snatched a spear from the goblin's hands. Standing over top of the bear, he killed it. Together, the gnolls dragged the bear down to the bottom of the hill. The goblins got back to work, jabbing and prowling the caves again. Soon, darkness fell, and small torches were lit.

The biting chill of early winter came quickly. Nath's breath became frosty.

Maefon hugged his arm more tightly. "I really could do without the cold," she whispered.

Nath nodded, but his attention was on the goblins, who prowled the hills like black devils. He understood how they worked now. They had a system, apparently an effective one, and they seemed to target smaller dragons, not bigger ones. Of course, the bigger ones were rare, and on average, most dragons were little bigger than men.

Don't find anything. Don't find anything.

No sooner had Nath thought it than the goblins started waving their torches. They shouted down the hill. "We found the dragon nest."

CHAPTER 58

THE GNOLLS AND THE GIANT men made their trek back up the hill. At the base, Sigourney, still on horseback, and the Caligin remained. Their eyes were fixed on the scene that unfolded up the hill. At the cave, the gnolls were in a heated discussion with the goblins, but the goblins assured them that it was a dragon. They handed over the iron cord to the gnolls, but Reaver took it away. He handed a length of the rope to Slaughter.

"The moment of truth," Darkken said.

As Reaver and Slaughter tugged the rope, Nath's throat tightened. The big men put their weight into it and towed the rope down the hill. Something was coming out. All Nath could hope for was that the dragon wasn't in a deep sleep. He wanted it to come out in full attack mode and tear the hunters to pieces. He wasn't so lucky. On tiptoe, he watched the dragon being dragged out of the cave. It was hard to see because it was balled up.

"Sorry, Nath, but it looks like they got one." Darkken gave him a firm pat on the shoulder.

Nath crept closer, staying low in the field of tall grasses just a few dozen yards behind Sigourney and the Caligin. The others in his party came with him. Squinting, he could see the goblins poking at the dragon with the butts of their spears. With the help of the gnolls, they stretched out the dragon's body and strung it up by the neck. Its scales reflected a citrine yellow against the torchlight. There were broad yellow stripes running down the length of its back. It was about eight feet long from snout to tail if he had to guess. Hornless, its wings were folded tightly over its back. Its eyes were closed, but Nath's keen vision could make out eyelashes in the dark. It was a female. He reached over his back for the handle of his sword.

Darkken stayed his hand. With the chilly wind in their faces, he whispered, "Be patient. Otherwise, they might kill it."

Nath ground his teeth. This was a bad scenario for the dragons. He'd never thought about it before, but capturing dragons while sleeping, if one could find them, could be easy. Dragons were very hard to wake from a hibernating slumber that sometimes lasted for years. It was no wonder that the poachers took advantage of them. A sleeping dragon was an easy target. A dangerous one too.

Ahead, Sigourney sat up in her saddle. There was a stir coming from the cave. A goblin crawled out and stood up, holding small baby dragons by the tail. They were two feet long and wriggled and nipped at the goblin with their little jaws. The Merchant Queen clapped her hands. "Yes. Yes. Yes."

It all became suddenly clear to Nath. Baby dragons would be worth a fortune in hopes that they could be domesticated. And these dragons, the yellow streaks, were fairly docile compared to the more aggressive sorts.

Come on, dragon. You have to wake up. Save yourself!

Reaver gathered the dragon up in his long arms. The goblins gathered around him, holding thinner coils of rope. They started hog-tying the bigger dragon's top and bottom legs. The goblins holding the fledglings stuffed them into burlap sacks. One of the fledglings let out an ear-splitting shriek that carried down the mountain. The mother yellow streak flexed in Reaver's arms. The dragon lashed out, jaws wide, snapping down on the nearest gnoll's hand. The gnoll let out a howl, staring wide-eyed at the stump that was once attached to his hand.

Slaughter shoved the one-handed gnoll aside and helped Reaver control the wriggling dragon. With mighty hands, he clamped the dragon's snout shut. Reaver held the dragon fast, squeezing it tightly. It thrashed against the two men, twisting and rolling. They lost their footing and went down to the ground. Flames shot out of the dragon's mouth, scattering the goblins and gnolls.

Nath jumped forward.

Darkken tackled his legs. He pushed Nath down in the grasses. "Not now. We don't have a good position." Nath wrestled against him. Darkken locked up his legs and said, "You are going to give us all away and get us killed. Stop this madness."

The elves and Sigourney's attention remained fixed on the scene above. Reluctantly, Nath pulled back. On the hillside, Reaver and Slaughter had the dragon mother contained. Her snout was bound up, as well as her arms, legs, and wings. The fledglings had both been stuffed into the sacks and slung over the goblins' shoulders. The group made its way down the hillside.

With a tug from Darkken, Nath slunk back into the woodland. At least the dragons were alive. Back inside the safety of the forest, he grabbed Darkken by the collar and shook him. "What are you doing? This is not how we save dragons. What are you wanting to do, wait for them to take the dragon back to the fort and then get them out?"

Darkken grabbed Nath by the wrists and jerked them from his clothing. "Don't be a fool, Nath. We don't have position or advantage out in the open. Think about it, will you? They will move down the path, and there are plenty of advantageous places to ambush them. Huh? Can you see it?"

Nath gave Darkken a little shove to the chest. "I see it, assuming you don't change your plan and decide to wait again. You do that a lot."

"That is because I am patient, and that is why we live. I give you my word. Those dragons won't make it back to the fort. We will free them. But we have to do it the right way." Darkken slammed Nath hard on the shoulder. "Just trust me. Can you do that, Nath?"

Chin down, he replied, "I suppose."

Chapter 59

Darkken led them to a spot along the path that bottlenecked. It was a good location for an ambush. They walked through the night to get there, and it was morning when they arrived. The trees were thick, and large moss-covered rocks sat on the ground alongside the path. On both sides, in threes, the Brothers of the Wind were poised to attack with their bows. Maefon remained out of sight, but she had plans to wall off the rear in case the dragon hunters retreated. Nath and Darkken waited on the side of the road where the bottleneck started. The idea was to give the enemy nowhere to run unless they scattered in the woodland.

Nath's heart pounded like a tap hammer in his chest. There were a lot more of the dragon hunters than them, but with any luck, the hunters wouldn't know that. He agreed to let Darkken do the talking. Darkken leaned against a tree, patting his sword pommel. Looking down the road, he said, "The anticipation is often the worst part. Once the enemy shows, the mind takes another course of action. Survival."

"So, do you think you'll be able to talk them into releasing the dragons?" Nath asked.

"Heavens no. Not unless we have a bag of gold that outweighs the both of us."

"Then why are we doing this?"

"Because you are determined to. That's why. We discussed this, Nath, but we can take another course. It's not too late." Darkken shook his head. "Blood will definitely be shed if we continue on the path we are on."

"It's the right thing to do. They are evil. They must be stopped."

Shrugging, Darkken replied, "On that, I agree with you, but there will be a price." He pushed off the tree. Quick as a wink, he snaked his sword, Scalpel, out of the scabbard. He twisted it with his wrist. "But I am itching for a fight. I think you are as well."

Nath thought of the old knight, Hacksaw. He missed the man. And with goblins in the mix, now would be the perfect time for him to be there, fighting by Nath's side. He pulled his own sword and stepped out into the middle of the road. He stuck the sword tip in the ground. "We can handle them."

Darkken stepped out into the road with him. "Yes, I know we can. I feel the two of us together are an unstoppable combination."

"Really?"

"Really. Really."

"Huh. That's an odd answer," Nath said.

"An ogre said it to me once. I thought it was catchy." Darkken bent his ear. "Ah, I hear the enemy." He took a deep breath. "For the dragons."

"For the dragons."

The small group of dragon hunters made its way around the bend in the path. Reaver and Slaughter rode in front of Sigourney, a wall between her and harm. Four Caligin walked in pairs on both sides of her horse. Behind the horse, the two gnolls carried the dragon, who was tied up on a long branch. One gnoll's hand was a crudely bandaged-up stump. It walked on the front end of the pole, grimacing with every step. The remaining goblins walked behind them. Sigourney looked right at Nath and Darkken. The giant men did too. They didn't slow their pace.

Nath noticed the burlaps sacks with the little dragons inside hanging over the side of Sigourney's saddle. Like snakes in a sack, they didn't move. He looked back up at the confident woman sitting tall in the saddle. Her dark hair was full and wavy. She showed the slightest smile as her eyes hung on his own. He swallowed.

Reaver and Slaughter kept their massive swords resting on their shoulders. Their heavy stares could have knocked an ordinary man over. Their fingers flexed on their sword handles. About twenty feet away, Sigourney lifted her hand. "Whoa."

The dragon hunters came to a stop. The goblins in the back fanned out. As they got a good look at Nath and Darkken, they chattered back and forth with one another. The Caligins' hands remained empty. They stood stark and silent, with a frozen demeanor. Their eyes were black as a coal mine.

An awkward silence fell over the forest as the two men exchanged glances with the dragon hunters. Finally, Sigourney leaned over her saddle horn and said, "Will you kindly get out of our way? It's either that or we kill you."

Nath looked at Darkken, who stared at the Merchant Queen, transfixed. Nath nudged the man.

Darkken blinked rapidly. "Apologies, Merchant Queen." He quickly bowed. "I was momentarily captivated by your enchanting beauty. Please, allow me to introduce myself. I am Darkken, and this is my very dear and young friend, Nath."

"I don't care who you are," she said. "I just want you to get out of the way. And mind you, this queen is being very merciful, or else you would be dead already." Her horse nickered, and she petted its neck. "Easy, girl. See, you have unsettled my horse. I don't like that. It's not safe having a nervous beast underneath your legs. But I take it the both of you are only here to cause trouble." She looked right at Nath. "You would think that you had learned your lesson when you crossed me in the Merchant's Cove."

Nath opened his mouth, but Darkken cut him off. Hand up in a peaceful gesture, he said, "Allow me a moment to speak on behalf of my friend. He overheard your conversation about the dragons, and in truth, he is very passionate about their condition. He cannot stand the thought of someone harming a dragon. Imagine, Sigourney… may I call you Sigourney?"

"No," she said.

"Disappointing," Darkken continued in a very warm and open manner. A top-notch merchant couldn't have done it any better. "We certainly admire what you do and respect your trade, but imagine if someone butchered your beast and put its parts out on the market. Wouldn't that disturb you?"

"It's a horse. We do that all of the time." She gave an eye roll. "I'm losing patience."

"Yes, sorry, but I suppose that was a bad example," Darkken replied.

"It was a horrible example. Dragons aren't any different than any other animal, aside from their mystical and invigorating properties. So far as I am concerned, they are just dumb animals, like all of the others."

Nath's ears heated up. He started to reach for his sword stuck in the ground. Darkken pushed Nath's hands away from the hilt. "Merchant Queen, we would like to make you an offer on your dragons."

Chapter 60

Sigourney tossed her head back and laughed. Her contagious laughter brought forth a solid chuckle from Darkken. He started to laugh harder and backhanded Nath in the chest. Nath, for some reason, began laughing too. The goblins were howling with chortling and clucking in the rear, but it was very clear they didn't know what they were laughing about. Finally, Sigourney produced a silk handkerchief and wiped her eyes. "Oh my, I haven't laughed so hard in such a long time. Go ahead, Darkken, please, shame yourself with your ridiculous offer."

Darkken caught his breath and patted his stomach. "Our offer is this. Give us the dragons in exchange for your lives."

Sigourney's expression turned cold. With narrowing eyes, she said, "I was afraid that you would say something stupid like that. A shame. I find you both very charming, but—"

Darkken lifted a finger. "Before you command your goons to attack, let me inform you that you are surrounded by our men. Many, many men. And they will get you out of that saddle if they have to, but I'd hate to do that. I truly enjoy your warm and radiant personality."

Sigourney and the giant brothers scanned their surroundings. "I don't see any men," she said.

Darkken made a sharp whistle. A concession of bowstrings snapped. All six goblins in the rear dropped dead as stones with feather arrows protruding through their chests. Quick as a cat, the Caligin slipped arrows from quivers and loaded their own bows. They aimed into the forest.

"Are you convinced now, Sigourney?"

The woman's fingers toyed with the chain of a necklace that hung over her chest. It was an ankh-shaped medallion. Nath recalled seeing her wearing it in the tavern. He eased closer to his sword.

"A very brave play," she said. "But bravery is often the mark of fools. You see, I've known that you've had eyes on me the entire time. You have seven elves in the forest, one of which is a woman. And though you've evened the odds up in your favor, I think it's important to know that even if there were one hundred more of you, it wouldn't be enough."

"Is that so?" Darkken said, paling.

"Oh, it most certainly is. You see, I didn't become the Merchant Queen just because of my stunning smile and personality." Sigourney twisted her amulet. "No, I became the Merchant Queen because I command the minds of other people."

Nath felt a probing presence invading his mind. He reached for Fang, but his limbs seized up. Straining, he looked at Darkken. The man's sword quivered in his hand. His jaw hung open.

In full control, Sigourney smiled. "I have a suggestion. All of you surrender your weapons and surrender yourselves."

At the same time, Nath and Darkken dropped onto their knees. Darkken's sword slipped out of his fingers. The Brothers of the Wind came out of the forest empty-handed, with their hands on top of their heads. The Caligin fully disarmed them. Maefon stepped from behind, walking toward the front with eyes as big as saucers and shaking like a leaf. She kneeled down beside Darkken. All of the Brothers of the Wind took their places alongside of them. Everyone's hands were on their heads. Their freewill was no longer their own.

Sigourney looked down at the group. "That is much better. And now that I have your full attention and cooperation, it's time to say goodbye, before my colleagues kill you. Goodbye, Darkken and Nath. Thanks for the laugh."

CHAPTER 61

NATH, DARKKEN, MAEFON, AND THE Brothers of the Wind were disarmed, bound up, and marched all the way back to the dragon poachers' fort. The woodland fortress made from log and stone was solidly built and covered in moss and vines on the outside. On the inside was an open courtyard. Nath counted another thirty goblins and at least eight more gnolls, well armed and leering at them from all angles the moment they entered. Small log stables and stone buildings covered the ground underneath the catwalks of the fort.

They were taken into the back end of the fort, where the mouth of a cave opened, leading inside the forest hill. In the damp confines, all of them were locked up in dungeon cells and chained by the ankles to the chiseled-out stone walls.

"Interesting," Darkken said, eyeing their surroundings. It was a dim and dank cell, with water running down the walls. "I thought she was going to kill us on the spot. Yet we live."

Nath pushed his hair out of his eyes. He bent over and tugged at the chain. "I was thinking the same thing, but I'm not complaining. I am pretty tired of dungeon cells and chains, though. Darkken, what did she cast on us? I lost complete control of my thoughts. She commanded them."

"Yes, it seems that we severely underestimated the Merchant Queen. She is more than she appears to be, and that is deadly." Darkken made his way over to the bars. In the cell across from his, Maefon sat with her face in her hands. "Dearest, are you well?" he asked.

Rubbing her temples with her fingers, she said, "I have a massive headache. I tried to resist what she was doing, and it felt like my head was exploding. She really dug deep and scrambled my head."

"Can you use your magic?" Darkken asked.

"I don't have anything that can tear these bars away, and to be truthful, my mind is fuzzy."

"Just rest."

Nath made his way over to the bars. The Brothers of the Wind had been put in the cell beside them, but he couldn't see them because of the wall between them. With his forehead resting between the bars, he said, "I'm really getting tired of losing my items and being shackled time and again." He looked at his bare hand where the Gauntlet of Goam used to be. "Really tired of it."

"It's my fault. We hesitated when we should have taken them down. I guess I thought I would be cute." Darkken's face sagged. "I knew better. Now not only have they captured the dragons, but they captured us as well."

"At least we have a better idea of what we are dealing with," Maefon said. "A merchant with otherworldly power. I never suspected her to be a sorceress."

Darkken nodded. "There might be a good reason for that. Perhaps she isn't. I think there is a special item that she wields. I noticed her toying with her medallion moments before all of this happened."

"I noticed the same thing," Nath added.

Maefon rose to her feet. A smile played on her face. "And like many powerful items, perhaps its use is limited."

"Either way, we need to see how this is all going to unfold. Sigourney said that she was going to kill us. The question is, when and how?" Darkken said.

Nath replied, "Well, I don't want to find out. We need to figure a way out of here before then."

Two gnoll guards carrying spears entered the hallway from underneath an archway that led to another room. They poked the tips of the spears through the bars at Darkken's chest. "Shut your mouth and get back!"

Hands up, Darkken and Nath backed away.

The gnolls rustled two of the Brothers of the Wind out of their cell and led them outside the dungeon. A few minutes later, a thunderous cheering erupted outside, echoing loudly into the dungeon chambers.

"Sounds like someone has a fight on their hands," Darkken said, making his way back to the bars.

Nath joined him. Across the way, Maefon's face was pressed against the bars. Her brows were knitted together. "What do you think is happening?"

Darkken clutched at the bars. "I have an ugly feeling that someone is making sport of the elves."

The cheering and roaring went on for several minutes, then a loud "Ew!" ended the revelry.

Nath's guts twisted. "That didn't sound very favorable."

"No, it didn't," Maefon replied, tapping nervously on the bars.

Moments later, the gnoll guards entered the dungeon room, dragging one of the Brothers of the Wind behind them. The elf's eyes were swollen shut, and his face was bruised all over. He made a ragged and wheezing breath.

"Where is your brother?" Darkken asked.

The elf looked Darkken's way and managed to shake his head before he was thrown back into his cell. Two more elves were led out. Within minutes, the howls of a blood-hungry crowd started all over. Not long after that, the beastly gnolls came back, empty-handed. They took the last two Brothers of the Wind with them.

Darkken shouted out after them, "Fight with might! Avenge your brothers!"

Nath paced the cell, clutching his head.

Darkken started talking to the elf in the other cell. "Brother, brother, can you hear me? What are you facing out there?"

Maefon shook her head with a frown growing on her face. "Darkken, I'm sorry, but our brother is no longer breathing." A tear went down her cheek. "This is horrible. Am I going to be beaten to death as well?"

"I think we all are," Darkken said. "And all for their amusement."

The dog-faced gnolls returned carrying one elf whose limbs and nose appeared broken. He breathed but showed no signs of pain. Sniggering, the gnolls put the broken elf in the cell and slammed the door. They came to Darkken and Nath's cell.

One opened the cell with the key while the other poked at them with a spear. "Get back! Try anything foolish, and I'll gore this little elven woman and feed her to the goblins."

The gnoll jailer entered with the keys and took the shackles from their feet. He shoved Nath and Darkken out the door. "Time to die. Reaver and Slaughter are waiting."

CHAPTER 62

Nath knelt in the center of the courtyard of the dragon poachers' fort with Darkken beside him. Their captors hollered and cursed at them. They passed jugs of wine back and forth. On the catwalks behind the fort's walls were dozens of goblins and more gnolls. Where Nath had counted only a few dozen before, now there were at least a hundred. On the western catwalks was a throne-like chair made from wood and stone. With the sun shining on her, Sigourney lounged in the chair, legs crossed, toying with her medallion. The Caligin stood coolly on both sides of her. She winked.

Fists balled up at his sides, Darkken spat on the ground.

Walled in by a circle of hard-eyed hunters, Nath scanned more of his surroundings. The portcullis was closed and guarded. Two goblins and one gnoll stood inside the towers next to the gate. On the eastern wall, the yellow streak dragon hung from the bottom of the catwalks. Two gnolls armed with spears guarded it. The back end of the fort was a steep cliff. Birds nested in the rocks. Scanning all angles, Nath's eyes led him back to the Merchant Queen. His sword and Darkken's sword were propped against her throne. Nath's backpack lay near her feet.

Finally, Sigourney raised her hand. The hunters fell silent. All eyes turned toward her. She straightened up in her seat and leaned forward. "Darkken. Nath. As I said, Reaver and Slaughter will kill you. Normally, I let them chop your heads off on the spot, but given that we recently captured such a fine dragon, I felt the hunters deserved some entertainment. The gnolls and goblins will find such joy in watching the sons of the giants beat the handsome out of you."

"And what if we beat the ugly off of them? What happens then?" Darkken fired back.

A gnoll slapped him hard on the back of the head.

Sigourney gave a confident laugh. "I assure you, that won't happen. The brothers have never lost, and they have killed dragons with their bare hands. I don't think they have anything to fear from the likes of you. Besides, you can't hurt them."

"If it was a fair fight, we could!" Nath shouted. The gnoll punched him in the back of the head, sending him sprawling to the ground. He pushed his face out of the hard dirt and wiped the grit off.

"What are you suggesting?" She stretched her hands out and motioned toward their swords. "Do you want to have a duel?"

"Yes!" Nath and Darkken said at the same time.

"How interesting," she said. "I'm not so certain that would be wise on my part. Why would I give you a fighting chance? You don't deserve it. After all, you were going to kill me."

Lifting a finger, Darkken said, "Correction. We were only threatening to kill you, not actually acting on it."

"You killed my goblins."

"True, but do they really count?" Darkken replied.

The goblin ring of men encircling them growled and clacked their teeth. The hackles on the hairy necks of the gnolls rose.

"Perhaps I should let you scrap with the hunters first. No doubt they want to take a piece out of you," she said, easing back into her chair. "It could be a warm-up."

"I'd prefer to save my energy for the brothers," Darkken said. "But you never answered my question. If we beat them, what do we get in return?"

The crowd turned its attention back to Sigourney. She tossed her head and started laughing. The gnolls and goblins cackled and howled with glee. With a wave of her hand, she silenced one and all. "If you defeat Reaver and Slaughter, I will let you go free."

"All of us? And our gear?" Darkken asked.

Checking her nails, she said, "Sure."

"And you'll free the dragon?" Nath added.

"Now you are getting absurd. You would think your life is enough, and now you want to barter for the dragon's." She shook her head. "No."

Darkken whispered to Nath. "It's all right. It never hurts to ask." He turned back to Sigourney. "And swear that you won't freeze our minds or something in case we are winning. That would be cheating."

"I make no promises. This deal is as good as it gets, and you are fortunate to have that. Not that it should matter." Sigourney eyed them both. "Are we finished chattering like gnomes now? I'm ready to get down to business."

Nath and Darkken exchanged glances. Nath's fingertips tingled. He was a dragon and could probably take a beating better than Darkken, a human. He wasn't certain how long the older man could hold up. He envisioned the broken bodies of the elves who had been dragged back into the dungeon. They were formidable fighters, he knew it, but Reaver and Slaughter made quick work of them. He nodded at Darkken.

"We are ready!" Darkken said.

The gnolls grabbed both men by their long locks of hair and hauled them to their feet. With a stiff shove in their backs, the gnolls walked back into the fighting ground.

Nath and Darkken stood side by side, facing the round wall of people. The giant men were nowhere to be seen. Then, from somewhere unseen, a loud gong rang. The hunters howled wildly. They pounded their chests and barked like dogs. Taking advantage of the chaos, Nath said to Darkken, "Do you have a plan?"

"Given their formidability, I suggest we probe for weaknesses. Every creature has a weakness. Now, what I'm about to suggest might sound crude, but take the best shot at their groins that you can." Darkken got head-to-head with Nath. "Anything goes, Nath. Anything."

"Ears, eyes, nose, and throat?" Nath replied.

"They have to hurt somewhere. I was thinking, using our small size and speed, perhaps we should go after them one at a time."

"Which one?"

"Reaver. I go high, and you go low. How is that for a plan?"

"Good, but Darkken, can you hold up against them? I know you are strong, but they are bone breakers."

"Hopefully, this suit of armor will keep me together. It's not a fine breastplate like yours but more than serviceable."

Nath and Darkken clasped hands. "We can win," Nath said.

Darkken replied, "We have to."

The goblins' and gnolls' howling reached another level of insanity. Flailing their arms wildly overhead, they started chanting, "Reaver! Slaughter! Reaver! Slaughter! Reaver! Slaughter!"

CHAPTER 63

MAEFON TREKKED BACK AND FORTH in her cell, nibbling on her nails. She'd spent time with Darkken before they ventured into the hills, but like on so many occasions, he was vague on the details. The goal was to help Nath out, save a dragon, capture a Caligin, and pressure false information about Chazzan from them. It sounded simple, but the plan became vastly more complex the moment the Merchant Queen dropped a mental explosion on them. She could still feel the overwhelming power dancing around in her head. That woman had power—a lot of it.

Maefon took a seat on the cot in the back of her cell and tried to collect her thoughts. It had become hard to concentrate. Bits and pieces of spells came to her, but the other parts were missing from her jumbled mind. Additionally, she didn't know if Sigourney was in on Darkken's plan or not. Perhaps this was all part of his plan to keep it all realistic. Just when she thought she had figured him out, something different would happen. *What do I do?*

The raucous cheering started up again. She came to her feet. In the cell across from her, the two elven survivors stirred. They were both bruised, bloodied, and mangled. Their sweating faces were covered by grimaces of pain. She'd never seen the Caligin so busted up before. They were the best-trained and deadliest of fighters, but the giant men had pounded them to death.

Over the years, Darkken had embedded a few thoughts in her mind. One of his sayings was, "You are no good to me if you can't save yourself."

Pondering the notion, she decided on a course of action. If Darkken and Nath didn't make it, then she would need to save herself. Either that or the giant brothers would beat her like a rug next. She reached outside of the bars and ran her fingers over the keyhole. Eyeing the entrance that led into her dungeon, she could see the back shoulder of one of the gnolls standing guard. He and the other gnoll were talking back and forth. It seemed clear that they didn't want to miss the fight.

She fished through her hair, producing a hairpin. She bent it into the shape of a makeshift key and started picking at the lock. It was a crude lock with heavy tumblers, making it difficult to move with a small piece of wire. Head aching, she went at it, feeling around the lock, bending her hairpin wire a few more times, and trying over and over again. The latch popped. She pushed the door slowly outward. The hinges squeaked.

The gnoll standing by the entrance looked her way. He stared hard with a wary eye.

Cocking his head to one side, he came into the room. "What are you doing, elf?" The door to her cell was about a foot open. "How did you do that?"

"Do what?" she said, hanging onto the cell-door bars. "I didn't open it, it just opened when I leaned on it. The lock is bad or something."

"A busted lock, huh?" the gnoll rubbed his canine jaw. "I told them these locks were old, but they don't listen. Of course, we don't use them so much these days, aside from keeping creatures, and they are too dumb to get out."

Raising on tiptoe, hands still clutching the bars, she said, "So, you believe me?"

"Believe you? An elf? Why of course I don't, you little pointy-eared fool. Now step back, liar! You'll be goblin food soon enough."

Maefon shoved the door hard. It cracked the gnoll in his snout. Fast as a striking snake, she pulled his dagger from his belt and stabbed him in the gut. Not stopping to watch him die, she raced for the exit. The other gnoll turned the moment she entered the room. Before he could let out a cry of alarm, she plunged the dagger into his heart and shoved him to the floor. She found the keys, went back to the dungeon, and tossed them to the Brothers of the Wind. The less wounded one scooped them under his body. Dagger in hand, she headed back out of the dungeon, searching for anything that might aid her in the quest to save Nath and Darkken.

Chapter 64

The crowd of gnolls and goblins parted. The towering Reaver and Slaughter marched out from underneath the catwalk, arms stiffly swinging at their sides. The huge men seemed bigger now. No longer covered in cloaks or dragon-scale armor, the gaunt-faced, hollow-eyed men were bare chested and thick with hard knots of muscle. Nath and Darkken looked up at both of them. The deep-chested men had hairy arms and fresh blood on their knuckles. A dark smile glimmered in their coal-black eyes. Slaughter smashed a fist into his hand, making a loud smacking sound.

Nath's hand ached from when he'd hit Reaver before. The man had barely flinched.

Sigourney called down to them, "If you like, I can just let them chop your heads off. That would eliminate the suffering."

"You wouldn't want to miss out on a good fight, would you?" Darkken said.

"I do delight in violent entertainment." She flipped her wrist. "Carry on with it then."

Reaver and Slaughter moved deeper into the circle. Nath and Darkken backed up. The hunters closed off the circle.

"Listen, Nath, they are big and slow. Use your speed. Fight smart. The longer we last, the better off we are," Darkken said. "Perhaps we can wear these brutes down."

Nath balled up his fists. "Agreed." His voice was a little shaky, however. He recalled the lessons that Master Elween had taught him in Dragon Home. He'd wrestled dragons; certainly he could handle giants.

Giants that kill dragons with their bare hands.

The unseen gong rang out again in a loud *bong!*

Reaver and Slaughter barreled toward them.

"High, low, Nath. High, low!"

With a sneer, Reaver thrust his clutching arms forward. Nath slipped under the man's long arms and punched the man hard in the groin. The giant didn't flinch. At the same moment, Darkken launched himself into Reaver's face. He punched him hard in the eye socket. The giant man wobbled backward, caught his balance, scooped Darkken up in his arms, and slammed him hard into the ground. "You can't hurt me!" Reaver snarled. "But I can hurt you!"

Nath unleashed a flurry of punches into Reaver's rock-hard belly. Reaver looked down on Nath with a look of amusement. Fists aching, Nath said, "Do you have a better plan? I'm pretty sure this one isn't working."

Slaughter picked Darkken up off the dirt and pressed him up at chest level. "Just keep hitting! They have to hurt somewhere!" Slaughter slammed Darkken onto the hard turf. He followed up by dropping down, elbow first, on Darkken's chest. "Oooof!"

Nath ducked away from Reaver, shaking his hurting fingers.

A goblin shoved him in the back. "Get in there and die!"

Nath punched the goblin hard in the jaw. The little yellow-eyed man sagged into the arms of the outraged crowd. Nath faced off with Reaver again. Nearby, Darkken had his hands full, rolling away from Slaughter.

Find a weakness, Nath. Find a weakness!

Head bobbing, Nath waded into the big body of Reaver. He ducked and slid away from the hard swings of Reaver. He landed a flurry of punches on the ribs, took a shot at the kidneys, and rammed a knee into the groin. The tireless man leaned on Nath, arms pumping in short powerful punches, landing a solid shot directly on Nath's chest. Nath stumbled backward into the arms of the hungry crowd. They spat curses at him, took cheap shots at his body, then shoved him back at Reaver.

He stole a glance at Sigourney. She had her hand over her mouth, yawning. Darkken, on the other hand, was hoisted over Slaughter's head, spun around, and flung hard onto the ground. Darkken crawled away, fingers digging into the dirt, only to have Slaughter grab him by the ankles and haul him backward. Nath took off at a full sprint, leapt over Darkken, and with a wild yell, pounced on Slaughter. He pushed his thumbs into the giant's eyeballs.

Slaughter let out a scream. "Nooooooooo!" The giant man locked his fingers around Nath's throat. The fingers were iron strong, sinking deep into the thick muscles around Nath's throat. At the same time, Slaughter's neck twisted hard side to side.

Nath pushed his thumbs harder into Slaughter's eye sockets. Slaughter choked, spit, and groaned. The huge hands around Nath's neck squeezed like a vise. Slaughter pushed Nath away from his body. Nath wouldn't let the man's skull go. It became a battle of one iron will against another. Neither man would let go. Neither would give. The hungry howls for death exploded from the crowd. Nath's vision turned hazy. A sea of blackness swam in his thoughts. His fingers loosened on the giant's eyes.

He was losing.

Slaughter pushed him down onto his knees, still choking him, and let out a triumphant howl. Nath hacked at the man's forearms. It was like chopping at a tree with a spoon. He looked up into Slaughter's watery eyes. Sheer evil filled the man's countenance. He was a killer, natural born.

I can't die like this! I can't!

With his air supply cut off, Nath's energy began to fade. A filmy darkness overcame his sight. He heaved once more against Slaughter's unbreakable grip. At that moment, two big bodies collided with Nath and Slaughter. The jarring impact allowed Nath to twist out of the man's grip. He found himself tangled up in a knot of battling limbs, sucking for breath.

Darkken and Reaver were engaged in a full-blown wrestling match. They sucked Slaughter and Nath into the fold. Darkken screamed, "I'm going for the eyes! I'm going for the eyes!"

Nath swept the legs out from under Slaughter. The man fell hard to the ground. Nath slipped behind him and put him in a chokehold. He locked his arms and cranked up the pressure on Slaughter's throat. The giant man got up on one knee. He tried to pry Nath's arms away with his fingers. "Put them in a chokehold, Darkken!"

Darkken had Reaver by the hair. He drove a knee into the man's face. "Good idea!" He kneed Reaver again, moved in behind the man, and embraced Reaver in a chokehold.

Nath and Darkken had both brutes locked up tight. "If they can't breathe, they can't live, right?" Nath said.

"Right!" Darkken agreed. His cheeks were red, and sweat drenched his face. "Don't let up, Nath! Don't let uuuuuup!"

Reaver and Slaughter stood straight up. Then, in unison, they fell flat on their backs, crushing Nath and Darkken beneath them.

Nath held on. So did Darkken.

Once again, Reaver and Slaughter did the same thing, all to the thrill of the crowd. Over and over again, they smashed Nath and Darkken underneath their broad backs. They shook limbs and knocked the wind out of both of them. Nath knew in his heart that if he let go now, he was going to die. The two juggernauts stood once more, on limbs as hard as steel, and executed the crushing blow once more. Nath's grip slipped. He lay flat on his back, arms sprawled out at his sides. Panting for breath, he rolled his head to one side. He saw some busted-out teeth. They were very white, probably elven. He ran his tongue over his teeth. *All there.* Darkken lay on the ground, the same as him.

The older man shook his head. "They are tireless brutes. I've never seen the likes of it. It's been good fighting with you, Nath. Very good. No matter what, just keep fighting."

Reaver and Slaughter lorded over the exhausted men. Beating their chests and letting out savage growls, they proceeded to pummel and savagely beat the life out of them.

CHAPTER 65

DAGGER IN HAND, MAEFON SNEAKED her way through the caverns behind the fort. At the moment, the caverns that consisted of a variety of rooms and caves were abandoned. All of the hunters were outside, watching the fights. The elven sorceress took advantage of her freedom, quickly rummaging through the supplies, searching for anything that could help. She would need an advantage, and at the moment, her mind wasn't clear enough to cast any spells. Whatever power Sigourney used had truly rattled her.

She wandered into a torchlit armory with racks of spears, swords, hatchets, and axes. There were bows, crossbows, bolts, and arrows. In their own section were suits of armor and a lot of piecemeal parts of full-body armor. Not a bit was a uniform match, but much of it appeared to have been traded for, acquired through raids, or stolen. That's when she noticed in another corner a pile of weapons that were very familiar. It was her gear, as well as that of the Brothers of the Wind. She put on her sword belt, grabbed a short bow and tested the string, and slung a quiver of arrows over her shoulder.

"That feels better," she muttered.

Her own personal gear was hardly enough to take on a small army, but she didn't feel naked anymore, either. Her eyes swept the room once more. She couldn't waste any more time if she was going to help Nath and Darkken. She just had to act. Lives were often lost from too much hesitation. Her eyes caught on a strongbox on the floor, tucked away between the weapon racks. The brass fittings were clearly fashioned by elven hands. It had a long and sleek design to it but was locked by a crude padlock that wasn't elven. She hustled over to it and took a knee. Using her hairpin, she picked the lock then tossed the padlock aside and lifted the lid. The box was lined with a sea-green crushed velvet. Inside was another black quiver full of feather-tailed arrows. A surging victorious clamor of blood-hungry voices rose outside.

Maefon grabbed the quiver, slung it over her shoulder, snatched up another bow, and headed back toward the entrance to the fort. She came across a stairwell carved out of the rock that curved upward. She took it. At the top, crouching down, she found herself staring down from a natural overlook. She had a full view of everything. The guard towers, Sigourney and the Caligin, and a living arena wall made of goblins and gnolls. Inside the arena were Nath and Darkken, getting the blood beat out of them by Reaver and Slaughter.

Heart racing, Maefon notched her first arrow from the black quiver. A red fire glowed inside the tip of the arrow. "You're a real beauty, but what in the world do you do?" She peeked up over the wall and targeted the giant men wailing on Nath and Darkken down below. Taking aim, she drew the bowstring back across her cheek. "Only one way to find out, I suppose."

CHAPTER 66

IF IT HADN'T BEEN FOR the breastplate armor that Nath wore, his ribs would have shattered like glass. Reaver and Slaughter were beating him and Darkken senseless. Nath slammed to the ground. He got kicked in the ribs. Reaver ground the heel of his boot on Nath's hand. His face was smashed hard into the dirt several times. The metallic taste of blood and dirt filled his mouth. He kicked, twisted, and squirmed only to have his head almost yanked off his shoulders by the hair. Any lesser man would have been dead by now.

Darkken wasn't faring much better. Slaughter had him in a one-arm headlock. He kneed Darkken repeatedly in the gut. The blows lifted Darkken off his feet. The giant man suddenly slapped Darkken on the back and hip-dropped him face-first into the ground. The ugly brother started laughing.

Together, the sons of the giants left their prey and gave one another a high-handed slap. Reaver took after Darkken, and Slaughter went back after Nath. At the same time, they flopped to the ground, driving their big elbows into Nath's and Darkken's backs.

Nath bellowed out a painful groan. The sound of his own voice startled him. He didn't think he had enough strength left inside to make such a noise, but it all came gushing out. As Slaughter pushed off of him, he stuffed Nath's face into the ground. It was clear that the brothers were just toying with them. They stood tall, pumping their arms and feeding the crowd. They flexed their brutish arms and monstrous shoulders. Nath pushed himself up to his hands and knees. Darkken did the same.

Blood seeped from Darkken's mouth. "This is not going very well, is it? And I'm bleeding. I don't ever bleed." He made his way to his knees and swayed. "Keep trying to find that weakness."

Panting, Nath said, "I swear I've hit them everywhere I can think of. Other than sticking a thumb in the eye, I don't think they have one." He combed his locks out of his eyes. "How does my hair look?"

Darkken shrugged. "It's as unrivaled as ever."

"Good." Nath planted a hand on the ground. He pushed up to his feet. Looking side to side, he lost sight of Reaver only to see Slaughter move in behind Darkken and scoop the smaller man up in his arms. Suddenly, arms like powerful pythons wrapped around Nath's body. Reaver lifted him up from behind, pinning his arms at his sides. Grunting, Reaver squeezed.

"Huuuuurk!" Reaver blurted out.

The breastplate armor was the only thing that saved Nath's body from shattering like a nut. Still, pressure behind his back was building. Across from him, Slaughter was giving Darkken the same treatment. Darkken's face started to purple like a plum.

"Nath!" Darkken managed to say. "Given the finality of our dire circumstance, I have to tell you something."

"Now? What is it?"

"I've been holding back. You see, I'm more than just a swordsman. I can control magic too."

Groaning, Nath said, "Any chance you can use some of that magic now?"

Darkken gave a stiff nod. His dark eyes became angry cauldrons of molten copper. "Nath," he said in a thunderous voice. "Duck!"

Nath tucked his head as far into his chest as he could. Two fiery bolts shot out of Darkken's eyes, striking Reaver in the face. The monster man's grip loosened. Nath dropped to his feet and looked up. Reaver's face was now a hollow, burning ring. He could see the tower in the background right through it. The gnolls and goblins shuffled back in awe-filled silence. Darkken's burning eyes cooled.

Slaughter, screamed. "Brother! Brother! You kill my brother! Now you die!" The enraged man cranked up the pressure on Darkken.

Darkken let out a painful moan.

A red missile streaked through the ledges hidden in the hillside. It buried itself inside Slaughter's head. He dropped Darkken and teetered around, pawing at the shaft protruding from his skull.

The wide-eyed hunters watched with fascination.

As he tried to pull the arrow out of his ear, Slaughter's head exploded with a muffled *pooompfh*. Like his brother, Slaughter still stood, headless and unmoving.

All eyes drifted between Nath, Darkken, and the Merchant Queen. Her beautiful face filled with rage. Her eyes flashed like lightning. With a wave of her hand, Maefon sailed out of the hillside rocks. Her arms were flailing like a wounded bird. A quiver and bow fell from her hands. She dropped from the air onto the ground, landing hard in front of Darkken and Nath.

Sigourney stood. She spread her fingers out and with a deep frown said, "Kneel."

Under a power that was not his own, Nath dropped to one knee. Darkken and Maefon did the same. Nath strained against the unseen forces that tangled his mind, but he could not resist the command.

Toying with her medallion, Sigourney said, "This is how you repay my hospitality, by killing my guardians?"

"We had a deal, Merchant Queen," Darkken shouted back. "We beat your champions. You gave your word that you would free us. You don't want word getting out that you broke with honor, do you?"

"You cheated, Darkken. It was a matter of hand-to-hand combat and not outside interference," she said.

"You never said that!" Nath said. He was amazed that he could talk. "It was our people against yours!"

"No, it was the pair of you against Reaver and Slaughter. This wretched elf woman intervened, hence breaking our agreement." Sigourney paced the catwalk in front of the throne. "The sons of the giants were precious to me. I raised them since they were boys. Now you have killed them."

Slaughter fell into Reaver, and both men hit the ground with a thump.

Darkken pleaded a new case to Sigourney. "You are the Merchant Queen. You know that all deals don't always work out. You have to cut your losses and move on. We both lost today. Let's have peace and go our separate ways. I swear on my life, we will never interfere with your affairs again."

Sigourney shot him a deadly look. "You speak as if you are someone with the power to negotiate. Let me assure you, Darkken. Your soothing words might carry weight with swooning women, but they have no sway here. Only I have power here. True power. And to make an example of you for all to see and to hear from one end of Nalzambor to the other, I'm going to have your heads removed with your own swords." She grabbed Nath's and Darkken's sword belts and tossed them into the circle. "Gnolls, fill your hands with steel. In honor of Reaver and Slaughter, remove their heads from their shoulders!"

CHAPTER 67

CALYPSA WOKE UP CLUTCHING HER stomach. Pain shot through her body. She could still feel Maefon's black daggers of energy plunging into her body. Calypsa gasped for air. Her face was drenched with sweat. Her damp, matted hair clung over her eyes. An icy breeze tickled her neck. Where was she?

Shaking, she wiped her sweaty, tangled locks out of her eyes and spit dirt out of her mouth. A stream of water flowed somewhere nearby. The soft sound of water trickled off the rocks. The moon hung in the sky above, a huge and massive orb. Maefon's hateful face invaded her mind again. The woman had stabbed her over and over. She ran her hands over her body. The holes that had pierced her flesh were gone. She crawled over to a massive hole that had been dug in the ground. It was a grave, her grave. The dirt hole was mostly filled, but it looked as if someone had crawled out of it. Judging by the grime that covered her body, it was her. Somehow, she hadn't died, but Rond was still lifeless.

Tears flowed down Calypsa's cheeks. She'd lost everything. For the first time in her life, she was scared. Maefon, the elves, and that awful two-headed vulture were true killers. They were an evil unlike anything she'd faced before.

Rubbing her arms, she warmed herself and raised up on her feet.

I have to help Nath.

Hugging her shoulders, she started the trip north.

"Where do you think you are going, daughter?" The voice was soft, womanly, and carried like a warm and gentle wind.

With the warmth touching her face like a morning kiss of the sun, Calypsa stopped in her tracks. "Mother."

A soft-white illumination glowed in the deeper woodland. It came right toward Calypsa. A woman who could be Calypsa's sister came forward, bathed in glorious light. Her flowing hair was as green as maple leaves, and her long locks covered her splendid figure. Her skin was white as snow. An army of varmints strolled alongside and behind her. Her piercing brown eyes were full of ancient wisdom. She reached down and stroked Calypsa's cheek. "I have missed you. You don't heed my calls."

Calypsa's mother's touch took all the shivers from her body. The radiant woman was pure warmth and brought a natural energy. She was the Mother Queen of the dryads, a goddess among nature's creatures and her kind. To the world of the races, she was known as Yasmela.

"Mother, I am not ready to give up my life to the woodland. I have friends that I care for. They need me."

"Like that bugbear who lies in the ground." Yasmela kept a warming smile. "You need to embrace your destiny and remain by my side. My throne is yours to have, yet you avoid it. I don't understand that, but it must come from that unruly man in you."

"I like being who I am, and I'd like it even better if I knew who my father was, so I could thank him."

Yasmela's smile faded. "Don't say such a foolish thing, daughter. And I am the one that you should be thanking. You were dead and buried. I brought you to life again." She pointed at the dirt hole. "Or would you rather be back inside that grave with a stinking and rotting bugbear?"

"Don't say that about Rond. He was a friend, and I cared for him."

"And you got him killed, did you not?"

Calypsa sobbed.

Yasmela put her arms around her and warmly said, "Daughter, I have told you about this deranged world of the races. All they bring is devastation, pain, and suffering. Embrace what you are destined to be, the Queen Mother of the Dryads. Care for your people." She glanced down at the critters. "These innocent ones. Stop wrestling with that beast inside of you, and be one of us. I cherish you, daughter." She stroked Calypsa's hair. "I miss you by my side."

"I miss you too." Shuddering in her mother's arms, she let out a long cry. She couldn't stop thinking about Nath. He didn't have anybody, and he needed her. "I have to help my friend. He would do the same for me."

"Daughter, you need to cut your losses. You need to be with me." Yasmela broke off her embrace but firmly held her daughter's wrists. "The world of the races continues to do the same thing, over and again. Believe me, I've been watching for centuries. No matter what you do, nothing will ever change. Be neutral, and care for your own. It is the way of the dryad." She looked at Calypsa dead on. "Now I've given you life, not once but twice. Don't waste it, Calypsa. We are part of Nalzambor, thriving from its grand eternal power, but if we drift away, we will lose our magic. You don't want that to happen, do you?"

Calypsa shook her head.

"Good girl." Yasmela kissed her forehead. "So, you will come with me?"

Calypsa nodded. She didn't want to abandon Nath, but her mother's words were so powerful and convincing. Nath would have to figure it out on his own. Finding a little spark inside her, she said to her mother, "On one condition."

"Oh?"

"I want Rond back."

"He's in a very deteriorated condition, but I'll see what I can do." Yasmela put her arm over her daughter's shoulder and marched her toward the forest. "Or perhaps, we'll see what *you* can do. I think you are ready for the next step in your learning."

Chapter 68

Inside the ring of the poachers' fort courtyard, the gnolls started a shoving match with one another. They were fighting over who got to chop off Nath and Darkken's heads.

Meanwhile, Nath continued to fight against the unseen force that controlled his body. It was as if Sigourney was inside his head, controlling his will and every move. The more he fought it, the more he sweated.

Beside him, Darkken's sweat dripped off his chin. The veins inside his neck rose. The man's cool composure was gone. An anger stirred.

"Can't you use your magic again?" Nath whispered.

"I can barely remember my name at the moment." Darkken squeezed his eyes shut. "This power she controls, I can't get a handle on it. It's not like anything I've encountered before."

Nath understood that Darkken was a seasoned adventurer, but the way he spoke about his current situation seemed to suggest more. The fact that Darkken wielded magic was another mystery. "I just wish you would have used magic earlier. Why didn't you tell me about it?"

"I hate to rely on it, and in truth, I didn't want to tip the Caligin off." Darkken shot a look at the elves standing on the catwalks with Sigourney. "Now our enemies prepare for it. Maefon, do you have anything?"

Nath was on Darkken's left and Maefon on the right. Her damp blond locks clung to her perspiring face. She shook her head. "I can hardly think myself. I'm sorry… I failed."

Sigourney held the medallion in her hand like a precious little pet. She shouted down at the gnolls, pointing at the two who currently had the sword scabbards in their clawed hands. "You and you! Take the swords, and be done with this. The rest of you back off! I have deals to make and dragons to sell. Get on with it!"

The gnolls holding the belts shoved the others back. One of them was the one that had lost his hand to the dragon's bite. He ripped out Darkken's sword, Scalpel. The elven steel shined against the sun. The gnoll squinted. The second gnoll had more of a wolfish face with dark fur covering it. He pulled Fang out of the sheath and held the blade high with two hands. The army of hunters broke out in more wild cheers.

Sigourney shouted, "Silence!" The hunters and poachers went quiet. With a pulling gesture of her hand, Nath and Darkken slid over the dirt, scraping their knees. "Bow your heads. It will be easier to remove them that way."

Nath felt a powerful grip pushing his head down. He pushed back against the monstrous force. He was nothing but a child compared to the awesome power.

In the same predicament, Darkken's body heaved backward, but he didn't have the strength to withstand the unseen power. His head was shoved forward, forcing his chin to his chest. Angrily, he muttered under his breath, "No woman can wield such power!"

Maefon pleaded to Darkken, "I'm sorry. This is my fault. All mine."

"No, it's not your fault," Darkken admitted. "It was my overconfidence."

They seemed to be talking about something else that Nath didn't follow. Still, he tried to steal a glance at the gnoll holding his sword like he owned it. All he could see was the gnoll's hard waistline. The sword flashed across the gnoll's feet. Nath couldn't stand the thought of losing the sword given to him by his father to a gnoll. All he had tried to do was the right thing. The gnoll flashed the blade back and forth and made some long arching slashes. Nath said, "Fang, I'm sorry. All I ask is that you free that dragon and my friends if you can. Don't worry about me. Just take care of them first."

"Any last words?" Sigourney asked.

"No, don't do this!" Maefon cried out.

"I wasn't talking to you," Sigourney replied. "Since you have nothing left to say, hunters, finish it. Start with the younger one first."

The gnoll with Fang stepped to Nath's side. The one-handed gnoll moved to the right of Darkken. The gnoll with Fang stuck it in the ground, tip first, spat on its hands, and rubbed them together.

Sobbing, Maefon said, "I will avenge you, Darkken. And you, Nath, I swear it!"

The gnoll pulled Fang out of the ground. The perfect blade was lifted out of Nath's field of sight. "I can't believe I'm going to die from the strike of a blade my father gifted to me. Darkken, Maefon, I guess this is goodbye."

Trembling from head to toe, Darkken said, "It can't be."

"Oh, it is," Sigourney said with a humorless chuckle. "It certainly is. What are you waiting for, gnoll? Finish him."

Nath squeezed his eyes shut.

Maefon gasped.

Darkken screamed, "Noooooo!"

As he fought with everything in him to move, the hairs on Nath's arms stiffened. The air shimmered. A loud awe-filled gasp came from the surrounding throng. A hot light, like the warmth of a fireplace, massaged Nath's neck. The gnoll standing over him let out a painful howl. The smell of burning hair and flesh wafted into Nath's flaring nostrils. Opening his eyes, he witnessed the gnoll's body turning into black char with glowing orange veins cracking out of the seams.

"What trickery is this?" Sigourney shouted. "How dare you?"

With his limbs still locked up, Nath watched the gnoll's body fleck away. Fang fell along with the ashes. The blade hit the hard ground.

Ting!

A sonic wave of energy blew into everyone and everything surrounding Fang. Nath was knocked aside into Darkken. His limbs were free. He sprang to his feet. Darkken rolled across the ground with the one-handed gnoll, fighting for his sword. The surrounding mob lay on the ground. Many held their heads. Others slowly came to their feet. On the catwalk, Sigourney sagged in her throne, rubbing her temples. Eyes sweeping the grounds, Nath searched for Fang. The sword lay where it had fallen, several feet away. He dove for it. The sword shot out from underneath his grasping fingers. It sailed up to the catwalk straight as an arrow and embedded itself in the fort's wood.

Sigourney stood back on her feet with four elves right behind her. Her eyes burned like shimmering lightning. The elves' eyes did as well. Like a woman possessed, she said, "Now you have angered me." Her face turned ugly. It contorted, flexed, and pulsed, changing into some unknown monstrosity. A crown of waving tentacles came out of her hair. Her voice amplified a dozen times. "I'm going to rip you all apart one bit at a time!"

CHAPTER 69

"WHAT IN NALZAMBOR IS THAT?" Nath said with awe. Sigourney continued to transform into a larger, hideous version of herself. Her clothing stretched and ripped. The skin on her face turned slimy. Nath's stomach twisted into knots. The gorgeous woman had become some sort of abomination that looked like it had crawled out of some subterranean netherworld. Her skin was fleshy. Her hands became talons with three fingers and one thumb. Her eyes were large, slanted orbs, pulsating with power. As the tentacles on her head grew out like waving snakes, her head bulged. "Darkken? Maefon?"

Darkken punched a goblin unconscious. He took up his sword. The moment his gaze fell on Sigourney, his jaw hung open. "That explains a lot."

Pushing off of her belly and onto her feet, Maefon said, "What are you talking about?" She got a good look at Sigourney. "Ew. I didn't see that coming."

"Neither did I, but I should have." Darkken stared at Sigourney with a wary eye. "You are awfully far out of your element, aren't you, flayer?"

"Flayer?" Nath asked. As he did so, the Caligin drew their swords. The goblins and gnolls stared at their grossly transformed leader with confusion in their eyes. They murmured with one another.

"What's a flayer?" Nath asked.

"One of the greatest abominations to see the light of day. Creatures spawned in the depths of the Faalum Sea, the sailors say, while others believe them to be otherworldly." Darkken crossed his sword in front of his chest. "They are not magic but beings that control the wills of others by thought. They are mind erasers. Will benders. Thought destroyers. Body possessors."

"So, Sigourney is possessed?" Nath said.

"She probably didn't even know it," Darkken replied. "The flayers lurk unknowingly in a body, empowering them for their own desires, only to reveal themselves when needed. They are infiltrators, subtle, very much like the Caligin."

"You are very knowledgeable for a human." Sigourney's toes lifted off the catwalk. She floated several feet high. "I'm curious to understand how you know so much about my kind. We kill those who learn about us. Now it's time to find out what you know, Darkken, and how you know it." Her eyes brightened.

Darkken dropped his sword, clutched his head, and cried out in pain. The hair on his head stood on end. "Get out of my head, star fiend!"

A twisted smile came across Sigourney's distorted face. With a triumphant voice that echoed in every living person's thoughts, she said, "Hunters, poachers, and elves, kill the others while I peel open the mind of this one."

Nath and Maefon exchanged a quick glance. Maefon dove for Darkken's sword, scooped it up, and bounced back to her feet. Nath grabbed the bow while snatching a handful of arrows out of a quiver. The tips on the arrows all glowed a different color. "Do you know what these tips do?" he asked.

The goblins and gnolls, weapons in hand, encircled them.

Gripping Darkken's sword with two hands, she said, "I have no idea. Just shoot them!"

A pack of goblins rushed Nath. He notched three arrows on the bowstring. The tips of the arrows burned blue, green, and red. He pulled back the string and fired into the rushing goblins. The green-tipped arrow punched right through one hunter after another, hitting the wall behind them. The red-tipped arrow sailed high, hitting the portcullis at the main gate. A thunderous explosion boomed. The wall shook. Wood and rock debris showered the courtyard.

A sharp whistle cut through the air. The blue-tipped arrow moved through the bodies of the enemies in a stream of vibrant blue light. It passed through goblins and gnolls, penetrating armor, flesh, and bone. It curved through the air, cutting a circle of death through the ring of surging bodies. The goblins and gnolls fell down, clutching the holes that burned through their chests. Several of them, seeing the massacre of the magic missile, fled toward the smoking remains of the front gate. The arrow left almost a hundred dead poachers in its wake. It chased after those that fled on foot, zigzagging and popping through body after body. The goblins and gnolls bled out in a staggered line. Dead. The blue-tipped arrow vanished into the forest.

Maefon looked at the ring of dead bodies surrounding them. "Good shot."

Suspended in the air above them, Sigourney and Darkken were interlocked in a tangle of limbs. A shield of golden energy surrounded them. The tentacles in Sigourney's hair engulfed Darkken's face. His arms and legs kicked and flailed.

Nath snaked another arrow out of the quiver and fired at the flayer. The arrow skipped harmlessly off the globe of energy. He drew another and pulled the bowstring along his cheek. The tip of the arrow was fiery red.

"Nath, look out!" Maefon shouted.

A Caligin blindsided Nath with a side arm chop into his body. The blow derailed Nath's aim. He released the string, sending the arrow streaking into the sky, missing the globe by a half dozen feet. Nath spun around the elf, shoving the attacker away. Now two Caligin flanked him. They carried a sword in one hand and a dagger in the other. Their fiery eyes were locked on him. One of the elves, with hair longer than the other, darted at Nath and slashed. Nath parried the blow. The sword cut deep into the hard ashwood that made up the bow. The elf kept hacking into it, taking chips out of the wood.

"This is not working!" Nath said.

The second elf, blades poised to kill, pounced right at him.

CHAPTER 70

WITH EYES SHINING LIKE LIGHTNING, two Caligin attacked Maefon. She parried one sword and ducked underneath the swing of the other. Part of being a Caligin was being able to sell a good fight and make it look real. However, these Caligin were possessed by the flayer's powers. Backpedaling in the heaps of the dead, she batted their attacks aside. The skilled fighters were quick, but their movements were mechanical. She looked for an opening with elven steel colliding in loud clashes and bangs.

If I only had my power, I could end this right now!

Something seized her by the leg. It was a goblin that had fallen to the arrow. It had survived. With yellow eyes full of pain and hatred, it jerked on her ankle. With a quick downward slice, Maefon cut the goblin's hands off. She dashed over the piles of bodies away from her relentless attackers. Stealing a glance at the sky, she witnessed Darkken's arms and legs spread eagle and shaking. Her heart quavered.

What manner of monster can handle Darkken?

The flayer clearly wasn't anything that she'd even imagined before. Its powers of the mind were awesome. It controlled the wills of men and scrambled the sharpest minds. Its abilities were foreign to Maefon. Worst of all, it surprised Darkken. The unflappable man had been unseated. Now he appeared to be dying. In Maefon's heart, she knew that this wasn't a game. Darkken's scream was the sound of something having its soul ripped out. He was suffering.

Maefon parried a sword aside then released a counterattack. She thrust Scalpel into the meat of the elf's exposed shoulder. The second elf made her pay, sticking a dagger into the back of her thigh. The elf raised its sword over its head. Maefon took one hand from her sword grip, yanked the dagger out of her thigh, and a split second before the sword descended, punched the blade into the attacker's heart.

The elf's sword fell from his fingers. As the blade hit the ground, the elf with a nasty wound in the shoulder slashed at Maefon's neck. She flicked Scalpel up. The blade, light in her hand, caught the heavy-handed blow. The dull back end of her sword cracked her in the forehead. Warm blood ran down her nose. The blood in her eyes sent a fire right through her. Taking Scalpel in both hands, she put her back into a mighty swing and unleashed it. The lengthy sword blade whistled through the air.

The Caligin parried. Scalpel slipped past the blade and ripped into the elf's flesh, cutting it clean through the abdomen.

Sucking for breath, Maefon looked at the long-handled elven sword. "Thanks, Scalpel." Limping over the dead, she added, "Let's go help Nath."

Chapter 71

The longer-haired elf chopped through Nath's bow. Nath flung the bow and string at the shorter-haired elf rushing him. The elf chopped at the broken bow and string, but the busted bow tangled around his sword. Nath jumped away from his first attacker, searching for a weapon. Not seeing anything of use, he said, "I'll just be my own weapon." He stopped and faced off with his attackers.

Both elves ran right at him. Two swords and two daggers were one step away from cutting him down. There was something labored about their movement. Nath dropped and rolled underneath the thrusting blades. He knocked the legs out from under one elf, and the other hopped over him. He grappled with the one on the ground. They rolled over the dirt, wrestling over the blades. Nath clamped his hands on the elf's wrists. He was stronger, bigger, but the elf was no weakling. He twisted out of Nath's grip, punched Nath in the jaw, and scrambled away.

"No you don't!" Nath dove for the elf's legs, driving the elf down. The elf turned underneath him and stabbed hard into Nath's belly with the dagger. The breastplate sent the elf's weapon skidding aside. "Enough!" Nath punched the elf squarely in the jaw. The elf's eyes rolled up inside his head. The rest of his body went limp.

The scuff of soft footsteps caught Nath's ear. He snatched up the fallen elf's sword and turned. The longer-haired elf cocked back to thrust. A sword tip burst out of the front of the elf's chest. The elf's glowing eyes went out, and he fell dead on the ground.

Maefon stood behind the elf with the blood-stained sword in hand. "Nath, are you well?"

"I am." He looked up. "It's Darkken I'm worried about." The globe of energy that encased Darkken and Sigourney had risen twenty feet high. Darkken's face could no longer be seen. His upper body was covered by growing tentacles like slimy strands of hair. "It looks like that thing is eating him. We have to help him!"

"I don't know how to help him!" Maefon said.

Eyes sweeping the fort, Nath looked for any weapon that could help. He saw the quiver on the ground, but there was no bow. He spied the yellow streak dragon hanging by the rope. "Cut that dragon down," he said to Maefon. "I'm going after Fang."

Maefon nodded.

Nath raced up the catwalk and stood by the throne. He noticed his small backpack lying underneath the throne. He grabbed it, reached inside, and found the Gauntlet of Goam. Stuffing his fingers into the leather, he watched Darkken's body quake inside the globe. The tentacles were eating him. On the other side, underneath the catwalks, Maefon cut free the yellow streak dragon. Its tail whipped out, striking Maefon full in the chest. She fell back on her rear, clutching her chest. The dragon darted into the tunnels where the dungeons were and vanished.

Nath went after Fang. He pulled the sword free from the wall. "Fang, see that thing up there? We have to kill it and save Darkken. Are you with me?"

The steel of Fang's blade hummed. With Darkken trapped in the globe just ten feet away,

Nath backed against the wall. With only ten feet of runway, he sped forward, leapt off the edge, and shouted, "Dragon! Dragon!" He chopped hard at the bottom of the mystic bubble. Fang's steel ricocheted off, and Nath landed feet first on the ground. Fang's shining blade dimmed. Nothing happened to the globe. There was no scratch, slash, or dent. Darkken and the thought flayer slowly ascended.

Holding her side, Maefon limped alongside Nath. "What are we going to do?"

Slowly shaking his head, Nath replied, "I have no idea."

Tugging on Nath's arm, she said, "Look."

The yellow streak dragon emerged out of the tunnels. The burlap sacks that held the fledglings were inside her mouth. She spread her wings, raced over the ground, jumped, and took flight. The dragon cleared the top wall of the fort. Without looking back, the yellow-scaled dragon disappeared over the forest.

"At least you saved some dragons. Now all we have to do is save Darkken." Maefon snapped her finger. "Grab that quiver. I know where another bow is. I left one on the ledge." Maefon led the way back, limp-running, inside the tunnel and up the stairwell to the natural balcony on the hill. She picked up a bow that still lay there. "Something has to work. Let me see those arrows."

Nath pulled the arrows out of the black quiver. There were many colorful tips that glowed inside the arrowheads. Emerald green, citrine yellow, fiery red, orange, volcanic blue, and purple. She took out the red-tipped one. "Try this one," she said. "I'm certain it explodes on impact."

"Why don't you fire it?"

"No, if something goes wrong, I don't think I could live with myself." She handed Nath the bow. "Please, do it for me?"

Nath nodded and notched the arrow. Pulling the bowstring along his cheek, he took aim and fired. The red missile streaked through the air. It hit true to the mark. Darkken and the monster flayer shook inside the globe. The ball of energy quivered, blinking in and out. It began to slowly sink toward the ground. "It's working. Ha ha! It's working."

"Fire another one," Maefon urged. She placed another arrow in Nath's eager hand. He fired again. The explosion rocked the fort, but the orb held. "Impossible. It still stands."

Darkken's hands came to life. The strong arms of the big man wrapped around the monster. Suddenly, black smoke filled the globe. Strands of coppery lightning spider-webbed all over the inside of the globe. Inside the smoke, the tentacles of the flayer batted around wildly.

We have to get down there!" Maefon said. Together, she and Nath rushed back into the courtyard, jumping over the dead, and raced toward the center. A screeching blast wave of mental energy knocked them both flat on the ground.

A loud, endless scream tore at Nath's mind. He covered his ears, rolling over the dirt, yelling, "Make it stop! Make it stop!" Maefon curled up into the fetal position. He couldn't even see her face. Her body shook like a leaf. Forcing himself to his hands and knees with the awful shrill sound tearing at his brain, Nath crawled toward the descending globe. Inside the ball, two forces battled like raging storms. The screaming became louder and louder. A coppery spiral of energy spun inside the black smoke. Two figures and countless tentacles thrashed back and forth. On trembling arms, Nath crawled on. The Gauntlet of Goam's gem burned brightly, feeding new strength into his numb limbs. The globe touched ground right before Nath's eyes. He leaned back on his knees, drew back, and hit it with all of his might.

Ka-pow!

The globe fell away. A bed of black smoke drifted over the courtyard like tar. Nath found himself buried underneath that blanket of smoke and flat on his back. The jarring screaming inside his head was gone. Teeth clacking together, he rose above the smoke. In the haze, he saw the strapping figure of a large man standing, stoop shouldered, with a woman in his arms.

"Darkken!"

Chapter 72

By the time the smoke cleared, everyone was sitting in a circle with numb looks on their faces. Darkken had dried blood underneath his nostrils. His eyes were cracked and red. He twisted the rings on his fingers. Sigourney lay on the ground, breathing in hard, rapid breaths. Maefon had her knees to her chest, and the lone surviving Caligin who Nath had knocked out had been bound up but was sitting up and wide awake.

Darkken spit. "I don't know why, but my mouth tastes like metal. Perhaps that's the result of a near-death experience."

Nath shrugged. "So, you killed that thing. How?"

"I assure you, it's dead, in flesh anyway." Darkken squeezed his eyes shut and scratched the top of his head. "I learned something when it tried to pick apart my mind. The flayers have flesh and a spirit. It hosted in Sigourney's body, but when we threatened it, its physical body manifested through hers. And this isn't magic, either. It's an alien power. That was my mistake. I thought that medallion Sigourney wore was the source of her power. Instead, it was a darker power that resided within, and not even she knew it."

Maefon moved closer to Darkken and snaked her arms around his own. "I'm glad you survived. I don't know what I would do without you."

Darkken touched heads with her. "Your quick thinking saved me. And your bravery too."

"But how did you kill it?" Nath asked. "I know you are a fine swordsman, but now you wield powerful magic too. Enough to kill that monster that could split our heads in two with its thoughts."

"You seem disappointed, Nath," Darkken replied.

"No, I'm confused. It's just been an extreme turn of events. And you even knew what a flayer was."

"I was fortunate to identify what is was from my studies in the past. As for beating it, once I knew what my enemy was, I had a way to combat it." Darkken sighed. "There's three forces in this world. The mind, magic, and the flesh. The flayer attacked my mind, but I beat it with magic and flesh. But only because you intervened. Your attacks shook loose its concentration. That was the only way I could get a grip on the host body and unleash the magic I had left within. Perhaps I can teach you more about magic later, Nath. Being what you are, I think you would be very adept at it."

"Nath, we all live when we could have died," Maefon said. "Why all of the suspicion?"

"I just don't like all of the lies and deception. It bothers me."

"He has risked his life for you! We all almost died saving your dragons, and some of our brothers did," she said. "You are ungrat—"

Darkken put a hand to her mouth. "Please, we are all we have left. Let's not argue with one another. The reason I have not revealed my powers is, as I said, I didn't want to tip off the Caligin. The less they know about our resources and powers, the better." His eyes drifted over to the Caligin prisoner. "Speaking of which. We need to deal with this one. I bet he knows where Chazzan is."

The elf narrowed his eyes on Darkken.

"Nath, you might not want to come along for our interrogation. I'd hate to subject you to something that you are not comfortable with."

"You're going to torture him, aren't you?" Nath said.

Darkken replied with an exhausted look. "I promise you that we will do no worse to him than he would do to us." He stood and lifted the prisoner to his feet. "Come along, Maefon. Let's extract what we need and move on. You'll keep an eye on Sigourney, won't you, Nath?"

He waved them off. "You take care of him. I'll look after her."

Chapter 73

Darkken and Maefon dragged the Caligin prisoner back into the dungeon. The two elves that had survived a beating from Reaver and Slaughter were still in their cell but had managed to prop themselves up against the wall. Darkken shoved the Caligin into it. "It hasn't been one of our better moments. That much is certain. Stay put." He looked at Maefon. "Come, let's talk."

They huddled in another cell and sat on a rotting wooden bench. Darkken rested his face in his hands. He started to chuckle.

Maefon gave him a funny look. "Are you all right?"

Darkken looked at her with a radiant smile. "I haven't felt so alive in a long time. That, my dear, was harrowing."

"So, this wasn't all part of your plan?"

"Everything was a part of my plan, except for the flayer. That I didn't see." He laid his hand on her knee and squeezed. "Remember, no matter how perfectly laid your plans are, anything can happen. We are fortunate to be alive." He rubbed her thigh. "Very fortunate."

Darkken's words gave her a chill. She'd never seen him vulnerable before. He was a titan among the races, fearless, wise, and strong. But the flayer shook him. "So, if Nath and I hadn't intervened, the flayer would have defeated you? Killed you?"

He shrugged. "I don't know. I haven't died before, so it's very hard to say. Nath's sword, now that was a gift that gave us the break we needed. It's a truly special gift that protected him. If not for Fang's intervention, I might have had to reveal my full power to get us out of the predicament."

"So, you were in control?"

"I could have called down Galtur and perhaps done a few other things. I held the line as long as I could. It was… risky."

"How did you know what a flayer was?"

"Ha, you would have known what one was too if you had only read more of the tomes back at Stonewater Keep. I've studied and compiled information about every living creature on Nalzambor I could find. The flayers, well, their origins are still strangely unknown. Some say they are spawned from the great krakens of the sea. Others say they came from the stars in the sky. Nevertheless, I hope I don't cross their path again. They are dangerous." He wiped the caked blood from his nose. "It made me bleed. I don't like that."

"It looked like it was swallowing you whole. Was it eating you?"

"The flayer started devouring my knowledge. That's how they conquer. They absorb our thoughts, learning our strengths and weaknesses." He coughed and tapped his chest. "It's a good thing I was able to kill it."

"How did you kill it?"

"My will was stronger. And physically, they are weak. Shooting those explosive arrows made a difference. It let me get a grip on it. A very good thing too. Had it absorbed my knowledge, it also would have absorbed my plans and all I knew about the dragons. With that sort of knowledge, they could destroy the world."

"Isn't that what you want? To destroy the dragons and the world?"

"No, I want to destroy Balzurth and rule the world."

They sat in silence. Maefon pondered all that he had said. She found another level of respect for Darkken. The flayer had showed power beyond anything she'd imagined. It shook her. With mere thought, it almost killed them all. Darkken defeated it. She had the feeling that he still held back to fulfill the deception. For Darkken to hold the line, risking his own death, meant only one thing. Darkken's quest was for true power, beyond anything she could ever hope for. She liked it.

"I think it's time to move on to the next phase in the plan." Darkken stood and helped Maefon to her feet. "Are you ready?"

"Always."

The small fort had become a graveyard. Already the flies were gathering over the fallen bodies. The wind died down. A new stink lingered within the walls. Nath gathered his sword and backpack. He added the black quiver and arrows to his armament. He twirled a black-tipped arrow between his fingers.

I can't believe we killed all of these people.

His stomach remained queasy. Part of it was hunger. The other part was the muffled screams coming from the dungeons. Nath tried to tell himself that the elf deserved it—all of them did for killing dragons. Regardless, it didn't sit well with him. He looked toward the tunnel and shook his head. A scuffle behind him caused him to turn. Sigourney was moving. He trotted over to her.

Sigourney sat up, leaning back on her hands. Her pupils were huge. Blinking, she looked at Nath. Her face, though beautiful, now sagged and was haggard, and her damp, curly hair clung to her face. She fished a long strand of hair out of her mouth.

Nath took a knee in front of her. "Do you know what happened here?"

Her head slowly swiveled on her shoulders. Surveying the corpses, she said, "You killed them all. Reaver. Slaughter. You killed them."

"You didn't give us much of a choice," he said. "We gave you a way out. You didn't take it."

With a lost look, she said, "I saw it all happen, but it wasn't me. I was something else."

"Something called a flayer took you over. Darkken killed it. It's gone now."

"It was powerful. I felt like a god. It let me do incredible things." Her fingers played with the medallion on her chest. "All of this time, I thought the power of this medallion gave me the additional power." She tilted her head. "It was the flayer?"

"Apparently so."

She shivered. "I feel invaded."

"Now you know how the dragons you poach feel. It's unsettling, isn't it?"

"I'm a merchant. It's what I do. You have a peculiar affection for dragons. I like your passion. It's a shame we aren't on the same side of the fight. We could work wonderfully together, and I could teach a young man like you very much." She reached for his face. "Very much."

Nath pulled back. "After all of this, you will continue all that you do?"

"I will unless you kill me, but I don't think you will do that." She looked over his shoulder, toward the tunnels. "Where are the others?" A loud, painful howl echoed out of the tunnel. "Oh, I see. So, am I going to be tortured?"

Nath shrugged. "You should be."

"I'm not very comfortable letting someone lay their hands on me if I don't want them to. And I am the Merchant Queen. Torturing me would be a crime."

Nath glared at her. "Torturing dragons is a crime where I come from."

Taken aback, she said, "You are a fierce young warrior. I like the fire in those beautiful golden eyes. I'm not sure what you are after, but I'm not going to stick around to find out." Her fingers quickly rubbed the medallion. She winked at Nath. "Goodbye, Nath. Perhaps we will meet again on better terms." Her body faded.

Nath reached for her. His arms passed right through her disappearing body. Sigourney the Merchant Queen was gone. "Gads!"

Almost an hour later, Darkken and Maefon emerged from the tunnel. They were alone. "Where is Sigourney?" Darkken asked.

Nath sat on the ground with his arms locked over his knees. "It seems that her medallion had magic powers after all. She rubbed it and disappeared."

"Sultans of Sulfur," Darkken said. "I should have known better. Certainly the Merchant

Queen would have extra protection. Regardless, Nath, this is not your fault. We saved the dragons, and now we can move on." He walked over to Nath, offered his arm, and helped him to his feet. He hugged Nath. "Thank you for saving me. Both you and Maefon are my heroes."

Nath hugged him back. Breaking off the embrace, he asked, "Now what? Did you learn anything from the Caligin?"

Darkken nodded. "He revealed to us the location of one of Chazzan's hideouts."

"Where is it?"

"West," Darkken replied, "in a place called Stonewater Keep."

CHAPTER 74

Dragon Home (aka the Mountain of Doom)

SLIVVER, NATH'S SILVER-SHADE DRAGON BROTHER, roamed the massive hallways of Dragon Home. Clawed hands behind his back, the slender dragon of brilliant silvery scales walked upright like a man, dragging his tail behind him. For over two years, he had been worrying about Nath. His brother, the one destined to take the throne, was out in the deadly wilderness of the world, all alone. He passed by a group of dragons wandering the same halls on all fours. None of them spoke.

After the fledglings had been killed, many dragons had taken sides, and they were not speaking to one another. The High Council of Dragons ordered silence about the matter too, until Balzurth returned. In the meantime, they had banished Nath for one hundred years, as all dragons within were forbidden to leave, and none were allowed to enter. Though time was fleeting for a dragon, and two years was a drop in the bucket, it had been torture for Slivver.

The long-necked eight-foot-tall dragon sighed.

"Must you be so depressing?" a voice asked from behind him.

Slivver turned his serpentine neck.

It was Master Elween, a dark-green-scaled forest dragon. She was built much like him, walking upright, showing the hard, pale-green scales of her belly. Her long black eyelashes blinked. "And you are making a rut in the halls. Why don't you come and train with me awhile?"

"Train for what?" he said. "Waiting for Balzurth to return?"

"He's not been gone very long at all. Why don't you nap or hibernate like the others? I'll wake you when he comes back."

"I can't sleep, not with Nath out there all alone with no one to help."

Master Elween let out a humph. "I have prepared Nath for many things. And you are the one that is always gone. Nath, I'm certain, is fine. After all, he was trained by a great weapon master. Me."

"It takes more than weapons to survive the world of men. It takes wisdom." Slivver's wings unfolded and closed. "The world of the races is nasty and devious. I've been among them, I know. And this sinister group that I learned about, the Caligin, are the very root of evil."

"Evil elves. Who knew?"

"Yes, who knew?"

A cavernous voice echoed down the hall. "*Slivver. Master Elween. Come.*"

Master Elween's eyes became saucers. "Balzurth has returned!"

Slivver spread his wings wide and flew down the hall, not stopping until he came to the throne room's gargantuan doors. One of the doors was open. The High Council of Dragons exited, one at a time, necks and heads low, and slipped away into the darkness of the halls.

"Enter."

Together, Slivver and Master Elween entered the throne room of Balzurth. The door closed behind them. Piles of treasure as far as the eye could see filled the massive chamber. Jewelry and gems twinkled within the golden piles. Straight ahead, on a backless throne, sat the monstrous red dragon, Balzurth. Even sitting, his massive frame was still over thirty feet high. His great jaw rested on his fist. The gold in his eyes burned.

Slivver and Master Elween stopped in front of the throne, and like tiny children in the dragon king's midst, they took a knee and bowed.

"Rise." Balzurth's powerful voice was quieter this time. He looked down on them with disappointment. "I return from the murals only to find Dragon Home in complete chaos. The High Dragon Council has informed me of all that has transpired, and I'm not very fond of their perspective on the matter. Nevertheless, they did what must be done and avoided chaos."

Balzurth's eyes bore down on both of them before fully landing on Slivver. Slivver's wings tightened over his back, and he averted his eyes.

"Slivver, you did well defending your brother," Balzurth said. "The High Dragon Council mean well, but sometimes they are blinded by their preconceptions. I can understand their prejudice against Nath, given what has happened in the past. If not for your defense, they would have made an example of him, and I would have been helpless to do anything about it. I thank you."

Slivver swallowed. "You're welcome, Father. I'm glad that you have returned."

"Yes." Balzurth leaned back and scratched his chin with his claws. His eyes swept the room as if he was searching for something he had lost. "I wish I could have returned sooner, but it didn't seem as if I were gone so long. Perhaps a day or two. The matters beyond the mural are quite different. But the past is the past. We must deal with the matters at hand. What can you tell me about Nath and the Trahaydeen that would be helpful? The High Dragon Council was not very forthcoming."

"I told Nath about your other son, the one like him who killed the fledglings the first time. I told him about a movement of dark elves I came across called the Caligin," Slivver admitted. "I fear I told him too much, or he might not have left, but he was determined to avenge the dragons and clear himself in the eyes of all of the doubters. I'm sorry. I should have kept those things to myself, but Nath seemed so confused."

Balzurth nodded. "No, you did the right thing. Nath needed to know. I just wish I would have seen this coming. The Trahaydeen even fooled me. I adored the one, Maefon, but I gave Nath one command. I told him, do not leave Dragon Home until I return. The circumstances don't matter. He disobeyed, and there is a price for disobedience that we all must pay. Sometimes we learn from it. Other times, we die first."

Slivver and Master Elween exchanged a quick glance.

"My king, Nath is not dead, is he?" Master Elween asked.

"No," Balzurth responded. "I can still feel him. He lives. Where he lives and his condition, I do not know. My heart feels him."

"Now that you have returned, can you let us leave to find him? I can bring him back. And if I could access the Chamber of Murals, it would make it quicker. The High Dragon Council has banned me from the use of them."

"Now that I have returned, all dragons are free to come and go as they please."

Slivver and Elween showed smiling dragon teeth.

"But Nath's banishment remains. He cannot return."

Shoulders slumping, Slivver said, "What? You can't undo it?"

"I have to respect the decisions of my appointed leaders, and Nath made a poor decision. He should have stayed. I knew someday something like this would happen, just like it happened before with my fallen son. I fear that he is behind this." Balzurth eyed Slivver. "I think you figured that out for yourself."

"It's a guess, but who else would have the knowledge to attack Dragon Home?"

"Yes, I see no other conclusion. I fear this all was a clever design to roust Nath out of his home." Balzurth rested his hand on the curled arms of his throne. "We can only hope Nath is not lost to his brother's causes."

"And if Nath sides with his brother?"

"Then Nalzambor and the dragons therein are doomed."

"Well, let's send out the dragons and put an end to this menace," Elween said.

"I have a dozen silver shades at my disposal, Father. We will leave at once," Slivver added.

"No!" Balzurth shook the great horns on his head. "It is not that simple. This is a matter of the heart, a test where Nath must choose between good and evil. He will be tempted and tried. This walk, he must walk alone. He made that choice when he left."

"But he has no help," Elween said.

"I would not leave my son abandoned without a helper. I cannot send an army of dragons, but I can send some of his dearest friends. If you choose, the both of you may go after him."

Slivver and Elween slapped their paws together. Their tails clapped on the floor.

"Can we use the Chamber of Murals?" Slivver asked.

"You cannot. This mission is a discreet mission. I don't want the High Council of Dragons knowing. My fear is that there may be more spies among our brethren, and I need to stay here and find out who they are." Balzurth lifted a clawed finger. "And you will need help from the world of the races. After all, dragons can't go wandering the streets of men. No, you will need to find someone that you can trust. Start with a family that the dragons have always been able to rely on. The Bolderguilds."

Slivver slapped his scaly face. "No, not Brenwar."

"Who is Brenwar? What is a Bolderguild?" Elween asked.

Letting out a long, disappointed sigh, Slivver replied, "Just the slowest, crankiest bearded curmudgeon the world has even known. Father stuck me on one mission with him before. It made the days seem like years."

"Brenwar's an acquired taste, Elween. I think you'll like him," Balzurth said.

"Sure, if you like boiling water poured in your ear canal." Slivver picked at his ear hole. "If it wasn't for Nath, I wouldn't do it. Is there any more notorious ilk who will be tagging along for the journey?"

"Hopefully, you will find more friends along the path."

"Ha. With friends like Brenwar, who needs enemies?" Slivver looked at Elween. "Let's get this over with."

"Dragon speed, children."

Slivver and Elween bowed. "Dragon speed, oh king."

Chapter 75

Quintuklen - The City of Crowns

HACKSAW LAY ON A STONE slab inside an infirmary. A royal blue towel covered his waist. The deep-chested man's upper body was covered in hair and scars that had been sewn up. On both sides of him, two legionnaires cleaned and dressed his wounds. Like Hacksaw, they were older, with gray-white beards neatly trimmed. One of them was missing his left eye. The other walked with a limp.

"Hacksaw always had a knack for surviving," the one-eyed knight said. "But I do not think he will survive this. His sleep is deep, his breathing shallow." He put an ear to Hacksaw's chest. "His innards gurgle as if something still leaks inside there."

"No potion or salve can save a man on the brink. His time has come," the knight with the bad limp said. Though old, he was the younger of the two with some black still showing in his beard. "Every knight's time comes."

"True, but this knight rode the thunder. And he carries the unicorn's horn."

"The pipe? I don't believe that's unicorn horn. None have ever seen a unicorn."

"None of us, that is." The one-eyed knight rubbed some salve into the stitches. Hacksaw had over twenty entry and exit wounds in his body. "How else do you explain that he arrived here from wherever he was? He appeared, out of nowhere, in the legionnaires' hall, spilling his own blood on the marble. That's the unicorn's power. There is no other explanation."

"Well, I don't know about things that I haven't seen for myself. Believing is seeing."

"I saw it. I stood there the moment he arrived. Feathered shafts filled him."

"Who do you suppose shot him?"

The oldest knight looked down on Hacksaw's pale face. "Only he can answer that."

THE ODYSSEY OF

NATH DRAGON

BOOK 5

HUNTED

CRAIG HALLORAN

Chapter 1

On a clear day in Nalzambor, two dragons flew beneath the broken piles of clouds. Slivver's silver scales glinted in the glowing sun breaking between the clouds. Beside him flew Master Elween. The forest-green dragon's serpentine figure did graceful barrel rolls through the air. She let out a cheery roar. Slivver spread out his wings, letting the air lift him higher, and dove quickly downward. He let out his own mighty roar that sounded like ten lions.

Elween's dark-green wings gently beat against the wind. She stretched out her neck to full length. She dove, like a missile, careening on a deadly path before it hit the earth.

"I see what you are playing!" Slivver shouted. He turned after her in pursuit, aiming at the long, slender tail that waved stiffly behind her. He caught up to her, pulling in right alongside her. "You can't outfly a silver shade."

"Oh, but can't I?" she said, eyeing him with supreme confidence. "Let's see who can skim the ground closest before crashing into it then, mighty Slivver."

"You're challenging me to a pull up? So be it then!" Slivver bore down toward the ground. The air whistled through his horns, making a sharp shrilling sound. Beside him, Elween's scale-covered figure made a whistling sound of its own. Her wings were folded behind her back, and her gemstone eyes were fastened on the ground.

A field of green peppered in colorful wildflowers waited to catch them below. A band of wild horses galloped across the plains. Only a thousand feet remained between the dragons and the ground.

"You better get ready to pull up," Slivver shouted.

"Never! You better pull up!" Elween edged past him.

Slivver counted the space out in his head. The pull up was a game that dragons played as soon as their wings let them fly. The entire goal was to see who would chicken out first. Whoever spread their wings first usually lost. Slivver never lost. *Three hundred. Two hundred. One hundred.* He glanced at Elween. Her eyes were set. *Fifty feet.* "Pull up!" *Twenty-five!*

Elween's wings sprang out.

Slivver laughed. Fanning out his wings, he pulled up just in time to let his belly skim the ground. He turned to see Elween skipping over the grasses like a stone being skipped across a pond. She made a trail forty feet long before coming to a stop in a heap. She didn't move. "Oh no!" Slivver dashed to her side.

Elween's body started to spasm, scales shaking all over.

Slivver gathered himself along her side. "Speak to me, Elween. Speak to me."

She sat up, laughing. Dirt covered her body, and clods of grass and wildflowers were stuck between her horns. With a cheery voice she said, "That was fun!"

"I'm glad you are well. You almost scared the dragon dung out of me." He eyed her horns. "I like your hat. It's very fitting."

Both dragons broke up laughing. Finally, Slivver helped Elween to her feet. She stood almost as tall as him, just over seven feet, with a tail that swished over the grasses. Both of them had long arms and legs, more like men. They walked upright just as comfortably as they did on all fours. In a way, they were dragon-like men, with wings. He dusted the dirt from her forest-green scales while she wiped the soil crusting over her long eyelashes from her eyes. "That was a very impressive maneuver for someone that has not stretched her wings in a while."

"I've been in the mountain so long that I'd almost forgotten the joy of flying. I'm not so sure I want to go back in the mountain again." She breathed deeply through her nostrils. "The air is much fresher here. Uh, Slivver, would you mind if we walked for a while? I love the flying, but being a forest dragon, well, you know I also enjoy the beauty of the earth."

"Certainly. I'm not in a rush for our rendezvous with Bolderguild anyway. But we can't remain exposed very long. The farther out of sight, and higher in the air, the better."

Elween pointed a claw at the forest line, not so far in the distance. Its outer layer was barricaded by shrubbery thick with thorns. "The willowwacks look as safe a place to roam as any. You are the seasoned dragon in worldly affairs. Please." She stepped aside. "Lead the way."

Elbows out and strutting like a man, Slivver led the way to the woodland. Finding a gap in the bush, he pushed some of it aside, letting Elween enter the shade of the green leafy trees.

Looking at him, Elween said, "You really do like acting like a man, don't you?"

Scratching his long neck, he said, "I find the races highly imaginative. They have amazing inventions in their cities and seem to live such robust lives. I really appreciate the grand efforts they put into their doings."

"I can understand that, but their imaginations are often wicked, and the unwise often mistake evil for good. Is that not so?"

"It's that way everywhere, I suppose. But it is exciting."

"Well, that isn't the kind of excitement I'm looking for. I just want to find Nath." Elween looked up into the branches. Two chipmunks were sitting side by side, looking down on her. They scurried down the trunk and hopped onto her shoulders. She giggled. "Look, I have followers. Cute ones too. I wonder what they taste like?"

"It's hardly a meal, but I've never had chipmunk before." Slivver opened his jaws wide.

Quick as a batting eyelash, Elween plucked both of the chipmunks into her hands. She tossed one of them into Slivver's open maul and chomped down the other. She clacked her teeth together. "Bland. Very bland."

"Agreed. We'll have to find you a plate of people food and see what you think about that."

She tilted her head. "Is people food made of people?"

"Don't be silly. People don't eat people, generally speaking. It's mostly food from livestock and farmed in gardens and trees." Slivver gave her a quizzical look. "Certainly you knew that? Are you teasing me, Elween?"

"Yes, but only because you are easy to tease." Her nostrils flared. She sniffed. "What is that horrid smell?"

Slivver's eyes narrowed. His tail stiffened behind him. The low branches rustled. He twisted his head toward the sound. Monstrous hooved beasts burst out from behind the tree, bearing down on them with murder in their eyes.

CHAPTER 2

ICY BITS OF SNOW STUNG Nath's cheeks. Dark-gray clouds floated slowly across the sky. The highland grasses were frosted with snow as he followed Darkken's trail. They were headed west toward Stonewater Keep, where Chazzan could be. Chazzan, the former leader of the Trahaydeen, from Dragon Home, turned Caligin, was Maefon's former love, but he had been killed by Lord Darkken. Nath was still under the belief that Chazzan was the leader of the Caligin and that he still lived. It was just what Darkken wanted.

Darkken moved with the grace of a brawny forest feline. His stride was easy, and his shoulder-length copper hair swept across his back. He was an imposing figure in his black leather armor, elven sword on hip, and arms swinging at his sides. Darkken glanced back at Nath, gave a nod, and kept going.

Stonewater Keep wasn't far from where they'd departed the poachers' fort. From what they gathered from the Caligin, it was a three-day walk at most. With the Brothers of the Wind who survived the battle with the half-giant brothers, Reaver and Slaughter, Darkken wanted to rally more forces. They spent the next several days doing so. Now a band of twenty more Brothers of the Wind joined them. They wore the leather clothing and fur of hunters. Swords and daggers dressed their narrow hips. Many slung a quiver over their backs and carried a bow in hand. They all had some feathers and braids in their hair and hardly said a word.

Nath turned and walked backward to face Maefon. She moved on silent footsteps right behind him, using his body as a shield from the wind. A heavy dark-green blanket was wrapped over her shoulder. Her short, wavy blond hair hung just over her sparkling eyes. Her soft lips had turned a little blue. "You look like you are freezing to death."

"I haven't been warm since the fire ended last night," Maefon said. "Achoo! I feel like an icicle."

"Don't you mean an elf-cicle?"

"Ha-ha," she said, shooting an irritated look at him. "That might be funny if it was you freezing and not me. Tell me, does your dragon blood keep you warm? I haven't ever seen a chill bump on your body."

Nath shrugged. "I suppose it does. As for you, the other elves and Darkken seem to be doing well. Not a one of them has shivered."

She narrowed her eyes on him.

"What?" he said. "It's just an observation."

She sneezed so hard she slipped on the grass and fell down.

Nath helped her up by the elbow. Chuckling, he said, "I never saw someone sneeze so hard that they fell. What is wrong with you?"

"I think I'm sick," she said, wiping her nose on her blanket.

"Sick? What do you mean?"

She rolled her eyes. "Yes, I can only imagine that you don't get sick either. I think being in that filthy dungeon made me sick. That's what happens when you are forced to lie in the grime and dirt. Illness comes. It can kill."

"You're going to die?" He wrapped her in his arms and held her tight. "I won't let you die. We'll find a cure for you!"

"No. I won't die." She sneezed into his chest. "It will pass. I just have to feel like I'm dying." She nuzzled into his chest. "You could let go of me, but it feels good. You're warm."

"Just stay put." His eyes slid to his right. The elves had formed a ring around them both, eyeing them with deadpan stares.

Darkken approached Nath with a raised eyebrow. "What's going on? Are we having a moment?"

"Maefon says she is sick," Nath replied.

She pushed out of his arms. "I can speak for myself. I am fine, Darkken. Just as chill as the bottom of a well. I can manage."

Darkken covered her forehead with the palm of his hand. "You're burning hot with fever. Dearest, I am so sorry!" His gaze slid over to Nath. "Are you well?"

Nath nodded.

"You shouldn't be walking, Maefon." Darkken scooped her up in his arms. "You need to rest."

"Darkken, no," she pleaded. "I feel silly."

"No arguments. We should make the river by dusk. We'll camp, set you by the fire, and hope your fever breaks." He gave Nath a nod. "Come along. I'll probably need you to share the load with me. My back has limitations."

"I'll help any way I can," Nath said, looking at Maefon. He'd never seen her in such poor condition. Cradled in Darkken's arms, she seemed to shrivel as she shivered, sneezed, and coughed. He reached out and touched her cheek. "We'll get you through this."

She gave a feeble nod and squeezed her eyes shut.

"Sultans of Sulfur, she sleeps," Darkken commented.

"Is that bad?"

"No, it should be good, but this fever took her quick. One never knows with sickness and disease. There are so many dangerous forms." Darkken's chin sagged. "The most danger lies in what cannot be seen. Remember that, Nath. There is much in this world that we do not comprehend."

"I will."

Pushing through the wind, they marched on, with the elves walking in rows in front of and behind them. Darkken and Nath exchanged Maefon between them a few times before they made it to the river. The Brothers of the Wind made a fire and pitched a small tent just big enough to shield her from the wind.

Darkken bundled her up in her blanket and lay her inside the tent. "Keep that fire going. She needs all the warmth she can get."

Chapter 3

"CENTAURS!" SLIVVER SHOUTED TO ELWEEN. Flattening to all fours, he scurried out of the half man, half horse's path.

The centaur had an extraordinary physique. Standing over eight feet tall, the bare-chested, coarse-haired brute's upper body was layered in thick muscle. The centaur reared around, glaring black eyes fastening on Slivver. The centaur carried a branch crudely fashioned into a spear. Horns like a ram's curled back out of his skull. The centaur reared up on its hind legs and chortled weirdly like a wild horse. Coming down hard, the brutish centaur's front hoof clawed at the ground. The centaur charged.

Slivver slipped away from the centaur's crude spear. The wood shaft snapped against the trunk of the tree. He'd collided in many battles with assortments of races and creatures. The centaurs were among them. They were a strange breed of brutes, like giants, known for exceptional cruelty and twisted imaginations. They would hunt, kill, and torment anything that was not their species. They were fierce warriors with a deep and devious code of destruction.

The centaur kicked Slivver, his rear legs catching Slivver full in the chest. He crashed wings first into a tree. He lifted his head up. The centaur came upon him horns first, crushing him into the ground. The centaur's massive arms pumped hard fists into Slivver's body.

Slivver roared in the centaur's bearded face. The wild-eyed centaur's eyes filled with new rage. The monster punched harder, knuckles as hard as rocks busting into Slivver's scales. The centaur chanted in broken, garbled speech. Spit flew from his wide mouth.

Slivver shook his long neck. "Enough of this!"

His mouth cracked wide open, and a strand of white lightning shot out. The bolt seared the monster's hairy chest. The centaur's eyes lit up like lanterns. The lightning raced through the man-beast's body, searing holes through his fur and skin. He backed off, bucking and flailing his arms like a man on fire. The lightning did its work. Silvery strings of energy worked through the man-beast's body, singeing hairs and turning them to ash. The centaur bolted away at a full gallop, crashed into a tree face-first, fell over, and died.

Slivver rose up on his hind legs. He rubbed the scales on his chest, wincing as he did so. "I felt every bit of that. Ugh." Gathering his senses, he hustled toward the spot where he last saw Elween. A second centaur had chased her into the woods. Following the disturbed ground, he quickly came upon her in the next clearing. Holding a crudely made spear that was broken in half, Elween stooped over a centaur that lay at her feet. It appeared to be dead but didn't have a mark on it. Crossing his arms over his chest, Slivver asked, "Is it dead?"

"Of course it's dead. I wouldn't want to let a centaur attack me and live to tell about it. That would be shameful." Elween tossed the broken spear to Slivver. It was the top half of the shaft. She looked down at a spot out of Slivver's view. "Come."

Slivver walked to the other side of the bestial creature. The broken front end of the spear protruded from the centaur's chest. "You hit the heart?"

Elween nodded. "A blow to the heart will slay most creatures."

"You killed it with its own weapon. How did you disarm it?"

Elween patted Slivver on the back. "You would know the answer to that if you spent more time training with me."

"I don't have need for the archaic weapons of the races."

"Says the dragon that wants to be a man," she replied.

"Touché."

Slivver and Elween abandoned the area. They walked in silence for a few miles then resumed an old conversation. "Elween, you know Balzurth as well as any. Do you suspect that he knows… things?"

"What do you mean?" She ducked under the low-hanging leafy branches and held them aside for Slivver.

"I've always had a suspicious feeling that Balzurth knows what is going to happen before it happens."

"So you think he knew that Nath would leave? Do you realize what you're implying? That would mean that Balzurth knew the fledglings would be slaughtered."

"No," Slivver replied. "I don't think Balzurth has that sort of foreknowledge. I believe he knew when he left that Nath would be tempted to leave. As eager as Nath was to spread his wings, it only makes sense. It was a test."

"I don't follow. You still imply that Balzurth knew something bad would happen. What else would tempt Nath to leave?" Elween sighed. "And if Balzurth knew that, wouldn't he know about the corruption of the Trahaydeen?"

Slivver shook his head. "I don't know. I just think that in life, there are things that are destined to happen, one way or the other. I feel Balzurth understands that, but he still cannot change the actions motivated by the hearts of others. And who can change one's destiny? The path might sway, bend, and twist, but it still remains a path."

"Hah, you are a deeper thinker than I've given you credit for, Slivver," she said.

"What is that supposed to mean?"

"I always thought you were aloof and well... stupid."

"Stupid!"

Elween let out a growling chuckle. "I'm only teasing."

"No, I don't think you are." He gave her a stiff shove. "Stupid. You've debased me into the class of the red rocks lizards and dwarves."

"I thought dwarves were stubborn, but very intelligent."

"I'll let you decide once you meet the Bolderguilds. Tell me, what is the difference between stubborn and stupid?" he asked.

"Stubborn has merit."

"Give me an example."

"Let me get back to you on that."

Chapter 4

It was morning. Nath kneeled down by the river and filled his water skin. Rapids flowed between the icy snow-covered rocks that jutted out of the cold black river, providing a constant roar. The winds whistled through the rigid grasses. It had been a long night without sleep, though he needed little of it. Maefon's wet coughing would wake him whenever he dozed off for a bit. He paced the riverbank, alone, while Darkken remained inside the small tent, keeping Maefon warm.

Whatever this fever is, I hope it passes soon.

Sickness was something foreign to Nath. Dragons, as far as he knew, didn't get sick. The other races, more fragile, were subject to a strange toxicity that could not be seen. He put the cap on his skin and headed back downriver toward the tent. He passed by two Brothers of the Wind who stood on the edge of the waters. Their hooded cloaks covered them down to their buckskin boots. Wrapped tight in their garb, they didn't acknowledge Nath's nod when he walked by.

"Good morning to you too," Nath said, shaking his head and moving on.

They have the personality of a dead tree stump.

The Brothers of the Wind were a lot more rigid than Darkken, Maefon, or any of the Trahaydeen he had known. It was unsettling. The worst part was that he hated to admit that maybe, just maybe, Hacksaw, the old knight from Huskan and Nath's departed ally, was right with his suspicions. He wondered how the old knight was. He missed him.

Hacksaw, I hope you are back in Huskan with your feet propped up by the fire. Drink some of that awful pumpkin cider for me.

Four elves were huddled over the campfire. They left a gap between them, allowing the heat to warm the side of the tent. Behind the tent, more of the elves stood in the grasses, eyeing their surroundings. Their piercing eyes passed over Nath like a chill wind.

Darkken emerged from the tent. He put his hands on his hips and arched his back. "That tent is barely made for one, let alone two." He found Nath staring at him. "She's doing well. Not out of the woods yet, but the coughing has subsided, and there is more color in her cheeks."

"So, she'll get better?" Nath asked.

"I'm confident she will. With any luck, the fever will break today. She's strong and has weathered far worse dilemmas, such as when Chazzan stabbed her." A deep frown crossed Darkken's face. "She was wrought with fever then. I don't know how she made it, such a small little thing, but she did. Her will to live is as strong as iron. I love that about her."

"Me too." Nath started toward the tent. "Can I see her?"

Darkken put a firm hand on his shoulder. "In a moment, Nath. I came out because, though I am loath to leave her side, I'm feeling antsy. I was hoping to stretch my legs and do some scouting while you look after her."

"Scouting? You mean, you're going to Stonewater Keep?"

"We need to get a glimpse. I was going to take half of the Brothers of the Wind with me and leave the rest with you. You can watch after Maefon while I'm gone. As I understand it, according to the Caligin we captured, we are less than half a league from Chazzan's threshold."

Not hiding his disappointment, Nath said, "We should stay together. Wait for Maefon to heal."

"It's just a scouting mission, Nath. We do this all the time. We'll depart immediately, find a safe place to cross the river, and return by dusk." Darkken patted Nath's shoulder. "You won't even have time to miss us."

"But—"

Darkken made a sharp whistle. Ten of the Brothers of the Wind moved out of their posts surrounding the tent. In a single column, they eased south down the riverbank, with Darkken falling in last. Turning and walking backward, Darkken smiled and waved. "We'll hunt for pheasant along the way. And remember, keep that campfire burning. I'm trusting the love of my life into your caring hands."

Nath's mouth hung open as the group of elves and Darkken walked along the river and vanished at the first westward bend. Slowly, Nath moved a strand of hair out of his mouth. He wanted to go. Instead, he'd been left standing in the cold. Two elves slipped along his sides, following his stare. Nath looked at the one on his left. The elf's penetrating dark eyes held his. With smooth and creaseless skin, the elf made a slender smile and said in Elven, "They'll return. Care if some of us hunt while we wait?"

"No, that would be fine."

The elf nodded. "The other half of us will stay behind." The two elves gathered three more. Bows in the hands of all five of them, they headed away from the river into the tall grasses.

Not used to the elves ever speaking to him, Nath said to himself, "That was odd." Though it gave him some comfort, a feeling a normalcy, that had been lacking for quite some time. He was getting used to them, and they, it seemed, were getting used to him. He moved over to the campfire and warmed his hands over the dying flames. He made a quick trip up the riverbank, gathered driftwood, and came back. He found Maefon, wrapped up in a blanket, huddled over the fire.

"Maefon!" He hustled toward her.

She didn't turn. Her lithe body quaked inside the blankets.

Dropping the driftwood in the fire, he kneeled in front of her. Her eyes were weak, skin pale, and lips cracked. "You need to get back inside and out of this harsh wind."

"No." Her voice was dry and raspy. "My toes are cold. I need to warm them."

"You need to stay inside until the fever breaks," Nath insisted.

She shook her head.

"Let me at least get you something to drink."

She nodded.

Nath found his water skin and helped her drink. "Drink a lot or you'll shrivel."

She gulped down several swallows then let out a gasp. "I'm still ice-cold but feeling a tad stronger."

"That's good."

Her eyes scanned the camp. "So, Darkken is gone?"

"They are scouting."

She took his hands in hers, pulled him close, got cheek to cheek with him, and said in his ear, "Nath, come into the tent with me and keep me warm."

CHAPTER 5

HIGH IN THE SKY, SLIVVER and Elween circled above Morgdon, the dwarven city. The vast city of stone and iron had been hewn out of the mountains, supported and also framed by massive beams of iron. It was perfectly fortified, a mountain castle full of mighty spires and watchtowers.

As they glided in the sky, Elween said to Slivver, "So, do we drop in and find this Bolderguild?"

Shaking his head, Slivver replied, "No, the dwarves wouldn't take kindly to a pair of dragons dropping in, or anyone else for the matter. Do you see those ballistae in the towers? I'm fairly certain they are loaded with moorite bolts that could shred us."

"If they can hit us."

"Can you dodge a hail of fifty missiles at once?"

"Probably."

"I'd rather not see that happen," Slivver replied. With his keen eyes, he could make out the dwarves milling about. The stocky, bearded men worked, marched, drank, ate, and reveled. Dedicated to their backbreaking engineering and laboring feats, they often ran for long hours over many months. Once they finished the task, they spent a great deal of time celebrating their hard work. Morgdon was a hive of activity in all shapes and forms. A well-organized, proud, hardworking unit.

"So, how are we supposed to find this Bolderguild? Do we knock at the front gate?" she asked.

"The dwarves are private, though known to have many guests, as they love to show off their accomplishments. But we want to use discretion. Two dragons stopping by for a visit will draw a great deal of attention. We just need to be seen long enough for the Bolderguilds to get notice of our presence."

"That's it, fly above them and circle a few times?" she said.

"That will do it. Follow me." Slivver beat his wings and jetted away in the skies. With Elween in pursuit, he dove toward the icy caps in the mountains, landing beside a guard tower made from stone in deteriorating condition that had been abandoned likely centuries ago. The tower had a clear view of the western valley that stretched out as far as the eye could see. "We'll wait for him here."

Walking around the base of the tower that stood on legs made from solid columns of chiseled stone, Elween said, "A very remote location for a rendezvous."

"Yes, and it will probably take days for Brenwar to get here. Hence, we wait on this bitter mountain, watching the snow fall around us." He shook his head. "Of all the people Balzurth had me team up with, why Brenwar? Why not a turtle or a sloth?"

"Certainly the dwarf has some merit if Balzurth is so fond of him," Elween said. She scratched ice from the tower's legs. "What choice would you have made?"

"Elves are quick and just as reliable. I've journeyed with them before, and I find them enjoyable. And they are willing to ride on the backs of dragons without having a tantrum." He flexed out his wings and folded them back in. "Of course, I'm not big enough to ride, but I'm plenty strong enough to carry them in my arms. Generally speaking, they are light. The dwarves are heavy as stones. Dead weight, just like their personalities."

A chunk of snow fell from the roof on the top of the tower, landing on the ground near Elween's feet. She glanced up. "Slivver, look out!"

Slivver looked up. An icy ball of snow hit him square in the face. Wiping the frozen grit out of his ice-blue eyes, he opened up his maw. A lightning bolt shot out of his mouth into the tower. Chunks of stone exploded from the guard tower's roost. A burly figure jumped out of the tower, landing deep in the drifts of snow. Slivver and Elween flanked the menace buried in the snow.

"Reveal yourself or die," Slivver said.

Deep laughter came from the snow as a burly bearded figure emerged. Short and stocky, a dwarf with a braided beard covered in snow came forward. He patted the belly of his breastplate arm and started laughing uproariously. He pointed a stubby finger at Slivver. "Bah-ha-ha-ha-ha! If you only could have seen your scaly face when I hit you. Ah, hahaha-haha!"

"Brenwar! You dare do a foolish thing at your own peril!" Slivver swiped his tail at Brenwar's feet, knocking him onto his backside. The dwarf landed in the soft snow but continued laughing. Slivver glanced at Elween. There was a playful look in her eyes. He pointed his clawed finger at her. "Don't you laugh too."

"Please, laugh, green dragon lady," Brenwar said as he pushed himself out of the snow. "It's always a chuckle to get the best of Slivver." Brenwar waded through the ankle-deep snow. He shoveled out the snow with his hands and picked up an oaken keg barrel that had busted open. "Ah! See what you did? You destroyed my ale!" Seeing the ale-stained snow, he packed it into a snowball and started eating it. "Hmm… all is not lost."

Elween giggled. "He's very resourceful, you have to admit. And humorous," she said. "I can see why Balzurth likes him."

"Don't be too elated. He's drunk. That's the only reason he's happy." Slivver packed a snowball in his paws and slung it at Brenwar. Brenwar swatted it down. "Brenwar, tell me, how did you get here so quick? We just flew over Morgdon. With those stumpy legs, it's impossible that you could get here so fast."

"Don't knock my stumpy legs." Brenwar marched in place in the snow. "They got me here before those wings of yours did, didn't they?"

"Out with it, dwarf. I know you didn't just run up here."

"No, I've been up here, waiting on you." Brenwar swallowed down his snowball and made another. The fine breastplate made from dwarven steel shined underneath the gaps between the braids of his beard. His bare arms bulged with brawny muscle. He packed up another ale snowball and ate it then winked at Elween. "I'm a good planner. That's why I beat you."

"Balzurth sent word, didn't he?" Slivver said with a snort.

"I knew I was going to be here before you even knew you were coming here," Brenwar bragged. "Bothers you, don't it?"

"Everything about you bothers me." Slivver walked up to Brenwar and swatted the snowball out of his hands.

Brenwar shoved him in the chest. "Don't test me, Slivver. I'll tear those scales right off of you."

"Then quit fooling around and pay attention. We have a mission, and we don't want to take a lifetime to complete it, like the others that you manage to delay."

"Dwarves don't fool around. Everything we do has purpose."

"Hitting me with a snowball had purpose?"

"Aye, it aggravated you, didn't it?" Brenwar picked up a chunk of rock from the ground and carried it over to the legs of the tower. With the heavy chunk in hand, he said, "I'm going to have to fix this before we leave."

"You aren't fixing anything. It was already in shambles!" Slivver's clawed fingers clutched in and out. "We need to leave."

"Don't let him get underneath your scales, Slivver." Elween narrowed her eyes on Brenwar. "He's only teasing you."

Brenwar dropped the rock in the snow. He walked over to her and extended his hand. "Brenwar Bolderguild. Very nice to meet you... er... what is your name?"

She took his hand. "Master Elween." She batted her lashes at him. "But you can call me Elween."

Brenwar offered her his elbow. "How about I escort you down this mountain?"

Slivver pushed between the two. "How about I roll you right down it?"

"I'd like to see you try, dragon!"

"Don't tempt me, dwarf!"

Chapter 6

INSIDE THE TENT, MAEFON LAY with her back to Nath, cuddled in his arms. She slept soundly with a gentle snoring. Her soft hair tickled Nath's nose. He didn't sleep at all. Instead, he remained restless, concerned about when Darkken would come back. It would be odd if the man came back only to find Maefon wrapped up in Nath's arms. Not to mention, Nath enjoyed her body against his. He cared for her, even loved her. It seemed like old times but still dealing with the same forbidden love.

What's done is done, I suppose. There won't be any secrets from the Brothers of the Wind, anyway. Whatever they see, I'm certain they'll tell him. Besides, he did tell me to take care of her. And she's sick. It's not as if anything is going to happen.

Maefon stirred. Her shapely body pushed into his. Her small hand gripped his. Suddenly, she turned. Her eyes fastened on his. Her teardrop face was beaded with sweat. Her body warmed.

"What is wrong? You're sweating like a waterfall."

She made an easy smile. Caressing the side of his cheek with the backs of her fingers, she said, "It's a sign. My fever must be breaking."

"Are you sure it's a good sign? It doesn't look good."

"No, it's good. Trust me. I can feel my body returning to me already."

"I can too."

"What is that supposed to mean? Nath, are you flirting with me?"

He couldn't hide the fact that he wanted her. "It's very cozy in here, making it very hard not to notice a beautiful elf lying in your arms. But I'm just trying to help."

"You are feeling bolder. I like it." She moved her lips toward his then broke out in a fit of coughing.

Nath gently patted her back. "Maybe we should take that as a sign not to spark our romance. Besides…"

"Besides what?" she said, rubbing her throat.

"Darkken. And this tent probably isn't hiding anything from prying eyes."

She took his hand. "Oh, they won't say anything. We are a brotherhood, but we elves also stick together, if you know what I mean." She kissed his cheek with very soft lips and whispered in his ear, "Our secret would be safe."

Nath nodded. "That's good to know, but wouldn't you feel guilty? I know that I do."

"I'm torn between the man I loved and the man that saved me. I love you both. Besides, can't a woman desire two extremely handsome men?"

"I see how it can be confusing, but I would never betray a friend." Nath pulled his hand free from hers. "I'm going to check the fire and fetch you some water. The way you are sweating, you are going to need it."

"Ha-ha, Nath. Charming and full of wit, but you can't evade me forever."

Nath slipped out of the tent and headed straight for the river. There were only a couple hours of daylight left. He stood on the riverbank, staring over the waters to the other side. He was burning up with passion. He began seeing him and Maefon together in his mind more often. Deep inside, he knew it wasn't right and not because she was an elf and he was a dragon but because he considered himself Darkken's friend. He grabbed a stone and skipped it over the surging waters.

Part of me wants to go home. But what am I supposed to do when I've been exiled for a hundred years? The only way to go home is to hunt down the elves who murdered the fledglings and bring justice.

He spent the next few hours sorting through his thoughts and pacing alongside the river. The elves who'd gone hunting returned, hauling back a young buck. They skinned it and began cooking the meat. They ate quietly, talking in Elven, adding some atmosphere to an otherwise gloomy situation. One of them offered a stick of cooked venison to Nath. With a nod, he took it and ate. He had learned from dealing with the orc slaver Prawl and from his time in Slaver Town that one should never pass up a meal, because you never knew when the next one might come.

Maefon poked her head out of the tent. Without looking at Nath, she came outside, sat down by the fire, and started nibbling on the venison.

Nath stood behind the elves across from her and said, "Darkken isn't back yet. Should we be worried?"

Chewing her food, she looked up at him. "It's early evening. Sometimes he runs late. It's hard to tell, but he'll be back, as he'll want to get some sleep. He's not elven like the rest of us. He needs his rest." The elves chuckled. One of them, sitting next to Maefon, bumped a fist on her thigh.

It was good to see the stoic elves show some personality. They seemed more like the Trahaydeen that Nath knew, who were very polite but also very entertaining.

They seem to really loosen up when Darkken isn't around. Interesting.

The clouds moved through the sky, blocking the full moon most of the time. A light snow fell on and off through the early evening. The elves had finished eating and packed up the food that could be saved. Nath kept his attention south, waiting for Darkken to return.

Coming along his side, Maefon put her hands around his waist. "I'm feeling better. Thanks for asking."

"I'm sorry. I guess I am preoccupied." Nath put his arms around her and gave her a peck on the forehead. "I'm glad. I was worried about you. I just never saw you looking, so..."

"Pitiful?"

"Yes. That's the word for it."

"Certainly you've seen sickly people in Slaver Town?"

"True, I've gotten accustomed to a lot of this world's cruel dealings, but none of those people were you. It's different."

"Ah, that is sweet, Nath." She put one hand on his waist and held his hand with the other. In silence, they watched for Darkken's return. That night, he never returned. By morning, Nath's heart was jumping.

Chapter 7

All of the way down the mountain, Slivver and Brenwar remained in a heated conversation. Brenwar wore a large, rough sack strapped over his shoulders. In his hands, he carried a magnificent dwarven-made war hammer. He was explaining the design of the weapon to Elween, who nodded with interest, and Slivver tried to get the dwarf to shut up about it. "We need to talk about the mission," Slivver said. "Not your hammer."

"It's a war hammer, and I'm almost finished."

"You said that two hours ago."

"Be quiet. Never cut off a dwarf!" In a showy fashion, Brenwar flipped the hammer in his hands. "I have the flat side and the axe side. I can bust through doors or chop through them, but it's grandly made to destroy giants."

Elween nodded with fascination. "May I hold it? Being a weapon master, I can't help but marvel at the unique design."

"Please don't encourage him," Slivver replied. He navigated through the trees, down the slope, to where the rocky woodland cleared at the bottom, opening to a prairie of snow-covered grass. "You'll regret it."

"It's heavy," she said, tossing the weapon from hand to hand before twirling it behind her back and to the front again. Brenwar's eyes widened. She handed it back. "Too hefty for me, but I do like it."

"You have to be dwarven strong to wield the war hammer properly." Brenwar rested it on his brawny shoulders. "I can crush a giant's bones with a single hit."

"Is that all?" she asked.

"Well, no, of course not." Brenwar clawed at his beard. "There's ogres, orcs, gnomes, lizard men, ettins, bugbears—"

"Gnomes?"

"They can be very annoying. Now let me finish." Brenwar went on to name over a dozen creatures and humanoids, and when he said "centaur," Elween stopped him.

"We killed two of those on our way to see you," she said.

"By Morgdon, you started a fight without me!" Unable to contain his anger and excitement, Brenwar stamped in the snow. "Tell me what happened. I want details!"

Elween recounted the battle.

With a hungry, glazed look in his brown eyes, Brenwar said, "Oh, I wish I could have been there. Them centaurs are an evil mix. Cocky too. Glad you got the best of them. Tough to kill."

"Not for us," Slivver commented. "But it would have been for you."

"I would smite them down with one stroke. You know that!"

"Uh-huh." Slivver stopped in the grass. "Now that we are all caught up, do you think we can discuss the mission and where we are headed?"

Brenwar looked at him. "Out with it then. What is the mission, and where are we headed?"

"Don't you know?" Slivver exclaimed.

The dwarf shrugged. "No. I thought you did."

"So, Balzurth didn't tell you the mission or anything about where Nath is?"

"No. Who is Nath?"

"Balzurth's son." Elween gave Slivver a lost look. Turning her attention back to Brenwar, she asked, "What do you know?"

"Nothing. I was told to be where I was. That was all."

"Don't play games, Brenwar. You really don't know who Nath is?"

"Dwarves don't lie!" He marched forward, gripping his hammer in two husky hands. "You aren't calling me a liar, are you? Because if you are, your life is over."

"No, of course not. I know better than that." Deflated, Slivver sat down in the snow. He looked at Elween. "Should I explain it all to him, or should you?"

Elween spoke. Brenwar listened intently. He pumped up his fist in a cheer. "I knew it! I knew it! I told everyone elves were evil!" He marched in the snow in his own personal parade. "A dwarf knows! A dwarf always knows! The elves are evil, and now we get to kill them all." He stabbed a finger a Slivver. "Let's go get them!"

"Nobody's killing any elves." Slivver's heart pounded between his ears. His mind ached. It often happened like that when he was with the dwarf. He called it the Brenwar effect. "Only some of them are evil, but not all, not by a long shot."

"We can't take any chances," Brenwar retorted. He chopped his war hammer in the air. "We have to take them all."

Slivver rolled his eyes.

Elween chuckled. "I admit, I like his fighting spirit."

"Yes, he's a real tornado of destruction. The destruction of common sense, that is."

"You better watch it with the insults, dragon. You don't want me to pop you one, but I will." Brenwar paced in the snow, weapon on his shoulder and stroking his beard. "So, we've finally confirmed that elves are evil. Ever since they stole the secret of dragon steel, I knew there were deviants among them. I can't wait to get a crack at them. So arrogant with their pointed ears and downward noses. Oh, I'm going to get them good."

"Let's not get all lathered up yet." Slivver looked to Elween. It was clear that she was amused by everything Brenwar was saying. Her eyes hung on the burly little man like a child seeing a sparkling toy. "There is still the matter of tracking Nath down. It's been over two years. He could be anywhere in Nalzambor."

"I can find him. I can find anybody. That's why Balzurth trusts me." The nostrils on the dwarf's broad nose flared. He sniffed loudly, wet his finger, and held it up to the air. He pointed northeast. "That way."

"That's absurd!" Slivver said. Why Balzurth was so fond of the Bolderguilds was a mystery to Slivver. He could think of a hundred other people who would be three times more effective. "You're just guessing."

Brenwar tilted his head to one side. "Dwarves don't guess." He marched east.

Elween followed, patting Slivver on the back of his wings as she passed. "Do you have a better idea?"

Chin dipping and with a defeated sigh, Slivver said, "No."

CHAPTER 8

"SOMETHING'S WRONG," NATH SAID. MAEFON huddled over the fire, rubbing her hands together, and yawned. They were alone. The Brothers of the Wind had moved out, making a quick search for Darkken. A few remained in the nearby fields, keeping watch over them as the sun slowly rose underneath the cloudy sky. Nath's fingertips tingled. "Don't you feel that something is wrong?"

"I've spent a lot of time with Darkken, and to be frank, I never worry, but now you are making me worry." Maefon rose, arching her back. "I'm just glad to feel myself again. That one day of fever felt like a week. Why don't you eat something? Take your mind off of it. Darkken can take care of himself, regardless of the situation. I'm sure of it."

"I don't know. He said that he would be back last night, early, and now it's the next day."

"Don't overthink it, Nath. We are in new territory and there are bound to be some hazards. My guess is that they got sidetracked or needed to rest in the night. It's too soon to panic, which is something the Brothers of the Wind never do."

"How can you be so nonchalant about it?"

"This isn't the first time that Darkken has been late. It won't be the last either. Just be patient. Everything will work out." Maefon took a stick and began moving the logs in the fire closer together, bringing forth a new flame. "Fire, fire, what would we do without you?"

Nath could see Maefon's eyebrows knitting together. Something was on her mind. He knew what it must have been and ventured to ask. "Tell me, are you worried about the possible confrontation with Chazzan?" he asked. Maefon froze. "I'm sorry. I shouldn't have asked that. It just came to me and I said it. I think it would be hard to face someone that tried to kill you."

Maefon turned to face him. She bit into her bottom lip as her eyes narrowed. She seemed to go deep into thought, and then finally she said, "I've thought about this many times, thinking that I would kill him. But we've tried to track him down before only to learn that he's not where we thought he would be. He's a ghost, Nath. And just because we have another lead doesn't mean that he will be there. He probably won't be. I suppose that is why I don't worry. Every time I think we are close and I can have my vengeance, I end up disappointed."

Nath walked over to her, put his hands on her shoulders, and looked down into her beautiful eyes. "We will find him. Both of us will have vengeance." He hugged her. "I promise."

She squeezed him tight. "Thank you. Your reassurance comforts me. It eases much of the guilt that I carry. I'm so glad to have you back, Nath. It means the world to me."

"Now that you are feeling better, would you object to going after Darkken? It's early in the day, and there is nothing else to do."

"It seems we are headed in that direction. I don't see why not." She broke off the embrace and whistled. Three elven warriors appeared, coming from different directions with a dusting of snow on their shoulders. They moved with the graceful ease of snow leopards. They stopped in front of Maefon. She swept the snow from their shoulders and said, "We are packing up. Nath has convinced me that Darkken might be lost and we should find him."

The elves smiled. The one in the middle chuckled, but in Elven he said, "I agree. Moving is better than standing. Right away, then."

"Right away," she said. Already dressed in her traveling cloak, she said to Nath, "Lead the way."

As good as the Brothers of the Wind were at hiding, they weren't difficult to follow in the fresh snow. Nath moved at a brisk pace, not seeing any reason to be discreet. Darkken's absence ate at his gut. He felt compelled to find the man. In truth, he was worried about him as well as the others. Something told him that something was wrong. They traveled three miles downriver before he eyed the first crossing. A weathered bridge with a roof covered in inches of snow crossed the icy waters at a narrow spot in the river. The faint traces of an abandoned road could be seen leading away from the bridge in another direction. Nath pointed at it.

"Seems like an obvious place to cross," Maefon said, regarding him with approving eyes. "You will make an excellent tracker with those golden eyes of yours."

"Yes, I will, won't I? Heh-heh."

With the rest of the elves filed in behind him, he headed for the distant bridge. The covered bridge's outer rails were missing some of their planks. It groaned in the wind as the waters splashed over the rocks beneath it. Daylight crept through broken holes in the roof, casting light on the bridge's broken floor. Nath was looking across to the open end of the other side when Maefon let out a sharp gasp.

Slumped against the bridge's wall was an elf. His body was frozen against the planks. He sat on the floor, holding his belly. Nath's heart jumped in his chest. His eyes swept over the covered bridge. The elves pulled their swords and notched arrows on bowstrings. There wasn't just one elf lying dead inside the icy darkness of the bridge. There were many.

Chapter 9

Seven Brothers of the Wind lay dead on the bridge. They were the ones who tracked after Darkken and the others. Many of them had crossbow bolts stuck inside their bodies. There were wounds from a blade too. Nath inspected one of the elves, looking at the frozen, bloody gash in his chest where a sword went in and out. "Whatever hit them was good. All of these wounds were made with precision." He found Maefon kneeling over another fallen elf. "I'm sorry, Maefon."

"It was an ambush." Her voice was dark with rising anger. "Many of the enemy were in the rafters, lurking on the beams, waiting to strike. This bolt went through my brother's back. Cowards!"

It was clear that the Brothers of the Wind were taken by surprise, however unlikely that seemed. One of the elves lay on his side, cold as ice, with a short sword half drawn from his sheath. A bolt was in his back as well. But not all of the Brothers of the Wind were taken by surprise. Spots coated parts of the covered bridge's deck. The fighting had moved toward the other side. There, across the river, Nath could see the shuffle of feet in the snow where the fighters fenced.

Two of the living Brothers of the Wind were talking together. Palming his hand inside one of the shoe prints, he said, "The tracks are elven."

Maefon came up on Nath. "Caligin. They were waiting." With a white-knuckled grip on her sword, she followed the path made in the snow. Her simmering eyes moved side to side, inspecting every detail. "If they knew we were coming, then they must have Darkken and the others."

"Or they are dead," one of the elves said with a long face. "We need to bury the dead and avenge them."

"You can't bury them now! The ground's too bloody hard!" Maefon said. "But we can avenge them! And we need to find the others. The burial can wait, but we are going to be burying more Caligin than Brothers of the Wind." She ripped out her sword. "I swear it!"

Uncertain what to say, Nath followed Maefon over the snow-covered ground. He wanted to tell her that they needed to proceed with extreme caution because the Caligin probably knew about them as well, but he held his tongue. Her mind was made up, and he saw no reason to talk her out of it. To some degree, it gave him comfort that he was right about the danger. His friends were out there, and he needed to help them.

As they moved, Nath noted the tracks in the snow. A tight-knit group walked in a bunch together, where they were flanked by many sets of feet. Darkken's force was nothing small, but the other surrounding footsteps were vaster in number. It appeared as if they stepped within their own prints, but he gathered there must have been two dozen of them. He had faith that Darkken could handle many men at once, but there wasn't much that could be done if they had crossbows bearing down on him.

Of course, he could have used his magic. Why didn't he?

The snow came down harder as they continued. In the distance, Nath could see icy cliffs rising out above the river. A fortress, several stories tall, had been chiseled out of the rock. Hundreds of feet above it, a bird circled with its wings spread wide. It glided toward them.

Nath caught up to Maefon and pointed. "What is that?"

Face to the wind, she squinted. "It looks like a vulture. Does it have two heads?"

"Yes. I've got a bad feeling that it's watching us, and it seems familiar."

"What do you mean?" she said.

"Just a feeling," he replied. The bird flew not more than a hundred feet over top of them. It was an ugly thing, with feathers covering its neck and head. Its emerald eyes pierced Nath's soul. Wings spread out wide, it flapped once like a great dragon, shrieked, and flew on. The elves' eyes followed after it. "You don't think it's going to eat the others, do you?"

Maefon resumed her trek. "If it does, we'll kill it too."

With the wind and snow picking up, Nath shielded his eyes. They were still moving right at what he believed was Stonewater Keep. It was an ominous structure, stark and cold, ancient, mysterious, and a place that appeared to be where hope was abandoned. "Maefon, we are getting closer. Don't we need a plan?"

"What do you suggest? Darkken is in there, and we are out here. We have to get him."

"Yes, I know, but certainly, if it is indeed Chazzan in there, he knows that we are coming. We are walking into a trap, just like the others did, aren't we?"

"Perhaps. But maybe they don't know. I'm gambling they don't, or they would have come for us by now."

She made a good point, but Nath still wasn't liking it. "But wouldn't the Brothers of the Wind move about in a stealthier manner? We should at least wait until nightfall."

"Let's just keep following the tracks. Maybe they turn somewhere else, and I don't want to lose them." Maefon moved with fiery determination. Nothing was going to stop her or change her mind. She followed the trail between two mounds of snow. With the snowy sleet in her eyes, she said, "Come on. The tracks are filling up."

She made it between the piles before Nath noticed the heaps shift. Tiny snowballs rolled over the top. The caked snow cracked and split. Fur peeked from underneath the snow. He reached for his sword. "Maefon!" A giant-sized arm shot out of the snow and snatched her up.

Nath tore Fang out of his sheath. He turned loose a downward-arcing chop. The blade sliced through the snow-white hairy arm of the monster, cutting its hand off at the wrist. Blood streamed out from the wound as the massive creature exploded out of the mound. Nath pulled Maefon behind him. The massive brute was a ten-foot-high yeti-like beast with coarse white hair hanging from layers of primordial muscle. It had a bare, hard chest and belly, colored like granite. It beat its chest with one fist and let out a savage howl.

"Stay behind me," Nath said.

Two of the Brothers of the Wind jetted over the snow, launching themselves fearlessly at the beast. They hacked into the ferocious monster. One elf stayed back, firing arrow after arrow into the brute's body.

Nath turned to ask Maefon if she was all right. She was clutching her ribs and wincing. "Stay put while we finish this," he said, brandishing Fang with two hands. He charged after the monster, oblivious to the other snow pile that came to life and pounced on top of him.

CHAPTER 10

THE MOUNTAIN OF FUR THAT piled on Nath tried to make a snowball out of him. The heavy-handed monster crushed Nath inside its grip and slung him across the frozen landscape. Nath hit hard and rolled. Fang slipped out of his fingers, disappearing into the snow.

The yeti bounded toward Nath. It leapt high, mouth wide open, revealing hungry, slavering jaws. Sailing an impossible distance that defied ordinary boundaries for such a hulking thing, it landed right in front of Nath. It pounded its chest and roared.

Nath stepped backward, searching for his sword. Not seeing it, he reached for the bow that was slung over his back only to come up empty. Only then did he notice it somehow found itself in the yeti's grip. The yeti snapped it in half like a twig. Nath swallowed the lump in his throat. He slowly stuck out his right hand and said to the shaggy white beast, "Perhaps we can talk about this. Let's start with an introduction." He touched his chest politely with his right hand. "I am Nath. And you are?"

The yeti's head cocked. Drool dripped from its teeth—big sharp teeth that could chew through bone. Hot breath came out like steam. It lowered itself, stuffing its fist in the snow, and ambled forward. It roared.

Nath fanned his nose and coughed. "That's awful. Not your strange name, but your breath. What did you say your name was again? Rower?" He spied an impression in the snow where Fang was buried. It was right in front of the yeti's fist. It stepped over top of it. "Gads." Weaponless, Nath backed farther away. Still holding his left hand out, a twinkle caught his eye. It was the gemstone on the Gauntlet of Goam. He clenched his fist. The gemstone shined bright. New strength and warmth filled him.

The monster's eyes locked on the bright gem. Its heavy brow furrowed. Snarling, it charged.

Embracing the surge of energy, Nath ran right at the beast and jumped. He sailed over top of the yeti's clutches, swinging with all his might, and punched it in the nose. The yeti's head snapped back. Staggering, it stumbled in the snow. Landing softly on his own feet, Nath watched the brute with wary eyes. It stumbled through the snow, nose bleeding as it shook its head.

"Blast, I was hoping that would knock it out." He looked at his balled-up fist. "Can't let up now." He charged the beast again, yelling, "Dragon! Dragon!"

Wincing as she clutched her side, Maefon turned in time to see the yeti that attacked her grab a Brother of the Wind in its great hand and bite the elf's head off. The savage death left her eyes wide and blinking as her mind fumbled to find a spell that would help. The remaining two elves slashed their elven steel in the yeti's legs. Its good hand swatted them away like children.

The elven warriors sprang back, stabbing with deadly ferocity. Fur, blood, and skin mixed with the falling snow. The beast's angry howls carried on the wind. One elf darted behind the yeti, climbed onto its broad back, and stabbed its neck. The yeti turned its attention to the second elf, who stood in its path, stabbing it in the gut. The yeti slugged the elf in the face with its stump. The savage blow flattened the elf in the snow. The yeti, with the elf on its back, jumped high. It came straight down on the elf in the snow. The elf's bones snapped under the yeti's feet.

"Nooooooo!" Maefon flung her arms forward. A swell of radiant lavender energy shot out of her hands. The beams of light slammed full force into the monster's body, knocking it down. It popped back up. Its smoking fur turned black. Smoke rolled from the dark spots of the energy blasts. It shed the elf that clung to its back like a dog shedding water and came at Maefon. Eyes blazing like purple wildfires, she hit it again with another blast, focusing on a tighter beam of energy as she did so. The yeti's chest slammed against her power. It pushed forward, a wild, raving animal, hungry to kill. Maefon let out another scream. "Diiieeee!"

Nath closed in on the yeti with his hand glowing like star fire. The ten-foot hulk didn't see him coming from its blind side. He heard the words of Master Elween speaking in his head. *Every creature has a weakness.* He decided to aim for the temple. When he was two steps from launching himself, the yeti caught him out of the corner of its eye. Instinctively, it lashed out. The blow caught Nath mid-launch and sent him sprawling into the snow. "Ooomph!"

The yeti growled and came at him.

Nath spit snow from his mouth. He braced himself for the impact of the ten-foot-high brute. Dragon man and monster collided. Clinging to the beast's fur with one hand, he punched as hard as he could with the other. *Wham! Wham! Wham!* The yeti's hard bones broke against the fury of Nath's magic-enhanced punches.

The wounded creature ripped Nath from its body. With two arms, it hoisted Nath overhead.

Nath let the creature's fur that he'd ripped out fall from his fingers. Seized in the monster's mighty grip, he said, "I suppose it's too late to talk about this!"

The yeti flung him head over heels.

Twisting in the air, Nath manage to land on his feet. It would take more than the Gauntlet of Goam to stop the savage creature. The sound of gentle humming vibrated at his feet. He glanced down. Fang lay there in the snow. "Lucky day!" Nath snatched up the magnificent blade. It glimmered blue as ice.

Once more, the yeti charged, bent on tearing Nath limb from limb.

"Let's try this again. Dragon! Dragon!" Racing through the snow, Nath met the yeti with a full-on swing. Fang sliced right through the brute's abdomen. A second swing took an arm from the elbow, and the third cut out the hairy savage's knee. It died, bleeding out in the snow. Huffing hot breath, Nath turned his attention to the bestial screams of the last yeti.

Maefon stood in front of the yeti, pushing it backward in the snow. Thick yellow-white smoke rolled from its charred limbs. Suddenly, Maefon's beam of light burst clean through the yeti's body. It died, standing upright and burning in the snow. The elven sorceress sagged to her knees.

Nath arrived a moment after. "That was amazing," he said. "What were those bumbling beasts?"

She looked up at him with a face glistening in perspiration and said, "Not sure. Giant yetis or mountain giants perhaps. I was pretty amazing, wasn't I?"

Clasping her outstretched arm, he helped her to her feet. "Yes." The hairs on his neck rose. Maefon gasped. The last Brother of the Wind stumbled toward them with a glassy stare. He fell facedown in the snow with at least a dozen arrows in his back. Appearing out of the snow, over fifty elves in dark cloaks and black leather armor surrounded them.

Nath looked at Maefon and joked, "Friends of yours?"

CHAPTER 11

SLIVVER AND ELWEEN WAITED IN the woodland for the dwarf to return from a trip to a small town east of Morgdon. Slivver could make out the town from the overlook where he sat. Smoke spiraled out of many chimneys from the small buildings and surrounding hut-like homes. Even though it was a cold day, the people remained busy, trekking through the snow, feeding the livestock in the barnyards and stables, and carrying sacks of meal on their shoulders to the kitchens.

Elween's eyes were closed. Her clawed hands were clasped together. She hummed in some sort of meditation. It was a soothing trilling sound that came from inside her long neck. She'd tried to teach the practice to Slivver long ago, but he didn't care for it. If he wasn't sleeping, he'd rather keep his eyes open.

"He returns," Elween said as she opened her eyelids.

"How could you know that he returns?" Slivver replied. "Your eyes were closed."

"You would understand if you let me teach you." She pointed a clawed finger toward the small, bustling town. "See?"

A stocky man rounded the corner of a wooden barn that had been painted red. It was Brenwar, marching through the snow, stocky arms swinging at his sides like hammers. The dwarven warrior had left his weapon with Elween.

"Great Guzan, he moves at an agonizing pace. Couldn't Balzurth at least match us up with an elf?"

"The elves betrayed us, hence the need for caution," she said. "It seems that Balzurth has more faith in the dwarves than the rest of the races. They are easy to predict. Perhaps that is why. Why do you begrudge Brenwar so much? He seems pleasant enough to me."

"He's slow. I'm fast. Isn't that enough of a reason?" he said.

"I think it's more than that. Besides, we are dragons, patient creatures. If you don't want to tell me, I understand and respect it."

"I just have a sense of urgency in regards to finding Nath. For all we know, he could be imprisoned somewhere and suffering. The races are cruel people. They commit horrible acts." He flexed his wings, knocking the snow free. "Horrible. And we have an entire world to search, led by a stumpy-legged dwarf."

"Perhaps we should purchase him a horse?"

"Feel free to make that suggestion, and prepare for a thousand reasons why he doesn't need a horse."

"Are they too tall? How about a pony?"

Slivver eyed her. "Go ahead, insult him, and see how quickly you fall from his good graces."

Her eyes lit up. "Ah, I see. Thanks for the warning."

They watched Brenwar disappear into the woodland and waited for him to make the journey up to their position. He stepped out from underneath the low-hanging pine branches, put his fists on his hips, and looked at them.

"Well?" Slivver said with an impatient tone.

"Well, one thing is for certain. Those men down there make awful, just awful ale. It's very light, and I had to drink a small barrel before I lost the feeling in my toes. Very bland too. I think the word 'robust' doesn't have any meaning to them."

"I didn't ask for a critique on their mead."

"Ale."

"Whatever," Slivver responded.

"No, there is a difference in meads and ales." Brenwar walked over to Elween and retrieved his war hammer that was propped on a rock beside her. "Just like there are differences in war hammers and war axes. You see, a war axe doesn't have a hammer—"

"Will you stop with the comparisons on these inconsequential matters? Did you find anything about Nath or not?"

"I'm getting to it." Brenwar grumbled as he clawed the snow out of his beard. He leaned back on the rock where the hammer was. "So, those townsfolk don't have much in regards of a true tavern. It's basically a house with four walls and a fireplace. And you ought to see that fireplace. Why, it wouldn't surprise me one bit if it collapsed or the tavern caught fire because of the lack of engineering. The mortar in the joints was cracked." He held out his arm at an angle. "And it leaned. Why, I've never seen such bad masonry unless an orc did it. And that's what I told them. First, I told them about the ale issues and how it should be fermented longer and they need more hops and barley in the mix. I offered to write it down, but none of them read Dwarven. I don't think any of them could read at all. Come to think of it, they were some pretty stupid-looking people. Smarter than livestock, but not by much." On a roll, Brenwar kept going.

Slivver noticed Elween looking right at him with one eyebrow lifted higher than the other. He mouthed the words, "Now do you understand what I mean?"

She gave an affirmative nod.

Over three hours later, Brenwar stopped speaking. Speaking to Slivver, he said, "No, I didn't learn anything about Nath."

Slivver gripped his horns. "What are you doing? It seems to me that all you are doing is going from town to town, sampling their ale and criticizing their engineering. That's a horrible strategy when you want strangers to open up to you. How does this help our cause at all?"

Brenwar pulled out a dagger that was tucked in his belt and thumbed the keen edge. "They are thankful for the help. And they should be, being such stupid people. Or ignorant. Or dumb. Well, all three of them."

"They mean the same thing," Elween assured him. Moving closer to Brenwar, she said, "So, you didn't learn anything. Did you even ask?"

Brenwar's eyes got big. "Oh, now you're both interrogating me, are you? Well, why don't you bother just flying down there and asking them yourself. See if you fare any better!" He produced an apple from his pack and began peeling the skin away with his blade. "And while you are down there, tell them their food is horrible too. The biscuits didn't have enough salt, and what is gravy without sausage?"

In a soothing voice, Elween said, "I think we all know that won't work, Brenwar. I'm sure you've gathered something useful from your constructive conversations. Isn't there anything helpful that you can share?"

"I have plenty of helpful. Just ask those villagers down there." He flicked the spiral-shaped skin to the ground and took a bite of apple. "I asked about Nath and gave a description. No one knew a thing. I've been at this a while, and the moment an eye bats at something, I know if I'm onto something. My process might not be fast, but we'll find Nath. Stories carry from one town to another. It just so happens this town was full of dullards, so I thought I'd have a little fun with them." He narrowed an eye at Slivver. "I know what I'm doing. I always do.

This one is just impatient. Did he ever tell you about his elven lady friend? What was her name? Ericha, wasn't it?"

With a growl, Slivver pounced at Brenwar. "You will be silent!"

Brenwar rocketed a punch in Slivver's open jaw, flooring the dragon. Slivver got up, shaking his head. His eyes were lakes of fiery blue ice. Dragon and dwarf squared off on one another. They circled with side steps. "Come on, Slivver. See if you can take me this time. I can't wait to wrestle those wings right off of you."

"I'll turn you into a burning toadstool!" Slivver fired back.

Elween stepped between them with her paws stretched out. "What is this madness that comes upon the both of you? Huh? What wounds are so deep?"

Wagging his finger at Slivver, Brenwar said, "He's in love with an elf. Of all the ridiculous things. She's probably one of those Caligin!"

"Shut your bearded mouth, Brenwar! Speak one more ill word of her and I'll tear your beard off!"

"Try it and I'll stuff your wings in those flaring nostrils! Elf lover!"

Elween shoved Slivver back. "Control yourself. This is not like you, Slivver. Who is this Ericha?"

Slivver shot her an angry look and moved back. "None of your business." He spread his wings and flew away.

She looked down at Brenwar. "You hurt him. Why did you do that? Did you not see the hurt in his eyes? By the dragons, his polished voice was cracking."

Brenwar grunted in his throat as he shrank away from her heavy stare. He sheathed his dagger. "It's for the better."

"How do you know what is best for him? Are you a dragon?"

"No."

"Is he a dwarf?"

"No. But he's not an elf either." Clawing at the braids in his beard, he said, "He wants to be a man or an elf, I don't know which, but he's only going to get hurt. Elves can't be trusted."

"You know better than that, Brenwar. The elves have their flaws, but they are ambitiously good-natured," she said.

"Ambitious for their own good and needs, that is. They are self-serving, putting themselves above all others." Brenwar started eating his apple again. "And their ale is fruity."

"Well, you should have mentioned that to begin with. Clearly, they are a devious race. Who would dare mix fruit with ale?" Elween added sarcastically.

"And a lemon at that. I tell you, it ruins the taste of a perfectly good lemon."

"Brenwar, I respect you. But we have a long journey ahead, and it's best that we all get along the best that we can. With Slivver, I think you should make things right."

He finished the apple, core and all. "I'll think about it."

CHAPTER 12

WITH THE SNOW FALLING AROUND them, Nath, back to back with Maefon, studied their enemies. A quick count revealed fifty Caligin fighters. They all looked similar in their fashionable black leather armor and long ponytails hanging down their backs. The ones that weren't aiming a bow or crossbow at them filled their hands with steel. Their expressionless faces were cold and deadly.

Feeling Maefon's heel against his, Nath said, "What do you want to do, fight or surrender?"

"Fight," she said, "but I don't think I can survive a hail of bolts and arrows, and I want to find Darkken. But I'll fight if you want to."

"I'll risk my life, but I won't risk yours. Like you, I want answers." Slowly, Nath stuck Fang back in his scabbard and dropped it in the snow. "I'm getting really tired of losing Fang."

A small group of Caligin slipped toward them. They took Fang, his backpack, dagger belt, gauntlet, and the quiver that he carried holding the magic arrows. They did the same with Maefon, leaving them both weaponless and empty-handed. The Caligin kicked them behind the knees, dropping them kneeling into the snow. They faced the keep that was still a mile away. Appearing through snow and drift dust, like a shadow, a horse on a rider approached with two more columns of riders on each side.

The snow-distorted image of the horse and rider cleared as they approached. The rider wore a metal helmet, bright with chrome, fashioned with the sharp features of an elf. He wore the same standard black leather armor. A red cape flowed behind his shoulders. The horse beneath him was a white stallion that appeared too big for the man on its back. It snorted hot breath from its nostrils.

The rider bent forward, staring at them both through metal eyelets in the full helmet. The eerie stare hung on them a long time. Nath studied the onlooker. The elven features of the helmet were heavily pronounced, with larger sharp, pointy ears and chiseled cheekbones. The helmet was twice the size of an ordinary head, and wavy hair was fashioned in it. It did, indeed, remind him of Chazzan, in a demigod-like form. Finally, the rider spoke in a voice that carried like it was in a deep chamber. "You are trespassing, strangers. What do you have to say for yourself?"

"My, what big ears you have," Nath replied.

In a lofty voice, the rider said, "Careful, or you will be wearing no ears at all. Or a tongue either."

"Chazzan! Is that you hiding behind that helmet? Are you behind all of this treachery?" Maefon demanded.

"It is I that asks the questions, not you. Now rise. It's time to take you to the keep, where you will be my prisoners for all eternity." The rider turned his horse. The Caligin accompanying him did a uniform turn and marched for the keep.

Walking side by side with Maefon, Nath said, "Do you really think it is him?"

"I don't know who else it could be. And that creepy helmet does remind me of him. It wouldn't surprise me one bit if he designed it for himself. He was very arrogant."

Nath always found Chazzan to be the extreme of everything elven. He was overly polite, primped and polished in all regards, and stood out from the others. Even the build of the person in the saddle seemed right. "What do you really think he wants with us?"

"It's hard to tell."

Maefon's thoughts were rattled. Before she pretended to be sick, her and Darkken had hashed out what would happen. She would fool Nath while Darkken departed. That would give him time to set up at the keep. What he hadn't mentioned was that many of the other Brothers of the Wind, or Caligin, would die in the process. And the yetis. That was beyond comprehension. They very well could have been killed. Anger stirred inside her.

Darkken must be mad to kill so many loyal to him just to fool Nath. I could have died too! I'll get to the bottom of this. But who in the world is wearing that elven helmet? Chazzan is dead. Lunacy!

As much faith and love as she had for Darkken, she didn't understand his methods. The Caligin were loyal to the Lord of the Dark in the Day, to the point of giving their own lives, but to see so many slaughtered over and over again became worrisome for Maefon. She rubbed her throat.

When will my time be? Is a certain death awaiting me inside the walls of the keep?

She trudged on, reaching over and taking Nath's warm hand. She gave him a worried look. He squeezed her hand for a moment before one of the Caligin pulled them apart.

They followed a road in the snow that wound back toward the river. A waterfall upriver crashed into the ice-cold waters. The road led back up the hill, to the level of the waterfall, where another stone bridge waited for them to cross. The elven-helmed rider stopped. He pointed to the top of the keep. Looking back at Nath and Maefon, he said, "Look up, comrades of yours."

Large square and rectangular stones were stacked up several stories high. The rest of the keep was built back into the rocky cliff. A sheet of ice coated the blocks, and glassy waters trickled down the sides. On top of the keep, behind the battlements, stood a monstrous ogre, bull necked and covered in coarse hair and natural muscles.

Maefon let out a sharp breath as the ogre slung an arm over the side of the keep down into the surging river. A moment later, the ogre had a one-armed elf wearing the garb of the Brothers of the Wind lifted over its head. The ogre let out a guttural roar and heaved the elf over the side. The elf did not scream or swim in the air. His body dashed against the rocks and bounced into the surge.

The elven rider looked over his shoulder. "That is Monfur. I suggest you don't try to do anything foolish if you want to avoid him. There's nothing worse than having limbs ripped off when you are still breathing."

Nath swallowed. The Caligin, led by the rider, crossed the stone bridge. He watched the bodies floating away before disappearing over the falls. Stopping in front of the metal portcullis, the rider said with a hollow chuckle, "Welcome to Stonewater Keep. Hahaha."

CHAPTER 13

MONFUR APPEARED ON THE OTHER side of the gate minutes later. He took out the iron pins with his bare hands then, with a single hand, lifted the portcullis. The gate groaned and made a grating rubbing sound of metal on metal that would wake the dead. All of the Caligin entered. Monfur lowered the portcullis, saying, "Yum-yum."

Nath found the heavy glare of the ogre. Monfur was even bigger than the one at Slaver Town. Though not nearly as big as the yetis they just encountered, he carried a dangerous intelligence. The ogre licked his lips with a thick black tongue then drew his forearm over his huge mouth. "Yum-yum. New marrow good. Yum-yum."

The rider dismounted. Monfur took the horse by the reins and led it away through the archways below the keep. With snow falling in the small courtyard, the rider led them inside. "Follow me. It's time to eat."

With a small escort of Caligin in front of them and one behind, the rider led them up the stairs that crossed back and forth, passing one landing and doorway after the other, until near the top they entered a grand dining hall with a wooden table that would seat fifty. Hundreds of candles burned from the chandeliers that hung above them. Heavy curtains made from dark velvet of many colors covered most of the stone. Empty fireplaces surrounded the chill room.

The rider sat at the end of the table. His head wobbled as the helmet he wore rested uncomfortably on his slender build. In a hollow voice he said, "Sit down. One to the first chair to my right and the other to my left."

Nath walked the length of the table and sat on the left, while Maefon took the right. She gave Nath an uncertain glance as she sat down. As they did so, the rest of the Caligin spread out along the walls of the room.

The rider clapped his leather-covered hands together. The fireplaces came to life with roaring, crackling flames. "That's better. Now, how about some wine and food? And I give you my word, it won't be fresh elven blood or meat. I save all of that for Monfur."

"We aren't hungry," Nath stated.

"Oh, you will be." The rider waved his hand. The doors opened, and one Caligin entered with a platter of food and the other a platter with jugs and goblets of wine. The elves gave all three of them servings of food and wine.

"Enough of this charade!" Maefon blurted out. "Chazzan, is that you inside that helmet or not?"

The rider held up one finger and made a quick nod. "I might as well reveal my identity. I can't eat or drink if I don't, and this helm does make me very thirsty." One Caligin came behind him and helped lift the helmet from his face by loosening the bindings in the back. The Caligin carried the helmet away and set it on a pedestal behind them near the fireplace. The rider's head was down, and his long hair hid his face. He started laughing.

Nath exchanged a glance with Maefon.

"Yes, Maefon, your suspicions are correct." He revealed his face. "It is I, Chazzan." He was a handsome elf with very distinct and pronounced elven features that almost gave him an unnatural and mischievous look. "Did you miss me?"

"You tried to kill me!" She lunged at him. Before she could cross the table, serpentine coils of magic slithered out from underneath the arms of her chair and snared her. The same happened to Nath. The coils seized their wrists and ankles, holding them fast to the chairs. Maefon strained against her bonds. "You are a coward!"

"And a killer!" Nath said with a sneer. "Slaying fledglings. You sicken me!" His muscular arms heaved against his bonds. The strands of mystic rope tightened and burned. "Gah!"

Chazzan waggled fingers at them both. "I wouldn't do that unless you have a penchant for severe pain." Chazzan picked up his red wine, swirled it in the glass, and smelled the bouquet. "I love the smell of wine in the evening. The aroma is mouthwatering." He drank. "And elven too. It's from my own family's vineyards."

"You dishonor your family and the Trahaydeen. You betrayed us all!" Maefon said, fighting against her bonds. Her eyes enlarged. She sagged back in her chair. "Guh…"

"I did what needed to be done. The dragons had it coming, and you had it coming too, Maefon, when you betrayed me." He took up a fork and knife and started cutting up the meat on his plate. "But I give you credit for finding me. Not an easy task. With that said, I've been onto you for quite some time. I keep my eyes open, and my Caligin don't miss much. You should know that. It's obvious that you've been coming after me for a while."

"I'm sure that big bird of yours was a grand help," she said.

"Galtur the vulture is another resource, just like the yettin, that, sadly, you slew. They were only there to capture you. You didn't have to kill them. They don't grow on trees, you know."

"I'm glad they are dead, and soon you will be too," Maefon said.

"Please, spare me the empty threats. You are both smart enough to know that I have it all under control, always. My elven army, everything." Chazzan swallowed his food and washed it down with wine. "You really should try the veal. It's exquisite and quite a rarity this time of year."

Glaring at the arrogant elf with smooth skin and perfect features, Nath said, "Why did you kill the fledglings?"

"Revenge. Isn't that reason enough?"

"What are you talking about? They were babies. They did no harm to you," he said.

"No, but their parents did. Their ancestors did. You see, Nath, you are very naïve about your king. The dragons have warred with all of the races and killed many women and children. Members of my own family." Chazzan looked at Maefon as he sliced his food. As he brought it to his mouth, the juice dripped on his chin. "An eye for an eye and a tooth for a tooth."

"You are mad!" she fired back.

"You've read the histories, Maefon. You know what I say is true. The dragons had it coming, and we hit them where it hurts."

"What is he talking about, Maefon? Do you know this? Is it true?" Nath asked. He was flabbergasted. Worse yet, Chazzan's words had a ring of truth to them. It stirred in Nath's belly.

"You look hurt, Nath, and you should be. Your kind is very evil."

Chapter 14

As Chazzan talked, Nath sat in his chair, fuming. Everything the elf said went against the grain inside him. He talked on and on about how the dragons warred with all the races at one time or another. Nath refused to believe any of it, but it was the look hanging on Maefon's face that caused him to doubt. Finally, during a break in Chazzan's words, Maefon interrupted.

"Don't listen to him, Nath. He's only trying to upset you. After all, the Caligin are full of lies." She looked right at Chazzan. "Where are the others?"

Chazzan raised a brow. "You mean the rest of the Brothers of the Wind? Those elves were given a choice. We killed most of them, while many of the others are imprisoned. Actually, they are more like pets that Monfur likes to fatten up and eat. Now, one of them, the man, he is interesting. How did you come to be with him? An inferior human, no less."

"He is a human with excellent timing. You thought me dead, but he saved me. And now I'm here, right before your eyes, to let you know that you will pay for all that you did."

Elbows on the table, Chazzan tapped his fingers together. "I see this man is very precious to you." He reached over and touched her arm. "I was very precious to you once. It could be so again."

Drawing a frown on her face, Maefon tried to pull away.

Chazzan tossed his head back and laughed. "Ah-hahahaha!" His voice cracked and dropped deeper. He cut the laughter short and drank a sip of wine. "Pardon me. It's been a time since I laughed so heartily."

Darkken's alive. A good thing. Reflecting on what happened at the Merchant Queen's fort, Nath hoped Darkken managed to keep his powers hidden until it was time to strike. For the time being, as much as he hated Chazzan, it was time to play along. As fortune would have it, his belly moaned. "As much as I detest your company and services, I would like to eat now."

"So be it." Chazzan twiddled two fingers. The mystic coils slid away from Nath's and Maefon's wrists but remained fastened to their waists and ankles. "I'm glad that you are taking advantage of my hospitality. After all, we are all old friends. I say we make the most of it."

Nath, along with Maefon, took up silverware and began to eat. The warm food was full of flavor and fit for a king. It seemed out of place at the dreary fortress.

"How did you come about all of this, Chazzan? The keep, the Caligin, it couldn't have all just happened," Maefon asked.

"I've had several centuries of life before you came along. Many stops before I became a Trahaydeen." Chazzan dabbed the corners of his mouth with a napkin. He took in a sharp breath. "When I came upon this keep and the knowledge within, I came upon a vision. A vision that would change the world." He peered about the room. "For this keep, long abandoned, revealed many secrets to me, and I formed the Caligin. We are a secret group devoted to making the world a better place."

"By killing children?" Nath said.

Chazzan leaned toward him. "As I mentioned, all wars have casualties. Vengeance shows no mercy."

"You do realize that once the dragons discover where you are, they will destroy you?" Nath added.

"The dragons will move on. Besides, most of them believe that you are responsible, don't they?"

Nath shot a dangerous look at him. "So, you did set me up?"

"I bought time so that we could make a clean escape. It worked out well, didn't it?"

Nath pushed his plate away. "I've lost my appetite."

"Good," Chazzan said with a smile full of perfect white teeth. "Caligin, take Nath to his new quarters."

"I've lost my appetite as well," Maefon said.

"That is fine," Chazzan replied, "but you are staying with me."

Chapter 15

The Caligin cleared the room as soon as Nath was taken away, leaving Maefon and Chazzan alone. Maefon took deep breaths through her nostrils. Her chest expanded. The tight leather armor she wore creaked. With a hard stare that could drive nails through a board, she said to the imposter elf, "Darkken, I know it is you, and you have some explaining to do."

"I beg your pardon," Chazzan teased. He brought the goblet to his lips. "Whatever do you mean?"

She grabbed him by the wrist and held his arm fast. "I could have died out there! Yettin! Really? My ribs are cracked, Darkken."

His dark eyes began burning with a coppery fire. His voice deepened into a threatening force. "Do I need to remind you who you are dealing with? I am the Lord of the Dark in the Day, and you would be wise to unhand me."

Maefon held him firm. "You will explain. I've earned the right to be treated like something better than a puppet. I've been stabbed, poisoned myself to fake a fever, then you allow snow beasts to almost tear me in twain. How loyal must I be to receive proper station?"

Darkken grabbed her wrist with a grip of iron and squeezed. The leather in his glove-covered hands groaned. "You'll be as loyal as I need you to be."

Wincing, Maefon finally let go. "Guh."

Darkken, in the transformed form of Chazzan, released her. The mystic coils that bound her waist and ankles fell away as well. "You survived, Maefon, as I knew you would. You are far more formidable than you realize. But let me make this perfectly clear: question me once more and I will destroy you." He drank his wine. "I'm actually glad that you were not foolish enough to do this in front of our brethren. It would have been instant death for you."

"You hurt me worse than those yettin did. And you are killing your own army of loyal men."

"I have to—"

"Sell it. Yes, I know. But it seems extreme to me."

"You must believe me; one Nath Dragon is worth more than an army of Caligin. And now we have him right where we want him—safely tucked inside Stonewater Keep."

"He's not going to be fooled forever," she said, rubbing her wrist. If Darkken had squeezed any harder, he probably would have broken it. Her ribs were sore too. "You could have given me some idea what to expect."

"No, you needed to be as surprised as he was. Nath will see through some of this. He's young, but he will become wise." Darkken rubbed his hands together and smiled. "Besides, I needed to test Nath and get a feel for that sword, Fang. I was curious to see what sort of other powers it might reveal. It's very... mysterious."

"I have no answers to that. Perhaps you will give some answers to me."

He arched an eyebrow. "Such as?"

"What is our next move? Or will you leave me in the dark again?"

"No, I will tell you what will happen next, but there is no reason to rush it now that Nath is safely confined." He resumed eating.

"And?"

"And what? I said that there was no reason to rush it."

"Darkken, I can't do this anymore. You have to give me some idea what to be prepared for, please?" She grabbed his forearm and rubbed it. With pleading eyes, she said softly, "Please, my lord?"

"What do you think should happen next?"

"I would place myself in the dungeons with him. Continue to gain his confidence. At some point, we would manage to escape and come after you, or Chazzan, to destroy him. But I don't know how you could be in two places at once."

Darkken nodded. "That's a very good plan, but it would be difficult to pull off. No, I have a better way, and a way that will keep you out of danger, if that makes you feel any better." He put his warm hand over hers. "That was what you wanted to hear, wasn't it?"

Darkken's strong, handsome features and soothingly warm touch started to melt her. He had a dark, charming, and hypnotic effect that drew her to him. He was an older, more mature and powerful version of Nath. He angered her, but at the same time, she found him irresistible. Her heart began to speed up. She swallowed. "That gives me comfort, Lord Darkken."

"Maefon, I have missed our intimate time together. You must know that I cherish you as much as the air that I breathe. I need you, and I'd never put you in a situation that you could not handle. Ever." He let go of her, scooted his chair back, and helped her out of hers. He scooped her up in his arms and gave her a long kiss. "Why don't we continue the rest of this conversation in the comforts of our chambers?"

"What about Nath?"

"He'll be plenty fine right where he is. He's used to it."

Nath huddled in a dingy gray cell, sealed in by a steel door fastened together with heavy bolts. The walls were slick with water and ice from the rain that trickled between the cracks. It was a six-foot-by-ten-foot cell with a wooden bed that was broken and covered with rotting straw. There was a foot-wide portal window that allowed him to see outside, across the river and frozen prairie. He had to pull himself up by the sill to look through it. He hung then let himself down. He gathered the busted bed and straw and shoved them out the window. It actually got rid of the stale, rotting smell. He dusted the strands of mildew-covered straw from his fingers. He sat in the corner and pulled his knees to his chest. A small rodent squeezed underneath the door.

"Rats."

Chapter 16

Slivver, Elween, and Brenwar spent the next several days moving from town to town, gathering the same results and mind-numbing stories from Brenwar. Though it irritated him, Slivver had gotten used to it, even though he secretly wished Brenwar would never come back from one of the many towns they visited. Currently, they were on a journey off of the well-traveled roads and paths into a rocky, unforgiving terrain called the Shale Hills. It was a twist in direction. After the last town they visited, Brenwar became determined to go there, leading the way and picking up large chunks of shale along the way.

"Some of this black rock has valuable minerals in it if you know what to look for," Brenwar said as he inspected a stone bigger than his hand. He touched it to his tongue and tossed it away. "But not this one."

The Shale Hills were covered by a rich green forest filled with many varieties of pines and fir trees. It had many hills and valleys, streams and creek beds, but the forest floor was almost completely covered in slippery shale. It defied reason how anything grew underneath the slick bits of flat black rock, but somehow life thrived.

Brenwar stopped at a high spot on the hills, sat on a fallen log, and began taking off his boots. He poured chips of stone out of them.

"What's the matter, Brenwar? Were your stinky little feet hurting?" Slivver said. His own feet were half buried in the shale.

"Shaddup." The dwarf took off a woolen sock and wiggled his broad, calloused toes, which had scars and burns all over them.

Elween exchanged a glance with Slivver then said to Brenwar, "What happened to your feet? It looks like you walked barefoot through the shale with them."

"I've done that and worse." He rubbed his toes, flapped the shale from his socks, and jammed his stumpy feet back into the socks. "This shale makes it hard to track. The loose rock hides the footing, but I can figure it out with my keen eye."

"Pardon me, but are we tracking someone or something?" Slivver said. It was news to him.

"No," Brenwar said. "If you have to hunt, you have to know what to look for." He put his boot on, strapped up the laces, and checked the seam between the leather and his calf muscles, making sure there was no crease in it. "That should do it. Let's move."

They traipsed through the hills and valleys, only stopping when Brenwar stuffed his hand in the shale and studied, sniffed, and tasted rocks that he picked up. They continued all day until they snaked through a gulch with a rather large cave mouth at the end. The opening was twelve feet high and half hidden by gargantuan snow ferns that grew alongside it.

Elween fanned her nose. "What sort of rank smell is that?"

"I better go check it out." Brenwar gripped his war hammer by the handle with two hands. "The both of you be ready."

"Ready for what?" Slivver said. "Certainly Nath is not in there?"

Brenwar eyed him. "Have you been in there?"

"No."

"Then how do you know?"

Slivver snorted a puff of smoke through his nostrils. With a self-assured harrumph, Brenwar marched toward the cave.

"I hope something eats him in there," Slivver said.

"I heard that," Brenwar fired back in Dwarven.

Rolling his eyes and shaking his head, Slivver said to Elween, "This is what I am talking about. There is no reason to be searching out the cave of some wild flesh-eating beast. It's just a waste of time."

"I'm enjoying the journey. To me, it's the best part of the trip." Elween reached over and combed her fingers through the hoary petals of a fern as tall as her. "This land is rich in wonders. As much as I enjoy Dragon Home and all of the ancient splendors that it offers, I find myself more fascinated by nature itself."

"I guess you haven't been out as much as me. Perhaps I take it for granted, but I can't help but worry about Nath."

"Worrying won't do you any good. You know that. Nath made his choice, and he has to learn to take care of himself."

"True, but he is my brother, and we all need help from time to time."

Elween nodded. "I agree."

Brenwar's stocky form was swallowed up in the mouth of the cave. The wind that whistled through the rustling pine branches died down to an eerie silence. Shale slid down the hillsides in various spots, toward the gulch. Slivver shrugged his wings. Whispering, he said, "Do you hear that?"

She tilted her head. Her bright-green eyes scanned her surroundings. "It sounds like breathing." She locked her gaze on a spot a few dozen yards up from them. Her long tail stiffened behind her. "It's coming from underneath the shale."

"Agreed."

A loud moan echoed out of the cave mouth, stirring the shale all around. It made Slivver's scales stand on end. "What was that?"

Brenwar ran out of the cave with his short legs pumping at full speed. He had a smile on his face. "Giant!" he yelled. "Giant! Ho-ho!"

At that same moment, men buried underneath the shale burst out of their graves.

Elween gasped. "By the mountain, what are those things?"

Chapter 17

Slivver and Elween turned tail to tail as a small army of strange humanoids formed around them. The mannish creatures that burst out of the shale were covered in black and white war paint. Their savage faces were painted pitch-black. They had bright yellow eyes and moved with slumped shoulders and an animal's grace. Their nostrils flared as they crept closer, snorting the air. "I believe they are orcs or some sort of orc."

"I think you are right." Elween took her own snort of air. "They have the scent of one."

The braids in the orcs' hair looked like black snakes, as the ends had white eyes painted on them. Their big hands had been painted white, and they had long fingernails that were hard and blackened. With drooling jaws that dripped saliva like starving canines, they chomped the empty air.

"I'm not sure what language they are speaking, but I believe that they want to eat us," Slivver said, fighting the urge to roar at the orc savages. There were a dozen orcs, and their ranks were growing as more emerged from the shale. They looked at the dragons like they were meat on a stick, oblivious to the dangers that the dragons brought on their own.

A moaning cavernous voice carried from out of the mouth of the cave. "BAAHHRRR!" The orc savages hunkered down. Something came out of the cave saying, "MONTOOTHA OMOHAROOOMTOM!"

A giant as broad as the side of a barn appeared from the shadowy inside of the cave. It bent over, lowering its head and peeking outside. It was an orc, almost ten feet tall. Black shoulder-length braids like snakes hung down to the middle of its back. Around its thick, greasy neck was a necklace made from skulls and bones. Deep scars showed all over the giant's body, painted white and black like the others. The giant was not only the orcen savages' leader. He was their god.

The giant orc's hungry yellow eyes landed on Brenwar. A mouthful of rotting teeth smiled. The burly, big-bellied orc sauntered out of the cave. He carried a deer skull and crushed it in his grip.

Brenwar looked over his shoulder at the dragons. "I'll handle this one!"

"He looks to have his hands full," Elween commented.

Slivver shook his long twisting neck. "Welcome to Brenwar's world."

The giant approached Brenwar, towering over the smaller man by over six feet. He balled up his fists and let out a wild roar.

Brenwar's own voice echoed through the canyon. "Challenge accepted!"

"So, how do you want to handle this?" Slivver said to Elween. "The quick and easy way or something more archaic?"

"I prefer to save my breath unless the situation demands. Besides, you know how much I enjoy hand-to-hand combat."

"Have it your way then!"

The giant orc rushed Brenwar with startling speed.

All at once, the savages attacked.

Hand-to-hand combat. Over centuries of training, Master Elween studied with great discipline the plethora of fighting styles that the races had created. The creativity of the world of men fascinated her, especially in terms of how to destroy one another. Apparently, the pursuit of peace wasn't a concern. The challenge for her, however, was learning how to use her unique body to master the styles of men. It made it difficult to execute many of the moves designed for the lesser races, but Elween's determination wouldn't let her walk away without mastering it. Like a man, her arms and legs were long. Many dragon breeds had shorter arms and legs, but not her or the likes of Slivver. They could walk upright. She delighted in it. So when the first orcen savage arrived in her face, she let out a triumphant roar and punched the teeth out of his mouth.

The savages hurled themselves at her like a hive of bees. They flung themselves fearlessly at her. She went to work. She boxed. Her thick hands peppered an orc's face. She slid her neck away from a punch. Her tail coiled around a savage's neck and flung him aside. She was strong, fast, striking quick like a snake, hitting with fists that busted bones.

"Come at me then!" she said.

Two savages jumped on her back. Their strong fingers pried at the wings on her back. They pummeled her, ripping away like hungry, starving, savage things. The beastly orcs piled on, one atop the other, striking hard and fiercely.

Elween had sparred with most of her opponents. Now she faced true killers that would die before they gave in. She latched her hand behind one savage's skull and head butted him with her horns. Before the knocked-out savage hit the ground, two more savages came on her in a blistering rush. She landed short, stiff, jarring punches, busting jaws and ribs. The swarm of rank-smelling fiends grew, piling up on her and dragging her down to the ground in a tangle of flailing limbs.

Showing a battle grin behind his heavy beard, Brenwar put his hips into his swing. His war hammer blasted into the giant's knee. The giant orc let out a pained moan and crashed to the ground.

Brenwar dove out of the way.

The giant's hands swatted at Brenwar on the way down. He upended the dwarf, sending the bearded little man sprawling to the ground. The giant got ahold of Brenwar's legs and pulled him into his clutches.

"No you don't!" Brenwar sat up with an overhead swing, busting the giant in the nose. Bone cracked like the sound of snapping timber. Blood dripped from the giant's nose. Brows knitting together above watering eyes, the giant let out an angry cry. Fastening both hands on Brenwar's legs, he slung the dwarf head over heels into a nearby tree.

Brenwar bounced off the tree's trunk. The nuts in the branches showered down on top of him. He lay still with his head swimming in pain. Tingling fingers groped the air, searching for his war hammer that lay half buried in the shale. He rolled to his hands and knees, looking left and right.

The giant jumped on top of him. Blow by blow, the giant punched Brenwar into the ground.

CHAPTER 18

ALMOST INSTANTLY, SLIVVER REALIZED THAT fighting like a man wasn't in his wheelhouse. Fighting in general wasn't. He preferred the power of flight and breath as his main avenue of attack. Before he could blink, a surge of bodies overwhelmed him. The stinky savages covered him up in a living blanket of powerful limbs. Their long, claw-like fingernails sank underneath his scales. They ripped at his eyes, grabbed onto his horns, and tried to twist his neck from his shoulders.

These savage fools don't realize they are fighting with a dragon!

A savage punched him in the eyeball.

The dragon came right out of Slivver. He clamped down on the savage's arm, biting clean through it. He twisted and barrel rolled like a gator. The relentless horde dug their fingers deeper beneath his scales. They pulled at them like hungry animals.

Being pummeled, bitten, yanked, and tugged from all directions, Slivver found himself overwhelmed by the smothering effect. His ice-blue eyes flashed. "Enough of these games!" Slivver summoned his inner magic. His scales charged up in a shield of living lightning. "Taste my sting!"

Zzzzzzap!

The lightning charge jolted every savage in contact with him. The orcs let out wild, pain-filled cries. Coarse, stinking singed hair stood on end as they scrambled away.

Slivver rose to his full height. Another wave came at him. "No more games!" He opened his jaws wide. Lightning streaked out, hitting the nearest orc savage then forking out into another and another. The bolts of energy punched black, smoldering holes through one after another. They dropped to their knees, mouths gaping open.

Slivver huffed out a breath of smoke. Many savages on shaky limbs crawled at him. He clobbered them with his tail. A handful of orcs, unmarked by the silver fire, stared at Slivver with eyes like yellow moons then turned tail and ran.

"That's more like it."

Elween struggled underneath the pile of savages trying to tear her apart one scale at a time. The tangled knot of fierce fighters didn't let up. Their punching, kicking, and clawing did little damage against her armored body. It was her pride that hurt the most. Like a fool, she'd been overtaken by a horde of mindless fiends that had the sense of an insect. She coiled her tail around an orc's arm. Constricting the serpentine appendage, she applied more pressure until the bones in the orc's arms snapped. The orc let out a furious growl but kept swinging with his good arm.

This is outrageous. Wriggling and twisting, she fought to escape from the savages' clutches. She was stronger and faster, with scales that absorbed their scratches and blows. Not just any weapon could hurt a dragon such as her. It took magic or a mystic blade. Yet the orcs managed to overwhelm her by sheer force of numbers. She was losing. Her anger turned her emerald eyes into flames.

No more holding back!

Elween unleashed her claws. Aiming for the neck and guts, she ripped into the war-painted orcs. In moments, blood smeared the bright white and mixed with the black paint on their chests. Savage after savage fell in their own blood. Her jaws clamped down on an orc's neck, trapping the flailing brute then slinging it away, hard. The orc collided with another, bowling them both over. The toppled orc regained his feet. She leapt high in the air, landing on top of him. She raked through his body, killing him on the spot.

One after another, she slipped into the onrush of brutes and killed them with no mercy. Blood soaked into the shale. No living orcs were left. Elween sighed after she caught her breath. She flicked the blood from her claws. "That was embarrassing."

In his armor, Brenwar was as hard as a turtle in the shell. He took the beating. It was just what he wanted. Before long, the thick-skinned giant's punches slowed. Brenwar slipped his dagger out of his belt. The layered dwarven steel was designed to be sharp enough to slice open the thick giant flesh. In a quick move between the punches, he rolled onto his back. "Heh-heh." The giant's boulder-sized fist came down. Brenwar jabbed his sword hilt deep between the giant's knuckles.

Hopping backward, the orcen giant let out a tremendous howl. He shook his monstrous head, letting out a moan that filled the forest.

Brenwar scanned the shale, locking on his war hammer nearby. He skittered through the slippery shale and snatched the great hammer up. He faced the enraged giant. Winding the hammer up like a windmill, he said, "Say goodnight, giant!" He let the hammer fly. Sailing through the air, straight and true, the war hammer's steel smote the giant in the forehead.

CRRRAAACK!

The giant orc stumbled backward on wobbly legs. Swaying side to side and rubbing his skull, he teetered toward the mouth of the cave. Two giant steps from the threshold, the giant fell face-first to the ground. Brenwar moved in. He retrieved his dagger and war hammer then climbed up the giant's back. He stood proudly on the giant's head with the war hammer slung on one shoulder.

Brenwar found Slivver and Elween looking right at him with looks of astonishment on their serpentine faces. He winked at them. "By Giimliin's hoary beard, that was fun!"

Furious, Slivver said, "You did this on purpose, didn't you?"

"I spoke to some folks in town. Seems these freakish orcs were giving them trouble."

"Since when do you care about people?"

"Maybe he has a soft spot for them," Elween suggested.

"Dwarves don't have soft spots."' Brenwar beat his breastplate. "Hah-hah-har! Unless they can lead me to giants."

CHAPTER 19

SITTING QUIETLY WITH HIS BACK against the wall, Nath heard a scuffle of feet on the other side of his cell door. Slowly the door, groaning on its hinges, swang inward. Two Caligin stepped inside and pointed short spears right at Nath's chest. A third Caligin set a metal plate of food and a bowl of water on the floor. The Caligin took the empty bowl and tray and backed out, and together, the three elves closed the door. The bolt on the outside of the door slammed shut. The scuffle of feet moving away followed. Nath was alone again.

His nostrils flared as he took in the aroma of the bland bowl of a milky soup with chunks of something like potato in it. Nath had been fed a bowl once a day. It was barely enough to sustain him. His stomach groaned day and night. He pushed off the cold wall and crawled over to the food. He started with the water, gulping half of it down.

I suppose I should be thankful for it. They could be feeding me nothing at all. May the great dragons bless it.

Trying to stay positive, he slurped the bowl of milky stew. Starving, he drained the bowl, spooning the gruel out with his finger and fighting not to smell it. He needed sustenance, no matter how bad it was, to keep his strength up for when he made his escape. He tossed the bowl aside, scooped up the bowl of water and washed the yucky soup down. "Gah! Who am I kidding? That is horrible. I can't possibly be thankful for that!"

Nath had been locked up in the cell for several days. There had been no word from Chazzan or Maefon. The only people he'd seen were the guards. Sometimes, he would pull himself up to peek out the window, thinking that he heard signs of life, but all he saw was the frozen landscape, getting buried deeper in snow. The howling wind outside the walls tricked his mind, making the sound of voices, only to turn up nothing. The days were long, uncomfortable, and dreadful. The nights were even worse.

Given Nath's last casual encounter with Chazzan, he was of the impression that he would be treated better. He didn't expect such a long isolation. He thought he might have been used to it by now, but one never got used to misery.

He moved back to his dry corner against the wall, where the wind didn't cut into the cracks. Just like in Slaver Town, he started to work out a plan to escape. He told himself to be patient, that Chazzan would let him out soon enough, but what if the evil elf didn't? Worse yet, what about Maefon and Darkken? Were they safe or in danger? What if Chazzan killed them? What if Nath needed to save them?

Action was better than no action. It was time to act.

The longer I sit here, the weaker I'll get—at least with this awful food they are serving. That's probably what Chazzan wants.

At the same time, Nath wondered what Darkken was thinking. The strapping wizard warrior with rust-colored hair would probably be playing possum with his powers. If Chazzan didn't know about them, then Darkken would probably strike at the opportune moment. Darkken had to be nearby, in a cell just like Nath's. But Nath had heard very little outside of the thick stone walls. Just the chittering of rats. And the Caligin were very cautious when they brought him to his cell. They put a red hood over his face. Nath stretched with his senses to get a feel the best he could of his environment. Stonewater Keep was about ten stories high, and he went up five levels when they brought him here.

Nath popped his knuckles one by one and sorted through everything he knew about Chazzan and the keep. Back in Dragon Home, he didn't know Chazzan very well, but the dark elf did seem different now. Nath wasn't sure if it was the elf's clothing or not, but his movement and build were off. There was something about him that Nath could not put his finger on.

Sitting long hour after long hour, he reflected once more on all that had happened. He stayed focused on what the dark elves did. They killed the fledglings. Nath ended up banished from Dragon Home as he hunted the murderers down. They all deserved to die, for in their death, there would be justice.

He longed to see the half dryad, Calypsa's, warm and beautiful face. He missed Hacksaw's hearty and rugged laughter. Seeing Homer again would have been nice too. They were all true, trustworthy, and loyal friends. He embraced them, but with Maefon and Darkken, he didn't feel quite the same. Something held him back from fully trusting them. Like Chazzan, it was something that he couldn't put his finger on.

A field mouse squeezed underneath the doorway. The mouse's big brown eyes, nose, and little whiskers twitched as it eyed Nath.

Nath flicked his fingers. "Go ahead. Enjoy what is left of that awful gruel, even though I don't think it's fit for a rat. I'm only warning you because at this moment, you are the only friend I have."

CHAPTER 20

"DID YOU GET YOUR BELLY full?" Nath said to the mouse that he held in the palm of his hand. With his thumb, he stroked its head. "You probably have a sick belly. I know I do." His stomach gurgled. The food was awful, but he started to worry that Chazzan might have added something to it to make it worse. It wouldn't have been the first time that he had been served bad food. They did it in Slaver Town too. He released the mouse. It dashed across the cell, pushed underneath the door, and vanished over the threshold. "I wish I could do that."

Nath stood. He jumped up, grabbed hold of the windowsill, and peered outside. The only things that moved were the snowflakes and icy river. Otherwise, the fields beyond were a sea of white. He dropped down.

"Enough of this. It's time to get out of here."

Rubbing his chilly cheeks, he suddenly thought of the hermix, Ruffle. For some reason, he said, "Ruffle, where are you?"

The strange little varmint-like man that resembled something like a giant gopher or beaver had the power to teleport the both of them from one place to another. Granted, Nath didn't miss the hermix, but he could use the strange man's help now.

"Ruffle, if you get me out of this, I'll owe you one."

Nath waited several minutes. Finally, he shrugged and began to pace. He'd hoped that he would have a chance to make it outside to see Chazzan and Maefon. There he would have a better chance to escape, or at least take a shot at Chazzan. The biggest obstacles were the Caligin. They weren't ordinary elves, by any means. They were extraordinarily trained assassins and hunters, alert and seasoned fighters. Overtaking scores of them would be impossible. At the moment, the only thing that Nath had protecting him was his breastplate. He considered himself lucky that he hadn't been stripped of that protection. When the guards came again, he would use it to his advantage.

Every day at the same time, the elves brought his food. Two of them brandished spears. The third dark elf carried the trays of food. Though they were quick and armed, Nath felt he could take them. He ran the scenario through his thoughts over and over again.

I can do this. They will open the door. I'll pretend to stir from my slumber. As they step inside, they will catch me covering my mouth and yawning. While sitting, I'll have one leg braced against the wall. I'll push off to propel me the moment the third elf enters. The moment he starts to switch out the bowls, which I'll leave just a little farther out of reach, I'll strike.

The first elf, on the left, will spear me in the chest, while I grab the spear from the second elf on the right. I'll pull him inside. As the first spear skips off my chest, I'll slug the first elf in the jaw and stuff him inside. Still moving as fast as only a dragon man can, I'll kick the third elf hard in the ribs. I'll shut all threats inside the cell with me and beat the living daylights out of all of them. I'll take their weapons, lock them inside, and find Maefon and Darkken. It will be perfect. It has to be!

Now all Nath had to do was wait. As he did so, he went through the many lessons taught to him by Master Elween. He stretched, did calisthenics, and practiced his attack. He started on the floor and burst into action, fluidly going through every move. Master Elween called it an action plan. She always critically stressed the importance of it.

He sat down in a half-cross-legged position, with his foot against the wall. He faked a yawn, pushed off toward unseen assailants, and ghost-fought through them all. He envisioned every tactic they might try. They could drop their spears and go for the sword or dagger. They might shout out for help.

"Hmm…" Nath rubbed his chin. "I better go for the throat punch. Knock their loud jugulars out. The question is, will there be more of them outside the door?" He pushed his ear against the door. There was a hollow sound that seemed to vibrate with the howl of the wind. He didn't hear anything on the other side, not even the slightest stir from another cell. He also found it odd that his dungeon cell was higher in the tower and not below the ground like most dungeons were. He pecked on the door's metal, making a soft clinking sound. "Come on, someone knock back."

He heard nothing new.

So far as he could tell, wherever he was, it wasn't guarded. He moved back to his dry spot in the corner, put his back to the wall and hands around his ankles, tucked his head into his knees, and waited. The day's light turned to a moony, snowy darkness. "Save your energy, Nath. Save your energy."

He made a real yawn, shuddered, and fell asleep.

Nath dreamed that he was in a river of black water, swimming against a rapid current. Dark, unseen forces pulled at his feet. He swallowed water as he was pulled under, only to swim desperately back to the surface. He fought his way onto a rock and hung on for dear life. He stared into a deep-purple skyline. A dragon came, a huge beast with copper scales and thick ridge plates all over its body. It had great horns and eyes bright and molten. It landed on a natural bridge of stone right in front of him. Spreading its great black wings from one side of the bridge, it let out an earth-shaking roar. Mouth wide open, it struck at Nath, swallowing him whole into its belly full of darkness.

Nath's eyes popped open. "Guh!" He sat upright. Cold sweat beaded his face. His panting was the only sound in the eerie silence. The chronic winds of the seasonal snows had stopped. Daylight peeked through his portal into the dreary cell, shining dully on the door. The only other sound he could hear was the pounding inside his ears. He wiped his eyes and the drool from his mouth. He'd never had such a vivid and intense dream in his life.

A scuffle on the other side of the door caught his attention. His mind went blank. His action plan seemed to have mystically evaporated from his memory.

Gads!

The door's bolt scraped across the metal.

Nath coiled to spring, completely oblivious to the plan he ran through his mind one hundred times, so shaken from his nightmarish slumber there was only one thought pounding through his mind.

Escape!

The door swang inward.

Nath closed his eyes. Fragments of his plan came together.

Two figures emerged through the doorway.

Nath opened his eyes and launched himself at them.

CHAPTER 21

"UH-HUH. UH-HUH," BRENWAR SAID TO the townsmen gathered around him. They wore long woolen shirts and had knit caps on their heads. They were farmers and tradesmen mostly, drinking from wooden tankards filled with ale. They were the hardworking leaders of the town. Before when Brenwar came, they clammed up, but now information came from their mouths like early-spring water from the melting snowcaps of a mountain. They talked about everything, revealing some very important and telling information. Brenwar listened. "Uh-huh. Uh-huh."

They all shared a long table. One of the townsmen's eyes kept drifting to the table's center. In the middle of the table was the skinned skull of the giant orc Brenwar had killed. The massive head filled the table from one side to the other. The white bone at the top of the beast's crown shined in the candlelight. The older townsman reached out to touch the bottom fangs on the skull's lower jaw.

Brenwar hammered his fist on the table. "Gootah!"

The men jumped backward. One white-bearded man fell off his chair.

Bursting out in laughter, Brenwar helped the man back into his chair. "It's dead. Trust me, I'm just teasing with you."

The surrounding men let out some guffaws and clanked their tankards. More stories spilled into the evening. Brenwar drank what they considered their most potent ale, though to him it was just watery stuff, early into the morning. All of the patrons passed out on the floor or on the table. Brenwar, who hadn't moved from his spot in hours, got up, tossed a couple of logs on the fire, and pointed a finger at the ugly skull. "Can't wait to find more of your brothers and kill them." With that he headed out into the blustery weather, stomping out of town through the ankle-deep snow.

Heading back to his rendezvous point with the dragons, he stopped on a small bridge that crossed over a wide creek. He'd been holding his water for over a week. Dwarves were known for holding their movements for what seemed like an impossibly long time to a human. Leaning over the bridge with his back to the wind, he peed. As he did so, he sang an old dwarven hymn.

Beyond the dwarven gloom,
Concealed from common sight,
Was a troll so big its arms were long as trees.
Canavaas the Slayer climbed the troll's mountainous body,
With his axe, he slayed him, with his hands, he chopped him. Whack! Whack! Ho! Whack!
Eight days later the troll was dead. Its head fills the great gulch in the mountain.
The lonely sky stares down with bright stones for eyes, singing,
Whack! Whack! Ho! Salute, Canavaas the Slayer!

Fifteen minutes later, Brenwar finished peeing and singing. He scuttled up into the hills, where he met up with Slivver and Elween. Both of them were nestled under an umbrella of pine branches, free from the building snow.

Slivver was the first to sit up. "Well, look who is back. And so soon. Did you dazzle the local townsfolk with the giant ogre-head bauble?"

"I dazzled them right out of their shoes. It's always nice to see little people like them happy." Brenwar peered about. "Why didn't you make a fire?"

"What is the matter? Is it too cold for you, Brenwar?" Slivver said.

"I'm not cold. I just wanted to melt this frost from my beard." Brenwar shook the snow out of his braids.

Elween moved to a stack of branches. "We didn't know when you would return. I have to admit, even I am surprised that you came back so soon." She breathed a narrow stream of flames into the wood, setting it ablaze. "Here is your fire."

Brenwar rubbed his hands together over the flames. "Much obliged. I truly enjoy the flames. It makes me think of my forge in Morgdon. I'll have to show it to you sometime. As a matter of fact, I can give you a very apt description." He flapped his braids. "I'll start with the tool benches. I have five, made from wood, iron, granite, steel, and marble. Made them all myself. I have sixty favorite tools that I use, and I've named them all. My oldest anvil was passed down to me by my great-grandfather. His name is Frank."

"Frank?" Elween tilted her head from side to side. "That is a curious name."

"Frank the anvil. What a shame you didn't bring this anvil with you," Slivver replied.

"Oh, I thought about it many times. A good anvil is always handy." Brenwar held his stubby fingers out over the flames. "Did I ever tell you the first time I used that anvil? I was wee high, got my first smiting hammer named Gildon. The moment that steel struck steel—"

"Brenwar!" Slivver exclaimed as he fought the urge to coil his tail around the dwarf's throat. "I don't want to hear any more stories. I just want to know whether or not you found out anything about Nath."

"You don't have to listen," Brenwar replied. "Besides, dragons are as long-winded as any. I thought you enjoyed my stories."

"No, I hate them, and I've told you that every time you've told them. And what dragons have you been conversing with?"

"Balzurth." With a twinkle in his eye, Brenwar added, "Talk about long-winded. My stories are as short as a headless halfling compared to his. You should thank me."

"Any news, or are we going to move on to the next town filled with simpletons that slaver over your stories?"

Brenwar looked Slivver dead in the eyes. "I talked long with a man who swears by the hair on his chins that he saw an unforgettable man who matched Nath's description." Brenwar reached into his pack and pulled out a rolled-up parchment. "As a matter of fact, his wife even painted a picture of him." He unrolled the parchment and held it before their eyes. "Is this him?"

Chapter 22

Slivver and Elween's long necks bent downward. They turned and exchanged befuddled glances between them, then fixed their stares back on the picture.

"Hah!" Brenwar said with great mirth. "I don't think I've ever seen a dragon look so surprised before. And you thought that I didn't know what I was doing, didn't you, Slivver?"

"I had my doubts about your tactics," Slivver admitted.

"Never doubt a dwarf."

"There is no doubt that this is Nath. It's an excellent resemblance painted with a relatively skilled hand." Elween's long eyelashes blinked. "And the man painted this? A farmer?"

"No, a tradesman. A fine bearded fellow, but a bit bushy, not as neatly trimmed as it should be," Brenwar replied.

"Seems like a strange fascination for a man," she said.

"No, no, not him, his wife. He told me that he and his wife made a trip to a town called Riegelwood. It's known for its festivals, especially the ones in the winter." Brenwar handed the pictured to Elween. "As he tells me, they go there to celebrate their anniversary annually. At the same time, his wife will shop, and he'll do some business. You see, he makes duck calls, taps for the wooden kegs, skinning knives, and such. A good tradesman, not as good as a dwarf, but a solid man of good repute. Well, as things would have it, his wife saw Nath. I spoke with her as well, briefly, but she said his golden eyes melted her heart. Then she rushed off to do more painting but wished me well in finding him and hopes I bring him by someday.

"You should've seen the scowl on the husband's face. Well, not so much of a scowl as a deflation of ego. This is a prominent man in town, yet his lifelong love is forlorn. He says his wife can't stop thinking about Nath, but he was thankful that his wife learned what his name was. He was tired of her guessing it." Brenwar turned back toward the fire. "He hoped that maybe that name would bring her some closure."

Looking at the painting while talking to Brenwar, Elween said, "Won't she miss this painting? It is a fine piece of work."

"No. As it turns out, she's painted dozens of portraits of Nath. She's filled a separate storage room with them. Ha. Poor fella, he seems lost. He got a good look at Nath himself, and he admitted that for a man, Nath was very striking but not so much that a person would lose their mind over it."

Looking at the picture, Slivver said, "A dragon's charms can be very powerful. There is no telling who it might affect. It seems this simple country girl was truly smitten. It happens with elves too."

"And dwarfs," Brenwar stated.

"I don't think humans have ever been smitten by dwarves," Slivver fired back.

"Have too."

"Have not."

Elween rolled up the painting. "So, where is Riegelwood?"

"A few days' walk from here," Brenwar said.

"Or half a day flying," Slivver added.

"You are more than welcome to fly, Slivver. You can just wait until I get there. And you'd think being such a high-minded and graceful dragon and all, you would show some appreciation for the find. You don't get much more proof positive than what I got you."

Slivver stiffened. It was true, Brenwar had more than delivered some vital information. He brought actual proof. Slivver put his hand on the dwarf's shoulder. "You are right. Well done."

Brenwar pushed Slivver's hand off. "Eh, don't get all mushy on me. A simple 'well done' will do."

"I don't mean to rush things," Slivver said, "but if we know where Nath is, we should get there right away."

Staring into the fire, Brenwar clawed at his beard. "It was two years ago when they saw him last. There was a fire at the inn where they stayed. The entire place went down in flames. They've been back once since but never saw him again. And trust me, according to the husband, they looked. Well, she looked. I'd say that Nath has moved on. The trail is cold, but it's certainly worth a look. And with that said, I'm ready to get going as soon as you are. But if it makes you feel any better, fly for Riegelwood. See what those keen dragon eyes of yours will see. I'll meet you there in a few days."

"You're serious?" Slivver said. Brenwar wasn't in charge, per se, but he was in the lead in tracking down Nath.

With a shrug, Brenwar said, "I don't see why not."

He looked at Elween, who said to him, "I'm ready to stretch my wings if you are." She rolled up the painting and gave it to Brenwar.

Brenwar gave them clear and concise directions.

"Dragonspeed to you, Brenwar." Together, he and Elween stretched out their wings and launched themselves between the trees and into the sky.

Brenwar kicked snow over the campfire, extinguishing the flames. "Dragonspeed to you, heh-heh." He picked up his war hammer and slung his pack over his back. "But I've got another thing to do."

Chapter 23

Nath crashed into the two figures entering his cell. He punched the tallest in the jaw. The elf dropped to the floor, out cold. He seized the second elf by locking his fingers around their throat. As he started to squeeze, his eyes locked on hers. "Maefon!" He released her.

Rubbing her throat, she said in a raspy voice, "That's a fine way to thank your liberators."

"I'm sorry. I thought you were the usual guards. So, you are here to rescue me?"

"*We* are here to rescue you, but it doesn't look like he's going to be of much help now." She looked down at the elf that had been knocked out. He wore feathers and narrow braids in his hair like the Brothers of the Wind. "Grab his sword. We need to go."

Nath slid the elf's sword and dagger out of the sheaths. "What is happening?"

"All chaos has broken loose. That is what." Maefon moved out into the hallway and walked at a quick and quiet pace down it. All of the doors were open, and many of the rooms had abandoned furnishings, such as beds, chairs, and chests of drawers in them, all common for typical guest rooms.

Nath peeked in each and every one that they passed. It seemed strange that the much more livable cells had been abandoned. "Where are the other brothers? And Darkken?"

"That's why I am here," she said, making her way farther down the hallway to the end, where a stairwell led up and down the tower. "Darkken escaped, freed me and the Brothers of the Wind, and now he is going after Chazzan. He sent us after you."

Nath could hear the distinct commotion of a battle raging echoing through the stairwell. "It sounds like a war going on up there." Following her, he crept into the stairwell. "Where have you been all of this time?"

"I spent a day with Chazzan, trying to win him over. He went into a typical fit when he saw I wasn't cooperating and threw me in a room much like yours." They moved up the stairwell two steps at a time until they made it to the next landing. "The rest of our friends were in the dungeons below, at least that was what Chazzan said. He planned to kill us all, though he hoped I would join him and possibly he would convince you too."

"I'd never do that."

"That's what I said. However, Darkken escaped within the last hour. With a handful of the Brothers of the Wind, he managed to sneak through, find me, and free me. Chazzan mentioned where you were. I got that much out of him. Now you are free, but we need to help Darkken and the others." She turned and gave Nath a firm hug. "Nath, there are so many. Perhaps we should escape. Darkken suggested that. But isn't it awful for me to consider it?"

"We came here to put an end to Chazzan, didn't we? We won't get a better chance than this."

She gave an approving smirk. "I was hoping you would say that. I needed your strength." She started back up the stairwell. The clash of steel on steel resounded from above. Both of them backed against the wall as a Caligin fell down the gap between the stairs, smashing to his death on the stone floor below. "That's one more for us, but there are so many, Nath. We need more power to take them."

"If I only had Fang," he said.

"I know where it could be, but time is fleeting. We need to help Darkken and the others."

"Is it on the way up, or is it down?"

"Up, in Chazzan's chambers. He took me to his library, showing off his prizes, trying to woo me over again. Can you believe that? He tried to kill me once."

"Then I wouldn't doubt that he would try to kill you again." With the battle raging above, Nath's blood churned faster. Another elf was pitched down the stairwell. This time it was a

Brother of the Wind. "No!" Nath bounded past Maefon, passing by the sixth, seventh, and eighth levels.

"Nath, you are passing Chazzan's chambers." She halted at the door to the eighth level. "You will need your sword."

"I feel there is no time. This one will have to do." The sounds of battle filled his ears. He couldn't stop running toward it. His friend was in danger. At the ninth floor, just outside the door, two Caligin were waiting. They lunged at Nath. He took a shot in the chest. The blade skidded off his plate. Nath cut the second attacker down with his sword.

Maefon slipped behind him, stabbing the first attacker with her dagger. She hit him square in the chest. The dark elf groaned and took a whack at her. She ducked underneath the wild swing.

Nath shoved the wounded Caligin into the stairwell. Maefon tripped the elf. The light-footed elf's sword arm flailed about as the strong push sent him off the edge of the stairs and plummeting down below.

They entered the grand chamber of the ninth floor. It was decorated much like the dining room but with a smaller, rounder table in the center. A gang of Caligin had three Brothers of the Wind backed against the wall. They tangled in a furious fight of steel on steel.

Nath lifted his sword and charged. "Dragon! Dragon!"

As soon as he spoke, more Caligin, hiding behind the curtains, emerged.

Maefon shouted, "Nath, watch out!"

Chapter 24

Five Caligin came at Nath, bull rushing him at full speed. The dark elves were nothing short of highly skilled and deadly fighters. He'd seen them in action enough to know that. Each carried a longsword made from the finest elven steel. Not seeing a way out, Nath dashed for the round table and dove under it.

The elves closed in, crouching down and taking quick stabs at them. But the table was big, allowing Nath to stay out of reach in the center.

With a flick of the wrist, Nath flung his dagger. The blade pierced an elf deep in the chest. In a burst of strength, Nath rose, moving the heavy table upward, carrying its momentum toward the elves and cracking two of them in the forehead with the hard edge. He shoved it all the way over top of the two reeling attackers. He jumped on top of it, facing off with the other two attackers.

The elves attacked him from both sides. The steel in their hands flicked out like striking snakes. They stepped in and jabbed.

Nath parried the first striker with a hard backhanded swing. With a loud clang, he knocked the sword aside. At the same time, he leaned forward, away from the second attack. "Augh!"

The dark elf sliced across his shoulder. Triumph filled the elf's dark eyes. It attacked again, drawing back for a lethal swing.

Nath stepped into a backward kick, catching the elf square in the belly. A gust of air burst out of the elf's lungs. Just in the nick of time, Nath parried the other attacker's deadly thrust. The elven steel slid right across the metal that covered his abdomen. Nath spun his sword behind him, catching the elf in the neck and taking the head from the shoulders.

He took no pleasure in the gruesome feat. The table stirred underneath his feet, jostling him. He ducked as the other elf unleashed his own decapitating swing. The blade swished right over top of Nath's head, clipping strands of hair. Nath thrust hard, stabbing the elf and killing it.

The victory was short-lived. The Caligin who cornered the Brothers of the Wind had slain them all. Now, in a rush, they came for Nath.

"Nath," Maefon shouted. "Jump!" The woman was crouched down between him and the doorway, with her hands planted on the stone.

Nath leapt so high his head almost touched the ceiling. The floor beneath him lit up with white fire that matched up with Maefon's blazing eyes.

The Caligin stopped in their tracks with their hair standing on end. Weapons fell free of their grips as their once-limber limbs twitched and convulsed like rickety things. With their garbs smoking and their hair singed, each and every one of them hit the ground.

Nath landed in the same instant. A powerful shock went through his body just as the glimmering white floor turned gray again. He tingled from head to toe. He shook his head. "Whoa…"

Maefon rushed over to him. She wrapped him up, steadying him. "Are you all right?"

"My lips feel really funny, and my teeth tickle, but I'm well. What did you do?"

"It's a spell I've had in my sheath for quite some time. This was the perfect opportunity to use it."

Surveying the fallen elves in the room, he said, "It did the trick. You continue to astound me."

"You haven't seen anything yet," she said with a smile.

"Glad we are on the same side." There was still a commotion rocking the ceiling above them. On the opposite side of the room from where they entered was another set of stairs that appeared to be something that the Caligin were guarding. "There!"

They made a break for the stairwell and headed straight for the top. Nath pushed through the wooden door at the top. A blast of icy wind greeted him like a slap in the face.

The beastly ogre, Monfur, stood at the rim of the keep's rooftop with an elf hoisted high over his head. The ogre's broad back was to Nath. On the rest of the deck, more elves battled against elves in a whirl of striking steel. Nath took off at a dead sprint, bearing down fast on Monfur. He rammed his sword straight into the ogre's back.

Monfur dropped the elf on the side of the wall. He twisted around, ripping the sword out of Nath's strong grip. "Did you stab my backside?"

Nath looked up into the lazy brute's eyes. "Uh-huh."

With a neck as thick as a horse's, Monfur bent his head down toward Nath. "You will die!" Monfur tried to wrap his big arms around Nath.

Nath skipped away. He scanned the rooftop for a blade. The only one he saw as he evaded Monfur's advances was the one stuck in Monfur's back.

Perhaps I should have gotten Fang after all! If elven steel won't kill this monster, what in Nalzambor will?

The long-armed brute kept coming after Nath, who skittered away like a critter. The ogre knocked aside the elves who waded into his path, striking them dead, Caligin or Brother of the Wind. He tried to corral Nath, closing him into the corner.

Nath made a move, dashing away from the ogre's grasp. His foot slipped on the icy, slick surface, slowing his escape.

The ogre's unusually quick hand caught Nath underneath the back collar of his armor. "I got you!" He flung Nath into the hard stone of the corner battlement.

With stars in his eyes, Nath watched the ogre advance while saying, "Yum-yum, your succulent bones are mine."

CHAPTER 25

SAGGING AGAINST THE HARD WALL, Nath fought to straighten his legs.

Monfur snatched him up in a bear hug. "I have you now."

Muscular ogre arms as hard as tree limbs constricted with crushing power. Nath's spine popped several times. The only thing keeping his bones together was the breastplate armor absorbing the punishing damage. Feeling his face redden, Nath manage to blurt out, "May I tell you something before you kill me?"

Pushing his big, ugly face into Nath's, Monfur said, "Sure."

"You have really, really, really, really, really bad breath, and you aren't the first ogre I've known either. Perhaps it's that rotting flesh that still hangs inside your mouth. Clean that out with a broomstick or something."

"Yum-yum. You are full of wit, human. I think I'll eat your head first and shut you up for good." Monfur's great jaws widened.

Nath kicked and wriggled with all of his might, but even his strong body was muted by the ogre's monstrous strength. With wide eyes, he watched the monster's jaws descend.

Bzzzzt!

Monfur's jaws gaped open even farther. Nath dropped out of the brute's hands. He found Maefon standing behind the ogre, winging balls of blue energy into Monfur like snowballs. The blue flame-like balls knocked the ogre into the wall where Nath was once pinned.

"Take him out, Maefon!"

She threw her last energy ball into the ogre, who ducked behind his arms. Her chest expanded in and out. "I think it's going to take more energy, and I don't have much left."

In a rage, Monfur came to his feet and fastened his stare on Maefon. "You will die!" He charged. Maefon ran.

Not seeing another sword on the deck, Nath dashed after Monfur. As the ogre chased

Maefon toward the wall, she quickly turned in another direction. Monfur started to turn after her.

"No you don't!" Nath gathered steam, ramming into the backside of the ogre. The momentum sent them both sliding toward the battlement. Nath grabbed onto his sword that was plugged in the ogre's back and pushed the beast like a sled.

Monfur slammed hard into the wall between the battlements.

Nath drove the blade in farther.

The ogre jerked and screamed. Like a mindless beast, he crossed too far over the edge. He twisted at the last moment, long fingers stretching for purchase. It was too late. He fell, screaming, "Nooooooooooo!" His body busted on the rocks and bounced just like so many victims before him.

Maefon looked over the edge with Nath, panting. "We got him. Thank goodness we got him."

Nath leaned against the stone with his arm stretched over the edge. "That's twice in a day you bailed me out. I owe you."

A thunder clap exploded somewhere on the rooftop.

At the same time both of them shouted, "Darkken!" Nath hadn't seen or heard the man, but instinctively he knew Darkken battled on the roof. There was a higher landing on the southern face of the wall. It was there he spied a bright ball of illuminating energy surrounding two men locked in mortal combat. The brightness of the glowing light obscured the view, but Nath could see the larger-sized Darkken locked up with an elf wearing a chrome helmet, all black leather armor, with the red cape covering his shoulders and black gloves over the hands. It was Chazzan. In a rush, Nath sped up to jump onto the landing.

Maefon hooked his arm. Squinting, she said, "You can't go in there, Nath. That energy will cut you to pieces. It might tear your mind apart."

"I must," he said, pulling away.

"No, Nath, no!"

A shockwave of energy blasted out from the two men fighting, lifting Nath and Maefon from their feet. When Nath looked up again, Darkken was down on his knees with his fingers locked with Chazzan's, who stood above him. The chrome helmet glared down on the man. Pain wracked Darkken's fierce expression.

"Noooo!" Maefon fired bolts of energy from her fingertips. They skipped off the elven helmet, knocking his head aside.

Nath burst into action, running at full speed. He leapt on the landing and rushed into the globe of swirling energies. Painful shards ripped through his body. With an agonized scream, he forced himself toward the men. "Darkken, don't quit!"

The older warrior lifted his chin. Once defeated, a new fire flowed through his eyes. Growling, Darkken started to stand. With fingers locked with fingers, he rose back to full height.

Chazzan's arms trembled. He shrank underneath Darkken's burning stare.

Darkken pushed the elf two steps backward and shouted, "Hit him, Nath. Hit him with all you have. I weaken!"

Empty-handed, Nath had nothing to deliver the finishing blow. Over the roar of surrounding energy, he heard Maefon's voice. He turned. Maefon hurled a longsword through the air. Nath snatched it and in the same motion stabbed Chazzan right through the heart.

The elf let out a loud sighing moan that had a different ring to it than Nath had expected. At that same moment, Darkken's ring-covered fingers glowed bright with copper. Like a forest catching fire, the elf's arms burned and crackled. In a few moments, Chazzan's body was burning cinders.

Nath pulled his sword from the body of ash. The skin and flesh, now charred to the bone, turned to dust as the skeletal remains collapsed to the ground. The elven-faced helmet bounced with a hollow *thunk* on the ground. Smoke rolled out of the neck and eyes. Darkken stumbled, exhausted, into Nath's arms.

"It's over," Darkken said as Maefon came to prop him up. "It's over."

"It's not over until it's over, I fear," Nath said. Caligin surrounded them, armed with swords and bows and arrows pointed right at them. He stepped out in front of his friends. "Stay behind me."

Chapter 26

With the icy wind tearing through their hair, everyone on the top of the keep stood at a standstill. The Caligin had six bowmen with arrows aimed right at Nath. Another dozen swordsmen stood at the ready behind them. They all stood with grim, stark looks in their dark eyes.

Sword gripped in his hand, Nath eased forward. The bowstrings stretched farther along the dark elves' cheeks. Their swordsmen took two quick steps forward. Nath lowered his sword. "Your leader is dead. So, who is your leader now?"

The dark elves exchanged uncomfortable glances. The bowstrings pulled along their cheeks eased. One of the elven bowmen at the forefront came forward. "Our leader is the one that vanquished the last."

Nath cast a look at Maefon and Darkken. "Us?"

Darkken shrugged. The drained look in his copper-colored eyes was replaced with new strength. He stood upright while clinging tightly to Maefon, who cradled his side. He came forward and said, "What do you mean?"

"It is our custom. Any Caligin can challenge another and take his station," the dark elf replied. "You have been victorious over our leader, Chazzan."

"Let me correct you, *we* have been victorious," Darkken said.

"Sire, it was you who engaged him. It was your magic that turned him to dust. It is a victory that you led." The elf's lips twisted. "Even though you are a human."

Darkken whispered in Nath's ear, "I'm not really sure what to make of this. Your part in this is as big as mine. Any thoughts?"

"I say go with it," he replied. It was an unexpected twist for Nath to follow, but the Caligin's words seemed sincere.

"What about you, Maefon? Any ideas?" Darkken said.

"Beware of treachery. We don't know these people," she replied.

With a thoughtful expression, Darkken chose his next words carefully. "According to your customs, then, if I am your leader, then I ask, do I have any challengers?"

The elves exchanged quick looks with one another, then their spokesman said, "You have no challengers. You are now the head of the Caligin."

"Then prove your faithfulness. Lower your weapons to the ground," Darkken said.

Bows, arrows, swords, and steel were lowered to the ground.

"Hands on heads," Darkken added. The elves complied. "So far as I am concerned, each and every one of you is guilty of evil, either by your actions or by association. I'm not one to murder in cold blood, but you have much to give an account for. You will spend your time in the dungeons while we sort through your ways and your dealings and decide on what must be done. Do any of you question this?"

The elven spokesmen replied, "No, you are the new Lord of the Dark in the Day. Your words must be heeded."

"I am no such thing!" Darkken's brows buckled. "Don't you dare call me that again," he said, softening his voice.

Nath felt the anger in Darkken's words. The sudden anger surprised him. He looked away, gazing over the top of the tower, and noticed elves on fleet feet running away in the snow. "Look."

Darkken leaned out over the wall. "It seems that many of the Caligin have abandoned the cause. Let them run. We have enough to sort out as it is." When he turned his attention back to the Caligin, two of the Brothers of the Wind were among them, holding swords to the Caligin's backs. "Thank the winds not all of our brothers are lost. Brothers, take these Caligin to the dungeons. Nath, will you help see them to their new station as well while Maefon and I check the rest of the keep for survivors?"

"I'd be glad to," Nath said.

Alone on the top of the keep, Darkken and Maefon engaged in a long embrace. As she smiled up at him, he kissed her on the forehead and then said, "We are home."

"That was brilliant, my lord. Costly, but brilliant. Are you wounded?"

"I still feel plenty of sting in the inside of my organs. Arteses fought well for the cause. He gave me a true fight as if his life depended on it."

"You trained Arteses well. He died with honor," she replied. Breaking off the embrace, she went over and picked up the chrome polished helmet. An elven skull fell out of it. "Poor Arteses. He made a fine Chazzan during his final stand. He'll be missed."

"Yes, they all will." Darkken took her by the hand and walked her to the end of the roof. He stared out over the frozen plains. "You were brilliant as well, my sweet. I couldn't have done this without you."

"Do you really mean that?"

"No, but I wanted you to feel good about yourself. After all, you did work hard."

"Ha-ha, but I'll take it. So, you feel that we have completely fooled Nath?"

"He cares deeply about us."

"I agree. So, what are we going to do next?"

"We've avenged the dragons, yourself, and all that the Caligin have wronged. I say we get him very comfortable here and start a new role in the world, with the Caligin playing heroes."

"Don't you mean the Brothers of the Wind?"

"Exactly."

CHAPTER 27

AS MUCH AS BRENWAR WANTED to help Slivver and Elween, there was something else he needed to check out first. According to the townsfolk he spoke with, some dwarven silver miners were feuding with the men of Quintuklen. Apparently, it had gotten bad, because Quintuklen had sent down their very best, the legionnaires, to settle the dispute. That didn't sit well with Brenwar. The dwarves had been mining the same holes in the hills for centuries, and it didn't make sense that the humans would take issue with it now. Something stank, and he felt obligated to check it out.

Ankle deep in the snow, he trudged along at as brisk a pace as he could, not stopping day or night. His black hair and beard were snow-white when he arrived at the dwarven mining camp. Southwest of Quintuklen, also known as the City of Crowns, he entered the tent city on a plateau tucked away in the hills.

It wasn't Brenwar's first trip to the small mining settlement of his brethren. He'd been there when he was younger, putting his back behind a pick and mining silver streams. It was late in the day, with darkness settling in, but the sound of metal ringing on stone could still be heard coming out of the mine shafts. He found the biggest tent in the center of the camp, stomped the snow from his boots just outside the threshold, pushed back the canvas flap, and entered.

The inside of the tent was roomy, with a high pitch, plenty big enough for men, but almost barren. In the middle was a circle of rocks, like a campfire, with orange stones with a fiery glow within. There were no cots, blankets, or bedrolls, just the hard ground underneath. Aside from some picks and other digging tools, there were two barrels and some cups crudely chiseled from stone. A lone dwarf, bigger than even Brenwar, with a hump in his back and a white beard down to his waist, had his back to Brenwar.

"Do you have any ale that's not as frozen as my beard?" he said.

The old dwarf's head tilted. In a strong but soft voice, he said, "It's no surprise that my old friend has forgotten that dwarven ale never freezes. It sounds like you've been drinking those watered-down brews again from the fragile cities of Nalzambor."

"I've had my share, to my disappointment, and it freezes within me. But I can still drink more dwarven ale than any, Varluun."

With heavy garb covered in debris from the mine, Varluun turned. Both of his eyes were smoky white. He showed a smile of perfect teeth capped in silver. "We'll see about that. Get over here, old friend." He opened his arms.

They gave one another a strong dwarven embrace, hitting each other on the back with hard fists.

"It's good to see you." Brenwar broke off the embrace and held his old mentor by the shoulders. Varluun had taught him everything he knew about mining and much about life too. Like many of the aged dwarves, Varluun was a great warrior, a general who retired to run the mines after his fighting days were over. Now, the old dwarf was going blind and had been since Brenwar left him. "How about that ale?"

Varluun pointed a slightly shaky hand toward the keg barrels. "Help us both out, will you?" While Brenwar filled up the cups, Varluun continued speaking. "So, what brings you about?"

"I've heard that the legionnaires are bringing you trouble. That seemed odd to me. We've always had good relations with the humans." He handed Varluun the cup. "To Morgdon." Together, they drank. Brenwar refilled the cups and repeated the gesture three more times. "For Morgdon. Ah, that's good. Dwarven ale is always worth the trip when walking through leagues of chest-deep snow."

"Ho-ho, chest deep, aye. Are you sure it wasn't above your head?"

"No, I'm no braggart. It was only a little snow."

"I see." Varluun ran his fingers through his cottony beard. "It seems that the humans have suddenly become stingy."

"Stingier than a dwarf?"

"It would seem so. We've mined without issue for centuries. The land has never been in dispute. We mine, keep our share, and give to them. That's the agreement." Varluun got a little wheezy. "It's a written agreement. Now, they say they want us off their land. This land is as much ours as theirs now. Not to mention that these silver fields are at the end of their profit. We just mine to keep busy."

"So, you've met with these men, I take it?"

"We've been going back and forth. Here we stand, little more than a hundred dwarves, breaking their backs, and Quintuklen sends their finest army. I fought side by side with the legionnaires in the Great Dragon Wars. Never would I have expected they would turn on me. Of course, all of the ones I knew are long dead. My past relationship carries no weight with them."

"Have they threatened you?"

"It's the old 'move on or else' speech. I think they are trying to provoke us, and I'd be a liar if I wasn't ready to fill their chests with my pickaxe. It's the elves that really irritate me."

"Elves? What elves?"

"Oh, you know the type. So clean and fanciful, staring down at us while at the same time their little noses are upturned. They shake with those soft hands that would fall off if they had a callus on them." Varluun's frown showed his great displeasure. "They think we are so stupid that their butterfly words can talk us out of what is rightfully ours. I don't like them, these especially. My gut tells me they are trying to provoke a war between us."

Brenwar wiped his arm across his mouth and stared into the coals. "You may be onto something."

CHAPTER 28

SEVERAL DAYS HAD PASSED SINCE the takeover at Stonewater Keep. Darkken and Maefon spent a great deal of time in the library. Nath was there with them now, among the large books and tomes that filled the walls of an inner tower-like sanctum. He leafed through the pages of one such tome, bound in leather, with brass clasps that buckled it shut. The book was half as big as his chest, written in Elven, describing the long history between the elves and the dragons. There were drawings and colorful pictures within.

Darkken and Maefon had spent countless hours working with a device on a stone pedestal, with a bowl on the top, called the Pool of Eversight. They both stared into it with a glow on their faces. Darkken looked deep into the waters, while Maefon read words from another tome. The waters glowed, casting warbling blue light on their faces.

"I think that I understand this device now," Darkken said, stepping away from the pedestal. "We don't see through our own eyes. We see through the eyes of something else. I believe it is that vulture that's been circling. I swear, I saw through its view. I think I can summon it."

"That's marvelous." Maefon closed the book and set it down on top of a nearby table. "I too hope to master it."

Rubbing his eyes, Darkken said, "This explains a lot. Now I understand how the Caligin have been able to stay a step ahead of us. But we turned the tables, didn't we?" He looked at Nath. "Didn't we?"

"Huh?" Nath had been studying a dragon that looked much like his father. "Oh, I suppose we did, and now we have the run of the mill in this cold, cold tower as dreary as the bottom of the well."

"I'm sure Maefon will spruce the place up. Besides, we conquered it, and I think it makes for an ideal base of operations for the Brothers of the Wind." Darkken had a proud and glowing look. "We can turn the world around from here."

Over the last two days, Darkken had been pressing the idea of recruiting the Caligin to expand and rebuild the Brothers of the Wind. It was a good idea, as he wanted to undo all of the damage the Caligin had done. The problem was prying the information out of the prisoners in the dungeons about what the Caligin were doing. That wasn't Nath's forte. The thought of torture appalled him. There were some records of their actions, but it was very little. The Caligin seemed to primarily operate by word of mouth. It was the same with the Brothers of the Wind, Nath had surmised. It was a concern that he kept to himself.

"You are awfully quiet over there," Maefon said. "What is on your mind, Nath?"

"In Dragon Home I never read about the elves warring with the dragons before, but this tome is full of many incidents. I just don't understand why I heard nothing about it. You would think that I would have been told."

"Perhaps your father was protecting you," she said.

"He protected me too much."

"Nath, I think all of the races have warred. After all, this world has been here who knows how long," Darkken added. He moved to the bar in the study and poured a glass of wine. "You have to admit, Chazzan did keep an excellent stock of wine in the cellar. It's the best I ever had." He sniffed the goblet. "Remember, friends, sometimes you have to take time to smell the rosy wine. Can I pour you both a glass?"

"No thanks," Nath said.

"I'll have one." Maefon took a seat in a small chair beside Nath. "As I understood it, the Trahaydeen were sent as peacemakers, a sign that they would be friends with the dragons. I believe that was part of the reason we were there."

"But wouldn't this treachery start a war between them again?" Nath asked.

"I think you might have prevented that," she added. "You've found the murderers who admitted to it. All you need to do now is let the dragons know."

"But I'm banished," he said. "They won't take my testimony for another ninety-seven years, and only then can I try to clear myself."

"You can do a lot of good in ninety-seven years. You've done plenty of good already." Darkken brought two glasses of wine over and handed each of them one. "I know you don't want a drink, Nath, but this is worth it. I say we make an oath to one another, agreeing to help one another and others the best that we can."

They exchanged glances and nods of approval, brought their glasses together, and before drinking, Nath said, "To the Brothers of the Wind."

"To the Brothers of the Wind," Darkken and Maefon repeated.

All of them drank. Nath's brows lifted. "You are right, this wine is excellent."

"It's one of my favorites," Darkken said.

Nath gave him a curious look. "How so?"

Darkken blinked heavily. "Oh, well, it's clearly elven, and they do make the best wine. Also," Darkken said, changing the subject, "I came across these bracelets in the treasury." From his pocket, he revealed copper bracelets with strands of silver woven in. An assortment of tiny gemstones ran through the middle. "They don't look like something you would find from a common peddler, but they have a mystic quality. They are locaters. As long as we wear them, we will be able to find one another and never be lost. Try them on."

Nath complied. Eyeing the dull jewelry, he said, "They go well with the rest of our assortment."

"Well, I've never been rich, so I settled on copper. I always felt it was a humble metal that didn't garner much attention. Do you like it?"

Compared to all Nath had seen in Dragon Home, it was hardly worth noting, but he said with a friendly smile, "I'll wear it with pride, my friend."

CHAPTER 29

RIEGELWOOD, THE CITY OF FESTIVALS, was covered in snow the day Slivver and Elween arrived. From a great distance high in the sky, they circled. The residents of Riegelwood were a hard-charging community that stayed as busy in the winter as they did in summer. The bundled-up residents traversed the streets, walking arm in arm and exchanging greetings with one another. Hungry bonfires burned on almost every corner. They had parades with drummers drumming and pipers piping. Men and women twirled batons of flames. It seemed one and all persons moved with flair and zeal.

Every morning, the porches and streets were shoveled clean. The winter traders and trappers were in full force, bringing furs and pelts by the wagonload. At nighttime, the citizens were as rowdy as ever, singing, drinking, and dancing all night long.

Late in the night, under the cover of a dark and moonless night, where the snow fell like white rose petals, Slivver and Elween landed on the rooftop of a three-story-high inn. They concealed themselves by pressing their bodies along the chimney. Smoke spewed from the chute into the sky. It was the second night they had come so close to the people in search of Nath.

"They are heavy revelers, are they not? Drunk with too much wine and their own stupidity," Slivver remarked. He eyed a group of trappers, decked out in wolf fur, that swayed through the streets, fell down in the snow, and erupted in laughter. They helped one another up only to fall down again. "Just stupid."

"As foolish as they may seem, they seem truly jovial and relatively harmless," Elween replied. "I thought you enjoyed watching people. Are you not fond of being one of them?"

"I suppose I'm more used to the elves, who aren't so… brazen. They show more self-control than these wild ones do."

"They are celebrating good news. They are happy with the new lordship, it seems. Let them revel. Life is hard." Elween soaked in the smell of spiced meat that was put on huge spits that twisted over the fires. A concert of stringed instruments had begun, and the music carried through the city. People were happy. "I like it."

"I don't hate it. I just can't filter out any conversations. I'd like to understand more, and I don't like waiting on Brenwar. He'll take forever to get here. He always does."

"Why don't we just ask someone what is happening?" she said.

"I've thought about that. After all, I've had friendships with several humans, but they don't last long, being so short-lived. Still, we don't want to start a panic. Not when they are like this. Someone could get hurt."

Elween nodded. "Then we will just have to wait. I'm fine with it. I just would like to see you more settled. In the meantime, I'm going to enjoy the music. This man that is entertaining, well, he is fantastic. I caught his name. Rome."

"Yes, his mastery of the strings is as good as the finest of the elves. Sings like a bird too." Slivver had been watching men for centuries and longed to walk among them. He didn't understand why, but he did. He had no aversion to what they did or how they acted. If anything, he was jealous that he couldn't be down in the streets and joining in. He admired their spirit. They lived life to the fullest even though, a lot of times, their actions could be detrimental.

They gathered bits and pieces from conversations. Not so long ago, Princess Janna had married Edwin Shirlwood, and they were the ruling power in Riegelwood. Life was good. Also, a new tavern had been built. Slivver could still smell fresh oak from the lumberyards. There was a workshop behind the taverns and stables that had been half burned down, and they were being rebuilt as well.

"Do you ever get the urge to scare them?" Elween said.

"What do you mean?"

"Well, I can't help but think that buzzing off the ground, silent as a shade, would put their ale-addled minds into temporary perplexity." She laughed. "I would just like to see the look on their faces when they saw a dragon. Would they not think it's a vision?"

"You have a devious mind."

"I don't mean any harm, Slivver."

"No need to be so defensive. I'm actually guilty of such an act myself. More than once that is."

Elween slapped him with her tail. "You sneak."

"It wasn't in front of a large crowd that likes to play with fire. It was more or less an early introduction." He managed a telling smile. "Seeing their faces, well, it was worth it."

A hunk of snow broke from the top of the roof. It slid down, creating a clean stretch, and fell to the ground.

"Hey!" A man teetered out in the street with a wine jug in his hand. His clothing was covered with snow. He stared upward, eyes scanning the roof. His stare locked on the chimney. He pointed. "Hey! Who is that up there?"

"It seems that we've been spotted," Slivver said. "We better leave before this reveler draws attention. But on the way out, why don't you say hello to him?"

Elween gave him a surprised look. "Do you mean it?"

"They are having a lot of fun. Why can't we? Besides, none of this would have happened if we didn't have to wait for Brenwar." He winked at her. "Just make it quick."

Belly first and wings spreading, Elween slid down the roof and dove right at the man. His eyes grew to the size of plates. He dropped his bottle in the snow. Just before she soared right over his head, she said, "Boo!"

The man cowered down. When he looked up again, Elween had vanished in the night sky, but she could still see him clearly. He picked up the bottle and chucked it into the nearest bonfire. She let out a cackling roar, caught up with Slivver, and they headed back into the woodland to wait.

CHAPTER 30

BRENWAR BOLDERGUILD CAME FROM ONE of the most respected families in all of Morgdon. The Bolderguilds' lineage could be traced back as far as any other dwarven family, yet, unlike many of the clannish, thickset, and short-sighted race of people, there were not so many of them. A lot of that was accounted to the losses in battle. The Bolderguilds were notorious for being the bravest and fiercest of fighters.

Oscaar Bolderguild, Brenwar's great-great-great-grandfather, had led all of his sons into a raging battle against the Hunsuk trolls, a fearless tribe of killers who had targeted dwarves for decades. They would strike and run. Oscaar and his sons eagerly volunteered to take on the task of ending the Hunsuk trolls. There were over five hundred of the Hunsuks. Oscaar and his sons were only four. Day by day, month by month, the dwarves took out the Hunsuks. Using traps—such as massive avalanches—sharp steel, and blunt-force trauma, the dwarves prevailed. But only one of the dwarves, Brenwar's great-great-grandfather, Moorlun, survived.

Those stories about his family had inspired Brenwar his entire life. He himself was on track to become a reputed dwarven warrior, ready to die in glory, until fate intervened and changed his life forever. He learned a telling secret about his family.

Long ago, when the races lived in peace with the dragons and Dragon Home's borders were open to all, a betrayal took place. Inside the boiling molten veins of the great mountain, a precious metal could be forged into what was known as dragon steel.

Dragon steel was the strongest metal in all the land. It could only be forged by fire, iron, and magic. Only the finest smiths that ever lived understood its secrets. Those secrets were trusted to the elves and the dwarves, which had no great love for one another. Betrayal ensued. The secret of dragon steel was stolen. Trust was lost forever.

Unable to pinpoint exactly who the culprits were, the dragons banished all of the races from Dragon Home. In an effort to appease the mighty race of dragons, the elves created the Trahaydeen to serve the dragons in any fashion that they could, but they would never work alongside the dragons in the forges again. The dwarves would never admit to having anything to do with the treachery, but not wanting to be outdone by the elves, they too swore their lives to serve the dragons. Those volunteers were the Bolderguilds, of course.

Brenwar didn't know the history until he was working in the mines. Late in the day, when the sun set behind the mountains, his grandfather, Oakwar, paid him a visit. Oakwar was a great dwarf who wore a horned giant's skull that was dipped and gilded in dwarven steel. They moved up the mountain, through the ice and snow, a mile high, until they reached the top.

It was there, on the top of that cold mountain, where he met the mighty king of the dragons, Balzurth, face-to-face. The great dragon was the only creature he'd ever met that made his toes tingle. The warmth from Balzurth's great body, covered in rich red scales flecked with gold, melted the snow, revealing the grasses all around him. With a head bigger than a horse, the dragon spoke in a voice that could be felt in Brenwar's sturdy bones. Balzurth told him all about dragon steel and his family's charge and commitment to the dragons. Brenwar, like his fathers before him, accepted his destiny, but not eagerly. After all, dragons were dragons, and dwarves were dwarves.

It was long after that, when his plans for the renowned life of a dwarven warrior were interrupted, that he was paired up with Slivver, one of Balzurth's many sons. They had been charged to find the culprits who had stolen the scrolls with the secrets of dragon steel. Over the decades, they worked together, and at times he and Slivver went their separate ways, only to take up the quest again later.

Trudging over the frozen prairies and crossing icy river streams, Brenwar found himself on a different quest, to find Balzurth's other son, Nath. Deep in thought, he said, "On this quest, I will not fail."

With a frosty beard, he spied the festival city of Riegelwood on the horizon. He looked to the skies. Two dragons circled high above. He put up his hand and waved.

CHAPTER 31

FAR AWAY FROM RIEGELWOOD, IN the hills where the men never came, Slivver paced while clutching his horns. "It's been seven days, Brenwar. Seven days. Even as slow as you are, it should take only four."

"And you should be glad of it, seeing how you don't care for my company." Brenwar huffed out an icy breath. "Besides, I had some business to attend to."

"This is your business. Your word to Balzurth. You are putting much on the line in regards to your family name." Slivver's tail flickered behind him. "I ought to smite you."

The dwarf, glaring up, stood chest to chest with Slivver. "Please try, and I'll stick that tail of yours in your nose hole and pull it out of your—"

"Enough!" Elween pushed them both apart. "Slivver, we haven't even heard a word about what Brenwar's been doing. I'm confident that he would not be wasting time if it wasn't pertinent to the mission."

"Are you taking his side? Why don't you just grow a beard while you are at it?" Slivver spread his wings, bending at the knee as he did so.

Elween hooked his arm. "You aren't going anywhere. Stop being so childish."

"Aye, stop being childish," Brenwar agreed.

Arching an eyebrow in Brenwar's direction, she said, "I meant that for the both of you. Now, where have you been?"

"I would have got around to what I was doing if he didn't start huffing and puffing like a fire-breathing warthog."

"Brenwar..." she said.

"In the same villages where I learned about Nath, I picked up word about trouble in the dwarven silver mines just beyond the Shale Hills. I used to mine there, back when I was younger, and word had it that the legionnaires from Quintuklen are hassling the dwarves. It's a territorial issue, and I felt obligated to check it out. My old mentor, Varluun, a warrior's warrior among the dwarves, and all mankind for the matter, filled me in on the details."

"And?" Slivver said.

"There are elves involved. Haughty in their glamorous robes that would make a peacock puke. Turns out, just as you've mentioned, they bear a standard on their fingers—the elven face carved on a black onyx."

"Are you sure?" Slivver said.

"I saw it with my own two eyes. I met with them and the dignitaries of the Quintuklen crown that was with them. They want to squeeze the dwarves out of the land that they've mined for centuries. That territory is practically empty, but the dwarves are content. They've settled in, they have families. They won't budge unless you kill them. They claim the land is theirs as much as any."

Slivver had his own beard, a flap of silver skin underneath his neck, that he stroked with his clawed fingers. "This is how the Caligin do it. Pretending to be wise, they use their subtle words and devilry to turn one group against another. They want the men and dwarves to skirmish, if not war. What did you do, Brenwar?"

"I told Varluun that he needed to hold the line, but he's already called on Morgdon to send more dwarves. It would be a shame to see the dwarves and legionnaires go at it after they've worked so well together in the past." Brenwar moved his war hammer from one shoulder to the other. His fingers tightened on the wood. "I'd want to be there one way or the other, but I won't abandon the cause."

"No, but you sure are taking your liberties about how you go about helping," Slivver said.

"Balzurth would understand. Besides, I needed to see with my own eyes if this tale about Caligin had any salt to it. If anything, I'm glad these elves have proven to not be worth their feathery weight." He crossed his arms over his chest. "It proves I was right, just as I knew it. So, have the two of you learned anything at all since you've been here? Any signs of the boy?"

Elween moved down the hill to a spot where she could see the town nestled peacefully in the snow. "Even for us, it's been difficult to gather any information when we can't be one of the crowd." She looked to Slivver. "But we've had our share of fun, haven't we?"

"Indeed," Slivver replied.

"How so?" Brenwar asked.

"For one thing, we've been flying overhead at night and throwing snowballs at them," Slivver said. "The best part is when they look up and we hit them square in the face."

"You're making trouble that you shouldn't be," Brenwar warned.

Elween replied, "Only the ones that are in a stupor. Sorry, Brenwar, but it's a tad boring waiting for you to arrive. We needed to have some fun. And it's difficult watching from the outside. The people are very fascinating. I tell you, I wouldn't mind walking the streets as men do, just to take it all in, just once."

"You really mean that, do you?" Brenwar said.

"Even you seem to take pleasure in it, so why wouldn't I?" she said. "To be honest, I've come to understand Slivver's disposition better during the short course of our adventures. He is jealous of you."

"I am not!"

"Oh, yes you are, and so am I. Brenwar is able to walk the streets and have all of the fun. Who wouldn't want that? And what a shame the dragons can't walk in peace with all mankind." She put a tail over Brenwar's shoulders. "Go, quickly now. I eagerly await the exciting news you'll bring on your return."

Brenwar massaged his chin and mumbled, "You can come if you want to."

"What was that?" she said.

"You can come," he said.

"Brenwar, stop being so daft," Slivver said. "You know we can't waltz right into town like people. They'd kill us."

Brenwar unslung his backpack, took a knee, and opened it up. Stuffing his fingers inside, he produced a pair of slender tube-like potion vials.

Slivver and Elween leaned over him, and Slivver said, "What do those do?"

With a twinkle in his eyes, Brenwar replied, "Polymorph for dragons."

Chapter 32

A hungry look built in Slivver's ice-blue eyes. "Brenwar, you better not be teasing me."

"Dwarves don't tease," Brenwar replied as he held up the vial. "Do you want to try the potion or not?"

Reaching for the potion vial, Elween quickly said, "I do."

Slivver snatched his potion away first. "How long have you had these potions? We've had many assignments together, but you've never mentioned having this. It would have been helpful, back when."

"No sense in looking backward when only forward matters. It will help now, but not unless you drink it." Brenwar handed the other potion to Elween. Clawing at his beard, he said, "I'd be very curious to see how this turns out."

Slivver scratched the side of his face. His blue eyes sparkled as he watched the orange-and-yellow concoction swirl and bubble mystically inside the clear glass of the vial. In a soft voice he said, "How long will it last? I don't want to use it if the duration is limited."

"As I understand it, seeing how the both of you are creatures of magic, the potion should have a long-lasting effect, so long as you do not use your dragon powers."

Slivver raised his bare eyebrows. He held up the vial to Elween and said with a grand smile, "Cheers!"

Both dragons drank at the same time.

Slivver transformed into a tall, lean, handsome man with bright-blue eyes, silver-gray hair, and a big smile. Normally naked on account of his scales, he now wore a dark-blue tunic over a full suit of ring-mail armor.

Elween became a tall, beautiful woman with emerald-green eyes and flowing forest-green hair that hung over her shoulders. A black headband held it back out of her eyes. She wore a rich green tunic over a dark-green suit of leather armor. She'd become a gorgeous human warrior queen. Her voice hadn't changed, but it was almost a purr when she said, "How do I look, men?"

With his bushy brows lifted high on his forehead, Brenwar replied, "You make as fine a human as you do a dragon."

"Thank you," she replied as she inspected her body. She had long, black-painted fingernails on the tips of her slender fingers. She clenched her fists, shadow boxed, then suddenly jumped up and did a double-ended backflip. "I like this body! It has a different agility, perfect for hand-to-hand fighting. I can fully execute all that I have learned."

Feeling his face and running his fingers through his silky locks of hair, Slivver said, "I admit, it is very nice, though I feel somewhat exposed." He peered at Brenwar. "I thank you."

Brenwar managed to say, "You are welcome. Now, what do you say to us strolling down into town and seeing what is going on?"

"I'm ready!" Elween said.

"So am I!" Slivver took off in a dead sprint down the hill. Elween chased after him.

Brenwar could hear them giggling like children all the way down the hillside. "Hey, wait for me." He finally caught up with them less than a mile from town. Elween was fixing Slivver's hair, while Slivver dusted snow from her shoulders. Stabbing a stubby finger at both of them, he said, "Listen to me. I lead. You follow. And don't start talking the people up fast. You have to let them warm up to you."

"Really, well then you must be really awful at this," Slivver said.

"Har-har. Anyhow, we eat, we drink, I'll ask most of the questions. You might get a lot of stares. Even though you are dragons, your features are far above these homely people." He gave them both a once-over. "Let's go."

Riegelwood had no walls, but like most cities in Nalzambor, it had many roads leading out of it that were surrounded by cottages and miles of rich farmland. It was late in the day, and the dragons, now men, strutted into town with their elbows swinging.

Brenwar scowled at them. "Will you cut out that brassy behavior? You'll draw unwanted attention to yourselves."

Men brought in wagonloads of logs cut from fresh timber to keep the bonfires going. Children ran the streets, engaged in snowball fights. Most of the people were heavily bundled up and cast more than a few wide-eyed glances at the striking Elween and Slivver.

"Will you keep your heads down? And wipe those smiles from your faces," he said.

"We just want to fit in. Aren't festivals supposed to be fun?" Elween said, smiling at a group of rugged lumberjacks who walked by and tipped their knit caps at her as they bowed. "Very fun?"

"You can have fun when I say so." He turned and faced a busy tavern that had been recently built with new wood. It had a long porch front and three levels, taller than most of the other buildings, aside from the outlying castles. The warm glow of candles showed inside the windows, where people were eating at tables within, their own happy glow on their faces. The sign that hung in front of the balcony railing read "The New Oxen Inn." "Follow me. We'll go in here."

Together, they marched up the stairs. They entered to a lively room, fragrant with cooked food and wood crackling in the fireplaces. A waitress wearing a rose-colored apron saw them to a table near one of the four fireplaces. She couldn't take her eyes off Slivver and blushed when he glanced at her. "Uh, I'll be right back with some drinks."

"We didn't ask for any drinks," Brenwar said. "But we are thirsty. What kind of ale do you have?"

Tearing her eyes away from Slivver, she said, "Oh, we have dwarven. Would you like that?"

"Yes!" Brenwar rapped his fist on the table. "Bring the finest flagon for them and one big enough for me."

"I'll be right back. Don't go anywhere." The moony-eyed waitress bumped into another table. "Ooops."

Slivver sat tall in his chair. "I think I'm going to like this place."

Chapter 33

Having the run of Stonewater Keep, Nath kept himself busy exploring the ancient facility. It was difficult to tell what the origins of the building were, but being far away from the dwarven kingdom of Morgdon and the elven kingdom of Elome, he assumed that men made it and abandoned it a long time ago. The thick stone walls showed many cracks and deep creases, but otherwise, it was a sturdy facility.

The Caligin used it for training, and there were two levels dedicated for the use of weaponry. The stone floor of one of these rooms was covered with a large wooden platform in the center. There were wooden benches backed against the wall and weapons racks on the opposite ends. It reminded Nath of Master Elween's training room back at Dragon Home. With no fires burning behind the mantels, the room had a cold and dreadful appearance. The wind howled outside, whistling through the cracks. It gave Nath a constant chill that he couldn't shake since he'd been in the keep.

He picked up a spiked flail that hung off the end of the rack and spun it around several times, whipping it fiercely over his head. He stopped the windmill and put it back. "Crude."

Over five decades, he'd trained with all manner of weapons with Master Elween, yet he still felt like a novice with many of them. The truth was, he didn't pay as much attention as he should have, and without routine practice, his timing and skill were off. Still, out of boredom, he tested one weapon after the other.

Elween's stern words echoed in his mind. "When you fight, be ready to fight with anything."

Shirtless, Nath went at it hour after hour, working up a good sweat. Fang lay inside his sheath on one of the benches, along with his pack. He'd been separated from them so many times that he was determined to keep them close. Still, he needed to be better prepared to live life without them, just in case. Ever since he came into Nalzambor, he felt unprepared for everything. That needed to change.

Chopping a two-handed battle axe hard and fast, he said, "I will not be taken by surprise. I will not be taken by surprise."

"Boo!"

Nath jumped away from the sudden voice. He spun in the air and landed on his feet.

Maefon chuckled as she approached with an off-white terrycloth towel.

He faced her. "Don't do that!"

"Were you surprised?"

"Yes! Gads, how do you get me every time? You are the only one," he said.

She tossed the towel in his face. "Am I truly the only one?"

Wiping his face, he said, "You know what I mean." He draped the towel around his neck. "You're sneaky."

Her stare swept over his muscular arms and chest. The corner of her mouth rose. "You are very sweaty. I like seeing you sweat. It reminds me of the time we spent in the dragon forges. It seems like such a long time ago, doesn't it?"

"It was another life."

"You sound sad." She grabbed the ends of his towel and pulled. "What is wrong, Nath?"

Her breath was fresh as apples and her face as warm as the sun. Maefon stole his breath momentarily as he tried to speak. Finally, he managed to say, "Now that I've had time to think about it, I miss home. What am I going to do over the next ninety-seven years?"

"You are going to become the greatest hero that Nalzambor has ever known. That is what you will do." She pulled him down to her eye level and kissed him with lips as soft as rose petals. "The time will go by before you even know it, but you can make the most of it with me."

"What about Darkken?" He pulled away a little, but his hands still found themselves attached to her small, curvy waist. "Wouldn't you rather be with him?"

"Since we've arrived here, he's become obsessed with the treasures in this keep. He's been working on corralling the hideous vulture. He even found a name for the blasted thing. Galtur." She started toweling off his chest. With a playful smile, she said, "I too miss the hot springs of Dragon Home that we spent so much time in. If I close my eyes, I can envision it, just me, you, and no one else around."

Nath took her face in his hands and kissed her with passion. He lifted her from her feet into his arms, and she kissed him back with the same hunger. Somehow, he broke it off, set her down, and walked away. "I'm sorry. I shouldn't have done that."

Just then, Darkken's voice filled the room. "No, you shouldn't have."

Chapter 34

If Nath's heart was pumping fast before, it was pumping ten times faster now. He twisted toward the entrance. No one was there. Maefon stood in front of him, breathing heavily. She locked her hands behind her back. Darkken, carrying an open tome in front of him, entered the room. His coppery eyes were glued to the pages. Maefon and Nath exchanged a quick look with one another. Nath's limbs were frozen.

Darkken slowly entered, eyes sliding left and right, and stopped when he came to the edge of the training platform. He slapped the book shut and looked right at both of them. With a puzzled look, he glanced between them, and in an aloof tone, he said, "So, what is it that you shouldn't be doing, Nath?"

"Er..."

"And pardon my eavesdropping. I was trailing after Maefon when I caught your words carrying through the stairwell."

He doesn't know that I kissed her!

With a raised brow, Darkken said, "Well?"

Nath was a moment from blurting out a lie when Maefon said, "He misses home and regrets leaving his family. I was trying to console his guilt, but he is eaten up with it."

"Oh, is that so?" Darkken set the book down and stepped onto the stage. "Nath, you can't carry guilt. Like Maefon said, it will eat you alive. I want you to think about all of the good that you have done. You have helped put an end to the Caligin. Your dragon family is avenged. Someday, they will thank you. I know that is a long time away, but they will, believe me." He gave Nath a friendly pat on the shoulder. "I just hope somehow I live long enough to see it."

Nath nodded. "I do too."

"Excellent!" Darkken spun on his heel. "Ah, I'm glad that we are all together, as I have good news to share. I've mastered the Pool of Eversight and now have control of Galtur. Soon, we will be able to track down our enemies so that they don't see us coming. I've made some other notable discoveries, too. It appears that Chazzan truly did have grand ambitions. He searched for great artifacts and weaponry."

"Like what, my love?" Maefon said.

"A few items that were marked in his research were called the Ocular of Orray, thunderstones, the Star of the Heavens, dragon steel, and the Elderwood Staff. It sounds like if they fell into the wrong hands, they would bring grave danger to everyone, including the dragons."

"With Chazzan gone, there shouldn't be anything to worry about." Nath moved over to the weapons rack and secured the battle axe. "Those items are safe where they may be."

"It's the knowledge that I am worried about." Darkken tied his hair back in a ponytail and stroked it. "Just because Chazzan is gone doesn't mean that all of his knowledge and ambition have died with him. He commanded an army of Caligin, and though we captured many, we certainly didn't capture them all. Don't think for one moment that those dark elves don't have their own ambitions. And though loyal, not everyone would agree with Chazzan completely. I think they will seek out these items to further their own ambitions. We should stop them."

Nath's shoulders sagged. He had no desire to chase after more Caligin. He'd chased enough of them to last a lifetime.

Darkken's head tilted. "You don't like the idea?"

"It seems like we are chasing our tails. Either we have defeated the Caligin or we haven't." He jumped back on the platform. "And the truth is, I'm not very eager to help a bunch of people that have for the most part lied to me at every turn. I just wanted to put an end to the Caligin and avenge the dragons. I didn't leave Dragon Home to save the rest of the world. I think my part is done."

Disappointed, Darkken said, "I see." He picked up his tome and hopped off the stage. "I can tell by the edge in your voice you aren't interested. Perhaps I am being too hasty. Nath, take some time, think about what it is that you want. I'm sure it's confusing, and we can discuss the matter again at another time."

Nath reached out as if to grab the man. "Darkken, I…"

Darkken opened up the book and quickly departed.

"I feel as if I offended him," he said to Maefon. "But you've both been doing this for years. Certainly, you are tired of the chase, aren't you?"

"Yes, I am, but when the hunt gets in your blood, it stays there. I don't think Darkken would stop chasing even if there wasn't anything to chase. It is who he is." She glided away from Nath and hopped from the stage. At the weapons racks, she picked up a pair of wooden swords and returned to the platform. She tossed him the wooden weapon.

"What's this for?"

"If you have to ask, then you certainly shouldn't be using it."

"Ha-ha."

"I think we both have some pent-up frustration that we need to work out." She unbuttoned her leather armor vest, opened it up, and tossed it aside. She wore a gray cotton shirt underneath of the same elven make used by the Trahaydeen. "I think this is the best way to do it."

"I agree." He stole a quick glance at the entrance. "Though I think the other way was much better."

She giggled. "True, but this is safer." She got into a fencer's stance, with her free hand poised gingerly over her head. *"En garde!"*

Nath knocked her step jabs aside. As quick and skilled as she was, he didn't have any trouble keeping up with her movements. He pressed forward, counterattacking just slow enough that she could parry. The wooden swords, hardened from decades of time, *clack-clack-clock-clock*-ed together noisily throughout the room.

"You are very good," Nath said.

"So are you," she replied.

Nath struck downward, adjusted the sword direction mid-swing, and gave her a swat on the thigh. "But you aren't that good."

Panting, she backed away with her eyes watering.

Nath dropped his guard and rushed toward her. "Did I hurt you?"

Maefon stuck a wooden dagger against his throat. Triumphantly, she said, "No, but I could certainly hurt you."

She had Nath dead to rights.

"Never let your guard down, Nath. I win. Now kiss me."

CHAPTER 35

A PETITE WOMAN DELIVERED THE TWO large flagons of ale to Brenwar's table. She was older, with smooth skin and an innocent teardrop face like a child. She set the platter down and poured each of them a tankard full of ale. "Welcome to the Oxen," she said, showing no expression at all. "They call me Little Shirl, and I own this establishment."

"It's well built," Brenwar remarked. He started to drink then said, "I am Brenwar, and these are my friends, Elween and Slivver."

"It's nice to meet you. So, what brings you to Riegelwood?"

"We are passing through." Elween took a drink of ale and made a bitter face. She stuck her tongue out of her mouth. "You drink this? For refreshment?"

Brenwar slapped his knee. "Ah-hahaha!"

Slivver gulped a big swallow of his dwarven ale. His eyes clenched. "It must be an acquired taste."

"I'd be happy to serve you wine or another one of our seasonal ales. We have a fine one that Edmund makes called Fitzgerald. It's very popular this time of year."

Brenwar poked a finger at Slivver. "It's rude to not eat or drink what you are served."

"Yes, you are right," Elween said. "I'll adapt to the bitter taste… somehow. Little Shirl, I'll be fine."

Staring, Little Shirl said, "You are very beautiful. You have eyes that shine like stars. The both of you. It reminds me of a friend of mine." She tugged on Brenwar's beard. "But don't you get jealous, you handsome thing. Where their eyes are radiant, your finely woven beard is glorious."

Brenwar pulled his shoulders back. "Oh-hoho, it is, isn't it?"

Little Shirl made a thin smile. "Absolutely. I see many people that come from all walks of life. Do you care to share where you are from?" She was looking right at Slivver when she said it.

"South, near Dragon Home," Slivver replied. "We are on a journey, just passing through."

"Interesting. I hope you stay long enough to enjoy the festival life that we offer. This year's is one of the best ones," Little Shirl said. "So, tell me, are you hungry? We have the finest food in town and pie that you will never forget."

Elween cast an awkward glance at Slivver. He shrugged. She then said to Little Shirl, "We'd like to try your best."

"I'll have it out right away. And for you, Brenwar, I think I know what a dwarf likes. Will that be all right with you?"

He winked at her. "Right as raindrops falling on my head."

Quietly, Little Shirl scuttled away, disappearing into the bustling crowd. A band played on stage, strumming strings and tooting small flutes and horns. Many in the crowd sang along and danced.

Slivver tapped his finger on the tabletop to the rhythm. "I'm impressed, Brenwar. You seem to have a better way with the people that you encounter than I expected. I figured you for a grumpy bearded lump that pried information out of people by grabbing their tongues with pliers."

"I know what I'm doing." Brenwar guzzled down his flagon and wiped his mouth across his forearm. "The little gal, Shirl, is vetting us. I'd be careful what you say. The townies can be very protective of their people and often swap information about others. Say the wrong thing, and it will set alarms off and they'll clamp up like a vise."

"Perhaps she'll do the talking," Elween said. "Did you catch the comment about our eyes? She said they reminded her of a friend. What do you think she meant by that?"

"She's prying. Be careful," Brenwar added. "Let's wait and see who brings our food out. If it's her or the other."

As they settled into the lively atmosphere, the dragons drank little, and Brenwar helped himself to their flagons. Fifteen minutes later, the first waitress approached with swaying hips. Her eyes were locked on Slivver as she unloaded their plates of steaming-hot food. "Enjoy," she said in a flirting tone to Slivver. She took her time walking away.

Leaning on his elbows, Slivver followed her with his eyes.

"Get your elbows off the table and your eyes off the gal's rear end. Show some manners," Brenwar said. He hungrily dove into the slab of steak and potatoes on his plate, sawing them up and sticking them with his fork. "Turning you into flesh and blood might not have been the best idea."

Slivver moved his elbows off the table. "Yes, manners. I'm not sure what overcame me, but that fetching dish of a woman was tantalizing." He looked at his food. "What do we have here?" He fanned the steaming aroma into his nostrils. "Savory. I'm not used to eating food that is cooked."

To the awe of the men that Elween captivated the moment she walked in, she ate the steak by holding it with two hands.

Brenwar held up a fork. "Er, you might want to use your silverware."

"Oh, I see." Elween picked up her fork and knife. "I thought they were tiny weapons. I should have known better, as there aren't any tiny people around." Like Brenwar, she began sawing into her food in a rugged manner.

"It's already dead, you don't have to kill it again." Brenwar cut up his food in a gentler way. "Nice and easy. Like a lady."

Once the plates were empty, the table was cleared, and Little Shirl brought two pies out. The crust was flaking and golden on top. "The strawberry and blueberry are out of season, but these are both pecan pies roasted with cinnamon. Would you care if I joined you? I like to learn from people that have been to other places. It fascinates me."

"Certainly." Slivver quickly stood up and pulled back a chair, beating Brenwar to it. "And we would love to learn about you and more about this fantastic tavern."

"I'd be delighted, but I must warn you, it is a tale of tragedy not meant for soft ears." Little Shirl took her seat.

Slivver scooted her in.

"You first," she said.

CHAPTER 36

"I FEEL IT'S ONLY FAIR TO warn you that Brenwar will talk your ear off about Morgdon. You might not want to open that gate," Slivver said as he resumed his place at the table. "He's more than fond of his home of iron and stone."

"Aye. It is something that everyone needs to know about." Brenwar drummed his fingers on the table. "Where should I start?"

"Actually, I would really like to know more about the two of you," Shirl said to Elween and Slivver. She continued to search their eyes. "You say you are from near Dragon Home, and I'm curious whereabouts. Do all of the people there have eyes like that?"

"We are just passing through. You're being nosy, ain't ya?" Brenwar said. "Are you fishing for something in particular?"

"You don't have to answer any questions if they make you uncomfortable. I only ask out of a deep curiosity, and it's the nature of my business." The little woman with straight brown hair pulled back behind her ear offered a winsome smile. "I look out for what is best for my tavern. The old one burned down not so long ago because of some unruly adventurers." To Brenwar she said, "And you carry a war hammer as big as me. Yet the two of you carry no weapons at all but wear very unique armor of a craft I've never seen. The moment you walked in here, I had a tingle."

"We certainly don't mean any harm," Elween added. Picking up on some habits from others, she pushed her hair back over her shoulders. "We are just looking for a friend. A friend who is from the south too."

"Elween. She doesn't need to know all of our business." Brenwar started into the pie on the table, cutting out a really big slice. "Keep our business among us."

"No, I like this woman. She has an intuitive spirit about her. I see no harm in letting her know why we are here."

"I'd advise against it," Brenwar said.

"I agree." Slivver made a face like he wished he could take his words back. "Oh, that was painful. I just agreed with Brenwar."

"'Cause you're getting smarter." Brenwar devoured his pie. "Very good."

"Please tell me who you are looking for. I'm familiar with many faces, as this is a popular place for travelers, though we focus on tradesmen and merchants, and not the adventuring sort such as you."

Elween looked for approval from her friends.

Brenwar said, "Go ahead. You've let the halfling out of the bag. You won't put him back in there now."

Elween nodded. "Through the grapevine, we learned that our friend was last seen here, before the fire. It's been some time, but we hoped to find him here, or at least someone that knew him."

Little Shirl nodded. "What is his name? What does he look like?"

Brenwar fished out the painting of Nath. He handed the rolled-up picture to Little Shirl.

Little Shirl's eyes grew the slightest bit. She rolled up the scroll and handed it back to Brenwar. With her attention on the others, she said, "Like you, this young man is very handsome. His eyes are striking like metal. I can tell you are of a similar descent. What is his name?"

Brenwar leaned forward. "Listen, Little Shirl, do you know him or not?"

"What is it worth to you?"

"What do you mean?" Elween said.

"If I've seen this man, how much will you pay me to know what I know?"

"Brenwar, is this customary?" Elween asked with a perplexed look. "Do you pay people for information?"

"No. She is shaking us down."

"That is not honorable." Slivver leaned back in his chair, crossing his arms over his chest. "Another deplorable tactic of humans."

Little Shirl sat up in her seat. "Humans? You called me human as if you are not a human yourself." With Slivver and Elween on her left and right and Brenwar across from her, she grabbed the dragons' hands and whispered. "I know what you are. You are dragons, aren't you?"

Elween and Slivver exchanged nervous glances. "Uh, er, how did you come by that?" Elween said.

"I know now that you are good people. You didn't accept the what I offered. Good people don't do that. And yes, I know your friend. I am a friend of Nath Dragon."

"Nath *Dragon*?" Slivver asked.

Brenwar let out a mirthful chuckle.

"I'll tell you what I know. He is not here, but I know another that can help." Little Shirl signaled for the buxom waitress, whispered in her ear, and sent the woman quickly away. She went on to tell them about Nath's dealings with the Black Hand, the wedding at Castle Janders, her relationship to her brother, Edwin Shirlwood, his wife Princess Janna, and the old Oxen Inn burning down.

When she finished, Brenwar leaned back in his chair and diddled his finger in his ear. "That was an earful."

"An awful earful," Slivver said, not hiding his displeasure. "Nath was imprisoned for over two years?" He buried his face in his hands. "How could this happen? Nath did nothing to deserve this." He started up out of his seat. "Where did he go?"

"Sit down," Brenwar said. "I think Little Shirl has more to say."

"Not me," she said, "but a friend of his named Homer." She looked back over at the front door. "There he is."

"What is so special about him?" Elween asked.

"He was in prison with Nath."

CHAPTER 37

"EVERYONE, THIS IS HOMER," LITTLE Shirl said.

"How do you do?" Homer said. The pleasant-looking fellow was pushing forty. He shook hands with everyone and pulled a seat over to the table. "Interesting company that you are keeping, Little Shirl. They are friends with Nath?"

"Aye, and we understand that you are as well," Brenwar said.

"Yes, we were cellmates in Slaver Town. I owe a great deal of gratitude to Nath for getting me out of that hole." Homer couldn't keep from staring at Elween and Slivver. "You really are like him, aren't you?"

"Yes and no," Slivver said.

"Your voice sounds very familiar," Elween stated. "Why is that?"

Homer politely leaned back and put his elbow over the back of the chair. "As an entertainer, I use the name Rome. You may have heard of me."

"Ah, you are the one that we heard singing. That explains a lot," Elween said. "You have a beautiful voice."

Homer nodded. "I thank you."

"So, how well do you know Nath?"

"Quite intimately. He saved my life, as I mentioned. He and many others helped me escape. I can't express how much Nath means to me. Without him, well, I'd still be doomed."

"Tell us about the others?" Brenwar asked.

"Certainly. There were two other prisoners that came out with me." Homer looked at the pies. "I don't mean to be forward, but may I indulge? I haven't eaten a bite all day." He wriggled his fingers. "I've been practicing, writing new songs and poetry, and sometimes it gets away from me."

"Of course you may," Elween said.

Homer pushed his sleeves up and took a couple of quick bites. "That is wonderful, Little Shirl. As always. Now, where was I?"

"Leaving Slaver Town." Brenwar half growled when he said it.

"Yes, I wasn't alone. The other prisoners were Calypsa, a ravishing woman, and a four-armed bugbear named Rond. Quite the unforgettable brute. There was an elf, fair-haired and pretty as snowfall, named Maefon."

Elween's hand locked on Slivver's wrist. "We know this elf."

"Yes, we do," Slivver said. "Please continue."

"I, well…" Homer frowned. "You don't care for this Maefon?"

"Let's just say that there are a great many questions that surround her. And this news is a surprise," Slivver said. "But this might be a positive thing."

"She was very nice and quite fond of Nath. I felt very comfortable that Nath was in good hands when I departed from him in Advent. I had my own journey of courage to make, which is why I've wound up here. Nath told me about his friends here, and I linked up with Little Shirl the day I arrived. I'm on my way to Quintuklen."

"We don't care about that," Brenwar stated. "Who else was with you?"

Homer stretched out his arm. "Ah, yes, there was a legionnaire, bearded and gruff, your sort of fellow, I'd presume. The old knight was named Hacksaw."

Brenwar's eyes brightened.

"Is this Hacksaw familiar to you?" Slivver asked.

With a grumble in his throat, Brenwar said softly, "I know the name." The fire returned to Brenwar's voice. "Is that all of them?"

"No, there were other elves. The Brothers of the Wind and the man, Darkken. He was a warrior's warrior, striking in every aspect." Homer ate another piece of pie. "Shirl, could I have—"

"Coffee coming, right away." She snapped her fingers.

"Anyhow, Darkken clearly was the one in charge of things. He was right in every manner, yet somehow wrong at the same time." Homer showed a puzzled look. "I didn't know what to make of him. He did nothing wrong, seemed inspirational but somewhat uncomfortable in his own skin. But, all in all, I felt that when I departed, Nath was in good hands. They were off to find the Caligin, and there was nothing that I could offer there. I'm a master of strings but a far cry from the master of any kind of weapon aside from a fork and knife."

The coffee arrived, and the waitress poured everyone a cup except for Brenwar. He rested a flagon on his thigh and steadily drank from it.

"So, where were they headed?" Elween asked.

"North, south, east, or west. I don't know," he said. "I just know that they were dealing with the merchants who were selling dragon parts. They believed those dark elves were behind it."

Scratching behind his ear, Slivver said, "I'm curious about the man named Darkken. Can you tell me more about him?"

"Easily enough. Darkken was a man that looked like a seasoned version of Nath. He stood taller and broader, with a strong, angular jawline. His hair was the color of leaves that turned in the fall." Homer straightened his back and looked at the dragons in human form. "Hmph."

"Hmph, what?" Brenwar asked.

"His eyes, though not as bright as the two of yours, were unique."

Slivver leaned forward on his elbow. "Unique how?"

"Well, I've never seen a man with copper-colored eyes before."

"What did you say his name was?" Slivver quickly asked.

"Darkken."

Elween's fingers locked on Slivver's wrist squeezed tighter. She said, almost in a hiss, "It's not Darkken. It's the Dark One."

Chapter 38

"The both of you look as pale as snow," Homer said to them. "Is this Darkken that bad of a character?"

"He's like you, isn't he?" Little Shirl said.

"No, he's nothing like us. He's evil incarnate." Slivver let out a long sigh. Nath's situation had been bad enough, but seeing how Darkken was involved only magnified the problem. It explained a lot as well. "Brenwar, if you didn't feel a sense of urgency before, then I pray that you believe me now. We have to find Nath, soon, and hope that it's not too late."

"Too late for what?" Little Shirl asked.

"Darkken will turn him to the wrong side. He's a clever twister of words, with all the charm and spellbinding capabilities of a dragon. He deceived us all, even his father, until the villain in his heart was discovered and he lashed out."

Rubbing his bearded mouth, Brenwar mumbled Darkken's name. "Hmmm…that name is dwarven. A very old dialect, but it has meaning. Dark in the day."

"That describes the Caligin perfectly," Elween said. As the mood soured, she took a long sip of coffee. "We have to act quickly."

"So, Darkken really isn't Darkken? He has another name?" Homer patted himself down, searching the small pockets on his shirt. "Shirl, can you fetch me a feather and quill? I have a song idea."

"Song? You are thinking about a song at a time like this?" Brenwar asked.

"Tragedies often make favorable music. We all live through pain and suffering, but soothing, relatable words help us all to cope with it." Little Shirl called a waitress, caught her attention, and gave a handwriting signal. "And it's very good therapy for me."

"I see no harm in it, so long as you promise to change the names," Slivver said. "His dragon name would be far too long to say with the human tongue, unless you were fluent in Dragonese. But, on the short, we call him Crixis."

"Crixis." Homer looked up at the ceiling beams. Appearing to be pondering the name, he said, "It would be hard to rhyme with that one, but I have many songs written about Nath Dragon, and I only use his name in one of them."

The waitress came with the pen, parchment, ink bottle, and quill.

"Thank you." Lost in his thoughts, Homer started writing with a fluid hand.

"Is there anything we can do to help?" Little Shirl asked.

"We'll have to pick up Nath's trail at Advent," Brenwar stated. "I can't get there as fast as dragons, even though my trip would be more meaningful. Do you want to fly?"

"Crixis, or Darkken rather, is no fool. He'll be looking for dragons coming after Nath, but he won't be looking for men. I say we stay as we are, but it would be helpful if we took horses. Will you consider that?"

"Given the circumstances, aye," Brenwar said.

"I'll set you up with my finest beasts," Little Shirl said. "Just come to the stables with me. Is there anything else that we can do?"

"Yes," Slivver replied. "Don't talk to any elves."

"Sound advice," Brenwar said.

As a group, they left for the stables, leaving Homer behind. Little Shirl set them up with two horses and a black pony for Brenwar. He saddled it like he'd done it a hundred times before and climbed on with a grunt.

Exchanging a hug with Little Shirl, Slivver said, "I've never ridden a horse before. This will be odd."

"They are good stallions. Be gentle, get familiar, and they will take good care of you," Little Shirl said. "Farewell, friends, and don't forget to come and see me again."

"Farewell, Little Shirl, and thank you for your kindness," Elween said.

With Brenwar leading the way, they headed south toward Advent to find Nath Dragon.

CHAPTER 39

MAEFON WAS INSIDE DARKKEN'S STUDY, replacing the candles that had burned down too low. Two weeks had gone by, and she occupied herself by keeping Nath comfortable and settling him in. In the meantime, Darkken had resumed his charge of the keep, running matters the same way he always had, preparing the Caligin that he now referred to as the Brothers of the Wind. It was a risky deception, but it appeared to be working. In the meantime, she stayed close to Nath, but the closeness was growing to a dangerous level, where guilt began to swell inside her chest. As she worked, she couldn't stop thinking about Nath.

Darkken entered the chamber with a smile on his face and gave her a kiss. "So, how is your seduction of Nath going?"

The words were like an icy hand clutching her heart. They hadn't openly talked about her seduction of Nath, but without saying, they both knew what was going on. The less they shared, the more real the twisted romance would appear. Replacing a dull green candle with a new one, she said, "According to plan."

"Interesting, seeing how we don't have a plan." Darkken took a seat on a small, padded, throne-like chair. It was one of four in front of the burning fireplace. "What plan are you following?"

Maefon moved to the chair across from him and gave him an inquisitive look. "The plan without planning. The one where I do what I think you want me to do."

"I see." Darkken twisted at one of the rings on his fingers. His eyes were intent on hers. "So, I can assume that a budding romance is building?"

"I don't think you should assume anything."

"Or you could tell me."

"That might endanger the deceit."

"You've come a long way. I'm proud of you." The warm smile that could melt the snow returned to his handsome face. "It's important that you know that you are proven in my eyes. With that said, do you think Nath is ready for another conversation about the Caligin?

I've spent time training the Brothers of the Wind. He seemed convinced when we swore the Caligin into the Brothers of the Wind. I think he's ready."

"Perhaps, but I think another tactic might be better," she said.

"Oh, and what might that be?"

"Take him on a quest. An adventure. Something that Nath can enjoy and taste the world. At the same time, let him know our eyes will be peeled for any suspicious behavior. After all, he really hasn't had time to catch his breath since he arrived. The victory over Chazzan, I feel, rang hollowly with him. He is lost. He needs a purpose."

"Yes, I see. A fine idea. It's so good that I'd swear I thought of it myself."

Maefon moved out of her seat and cozied into his lap. "You have something planned, don't you?"

Darkken let out a low and wicked chuckle.

Nath spent most of his time in the training room. Like he did back in Dragon Home, he worked with the elves, rededicating himself in the use of many weapons. It also included martial arts and wrestling. It reminded him of the days with Tevlin and Pevly, the elven brothers, who were also Trahaydeen. They had busted one another up on many occasions.

Now, wrestling on the mat with an elf, he found himself thrown by a hip toss. Landing on his feet, Nath quickly countered. He snatched the elf's leg, twisted, and put the elf on his back. The elf fought to twist out of Nath's grip. Nath locked up the elf's arms behind his back and rolled over, pinning the elf's shoulders squarely on the mat.

It wasn't a move that inflicted pain, but the elf tapped out by flipping his fingers into Nath's belly.

Nath released him. They shook hands and bowed. "Well fought," he said.

"Well fought," the elf said.

There were more elves in the room, sparring with one another, using bare hands and weapons. He heard applause and turned to see Darkken sitting in the wooden bleachers.

The elves stopped what they were doing. They all gave a slight bow.

"Please, continue, brothers," Darkken said. "Though I am your leader, there is no need to be so formal with me. Resume your fighting and preparation. You will need it. Nath, a word, if you have a minute to spare."

Nath jumped off the platform and landed lightly on his feet.

"You spring like a deer. A gift I wish I had."

"I've seen you move. Don't think you can deceive me. I know better."

"Well, perhaps I'm understating my ability." Darkken handed Nath one of the towels that was stacked up on the bench. "I've been so absorbed in my studies that I haven't practiced the sword craft. That's to my shame. I think I'll be looking to you to hone my skills in the future. The keep's chill is warming up, isn't it?"

Nath patted the sweat from his face. "Yes, Maefon and the brothers have been giving it warm life again."

"Walk with me. I like to walk and talk. It keeps the winter chill from me."

"You sound like an old man. Shall I fetch you a blanket?"

"Would you?" Darkken threw his arm over Nath, put him in a headlock, and rubbed his knuckles on his head. "You think you are funny, do you, whippersnapper?"

"Only because of the sounds of your bones creaking."

Moving out the door, Darkken broke out in boisterous laughter. "Nath, you have a wit about you that is delightful. You are the younger brother I never had. The elves are a bit prickly, in case you didn't notice. It's good to have another man around, even though you're a dragon."

They moved down the torchlit stairwell. "You are like a big brother to me, even though I do have brothers, but they have scales all over them and didn't talk with me much."

"Well, we are all brothers now. There is something I wanted to talk to you about."

"The Caligin?"

"Yes. I understand that you are tired of that chase. The truth is, I could move on, though I love the hunt. But the elves, Nath, they can't just let one of their own race go to freely create murder and chaos. They've been loyal to me, and I need to be loyal to them. The Caligin are a stain that needs to be washed from the world. They want to redeem themselves."

"I never thought about it that way."

"You wouldn't be expected to. You are not an elf. All races have a different sort of honor, but I think this one is common. You are just as passionate about dragons, are you not?"

"I'm destined to save them."

Darkken's nose crinkled. "Yes. I was thinking, we could move southeast, below Dragon Home, where the weather is warmer. It seemed that Chazzan had plans in a place called Old Hen. Have you ever heard of it?"

"No."

"Good. Neither have I, and that is what will give the journey more intrigue. We'll take our time about it. See the countryside." They made it to the main floor of the keep and moved outside into the courtyard, where the snow was falling. "How does that sound?"

"What was he looking for?"

"The Star from Heaven. I believe it's a diamond with mystic powers that can control minds among other things. That would be very dangerous in the wrong hands."

"Maybe it's in the right hands."

"That's what we are going to find out. We won't know until we get there, and I like to have some assurance." Darkken moved toward the portcullis, where two elves were stationed. With effort, they turned the crank that operated the chains lifting the gate, and the jaws of metal lifted off the ground. Darkken led Nath outside. The snow was up to his knees. He moved down the rocks that lined the keep in front of the river. Monfur, the huge ogre, lay covered in the snow. He breathed ragged breaths.

Aghast, Nath said, "He's been out here this entire time? Alive!"

"Naturally, we thought him dead, but ogres are resilient."

Monfur's drooping eyes hung on them both with a pleading look. He snorted in a low, groaning misery.

Nath felt pity for the monster. One arm was bent backward at the elbow. "What do we do with him?"

Darkken handed him an elven dagger. "You kill him."

CHAPTER 40

NATH'S STARE HUNG ON THE finely crafted blade. A chill went up his arm and down to his heart. His jaw hung. He swallowed. His eyes drifted to the mangled ogre that lay helpless in the snow. The brute had no redemptive quality in him. He was an evil, cruel, merciless flesh eater. Monfur gave Nath a burning stare. He saw Nath as an enemy. If he could strike, he would.

Still, Nath said, "I can't do this."

"This monster would not hesitate to crush our skulls if we were in his situation. He would do it with pleasure and laugh all the day long," Darkken said with a disappointed tone. "Nath, you cannot show mercy. Let your enemies live and they will come back to bite you. They must be put in the grave. You need to do this."

"I understand your point, but I can't. It doesn't feel right."

"Did it feel right when you killed those elves in the keep?"

"That was different." Nath thought of the ogre, Torno, that he battled in the quarry back in Slaver Town. Torno was a dumb brute, but he was kept under tight control with a collar. He just shook his head.

"He's going to starve to death eventually. Wouldn't that be a worse fate? This act is a show of mercy." Darkken turned away and faced the keep. "And the ogre is as worthless as sandstone."

Monfur stirred in the snow, making an angry garble. His eyes shot a knowing glare at Darkken. Nath got the feeling that if Monfur could tear the man's head from his shoulders, he would. It was as if they knew each other.

Darkken spun on his heel back toward them. He took the dagger from Nath. "I'll handle this. Look away if you can't stomach the sight of me showing mercy to evil."

Nath didn't look away. He watched Darkken bury the dagger to the hilt in the ogre's chest. Monfur died without a gasp. His hot glare remained frozen on Darkken.

Darkken cleaned the blade in the snow and tucked it back in his sheath. "That wasn't so bad, was it?"

"I don't suppose. It was quick."

"Nath, you can kill with mercy in situations like that, and now you've seen how it can be done. I should have instructed you better, but we did lose a lot of men to the ogre. He didn't deserve the quick death I gave him. I hope you learn to understand that."

There's a lot I wish I understood better. Something just isn't right.

For the next couple of days, Nath kept to himself. He spent a lot of time in the solitude of his room, staring out the portal window. Stonewater Keep could be a lonely place, even with a hive of activity in some places. The Brothers of the Wind spent time training and preparing. They brought in wood from chopped-down trees. There was a tunnel in the backside of the keep, in the subfloor levels, that lead to mines of coal that kept the keep fires burning. The keep had warmth churning through it now, yet it was cold at the same time.

Even Nath's hot blood kept a chronic chill. Something about the relationship with Monfur and Darkken continued to dig at Nath. He swore that if he didn't know better, they knew each other. He peered through the portal window, looking down at the spot where Monfur lay. There was a huge bulge in the snow. Monfur's grave. For some reason, Nath didn't think the ogre was as bad as he was made out to be. There was a knowing intelligence that looked behind those droopy eyes. Monfur, the gatekeeper, knew secrets. Those secrets died with him.

I wonder what other secrets the former Caligin know that they aren't telling.

Moving away from the window, Nath sat on his small bed and brooded. He contemplated leaving, but everyone he'd known had let him down. Hacksaw and Calypsa left him. Homer had a life of his own. Just about everyone else he knew had been bad to him. He felt no desire to go out and save the people who were so content on making life miserable for one another and themselves. The only people that had been with him since he'd met them were Darkken and Maefon. He trusted them, even though questions that he didn't know how to ask still swirled inside his head.

Rubbing the tops of his thighs, he said to himself, "I need to do something."

The field mouse that comforted him before in the cell squeezed underneath his room door. It scurried up the footboard of the bed and into Nath's waiting hand. "Well, look who is back." With his thumb, he stroked the mouse's winter-gray pelt. "If you keep coming around, I'm going to have to name you. Hmmm… what would be a good name for a rat?" The mouse's whiskers stopped twitching. "Pardon me, I meant for a mouse. How about Melegal? That's a clever name." He tilted his head from side to side. "No, I think that might be too complicated. Besides, I overheard it in a tavern full of drunks and swindlers. You deserve better than that. Let's just stick with Mouse. Would you like to take a walk with me, Mouse? I'll find you some cheese. And Maefon says I need to practice my new craft."

Maefon had spent time teaching Nath how to use his dragon-given talents to develop subtler abilities. She taught him about spying, observing, watching for habits of other people. They even dabbled with picking locks, climbing the high walls of the keep, and concealing weapons. That was the trick she pulled on him when they sparred in the training room. He swore he'd never be fooled like that again.

He got up. "Let's go, Mouse. I've been through almost every nook and cranny of this keep, but there are a few that I haven't been in yet. They are locked, and Darkken has the keys. I could ask, but I'd rather make it a challenge. Let's see what I can do on my own."

CHAPTER 41

AT THE COURTYARD LEVEL, NATH slipped beneath an archway. Back pressed against the wall, he watched a pair of elven sentries pass by. All of them had duties, and one of those duties was keeping watch over the keep from inside and out. Nath didn't really see the point in having guards inside the keep. If they were a brotherhood, that wouldn't be needed. But Darkken said, "When you have something worth protecting, protect it. And it's good soldiering for the group."

Once the elves were out of sight, Nath used the keep's inner walls, avoiding the portal views above, and crept to another archway. Inside was a separate stone stairwell that led to the subterranean levels below. He took the steps down, as silent as a cat, out of the icy winds that howled through the archways of the keep.

Small iron torch brackets were spread throughout the corridor at the bottom. Aside from getting lumps of coal, there was no other reason to be down there. At the landing, he stopped and listened. Hearing nothing, he moved on with the mouse still cupped in his hand.

Twenty yards down the corridor on the right was the entrance to the cave that led to the coal. There were more coves and storage rooms beyond. He passed the room that led to the dungeons where the Caligin were once kept. At the end of the corridor was a cast-iron door that had been locked. Nath kneeled down and put his hand over the threshold. Wind whispered through his fingertips.

He looked at his pet. "I wonder what is in there." The door had a key lock that was nothing unusual. However, the mechanism was big, requiring a large key. Maefon taught him that it wasn't the size of the lock that mattered. He only needed the right set of tools to open it, a delicate touch, and nimble fingers. From inside the pocket of his trousers, he removed three slender lock picks. He set the mouse down. It vanished underneath the door. "See you on the inside."

He put his ear to the door and began picking the lock one-handed. Back up the corridor, he heard the faint scuffle of soft footsteps.

Oh no! The patrol is coming down here!

Nath had several options. Hide. Hide and run. Play dumb.

What have I got to lose?

He put the tools away and casually leaned against the door.

Two elves, with heavy cloaks covering their shoulders and their black leather armor showing underneath, approached. Their elven eyes widened the closer they came. Slender hands went to the swords underneath their cloak.

"Good evening," Nath said. "What brings the two of you down here?"

"We are on patrol," the taller of the two said. He had a small scar in the middle of his chin. The other elf was shorter, built on a sturdier frame, and darker skinned. "What are you doing down here?"

Nath said in a nonchalant manner, "Just doing my duty." He rapped his knuckles on the iron door. It made a hollow echo in the tunnel. He faked a yawn. "Can you believe Darkken wanted me to maintain a post all the way down here? Guarding this door until tomorrow? Of all the ridiculous things. It's me, for dragon's sake. But I agreed."

The taller of the two said, "I wasn't told about this."

"Me either," the other one said.

"Well, I don't think Darkken needs to clear anything with anyone. Or Maefon either, but you can question them if you like, like I did, about some other duties I didn't like, and be put down here like me."

"If you are guarding the door, then why don't you have any weapons?"

Quick as a cobra, Nath took the shorter one's dagger out of his sheath. "Oh, but I have one now, don't I? How about that. I disarmed you. I bet Darkken would love to hear about that. After all, I'm here to test you."

The elf's eyes grew big.

Nath handed the dagger back. "Listen, it's my word against yours, but I think I have the advantage. So you patrol and I'll guard, and we keep this between ourselves."

"The whole purpose of patrolling is to report suspicious behavior." The taller one's fingers started fidgeting. "I think you should come with us."

Nath stared him in the eye and said with a wave of his hand, "You don't want me to come with you."

"What are you doing, some sort of a mind trick?" the other elf asked.

Changing the subject, Nath said, "I don't know what you are so worried about. It's not as if there is something important behind this door, is there?"

"How would we know?" the taller elf said.

"I think the both of you know what is in here. You were here before, being former Caligin. You know things, don't you?"

"What is in the past is in the past." The shorter elf stood upright and chest out. "We are sworn into the Brothers of the Wind. Our knowledge is your knowledge. But we don't know what is behind that door."

The other elf elbowed him.

Nath was surprised to see some color coming out of the elves, who were typically very stoic. But they weren't stupid either. One was as crafty as the other. Yawning again, Nath said, "You want to know what is in here as much as I do, don't you?"

They shrugged.

Nath fanned out his lock picks and smiled. "Then let's find out."

Why not bond with them a little?

With the elves leaning over his shoulder, Nath picked the lock. He fished through the mechanism until he found a pinhole that allowed him to flip the tumblers one at a time.

"You're doing good," the shorter one said.

Although it was harder than threading a needle more than once, Nath finally unlocked the door.

"Impressive," the taller elf commented.

"Hand me that torch," Nath said as he pulled the door open. To his surprise, it swang silently on the hinges.

The shorter elf handed him the torch. He peeked inside. "Interesting. Uh, can I see those tools? They are a nice set."

Nath handed them over and entered a large treasure chamber that gleamed from one side to the other. "Great dragons," he said with awe.

The two elves slammed the door shut, locking him inside.

CHAPTER 42

"GADS!" NATH POUNDED ON THE door. "Let me out of here!" He knew they were gone. Like a rat in a trap, he was imprisoned. "I can't believe I was so stupid."

He wasn't close with any of the elves, so why all of a sudden did he trust them? He didn't know, but there was something unique about those two that he liked. He managed a faint grin. "I'm going to have to remember that one."

Turning to search for another exit, he discovered the marvels that lay within the room. From one corner of the chamber to the other was a trove of treasures. "Will you look at that?"

Nath hadn't seen so much treasure since he left his father's throne room. Even the Black Hand's war chest was not so full. Sacks full of coins lay on the floor and against the wall. There were paintings, swords, shields, gleaming suits of armor, and fur cloaks and coats on racks in the corners. There were long tables with unique devices. Wands, leather gloves, tiaras studded with precious stones, small mirrors and brushes, suede boots and other shoes underneath the tables. That was just what Nath could see with the quavering torchlight that nullified his dragon vision in the dark. Still, it was ample. The breeze that stirred the room came from a grate on the floor. The mouse scurried across it.

"If only that grate were bigger, I might just squeeze out of here like you did, Mouse."

Nath rummaged through the treasure. Clearly the Caligin had taken the best from all those they had stolen from. No three of any of the items went together. The sacks of coins were marked by the money lenders and merchants that they came from. There were wagonloads of them. Gold, silver, copper, and pewter. He scooped up a handful of coins and laid them on the table.

"Interesting, a little something from all of the races. How about that?"

It only made sense to him that this would be how the Caligin operated. They would need to fit in wherever they went, and that explained many of the outfits that were piled up inside the chests. Maefon explained a good bit about disguises and blending in. There were fine hats, knit caps, and fur ones too. Something for all seasons could be found.

Mouse darted across the table. He hopped from one table to the other, ran down a table leg, and disappeared between the sacks and chests.

Nath followed Mouse's path, wondering if this was where Fang and his own gear was originally brought when Chazzan overtook him. Getting over his fascination, he realized that if anything, he needed to get out of the room before he starved. Nath started looking for anything that he could find that would help him get out.

"Come on. Come on, there has to be something I can use to get out of here." He hastily rummaged through the room, looking in every nook and gap. Many items were wrapped up in cloth, but he came across nothing useful. He found one item, wrapped top to bottom, with a long handle. It was heavy. "What is this?"

He undid the bindings. Pulling the cloth from the object in hand, he gasped. The sledgehammer Stone Smiter filled his hands. It was the weapon that he took from the orcen slaver, Foster, and gifted to the bugbear, Rond. Nath's heartbeat pounded like war drums inside his ears.

"If Stone Smiter is here, then where is Rond?" His chest started to heave. It was obvious. The Caligin killed Rond. Did Darkken know about this? Certainly he didn't miss it. The gemstone on the top of the hammer's head started to burn bright, matching the intensity of Nath's rage. Someone was lying. He looked at the iron door. He had the hammer. One swing would take it off the hinges.

Nath raised the hammer back over his shoulder. "It's time to get to the bottom of this! Stone Smiter, do your thing!" He turned his hip into his swing and stopped, hammer head just inches from blowing the door wide open. Gathering his thoughts, Nath said to himself, "No, there must be a better way to get the answer to this."

He put his ear to the door. Footsteps echoed toward him. There were many, coming in a hurry.

Gads!

Chapter 43

Darkken had his powerful fingers locked around an elf's neck. The elf, a Caligin, was down on his knees, choking. His smaller hands chopped and clawed at Darkken's wrists and hands. Futilely, the elf tried to pry the man's strong fingers away. With a raspy sigh, the elf died. Darkken slung the elf's corpse across the dining chamber table.

Maefon swallowed hard. Memories of when he killed Chazzan surfaced. The dangerous look in Darkken's eyes had her heart shooting through her throat.

He's mad.

It was those unpredictable outbursts by her lord that frightened her. She rubbed her neck. Would the time come when she would disappoint him and he'd crush her throat like fallen leaves?

"I should have killed him sooner," Darkken muttered. He was staring into a burning fire with a glazed look in his eyes. "I knew he was dangerous."

"Perhaps he didn't survive. Our brethren said that he was gravely wounded." She wanted to be helpful. Appease him. She slowly approached and put a hand on his shoulder. "They filled him with over a dozen arrows. What man can survive that?"

Coldly he said, "Never assume anything. That is why I kill Nath's allies. Good people look out for one another. They have instinct. Especially that one. Like a loyal hound, he would watch out for Nath. His living would always be a thorn in our side. That is why he started back. He was on to us. He had to perish. Nath must trust us. No other. He needs to forget about the very existence of them." He clenched a fist. His knuckles cracked. "And take your hand off me."

She jerked her hand away. Goose bumps popped up on her arms. *He is insane. Paranoid. Is such a violent death reserved for me?* "Do you want me to go and try to discover what happened to Hacksaw?"

"He vanished into thin air. How, I do not know, but I should have been informed sooner." Darkken looked back at the dead elf on the floor. He shook his head. "The delay is what angered me more than the failure. I should have had word of this weeks ago. It seems there is a flaw in my chain of command. I can't have that."

"I will find him. If he lives, I'll kill him."

"No, I need you here with Nath. The Caligin are still searching. You heard our brother. They've been casting their eyes all about Huskan and Quintuklen. If Hacksaw has been there, news of him will surface, I'm certain of it. Let's just hope they discover proof of death. It's imperative that he took our secret to the grave. But if the secret is out…"

"Who would believe him, Lord Darkken? It's a hard sell. We always have that advantage," she said. For the first time, she saw a crease in the smooth skin of Darkken's brow. It was a crack in his impenetrable armor. There was worry.

A heavy knock started on the chamber's doors.

"I'll send them away." Maefon hustled to the door and cracked it open. It was Roday and Dule. "What do you want?"

Roday whispered in her ear.

Maefon's eyes widened.

Darkken caught her surprise and said, "What happened?" He stormed to the door and flung it open. "Roday. Dule. Out with it!"

"We trapped Nath inside the treasury."

Darkken's eyes showed an angry bright-copper shine. They filled with energy that could shoot holes through the both of them. "Come with me, and explain on the way down."

The elves finished the story just as they made it to the subterranean level. Darkken took out his ring of keys and opened the iron door.

Nath was sitting on the end of the table, kicking his legs, and with a sheepish smile, he said, "Am I in trouble?"

With her fingernails digging into her palms, Maefon gave Nath a warning look.

Darkken entered the chamber. His eyes quickly swept the room. He fixed his attention on Nath. "What are you doing?"

"Just looking around. The keep is ours, is it not?"

"Order must be kept to some degree, but of course, you are not in trouble per se, other than the fact that you are ignoring your sworn-upon duties." Darkken moved deeper into the room. He walked along the tables. "It's such a fortune that I've not had the time I needed to figure out what to do with all of it."

"We could return it." Nath suggested.

"Yes, but to whom?"

"I bet those two might know where to start." Nath shot the elves an angry look. They grinned at him and pumped fists. "And it seems that these two twits on patrol did a very bad job by letting me in the chamber."

"And trapping you too?" Dule said.

"Silence. There is plenty of blame to go around." Darkken picked up a scimitar that lay on the floor. He slid it out halfway. "A pirate's blade from the Faluum Sea. The Caligin clearly have a very long reach. We'll discuss and use these resources as needed until we can come to a reasonable conclusion, but it's hardly worth addressing now. We have a journey ahead." He set the sword down. "Nath, I understand what you are doing." He smiled and gave Nath a pat on the back. "Well done picking the lock. Let's depart and talk over something hot to eat. Roday, Dule, you performed well. You may join us." He saw Nath out.

Nath might have been playing along, but he was still simmering inside. Rond's war hammer was in there, and he wanted an explanation. And if Rond was dead, then what about Calypsa? He stared at Maefon. She was pale when she arrived, but now the color returned to her face.

Darkken started to close the door and said, "Maefon, the three of you go ahead. I would like to speak to Nath alone."

"Certainly," she said.

Roday and Dule nodded their heads so low it was almost a bow, but they caught themselves before bending too far and moved on.

Once they were out of sight, Darkken pushed the door back open. "Nath, come inside. There is something I need to show you."

Nath followed him inside.

"This is where I found your sword and backpack, quiver, and arrows. That wasn't all that I found either." He frowned at Nath. "What I'm about to show you, I am not proud of, but I was not certain what to do." He went to the spot where Nath found Stone Smiter and pulled it out. It was wrapped up in cloth. He handed it to Nath. "I'm sorry, but I'm afraid that your friend might be dead."

Chapter 44

It was late in the day. Brenwar and Slivver were in the woods, chopping up the dead branches that had fallen from the trees. Slivver carried a bundle of sticks in his arms. His teeth chattered as he said, "I never realized that people were so thin-skinned."

"In more ways than one." Brenwar cleanly cut the dead branches off in quick, accurate strokes. "Now, if you turned into a dwarf and not a man, you would fare much better in the depths of this chill weather. The weather makes no difference to us. Our skin is as thick as a winter hound's fur."

"Sure it is. I see you warming your hands by the fire the same as us."

"Just because I like a fire don't mean I need it. Now, gather up this bunch. If you're going to be a man, you need to learn to survive like one." Brenwar cast a look at him. "Feeling vulnerable without your scales, aren't you? And I thought you wanted to be a man."

"The cold will pass. I'll adapt," Slivver said. "And I don't want to be a man. I like being a dragon. I just enjoy the world of the races."

"You need to be satisfied in your own skin. You are what you are. You are just twisted up inside on account of that elf."

"It's something that you wouldn't understand."

Brenwar stopped chopping, put his foot up on the log, and with a wary eye said, "What wouldn't I understand?"

"You know, love… affection."

"Harumph! Who are you to say what I might or might not be feeling? I do what I do not just out of duty but because of those very words you say. It sounds different in dwarven, the way we call it, but it's all the same. Don't let this bristling stump of bearded brawn fool you. The torch burns bright within me."

"I guess that is possible."

"I don't let my feelings guide me. Particularly on a mission like this. It's too dangerous to hesitate. Emotions can give one fire in battle, but they can be destructive too if you can't control them." Brenwar lopped off a branch with another clean cut. "You can learn from me."

"You are a difficult person."

"To you. You aren't a dwarf, you're a dragon. I'm hardly difficult by my bearded brethren's standards."

Brenwar made a good point, but Slivver wasn't about to admit it. He gathered up the small logs made from the branches and started toward the camp. He couldn't believe he was actually cold. Even in the highest elevations, he never got a chill, but the polymorph potion made him vulnerable. He walked and talked as a man, enjoyed it all, but he was out of his skin. Walking away, he muttered, "If only we could all be accepted as we are."

"That won't ever happen. What matters are the ones that do accept you as you are, and still, whatever that soft word is that you have for it."

"Love?"

"That's the one." Brenwar caught up to Slivver. Walking with him back to camp, he said, "Listen, I know I've been hard on you in regards to Ericha. I think you know that I'm not fond of elves. It's just my way of looking out for what is best for you."

Slivver raised a brow. He could see the sincerity beyond the hard lines in Brenwar's face. "I appreciate that."

"Don't get all mushy on me." Brenwar moved along.

Back at camp, Elween sat on a log in front of a dying fire, skinning a rabbit. She smiled at them contentedly. "I'm really enjoying this different sort of hunting. The craft that the races practice is unique. It's extra work, but more work is more learning."

Slivver dropped the bundle of wood. He tossed the small logs on the fire, getting the flames crackling with new life. "Yes, and hopefully you won't eat another chicken, bones and all, in a room full of people."

She ripped the skin from the rabbit and tossed the meat by the fire. "Not all of them were appalled. That hulking northerner with volcanic blue eyes and a cimmerian mane of wild hair seemed to enjoy it."

"The barbarian?" Slivver said. "He was as out of place as you were. Talk about otherworldly."

"He was handsome."

Slivver shook his head. Brenwar scoffed.

They'd spent time in Advent, gathering what information they could find about Nath and company. It took some time, but after several zealous purchases they learned more about the group. Nath, Maefon, and Darkken had been there and moved on. They learned about the battle at the merchant fort too. By the time they arrived, it had been overtaken by a full host of goblins. They moved on.

Elween pointed to a pile of berries by her feet. The size of cherries, they were a mix of bright red and plum purple. "Brenwar, are these the anglon berries that you were talking about?"

Brenwar took a knee and looked at them. "That's quite a haul. There must be two dozen of them there. You have to have a good eye to locate them, especially this time of year. Well done."

"I couldn't help it, but I had to try one. They certainly enrich the blood."

"Aye, they'll do that."

With the fire's new life and the sun falling into the night, they sat quietly and ate. Once they finished, Brenwar broke the silence. "We've talked about a lot of things on this journey, except one." He held up his sausage-sized finger. "I need to know more about our enemy. Just how dangerous is this Darkken?"

Sliver replied, "Dangerous enough to destroy the world."

CHAPTER 45

BRENWAR PULLED UP A LOG, sat, and folded his arms. "How so? Let me hear it."

Slivver took a seat beside Elween. Frosty smoke came out of his nose as he shook his head. "The day Crixis came was a day of jubilation. Balzurth had a true heir. I'm older than Crixis, and I too was thrilled by the arrival of my brother. At that time, I only knew about what it was to be a dragon, having never left Dragon Home myself. There was one glorious celebration after another as Balzurth's heir had become apparent." Slivver's eyes drifted to another place and time. "I'll never forget all of the excitement. At the time, I didn't realize the significance of what was happening. Naturally, I assumed that Balzurth would be around forever. It would only be later that I would come to know better.

"You see, Balzurth too was born a man who later became a dragon. It had been that way with his father before him and so on. Now, all of the past lineage has moved on to the Land Beyond the Murals. As I grew older I came to understand that the dragons have a bigger role in life on Nalzambor. They are the guardian race of this world, but in order to protect it, they must understand it, and that is why the king of the dragons must walk as a man, to learn the ways of the people."

Brenwar edged closer to the fire. "I thought dragons protected the dragons."

"We do," Elween said, "but that is only part of the bigger picture."

Slivver agreed. "Yes. There is a delicate balance. The dragons are a race, just like all of the others, but they have greater powers and responsibilities. The dragons must have a leader and an heir to that leader. If Balzurth were to fall, it would leave unrest among the dragons. Without a clear king, they would fight with one another for power."

"But you are Balzurth's son as well. Why couldn't you claim it?" Brenwar asked.

"A good question. I have many brothers and sisters, but only a dragon born a man can be the rightful heir to the throne. If there was no such man—or dragon, rather—then any dragon would have a right to the throne. This would only lead to many thrones, or so they say. You see, according to dragon lore, long, long, long ago, the dragons were divided all over the world. There was no dragon born a man, but there was a prophecy."

Staring deep into the fire with his arms crossed over his chest, Brenwar said, "I see. It would have been better if you were born a dwarf. You know that, both of you, don't you?"

"Yes, we know that," Elween said with a giggle. "Please, continue, Slivver. I enjoy the sound of your voice so much."

"Of course." Slivver shifted in his seat. "My backside is freezing to this stump. It's a new experience." He wiggled his bottom on the cold seat then sighed. "Oh well, where was I?" He lifted a finger. "Ah, so, we have had a king to unite us and give us purpose. To do without would be chaos. All of the dragons who weren't so ambitious could breathe a sigh of relief. But the ambitious ones, those who make up the High Council of Dragons, are the ones that need to be watched out for. They, though faithful in all appearances, stand to gain the most if Balzurth was lost. Not all dragons want to protect the races, and not all dragons want to protect the dragons. We have wicked serpents among us.

"This is where Crixis came in. He brought a great unifying effect. The lineage of the dragon king had been strengthened. And as the men of this world say, 'He was the apple of Balzurth's eye.' All was well in Dragon Home. Crixis was embraced and fawned over by all. He was being groomed for the throne, as Balzurth spent more time in the Land Beyond the Murals. Crixis was being prepared for life to walk among men."

Elween lifted a hand. "I had a strong part in that too. I trained Crixis. So did the Trahaydeen. He was such an apt and eager pupil." Her voice soured to go with her frown. "But when he trained with the elves, he was merciless. Dragons too. He beat more than one elf half to death."

Slivver pointed at Brenwar. "Don't say it."

"I didn't have to." Brenwar made a grumbling, "Ho-ho."

"The bottom line was that Crixis was devious," Slivver continued. "And as he grew in strength and knowledge, it became worse and worse. He started to become demanding and arrogant. To our shame, no one said a word to him. Considering what he was, who was to say anything? Of course, most dragons only saw the better side of him, but the ones closest to him knew better. He was a problem child."

"An evil seed began to blossom in him," Elween admitted. "There was no turning back once it sprouted."

"No one knew how to deal with it either. We overlooked it. I think Balzurth did too, at least for a while. Then the time came when the eager son began to make demands of his father."

"What sort of demands?" Brenwar asked.

Elween answered, "He wanted to know the secret of dragon steel. I think there were many dragons encouraging his behavior. That we didn't see coming either."

"Puffed up with pride, Crixis confronted Balzurth and made his demands. Balzurth, now fully aware of Crixis's behavior, gave the power-hungry boy an answer he hadn't heard before. All of Dragon Home shook that day, so angry Balzurth was with his son. *No* was a very powerful answer. Rejected, Crixis stormed out of the throne room against Balzurth's orders. They did not speak for years, despite Balzurth's attempts. Crixis isolated himself, but his rage still simmered. Then the darkest day of all days came. It was the unthinkable." Slivver's chin dipped, and his shoulders sagged. "Crixis, in a fit of rage, slaughtered the fledglings."

The forest became dead quiet. Not a branch rustled.

In a low voice, Brenwar asked, "Then what happened?"

"Balzurth cast judgment on his own unruly son. Death. The High Dragon Council convinced him otherwise, and the rest is history."

Chapter 46

DARKKEN LED THE BROTHERS OF the Wind southeast, following the snowless and warm back trails toward Old Hen. They moved on foot, spending a few days in a massive tent city, much like the settlements west of Dragon Home, but smaller. It was there they warmed themselves, near the massive lakes of fire that oozed from Dragon Home. The tent city was a mishmash of the races, passing through during their travels. The commoners had dusky skin, light hair, and a swarthy style about them. They wore robes and sandals, and many of the broad-chested men walked shirtless.

Using funds from Stonewater Keep's treasury, Darkken bought another wagon and a pair of horses to pull it. He also got horses for Nath, himself, and Maefon to switch out on, while the elves kept up on foot. They spent two nights there, looking for any signs of the former Caligin, but they didn't come across any disturbing news, and they moved on.

Nath remained amiable throughout the journey. It was difficult. When Darkken showed him Rond's hammer and admitted his shame for not telling him sooner, Nath was both angry and relieved. He was angry that something had befallen Rond. Worse yet, Calypsa might have been in danger. However, he was relieved that Darkken had been honest with him. They talked about Darkken's decision. It made sense, and Nath couldn't rule out that he might have made the same decisions if he were in Darkken's shoes.

But what about Calypsa? That was what bothered him most. He wanted to track her down, but at the same time, he knew she could handle herself. She'd made a decision, and he couldn't worry about everyone all of the time. That would distract him. At least, that's what Darkken and Maefon told him.

A little squeak caught his ear. He looked down at the horn of his saddle. A little brown-gray mouse sat on the horse's saddle, looking up at him. "What is it, Mouse? Are you hungry again?"

The mouse's fur had begun to change into a richer brown color. It seemed that the warmth of the southern hemisphere helped the mouse to quickly shed his winter coat. Watching the little whiskers twitching, Nath fed the mouse bits of hard cheese and breadcrumbs that he kept in a small pouch. He sprinkled them on the horse's mane. "That should keep you busy."

Roday and Dule ran up alongside him. They eyed the mouse. "Will you look at that, Dule, our friend has a pet rodent," Roday said. "Or is that beast your familiar?"

"Could be." Dule gave the mouse a curious look. "Does it have magic powers?" Dule and Roday sniggered.

"Maybe," Nath said. "Probably more than you."

Dule gave an offended look.

"So, tell us, what can this magic mouse do?" Roday asked. "I'd be curious to know. Can you communicate with it? Will it lead us to a treasure trove of cheese?"

"I love cheese." Dule made a big smile. "Mmm-mmm, as a matter of fact, I'm a cheese connoisseur. I've sampled over three hundred different kinds of cheese, and those are just in Elome."

"It's true, he knows his cheese. That's why he has that constipated look all of the time."

"You know that's right. Wait, I don't have a constipated look." Dule shoved Roday. "You have a constipated look, and you look like a rat."

"I don't look like a rat." Roday pushed Dule.

"A possum. You do look like a possum."

Dule and Roday exchanged quick punches into one another's arms and shoulders.

"Possum head!"

"Pineapple face!"

"What does that even mean?" Dule caressed the buttery skin of his unelven, round face. "My face is more of a saucer of fine china."

They took a few more shots at one other before breaking it off.

Nath couldn't help but laugh. The strange Brothers of the Wind, unlike the others, had a way of keeping the atmosphere light. It was such a change from the frosty demeanor that he didn't know what to make of it. They were friendly yet devious. Nath remained wary but played along.

Mouse stared right at both of them and hunkered down on all fours with his hackles up.

Seeing the mouse's look, the elves stiffened.

"That's a mean-looking mouse," Dule said. "Is it going to attack us?"

"Perhaps," Nath replied.

"Well, I like your little familiar. It shows spunk." Roday looked up into the sky, where the two-headed vulture circled above them. "And it's not horrid looking, like Galtur. Why would a bird be so ugly?"

"It has two heads. It's double ugly."

"So, the both of you are used to seeing Galtur in action?" Nath asked.

"We've spent most all of our time in the keep. But it comes and goes. Spooky thing," Dule said. "I don't care for spooky. That bird sends spiders crawling up my back."

Roday pointed a finger at Dule's shoulder. "Like that one."

Dule hopped and swatted at his shoulder furiously. "Get it off me!"

"There's no spider," Nath said. When the former Caligin agreed to become Brothers of the Wind, all agreed to leave the past in the past, but Nath saw an opportunity to probe a little deeper. "How are you adapting to the change in venue?"

"What do you mean?" Roday asked.

"Working for Darkken as opposed to working for Chazzan?"

Roday and Dule looked at one another, and Roday said, "It's good to get out of the keep. Otherwise, it's not so different."

"I see." He was about to dig deeper when he caught a streak in the sky out of the corner of his eye. Galtur dove. A sharp whistle followed.

Up ahead, Darkken, riding with Maefon by his side, called out, "Trouble ahead." He snapped the reins. The horses pulling the wagon shot forward. All of the elves were off and running down the path. Roday and Dule sprinted.

Nath spurred his horse on. "Eeeyah!"

CHAPTER 47

THE GROUND BURNED. THE SMALL trees in the prairie field were cinders. Plumes of smoke went up in the air. A big, black, charred spot that went on for several yards had been burned into the ground. Bodies covered the ground. Fire had taken the flesh from their bones. Horses and pack mules were roasted just the same, and three wagons were ablaze. Whatever was passing through had been totally wiped out.

Vultures picked at the dead bodies. With a squawk from Galtur, the ugly birds scattered, landing no more than a hundred feet away.

Down among the waste and flames, Galtur landed. The black-feathered bird's neck cocked side to side. One head picked at a dead body on the ground. Darkken led his wagon right up to the devastating scene. He and Maefon had climbed out by the time Nath and the elves caught up with them.

The appalling smell of burnt flesh and hair burned Nath's nostrils. He covered his nose and looked down to see what was left of a man on his back with his mouth open. There was at least a score of bodies. He dismounted. "What did this?"

"I'm not sure." Darkken reached down and picked up a small golden broach that had somehow withstood the flame. "Fan out. See what you can find, brothers."

Maefon gave Nath a worried glance. She kept close to Darkken. It didn't take long for Nath to find an assortment of footprints on the ground. The men's prints were heavy, as if they wore armor. There were smaller prints too, women and children. He spotted Roday and Dule looking down at the ground just south of him. He approached.

"That's a big foot," Dule said.

"That's not a foot, it's a paw," Roday said. "I've never seen one that big either."

"It looks like a dragon's paw. A very big dragon's paw." A crushed trail could be seen through the grasses where the attackers had passed. There were dragon footprints and a long, heavy trail through the grasses. Nath bent over and picked up a scale as big as his hand. It was red and shined like armor.

With big eyes, Roday and Dule hung over his find. "What is that?" Roday said.

"It's a bull dragon scale."

"A bull dragon. Are you serious?" Dule said. "Those are really big, aren't they?"

Nath nodded. "Bigger than elephants. This one must be old for him to have lost a scale. Either that or he lost it in a fight, but it didn't look like there was much of a fight. The question is, what would a dragon be doing with men? Bull dragons are huge, but they spend time in the sky. This dragon's on his feet. It makes no sense."

With a heavy beating of wings, Galtur took to the air. The two-headed vulture took a flight path the same direction as the trail.

Nath looked back to see Darkken standing beside Maefon. Both of them had eyes to the sky. Nath walked back to them. "What's going on?"

"Galtur will give us an idea of what lies ahead," Darkken replied, "but I'm not sure that this is something that we need to fool with. Aside from checking for wounded and survivors, which I don't see any, I'm not sure what else to do."

"Whoever it is has a dragon." Nath held up the scale. "That's a problem for anyone. Particularly the dragon. Something foul is afoot, and I want to see what is going on. I'll go with or without you."

"If you feel strongly about it, then who am I to hold you back? Please, lead the way," Darkken said.

Nath gave a quick nod. He started to run, but when his horse nickered, he jumped on. With many of the Brothers of the Wind gathering around, he said, "Follow me, brothers. Follow me!" He galloped off. The elves sprinted after him.

Maefon shouted, "Don't get too far ahead!"

The wind roared through Nath's hair as he thundered down the trail. The attack couldn't have been more than several hours old. If the attackers took prisoners, they would be moving slowly as well. The trail was easy to follow. They were deep in the countryside and not trying to hide where they were going. If Nath was going to take a quick count, he'd guess that it was about thirty men plus the bull dragon.

What manner of men can control a bull dragon?

Perplexed, he rode on, trying to envision the foes he might face. A bull dragon was more than a match for a small band of men. It would take a formidable group to defeat it. And no ordinary weapon could harm a bull dragon.

After over an hour of hard riding, he crested a high point on the prairie hill. Way down in the valley, he heard a mighty roar. His horse reared up and whinnied. "Easy, easy." Nath stroked the horse's neck. "Who are they?"

A small army marched alongside a huge dragon. The foot soldiers wore heavy armor, and all of their faces were covered with great helmets. One warrior rode on top of the dragon, holding a black banner with gold lightning streaking across it. The soldiers walked alongside the dragon, carrying chains that were cruelly tethered to the dragon's paws and attached to spikes that somehow penetrated the body. Nath's stomach turned further the moment he caught sight of another abomination. The dragon's wings had been shorn off. His jaws clenched.

How dare they!

Chapter 48

Tracking during the winter snowfall could be easy or it could be hard. Brenwar had seen it all. Unless the tracks were wiped out by magic, he would find them. Tracking down Nath, however, proved difficult. There had been steady snowfall and melting only for the path to be covered by fresh snow again. He'd moved them on, out of the forest, away from the brigand fort, going west toward the open countryside.

With small flakes falling from the dreary sky, Elween and Slivver remained a few steps behind. Their eyes swept across the ground, searching, probing for any signs of men passing through. In the forest, Brenwar pointed out several unnatural disturbances on the hard ground. There were signs of boots sliding over the debris. All Brenwar said was, "This way."

Brenwar led his small horse away.

Now they stood in front of a great field of snow where no single spot looked any different than the other for leagues. Not saying a thing for the longest time as he stared out over the field, Brenwar finally pointed west. "That way."

Slivver stood beside him with his arms crossed over his chest. "Why that way?" He pointed southwest and northwest. "Why not that way or that way?"

"'Cause I said so."

"You are guessing, aren't you?"

Brenwar marched on with the prairie winds tousling his beard. His voice carried with the wind when he said, "Dwarves don't guess."

Slivver made a disappointed look.

Elween tugged on his cloak. "Come on. He's been right so far."

"Yes, yes indeed. I should give him some credit, shouldn't I?" Slivver said.

"It couldn't hurt." They rode on. "I never really could understand why the High Council of Dragons wanted to let Darkken live. But now it makes sense. Perhaps they knew that

Darkken would strike. That he would be Balzurth's weakness. It's hard to think about it being so."

"It would make my scales shudder if I had them," Slivver said. "I hate to be so critical of Brenwar, but he can be wrong and never admit it. I swear, we were close in our prior adventures to finding the scrolls on dragon steel. We missed our chance. He blames me for being distracted by Ericha, and I blame him for being bullheaded. I think we were both wrong."

"If you were so close, then what happened?"

"Magic. Teleportation. Something powerful whisked them away. The trail went cold, like this one."

They came to a river with chunks of ice flowing down its rippling waters. Brenwar walked along the bank. "Ah-hah!" He held a chunk of charred wood that fit between his thumb and index finger. "They came this way, following the river south."

"How do you know it was them? It could have been anyone," Slivver said.

"They tried to cover their tracks by sending the campfire downriver. It's an old trick, a good one. Passersby wouldn't have bothered. They cleaned up well, but this piece didn't quite make it out."

Taking the wood bit from Brenwar, Elween said, "Why would Nath hide his tracks?"

"It's what this group does. Besides, someone is cleaning up after they go. It's clear to me." Brenwar mounted his horse and followed the river south.

The land of the west had a lot of open territory. Most of the main cities of the world were in the middle and east territories. It was sort of a no-man's land on the other side of the river. They came to a downtrodden covered bridge in disrepair. Shingles were missing from the roof. The wind passing through it howled like a banshee. The timbers creaked and groaned. Brenwar stopped just outside the bridge. He dismounted and led his pony inside by the reins, casting a wary eye at them as he did so.

"Perhaps he thinks the bridge won't hold that big beard of his," Slivver said. They came close enough to look inside the dimness. The heavy planks of wood had rotted in many places, but passage looked safe enough. Brenwar was down on a knee, brushing away some of the snow that had fallen inside. He leaned downward. His shoulders bounced. He scooped something up in his hand.

Slivver and Elween dismounted and led their horses in. Elween slapped Slivver on the shoulder and showed him a dark stain in the wood. It was frozen blood. Dead bodies, frozen like ice, lay half covered in snow drifts. Arrows stuck from their bodies. "They are elves," she said. "The ones we track?"

"It's them all right," Brenwar said.

"But that doesn't make any sense." Slivver broke an arrow out of a fallen elf's body. His shoulders sagged. "No, it does make sense. The Caligin kill the Caligin, or the Brothers of the Wind. The Lord of the Dark in the Day is that devious. He killed fledglings. He cares for nothing but himself. Clearly, Darkken will stop at nothing to convince Nath. My, his mind is twisted like a gnarled root of a willow tree."

"Why doesn't he kill Nath?" Brenwar said.

"Because he wants Nath to help him kill our father," Slivver replied, casting the arrow aside. "Together, brother and brother would be invincible, so to speak. If Darkken controls Nath, then he can control the dragons and the world of men and shape it into what he wants it to be."

Elween agreed and added, "There are countless possibilities, one as dangerous as the other. Darkken's seduction is clearly powerful."

"Nath was not ready for this. We must find him quickly." Slivver mounted up and rode out of the covered bridge. "Let's move."

Even with the falling snow, the road south could still be found. Eventually, Brenwar took the lead, and long hours later, after the sun set, they stopped, facing a keep waiting eerily in the distance.

"That's it, isn't it?" Slivver said, looking at the ominous structure.

"Only one way to find out," Brenwar said.

"What's that?" Elween asked.

"We knock."

CHAPTER 49

NATH STARED AT HIS COMRADES. Darkken sat in the wagon with his fingers to his temples. Maefon had a hand on his thigh. His face began to perspire. Eyes rolling up in his head, they gave off an eerie copper glow. Nath's eyes hung on the man's bizarre look. Looking deeper into Darkken's eyes, he could see floral scenery moving. If Nath had not flown on the back of his father before, it would have been confusing. It was an aerial view from something that soared about. It only took him a moment to put it all together. Darkken had connected to Galtur.

"Guh!" Darkken gasped, his head snapping back. He blinked several times then rubbed his eyes with his fists. "There is a small town. Those soldiers are headed right for it. It's not our problem if we don't want it to be."

"Who are those soldiers?" Nath asked.

"Judging by the helmets and heavy armor, I'm certain that they are part of the Guul raiders." Darkken let Maefon rub his temples. "In the south, away from the armies of the five main cities, they roam free, battling with other brigands. The Guuls are one of the mightier groups of nomads who roam the territory. They're a mix of many races led by an undead leader. Strong and well-armed. They are not known for mercy. They will pillage that village, take more slaves, and possibly wipe it out."

"We can't let that happen." Nath opened up his backpack and slid on the Gauntlet of Goam. He slung his quiver of magic arrows around his hip, tied it on, and patted the handle of Fang that was strapped to the saddle. "I'm not going to let them enslave those women and children and abuse that dragon. He's my kind, and I'll free him."

Pushing Maefon's hands away, Darkken leaned forward and gave Nath a stern look. "That is a superior force compared to us and twenty brothers. We will not all survive the skirmish. Our mission is different at the moment. We want knowledge. There is no reason we can't send word to a higher authority. The leaders of the south have their own way of doing things."

"And I have my own way of doing things." Nath pulled the reins, turning his horse away. "I'll go it alone."

"At least have a plan, Nath! What do you expect to do, storm down the hill and frighten them? The Guuls do not flinch. They yearn to die with dwarven zeal."

Nath's blood ran hot. He itched for a fight. His jaw clenched. What Darkken said made sense, to play it safe and not risk his fellow brothers. But there was injustice. He could not let that stand. "I'll come up with a plan on my way down. If you come, I'll let you know what it is on the way." He led his horse down the incline, leaving the others behind him.

"We can't just let him go on a one-man mission," Maefon said. "He'll be executed."

"Perhaps, but maybe he can defeat them all."

"You are jesting," she said.

"Am I?"

"Don't toy with me, Darkken. I can't stand by and watch him ride to his doom. You did not even warn him about the ghouls."

"He should have asked, but surely he knows what a ghoul is."

Maefon's eyes were fastened to Nath riding away. Her heart twisted inside her chest. At the same time, she wondered what Darkken was thinking. The Lord of the Dark in the Day had power. Perhaps he could handle the Guul raiders, but that didn't mean that Nath could. Not to mention, they were flesh eaters, known to paralyze men and turn them into abominations. "I can't watch this, Darkken. We have to stop him or help him." She reached for the reins.

Darkken seized her wrist. "Don't you trust me?"

She wanted to give him an answer that was a better option. A quick thought passed through her mind. Perhaps Darkken set the entire encounter up. If he did, somehow, someway, she needed to let what he had in mind unfold. She leaned back in her seat and said, "Yes, of course I do."

The Brothers of the Wind had gathered around the wagon. Wearing their dark leather armor, some stood, others kneeled. They were relaxed, stoic, with their fingers at their sides, watching intently.

Maefon chewed on her lip. This was the way of the Caligin. They were a reflection of Darkken's cool and calculating demeanor but capable of blending in with any crowd with warm and welcoming behavior. On her side of the wagon, to her left, Roday and Dule watched the same as the others. They were two of the best actors and deceivers and doing an excellent job bonding with Nath. Now they stared on, cold as the others, watching Nath Dragon ride into the certain jaws of death.

Nath closed the distance, and halfway between him and them, the back end of the Guul raiders turned. In their heavy metal armor and helmets, they appeared as big as a horse and rider. The largest of the three stepped forward, carrying a two-headed sword that was every bit of six feet long. Maefon could not tell what race the raider was other than that he was big. Her fingernails bit into her skin.

Please turn back, Nath. Turn back now!

Nath unslung an arrow from his quiver. He loaded his bow and fired. A red missile streaked over the plains, hitting the huge raider square in the chest.

Boom!

Large pieces and bits of Guul raider went everywhere.

"That was… awesome!" Darkken held his gut, tossed his head back, and started laughing. "Ah-hahahahaha!"

Chapter 50

STANDING IN FRONT OF THE iron portcullis of Stonewater Keep, Brenwar said to Slivver, "Go ahead. Knock."

Slivver shook his head. "I'll leave the honor to you."

Brenwar pulled back his hammer and banged on the portcullis, making a lot of noise.

Elween stood outside the archway at the end of the bridge. Her green eyes moved over the tower. "I don't see anyone, but I know that someone is in there. I can feel their eyes on me."

Taking a position beside her, Slivver agreed. The portals to the tower were dim, but they had seen smoke coming from the chimneys. "I'm sure they don't want visitors, but we are going to have to be persistent. Worst-case scenario, we can always fly up there."

"True," she said.

Brenwar paced in front of the portcullis. He shouted hello out in Common, Dwarven, Elvish, and a few other languages. He rapped on the portcullis with his hammer more than once too. He yelled through the straps of iron, "It's very rude to have a door and not answer it!"

"It might take them some time to journey down from the top if that is where they are staying," Elween suggested.

"My behind. They are in there, watching, hoping we are going away," Brenwar replied. "We aren't going away! And I can knock on your door all night and all day."

An hour went by followed by another. Brenwar knocked at least a hundred times during that span. Slivver and Elween gathered some wood and started a campfire underneath the portcullis's archway to stay out of the bitter wind. Like normal people, they rubbed their hands in front of the flames and did their best to talk about ordinary things, making up information about where they were going. Once night came, they sat with the warming orange glow on their faces. "It's going to be a long night," Slivver said, referring to Brenwar hitting the metal time and again.

Brenwar let out an elated, "Hoo-hoo. Someone comes."

Sure enough, a person covered in a hooded robe and carrying a lantern approached. He stood several feet away from the portcullis, keeping most of his face hidden in the shadows of his hood.

Elween and Slivver stood up just as Brenwar said, "It's about time someone showed. Let us in. We are hungry and cold."

"You don't look hungry," the man said in a bitter Elven accent. "But you do look old. That is not something I can help you with."

"I didn't say old. What's wrong with you, are your ears filled with snow? I said—"

"Pardon my comrade. He is very cranky when he is hungry." Slivver stood with his nose almost touching the metal. "We are low on supplies for the rest of our journey, and my, er… wife is getting a nasty head chill. We hoped to resupply and have a good night's rest in your sanctuary. We have more than sufficient gold to pay you." He put his arm over Elween's shoulder. "You will make it, darling." He gave her a strong one-arm hug. "My sick darling."

Elween started coughing. Weakly she said, "I will remain strong for you." *Cough-cough.*

"You aren't welcome here, and we don't want your sickness. Go away," the elf said.

"Who is the lord of this keep? I would wish to speak with him." Brenwar made it more of a demand. "Right away, elf."

"I speak for the lord of the keep, and he does not care for any new company. Particularly an obnoxious dwarf that has been damaging his gate. That is most impolite."

Brows knitting together, Brenwar said, "You should answer when you are called!"

"There are no requirements out here in the wild. We are in a keep, protecting ourselves from dangerous elements."

"What is an elf doing out here anyway?" Brenwar asked.

"Just stop," Slivver said. "I apologize for my friend."

"Don't apologize for me."

"As I was saying," Slivver continued, "we will pay you well for any supplies you can spare and possibly a night or two of shelter. You appear to have a lot of room in your keep." He rubbed the stone walls of the archway. "And I do enjoy studying different architecture."

"Without apology, I say, go about your business and remove yourself from our archway." The elf remained in the same spot the entire time, holding the lantern out from his chest, making it difficult to get a good look at him. "Immediately."

"I told you elves weren't friendly." Brenwar eyeballed the elf. "They only pretend to be when they can get something out of it. The race of peace." He spat. "A farce."

The elf sighed. "As if a dwarf would know anything about peace."

Wagging his finger in the air, Brenwar said, "See, see. The pointy-eared devil is starting something. They just can't help but take a poke while looking down the length of their nose at you."

Addressing Slivver and Elween, the elf turned the slightest bit their way and said, "Sorry to hear about your condition, but respectfully, you must move on. I cannot emphasize that enough. Leave, or else."

Brenwar pushed his face into the portcullis. "Or else what?"

Chapter 51

Riding down the hill, Nath cast a backward glance over his shoulder. The Brothers of the Wind hadn't budged. His gut told him that Darkken and company expected him to turn back. It would be the wise thing to do, but he wasn't going to. Whether it was his business or not, the Guul raiders had to be stopped.

With no more than one hundred yards between them, the raiders bringing up the rear turned. There were three in all, massive fighters in metal armor with a formidable look about them. The biggest one, standing in the middle, readied a two-handed sword bigger than most men. There was something unearthly about the towering warrior. Nath readied his bow and nocked his first arrow, which had a gleaming red tip.

Let's find out how nasty you really are.

He pulled the string along his cheek and released. The arrow, straight and true, sailed fifty yards, hitting the big raider square in the chest. The explosion of flesh, armor, and bone blew the other two raiders from their feet. The rest of the raiders jumped and turned. The hardened fighters drew their weapons and faced the rider bearing down on their position like an angry wind. The leader on top of the dragon called out orders while waving a spiked flail round and round over his head. He started to turn the dragon.

Half of the army of fifty raiders advanced toward Nath. The rest set up a perimeter around the dragon.

Not slowing his mount, Nath drew his own sword and let out his battle cry. "Dragon! Dragon!"

Eyes grew big inside the ugly full-metal helmets of the raiders. The closest one, holding a spear, set his feet to take the charge.

Nath's horse leapt over top of the raider. Hooves cracked into the foot soldier's helmet, flattening the man. Nath stretched out his sword, cocked back, and hacked. The swipe killed one of the raiders tethering the dragon with chains. With a horde closing in, Nath took aim on another raider. Fang cut the fighter down.

Rage-filled cries erupted from the ranks of the dangerous company. Nath had killed three of them in a matter of seconds. They attacked with vigor.

Moments from being hemmed in and gored to death, Nath chopped his sword clean through one of the dragon's chains. He hopped out of the saddle and slapped his horse on the hindquarters. "Go!"

The horse bolted away from the surging horde, leaving Nath hemmed in between the raiders and the dragon.

Gripped in both of his hands, Fang burned with blue energy. The raiders slowed the charge, coming at him one slow step at a time. Their full helmets covered their heads but in some cases showed their faces and eyes. Many raiders were pasty skinned and white eyed. The others were part of the evil races—orcs, gnolls, bugbears, and goblins—with a few men among them. "I guess you've never seen a sword like this before. Come, take a closer look, demons!"

A raider wielding a battle axe charged.

Nath cut him down in one stroke. He spun his sword in his hand by the handle. "I can do this all day."

A gruff-voiced gnoll said, "So can we." He raised a sword. "Kill him!"

All at once, every Guul raider stormed forward.

Perfect.

Nath dropped and rolled underneath the belly of the dragon. Where the tail started from the body was a soft spot between the scales of the underbody. It was like the skin between a man's toes. Very sensitive. Nath reached up, slipped his hand in between the scales, squinted his eyes, and said, "Here goes." He pinched a fleshy part of dragon skin.

The bull dragon reared up. It let out an eardrum-shattering "ROOOOOOOOAAAAAR!"

It came back down on all fours and thrashed like a wounded wolverine.

Nath sprinted away from the dragon.

The raiders holding the chains that were cruelly fastened into the dragon's writhing body were yanked from their feet. The dragon's tail lashed out. Three raiders went flying through the air. The dragon's jaws opened. Striking as a snake, it crushed a raider in its jaws. Metal and bone popped and busted. The dragon spun around, striking out at its foul captors. Raiders were trampled and stomped deep into the ground. Dragon claws peeled them out of their armor.

Somehow, the leader kept his hold on the back of the dragon. The raider held on like a man breaking a bucking wild bull. All the while, the Guuls fearlessly flung themselves at the dragon. With swords hacking and axes chopping, they fought to slay it. Spears shattered against scales. Bodies were torn asunder by great teeth and dragon claws.

Nath hung back, keeping far from the dragon's raging path, watching the raiders fall in ones, twos, and threes. It was just what he wanted.

Let them have it, red bull!

The bull dragon spewed out flames, turning the hardened raiders in its path to smoke, molten metal, and cinders.

Suddenly, the lead Guul was flung from the top of the dragon. The large warrior landed hard on his knees and rolled away from the danger. Spiked flail in hand, the leader backed away, eyeing the massacre. It was more than clear that the dragon was going to win. The Guul leader took a look at his flail, at the dragon, at the flail again, and shook his head. Finally, he pointed a finger at Nath. "You! You will pay!"

Nath narrowed his eyes and waved the raider over. "No, you will!"

At the same time, they both charged each other.

The Guul, bigger, taller, and broader than Nath, came on like a juggernaut in plate-metal armor. Weapons collided. The chain of the flail wrapped around Fang. A tug of war went back and forth. The raider tried to rip Fang from Nath's grip. Nath tried to free it. Locked up, face-to-face, he got a closer look at his opponent. He was pasty skinned and white eyed and breathed out the cold and fetid breath of the undead. His strength was not natural.

"You are strong. But you are not dead! Nothing can kill me, for I am already dead. My touch is death!" The Guul leader yanked Fang out of Nath's hands.

Nath's fingertips caught the bottom of the sword's pommel, pulling free a concealed dagger that lay within. The blade glowed bright purple. Without thinking, Nath punched the dagger into the Guul's exposed chest.

"No! Impossible!" The Guul's body crumbled into ash, leaving nothing but armor and the ugly metal helmet.

Chapter 52

The elf inside the walls of Stonewater Keep tartly answered Brenwar's question. "Step back, look up, and see for yourself."

All three of them backed up in the snow. They cast their eyes upward. Two levels up on the high outer wall of the keep, elves armed with crossbows took aim between the battlements. Slivver counted ten faces.

Brenwar growled as the three of them took cover once again underneath the stone archway.

"Well, I just want to go on the record and say that you are the least hospitable elves I have ever met," Slivver said.

"Agreed," Elween added as she shivered underneath her cloak.

Showing a tight smile behind the lantern's light, the elf said, "I take it you'll be going then."

Slivver huffed. "Indeed. But you are going on the record. Let me say that again."

The small group moved out of the archway, beside the horses, and into the wind. Using the wind to conceal their whispers, they spoke of Nath.

"If he is in there, then we need to find out," Brenwar insisted. "And if we cross that bridge, we won't be coming back without them carving us up with those bolt throwers. I can get us in there now." He gave his war hammer a little shake. "Trust me."

"I have another suggestion," Elween said. "We can wait them out. They are bound to exit, possibly to patrol or something. We shall be waiting. We'll interrogate them. That will give us what we need."

Slivver rubbed his chin. "Hmmm... we can't risk the wait. It could be weeks. No doubt they are well supplied. I have another idea right along those lines. Let's go."

"We might not get this close again. We have to take it right to them," Brenwar demanded.

"Brenwar, trust me."

"Pah!"

Slivver led them over the icy bridge, feeling more vulnerable than ever. The cold, dead, penetrating stares of the elves seemed to dig into his back. It was as if he could feel their fingers pulling on the triggers of their crossbows, waiting to release. He had no idea if those bolts would hurt him or not without his scales. He had the feeling they would.

In silence, they trudged through the snowy night until they were far enough out of sight that they couldn't see the keep anymore.

"So, what is your brilliant idea?" Brenwar asked.

"Simple. Elween and I can fly in. We'll start at the top of the keep and work our way down from there. I don't think they'll be expecting any dragons."

"I don't like it," Brenwar said.

"We could take you with us," Elween suggested. He eyed her. "I know, dwarves don't fly, but who's to know when it's only us around?"

"I'm not flying."

"Why don't you close your eyes and imagine that it's teleportation?" she said.

"No."

Slivver snapped his fingers. "I have it. I just need to change back into a dragon."

"Are you sure that you want to do that?" Elween said. "I know how much you enjoy being a person."

Slivver looked at his spread fingers and wiggled them. "I wouldn't mind holding on a little longer, but we need to do this—"

Elween huffed fire out of her mouth. She quickly transformed from a beautiful woman into a beautiful dragon, green scales and all.

"You didn't have to do that," Slivver said.

"But I did," she said. "Now what is your plan?"

"Simple." Sliver spread out his arms like a great bird. "Swoop in and pluck an elf from the walls. Bring him back here, but be discreet about it."

Brenwar nodded, and said, "Aye, discreet like me."

She winked at Brenwar. "I'll return shortly." Launching herself into the sky, wings beating, she barrel rolled a few times before vanishing behind the falling snow.

"This better work," Brenwar said.

"It's a much better plan than watching you smash the gate in with your hammer. Talk about a lack of subtlety."

"At least it's a better plan than me flying."

No more than ten minutes passed before Elween appeared. Her bottom paws were hooked into the shoulders of an elf. His head sagged into his chest. From twenty feet up, she dropped the elf. He plummeted back-first into the snow right between Slivver and Brenwar. Elween landed.

"Well done. Did you draw any attention?" Slivver asked.

"This one was on the roof, a lone guard, so I believe we have time."

With one hand, Brenwar pulled the elf up by the collar of his armor. The elf's neck rolled. "Did you kill him?"

"No, I knocked him out first with a quick swipe from my tail to the chin. I didn't want him yelling and alerting the others."

"Well done," Slivver said as he took the elf's sword belt away.

"Pat him down better than that," Brenwar said. "I'm sure he'll have more weapons. These Caligin are devious."

Slivver's search revealed three small knives, one in a boot, one under the sleeve, and one behind the lower back. "That should do it. He's not going to talk, so how do we do this?"

Brenwar looked at him. "Don't worry about that. I'll make him talk."

CHAPTER 53

THE BATTLE SCENE HAD COME to an end. The Guuls were dead. The bull dragon ground them into the dirt. Others were wiped clean off the face of Nalzambor by the dragon's flames. There were many survivors with sense enough to flee the fray. That was when the Brothers of the Wind swept in and finished the remaining ferocious men off. Sitting atop its hind legs, the dragon, reaching thirty full feet in height, let out a victorious yell. A snort of smoke rolled out of its nostrils. The hulking dragon, chains and all, sauntered across the prairie into the woodland.

Nath sat on the ground, studying the dagger that he found inside Fang's hilt. His father told him that Fang wasn't complete. Nath wasn't certain what that meant in regards to the sword, but he was baffled that he missed this. As Darkken and Maefon pulled up in the wagon, he reached over and grabbed Fang.

Maefon jumped out of the wagon. "That was the bravest thing I ever saw!" She tackled him with a fierce hug. "Did you get hurt?"

"I have some scrapes. I'm going to live, however, no thanks to either of you."

Getting out of the wagon with a surprising smile on his face, Darkken said, "Do they not say that fools rush in where angels fear to tread?"

"Oh, so you are angels now, are you?"

"Of a sort." Darkken's eyes swept over the smoking carnage. "My, that was a fantastic battle. I really thought that you would turn back, but when you didn't, it was too late. You executed quite a fantastic plan." He looked at the dagger, brows lifting. "What is that you have there?"

"It's a dagger, hidden in Fang's hilt." The dagger was the bottom part of the sword's double-handed handle. When he pulled it out, the cross guard flipped down. With his hand, he locked it into place. "Quite a device."

"It seems that Fang has a dragon claw of his own," Darkken said.

"Dragon Claw. I like that." Nath folded the cross guards closed and fit them back into Fang's handle. With Maefon's support, he stood, looking at the dead Guul leader. "He said he was dead and I couldn't kill him. He said his touch was death."

"Guul leaders have a paralyzing touch. So he was right. Once you're paralyzed, it would be easy to kill you." Darkken extended his hand. "Nath, we should have ridden down that hill with you. You could have died, but for some reason, I was not worried. You are truly... special. I won't let that happen again. So, the dragon, it's going to be fine?"

"Trust me, that bull dragon is not going to want anyone's help. He'll be fine on his own. Though, I wish I could have at least cut off more lengths of chain."

People from the distant town showed up, thanking the elves, offering them food and flowers as well as their daughters. Nath fetched his horse, and the group moved on toward Old Hen. Nath switched with Darkken and rode with Maefon, who refused to leave his side. She'd become clingy. When Darkken scouted ahead with the Brothers of the Wind, she talked a lot and pawed all over him.

"You truly are brave, Nath. I mean that. There is deep good in you. You are rich in it. I wish I was."

"Why would you say that?"

"I just feel incomplete. I'm rife with guilt about the fallen Trahaydeen. I'll always be one of them."

"Let it go. We've moved past that now."

She wrapped her arms around his. "I'm trying."

He whipped the reins, urging the horses up the hillside. "Since we are alone, I'm getting more curious about Darkken."

"What do you mean?"

"For a man, he's very formidable in fighting and magic. Where did he learn all of this?"

"The elves, I suppose. The ones who raised him." She shrugged. "So far as I know, he's a bit of a rover that has dabbled in many things."

"He's done more than dabble. Now he controls that big ugly bird that flies above us. That couldn't be easy." Nath shooed away a mosquito. "I've been thinking about all he has done. He's very strong."

"Does that concern you?"

"In the keep, he had access to all of those mystic tomes and the treasure. It was much to behold. An arsenal of items and information. Wouldn't it take decades to comprehend many of them? In Dragon Home, they studied for decades, even centuries, to understand magic."

"I'm just as guilty, am I not?" she said. "Don't you think I am powerful?"

"Yes, but you are an elf and live much longer." He studied her face. "How old are you?"

"You aren't supposed to ask that."

"True, but you would be much older than Darkken. That is my point. I can understand all you know, but he is different. Special."

Maefon squeezed his knee.

Nath laughed out loud. "Will you stop that?"

"No, you need to stop thinking so much. I'm trying to enjoy riding in the countryside with you." She kept tickling him. Nath tried to get away but couldn't. "I won't stop until you change the subject. I just want it to be me and you."

"Fine. Fine!" he blurted out. "I'll stop."

"Do you promise?"

"I promise."

She pulled her hands back. "Good. Let's enjoy nature and the quiet together then."

"Agreed."

Without any further delay, they made it to Old Hen. It was a charming area, with small stone homes spread out all over the countryside. A main road led them straight toward the city itself, where similar but larger buildings were nestled together.

The Brothers of the Wind broke away before Darkken, Nath, and Maefon rode in. The wagon wheels rumbled over the cobblestone road. Unlike the other towns, there were no porches in front of the stores. All of the buildings were made from stone blocks that appeared to have stood for centuries. They were weathered by time and the elements in many places.

The people scuttled about, paying them no mind, but a few offered an amiable greeting. It was a nice place.

Darkken leaned forward and looked to Nath. "Welcome to Old Hen. What do you think?"

"This is it? I expected something else."

"Good. I fooled you then. Let's settle in with some eats and drinks. I'm thirsty."

Chapter 54

Brenwar stuffed a cold handful of snow into the elf's face. The elf shook his head and opened his eyes. He got a full look at Brenwar staring right in his face. His lips tightened over his chin, and he looked away.

"Heh, this one is going to be difficult," Brenwar said. "Hold him still."

Elween had hooked the elf's arms behind his back. She had a good hold on the elf. "Get on with it."

Slivver stood beside Brenwar, holding open the picture of Nath.

Brenwar pointed at it. "Is this man inside the keep?"

The elf turned his face.

Grabbing the elf by the head and chin, Brenwar twisted hard, forcing the elf to look at the picture. "Answer me!"

The elf squeezed his eyes shut.

"Will you look at that? I told you he would be difficult." Brenwar slid a dagger out of its sheath. "I'll poke you with so many holes you'll bleed to death. Now look at the picture!"

The elf refused to open his eyes.

Brenwar drew back to wallop the elf in the gut with his fist.

"No, let's not be inhumane," Slivver said. "If we torture him, then we are no better than Caligin."

"I told you we should have gone in for a straight-up fight. That way we could have found out for ourselves." Brenwar glared at Slivver. "If you can't stomach it, look away."

Slivver looked away.

Brenwar popped the elf hard in the sternum, causing the elf's mouth to drop open. He stuffed a handful of snow into the elf's mouth and clamped it shut with his own hands. "See how much you talk with a mouth full of snow!"

Squirming, the elf tried to spit out the snow. Glaring at Brenwar, he swallowed it. "You are torturing me with a snowball. Have you even done this before? Ignorant weaklings!" The moment Slivver turned his head back, the elf opened his eyes and started laughing. "You fools are doomed," the elf said. "You take me prisoner to what, tickle me to death?" He puffed out a laugh. "You will all die by morning, for you have made a fatal mistake. The Lord of the Dark in the Day will forever punish you."

Brenwar gave his comrades a knowing look. He said to the elf, "Feeling chatty all of a sudden, are we?"

"Of course not, you bearded mountain goat. I don't speak with imbeciles," the elf said. "You cannot break me, so do not attempt it. I am Caligin. My will is harder than iron. I will take my secrets to my death."

"So, your name is a secret, is it?" Brenwar asked.

Elween and Slivver exchanged a perplexed look.

Haughtiness surfaced in the elf's tone. "Of course my name is a secret, you fool! All we do is secret."

Brenwar looked at the elf. "Tell me, elf, what is your secret name?"

"Garalan." The elf's eyes became bigger than saucers. "No, that is not my name. It's Garalan. Garalan. No, it's not. It's Garalan."

"Heh-heh-heh." Brenwar pointed at the picture of Nath again. "Is this man inside the keep?"

"No," the elf said clearly. His face became white with horror. "What have you done to me, dwarf?"

"You just swallowed a mystic pellet of truth this big." Brenwar made a gap between his finger and thumb the size of an acorn. "And you'll tell us all we want to know. How many elves are in the keep?"

"Twenty-two."

"Who else is in the keep?"

"None but the Caligin," the elf said, shame-faced.

"What is this man's name?" he said, pointing to the portrait again.

"Nath."

"Where and who is he with now?" Brenwar asked.

"He travels with Lord Darkken, Maefon, and twenty Brothers of the Wind to Old Hen."

"Why?"

"Lord Darkken does not say why. The Lord of the Dark in the Day does as he wishes. You might have tricked me, dwarf, but you will not win." The elf's voice became poison. "Lord Darkken is a god!"

"What does he want Nath for?"

"To make him one of us. Destroy the dragon king. Rule the world. He has the power to do it too!" The elf started offering up more information. He told them about the keep, the hundreds of Caligin that infiltrated the cities. He went on a tirade about Darkken's great deception turning all against one another. "Lord Darkken is already invincible. He knows all. He sees you. His eyes are Galtur. His thoughts the wind. He'll tear your hearts from your chests."

Brenwar asked, "How long ago did they leave the keep?"

"Five days ago." The elf spit on Brenwar. "You will die. All of you will die! Nath will succumb, or he will die if he has not died already. Perhaps he is eaten by worms. Perhaps he is joined at the hip with us. Lord Darkken will know that you come! You are doomed!"

Brenwar punched the elf in the jaw. The elf's chin sagged.

"Well played, Brenwar. You, too, are tricky. But what do we do with this elven bag of wind?" Slivver rolled up the picture. "He'll warn the others unless we kill him."

"No, he won't remember the last hour. That pellet will wipe his memories of the last hour. It's a side effect. Can be good or bad." He looked to Elween. "Take him back where you found him. We need to get going."

CHAPTER 55

NATH AND DARKKEN SAT AT a small table in a candle-lit tavern eating a late dinner. Maefon had retired to her room for the evening, leaving them alone to finish their meal. Darkken sawed into a slab of baked roast. "Old Hen is interesting, is it not?"

"On the contrary, it is, well—" Nath looked about. "Ordinary."

"Yes, it is a peaceful place, very quaint and simple, but you need to know that is also called the place of secrets."

Nath raised a brow. "What kind of secrets? I don't think there is anything worth hiding here. The people I see are gray and silver haired. Even the halflings sport white heads that look like cotton."

"Old people like the warmth in the south. This is where they come and live out their final days in peace."

"I see. So are you thinking about moving down here? I thought I saw some frosting growing out of your sideburns."

"Very funny." Darkken chuckled. "I'm sure that I still have a ways to go, assuming I survive the next engagement."

"You will. We will." Nath nodded to the waitress, who refilled his mug with water. She wore an ankle-length blue skirt and a white blouse that was untied at the top. The mature woman, much older in appearance, gave him a warm smile. "So, what is it that we are looking for in this elderly community?"

"Chazzan believed that some of the items' locations could be revealed from here. The Star of the Heavens, the scrolls of dragon steel, and the thunderstones. You saw his trove. He had a knack for acquiring many items. But since Maefon is gone, I wanted to follow up on something that I meant to touch on earlier."

With a mouth full of red potatoes, Nath said, "What is that?"

"I want you to take care of her, closely, when I'm absent."

Nath swallowed his food and looked up. "Pardon?"

Darkken wiped his mouth on his napkin. "Face it, Nath. She adores you, and I've always known that my future with her would be limited. She is so fond of you. It would be better if I broke off our relationship and see if yours blossoms. It would be best for her and you, I believe."

"No, I don't, well—I can't be a part of that." Nath fumbled to find the words. On the one hand, he wanted to be with Maefon, but on the other, he felt he'd betrayed Darkken. "I feel that I have come between you. That isn't right. If anything, I should step away."

"Search your heart. You know this is right. In truth, I should search out someone more like me. Someone that I can become old and gray with. Again, that is if I live that long." Darkken lifted his goblet and took a sip of wine. "I feel tension, but I need focus. I love Maefon, but I feel that I am holding her back and that she needs to be set free."

"Don't do this."

"So far as I am concerned, it is done. It was done the moment that we found you. Let what will be, be."

Numbness washed over Nath. He stared at the candle flame on the table. His heart throbbed with guilt. He wanted Maefon, but he didn't want to lose his friendship with Darkken. He thought back to her fawning over him on the wagon ride. "Does she know this?"

"Yes, she knows. We've... discussed it. It's mutual. No feelings hurt."

Nath sank in his chair. "I feel awful."

"Don't." Darkken got up from the table and set the napkin on his plate. "Go to her. Discuss your feelings. I'm going to take a stroll, like the elderly. Let's catch up in the morning." With a nod, he left.

Nath sat for the longest time pondering what happened. Finally, figuring the best thing to do was to talk about it with Maefon, he headed upstairs on heavy feet. Softly, he knocked on the door. *Rap. Rap. Rap.*

Maefon opened the door. Her soft fingers took him by the wrist and led him into the room. He stayed with her all night and into the morning.

CHAPTER 56

THE BROTHERHOOD OF THE WIND met up south of Old Hen. It was business as usual as Darkken discussed his plan to locate the artifacts. Nath and Maefon stood quietly side by side, listening. Occasionally, the back of her hand would brush against his.

"The secret of Old Hen is the records that they keep and the crypts that they maintain. There are countless graves where the dead are buried from all over the world. That is where the Caligin searched for the artifacts. But there are guardians too in those haunted hills, and we need to know what to look for. I'm going to spend the day searching the library back at Old Hen. We could all search, but that would draw attention. However, a couple of elves would be less conspicuous, unless the two of you would rather join me," he said, looking at Nath and Maefon.

"What else would we do?" Nath said.

"Why, check out Old Hen's infamous graveyard. They say it's best to see it in the day, before the guardians come out at night," Darkken replied.

"What sort of guardians?" Nath asked.

"That I am not sure about. I've never been here myself. It could be anything." He looked at Dule and Roday. "Why don't you accompany them?"

"I would like to search with you, Darkken," Maefon said.

"No, I think you should stay with Nath. The search will be lengthy. Perhaps tomorrow." With a nod, Darkken led a handful of elves away, leaving Nath and company alone.

"I suppose all is well," he said, even though he didn't feel that way. "South is it?"

"Come on. Let's walk. He said it's not that far away. We can talk about last night if you like."

"How about we just walk?" His eyes followed after Roday and Dule, who began the trek. No other elves came with them. "I'm a bit tired of everything that has happened. It has all happened so fast."

"I know," she said softly. "But I'm glad that it happened." She bumped into him. "Silence it is."

The southern terrain was rich in flourishing vegetation and wildlife. The forest and woodland were green, and prairies and grasslands ran around and between them. It was a great spot for hunting. Nath spotted a great white horned elk on a grassy bluff. It had a broad fur chest and jumped out of sight into the woods.

For miles, Dule and Roday moved at a quick and easy pace, maintaining a straight direction through the fields. They talked back and forth in Elven, making comments one to the other.

Maefon laughed at what they said. "They are a funny pair, aren't they?"

"I'm just glad that some of the elves have finally warmed up around me. They've been stone-faced for so long that I'm not sure what to make of this pair. Do you trust them?"

"Yes, just not as much as you. I knew Chazzan well, and he was very demanding," she said. "I think the new Brothers of the Wind are able to loosen up without him."

"That makes sense."

"Of course it does. I said it."

Roday and Dule stretched the gap between them by jogging up to the top of the hill. They stopped at what appeared to be a drop-off and waved. Dule pointed downward.

"It looks like we've arrived at our destination," she said.

Roday scratched his head as he stared outward with his head tilted. Dule's jaw hung half-open. Their hands fell on the pommels of their swords.

"That doesn't look good." Nath's eyes narrowed as he marched to meet them. He stood beside them and stared down the hill. "Whoa. So, this is Cemetery Valley."

The entire valley was filled with tombstones and markers by the tens of thousands. There was a stark transition in the landscape too. The trees were bare and looked like ugly hands bursting out of the ground. The ground had no grass, but a yellow, spongy moss. A sour smell lingered in the air.

Maefon's nose twitched.

Amongst the tombstones were small caves that appeared to be used for tombs, carved out of the rock walls that made up the huge valleys. There were obelisks, thirty and forty feet high. On the backside of the valley stood a mausoleum, made out of blank granite, that could have been its own city. It was a huge rectangle, hundreds of feet long and dozens of feet high. Black crows nestled on the ledge of the tremendous building. More birds pecked at the worms on the ground.

"I've seen my fair share of graveyards," Roday said, "but they had flowers and soft grasses. They didn't smell either."

Dule replied, "It's a graveyard. We shouldn't expect any different. It's full of thousands of dead. And maybe their spirits. I can see why it wouldn't be safe at night. It doesn't look safe in the day."

"Let's go." Nath took the lead down the hill. The closer to the graves they got, the more expansive it all became. It seemed like the burial had started at a single spot and spread out for miles in every direction. Entering the field of graves, his feet squished down on the spongy yellow moss-like grass that covered the field. "If something is hidden here, it will be impossible to find."

"It wouldn't surprise me if many treasures rest beneath our feet." Maefon squatted in front of a stone tombstone. The chiseled-out lettering had faded from years of wind and rain. "This common lettering is not even used anymore. This person is from a time long forgotten."

"Not all are forgotten." Nath spied some sunflowers that were wilting lying on top of a grave. "I guess there are people that still come and remember." West of his position, he noticed a small group of men and women standing over a hillside grave. They were so far away he didn't notice them at first. "What sort of lives did all of these people lead?"

"Being human, they don't have much of a life. It all ends quickly," Roday said. "That is why this graveyard is so vast. Elven cemeteries are small. We live much longer."

As they walked about, Nath said to Maefon, "You said that many people buried their treasure with them. What would keep grave robbers out?"

"The guardian," Dule said. "That is why so many dead are buried here. They are protected by a guardian who keeps grave robbers out."

"How do you know this?" Roday asked.

"Because, I read."

"I read," Roday fired back.

"I've never seen it."

"That doesn't mean I don't."

Dule looked at Roday and said, "Yes, it does."

Traipsing through the creepy field of the dead, Nath didn't pick up on anything extraordinary. If Darkken was going to try and find something, he would need a map of some sort, and that hardly seemed likely. The graves were scattered all over in no particular order. The tombs dug in the ground and around the outlying hills were just the same. The layout, it seemed, was no layout at all. The only thing that appeared to be in the right and proper place was the mausoleum. With Maefon tailing behind, he approached the massive structure.

The gargantuan mausoleum had been made from smooth granite stones, each bigger than a man, stacked up brick by brick with hardly a seam between them. All across the front were archways that led inside.

Nath entered the nearest archway. Ten feet inside, a slab door sealed the exit shut. It had no handles or a mechanism to open the door. With Maefon right behind him, he said, "How do you get in?"

"Maybe another one is open," she suggested.

They checked several. The elves did the same. All of the entrances were sealed.

Standing back outside, staring at the mausoleum, Nath said, "Whatever it is we are looking for, I hope it's not inside there."

Roday replied, "Knowing Darkken, it probably is."

CHAPTER 57

LATER THE SAME DAY, MAEFON and Darkken met privately in his quarters. Darkken sat in an upholstered chair in the corner, reading a scroll.

Maefon sat on the bed. "I'm not going to lie to you. I'm not very comfortable with this relationship with Nath. I feel strongly about you."

He quickly rolled up the scroll, tied a cord of leather around it, and tossed it onto the bed. He gave a quick smile. "I don't care. Fall in love with him, for that matter, just leave me out of it. He needs to be close to you. His guilt will keep him closer to me. You are both young. Just work with what comes naturally."

"I feel guilty."

"You are Caligin!" He quickly lowered his voice "We live without regret. I'm disappointed, Maefon. I thought this would be easy for you. I believed that you were stronger."

"You are confusing him and me," she said.

"It astounds me how emotions can easily make a wreck out of the best-laid plans. Emotion is instability. Fear, anger, love, joy, sadness, lust—they control the very air that people breathe, but I am above that. Our kind is above that." He reached over and lifted her head by the chin. "There is no true future for you and Nath. You know that, don't you? He is a dragon. You are an elf who murdered his friends. If he finds out, he will not forgive you for it. It would be the ultimate betrayal. But if we win him over, well, then it will all change. He'll be one of us. You want that, don't you?"

"I want what you want, truly."

"Perhaps it would be best if we work toward a stronger platonic relationship among the three of us. That might be less confusing. What do you think?"

Maefon carefully chose her next words. "No, I want him all to myself."

"Good thinking." He kissed her forehead. "We are close, very close, to locking it all in." He started to leave.

"Where are you going?"

"Downstairs. Round up Nath, Roday, and Dule. It's time to discuss what I have discovered."

Inside the tavern, away from prying ears, the five sat at a circular table. By candlelight, Darkken addressed Maefon, Roday, Dule, and Nath. "Cemetery Valley is more ancient than the dragons. As you have seen, it is a chief burial place for the dead. It is also the chief burial place for secrets and treasure. The problem is, well, there are guardians who roam the gravesite at night. That's when the mausoleum doors open, and the guardians come out to prowl the night."

"What are we searching for?" Nath asked.

"The records list the name of every man, woman, and child buried there over the past several centuries," Darkken replied. "Chazzan had a name in his own records. Afflana Shannreer. An elf. An elf conspirator that was rumored to be the one who stole the secret of dragon steel. His name is in the books. He is buried here and the secret with him."

Nath gave his friend a curious look. "I thought we searched for the Star of the Heavens?"

"Perhaps I spoke flippantly when I was laying out the artifacts. Please, forgive me. I am only human." Darkken shook his finger. "But that is still a possibility. You see, Afflana Shannreer was a great preserver of many precious items. He considered himself a guardian of dangerous treasures. It is very possible he brought many antiquities to his tomb, knowing that Cemetery Valley was the ideal place for safekeeping."

"If it is safe, then we should leave it as is," Nath said. He noticed Roday and Dule nodding. At the same time, he'd been thinking about what Roday said earlier about Darkken. Roday said, *"Knowing Darkken, it probably is."* It suggested a much deeper relationship than two people who had only recently met would have. Nath watched for anything else that stood out. "Why the chase?"

The large man rested his muscular forearms on the table. His chair groaned when he moved. "Let me remind you that we are here to verify all is in place. The Caligin might have it in their hands as we speak."

"Wouldn't the guardians stop them?" Maefon asked.

"We need to find out. Perhaps the Caligin are buried in the graveyard, but I would sleep better if I knew for sure," Darkken said.

"So, Afflana Shannreer is buried inside the mausoleum?" Nath said. Darkken nodded. "And we can only go in at night?"

"Precisely." Darkken leaned back in his groaning chair. "But before you let that chill sink into your bones, there is a caveat. The guardians won't attack unless the tombs are disturbed. However, I'd imagine that they will make us very uncomfortable."

"Uncomfortable how?" Dule asked.

Darkken drained his goblet of wine and stood up. "I guess we will find out when we get there."

"We are leaving now?" Maefon said. "We just returned."

"We don't all have to go, if you would like to stay back," Darkken said.

"No." Nath stood up. "We are ready. The sooner we leave, the sooner we come back."

CHAPTER 58

DARKKEN RODE ON HORSEBACK WHILE Nath and Maefon drove the wagon back to Cemetery Valley. They stopped at the same spot Nath and company entered earlier that day. The horses whinnied, nickered, and snorted. Hooves stamped at the ground. Nath tugged on the reins in an effort to settle the nervous horses. "They don't care for this place."

Getting out of the wagon, Maefon said, "I don't blame them. I don't like it either."

Two of the Brothers of the Wind remained with the horses and wagon while Nath and Maefon made the trek up to the top of the hill that overlooked the cemetery. On horseback, Darkken waited at the top. Tall and formidable in the saddle, he had a powerful, foreboding look about him. The Brothers of the Wind kneeled around him, blending in like part of the land.

Covering his nose, Nath said, "There is that smell again. It's worse in the night winds."

"Agreed." Maefon's fingers toyed on the handles of her sword and dagger. "I don't care for this. Invading a grave seems... foul."

"I'll protect you."

"Then who is going to protect you?"

Nath patted her lower back and smiled. "Darkken." Joining the group, Nath studied the vast cemetery. The valley was pitch-black on the star-filled night. The wind howled throughout the tombstones like an army of banshees. His eyes adjusted, and he could make out the graves much better. There was movement behind and between the tombstones and small mausoleums. "It looks like we aren't the only ones that want to take a stroll through the valley tonight."

Darkken dismounted. He handed the reins to one of the brothers. "Those are guardians, I would assume. Don't anyone do anything suspicious. Keep your hands off the stones. We head for the mausoleum. Follow me."

As soon as they crossed the first grave, a low, deep, animal-like growling carried over the valley. Huge night hounds with glowing eyes and slavering jaws appeared among the stones by the dozens.

Darkken's pace didn't slow. He moved steadily toward the gargantuan tomb as if he didn't hear the sound. In addition to the dogs, the branches rustled. Crows filled the dead-looking limbs and squawked in the night. Their dark eyes followed every person's move like flesh-hungry vultures.

Nath fought the urge to draw his sword. One thing was for certain. The cemetery was truly well guarded. Only a fool would rob a tomb. The guardian dogs would rip flesh apart. The crows would help eat them. He glanced up and saw Galtur circling. The great vulture glided down and landed on the distant mausoleum. It sat perched, emerald eyes watching them as it waited.

Lengthening his stride, Nath caught up to Darkken. "How can people bury their dead within when the doors are sealed shut? Do they do this in the night, with all of these predators around?"

"No. I spoke with the seer that handles the records in Old Hen," Darkken replied. "He said that the doors open for the dead."

"I don't follow."

"You have to have someone to bury or entomb." Darkken stopped just twenty feet away from the mausoleum. "A fitting place for the dead."

"So, this building is enchanted?" Nath asked.

"There may be other explanations for it," Darkken said, staring into the blackness inside the archway on the front of the building. "I didn't realize that it would be so huge. This might take a while. Shall you go first, or shall I?"

"This is your mission. I'd just as soon stay back in Old Hen and watch the people sprout more wrinkles."

Rubbing her goose-bump-covered arms, Maefon said, "This place is giving me more wrinkles."

Darkken and Nath shared a quiet laugh. Darkken then said, "Dule, Roday, light some torches. The two of you can lead the way."

The elves exchanged a look and a head shake to one another, readied lit torches, and headed inside. They passed underneath the archway. The torches showed that the slab doorway was open. A tunnel waited. The pair entered the mausoleum. Slowly, they walked down the hallway. Like a falling butcher's knife, the slab door dropped behind them, sealing them inside.

Maefon let out a quiet gasp. Then the slab door slowly opened again. Stone scraped against stone on its ascension. The torches lay burning on the corridor floor. Dule and Roday were gone.

With something that felt like insects crawling up his back, Nath said, "What just happened?"

"I'm not sure, but the answer must be inside the mausoleum." Darkken took a deep breath. "Stay together and follow me. The rest of the brothers stay outside. We'll handle this."

Maefon gave Nath a nervous glance. His back straightened and jaw muscles clenched. They stood inside, crossed the threshold, and picked up the torches. The slab door stayed open. The Brothers of the Wind stood outside, peering at them. On the inside, hanging on the walls, were torches and brackets. Before Nath could light a torch on the wall, all of them suddenly lit up on both sides from one end of the hall to the other. Small insects scurried away from the light.

"Impressive." Darkken walked down the wide corridor, looking from side to side of the massive crypt. There were countless shelves made from stone lining the walls of the cobweb-laden facility. Inside the shelves, coffins were stuffed in lengthwise. There were markers carved in the stone, written in many languages, where the dead had been laid to rest. "Very impressive."

They ventured deeper inside. The crypts appeared to be carved out of stone. Stone staircases led to the higher levels, with walkways leading past the crypts. There were thousands of slots for the coffins. Some of the shelves were bigger, revealing as many as twelve to twenty coffins inside.

Maefon stopped at one where the coffins had been paired up. "Husband and wife," she said.

"Probably," Nath said. The coffins were all shapes and sizes. Many were ornate and majestically fashioned, but most were boxes of wood. The entirety of the facility held just as many graves inside as the outside. Possibly more. In wonderment, Nath said, "Searching for Afflana Shannreer is going to take forever."

"Yes," Darkken replied. "Isn't it exciting?"

CHAPTER 59

NATH RUBBED HIS EYES. HE'D been staring at the markers so long that he'd lost track of time. Aside from the search for Afflana Shannreer's crypt, there was still the matter of Roday and Dule being missing. Part of him believed they might be playing a trick. The other part of him wasn't so sure. Darkken moved to the higher levels, simply stating they needed to keep an eye out for the two missing elves.

On the other side of his corridor, Maefon did her own search. They hadn't spoken in what must have been hours. It wasn't because of any tension, but rather, the exhaustive search had drained her energy as much as his. As the search went on, the pace became quicker, their keen eyes adapting to the markings.

Breaking the long hours of silence, Nath sat down and leaned against the stone shelving. "We are not going to find this crypt. This is stupid."

"I find it interesting," she said. Her hands dusted over the markings chiseled in the stone. "I've learned so much about history. The different races and their marks. How they valued their families. They cared deeply for the ones they loved and safely put them inside here."

"I'd rather be buried underneath a bed of flowers where the sun feeds the fragrant petals."

"No doubt your body would make the soil very fertile." She crossed over to his side and put her arms around his waist. "But I prefer you living and breathing above the ground."

"Me too." He kissed the top of her head. Looking back down the corridor, he said, "Gads. The doors are closed again. We are sealed inside."

"It probably just does that," she said. "I'm sure they will open when it's time to leave."

"Or not," Nath said. Suddenly, he regretted not bringing Stone Smiter along. He'd left it in the wagon, but he'd thought it might be helpful in case they had to bust in or out of there. "And you said it as if this place was alive."

"I think it does live, magically, somehow. You can't feel it?"

"I just feel like I want to get out of here. That's how I feel."

"Huh. I'm getting used to it," she said. "It feels safer inside than outside with those night hounds and whatever else was out there."

Nath shook his head. "How does anyone know where to bury their dead in this place? There must be a system of sorts. A guide."

"You mean a crypt keeper?"

"Yes, that would make sense." Nath cupped his hands over his mouth and called out, "Calling all crypt keepers. Calling all crypt keepers. We need you to take us to Afflana Shannreer!" His voice carried down the corridor and faded. "That should do it."

"You are silly. If a guardian lurks here, certainly you have woken it." She slapped his arm. "Stop drawing attention to us. We come quietly. We go quietly."

"Sorry, but I don't think anyone is listen—" Nath stiffened. A smile played on his lips. He took off his satchel and reached inside. "I just thought of something." He pulled out the small hooded lantern that fit on the palm of his hand.

"Winzee's Lantern of Revealing. Perhaps it will aid in our search." Nath gave it a shake. A green flame flickered on inside. It cast a strong green hue all around them. "Now, if I can make it work to our benefit."

The lettering on the markers that were lit by the green light appeared sharper and clearer. Its radius stretched out like a blanket for several yards. Maefon walked with Nath and said, "It's helpful, but this is still going to take forever. Do you know how to use that lantern?"

He held it higher. "I'm not sure what else I should be doing."

Studying the flame intently, Maefon leaned closer. "That flame. It looks like a little person."

"What?" Nath took a closer look. Sure enough, a tiny little person or fairy creature of some sort danced inside the flames. "I'll be." He tapped on the glass, getting the tiny fairy's attention. It kept dancing. "Why would a fairy be inside there?"

"That's the magic." She held out her hands. "May I?"

Nath handed the lantern over.

"Let me try something." In mystic words, Maefon spoke in a rhythmic fashion. She repeated the same words over and over. The fairy stopped dancing. It tilted its head to one side. Then, without warning, it shot out of the lantern.

"What did you do?"

"I connected with it. I told it to find the man, Afflana Shannreer. We must follow it!" She and Nath gave chase, but the fairy was too fast. It streaked down the corridors and different levels in all directions then ran one way, only to turn another. Up the stairs they started, only to come down again. Finally, the fairy stopped on the third level. Winded, Nath and Maefon caught up to it. The fairy hovered in front of a crypt. It pointed then jumped inside the lantern.

Nath and Maefon gave the crypt a hard look. "If this is it, I could kiss you," Nath said, setting the lantern down.

"It's your lantern. I should be kissing you."

Dust and debris fell on Nath's shoulders from above. Tiny, hard feet scratched on stone. He looked up. A strange centipede-like creature crawled down the wall. Big enough for a halfling to ride, it had a skull face and the body of a serpent. A small, pale white man rode on the creature's back. Slowly, moving hundreds of small insect feet at a time, it made its way to the floor.

Nath pushed Maefon backward. Shielding her with his body, he drew Fang. "Watch out!"

Butterflies fluttered in Nath's stomach. His lips twisted under his nose. Gripping Fang with white knuckles, he said, "Stay back!"

"Noooo," the rider said in a voice that cracked and bubbled. Short with a stout build, he stared at Nath with big eyes blacker than coal. Bare chested, with warts all over his body, the creepy gnomish figure wore only trousers. His feet were big and bare. He pointed a stubbed finger at Nath's glowing sword. "Noooooo."

The gnomish man clacked its human teeth together. The thing it rode lifted its tail high, showing a stinger.

"Is that a gnome?" Nath said to Maefon.

"It looks like one to me."

"Noooooo," the gnome said, still pointing at the sword. "Nooooo."

"Perhaps you should do as he says," she suggested.

Nath put Fang back inside his sheath. "I hope I don't regret this."

The gnome lowered his hand. He studied them both with black, spacy eyes and tilted his head left then right. "Nooooo. Nooooooo." His dark eyes were fixed on the lantern. He made strange, nibbling noises with his mouth. "Noooooooo."

"I think he is the crypt keeper. I think he wants us to heed him and stay away," Maefon said. "We must have unsettled him."

"I think he wants the lantern." He caught a glimpse of Darkken down on one of the lower levels, looking up at them. Nath yelled, "This way. I believe we found it."

Darkken spun on his heel, waved, and headed for the stairs. "Right away!"

The crypts on the higher levels were no different than the lower levels. Unlike the honeycombs in a beehive, they were all shapes and sizes. Darkken caught up with them. He was puffing for breath. His eyes got really big when he caught sight of the crypt keeper. "How did you wind up with this hideous thing?"

Nath dusted off his hands. "We used the Lantern of Revealing. A tiny fairy led us here, and this bullish creature came."

"A magic lantern. How interesting. It seems you drew a skelapede and a gravel gnome from the bottom pit of life itself. Well done, Nath," Darkken said with a smirk.

"Are they not dangerous?"

"Uh, ugly yes, dangerous, eh, depends on how many. Well, except the skelapede's stinger. It isn't known to kill, but it will definitely hurt a lot." He lifted a finger. "Oh, and they do have excellent memory—so refined that they even name their gravel, which I think is a massive waste of time. All gnomes are quirky. I think this one really likes your lantern. Like a moth to a flame."

"They look more dangerous than that," Nath said.

"Looks are deceiving. But they don't attack unless provoked. And when they do, you don't fight one. You fight dozens of them. Possibly hundreds," Darkken said.

"How do you know this?" Nath couldn't put his finger on why, but he felt as if Darkken had been there before.

"The seer told me."

"Why didn't you tell us about this seer's comments before?" Nath said.

"I didn't think we would see one. The seer in the records room said… how did he put it?" Darkken scratched his temple. "You might find help, but it won't be what you expect. According to him, the dead wander the halls, and I think he thought that might be what helped us. He was very skittish when he talked about it."

The gnome stopped in front of a nondescript crypt covered in cobwebs. He pointed at the crypt. In his raspy, bubbly voice, he said, "Afflana Shannreer." He reached for the lantern.

Nath snatched it up. "No, no, no to you. This is mine, gnome." He held the lantern to the marker. He could read the language. "Afflana Shannreer. Plain as day."

"Excellent," Darkken said. "The gravel gnomes are very knowledgeable when it comes to the vaults. They are the crypt keepers and guardians. Now let's open it."

Nath's neck hairs rose on end. "What?"

CHAPTER 60

"I'M ONLY JESTING, COMRADES," DARKKEN said. "You should know better than to think that I would call an entire army of the dead upon us." He approached the crypt of the dead elf, Afflana, and peeled away the cobwebs that partially concealed the coffin from view. "Hmmm, a very modest arrangement. Most treasures are kept in something more flamboyant. People like to be showy at funerals."

Nath breathed a sigh. "All seems to be in order. Can we go now?"

"Wait." Darkken dusted away the marker's covering of decades of dried grit. "I want to be absolutely sure that we are not missing anything. And that this gravel gnome is not making a mistake. They aren't beyond trickery. Let me see your torch."

Maefon handed him hers.

Holding the flame to the marker, Darkken said, "It's written in Elven. Not my best subject. Maefon, will you take a look?"

She moved toward the marker. "Afflana Shannreer. This is him."

Darkken turned to the crypt keeper and asked, "May we take a look inside the coffin and verify that it is indeed him?"

The crypt keeper furiously shook his head.

"Darkken, what are you doing? Let's go. There is no need to upset them."

"Just a moment. We came this far. We need to be absolutely sure." Darkken stuck his hand inside the coffin's crypt. The gnome growled. "He's a fierce one." He retracted his hand. "Has anyone else come here to see this crypt?"

The gnome shook his head.

"You are certain?" Darkken asked.

"Noooo," the gnome said.

Darkken faced his friends and said, "I am satisfied. Our journey comes to an end. How relieving."

"We need to find Dule and Roday," Nath said. "They have to be around here somewhere."

"Why don't we ask your friend?" Darkken said. "What happened to the other two elves who entered just before we did?"

The crypt keeper shrugged.

"That's ridiculous. He has to know where they are. He knows where all of the tombs are," Nath said.

Holding out a calming hand, Darkken said, "Easy now, or you will be the one to get him and all of his brothers riled up. My guess is that this gnome would like a tribute. Something unique." He patted himself down. "I don't have anything on me. Do either of you?"

"Nothing I'm willing to part with," Maefon said.

"Me either." Nath had lost enough, and he wasn't about to part with anything else that was his.

"Tell you what, go and fetch something from the others. Perhaps Roday and Dule have departed from the crypt without us knowing. I'll follow you down." Darkken reached out a hand. "May I use the lantern while I wait? It's comforting."

"Sure." Nath led the way with the others, including the crypt keeper, in tow. He couldn't shake the tightness in his chest, however. The way Darkken handled himself, supremely confident in the midst of such a place, seemed off.

Darkken stopped in the hallway a good fifty yards from the entrance they came through. "I'll wait here. Someone needs to keep an eye on our friend," he said of the crypt keeper. "Make it quick. I'm getting hungry."

"What should I fetch him?" Nath asked.

"Anything shiny that we don't need. Gnomes like shiny, but make it more original than a coin. I'm sure they've seen plenty of those lying around. Hurry now."

The slab doors opened on Nath's approach. He hustled outside into a very bright moonlit sky. Shielding his eyes, he said, "How long were we in there?"

"Three days." It was Roday that spoke. His face was ashen. "We made it out after two."

"Two days that felt like ten," Dule said. "My spine is still tingling."

Nath looked back at the door. It was a different door than the one that they exited, farther toward the eastern end. The slab slammed shut, leaving Darkken trapped inside.

Nath rushed to the door, pounding on it. "Darkken! Darkken!"

Chapter 61

"Well, gravel gnome, it seems that it is just you and I," Darkken said, with a froward expression. "And your pet. Come, I would like to see that crypt again." He led the way back up the stairs to the third level, and with great strides he made his way down to the rock landing. Inside the crypt was the coffin of Afflana Shannreer. It had lain there undisturbed for centuries. Darkken twisted at the copper rings on his fingers. "So long I have searched. And now I find. Let's see what this elven earth digger has to offer." He reached inside the shelf.

"Nooooo." The crypt keeper started clacking his teeth. "Noooooo!"

Without looking at him, Darkken said, "Excuse me, did you say something?"

"Noooooo—*gurch!*"

In the wink of an eye, Darkken drew his sword Scalpel and stabbed the gnome in the throat. The skelapede struck out with its stinger. Smooth as silk, Darkken cut off both the stinger and the ugly monster's skeleton head.

Darkken leaned his blade against the shelf. He pulled the coffin out. The lid was nailed shut. Fingers digging between the cracks of the wooden resting place, he pried it open. With a heave, he ripped the top off. Flipping the door casually aside, he said, "There you are, you troublesome elf. It's been very difficult to find you."

The body of Afflana Shannreer was dressed in modest elven robes that showed little deterioration. Long locks of what was once a lustrous head of full gray and red hair were now dried and stringy. Tight skin like baked leather showed the sharp elven features of his face. The eyes were long gone from the sunken sockets. His hands, below the sleeves of his robes, had withered to the bone. In those hands was a black scroll case carved out of black ivory with brass caps on the end.

Darkken ran a gentle finger over the raised runes of the narrow scroll case. He read what he felt. "'Let he who steals this be accursed.' Hah, too late for that." Darkken pulled the scroll free of the bony fingers. One hand broke off at the wrist, still clinging firmly to the scroll. He wacked it against the floor, busting the fingers off. "Let's see what else we have in here."

With rough hands, he rummaged through the coffin, searching the dead elf's body. He picked up the dried-up body and gave it a fierce shake. The head fell from the shoulders, hit the landing, and rolled off the ledge. He tore through the clothing and patted the corpse down before slinging it aside. Exposed to the air, hunks of flesh and dried skin and hair fell off.

"I will not be fooled, Afflana Shannreer." Darkken searched through the nooks of the coffin. He knocked on the bottom and heard a hollow sound. He punched through the wood and ripped out the boards. Inside the hidden compartment, he found a black velvet pouch. He emptied it into the palm of his hand. A pink diamond, oval shaped, the size of an egg, burned with its own inner fire. "The Star from the Heavens." A broad smile formed on Darkken's face. "Now I have it all."

A scuffle of tiny legs caught his ear. He put the Star back in the pouch, tucked the scroll into his belt, and grabbed his sword. The stone walkways began to fill with dozens of skelapedes ridden by the gravel gnomes. "Shouldn't you be chiseling out more crypts?" Darkken said.

"Put it back," said a deep voice that carried throughout the great chambers.

There was no source to the sound that Darkken could see. "If you want what I have, you will have to take it."

"There is no way out unless you leave it."

"We'll see about that, won't we, guardian." The rings on Darkken's fingers glowed with radiant energy. His eyes shined like the stars. "Come. Test me."

"Foooolish one!" The unseen speaker's voice continued to resonate throughout the chamber. "Slay him!"

"Ha. Do try, fools!"

The crypt keepers attacked in a surge of skittering speed. Darkken's elven sword became a glowing and living thing in his hand. He sliced through the faces of the skelapedes faster than they could strike. With his own sorcerous powers, he flung them from the ledges with a flick of his hand. The gravel gnomes attacked with spears made out of the crypt's own rock. They stabbed hard into Darkken's body, only to see the shafts shatter against his glowing skin.

Darkken laughed maniacally as he released his own power. So long he had held in his omnipotence. Now, away from his comrades, he could cut loose his god-like powers and not hold anything back. As a sea of gnomes and skelapedes loaded up and blocked his passage, he cast fire out of his eyes. The beam of energy ripped through every living thing in its path.

Darkken cut his closest aggressors down. The walkway filled with sticky insect guts and oily gnomish blood. His attackers fell in heaps as he made his way down to the lower level. He left a path of carnage behind him. Dozens of the gnomes and their bizarre mounts were dead. Still, more came on. Darkken reveled in the frenzy. He controlled power they could not comprehend. No one could but him.

Since being banished from Dragon Home, Darkken had acquired more knowledge and power. He'd studied with great mages renowned in the land. He'd learned from tomes he'd stolen and read. He'd used the dragon magic within him to master the mystical elements of the world of Nalzambor. Decade after decade, century after century, he stored those powers in the rings on his fingers. Copper was the perfect resource to conceal magic energy. His rings were rich in spells of his craft that he could recall instantly. With two on one hand and two on the other, the bland jewelry drew no attention and deflected desire. Combined with his own dragon lineage, he was all but invincible.

He split open the face of a skelapede. The gnome rider dove away. Darkken gored the hairless gnome in the back.

After the fatal blow, the sea of the enemy survivors parted, scrambling up the walls, leaving only a few in sight. From down the hallway, the sound of heavy feet came his way. A big-boned skeleton, standing twelve feet high with eyes that burned with blue flames, rounded the corner. It carried a studded ball-and-chain flail in one hand. The other hand was covered in fingers of blue fire. Its burning eyes set on Darkken.

"YOUR ACTS ARE SACRILEGE! YOU MUST DIE!" the crypt guardian said. "THERE WILL BE NO ESCAPE!"

Darkken pulled his shoulders back. His nostrils flared. "Clearly, you don't know who you are dealing with. I am the Lord of the Dark in the Day."

"I AM AZOR THE GUARDIAN. I RULE HERE. YOU KILL MY SERVANTS LIKE INSECTS, BUT YOU CANNOT KILL ME. I AM DEAD. SOON YOU WILL JOIN. SOON YOU WILL SERVE ME."

Darkken shook his head. "Let me go, guardian. I am a god."

"I AM THE GOD OF THIS DOMAIN. PREPARE TO PERISH." The skeleton came forward.

Darkken summoned his own power. His body grew, matching the height of the skeleton. He shot fire from his eyes.

Azor knocked aside the bolt with his flail. "YOU HAVE NO POWER OVER ME." The skeleton swang.

Darkken parried. The blow shook his arms, sending stinging pain through his fingers. The unnatural strength of the skeleton was greater than that of a giant its own size.

With a cobra's speed, Azor locked his burning hand around Darkken's throat. "SEE YOUR DEATH. YOU THIEF. YOU REAVER. YOU VIOLATOR. MY FLAMES SHALL CONSUME YOU."

Blue flames spread all over Darkken's body. Bony fingers dug into his neck, pinching harder and harder. Darkken stabbed into Azor's body. The sharp edge clipped into bone. Fighting against the blistering mystic heat consuming his body, he grabbed Azor's spine and squeezed.

Spitting through his teeth, he said, "Two can play at this game, titan!"

Azor's jaw snapped open, letting out a gusty groan.

Darkken sent a charge of fire out of his rings and through his fingers, coursing right up Azor's spine. The skeleton's face started smoking. Azor dropped his flail. His bones rattled. The blue flames covering Darkken extinguished. Pouring on the power, Darkken warned with fervent speech, "Do you still think you can consume me, little guardian?"

Fighting to speak, Azor said, "I YIELD."

Darkken shook Azor's spine. "Yield to who?"

"THE LORD OF THE DARK IN THE DAY."

Darkken let go. Azor fell on his hands and knees. His bones were smoking. Diminishing back to his normal size, Darkken patted the skeleton's smoking head. "You have a simple job. Keep it simple. Now open this crypt so I can fill the rest of this mausoleum with more dead."

CHAPTER 62

NATH POUNDED ON THE SLAB door to no avail. He screamed at the wall.

Maefon tugged on his arm. "It's no use. It will open when it opens. It's a strange place, Nath. I'm sure that all will work out well."

"I don't know about that." Nath's arm hairs stood on end. "I felt something evil stir the underside of my skin. It came on all of a sudden. I need to fetch the hammer."

"This hammer." Roday held Stone Smiter with both hands. "I tried to break through the door with it, but you might try again. It barely left a mark on the stone."

Nath snatched it away. "What are you doing with this?"

All of the rest of the Brothers of the Wind formed a half circle around the others.

"I was only trying to help," Roday replied.

"Yes, we both were," Dule added. "Show a little gratitude."

"For what, stealing my hammer?" Nath said with disgust.

"We are a brotherhood, Nath. It is you that is acting impolite. We are trying to help you," Roday fired back.

"I am sure that all will be well," Maefon said to Nath. "Focus on finding payment for the gnome. Perhaps that tribute will open the door when we offer it. What do we have that a gnome might—"

The valley filled with hungry growls. From the valley of tombstones, the night hounds crept forward. Heads low and teeth bared, they surrounded the group. There were dozens of them. Shrill howls started from an unseen voice. Ghostly spirits, like small wispy mannish clouds, glided over the grasses and around the tombstones. They rose high then dove like birds at the elves' heads. The elves ducked as they drew sword and dagger.

"This isn't good." With a flick of her fingers, Maefon's hands radiated with mystic fire. "I suddenly get the feeling that it was safer inside the crypt."

The night hounds grew in number, eyes glowing, saliva dripping from their hungry jaws. Nath reached behind his back and drew Fang. "Where do they keep these things?"

Roday and Dule stood beside Nath and Maefon, ready to fight. Nath handed the war hammer to Roday. The gem on the hammer started to burn. "You might want to give this a try."

"It's not my style, but I have trained with just about everything." Roday sheathed his blades and took the hammer. "I really like that gem on the top. Does it go well with my eyes?"

"No," Nath said. Fang in hand, he summoned the power of the Gauntlet of Goam. New energy fueled his blood. He took a deep breath. "Time to fight. Maefon, focus on those spirits. I don't know what they are."

"Me either," she said, "but I'll do it."

A night hound bayed at the moon. The dogs attacked. Stabbing steel flickered in the moonlight. The hounds made ferocious sounds as their canine teeth tore into flesh. The Brothers of the Wind, one and all, battled hard.

More hounds split through the gaps between the ranks of elves, bearing down on Nath. Out of the corner of his eye, he caught Roday charging, swinging, and connecting a bone-shattering blow that sent a hound flying. At the same time, Fang struck off the head of a dog lunging for his throat. He stabbed another in the body. "Get your back to the archway, Maefon. Roday, Dule, protect her!"

Nath, Roday, and Dule made a defensive half circle in front of Maefon. She stood behind them, firing glowing missiles from her fingers. Like mystic bees, the missiles chased after the spirits that attacked from the sky. One spirit plunged into the body of an elf in the outermost rank. The elf's arms flung wide. His body seized up. Horror-stricken eyes grew like moons. The night hounds bowled him over. Teeth and claws ripped away armor and tore into flesh.

"Noooooooooo!" Nath yelled. "Maefon, kill those things!"

"I'm trying," she said.

"Try harder!" Clenching his jaw, Nath matched the fearsome beasts' savagery with savagery of his own. Fang cut through every hairy beast he came in contact with. Hound after hound went down. Fur and blood flew. The hounds, fast, powerful, and quick, were no match for the angry fighter. Ravenous, they threw themselves against a mystic hurricane of steel. A hound slipped around Nath's side. Jaws wide open, it jumped at Nath. He caught it by the throat. Using the gauntlet's power, he squeezed, crushing the wild beast's throat. With one hand, he slung it into an oncoming swarm of others. In turn, some of them started devouring it.

The battle raged on. Elves and hounds. Steel and teeth. Both sides fell. With the graveyard spirits swirling through the airways, Maefon shouted, "Nath, I can't hold them off. There are too many!" She fired a missile of energy. A spirit twisted away and plunged into her body. Maefon stiffened. "Guh!"

All at once, without the magic of Maefon's power to keep them at bay, the spirits attacked Nath, Roday, and Dule. Dule's sword sliced through the wispy spirit, passing right through its airy body. It, in turn, passed through him, paralyzing the elf. Roday's swing of the sledgehammer was not fast enough. Two at once went right through him. As the spirits came at Nath, he twisted Fang through the air, keeping them at bay. He pulled Dragon Claw out of the hilt. He punched and poked at the spirit demons in the sky. Dragon Claw bit into one. It shrieked and exploded in a *poof.*

More came. It was no wonder Cemetery Valley was safe from grave robbers. The guardians would overwhelm them. They were the masters of the sacred grounds. Now, a swarm of screeching spirits rushed right at Nath. It would be impossible to stop them all. He swang. He stabbed. They passed through his body, turning his blood to ice. His pumping muscles seized. It was over. A night hound charged, eyes burning with angry fire. The dog leapt onto his chest. He tumbled helplessly backward.

CHAPTER 63

HACKLES RAISED, THE HOUND HAD Nath pinned down. Hot saliva dripped onto his face and chest. He fought against the unseen force that locked up his body. Not even a finger budged. Prone as a statue, he lay still, awaiting his doom. As his life flashed in front of his eyes, he felt regret. He saw his childhood. A caring father. An unknown mother. Yet something else remained. The dragons. They were not kind. They'd shunned him. He left on their account. He'd met with nothing but betrayal. Liars. Cheaters. Murderers. He wasn't welcome in Dragon Home. He wasn't welcome in Nalzambor either. He made few friends that he could trust. It was all a mishmash of confusion. Now, he was going to be eaten by a dog.

Perhaps this is the fate that I deserve. Gads. At least I'm already in a graveyard.

He looked into the burning, glowing stare of the night hound, its fetid breath heavy in Nath's face. It was death.

Go ahead. What are you waiting for? Saliva dripped on him. *Gross.*

Ears pinned back, the hound growled in his face once more. Suddenly, it pulled back. The hound's ears perked up. It panted, and its tongue hung from its mouth. It slunk away.

Nath's eyes moved from side to side. He could see above him and catch glimpses of the tombstones on the hills. Galtur remained perched on the ledge of the mausoleum. The vulture's four green eyes followed movement on the ground. There was the sound of the dogs padding away into the cemetery. The shrieking of the guardian spirits had come to an abrupt stop. Stone scraped against stone. It was the sound of the entrance to the crypt. A boot scuffle captured Nath's attention.

"Oh my." It was Darkken's voice. "Maefon! Nath!"

Nath saw Darkken standing over him with Maefon in his arms. The woman was as rigid as a statue. Darkken gently laid her down. The copper-eyed man ran a finger in front of Nath's eyes. He followed it.

"Thank goodness you are well. Nath, I take it you can hear me. The paralysis should wear off soon." Darkken got face-to-face with him. "You will be fine. I'm going to check on the others. Don't exert yourself. That might make it worse. Try to relax."

It was easier said than done. Nath could hear Darkken tending to the elves. There were some sad sobs too. Darkken passed by him several times. His eyes were wet. It sounded as if he went back into the mausoleum and came out again. During one pass, Nath saw a shovel in Darkken's hand. Blood stained his hands.

At the crack of dawn, Nath could move his fingers and toes. Once the sun rose, he was able to sit up again. Every fiber of his being felt like a piece of dried oak he was trying to bend. His mouth was dry. His neck hurt to bend. With his blood warming again, his arms and legs started to burn from gashes the hounds' claws had inflicted. The wounds were ugly and sore.

Maefon moaned. She blinked long, slow blinks as Nath helped her into a sitting position. "Can you speak?"

"I can't feel my tongue, but I think I'm speaking, or thinking. I thought so much, I can't tell the difference from death or living." A rosy color returned to her bone-white cheeks.

"You live. We both do." The door into the mausoleum had closed. "That was bizarre."

She let out a lengthy sigh and leaned against his chest. "I was worried you had died. I didn't know."

He put his arm around her. "I felt the same way."

Many hours had passed since they had been paralyzed. The sun was warming. He could see Darkken far away, digging into the hillside. He wasn't alone. A handful of the Brothers of the Wind were with him, as were some tall, lanky, gaunt men with shovels. Several graves had been freshly dug and filled in. One of the gravediggers patted the new dirt down with a shovel.

Nath searched for Roday and Dule. They had fallen by his side, he was sure of it. Now, their bodies were gone. The sledgehammer lay alone in a bed of bloodstained grass. Fighting against the sluggishness that wanted to hold him down, Nath stood. Eyes knitted together, he stormed over the graveyard, making a straight path toward Darkken. Something smelled. It wasn't night hound excrement either.

"What in Nalzambor happened, Darkken?"

With a sad look in his eyes, Darkken somberly replied, "We didn't all make it. I fear Roday and Dule are gone, along with many more of our brethren. Only ten of us remain."

The loss shocked Nath's sinking heart. He liked Dule and Roday. They were the only brothers he was close to. "You could have waited until I was revived!"

"The dead are dead." Darkken took a knee in front of one of the graves. An elf lay inside the dirt hole. The odd gravediggers began shoveling in more dirt. As they buried swords, armor, and all, the elf's broken body was covered in rich brown soil. "A quick burial is our way." He sniffled. "Though I've never dug so many before at once."

"I bet." Nath couldn't hide his anger. "What happened in there, Darkken? What happened? We were safe until that door closed."

"The gnome and I spoke longer. I tried to negotiate over Afflana Shannreer's crypt." He patted the scroll case tucked inside his belt. "The gnome didn't take it too well at first."

"What you did got our brothers killed!"

"No, that is not what happened. The gnome agreed. As it turns out, what the legends say is not always true. The crypt keepers can be reasonable, even bribed. They just have a reputation to uphold. Hence the legend. And I thought their price was worth it for a look inside Afflana Shannreer's crypt."

"What did you give the gnome?"

"This part you won't like. I gave the gnome Winzee's Lantern of Revealing. Actually, he was so fond of it that he threatened that I couldn't leave, but that is when I struck the bargain. I not only have the scroll, but I also have the Star of the Heavens."

Nath shoved Darkken. "While you were in there, haggling, we were attacked!"

Darkken shoved Nath backward. "Don't do that again! I did not have a choice. And I was unaware of any peril on the outside. I did what I could. As for the night hounds and the guardian spirits, I can't say what provoked them."

"You provoked them! We don't need a scroll or a star. You should have left it all alone. We found what you were looking for. Its secret was safe. We needed no more!"

Darkken stood up. "Listen to me, if you will, please. What happened, it's in the past, and the Brothers of the Wind move on. We have many enemies out there. We have to be able to find them and fight them."

"Well, you just gave away the one item that could help us find them." Nath snatched the shovel out of the lanky gravedigger's hands. The man was old, but his forearms were corded with muscle, and he had hard muscle bulging in his shoulders from decades of digging. "I'll finish this one," Nath said.

The shabbily dressed old digger said in a quiet, raspy voice, "I'll get another shovel and help you."

"We'll all help," Darkken said.

Nath wiped the falling tears from his eyes. "Just go away."

Chapter 64

It was a long wagon ride back to Old Hen. Nath brooded. Maefon sat beside him, quiet. She agreed with his frustration, but not for the same reasons. Darkken had allowed too many of the Caligin to die. In her opinion, it made Nath suspicious. It drove him away. It would be up to her to convince him otherwise, but for now, she needed to leave him be. Not pry. That would make it worse.

As they passed by the inviting cottages of Old Hen, Nath mumbled, "I can't believe they are gone."

She knew he was talking about Roday and Dule. They'd formed a kinship with Nath, which made their untimely deaths harder to understand. She opened her mouth then closed it. *Let him do the talking.*

"They were different," he continued. "Unlike the others, they had showed more teeth, I guess. Everyone but the two of them is so stoic. No. They were too young to die."

"I know," she said softly. "I'll miss them too."

"I really don't understand how they became Caligin to begin with. They didn't seem like the sort. They reminded me of Pevly and Tevlin. Remember them back in Dragon Home?"

"Of course I do," she said. "They were ornery too, weren't they?"

He nodded. "I hope they are well, and I hope they weren't Caligin either. That would stink." He looked at her. "You are very quiet."

"I'm empty inside, yet I hurt for them, for you."

"I had a conversation with one of those gravediggers when Darkken wasn't around. He made some revealing comments."

"You did?" She sat up. "What did the gravedigger say?"

"I asked him about the night hounds and spirits. He said that normally they don't attack, but anything can set them off." Nath let out a long sigh. "He went on to say that they are wild beasts, and only a fool would stay there at night. He was surprised that when the elves were outside for three days, they didn't attack sooner. That was a long time. Only a fool stays with a beast too long. We overstayed our welcome."

"That makes sense. But the time that was lost in there, I'll never understand that. They say 'The dead know no time.'"

"We should have been more careful," he said. "I feel bad. I shouldn't have attacked Darkken."

"What?" Maefon was astonished. "You have a right to be upset. I am."

"Yes, but we all hurt. We are all of the brotherhood. I have to be committed to our cause. Instead, I went against the grain. I think that made it worse. I created division. That endangered us all."

"We were unified," she said. Nath's statement astounded her. He was truly loyal to them. To Darkken. Perhaps the Lord of the Dark in the Day knew exactly what he was doing after all. "It's fine to be angry that we lost our brothers. If I had died, I'd hope you would have been angry."

"Of course. I'd be angry and lost. You are the person I'm closest to in this world. I know I can trust you."

A pang filled Maefon's heart. She fought back the tears as her tongue clung to the roof of her mouth. She was not what he thought she was, and she was ruining a very, very good man. Swallowing the lump in her throat, she said, "I'm grateful for you, Nath. So, you are going to talk with Darkken?"

"I'll apologize later. I just want to make sure I say the right thing." Nath's eyes were fixed ahead. Darkken rode on horseback nearly a hundred yards ahead of them. His shoulders were slumped over the saddle. The elves walked behind him with chins dipped. "I think we are all hurting right now. Besides, I still have some questions that I'm compelled to ask."

"Care to run them by me?"

"What does he plan to do with the secret of dragon steel? Or the Star of the Heavens, whatever that is? So far as I am concerned, the scroll should be destroyed."

"My guess is that he wants to study it. He is very passionate about magic." She got hip to hip with him. "I'm sure he'll listen to what you have to say. Nath, he is not in charge of you. You know that. Either you choose to follow or you don't."

"I don't mind following him," he said. "I just don't think I've ever followed anyone before."

"I've always been taught that to be a good leader, you have to be a good follower. You will be a good follower, but I know you will be an even greater leader." She wrapped her arm in his. "I know I would follow you anywhere. Also, I think Darkken is grooming you to lead the Brothers of the Wind. He becomes quite dreary when he discusses his mortality. I think he is jealous that you and I will live much longer. At the same time, in his wisdom, he wants to secure a future for us all. He's responsible like that."

"The man's not ancient. He still has a few decades left in him." Nath laughed. "Huh, I suppose that is why he forged ahead with such zeal."

Maefon's eyes brightened. "I never thought about it before, but I think you hit the nail right on the head."

"You do?"

"Think about it. It makes perfect sense. Darkken is pressed for time. He's forging a legacy. Being a man, that is not something we can relate to. We are different." She leaned her head on his shoulder. "Try to walk in his shoes."

"That's helpful," he agreed. "I'll do it."

CHAPTER 65

APPROACHING FROM THE EAST, JUST inside the sweeping hills where the outlying cottages of Old Hen began, Brenwar, Slivver, and Elween arrived, trotting on horseback. Like many travelers who passed through, they stayed on the main roads. Brenwar led the way, while Slivver and Elween followed. Elween, with the aid of another dragon polymorph potion, appeared as a beautiful woman in traveler's clothing again. The only difference was that she was armed with a fashionable sword that she picked up along the way. Now both she and Slivver sported sword belts, but Slivver seemed a bit uncomfortable with his.

"Lay low and let me do the talking," Brenwar stated on more than one occasion. "The folks here are older and will probably relate to a seasoned man like me better."

"You mean old," Slivver said.

"I mean I'm experienced, not old. I don't have a strand of gray on my head, not that there would be anything wrong with that. The older I get, the stronger I get." He lifted a proud chin. "And better looking. The two of you look like you were drawn up in an elven kingdom. Slap some dirt on, and mess up your hair or something."

Elween tousled her hair with her fingers, making her greenish-brown locks a mess. "Like this?"

"Er… just comb more of your hair over your face and try not to smile so much. A pretty girl like you will likely attract the wrong kind of men," Brenwar said.

"Wrong kind?' she asked.

"The point is, lay low. Don't make that polymorph potion I gave you go to waste either." Brenwar slowed his horse to a walk.

"I think it would be best if we split up but have a meeting place," Slivver suggested. "Darkken is no fool. If he is here, he'll have eyes watching for us, or at least, something out of the ordinary. That Caligin we interrogated warned us of that much. It's best that we see him before he sees us."

"We don't even know that he will be here, but I don't disagree," Brenwar said. "Let's settle, and then we can discuss it. It's best to think over a flagon of mead."

"What happens if we are quaffing a flagon and we run right into Nath? Chances are he might be where we are," Slivver said.

"Don't stare. Don't speak. Nath doesn't know who we are or what we look like, so act natural." Brenwar looked them up and down. "Or just be rude like me. Make sure we are all in the loop if we spot him." He noticed Elween studying the sky. A huge bird circled farther east of them, over the heart of Old Hen. He squinted. "Is that a dragon?"

"No, that's a vulture. It has two heads like the Caligin described," she said. "Eyes in the sky. I think it's Darkken's pet."

"Then quit staring at it, and let's just assume that Darkken is here. We are passing through, if anyone asks. Looking for a calm spot to relax," Brenwar said.

"Two humans and a dwarf seems odd for a set of travelers," Slivver said. His hands were on the reins. "We will need a better story than that. Why would people relax with a dwarf? It seems unlikely. I think we should separate. Elween and I will pair together. You go it alone, but we can stay in close proximity."

"Hum-har… That's exactly what I've been saying," Brenwar said. "Why'd it take you so long to understand it? Just find me at the biggest inn."

Slivver looked at Elween, smiled, and shrugged. As Brenwar forged ahead, she started laughing. "It is a good idea, Slivver. A very good one." She rode closer and hooked her hands in his elbow. "We can pretend to be a couple. You know the world better than I do. Where should we be from?"

"That's a good question." Slivver rubbed his chin. "If a place is too small, if you run into someone from there, they'll expect you to know what they know. Quintuklen is a vast city of humans, a great place to blend in, but they have a hierarchy and lineage I'm not so familiar with. The best place would be Narnum, the Free City. All races come in and out. It's very active and moving. That would be the best place to be from. There is no structure there." Slivver took a great deal of time to name off many places that he knew about in Narnum.

He actually had walked in the city with Brenwar, fully cloaked as a man, for a brief time. He looked at her. "How old do I look for a man?"

Studying his face with bright-green eyes, she replied, "Hmm... perhaps a young man in his thirties." She batted her eyelashes. "And me?"

Showing an inch between the span of his fingers, he said, "Just a tad older."

"I should swat you."

"Well, you are much older," he said.

"True, and shame on me and my vanity."

Slivver shared several more details about human settlements, and they decided they were a wealthy couple that did not work in need of a vacation. They made perfume but didn't know much about it, agreeing to act spoiled. "I tell you, I like the way you think for a weapons master. You can be deliciously conniving."

"Well, it's just good fun talking about it. I've never put so much thought into being human before. At least not outside of the terms of using their creative weaponry." She had a pleasant smile on her face as warm as the sun. "I know this has been hard on you, Slivver, but I am enjoying this adventure. Remember, love will prevail. No matter what. It always does."

"I wish I had your faith. Darkken is so very devious. And the god speech that Caligin gave didn't sit well with me. It sent a shiver through me. Clearly, Darkken has amassed far greater powers. He's more than what I once knew. He's worse."

As they penetrated deeper into the boundaries of Old Hen, the cottages with whitewashed stone became more prevalent. Deep in the heart of the wall-less city was a massive lodge with a great banner billowing on top. Its highest level rose above all other structures.

They weren't the only ones coming or going. Other travelers were on the move. Two riders rode a wagon pulled by two horses. Brenwar went right by them without so much as a nod, even though the occupants in the wagon waved. The wagon rumbled over the dirt road, right at them. Slivver's keen sight picked up instantly on the riders in the seat. He blinked. What he saw was confirmed when Elween silenced a quick gasp. Riding in the wagon were Nath and Maefon.

Chapter 66

Nath sat in the wagon to Slivver's left, and Maefon rode on the right side. With his heart thumping in his chest, Slivver split away from Elween, leading his horse to the left, and she went to the right. Nath and Maefon were talking, not paying them any mind. Slivver did his best to avert his eyes, but he couldn't. A moment passed when they both locked eyes. The closer he came, the more thoughts raced through his head. Nath lived. He appeared in good health. His conversation with Maefon sounded light.

Should I warn him now or later?

Casting a sideward glance to Elween, he gave her a subtle nod, hoping that she would keep going. He would do the same, but something gnawed at his stomach. It wasn't like him to feel uncomfortable, but all of his senses were tingling as if on fire. That was when he spied another horse and rider bringing up the rear, followed by a troupe of elves on foot. Riding high in the saddle was Darkken. Sturdy in build, with a full mane of rust-colored hair, he stood out in his black leather armor. He was thicker limbed than when Slivver saw him last. Darkken's stare drifted toward Slivver.

Slivver looked away as he was passing the wagon. He found Nath's eyes on him. There was a hardness in Nath's face that wasn't there when he left. His arms and chest were more muscular. Unable to break the young man's probing stare, Slivver came to a halt. "Greetings. Do you mind if I ask how your time in Old Hen was? We've never been, but we hope to enjoy all of the pleasantries that it is rumored to offer."

Nath and Maefon offered warm smiles, and Maefon, with her arms around Nath's, said, "We found it to be everything we expected, but we were on business, so it wasn't so pleasurable as I am certain you will experience."

"We hope to come back when time permits." Nath looked back and forth between Elween and Slivver. "I'm certain we haven't crossed paths before, but I feel we have."

"We get that often," Elween quickly said. "I am Lydia, and this is my love, Apollos. We do a lot of traveling but hail from Narnum. We make many friends. A shame you are leaving. We could have dined together."

Darkken rode right up alongside Nath with his eyes locked on Slivver. Without a smile, he said, "I'm certain that you will find many friendly faces that will enjoy your company." He looked at Nath. "Let's keep it moving. We have a delivery to make by nightfall with a long day ahead. Pardon us, but once they start talking, eh, Apollos, they tend to not stop."

"Understood." Slivver dipped his chin. "Nice to meet all of you. May your journey bring you much fortune."

"And you as well." Nath snapped the reins. The horses moved forward. The wagon rolled down the road again.

With his horse nickering, Darkken gave Slivver and Elween both a lasting glance. "Good day."

The elves, dressed in woodsmen garb, with feathers and braids in their hair, walked right by the both of them as if they weren't there.

Slivver shrugged at Elween. He led his horse toward hers and didn't look back as they urged their horses forward. He reached for her hand affectionately. She took it.

He said, "That was intense."

"Agreed, but you did well." She put her hand over her heart. "My heart pounds like thunder. It took everything I had to not try and rip Darkken's eyes out. He carries an air about him. Do you think he suspects what we are?"

"I think he suspects everything," Slivver said. The encounter rattled him. Worse, the nagging feeling was still there. They had the element of surprise. Perhaps that was the very moment to do something. But they didn't. He hoped it was the right call. "Without looking back, do you feel a burning eye on your back?"

"Yes, I do. But let's not overthink it. Let's catch up with Brenwar."

At the huge lodge in the center of the city, they checked their horses into the stables.

Brenwar waited, standing with his arms crossed over his barrel chest and fingers tapping. "The two of you are as dumb as a pair of mute halflings. What were you thinking?"

"They were staring," Slivver said as he dismounted. He lent Elween a hand. "I didn't want to draw suspicion and seem, er… shady."

"Those eyes of yours practically glow in the dark," Brenwar said as he paced. "Stupid. Stupid. Stupid."

"I don't think we made that much of an impression. The conversation was brief."

"Conversation." Brenwar threw up his hands. "You don't need to have conversation." He tapped his chest with his thumb. "I do that."

Elween led her horse into a stable. "There is no sense in arguing about it now. And I think Slivver handled it well. We both did. The question is what do we do now?"

"As we wait, we'll poke around and try to find out what they did. We know what direction they went, and my guess is that they are heading back to the keep. We can't follow them, but maybe we can go north, around Dragon Home, and cut them off."

"And what if they aren't going back to Dragon Home? Can we afford to lose the trail? You are suggesting a very long way around."

Brenwar scratched the side of his beard-coated cheek. He continued to pace from one end of the covered stables to the other. He did it for over an hour. Finally, he said, "Let's eat, drink, and discuss over a few flagons of ale."

Slivver and Elween rolled their eyes.

CHAPTER 67

THEY WERE TWO DAYS OUT of Old Hen, following the main road under a clear blue sky. Leagues away, Nath could see the faint outline of the top of Dragon Home. Its sawed-off peak stood higher than any that surrounded it. The very top almost kissed the clouds. He remembered spending time playing on that plateau and lying on his back, watching the clouds pass by. Sadness overcame him.

"You miss it, don't you?" Maefon said. "I miss it too. I'm sure we will both be able to go back one day."

"If only that day wasn't forever away," Nath said.

"Time will pass so long as you fill it and don't sit and brood about it," she said.

"I'm not brooding."

"Yes, you are brooding. Just admit it, or I won't leave you alone about it."

"Fine, I'm brooding." Nath looked for Darkken and the elves. Only five of them were trailing them, fanned out and walking behind them like guardian hounds. "I don't understand where Darkken went. I thought he was in a hurry to return to Stonewater Keep. Now that he has what he wants, he should press on and stop backtracking. He said he was hunting, but he's doing something else. I know it."

"Perhaps Galtur spotted something that disturbed him. They are very connected now," she said, fighting a yawn. "I still feel bushed."

"I've had better days myself. Those spirits took it out of me." He eyed the sky. "That vulture is such an ugly bird. I don't see how it can be a good thing."

"It is what it is, I suppose. Darkken is not one to judge something by how it looks. He always said that you have to look to the inside of a person in order to understand what they are about. Judge the heart, not the body."

"That ugly buzzard has no heart. That much I can tell."

Maefon giggled. "You'll get used to it."

"I hope that I never do. Nothing against ugly, but well… so, maybe I don't like ugly. Nobody is perfect."

"I agree."

"Speaking of ugly and not ugly, do you remember the people we met on the way out? Apollos and Lydia? They weren't ugly." He pictured them both in his mind. "Their eyes were striking."

"She had a fetching figure, as well did he. Does something still bother you about them? There are many beautiful men and women in the world. Darkken is a good example."

"Huh? You know, that is true. They weren't so imposing, but yes, they were very comely. Still, those eyes. I just feel as if I've seen them before."

"They had unforgettable eyes, I'll grant that, but so do you."

"Yes, but my eyes are gold, and I'm a drag…" Nath's voice trailed off. Those people were not people. They were dragons like him. He didn't know how he knew, but he did. It had to be.

With a concerned look, Maefon said, "Nath, are you all right?"

He coughed and swallowed. "Sorry, my throat got a little dry. I suppose I'm not as used to the dry heat as I used to be." He made a backward glance. Darkken was riding hard with a cloud of dust behind them. Nath stopped the wagon. "Look."

Maefon turned in her seat. "He seems to be in a hurry."

Darkken rode up to them. "We have trouble."

"What sort of trouble?" Nath asked.

Darkken's lathered-up horse snorted heavily. He took a deep breath, causing his leather chest plate to groan. "I take it that you haven't forgotten about the Guuls you slaughtered."

"No, of course not," Nath said.

"Well, they are tailing us. It seems that they were only a smaller detachment of a bigger army. I can only imagine that someone from the band, a survivor, caught a glimpse of us in Old Hen. Now, they pursue." He looked to the sky, where the vulture soared above. "It is a good thing Galtur spotted them. He's quite a gift. They move fast, on steeds. This wagon and the elves won't be able to outrun them. We'll have to hide."

"Hide?" Nath shook his head. "Where will we hide a wagon?"

"It's possible that we might have to ditch it. Listen to me, the both of you." Darkken pointed northwest. "We can make it to the Sultan's Lake of Fire before they catch up with us. There will be sanctuary in the rocks, as it's hard and dangerous to navigate. But the two of you, take this horse." He jumped off and handed Nath the reins. "Take it!" He pulled Nath and Maefon out of the wagon. "Now get on, the both of you. I'll stay with you, but when I say go, head for the keep. We should be able to lose them in the mountains surrounding Sultan's Lake."

Nath had never seen Darkken so nervous before. He kept looking back to where the remaining elves were catching up. Nath and Maefon climbed into the saddle.

"Thank goodness," Darkken said of the Brothers of the Wind who had caught up. Their hands were on their hips. He huffed as he smiled. "They saw us, and the Guuls know they can close the gap."

"Where is this lake?" Nath said.

"It's right between us and Advent." Darkken pointed with a flat hand. "You won't miss it." He slapped Nath's horse on the hindquarters. "Now go!"

The horse bolted forward. Darkken jumped in the wagon, snapping the reins and yelling, "Yah! Yah!"

As Nath galloped ahead, he took a look behind him. Far off, over a mile away, there was a huge cloud of dust. Maefon was pointing at the same thing. "Great Guzan, they really are coming. This is madness!"

CHAPTER 68

AFTER CAREFUL THOUGHT AND A few flagons of ale, Brenwar opted to head back out after Nath before the crack of dawn the next day. He decided it was less likely he'd be noticed following right on Nath's trail as opposed to Slivver and Elween. They would make haste and travel north, around Dragon Home. Figuring that Darkken was leading Nath back to Stonewater Keep, they would meet south of Advent on the trail they'd taken before.

Slivver was on edge. Riding in the saddle became uncomfortable. It would have been easier to fly and track Darkken from a high elevation. The problem was the two-headed vulture, Galtur. The two-headed bird would easily sniff them out. So, in the meantime, they opted to ride as men, keeping their low profile, hoping to find an angle on how to grab Nath. It ate at him that they were so close and didn't say anything. It was awkward, and he hadn't convinced himself it was the right call. Nath seemed fine, but the last thing they needed to do was strike when Darkken was there. He would need to separate the two, and in order to do that, they needed to be dragons.

"The worry you carry shows on your human face," Elween said. They'd slowed down and stopped at a creek to water the horses. The beautiful beasts were lathered up. She dismounted, as did Slivver. "It must be hard for people to hide their feelings. Ours are hidden behind our scales."

"Is it that bad?" Slivver said, petting his horse's mane.

"Don't regret our decision. We have a better plan. Before Nath makes it to the keep, we'll snatch him up. The issue is getting past that vulture before it alerts Darkken. We should just kill it."

"Agreed, but maybe we can distract it." He looked to the sky. "The vulture tells us where he is as well. So we should know where to look and find the opportunity."

"I think it's a sound plan, Slivver. Regardless, we make our move to alert Nath one way or the other. He'll have to make a decision then."

Slivver nodded. "Yes. Let's just hope it's the right one and we have not lost him entirely. He seemed very content. That bothered me."

"We'll know soon enough."

Riding at a trot, Brenwar closed the distance on Nath. His eyes weren't as keen as a dragon's, but his vision was still sharp. He could still see the two-headed vulture circling far away in the sky. That wasn't all he noticed either. He heard a rumble of horses galloping behind him. He steered the pony into the nearby wood line and waited behind the bushes.

"By my beard, what is this?"

Over twenty riders charged down the road. Each and every one wore a full battle helmet, made with terrifying faces upon them. They were led by a rider who had no helm but the shriveled face of a man who was dead. The fierce glow of fire burned in his eye sockets. A head of thinning white hair trailed behind him like a banner. Brenwar spat.

"Guul raiders. That's a problem. As if there weren't enough."

Waiting for the gap between them to grow, he followed from a safe distance. The Guuls would destroy anything and everything in their path. Whether or not they pursued Nath and Darkken, he did not know, but there would be fighting anyway. Whoever was in their path would need help. He scanned the ground. He could still make out some of the fresh grooves in the dirt that the wagon had made. No doubt the wagon would slow Nath's group down. They would be overcome soon.

Seeing the raiders stretch the lead, he gave his pony a kick. "Yah!" The pony lunged ahead. It was a quick beast but not a match for the bigger horses. It was clear Brenwar would not catch up before the Guuls crossed paths with Nath. Face set to the wind, he rode hard. "Come on, mule. Run quicker. I at least have to get there in time to finish it."

Chapter 69

Sultan's Lake was a fiery pit of lava leagues wide that bubbled and churned. It was surrounded by jagged rocks and cracks and the most rugged terrain. Within that harsh terrain were giant crevices and cracks, forming pathways and channels that had been bored out by nature ages ago.

Sweat drenched Nath's face. Maefon's damp hair clung to her skin. The heat near the lake, trapped by the sheer rocks and rolling steam, made the temperatures excessive. The sulfuric air had a foul taste and overwhelming smell.

"The wroth heat steals my breath." Maefon's arms were wrapped around Nath's waist. "Your breastplate feels like a hot plate. How can you stand it?"

"I'll be fine." He looked behind him. Darkken was leading the wagon up a steep incline covered in hunks of fallen stone. The wagon bounced hard, jostling the determined man. Behind him were the elves, pushing the wagon as its back wheel wedged against a rock. As one, they lifted and shoved. The horses pulled. The wagon popped up over the rock, bouncing hard on the ground, and rumbled forward. "We need to move faster."

She followed his stare. "I don't think we can outpace them now."

From their elevated positions, he could see the Guul raiders charging into the lakeside terrain. Waving swords and all sorts of weapons, they shouted at the men and elves they pursued. The leader's eyes shined like burning pearls. Like death, he carried a sickle in his bony, withered hands.

"Don't gawk. Ride!" Darkken's voice was loud and tight. Perspiration soaked his body. "Lead us to as high a ground as you can. We need to get to the top of these hills. It's our only chance."

Nath galloped ahead, scouting the paths that diverged in many directions. Most of them were too narrow for a horse to ride through. A couple might barely fit a wagon. He agreed with Darkken. They needed a high spot where they could defend themselves, but he didn't see it happening. The Guuls would have them trapped long before they got there. He slowed to a trot, noticing some wild brush and overgrowth hiding an old pathway big enough for a wagon. It wound upward at a steep angle. He waved his arms at Darkken. The man led the two-horse team right at him.

"You go first, Nath. This will have to do," Darkken said, eyeing the trail. "Perhaps it will lead us to safer ground."

Nath led the way up the winding channel. The surrounding rocks rose thirty to seventy feet high, making a jagged line of walls surrounding him. Behind him, the wagon churned on. The Brothers of the Wind pushed when needed. Others walked backward with bow and arrow ready. He hit a long stretch, over fifty yards deep, that widened enough for three wagons. It bottlenecked again at the end. As soon as he reached the end, a wild howl carried through the channel.

The Guuls spilled into the other end.

Darkken shook his head. "This is it. The battle starts here. We don't have a dragon to turn against them this time."

"We?" Nath said.

Darkken managed a smile as he wiped the sweat from his eyes. "Yes, you. Perhaps you can take all of them down again."

"I'm thinking." Nath had seen enough of the Brothers of the Wind die, and if they engaged in combat, more would die. He started counting the Guul raiders. At least thirty barreled into the channel. They were a sordid lot of what could be man, orc, gnoll, or bugbear. The leader with the sickle was the most terrifying of all. He appeared as a weathered old man with the strength of the elements in his pearl-white eyes. His armor was plates of metal, half covered in a rotting cloak.

On horseback, the Guul leader approached with two defenders on each side of him. His voice was that of a chill, howling wind. "Your path in life ends. A new path in death begins. Put down your weapons, surrender, and swear allegiance to the Guul and live. That will be payment for the brethren you took. Otherwise, you will certainly die, for I am the Guul master. My touch is death." He raised his sickle. "I cannot die."

Nath's hand went to Dragon Claw. It worked before, and he saw no reason why it would not work again. He got off his horse and started toward the Guul.

"He's baiting you, Nath," Darkken said. "Surely he knows that one of us killed his brother. They'll ride you down before you get within ten yards of him. He tests us. Let us test him. Brothers of the Wind, take a shot," he commanded.

Four elves fired a volley of arrows into the Guul master. All four shafts bounced harmlessly away from the leader's body.

The Guul leader dusted his chest with the back of his hand. Casually he said, "I cannot be killed as my brother was. Now, do you choose life or do you take death?"

Darkken held up a finger. "A moment, please." He said to Nath, "So, do you want to join them? They have very intriguing helmets."

"No, but I have a better idea that might tip the odds in our favor. Look up over my shoulders, in the rocks. Do you see the neck of rock?" Nath slid a red-tipped arrow out of his black quiver. "I think it's worth a shot. Keep him talking."

"You are full of creativity. I like it." Darkken straightened his back and looked to the Guul master. "Can you give us more information about the benefits of joining your group? For example, do you supply the helmet, or do we need to purchase one ourselves? And what about the rate of pay? Do we share in the spoils, or is there an agreed-upon daily wage?"

The Guul master sneered. "You seek to enrage me. Fool! Offer rescinded." He lifted his scythe high in the air. "Guuls! Attack! But save that one's head for—"

From a knee, Nath fired the red-tipped arrow at a neck of rock that held up a crag of overhanging boulders.

All eyes in the chasm watched the missile streak through the sky. A bright explosion followed with a loud thundering *boooooooom*!

Horses reared up.

The Guuls' eyes froze on the blackened and damaged rock face. Only a few small stones fell.

The Guul master made an evil grin. Quickly he said, "You tried. You failed. Kill them!"

CHAPTER 70

TEETH GNASHING, THE GUUL RAIDERS surged forward, the sound of thundering hooves echoing in the tight space like thunder. Darkken looked at Nath. "It was a good idea. You've proven to be quite resourceful." He drew his sword. "Too bad it didn't work. Let me handle the Guul master. Just keep the others off me." He jumped out of the wagon and stood before the Brothers of the Wind. "Stand your ground!"

Nath dropped the bow and pulled Fang free of the sheath. He joined them.

A loud crack that sounded like a great oak snapping started above. Heavy stone scraped on stone. The horses halted. Many reared up and staggered back. One member of the raiders pointed a great sword at the rocks. "The rocks cry! The rocks fall!"

The huge boulder that Nath struck broke free from its perch. It smashed down into the lower shelves, rapidly bringing an avalanche of boulders, clay, dirt, and debris with it. The avalanche spread, widening as it came down. The massive, wagon-sized rocks bounced from the rocky ledge, spun in the air, and slammed into the raiders.

"Get out of the way!" Darkken screamed. He and the elves scrambled up the hill.

Nath, gleaming sword in hand, followed.

Underneath the tide of stone, helmets were mashed and skulls crushed. One of the largest boulders, bigger than a man, caught the Guul master full in the chest with a sickening smack. In seconds, the wave ended. The Guul raiders were buried.

Coughing and fanning the dusty debris from his face, Nath called out, "Maefon. Maefon."

"I'm here," she said.

He couldn't see her through the thickness of smoky brown dust that clouded his vision. Reaching out, he found her hands searching for his. "How are you?"

"Not a scratch," she said, coughing softly. "I see your improvisation worked again. I think you've made a lifetime enemy with the Guul."

"Ah, well, they are stupid. They are the enemy of themselves."

Darkken approached with a big smile on his face. Momentarily his expression soured, and he had to spit. "Aside from dirt soup that I'll taste in my mouth for days, your plan was well executed. Words cannot express how impressed I am with your quick thinking. You saved us from grave danger." He slapped a heavy hand on Nath's shoulder. "You are something else, brother."

"You would have done the same."

"Only if I would have thought of it." Darkken whistled. "We need to go in and see if there are survivors. There are always survivors. Never hold back on those pesky remnants of evil, eh?"

"Of course not," Nath replied.

It took over an hour for the dust to finally settle. The bodies that could be seen jutting from the grave of boulders were mangled. None of the evil army stirred, but a few horses were rescued and set free. The channel that they had passed through was filled with eight to ten feet of rock. The wagon's wheels were half buried. Crushed underneath a boulder, the Guul master lay with his body and face smashed. His feet kicked inside his rotting boots. The bony fingers on his hands twitched.

"He still lives," Nath said with an incredulous look. "How can that be?"

"Like he said, he was dead already," Darkken replied. His armor and hand were frosted with dirt and debris. Dust coated his face. "These men are a strange breed, brought back by dark magic." A finger stretched toward Nath's toe. Darkken pushed Nath back. "I'd say that touch still has death in it." With his sword, he hacked off the hands and feet. "Bury that," he ordered one of the elves. He looked at the wagon. "I hate to leave a fine piece of equipment behind. I have a thing for wagons, and most of our supplies are in it." He walked over a dirt pile to the wagon and fetched a canteen. He drank then shared with Nath and Maefon. "Ah, that's good."

After a drink, Nath said, "So now what?"

"I suggest that you and some of the elves move on to Advent. The danger has passed, and I think we should, well, celebrate. Besides, this journey has been a rough one. We need to remember those we lost, and I've been cold about that. What do you say?"

"We should stay together," Nath suggested.

"Nonsense," Darkken replied. "We only have two shovels, and it shouldn't take more than a few hours to dig out. Ride ahead, and just think of it as a scouting assignment if you feel guilty. We should all be back together by nightfall."

"I think it's a good idea," Maefon said. "Not that I don't want to help, but this heat has sapped the energy out of me. I want to smell the fresh air again."

"It's still the cold season, but eating snow is better than eating dust." Nath reached out and shook Darkken's hand. "All right then. We'll *scout* and you can *dig*. Here's your canteen. You'll need it more than me."

Darkken laughed. "Ha-ha, excellent. It sounds like the perfect plan."

Chapter 71

GALTUR SOARED OVER THE SULTAN'S Lake of Fire. Slivver and Elween rode closer. The vulture had been hanging in the air for a very long time, circling the same spot. It wasn't alone. Small birds of prey had formed circles beneath it.

"Something died," Slivver said, "and it looks like a lot of it." He watched the birds dive and swoop back up in the air. "I hope Nath is well. I can't imagine what would draw this creature to this burning lake."

"True," Elween agreed.

They rode until the green grasses turned brown and hot steam smacked them in the face. Keeping their distance from the shoreline, they moved along the rim. Steamy haze bubbled up from the lake. Slivver's clothing clung to his body, damp and sticky. "I believe I'm sweating. Dragons don't sweat."

"You sound like Brenwar," she said.

"Oh, that's bad. I really need to change back soon then. Apparently being a human has gotten to me."

"I thought you wanted to be human."

"I just want to be with my love, Ericha. I'll do anything for her." High above, the vultures, including Galtur, started to dive and land in the rocks out of sight. "I think we may have caught a moment. It seems the vulture is distracted."

Urging her horse into a trot, she said, "Let's make haste then."

The fiery lake was expansive, the terrain rugged, and it took a great deal of time to navigate to the spot where they saw the vulture drop. But it was a break to move in without the prying eyes of Darkken. Now, they just needed to see what condition Nath was in. Perhaps he needed help. Riding through the veil of hot fog that rolled from the bubbling red-orange waters, they entered a glade where the leafless trees stood petrified. A figure sat on the rocks that made a wall along a path. He wore a cloak, and his flame-red hair covered his face. He looked up and saw their approach. His hand went to his sword. "Who goes there?"

Slivver and Elween brought their horses to a halt. "Hail," Slivver said. "Sorry, but we did not mean to startle you. We saw the vultures circling and thought that there was danger. Are you well, friend?"

Nath had half of his sword out. He stuffed it back into the sheath. Obscured in the fog, he walked closer, squinting his eyes. He wore his breastplate and was drenched in sweat. "We ran into some raiders. All is well now, but many are dead. Did you say vultures?" He looked back over his shoulder into the sky. "They come quickly."

Nath and Elween dismounted. Slowly, they came forward. "Are you alone? Do others need aid?" Elween asked.

"I'm fine. I just wandered." His damp hair covered his eyes. He swept the sweaty locks aside. "Say, didn't I meet you outside of Old Hen?" He grabbed the sword at his hip and stepped back into a fighter's stance. His eyes narrowed. "You said your names are Apollos and Lydia. What are you doing here? Are you spies like Darkken said?"

Hands up, Slivver said, "No, no, Nath."

"Nath? I did not tell you my name. You are spies!"

Elween took a step forward. "We are not spies. We are friends, Nath. It is I, Master Elween, and your brother, Slivver. We've been looking for you. Today our search ends."

Nath cocked his head. "How could you know who…" He looked deep into their eyes. His tight grimace began to loosen. "When I saw you, I knew there was something familiar. I knew it. But how can you be…"

"Human?" Slivver said. "Magic, of course. We can change back in a moment, but we had to get close to warn you."

"Warn me about what?"

"Darkken," Slivver continued. "He is not who he says. He is the leader of the Caligin. He is the Lord of the Dark in the Day. He is… your brother."

Nath's face sagged. "That can't be. He's been my friend."

"He is a grand deceiver," Elween said. "You must listen to us. It was he that had the Trahaydeen kill the fledglings. It was him, Chazzan, and Maefon behind it all. I'm sorry to tell you, but his goal has been to win you over and turn you against Balzurth. We've been sent to find you and put an end to this. You must trust us."

"I don't know," Nath said, shaking his head. He staggered backward. "It's all been very confusing. I want to believe who you are, but I-I can't. Darkken is a good man, and you are pretending to be my friends. But it's been so, so long. You're confusing me."

Slivver reached out. "Nath, search your heart. You must believe us. It is imperative. You are in danger. All of Dragon Home, including our father, is in danger. Let us take you away from this place."

"I can't just leave them. They need me." Nath's eyes were big. "And you said Maefon killed the fledglings. How do you know this?"

"Blood is on her hands." Elween clasped her hands together. "Nath, just come with us. Let us go now before Darkken comes. He is dangerous. A killer. We don't know the power he wields."

"If you say you are who you are, then turn into a dragon." Nath's hand still gripped his sword's pommel. "I need proof."

Slivver huffed out a small charge of lightning from his mouth into the fiery lake. Quickly, his body transformed into a slender, seven-foot lizard. He did his customary arms crossing over his chest. With a glimmer shining in his ice-blue eyes, he said, "Now are you convinced?"

Gaping, Nath slowly came forward. "Yes, yes, I'm fully convinced." He came right at Slivver for an embrace. Three steps away, he whisked his sword out of the scabbard and lunged, stabbing Slivver deep in the chest. "Disguises. Two can play at that game!"

Chapter 72

Brenwar Bolderguild rode after the Guuls and followed them into the Sultan's Lake territory. He abandoned his pony, tethering it to the trees, before he traversed into the barren landscape. On foot, he took after the Guuls, war hammer at the ready. He kept his eyes wide open, head turning side to side. Loose lava stone crunched beneath his feet. He moved quickly through the natural channels that stirred with rock dust and hoof prints from the enemy's travels.

Bulky arms glistening with sweat, he followed after the sounds echoing down the canyons. There was a loud explosion and a bright light in the rocks above. A momentary silence. Wild cries of the chortling Guuls reached blood-hungry levels. He started to run.

"Smells like a fight!"

A distinct crack of stone splitting captured his attention. He'd cracked thousands of stones in his mining days and knew exactly what it was. The boulders rolled down from the tips of the ledges. An avalanche came down. A gust of dusty air and debris washed over him in the channel. Covered in a new layer of grit, he crept forward until he saw the Guuls buried in a stone grave. He concealed himself in the clefts. The elves methodically killed the wounded survivors with lethal use of their blades. What he didn't see he heard. Voices.

He bent an ear. Darkken's authoritative voice carried well. So did Nath's. They talked about digging out the wagon and moving on to Advent. It was perfect. He could catch up with them between there and Advent. He heard Nath ride away and peeked out of his spot at the sound of the scuffle of soft boots. A pair of elves, patrolling, was coming down the channel. Brenwar backed deeper into his nook.

Time to be a boulder, Bolderguild.

Relying on his battle-hardened instincts and senses, he listened to every soft elven footfall. They moved on cats' feet. Prowlers. Killers. Looking for survivors from the Guul raiders. They wouldn't find any. Brenwar would have seen them. They stopped just a few yards from his hidden location, lingering. In Elven, they whispered to one another. They called back up the channel. Another voice hollered back. Brenwar knew enough Elven to understand that they were ordered to sweep back out to the plains.

Not good.

Finally, they moved on, south, toward the plains. There was a chance, however, that Brenwar's own tracks would be found. He hadn't been careless by any means. It was a habit to tread lightly when he traveled, but he'd moved with haste as well. He hoped that the smoke and dust covered any traces of his presence. He snuck out of his spot and pressed on, toward the avalanche. From another niche, he spied Darkken. He got a decent look at the man when he passed him on the way to Old Hen.

With the elves digging out the wagon, he saw Darkken sitting in the back. He crossed his legs and closed his eyes. He rubbed his fingers and thumbs as he quietly chanted. His well-honed body shimmered. A slow change began. His rust-colored hair shortened. His dusty black leather armor transformed into a breastplate. In seconds, he was the mirror reflection of Nath Dragon.

The hair rose on Brenwar's arms. *What is this all about?* A shadow crossed over him. He glanced upward to see the huge vulture circling. Something wasn't right. They were waiting on something. While they did, they still worked on digging out the wagon. At least until Darkken stopped them. The Caligin stepped aside on his word. He stood in the wagon, and with the horses beginning to nicker and whinny, the dust and gravel beneath them trembled and stirred.

As if moved by a harsh wind, the gravel and debris were shoveled away by an unseen force. It took many minutes, but finally, the wheels of the wagon were free. Darkken, disguised as Nath, had a satisfied smirk on his face. There, they waited for a couple of hours. The two-elf patrol came back empty-handed. Above, smaller vultures began to circle, then Darkken left, followed by the elves, heading down toward the lake.

Brenwar gave them a few minutes. Then he climbed toward the wagon. There were routine supplies in it, but nothing special, until he found and unwrapped the sledgehammer. "Now, ain't that something?" He'd been trying to figure out what Darkken was up to. Why did he transform into Nath? Who was he trying to fool? He wrapped the hammer back up. Then it came to him the moment a familiar soft scuffle caught his ear. Elves entered the channel with knowing looks on their faces, swords drawn and murder behind their eyes. Darkken knew Brenwar was there. He was probably leading Elween and Slivver into a trap too. He looked up and could see the icy glare of the vulture's eyes above him. *He's known all along, hasn't he? I should have known.* He stepped away from the wagon and faced the elves.

"It looks like you elven maidens came to dance." Brenwar tightened his grip on his hammer as the elves encircled him.

With a froward expression, one of the elves said, "I didn't think dwarves could dance."

"Dwarves don't dance. At least, not in the way that you little girls prance. But we do fight." He set the hammer down, spat in his hands, rubbed them together, and picked the war hammer up again. "I've been itching to bust up elves for a long time. I always knew they were rotten. Now, I get to pulverize them."

With a sword and dagger in hand, the dark elf advanced on Brenwar. His blades sliced through the air in whistling chops. With haughtiness, he said, "Let's see what a clumsy dwarf can do with such a clumsy wagon. As you say, dwarf, 'Let's dance.'"

"I didn't say that, but you're welcome to try."

The elf thrusted.

Brenwar parried. The weapons banged loudly. The elf's sword came clean out of his grasp. The elf backpedaled, but not before a stiff, shorthanded counterswing busted the elf in the face. *Crack.* The elf dropped dead from the fatal blow.

The remaining five elves converged. Brenwar scrambled to the high ground of the avalanche. Like a bearded ball of armored fury, he faced them all. He put all he had behind every swing, while singing the song, "Home of the Dwarves, Morgdon!"

His war hammer busted knees. Cracked ribs. Jarring blows shattered the bones in the Caligins' bodies. True to his name, Brenwar Bolderguild was as hard as rock and as tempered as steel. The elves could match his speed with jabs and strikes, but that could not match his ferocity. Bleeding from several slices on his arms and legs that would cripple most fighters, Brenwar swept their weapons aside, knocking them free of their hands. Strong and powerful, he overwhelmed them with a furious assault that sent them to an early grave. They underestimated the dwarf, tempered by centuries of war and hard-fought battles. Four fell among the dead to his war hammer, leaving only two.

Drenched with sweat, the dark elves kept their distance, picking, jabbing, and thrusting at Brenwar. His dwarven breastplate saved his life more than once as the blades skipped off the metal. The elves went after the meat on his arms and legs, slicing at the muscle and tendons. Brenwar fell hard to a knee.

With eyes growing intent on Brenwar's death, they seized the moment, lunging forward, thrusting as hard as they could. At the last possible moment, Brenwar slid his head aside. A sword thrust passed over his shoulder. One elf stabbed the other through the heart. The stabbed elf's eyes rolled up in his head.

"You just fell for the sixty-eighth-oldest trick in the book," Brenwar said to the last remaining elf. Without hesitation, he swang this war hammer into the exposed body of the last standing elf. Bone snapped. The elf hurtled backward off the pile, landing hard on the rocks below. The elf moved no more.

Brenwar took a long, deep breath and lifted his arms in the air. "For Morgdon!" He climbed down the pile of rocks and rubbed dirt into over a dozen lacerations. On throbbing legs, he headed down the narrow channel that Darkken took earlier. Through the hot, hazy fog, he made out Darkken, Slivver, and Elween speaking on thc fiery lake's bank. Just as he started to shout a warning, Darkken, disguised as Nath, stabbed Slivver.

CHAPTER 73

SLIVVER FELL AWAY FROM THE sword, clutching his chest as he hit the ground. Dragon blood seeped through his fingers.

Elween's sword snaked out of her scabbard. She shielded Slivver with her body by stepping between him and Nath. "What madness is this? Why, Nath? Why?"

Nath stepped back, tossing his head back and laughing.

Brenwar emerged from the rocks. "That is not him! That is not him!"

Nath's body and armor transformed into the full body of a man in black armor with rust-colored hair and eyes that burned like molten copper.

"Darkken!" Elween exclaimed. "Such treachery! You've attacked your own brother!"

"I like to think of Slivver as more of a half brother! But yes, I not only attacked him, I should have killed him." Darkken had the dangerous look of a cold-blooded killer. "It is, however, a nice surprise to see you again, my former weapons master." He flipped his elven sword a few times. "If you would have been paying better attention, you would have noticed I did not carry the same blade that Nath does. This is one of another fashion, but very, very deadly, as you can see." He looked at Brenwar. "Ah, I see the bearded pest outfought my Caligin. How disappointing from them. Let me guess, you are one of those Bolderguilds, my father's stumpy henchmen."

The battered Brenwar cocked his war hammer back over his shoulder. "I'll turn you into a stump."

"It would take a miracle," Darkken replied.

"I'm full of miracles!"

"Brenwar! Tend to Slivver," Elween ordered.

With a grunt, Brenwar hustled over to the silver dragon. "The wound is grave."

"That was a cowardly attack," Elween said. "Even for you. I thought you would at least face us with a straight-up fight."

"If it's a straight-up fight that you want, Master Elween, I would be happy to oblige." He twisted his sword by the pommel. "Even when I was a boy, I dreamed about fighting you to the death." He eyed her up and down. "By the way, I like your new body. It's attractive yet shows off all of your vulnerabilities."

"So does yours. You wear that froward countenance of yours so well. It complements your arrogance." She moved forward. Darkken backed away. "I am willing to give you what you wish for and end your reign of insanity here. It's time that your twisted vileness comes to an end. You're not worthy of the skin of a rattlesnake."

"I am the worthiest and will be the worthiest of all things. I will take over Dragon Home and rule with an iron fist." Darkken stuck his sword in the ground and tied his long hair into a ponytail. He picked the sword up again. "You see, you made a fatal mistake. When you encountered us at Old Hen, you flinched. At that moment, you should have taken him, but you hesitated. It was enough to alert me to watch you and sink my claws deeper into Nath.

He, I assure you, is one of us now, a Caligin, a dark Brother of the Wind. And soon, together, we will slay our overbearing father and shatter Dragon Home from within."

"You are cursed. Insane. You will never rule the dragons because you can never become a dragon. Your wings are clipped, Crixis."

"I prefer Darkken. Or Lord Darkken. Or Lord of the Dark in the Day."

"It does not matter," she said, marching right at him. "You will always eat the dust of men and never taste the air of the skies. Again, you are cursed. And it is my duty to end you right here."

"So, the master challenges the student?" Darkken made a nasty grin. "I accept. And please, feel free to fight in whichever body you are the most comfortable with. I highly recommend you add the scales. You are going to need them."

"Not as much as you will."

With her arms wrapped around Nath's waist, Maefon said, "I know that times are sad, but I am starting to look forward to a short stay in Advent. It is a shame that we were unable to take advantage of our time in Old Hen. Let's return sometime, shall we?"

"Uh-huh," Nath replied, rather listlessly. The horse moved at a trot, four of the Brothers of the Wind jogging behind them.

"You are in very deep thought. Tell me, what is on your mind?" she asked. "If I am prying, you can tell me to keep silent. Sometimes, a person needs to be alone in his thoughts."

Nath shifted in the saddle. "I don't know. I just feel something. I don't know what it is, but it's some sort of alarm going off inside of me. We've separated, and it leaves me uneasy."

"You are war-torn," she said.

"What is that?"

"Well, you've been through so much torment that you can no longer relax. Your mind is very restless. Let me try something." She started rubbing his temples with the tips of her fingers. "This should ease your worries."

"It's nice, but"—he pushed her hands away—"I can't really enjoy it at the moment. Probably because I don't want to." He turned the horse. Miles away, the rock hills surrounding Sultan's Lake seemed to call him. He could make out more birds of prey in the air. The Brothers of the Wind were looking at him and casting backward looks over their shoulders. All of them were covered in dust and grit. "I'm going back."

Startled, Maefon said, "What? Nath, you need to stay with me. Darkken is fine."

"We can all go. After all, isn't this a brotherhood? Besides, I worry. I've a feeling that there is another foe that we might have missed. Maybe there are more Guul? I can't take that chance."

"But," she said. Nath started to dismount. "No. If you have to ride, I will ride with you."

"Are you sure?"

She tried to fight off a frown by positively saying, "I don't think I have a choice."

CHAPTER 74

BRENWAR APPLIED PRESSURE TO SLIVVER'S wound. With a ragged groan, Slivver said, "Stop doing that."

"What do you want me to do? I don't have much experience applying aid to dragons. Oh, wait." Brenwar unslung his backpack. Opening the flap, he reached inside. Bottles rattled. He produced a handful of clear cylindrical potion vials with corks in the tops. Looking at them one by one, he said, "Not it. Not it. Not it. Not it."

Slivver's eyes fluttered. "Brenwar, you've been a friend. Not the best but a friend nonetheless."

"Don't get weepy. I don't like weepy."

"Tell me that you'll be kind to the little creatures of the world. That you'll use a softer voice, and never attack innocent flowers."

"What? No. If you want me to bury you, I'll bury you."

"I want to be buried beside you, Brenwar. I want a dwarven funeral. Promise me."

Brenwar gaped. As he did so, he watched Slivver's ice-blue eyes burn like crystal coals. The wound in his chest closed. His scales mended. "What's this all about? Are you well?"

Slivver rose to his elbows. "Yes, fortunately. But I truly was a hair's breadth from death. I could feel Darkken's blade slide right past the edge of my beating heart. If he hit me, I would have been killed."

"And you heal from such a fatality?"

"Centuries of stored-up healing magic that is drained now. But I live." Slivver's eyes slid to the battle between Darkken and Master Elween. Their shining steel flickered like striking snakes. Blades flashed quicker than the wink of an eye. He came to his feet. "Darkken baited her, the same as he baited me. We must stop this."

"I'll stop it!" Brenwar said.

Soaked in perspiration, Elween broke away from the fight. So did Darkken. "No!" she said to Slivver. "I've made the challenge. I live and die by it. Slivver, go find Nath."

"Do not honor Darkken with a fair fight, Elween. He will deceive you," Slivver warned. "It should be me fighting him, not you."

With a look of disgust, Darkken glared at Slivver. "You live! You always were as slippery as an icicle. Regardless, I'll not miss your heart a second time. I'll dispatch the eroding Master Elween, then I'll dispatch you."

Elween rolled her shoulders and made windmills with her arms. "I'll be fine, Slivver. Take advantage of this time and go after Nath. Warn him." She spun her sword in her hand and faced Darkken. "It's time to finish you."

There was no changing Elween's mind. Slivver knew that once a challenge was made, she would not back down, no matter how grave the danger. As painful as it was, he said, "Brenwar, keep an eye on them."

"I'm not going anywhere, but she better realize I can't restrain myself forever," Brenwar replied.

Slivver launched himself into the air. With a downward glance, he spied Darkken and Elween going at it again. "May the dragons be with her." Wings flapping, he jetted toward the rocky hillside. The two-headed vulture flew directly into his path. Aided by a host of vultures, they swarmed Slivver. "Certainly you don't think you are a match for me?" Flying, he punched right through the flock.

Galtur proved quicker than anticipated. In midair, the hostile bird smashed into Slivver with the force of a charging bull. The vulture's talons latched into Slivver's body and ripped at his scales. The bird, little bigger than Slivver, with much more girth, snapped at Slivver's face.

Wings beating hard in the wind, Slivver head butted one head with his horns. "What manner of creature are you? You are no simple bird." He clawed into one head's neck. The vulture made a very dragon-like roar. Writhing in Slivver's clawed clutches, Galtur shed his feathers and transformed into a featherless, dragon-like creature with a serpentine body and bat-like wings. A tail and stinger sprouted out of Galtur's tail feathers.

With pure hatred, Slivver said, "Wyvern!"

Wyverns were an abominable form of dragon and serpent, spawned from the lowest depths of Nalzambor. Pure evil, they were detested by all dragons, good and bad.

Galtur's tail struck, driving a stinger home into the meat between Slivver's scales. The smaller vultures' illusions fell away. They were all smaller wyverns, the size of turkeys, with brown-and-black serpent skin like Galtur. One by one, they latched onto Slivver. Each one bit, clawed, and stung.

With burning poison coursing through his body, Slivver had to rely on the hard scales of his body to protect him. The smaller wyverns couldn't tear him apart, but they could drag him down. Fighting, straining, twisting to break free from his captors, he only found himself face-to-face with Galtur. The jaws of the wyvern opened. A hot, acid-like spit shot out. Slivver coiled his tail around one of Galtur's necks. He sank his clawed hands into the other neck. With rage swelling, he said, "I've had enough of this." He breathed out a blast of lightning. Tendrils of energy twisted all over Galtur's body. The smaller wyverns sizzled and shrieked.

Plummeting toward the ground, Slivver spewed out all of the fire he had in him. Galtur's claws ripped at his chest. His strong necks writhed in Slivver's clutches. The silver dragon held fast. Galtur's skin steamed and crackled. His body spasmed. The emerald fire in his eyes turned into smoking pits. Spiraling downward, they hit the beach of Sultan's Lake with a crash. Galtur's smoldering body broke the fall. The rest of the smaller wyverns, stung by Slivver's lightning flame, perished.

Slivver rolled off the dead wyverns. With the fire of poison still burning inside him, he said, "I hate wyverns. I hate vultures."

Chapter 75

With quick, hard, and fierce sword strikes and thrusts, Master Elween backed Darkken down the path. Drenched in sweat, he parried furiously.

"You are as rusty as your hair," she said. "And you never were a good student."

The larger swordsman didn't pant or puff for breath. He parried and countered with a lethal strike that would have downed the finest of swordsmen. Elween blocked his counter and countered with a slice across his exposed abdomen. Only a quick hop back saved him from being disemboweled.

"There is no questioning that you are a true master. And here I thought I'd mastered everything," he said. "And the taunting. You've added another weapon to your arsenal, but it won't work on me. I don't care what you think, and I never did."

Elween advanced. She stepped, jabbed, and lunged, and repeated. Darkken danced away, only to come back with tomahawk chops. She jumped aside from the new offensive tactic. Fighting for long minutes, by her count, Darkken used over eleven different sword-fighting forms with total mastery. As big and fast as he was, he would destroy the finest swordsman. But Elween had seen it all, done it all, was still quicker by a lick, and despite her small size, she retained the full strength of a true dragon. Now, the time had come to cut Darkken down and end his reign of madness. She pressed.

"Goodbye, Crixis!"

With both hands on his handle, he battled her across the crusty beach, swinging hard from side to side. Her longsword beat hard into Darkken's cross guard. She clipped at his knees. Fighting to keep his balance, he jumped back. Putting more weight behind her swing, Elween knocked Darkken's sword out of his strong grip.

Flushed with rage, Darkken said, "Impossible!"

Elween delivered a life-finishing strike that would have split his skull. An unseen force checked her swing. Her body locked up. Darkken rose to full height. Towering over her, he said, "I underestimated you. No matter. You won't be around to underestimate again!" His sword flew back into his grip. "I've toyed with you long enough, but thanks for the practice. I almost feel winded. Goodbye, Master Elween."

Brenwar charged Darkken. "Honor your fight, you black dog!"

With a flick of his wrist, Darkken lifted Brenwar from his feet and sent him skidding across the stony beach. "Dwarves, such a nuisance."

Despite her struggles, Elween could not break free.

Darkken looked her in the eye. "Now, where were we? Oh yes, it's time to kill you."

Against the unseen bonds that held her, Elween summoned her inner strength, bringing forth flame enough to spit in Darkken's eyes.

"Aaaargh!" His anger sent her flying back into the rocks. She transformed back into a dragon. Sword still in hand, she charged Darkken again.

Darkken wiped the burning spew from his face. With a look, the sword was torn from her fingers, and his stare froze her where she stood. He closed in, five steps from delivering the finishing blow.

The moment Nath caught a glimpse of Galtur battling in the sky with a silver dragon, he urged the horse into a gallop. It was too far to see, and the battle frenzy in the sky was ugly, but he swore the silver dragon had to be Slivver. The horse raced back up the ridges, through the rocky spires, and into the hills that surrounded Sultan's Lake. Ahead, he saw the spit and lightning of the interlocked dragons clawing the life out of one another. In a smoking spiral to the ground, they dropped out of sight.

He passed the wagon and took the narrow channel in the rock toward the lake. He made it to the beach, eyes searching for Slivver and Galtur. He found something else that made his heart jump a beat. Darkken was three steps away from slaying Master Elween. Nath shouted at the top of his lungs, "Darkken, stop!"

Darkken slowed his stormy advance only for a moment as he glimpsed Nath. He moved in on the prone Elween, who appeared frozen in time.

A war hammer hurtling through the air smote Darkken with the sound of a clap of thunder. The powerful man stumbled away. Behind him, farther up the beach, Slivver appeared. He clutched his side. "Elween, get Nath out of here. I'm too weak to fly."

Elween's wings spread out. She launched herself into the air, arms outstretched, making a beeline for Nath. He reached up for his old friend. Maefon tried to pull his arm down.

Darkken appeared in his view. He uttered a word. The wristbands he'd given Nath and Maefon glowed with twinkling light. A foot away from Elween's outstretched fingers, the scenery suddenly changed as Nath's body faded and disappeared. Body spinning through time and space, he found himself back inside the library of Stonewater Keep. Darkken and Maefon were there. She helped him up from his hands and knees. Darkken, with a hard grimace, stood peering out the window.

Nath rubbed his wrist, which had a fiery burn from the teleporting powers of the bracelet. With his eyes set on Darkken, he said, "That was Slivver and Elween. You tried to kill them, didn't you?"

"Actually," Darkken said as he faced Nath. His face was as hard as stone. "They were trying to kill me. I was trying to protect you." With one hand up, he said, "Let me explain, as there is something very important that you should know."

With fire building in his golden eyes and unable to contain the disdain in his voice, Nath said, "Let me guess: you are my brother." He hoped Darkken would say no.

Darkken calmly replied, "Yes, Nath, you are my brother. And I have a lot of explaining to do."

Chapter 76

Slivver, Elween, and Brenwar sat on the gritty banks of the burning lake with their heads downcast. They'd been so close to saving Nath, but they'd failed. The wyvern's poison took a toll on Slivver, partially paralyzing him, but he'd make it.

"Vanished into thin air," Brenwar stated. "That's cheating. No telling where they might have gone."

"No, but we can't give up," Elween said. "We can only begin again. I say we start at the keep."

"Agreed," Slivver said with sluggish speech. "At least Nath knows that we come for him. We have to hope that Darkken's lies won't win out over the truth."

"I saw confusion in his eyes when he reached for me." Elween tossed a lava rock into the lake. "But I think he knows. The danger is, will Darkken kill him if he resists?"

Stretching out a hand, Slivver said, "Sadly, I think we all know that he will. Help me up. I can't fly yet, but I can walk. Let's forge on."

The group moved through the channels to where the wagon lay. Brenwar retrieved the sledgehammer, and they searched for anything that would tell them more about Darkken. They found some maps inside and took them.

Brenwar gave the maps a once-over. "It's not much to go on, but it's something."

"Are you ready to ride?" Slivver said.

"Aye. Let me fetch my pony."

EPILOGUE

In Quintuklen, the City of Crowns, inside the legionnaires' barracks and training ground was a circular sanctuary called the Hall of Knights. The walls and floor were made from white marble. A dome with knights battling the forces of evil was painted on the ceiling. All of the races battled at one time or another, men, dragons, orcs, elves—not one race was missing. The painting was a reminder that no one could be trusted all of the time unless you were a legionnaire. Supposedly.

Hacksaw studied the figures painted on the ceiling that had been made with such realistic detail. He studied the elves mostly. On the painting, which must have been centuries old if not millennia, he did not see evil in them, but now he knew better.

He was on both knees, surrounded by a ring of statues towering over him on their podiums against the wall. They were known as the Lords of Thunder, the greatest knights who ever lived. Each statue had been chiseled out of stone by hand with realistic detail. There were twenty in all, but there was room for more.

Hacksaw let out a ragged breath. He grimaced. The Caligin had filled him with arrows. He had scars for every one. He saw their cold, dead stares boring into him. Wearing only a towel around his waist, his fingers ran over those scars on his chest. *I should be dead.*

The old knight had escaped death once again. It was the unicorn pipe that saved him. Its magic was powerful, and he knew that. It was what transported him back to the Hall of Knights, where he lay in the circular ring, dying. His blood had been scrubbed from the floor. The wounds he suffered patched up. The legionnaires' healers went to work on him, keeping life inside his body. With the tingle of life coursing through his limbs, he was ready to enact revenge and save his friend, Nath.

Now, he prayed in the sanctuary among the Lords of Thunder, faithful fighters one and all, renowned for fighting the good fight, giving thankfulness, and asking for direction. It seemed that his battle was not yet over.

"It's time to find Nath." He stood up just as a white-haired man entered. Like Hacksaw, he was older, not burly, and had a neatly trimmed beard. He wore a ceremonial legionnaire tunic. "Everett, don't try to talk me out of this."

"Talk you out of what? You haven't even told me or anyone what happened," Everett stated. "You just show up and make a bloody mess of the floor."

"It's for your own good."

"Bloody floors?"

"No, not knowing what happened. This is my fight, not the legionnaires'."

"Yet you wound up here? That makes it our business." Everett looked Hacksaw up and down. "You had twelve arrows in you. Twelve. It's a miracle that you breathe. Even the healers said so."

"Do you have my gear ready?"

"Yes, of course, old friend. And you are very fortunate that the Council of Knights has been preoccupied with the dwarves. They would scour you with questions."

"No, they wouldn't. They don't care about an old man like me." As they walked out, Hacksaw gave the statues and painting one final look. He nodded. "Where did you say my gear was?"

"Your gear is ruined, but you'll have something more suitable for your travels that isn't thirty years old." Everett led him to a room in the barracks, where a tunic of chainmail and new traveling garb lay on the bed. Hacksaw's sword, Green Tongue, lay sheathed in its scabbard. "If there is any sort of threat to Quintuklen, you must tell me about it."

Hacksaw started dressing. "There is always a threat, and you wouldn't believe me if I told you."

"Try me."

"This part is between us. Knight to knight. How you handle it is up to you, Everett."

"I'm all ears."

Without getting into all of the details about everything he'd been through with Nath, Hacksaw briefly explained what he knew about the Caligin.

Everett hung on every word, and when Hacksaw finished, he said, "I don't believe it."

"I didn't think you would." Hacksaw buckled on his sword belt. "You were always one who had to see to believe."

"But elves have been nothing but noble in their relations with us. I'm sorry, I don't mean to discard your word, friend. You know that. But your tale is a stretch. Dark elves. I'm glad you only told me, because the council would laugh at that."

"Did you not see the arrows in my body? They were elven shafts."

Everett scratched his chin. "Yes, that was perplexing."

Hacksaw sat down and tugged his boots on. "Again, I appreciate you and the knights and healers stitching me back together, but this fight is my fight. I didn't expect anyone to understand. Keep word of my coming and going to yourself, and most of all, away from any elf. Just pay closer attention, friend." He stood up. "And fight the good fight."

Everett nodded. "I really wish you would have taken a station with me here in Quintuklen. You have many friends. They and my family would cherish you."

"And miss out on all of the fun I'm having now?" Hacksaw stuck his white pipe in his mouth. "I don't think so. So, where's my horse?"

"Outside the wall as you requested." They exchanged the knights' handshake. "Ride the thunder, brother. Ride the thunder."

Calypsa, the daughter of the mother queen of the dryads, sat on a tree stump shaped like a throne. A host of pixies, with wings buzzing behind their backs, attended to her needs. The size of birds, each pixie had soft skin the color of different rose petals, and their eyes were as bright as gems of the same color. They trimmed Calypsa's fingers and toes. They painted them with nature's paint. They fixed her hair in braids and flowers. Not once did the pixies' feet touch the ground.

The entire time, Calypsa's frown deepened. She was a sultry, happy vixen, with an hourglass figure, mounds of wavy brown hair, and sun-browned skin as soft as butter. A glorious beauty but far from happy.

"Oh, will you stop this pampering!" she said, shooing the pixies away. Like flies on honey, the pixies returned and went to work again. Stomping through the forest, she couldn't shake their tiny little hands. Dressing in nothing more than a white woolen tunic dress that showed her shapely figure, she shouted, "Mother! Get these insects off me!"

A pink pixie hovered right in front of her, tilted her little head to one side, and frowned.

Calypsa flicked it with her finger. "Go away!"

The pixies made wicked chattering remarks that only their kind could understand. Propelled by buzzing wings, they vanished into the leaves of the forest.

Sighing, she said, "Finally." Ever since she'd battled Maefon, she hadn't been the same. The evil elf woman had buried her for dead. Calypsa's own mother saved her. Trying to follow her mother's wishes, she tried to move on and forget about Nath Dragon, but with every passing day, it only got harder. At first, there was the fear of dying again, but with time, that fear began to fuel anger. A fire burned inside Calypsa like it had never burned before. She was ready to take her revenge.

Ripping the flowers out of her hair, she tousled up the wavy locks, giving her the frizzy look of a wild thing. She undid her braids and clawed them out. "Mother! I know you can hear me. Don't try to stop me. I'm leaving!"

Her bold statement was met with silence. She knew what that meant. Calypsa's mother wouldn't be around to save her the next time. This time, she would be all on her own. Looking to the trees, and as if speaking in her own inner private communion with some unseen person, she said, "Thank you, dear mother."

A gentle breeze rustled through the leaves and branches, kissing her face. A tear streamed down from the corner of her eye. She wiped it away. "I love you too."

Now the other hard part came. Looking into the woodland, with a trembling heart, she said, "Come on, Rond."

A hulking, four-armed brute pushed his way out of the overgrowth that covered him. With vines of ivy snapping, Rond emerged. No longer did the bugbear's veins pulse with the lifeblood of his breed. Already considered an abomination to many, he had changed into something worse—a gray-skinned golem of flesh and brawn, with his jaw half hanging open. What little gingerness he walked with before was gone, replaced by a rugged stiffness. His eyes were as white as snow as he looked outward, beyond Calypsa's position.

She sobbed. She'd tried to convince herself that it was the Caligin's fault, but deep down, she knew it was hers. She never should have left her loyal friend's side. He never left hers until the end, and he died for it. She reached out and grabbed his lowest cold and clammy hand. "Rond, I know you can hear me. Do you want to go with me? We'll hunt down and kill the ones who did this to you."

He looked down on her lithe body with a raincloud-heavy stare. For a long time, he stared, drool dripping out of his mouth. With a deep fire hidden somewhere inside, he roughly managed to say, "Kill elf."

"Come on then," she said. She started out of the forest, leading him by his big paw. "Together, we will kill many."

THE ODYSSEY OF

NATH DRAGON

BOOK 5

STRIFE

CRAIG HALLORAN

Chapter 1

The air inside Stonewater Keep was chill despite the fireplaces blazing within Lord Darkken's study. Wind whistled through the small open portals above the rafters, stirring the floor-length curtains that softened the otherwise dreary room. Flat-footed, his heart shooting through his throat, Nath stood beside Maefon. When he'd made the suggestion that Lord Darkken was his brother, he'd hoped he was wrong even though he knew, deep down, that he wasn't.

Now, he looked at his older brother as though for the first time, numbness spreading throughout him. His knees weakened, but he fought and stood upright. "If you're going to talk, then talk, Darkken. I'm willing to hear you out."

Darkken's copper eyes brightened. An eyebrow arched. The formidable man in a suit of black leather armor could not hide his surprise the way he did with all his other deceptions. Instead, the hard expression in his angular jawline softened. He unbuckled his sword belt and set it aside on a table beneath the window that shone glumly on the Pool of Eversight. He eyed Fang, which Nath held tightly in his grip. Nath leaned the sword against a wall.

Twisting the copper rings on his fingers, Darkken said, "Let's have some wine and sit." His eyes slid over to catch Maefon's gaze. "Family only."

Maefon's suit of black leather armor groaned softly as she stiffened. Her short damp blond hair clung to her forehead. The beautiful elf still had new sweat on her face and neck from the humid heat of the Sultan's Lake of Fire. They'd only been transported from that location minutes before by the magic bracelets Darkken had given them as tokens of friendship. Maefon laid her gorgeous eyes on Nath's for a fleeting moment. Then she bowed to Darkken and quickly departed.

Darkken moved over to a small study table and pulled out one of its four wooden chairs. "Please, have a seat, brother."

As Darkken moved to the other side of the table, Nath took a seat in the chair. All the while, his mind rifled through images of everything that had transpired at the Sultan's burning lake. Riding back to aid Lord Darkken, he found himself facing his old friends, his brother Slivver and his former weapons trainer, Master Elween. His joy of seeing them was fleeting, however, as he discovered Darkken battling the both of them. Darkken was a moment away from slaying Master Elween. A grisly dwarf hurled a hammer that smote Darkken and saved Elween. Darkken shrugged off the mighty blow of the hammer like a dog shed water. Master Elween flew toward Nath, arms outstretched. Her eyes were filled with desperation and worry. Nath reached for her grasp only to find himself teleported back to Stonewater Keep. That was when it all came together, and in his heart, he knew Darkken was his brother.

A bottle of wine shaped like an hourglass waited on the table with four cherry-colored glass goblets.

Darkken filled two goblets halfway to the rim. "This wine is made beneath the ground in the vineyards of the crystal gnomes. It has a very unique flavor, but I think you'll find it delicious."

Nath thirsted. He leaned over the table, took the goblet, and drank. He didn't stop until he finished the glass. He didn't recall being so thirsty, but he was. He was hungry too—for answers. "You said that you were trying to protect me from Slivver and Elween. What did you mean by that? They are my friends. My family. They are your family too."

"Pfft!" Glowering, Darkken refilled Nath's goblet. "They are not my family. What sort of family turns on their own brother? No, Nath, the same as the rest of the dragons, they cannot be trusted. At least not by the likes of us. We are different. Are we not?"

Nath shrugged. He liked Darkken and adored him like a brother. Darkken had been there for him since the beginning, and now that he knew that the man was indeed his brother, he found the bond between them strengthening. For the first time in his life, he felt that he wasn't truly alone. He wasn't the only one that was a dragon born a man. He drummed his fingers on the table with one hand and drank again. "So, you are the one that slaughtered the fledglings? The one that the dragons told me about. You are the reason that they don't like me."

Darkken smiled easily. His head tilted slightly to one side, causing his rich rust-colored locks to fall over that shoulder. Narrowing his eyes, he said, "That is what they told you, didn't they? But how do you know the truth, huh, Nath? The truth is this. The dragons framed you the same way that they framed me. You see, dragons consider us to be abominations. Dragons born as men are a curse. And for the likes of us to rule one day"—he rapped his fist on the table—"ha!"

"But we are supposed to rule," Nath said, "aren't we?"

"Of course we are. Actually, I am supposed to rule, being the older of the two brothers, but they managed to banish me. Don't let the dragons fool you. They are very clever. Sure, Slivver and Elween seem honest enough, and they can be your friends, but they are not the ones that pull the strings. It is the High Dragon Council that does that. They weren't very approving of you, were they?"

"They seemed eager to condemn me, but Slivver bailed me out." Nath combed his fingers through his hair. "His intentions were good. I know it."

"Slivver is a babysitter. That is all. I assure you that he is as jealous of you as he is of me." Darkken propped an elbow up on the table and leaned over it. "Tell me. You spent time with Slivver, didn't you?"

Nath nodded.

"And he talks very much, doesn't he?"

Again, Nath nodded in agreement.

"Now, think about this. Don't you find it odd that Slivver wants to walk like a man—even admits that he is a man? When you met him along the road, coming from Old Hen, was he not disguised as a man?"

Nath sat back. "That was Slivver, wasn't it?"

Darkken nodded. "And Elween. They were following us, but I caught on to their little game. For me, it was their eyes that gave it away. And there was a tightness in their speech that also alerted me."

Nath was well aware of Slivver's desire to be a man and act like a man. He'd been that way ever since he'd known him. But he'd also been kind. "So, why didn't they reveal themselves on the road from Old Hen?"

"They were sizing us up. I don't think they want to harm you, Nath. I think they want to keep you controlled. But it is me that they fear. And, no doubt, they recognize me." He took a long drink. Staring at the cherry glass goblet, he said, "Ah! By the Horn of Guzan, that's good. Isn't it?"

"I suppose."

"Just so you know, there was a reason that I insisted on sending you and Maefon ahead toward Advent. I wanted to verify that we were being followed. The Guuls were one matter to deal with. But when we dispatched them, I still wasn't settled. Thanks to Galtur—" His voice cracked, and he sobbed then recovered. "May peace be with him. He was a fine servant." He cleared his throat. "Well, thanks to his final efforts, I detected Slivver and Elween coming. To spare your confusion, I chose to confront them myself. That's when they attacked me. My actions were self-defense. Believe me when I say they were intent on killing me."

"What about the dwarf? Who was he to keep company with dragons?" Nath asked.

The fierce-looking, as-stout-as-stone dwarf had slung a heavy-headed war hammer like a stick.

"A henchman of the dragons, nothing more, nothing less. I have to admit that his weapon stung me." Darkken rubbed his chest. "If not for the shield spell I'd cast, no doubt my ribs would be showing on the other side of my back."

"I noticed that you didn't seem too fazed. It was uncanny."

"What can I say?" Darken raised his fingers, and mystical sparks danced between the tips. "I'm quite the magician. And so can you be, Nath. There is so very much that I can teach you about the deep magic that dwells within you."

Once again, Darkken was proving to be as charming and reassuring as ever. His words were so smooth that not believing everything he was saying was difficult.

But Nath didn't want to get off track. More questions burned inside of him. "I'm not interested in magic right now. I still have more questions."

Darkken nodded. "You'll have to forgive me, Nath, but if you only understood how excited and relieved I am to have you by my side. The way it should be. I know that I should have told you sooner, perhaps, but would you have believed me?" He reached across the table and gripped Nath's hand in his. "I felt strongly that I needed to earn your trust first. After all of the trouble you'd been through, I'm grateful that after all we've been through, you are willing to listen to my side of the story." He squeezed Nath's hand harder. "Grateful!"

Nath squeezed back and pulled his hand free. "Your words are as welcoming as a warm waterfall, but I still have many doubts." He looked Darkken right in the eye. "You are the reason that I was banished from Dragon Home, aren't you?"

"It was for your own safety, Nath. Please, hear me out. I had to reach you, and I've been trying for decades." He eyed Nath, looking for approval. "I swear it."

Crossing his arms over his chest, Nath said, "You still have my ear."

"Thank you, brother." Long-faced, Darkken eased back into his chair. "Being the only man in Dragon Home… It was lonely. But probably like you, I built strong relationships with the Trahaydeen. Even after I was banished, I found a way to stay in contact with them as they came and went on occasion. Chazzan was a close friend, and I told him if another like me were to arrive, we would have to set him free. I set forth carefully laid plans that literally took decades. And they might have taken decades longer. But…" Darkken pointed at Nath. "Chazzan took matters into his own hands. He wanted to rush the timetable that might take another fifty years. Hence, he acted on his own." Darkken's voice started to rise. "The fool set you up the same way that they set me up, by slaying the fledglings. With that, the full weight of the dragons would come upon you. Knowing that Balzurth would spare you, he was certain that you would be banished." He shook his head sadly. "I never wanted a single drop of fledgling blood to be spilled. The older ones that can defend themselves, well, I could live with that, but not the loss of innocents." He wiped his eyes. "I was angry when Chazzan returned, and I could not let his callous actions go unpunished. So I punished him. Actually, I humiliated him. I don't think it sat well with him. When I wasn't watching, he turned against me."

Nath sat up. "So, he took over the keep."

"In a manner of speaking, yes." Darkken sobbed. "And he died by my own hand. It was hard to lose a brother like that."

Nath's own heart sank. More lives seemed to have been lost on account of him. His core was shaken by Darkken's sorrowful tale. "I hate to hear that."

"Listen to me. I've made my mistakes. I admit it. And don't think that their blood lies on your hands, Nath. Countless innocent lives will be saved because of our reunion if we work as one. You see, Nath, as one, no power on Nalzambor can stop us."

"What do you mean? Stop us from what?"

"Nalzambor is not meant to be ruled by dragons. It never was. But it is destined to be ruled by the next generation of dragons. Dragons that walk as men. That is us. If we are united, no one, not dragons, not the elves, men, or dwarves can stop us. Not even our father, Balzurth. We are the future."

CHAPTER 2

WITH A FURROWED BROW, NATH tried to soak all he discussed with Darkken in.

"You are thinking deeply, Nath," Darkken said. "I know you well. I've seen that furrowed brow before. Tell me, what is on your mind?"

Nath looked at his brother and asked, "Do you hate our father?"

Darkken sank in his chair and sighed. "Balzurth was very good to me. He treated me like a prince. I was showered with his adoration. But he has a blind spot, it seems. I tried to tell him how the other dragons would treat me, but he would just say, 'Not all of them will accept you. But give them time. Most of them will.' Most of them." He finished in a whisper. His gaze looked right through Nath. "I'm certain that most of them didn't like me. I tried to explain their ugly disposition to Father, but he turned his ears away. It was hurtful. But inside those grand cavernous halls, I heard the dragons' whispers echoing through the channels. 'Beware of Crixis. The son of Balzurth is evil.'"

Turning his head, Nath said, "Crixis?"

"Crixis is my birth name. I changed it to Darkken soon after I was banished. I had to start all over again. Alone in the world, I had to forge my own path, never to return to the Mountain of Doom again."

"You mean Dragon Home?"

"It is the same, but I call it the Mountain of Doom, for that is what it is. For me and many others, anyway." Darkken fixed his confident stare back on Nath. "What are you thinking? I can see doubt lingering in those golden eyes. Tell me, what bothers you?"

Nath heavily contemplated everything Darkken had said. He'd given nearly perfect explanations and answers to Nath's questions. Still, deep inside, Nath was troubled by what the Lord of the Dark in the Day said. But he still yearned to believe him. He wanted to give in. "So, your goal is to rule Nalzambor? And you want me to help you? I don't see how this can be done by the two of us. And what about the dragons? They certainly aren't going to step aside."

Darkken stretched out his hand like a ringmaster playing the crowd. "That's exactly my point. What are the dragons doing? Nothing!" He hit his fist on the table. "They claim to have saved Nalzambor during the Great Dragon Wars hundreds of years ago, but in truth, they were the cause of it. If there were no dragons, there wouldn't be great wars. They draw strife. And their interactions with people—ha! Why, they have no relations with people. They stay in the sky, aloof, turning a blind eye to the chaos beneath them."

Nath scratched in front of his ear with his finger and asked with incredulity, "What are you proposing? That we kill the dragons? There is no army that can stop them. It would be impossible. It's madness."

"No, brother, you are misunderstanding my intentions." Darkken's voice softened. "I don't want to fight the dragons, but I do want to be rid of them. You see, their time on Nalzambor has long passed. Their purpose has been served. They have evolved, and we are proof of that evolution. We are the link of change. They don't want to admit it, but now the time has come for them to depart this world to the Land beyond the Murals."

Nath leaned back in his chair and squeezed the ends of its arms. Darkken had given him another matter to consider. The last time he'd seen his father was just before he moved into the Land beyond the Murals. Balzurth had never spoken much on what that was, and perhaps now was the time Darkken could shed more light on the matter.

"I don't know much about the Land Beyond the Murals," Nath said. "I guess I never paid that much attention. I always thought that it was a place where dragons went when they died, but that was never the case with Father."

"No, it's not a place where dragons go to die. It's a place where dragons go to live," Darkken said. "Forever."

"You mean they can't die in there, at all?"

"As I understand it, it's not a place of strife but a place of tranquility. The dragons live in peace." Darkken shifted in his chair and twisted his rings. "It's a real world, the same as this, but only dragons exist there. You see, though dragons live a very long time, they are still mortal in this world. They can die or be killed, as we both know. But once they've served their purpose here, they can move on to another sanctuary. You see, dragons are not originally born of this world. They are from another plane, in the Land beyond the Murals. To Nalzambor, they are invaders, pretending to be protectors."

"I don't understand."

Darkken rose from his chair and walked through the chamber. His voice became that of a master storyteller, captivating and rich. "If you search the ancient texts, you will discover that Nalzambor was a very dark and dangerous place. Only the two-legged races existed, and the giants ruled. It was a world of devastation and destruction. There weren't very many good people in those dark times—mostly the elves, but even they could be jaded. But the time came when the finest of the races, desperate for salvation, put aside their pride and gathered. As one, they chose to combine their abilities to find someone or something to combat the strife and darkness that consumed them. They journeyed into the hot belly of the Mountain of Doom to seek sanctuary and work together in a collective peace. It was there that they discovered the Land beyond the Murals and opened it.

"The dragons—strong, sleek, and mighty—came forth. They battled against the terrors that ruled this world. Giants, titans, ogres, and their hordes of orcs, gnolls, and goblins were flung from their lofty perches. The ground quaked. They waged war for centuries, but the dragons finally wore the dark enemy down. Peace spread throughout the world. The land's rich soil became fertile. The hordes of evil had been pushed back into the darkness whence they came."

"Well, not all of them," Nath said. "I still see one too many orcs running around. If I were a dragon then, I'd have wiped out all of them."

"There are bigger problems than the orcs. They are just difficult, stubborn, and stupid people." Darkken stood behind Nath and patted his shoulders. "But there is more to the story."

Hanging on every word, Nath thirsted for more. He drank more wine. "I'm listening."

CHAPTER 3

Darkken and Nath moved over to a window that looked over the river to the wind-tousled grasses on the other side of the waters.

Darkken stood with his hands behind his back, chin up and a grim expression on his face. "Little brother, you need to remember that the dragons are not of this world. And Nalzambor has a strength all of its own. For it is a land rich in magic, and the magic can be used for good and evil. You see, many dragons were tainted by the temptation of evil. They moved apart from the others and lurked in darker places. They enjoyed the attention that the wicked races showed them. Many of them were worshipped as gods."

"That led to the Great Dragon Wars, didn't it?"

Darkken smiled at him. "Yes. Though the histories you read probably didn't mention that was the actual cause. One has to be careful with who wrote the history that you are reading. And that was a very dark time for the dragons. But thanks to our father, Balzurth, and his strong leadership, the black dragons that became a scourge upon this world were defeated. Nalzambor has been safe ever since. And I strongly believe that the dragons' purpose has been served. Now, the time has come for them to move on. It would be for the better."

Nath looked directly at him and asked, "For them or you?"

"For all of us." He moved to the Pool of Eversight and beckoned Nath over. He waved his hands over the clear waters of the pool, which rippled, colors taking shape within. "This is my fear, brother. The dragons have succumbed to darkness before, and I believe many are still tainted by it. They conspired against me and you because they know that we are the future of this world. As the knights in Quintuklen would say, 'It's a changing of the guard.' But they want to rule this world and not protect it. For dragons are not without their own ambition."

Nath gazed into the Pool of Eversight. The swirling image within started to sharpen into a living picture of dragons flying the skies and breathing hellish fires that scorched the earth.

"If the dragons do not depart back into the Land beyond the Murals whence they were summoned, I'm certain that history will repeat itself." Darkken's copper eyes glowed. "The black dragons will rise again, stronger than before, and if they are not defeated, what then? They will destroy the world. Nalzambor is at peace now. Order has been brought amongst the races. They've been shown how to defend their world, and thanks to the dragons, they are stronger for it. The danger now is grave. The longer the dragons stay, the more likely the races will depend on them to bail them out of their troubles, and they won't be ready for the next conflict that could consume them. Look for yourself. See what I have envisioned."

The pool revealed dragons fighting one another in the skies. Cities burned beneath their beating wings. Men, women, and children marched in desperation from the devastation that had been wrought by war. Farmlands lay in rot and ruin. Mass graves were dug in cold and clammy soil. Towns large and small burned like an inferno. The giants teamed with dragons to enslave mankind once more.

"We can't let this happen again," Nath muttered. The picture in the pool was so vivid that it made his brow sweat. "But how can you be certain that it will happen?"

"I am certain because I can see the future, and I understand the nature of men and dragons. What I have shown you is inevitable, but I am trying to prevent it." He passed his hands over the waters. The image faded back to a clear pool of water that rippled gently then stopped. "I need your help, Nath. Together, we can do this and avoid the coming bloodshed." He reached over and grabbed Nath's wrists. "Join me! We can make Nalzambor a perfect place."

Nath shook his head. He yearned to believe his brother and wanted to join his cause. Not fully convinced, he asked, "But how?"

CHAPTER 4

WITH HIS BEARDED FACE SET against the southern winds, Hacksaw traveled all day and late into the night. The old knight slept away from the road, underneath the trees, rising before the call of the morning birds and heading down the roads again. The grizzled veteran of countless battles rode a chestnut steed with a shiny coat. He wore his one shirt of ring mail underneath a leather traveling tunic. On his hip, his sword, Green Tongue, the goblin slayer, rested in its scabbard, ready to go.

Hacksaw puffed on his pipe made from unicorn horn. An airy smoke was quickly taken away by the winds. He was not certain whether or not the pipe had been made from a unicorn's horn. After all, only a few men and women ever claimed to see them. But one thing was certain: the pipe had magic within, and it saved him.

He took a deep breath and let out a stiff cough. Despite having been saved by the knight clerics of Quintuklen's Legionnaires, Hacksaw was still sore and tender. The dark elves calling themselves the Brothers of the Wind had butchered him with a dozen arrows. Certain his fate was sealed, the last thought Hacksaw had was of going home. Instead, he was taken to the Legionnaires' Hall of Knights and brought back from the brink of death.

Cardinals and blue jays flew across the road before him and vanished in the forest. A stir started in the branches. A sharp chirping and angry fluttering of wings followed. Hacksaw's shoulders slumped, and one hand on the reins, he swayed gently in the saddle. Then he sped the horse to a trot, thinking once again of the death he'd dodged.

Thanks to the power of the pipe, he'd fooled old man death once again. The pipe, a gift from his father passed down from his grandfather, had been little more than a toy that lit tobacco on its own. But he remembered that when he was a young fella, able to sit on his grandfather's knee, his grandfather talked about the unicorn he felled. His grandfather said he'd killed it with an arrow that would slay anything and that he made the pipe himself. Of course, he had no proof to the story—no unicorn hide or mane, no hooves or teeth, just a story. But his grandfather swore up and down the pipe had a very deep and special magic. His grandfather died when Hacksaw was young. That story was the last thing he remembered of his grandfather, who had hard hands, a bushy beard, kind eyes, and a smile that warmed the cold taverns of Huskan.

Hacksaw blew out a ring of smoke, looked to the sky, and said, "You were right, Grandfather."

As for his father, a hard-working man who never smoked nor carried the pipe, he passed it on to Hacksaw when he became a legionnaire. His father, a stalwart laborer that cut down trees for a living, said, "Take this pipe of your grandfather's. Keep it with you for safety and comfort on your journeys."

Hacksaw never saw his father alive again after that. He perished in a logging accident. Hacksaw, on a mission at the time, didn't get word until long after it happened, and his father's body was burned to ash along with the wood that took him. In Huskan, such burials were often customary.

Now, Hacksaw rode alone with a dreadful feeling hanging over him like a great shadow. He'd abandoned Nath when he should have stayed close to the young man. As a result, he'd almost died for it. But now, he still lived, thanks to a mystic bauble that his family had blessed him with. It saved him once before, but he doubted it would save him again. In his gut, he felt it had saved him so he could complete his mission. He had to find Nath and warn him. He just hoped he wouldn't be too late when he found him.

Traveling at a brisk pace, he finally made it all the way down to Advent. The time was midday, and the winter frost had left the city, but the early-spring winds still had a bite to them. He led his horse through the streets, spying all his surroundings, keeping a sharp eye out for elves. Not seeing anything out of the ordinary, he moved block after block through the sizeable city, passing the storefront porches. Singing and string playing caught his ears.

He tied his horse to a hitching post, walked up the steps to a porch, and entered a tavern filled almost to capacity. Hacksaw pushed his way in, took a stool, and sat at the bar. He ordered a pint of ale and took a look over his shoulder. On a low stage, Homer, now called Rome, sat on a stool, singing a love ballad and playing a twelve-stringed lute. His fingers moved over the strings with the nimbleness of a pixie. His soprano voice, as enchanting as a dove song, carried through the tavern, where dreamy-eyed women swooned.

Hacksaw grunted. Homer was a pleasant-looking fellow, slight in build, with soft eyes and elegant features. His short tousled hair was light brown, and he'd grown sideburns to the bottoms of his ears. The bard was not alone. On either side of him was a pair of elves. One strummed a cello with his bow, while the other blew into a wooden flute. Luckily, he did not recognize their faces. They weren't the ones that had tried to kill him on the river. Them, he would've recognized. But he was certain of one thing: judging by their dark eyes and hair, he knew they were Caligin.

He guzzled half of his ale and wiped a sleeve across his mouth. He drank again. After days of riding on little more than water, the ale tasted very good. He ordered another, kept his back to the stage, and contemplated.

I need to separate Homer from the elves. He patted the pommel of Green Tongue. *If I have to kill them, then I'm going to.*

Chapter 5

Back inside Lord Darkken's study, he and Nath continued the discussion back at the table.

Darkken pulled back Nath's chair, seated him, then sat down himself. "You see, Nath, this is where the Brothers of the Wind come into play. My time in Nalzambor has been well spent. Here in the keep, I've found the elves most devoted to Nalzambor to serve my cause. Over the decades—well, centuries, actually—I've built up my own army. They serve as common citizens, serving among the people, offering assistance. They help the needy and downtrodden, and they are watchdogs for trouble. Ultimately, they are where they are to be peacekeepers. Would you like more wine?"

"No."

"Something else, perhaps? I'm getting hungry, and after that last ordeal, I think I'm getting famished."

"Do what you will, Darkken. I'm just listening." Though hunger was nagging Nath's gut, he still wanted to hear everything Darkken had to say. His brother was putting all of the larger pieces of the puzzle together, but some small pieces were missing, and Nath didn't want to miss anything. "Go on."

"The objective is simple, assuming that it is well executed. We are the glue that keeps the races from fighting and warring with one another. We divert them from travesty by being a positive influence." Darkken smiled. "What we need to do is strengthen our position with the higher cities and influence the smaller ones. When we have determined that all is in order, we can present our work to Balzurth."

Nath disagreed. "But we are banished. He will not hear a word that we say."

"You are banished one hundred years, correct?"

"Yes." Nath nodded. "But three years have passed."

"Little brother, what I am talking about might take one hundred years, and at that point, then you can show our work to the dragons. After all, what is one hundred years in a dragon's lifetime?"

Nath raised an eyebrow. "You are willing to wait that long?"

"I waited one hundred years to get you out. I can wait another." Darkken lifted a finger. "Though I would like to see this mission completed sooner. I just feel the longer the dragons are here, the more subject they will be to temptation. That's why I've sought the artifacts so that we can use dragon steel. If dark dragons rise, we can use it as a weapon against them. We are going to need every resource available to use if we are to match the dragons." He rubbed the copper rings on his middle and index fingers. "I would be lying if I said that I didn't have a sense of urgency, but I feel a tingle all over when I talk about it."

"Do you really think we need dragon steel?"

"Even my elven-blade scalpel is not a match for all dragons. Some of them have scales too hard to be cut even with enchanted weapons. Other dragons are like ghosts and shadows. They walk between one world and another. Few weapons can touch them, but dragon steel can. Fang is made from the rarest metals"—his eyes hung on the sword—"but that is your gift to bear, not mine."

Nath glanced back at Fang, propped up against the wall. Like the lone burning candle in the room, it outshone everything else. He fastened his eyes on Darkken. "Father made that sword for you, didn't he?"

Darkken smirked. With a slight shrug, he said, "Let's just say that Fang was under construction long before you were born. Whether or not the sword was made for me specifically, I cannot say. But the sword is yours now, brother. I'd never try to lay claim to it." He wagged a finger. "However, I would desire to have a similar sword made from dragon steel, myself." He moved to Fang and leaned over the blade. Stretching out his hand, he asked, "May I?"

"Certainly."

Darkken lifted the sword by the handle and grimaced. His eyebrows knitted together. He moved away from the wall and spun the sword by the pommel. He turned the weapon, ran his fingers over the wide blade, and flicked the sharp edge of the metal. *Ting.* The sword hummed.

He smiled. "It's a living weapon that sings. I can feel great magic within it. It flows into me from the warmth of the handle. I've never held nor seen the likes of it." He held the blade out before himself and gazed upon it with hungry eyes. "Simply marvelous."

"It's a true friend," Nath said and swallowed. His fingers flicked at his sides. Watching Darkken holding his sword made the hairs on his neck rise, but Fang did not bring Darkken any harm as he'd suspected. He'd figured only he could hold the blade, but perhaps others with the right hearts and minds could as well. "You should have one like it."

Darkken spun the sword behind his back and switched to the other hand before leaning the sword back against the wall. Rubbing his hands together, he said, "In all honesty, I'm not the swordsman that I once was. Master Elween exposed that of which I am ashamed."

"Well, she is the master."

"True. I could have done better, but over the last few decades, I've been focusing more on the mastery of magic." A blue glowing ball of energy formed in his hand. It turned from one ball into four, and he started juggling them. The balls made trails of wispy flame behind them. He caught them all in one hand, and they disappeared. "Because we are creatures of magic, like the wizards of this world, manipulating it is not so difficult. That is where I have concentrated my efforts the most of late. And I've taught Maefon a great deal too. I'm an excellent teacher." He walked over to Nath and put his arm over his shoulders. Darkken turned Nath toward the books in the shelves. "What will you use when you don't have a sword or a weapon of another sort? Hmm?"

"My wits," Nath said.

Darkken tossed his head back and laughed. "Ha! There isn't a sharper weapon in the armory than the mind. But with magic, you can amplify it a hundred times. What do you say, Nath? How about I teach a little bit about yourself that you didn't know you had in you."

Nath looked at his empty hands. He envisioned balls of fiery energy forming inside of them. He nodded and said, "Let's do it."

CHAPTER 6

HACKSAW DRANK AND ATE AT a steady pace while Homer kept singing for another two hours.

The bustling crowd cried out, "Encore! Encore!"

That led Homer to belt out three more songs, which took another thirty minutes. By that time, Hacksaw's belly had begun to bulge farther over his belt as he finished half of a lemon cream pie. If he had one weakness that assailed him in his older years, it was enjoying good food. The ale and pumpkin cider, he managed to hold off on, but tasty food was a different story. That was why he kept himself busy.

Finally, Homer and the two elves gave their final farewell to the crowd, and a sea-blue curtain was pulled closed in front of them.

Hacksaw gulped. He hadn't accounted for decorative curtains to be closed. As the cheerful crowd dispersed, he left his payment on the bar and made his way up to the stage. Moving to the side, where the men were drawing the curtains shut, he moved up the steps and peeked behind the veil. Homer and the elves were long gone. They'd left their instruments on the stage. The strange thing was that Homer didn't see any exit from the stage except for the curtain. He hustled across the small stage, where he saw an outline in the floor. He knelt and traced his fingers along the edges.

"I'll be. A trapdoor."

Hacksaw considered his options for a couple minutes. He figured there was a back way out through the cellar. His best move might have been to move outside and track them from the back end. His other option was to drop down the hatch and see if he could catch up to their tracks. Either way, he just didn't want to spook them. And at least now, he knew what to expect. Seeing how Homer was so popular, catching up with him later shouldn't be hard. He shook his head.

"No, time's a-pressing."

He grabbed ahold of the finger holds in the trapdoor and lifted it up. Quickly, he slid into the opening and climbed down the stairs, letting the trapdoor shut above him. The tavern cellar wasn't a very deep room. Its ceiling was only about six feet high, and he had to stoop. The walls ran the width and length of the tavern. Shelves stood along the walls, deep and stocked up. Barrels of wine and ale, large and small, lay stacked on the floor. Oil lanterns hung from the support posts, flickering with low-burning flames. He didn't see any sign of Homer and the elves.

He scratched his scruffy beard, let out a burp, and sauntered deeper into the cellar, looking for the way out. At the back end, he saw a loading ramp and a wooden set of stairs running alongside it. A double cellar door waited at the top, one side still open. Hacksaw nodded to himself and started up the stairs. A lower step groaned beneath his foot, and the sharp pressure of a dagger point dug into his back.

"Lords of Thunder," he murmured.

"Fasten those hands to the rafters," a male elven voice said.

Hacksaw locked his fingers on the wooden beams above his head. Without seeing who was there, he was certain they were the elves accompanying Homer. While one elf kept a dagger on his back, a second elf patted him down and took off his sword belt. He locked eyes with the second elf, who had a rounder face and darker skin than most of the ones he'd seen. The elf glared at him then darted out of sight.

"What are you looking for?" asked the elf holding a dagger at his back.

"I just wanted to meet the great bard, Rome. I'm a tremendous fan of his talents. I came a long way just to hear him."

"Men are such bad liars," the elf behind him said to the other.

"You have the right," the other elf replied. "Bad liars."

Not wanting to beat around the bush, Hacksaw called out in a strong voice, "Homer, I know you are in here. Are you going to let these elves speak for you, or are you going to speak for yourself? Huh?"

From a position deeper in the cellar, Homer spoke out and said, "Actually, I was going to let them do the talking for me, as my throat is dry from all of the singing. I think I can manage now. Dule and Roday, I want you to meet a, well, a former colleague of mine."

The elf behind him said, "I'm Roday. Make sure you get it right."

The darker-skinned elf leaned in front of his face and said, "And I'm Dule. You know that's right."

"Turn him around," Homer said. "I want a closer look at my old ally that has returned from the dead." His eyes widened when he got a closer look at Hacksaw. "This is Hacksaw, a retired legionnaire and former friend of Nath."

"I'm still his friend, and clearly you are not if you're in league with elves that smell like Caligin," Hacksaw replied.

"We prefer Brothers of the Wind now," Dule said.

"Yes, Caligin isn't very warming," Roday added.

With his slender hands clasped together, Homer said, "Brethren, it doesn't matter, and I'm certain that Hacksaw doesn't care."

"You are right about that," Hacksaw said. "A snake is still a snake no matter what you call it."

"Ew, that stung a little," Roday said. "And you don't even know me."

"You're the one with a dagger in my back."

"Touché," Roday replied.

With a serene look, Homer came forward and said, "As much as I would like to embrace your gruff exterior, I won't. You'd probably bite my ear off." He shook his head. "You shouldn't have come back to Advent, Hacksaw. What were you thinking? Did you really think the Caligin would let you slip through their fingers and just forget about you? Wherever you were, you should have stayed there. Now, I have to get my hands dirty. My own neck is at risk."

Snarling, Hacksaw said, "You little worm. Nath saved you from Slavertown."

"No, you were there. Lord Darkken is the one that did that, not Nath."

"It was Nath's money that brought your freedom."

"No, it was Darkken's moxie and persuasion. It would have boded you well to embrace it." Homer sighed. "I hate to be the one to do this to you, but what must be done must be done." He gave a quick nod.

Hacksaw sprang at Homer, but the elves were quicker. The well-placed pommel of a dagger cracked him in the back of the head. He saw stars, then the cellar turned black. He hit the ground hard with a thud.

Chapter 7

Brenwar, Slivver, and Master Elween traveled together underneath gray skies toward Stonewater Keep. Brenwar rode on his pony, while Slivver and Elween were in full dragon form. Standing a full seven feet tall, they walked afoot like men but with an awkward gait in their otherwise serpentine bodies. Slivver's scales were a coat of shiny silver coins, and Elween's scales, in contrast, were a rich evergreen reminiscent of the forest. Slivver watched with a map unrolled in his hands. It was one of the maps they'd found in an abandoned wagon. Elween led the way, with Brenwar bringing up the rear.

"You've been consumed with that map since we started walking," Brenwar said. "But you haven't said a word. Perhaps I should take a look at it."

"No, I assure you, I am plenty astute in being able to interpret them myself," Slivver replied. He didn't even lift his head when he spoke. "It seems that they are marking spots in search of treasure and artifacts. Back at Old Hen, they sought out a great mausoleum at a place called Cemetery Valley. There is another place, a small island in the Faalum Sea. The Ruins are marked, and so is another southern town called Bergion. At least there is a symbol of a staff there. It seems that Darkken likes to hoard special items. It makes sense for a sorcerer to pursue such things."

Elween drifted back and asked, "What do you mean?"

Slivver rolled up the scroll and tucked it underneath his arm. "It's only a theory, but I would assume that since Darkken had his wings clipped, so to speak, he would choose to strengthen his own natural powers. Since we are creatures of magic, it would not be difficult for him to master it himself. I see no reason why he couldn't become one of the greatest sorcerers that ever lived. After all, he'll live as long as a dragon, and time is on his side. I can only imagine that, over the last couple of centuries, he's been strengthening his magic."

Elween gave him a worried look. "Come to think of it, he did teleport Nath and the elven woman out of your sight in a blink of an eye. He slung me aside like a child's doll. I felt great power in him."

"I felt it too," Slivver admitted.

Brenwar jumped back into the conversation. "And I smote him with my hammer! I've leveled giants into their graves with a blow like that. He withstood it." He grumbled. Clawing at his beard, he said, "Perhaps I just glanced him."

Slivver shook his head. "No, we cannot underestimate Darkken and his powers. This is not some mortal but a dragon that, one could argue, has immortal blood in him. By the dragons, if he were to win Nath over, it could be catastrophic for Nalzambor. They would be men without limitations."

"I agree with your concern," Elween said, "but even their own bodies have limitations.

They would need a vessel to control omnipotent magic. I didn't see Darkken wielding anything but a sword, and there was no magic in that. It was just elven steel."

"True," Slivver said.

"You make it sound like Darkken doesn't have a weakness," Brenwar said. "Everything has a weakness."

Slivver nodded. "Again, true, but Darkken has been a step ahead of us at every turn. To beat him, we are going to have to get a step ahead of him. We need to find out what he is trying to do."

"Are you suggesting that we don't move on Stonewater Keep? Certainly, we will find some answers there that we need," Elween said.

"Darkken is going to fully expect us to head right for the keep. He'll be watching." Slivver glanced upward as Brenwar did the same. "He probably has eyes on us already. I'm all for heading toward the keep, but before we do anything else, we must plan carefully. Darkken's fooled us once by shapeshifting into Nath. It wouldn't surprise me if he tried the same trick again."

Brenwar urged his pony ahead and said in a gusty voice, "Well, I guess I'll just have to capture all of Nath's dragons, and you'll have to sort them out later."

CHAPTER 8

NATH KNOCKED ON THE DOOR of Maefon's private quarters. She was standing inside, changing the sheets on her bed. She didn't look at him as she spread the woolen comforter over the top and set the pillows.

"May I come in?" he asked.

She shrugged. "I guess. Is your private meeting with Lord Darkken over?"

Stepping into the room, he said, "Are you upset?"

"Why would I be upset? After all, I'm not part of your family. I've only been serving it faithfully for over fifty years."

He gently took her by the elbow and turned her toward himself. "Now, that isn't fair."

Avoiding his eyes, she wiggled her head a little and said with her bottom lip out, "I suppose not."

"You're pouting."

"I don't pout."

He bent his head down and raised an eyebrow.

"Perhaps I'm pouting. So what if I am? I just don't like being left out." Finally, she looked up into his eyes, a smile warming her beautiful face. Her fingers crawled up his chest and fastened around his neck. "It's not fair," she said with bated breath.

"What isn't fair?"

"Your eyes melt my heart like the flame above a candle." She rose up on tiptoe and kissed him fully.

Nath caught her up in his arms. The long kiss started his heart racing. He tossed her onto the bed.

Maefon let out a delightful squeal as he climbed on top of her. He kissed her all over her neck. She started giggling. "Will you stop that? It tickles me."

"What does? This?" He kissed her again and again.

"That's enough!" she said while laughing. "Enough, Nath. I didn't want to do this now."

He was over top of her with her body pinned beneath him. "You started this, not me. What did you expect?"

She brushed her hair from her eyes and said, "I know, I know. But I haven't even bathed yet." Staring deep into his eyes, she caressed his face with her fingertips. "So tell me, why did you come down here? I figured that you and Darkken would be talking much longer."

"We decided that we needed a break. He filled my ears plenty."

"Oh," Maefon said, sliding out from underneath him. She sat on the side of the bed and patted the spot beside her, where Nath took his place. She held his hand in both of hers. "Go on."

"I don't think there is anything secret that you don't know. He wants to teach me magic, like you. He answered all of my questions fully, but I still have concerns that are lingering."

"Really? Like what?"

"It wasn't so long ago that we took this keep from Chazzan. I thought that he was the leader of the Caligin, but it seems that Darkken has been leading them all along. The entire time, I was led to believe otherwise. But I didn't confront him on that point."

Maefon nodded. "I think Darkken is embarrassed by his failure with Chazzan. And I think Chazzan was mad at him. Chazzan, to say the least, was cocky. It didn't surprise me a bit that he would try to take over the Caligin when Darkken and I pursued you. He had many elves that were very loyal to him. And even though he was no match for Darkken at face value, the acquisition of artifacts could swing fortune in his favor."

"So, you think that Chazzan wanted to get the artifacts before Darkken did? So that he could take over the Caligin?"

"It doesn't seem unlikely." She squeezed his hand. "Listen, Darkken is a lonely man, a spurned child, you might say. That is why he is so passionate about his mission. He needs elves that he can trust. When Chazzan deceived him, I can only imagine how much it must have hurt him." She leaned into him. "Just between the two of us, Darkken isn't perfect, but he thinks he is. He's very hard on himself when he makes mistakes."

"I know that feeling." Nath's stomach growled. "And that feeling."

Maefon giggled as she got up. "Why don't you lie down and relax, and I'll get us some food to eat."

"I don't know." He started to get up.

She pushed him back down. "Stay." She lit some candles and incense that were on the dressers in the room. "Close your eyes, and I'll be back soon." She kissed his forehead. "Rest."

With a heavy heart, Maefon took the steps up to catch Darkken in his study. Though she wasn't entirely certain, Nath seemed to be buying into her and Darkken's stories. What worried her was that what she had said and what Darkken had said didn't match. She found him waiting in his study chamber, standing by the window and drinking wine. She knocked on the open door.

"Please, Maefon, come in, and close the door behind you," he said.

She closed the door, walked up to him, and bowed.

Darkken wrapped her up in a bear hug. "I don't think that I've ever had to lie as much in a conversation as I did today. Even for me, it was exhausting."

Hugging him back, she replied, "I did the same. I just wanted to size up our stories." She gave a quick review of her and Nath's conversation as the hugging broke off. "I hope I said the right things."

Darkken pinched her chin between a thumb and finger and said, "I couldn't have said it better myself. So, do you think he is buying into my story?"

"There's plenty of truth to sell the lie."

He smiled at her. "I taught you well."

"So if he keeps asking questions?"

He placed her small face in the palms of his big hands, looked her right in the eye, and said, "He is still young and naïve. He'll believe. Just lie your rear end off."

CHAPTER 9

HACKSAW REGAINED CONSCIOUSNESS. HE'D BEEN hog-tied. The bindings on his hands and feet dug deep into his ankles and wrists. That wasn't the worst part of it. Covering his head was a burlap sack that smelled like manure. The air he breathed in was hot and rank. Also, he was jostling, being tossed roughly from side to side. He was in a wagon riding a rough road, and he had enough of his senses to know they were going upward.

I can't believe they got me. I should've gutted them the first chance I had. Bloody elves. I swear they must have goblin in them.

He had to wrestle with his failure the entire ride, which became more agonizing by the minute. The only comfort he had came from the stiff breezes from the north, which rustled the branches in the trees. At least he was outside, in the open air, and not buried alive in a grave. He was thankful for that even though that might be where he was headed.

I should have made my move later, but I hate second-guessing myself. I went with my gut. It failed me.

He listened for voices but was met only with silence. The stench from the sack on hi head blocked out any other smells around him. If he had to guess, he was probably cap of at least a half dozen of the spooky elves. He could imagine the stone-grim expressi their cold faces. He hated them. From the moment he'd seen them, he knew a dark evil lurked within them. He should have trusted his gut then. Instead, he stood by Nath and was too late when he tried to depart. That was when the elves came to kill him. Now, they were going to kill him again. Probably make an example out of him.

I probably should have died the first time.

The wagon rocked and rolled. Finally, it came to a long stop. He heard the wagon groan as it teetered to one side. The sound of footsteps caught his ears. Whoever it was wasn't being quiet about their business, but they weren't talking either. Someone he couldn't see climbed into the wagon. Strong hands grabbed him by the legs and started to pull him out of the wagon.

Hacksaw felt his legs dangle off the edge, then rough hands pushed him out of the wagon. He hit the ground with another loud thud. He stayed limp and didn't moan, wanting them to think he was still out cold. His best chance to get the jump on them would come if he lay still. Overconfident, his captors might let their guard down. Then he would spring. If he was going to die, he was going to die fighting. He vowed to kill at least one. That would serve to make the world a better place.

Two people hooked his arms and dragged him facedown over the rough terrain. Hacksaw fully expected to be pushed off a cliff or dropped into a grave. Instead, whoever had him propped him up against the hard bark of a tree. Someone ripped the sack off the top of his head. He let his chin sag into his chest but breathed deeply through his nostrils.

"Oh, come now, we know that you are fully awake," a voice said. It was the elf, Roday, speaking in a sarcastic and distinct voice. "Don't play games, Hacksaw. We have some more chatting to do."

A moment of silence passed.

"Dule, do it."

"I'd be glad to," Dule replied in a cocky voice.

Sharp fingernails bit into the skin on Hacksaw's forearm. It hurt like the dickens, but he didn't move.

"Pinch him again," Roday said.

Another fierce pinch came. Still, Hacksaw remained still.

"I think he's dead, Roday," Dule said.

When the elf spoke, Hacksaw felt his breath on his face. Unable to contain his emerging rage, he lunged forward and busted the elf in the side of the jaw with his skull, which made a loud smack. Hacksaw popped his eyes open and yelled, "You better believe I'm not dead! But the two of you are going to be!"

Dule rolled away. He popped up with a sword in one hand, holding the side of his face with the other. "What did you do that for, bearded geezer?"

It was night, and Hacksaw's eyes adjusted to the dark. "I'm not going to go down to the likes of you without fighting! I challenge the pair of you! I'll fight you barehanded if I have to. I'll kill the both of you!"

Roday came to his feet and said, "Just hold on, Brisky Britches. First, you aren't going to be fighting anyone."

"Because you are cowards!"

"No, because then, my partner, sweet sabre, and I would have to kill you."

Dule and Roday bumped fists. Smiling and thumbing his nose, Dule said, "You know that is right."

Roday continued. "And second, we didn't bring you all the way out here to kill you when we could have just done it back in Advent. By the way, you are very heavy. An older man like you should really watch his weight. It felt like we were lifting a pregnant heifer into the wagon. Poor Dule strained his back."

Rubbing his back with his free hand, Dule said, "It's still sore. You're too heavy."

"What are you two pointy-eared lunatics talking about?" Hacksaw wriggled in his bindings. "I'll not be slaughtered by two babbling fools. Let me out of these bonds. I'll just bury myself."

Roday waved his hands. "No, no, no, you don't understand, Hacksaw. We aren't going to kill you. We don't like blood on our hands. It's too sticky."

"And messy," Dule added.

"Yes, our job is done here," Roday said.

A stir in the woodland behind him caused him to turn his head. Someone or something was coming. It was big and moved slowly, and the brittle branches that had fallen in the winter crunched underneath heavy feet.

Roday stepped aside. "Now, it's his turn."

From the darkness, a hulking seven-foot monster emerged.

Hacksaw's jaw dropped. His hot blood ran cold. "Impossible."

Chapter 10

"Nath, words cannot express how elated I am that you've decided to come with me," Lord Darkken said.

Early-morning sunlight shone through the windows of his study chamber. He was leaning over a table and rolling up the scroll they'd recovered from Cemetery Valley in the gargantuan crypt. It had the secret of dragon steel inscribed on it. He tucked it underneath his arm. "I swear you will not regret it. It shall be a great learning experience."

"It's *been* a great learning experience," Nath said.

He and Maefon were together. Both had had a light meal for breakfast before Darkken summoned them. Maefon and he had talked at length during the night, and she eased his concerns.

He put Fang in a scabbard and slung the weapon over his shoulder. "But I don't want to see anyone else getting hurt if I can avoid it."

Darkken gave him a concerned look. "I don't take your meaning."

Nath cast a knowing look at Maefon. He held her hand and said, "Well, last night, we had a long talk about many things. Maefon seems to believe that if Slivver and Master Elween were to show up at the keep, you would try to kill them." He locked eyes with Darkken. "You would, wouldn't you?"

"I wouldn't have a choice. And they are very dangerous." Darkken grabbed his sword belt from the table and buckled it around his waist. "They aren't going to listen to me, and they want to take control of you. I'm not about to let that happen when we are so close to an excellent opportunity to bring peace. I want all of us to get along, but I know in my heart they won't listen."

"You shouldn't have to kill them," Nath said. "That would be wrong."

"I could imprison them. I'm just not that certain that these walls could hold them." Darkken calmly walked up to Nath and rested his hands on his shoulders. "Assuming that they seek us out at the keep, I'd be willing to wait. We could have a negotiation. But it will prove a waste of time. And if words become weapons, I'm not going to hold back against them."

Nath held his brother's gaze and nodded. He and Maefon had thoroughly hashed out several scenarios. One thing he'd learned from Darkken was that he was merciless when threatened. And he had the power to back it up. He'd seen Darkken wipe out a mind flayer. He'd had Slivver and Master Elween defeated. A blow from a hammer had barely jarred the man. No, Darkken had great power, and Nath didn't understand the source of it, but it was scary. Not to mention that he teleported himself, Nath, and Maefon leagues away from danger with ease. He came to the conclusion that the best way to keep his friends out of harm's way was to get Darkken as far away from them as possible.

"And if they come to the keep," Nath asked, "are the Brothers of the Wind going to stand against them?"

"Our brothers are going to defend the keep with their lives. It's what they are sworn to do. It's no different from the dragons defending the Mountain of Doom." Darkken sighed. "As long as they don't pose a threat, no harm will come to them. I can assure you of that. But I don't think Slivver is going to take their word for it. At best, the brothers can tell them we are not here, and if they want to find us, they'll just have to start looking elsewhere."

That was the best Nath could hope for. As dangerous as the Brothers of the Wind were, he was confident that Slivver and Elween could handle them. And the dwarf seemed plenty formidable on his own.

Nath nodded and said, "I don't want any harm to come to them."

Darkken walked over to the table and found some parchment, a quill, and ink. Sarcastically, he said, "Why don't you write them a note, then? It could say, 'Dear Slivver and Elween, I am not inside. Please go away. Sincerely, Nath Dragon.'"

"Fine. Fine," Nath said with a frown.

Maefon gripped his hand. "We have to live or die with the choices we make. It's no different with them."

Darkken set down the quill and parchment. "Well said. Shall we get on with it, then? We have a very long journey ahead. But hopefully, the trip won't take that long."

"Where are we going?" Nath asked.

"North. To the Faluum Sea."

Nath's eyes grew big. "That's going to be a long journey. And if we travel by horse, Slivver and Elween won't have any trouble finding us."

"No doubt. That is why we won't be traveling by foot, horse, or wagon, like some sort of commoner. We'll be teleporting there the same way that I teleported us all here."

Looking at the bracelet Darkken had given him, he said, "You can take us that far with one spell." He noticed even Maefon's eyes had grown big.

"It's not the distance so much as it is a matter of having a clear picture of where we are going." Darkken moved over to the Pool of Eversight. "And I have the pool as well as this little bauble that enhances my power." From a pouch hanging from his sword belt, he fished out something wrapped in black silk cloth. He let the object slip from the silk into his hand and held it up for all to see. An oval diamond shone like a bright and pink star. "Behold, the Star of the Heavens."

Nath squinted. Maefon shielded her eyes. He caught her as her knees buckled. The hairs on his arms stood on end. He lost his breath. The diamond contained magic that tickled the marrow in his bones.

"It's marvelous," Maefon said in awe. She eased toward it with her hand outstretched.

Darkken gave her hand a smack. "No, no. You aren't ready for this yet." He covered it up and tucked it away. Then he wiggled her chin. "Be patient."

Nath caught his breath and said, "I've never felt something so beautiful."

Rubbing her eyes, Maefon said, "Me either. No offense."

"It's very special. Now, let's get down to business." Darkken waved a hand over the Pool of Eversight.

The calm waters rippled and colored, and an image took form, of an island set against the punishing waves of the sea.

"Because it's such a long distance, I'll exercise caution and do this one at a time." He grabbed Nath and Maefon by the hands, forming a circle.

His eyes glowed with radiant intensity. The bracelets glowed on all of their wrists.

"Ladies first."

With his blood racing as if charged by lightning, Nath watched Maefon disappear in a wink.

"See you in a moment, brother," Darkken said.

With his eyes locked on Darkken's, he felt a charge shoot through him. Darkken vanished. Nath stood empty-handed in the stinging rain and gusting wind, searching for Maefon.

Before Darkken departed, he summoned one of the Caligin. One swarthy elf armored in black leather entered, took a knee, and bowed.

"Deterus, I leave you in charge. If the keep has any visitors, destroy them with any means necessary I have left at your disposal. Don't leave a speck of them to be found on this earth."

Deterus nodded. "As you wish, Lord of the Dark in the Day."

Chapter 11

With his heart shooting inside his throat, Hacksaw watched Roday and Dule step aside as the four-armed abomination came. The monster lumbered closer, heavy arms slowly swinging at its sides. The eyes of the hairless creatures were sunken. It had big pointed ears and pale, pasty skin, with black lips revealing decaying teeth. Partially covered in forest overgrowth, it was something Hacksaw had never seen before.

"At least give me a fighting chance at this thing, you cowardly elves!" he yelled.

The monster stood over Hacksaw, looking down on him with dull eyes. The muscles bulged in its massive shoulders. Its breath was heavy and wet. Drool dripped from the corner of its mouth onto Hacksaw's leg.

Hacksaw tried to scoot away. Instead, he fell over on his side. Strong hands picked him up from behind, lifting him up to his feet as if he were a child. He faced away from his assailants and could feel four hands locked onto his body.

"If you're going to kill me, then get it over with. I don't have time for all of this drama! But I'd like to look my enemy in the eye before I…" His voice trailed off.

Another person approached from the dark folds of the forest. It was a woman with a bewitching figure and a head full of wavy hair down over her shoulders. Her captivating eyes drew him in and stole his breath.

Still, he managed to say, "You."

The woman stood right in front of him with her hands on her curvy hips. All she wore was a revealing tunic-like dress made from grasses woven like armor. Her eyes burned into Hacksaw when she said, "Have you forgotten my name so soon?"

"Calypsa," he said, blinking hard. "So you are one of them. And you've come to feast on me." He whipped his head back. "This is that bugbear, Rond, isn't it? I thought he looked familiar, but his body shambles, and that rodent hair of his is gone. I guess I'm tribute to your Lord of the Dark in the Day."

She filled her hands with both sides of his beard, looked him dead in the eye, and said, "Hacksaw, that's not a very fond greeting, but it's good to see you too." She rubbed noses with him. "I could kiss you, but you might not wake up for days."

"What?" he said with a furrowed brow. "You aren't going to kill me?"

"Kill you? I'm elated to see you in this dark time." She let go of his beard and stepped back. "Rond, loosen our friend's bonds."

Rond moaned.

"Do as I say, please. Hacksaw is a friend," she said.

Rond held Hacksaw with two hands and undid his bindings with the others. His tugging was fierce and painful.

"It would be easier if you would cut it with a knife!" Hacksaw said. "He's about to rip my hands off."

"Apologies," she said with a pleasant laugh. "Rond is not as able as he once was, having been brought back from the dead. I sometimes forget about that."

Dule and Roday slipped over and untied the bonds. The ropes fell free, and the elves stepped away. Roday started coiling up the rope.

Rubbing his wrists, Hacksaw moved away from the group. His fingers stung as blood started to flow into them. He eyed the group standing right across from him. Rond was a mountain beside them all. The bugbear, once a creature rich with vibrant life, now existed in a deteriorating condition. He moved but did not seem to live. Calypsa was the same vision that she had been before, but she had a hardness about her that hadn't existed before. Roday and Dule, he just didn't know what to make of. Eyes sweeping across his surroundings, he looked for his sword or anything that he could defend himself with.

"Tell me what is going on," Hacksaw said.

"We are going after Nath." Her eyes narrowed. "And taking vengeance on Darkken and that witch, Maefon. She killed Rond and nearly killed me. It was my mother, the Mother Queen of the Dryads, Yasmela, that breathed life back into me, but I can't say the same for Rond. He lives but not as he did."

"When did this happen?" Hacksaw asked.

"As soon as I departed from Nath, the Caligin came right after me." Anger filled her voice. "Maefon will pay. I swear it. I'll rip her head off myself."

"Well, the same happened to me, the moment I left Advent," Hacksaw said. "I don't think they were going to kill me, but when I turned back toward the city, they held nothing back." He eyed the elves. "Which doesn't explain why you are in the company of these two fiends. They are Caligin, through and through."

"Former Caligin," Dule said.

"Ha! If that's the case, then why did you snatch me out of Advent?" Hacksaw said.

Rolling his neck, Dule replied, "We were saving you, grandpa. And it's a good thing that Homer saw you too, or first, because the Caligin are looking for you. We had to get you out of town before you contacted Homer. Lucky for you, none of our efforts were spotted."

Hacksaw looked at Calypsa and asked, "You trust them?"

She nodded. "I too went to Advent in disguise and made contact with Homer. Homer is still on Nath's side but not saying so. The Caligin watch him. Darkken told him so long as he stays in line, no harm will come to him, but if he does anything he shouldn't, it will be the end of him as well as the people that he cares about."

"That's why he stayed in Advent," Roday said. "He's playing along. Lord Darkken sent us away from Nath and assigned us to Homer in Advent. We're supposed to report anything suspicious back to Darkken. But we don't follow Darkken anymore. We like Nath."

The pair of elves fist bumped.

"That's right," Dule said. "Darkken is insane. And I'll die before living another day to serve him. On my elven blood, I swear it."

"We both do," Roday added.

"Your words mean as much as an orc's." Hacksaw looked around. "Where's my sword?"

Dule fetched the sword belt from the woodland. He handed it over to Hacksaw without a word.

"And my pipe?" he added.

Roday fished the pipe out of his clothing and hand it to Hacksaw.

Hacksaw put the pipe in his mouth and buckled on his sword belt, then he eyed his new companions and asked, "Where's my horse?"

CHAPTER 12

BY THE TIME DARKKEN ARRIVED, Nath and Maefon were soaking wet from the drenching rain splattering against their bodies. The heavy winds made the trees bend and sway. The surrounding thickets rustled. With the icy rain hitting his face, Darkken spoke over the thundering wind. "A beautiful place, isn't it?"

"Where in Nalzambor is this place?" Nath asked as he turned his back to the wind and rain and flung his hair out of his eyes. "It's miserable!"

"It's only a storm. The winds will calm, one day," Darkken replied. He grabbed Maefon and Nath by the arms, tugged them after himself, and said, "Follow me!"

They fell in line, with Nath towing Maefon behind him. The sloppy, slippery ground made the sure-footed warrior stumble more than once. Darkken slipped as well. He grasped at trees but maintained a steady pace. He didn't stop until they found a break in the trees, where the high grasses ran to the edge of a cliff. Nath joined him looking over the edge. Two hundred feet below, stormy waters crashed against the jagged cliffs. Out at sea was nothing but white bluffs and high waves.

Through the rain, Nath could make out a black coastline. He pointed. "What is that?"

"The northeasternmost part of Nalzambor!" Darkken pointed. "That's the Mountains of Urslay. Giant Home. This, the island we stand on, is called Cold Cliff. It's sparsely inhabited by strange sea peoples and monsters."

"What kind of monsters?" Maefon shouted.

"The kind that we hope we don't run into," Darkken fired back. "I swear it's not so gloomy when the storms pass, but storms are frequent over these seas. And the cliffs and shallows are too dangerous for the fishermen to cast lines and nets. It's not friendly territory. Come on. We have some walking yet to do."

"Why didn't you teleport us where we needed to go?" Nath said.

Leading the way, Darkken cast a backward glance and said, "Too risky. There are guardians where we are going. They don't take kindly to strangers… or anyone, for that matter."

"So, you've been here before," Nath said.

"Once, but it was a very long time ago." Darkken made his way toward the trees. "Let's get within the trees. There are great seabirds big enough to snatch men from the banks and carry them out to sea. I'd rather not cross them. It's imperative that we save our energy. Only use your powers when it's absolutely needed."

Shielding her eyes from the rain, Maefon asked, "How are we supposed to know when that is?"

Darkken replied, "You'll know because your life will depend on it."

Nath and Maefon kept a fierce pace with Darkken as they traveled over the treacherous terrain. They slid down into gullies and waded through waist-high washouts. They climbed over moss-covered rocks and snaked through channels of stone that lingered among the trees. Finally, they climbed a grass-slickened hill, where strange trees, with leaves only on the top, bent against the wind.

His hand shielding his eyes, Darkken pointed at a valley of fog that resided at the base of the hills. It was miles wide and long. Huge trees stabbed their way out of the mist, but the trunks disappeared below them.

"We are going in there?" Nath squatted and studied the fog. He saw treetops sticking through the cloud of fog.

The treetops shook, and the ground beneath him trembled. A loud, moaning roar rose out of the foggy valley.

Nath's heart started thumping. He looked at Darkken, pulled his sword, and said, "Lead the way."

CHAPTER 13

IN THE EARLY MORNING, THE fog had begun to rise from the high grasses of the plains. From a mile away, Slivver had a hazy view of Stonewater Keep. The formidable ten-story structure blended into the high cliff face behind it. Travelers could pass it by and not even notice without giving it a hard look. The snow and ice in the cliffs had started to melt, sending rivulets of water streaming down the sides. The churning river swallowed up the trickling water.

Slivver's heart was heavy. He felt that time was pressing for his brother Nath. He needed to find him soon. He turned to Brenwar and Elween, who were standing behind him. "Now that we are here, do we have any ideas?"

"Trap," Brenwar said sternly.

"I think that goes without saying," Slivver replied. "No doubt, Darkken knows that we are coming. That's why I'm asking for ideas."

"We don't know for certain that Nath is in there. I think we need to sneak in and find out," Elween suggested.

"Agreed, but we aren't the thieves that blend in with the walls. We are dragons," Slivver said. He looked at Brenwar. "You wouldn't happen to have anything that could change us into something else that is more… eh, discreet?"

Brenwar's pudgy fingers rummaged through his pouches. "I don't know. Perhaps I might have something. But I don't like potions. They make my stomach turn inside itself. Besides, this magic is for emergencies."

"This is an urgent matter," Slivver replied. "The fate of Nalzambor could be counting on it."

"Nalzambor will be just fine so long as dwarves are on it." Brenwar produced two corked vials in his calloused hands. One vial was as green as spring grass and the other sparkled yellow like the sun. He clawed at his beard. "Sometimes, I forget what they do."

"There are inscriptions on them," Elween said. She extended her hand. "May I?"

Brenwar handed them over.

"How did you come by all of these potions, Brenwar?" Slivver asked. "I didn't think that dwarves dabbled in this sort of magic."

"Balzurth gave them to me."

Slivver couldn't hide his widening eyes. "Really? That's a very special trust."

Brenwar snorted. "That why he gave them to me. Dwarves are the most trustworthy race in all the world, unlike elves, orcs, ogres, men, gnomes, dragons, pixies, sprites, elves, orcs—"

"You mentioned elves and orcs once already," Slivver said.

"So? They are worth mentioning again because they are twice the trouble."

"I don't think elves present the same problems that the orcs do," Slivver said.

Brenwar lifted a brow. "Is that so? Then what are we dealing with now? Those aren't orcs in that tower. They are elves."

"Well, I just think it's an unusual circumstance."

"You're just saying that because of a special elf that you are so fond of," Brenwar replied.

"Perhaps, but the Caligin are few. Besides, all races have good and bad in them—even the dragons, admittedly."

"Dwarves don't." Brenwar moved closer to Elween, who was inspecting the vials.

Slivver knew he was correct. Even the best of the races had some of the worst characters in them. But the dwarves, as a whole, were as good as good could get. He just wasn't going to admit that to Brenwar.

Elween traced a fingernail across the length of one vial. "Ah, I found tiny lettering inscribed on the bottle. It's written in Dragonese."

"Well, I can't read Dragonese," Brenwar said.

Elween giggled. "I'm certain that's why Balzurth color-coded them for you."

"I'm not stupid." Brenwar poked the yellow vial. "I know that one heals. I just forgot the other one. What does it say?"

Eyeing the green vial, she said, "There is plenty of room in a bigger world for you. Try a mouse's point of view."

Brenwar tilted his head, as did Slivver. Brenwar grunted. "I'm not turning into a rodent. That would be stupid. Dwarves aren't rats."

"No, I think I know what this is," Elween said. "I'll try it." She sipped down a third of it and handed it to Slivver. "It has a very minty taste." As she finished the last word, she started to shrink. Elween disappeared into the grasses.

"Where did she go?" Brenwar said.

"Don't move," Slivver said. "You might step on her and crush her."

"I'm not moving!"

Elween flew up out of the grasses. She was no bigger than a mouse. She hovered in front of Brenwar and waved.

"That's small." Brenwar shook his head. "I'm not doing this. Dwarves don't shrink."

"You're going to miss out on all of the fun," Slivver said.

"Hold on," Brenwar said with a grunt. He went to his pony and grabbed his sledgehammer, Stone Smiter. He tucked it behind his armor. "If I'm going to do this, I'm bringing backup." With his war hammer in one hand, he took the potion in the other and drank a third. Then he gave it to Slivver. "Hurry up. Let's get this over with."

Slivver drank. A moment later, he and Brenwar shrank and stood hidden in the now-enormous grasses.

Scratching his head, Brenwar said, "My, it's going to be a long walk."

Slivver and Elween hooked Brenwar by the arms and took flight.

Kicking his legs, Brenwar bellowed, "Dwarves don't fly! Dwarves don't fly!"

Slivver smiled. "They do today."

Using the cover of the lifting fog, they flew just over the top of the short grasses, crossed the river, and made their way over the rocky bank that led up to the keep, where they landed in the rubble. Slivver could see the entrance gate. Two elves stood guard inside it.

"We are still too big to walk right by them," he said. "We need to seek out another way in. Come on."

As one, they moved toward the keep. The old structure had cracks big enough to slip through.

"We enter here. Let's go." Slivver led the way through one crack, which was more like a tunnel, to a courtyard inside. "We're in," he said, eyeing the gargantuan surroundings. At their current size, the search might take forever, but that wasn't the only problem. He looked at the dwarf. "Brenwar, how long will this potion last? Will it stop if we act aggressive like the polymorph, or does it only last a certain length of time?"

"Can't remember for sure, but it's one or the other."

Irritated, Slivver said, "You knew how the polymorph spell worked."

"That's only because I'd seen it used before. And you'd seen it used before too."

"I can't believe Balzurth gave the potions to you. He should have given them to me."

"True, but you don't have any pockets, do you?" Brenwar smirked.

"Friends, stop bickering," Elween said. "I don't think it really matters anymore."

Slivver gave her a strange look. Either he was shrinking, or she was growing. "Great gooseberries."

"What?" Brenwar growled. He looked up. "Oh."

Elween had become gigantic.

"I guess that potion didn't last very long. I'll be certain to remember that the next time."

"Let's hope there is a next time." Slivver started growing, realizing they were in full view of the courtyard. "Gads."

CHAPTER 14

DARKKEN LED THE WAY INTO the fog-filled valley. The mist was thick, so they remained in a tight group. Even Nath's keen vision could only see several feet in front of him. The men kept Maefon between them. She held elven daggers in her hands. Once they entered the fog, they walked around the rim until they found a slope leading down into a deeper valley. Like a shallow cliff, it hugged the inner rim of the strange valley. Birds' wings flapped, and strange calls echoed in the valley. The ground shook from time to time.

The last roar that Nath heard before they'd entered had not repeated itself. But tension lay in the creepy stillness of the fog. Maefon looked back at him. He gave her a reassuring nod. Nath found a fear of the unknown lurking in his heart. He was in a foreign landscape unlike anything he'd seen in Nalzambor. The air was soggy. His surroundings made his skin itch. He was ready to spring at any moment, to hack down unseen aggressors that he knew must be waiting on him.

A bat-like pelican with sharp nodule teeth in its beak dropped out of the mist and pecked at Maefon. She stabbed the nasty bird in the neck, and it flopped loudly on the slope. She kicked it away.

Darkken turned to her and put his finger to his lips. She shrugged and glared at him.

Finally, they made it to the bottom of the valley. Great trees wide enough to drive wagons through were rooted in the ground, with smaller, normal trees among them. At the bottom, the mist had risen higher like a dim gray cloud above them, giving Nath a clearer view of his surroundings. The murky forest was filled with giant ferns and shrubbery. Wildflowers bloomed as big as Nath's head. The ground was packed with rich brown soil.

The valley tremored again.

Nath broke the silence. "What is that out there? I know that you know what it is."

"The guardian," Darkken said in a low voice.

"Guardian of what?" Nath asked.

Moving his head from left to right, Darkken said, "It's the guardian of where we are going."

"And where are we going?" Nath asked. He looked down and saw a two-foot-long centipede crawling over his foot. He kicked it away. "Tell me everything isn't so big in this place."

"Cold Cliff is rich in wildlife. Its climate is much different from the rest of Nalzambor. Inhospitable for people, it's thrived for millennia on its own. The nature here is not very fond of outsiders, so I suggest, don't touch the plants or the critters. Just stay close to me."

"*Maaahrooo-Maaah!*"

The ground trembled.

Thoom!

Rain dropped in sheets out of the shaking branches. Unseen birds flapped from their perches and flew higher into the fog.

Nath gave Darkken an incredulous look. "Even bull dragons don't stomp the ground like that. Whatever it is, it's getting closer. Darkken, what is going on? What is that thing?"

"It is a behemoth," Darkken answered.

Thoom! Thoom!

Darkken continued, "I believe it smells us, and he's coming this way." His look swept from Nath to Maefon. "Follow me. It's time to run."

Just as Darkken said that, a head like a snapping turtle's popped out from behind the trees. The head of the creature was bigger than a pair of oxen. It had a long neck like the trunk of a great cedar. Its orange eyes fastened on the group. It opened his great jaws and roared. "*Maaahrooo-Maaah!*" Pushing through the trees, it came after them.

The company fled with the speed of a gazelle. They hopped fallen limbs and pushed through the thickets. The behemoth, tremendous in size, also moved with alarming speed. It closed in on them.

Following Darkken, Nath wished he had some idea where they were going. But at the moment, they were running for their lives. Nath couldn't help but steal a backward glance. He'd never seen a creature like the behemoth before. He hadn't read about one, either. It stood over thirty feet high at the top of its back. It was built like a turtle but without a shell. Instead, it wore thick plates of flexible hide for armor. Its clawed fingers tore up the soft dirt behind it. The trees that it bumped shook as it passed. Its orange eyes were locked in on him. It hungered. It hated.

"Up here," Darkken said as they reached a tree with low-hanging branches. He climbed up into it. Reaching down, he aided Maefon.

Nath jumped into the tree, and they all scrambled up higher and higher.

The behemoth plowed into the tree, shaking it hard.

They were trapped in the tree like varmints.

The monster put its claws to the bark and started ripping it off.

"*Maaahrooo-Maaah!*"

Sitting in the branches with nowhere to go, the group covered their ears.

"Gads, that thing is loud!" Nath said.

"*Maaahrooo-Maaah!*"

The monster started biting the tree and ripping large chunks of wood out.

Nath shouted to Darkken, "Blast! It's eating the tree. We're going to have to kill it!"

"That's the problem!" Darkken shouted back. "I don't think it can be killed!"

Chapter 15

Slivver froze. The outer courtyard of the keep was surrounded by a two-story-high wall. Caligin elves were posted along the wall, but luckily for them, they were facing outward. With his stomach twisting from the effects of the potions, he checked out his companions. Elween and Brenwar were back to normal size. Both of them had their hands on their guts.

"Well, that went awful," Brenwar said.

Slivver shushed them. "Follow me." He crept along the interior wall, away from where the guards stood at the portcullis. His eyes were fastened on the guards on the other side of the courtyard. He had seen six, and based on their positions, their number must have been at least twelve, including the two at the portcullis.

One of the Caligin started to turn. Slivver and the group stood like statues. The elf turned halfway around and stretched out his arms. Then he glanced down into the courtyard.

Slivver's heart pounded inside his throat. *Look away. Look away. Look away.* The elf's piercing eyes started to slide his way. That was when another elf called out, catching the attention of the elf looking. He turned back around and stood at attention.

The second elf approached and smacked the first elf in the back of the head.

"Let's go!"

With the elves' backs turned, they hustled into an archway leading into the bottom of the keep. Slivver took a peek outside. The elf that had disciplined the other took a quick look into the courtyard and moved on.

In a low voice, Slivver said, "That was close."

"I say let them find us," Brenwar said. "I don't like all of this sneaking around and being tiny. It's not natural."

Slivver looked down at him and asked, "Are you sure being tiny isn't natural?"

Brenwar glowered at him. "Watch it, lizard face."

"I'm all for fighting, but there could be over a hundred Caligin in here," Elween said. She looked up at a nearby set of stairs and pointed at another that led down. "Which way? Up or down?"

"Down," Brenwar said.

"Up," Slivver replied. "You break the tie, Elween."

"I don't think Nath will be in the dungeon level. My guess is that if they are here, Darkken keeps him close. And knowing Darkken, I'm sure he lives on the top, where he can see everything." She stepped aside. "Lead the way."

"You can lead the way if you like," Slivver replied. "After all, you are the seasoned fighter."

"Don't mind if I do. We'll take it one level at time. The courtyard is cleared, so let's proceed to level two."

Elween headed up the steps. At the top of the stair shaft waited a closed door. Three steps short of the next landing, the doorway popped open. A Caligin wearing black leather armor and cleaning his fingernails with a file stepped out. Before he could let out a whistle, Elween's tail cracked him in the middle of the face.

The elf staggered back into the wall, holding his bleeding nose. His free hand went for his sword. Elween smacked him hard in the face with her fist, knocking the elf out cold.

She peeked inside the second-level room. "Quickly. The room is clear. Drag him inside."

Brenwar took the elf by the arms and followed her into the second level. It was a barren room, bereft of any interior walls. Barrels and sacks of food were piled up on the floor.

Brenwar dragged the elf deeper inside and propped him against a wall. "This elf is still breathing. You should have killed him."

"I didn't want to get blood everywhere," Elween said as she made her way around the room.

Slivver did thc same. Nothing was extraordinary about the room. It was typical of any storage house in a castle, keeping the dry goods aboveground, away from deteriorating elements.

He said, "Secure that elf. And let's see what awaits us on level three."

"Aye." Brenwar punched the elf in the jaw. "That should do it."

The elves on the keep's wall maintained their posts. The Caligin commander, Deterus, walked the parapet behind them. He returned to the guard he'd pretended to reprimand earlier. "Brother, tell me what you saw once more."

Eyes outward, the elf gave a quick nod and said, "My eyes swept over the courtyard. I captured the sight of two dragons—one green, the other silver—and a dwarf. It was the same dwarf that came to our gates days ago."

Commander Deterus smiled. "Yes, I saw them as well. You did well not to let on with it. That is the Caligin way." He patted the elf on the back. "Grab one of your brothers. Head into the sublevel and let out the Creeper of the Deep. I'll alert the others of the trespassers and meet you back down there."

The elven guard nodded. "Death to the dragons."

Deterus smiled. "Death to the dwarf."

Chapter 16

"Teleport us out of here or something, Darkken!" Nath yelled.

"That's a once-a-week trip, I'm afraid," Darkken replied.

The tree they clung to shook from top to bottom. Below them, the behemoth bit larger chunks out of the tree and spat them out.

"What kind of monster eats trees?" Maefon yelled.

"I don't know. So, Darkken, is this one of those life-or-death situations? Cast a spell at it!" Nath said.

"I don't think I have a spell that will do any good. All I can suggest is that when we hit the ground, run," Darkken replied.

"That's assuming the fall doesn't kill us," Nath said.

The behemoth had eaten halfway though the tree's trunk. The tree started to teeter toward the monster. If they fell, they were going to fall right on top of the awaiting behemoth.

"This isn't good." Nath shoved Maefon. "Climb! Climb! To the other side!" He hoped the tree would fall on the ignorant flesh-hungry beast. If the tree didn't kill it, perhaps it would pin it to the ground.

Maefon climbed around the branches, and Nath followed her.

Just then, the monster lunged shoulder first into the half-eaten base of the tree. The tree bent away from the beast then snapped back, flinging Maefon from the branches.

Nath reached out to save her. "No!"

The elven woman tumbled down through the branches and caught herself on the lowest set. Her legs dangled over the ground. The behemoth locked its eyes on her, rose on its back legs, and opened its jaws wide.

Nath wrapped his fingers around Fang's pommel.

"Nath, don't!" Darkken yelled.

He dove sword first at the behemoth. Dropping straight through a crease in the branches, he aimed for the behemoth's eye. The monster swung its jaws right into Nath's path. Nath went straight into its widening throat and struck something soft and gooey. He turned in time to see the great jaws snap closed over him.

The moment the behemoth's jaws closed up on Nath, Maefon let out an enraged scream. "Nooo! Nath! Nooo!"

She dropped out of the tree and hit the ground with her hands filled with magic fire. Tears started down her face as she slung one ball of flame after another at the monster's head. The bright balls of energy exploded on the monster's face. Its neck bent backward. Rolling its long neck, it set its eyes back on her.

"Come and get me, monster!" She threw more balls of fire at it.

The behemoth reared up on its hind legs. Its massive clawed hands came down at Maefon.

Still throwing her searing explosive magic at its belly, she didn't budge. She stared death in the eye, waiting to be crushed. "I hate you!"

Out of nowhere, Darkken knocked Maefon out of the way just before its great paws pulverized her.

Thoom!

Shaking the disheveled elven woman, he said, "Maefon, we must run!"

Sputtering, she said, "I can't leave Nath. I can't. I don't care."

The angry behemoth pulled back its neck like a striking snake. Its burning orange eyes locked them in its sights. Its tremendous body crept toward them.

"We must go!" he said, pulling her to her feet. "We must!"

Suddenly, the behemoth's limbs became sluggish. Its great advance slowed. A crackling sound came from within its humongous body. It opened its great mouth and moaned, "*Maaarooo—*" Then its thundering voice was choked off. The hard scales on its reptilian flesh crusted over with spreading ice, which started in the neck and ran its freezing course through the head and body. The behemoth turned from flesh into an ice statue.

From out of its half-open mouth, a flame-haired young warrior crawled. Sword in hand, he rolled out of the behemoth's mouth and hit the ground, gasping for breath.

Maefon rushed Nath and peppered him with kisses. "Nath! You live! You live!" She pulled back and pinched her nose. "And you stink."

Nath looked behind his shoulder. "That thing is nasty."

Darkken helped Nath to his feet. Looking at the behemoth with awe, he asked, "How did you do that?"

Lifting his sword, Nath casually said, "I'm pretty sure Fang did it. I stabbed hard, and then came a crackle."

Darkken walked to the behemoth and ran his hands over the sculpture of ice. "This is astonishing."

"You said that the behemoth could not be killed," Nath added as Maefon still clung to his side.

"Well, not by ordinary means. Blades are useless against its hide, and even fire and lightning do little more than slow it. It's a juggernaut." Darkken pressed his ear to the iced-up monster.

"What are you doing?" Maefon asked.

Darkken put the finger of silence to his lips. One eyebrow rose. After about a minute, he pulled his head away. "It's not dead. The heart still beats. Come." He motioned to them. "Feel."

Nath put his hand on the ice. A few seconds later, he felt the slow *thump-thump* of a heartbeat. "It does live."

"I cannot say for sure, but if I were to guess, I think the brute beast will end up thawing. We'd better go," Darkken said. "Your sword, Fang, has given us a tremendous advantage. Follow me."

Before Nath had a chance to let out another word, Darkken was off and running. Nath had barely had time to catch his breath before he was on the move again. Questions still lingered in his mind. The behemoth had almost killed him. Darkken seemed to know a lot about the creature as well and needed to give a better explanation. As they raced through the jungle, Maefon caught up with him and took his hand.

"Nath, you are the bravest man I've ever known. I can't thank you enough for saving me," she said.

"I'll let you thank me later. Right now, I just want to figure out what in the wild world we are doing."

Traveling through the heavy jungle with monstrous trees covered in vines, they startled more strange creatures that jumped out of their path. They saw gazelles with three horns and black lizards as big as men, with long red tails. The cawing of birds never stopped in the fog above. They seemed to be sending a warning of the strangers. Darkken pressed on, moving from the side that they'd started on toward the other side. Finally, they arrived in front of a sheer cliff that stretched up into the fog.

Darkken stopped and pointed. "There is where we go."

Carved into the cliff face was a towering temple with round stone columns guarding a smaller cave entrance. Thick brown-and-green vines twisted up the walls like snakes. The entrance was partially covered in more low-hanging vegetation.

"This is what the behemoth was guarding?" Nath asked.

"The behemoth guards against all strangers in its natural habit. That's why I chose this location. Thanks to the behemoth, it is long abandoned." Darkken started the walk up the stairs. "Let's go. The guardian's worshippers will be curious once they discover that their god has been frozen."

"What worshippers are you talking about?" Maefon asked. "I didn't think people lived here."

Standing outside the entrance, Darkken replied, "Well, they aren't really people because they are so primitive. Primarily, they are savages that feed the behemoth. Come on, though. We don't have time to concern ourselves with such trivialities. They won't follow us in here."

Topping the steps and looking around, Nath asked, "Why not?"

"Because this temple is haunted."

CHAPTER 17

THE CALIGIN WERE A BROTHERHOOD devoted to the Lord of the Dark in the Day. Among them were no formal ranks. Lord Darkken gave them their assignments, and they obeyed without question. Deterus was in charge of guarding the keep and unleashing the Creeper of the Deep. The swarthy elf could barely contain his rail-thin smile as he made his way down into the subterranean levels. He'd served Lord Darkken faithfully for more than one hundred years. Now, he had an opportunity to prove his worth once more. He would do anything for Darkken—anything large or small.

Stonewater Keep had several subterranean levels. They were decrepit and long-abandoned places with old goods ruined by rot. The walls of stone were long deteriorated, revealing the original caverns, which had been dug out centuries before. It was cool and damp. The air reeked of stagnation. But something else lingered. An ancient evil pulsated in the darkest depths. A foul spirit had resided in the keep when Lord Darkken discovered it.

With no torch or lantern, Deterus navigated his way through the dark catacombs. He came upon a quivering light and approached. Ahead, two elves stood by a great iron door. A lantern hung on a post behind them. They nodded, and he returned the gesture.

"Today is a grand day, brothers. After all of these decades of service, we get to release the monster that we have learned so much about." Deterus stepped to the door and put his hand on the cold metal.

Something on the other side breathed heavily. The air chilled his toes. The elves gave Deterus a curious look.

"The Creeper hungers."

On the other side of the door, claws scraped over the metal with a screeching sound. The cold breath huffed again.

From inside his armor, Deterus removed a medallion set in a golden necklace. The coin was a solid piece of pewter with three devilish eyes and claws stamped into it. It illuminated the area with burgundy light.

"The Medallion of Darkness," he quietly said. "Our revered Lord of the Dark in the Day discovered the existence of this charm in the lost Annals of Elvenkind, which he had stolen. It allowed him to control the Creeper that the Stonewaters builders discovered by accident. They dug too deep. The Creeper came from the bowels of the earth and slaughtered them all." Staring into the medallion, he smiled. He couldn't wait to see the creature in action. It had slain the formidable peoples that lived there long ago. "Today, history unfolds. Open the door."

Together, the elves slid back the huge iron bolts that sealed the door shut. Then, as one, they grabbed an iron rung and pulled the door open.

Deterus stood with the medallion hanging over his chest. In the darkness of the Creeper's den, he saw two pairs of red eyes fixed on him. A snort came from the darkness. The Creeper crept out. It was bigger than a horse, with a jackal's face and a feline figure. Its coat was a patchwork of black and pinkish-red skin. Muscles heaved all over underneath its strange pelt. Its shoulders were huge, the face tigerish but monstrous. Its lips curled back, showing an oversized mouth full of flesh-eating teeth. Body lowered, it slunk all the way out of the den on eight legs and black paws with claws like talons at the ends. The claws on the front legs slowly drummed on the floor. It stood nose to nose with the inferior Deterus. From its jaws, saliva dripped to the floor and sizzled on the stone. Deterus's hand went over the medallion.

Swallowing the lump that formed in his throat, he said, "Slay the dwarf. Slay the dragons."

With an easy gait, the Creeper silently skulked down into the tunnels and out of sight.

Chapter 18

Slivver and company had cleared every level, all the way up to the fifth floor. They hadn't seen any signs of anyone since they'd encountered the last Caligin on the second floor. It was as if the keep had fallen silent—too silent. They were entering the sixth level, into what appeared to be a training ground for the elves. Arenas were there, for practicing swordplay and wrestling. Weapons racks were lined up along the walls. They swept through the room and, again, didn't see anyone.

Crossing his arms over his chest, Slivver said, "I'm not sure what to make of this." He stole a peek out of one of the portal windows, to see the guards still posted on the exterior wall of the keep, looking outward. "They couldn't possibly be the only ones here. I expected at least fifty of them."

"Perhaps they are just a skeleton crew," Elween suggested. "Don't lose heart. We came here to find out if Nath was here or not. If not, we can find him by other means." She sifted through a weapons rack, grabbed a spear, and twisted it around her body. "Very interesting. This training room has remarkable similarities to mine."

"So, you are thinking that everything you taught Darkken, he's passed on to the Caligin?" Slivver said.

"A scary thought, but I'm certain that is the case." She frowned. "All of my great secrets shared with these fiends. Disgusting."

Slivver took in a snort of air. "Elween, do you smell what I smell?"

Brenwar's own prominent nose started sniffing. "I smell the stink of elves. Their sweat smells like fear." He waggled his hammer. "They must know I'm here."

Fanning air into her nostrils, Elween said, "Nath has definitely been here. But even with our keen noses, the scent is faint. It could be weeks old."

"At least we know that he has been here. We just need to find out if he is still in here." Slivver headed toward the door. "Let's see what we find on the next level."

Brenwar cut into Slivver's path. He extended his war hammer, shielding the dragon, and murmured, "Trap."

Slivver's eyes narrowed on the doorway leading out. Elween came to his side, brandishing a pair of swords. The training room fell stone-cold silent. He didn't see or hear anything out of the ordinary, but he could have sworn he felt an unnatural chill in the room.

"Elween, I remember when you used to tell me that you cannot always trust your senses. Sometimes you have to trust yourself." Slivver cast a sideward glance at her. "I think this is one of those moments."

"Agreed," she whispered.

From the corner of the room behind them, they heard the soft mewing of a cat. All of them turned in that direction. Nobody saw any sign of a cat, but it could have been hidden underneath the bleachers.

"It might have been overlooked before. I'll go check it out," Elween said.

"Trap," Brenwar said sharply.

"Brenwar, we won't know until we confirm it. Let's not outthink ourselves." Elween started away from Brenwar, but the dwarf snatched her arm. Turning, she said, "Don't do that..."

While they had turned, the Creeper had slipped into the room from the front door. The jackal-faced catlike abomination was unlike anything she'd seen before. As the wicked thing's icy stare made her blood turn cold, she said, "Trap."

The Creeper from the Deep would have slaughtered ordinary fighters in an instant. Its terrifying gaze froze the sturdiest men in their tracks.

Jaws slavering and dripping sizzling saliva, it pounced at them. Hungry jaws and razor-sharp claws came right at their necks.

At the last second, Slivver's frozen instincts kicked in. He snaked his neck out of the way from the swing of the claws. Brenwar crouched low and balled up underneath the massive jaws. He jammed his hammer in the monster's mouth. The Creeper bit down on the hammer and flung the dwarf and war hammer aside like a child's toy.

Elween chopped her swords into the hard flesh of the beast. The blades skipped off the creature's hide.

"It's impervious to metal!" she shouted.

With a deep breath, Slivver summoned a charge of his lightning. The beast moved with the speed of a dragon. Before he could get a breath out, the beast jumped on top of him and started mauling him. The sharp claws tore at the scales of his silvery body. In that instant, Slivver found himself in the fight of his life. The ravenous Creeper was trying to tear him to shreds.

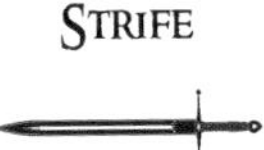

Brenwar skipped over one of the training arenas and rolled up to a knee. He immediately saw Slivver underneath the beast with its claws ripping into him. On the monster's back rode Elween. Her claws had sunk into the beast's hide. She spat small balls of fire into the back of its head. The Creeper bucked her off like a human.

"Enough of this!" Brenwar raised his war hammer and charged. The monster was unlike anything he'd seen before, and he'd seen plenty. But he'd met nothing that couldn't be killed. Closing in like a charging bull, he cocked his hammer back and swung. The blunt end of his weapon connected with the beast's shoulder.

Krang!

The power of the resounding blow shook the entire room. The monster let out a yelp as it detached itself from Slivver. The dragon scrambled out from underneath the beast's belly. Cuts were all over his silvery scales. Brenwar stood his ground beside his two friends, who gathered at his side, and said, "What in Morgdon is that thing? My strike should have slain it."

"I have no idea," Slivver said, sucking breath. "But if we don't find a way to kill it, it's going to kill us."

The Creeper squared up on the group. Sizzling streams of saliva dripped out of its jaws. Head low, it started to advance.

With a huff of breath, Slivver hit it with a bolt of lightning. The beast from the darkness shivered as the lightning coiled around its body and faded in a wisp. It came on.

Slivver gulped. "I think we're in trouble."

Chapter 19

"This is a horrible idea," Hacksaw said.

Dule had bound his hands and tethered him to his own horse. Roday rode in the saddle.

"I don't trust either of you that much."

"It's the best idea that we could come up with." Roday replied. "Unless you have a better one?"

The group was only a couple of miles from Stonewater Keep. The plan was for Roday and Dule to approach with Hacksaw captured. After all, the Caligin were looking for him.

"I suggested that Dule and I go in alone to see what is going on, but you didn't like that plan either. So this is the only option."

Hacksaw grumbled. "I'm more comfortable having you in my sights than out of my sights. Besides, the closer I can get to help Nath, the better."

"I'll be close, Hacksaw," Calypsa said. "I swear that you can count on me and Rond."

He looked over at her and up at the big goon of a bugbear. "I guess I'll have to take your word for it."

Roday gave Hacksaw's horse a kick, and they were on their way toward the keep. Calypsa and Rond stayed behind. The elves whistled a slow and dreary tune.

It was a do-or-die mission. It wasn't Hacksaw's first, either, but he had the sinking feeling it would be his last. All he wanted to do was get face-to-face with Nath and warn him one last time about the Caligin. Now, he'd placed his trust in two former Caligin that were leading him straight into the jaws of death. They didn't even know if Nath was in the keep or not. All Roday and Dule knew for sure was that Darkken would be heading back with Nath and Maefon eventually. For now, Hacksaw was going with his gut with his new companions. At least he was going to figure out where Darkken lived. A hundred yards into the journey, he glanced backward. Calypsa and Maefon were gone.

Dule caught him looking back, stopped whistling, and said, "That's one slippery woman. Be glad she's on our side."

"What do you mean?"

"I mean that I wouldn't want to be Maefon when those two cross again. That dryad wants vengeance," Dule said with a serious look. "Listen, Hacksaw. Just let us do the talking when we get there. We are sticking our necks out too. Lord Darkken doesn't like failure, and technically, you should be killed on sight. The last thing he wants Nath to see is you, dead or alive. But we have to try something."

"Aye, doing something is better than doing nothing. I just wish I were with a host of legionnaires and not two squirrelly elves."

"Squirrelly?" Roday said. "I've never thought of myself as a varmint. I think if I were, I might be a badger. Yes, I'd make a fine badger."

"The two of you don't come across the same as your spooky brethren," Hacksaw said.

Half turned around in the saddle, Roday said, "In our defense, we are trained to control our personalities. It's all part of the deception as we are expected to blend in with our communities. But remember, we are still elves that are friendly, even jovial, by nature. Darkken just has a way of subduing it. I like to think that you are seeing the real us now. Dule, wouldn't you agree?"

"I do," Dule said with a growing smile. "It's as if, since we met Nath, we've had an awakening. I can't explain it, but his goodness lifted a veil from my eyes, and I could think clearly for the first time."

Roday was nodding.

Hacksaw knew the feeling they were speaking of. He'd felt it before himself, at least in regard to the goodness. Something about Nath's presence raised the spirits of a man. He was good company, as good company as any.

Hacksaw got his first good look at the keep, half a mile away. It was a dreary-looking place with dark clouds hanging overhead. He couldn't shake the ominous feeling clutching at his heart. He could make out the exterior watch wall that guarded the keep. Tiny figures could be seen stationed at the parapets.

"Well, they know we are coming," he said. "Will they send riders?"

"No, not likely," Roday said. "We are almost close enough where they will recognize us. They'll wait. If they don't like what they see, then they'll most likely shoot us on the bridge. Actually, assuming Darkken is in there, then he'd already be notified. So he either slays us, or lets us in. One way or the other, it will be interesting."

With the grass rustling by his knees, Hacksaw walked on. Bereft of his sword and pipe, he felt as naked as ever. A quarter of a mile away, a bright light flashed halfway up the keep's tower from a portal window. A sound like thunder rumbled from the ancient structure.

Roday pulled the horse to a stop. He looked at Dule and said, "That's not normal."

With a nervous look, Dule replied, "It certainly isn't."

"We need to move," Roday said as Dule jumped on the back of the horse. "Hacksaw, do your best to keep up. Eee-yah!"

"Don't you dare! Don't you dare!" Hacksaw started running.

The horse started galloping. Hacksaw kept up for the first fifty paces before he lost his footing. He landed belly down in the grasses, and the horse dragged him, filling his mouth with grasses.

Dule yelled, "Sorry, Hacksaw, but we have to sell it!"

Hacksaw tried to yell back, but all he could manage were a few curses as he fought to spit the grasses from his mouth. Suddenly, the grass turned to dirt and stone. They dragged him across the bridge. He fully expected to see arrows or crossbow bolts flying. Instead, they stopped on the other side of the bridge. Roday and Dule jumped off the bridge and raced to the portcullis. Hacksaw, fighting his way to his feet, groaned.

A clamor of explosions and falling rocks and debris came from within the walls of the keep. The ground trembled slightly beneath them.

Dule and Roday banged on the portcullis gate. The elves that normally guarded it had abandoned it.

Hacksaw loosened his bonds and caught up with them and peered through the iron grate. He could still see bright flashes inside the tower. His neck hairs stood on end. "We have to get in there now!"

CHAPTER 20

WITH MAEFON IN TOW, NATH followed Darkken deeper into the belly of the temple. Using the blue glimmer of Fang for light, he surveyed his surroundings. The stonework and architecture of the temple was that of an advanced and ancient people. The walls and columns were cut in squares and rectangles. The archways weren't round at the top but triangular. The walls were not marked with symbols, language, or arcane letterings. They were plain in design, as if made by intelligent but simple people.

If Nath were to guess, he'd think men had done this. Humans tended to take a little bit of everything from the races and adapt it to their own culture. The people that had once lived on Cold Cliff Island probably didn't have much contact with the rest of the world.

They'd moved less than a hundred feet into the spacious chambers. The fifty-foot-high cathedral ceilings made the space look much bigger than it was.

Darkken moved to one of the rectangular columns, where a torch hung in an eroding brass bracket. He lit it with a touch of his finger. "I've found that this is a very interesting place. It reminds me of Stonewater Keep. The only difference is that it's devoid of life."

"I thought that you said it was haunted," Maefon said.

Darkken ventured deeper into the temple, where the modern architecture turned into dug-out tunnels and caves. "Aside from us, there are none living within here. But there are spirits. They won't disturb us if we don't disturb them."

Nath felt cold breath on his neck, though no one was there but Maefon, who stood to his side. "Do you have any idea who used to live here?"

"Well, sort of. The Annals of Elvenkind were written by elven explorers determined to map the entire world, down to the last detail. They are accurate in regard to landscapes, but because of war, famine, and disease, the peoples of the world change. At one time, men, eh, like monks, lived in this place. But the annals say that they were turned to savage beasts. But those annals were written millennia ago. Times change."

The cavern tunnels wound through the rock. The path sloped up and downward. They passed several coves, big and small, the deeper they went. Those appeared to have been living quarters at one time, where the people with their families slept. It was hard to tell because no tables, chairs, or linens of any kind were there—no signs of tools either. The temple seemed to be abandoned, and everything the inhabitants had was taken. It didn't make sense to Nath.

"Tell me, Darkken, how did you come upon this place?" Nath asked. He looked at Maefon, who shrugged.

Moving into a bigger tunnel, Darkken said, "Well, I was looking for a safe spot to hide a treasure of mine. It had to be a place out of the reach of thieves and raiders… and a place for meditation and privacy. I read about Cold Cliff in the annals, which have proven to be priceless resources in my journeys. And this temple, well, seeing how it's the home of spirits, it wasn't likely that any brave souls that made it this far would come any farther."

Nath felt the cold breeze on his neck again. Something invisible plucked at his body like fingers touching the hair on his arms. Maefon gripped his free hand and wouldn't let it go.

"So, the spirits don't find you a threat," he said.

Darkken stopped and said, "I told you if we don't bother them, then they won't bother us. Just stop with the questions. You'll understand soon enough."

After another hundred yards of walking, the tunnel opened up into a massive cavern. It was illuminated by glowing white insects that crawled along the walls and ceiling. All of the cavern was natural, but the floor had been chiseled out, making tiers and steps to many levels, dozens of platforms. On most of the platforms were vases and urns, each painted with different pictures of nature and some inlaid with metal. They were all different shapes and sizes, squat and slender. Thousands of them must have been there.

Also, in the center of every platform was a stone sarcophagus. Darkken took the steps from tier to tier and said, "Don't disturb the urns. I can't say for sure, but they are filled with either the dust of the dead or their treasure." He stood by a sarcophagus. It was a stone rectangle with a heavy lid and no notable markings. "I believe this is the family patriarch within. And the urns and the rest of the expired family." He scanned the chamber. "I believe it is their ghosts that lie within."

"So it's another burial chamber?" Nath asked. He glanced at all the urns at his feet. "Great."

"Filled with the riches of the dead." Darkken handed his torch to Maefon. He got on one end of the sarcophagus and motioned Nath to the other end. "Help me remove this lid?"

Aghast, Nath said, "What? Won't that set off the spirits?"

Darkken inadvertently kicked over an urn, shattering the pottery. Sand and dust spilled out. Darkken looked at Nath with wide eyes. "Oops."

A cold breeze howled through the chamber. The torches' fire extinguished. The illumination from the bugs crawling the walls went out.

CHAPTER 21

BRENWAR POUNDED HIS WAR HAMMER into the nose of the striking Creeper. It shrugged the weapon off like a stick. Of all the creatures he'd fought in the world, he'd never faced one like this. It was unearthly, fueled by an ancient evil in the bowels of the world, which time had long forgotten. He swung hard into the monster yet again. It slipped away and took a swipe at him. Brenwar ducked but not before the Creeper's claws caught him upside the head and sent him spinning to the ground. Blood started to run into his eyes.

Slivver breathed bolt after bolt of lightning into the jackal-faced beast. Its body lit up the cracking dawn. Its tail flicked out like a snake's tongue and took Slivver from his feet. It flipped around to face Elween. She blew balls of fire into the monster's face. Parts of the training room began to burn, and the fire spread.

The Creeper lunged at Elween. She sidestepped, grabbed the brute by the neck, and shoved it headfirst into a stone wall. Its back paws kicked back into her chest, knocking her back into the stands. Before she could recover, the Creeper closed in and pinned her down with its claws, trying to tear the weapons master to pieces.

"For Morgdon!" Brenwar yelled. He charged alongside Slivver to save the overwhelmed Elween.

Her skill kept her alive as she twisted her neck away from its biting death. Burning saliva dripped onto her face. She held its jaws back by pushing up underneath its chin. Slivver flew right into the side of its face. Brenwar smote its rear haunches.

All fire broke loose.

The Creeper, bigger and stronger than all three of them put together, turned into a tornado of claws, teeth, and hatred. It sank its claws into Slivver's and Elween's backs and tore the membranes of their wings open. It absorbed and shrugged off everything they threw at it.

Brenwar hit with all his might, testing one spot then the next. "Keep attacking! It has to have a weakness!"

The longer they fought, the more damage the Creeper of the Deep did. Slivver, Elween, and Brenwar were all bleeding. Loose scales had been ripped from the dragons' bodies. Drops of dragon blood were sprayed on the floor. They were clearly losing, but Brenwar wasn't about to die without a fight. The dragons weren't either. They fought like wildcats, clawing at the monster's eyes and sinking their teeth into its neck. The Creeper rammed them into the walls. It slung them off with its claws. It attacked tirelessly, again and again.

Brenwar was knocked down to a knee, puffing for breath.

Slivver lay flat on his back, fighting to get back up again. Elween was cornered against a wall, fighting off the Creeper's slashing claws.

Battered, bruised, and bleeding, Brenwar and Slivver set themselves for another charge. "For Nath," Brenwar mumbled.

"To the end," Slivver said. "It's been an honor to fight beside you." He took a deep breath and readied to charge.

Brenwar heard the sharp snap of bone. Elween's body was in the jaws of the Creeper.

Running at full speed, Slivver screamed, "Elweeeen!"

Hacksaw retrieved his sword, Green Tongue, and attacked the portcullis. Roday and Dule looked at him as though he were crazy. Determined, he chopped away. The faintly glimmering green blade shone as the sword flashed down and bit deep into the inferior metal. Regardless, at the rate he was whacking at it, an hour would pass before he cut through.

With a head full of steam, he said, "Well, help me out, will you!" He stopped cutting.

The elves were gone.

"Huh?"

On the other side of the portcullis, someone whistled.

Hacksaw whirled around. Roday and Dule were standing on the other side of the gate.

"How'd you do that?" he asked.

"There's a secret entrance," Roday said.

"Why didn't you tell me?"

"Well, you were so lathered up that we didn't want to bother you," Roday replied.

"Let me in there!"

Roday pointed to the right. "Thirty paces—take a right. Look for the stone with a crescent moon on it."

Hacksaw took off, found the entrance, and slid into the keep. He caught Roday and Dule in the courtyard. Smoke was rolling out of the portal windows of the keep. "How do we get up there?"

Roday pointed toward the opposite end of the courtyard and said, "Those stairs are the only way up. Follow me." He hadn't made it ten steps when a swarm of Caligin came out of the stairwell. Each of them had a sword or dagger in hand. At the front of the pack stood the swarthy Caligin commander, Deterus.

"Greeting, Deterus. It seems that things are in great order, assuming that you are in charge," Roday said as he looked at the smoke rolling out of the upper portals. "Did you let Darkken know that his fortress is on fire?"

Deterus smirked. "Well, if it isn't the black sheep of the Caligin, Roday and Dule," he said in a scoffing tone. "And look what they've brought with them. A fully armed prisoner." He tilted his head to one side and stared at Hacksaw. "My, you are the man that we filled with arrows, who disappeared, aren't you? I promise we won't miss the heart a second time."

The smug sneering of the dark elf went right through Hacksaw. His jaws clenched as the stone-faced elves surrounded them. He hated them. He had since the very moment he'd met them. And now, they had him surrounded again.

All he could think to do was yell, "Nath! Nath!"

"Save your breath, brawny fool. Nath is far away from here," Deterus said. He was the only one that hadn't drawn his weapon. His hands rested on his pommels. "But we do have other guests that have been introduced to the Creeper."

With shocked voices, Dule and Roday said, "You let the Creeper out? Are you mad?"

Deterus showed them the medallion hanging on his neck. "No, I'm following orders and in control of everything. Darkken said to wipe the likes of you off of the face of the world. I intend to see that done." His expression darkened. "Caligin, slay them!"

CHAPTER 22

THE CALIGIN CLOSED IN. HACKSAW, Roday, and Dule moved back-to-back, forming a tight circle. Before Hacksaw could blink, he parried a vicious cut. The sharp ring of steel started the beginning of the battle. It was twenty against three, and the Caligin were highly skilled fighters.

Hacksaw belted out his battle cry. "Ride the thunder! Ride! Argh!"

A second attacker's sword cut into his arm. Green Tongue flashed back, countering with a backswing that clipped open the new attacker's leg.

"Take that, elven demon!"

Deterus stayed behind the ranks, gloating. He laughed aloud and said, "Make them bleed. Then slaughter them!"

The quick-handed Dule and Roday fought with their own ferocity.

Roday shouted, "Left strike!"

As one, they teamed up on a Caligin engaged with Roday. Their swords overwhelmed the dark elf and put him down as he blocked one sword only to catch another in the chest.

"Well done, brother!" Roday said.

Roday and Dule managed to parry the stinging blows of their attackers a few moments longer. They were fine swordsmen fighting with purpose and vigor. They killed two more Caligin before the superior ranks got to them. Sword and dagger cuts whittled away their armor. Both elves started to bleed heavily from their wounds.

Hacksaw battled away with everything he had. The only thing keeping him together was his chain mail. He blocked a slice to his throat. He countered with a downward chop that cleaved into his attacker's shoulder. A dark elf stabbed into the chest of his chain mail. The point of the sword stuck him in the flesh. He groaned as he batted away his attacker with Green Tongue. "You fools are lucky I'm old, or I'd have put you in the grave by now!"

A shadow passed overhead.

If Hacksaw were to guess, he would've thought death had come to get him. No doubt, time was running short. He'd slipped death enough in his lifetime. He wasn't likely to slip it again. Over the clamor of clashing steel, he heard the distinct screech of a bird. A shadow passed over his eyes. "Death circles!"

Something dropped from the sky.

Thud!

From the air, Rond, the four-armed undead bugbear, dropped behind the dark elves. His dark brows were buckled. He locked eyes on the elves and charged into the shocked brood like a charging bull. Rond snatched up an elf with his upper hands and broke its neck with a snap. His lower fists grabbed and whaled on another surprised elf.

"What is this abomination?" Deterus shouted. He pointed at four of his elves broken from the fray. "Go kill that thing!"

The four dark elves zeroed in on the bugbear. They stuck him with their swords high and low. The undead bugbear didn't flinch. Rond grabbed elves by their hair and smashed their faces together. His face was a countenance of rage. He picked another elf up overhead, took a sword right into his chest, and flung the elf into the other.

"Ha!" Hacksaw yelled with a renewed spirit. "Death does circle!"

As they still fought, Roday joined in the conversation. He pointed his sword at the shocked Deterus. "Yes, it does circle. It circles for you!"

"Fools!" Deterus said. He waved the medallion at them. "I control the Creeper! Nothing can stop that! I'll just call it down to kill y—ulp!"

A huge hawk snatched up Deterus, its talons sinking deep into the elf's shoulders. With a wingspan beating at over twenty feet, it flew out of the keep's courtyard. It went higher and higher.

Hacksaw lost sight of the great bird. He was still fighting, but now, he was on even terms. The dark elves' ranks diminished. They fought two on one, but that was good enough odds for the old swordsman. Green Tongue, a blade as fine as any, gave the knight the advantage. It was time to take the Caligin to school. Using his superior weight and strength, he unleashed a fierce downward chop. One dark elf parried and saw his sword break from the blow on the hilt. Hacksaw punched his dagger into the shocked elf's chest.

The second elven attacker sideswiped at Hacksaw's ribs. Hacksaw stepped into the swing, locked up the elf's extended arm with his own, and head-butted the elf square in the nose.

"That's from the old school of swordsmanship!" He stabbed the staggering elf in the chest.

Now, the four of them were equal in number to the four dark elves remaining. The Caligin fled.

Hacksaw, Roday, and Dule held up their blood-coated blades and let out a triumphant shout.

Glancing upward, Hacksaw noticed smoke still coming out of the higher levels, but the explosive sounds had died out. He had a sinking feeling. "We need to get up there!"

The great hawk came from the sky and landed in the courtyard. It stood taller than a horse. Quickly, it changed from a hawk to the petite form of Calypsa the dryad.

Roday and Dule rushed over to her. "That was something, but what did you do to Deterus?"

Calypsa gave them a curious look. "Who?"

"The elf you took. He had the medallion that controls the Creeper," Roday said. "Where is it?"

"I dropped him off," she said with a curious look. "Did I do well?"

"No! No! You have to go back and get that medallion. Change back into a big bird," Roday demanded.

"Yeah," Dule agreed, "'cause I want to ride on you."

"I can't change back," she said.

"I can't wait any longer!" Hacksaw ran to the stairwell, calling out, "Nath! Nath!"

Everyone followed Hacksaw up the stairs into a training room, which was smoking from fire. Once all were gathered inside, they caught their first terrifying look at the Creeper through the smoking haze. It had a bloodied-up dwarf in its jaws, and two dragons lay unmoving on the ground.

Hacksaw called out, "Hey! Get away from that dwarf."

The Creeper turned. Its slavering jaws dripped. The saliva sizzled and burned.

"Lords of Thunder," he said in awe. "What is that thing?"

"Certain death," Roday said quietly. "Certain death for all that cross it."

Chapter 23

The only light in the burial chamber was the glow of Nath's sword, Fang. His golden eyes scanned the chamber as he waited for ghosts or spirits to attack at any moment. Then the crawling cave bugs' glow renewed. The chill wind died. They had full light again, and the tension in the air started to fade. "What is happening?"

"Nothing," Darkken said nonchalantly. He scooted the broken urn and dust away with his foot. "These urns are filled with the dead."

Nath and Maefon tilted their heads. "I don't follow."

"Well, you see, when I came here long ago, I discovered that some of these platforms were indeed the burial sites for the people. But"—Darkken held up a finger—"some of these platforms, coffins, and urns were vacant, meaning there were no dead in them. The people of this area certainly kept their dead in high regard, so much so that they prepared their burial chambers early." He scratched the beard that had started on his chin. "I actually think that this burial chamber worked as a business. These urns were prepared well in advance, and I assume families would pay for their site in advance. These abandoned ones made for a perfect hiding spot."

"Hiding spot for what?" Nath asked.

"Help me lift this lid off of the sarcophagus, and I will show you," Darkken replied. He braced his arms on the end of the coffin opposite Nath.

"That looks heavy. Are you sure that you can lift it?" Maefon said.

"We're going to find out." Nath fastened his arms on his end. Looking about, he asked, "Are you sure the spirits will be fine with this? Something is here. I can feel it. And the bugs… Why else did they and the torches go out?"

"Well, the spirits don't want us to be too cocky, I presume. After all, we are invaders." Darkken's gaze drifted toward the ceiling. "But so long as we honor the dead, then we have nothing to worry about."

"Are you certain?"

"Yes, I'm certain. I almost died the last time I was here, but I figured it out. Come on now. Let's put our backs into it." Darkken started to lift and grunted.

With the muscles in his arms bulging and back straining, Nath put his might into the lift. Across from him, veins bulged in Darkken's neck. The man's face turned red. The stone lid scraped against the coffin.

Nath straightened his back, and they shuffled over to one side and set the lid down. "Ooof!"

Panting, Darkken fanned himself. He arched his back. "That seemed heavier than it did the last time. I guess I'm getting old."

"Who helped you last time?" Nath asked.

"Good question." He lifted his fingers, and the tips glowed. "I used magic."

"Why didn't you use that this time?"

"I told you we needed to save our energy. Besides," Darkken said, "you could have used the Gauntlet of Goam but didn't. And I was curious to see if you could lift it."

Nath looked at the leather gauntlet on his hand. He'd gotten so used to it that he'd forgotten it was there. He opened and closed his fingers. "Huh, I suppose I could have, but like you said, I need to save my energy." He peeked into the coffin. A blanket was there, covering something. "So, what's in here?"

The coffin was big enough for Darkken to climb in. Maefon leaned over the side. Darkken looked at them both and said, "Feast your eyes on this." He lifted the blanket, revealing a chunky block of metal bigger than an anvil.

Nath cocked his head. "That's it? Metal?"

Darkken showed his winning smile. "Not just any metal. Nath, touch it with Fang."

He whipped out his sword and banged the blade on the chunk of ore. *Tang!* Radiant pulsations of blue ran through the chunk of metal and faded.

Maefon gasped.

Darkken said, "Dragon steel."

"Whoa," Nath said. Fang's blade shimmered with an icy-blue sheen. "Where did you get this? It can only come from Dragon Home. I don't see how it's possible that you have it."

"Well, I have a hunk of it. Consider it my inheritance." Darkken bent down and picked up the block of dragon steel with both hands. With a grunt, he set it on a top corner of the coffin. "Luckily, it's not as heavy as real steel. It's less than half the weight of common ore."

"Seriously, Darkken, where did you get this?"

Darkken climbed out of the coffin and said, "I don't think that really matters at this point." He started to pick up the ore.

Nath stopped him. "If we are going to trust one another, then you need to tell me."

"I didn't steal it. Not that it should matter if I did." Darkken sighed. "Well, that's not entirely true, either. Actually, this hunk of steel was stolen by the elves long ago. I discovered their treachery and stole it from them."

Nath shook his head. "Are you certain that you didn't have the Trahaydeen steal it for you?"

"No, brother. I did not. This dragon ore was taken long before I came along. It was part of the reason why the elves and dwarves were sent from Dragon Home. Remember the stories. The dwarves and elves wanted the ore for themselves, and the dragons kicked them out. Well, this is part of that stolen steel. Now it is mine."

Nath knew the story, and what Darkken said made sense. Some dragon steel had gone missing. How much, no one knew for certain.

"That hunk of ore is worth more than its weight in gold," Nath said.

"More. Ha, it's worth a thousand times more." Darkken patted the chunk. "That is what your precious Fang is made of." He looked at the sword with a flicker of desire in his eyes. "That sword can cut through anything. Not to mention its other unique powers. But that's a special enchantment on the metal itself. Only our father knows what it does for sure because clearly you don't. But there are other weapons of its kind out there—not like Fang but made from the steel. They were so formidable that, after the dwarven and elven fallout, Balzurth had the dragons retrieve all that they could and melt them down."

"It sounds like Balzurth didn't want it falling into the wrong hands," Nath said.

"True, he took precautions. The only weapon I'm aware of that contains the metal is the Spear of Barnabas. I never found it or another the likes of it, and believe me, I searched them out. But I did find the scroll, and I did find this ore in the vaults of Elome. The elves are too embarrassed to admit they lost it. But there are those that search for it, only to never find it." He tapped his rings on the ore. "It's mine now."

"And what do you intend to do with it?" Nath asked.

"Why, I'm going to make a sword, like Fang, of my own."

Chapter 24

The Creeper fixed its four eyes on Hacksaw and the others. It seemed to be able to see all of them at once. Hatred burned in its eyes. Hacksaw's heart pounded in his ears. He'd never seen the likes of the monster. It now walked toward them with the dwarf in its jaws.

The dwarf punched the creature in the side of the head, saying, "Nothing eats a dwarf!"

Dule and Roday moved to Hacksaw's left as Calypsa and Rond moved to his right.

"It's seen us now. It won't stop until it kills us or we kill it," Roday said. "Which is virtually impossible without the medallion."

Dule punched Roday in the shoulder. "I told you I didn't want to join the Caligin. But you talked me into it."

Roday smugly said, "Dule, you said you wanted more excitement than selling herbal toxins and healing ointments. It doesn't get any more exciting than this."

Dule shook his head. "I hate you, Roday."

The Creeper half slung, half spat the dwarf out of its mouth. The dwarf rolled over the training-room floor in front of Hacksaw's feet.

Hacksaw looked down at the battered dwarf and said, "Brenwar?"

"What's left of me. Ha. A fine time to meet, Hacksaw." Brenwar rolled up to a knee. "Help me kill that thing. Fetch that sledgehammer out of my back. I misplaced my warhammer."

"Certainly," Hacksaw said with a dozen thoughts rushing through his mind. He hadn't seen Brenwar in decades. The dwarf was the fiercest fighter he'd ever met. Now, he looked like a dog's chew toy. Immediately, he recognized the sledgehammer. It was Stone Smiter. Before he could grab it, Rond reached over and snatched it away.

Stone Smiter's top gemstone flared.

The Creeper charged.

Arms and sledgehammer high, Rond rushed right at it. His overhanded swing missed the Creeper's head, but he hit it square in the shoulder. *Crack!* The Creeper shook. Its claws tore into the bugbear. They went at it like a giant four-armed man fighting an eight-clawed grizzly.

Wiping the blood from his nose, Brenwar asked Hacksaw, "Who's your friend?"

"Not a friend. Just an undead bugbear."

"Well, we can't let him have all the fun!" Brenwar got to his feet and fixed on his warhammer, which lay on the other side of the platform. "Keep that thing away from me." He ran, jumping the Creeper's swishing tail as he did so.

"Whoa, that stumpy little dwarf can scoot," Roday said.

Hacksaw shook his head, put both hands on his sword, set his eyes on the Creeper, and said, "Ride the thunder!"

A quick flip of the Creeper's tail sent Hacksaw to the ground.

Roday and Dule helped him up and said as one, "Get back in there, elderly one. Don't take that from the beast!"

"And what are the both of you going to do?" Hacksaw replied.

"We'll distract it," Dule said. They started running around the room, waving their blades, trying to catch the monster's attention. "Over here! Over here!"

The Creeper stood on its hind legs, wrestling against Rond. The bugbear had a good go at it, whaling away with his fists and hammer. The monster's claws ripped up the bugbear's skin.

The saliva in its mouth sizzled flesh. The bugbear hammered away while Calypsa drew near to him, shouting encouragements.

Hacksaw moved to the dryad, shielding her with himself. "Lady, that thing will rip you open if you don't turn into something else. Let us handle this." Looking for an opening to attack the monster, he caught Brenwar out of the corner of his eye, warhammer in hand and charging from the rear, shouting in dwarven. Hacksaw darted in and speared the monster right through the ribs with his sword. "Die, beast!"

The pinkish-brown skin of the monster was sliced open, but no blood came from the wound. It quickly healed over.

"It does not bleed! The wound closes!" Hacksaw yelled. He stabbed Green Tongue deeper into the flesh.

At the same time, a loud sound of metal on hide hit the Creeper square in the back. It reared up higher on its back legs. Its head twisted around, and it snapped at Brenwar. The dwarf hopped backward, missing his head being bitten off by twelve inches.

Rond ripped out of the Creeper's hold. He brought the sledgehammer around and hit the Creeper full force in the back of the skull. Bright-purple light sparked out of the hammer, making a clap of thunder. The Creeper's entire body shook.

"It felt that one! Keep hitting it! It has to have a weakness!" Brenwar crashed the bladed side of his hammer into the Creeper's snout. The hard shot snapped its head around. All eight legs wobbled underneath it. "Don't let up!"

Crack! Rond hit it again with his hammer.

Clang! Brenwar busted its iron-hard ribs.

Slice! Hacksaw cut the monster in the neck.

Chomp! The Creeper bit down on Hacksaw's leg.

He let out an anguished cry.

Dule and Roday came to his aid. Their swords jabbed into the Creeper's face.

"Kill this bloody thing!" Hacksaw roared. Hands overhead, he chopped into the monster's nose like a log. It slung him aside so hard that he could have sworn his leg must have ripped off. When he landed, he still had his leg, but blood coated it. The burning saliva sizzled on his flesh. He tried to fight his way upright, but Calypsa pushed him down.

"Stay put," she said, using her hands to put pressure on his legs. "Be still."

"I'm not going to die sitting on my rear end. Get me to my feet!"

Brenwar and Rond exchanged blows with the beast. They hit, and it hit back with claws and tail. It knocked them down only to see them get back up again. The creature's head hung low. The holes, which Hacksaw had poked in its side, reopened. It started to bleed.

"It leaks! It leaks!" Hacksaw yelled. "Keep hitting it!"

Fighting as a single unit, with hammers that hit like battering rams, the dwarf and the bugbear gave it their all. They worked their way to the front of the beast and struck its skull at the same time, making a resounding *kraakow!* The Creeper's legs buckled. Its belly flattened on the floor.

Sucking for breath, Brenwar hit it again. "For Morgdon," he half yelled, half mumbled.

The tireless Rond's hammer rose up and came down in a slow and steady fashion. Metal smacked against bone and flesh. *Wham! Wham! Thud! Pow!*

The Creeper fought its way to its feet, only to fall back down again. It bled. It breathed. It took punishment, but it would not die.

Calypsa reached for Hacksaw's sword. "Can I borrow this?"

Hacksaw shook his head. "I know what you are thinking. Help me up." Using her for strength and his sword for a cane, he hobbled over to the Creeper. Its paws scratched over the floor as it pushed to stand. Hacksaw pushed his sword into the middle of its skull. He didn't stop until it was all the way to the hilt. The monster's jaws opened. Its head shook. Finally, its tongue juddered out of its mouth, and its teeth collapsed on it. It lay still.

"That should do it," said Hacksaw.

Leaning over the monster's body, Roday coughed. The room was still smoking, though the small fires that had started were going out. Fanning his face, he put his pointed ear on the creature's hide. "I think the heart is still beating." His eyes widened. "Well, was beating. Nope, it's still beating. Really slowly, like dripping water from an early thaw."

Wincing, Hacksaw let out a ragged sigh.

Rond kept striking the Creeper until Calpysa stopped him by saying, "Friend, you did well."

Eyeing the dragons lying on the floor, Hacksaw asked Brenwar, "Are your friends gone?"

Brenwar's moustache ends billowed out with a huff. With a worried look in his eye, he marched toward the dragons and said, "I'll check."

CHAPTER 25

NATH KEPT QUIET AS THEY headed out of the temple while he pondered Darkken's words about making his own Fang. The mere mention of it instantly irritated him. Fang was a special sword made for him. A true one of a kind. He couldn't bear the thought of there being another. He wasn't sure why, but he just couldn't.

As they wove through the catacombs, he finally broke his silence. "Are you going to make a sword *just* like Fang?"

Darkken's hollow laughter echoed through the tunnels. "No, not just like Fang, at least in regard to the shape and form. Fang is certainly a marvelous blade, but I prefer single-handed fighting. That pommel on Fang is made for two grips, and I don't have the need for that." He chuckled. "No need to be jealous, little brother."

"I'm not jealous. But I don't see the need for it, either." He ducked into another tunnel. "I thought that you were fond of Scalpel."

"I am. Its elven design is of the finest craftsmanship, and because I am so accustomed to it, I plan to fashion my new sword very much like it. I'll probably call it Scalpel. Maybe Scalpel Two."

Frowning, Nath said, "That would be a silly name."

"Agreed," Maefon added.

"So will you be able to give this new sword powers?" Nath said. He wanted to keep the conversation going while he tried to think about things. He didn't like the idea of the sword having powers, either. But he was relieved that it would not look like Fang. The deeper question was, why did Darkken really need a sword when he boasted that he was more of a sorcerer these days?

"Like Fang, I would like to try to enchant the metal with special powers. But I really don't know how Balzurth managed to do that," he admitted. "But I have theories. Well, I mean, I've studied, and there aren't many swords out there that have powers." With the hunk of ore underneath his arm, he caught up with Nath when they cleared the tunnel leading into the back end of the temple. "Listen, brother, I want this to be a project for us to do together. And I've never made my own sword before. Though I have been seasoned by the fires and the furnace, I've held off until this very special time."

Nath played along. "Fine. I'll help, but it better not look like my sword. Do you understand?"

Darkken nodded. "You can inspect my mold yourself."

"Don't we need dwarves and elves to shape the dragon steel?"

"We have an elf—well, plenty of them, actually—but we don't need either one of them," Darkken said. "Why? Because we are dragons. And we have the scroll, not to mention the Star of the Heavens. Once we get to the forge, we'll have more than enough power to melt the finest metal ever made."

"I'll take your word for it." Nath started out of the temple.

Darkken hooked his arm. "Not so fast, my brother."

Outside, a lot of strange hooting and chirping was coming from the fog in the trees.

Maefon gave Darkken a troubled look.

"What is it now?" Nath asked.

"Do you remember how I told you that we needed to save our energy?" Darkken said.

Nath replied with a drawn-out "yes."

"Well, this is where the wagon wheel meets the road." Darkken hefted the ore up onto his shoulder. "You see, there was always a chance the spirits would attack, which, thankfully, they didn't. And we bypassed the guardian to get here. And that's excellent even though he is bound to thaw out eventually. But there is a third obstacle that I have not mentioned. The only way out of here is to fight our way out past the creatures that fill the trees. You see, none that enter the temple are ever supposed to leave. If the spirits don't take us, or the guardian behemoth, then the smaller guardians will."

"Can't you teleport us out of here?" Maefon asked.

"My, such confidence you have in me. But no," Darkken said. "I can't, not without much additional rest."

"Let's just wait it out, then. We can stay in the temple until you are ready," Nath suggested.

Darkken slowly shook his head. "The spirits only let us pass because they know that, most likely, we will not leave. They fully expected the winged beast men to drag our dead carcasses back inside. It's entertainment to them. But if we go back in, their grace will run out, and they'll put an end to us. The screaming is awful. Trust me."

Nath looked back inside the temple. The wind had picked up and was whistling through the columns. The stale scent of death tickled his nose. "You knew this the entire time and did not tell us?"

"I didn't want you to worry."

"Well, we could have had a better plan." Nath stared out into the wilderness as steady drops of rain still fell from above and more rustling sounded in the trees. "How did you get out the last time?"

"The last time, I slipped past the behemoth. Well, barely. But I outran him."

Eyeing the ore, Nath said, "Carrying that?"

"I have very strong and fast legs. Surely you understand. Anyway, I ran in, and I teleported out. I hoped to have the same success this time, but it turned out backwards."

"You sure went to a lot of trouble over a block of metal. It doesn't seem worth it."

"Don't you think that Fang is worth it?"

Nath held up his sword. "I suppose."

Fang's pommel heated up.

"Er... definitely."

The pommel cooled back down.

"So, what are these winged beast men?"

"The beast-birds are not monstrous in size. They are smallish, like a halfling, feathered darkly, with talons for fingers and feet. They look like men but with beaks on their faces and black fur around their neck. In a way, impish."

"Doesn't sound so bad," Nath said, easing his way farther out of the temple. "How bad can winged halflings be?"

Darkken moved alongside him and said, "Pretty bad when they are flesh-eating halflings. Stay close, and run with me. We'll have to fight our way up the slope, but if we break through the fog, we should be safe by then."

Nath looked at him and said, "You can't fight and carry that thing. Put it in your pack."

"I'd rather hold onto it."

"Don't be silly," Maefon said. She unbuckled the straps on his pack and flipped the flap open.

Nath took the ore from Darkken. "This isn't exactly light." He stuffed it into Darkken's pack. "Still cumbersome."

"It won't be once it's a sword and a few other things."

Together, Nath and Maefon buckled the straps.

"I hope your stitching holds," Nath said. "It should. It's dwarven." Darkken stepped all the way out of the temple's entrance, eyed the fog above, and said, "Let's go!"

He took off at a dead sprint with the pack bouncing on his back. Nath brought up the rear. He and Maefon didn't have trouble keeping up with him as they snaked past the brush and around the great trees.

Above, a clamor of beating wings started. The strange bird-calling began and grew louder.

It sounded like giant locusts come to life. Then they came. Just as Darkken had described, the beast-birds dropped out of their fog-covered perches and swarmed them from all directions.

Nath's sword flashed through the air. He split a beast-bird in half then cut loose on another. They were ugly little things with hooked beaks and sharp teeth. Dozens must have been there. While running, Darkken swung his sword with fatal accuracy. Maefon did the same. No matter how good they were with swords, that wasn't going to be enough. The superior forces that made it past their defenses latched onto their bodies like leeches. Claws and teeth bit into armor and flesh.

Maefon let out a blood-chilling scream.

Chapter 26

The fires in the training room were extinguished, and the smoke began to clear. Calypsa, Dule, and Roday used towels stored in the Caligin training room to give aid to Brenwar and Hacksaw.

"We'll get you stitched up," Roday said. He broke off some stitching with his teeth and threaded a needle. "It's not as if this room hasn't seen blood drawn before. Just not this much."

"I've bled worse," Brenwar said.

"Really? Somehow, that seems impossible," Roday responded.

Brenwar's arms were gashed up from the Creeper's talons. His hair was matted with blood, his burnished breastplate stained with blood. He looked at Hacksaw. The battered knight was in as bad a shape as him, if not worse. Blood soaked the man's leg through the trousers. The deep teeth marks were visible.

"That's a fine scratch," Brenwar said. "Probably best that you take the leg off."

Grimacing, Hacksaw managed a chuckle and replied, "You best take that head from your shoulders too. It's a mess."

"A headless dwarf, now that would be something. I like it," Slivver said. The silver dragon lay nearby on his belly. His fine scales had been torn open in many places, revealing the muscles and flesh underneath. The membranes on his wings were tattered. One wing hung lower than the other. It was either disjointed or broken. He breathed heavily. "That was the first time that I even thought I might not make it. You came just in time," he said to Calypsa, who made her way over to him and checked his wounds.

"Try to remain still," she said.

"I will, but if you would, check on my friend." Slivver looked at Master Elween, who was in as bad a shape, lying still with only a choppy rise and fall to her chest. "It's hard to see her down. I don't know of a more resilient dragon." He looked at the dead Creeper. "That thing is not of this time or age. We exhausted our powers against it. It seemed to absorb them."

"I wore it down just enough for the newcomers to finish it," Brenwar said. "But I agree. That is not of this age." He eyed Hacksaw. "You look much older than our last encounter, Legionnaire."

As Roday worked on the wound on his leg, Hacksaw said, "I wish I could say the same for you, but you have not aged a day."

"The dwarven constitution brings longevity. A shame that men don't have that. The world would be a better place if it were all dwarven."

"Oh please," Dule said.

"Don't start, elf," Brenwar warned. "You don't see dwarves trying to take over the world. We mind our own business."

Dule shrugged. "Eh, I see your point. So, the two of you know each other."

"Aye, from a campaign against the goblins decades ago," Brenwar said. A smile formed underneath his bushy beard. "That was my kind of scrap. Five hundred goblins ambushed a host of dwarves and legionnaire riders."

Hacksaw's haggard expression brightened somewhat. "Yes, we stacked those yellow-eyed fiends up like split wood." He pointed at Brenwar. "I'd never seen anyone fight like Brenwar Boulderguild. How many did you take down that day? Twenty?"

"Thirty-two." Brenwar almost grinned. "One of my best days in battle. But I don't think it would top this one."

"No, I'd rather fight a thousand goblins than face the likes of that thing again," Hacksaw said. "It's good to ride the thunder with you again, Brenwar Boulderguild."

"You as well, Hacksaw."

"If you are finished gushing all over one another, I'd like to address a bigger problem." Roday leaned over Hacksaw's leg and applied pressure to the grave wound. "This leg won't stop bleeding. And Hacksaw's skin is starting to pale." He looked in the man's eyes. "It might have to come off. But for now, I need your belt to make a tourniquet."

"No," Brenwar said. He had a potion vial filled with golden liquid in his hand. "Use the entire bit." He tossed it to Hacksaw.

When Hacksaw opened his hand to catch it, Roday plucked it out of the air. "Should he ingest it or apply it?"

"Half and half," Brenwar said.

Roday took his bandage from the wound and applied half of the potion by dripping it on the gashes. The bleeding stopped, and the flesh started to mend. Hacksaw's graying flesh started regaining its luster.

Roday handed the vial back to Hacksaw and said, "Bottoms up."

Hacksaw shook his head. "I think this would best be served on that dragon over there." He eyed Elween closely. "That's a lady, isn't it? Lighter scales on the chest. Eyelashes."

"Aye," Brenwar said.

"I haven't been so close to dragons—well, at least living ones. They are different from the ones I've seen." His eyes drifted to Brenwar. "They seem like people."

"We *are* people," Slivver said.

Calypsa came for the potion and took it from Hacksaw. "Thank you."

"I didn't mean any offense," Hacksaw said, "but I'm not used to seeing a dragon talk, either. It's a new experience."

"Think nothing of it, Hacksaw. Again, I'm thankful that you arrived when you did. All of you," Slivver said.

He looked across the room, where Rond was standing guard at the entrance to the training room. The bugbear had wounds so bad that one could see to the bone, but he did not bleed.

"Even him. Especially him. What is the story behind that one?"

"A sad one," Calypsa said. She had rested Elween's head on her lap and began to empty the potion into the dragon's mouth. "But he was my dearest friend. The Caligin destroyed him, courtesy of Lord Darkken and Maefon's betrayal. But the wound in his heart, I fear, came by my own hand."

"Well, now that our paths have crossed, let's clear the air about something," Slivver said. "Are all of us looking for Nath?"

As the room filled with nods of agreement, the group swapped information about what they knew of Nath, Darkken, and the Caligin. Once they wrapped up, Brenwar glanced about. He fought his way to a knee. "I suppose we need to clear this keep and resume the search for Nath. But my gut tells me that he's not here. But there should be some clues here about where to find him." He looked at Dule and Roday. "Well?"

"Well," Roday said, "first things first. We may have killed the Creeper, but I'm certain that this keep is still filled with Caligin waiting to kill us. And it wouldn't surprise me one bit if more were coming."

CHAPTER 27

Swinging his sword at anything that moved, Nath fought his way toward Maefon. The beast-birds were smaller and lighter, but they still stood above his waist. Strength was in their wiry limbs. Attacking in superior numbers, they became stronger. Claws pulled at Nath's mouth, and sharp beaks pecked the back of his head and body.

He screamed, "Hang on, Maefon!"

The elven woman was buried underneath a tide of fierce little bodies. The blades in her hands kept striking until they struck no more.

The beast-birds clung to his legs, stopping his efforts to move forward. Outraged, Nath said, "This is ridiculous. Darkken, do something!"

Hacking at the monstrous little men with overhead chops, Darkken said, "I'm trying. Nath, invoke the Gauntlet of Goam!"

Nath had become so accustomed to it that he'd forgotten to summon the magic gauntlet's power. With the feathered fiends fighting to pull him to the ground, he called forth the item's magic. The gemstone on the back of the hand brightened with a new life. A spring of energy spread up Nath's arm and through his extremities. His natural strength doubled, if not tripled.

He let out a triumphant "Yes! That's better!" He grabbed a beast-bird by the wings and flung the screeching thing aside. Hacking away with a surge of energy, he stormed toward Maefon. "Hang on!"

Maefon kicked a beast-bird away. "I am!"

Nath snatched one beast-bird after another by whatever he could grab. He pulled them free from his arms, back, and legs. Their talons tore his skin. They let out earsplitting screeches. Nath went to work on Maefon's attackers. He stuck his sword into the ground and grabbed two beast-birds at a time.

"I hate bird-beasts!" He slammed their beaks together. *Crunch!*

Maefon wiggled her way from underneath of the pile. Using her sword and dagger, she stabbed two different beast-birds in the chest at the same time. "I hate them more than you! And it's *beast-birds*!"

"What?" he asked as he punted a beast-bird away from him.

"Nothing!" Maefon killed another with her sword.

With dead beast-birds piled up at his feet, Darkken yelled at Nath and Maefon, "Get up the slope!" He pointed his sword, which was caked with blood and feathers. "Up the slope. Toward the fog!" He ran toward the slope, fighting his way through the beast-birds that had landed.

By the dozens, the beast-birds dropped from the fog and landed in their path. An army of them was growing.

Nath and Maefon, still fighting the beast-birds that rushed them, caught up to Darkken.

"There are too many!" Nath said. He swung his sword through two of them. "We have to kill them faster. Maefon, can't you shoot them with something?"

"I spent my energy on the behemoth!" she said.

A beast-bird landed on her and sank its bottom talons into her shoulder. She let out a fierce grunt and stabbed its chest. With it skewered on her sword, she flicked it away.

Nath mowed down every feathery thing that moved. Fang sheared the feathered monsters in two. For every one that died, two more dropped from the foggy sky like new rain. He was bleeding. They were all bleeding. Their blood mixed with the rain and soppy ground.

Protecting Maefon the best he could, Nath kept swinging. "Great Guzan! Will they all just die?"

A beast-bird flew into Darkken's face, making a loud smack. He stumbled on the slick ground. The beast-birds piled on, driving him to the ground. He roared and thrashed in the heap of wild things.

Darkken bellowed in a resounding voice, "Enough of this!"

A blinding flash of coppery light exploded from his body. Every beast-bird that touched him vaporized.

The forest went still. Darkken came to his feet, his eyes glowing. His countenance became a snarl. Copper strands of lightning gathered on his hands and started to build. Gaping, Nath and Maefon backed away.

With a deep frown, Darkken opened his hands. A globe of mystical light formed around him. The savage beast-birds flew right at him and hit the globe. The moment they hit, they crackled. Feathers flew. Without warning, Darkken cast strands of lightning from his fingers like a net. It slammed into the wave of beast-birds. They squawked, screeched, convulsed, and spasmed. Feathers exploded from their bodies. Their skin crinkled and blackened. All over the forest, the beast-birds started to die in waves. They fell from the fog and crashed through the branches of the trees. Smoking, they bounced and burned on the ground.

Nath felt Maefon's hand grip his as Darkken's powers cleared the forest of the flying vermin. The beast-birds died in droves. The ones that survived the wave of fiery magic fled. The wounded that Darkken caught moving were turned to a crisp by fire from his hands.

The forest reeked of burned skin, fried feathers, and death.

The brilliant coppery light on Darkken's fingers extinguished. The glow in his eyes faded. His damp hair clung to his forehead. Sweat dripped from his brow. The hard lines in his face eased. He looked at the damage and said, "I didn't realize I had that kind of power within me." He glanced at Nath and Maefon. "I have no idea if more will be back." With a sigh, he trudged toward the slope. "We'd better go."

Nath looked at Maefon. Her eyes were bigger than saucers as she surveyed the dead beast-birds covering the forest floor. Her body shuddered.

Nath put an arm over her shoulders and said, "The danger is over."

She looked at him and quietly said, "I don't think so."

CHAPTER 28

ESCORTED BY RODAY AND DULE, Hacksaw and Brenwar resumed their search for the Caligin. Rond stayed behind, keeping watch over Calypsa, Slivver, and Elween. Being in such close proximity to dragons was strange to Hacksaw. He wondered if that was what Nath would one day turn into. He ambled after the elves, up the stairs, keeping pace with Brenwar. His wounded leg felt as stiff as a board, but he managed. "And I thought my adventuring days were over. Ha. This is the worst one of them all."

"It's been a scrap, that's for sure," Brenwar grumbled.

They found the seventh level clear and moved through the doors on the eighth. It was a barracks, with bunk beds and cots lined up uniformly. Each set of beds had a wooden chest at the foot and the head. All of them were locked. Dule and Roday glided into the room on cat's feet, swords and dagger ready to strike. They didn't take long to make a clean sweep of the room.

Roday came back and said, "I swear, there have to be more dark elves in the keep. Just keep your guard up."

Holding up his warhammer, Brenwar firmly asked, "Does it look as if my guard is down, elf?"

"I'll be back. I'm going to take a closer look around." Roday joined up with Dule on the other side of the room. They vanished into the alcoves built into the walls behind the beds.

Hacksaw slowly limped through the room, fighting the urge to lie down on a bed. Brenwar's dark eyes scanned the room like a hawk's. The dwarf looked as solid as a great oak. Blood and bruises were a part of the dwarf's rugged exterior. He wore them naturally. By comparison, Hacksaw felt like he'd literally had the life beaten out of him. Leaning on a bedpost, he asked, "So, how did you come to be in the service of dragons, if you don't mind me asking?"

Brenwar clawed at his beard and said, "The Boulderguilds and the dragons go way back. Serving their causes is part of our heritage."

"So, you know Nath?"

"No. Never met the boy."

"Darkken?"

Brenwar shook his head. "Never knew he existed until word came to me. Slivver and I go back. They needed me to track Nath down. So, you know Nath well?"

Hacksaw nodded. "Well enough, I suppose. I'll tell you this: I've never met the likes of him. He's good, just naïve to the ways of the world. I never should have left him."

"You aren't his nursemaid. The boy has to learn to live by his decisions, the same as we all do."

"I agree, but he came a babe in the wilderness. Now, he's being raised by the wolves."

Hacksaw's heart sank. If he never saw Nath again, that would be hard to live with. He wanted to help him. "He needs guidance. This Darkken—and the Caligin—I've never encountered the likes of them. They are so eerie for elves. Cold-blooded. They shot me full of arrows. I'm still not sure how I made it out alive."

"What about those two little windbags that are leading us through this tower? You've put your trust in them?"

"Nath can have a profound effect on people. He brings out the good in them." Hacksaw looked for the elves but didn't see them. "I think they were on the wrong side of things, but Nath turned them. I wouldn't normally say that, if I hadn't seen it happen with Calypsa. She's a dryad, or part of one, I think. He changed her heart too."

"The woman is a dryad, you say?" Brenwar asked.

"Yes, as I understand it. Of course, I've never met a dryad before, so what do I know? I've never met dragons, either." Hacksaw searched the room again. "Where are those elves?"

"Probably setting a trap that we are about to be led into."

"What sort of trap, do you think? A pit of spikes? Poisoned arrows? Sleeping gas?" Hacksaw said playfully.

"I think we can rule out a rockslide." He glanced up. "But maybe a ceiling might drop on us. Maybe the sheets on these bunks will envelop and suffocate us. I can only imagine this keep is full of traps. Dwarves make the best traps. In Morgdon, we have catapults that hurl people off the wall."

"Yes, that is well-known in Quintuklen, but that's not a trap."

"It is so."

"But it's not secret. Traps are secret," Hacksaw said.

Brenwar grumbled.

Roday and Dule returned with a swagger.

"I can't explain it, but I can't find any more of our former Caligin brethren. But"—Roday lifted a finger—"we did disarm some traps. A poisoned needle jettisoned out of a small cupboard and struck my good man Dule in the buttocks."

Dule made a frustrated face. "You opened the door when I told you not to. And no, the needle wasn't poisoned. It just stung. It was meant for the eye, not the butt."

Brenwar exchanged a look with Hacksaw. Then with a huff, he said, "We're going up."

Roday and Dule scooted right by them.

"Let us lead the way!" Roday said.

The eighth floor was cleared as well as the ninth. Dule and Roday were left scratching their heads by the time they made it to the tenth. Standing outside the tenth-level doorway, Roday said, "I honestly thought we would have encountered the Caligin by now. They are supposed to protect the keep and everything within with their lives."

"Perhaps they are in the dungeon levels," Hacksaw suggested.

"That wouldn't be protocol. The Caligin are called to defend from the top down, keeping the enemy on the lower levels," Dule said knowingly. "It's in the book."

"So, what's behind this door?" Hacksaw asked.

"Lord Darkken's quarters, designed for meetings, dining, sleeping, and study. We've only been inside a few times before," Roday said. "Honestly, I'm very eager to get a closer look at it."

"Quit standing around, and let's go in," Brenwar said.

Roday opened the door. A spear lanced him in the chest.

Chapter 29

Nath and company walked the rim of Cold Cliff Island with the rain stinging their faces. Darkken led that way with his shoulders slumped. The battle with the beast-birds had taken a toll on all of them. Fortunately, the wounds, though bloody, were superficial, not grave. All of them had cuts, some they might not ever forget. Nath was just glad to be out of the fog. The salty wind was doing his wounds some good.

Ahead, Maefon looked back and caught his eye. She held her shivering shoulders, as Cold Cliff was as cold and wet as it could get without any snow. She drifted back and let Nath put an arm over her shoulders. "Oh, your warmth feels good."

He kissed her head. "Stay close. Stay warm."

They had been walking for hours without Darkken having said a word. Nath couldn't tell if his brother was exhausted or brooding, but he had the feeling that leaving him alone was best. He'd been following Darkken like a blind man all along and didn't see any reason to stop. He wasn't in any hurry to do anything. He just needed to keep Darkken close and away from his friends—the farther away, the better.

The waves of the Falluum Sea crashed into the cliffs. It was one of the views Nath could watch for hours. He'd never been to the sea before. The closest he'd ever been was at the Nameless Temple, in the west, where the view of the sea was distant. Now, he was right on top of it. Cold Cliff Island would be a great place to escape to, a place to watch the churning sea.

Like the sea, something else was brewing inside him: Darkken. His eyes fell on his brother's wide shoulders.

He wiped out the beast-birds in seconds. Such power he wields. It's frightening.

Even though the beast-birds weren't the most formidable monsters, they were sturdy, for living things. Darkken had killed dozens of them, if not a hundred or more, which shook Nath. He could tell it also shook Maefon. Darkken had been angry when he did it. A fierce storm brewed deep in the man's eyes, reaffirming that Nath's decision to get Darkken away from his friends was the right thing to do. He didn't think either Slivver or Elween was a match for Darkken. He himself had no idea what stopping him would take. He liked Darkken, and they were brothers, but the methods of the man were giving him growing concerns. He didn't know whether to believe him or not.

Darkken stopped walking, turned back toward them, and pointed outward. "There," he said. Below the cliffs at sea level, a jetty of rocks stuck out into the waters like an arm. Small fishing boats were turned upside down on the stones. "We'll take that boat to the main shore."

Nath looked over the ledge. "How do we get down there?"

"The island slopes downward at this point, and you can see an outline of a beach among these cliffs," Darkken said, "so the island isn't impassable. If I were to guess, sea pirates use this island for sanctuary. Perhaps they hide their treasures in the valleys."

"Like the one we were in?" Nath said.

"Naturally not that one," Darkken replied. He straightened his back, took a deep breath, and started his march down the slope.

Once Darkken was out of earshot, Nath asked Maefon, "Does he seem well to you?"

"His moods are very unpredictable," she replied, "and to be honest, I've never seen him lose control, but down in the valley, that look in his eyes…"

"I know," Nath said.

"I'd hate to see what he would do if he fully lost his temper." She started walking while at the same time holding his hand, which was over her shoulders. "I'm glad I'm with you."

Nath squeezed her hand and nodded. "And I'm glad I have you." Once again, Nath started to sort through his thoughts on Darkken. The man—or dragon, rather—continued to reveal more power from his arsenal. That made Nath wonder if there was anything that Darkken couldn't do. He hadn't dealt much with wizards in his lifetime, aside from Virgo of the Black Hand. But Darkken's powers, compared to hers, were extraordinary. *I know all that I've seen, but what scares me is what I haven't seen.*

The island slope became more treacherous on the way down. The rocky ledges required slow climbing, but finally they made it to the beach, which was half covered with seaweed. On a nice day, it would have been a good place to bask in the sun and fish. It was a private cove below the sheer face of the cliff.

Darkken quickly moved on to the jetty of rock. He gave it a thorough inspection, knocked on the wooden hull, and said, "It's sound. Help me turn it over."

Nath complied and found two oars underneath the boat, which was plenty big enough for three. "Whose boat do you think this is?"

"Possibly some seamen that lost their way on the island. It happens." Darkken pointed at the beach, where wooden debris had gathered in many places. "At least they made it on the island. Much luckier than some, who ended up dashed against the cliffs. We are lucky to find a boat."

"So, we are going to row to shore," Nath said, looking out to sea. "I don't know much about the open water, but it doesn't look easy."

"We'll go out with the tide. It will be an adventure."

"Can't we wait and you teleport us tomorrow after you've rested?" Nath asked. He was fishing to get a feel for Darkken's abilities.

"No, we don't want to be stranded on this island for days." Darkken shoved the boat into the water. "At least, I don't want to be. Do you?"

Nath took a look back at the dreary island and said, "No. I'm ready to go."

Darkken helped Maefon into the boat. Then he climbed in with her and patted the bench where the oars were stationed. "Come on, little brother. Start rowing." He let out a gusty laugh. "The sea is waiting."

Nath climbed in. *Gads. My brother's crazy.*

Chapter 30

WITH A STRONG THRUST OF his sword, Hacksaw killed the dark elf that had speared Roday. Before he could think, he and Brenwar barreled their way inside the large dinner chamber. Ten more Caligin faced off against them. They carried swords and daggers and wore red hoods that had the eyes and mouths cut out, showing different expressions.

"Let's end these demons," Hacksaw said.

"Aye! For Morgdon!" Brenwar charged the elves nearest him. With a sweep of his war hammer, he knocked aside their lighter weapons striking at him. He plowed over the elves with boots and hammer blows.

Hacksaw struck hard and fierce. He downed two Caligin before the others got a clip at him. His armor absorbed their strikes. He used his superior length and strength to whittle them down one by one. Seconds into the fight, he realized the Caligin were novices, yet he didn't spare them.

The last elf, killed by Brenwar's hammer, fell dead onto the ground. Nobody was left living but them. Outside the entrance, someone was sobbing. Dule had Roday cradled in his arms. It was Roday, who'd taken the spear in the chest, that was crying.

"It hurts! It hurts!" Roday moaned. His neck rolled, and his eyes were big. "I'm dying, Dule. I'm dying." He clutched his friend's collar. "Avenge me."

Dule rolled his eyes. "You aren't dying. That spear didn't even break the skin, Roday. You have that shirt of feather chain on underneath that leather, don't you?"

Roday's tears stopped flowing. He fingered the gash in his armor. "Oh yes, I think I do."

"A real fierce fighter, this one is." Brenwar scoffed.

"Yes, I'm starting to suspect that they were never Caligin," Hacksaw added.

Roday and Dule hopped up. "We are, or we were, Caligin. I can assure you of that," Roday said. He winced and clutched his chest. "Ow. It still hurts."

Dule made an aggravated nod. "You'll live. Now, let's see what is on the inside. I've never made it past Darkken's dinner table, but I've heard stories."

Once all of them were in the room, Hacksaw motioned to the dead and asked, "Who are they?"

"Caligin in training," Dule replied smugly. "Usually, there are many more, but Darkken recently graduated and dispatched all of them. These elves were holdovers for guardianship of the keep. It seems that we've run out of Caligin to fight, which is strange."

"Why is it strange?" Hacksaw asked.

"I just don't think that Darkken would leave this place unprotected," Dule said as he ventured deeper into the room. "I mean, it was protected, but by a small force."

"A small force plus the Creeper," Roday injected. "That should have been more than enough to handle anybody. I would hardly say that the defenses were weak. We faced off against over thirty Caligin." He moved to a window and looked out. "And it's possible that some of them fled elsewhere. Perhaps they go to warn Lord Darkken."

"Please. Lord Darkken knows everything. He had to know that they would be coming here to find Nath. Why else would they have let out the Creeper?" Dule asked. He opened one of the large double doors leading to another room. "Well, what do we have here. It's Darkken's study. I've been dying to get a closer look at this place."

Just as Dule started inside, Roday hooked his arm. "Cross that threshold, and you might just die." He looked about, head turning in all directions. "Looks clear." With a nod, he and Dule entered together.

Hacksaw followed them inside. The study was big, with stone archways holding up the ceiling. Heavy curtains covered the windows. Tall shelves loaded with books lined the walls. The fireplaces in the room were cold, leaving a dampness in the room, much like the rest of the keep. He parted the curtains to see a fine view of the plains on the other side of the river. "Not a bad view. Peaceful. Get those fires blazing, and it could be very cozy." He stuck his pipe in his mouth. With a few puffs, smoke started to roll out of the pipe. "I could look out of this window all day."

Brenwar set his hammer down headfirst on the floor. "I find this place spooky. And my nose is tickling."

Leafing through a book he'd taken from one of the shelves, Roday asked, "Is your dwarven sense tingling?"

"Don't be a smart-alecky elf," Brenwar said. "We still need to check the roof and the dungeons. It's possible that they might be lying in wait."

"Do you really think so?" Hacksaw asked. He picked up a chair, took it to a window, and sat down. "I don't sense any danger. I think that Darkken didn't think we would make it this far. I mean, he knew we would come and was ready for that but was certain that if the Caligin didn't kill us, the Creeper would." He propped his stiff leg up on the window ledge. "But we survived. We won." He managed a smile. "Darkken is overconfident."

Dule slapped a book shut and tossed it onto the table. "So you think that he thinks we are dead." He nodded. "I can believe that." He wagged his finger. "Because I think he anticipated the dwarf and the dragons coming but did not know about us."

"Whoa," Roday said. "We blindsided Darkken's plans." He lifted his hand. "Hi-ho!"

Dule slapped Roday's hand. "Hi-ho!"

As much as Hacksaw would have liked to share in their jubilation, he couldn't help but say, "We may have won the battle, but war will be coming. Darkken will come back, and what do you think he's going to do when he finds us here?"

Dule and Roday stopped smiling.

Brenwar kicked his hammer up to his hands with his toes. "I'll be waiting."

Chapter 31

Nath's first rowing experience left his back aching and burning. One thing he learned for certain was that the old saying, "The sea has no master but the sea itself," was true. At least Darkken and Maefon got a chuckle out of his efforts as he fought the sea with the oars. He just kept rowing until he mastered it. When they made it to shore, drenched by chilling seawater, he was exhausted. The waves had taken more fight out of him than the beast-birds had.

Darkken gave him a hearty slap on the back and said, "I would have helped, little brother, but you were doing so well. I just didn't think I could do better myself."

"Ha ha," Nath said.

They dragged the boat up onto the beach.

"What do you have in store for us now?" asked Nath. "Are we going to march all the way back to the keep?"

"Perhaps." Darkken put his long arms over Nath's and Maefon's shoulders. "I want you both to know that I am grateful that you made this journey with me. And I promise it will all be worthwhile shortly."

"Shortly?" Nath said.

Darkken pointed over the tall wind-bent grasses behind the crusty sand of the beach. "We are not far from the sea town of Artus. It's a short march from here. There, we will feast like the Sultans of Sulfur."

Nath's stomach moaned the moment Darkken mentioned the word *feast*. He was famished. "That sounds good to me. Lead the way."

The arrived at the sea town of Artus in the middle of a misty rain. It was a cozy town sitting high on the coastal plains, surrounded by muddy roads that ran by hundreds of rock or wooden cottages. The heart of the city had more durable buildings, made from stone, standing no more than three stories tall. Smoke billowed out of chimney stacks. The hardy people lumbered along, wearing woolen coats and trousers. The women would smile, and the weathered men would grunt a hello when they passed. Some of the folks standing and sitting on the storefront porches waved at them. Artus reminded Nath of Riegelwood, just smaller.

Darkken strode through the town with a smile on his face. "You'll like Artus. They aren't opposed to strangers in their seafaring town. As a matter of fact, they like to talk you up and make you feel welcome. They are hard-working fishermen and ranchers. And given the frigid climate, it's not so desirable to threatening peoples. Plus, they are excellent traders and able to keep the peace."

"Thanks for the history lesson," Nath said.

When Nath grew up in Dragon Home, he'd spent time reading about Nalzambor's different places and people. On the surface, the books were accurate, so he knew what to expect. He read descriptions of the towns and cities and information about what they traded and thrived on. They even mentioned population. However, what dwelled within those towns, cities, and provinces could be a different matter from the simplicity of what he had been led to believe. What he thought were simple people could be complicated. He learned that hard lesson in Riegelwood. Thanks to Riegelwood, no people, no matter how friendly, could be trusted.

"So, are Caligin posted within?" Nath asked.

"Ah, good question. Don't be surprised if we cross some of our Brothers of the Wind. But they work hard to keep the peace at all of their stations." Darkken led them up the steps into what looked to be the largest tavern in town.

The sign hanging from the porch read The Black Fin.

Darkken open the door. Two townsfolk with their coats clutched at the neck slipped by him and hustled down the steps.

Maefon entered first.

A strong aroma of cooking fish hit Nath like a slap in the face. His nostrils flared as he stepped inside the warmth of the tavern.

"That smells good," he said.

Darkken closed them inside and said, "Wait until you taste it. Uh, is this your first time eating seafood?"

A robust waitress with her hair in a bun strode up to them and said, "Welcome to the Black Fin Inn, the best seafood in all the world." Her eyes widened when she saw Darkken. "Well, look who's back." She gave him a hug. "You've been a stranger too long. And look at all of you, soaking wet and underdressed. I'll have some towels and blankets fetched and seat you by the fire." With her hands on her hips, she gave Darkken and Nath a good look. "Mmm-mmm-mmm. Tell you what—the pleasure is all mine. Is this your son?"

"No, little brother," Darkken said. "It's great to see you, Rhoda."

"Not as great as it is to see you. And this is your little brother. I'll be. Well, he's as cute as you." Rhoda snapped her fingers. In a gusty voice, she said, "Girls! Towels. Blankets. Fireside table. Now!"

CHAPTER 32

FOR THE FIRST TIME IN his life, Nath ate until his belly popped out. It was so much that he removed his breastplate so that he could continue eating. In Dragon Home, food wasn't a big deal. Dragons, for the most part, ate cattle and didn't eat often. Only the Trayhaydeen elves ate normal food. It was good and simple when Nath dined among them, but it was nothing like fish.

He patted his belly and eased back in his chair. "After all of that rowing, I never would have imagined that what the sea offered could taste so good."

Darkken and Maefon both chuckled. All of them wore bright-orange bibs with blue swordfish on them.

Darkken said, "No race on earth takes greater pleasure in preparing food than the race of men. The put a lot of zeal into it, whereas the other races see food as little more than a necessity. To humans, it can be a way of life."

"I don't know that I agree with that," Maefon said as she nibbled on the meat of a crab leg covering her plate. "The finest fruits and vegetables are harvested in the elven gardens."

"Oh, so boring." Darkken rapped his fist on the table. "There's nothing like succulent fish meat that is slathered in butter. There is nothing better, when matched with a delectable wine." Raising a pewter goblet, he asked, "Nath, what do you fancy most from this fine feast?"

Nath tapped his chest and let out a loud belch. Patrons at a nearby table let out a cheer and applauded. Studying the table, he took a long drink of ale. The dishes and platters were covered in broiled creatures that he'd never seen before, ugly creatures with hard shells. He saw lobster tails and claws, crabs, shrimp, mussels, scallops, and clams. A big bowl of steaming-hot stew sat in the middle of the table.

"I really like this sea stew," he said, pointing at the pot, which had sea creatures engraved on it. "What do you call it?"

"That's sea gumbo. It has a little of the best of everything in it." Darkken poured hot butter on a hunk of lobster tail as big as his fist. He picked it up with one hand and stuffed it in his mouth, grunting with pleasure.

Nath laughed. "You're eating more than me."

"I've had more practice at it." Darkken chewed his lobster and swallowed. "Seafood passes through the system rather quickly, so give it some time, and you'll be able to down more."

"No, I think I'm ready now." Nath scooped up a handful of boiled shrimp. Each was bigger than his finger. He dipped them in a spicy red sauce and quickly devoured them one by one. He let out another burp, not as loud as the last one.

Pushing her plate away, Maefon said, "You both eat like savages."

"At least we don't eat like birds," Nath said.

"Yes, like beast-birds," Darkken said.

All three of them burst out laughing. When they'd walked into the Black Fin Inn, they couldn't have been any worse off. Now, they were dry, patched up, and in high spirits. Rhoda was taking great care of them as if she'd known them all of her life. Aside from a little aching here and there, Nath felt as good as he'd felt in quite some time.

"So, are we staying the night," he asked, "or are we moving on?"

"I'm not one for much sleeping, but I certainly think that a good night of rest is due. My eyelids feel as if they are made of sandbags," Darkken said. "And I don't see any need to rush out of here tomorrow. We'll have a great breakfast. Wait until you eat scrambled pelican eggs and shark meat served like bacon. You won't forget it. Oh, and their biscuits are wonderful."

Nath wiped his hands on his bib. He tilted his chair back on two legs and stretched his fingers toward the fire. "You know, I think I could get used to living in this sea city."

Maefon shivered. "It's too cold for me. And wet."

"You just have to bundle up," Nath said. "So, Darkken, if you aren't in a hurry, I'm not either. I wouldn't mind visiting here for a while."

"Why's that?" Darkken said.

"Well, I haven't stayed anywhere very long. At least outside of Dragon Home. There's Stonewater Keep, but that is about it. It would be nice to settle in somewhere for a bit. You know—get the lay of the land."

"I hope my eagerness doesn't seem unfair, but now that I have the dragon steel, scroll, and star, I'm ready to fashion my sword. It's been a very long time."

"Yeah, about that… Uh, where are you going to make the sword? Is the smithy back at the keep even sufficient?" Nath asked. "I mean, it's good for repairs and working small weapons, but you're talking about making a sword like the one that was forged in the huge furnaces of Dragon Home. I'm not sure that you can stoke a fire hot enough to melt down that ore."

One of Darkken's copper rings slipped from his finger and landed on the table. He smashed his hand on top of it. Quickly, Darkken wiped his hands on a cloth napkin and replaced the ring on his index finger. He had four of them, each different in design but simple. They dressed his middle and index fingers.

"All of that butter made my hands a bit slippery," he said. "You raise a good question. Lucky for you, I have a location picked out that will serve my purpose."

"Is it far away?" Nath asked.

"I guess that depends on whether or not we are going to walk, ride, or teleport." Darkken covered his mouth and yawned. "But if you want to see more of the countryside, we could consider walking."

"You don't want to carry the ore. I think we should ride," Nath suggested. "I like the idea of seeing the countryside."

"We'll see how I feel tomorrow." Darkken got up and left.

Nath and Maefon watched him head up the stairs.

"That was abrupt," she said.

"I don't think I said anything to upset him. Do you really think he's tired?"

Maefon looked Nath dead in the eye and said, "No." She grabbed his hand. "But at least the two of us are alone."

"Yeah," Nath said with distance in his voice.

Darkken was up to something. He wondered what. *Tonight, I'm going to try to keep an eye on him. I just hope I can keep my own eyes open.*

CHAPTER 33

ASIDE FROM THE DEAD, STONEWATER Keep was clear of Caligin. Led by the elves, Roday and Dule, Hacksaw and Brenwar made their rounds, high and low. They took the dead to the burial chambers below the keep and sealed them away in the tombs. Now, they were alone with the dragons, Calypsa, and Rond, having the run of the keep.

Rond stood guard on top of the parapets of the outer wall. The rest of them took turns watching with him. They rotated on the roof level as well.

Currently, Slivver, Brenwar, and Elween were touring the sublevels with Roday and Dule. Elween had finally woken up but walked with rigid stiffness. She had a heavy look in her eyes. Slivver didn't feel much better. He needed his wing snapped back into place but let it lie for the time being.

"Where are you taking us?" Slivver asked Roday.

They stopped at a vaultlike door at the end of the hallway. Using a big key that hung from his neck, Roday unlocked it. With Dule's help, they pulled the door open.

"This is why we are certain that Lord Darkken will be back," Roday said.

As soon as the door swung open, the dark room's lanterns lit up.

"By the Beard of Varlaan!" Brenwar exclaimed.

The vault was filled with sacks of coins and treasure chests on the floor. Tables were covered in precious coins stamped by races from all over. The shelves on the walls were filled with goods. Racks of clothing of all sorts and sizes half filled the large treasure room. Staffs and canes were there, along with scrolls rolled up on tables, swords, hammers, spears, and knives.

Roday slipped inside and opened a chest half as big as him. Racks of potions in vials sat inside it.

He smiled. "I don't think Lord Darkken will leave any of this behind." He plucked out a clear glass vial with golden liquid in it and tossed it to Elween. "That should get rid of your stiffness."

"Much obliged," she said then drank it down.

From a table, Slivver picked up a diamond as big as his knuckle. "This reminds me of Balzurth's throne room, but on a much smaller scale. Hmph. It seems that Crixis has been working very hard these past few centuries. To do what, I'm not so sure."

"Who is Crixis?" Hacksaw asked.

"Crixis is the birth name of Lord Darkken," Slivver replied.

"Ah," Hacksaw answered.

The formidable old knight couldn't stop ogling the treasure. It was everything that he dreamed about finding back when he'd started adventuring. Now, it all lay at his feet. The silver and gold coins twinkled in his eyes. The gemstones and jewelry made him salivate. He rubbed his mouth. The treasure there was more than enough to last him a dozen lifetimes if not one hundred.

"You said that this is nothing compared to the Dragon King's throne room?" Hacksaw said.

"Balzurth's treasure room could fill this keep a dozen times over," Brenwar said.

"I can't imagine." Hacksaw took a knee and stuffed his hands into an open chest filled with twinkling coins. "I could bathe in this."

"Aye, me too," Brenwar said. He picked up a gold coin and flicked it high in the air. "Gold—there is nothing more beautiful than it in the world. The only sorry part is that it's not useful for weapons. I'd like a hammer of gold. That would be something."

"So, is this going to be ours?" Hacksaw said.

Slivver was rifling through the racks of clothes. "Only if you live to spend it, but I suppose."

"What are all of the clothes for?" Hacksaw asked.

"We can answer that," Dule and Roday said as one.

Dule had slipped on a dark-purple vest over a yellow satin shirt. On his head he placed a floppy gray cotton cap that hung over the side of his face. Roday wore a warrior's helmet with a cruel spike on the top and menacing eyeholes. It was far too big for his head. They looked ridiculous but somewhat dangerous at the same time.

"This vault also works as a staging room," Dule said. "The clothing is used by the Caligin when they infiltrate other cities. Hats, coats, boots—you name it. The jewelry is part of the costume, and having the right coins for currency makes the Caligin more acceptable. The Caligin have a presence in every city."

"That's scary," Hacksaw said.

"Just imagine," Slivver said. "Darkken has been doing this for hundreds of years. Dule and Roday, you need to tell us everything you know. We have to figure out what he's doing."

"We'd like to know too." Roday pointed up. "The most likely places to find answers will be upstairs."

Slivver scanned the room. "Everyone, take whatever you think you might need. When Darkken comes, we must be ready."

"Aye," Hacksaw said.

With a grunt, Brenwar agreed. "Aye."

CHAPTER 34

NATH LAY IN BED WITH his head propped up on a pillow. The steady sound of rain danced on the roof above them. Maefon rested on his chest. She'd fallen asleep on top of him shortly after they climbed into bed. She slept deeply, making a faint whistle through her little nose. He also hadn't budged since they'd lain down, which had been at least two hours before. However, Nath couldn't sleep, even though he was weary. He'd closed his eyes only to open them again. He sighed.

Can I trust my brother or not?

Since the day he'd left Dragon Home, he was lost. That was years before. Now, he still felt as lost as ever. He'd become so close with Darkken and Maefon that he couldn't imagine a day without them. In truth, he would give his life for either one of them. That was how much he loved them. They'd all risked their very lives for one another. That was real, but something inside him was not right.

I wish Hacksaw were still around.

He missed the salty attitude of the old knight. He could count on the seasoned warrior for a straight answer even if he didn't agree with it.

Maefon's eyes cracked open. She looked up into his and smiled. Her hand brushed his hair behind his ear. "Your eyes shine in the darkness. Do you know that?"

"No. Did they wake you?"

"Of course not, silly dragon. But they do stir my heart when I see them." She made a relaxed smile and closed her eyes. "Can't you sleep?"

"You know I don't sleep much. And I, well… need to relieve myself. I just didn't want to wake you," he said. What he said was the truth even though it wasn't an urgent matter. He just wanted Maefon to move. "Do you mind?"

"Certainly not." She slid off his chest and snuggled into another pillow. "Be quick. I miss your warmth."

"Oh, I felt it was a bit stuffy in this small room. I was going to crack open the window."

"You weren't going to pee out the window, were you?"

"It is rainy. I don't think anyone will notice," he joked.

"You crude little jester."

"I tease."

He kissed her and moved to the window and cracked it open. Then he departed the room, closing the door quietly behind him. Alone in the hall, he moved in front of Darkken's door at the end of the hall. He listened, wondering if his brother was in there. He heard the creak of a floorboard inside. Another groan of the floorboards sounded closer. *He's coming out!*

Nath hustled down the hallway on cat's feet. He hurried down the stairs that led down into the heart of the tavern. The sea people, merchants, and travelers bandied about in excited conversations.

Nath caught a waitress by the arm and asked, "Where are the facilities?"

The young woman with tired eyes but a smile on her face said, "Take the back door. Come, I'll show you."

"I'm really in a hurry."

"Drank too much, did you?" She giggled as she took him by a hand and led him to the back door. She pushed it open, propped her body against it, and asked, "Do you need a blanket for cover? It's a steady rain. You'll want to keep dry."

"Sure." He stepped out onto the porch, which wrapped around the end of the building.

A husky old man teetered up the steps. He looked at Nath, pointed at the distant outhouse, and said, "I wouldn't go in there for a spell, young fella."

Nath looked at the man, who reeked of ale and fish, and said, "I'll mind your advice."

He opened the door for the man and noticed Darkken coming down the steps. He closed the door and took a peek in the windows. Darkken slipped out of the front door quickly without a word of greeting to anyone.

"Huh," said Nath.

The servant girl came through the door, saw him peeking through the window, and asked, "Looking for me?"

"Of course." He took the blanket and smiled. "Thank you."

Twirling the curls in her hair with a finger, she said, "If you need anything else, please tell me. You should try our hot saltwater baths. I can prepare one for you. They help you sleep well."

"Uh, maybe tomorrow." Nath covered himself with the blanket and headed into the rain. As soon as the servant girl entered the building, he moved to the side of the building. He spied Darkken walking down the street and out of town. Nath followed.

Where in Nalzambor is he going?

The constant sea breeze and steady rain made for excellent cover. Nath managed to stalk his brother from a distance. He ducked low in the grasses when Darkken turned around, but the bigger man didn't break his stride. Darkken kept moving past the cottages, which became less frequent the farther they went. Finally, he veered toward a lone cottage, far separated from the others in deteriorating condition. He entered.

Once Nath lost sight of his brother, he started to creep closer then froze and squatted down in the tall grasses. Four figures, clad in black, north of his position, also descended on the cottage. Nath could tell by their frames and builds that they were elves. The hairs on his nape stood on end. They entered the cottage. *Caligin.*

Nath gave it a few minutes then padded toward the cottage. He knew enough about the Caligin to know that they traveled in fours. That was also the practice of the Brothers of the Wind, so he didn't fear that anyone else would see him. He sneaked alongside the building and moved with his back to the wall. He made his way to a broken window, hunkered down, and listened.

Not all the voices inside could be heard easily over the wind and the rain. Even with Nath's keen senses, hearing was difficult, but he still picked out phrases and words, for Darkken's rich voice carried well. "Ready the furnace… set the trap for the infidels… the time nears when the dark shall rule the day."

The sinister inflections in Darkken's voice chilled the marrow in his bones. Nath had heard enough. His heart pounded. He raced back to the Black Fin Inn.

The girl met him on the porch with a dry blanket. "You're new to seafood, aren't you?"

"Yes." He patted himself down and headed up to his room. Inside, he found Maefon sitting on the edge of the bed, waiting.

CHAPTER 35

Maefon paced the room, her arms crossed over her chest. "You shouldn't have followed Darkken. That was a foolish thing to do, Nath. That shows a lack of trust."

"A lack of trust?" he said sarcastically. "I'm not the one running around in the middle of the night. He is."

"Don't raise your voice," she said.

Nath moved to close the window. He'd left it open before in case he needed to slip out. He should have known that it wouldn't go unnoticed. Maefon, despite her fatigue, was still a Caligin and as alert as a night owl. With a quick look outside, he could see the outhouse. Another man was stumbling up the hill to the wooden structure, which groaned against the wind. He closed the window. "Honestly, I don't care if he hears me or not. Darkken needs to be held accountable."

"For what?" Maefon said. "Taking a stroll and meeting with our Brothers of the Wind? I don't think that is anything that should draw your suspicion. He told us there would be elves about and we might run into them." She poked him on the chest. "You need to stop being so jumpy."

"I'm not jumpy!" he said in a loud whisper. "And Darkken said he was tired. So why would he get up in the middle of the night to meet them at a withering cottage?"

She took him by the wrist and led him to sit down beside her on the bed. Rubbing his hand, she said, "We are building a strong bond. We don't need to break that. Aren't you happy with the way things are going?"

"So long as no one is getting hurt, I am happy."

"Listen to me. You know that Darkken will have a good explanation for his actions."

Nath scoffed. "Doesn't he always?"

"What is that supposed to mean?" she said.

"He always has the perfect answer for everything. That's what it means."

"Well, he is very smart. And an excellent planner." She looked him in the eye. "You sound angry. Why are you angry?"

"I'm not angry. I'm just… Have you ever had that feeling that something wasn't right but you couldn't put your finger on it?" He tapped his chest. "It's right in here. Like a warning drum pounding in my breast."

"I respect your instincts and feelings, but I think you are getting all lathered up over nothing."

"You didn't hear his voice, Maefon. You weren't there. I was. When he said, 'The time nears when the dark shall rule the day,' my heart skipped a beat, and ice ran through my veins."

"Was it not hard to hear in the wind and rain?"

"I know what I heard. And you know how well his voice carries."

She nodded. "So you heard the entire conversation?"

"Well, no."

"Then stop jumping to conclusions. I'm tired enough from fatigue, and now you are adding worry." She quit rubbing his hand. "I trust Darkken, Nath. You should too. If you don't by now… Well, I don't know. All I know is that he saved my life on more than one occasion."

Disappointment showed in her eyes. Darkken had saved them both. And Nath had considered all of that. Whatever was nagging him inside, he just wished it would stop.

"Just don't say anything to him before I see him. If I tell him, I'll tell him myself." Nath pulled back the covers. "I'll do my best to sleep on it."

"That's a good idea." Maefon slipped under the covers and turned her back to Nath. "Good night, finally."

Nath covered himself in the blankets. "Good night," he said softly as he touched her shoulder. She pulled away. He fluffed up his goose-feather pillow. All he wanted to do was keep Maefon in the room before she saw Darkken. It was important that he saw Darkken before she did. Darkken was intuitive, almost all-knowing. Tipping off Darkken would be easy for her, telling him Nath was bothered by something. Keeping it to himself would be hard enough. Darkken could see right through people.

Nath lay awake in bed until morning, when the first rooster crowed. Maefon stirred. She rose up, stretched her arms, and yawned. She caught Nath looking right at her and said, "Go on."

"What do you mean?" he said with a guilty look.

She put her feet on the floor. "I know you've been up all night. You were as rigid as a board. So go on. See Darkken. I'm staying out of it."

Blustering, Nath said, "Well, I… uh, don't know what you—"

"Shush and go. I'll see you down there shortly."

Nath put on his clothing and boots and headed into the hall. He walked by a couple of patrons, who greeted him and said good morning. Slowly, he made his way down the stairs. Darkken was sitting at the same table they'd sat at the night before. With a cheery smile, he flagged Nath down. The table had been filled with hot plates of steaming food. The eggs were scrambled and the hot biscuits buttered, and two carafes of coffee had been brewed. That wasn't the half of it. Nath's stomach grumbled again. He pulled up a chair and sat.

"I hope you don't mind, but I went ahead and ordered," Darkken said. He looked refreshed, as if he'd slept for a week. "Did you sleep well?"

"Not bad. I think I'm still used to sleeping outside." Nath started eating a strip of bacon. "Is this the shark meat?"

"The best."

"So, how did you sleep?" Nath asked.

"Like a baby."

"Through the night, huh?"

Darkken sipped his coffee from a large mug. "I can't say that I remember, but I assume so."

Nath stuck a fork in his eggs. *Liar, liar, trousers on fire!*

CHAPTER 36

SLIVVER, BRENWAR, CALYPSA, RODAY, AND Dule were all gathered in Lord Darkken's study. Hacksaw, Elween, and Rond kept watch outside. The group in the study had spent long hours looking for information that would be helpful in aiding them with Darkken's plans.

Roday and Dule filled them in on everything they knew. They made it clear that Darkken wanted to win Nath over to his side. After all, they were part of that deception. They spoke about the gathering of magic items, which included the Star of the Heavens and the Dragon Steel Scroll.

Dule had a tome in his hand and was leafing through the pages. "Darkken also mentioned the Elderwood Staff, the Thunderstone, and the Ocular of Orray. He's very private, but he was definitely obsessed with magic."

Brenwar and Slivver stood side by side, looking at scrolls and the maps they'd recovered from the wagon and the Sultan's Lake.

"I don't know much about the kind of magic that is wielded by the races," Slivver said. "It's never been a concern of mine. But do you think that he wants all of them? Is he making a weapon?"

"I'm certain that he is," Brenwar said. "The question is: where is he going to make it?"

"And what is he going to use it for?" Slivver said. "You don't think that he's going to kill Nath, do you?"

"He will if he can't turn him," Roday said. The former dark elf stood with a boot on the window ledge. He was looking outward. "I've seen Darkken hurl elves from the keep's edges onto the rocks below. If they show any sign that they aren't coming aboard, he makes examples of them." He glanced at Dule—the dark-complected elf had his nose buried in a book. "I think I can speak for the both of us that we had doubts early on, but Darkken's, eh, merciless leadership convinced us otherwise."

"You know that's right," Dule said. "These books are fascinating. I wish I could have been trained as a magic user and not a swordsman. It's a waste of my talents. I could have been like Maefon or better."

Calypsa slammed a book on the floor, making a loud smack. "What did you say?"

Dule peeked over the rim of his book. "I said I could have been a magic user?"

"No, you said *Maefon*." With a simmering look in her eyes, Calypsa walked over to Roday and pushed his book down. "You sound like you know her intimately. Why is that, dark elf?"

"Listen, gorgeous, don't heat up on me. I—urk!"

Calypsa turned her hands into bear's paws and locked them on Dule's neck. "You are a spy! A traitor! A confidant of the elven witch!" She shook him like a blanket. "Admit it!"

Roday jumped at Calypsa and chopped at her arms. "Let go of him! Please! He's not a traitor! I swear it!"

Lifting Dule up off his toes, she looked the choking man in the eyes and said, "Admit it!"

"Slivver. Brenwar. Talk some sense into her. We are on your side!" Roday pleaded.

Brenwar stroked the braids in his beard and said, "I like the way Calypsa thinks. Maybe she's on to something. This big-eyed elf did talk the woman up."

Choking and spitting out words the best he could, Dule made his case. "I don't like Maefon. No one does. She's a seductress, Darkken's right hand. She's as evil as him. Just good with magic." His face turned purple as he snorted for air.

"Slivver, talk her down," Roday said. "Please!"

"I have no control over Calypsa," Slivver said calmly. "She has instincts of her own."

"All she has is a jealous bone!" Roday shouted.

Calypsa backhanded Roday so hard that he spun to the ground, and as she did, she dropped Dule, who fell to the floor, coughing and gasping for breath. Roday came to a knee, drawing his sword and wiping the blood from the corner of his mouth.

Brenwar stuck his hammer in Roday's face. "You'd attack a woman, would you?"

"Look at those hairy arms. You call that a woman?" Roday slammed his sword into his sheath. "Maybe a bear woman."

Still coughing, Dule came up to his hands and knees and managed to say, "She's all woman to men. Hairy arms or not. Calypsa, I'm sorry. I don't blame you a bit for hating Maefon. She's been helping Darkken pull the wool over Nath's eyes from day one."

Calypsa's heaving chest started to ease. Her bearlike arms went back to normal. "That woman tried to butcher me." She looked at all of them. "When she shows her face again, she's mine." She pointed at Dule. "You should be ashamed you wanted to be like her."

Dule put his hands up. "You're right. I just wanted to warn all of you that she may be small, but she's very powerful. But even with that said, she's nothing compared to Darkken. He's the biggest snake of all. Secretive. Shifty. Superpowered."

"*Superpowered?* That's an odd word," Slivver said. "What do you mean?"

Dule shrugged. "Even for a wizard, he exercises unimaginable capabilities. And that's just what we've seen. He can change form at will."

"I can do that," Calypsa said.

"Yes, but can you do it at will?"

She frowned.

"Of course there are shape changers in the world," Brenwar stated.

"Yes, but Darkken is still a dragon—well, by blood," Slivver said. "We need to note everything that Darkken can do and try to have a way ready to counter it. Let's see. He changes shape, teleports… He does all of this at will, that we know of. What else?"

"He can do anything any mage can do," Roday chimed in. "Cast lightning and fire. Hurl objects with his thoughts. I know that the Creeper was tough, but Darkken could make that thing look like a puppy if he wanted to. I'm telling you that he's one bad dragon."

Slivver looked at Brenwar. "Only Balzurth has such power. Darkken has to draw it from somewhere or something."

"If he's so powerful, then why does he need to create another weapon?" Brenwar asked. "Why does he need Nath? Nath doesn't have that sort of power, does he?"

"No, not yet." Slivver's clawed fingers scratched at his neck. "But if he were to win Nath over, they might become strong enough to overthrow Balzurth."

"And if he doesn't turn Nath?" Brenwar asked. His eyes grew big, and he snapped his fingers. "That's why he needs the dragon steel. It's the only metal in the world that can penetrate Balzurth's scales."

"You're right. We have to stop them. But where in the world besides Dragon Home is there a forge that can handle dragon steel?" Slivver asked Brenwar.

The dwarf grumbled. "I don't know, but we'd better find out."

CHAPTER 37

LATER IN THE MISTY, RAINING morning, Nath, Darkken, and Maefon journeyed south on foot. The backpack containing the dragon ore was strapped to Darkken's shoulders. He led the way with a long and easy stride. Nath and Maefon walked behind him. Since they'd departed Artus, no one said much of anything, although Nath was biting his tongue not to do so. He'd caught Darkken in a bald-faced lie. He let it be. He didn't say anything to Maefon about it, either. He just clammed up.

Every so often, Maefon would give Nath a questioning look. He would shrug at her, playing as though all was well, and he'd kept his mouth shut. And his silence was true. He had kept his mouth shut, but she didn't know that Darkken had caught her in a lie. What he was more curious about was whether or not she would tell Darkken what she had heard from Nath. He needed to decide whether or not he could trust her.

Can I trust her? Can I trust him? Can I trust both of them? Father, Balzurth, grant me wisdom.

"You two are very quiet back there," Darkken said loudly without looking back. "Is all well?"

"It would have been nice if we had horses or if you would tell us where we are going," Nath stated.

"Walking is better than rowing, isn't it, little brother?" Darkken replied.

"Well, that's true. I guess I shouldn't complain."

"We could have gotten horses, but once my strength returns, I might teleport us out of here." Darkken pointed to the high hills on the horizon. "It's rich country. You need to take time to see it for yourself. But the hills are not without their dangers. Orcs often patrol far north of Thraag, and horses would be difficult to hide. They'll just kill them for meat. They'll do the same to us as well."

"You aren't scared of a few orcs," Nath said.

Maefon bumped him.

"Ha. A few orcs, no, but a few hundred… That's a different story." Darkken moved on.

"So why are we taking the risk? Is where we are going in the orcen territory?" Nath asked.

Darkken tossed his head back and laughed. "Are we not the Brothers of the Wind? We should be able to slip in and slip out of anywhere unseen. It will be a good exercise for us.

After all, if you take the path of least resistance, you won't learn much of anything. And you need to learn more about the orcs. They are a dangerous enemy of all mankind."

"You don't have to tell me that," Nath said, recollecting his encounters with the orc slaver Prawl and the slave lord Foster. Back in Slaver Town, they'd made his life miserable. "I'd just as soon never see another orc again."

"That would be a blessing, but orcs are the notorious dragon poachers. I'd say there is a good chance that you'll cross them again."

Nath exchanged a curious look with Maefon, who shrugged her eyebrows. Nath caught up with Darkken and said, "I don't take your meaning. I thought you weren't concerned with the dragons."

"I might be bitter toward my brethren, but I don't like seeing their fates sealed by the likes of orcs. After all, they are the lowest form of humanity." Darkken tipped his chin toward the sky. "Look at that: a triple rainbow."

As the sun cracked through the rain clouds, three bright rainbows formed, rich in all seven colors. Nath had never seen a rainbow so brilliant before. Its quavering colors appeared magical.

"It's wonderful," Nath said.

Darkken swiped his rusty locks from his eyes. "The sea people believe that it is a sign of promise that their towns will never be flooded again. Half of the northern valleys were flooded by the Faallum Sea tides once. It was an age long ago, according the histories jotted down in the elven tomes of Alvareen. That's why the earth has so many peaks and valleys. It's where the ground was pushed up and washed away."

"Thanks for the history lesson," Nath said, but he was more concerned about the talk of the dragons. "I thought we were going to focus on getting the dragons to leave. I thought they were supposed to return to their world and leave this one to us."

"Chances are, even if our father leaves, many dragons will remain behind. If that is the case, they will be an even rarer commodity and hunted even more. I'd feel obligated to protect what remains of them. Wouldn't you?"

"Certainly," Nath said.

He was even more confused by what Darkken was saying. One minute, they were all about creating a sword made out of dragon steel, and in the next, they were touring the north, searching for dragon-snatching orcs. It was misdirection, plain and simple. Nath's frustration rekindled. His anger rebuilt. He stepped right in front of Darkken. Darkken stopped in his tracks.

Nath poked him in the chest. "I want to know what you are up to, and I want to know it now!"

CHAPTER 38

WITH HIS EYEBROWS KNITTING TOGETHER, Darkken asked, "Why so hostile, little brother?"

"Don't call me that!" Nath replied.

"Fine, Nath, why so hostile? Have I done something to offend you?"

Nath fought against himself, trying to keep what he knew to himself. He didn't want to tip Darkken off, but that was becoming more difficult to keep inside. "Are we going to build your sword or not? It feels like we are chasing the wind when we follow you."

"Are we not the Brothers of the Wind?"

Nath shoved Darkken. "I don't know what we are!"

Maefon jumped between them. "Stop it, Nath!"

Darkken pointed a finger at Nath and said, "You lay a hand on me one more time, and I will break it!" He wagged the finger. "I swear it!"

"Get out of the way, Maefon." He glared at Darkken. "I want to see him try to break my hand."

"No, I won't," she insisted.

"This is between blood. You wouldn't understand, Maefon. Move," Darkken ordered.

The elven woman's cherry lips parted. She slouched and stepped away.

Darkken dropped his sword belt. "If you want to take a poke at me, take off that sword and go ahead." He tossed his backpack aside. "Come on, *little brother*."

Nath unslung Fang and handed it to Maefon. He squared off with Darkken. "I said don't call me *little brother*."

"Fine, I'll just call you *big baby*," Darkken said.

Letting out a growl, Nath lowered his shoulders and charged. He reached for the bigger man's waist but found nothing but air as Darkken stepped aside and tripped him. Nath crashed into the grass and jumped back up. Before he could set his feet underneath him, Darkken slugged him in the face. He stumbled backward and fell on his butt.

With his fists still drawn, Darkken lorded over him and asked, "Have you had enough?"

Panting, Nath took a knee. He couldn't believe he'd become winded so soon, but he was mad. Madder than a hornet. He needed to control that. Darkken was a bigger, stronger, and more seasoned fighter. The prominent man had never shown any sign of weakness. He nodded at Darkken and extended his hand.

"Good," Darkken said, lowering his guard. "We don't have time for this foolishness." He reached for Nath.

Nath punched his brother hard in the side of the face, and Darkken staggered backward. Nath pounced. This time, he caught his stunned sibling off balance, drove his shoulder into his belly, lifted him off his feet, and slammed him down.

The brothers went at it like a mongoose and a cobra. In a tangle of limbs and flailing fists, they beat the snot out of each other as they rolled across the grasses.

Darkken head-butted Nath in the chin.

Nath drove a knee into his brother's ribs.

Back and forth they went, tossing and turning over the wet ground. Darkken's strong fingers wrapped Nath up by the head, but Nath squirted out. His brother might have been stronger, but Nath felt he was quicker. He slipped a hard punch from Darkken and clocked the man upside an eye. Darkken drove a boot into Nath's chest and sent him flying.

Nath jumped to his feet just in time to catch the full weight of Darkken coming down on top of him. Darkken locked Nath's legs up with his own. Nath couldn't break free. Darkken head-butted him like a ram. Bright spots burst in Nath's eyes. Darkken's strong arms seized his head. He put Nath in a headlock. The pressure built like a crushing vise. Nath started choking.

"Darkken, stop!" Maefon yelled. "Stop it, Darkken! You're going to kill him!"

Nath's eyes bulged in his sockets. He couldn't breathe.

Darkken spoke right in Nath's ear. "Listen to me, and listen good. I am delaying the journey for your sake. If we cross Slivver and Elween, there will be no choice but to kill them, or they will kill me. Perhaps it's for my sake. Hence, we wait them out, take a safer path, waiting for the Brothers of the Wind to report their whereabouts. I thought an adventure with the orcs would be a good distraction until the coast is clear to return to the keep. Do you understand me?"

With the lock on his neck easing, Nath choked out the words, "You could be more up front about it."

"You should trust me." Darkken tightened his grip. "Do you yield?"

Nath tapped out on the grass, and Darkken released his hold. Nath fell onto his back and caught his breath. He punched his kneeling older brother in the thigh.

"I just wanted to see what you were made of," he said.

"So this was an act. I don't believe it."

"Good. That means I'm getting better at fooling you."

"No," Darkken said, "it just means you are not getting any better. You don't trust me, then so be it. But you don't have to attack me." He helped Nath to his feet. "So, where do we stand?"

"I don't know," Nath said. "I'm tired of all the mystery. Can we just go and make the sword and get it over with?"

"That's what we were doing. I just thought that you might enjoy an excursion on the side." Darkken looked at Maefon, whose arms were crossed as she glared at both of them. "Are you all right?"

"I'm tired of the games too," she said. "And I don't like seeing both of you fighting. Either we are a team, or we are not. Darkken, I mean no disrespect, but I don't understand what you are doing, either. So I share Nath's frustration. You are going to march us into orcen territory? Why? You risk losing the scroll, the ore, even the Star of the Heavens. It just doesn't make any sense to me."

Nath's eyebrows arched. He was pleasantly surprised to see Maefon on his side. *That's my girl.*

Darkken spread his arms wide. "Dearest Maefon, I was only glamoring the adventure up, to make it sound exciting. Our southern destination is no more or less dangerous than any other direction. I'm only delaying Nath." He dropped his hands and slouched. "I don't mean to be soft, but I don't want the confrontation with Slivver any more than Nath does. I just want them to go away." He let out a long sigh and buckled his sword belt back on. "It is my hope to make the sword before we have further confrontation. Once the sword is ready and Nath and I stand side by side, I believe they will be willing to listen."

Nath's head started to ache as Darkken spun another web of words that served only to confuse him. "How is the sword going to change their minds about anything?"

"Once they see that we can craft a sword the same way that Balzurth crafted Fang, they will take notice. They will know that we harness a power that rivals his own. A new age will have begun. We will be the protectors of the Nalzambor. The dragons can then return home to the Land beyond the Murals. Brother, we can handle it. I just need you to be with me."

Nath looked toward the southern horizon. "Let's walk."

Chapter 39

Trailing behind Darkken and Maefon, Nath traversed the rocky and brush-heavy hills while sorting through his thoughts. His brother had said so much that it was difficult to keep track of. And he'd been so busy since they left Stonewater Keep that he hadn't taken time to thoroughly think through all that Darkken had mentioned. He was almost tired of trying to keep up with it. The story seemed to be always changing slightly.

I feel like my mind is going around in circles.

He pushed through some prickly berry bushes and found himself on Maefon's heels. She had stopped in place, and she reached back and touched his thighs.

He leaned down and told her, "Everything is fine. Just keep going."

In a quiet voice, she asked, "Are you sure?"

"I am certain. Believe it or not, this walk is doing me some good." He patted her on the rump. "Just follow my big brother's lead."

She gave him a backward smile. "If you insist."

Nath followed Maefon's graceful figure through the choppy woodland. He wasn't one for deceit, but he didn't want to let on about how he was truly feeling. He had concerns, grave ones. But he couldn't reveal them now. Darkken might have a great deal of power, but he certainly couldn't read minds too.

He'd better not be able to read my thoughts. Gads, there is no telling what that man can do!

Back in Stonewater Keep, shortly after Darkken had teleported them from the Lake of Sulfur, they had a lengthy conversation. Darkken explained the dragons were not from Nalzambor but from the Land beyond the Murals. The dragons had been summoned to Nalzambor by a gathering of the races during their darkest hours. The dragons drove the evil races of giants, trolls, ogres, orcs, and such back into the darkness. After that, peace reigned for a short time, but a dark element of dragons started to rise. They were the Black Dragons, who caused the Great Dragon Wars. They wanted to dominate mankind as gods.

According to Darkken, the dragons had served their purpose by liberating the races the first time. Now, he feared the dragons would eventually be tempted again and try to take over Nalzambor once more. The dragons were a threat. They needed to return home. Nath and

Darkken were proof of a new age coming to Nalzambor, where they, men that were dragons, would use their gifts and resources to maintain peace in the world.

But the dragons such as the ones on the High Dragon Council, who wanted to rule the world, would not return to the Land Beyond the Murals. They treated Nath and Darkken as threats to their order would eventually come after them and destroy them.

Some dragons were impervious to manmade weapons. Some had scales that could shed an enchanted blade. But none of them were impervious to dragon steel. If the dragon ore was properly enchanted, it could cut not only the flesh but the spirit as well. Dragon steel was the only way for them to protect themselves from the dragons that would eventually come to get them.

Nath climbed over a fallen tree. In his deep thoughts, he'd fallen farther behind Darkken and Maefon's quick pace. He jogged to catch up. Maefon glanced back at him and waved.

Adding up everything that Darkken had told him sounded very convincing. Even in his long talks with Maefon, it made sense. But was it the truth, part of the truth, or one big fat lie? Who could he trust that would know the answer to the question? What if the dragons were lying? After all, he was different, and the dragons had never really liked him. That he would be perceived as a threat to them made perfect sense. One thing was for sure: at some point, Nath would have to decide which side he wanted to be on. That was a matter of life or death, not just for him but perhaps the entire world.

Ahead, Darkken held up a fist and hunkered down in the bushes. Together, Nath and Maefon crept up to his position. Darkken pointed toward a pathway deep down in the ravine. Dozens of orcs were marching in a double-column line. At the back of the ranks, they were towing creatures bound up in thick ropes. Nath's nape hairs rose. He whispered angrily, "Those are dragons."

CHAPTER 40

THE SIGHT OF THE DRAGONS being dragged by the orcs started Nath's blood boiling. He wanted to run down the hillside and take Fang to the orcs. But from their elevated location, they were still far away.

He asked Darkken, "Did you know that this was going on?"

"No," Darkken replied. "But treacherous hills like these are good havens for dragons. I hate to say it about the orcs, but they are very good when it comes to hunting dragons."

"Dragons are smarter than orcs. They should never be caught by their filthy kind," Nath said, starting to draw his sword.

"Tuck that sword back in the sheath. We can't storm down there and take on an entire orc regiment. If you want to help the dragons"—Darkken leaned forward—"we need to be more clever. Hmm. Those look like yellow-stripe dragons. They are very docile. It's no surprise the orcs captured the likes of them. They wander the shrubbery too openly, devouring berries and leaves."

Maefon poked her head between the two men. "So, what are we going to do?"

"We don't have to engage. We can keep on going," Darkken suggested. He caught Nath's glare. "Only a suggestion. As much as I am for seeing this world move away from the dragons, I'm averse to seeing innocents suffer, particularly at the hands of orcs. We just have to be careful how we go about it."

"You have plenty of magic. Use it. Scare them or something," Nath said. He regretted not having brought a bow and the black quiver of magic arrows. They would have been of great help in this situation. He locked his eyes on Darkken. He knew by now that his brother was always holding back his powers. But he needed to use them now. "Well, do that lightning like you did before with the beast-birds."

"Don't you know that I wish that I could. The beast-birds are much smaller. It won't have the same effect on the orcs." Darkken ran his index finger across his lips. "I would take out some of them, but hardly all. Those orcs will fight for that dragon like a hungry dog protecting a juicy bone. They'll die for it. And look, those aren't poachers. Those are soldiers. They must have been in the middle of a military exercise or patrol when they came on the dragons. I do like your idea of scaring them. Perhaps I could cast something that will distract them while you and Maefon free the dragons."

Down in the ravine, the orcen regiment snaked down the path. The back end disappeared around the bend.

Nath fanned his nose. "Whew, I can smell them from all the way up here. Such a foul dander."

"Yes, they sweat a lot." Darkken stood up and said, "I'll go down. You wait for my signal."

"What sort of signal?" Nath said.

"I'm certain that you will know it when you see it or hear it." Darkken gave a casual wave and ran off, vanishing as he dipped behind the large shrubbery.

"I guess it's just us now," Nath said. "Let's get down there and await his *signal*." He rolled his eyes and started down into the ravine.

Maefon giggled. "You know that he will come through."

"Yes, I know, but once again, he makes everything a surprise. You'd think that he would just tell us," he replied.

"Depending on the situation, his initial plan might change, and he'll have to improvise." Her boots slipped down the hill on a steep part of the slope. "The Brothers of the Wind are notorious for improvisation. You know that."

Nath took her hand and helped her down onto the path. "Yes, I know. I'm just tired of secrets." They trotted down the path, trying to catch up with the orcs. They made it close enough to where they could hear footsteps marching ahead. Nath moved down off the path to the slope below it. He navigated them through the woodland. They followed along at the lower elevation, using the cover of bushes for concealment as the orcs glanced back from time to time.

The orc soldiers were a burly bunch of warriors, with coarse black hair on their heads and arms. They had flat noses and ugly, hard-featured faces. This regiment wore shirts of ring mail or breastplates of thick leather armor. They carried spears, heavy swords, and axes. They moved as one well-trained military unit while hauling the dragons behind them.

"So, what is the plan, or do you want me to come up with one?" Maefon said.

"Simple—when the opportunity presents itself, we cut the dragons loose and run. Or hide," Nath said as he slipped between a pair of giant red ferns. "We want to make it look as though the dragons did it on their own so that they won't be looking for us."

"How are you going to make it look like the dragons did it? Are you going to chew through the rope?"

He smiled. "No, I was going to leave that to you."

"Ha… ha."

The regiment of orcs came to a stop.

Nath and Maefon hunkered down by the bushes. Only two orcs were in the back of the ranks, guarding the dragons. No one else was behind them. As for the dragons, they weren't very big. They were the size of large dogs but bound up heavily. Their snouts were tied shut, and their hind legs and front paws were bound together.

"This shouldn't be too bad. Once the orcs are distracted, we'll move in, cut the cords, free the dragons, and run. We just need to be quick about it."

Maefon drew her dagger. "It sounds simple enough to me."

Behind the orcs, Nath crept up the slope.

The orcs started to rustle and murmur. All of a sudden, a loud sound like a giant blowing a blaring trumpet cut through the hills like a knife. The orcs dipped down and drew their weapons. Two orcs moved from the back ranks to the rear. Spears in hand, they formed a wall around the dragon just as the sound of the strange horn blasted again.

Nath looked at Maefon, shook his head, and said, "Blast."

CHAPTER 41

THE LOUD SOUND OF A horn blasted one more time. The orcs' hard gazes searched the sky. Nath wasn't sure what to make of it, himself. Perhaps the horn blast was supposed to scare the orcs, but it didn't. All it did was put them on guard. Then, without warning, the orcen ranks advanced down the path, leaving behind the four orcs guarding the dragons.

Nath and Maefon exchanged a look. Keeping his silence, he shrugged. Slipping by the orcs and freeing the dragons without setting off some sort of alarm would be almost impossible. Nath reached back to draw Fang. They were orcs, and he could handle four of them, he figured.

Maefon lifted a finger and shook her head.

Nath mouthed the word *What?*

I have this, she mouthed back. Maefon's hands drew intricate patterns in the air. A soft glow emanated from her hands. Suddenly, fluffy cotton balls of colorful energy grew inside her palms. She lifted up her fingers and blew. The balls of energy floated up into the air and drifted toward the orcs. Dozens of them, the size of eyeballs, blue in color, headed on a path toward the brutish men.

Seeing the balls of energy, the orcs' dark, beady eyes grew big. They made nervous grunts. One orc poked a floating fuzzball with his spear. It stuck to the tip of the metal.

"Unh," the orc said.

Slowly, like falling snow, the fuzzballs landed on the foursome of orcs. The arcane globes stuck to the orcs' heads, bodies, and arms. The orcs tried to pull them away, only to have the fuzz balls stick to their fingers. One orc propped his spear up against his shoulder. He studied the fuzzball inside his hand then clapped. *Zzzap!* The orc's head hair stood on end, and he collapsed.

The three remaining orcs stood with their jaws hanging. Speaking in orcen, they tried to dust the balls from one another.

Maefon whispered a word.

The orcs lit up like burning trees. Their legs buckled beneath them, and they fell to the ground.

"Now, that was clever." Nath climbed from the bank up onto the path, where Maefon joined him. Smiling, he said, "You are just full of surprises, aren't you?"

"I have a special talent for improvisation." Maefon started cutting away the ropes that bound the dragons. "I've really missed the dragons. They are such marvelous creatures."

Nath had his hand on the breast of one dragon. It wriggled in its bindings. Nath wanted to calm it. The yellow dragon's scales shimmered in the light.

"Easy, sister," he said. "We are here to help. Maefon, don't worry about the mouth. You don't want to take a chance that they nip you."

"I remember. I've been nipped at before in Dragon Home," she said. "Hmm… Male and female, I see. I hope they find a better place to nest this time. You don't think the orcs have dragon eggs, do you?"

"I hope not." Nath cut the last cords free from his dragon.

The yellow-streaked dragon, with two black stripes that ran the length of its body, stretched out his wings. As Maefon freed the other dragon, the dragons touched noses. Using their front claws, they removed the ropes that bound their mouths. Without giving Nath or Maefon a glance, the took off from the ground like birds and flew away.

Nath called out after them, "You're welcome!"

"What did you expect? A hug?" Maefon said.

"Some sort of acknowledgement would have been nice," he said.

"You know how aloof the dragons are, especially when you are not one of their kind. Remember, they are not of this world." She took the cut rope, bundled it up in her hands, and muttered an arcane word. The rope burned quickly and turned to ash. She dusted her hands off. "There, no evidence. How clever is that?"

"Very clever. I should have let you do this all by yourself."

"True, but it wouldn't have been as much fun without having a big, strong man to keep me safe." She rubbed his muscular arms, and like a rescued princess, she said, "I couldn't have done it without you, great warrior."

"I know you are being sarcastic, but in truth, you couldn't have done it without me. After all, I am your inspiration."

Maefon rolled her eyes.

"Maefon, do you really think that I'm not one of their kind?"

"What do you mean?"

"I always thought that I would become a dragon and be able to fly the skies one day. But now, I feel more like a man. And if dragons aren't from this world, does that mean I'm excluded from the Land beyond the Murals? Darkken said only dragons exist there."

They walked down the path in the direction the orc regiment had gone.

"I think that you and Darkken are both man and dragon. And you are the change of the new age in the world. You are part of that evolution. Yes, you are different, but you still have dragon blood in you. But it is blood that is meant for the new world, not the old one." She crinkled her nose. "How do orcs sneak up on anyone when they stink so badly?"

Nath shrugged.

"Nath, try not to think about it too much. It doesn't matter to me if you are a man or a dragon." She turned to him and took his hands in hers. "I love you. I hope that is all that matters." She rose on tiptoe.

Nath lowered his lips toward hers.

"Run!" Darkken sprinted right at them, waving his hands and arms. "Run!" He blew right past them. "The orcs are coming! Run!"

Down the path in the direction they were headed, a full regiment of orcs charged with murder in their eyes and a full head of steam.

A spear sailed right by Nath's head.

"Running sounds like good advice," he said.

"Agreed," Maefon said.

Side by side, they dashed after Darkken.

CHAPTER 42

NATH, DARKKEN, AND MAEFON RAN for over a league before they came to a stop. Collapsing by a trickling stream, they lay on their backs and shared a laugh.

"What was that awful sound that you made?" Nath asked of Darkken.

"Oh, that. Yes, it was an old one called the Horn of Thunder. I thought it would scatter them like sheep, but those stubborn orcs just hunkered down. It had the opposite effect of what I wanted."

"You can say that again. The orcs doubled the guard of the dragons." Nath rolled onto his side and faced both his friends.

Darkken's and Maefon's hair were damp with sweat, and they still breathed heavily.

"I don't think they can find us now, do you?" Nath asked.

"No doubt they'll chase after us until nightfall, but they'll give up the hunt once they lose the trail." Darkken looked back toward the path they had taken.

They'd dropped out of the hills and made it to the open plains that led south toward Riverwood.

"And they will lose it once the rain starts falling. I'd guess they'll cross the northern river, heading back east to their home of Thraag."

Rain was coming from the south.

Nath looked up at the storm clouds. "I'd say that we've put an hour between us. I'm ready to stretch the lead as soon as you are."

Maefon sat up, holding her sides. "I don't think I've ever run that far before. The two of you have longer legs than I. Even for an elf, it was a challenge to keep up. Perhaps I should lead the run from here on out."

"I say we make haste toward civilization. The orcs will let up once the storm hits, and they won't journey too close to the human cities. They won't think we are worth it." Darkken rolled onto his belly and pushed himself up. "Let's get at it."

"Aye," Nath said. "And thanks for helping out with the dragons. That felt good, freeing them."

"Do you feel better about things?" Darkken asked.

"It just felt good to do a good thing,"

"True, being helpful can be addictive. And the Brothers of the Wind have plenty of work to do." Darkken gave Nath a hard slap on the shoulder. He offered his hand. "Let's let bygones be bygones."

Nath shook his brother's hand. "Do you think you could at least tell me where we are going?"

"If you insist." Darkken took the lead, wading into the stream until he was thigh deep. He looked at Nath and Maefon, who hung back. "What? We are about to get rained on. A little water won't hurt you now." He sloshed through the waters toward the other side.

They followed.

By the time they climbed up the bank and moved away from the stream, a drizzling rain had started. The wind picked up.

"It's going to be a hard rain but not a storm," Darkken said. "Come on, let's walk briskly, and I'll tell you more about where we are going."

Wiping his damp hair out of his eyes, Nath said, "I'm all ears."

"Me too," Maefon said.

Darkken patted the scroll tucked into his belt. "Not just anyone can mold the dragon ore. It's not like ordinary steel. In order to use it, one must possess the power of great magic. Now, I have such magic, which will be aided by the Star of the Heavens. This will give me the ability to enchant the blade and keep the folds in the blade mended."

"Weren't the elves and dwarves able to make weapons of dragon steel before?" Nath asked as he marched by Darkken's side, his face to the wind.

"Yes, and those elves and dwarves possessed the ability to use magic, as well as the natural use of dragon magic, which aided them. And they were master weaponsmiths, the best of their kind." Darkken lifted two of his fingers. "Remember, though, they were also inside Dragon Home when they made it." He gave them both a knowing glance.

Nath about lost his breath. "You aren't suggesting that we sneak into Dragon Home and make your sword. That's insanity. Not to mention, I'm banished."

Darkken nodded. "A great unknown wizard once said, 'Only the ridiculous achieve the impossible.'"

My brother's insane.

CHAPTER 43

"IT SOUNDS MORE LIKE SOMETHING stupid that you would say." Nath couldn't believe what Darkken was proposing. *The dragons have the power to slaughter us.* "Now, I'm sorry that I asked."

"I didn't say that we were going to the Mountain of Doom, now, did I?" Darkken said.

"It sure sounded like that to me," Maefon said.

"First off, the both of you are jumping to conclusions." Darkken wiped the rain off his face with a stroke of his hand. "I'd never suggest a suicide mission. Now, if you would just listen, I'll finish explaining the point that I was trying to make. The dragon ore can only be melted by the hottest of fires, a special fire, actually. The molten lava that runs through the Mountain of Doom—"

"You do mean Dragon Home, don't you?" Nath said.

"It's not my home or your home anymore, but yes. I just like to call it the Mountain of Doom. It's more fitting, if you ask me." As the rain intensified, Darkken spoke up. "The dragon ore is gathered from those streams of lava, and it's by those same streams that the dragon ore can be melted. In all of the world, there is only one place where those streams run. That is the Mountain of Doom."

Nath started to open his mouth.

"But," Darkken continued, "I have discovered the Dragon Vein."

"I don't follow," Nath said.

"I have discovered that, south of the mountain, in the Lost City of Borgash, a vein of lava flows." Darkken's expression brightened. "I've seen it with my own eyes. There is a forge and armory abandoned by people long forgotten. It is a place of desolation and waste created by the fire of the dragons. You see, the dragons wiped out the strange people that once thrived and lived in that dwelling. Now, it lies in ruin and is said to be guarded by dragons."

"If the ancient people had access to the Dragon Vein, wouldn't they have access to the ore?" Maefon asked.

"Pure dragon ore is difficult to find, even within the Mountain of Doom. There might be fragments of the ore, but it would be difficult to turn them into dragon steel unless you had a substantial amount of it." Darkken reached behind his back and lifted his pack. "I have a hunk big enough to make at least five swords, but by the time we are finished purifying it, I hope we'll be lucky to have enough to make more. It's those impurities in the metal that are so difficult to overcome."

Nath felt the tightness in his chest subside. He couldn't have been more relieved to know that they weren't heading back into Dragon Home. The mission seemed much more manageable, but then he thought of something else Darkken had said. "Did you say that Borgash is guarded by dragons?"

"I seem to recall that I mentioned something about that," Darkken coolly replied.

"But you've been there before, so you would have had to have faced the dragons, right?" Nath added.

"If you are wanting to know if I fought dragons during my explorations, yes, I did. It was them or me, and the dragons don't have a special hold on the Lost City territory." Darkken stepped over a fallen tree, one of hundreds scattered over the open plains. "If it was Dragon Home, it would be different, but anything outside of the mountain is fair game. You do understand that, don't you, Nath?"

"I'm not going to kill any dragons," Nath replied sharply.

"First off, these dragons are copper sliders. They are part of an evil brood. And second, there is always a chance that they won't attack us because of you."

"Me?"

"You are the current Dragon Prince. I'm certain that there are orders not to harm you. Even though the copper sliders are very disobedient."

"It sounds like they wouldn't make very good guardians," Maefon said.

"Actually, they are perfect guardians. They have no respect for persons and won't hesitate to attack anything that comes into their valley. Even the poachers won't go into Borgash, and they know the dragons are in there. The poachers might be brave enough to capture one or two, but a hive of copper sliders… They won't venture into that."

"Yet we are," Nath said.

"Honestly, Nath, I don't think the copper sliders will pose a big problem. After all, there are other unknown terrors that could be lurking in the ruins." Darkken chuckled. "Fortunately, I didn't cross any of them. The point is, I don't think the dragons are guardians in the true sense of being a guardian—you know, like the skelapedes we dealt with in the crypt at Cemetery Hill."

"I don't want to even think about them," Nath said with a shiver. "Those things were creepy."

"Agreed. So bear in mind when we approach the Lost City of Borgash, we will approach with caution. If we don't bother the copper sliders, then chances are they won't bother us. Since it's been centuries—well, perhaps over a millennium—since Borgash was turned to ruin, I think most everyone has forgotten all about the Dragon Vein. There are all kinds of lost treasures from civilizations that were long forgotten. They are buried underneath the mud and sand." He stomped on the ground. "Why, there was probably once a great society right underneath our feet. I bet if we dug deep enough, we could find something."

"I'm so glad we don't have any shovels," Nath remarked. "Because it wouldn't surprise me one bit if you tried to dig to find one."

"I detect sarcasm," Darkken said.

"No, not me," Nath sarcastically replied.

Darkken threw his arm over Nath's shoulders just as the rain started pouring. "So, you are on board with this adventure, brother?"

"Yes."

"That's the spirit." Darkken gave him a firm shoulder hug. "I can't tell you how elated I am that you and I, together, will be forging this sword. It's going to be magnificent!"

Nath didn't share his brother's enthusiasm. He just didn't like the idea of the existence of another sword like Fang. But even in the rain with his lingering doubts and worry, he found Darkken's excitement contagious. "Are we going to walk the entire way? It's several days' journey from where we stand."

"You sound like a man that's in a hurry. I thought you'd like to see more of the countryside."

"If you've seen one tree, you've seen them all." Nath smiled at his brother. "Let's go make your sword."

Standing in the rain, Darkken smiled from ear to ear. "Brother, you just made my day."

He lifted his arms, and his eyes and the bracelet on his wrist glowed. Nath's and Maefon's bracelets burned with inner fire.

Darkken shouted, "To Borgash!"

Nath and Maefon lifted their hands with their bracelets high like a salute and said as one, "To Borgash."

In the wink of an eye, the world around them fell away. As one, they were launched through the portal.

Hurtling through space, Nath could hear Darkken's words from the night before still tumbling through his head. *"The time has come when the dark shall rule the day."*

I will get to the bottom of this.

CHAPTER 44

SLIVVER, RODAY, AND DULE HAD tirelessly searched the ancient texts and tomes in Darkken's study. The tomes consisted of world history, the craft of magic, and old stories written for entertainment. Despite all their efforts, they hadn't come across anything about where Lord Darkken would be able to craft a weapon from dragon steel. Their efforts had been fruitless. Now, Slivver was standing over a table, leafing through an elven history book. He slammed the tome shut. "I'm not getting anywhere."

Sitting in a chair with his legs propped up on a windowsill and a big leather-bound book in his lap, Dule said, "I find all of this fascinating. I'm reading how to make effective potions from a mixture of berries, roots, and flowers. It only makes sense since magic does come from the earth. I just never thought that it could be in anything that we touch." He shook his head. "I should have practiced magic."

"You're an elf," Roday said. He was standing with a different book in hand and tossed it on the table. "You have hundreds of years to delve into something else. It's not like we are Caligin now. You're free to do whatever you want."

Dule perked up. "That's right. I can be a wizard if I want to. I have plenty of books. I just need a good teacher."

"See, things are looking up," Roday replied. "That is assuming that we don't die by the hand of Lord Darkken within the next several weeks… or hours."

"Why did you have to go and ruin it, Roday?" Dule shook his head. "I don't understand why you have to be that way."

"I'm just thinking about things from all of the angles." Roday made his way back to the bookshelf and looked through the books. "It's how I process things."

Slivver flexed his wings halfway out. The membranes that had been torn by the Creeper had sealed back up thanks to the use of a healing potion. His wing that had been out of socket was back in place but still sore. He hadn't tried to fly yet either. "Roday and Dule, as much as your help has been beneficial to our campaign, you are under no obligation to stay. This is our fight, not yours."

Dule and Roday looked at Slivver as though he were stupid. "Are you trying to brush us off, Slivver?"

"That's a unique way of putting it, but no. You have proven to be a great help, and I am grateful, but it might be best that you consider more favorable options. Long-lasting options."

Dule got out of his seat and said, "First off, if Darkken isn't defeated, we'll be dead soon after you. I don't want to live life on the run. I want to live a free elf."

"We didn't come this far to turn away now," Roday said. "It's going to take every one of us to win over Nath and stop Darkken."

"It's your decision. But you can leave at any time. No one will think the less of you for it." Slivver opened another book. He liked Roday and Dule, but the elves were still former Caligin, and he wasn't entirely sure he could trust them. He needed to be sure. They had been very helpful—too helpful, perhaps. The fact that they were adamant to stay around made him a little more suspicious. "Well, except for Brenwar."

The doors to the study opened, and Brenwar marched into the room. "Find anything?"

Frowning, Dule said, "We found a dragon that doesn't want us to remain on the campaign."

"Smart dragon. You can toss a dwarf on the side of that line of thinking too," Brenwar said. He made his way to the table and started looking at the maps. "I don't like this waiting around. It's too quiet."

"Agreed," Slivver said. He crossed his arms and sighed. "The longer we do nothing, the more likely we lose Nath. We've been through all of these books, and we haven't found anything. Darkken is so secretive. I can't fight the feeling that we are right where he wants us to be."

"As far as I know, Darkken never opened up to anybody," Roday said. He climbed from bookshelf to bookshelf, tossing more books onto the floor. "We've been in the keep as long as any with him. He didn't take much company. He was weird like that."

"It's probably why he's so successful," Dule added. "He doesn't let anything distract him."

With his eyes fixed on the map, Brenwar said, "I'll distract him with a hammer strike upside his head when I see him again."

"Brenwar, how long does it take to craft a weapon?" Slivver said. "Considering the material, I would think that it would take days. Perhaps weeks."

With a hearty laugh, Brenwar said, "It would take *you* that long. Back in Morgdon, we could spit out a dozen swords in an hour—at least, if we cast a mold for the metal. Sometimes, we would hammer the metal out, but the molds are quicker. There's nothing like seeing the orange molten metal taking shape and form. It's beautiful."

"I have always been of the impression that Balzurth spent a great deal of time creating Fang," Slivver said.

"Balzurth takes his time when he goes about things. I'm sure he could do it quickly if he wanted to. The Dragon King is patient. Patience leads to perfection."

"Perhaps that gives us an advantage. Darkken might be rushing things. Hence, his sword might not be so perfect."

"It won't have Balzurth's touch, that is for certain. But once you put an edge on that steel, it will cut through anything, enchanted or not." Brenwar turned the map on the table. "It was dragon steel that helped end the black dragons in the Great Dragon Wars. It's tougher than dwarven moorite, and that's hard to say, for a dwarf."

Standing on the bookshelf ledges, Roday said, "This is interesting."

"What's that?" Slivver asked.

Roday was knocking on the back of the wooden shelving. "It's hollow behind this section. Dule, check some of the other spots. See if they are hollow too. There might be a concealed compartment behind the shelves."

Dule, Brenwar, and Slivver got in on the act. They removed the books from the shelves and started knocking. All the back panels were solid except the one that Roday had been knocking on. It was in the middle section of the bookshelf.

"I can't find a way to open it," Roday said.

"Get out of the way. I'll bust it open," Brenwar said.

"Will you just give me a moment? I'll figure it out."

"It might require a secret word, Roday. You know how Darkken is. If he hid something there, it's protected by something."

"No, no, I think I have it." Roday's jaw muscles clenched. "It's starting to slide."

A cloud of mist sprayed out of the bookshelf and filled the room. Roday dropped to the floor. Slivver covered his mouth, but his head swam. The walls of Darkken's room warped. Everyone fell, even Brenwar.

CHAPTER 45

HACKSAW AND CALYPSA STOOD ON top of the keep, overlooking the wall. The rolling hills and high grasses stretched as far as the eye could see. Hacksaw puffed on his pipe.

In his bones, something didn't feel right. They'd conquered the tower, yet victory eluded their grasp. All of them were still desperate to find Nath.

Hacksaw hoped he was somewhere out there, waiting to be found. "It's a pretty land, even though these skies seem to remain grim."

"The clouds seem determined to shield the keep from the light. It's a very odd thing to see," Calypsa said. She climbed up on the wall and leaned against the battlements. "Perhaps the clouds have a mind of their own."

"Even with those dark clouds, your presence has a way of brightening things," Hacksaw said.

"Are you flirting with me?"

Rubbing the back of his head, he said, "I've seen many women, but I haven't seen any as fetching at you. That's just the truth of the matter. And frankly, your beauty is distracting." He puffed out a ring of smoke. "I'm old. I've almost died and probably will soon enough, so I don't see any reason to hold back on what I'm thinking. You are something."

Calypsa showed a warm smile that could've melted butter. "Thank you, Hacksaw. And just so you know, I think you are charming. And I like a man that is rough around the edges. But I don't think there will be a future for you and me."

He let out a rusty chuckle. "Crickets, girl, I never thought such a thing. I was just admiring you. I'm too old and set in my ways to settle down with anybody. But if I wasn't, I'd be coming after you."

"You do know that I'm probably older than you by at least one hundred years," she said.

"Well, then maybe I should reconsider. You might need me to take care of you in your old age."

They shared a laugh.

Down below, Rond was standing guard on the outer wall built over the top of the front gate. The four-armed bugbear held the sledgehammer on a shoulder. He hadn't moved an inch since he'd stood there.

With his eyes on the large humanoid, Hacksaw said, "I'm sorry about your friend and what he's become. I can tell that it hurts you."

"Rond is the best friend I ever had. He's loyal." She clutched her chest. "My heart aches for him. I know he's suffering."

"We all suffer in one way or another. At least he's still with you. I think he's happy because he is even though he can't show it."

"Come here," she said.

Hacksaw walked up to her. Calypsa gave him a strong embrace. For a small woman, she was as strong as an animal. It made him think that he might be getting hugged by those bear arms she'd shown before. He hugged her back as tightly as she could. Her warmth took over his body.

"Whew, woman, you are as warm as fresh baked bread."

"I know." She kissed his cheek and let go. "Do you think we will find Nath?"

"Either we'll find him, or he'll find us. When he does, I hope that he's still the man that we knew and not someone else."

"That would be a tragedy," she said. "Nath is a sweet man, just naïve. I should have looked out for him the first time I met him, but I didn't. Instead, I robbed him. I basically did the same thing to him that people did to me. I wouldn't blame him for not trusting anyone."

"Yes, if Darkken deceives him… Well, I don't want to even think about it."

A shadow passed overhead. Master Elween had dropped out of the clouds and was circling above. She landed on the roof, and her wings folded behind her back. She nodded and greeted them.

"Any sign of anyone?" Hacksaw asked.

Master Elween shook her long serpentine neck. "No Nath. No Caligin. Only varmints and critters for over a league. I thought for certain that the Caligin would have regrouped somewhere, but I haven't seen any signs of them at all. It's lonely land out there. Any new developments on your end?"

"Aside from Hacksaw confessing a strong yearning for me, no," Calypsa said.

Hacksaw couldn't help but grin. But he said, "I think it's the other way around."

"I'm sure it is," Elween said. Her nostrils flared, and she started sniffing. "What is that odor?"

Hacksaw inhaled deeply through his nose and said, "I don't smell anything." Then he noticed white smoke drifting up from the stairwell leading to the lower level. Like a cloud, it was rising into the air. "What is that?"

CHAPTER 46

CALYPSA JUMPED OFF THE WALL. "Eerie. We'd better check on the others."

The three of them headed down the steps and entered the top level, into Darkken's study. Slivver, Brenwar, Roday, and Dule were out cold on the floor. "Oh my!"

"I told you something smelled funny," Elween said. She rushed over to Slivver and cradled his head in her arms. She started slapping him in the face. "Wake up, Slivver. Wake up!"

Hacksaw put his head on Brenwar's chest. "He's breathing but sleeping as soundly as a bear. What in the world do you think happened?"

Calypsa tried to stir Roday and Dule, to no avail. The elves were knocked out cold.

"A great sleep has befallen them," she said, "but I think I can wake them up."

"What are you going to do?" Hacksaw asked.

She rubbed her fingers together, creating sparks. "I'm going to charge them up." She touched Roday on the neck.

Roday's body jumped, and he let out a shout. His gaze found Calypsa. "What was that?"

Smiling, she said, "Just a little wake-up spark."

Roday pointed at Dule. "Do it to him!"

Calypsa touched Dule.

The elf jumped clear up to his feet with a loud yelp. He started dancing and swatting himself as though he were being attacked by a hive of bees. He finally stopped when he saw Roday and Calypsa laughing. "What's so funny?"

"You, dancing around like your pants are on fire," Roday said.

"Ha ha," Dule replied. He looked quickly at his shoulders and dusted them off as though a hornet were on then. "I still hear buzzing."

"It will go away. Let me wake the others," Calypsa said.

"Slivver is coming to," Elween replied.

"So is Brenwar," Hacksaw added. Looking at Brenwar's sagging face, he said, "Wakey, wakey, sunshine."

Brenwar jerked away, pushed himself up to his feet, and asked, "What's going on?"

"You tell us," Hacksaw said.

"Poison gas, well, a sleeping gas came out of the bookshelf," Roday replied. He stretched his arms and yawned. "I can only assume Darkken put it there for this very specific purpose, to knock out any intruders. It worked. And if the rest of you hadn't come along, we would still be asleep. And if Darkken had come along, we'd be dead in our sleep."

Rubbing his blue eyes, Slivver asked, "So what was he protecting?"

"A fine question." Roday climbed back onto the bookshelf. He reached inside a secret panel and pulled forth a leather-bound book that fit in both of his hands. "This!" He studied the cover, opened it, and read from the first page. "*Ancient Weapons Craft.* Interesting, it's written in elven."

"Let me see that," Elween said.

Roday hopped down from the bookshelf and handed it to her.

"There's no dust on the book." She leafed through the pages. "Huh, we have a manuscript similar to this in Dragon Home. I use it as a teaching guide. It teaches the variety of weapons, how to use them and make them."

"It doesn't sound so special to me, compared to all of these other books. That's quite ordinary," Slivver remarked. "So why keep it hidden?"

"I don't know." Elween's dexterous claws moved from one page to the next. As she slipped through the pages, a folded-up piece of parchment fell out.

Brenwar snatched the paper out from underneath Roday's hand. "Back off, elf!" He put the map on the table and folded it out. The paper unfolded to a three-foot-by-two-foot rectangle. "Strange parchment. Very flexible. Har. It's much bigger than it looks. It's a map of a city."

All parties present surrounded the table.

Running his finger around the lettering on the header, Brenwar read aloud, "Borgash."

"Borgash? Isn't that a gnomish casserole?" Roday said.

"No, that's gorhash," Dule replied.

"That is one intricate map," Slivver commented. "The details are incredible. But Borgash is a fallen city, a place of ruin. Not a single structure stands. It's all covered in overgrowth."

The map showed colored pictures of the well-constructed city, much like Advent or a smaller Quintuklen. It showed the rich farmlands, barns, and storehouses out on the range.

The streets were paved with stone. The buildings stood several stories tall. It was all drawn like a painting, with living detail.

"Are those little flags on the structures moving?" Hacksaw asked. Staring at the map made him queasy. He held his stomach and squinted. "I swear they are moving."

Brenwar nodded. "It moves."

"There is an ancient craft of cartography where the quill and inks are enchanted. I think you are seeing that effect," Slivver said. "It makes me think of the murals in Dragon Home. They are always moving, just slowly."

"So what happened to this city? Better yet, where is this city?" Hacksaw asked.

"It's south of Dragon Home. It was wiped out before my time," Slivver replied. "I just don't see the significance of it. Do you see anything in the book, Elween?"

"No." Elween closed the book and focused on the map. "But I know about Borgash. Its people warred with the dragons. They were a wicked brood. The dragons wiped them out."

"What kind of people were they?" Dule asked.

"Don't know," Elween replied. "Men, I always supposed, but I'm not sure."

Hacksaw fixed his sights on a bright-orange spot on the map that caught his attention. "My eyes aren't the best, and that lettering is so tiny. Not that I could read elven. But what is that burning mark or speck?"

Slivver leaned closer. "It says armory."

Elween also took a deeper look. Her head almost touched his head from the other side of the table. "That's not all it says. Look closer, Slivver."

"Oh my," the silver dragon said with awe in his voice. He pulled his head back and looked right at Elween. "That reads 'Dragon Vein.'"

CHAPTER 47

"DRAGON VEIN." WHILE LOOKING AT the map, Brenwar shook his head. "That would be a problem."

"Assuming they can access it," Slivver said. "Borgash is nothing but ruin. I can't imagine an armory still standing in the wreckage."

"In Morgdon, our forges run below the dirt. The same goes in Dragon Home, does it not?" Brenwar asked. "An old city like that, well, it might be buried in rubble, but it wouldn't surprise me a bit if there were tunnels below."

"Wouldn't Darkken have taken the map with him if that was where he was going?" Hacksaw asked.

"A good question," Slivver said. "Darkken, if he's anything, is a planner. If I had to guess, I'd think that he memorized the map and hid it away so that no one could see it." He looked at the elves. "He's strong because he keeps all of his plans locked up in his mind, all to himself."

"No doubt that his mind is a steel trap," Roday answered. "He's so successful because he's such an intricate planner. That's probably why he has such a strong following."

"That and because everyone is scared to death of him," Dule added.

Slivver spread out on the table the other maps they'd found in the wagon. "Of course, if he memorizes maps, then why did he have these in his possession? Many of them are marked with places that they have been."

"Perhaps these maps were a decoy to throw us off," Hacksaw said. "When I rode with the Legionnaires against the enemy, there were times when we spread misinformation into the enemies' hands. These maps could be the result of a similar ploy."

"The same could be said of the map we found in the bookcase," Elween stated. "Perhaps Darkken wants us to explore Borgash. It could be another trap or a ruse to lead us off the trail. After all, look who found the map. Former Caligin, or so they say."

"Whoa, now wait a moment," Roday said, lifting up his hands as Dule joined his side. "I don't understand all of the doubt. We didn't plant an ancient map in that bookshelf. We've never even been this far in here."

"That's what a liar would say," Brenwar said. "I say we toss these two pointy-eared saddlebags off the top of the keep. We can't afford to doubt them anymore. And it's too dangerous to let them breathe."

Roday shot a finger at Brenwar and wagged it in his face. "Just when I started liking you, Brenwar, you resort to this. We are not traitors. At least, I'm not as I can only speak for myself."

"Hold on. I'm not a traitor either," Dule said. He pushed Roday. "And if anyone was a traitor, it would be you."

"I think you're both traitors!" Brenwar said.

"You think all elves are traitors," Slivver added.

Brenwar rose up on his toes, pointed at the elves, and said, "That's because they are!"

"What you are proposing is insanity," Roday said as he and Dule walked back toward the bookcase. "We've risked our lives as much as you've risked yours!"

Master Elween jumped in and stated, "Caligin will give their lives for their cause. You would have died trying to fool us."

Roday and Dule drew their swords and daggers.

"Fine. You doubt us, then you'll have to kill us," Roday said. "But I'll cut you to ribbons before I fall. I'll take those braids right off of your beard, dwarf."

Hacksaw stepped between the elves and the dwarves and dragons that began to crowd them. In his strong voice, he said, "Enough of this. This is exactly want Darkken wants. This is how his wicked musing works. He sows seeds of doubt and discord wherever he goes. He does not want anyone to trust anyone but him. He's tripped us up so many times that we can't make a decision when the truth is right in front of our eyes. Maybe the map is a ploy. But at the moment, it is all that we have, and we are running out of time. We must make a decision. Do we trust these elves? Do we pursue that map?" He lowered his arms. "I know this isn't a democracy. I don't know what it is. But I don't have a problem with the elves, and I'm all for the journey to Borgash. I don't see any other choice but the one that is in front of us. It's that or do nothing."

Slivver backed away from the elves. "He's right. We can't start second-guessing our every move. We have to move forward on faith. We aren't going to find any answers or Nath otherwise."

Leaning against the window ledge, Calypsa spoke up, "I don't know about the rest of you, but I'm tired of the dreary walls of this creepy place. I think it's time to move."

Elween nodded. "I agree as well."

Brenwar huffed. "I'm fine with all of it. I just don't like the elves." He turned his back on them. "I'll meet you at the gate. I'm ready to go."

Roday and Dule let out breaths of relief as they sheathed their weapons. They patted Hacksaw on the back. "Thanks for believing in us, Hacksaw."

"I don't believe in you. I believe in Nath." Hacksaw followed Brenwar toward the exit.

"Grab anything and everything that you think we can use from the vault," Slivver said. "I have a feeling that we're going to need it."

CHAPTER 48

A LOT MORE HAD TRANSPIRED IN the sea town of Artus than Nath was aware of. When Lord Darkken met with the Caligin in the old cottage, they informed him that Slivver and Master Elween had overcome the Creeper in the keep. Word traveled swiftly north, thanks to the Caligin that fled, who sent their fastest ravens from city to city, sending word to Darkken. That was one way how Darkken operated. It kept him and his Caligin, who were spread throughout all the major cities, informed. It kept him a step ahead of everything.

But the news about the Creeper from the Deep hit Lord Darkken hard. It sent his head spinning so much that he took his anger out on one Caligin. With his sword, Scalpel, he cut down the loyal elf delivering the message. Darkken had felt with absolute certainty that the Creeper would wipe out Slivver, Elween, and the dwarf. That mission failed. And furthering his disappointment, he discovered that not only was the old knight, Hacksaw, alive, but so was the half-dryad woman, Calypsa, and her cohort, the four-armed bugbear, Rond. The news of their survival boiled his blood. His enemies were not being crushed. Instead, they were slipping through his fingers.

To Darkken, the heroes trying to reach Nath were nothing more than pawns. But now, they'd proven formidable, so he had to act quickly. At all costs, he had to see to it that under no circumstances did they encounter Nath again. He had to be rid of them once and for all. Thus, when he received word that the heroes were in the keep, he enacted a plan. He summoned his Caligin lurking in the cities and sowed discord in order to form an army. He had them dispatched near the Lost City of Borgash. Assuming that the heroes would somehow figure out that the lost city was where he was headed, the Caligin would be waiting for them there. If the Caligin couldn't handle it, then he would have to do it himself.

In the meantime, he had a sword to make, a sword capable of slaying his father, Balzurth. But he couldn't do it all on his own. According to the Dragon Steel Scroll, properly enchanting the blade would require a very special ingredient. It would require the blood of an innocent dragon destined to be the king. Either Nath would have to give it freely, or Darkken would take it—one way or the other.

CHAPTER 49

NATH, DARKKEN, AND MAEFON REAPPEARED on a stretch of land in the southern plains. A warm, welcoming breeze rustled their dripping-wet hair. The hot sun shone in their eyes.

Turning his face toward the sun, Nath said, "Ah, that feels good. So much better than the bite of the cold." He knees buckled. "Whoa!"

Darkken caught him by one arm. "The teleportation will turn your legs to noodles and your stomach into jelly. Stay still for a moment."

"I remember the feeling from the last time. It sneaks up on you, doesn't it?" he said.

"Every time," Darkken replied.

Maefon combed her fingers through her hair. Her eyes closed, she swayed in the wind. "I think living in the south would be so much better. Can't we build another keep down here? It would be more pleasing."

"Who knows. Maybe we will rebuild in the Lost City of Borgash. Certainly, the materials are available," Darkken said. He stood tall, eyes directed south, where the steppes spanned out as far as he could see. "Sorry, I didn't land us as close as I wanted, but we are about half a league from Borgash. But it was a safer option than landing in the middle of the ruins. A sudden appearance could cause an unwanted awakening. Shall we walk?"

"You know the way," Nath said.

As usual, Darkken took the lead, Nath guarded the rear, and Maefon was in the middle. On the way, Nath found a visitor on his shoulder, the small brown rodent.

He took it in his hand. "Mouse, have you been hiding in my pack this entire time?"

The mouse's whiskers twitched.

Nath had forgotten about the little creature that had stowed away with him on their journey to Old Hen. The field mouse must have slipped back into his pack after they took off to Cold Cliff Island. Holding the mouse in the palm of his hand, he said, "You must be getting hungry."

"I see you have your friend back. Interesting company," Maefon said.

"Well, I thought I might need more backup in case things become too dangerous." Nath reached into his belt pouch and grabbed a hunk of dried beef. He pinched off a nibble and gave it to Mouse. "There you go."

Mouse stuffed it into his mouth and waited for Nath to give him a bigger piece. Nath added another tiny hunk to his hand. Mouse took the beef in his mouth, scurried up Nath's arm, and crawled into his pack.

"So much for new company," Nath said. He shrugged his eyebrows at Maefon. "It looks like you'll have to do."

"I think I can best a rodent." She hooked her arm in his as they strolled the meadows together. "I really do enjoy the warmth. If you work with me, perhaps we can make a home here. Together, we can convince Darkken this is a better base for our operations. It's more fitting for the Brothers of the Wind than that damp keep."

"I don't know. I think Darkken is fond of it. Let's just get his sword made, and we'll see." Nath checked the sky—a brilliant blue with rolling clouds as white as snow. "I sure wish I could fly."

She leaned into him. "You will one day. I'm sure of it."

"I don't know. If the dragons leave, maybe I'll never become a dragon, and then I wouldn't have wings."

"Not all dragons have wings. What makes you think that you would?"

"Huh. I never thought about it like that. I always assumed I would."

Nath didn't care for what Maefon said about him not having any wings. She didn't mean anything bad by what she'd said, but it still stung. He'd always dreamed of flying. The thought that he never would suddenly became very disturbing. *I wonder if this is how Darkken feels.*

The group trudged along at a steady pace until the terrain took a sudden change. The landscape became lumpy and jagged. An outline miles in circumference made up a sunken valley. Huge stones and columns, toppled over long before, were half covered in thick vegetation and vines.

Darkken climbed up on a mound of wildflowers that heaved up from the ground. He looked back at Nath and Maefon and said, "Welcome to Borgash."

Joining his brother on the perch, Nath scanned the odd territory. Wildlife scurried over the city of ruins. A roar carried across the strange expanse. It had been made by a dragon, undeniably. A large one.

"So, you say that copper sliders made a home in there?" Nath asked.

"Aye." Darkken drew his sword. "Them and their mother."

Chapter 50

Nath drew Fang.

Maefon snaked out her sword and dagger.

The slipped into the lost city on cat's feet. Nath had knowledge of all dragons. The copper sliders were one of the worst breeds. They were ill-tempered, vile, and nasty, so much so that they didn't frequent Dragon Home except on rare occasions. They weren't big dragons, but they were some of the deadliest. They were hornless, with copper scales covering their bodies and black stripes that ran from head to toe in zigzag patterns. A long black prehensile tail ended each of their bodies. They used them efficiently to choke their prey. Their claws could rip through metal, and they spat black acid that would eat flesh. The only glaring weakness the copper dragons had was their size. They didn't become huge, like a bull dragon, but were mostly the size of people, sometimes bigger or smaller.

"Stay close," Nath said to Maefon.

Copper dragons were quick. From their concealment, they could strike like cobras. Nath's golden eyes slid from side to side.

"I know what a copper dragon is," she said. "I spent over fifty years in Dragon Home with you."

"True, but how many dragons did you wrestle?"

"None."

Nath caught a glimpse of a white flag being waved. It was held by an elf wearing black leather armor. The elf was hunkered down in some brush.

"What is he doing here?" Nath asked.

"I dispatched Brothers of the Wind here before we left for Cold Cliff Island. I knew we would be coming. After all, it was our final destination." He made a beeline for the elf. "Come on. The coast is clear."

"Why didn't you tell us this vital tidbit of information?" Nath said.

"First off, it's not that relevant. Second, you should have foreseen this for yourself. It's called planning. The last thing I wanted to do was lead us into a den of dragons. It was best to clear the road first. Especially after the last time."

Aggravated, Nath said, "I wouldn't be so surprised if you told us where we were going to begin with." He caught sight of the end of a long black tail slipping into the concealment of the brush. "How many of them are there?"

"A score, assuming that they are all still living." Darkken hustled over the short expanse and climbed up a rocky mound of vegetation, where the dark elf stood and bumped forearms with him. "Well met, Dalva."

Dalva was a tall, lean, slender-faced elf with dark-brown hair braided in spots, with small bird feathers woven into the braids. "Well met, Darkken." His eyes slid over to Nath and Maefon. "Well met. I fear that I have troubles to report. The copper dragons have proven to be very hostile to our presence."

Darkken arched a brow. "We've lost brothers?"

"Two. Come, I'll show you what we are up against." Dalva led the way down a steep bank leading to the edge of a gulch. Over a dozen elves, clad in black, were squatted down in the brush of both sides of the gulch. Their eyes were fixed on the bottom of the gulch. In the shadows, a large copper dragon bigger than a horse lurked over a creek. Two bodies lay in the waters, covered in black grime. The skin had melted from their bones.

Nath and Maefon covered their noses.

"It reeks," Nath said of the rotted skin and flesh chewed up by the acid.

Studying the copper dragon, he could tell by the lighter scales on its belly and eyelashes above the eyes that it was the mother. She was surrounded by smaller dragons, nestled in the ferns, still as big as men.

Nath counted at least fifteen of them. "That's quite a brood. What happened?"

"We were patrolling the ruins yesterday morning," Dalva said. "The dragons struck without warning as we traversed the gulch. We missed them entirely. Our brothers were covered in black spit before they knew what hit them. The screams. The gurgling. It was awful." His chin dipped. "We tried to recover our brothers, but the mother came. I believe she nested down there. I think we went into the wrong place at the wrong time."

"Don't be so hard on yourself, Dalva," Darkken said. He knelt, pulled a wildflower from the ground, and started pulling off the petals. "The coppers are some of the most slippery of servants. The problem is I don't think the mother is going anywhere."

"That sounds like a good thing," Nath said. "If she is down there, then we are safe up here. Right?"

"True," Darkken said to Nath. He flicked the flower away. "The problem is, the entrance we seek to access the Dragon Vein is in the gulch. The only way through that is through the dragons."

Sweat ran down Nath's cheek. He wiped it away and said, "Oh."

Chapter 51

Slivver took to the air. His wing ached, but flying again rejuvenated him. Elween glided alongside him. Since they could travel ten times faster, if not twenty, than their two-footed companions, they chose to scout ahead. The dragons would need only several hours to make it to Borgash, whereas the rest of the group would take a few days. They didn't have time to waste. Scanning the landscape hundreds of feet beneath his wings, he said, "It's good to ride the winds again."

"I've certainly missed it myself," Elween said. She had a bit of a smile on her scaly face. "The longer I'm in the air, the more I wonder how I managed to stay away. I was always content in Dragon Home, living in the caverns and conducting my training. The sky, I find, is a much more preferable climate. It's peaceful up here."

"I know. The gift of flight must be one of the greatest gifts of all. It puts the problems of life into perspective. From this view, our troubles seem so small."

"Yes. No more relevant than a blade of grass. Perhaps that is why dragons are so aloof to the problems of the world of men. It's so easy to escape them," Elween said.

"True. But we can't fly all of the time nor live in the clouds. That's the sad part. Of course, I'm very fascinated with people. I enjoy being involved with them. In a way, a dragon's life can be very boring."

"That's why we sleep so much," she joked.

With a fierce beating of his wings, Slivver jettisoned through the air. Like a lightning bolt hurled through the heavens, he flew. Exhilaration passed through him as the wind whistled by his horns. He went on for miles then slowed back to a glide and let Elween catch up to him.

"Show-off," she said.

"I had to make sure I still had it."

"Slivver, no one surfs the firmament like you."

"I know."

The dragons buzzed underneath the clouds. Their keen vision allowed them to see the activity on the ground with clarity. Herds of cattle grazed the farmlands. Small groups of antelope raced through the grasses. Wagons were being hauled by horses from town to town. Merchant caravans remained busy. Nothing suspicious was going on—just people and wildlife, going about their business as they always did. The only areas of concern were the forests. The dragons couldn't tell what might be lurking within the leafy cover of the trees. As far as Slivver could tell, for his friends, the coast was clear of any imminent danger. He saw no signs of elves or Caligin.

"Slivver," Elween said. "How are we going to defeat Darkken? We don't have any sort of weapon to use against him, aside from our claws and breath. I fear that, like the Creeper, he is immune to them."

Worried, Sliver shook his head. "I don't know. I think that he is going the expect us to fight him, but maybe that isn't the best strategy. We are going to have to focus on Nath. We have to convince him that we are on his side. The best way is to try to separate the two of them."

"We almost had him last time," Elween said. "If I'd been a moment quicker, I could have grabbed Nath and taken him to safety."

"You can't blame yourself. After all, Darkken teleported them away. Even if you grabbed him, I think the result would have been the same."

"Are you trying to make me feel better?" she said.

"We can't forge ahead with doubt. You shouldn't, most of all. I don't know a finer dragon than you." He gently clipped his wings with hers. "It's an honor to have you by my side."

"I feel the same about you."

Slivver's head hung low and moved from side to side. He saw nothing to be suspicious about below, which was disappointing because he hoped to spot movement from the Caligin. They were masters of concealment, and it bothered him that he might have overlooked them.

"There is one thing that bothers me," Elween said. "I don't understand where Darkken acquired all of his power. He is a fallen dragon. He doesn't have scales, he can't fly, and he does not have the use of a breath weapon. Either one of us should be able to handle him."

"I've shared the same thoughts. Darkken is still a creature of magic, and he has the ability to manipulate it. He has qualities superior to the other races as well. In the world of men, he is extremely gifted. And he's fueled by vengeance. He's spent hundreds of years preparing for this very moment." Slivver flapped his wings. "I do think that he has acquired items that enhance his power. I noticed in our encounter with Nath that a bracelet on his wrist glowed right before he disappeared. Darkken's did as well."

"Yes, I saw that bracelet. We need to separate Nath from it so they can't vanish on us again. We could cut it off."

Slivver nodded. "I'm sure it won't be as easy as just cutting it off. Darkken would be prepared for that."

"I'm sure Darkken is, but I wasn't talking about cutting off the bracelet. I was talking about cutting off Nath's hand."

CHAPTER 52

HACKSAW STOOD IN THE VAULT of Coldwater Keep, watching Roday and Dule load up backpacks. In his hand, he held more gold than he'd ever had in his life. On the floor, in sacks and in chests, was more treasure than he'd ever imagined. He could take what he wanted. He could live a good life and walk away.

Brenwar bumped against him. "Gold fever."

"What?" Hacksaw asked listlessly.

"Dwarves are notorious for their obsession with treasure. Why do you think we stay in the ground so much? We are digging."

"It's so much."

"Have you ever eaten too much food?" Brenwar asked.

"Many times."

"Too much food makes your belly sick. It's the same with gold. Only take what you need. The rest will spoil you."

Testing the weight of the gold coins in his hands, Hacksaw said, "Is this too much?"

"Ha! You can barely buy a good horse with that." Brenwar picked up a small sack that weighed a few pounds. "Take this. Make it last. There's plenty to enjoy."

Hacksaw looked at the bag. It was a fortune, more than he'd acquired in all his life. As a Legionnaire, he'd been supplied with a place to live and the finest armor and weapons. But when he retired, he turned all that in. Knights lived a humble life—at least, they were supposed to.

He tossed the sack on the table. "I need to be focused on Nath, not spending money."

"Suit yourself, but this expedition isn't going to pay for itself." Brenwar picked up the sack of gold and put it in another sack. "Don't worry. I'll cover you."

Roday had a black quiver full of arrows strapped on his back. He had a sack of goods in his hand. "It seems very strange to leave the keep abandoned. Shouldn't someone stay behind and guard it?"

"Are you volunteering?" Brenwar asked.

"No. I'm just saying that it seems strange. This was home for a long time, and now, anyone can waltz in here and take it," Roday replied.

Dule bumped Roday. "You have the key, so lock the vault. Besides, you don't really think that Lord Darkken is going to abandon this keep, do you? Would you?"

"No. But if we kill Darkken, who gets the keep then?" Roday asked.

"We'll worry about that after we kill him," Brenwar said.

"Did you find anything useful?" Hacksaw asked the elves.

Dule lifted up two sacks of goods. "I wiped out the potions and grabbed some other strange stuff. I don't think Lord Darkken left behind a secret weapon that would kill him. But these items might save our hind ends."

Hacksaw didn't see any need to rummage through the treasure. He would have to rely on his wits and his sword. He asked Roday, "You?"

"What is this? Inventory?" Roday replied.

"Yes," Hacksaw said.

"I have this quiver and arrows. It was Nath's. He left it, and he might need it again." Roday patted a pouch on his belt. "And I took a little heap of treasure for myself."

"Let's get out of here." Brenwar departed down the hallway.

Roday locked the vault and tucked the key inside his armor.

They all headed up to the courtyard, where Calypsa was fighting with Rond. She had a black Clydesdale horse by the reins. It nickered and whinnied while stamping its hooves.

"Rond, get on the horse!"

Rond shook his ghastly head.

The horse tried to rear up. Calypsa grabbed the horse's harness and pulled it down. "Be calm, beautiful. Rond will bring you no harm."

"Rond might break the beast's back," Roday said. "I wouldn't let the bugbear ride on me. Look at him. Would you?"

The bugbear showed strips of skin hanging from his body, exposing the muscles. His cheek was pierced by a hole that could be seen clean through. Part of his upper lip was missing, giving him a permanent ugly smile.

"You aren't helping," Calypsa said.

Holding the horse firmly by the harness, she whispered in its ear. The beast's snorting and stamping stopped.

Stroking the horse's mane, she said, "That's better. Rond, gently get on the horse."

A rumble came from the bugbear's throat.

"Now," Calypsa insisted.

"This, I have to see," Hacksaw whispered to Brenwar.

"Aye."

With his shoulders slumped, Rond reluctantly approached the horse. He put his top hands on the saddle and stuck one foot in a stirrup. The horse lurched. It broke Calypsa's grip from the harness and bolted. With Rond's big foot stuck inside the stirrup, the horse dragged the bugbear through the courtyard. Rond flailed his huge arms like a wild man.

Hacksaw, Brenwar, and the elves let out gusty laughs.

The horse galloped, trying to shake the lumbering undead body that was attached to him. The beast kicked and bucked.

Calypsa gave chase. Waving her hands, she yelled, "Stop! Stop!"

Holding his gut, Hacksaw couldn't help but laugh harder. Then the horse suddenly turned and came right at him.

"Sweet cider!" He dashed underneath the archway in front of the portcullis. Brenwar and the elves joined him.

Calypsa stopped in the middle of the courtyard and glared at them. With her fists balled up at her sides, she said, "Shame on all of you!"

"I guess that's our cue to help," Hacksaw said.

"Aye. I'll handle it." Brenwar stormed forward with his meaty fingers clutching the air. As soon as the horse rounded the courtyard, the dwarf charged into its path.

"Brenwar, what are you doing?" Hacksaw shouted.

The horse thundered right at the dwarf.

Brenwar hunkered down, and at the last moment, he exploded into the horse's leg. The horse let out a loud whinny and crumpled to the ground. Brenwar had tackled it.

Before the horse could get back up again, Brenwar grabbed the beast's harness, put a knee on its neck, and said sternly, "Be still!"

The horse didn't move.

Rond thrashed about before finally ripping his foot free of the stirrup. With clenched fists, he stepped toward the horse.

Calypsa jumped in front of him. "No!"

With a snarl, Rond stepped back and turned his back on her.

"Lords of Thunder, Brenwar! You just tackled a horse," Hacksaw said. "I've never seen the like of it before."

"Aye. No one tramples a dwarf."

"Well, it looks like Rond and I will be walking," Calypsa said with a frown. "The rest of you, grab your horses and go. Rond and I will catch up later."

Hacksaw nodded and said to the others, "Let's ride."

CHAPTER 53

"IS THAT THE ONLY WAY in?" Nath asked Darkken.

Darkken had moved inside the rim of the gulch. Standing in a position lower than Nath's, he said, "It's the only one that I know of. And we don't have the means to dig another entrance. That could take months."

"I thought you weren't in any hurry," Nath said.

"In the grand scheme of things, I'm not. However, our enemies are bound to catch up with us eventually." Darkken moved onto a small boulder and knelt. "This is a sorry situation. The last time I was here, the gulch was empty of these predators. Now, a mother dragon's nest is there. Nath, I'm confident that this is the only way in or out. We are going to have to go through her to get there."

Nath's jaw clenched. He knew that moving a mother dragon from her nest would be virtually impossible to do without killing her. She would defend her eggs, or fledglings, with every ounce of fight in her.

"I'm not killing a dragon," he said. "Especially a mother dragon. Her fledglings will need her."

"Not to mention that the other copper dragons will attack," Maefon said. She stood at the rim of the gulch beside Nath, sweeping her gaze over the area. "I can count nine coppers nestled in this ravine. There are probably dozens more."

"Darkken, you know as well as I do that a lone copper dragon is more than a match for a

Brother of the Wind. One wrong move, and we could all be ripped to pieces. Not to mention the rather extraordinary size of the mother," Nath said.

"Yes, I can see the clear evidence of that," Darkken replied. "Our fallen brethren at the bottom didn't suddenly become dead all by themselves."

"We're going to have to find another way."

"Why don't you go and talk to the mother," Darkken suggested.

Nath blanched. "Be serious."

Darkken looked up at Nath. "I *am* being serious. I didn't come all this way to turn back now. You should go and talk to the mother. You are the Dragon Prince. She should listen to you."

"First off, I've never had the best luck with dragons when it comes to having a conversation. Generally speaking, I think it's safe to say that they don't like me."

"But have they ever attacked you?"

"No," Nath said doubtfully. "Have they ever attacked you? You are just as much a dragon as I am."

"Huh. I've been attacked, just not in the traditional way of thinking about it. As for my Dragonese... Well, let's just say it's rusty." A long silence passed between them. "It's possible that the mother has not even laid any eggs. If she hasn't, you might be able to talk her into moving." Darkken gave Nath a hard look. "I'm not turning back. The dragon is going to have to go, one way or the other."

"We'll end up fighting them all. Our brothers will be slaughtered," Nath said.

"No, they can move out of harm's way. But one way or the other, I will be going in."

The determination in Darkken's voice shook Nath. He knew Darkken had the power to kill the mother dragon and take even more if he had to. Even though copper dragons had a poor disposition, he wouldn't let any harm come to them if he could avoid it. He started down into the gulch.

Maefon grabbed him by the arm. "What are you doing?"

"I'm going to strike up a conversation with my cousin. What does it look like?"

"Like you're about to die," she said.

"Thanks for the vote of confidence."

Slowly, Nath moved past Darkken and deeper into the gulch. He gave Darkken a lasting look and shook his head. His brother gave him a stiff nod. He'd made it halfway down into the gulley when the hairs on his arms rose. The dragons shifted in their places of concealment. Nath started whistling. It wasn't a sound made by the lips of a common man but instead a high-pitched melody too high for human ears to detect. It was a sound only dragons could make. The dragons creeping though the brush froze in place. Sweat ran down Nath's face until he made it to the bottom of the gulch.

A shallow creek ran down the deep gulch. The elven corpses lay on the other side of the trickling waters. Nath walked down the middle of the creek. The water reached his toes. He kept his head down, whistling as he walked. His heart beat in his ears.

Don't show fear, Nath. She'll eat you alive.

He'd been surrounded by dragons most of his natural life and had grown up with no fear of them. However, having lived among men for so long, that had changed. Even though he was an outcast before, he felt like an outsider walking into the dragon's den for the first time. Step by step, without eye contact, he moved close to the mother dragon, who nestled deeper down the gorge on the bank.

The mother dragon's teeth rapidly clacked together.

Nath stopped a dozen feet away. He'd made it as far as she was going to let him come. He lifted his head and met her glowering stare. More copper dragons skulked through the brush, surrounding Nath in all directions. He stopped whistling. He swallowed the lump in his throat. In Dragonese, he said, "I am Nath, son of the Dragon King Balzurth."

The mother dragon's black tail lashed out.

Nath was lifted into the air with his head flying over his heels.

Chapter 54

After landing facedown in the creek, Nath slowly pushed himself up. Water dripped from his face. The mother dragon stretched her neck out and snorted a hot blast of steam at him.

Hunkered in the brush of the gully's hills, the Brothers of the Wind drew their swords. Several others pulled arrows along bowstrings.

A growl rattled from the mother's throat, and her eyes narrowed.

Nath looked up the hillside. He caught Darkken quietly stepping down the trail, his sword in hand. Nath called up to him. "No, wait. I think that might have been a warning."

Darkken stopped in place.

From his hands and knees, Nath stretched out his hand, looked right at the dragon, and said again in Dragonese, "I am Nath, son of the Dragon King Balzurth. I come in peace."

The mother dragon's head tilted from left to right. She snorted at him again.

Nath remained still. Copper dragons, known for their ferocity and nasty streak, were far from being renowned for conversation. Most dragons didn't even speak Dragonese, but older ones, depending on where they were raised, would learn it. Judging by the mother dragon's size, she was centuries old, perhaps over one thousand. Nath had never seen a copper dragon as big as her before. With her as big as a horse, one blast of her breath could incinerate him. "We only want passage to the tunnel in this gulch. We will not harm you or your family."

The mother dragon's head slowly shook from side to side. The ridges on her back rose. Her tail curled up behind her, its tip like that of a spear.

At least Nath had made contact. She understood what he was saying, which was good. If she was listening, he might be able to talk her into moving. "Do you protect your fledglings? Unhatched eggs, perhaps?"

A loud rattle came from the dragon's throat. Nath peeked at her underside. A nest of dirt was dug out of the ground, but he didn't see any eggs or fledglings. Her belly covered most of it, so it was hard to tell.

Darkken shouted down to him, "Nath, are you communicating with her?"

"Yes. I'm not certain, but I think she is close to laying eggs. She isn't going anywhere." He smiled at her. "Ever."

"Ask her if she wants a gift."

"A gift?"

"Dragons like treasure. Try to buy her off. Or try flattering her. You're a man. She's a woman. Appeal to her with those gorgeous golden eyes of yours."

"Are you serious?"

"You're the dragon prince. What lady dragon wouldn't be flattered?" Darkken replied.

Nath kept his eye on hers. As silly as Darkken's suggestion was, it was worth a try. "You have beautiful eyelashes. And your scales are the most sensual that I've ever seen." He heard Darkken chuckling. *Here I am with my heart thundering in my ears, a blink away from being incinerated, and he's getting a laugh from it. I'd better not die from this.* "And your eyes, they are as spectacular as Balzurth's treasure room."

The ridges on the mother dragon's back lowered. The stiffness in her long neck eased. Her copper-colored eyes lingered on his as she waited for the next words from his lips.

"Uh," Nath continued. "Of all the breeds of dragons, I've always found the copper dragons the most enchanting. And believe me, I've seen almost every breed there is to be seen." Nath rose to one knee and smiled. "Did you know that there are many murals back in Dragon Home with coppers depicted fondly on them? If I had my paints and supplies, I would be honored to paint a portrait of you. Though I don't think I could truly capture your magnificence. Have you ever seen yourself, milady? If you haven't, I assure you that you would find yourself tantalizing." Nath tossed in several more flatteries.

The mother dragon's eyes softened the more he spoke. She huffed out a blast of air, covering him in a refreshing aroma. Her tail came around her body and snaked around his waist. She reeled him in close and licked his face. Gently, he hugged her neck. A rumble like a purr started behind the scales of her neck.

"Darkken, I think it's safe to come down. Just you and Maefon, at first. Take your time," Nath said with strain in his voice. "I don't want her tail squeezing me in half."

Darkken and Maefon entered the bottom of the gulch and made a slow approach. Darkken took a knee. He had a broad green leaf in his hand. He opened it up for the dragon to see. The leaf had valuable coins and small gemstones inside.

"A tribute," Darkken said in Dragonese.

The purring stopped. The mother dragon cast her gaze between Nath and Darkken. Her eyes narrowed on Darkken. She released Nath and coiled her tail around Darkken. She pulled him close. Looking him dead on, eye to eye, she started purring again.

"I think she likes you," Nath said. "Isn't that a fortunate turn of events?" Nath backed away and stood by Maefon. "Now what?"

"Er, well," Darkken said as he petted the dragon's neck, "take five brothers with you to the tunnel at the end of the gulch. It's only fifty feet away or so, probably covered by the brush. Go within. I'll meet you there." He looked up into the gulch. "Brothers, leave the dragon a tribute before you. Kneel. Take your time and go."

"Are you sure that you'll be fine?" Nath asked Darkken.

"I think so. Just go. If I'm not there within the hour, send a brother to check on me. But I think we know that I can handle myself if need be."

With Maefon in tow, Nath moved down the creek. The waters disappeared underneath the brush. He pushed through the foliage and found himself in the mouth of a cave. The walls were lined with solid blocks of stone. As his eyes adjusted, he saw the hard, angular lines of a tunnel.

"Welcome to Borgash," Nath said.

The Caligin leader, Dalva, approached Darkken twenty minutes later. He took a knee and set down a small tribute of coins on a leaf. "They are inside, Lord Darkken. The way is clear."

Darkken patted the mother dragon on the head. "You can release me now." The dragon's tail uncoiled. "Well done, sister," he said. "Nath fell for the entire act, hook, line, and sinker. Now, you and the brood keep this valley protected from any coming interlopers such as Slivver and Master Elween."

The dragon nodded.

"As for you, Dalva, are our forces prepared?"

"Over one hundred strong, Lord Darkken. No one will make it into the gulch without facing a certain death." Dalva stood. "Alongside your army of dragons, we are invincible."

Darkken nodded. "Caligin and coppers. Oh my."

CHAPTER 55

DARKKEN FINALLY CAUGHT UP WITH Nath, Maefon, and the five other Brothers of the Wind thirty minutes later. The Brothers of the Wind carried lit torches. The group had made it over fifty yards into the tunnel, where it met with a steep drop-off. All of them stood there, looking over a field of piles of rubble. The creek dropped into the ruins as a waterfall, splashing down into a pond a few dozen feet below.

"This is Borgash," Darkken said, "believe it or not. As I understand it, Borgash was built on the ruins of another city. When the dragons warred with the citizens of Borgash, a great quake shook the streets. The entire city dropped all at once, killing thousands of people."

"Was it a quake or dragons that took down the people?" Nath asked.

"I can't say for certain, but it would be within our father's power to do it."

"He could cause an earthquake?"

Darkken nodded. "It's well within the realm of his abilities."

Nath found that hard to believe. He had no doubt that Balzurth's strength was great, but to be able to make the ground shake and tumble buildings seemed outside the borders of reason.

"Maybe if Father dropped out of the sky and crash landed," Nath said.

Darkken gave him a slap on the back. "Nath, I like the way you think. Just picturing it makes me chuckle. Come on, then. I'll lead the way though this labyrinth." He took a narrow pathway that required more walking than climbing.

All of them arrived at the bottom level. They stood by the pool of water created by the creek. In a single line, they moved deeper into the underground city.

"I spent a great deal of time down here, searching for the Dragon Vein," Darkken said. His voice echoed when he spoke. "The city dropped into a seam, and the ground spilled over on top of it. Surprisingly, many of the structures remained intact. The dirt covers much of what once was, but somehow, a ceiling effect was created. All of this should be buried, but somehow it stands."

Nath studied the thirty-plus-foot dirt skyline. Somehow, the quake had created a giant cave. He could see the roots of the trees above growing through the ceiling. "I don't see how this is even possible."

Darkken made his way onto a broken stretch of road. To either side were buildings turned into rubble, but some of them remained halfway intact. "I think the people were trapped, but great wizards held the dirt up with a telekinetic dome of some sort. The place is expansive, but it could be done. They probably did it just long enough for them to escape."

"What do you think happened to them?" Maefon asked.

"The dragons must have killed them. Follow me. I want to show you something." Darkken quickened his pace and slipped into a collapsed building that had an opening. Inside, skeletal figures lay on the floor. "I can't verify it, but I believe these are the people that resided here before."

Judging by their size, Nath thought the skeletons must have stood eight feet tall. They had long oval skulls and very big eye sockets, mouths, and teeth.

"They don't look like any of the races I know," Nath said. "Their bones are not thick like a giant's." He took a knee and touched the silvery hair on top of one of the skulls. He rubbed it between his fingers. "It feels like silk."

"Yes, I noticed that too. It's not like anything I've seen before. Perhaps they were aliens from another world, like the dragons," Darkken said. "Hopefully, our presence won't reanimate them. I hate it when that happens. Let's go."

Darkken's statement left Nath with a sinking feeling. He didn't care to believe that the dragons were from another world. Darkken and Maefon had been reinforcing that lately. It gnawed at him. *Aliens. I don't think so.*

They walked what appeared to be several blocks before coming to a wall of broken stone that went from the floor to the ceiling. Two buildings appeared to have fallen across the street and into one another. In the rock were portals big enough to crawl through.

"We are close." Darkken was the first to crawl inside. The elves followed him in, leaving Nath and Maefon alone on the outside.

"You haven't been here before, have you?" he asked.

"Never. Why do you ask?"

"I guess I was hoping that you'd have some idea of what lies on the other side of this wall." He gazed about. "You don't really think there is a working forge, do you? This place is in ruin."

"This side is, but maybe not the other. With Darkken, I've learned there is much more to this world than what we've seen. And I enjoy adventuring to strange and unexplored places. Don't you?"

Facing the wall and rubbing the back of his neck, he said, "I like to know what to expect."

Maefon crawled into the hole. "You should know better than that by now."

That's what scares me.

Chapter 56

Crawling through the gap in the wall, Nath was surprised to find himself inside a building. The elves were inside with Darkken, waiting on him and Maefon.

"Glad that you made it over," Darkken said. "For a moment, I thought you'd gotten lost." He opened his arms wide. "Welcome to the Borgash armory."

Nath surveyed his surroundings. The room was large and rectangular, with vaulted wooden ceilings. The support beams were cracked and damaged but held in place by other support beams. It had everything one would expect to see in a blacksmith's shop. Hammers, anvils, and other tools customary to the craft were there. Heavy leather aprons hung from pegs on the wall. Thick gloves lay on the tables. Back against the wall was a furnace with no fire within. Otherwise, the armory appeared to be in good and working order.

"Strange. This place seems operational," Nath said.

"We've worked on it. Not recently but years ago, when I discovered it and we didn't have to deal with the dragons." Darkken paced the room. His fingers traced lines over the long worktables he passed. He sniffed deeply. "I can't wait to start working. There's nothing quite like the smell of boiling metal and the hammering of iron."

Nath recalled his first experience in the forges in Dragon Home. He'd sweated until he could sweat no more. His arms and back burned like fire. As the Caligin set their torches in the wall brackets, he asked, "So, the Dragon Vein is in the furnace?"

"No, not in the furnace, though we will stoke the fires of that one." Darkken waved him over. "Come, see this." He showed Nath a sword's stone cast, which lay on the table. "This sword mold is remarkably similar to my sword, Scalpel, isn't it?"

"I think you could fit Scalpel right in there," Nath said.

"I could, without all of the hardware on the handle." Darkken drew his sword and set it down in the casting. It was a perfect fit. "I wanted to show you this because I didn't want you to think that I would be copying Fang. As your sword is one of a kind, so will mine be."

"It would have been fine if they were similar, just as we as brothers are similar," Nath said, even though he didn't fully mean it. He'd never liked the idea of a sword looking like Fang. He just wanted to appease Darkken. Nath noticed the mold included the full shape of the grip, with a wraparound handguard. "The cast includes the handle?"

"Indeed. Unlike Scalpel, whose metal ends at the tang, this sword will be one complete piece. I'll fashion a new handle around it, made from giant bone, and bind it up with leather." Darkken tapped his rings on the mold. "The new sword will be a valuable prize."

Two of the Caligin started the fire inside the furnace. The coals came to life, burning with a red-hot glow. They brightened as one elf pumped the bellows with his foot. Maefon put on an apron.

"Won't it be difficult to hammer the metal into shape with the handle fully intact?" Nath asked.

"A good question. It might take two of us to hold the sword with tongs while I shape its edge on the anvil. *But*"—Darkken lifted a finger—"we'll be able to reheat the blade and not damage the handle if we are careful. Dragon steel has unique qualities that allow for reheating."

"So, where is the Dragon Vein?" Nath asked.

Darkken's eyes slid toward the center of the room and landed on a circular stone about three feet in diameter, which lay on the floor like carpet. It seemed out of place. He guided Nath over to it. "I stubbed my toe on this. When I discovered the belly of Borgash, I searched high and low for the vein. I dug in that furnace, covered in soot to my elbows. My face was as black as pitch. I screamed more than once. But that last time I screamed, I kicked this stone, which was in the middle of everything for no apparent reason. Then I cursed out loud. Great Guzan!" He chuckled. "Then I thought the stone couldn't be there for just no reason other than being a stumbling block." He squatted down. "That's when I touched it."

Nath squatted beside him, as did Maefon, and both placed their palms on it. His eyes brightened. "It's warmer than toast."

"You could cook an egg on it," Darkken said. "Come on, now. Help me push it aside." He hunkered down and put a hand on the heavy stone. "It's every bit of a thousand pounds. Like the lid of a sarcophagus but more shapely."

Nath got down on his hands and knees.

"Brace your feet in the stone lips in the floor," Darkken suggested. "Put your legs into it and—*urk*—heave!"

The slab ground over the floor. A crack of light, like the rising sun at dawn, burst out of the crease like a ray of sunshine. Nath could feel the heat on his cheek. He kept pushing. The gap opened. The burbling molten well of fire became brighter and hotter.

Sweat dripping from his chin, he pushed the stone away and gasped. "Whew!"

Darkken wiped the sweat from his face. "Heavy and hot, isn't it?"

A cauldron of bubbling lava—rich in bright gold, red, and orange—instantly heated the room. Nath scooted away and stared into the square well in the floor that contained the Dragon Vein.

For some reason, Nath's heart clenched inside. "It's just like home."

CHAPTER 57

NATH FOUND HIMSELF SUCKED IN by the glow of the Dragon Vein. In Dragon Home, the molten lava flowed through the tunnels and channels. It made the darkness of the caves warm, inviting, and cozy. He found himself longing for home. He missed his father but still had close to a hundred years before he could ever return.

"You have a concerned look about you, brother." Darkken said. "Are you well?"

Choosing not to share with Darkken what he was feeling, he said, "How does it work?"

Darkken's expression lit up. "Ah, that's the million-pieces-of-gold question." He pulled the Dragon Steel Scroll out of his belt. "In my review, I learned something that surprised me. The fire from Dragon Home is the only fire that can interact with the dragon steel. No other fire's touch or heat can melt this metal." He unslung his pack from his shoulders and dumped the hunk of ore on the table. "It's special."

Gazing into the Dragon Vein's well, Nath asked, "Are you going to drop it in there?"

"No, that would be irresponsible. We are going to melt it in that jaxite cauldron. It can conduct the heat, whereas metal would melt and stone would crack."

The jaxite cauldron was an icy-blue mineral, shaped into a deep bowl with a spout or lip on both ends. It sat in the floor by the furnace. It had a handle on the top, made from steel. One of the Caligin picked up the cauldron and hung it on a chain suspended over the Dragon Vein. The chain was attached to a pulley. Once the elf lowered the cauldron to chest level, Darkken dropped the hunk of ore inside.

"Here we go," Darkken said.

Nath backed away from the fiery pit.

Hand over hand, Darkken used the chain to lower the cauldron into the pit. As soon as the jaxite hit the vein of fire, it let out an angry hiss. The cauldron's sparking minerals soaked up the fire's colors in a spectacle of tiny sunbursts that filled the cracks. The pot pulsated with its own life as Darkken sank it down, right to the rim. He set the chain in place. The elves locked the pulley mechanism. The quavering lights in the room cast shadows on Darkken's intense face, giving him an omnipotent look.

Maefon grasped Nath's hand.

His grip tightened on her. With his throat turning dry, he asked, "How long?"

"That, I can't answer. It might take hours. It might take weeks, though I think that might be a stretch." Darkken sat down on a nearby stool and readied his flask of water. "My, this place makes you thirsty, doesn't it?"

"Parched." Nath opened his own waterskin and drank. He offered it to Maefon.

"It's much cooler outside." Darkken pointed to an askew opening that must have been the front door. "Go where the smoke goes."

"Where does the smoke go?" Nath asked.

The Dragon Vein didn't give off any smoke, but the torches and fire in the furnace did.

"I imagine the dirt soaks it up through tiny holes. I'm sure there is more than one way to get out of here, but I haven't explored enough to find it. But while we wait, feel free to roam the caverns." Darkken set his waterskin on the table. "I'm going to start shaping my giant bone handle. Don't wander off too far. There could be monsters."

"If we see any of them, you'll be the first to know," Nath said, smiling. He grabbed a torch and led Maefon outside into the coolness of the cave air. "Whew! That feels better."

The cavern was more of the same as what was on the other side of the walls. Stone buildings and other wooden structures had toppled over and lay where they'd fallen, partially buried in dirt. He ventured farther away from the armory.

"It's not Dragon Home, is it?" she asked.

"No, but I think that there would be many dragons that like it here. They love cold, damp places." He lifted the torch above his head, where a very gentle breeze rustled the flames. "Interesting."

"What, the breeze?"

"Yes, it's not the same breeze we came in with. It's passing in another direction. I'm sure there are many critters that have made a home down here. Like giant bears." He tried to scare her with a loud growl.

Maefon rolled her eyes. "That's a really horrible imitation of a scary bear."

"Worse than my songs?"

"No, not that bad." As they traversed the broken ground, going deeper into the cavern, she said, "You seem to be at ease with all that is going on."

"Eh, I think I've settled in with everything." Nath wasn't lying, just putting a positive twist on how he felt. "If Darkken wants a sword that will protect him from the dragons, then so be it. Who am I to say no? After all, I have a sword of my own."

"Aren't you concerned about a conflict with Slivver and Master Elween? No doubt they won't stop coming after you."

"It's my choice. I'll have to live with it." Nath bent over, scooped up a chunk of busted rock in his hand, and tossed it down the cavern. "Besides, I'm getting used to my independence. I'm banished for a long time, so I might as well enjoy myself."

"They'll try to separate us," she said.

Nath put her arms over his shoulders, looked into her eyes, and asked, "What do they have to offer me that is better than being with you?"

Maefon's eyes watered. She rose on tiptoe and kissed him.

Though Nath still had doubts in his heart, he thoroughly enjoyed Maefon's soft lips. She sent tingles right through him. They finished the kiss.

He hugged her tightly and said, "I always want to be with you, Maefon."

CHAPTER 58

WITH THEIR WINGS SPREAD WIDE, Slivver and Master Elween glided in a slow spiral over the top of the Lost City of Borgash. Dawn was cracking, the first light of the new day peeking out from the distant mountains. Over a thousand feet in the air, Slivver could still make out the critters beginning their day, hunting for food. His keen eyes detected the slightest movement in the brush covering the fallen city. However, they had a lot of territory to cover.

"Don't you think that it would be best to explore at the ground level?" Elween suggested.

"I'm considering it. If Darkken and his Caligin are down there, they will be watching for us. I'd rather that we see them before they see us."

"We have our senses. *If* they are there, we can find them before they spot us if we stay downwind. Like hunters," she said.

"I'll take your word for it. You lead."

Elween dove toward the forest tree lines downwind from the lost city. On foot, they moved through the forest, not stopping until they made it to the border of the fallen city. It had become a sunken valley covered in trees and brush. Parts of it, covered in ankle-thick vines and ivy leaves, looked like temple ruins, with mounds and even slopes. The brush would snag their clawed feet. It became thicker the farther they crept in.

Elween's nostrils flared. Her tongue licked the air. "Do you smell that?"

"Elves," Slivver replied.

Dragons, generally speaking, also had a very keen sense of smell. To them, just about every living thing had its own unique scent. Advanced dragons like Slivver and Elween could pick up the scent of something and, if they were familiar with it, identify it immediately. That was the case now. The smell of warm flesh and blood was in the air—creatures with fur and skin. They'd been around enough Caligin and could easily detect their elven sweat and dander.

"They could be tucked in anywhere in this valley," he said. "I suggest we hunker down and watch."

"That's probably a good idea since you shine as brightly as a tree ornament," she said.

"A tree ornament?" He looked at his chest. His scales did have a sheen to them that attracted the sunlight. "Oh, I see your point. I am attractive, aren't I?"

"For a silver dragon, yes."

Using a chameleonlike power that certain breeds of dragon could command, he toned down his scales to a dully finished steel. Looking at his arms, he said, "This is hideous."

"It's better than looking like polished tableware."

She scrunched into the bushes, and quietly they sat for the next few hours. The local wildlife, such as squirrels and chipmunks, crept through the bush right in front of their faces. A possum and her babies waddled by. Finally, she said, "I don't see anything, but I can smell them. I say we follow the scent."

Slivver gave a nod. "I trust your judgment."

Staying low and carefully navigating the terrain, they moved at a creeping pace. It took an hour to travel one hundred yards deep into the sunken valley, which was miles wide in all directions. Finally, they came upon two elves dressed in black armor, nestled in the willowhacks. The elves had their bows in hand. Their heads moved left and right, eyes seeking any movement.

Slivver tapped Elween and gave her a thumb-claw-up. Seeing the Caligin was confirmation that Nath and Darkken would be near. Together, they crept backward, out of earshot of the elves, and talked quietly in Dragonese.

"You know there must be more of them spread out all over this forest," Slivver said. "Do you want to draw them out? We need to get a better idea of what we are up against."

"I say we take these two out," she suggested.

"That will create nothing but a stir. We have to deal with this situation more tactfully."

Elween shook her chin. "What are you going to do? Throw a rock to draw their attention?"

"Well, it could work."

"Or it could be a disaster. Look around. There is no sign of a city. And if there is no city, then there is no forge. My guess is that the forge is below."

"Below?" Slivver shrugged his eyebrows. "That's a stretch."

"Unless they are invisible, they aren't here, so where are they? We need to find out where they are stationed. Those elves are guarding something." Elween's small nostrils snorted deeply. "Do you smell that?"

"Elves?"

"No, dragons." Her eyes narrowed. "I'm not sure which sort, but one of our brethren lurks in these woods."

"Funny, I didn't see any sign of them."

Elween clamped her claws over his mouth as her eyes widened.

Slivver's earholes picked up the sound of four-legged creatures rustling quietly through the bush. The sound came from all around them. Elween was right—they were dragons. What kind, he was not sure. Unlike people and animals, dragons' cold blood and scaly makeup made their scents very similar. His eyes widened on hers.

Elween slowly shook her neck and silently uttered, "We are surrounded."

Moving back to back, they rose from the brush. A ring of copper sliders standing on their hind legs had them surrounded. Each dragon was as big as them. Their eyes were coppery slits of evil. As one, their necks swayed from side to side. Long black tongues flickered out of their mouths. The bared their teeth. Acidic venom dripped from their jaws like saliva.

The tallest of the brood spoke in Dragonese. "Slay them!"

As one, they lunged.

Chapter 59

Slivver breathed out a bolt of lightning. The shard of energy blasted a hole clean through two charging copper sliders.

"Elween, take to the sky. There are too many of them!"

At his back, Elween spewed out a stream of fire. A copper dragon countered with its own breath weapon. It spewed black acid right into her flames. The collision of the elements created a loud, angry hiss. A nasty-smelling yellow smoke was created, which stank up the valley. The air made the rushing dragons gag.

"Now, Elween, now!" Slivver shouted as he launched himself into the air. A mushroom cloud of mustard-yellow smoke covered the battle below him. He heard a fierce commotion of dragons fighting. "Come on, Elween. Get out of there!"

Master Elween burst out of the nasty cloud, copper-dragon spit all over her. "I'm out! Go!"

With his wings lifting him higher in the air, Slivver kept his gaze downward. In the green foliage were at least a score of dragons. They were accompanied by a dozen elves pointing right at them. The copper dragons' heads reared up. They locked their stares onto Slivver and Elween. As one, the coppers launched themselves skyward.

"We have company!" Slivver warned.

Elween's dark-green wings had many small holes burned in them, and the coppers' talons had ripped open some of her scales. Her head drooped.

"You go ahead," Slivver said. "Find Brenwar! I can handle these coppers!"

"There are too many of them," she warned.

Slivver counted six of the enemy. The coppers weren't the best flyers. They roamed the ground more than they did the sky.

"Don't you worry about me. In the air, no dragon is a match for me!" He curled away from Elween's tail then unleashed a spray of lightning. The bolts hit the leading copper square in the face. Its skull smoked, and it spiraled to the ground. Slivver pulled up just in time to avoid the rest of the dragons.

Three coppers chased after him. The other two pursued Elween. The coppers let out nasty roars. With open jaws, they nipped at Slivver's tail.

"You fools don't seriously think that you can keep up with me, do you?" Slivver asked, laughing.

He enjoyed nothing more than a fight in the sky. Silver shades were arguably the fastest dragons in the air except for the notorious blue-streak dragons. The blue streaks used their own special magic to make them faster, but they weren't very formidable fighters.

"Tell you what," he said. "If you can catch me, you can kill me."

The dragons screeched.

Slivver increased his speed. He barrel-rolled and looped. He slashed between their ranks. In a desperate effort to cut him down from the sky, two coppers collided.

He let out a gusty laugh as the dragons descended toward the ground. "Perfect."

That left only one attacker against him. He flew circles around it. Using his sharp talons, he jumped on the dragon's back and turned its wings to shreds. He pushed off of the dragon, which flapped wildly in the wind.

"Happy landing!" he called.

The last two copper dragons were closing in on Elween.

Zeroing in on the chasing dragons, Slivver kicked his wings into full speed. Like a silver rocket, he streaked right up behind them. He shot two lightning bolts from his mouth one at a time. The bolts blasted the copper dragons squarely in their backs. Their wings curled up, crackled, and smoked. They spiraled downward in two twisting trails of smoke. The earth greeted them with the kiss of death.

"Thank you," Elween said. She was laboring for breath. Her front hand clutched at her chest. "My wounds slow me."

Upon a closer examination, Slivver realized Elween's wounds were even worse than he'd estimated. She had torn scales all over her, and her own blood dripped from her scales. Slivver glanced backward. They had no pursuers.

"Can you make it very far?" he asked.

"I can fly, just not at full speed. Let me drift behind you. Let's find Brenwar."

Chapter 60

Brenwar was the first one to catch sight of the approaching dragons. "Ho. It's Slivver."

Slivver made a gentle landing. Elween made a rougher landing behind him. Her neck sagged. She labored for breath and was bleeding.

Brenwar dismounted his pony. Hacksaw, Roday, and Dule jumped off their horses and rushed over to the dragons. Brenwar hustled over on his stumpy legs and caught up with them. "You look like you've been in a nasty scrap. What happened?"

"We made it to the Lost City of Borgash," Slivver said. "We discovered Caligin and were ambushed by a brood of copper dragons. They were either waiting for us or protecting something."

"I'm certain they are guarding Darkken." Elween groaned. "They about got us, or me, at least."

Dule fished out a healing potion from his pack. He offered her the vial of golden liquid. "Take this."

"I feel fragile, having to rely on this sort of means," Elween said. She took it in hand and drank it. "But copper dragons and forest dragons, like me, don't mix well. Their claws can do much damage to our scales. They are as sharp as steel. I should have been better prepared for it."

"You will be the next time," Slivver said. "I'm certain of it."

"How many dragons are there?" Hacksaw asked.

"There was only a score or less that I saw, but there could be more. Possibly more Caligin. I noticed twelve." Slivver crossed his arms over his chest. "I have a bad feeling about this. Worse yet, Darkken will have been alerted to our presence. The element of surprise is lost."

"We're about a day's ride away. We'll have to think of something on the way," Brenwar said.

"Where are Calypsa and Rond?" Elween asked.

"They couldn't get Rond on a horse," Dule said. "It got ugly. She says that they will catch up somehow."

"Well, at least we know what we are up against, for the time being. Let's keep moving." Brenwar climbed back in the saddle. "Onward."

Chapter 61

Outside the forge, Nath sat with his back against the wall. Maefon lay napping at his feet. He ran his fingers through her hair. She'd been his best friend for the longest time, and he appreciated her. Even though he'd become closer to Darkken, he felt that she was the one he could trust the most. The time together had brought them closer. He wondered, if he were never to become a dragon, if he could be with her for the rest of his life. That might make the sting of not ever flying easier. Still, deep in his thoughts, some doubt lingered. All his life, he'd felt that he was destined to become a dragon. Now, all that seemed to be a lie.

Maefon stirred. Her eyes cracked open, and she met his gaze, an easygoing smile spreading across her face. "Have you rested any?"

"It's so cool and quiet down here that it's almost like resting. Seeing you slumber so well gives me peace." His fingers gently caressed her cheek. "Even though you snore."

She stiffened. "I don't snore."

Nath made some loud imitation snorting sounds, like a pig gobbling at a trough. "Well, if you don't think that sound is snoring, then I guess you weren't snoring."

She popped up, drew her fist back, and straddled his legs. "You smart-mouthed man. Shame on you. You're going to get a throttling."

"If it's with your lips, I'll be just fine with that."

Maefon dropped her fist and cozied up to him some more. "You know, you are too charming and handsome to be mad at. I accept your little jest." She leaned in to kiss him.

Nath parted his lips. "Ow!"

Maefon had sunk her sharp nails into the meat of his arm and pinched the snot out of him. Holding fast, she twisted his skin.

"Owww!" Nath called out. "You are the meanest snorer I've ever heard."

"Take it back!" she said, pinching harder. "Take it back!"

Nath wobbled his head and insincerely said, "Fine, I suppose I might have been hearing things."

The pretty elf dropped her hands to her hips and said, "What, a half-hearted apology? I thought you were one for honesty and sincerity."

"Me? Why, I'm a Brother of the Wind, the same as you. Can't I be sneaky and subtle too?"

Maefon's playful smile dropped from her face.

"What's wrong?" he asked.

"Nothing."

"Maefon?"

"I, well, I've always adored your honesty and innocence, Nath. I would hate to see you lose that."

"Well, we are only playing. It's not as if I've purposefully fed a bald-faced lie to you." He lifted up her sagging chin. "Only joking?"

"I know. But you're special, and I admire that." She held his face in the palms of her hands. "I like knowing that I can count on that."

"You can. What about Darkken? Don't you feel the same way about him too?" Nath asked.

"I do, but with you, it's different. I can never tell what Darkken is going to do or what he's thinking. With you, I just feel I always know where I stand. You don't keep anything to yourself."

"Right," Nath replied.

That was only a partial admission of truth. He kept his concerns about Darkken to himself while letting himself be fully distracted with Maefon. Paying attention to her kept his own trepidations at ease. He hugged her.

"Well, it's warming to see the two of you shining in such a dreary setting," Darkken said.

Nath and Maefon broke it off. She couldn't contain a giggle. Darkken dabbed sweaty drops from his face with a towel and wiped down his short beard. He slung the towel over his shoulder.

"I know it's taken some time," he said, "but the good news is that the dragon ore has melted."

"Really?" Nath asked excitedly as Maefon stood and helped him to his feet. "So we can make your sword now?"

"Unless you'd rather snuggle some more."

Nath looked for an approving glance from Maefon.

"Will you go in there?" she said.

Nath kissed her cheek and hustled inside.

Alone with Maefon, Darkken took a peek through the forge's door and asked her, "How is he?"

"Content enough to eat out of my hand," she said with a wry smile.

"I have to admit even I sense that much of his edginess has worn off recently. So you concur?"

"I do, but I really enjoy his company. It's easy for me." She stepped up to Darkken and patted his cheek. "Though I miss what we've had together. I hope that isn't all gone."

"You have been my most treasured servant ever." He took her hand and kissed her fingers. "There will always be a place for you with me. With that said, I've been informed that we've had an intrusion above."

"Is that so? Who?"

"It seems that our dear friends Slivver and Master Elween are back. I suspected this. The trap was sprung, but their formidableness proved enough to escape it."

"What can I do?"

"Stay alert. I don't want them getting close to Nath at all. But if they do get too close, I'll use the bracelet." He wiggled the serpent-patterned chain on his wrist. "Make sure Nath's stays on."

"You're always a step ahead, aren't you? But will the bracelet work? You just used it not so long ago."

"There is always that risk with magic. It may teleport, or it may not. That's why I always stay three or four steps ahead. Sometimes ten. One day, you will get there." He kissed her forehead. "The main thing now is getting the sword completed. Even I have to admit that I'm somewhat giddy with excitement. Having a sword of my own will change the game."

"Will it be anything like Fang?"

"Not in shape or form, but in purpose, definitely." He put an arm over her shoulders and led her toward the door. "Come on, now. Let's go and change the world."

Chapter 62

Inside the sweltering forge, Nath stared into the jaxite cauldron, which was immersed to the rim in the Dragon Vein. Inside, the dragon ore, once just a clump of metal, was boiling. The ore, once dull, now shone with the color of a burning sun. Inky vapors wafted up and out of the pot with a metallic stink.

Covering his nose, Nath said, "I take it that's the impurities coming out."

Standing beside Nath, Darkken put his hand on his shoulder and said, "Yes. I'm impressed with your knowledge."

"I did some weapons crafting myself, remember?"

"Of course. But I wasn't sure what sort of metal you worked with. Most metals used in weapons making have impurities in them." Darkken swiped his forehead with his towel. "To make true dragon steel, it needs to be purified like silver or gold. Its metal should cast a mirror image. It should be perfection. Once the smoke passes, it will almost be ready to feed into the mold."

"What else needs to be done?" Nath asked.

"There is one more ingredient. Come." Darkken moved over to the table where the Dragon Steel Scroll lay. He unrolled it. "Can you read this?"

Nath squinted. He didn't recognize the sweeping lettering, but it looked similar to elven. "No."

"It calls for blood. Only a few drops. The blood of a dragon."

Nath swallowed. He wiped the damp hair from his eyes. "Are you saying Fang has blood in it?"

"I'm saying Fang most likely has Balzurth's blood in it. It's a very special blood. Pure blood." His intense eyes searched Nath's. "You and I have a shared heritage with Balzurth, being his sons. But I'm not sure I'm as much a dragon as you. I've been gone a long time. Nath, will you help me?"

Nath rubbed the back of his neck. He glanced at Maefon and said, "Uh, I don't know. It's a strange and unexpected thing that you have asked. Are you really sure that you need it?"

"It's more of a precaution, for my one pitiful sake. I understand if you don't feel comfortable with it." Darkken quickly rolled up the scroll. "Never mind, then." He moved over to the cauldron and stared deeply into it with his jaw clamped shut.

Nath shrugged at Maefon. He felt certain that Darkken was angry with him. He didn't want to disappoint his brother, either. He wanted to help him. He searched Maefon's eyes for answers. She shrugged and lifted her hands as though it wouldn't be any big deal.

He wandered back over to the cauldron. "I guess I have plenty of blood to spare."

"Brother, I completely understand if you are uncomfortable, but you have given me great relief." Darkken embraced Nath. "I knew that I could count on you." He chuckled.

"Why are you laughing?"

"Because I don't need your blood. I need your trust. And now I know that I have it." Darkken tossed his head back and shouted, "I am elated! I have a true brother!"

Nath gave him a curious stare and said, "So Father's blood does not run through Fang?"

"No, it does, but it's more of a blessing. A ceremonial thing," Darkken replied. "I still plan to do the same with my sword. I hope you aren't angry, Nath."

"Uh, I'm relieved."

"Good. You should be." Darkken fanned his hand over the cauldron. The inky smoke was gone. "That was quick. The Dragon Vein shows no mercy to the tainted. It's ready."

Darkken drew a dagger from his scabbard. He cut the palm of his hand, made a fist, and squeezed. Blood dripped into the boiling metal. The blood sizzled out in a puff of smoke.

"That's that," Darkken said.

Nath extended his hand.

Darkken arched a brow and handed him the dagger. "Are you sure?"

"It would be an honor."

Nath cut his palm, made a fist, and held it over the cauldron. He squeezed until blood dropped from his fist. The drops hit the smelted ore and sizzled. There was no more smoke.

He handed the dagger back to Darkken and said, "Let's make this sword."

"You have brought me nothing but joy." Darkken wiped his blade with the towel and sheathed it. "Together, we will bring peace throughout all of the lands." He grabbed the chain that held the cauldron and pulled. The lava of the Dragon Vein dripped from the bottom of the cauldron. "I must go quickly now. The dragon steel will cool fast."

Nath helped him swing the cauldron over the table where the sword mold waited.

Darkken lowered the cauldron over the top end of the mold. He put on a heavy pair of gloves and tilted it over. A stream of red-hot metal poured into the cast. It snaked its way through the channel, forming the blade and splitting at the cross guard and handle until the two streams kissed at the pommel. The last drop of dragon ore dripped out of the jaxite cauldron.

"That's all of it," Darkken said. "It had more impurities than pure ore."

"Now what?" Nath asked as the molten metal cooled.

"It must be tempered with the strike of a hammer and magic." Darkken took off the heavy leather gloves and removed the Star of the Heavens from one of his pouches. The oval diamond glowed with pink star fire. "This is why it takes two to make the sword: one to read from the scroll and enchant with magic while another shapes the steel, using the Gauntlet of Goam."

Nath looked at his left hand. The gemstone on the top of the gauntlet burned with light. New strength coursed through his limbs. "You want me to shape the steel?"

"It's a two-man task that requires awesome strength," Darkken replied. "The steel cools and hardens. No mortal strength can temper such metal, but with the gauntlet, you can. Just flatten it out and put a nice edge on it. I trust you."

The molten metal had cooled to a dull shine in the cast. Nath grabbed a set of tongs and took the sword from the cast. He lowered it to an anvil, grabbed a hammer, and nodded at Darkken.

Darkken held the gem out over the scroll and read. Enchanted words flowed out of his mouth and stood Nath's arm hairs on end. The Star of the Heavens sparked. Tendrils of pink energy flowed from the gems to the steel in the sword. Darkken's words gained strength.

Nath hammered the steel. The blade soaked up the gemstone's energy and glowed like molten fire again. Sweat dripped from Nath's face as he hammered away, shaping the metal into a perfect weapon that would rival Fang.

CHAPTER 63

SLIVVER AND ELWEEN LANDED OUTSIDE the Borgash, where Brenwar, Hacksaw, Roday, and Dule were waiting. The people all had somber looks.

"Well?" Brenwar said to Slivver.

Parting his talons, Slivver said, "The situation is, well, infinitely worse."

Puffing on his pipe, Hacksaw asked, "What is that supposed to mean?"

"Whereas before, the Caligin and the dragons were hidden, now they patrol the city in the wide open," Slivver said. "Which tells me that Darkken is well aware of our presence, and I think he is daring us to strike."

"How many are there?" Brenwar asked.

"That's another problem. The numbers, it appears, have tripled," Slivver said.

"Triple!" Dule blurted out. "Triple as in three-dozen Caligin and three-score dragons?"

"No," Roday replied, "as in three-score dragons and three-dozen Caligin."

"That's what I said, Roday."

"No, it's not. You said three-dozen Caligin and three-score drag—"

"Enough of your silliness!" Brenwar slammed his hammer into the dirt. "I can handle two score, but the rest of you will have to do the rest of the work." He clawed at his beard and started mumbling.

"And there could be more," Elween added. The dragon weapon master sounded tired. "As much as I'd like a straight-up fight, we have to realize that Darkken is too sophisticated for that. He's always a step ahead of us. We need to get a step ahead of him. Let's run through all of the scenarios. Let's see what resources we have at our disposal."

Inside the edge of a forest line over a mile from the borders of Borgash, the group huddled in a circle.

Slivver initiated the conversation. "Darkken is creating a sword inside the ruins of Borgash. The Caligin and copper dragons are protecting him. Or they are protecting Nath from us. Once he has the sword, what is it that he will do? He'll have to come out or teleport out."

"If he teleports, he'll go back to the keep. That would be my guess," Hacksaw said.

"Mine too," Elween said. "And unlike him, we can't teleport from one spot to the other. He's going to keep moving Nath, or he will so long as he has to."

"We have to get to Nath now." Hacksaw puffed out smoke rings. "We haven't even had a word with him, but if we could get word to him, that would be better."

Slivver nodded then said, "The problem is there's miles of terrain to cover, and we don't have any idea where they entered or if they are even there. We are operating on assumptions. We're going to have to come up with a plan and give it all we have."

"I've been on plenty of campaigns, and the entrance will be where the enemy is the thickest," Hacksaw said. "Did you notice any place like that when you scouted the enemy from the skies?"

"A cluster of elves and dragons gathered in number along the rim of a gulch. There might have even been more down in there," Slivver said. "I could go for a closer look."

"No, that has to be it. I felt it in my gut the moment you said it," Brenwar said. "It is, or I'm a bearded gnome."

"Is there a difference?" Roday asked.

"Watch your mouth, elf," Brenwar warned.

Roday stuck his lips out and looked down at them.

Dule popped Roday in the back of the head. "This is easy. All we need to do is slip past the protection, ease into the gulch, and find Nath. But we need a distraction."

Brenwar's brows lifted. "Are you saying we need to engage?"

"Part of us attacks, and the other part goes after Nath," Dule said.

"And how do you propose to slip past them?" Slivver asked. "The Caligin and dragons will not overlook you."

Dule spilled out his pack. Several potion vials fell out, among a few other things. "Easy. We have magic. And I'm all about using magic."

Scratching one side of his beard, Brenwar asked, "Do you think we are fools? Darkken will probably let you two sneaks waltz right in there and leave us in the slaughterhouse. I don't trust them. Do you, Slivver?"

"As much as I like the both of you, like Brenwar, I'm not willing to take that risk. You're too close to Darkken."

Dule started shoveling his potions back into his back. Hacksaw stepped on his arm.

Dule glowered at him and said, "You'd better step off my arm, or I'm going to put a hole in your belly."

"Is that right?" Hacksaw asked.

The screech of a great bird turned every head toward the sky. A giant black hawk came in for a landing, carrying Rond in its talons. Calypsa rode on its back. The black hawk dropped Rond, and the bugbear plummeted twenty feet and landed hard. The bird landed, folded up its wings, and squawked.

The sultry Calypsa climbed down from its back. "I'm glad to see that you are all alive. What's the plan?"

Slivver brought her up to speed.

Calypsa looked at the elves, looked back at Slivver, and said, "I'll get the message to Nath. You do the rest."

CHAPTER 64

EVEN AFTER THE USE OF the Gauntlet of Goam, Nath's arms ached. He'd pounded on the dragon steel for hours. Now, muscle spasms started in his arms and shoulders. He sat down and drank his waterskin dry.

Darkken sat on a stool across from him, fanning himself with a leather glove. He'd read the words from the Dragon Steel Scroll for over an hour before his flowing words ended. The Star of the Heavens shone as bright as the sun and winked out. After that, Darkken guided Nath in shaping the edge of the sword. He demanded perfection. He got it. Now, the sword lay across Darkken's lap, catching the fire from the furnace on the metal. It gave the sword the appearance of a living thing.

"That was taxing," he said, "but I'm very pleased. I just need to mount the handle on it, and we'll be ready to go."

"Do you want my help with that?" Nath asked then groaned.

"No, I can handle it. But feel free to observe if you wish."

"Good, because I don't think I can stand." Nath leaned back against the wall.

Maefon wiggled her waterskin and said, "I think we've run dry. I might as well mosey over to the creek and replenish." She and the other five elves departed.

With a grunt, Darkken stood up. He twisted the sword in his hand. Like Fang, it was a superb piece of work. Much the same as Scalpel, the blade had a slight curve at the tip. The tip was sharpened on both sides. It was longer than a typical longsword. The lengthy handle gave it an even more imposing look. It fit Darkken's strong, rangy build perfectly. He twisted it from side to side. "You did wonderful work."

"I think it was a team effort. I'm glad you are happy."

"*Happy* is putting it mildly." Darkken spun it around his body. "I'm ashamed to say, but this sword makes Scalpel look like a piece of scrap iron." He moved to the worktable where he'd carved up the handle made from giant bone. It was in two pieces. He snapped them into place, then using a tiny hammer, he drove small pins between the handles. He tested the grips. "Firm in hand. I like it."

"Aren't you going to bind it with leather?"

"Now that I have a feel for it, I don't think that I will. You see, giant bone has a natural grip to it, which shouldn't be surprising, given their makeup." Darkken held the sword straight out and eyed the edge of the blade. "Perfect."

Nath stretched his arms, yawned, and asked, "So what will you do with Scalpel? It would be a shame to retire a sword like that."

"I'm sure I can find a willing brother big enough to swing it." Darkken fetched Scalpel, which rested in its scabbard against the wall. He slid the sword out of the sheath and pushed the new sword in. "An excellent fit."

"So what are you going to name your new sword?"

Darkken stroked the beard around his mouth and said, "I'm not sure. Do you have any suggestions?"

"Little Fang."

Darkken tossed his head back. "Ha!"

"Toothpick."

"Nath, you're going to make my guts hurt from laughter."

"Needle."

"Now you're being just plain insulting." Darkken drew his sword and said, "I have to admit that your four-letter name does pack a punch. I envy it. You did name it yourself, didn't you?"

With his hands on the back of his head, Nath leaned back again and said, "I came up with it all by myself."

"I don't think I need to name it now. There's plenty of time," Darkken said with a frown.

"I'm sure that you have something in the sheath. Let's try some real names out."

Darkken closed his eyes. "I'm thinking."

"While you are *thinking*, I am curious. Why didn't you tell me that you needed the Gauntlet of Goam? I have to admit I feel a little used."

With aloofness in his voice, Darkken said, "You know me, Nath. I like surprises. Besides, I wouldn't want you to obsess over the gauntlet. Sometimes when you try to hold something too tight, you lose it."

"What would you have done if you didn't have the gauntlet?"

Darkken lined his sword up over top of the anvil. "It's just a matter of strength. I would have come up with something. There are spells and elixirs that would suffice. But the Gauntlet of Goam is what the dwarves and elves that worked the forge in Dragon Home used to use." Without looking at Nath, he added, "You didn't know that, did you?"

"Every day with you is a learning experience," Nath said mirthlessly.

Darkken lifted his sword over his head and chopped hard into the anvil. The blade cut the hunk of metal from top to bottom and buried itself in the block of wood. Darkken's copper eyes lit up like burning candles. "Mercy!"

Nath snapped his fingers. "Turn out the lights. I think you found the name you've been searching for."

With ease, Darkken pulled the blade free of the anvil. His teeth showed white in the dimness of the torches. The sword hummed like a tuning fork. The well-honed blade carried a blue shine in the metal. He ran two fingers down the length of the blade, and the humming stopped. He touched his cheek to the dragon steel and uttered quietly, "Mercy, I like it. Death will come quick and clean."

Maefon and the five Brothers of the Wind returned. Their concerned eyes fell on Darkken.

"What ails you?" Darkken asked.

"We've discovered that some of your brothers are dead," Maefon said.

"Was it the dragons?" Darkken asked.

"No, not them." She looked at Nath. "The others."

Mouse crawled out of Nath's pack, which lay on the table. He stood up on his hind legs with his whiskers twitching.

"Hey, little fella," Nath said.

"Is that your rodent?" Darkken asked with an arched eyebrow.

"He cozied up to me in the keep and has been living in my pack." Nath reached for the field mouse, which ran down the table leg and darted into a hole at the back entrance of the room. "Hey, Mouse, where are you going?"

"I'm sure your rat will be fine," Maefon joked.

"Maybe he got thirsty." Nath hollered into the tunnel, "Mouse!"

"We have more important issues to deal with at the moment." Darkken sheathed Scalpel and kept Mercy in hand. "Slivver and Elween have caught up with us, it seems. They are going to try to kill me. I am going to try to kill them. That's where I stand."

"No one is going to kill anyone," Nath said. "Not on account of me, you, or anyone. I've made my decision, and I'm going to stand by your side, Darkken. But this bloodshed has to stop."

Chapter 65

BRENWAR SHOOK A VIAL FILLED with a deep-blue magic elixir in front of his eyes. "What's this one do?"

"That's invulnerability," Slivver said.

"I'm already invulnerable."

"I'll take it," Hacksaw said.

Brenwar pulled the vial down. "No, I think I'll hold onto it."

"We have more than enough potions for everyone," Roday said as he fanned his hands over the tubular corked bottles. The liquids were a variety of brilliant, bubbling watercolors that swirled in lifelike patterns of their own. He picked them up one by one and tossed them aside, saying, "Giantism, invisibility, more invulnerability, healing, polymorph, eh"—he squinted—"fire-breathing. Huh, I think I might try that one and this one." He grabbed an invisibility potion. "And this one."

"Breathing fire and invisible," Dule said with admiration. "Now, that's thinking."

"You can't mix potions," Slivver warned.

"We're pulling out all of the stops. This is war," Roday said. "We'll do what we have to do to win it. Maybe once it's over, you'll believe we're on your side. Hopefully, we won't have to die to prove it."

"I believe them," Calypsa said as she squatted down between the elves. "Now is the time when we have to have faith in one another and other things." A brown-gray field mouse squirted out of the grass and crawled into her awaiting hand. "Hello, little friend. What news do you have for me?"

"Is she talking to us or the rat?" Roday asked Dule.

"I think the rat," Dule replied. "Geez, why do the rats always get the pretty girls' attention."

Calypsa rose. "He's a mouse and a good sign. If this mouse is here, then Nath is near. You see, when I left, I assigned the little creature to be Nath's guardian."

"You don't think that rat can protect Nath, do you?" Brenwar said.

"He is my eyes and ears." She put the mouse on her shoulder, where it stood on its hind legs and chattered into her ear. "Uh-huh. Uh-huh," Calypsa said. She addressed the others. "You are right. Nath and Darkken are underground, where the gorge leads into a tunnel that is guarded by a full-grown copper dragon and the others." Her brows knitted together. "Maefon is there too. No one lay a hand on her. She is mine. I'm going in."

"How are you going to get past that army?" Slivver asked.

"Even though my shape-changing powers are drained, I can use one of your polymorph potions. I'll go back in as the mouse. From there, I can warn Nath."

"The rest of us will provide the distraction," Slivver said. "Darkken will anticipate the battle. And a battle he will get. Calypsa, be careful."

"I will be." She grabbed a potion vial and then slid a dagger out of Dule's scabbard. "I hope you don't mind if I borrow this."

"Not at all," Dule said with a heart-warming smile. "You can borrow anything of mine anytime."

Calypsa approached Rond. She stood barely chest high to the brawny bugbear. "Rond, listen to me. I must go. I'll be back. Fight with them."

"Noooo," Rond said. His pointed ears wiggled when he spoke, and saliva dripped from his mouth. "Nooo go."

"He might chase after me," she told Slivver, "which means when I go, you better get ready to fight. Because he's likely to charge those thickets like a rhino. Are you ready?"

Dule passed out potions.

Brenwar, Hacksaw, Calypsa, Slivver, and Master Elween, plus the elves, lifted them up in a toast.

"For Nath," Slivver said.

They all drank them down. "Aye! For Nath!"

Calypsa shrank down into a field mouse. She darted toward the city. Rond made a disturbing grunt. His heavy-lidded eyes searched the landscape. He rumbled after her.

Roday and Dule turned invisible and said, "See you later." Their footsteps left in the grass chased after Rond.

"We've been hoodooed!" Brenwar spiked his vial on the ground. It didn't break. He stomped the vial, crushing it. "After them!"

"Remember, men, that potions only are effective for a limited time!" Slivver said. "Be wary!"

Hacksaw drew his sword and said to Elween, "I don't know about you, but I feel great!"

"How great?" Elween asked.

"Invincible!"

"Yes," she said. "Me too. Now, extend your arms like a bird."

"Why?" Hacksaw asked as he slowly raised his arms.

Elween spread her wings and lifted off. She wrapped her talons around his arms and took flight. "Because we are going to strike first!"

Brenwar glared at Slivver and asked, "Well, what are you waiting for? No one beats Brenwar Boulderguild to the front of the battlefield!"

CHAPTER 66

As a mouse, Calypsa ran as quickly as her tiny little legs would carry her. Caught up in the excitement, she'd forgotten that the distance between her and the Borgash, over a mile, would now be ten times longer than before. Mice were fast, but they weren't as fast as people. It was a problem. Not even one hundred yards into the trip, she started panting for breath.

What was I thinking?

The other mouse ran by her side, laboring on his own. His whiskers twitched. He froze as the ground shook beneath them.

Calypsa looked back. Rond's gargantuan feet were coming right at them, his heavy gaze focused far ahead of their position.

She squirted out of the bugbear's path and shouted to the other mouse, "Jump on!"

Rond's foot stomped the grasses right in front of their faces.

She leaped onto his foot and scurried up Rond's leg. Rond plowed over the rugged terrain with a full head of steam.

He called out, "Calie! Calie!"

Climbing as quickly as she could, she made it all the way up his chest and onto his shoulder. His gaze still scanned the thickets as he called out for her again and again.

She grabbed hold of his earlobe and shouted in his ear, "I'm here, Rond!"

Rond kept running.

She didn't know whether or not he could hear her. She understood what she was saying, but maybe Rond didn't. She was too small. Even her shouting was pointed. She crawled around his back to the other shoulder. The other mouse had his claws dug into Rond's tattered clothing.

"At least he will save us some time!" she said.

Overhead, two dragons streaked through the sky, Elween and Slivver, carrying Brenwar and Hacksaw. Slivver raced to the front as they crossed the border into Borgash. They didn't make it a hundred yards in before copper dragons' heads popped up out of the weeds—many of them.

"Oh my," Calypsa said.

Slivver and Elween dropped Brenwar and Hacksaw into the midst of the copper-scaled brood. The man and dwarf hit them like flying juggernauts.

Rond turned toward the battle scene. He lifted his sledgehammer over his head and charged. Two copper dragons snaked into his path. The sledgehammer flashed downward in an arc of purple energy. Metal collided with dragon skull.

Kraakk!

The second dragon tangled up Rond's legs. He tripped and fell toward the ground.

Calypsa leaped free of his shoulder and, with a quick glance back, said, "Get them, Rond!"

She and the other mouse darted for the gulley. The clamor of battle filled her ears with screams, roars, sizzles, and hisses. It sounded like a thunderstorm rising up from the ground. All chaos broke loose. She kept running, following the other mouse's lead. Down into the gorge, they went.

They bottomed out at creek level and hopped from rock to rock. The eyes of the Caligin lining the banks were up on the channel's rim. No one was paying any attention to the varmints scrambling into hiding.

Calypsa got a good look at the tunnel waiting ahead of them. They only had a few dozen yards to go. *Almost there!*

Out of nowhere, a huge copper dragon's head struck and gobbled up Mouse.

CHAPTER 67

HACKSAW LANDED ON TOP OF a copper dragon sword first, pinning it to the ground. By the time he yanked his sword free, he was peppered with arrows and covered in suffocating dragon spit. He didn't feel a thing.

He slung the black spit from his face and bellowed, "Ha! Taste the thunder, demons!" He stuck his sword, Green Tongue, through a Caligin's chest.

The dragons backed out of the fight and took to the sky. They chased after Slivver and Elween, who soared through the air.

En masse, the Caligin converged on Hacksaw. With their swords and daggers in hand, they rushed Hacksaw with military precision. Swords chopped into his limbs. Daggers gouged his body. Every strike of elven steel was deflected away harmlessly.

Green Tongue shone like a flame. It flashed downward, cutting an elf's arm from the shoulder.

"You lost one arm!" Hacksaw shouted. "Do you want to lose two? Don't be a fool! Surrender!"

The elves fearlessly flung their bodies into Hacksaw. The attached themselves to his legs, put their shoulders into his ribs, and drove him to the ground. They smothered him.

"Get off of me, cowards!"

Hacksaw hated the Caligin. Their dark eyes and creepy stares sent a jolt of anger right through him. They'd almost killed him once before. He wasn't about to let them do it again. This would be payback. Using the greater weight of his body and heavy armor, he rolled right over them. His girth pushed the air out of one that got crushed under his chest. He backhanded another with his sword pommel, cracking the Caligin in the jaw.

"Worms! I'll shed you all!"

A Caligin chopped Hacksaw in the middle of his head. The blade bounced from his face.

Hacksaw punched that elf in the belly. He grabbed another by the dark hair of his head and yanked hard, pulling the elf free of his back. He killed the elf with a thrust of steel. "You had it coming."

The elves lassoed him with three separate coils of rope. They ripped his legs out from underneath him and pinned his arms to his side.

Wriggling in his new bonds, Hacksaw yelled, "Sour cider! What kind of fighting is this?"

A Caligin stepped on his chest. With a cocky smile, the elf looked down at him and said, "It's smart fighting, stupid. Now that we have you tied up like a hog, we'll just wait for the enchantment to wear off of you." The elf knelt down and got face-to-face with Hacksaw. "I was there, at the river, when you should have died the last time. I put two arrows in you then." He took an arrow from his quiver and twirled it around a finger. Then he put the arrow tip below Hacksaw's eye. "This time, death will be your only escape."

"For Morgdon!" Brenwar bellowed. He dropped out of the sky like a bearded juggernaut. A copper dragon waited with jaws open, spraying at him with spit. Brenwar stuffed his hammer inside the dragon's jaws. He crushed the scaly beast underneath his dwarven girth and broke its neck. Arrows whistled through the air right at him. They ricocheted off his face and elbows. "I like this elixir! Come on, elves! Come and face the wrath of Brenwar Boulderguild!"

Clad in their black leather armor, the dark elves converged on Brenwar as a single unit. With swords and daggers made from razor-sharp elven steel, they chopped and thrust at Brenwar. The tips skipped off his breastplate, arms, and chin.

Brenwar laughed at them. Swinging his warhammer in a broad arc, he knocked two elves out of their boots. He laughed heartily then began singing, "Home of the dwarves, Morgdon! Home of the dwarves, Morgdon! We make the finest steel and ale! Our weapons never fail! Home of the dwarves, Morgdon!"

The elves came at him one by one, two by two, three by three. The stout dwarf with bulging arms as hard as metal, braids whipping beneath his chin like snakes, became a maelstrom of fury. He pulverized the elves. Bones cracked. Legs wobbled. The Caligin that fled tried to crawl. Brenwar showed them no mercy. His warhammer came up and then down.

Wham! An elf's chest caved in.

Crack! A jaw busted.

Boom! A Caligin flew head over heels.

Brenwar had little care for elves, but the thought of wicked elves set his blood on fire. He had more contempt for them than orcs and giants. Simply being evil was one thing, but nothing was worse than good twisted into evil.

As the elves scrambled to regroup, he chased after them on his stubby legs. "Where are you going, cowards?"

A copper dragon swooped down out of the sky, locked its talons onto Brenwar's shoulders, and lifted him into the sky.

With the ground falling away beneath him, Brenwar shouted, "Put me down, lizard! I'm not your dinner!" He swung his hammer backward over his head, though the copper dragon's head slid away from the strikes. "Be still, scaly varmint!"

The dragon made it a few hundred feet in the air, hissed mercilessly, and dropped him.

Plummeting toward the ground, Brenwar shouted, "Nobody drops a dwarf!" Then realizing the finality of his situation, he yelled, "Slivverrrr!"

As soon as Slivver and Elween dropped Brenwar and Hacksaw, the copper dragons launched themselves from the ground in pursuit. Slivver and Elween flew side by side.

He said to her, "What elixir did you swallow?"

"Fleetness," she said. "I feel the effects coming on now." A little charge of lightning flickered through her emerald eyes. "What about you?"

"Well, I couldn't let you be faster than me, now could I? I took the same elixir too. I couldn't resist the temptation to be faster than I already am." He made a quick smile. "Remember, the effects are only temporary."

Elween glanced back at the pursuing flock of blood-hungry dragons gaining on them. "Then let's not waste any time. Happy hunting, Slivver!" She peeled off to the right at startling speed.

"Whoa," Slivver said in awe. His own dragon blood churned with a resurgence of new fire. "Let's see what this potion can do." He looped upward and flew upside down right at the copper. With a fierce beat of his wings, he sliced through the air as if he'd been shot out of a bow. He stretched out his sharp talons. As the dragons veered away, he cut one set of wings to ribbons, sending the copper toward the earth, screeching loudly as it fell. "I like this!"

The coppers spread out. One by one, from different angles, they made runs at Slivver. They spat acid, screeched, and clawed at him.

Slivver flew circles around the brood. He dodged one copper's stream of acid and ripped into the wings of another. He squirted between two that had him dead to rights. The coppers' heads collided together with a loud crack. He showed the fiendish dragons no mercy. His talons shredded the membranes of their wings. He mutilated them. In the sky, he was king. One by one, the coppers were being humiliated. They wanted him on the ground, where they could pin him down. Slivver wouldn't let that happen.

A copper dragon slipped in behind Slivver and hooked its talons into his tail.

It slowed Slivver. He turned his head around as two more coppers closed in, and he said, "No, you don't!" and shot a bolt of lightning out of his mouth.

Bzzzat!

The copper dragon's scales lit up so bright he could see the bones. It fell away in a dying spiral. Slivver ducked the other two dragons coming at him and jetted away. That was when he caught the sound of Brenwar screaming, "Slivverrrr!" Slivver pushed through the air with all he had.

Master Elween wasn't a better flyer than Slivver, but she was a better fighter. As she split away from her friend, she used another tactic. She caught sight of two Caligin charging through the fields and dove after them. The dark elves had their swords raised high as they rushed after Rond. She sneaked in behind them, knocked them down, and stole their swords. She took back to the sky and raced high above the ground.

The copper dragons chased with furious roars.

Feeling as spry as a pixie, Elween stretched the distance between her and them. She hovered, held out her swords, and watched the coppers close in. If there was one breed of dragon she couldn't stand, it was the coppers. Her kind, the forest dragons, feuded with them over territory in Nalzambor's forests. Many lives were lost in their feuds. Now was the time for some payback. She flashed her swords across her chest.

Glaring down at her enemies, she said, "It's time to eat steel, you idiots!"

The coppers let out a unified screech.

Diving, Elween barrel-rolled through the air, twisting like a cyclone right at the brood. Her spinning blades turned the first copper dragon she hit into giant food. Her swords twisted through wings and lopped off arms and segments of tails. The armored chests of the copper dragons were gored. The coppers were used to fighting claw against claw. They were overwhelmed by the expertly wielded strikes of spinning steel that decimated their efforts.

One of the copper dragons' superior numbers got the drop on Elween and plastered her with acid. She let out a moan. Striking like a snake, she chopped the copper dragon's head off with her sword. Burning acid ate into her scales. She spun like a whirlwind in the air, shaking the sizzling black flakes from her body.

Wiping the last bit from her face, she looked at the enemy gathered around her and said, "You're going to pay for that."

The relentless coppers' jaws all opened as one, and they let out evil hisses.

CHAPTER 68

WITHOUT SLOWING, CALYPSA RAN AS quickly as her tiny mouse legs would take her. Mouse had been gobbled up by a full-grown copper dragon. She could do nothing to help him now. She had to save herself. Racing toward the tunnel entrance, she heard a loud huff and glanced backward.

The copper dragon's hard stare was tracking her like a hungry hawk. Its neck started to coil back. The dragon was no fool. It had instincts and wisdom. She could tell by the intelligence lurking in its eyes that it knew they were intruders. After all, a tiny little mouse would not feed a dragon's monstrous appetite. Filling a dragon's belly would take a thousand mice. The copper dragon moved down the bank with the grace of a panther. In four great strides, it overtook Calypsa.

She wove between the creek stones and scurried through the shallow waters, saying to herself, "No, no, no!"

The copper dragon's head lashed downward.

Calypsa jumped left, but it didn't do any good. The massive jaws of the dragon closed in around her, scooping her up with the dirt, rock, and water. She was sealed inside the dragon's mouth in total darkness.

Fighting and clawing to keep herself from being swallowed into the rancid throat of the monster, she desperately screamed, "No, no, no, no! I have failed!"

Crack!

The dragon's head shook like an earthquake. Opening its jaws, it let out a roar, spitting out Calypsa at the same time. She tumbled out of the monster's mouth and splashed into the water of the creek. Wearily, she looked up and gaped. Rond, with the sledgehammer Stone Smiter in his hands, was taking it to the dragon. Caligin arrows were sticking out all over his body, but Rond fought with a berserker's fury. The purple gemstone flashed with fire. It hammered into the dragon's armored hide.

Wham! Wham! Wham!

"Kill her, Rond!" Calypsa screamed futilely below the clamor of battle.

Caligin elves crept in after Rond. They filled him with arrows. The copper dragon unleashed her fatal breath weapons. The stream of acid scorched Rond's rotting flesh.

With fire in his eyes, Rond continued to hammer away. Somehow, he glanced at Calypsa and said, "Go!"

Cowering back toward the tunnel, her rodent eyes swelling with tears, she said, "I love you, Rond. You are my best friend." With her heart breaking, knowing that Rond was giving his life for her again, she made her way into the darkness. The deeper she went, the more the commotion of battle fell away. After she ventured deep enough, she realized she had no idea where she was going. She was in a humongous cavern with no sign of life anywhere.

Behind her, a rodent squeaked.

She turned. "Mouse! You survived. The dragon must have spat you out with me."

Mouse ambled toward her, his left front paw limp. He bumped noses with her. Whiskers twitching, he made a series of squeaks and led the way, limping deeper into the cavern.

Down inside the buried city, they found the back entrance to the forge. Calypsa patted Mouse on the head. After he told her what to do and expect, she went in alone. The forge was sweltering. Her heart leapt the moment she saw Nath. He was in a heated conversation with Darkken and Maefon.

She started grinding her teeth the moment she saw Maefon. *I hate you.* In the background, five Caligin were in the room with them. Nath grabbed Maefon's hand and squeezed it. Calypsa's heart jumped. *What's this? I'll not have this. It ends now!*

"Darkken, as my brother," Nath said, "you must promise me that you will not harm my old friends. I mean it. This feud between you and them must end now."

Calypsa was about to reveal herself and call Maefon out, but she froze. Now was the time for listening, not for action. She needed to understand what was going on. She scurried across the floor and crawled up Nath's pant leg, up his back, and onto his shoulder.

"Oh, there you are," Nath said, eyeing her.

Darkken had his back to Nath. He was shaking his head. "It's us against them now, Nath. If you stand with me, then you must stand against them."

Calypsa did not like what she was hearing or the direction it was headed. An eerie feeling crept over her. At the same time, she couldn't stop glaring at Maefon.

The elven woman stiffened against Calypsa's intense stare and said, "Nath, your little rodent is glaring at me, I think."

Yes, keep smiling, witch. This little rodent is going to gnaw your face off when the time comes.

Nath picked up Calypsa by her tail and said, "Mouse, be good." He eyed her closely then took a long look. He tilted his head. "Uh, he does look kind of angry." He stuffed her inside his belt pouch.

Calypsa kept her head popped out.

"Darkken, Calypsa," Nath said sincerely, "you know I love you both dearly, but for now, we have what we want. There can be no more bloodshed. Not today. I say we negotiate."

Darkken spun on his heel and looked Nath dead in the eye. He placed his hands on Nath's shoulders and said, "Fine, brother. You have my word. But if they attack, I'm not holding back. Agreed?"

"Agreed."

No, Nath, no, he's lying! They are trying to slaughter your friends up there!

"Excellent. Let's cover the Dragon Vein, and let's get out of here," Darkken said.

"You are a very wise man, Nath. I look forward to being with you forever." Maefon gave Nath a passionate kiss.

Calypsa's temper boiled over. She screamed aloud, "Nooo!" Then she started growing.

CHAPTER 69

"ONLY A COWARD WOULD FIGHT with a rope," Hacksaw said as he wriggled against the ropes holding him fast.

The potion of invulnerability gave him incredible power in terms of defending himself, but it did him little good when he was immobilized. The elves stretched his arms and legs wide, making a cross pattern with his body on the ground. One lone dark elf still stood with one foot on his chest.

"Let's you and I settle this, sword against sword."

With a cocky smile, the slender-faced elf said, "There's no need for that. I have you right where I want you."

"You had me right where you wanted me the last time, and that didn't work," Hacksaw said. He found himself wishing he had his pipe in his mouth, but it was tucked away.

The dark elf said, "My name is Dalva. I'm only telling you that so that you can know who is your slayer, legionnaire." Dalva pocked his longsword into Hacksaw's thigh. The tip of the blade skipped aside as though hitting stone. "Magic is fascinating, isn't it? The problem is it always wears off. Brothers, join me. Let's see if we can find a weakness in this mortal."

Two more elves started poking at Hacksaw with their swords. They poked at his eyes, cheeks, neck, arms, belly, and legs.

Hacksaw felt as though he had on a suit of full plate armor, protecting him. But he knew it would wear off in only a matter of time. "Since you have me at a disadvantage, all I ask is a quick death. I don't want to be poked and prodded like a skewered pig."

Dalva took a knee beside Hacksaw's head. With a creepy stare, he said, "But you are a pig, human. It is the Caligin that will soon rule the world, and we shall make slaves of all of you. And the ones that resist shall be killed. For the time comes when the dark shall rule the day."

Giving the elf a hard look, he said, "That will never happen." He noticed the dragons fighting in the sky. Elween ripped through three copper dragons and sent them to their deaths. She was hovering in the sky, wings beating, chest heaving, when she looked down and caught Hacksaw's stare. "Elves are such a cowardly lot. Small and frail. It's no wonder that you couldn't kill me before. Each of you could hardly pull a bowstring back. Back at the river, all it felt like was that I was getting hit by a flurry of pine needles."

Dalva snarled. "I think we are going to kill you a little bit at a time. And we'll do the same to others." He started tapping his blade on Hacksaw's chest. "I'm sure your magic will fail any moment now."

Hacksaw's own sweat stung his eyes. He couldn't tell for sure, but the confidence the potion was giving him seemed to be wearing off. Above, Elween dove right at him. Her jaws opened, revealing the fire within. "Hurry up, will you!" he shouted.

Dalva looked surprised. His head whipped around just in time to see Elween unloading a geyser of orange-red flames.

The dragon fire consumed man and elf. The elves' skins turned to ash. Hacksaw screamed until the intense heat suddenly took his breath. He felt as if he were in an oven, suffocating. The burning elves collapsed.

Elween landed, helped Hacksaw to his feet, and moved him away from the flames. "Are you well?"

He coughed hard several times, caught his breath, and said, "Pan seared, I'd say, but alive." The scent of his own singed hair tickled his nose. The hairs on his arms were all curled up. "Thanks for saving me. If it had been a moment longer, those elves would have gutted me. I'm pretty sure that elixir has almost worn off."

"Mine is fading as well," she said. "Let's find the others." At about that time, they heard Brenwar screaming from high in the sky. He was plummeting right toward the earth. "Oh my!"

Slivver streaked through the sky with his clawed fingers outstretched, making a beeline for Brenwar.

"That's fast," Hacksaw said with awe.

Slivver reached for Brenwar's outstretched fingers. The dwarf was only thirty feet from the ground. Slivver missed. Brenwar hit the ground a split second later. He landed hard on a rock, bounced, and fell into the surrounding shrubbery.

Hacksaw and Elween ran after the fallen dwarf. By the time they got there, Slivver had already landed. Brenwar lay flat on his back, eyes closed, unmoving, with his war hammer still clutched in his grip.

Shaking his head, Slivver said, "I can't believe I missed. I'm so sorry, dear friend, Brenwar. You will be missed."

Brenwar's lips parted. "I ain't dead, you shiny lizard. Now help me up so I can finish throttling those elves."

Smiles broke out on everyone's faces.

Hacksaw helped Brenwar back to his feet. "I take it the elixir spared you."

"No, dwarves bounce really well." Brenwar's eyes narrowed. "Let's get after the rest of them." He limped forward.

Aside from their dead, no signs of the Caligin or the dragons remained. The group made it over toward the rim of the gulch. One hundred feet away, copper dragons and dark elves slunk out of the ravine, dozens of them in all. Marching forward, the regiment encircled the heroic group. They were outnumbered at least a dozen to one.

Hacksaw put his pipe in his mouth and said, "I don't suppose anyone has any more elixirs left."

Brenwar's hands wrung the leather grip on his hammer's handle. "I've got all I need. Now, let's make them bleed."

Hacksaw had never faced greater odds before. He knew this battle would be it. He said, "Let's ride the thunder." He stabbed Green Tongue high. "For Nath!"

Chapter 70

Nath couldn't believe his eyes. With a pounce, Mouse had transformed into the half-dryad, Calypsa. The petite woman's arms were like a bear's. She jumped on Maefon, shoved the elven woman to the ground, pinned her underneath her body, and locked her claws around her throat.

Astonished, he managed to spit out the words, "Calypsa, what are you doing? Stop!"

"I'll tell you what I'm doing," Calypsa fired back. "I'm going to kill this evil witch that tried to kill me!" Her eyes were locked on Maefon. She snarled, "Now it's payback!"

Maefon's eyes bulged in her sockets. Her face was turning as red as a beet. Gritting her teeth, she locked her hands on Calypsa's furry arms. Mystical energy burst from her forearms and flamed up her hands.

Calypsa groaned, but her grip held firm. In a voice full of wrath, she said, "You will not escape me! Not this time! Nath, she is a liar! Every word that comes out of her mouth is twisted! So is Darkken. They want to control you, and the entire time, they've been trying to kill us. They killed Rond." Her gaze landed on the Caligin. "Those shifty fiends tried to murder Hacksaw. It all happened after they tricked us to leave you! You have to believe me!"

Darkken stepped forward with one hand glowing with copper fire. "Enough of this nonsense. The dryad is insane with jealousy. That is all that this is."

Nath didn't know what to say. He'd been willing to buy into how Darkken wanted him separated from the dragons. Now, however, Calypsa claimed that they were willing to commit murder in order to convince him.

He stepped in front of Darkken. "Is this true?"

"No, of course not. Nath, she is another agent of Slivver and Master Elween. And remember that dryads, pixies, and fairy-kind are all notorious tricksters and liars." Darkken's hands burned bright. "Now, step aside before this deluded dryad kills Maefon."

"I'll handle this." Nath turned around and put his hand on Calypsa's shoulder. "My friend, I know most all of what you speak. Please, let Maefon go."

Calypsa glowered at Maefon. Sweat dripped down her face as the fires coming from Maefon's hands burned brighter. "No. She deserves death, and I'm going to give it to her." She put all her weight on Maefon, and her claws sank deeper into her neck.

"No, Calypsa! No! You are not a murderer!"

Seething, Calypsa said, "No, today I am vengeance!"

Maefon's eyes rolled up in her head. The fires on her fingers began to fade.

Nath dropped down to his knees and yelled at Darkken. "Get her other arm!" Straining, Nath used his hands to try to break Calypsa's mighty grip. She didn't budge.

"Let me do this, Nath!" Calypsa said. "It is the right thing! It is—"

Chok! Darkken smote Calypsa in the back of her head with his sword pommel.

Calypsa lost her grip and fell sideways onto the floor.

Maefon scrambled away. She rubbed her throat and gasped for breath.

The Brothers of the Wind went right after the dryad with their swords poised to kill.

"Back off!" Nath warned the elves.

He shielded Calypsa's body with his. The woman was out cold, the back of her head bleeding.

"You cracked her good, Darkken. You might have killed her."

"I wish he had," Maefon said. She was sitting up with her back against a table leg. "She's insane."

The sinister inflection in Maefon's voice, matched with the intense hatred burning in her blue eyes, caught Nath off guard. For a moment, Maefon was not who he thought she was.

"Thanks for checking on me, Nath." Maefon stood up. "But I'm fine."

Nath scooped up Calypsa. Carrying her in his arms, he said, "I'm leaving."

Standing beside Maefon, Darkken said, "You swore that you would stand by us, brother. And now, you've suddenly had a change of heart on account of this woodland witch?"

Nath stopped at the opening at the back wall. Without looking back, he said, "I haven't changed my mind about anything. We are going out to put an end to this matter once and for all. The both of you are coming too."

"Brothers of the Wind," Darkken said, "get our things. It's time to get some sunlight."

Outside of the tunnel, Nath saw a scene where a grisly battle had taken place in the ravine. The full-grown mother dragon lay dead in the creek. The dragon's head had been crushed. Scattered around the dragon, five more Brothers of the Wind lay dead in the thickets, their bodies horribly mangled. They looked as if an anvil had hit them. Nath picked his way around the dead dragon and moved farther up the creek. Lying facedown in the shallow waters was a huge humanoid body. Draconic acid had eaten away most of the skin and muscles. One leg was missing, and two of the humanoid's four arms were gone, but it still moved forward, pushing up on its two good left arms and using a sledgehammer for a crutch.

"Rond!" Nath said.

The four-armed bugbear's charred ears wiggled. His head twisted around, revealing half of his ghastly face.

Nath swallowed the lump building in his throat. He'd never seen anything so grotesque. The bugbear's muscular body had been torn to shreds. Acid had eaten away most of his flesh, yet he still moved. That the monster could still be living defied reason.

"Rond, what happened?" Nath asked.

Rond's eyes brightened at seeing Calypsa. He reached for the woman.

On instinct, Nath set Calypsa down by his side. He wasn't sure what compelled him to do it, but in his heart, he felt it was right. Calypsa stirred. She saw Rond, and with growing eyes, she threw her arms around him. She started crying and said, "Oh, Rond, I'm so sorry!"

Fanning his face, Darkken said, "Phew. And I thought bugbears smelled bad before."

The clash of steel and roar of dragons sounded above.

"It's sounds fierce up there. Are you sure that you want to get involved?"

Nath told Calypsa, "I'll be back. Stay with Rond." He pointed at Darkken and Maefon. "Get up there and stop this now."

He raced up the hill. At the top of the gully, he stood on a high spot looking down into the valley. He was shocked to see Slivver, Elween, Hacksaw, and the dwarf surrounded by dozens of copper dragons and Brothers of the Wind. The elves hurled spears and shot arrows at Hacksaw and Brenwar. The dragons were shielding them with their bodies.

Nath yelled at Darkken, "Call this off now!"

Darkken lifted a hand and said, "Enough!"

The Brothers of the Wind and the dragons withdrew. The dragons hunkered down in the brush, and the elves all took a knee.

Slivver and his group cast nervous glances among themselves before finally settling their stares between Nath and Darkken.

"Well, brother," Darkken said dryly, "you have your audience. Now make your proclamation for peace."

CHAPTER 71

As Nath joined Maefon and Darkken, the other five elves made a half circle behind them. He sorted through his thoughts. So much had happened and so much had been said that keeping up was difficult. Seeing Calypsa, Rond, and Hacksaw was startling. They should have been far out of harm's way, but they had come back. *Why?*

A breeze picked up. The stench of death carried through the valley. The leaves were covered in bodies and blood. Nath counted more than one crushed body. He searched the faces of his friends, who stood no more than a hundred feet away. Slivver's ice-blue eyes were filled with worry. Elween's eyes showed growing concern. Hacksaw's jaw sagged as he puffed out streams of smoke. They all looked weary, even the dwarf, Brenwar, whom he didn't know well.

Nath cleared his throat. He glanced at Maefon, who gave him a nod. "Slivver. Elween. Hacksaw. Today, this fight has to end. I want you to stop pursuing me and my brother, Darkken."

"That's not going to happen, Nath," Slivver said strongly. "We did not come here to allow you to be taken by this predator. This murderer. Balzurth sent us to save you from him. Heed us when we tell you that Darkken is nothing but evil."

Darkken shrugged. "It's their word against mine. You have to decide, Nath. It's either us, the ones that have been fighting with you from the beginning, or them, who have done nothing but stir up trouble since all of this started. I thought you gave us your trust."

"I did. I don't need to be reminded of it. But as I've said before, this bloodshed must stop. I won't have it."

"We need to finish this, and it will stop," Maefon suggested. "A final battle is the only way. They are not your friends, Nath. Look at them: dragons, a dwarf, and a human. They are not the same as you and Darkken. They are not part of your evolution."

"I'm not going to fight my friends, and I'm not going to watch them die, either." Nath's fists clenched at his sides, his heart racing. The back-and-forth and double-talk was getting to him. "Slivver, we are too strong for you to overtake us. Elween, you must go. Hacksaw, go and live the rest of your years in peace. You need to forget about me."

"Who are you, boy?" Hacksaw shouted. "These shady elves tried to kill me the same day that I left you. They shot me full of arrows. What sort of friends do you call them? It was twenty against only one. They skewered me like a hog!"

"That's only his side of the story," Darkken replied.

"Nath, they've been manipulating you ever since you came out of Dragon Home," Master Elween said. "It started with the Black Hand, and it hasn't ended since then. I've known you all of your life, Nath. You know that I wouldn't lie to you. Darkken is dangerous. He's only using you to get what he wants. He wants to use you to kill Balzurth. That's why he wanted the dragon steel. It's the only way to slay your father."

"That's insane!" Darkken stabbed his fingers at Elween and said, "The time has come for the dawn of a new age. The dragons have served their time, and now it is their time to return to the Land beyond the Murals, from where they were summoned. It's Balzurth's time to move on, and he knows it."

Slivver and Elween exchanged dumbfounded looks. "This is outrageous," Slivver said. "Nath, you can't believe a word of this. Darkken tells nothing but lies!"

"You're the liar!" Darkken shouted. His eyebrows buckled. His fist clenched. "I'm not going to stand here and tolerate these accusations. I've had all that I can stand!"

Nath could see his brother's face flush. Darkken had murder in his eyes. Nath had been buying time, trying to sort out everything he was hearing. The words of Slivver and Elween rang of nothing but truth. Their body language and tone suggested the same. They'd never lied to him. But Darkken left too many questions. Nath remembered catching up with his brother in the shack outside of Artus. *"The time has come when the dark shall rule the day."* That wasn't all. Darkken had never said he would not try to kill Balzurth. That bothered Nath. Other truths were hiding in what Darkken was not saying.

Then, there was Maefon. The look in her eyes when Calypsa had come upon her was full of shock, hatred, and murder. His heart was breaking, but he knew Maefon was not what she said she was. She too was a liar.

The time had come when he couldn't ride out his feelings any longer. He had to decide and have faith in what he believed was right and wrong. The problem was that he did fully believe one thing: Darkken could kill them all. His brother showed no weakness, but he had to have one. Everyone had a weakness. That was what he'd always been taught.

I have to buy more time.

"Can we stop with all of the accusations?" he said.

"Aye." Brenwar spat in his hands and rubbed them together. "No one is as blind as he that will not see. I say we get back to the fighting."

"Are you talking about me, dwarf?" Nath said, deliberately buying time.

"No, I'm talking to the other idiot with golden eyes and his head up his hind end," Brenwar fired back.

"You remind me of the first dwarf. He was just like you. I didn't like him, either," he said.

"Yes, Nath, this dwarf is much like Cullen of the Black Hand. They are the same sordid ilk," Maefon said. She locked an arm around his. "You remember what you went through with them. They are no different."

He nodded. At the same time, he was still running through what he knew about Darkken. His brother seemed invincible. He'd mastered great magic, including teleportation, and controlled unearthly powers. He'd wiped out the beast-birds with lightning from his fingers. And Darkken had just created a sword called Mercy, which would make him the finest swordsman in the land. Darkken could control so much, not to mention his command over the Caligin and over a score of copper sliders. His eyes slid to Darkken. The man was ready to erupt. Nath could almost feel the heat rising from his brother's body. Darkken had a look that could kill. Nath felt in his heart that it would.

"Darkken, let's go back to the keep. Me, you, Maefon, and our brothers."

"I say we finish this," Darkken replied.

"That's what I say too!" Brenwar shouted.

"Dwarf, shut up!" Nath said. "Slivver, don't be a fool! Honor my request, and let me go. It's my life. It's my decision." Nath needed time to figure out how to stop Darkken. To do that, he needed to find his weakness. "Let me be!"

Spreading his wings, Slivver said, "Sorry, but if our dying is the only way for you to see the light, my brother, then so be it."

"Darkken, take us out of here now! I won't stand for this," Nath said. As he did so, he saw footprints moving in the grass toward Darkken. *What in the world?*

Darkken arched his back and cried out, a dagger lodged in his back. The dark elf, Dule, appeared, along with Roday. He'd slit the teleportation bracelet from Darkken's wrist and tossed it aside.

Roday said, "Nobody is going anywhere now. It's time to finish this."

His face contorted in rage, Darkken pulled Roday and Dule into his grasp with telekinetic power. His fingers locked around their throats, and fire surged into his hands.

Roday and Dule both choked out the words "Goodbye, Nath." Their screams were cut short as their bodies burst into flames, burned like cinders, and fell away in ashes.

Chapter 72

NATH'S KNEES BUCKLED. "NO."

Why would Roday and Dule, Brothers of the Wind and faithful servants of Darkken, attack their leader? He'd thought they were dead already. Now, they'd both given their lives for Nath. At that point, any morsel of doubt that he had left about where he stood was shattered. He'd been playing both sides, but the time had come to stand on the right side of things. The growing rage on Darkken's face sold the rest of the story. His brother was going on the warpath.

"That's it," Darkken said. "They are all going to die now!" He glared at a Caligin. "Get this dagger out of my back!"

A throaty chuckle erupted from Brenwar.

Darkken stabbed a finger at the dwarf and shouted to his followers, "Kill him first!" He turned his hot stare on Nath. "Well, brother, where do you stand? Because we aren't going anywhere."

Nath shoved Maefon into Darkken's arms. He drew Fang, pointed at his friends, and said, "I stand with them!"

Darkken showed him a wicked smile and said, "Not for long, sibling fool!" With a wave of his hand, Nath was lifted from his feet and hurtled over one hundred feet away. "Caligin, restrain him. I'll deal with him later, after I've finished off the rest of them."

With the ring of Caligin and copper dragons closing in on the group of heroes, Brenwar lifted his hammer and shouted, "I've had enough of this! Stay close!" He brought the warhammer up and then down with wroth force.

Boom!

The ground quaked in all directions beyond the head of the hammer. The copper dragons and Caligin lost their footing.

"Strike quickly!" Slivver ordered.

He breathed out a bolt of lightning that hit the nearest copper dragon. The lightning bored a black hole through the dragon, passing through it and into another, jumping from dragon to elf to dragon in a chain reaction.

Master Elween launched herself at the fallen dragons and elves, releasing geysers of flames. The fire jumped from body to body, consuming hair, flesh, and armor.

Hacksaw darted into the fray of Caligin missed by the dragons' attacks. He thrust his sword into their shaken bodies with deadly accuracy. "Ride the thunder!"

Many of the enemy fell underneath the lethal attack, but many more still lived. A single elf rushed Brenwar with deadly intent. The elf's sword thrust skipped off the hard armor of Brenwar's breastplate. Using an uppercut swing, Brenwar knocked the Caligin off the ground, sending him colliding with another. "Scrawny fools! I'll break all of you!"

With the odds evening out, the combatants battled on. Man, dwarves, elf, and dragons battled for their very lives with everything they had in them.

Nath landed on his backside and rolled back up onto his feet. Before he could swing his sword, Caligin locked up his arms and legs. They held him fast as he watched his friends battle without him. They were outnumbered. They were going to lose.

"Let me go!" he yelled.

"You aren't going anywhere, *brother*," said the elf locking up his right arm.

"I'm not your brother."

"Once a Caligin, always a Caligin. It is that or death. Didn't you see what happened to Roday and Dule? They are worm food now. Soon, you will be too."

Nath strained against the strong, wiry limbs of his captors. The Caligin were as fit as any man, but Nath was stronger than any two of them, possibly three. He pumped his arms, trying to shake them, but they held fast.

"It's leverage, fool. You cannot break our grip," the elf said. "No, watch your friends die at the hands of the Lord of the Dark in the Day."

Nath watched in horror as Slivver and the rest of the group fought for their very lives against the onslaught of attacks. There were still too many dragons and elves. He had to get to them. He looked at the Caligin spokesman and said, "You know what, brother? I think you forgot something."

"Really? What is that?"

Nath clenched his left fist. The gemstone on the back of the Gauntlet of Goam brightened like a star. Boundless strength coursed through Nath's body from head to toe.

"This!" Nath shouted.

Effortlessly, he punched the elf hard in the face. *Pop!* The elf fell over with his nose busted open. He didn't move. Nath twisted out of the other elves' arms. He hammered them away from him. They crumbled beneath his power. Kicking his way out of their grasping fingers, Nath retrieved his sword.

Nath let out his battle cry. "Dragon! Dragon!"

He closed the distance in a second. His first swing cut a man-sized copper in half. *Slice!* A split second later a second dragon fell. *Chop!*

"It's about time, Nath!" Hacksaw bellowed as he punched shimmering green steel into a Caligin chest. "Ride the thunder with me!"

Nath went to work. "Thunder! Thunder!"

With their hardened spirits broken, the Caligin and copper dragons fell more quickly. In only seconds, it was all over.

Dripping sweat and sucking for air, the victorious group turned toward the sound of clapping.

Darkken and Maefon stood on the risen ground, smirking. Darkken was the one doing the clapping. "Well done, fools. You managed to slay all of my retainers. I have to admit even I am impressed. The problem is you haven't slain me."

"Or me," Maefon said.

"Maefon, you've made my heart grieve," Nath said. "All of this time, I meant nothing?"

With a cold stare, she said, "I've always served the Lord of the Dark in the Day. You would have been wise to serve him too." Venom was in her voice, though a tear ran down her cheek. "You ruined it, Nath. You ruined everything we could have had. But now, we'll rule the world without you. You are such a fool." Her hands glowed.

Darkken tapped his mouth as he yawned. "I suppose the time has come to get this over with. Slivver, my brother, you should have walked away. I would have let you live… for a while. But now, you are going to have to experience ultimate suffering." He pulled his sword, Mercy, out of its sheath and pointed the tip at Slivver, Elween, and Hacksaw. "I challenge you, you, and you."

"No!" Nath yelled. "What about me? I challenge you!"

Nath was lifted up into the air as Maefon's hands gesticulated. Mystic bindings snared him in violet red.

"Put me down!"

CHAPTER 73

THE SAME CIRCLES OF RADIANT light that captured Nath also encircled Brenwar and Slivver, and they too were lifted from the ground. They hovered in the air with Nath. Helplessly, they watched Darkken draw his other sword, Scalpel, as Master Elween and Hacksaw marched to his challenge.

"It's a trap, Elween!" Slivver yelled. "Don't fall for his tricks. Stay back."

Elween picked up two swords from the fallen Caligin. Hacksaw followed her up the ridge toward Darkken. Elween turned, saluted them, and said, "A challenge is a challenge."

"Yes," Darkken said brightly. "And they would die one way or another anyway. I'm just looking forward to testing the strength of the new blade, Mercy. I'm curious to see how it compares to Scalpel."

"So that sword is made from dragon ore, I take it," Slivver said, concern in his voice.

"To my shame, I helped him make it," Nath replied. Suspended in the air, he could do nothing but watch as, once again, Darkken had all of them at his mercy. "I'm sorry, brother. I've been trying to put all of the pieces of the puzzle together, but Darkken always has an answer. He's prepared for everything. I just don't understand how he is so powerful."

"He's a crafty snake. He always was," Slivver replied. "Don't blame yourself. You have seen the light. That is what we hoped for."

"I fear I saw the truth too late. If I'd seen it sooner, I could have stopped him. Since I've doubted, I've been playing along, trying to find his weakness. I still don't see any. He's a master swordsman and omnipotent wizard. It's impossible to even lay a hand on him," he said.

"Nothing's impossible," Brenwar stated. He glanced at them. "For a dwarf, that is."

"Crixis put the veil over many eyes. It's nothing to be ashamed of. Just think," Slivver replied.

"I think it was Maefon that covered my eyes. I just don't understand how she could do this." He gazed at the elven woman that he deeply loved. Her eyes burned as blue as fire. "Did she really try to kill Calypsa and Rond?"

Slivver nodded.

Nath's head dipped along with his sinking heart. "I feared so."

Clang!

On the ridge by the gulch, Master Elween and Hacksaw engaged Lord Darkken. With a sword in each hand, Darkken parried their fast strokes with a grim smile of determination. Dragon and elven steel flashed in the sunlight. Hacksaw labored with strong hacking chops on one side. Master Elween weaved a path of thrusts on the other. Darkken parried with dazzling speed.

Maefon brought her captives in for a closer look. They hovered only twenty feet above and twenty feet away.

"One of you hit him, will you?" Brenwar shouted.

The dance of steel went back and forth for over a minute. Hacksaw's shoulders slumped, and his chest heaved. His sword thrusts slowed and turned to parries against Darkken's quickening strokes.

Master Elween fought with two swords, attacking Darkken's right hand, which wielded Mercy. He parried and countered with unrivaled grace, skill, and speed.

"You improved marvelously since we last fought," she said. "I can only imagine it's the sword."

"Yes, the sword has no rival," Darkken replied. "We are a perfect match, for neither do I."

He broke away from his attackers by leaping over Hacksaw, and the moment he landed, he attacked. "You would have been better off if you'd just died earlier as planned, Legionnaire."

"I never should have left Nath alone with you. I smelled the stink on you the moment I met you." Hacksaw used both hands on his sword to parry Darkken's blades licking at his face. His cheeks were as red as fire. "You won't win this!"

"I've won already." With his left-handed sword, Scalpel, Darkken knocked Green Tongue aside. He thrust Mercy into Hacksaw's heart. "Good night, old knight."

"Nooo!" Nath screamed. He swam wildly in the sky, going nowhere. "Maefon, please let me down!"

Maefon didn't even look at him. Her eyes were glued on the sword fight.

Wide-eyed, Hacksaw dropped to his knees. He looked at Nath, raised an arm, and sputtered, "Ride the thunder."

Darkken pulled his sword free and let out a victorious laugh. "'Ride the dirt' is more like it." He squared off with Master Elween. "You are next, old master. It's time to see who the master is now." He stuck Scalpel into the ground. "Take my sword. It's superior to that which you are using. It will be one blade against the other."

Master Elween tossed her two swords aside and took Scalpel in hand. She twisted it by the pommel, flipped it around, and sliced a Z-pattern in the air. "Fair enough."

Darkken chuckled in his throat, which stoked hatred within Nath. Anger stirred in his gut, not because of Darkken but because of himself. He should have seen the deception long ago. Now, his lapse in judgment had come to bear. He and his friends were doomed.

"Kill that slithering snake, Elween!" Brenwar hollered. "Show him no mercy!"

Elween flexed her wings in and out. She and Darkken circled. She poised herself in a sword-fighting stance. In Dragonese, she spoke. "En garde!"

Darkken came at her with a demonic expression. He slashed at her neck. She slipped her head aside and parried. Steel cried out against steel. She countered with a quick thrust and caught Darkken's dodging head across the cheek. He jumped backward.

Touching the bleeding gash on his face, he said, "First blood. Well done. It's last blood that truly matters."

"I know," she replied coolly.

The dragon steel in Mercy's blade shone like copper. Darkken chopped the deadly weapon back and forth. His eyes narrowed into slits as he rushed Elween. The master swordsmen went back and forth with metal clashing against metal.

Nath had never seen sword strokes so fast before. Every thrust and slash was masterful. Their footwork was outstanding.

He shook in the air. "Finish him, Elween!"

Darkken parried and thrust.

Elween riposted and slashed.

Suddenly, Darkken ducked low, and Scalpel slashed over his head. With blazing speed, he thrust Mercy's hilt deep into Master Elween's heart. Scalpel fell from her fingers. Her eyes fluttered a moment, then her neck sagged. She hit the ground, dead.

Nath let out an anguished scream.

Chapter 74

An emptiness grew inside Nath. More friends were dying because of him. Roday and Dule were incinerated. Hacksaw and Elween had died by a sword Nath had helped Darkken create. Tears rolled down his cheeks. Outraged, he screamed again.

"Pull it together, boy!" Brenwar said. The dwarf continued to fight against the violet-red restraints that kept him suspended in the air. "This is war. No time for crying!"

"Let him cry," Darkken said. He wiped the blood from his sword onto the grass. "He needs to get it out of his system. But save some for your father's funeral, in case I let you live to see it."

"What are you talking about?" Slivver asked.

Darkken floated up off the ground. He walked on air right toward the heroes. Standing several feet away from them, he addressed them all. "To be honest, I've really enjoyed all of this. It's been worth all of the decades that it's taken to plot it." He held out Mercy and touched the tip with his finger. His eyes slid between Nath and Slivver. "With this sword, I can finally kill our father, Balzurth."

"Pffft!" Brenwar said.

"Oh, but it's true, dwarf," Darkken coolly replied. "You see, now that Balzurth has returned from the Land beyond the Murals, I'm quite certain that he is sleeping. He always does, does he not, after that strange journey?"

Nath recalled his father's coming and going before. After a brief time of sorting things out with the High Dragon Council, Balzurth would slumber for years. He glanced at Slivver. The silver dragon's eyes suggested that Darkken's charge was authentic.

"The dragons will never let you near Dragon Home," Nath said.

"You mean the Mountain of Doom. Ha." Darkken twirled his sword around and slipped it into its scabbard. "I'm not going through the front door. I'm going to teleport right inside the great throne room. There, I will stab my father in the heart, the same way he did me. But this time, it will be more lethal. He will die, and I will become the new Dragon King."

"You can't teleport." Nath laughed. "Roday and Dule destroyed your bracelet."

Twisting the copper rings on his fingers, Darkken smiled at Nath and said, "Why, those bracelets were for you and Maefon. That way, I could track your whereabouts. As for me, I can teleport any time and any place that I want. I have that sort of power—powers that you can only imagine." Darkken blinked out of sight.

"Where'd he go?" Brenwar's head moved like a bird.

On a grassy knoll where a tree had fallen, a furry creature crawled up on the log. It looked like a giant woodchuck but had a human face. It waved at Nath. "Do you remember me?"

"Ruffle?" Nath said in astonishment.

The beast was the hermix that had teleported Nath after his escape from Slavertown to the Nameless Temple. He met him in the woodland shortly after he first met with Calypsa. The hermix had great power. Nath had forgotten all about him.

"Who is that?" Slivver asked.

"An acquaintance that aided me long ago," he said. He noticed the confused look on Maefon's face. "Ruffle, tell me you are here to help us. Did you make Darkken disappear?"

In a scratchy voice, Ruffle replied, "Of course I did. Would you like for me to make him reappear?"

"No, no," Nath said. "Just help us."

The furry Ruffle started to chuckle. Then he started to grow and quickly transformed back into Darkken. A sick feeling churned in Nath's stomach. Ruffle had shown extraordinary powers that even Darkken had not revealed. Now, the creature had turned out to be Darkken.

"That was you?" Nath asked.

Darkken chuckled and said, "Yes, isn't it frightening, knowing the amount of power that I wield?" He changed again from himself to Radigan, the heavyset cook Nath had been imprisoned with at Slavertown. He wore a smock, had a greasy head of hair, and asked in a cheery voice, "Would you like some cream cakes?"

Nath's jaw dropped.

"Nath, are you well? It looks like the blood has drained from your face," Radigan said. "I can whip you up something for that." He made a toothy grin. "It kinda makes you really wonder who can you trust, doesn't it?"

"Are any of my friends even real?" Nath said.

"We are," Slivver said.

"Aye," Brenwar added.

Walking up invisible steps, Darkken turned from Radigan into an image of Nath and stood eye to eye with him. "It really makes you wonder, doesn't it? Who is who and what side are they on? Just imagine, Nath, I kill our father, and the High Dragon Council sees you carrying the blade. Won't that be something? Then, perhaps, I return to save the day."

Nath was so angry he wanted to spit on Darkken. Instead, all he could say was, "You win. All I ask is that you spare my friends."

"You mean, what is left of them," Darkken replied. "No, little brother. I can't do that. You see, this is war, and I'm not taking any prisoners." He shifted from the image of Nath back into himself. He reached back for his sword, and without taking his eyes off Brenwar, he said, "I think I'll start with the dwarf first. Maefon, hold them still."

CHAPTER 75

MAEFON RATCHETED UP HER CONTROL over Brenwar, keeping the dwarf as still as a stone. She was still processing everything Darkken had been doing. She hated the thought that he might kill Nath. She sincerely cared for him, but she couldn't have cared less about the others. But whatever Darkken did, she would support. Soon, control of the entire world would be in Darkken's grasp, and she would share it. A scuffle in the brush caught her attention. She figured it was a Caligin making his way up the ravine bank.

Then someone with a very unpleasant and familiar voice said, "Yes, hold still." When

Maefon turned her head, the haggard Calypsa was standing behind her with eyes filled with murderous intent. Her arms were hidden behind her back.

"Well, look who it is. The critter woman. If you had any sense, you'd crawl back to your burrow. It's over. But stick around longer, and I'll finish you off too."

"The way I see it, you have two choices," Calypsa said with growing confidence. "Release my friends or face Stone Smiter." She brought the hammer out into full view. The bright gem on top of the hammer burned like a star. "Drop my friends."

With her heart shooting into her throat, the now big-eyed elven woman cried out, "Darkk—"

Calypsa put the full weight of her shoulders and hips into her swing. The hammer's head flashed in an arc of light. Stone Smiter's head collided with Maefon's chest, making the sound of a thunderclap. The elven woman flew off her feet high into the air and landed limp below the hovering men's feet.

Nath didn't even notice Calypsa entering the picture until he heard the sound of a thunderclap. As his head twisted toward the source, he saw Maefon's limp body sailing through the air. The moment the elven woman hit the ground, the rings of energy around his body dissipated. He was falling, and so was Brenwar. They hit the ground close to one another with their weapons drawn. He didn't have time to check Maefon. He looked up. Slivver flew into Darkken and tangled up his limbs. "Bring him down here!" Nath yelled.

"Aye! Let me get a crack at him!" Brenwar said.

Slivver's tail coiled around Darkken's neck. The warrior's face turned purple, and he rapidly drifted toward the ground. Darkken bear-hugged Slivver's neck. His arms glowed with copper fire. Slivver head-butted the man with his horns.

Before they hit the ground, Nath charged his two brothers. He jumped on top of the two combatants and sent them all crashing to the ground. They had Darkken in their clutches. Nath locked up the man's arms. Darkken thrashed like a wild beast. His unnatural strength started to break their holds.

Brenwar stormed over with his hammer gripped in his hands. He lifted it overhead and said, "Hold him still!"

Darkken's eyes shimmered like copper lightning. His muscles flexed as he grew. Twisting on the ground and fighting against Slivver's chokehold, he said, "Get off of me, insects!"

Fah-pooom!

At the sound of Darkken's commanding voice, an invisible force shield knocked all three of them far away from his body. They landed side by side. Nath crawled up on all fours, trying to shake off the stinging effect of whatever power had hit them.

Slivver rolled up to one knee. Brenwar's braids had come out of his beard, and his hair was all bushy.

Nath tasted metal in his mouth. He spat blood, having bitten his lips when his teeth clacked together. Trembling, he cast his gaze on Darkken. Over fifty feet away, a stiff breeze billowed his brother's coppery locks. His eyes burned with volcanic intensity. He reached over his shoulder and pulled Mercy from its sheath. A ray of sunlight reflected off Darkken's rings. Then, like a kick in the head, everything came together.

The copper rings! That is where his power comes from!

Memories flashed through Nath's thoughts like bright pictures: Darkken's copper hair and eyes; the copper-colored mystic powers he summoned; the copper dragons. He could see Darkken twisting and touching the ambiguous rings often. With a sideward glance, he whispered to Slivver, "I think I've figured out the source of his power."

"Now would be a good time to spit it out," Slivver responded.

"The rings on his middle and index fingers. That's it, I swear it," he said. "We have to separate him from them."

Brenwar crawled over toward them, "Easier said than done. Have you ever separated a bride from her rings before? This will be worse." He cast a look at the formidable Darkken. "I'll handle it."

Nath stood. Brandishing his sword, he said, "No, I will." He marched right at Darkken. "I challenge you to a battle. Fang against Mercy. Do you accept?"

At that same moment, Calypsa came charging down the hill on a path right toward Darkken. The sledgehammer she held seemed to lift her from her feet. With a flick of his wrist, Darkken sent her flying back into the ravine.

"Little brother, you alone are not a worthy challenge. I am too formidable. However, I'll gladly fight the three of you at once," Darkken said.

Brenwar and Slivver were both lifted off their feet and dragged toward Darkken by an invisible hand. Suddenly, they spun around like tops. When they came to a stop, the dwarf and dragon marched toward Darkken with wobbly gaits.

Nath rushed at Darkken full speed and launched a two-handed chop at Darkken's head. Darkken parried. Steel rang as loudly as a gong being struck. The blue magic in Fang's blade lit up.

Over the clashing exchanges of dragon steel, Darkken said, "Look at that. Fang and Mercy are like two brothers meeting for the first time. Don't worry, Nath. When you are dead, I'll find a worthy master for Fang. The Dragon Vein, perhaps."

"We'll see." Nath fought against Darkken with everything he had. He parried hard sword strokes that jarred his limbs. Darkken's strength and speed quickly started to overpower him. He shuffled backward, blocking and parrying, completely unable to counter or attack. His shoulders started to burn like fire. He focused on the rings. He needed only one shot at them.

Slivver and Brenwar charged as one. Their bodies were hurled together in a fierce collision.

"Quit running into me, you clumsy dragon!" Brenwar jumped back to his feet. A hunk of stone flew out of nowhere, knocking him back off his feet again. "Barnacles!"

Once again, Darkken had all the angles covered. He was a man among children, toying with their lives, with wicked delight in his eyes. With telekinetic power, he pummeled the dragon and dwarf over and over, with rocks and one another. At the same time, he fought Nath like a skilled champion.

Fatigue set in on Nath. His blocks became sluggish. Mercy licked at his eyes. Darkken made a sudden jab step. Mercy tore through Nath's breastplate at the shoulder. He gasped and dropped to a knee. He held Fang but couldn't lift it up.

"What is the matter, little brother? Are you tired? You aren't going to let a tiny flesh wound stop you from fighting, are you?" Darkken asked.

Nath stopped panting and said, "I'll never stop fighting you."

"Don't be silly. You'll be dead. You can't fight from the land of the dead. Well, perhaps you could if you were undead. Why, I could bring you back like the Gull. Would you like that? You could be my servant forever." Darkken wiped a forearm over his forehead. "I think I would enjoy having you around in that capacity."

"You're overconfident. Maybe not today, but one day, it will be your undoing."

"Confident, yes, but overconfident, no."

Darkken waved Slivver's and Brenwar's battered bodies toward himself. Both of them dragged over the ground. Brenwar didn't even have his hammer in his hand. Like dead things, they lay exhausted at Darkken's feet. "It looks like this is the end of the rebellion." His eyes still crackled with energy. "I'll let you pick, Nath. Which one goes first?"

Chapter 76

"Take me first," Nath said with a shuddering breath, his eyes downcast. "I cannot bear to watch another friend die. You have named your sword Mercy, brother. I ask that you show mercy on me." Nath hadn't quit. He was stalling.

Darkken would be ready for any move he made. He'd proven to be ready for anything. Nath focused on one lethal strike at the hands of Darkken.

Fang, if you can hear my thoughts, listen to me. Give me strength. Do something to help me. "Please."

"You are all heart," Darkken said. "It's going to be disappointing to not have you by my side in my moment of triumph. You know, Nath, if you earnestly swear your faithfulness to me, I'll let you live, but your friends will still have to die. I just don't like them."

Stirring on the ground, Slivver groaned. Brenwar lay as though he was out cold.

Nath shook his head. He envisioned his surroundings by making a perfect picture in his mind. He thought clearly about what he wanted to do. He saw himself striking Darkken's right sword arm at the wrist. He saw the hand with two of the rings fall away as he performed a counterstrike at the other wrist.

Fang, you are my only friend left standing. Give me strength.

The snap of a bowstring caught Nath's ear. An arrow whistled through the air, coming from the rim of the gulch. Calypsa had Roday's bow and the black quiver on her back. Her face was swollen and bleeding. The whistle of the arrow came to a stop inches from Darkken's back. The arrow tip glowed like red-hot embers.

Darkken chuckled wickedly. "She's a feisty one. This time, I won't fail to kill her."

The arrow flipped end over end and took aim at Calypsa. Darkken puckered his lips and started to whistle.

"Nooo!" Nath shouted.

At the same instant, Fang came to life in his hands. Faster than thought, the sword flashed right in front of his and Darkken's eyes.

Darkken's eyes grew as big as the sun. "Nooo!"

Slivver launched himself at Darkken with his jaws wide open. His sharp jaws bit down on Darkken's exposed left hand.

Chomp!

The red-tipped arrow dropped onto the ground.

Darkken staggered back while staring at his severed hands.

Nath rose up in front of his brothers and put his sword point to Darkken's chest. Chin quivering, he said, "I'm sorry, brother, but I can't let you live any longer."

Darkken sneered at him and said, "You don't have the guts to do it!"

Nath shoved Fang straight through Darkken's heart. Darkken gasped.

Watching his brother's dead body fall to the ground, Nath said, "You didn't give me any choice."

CHAPTER 77

As SLIVVER AND BRENWAR MADE arrangements for a proper burial, Nath sobbed uncontrollably. He had killed his own flesh and blood, a man that he loved as a brother and a friend. Now, he had to bury that man. At the same time, the dragon heart beating inside his chest continued to break. Maefon had not survived the blow Calypsa had delivered to her. The beautiful, bright-minded elf, whom he'd known more intimately than any other, was gone.

Calypsa squatted nearby with her arms wrapped around her knees, rocking back and forth. She too was crying. Rond had not survived. Whatever life forces he'd had within him had expired. His undead constitution wasn't enough to withstand all the damage he'd taken. They'd hauled what was left of him up the bank. Now, he lay alongside many of the dead, lifeless and cold.

High in the sky, great dragons appeared. Their shadows shaded parts of the valley.

Slivver and Brenwar stopped moving the dead elves that they were preparing for burial.

"Fetchers," Slivver said. "They come to take the fallen dragons to the Valley of Bones for burial."

The Fetchers were behemoths of the air, the size of bull dragons. They moved in a lazy pattern and had gray scaly skin like that of an elephant and a soft look in their eyes. They dropped down slowly, grabbed the copper dragons in their great talons, and two by two, lifted them away. The last Fetcher to land picked up Master Elween all by herself. Nath choked out an audible sob. Slivver waved as the Fetchers flew up and away, vanishing into the clouds.

Even Brenwar wiped his eyes as Hacksaw lay near his feet. "He was a true knight in every sense of the word. There aren't many men that I have so much respect for. He fought like a dwarf."

A cloud descended from the sky. The closer it came, the more it took form. A group of ghostly men took shape. They were knights wearing full suits of armor. All of them had content looks on their faces. The stalwart group surrounded Hacksaw. Their wispy figures lifted Hacksaw up from the ground.

Nath approached them. "Where are you taking him?"

In a hallowed voice, one of knights with a cross on the top of his helmet said, "To the Legionnaires' Hall of Honor. He is a legend that rode the thunder with great honor."

"But I will miss him," Nath said as he wiped his cheek.

One of the apparitions turned and said to Nath, "I will miss you too."

Nath gasped. It was Hacksaw, with a warm smile on his face.

"I'm proud of you, son. Take care," Hacksaw said.

The group of ghostly knights rose into the air, faded, and disappeared.

Listlessly, the battered company of friends spent the next several hours burying all the elves. The entire time, Nath couldn't stop thinking about Dule and Roday. He hardly knew them, but they'd given their lives in exchange for his. Every time one of the Caligin's shovels dug into the ground, it felt like a stab in the chest. How many had died because of him? He'd lost count. He was sickened by the thought that he couldn't keep track, and it had all started with the Black Hand.

They buried Maefon with the rest of the elves. Nath didn't have any tears left to shed after that. Now, only Darkken remained aboveground, lying beside a dirt grave that Brenwar had dug out for him. Amazingly, Darkken's strong features made him look alive somehow. He appeared more like he was frozen or sleeping.

Nath sighed.

Slivver stood to the right of Nath, with Calypsa on the left. "Don't have any regrets, Nath. He would have killed us all, including your father. Darkken, sadly, was evil. He would have turned this world upside down."

"He was the only other person in the world like me," Nath said softly. "Now, I'm alone again."

"You'll never be alone." Calypsa put her hand on the small of his back. "You have us."

Nath didn't say a word as he watched Brenwar sort through Darkken's belongings. Once he stripped the dead man of his gear, he rolled him into the grave. Brenwar grabbed a shovel and filled dirt into the hole. The last thing Nath saw of Darkken's face was quickly covered by dirt.

"Goodbye, brother," Nath said.

After the grave was filled, Slivver said, "There is the matter of these items." He opened his hand, revealing four copper rings and the Star of the Heavens in his palm. "I have to admit the copper rings were very clever. If you hadn't figured it out, Nath, we wouldn't have made it. I don't think anyone would have been able to come to the same conclusion that you did."

Nath blankly stared at the rings. He plucked one out of Slivver's hand. Whereas most rings had inscriptions on the outside, this one had arcane engravings on the inside. "I never learned much about magic or how it worked. What did they do?"

"Being one of dragon blood, Darkken had a natural gift for using magic," Slivver said. "But given that he was cursed, his powers were limited. You see, without the rings, Darkken really wasn't that powerful. Unlike you, Nath, he cannot grow in his dragon abilities. So he enhanced himself with rings that allowed him to teleport, change shape, cast fire, and shield himself. The Star of the Heavens enhanced his power. But I will say, to be able to wield them all at once was the true gift. Ordinary mortals could not do it. It was his dragon blood that allowed it."

Nath put the copper ring back in Slivver's palm. "We should destroy the rings and the sword."

"Agreed," Slivver said.

With heaviness in his heart, Nath picked up the sword, Mercy, and led them all down to the belly of Borgash. Back inside the forge, he and Brenwar pushed away the stone that covered the Dragon Vein. Slivver dropped the rings into the molten fire. Nath gave the perfect sword, Mercy, one final glance. He saw his image quivering in the blade. For a moment, he could have sworn he saw Darkken. He dropped it into the pit. The molten fires churned with anger as the sword melted into the lava.

"What about the Star of the Heavens?" Nath asked Slivver.

"I don't think it can be destroyed by the same means. It might be best to return it to Dragon Home, where the dragons can protect it," Slivver suggested.

"I can't go home," Nath said with his head hanging. "I'm banished."

"Given all that has transpired, I think the High Dragon Council will be willing to reconsider. I can bear witness, and so can Brenwar, of all that occurred. I think there is a strong chance they will change their minds," Slivver said.

"I just wish that I could forget all of this."

"It can be done," Brenwar stated.

Slivver stepped between Nath and Brenwar and said, "No, dwarf. Shame on you for even suggesting it."

Nath brushed by Slivver and said, "What do you mean?"

Brenwar fished a vial out of his pouch. He held it before Nath's eyes with his thumb and index finger. "It's the Elixir of Forgetfulness. Potent. It will let you forget what you want to forget."

Slivver pushed Brenwar's hand aside. "But there are risks, Nath. It will wear off, and sometimes, you lose memories that you might want to keep. Its effects are unpredictable. I know this is hard to bear, but you need to learn to live with all that will happen. With time, this pain will pass."

Calypsa's warm hand took his. "I will be here for you."

He squeezed her hand. With his free hand, he reached past Slivver and took the vial. A flood of memories spanning the last few years returned. His chest tightened. Nath wanted to live up to all that he faced, but having killed his brother and lost Maefon was too much. All he could see were their dead faces.

"Think about this, Nath," Slivver said. "Life is hard, but with friends, faith, and family, we can get through it."

"You said that it would wear off one day. For now, I just want to forget."

With his thumb, he pushed the cork off the ceramic vial. An inky substance was inside. He exhaled a shuddering breath and drank. His heavy thoughts lightened. The dark fog in his mind was gone. He blinked repeatedly.

He looked at the dryad, who was holding his hand, and said curiously, "Hello. You're very pretty." He leaned in toward her. "Who are you?"

Calypsa let out a sob.

Chapter 78

Back outside, in the fields of the Lost City of Borgash, Slivver, Calypsa, and Brenwar were talking while Nath wandered the area.

"I'm very sorry, Calypsa," Slivver said sadly. "It wasn't supposed to happen like that. Brenwar let him drink the entire potion when he was only supposed to drink a greater portion."

"I'm a dwarf, not a wizard. Balzurth should have given it to you, not me."

Calypsa gave them both a hug. "It's all right." Her gaze wandered toward Nath. "I think it's better. I'm not the one for him, and I'm glad he's not suffering. He's just too young to have to live with all of that. I just hope one day I'll see him again. I'm excited to meet the man that he will become. Besides, he still remembers the both of you well enough. He couldn't ask for two better friends. Goodbye, now."

She wandered over to Nath, gave him a hug and a kiss, said farewell, and left.

Nath walked back over to them with a smile on his face. He gave her another glance. "She was nice... and curvy." He scratched the side of his face. "So I knew her?"

"In passing," Slivver said. "Nath, what do you—"

Brenwar bumped Slivver.

"Never mind. Listen, stay with Brenwar. I'm going to Dragon Home. I'll make haste and try to return in several days." Slivver spread out his wings. "Brenwar, you have this, right?"

"Of course," Brenwar said. "We'll go hiking toward the keep. You can catch up with us there. I want to check something out. I have a feeling."

"Just stay out of trouble." Slivver took to the sky.

"You still know how to ride a horse, don't you?" Brenwar said to Nath as he climbed onto his pony.

"Of course." Nath mounted a horse. "So where are we going?"

Brenwar eyed Nath with an arched brow. "Stonewater Keep."

"It sounds intriguing. Lead the way."

Brenwar grumbled. The thought that Nath had forgotten all about Stonewater Keep was disturbing. Worse yet, he felt guilty for offering the potion in the first place. He didn't know how much that would cost Nath. It didn't seem right. He snapped his reins, and at a trot, they headed west.

Neither one of them said much the first several hours of travel. They both seemed content enjoying the open air and countryside. Finally, Nath broke his silence and said, "I have a hollow feeling inside. Have you ever had a feeling like that?"

"No." Brenwar wasn't sure what he should say to Nath. He wanted to find out how much he knew, but he didn't want to trigger any bad memories, either. Clawing his fingers through his beard, he said, "Since we are going to be traveling more together, we might want to get to know each other better. I'm Brenwar Bolderguild, from Morgdon. I come from a family that are the chosen servants of your father, Balzurth."

"That's good to know. And it's good to meet you." Nath almost looked as though he were lost. "I have to be honest. I feel as though I woke up from a dream. I remember leaving the Mountain of Doom because I was banished. Fledglings were murdered. I'm seeking out their murderers."

"Don't you mean Dragon Home?" Brenwar said.

"Yes. Why, what did I say?"

"The Mountain of Doom."

"Oh, that's odd. Anyway, I feel confused."

Brenwar stopped his horse as Nath did the same. "Listen. The murderers of the fledglings have been taken care of."

"They have? Why don't I remember that?" Nath pushed his hair out of his eyes. "I remember a lot of things, but they're hazy."

"What do you remember?"

Nath looked in the direction of Advent and said, "I remember being in cities north and south. I was a slave in Slavertown. I made a friend with a man named Hacksaw in Huskan." He squinted. "It's all so hazy. My head aches, thinking about it."

"Let's ride while you listen. Back where we started, there was a fierce battle. Many friends and enemies perished, but we prevailed."

"That's explains all of the graves," Nath said. "So I was there, and I don't remember it."

"You lost some people that you carried deeply about. Because your pain was so great, I offered you an Elixir of Forgetfulness. You took it."

"That sounds like a very simple solution to a very complicated problem." Nath rubbed the back of his neck. "It explains my haziness. There is emptiness in my chest as well. Whatever happened must have been horrible. I feel like a coward for not facing it. Do you think I did the right thing?"

"You did what most people could never do. It was a brave thing," Brenwar said, speaking of Nath killing his brother, not taking the potion. "It was a burden that you shouldn't have had to carry on your own, but you did."

"Can you tell me what I did?"

"No. It's in the past now. It's best to move forward and leave it all alone."

"I don't mean to sound glib, but I'd like that."

Brenwar nodded. "There's nothing wrong with it."

They arrived at Stonewater Keep. All ten stories of the building had collapsed. The stones dammed up the river, causing a flood in the valley. The entire area was in ruin.

Staring at the fallen heap, Nath said, "I lived here before, didn't I?"

"For a spell." Brenwar dismounted and started making a camp as night had begun to fall. "So you don't remember anything at all?"

"There is coldness in my chest, a feeling that makes me angry." He shrugged. "But that is all. Whatever happened there, I don't think I want to remember. It seems like a dreary place."

"It is." Brenwar started a fire. "We'll wait here for Slivver. Are you hungry? I'm certain there are some mighty fine fish in that river."

"Fishing sounds like a good idea to me."

Slivver landed the next morning, bearing good news. "Nath, you can return to Dragon Home. Your father looks forward to seeing you."

Back in Dragon Home, Nath was met with the same distance and disdain he was used to. The homes of the Trahaydeen were gone. He thought of Maefon and was sad that she was now missing. He had no friends he could relate to. While Slivver and Brenwar met with Balzurth, he listlessly wandered through the great tunnels. Not a single dragon welcomed him back. It was as if he'd never left at all, but he knew he had.

Inside Balzurth's treasure room, the King of the Dragons sat on his throne. The great and mighty red dragon with gold flecks in his scales sat three stories tall. Brenwar laid Nath's sword, Fang, at the king's feet.

"Thank you, Brenwar," Balzurth said in a voice that filled the massive treasure chamber. Coins slid from the tops of their piles as he spoke. "I need to make haste and finish my work on this sword. In the future, Fang can serve him even better. So tell me, how is my son?"

Brenwar explained all about the Elixir of Forgetfulness and the effect it'd had on Nath. "It is a shame, sire."

"Don't feel guilty. You and Slivver are fine servants. I wouldn't have given it to you if it hadn't been needed. You did well. When Nath is ready, the veil will be lifted from his memories." He sighed. "But Crixis knew what he was doing. He has planted a seed in Nath. One never knows for sure how that will blossom and develop. We need to take great care with him. I leave that charge to you, Brenwar."

"Aye." Brenwar bowed. "My service is yours, Your Majesty."

"And what of me, Father?" Slivver asked.

"Son, take to the skies and do what you do. I only want what is best for you. Now, please go and fetch me Nath."

CHAPTER 79

NATH SAT ON A PILE of coins with his legs crossed, facing his father. His chin dipped toward his chest. *Oh no, here it comes.*

"It's good to see you, son. How are you?" Balzurth asked.

"Restless. Lonely. The same as I was before I left. But it's good to see you, Father. It seems like it's been a very long time."

"As I understand it, you've been through a great ordeal. According to Slivver and Brenwar, you handled it exceptionally well. I'm glad to have you by my side again. I was worried." In his seated position, Balzurth lifted a finger. "I know about the Elixir of Forgetfulness, but do you remember the last thing I told you before I left?"

Nath nodded. "Don't leave Dragon Home until I return."

"And you left. Great trouble ensued. So much trouble that you could not bear to remember it." Balzurth sighed. "If I've told you once, I've told you a thousand times. Obedience is the key to knowledge. You must remember that if you ever want to earn your scales and fly. Do you still want that?"

Nath quickly stood up. "I do."

"In order to become a dragon, you must save the dragons. Find the lost. Bring them back home," he said. "But don't venture out until I say that you are ready. You need to rest, son."

"I would, but I'm having trouble sleeping. There is restlessness inside."

"Go back to your cove. Wait there until I send for you." Balzurth reached down and patted Nath on the head. "I love you, son."

"I love you too."

When Nath returned to his cove, heavy sleep fell over him. When he awoke, he was hungry for food and adventure. The dread inside him had subsided. He was ready for a fresh start. The time to become a dragon had come.

He made his way back to his father's throne room, where Balzurth was sleeping on the floor. "Great, he's never going to wake up."

He knocked on his father's eyelid. Balzurth didn't flinch. He searched the piles of treasure for Fang. He found it half buried underneath piles of coins near the throne. The sword was ready, scabbard and all. He patted the dragon-head cross guard. *It's time to save some dragons.* He slung it over his back.

Standing by his father's earhole, he said, "Father, I'm going to leave for a little bit. I'll be back soon." He knew his father would sleep for years, and he didn't feel like waiting. "Just don't move or say anything if that's fine with you."

Balzurth's chest barely expanded.

"Good." Nath patted his father on the horns. "I'll be back soon. I'm going to earn my scales and save the dragons." He crept out of Dragon Home and departed.

Brenwar Boulderguild entered Balzurth's throne room with his war hammer slung over his shoulder. Balzurth sat on his backless throne. Brenwar took a knee.

"It seems that Nath has slipped out on me while I was sleeping. I need you to go after him," Balzurth said.

"I will. Do you have a message for him that I should deliver?"

"Watch over him, Brenwar. Remind him of who he is and what is his purpose. The world of the races will still be very tempting. He still has to figure it out for himself. The encounter with Crixis made him stronger within, but I feel a greater evil invading from the darkness." Balzurth's clawed finger tapped one arm of his throne. "But at least now, Fang is complete. It should be an even greater friend to him this time around. He saved the world once. He'll need it to save the world again."

"At least he's had plenty of sleep. Over fifty years is a long time. What sort of lullaby did you sing to him?"

"The right one." Balzurth sighed. "Keep an eye on him, Brenwar. He's starting all over again. He has to get it right this time. He must become a dragon. Our future depends on it. He still needs guidance. Use a firm hand the best that you can. He'll not always listen. Show patience. My son is all the hope that we have. I fear that eventually that dark seed Crixis planted might surface. Be ready. Do your best. Bring him back home to me when you can."

Brenwar stood and saluted. "I will."

Other Books and Author Info

Craig Halloran resides with his family outside his hometown of Charleston, West Virginia. When he isn't entertaining mankind, he is seeking adventure, working out, or watching sports. To learn more about him, go to www.thedarkslayer.com.

Check out all of my great stories …

Free e-Books

The Darkslayer: Brutal Beginnings

Nath Dragon – Quest for the Thunderstone

The Odyssey of Nath Dragon Series (New Series) (Prequel to Chronicles of Dragon)

Exiled

Enslaved

Deadly

Hunted

Strife

The Chronicles of Dragon Series

The Hero, the Sword and the Dragons (Book 1)

Dragon Bones and Tombstones (Book 2)

Terror at the Temple (Book 3)

Clutch of the Cleric (Book 4)

Hunt for the Hero (Book 5)

Siegc at the Settlements (Book 6)

Strife in the Sky (Book 7)

Fight and the Fury (Book 8)

War in the Winds (Book 9)

Finale (Book 10)

The Chronicles of Dragon: Series 2, Tail of the Dragon

Tail of the Dragon
Claws of the Dragon
Battle of the Dragon
Eye of the Dragon
Flight of the Dragon
Trial of the Dragon
Judgment of the Dragon
Wrath of the Dragon
Power of the Dragon
Hour of the Dragon

The Darkslayer Series 1

Wrath of the Royals (Book 1)
Blades in the Night (Book 2)
Underling Revenge (Book 3)
Danger and the Druid (Book 4)
Outrage in the Outlands (Book 5)
Chaos at the Castle (Book 6)

The Darkslayer: Bish and Bone, Series 2

Bish and Bone (Book 1)
Black Blood (Book 2)
Red Death (Book 3)
Lethal Liaisons (Book 4)
Torment and Terror (Book 5)
Brigands and Badlands (Book 6)
War in the Wasteland (Book 7)
Slaughter in the Streets (Book 8)
Hunt of the Beast (Book 9)

The Battle for Bone (Book 10)

The Supernatural Bounty Hunter Files

Smoke Rising (2015) Free ebook
I Smell Smoke (2015)
Where There's Smoke (2015)
Smoke on the Water (2015)
Smoke and Mirrors (2015)

Up in Smoke
Smoke Signals
Holy Smoke
Smoke Happens
Smoke Out

The Gamma Earth Cycle

Escape from the Dominion
Flight from the Dominion
Prison of the Dominion

Zombie Impact Series

Zombie Day Care: Book 1
Zombie Rehab: Book 2
Zombie Warfare: Book 3

OTHER WORKS & NOVELLAS

The Scarab's Curse—Sword & Sorcery Novella
The Scarab's Power
The Scarab's Command

You can learn more about the Darkslayer and my other books' deals and specials at:
Facebook – The Darkslayer Report by Craig
Twitter – Craig Halloran
www.craighalloran.com

Made in the USA
Middletown, DE
14 May 2019